AZTEC

They stood like that, immobile, long enough for
me to capture a picture of them: Jadestone Doll
still on tiptoe, the two of them touching nowhere
but at lips and breasts. Then the girl reached to
the waist of the woman's skirt, and deftly undid
the fastening of it, so that it dropped rustling to
the floor. I was close enough to see the just perceptible ripple of the woman's muscles as she
tightened her long legs protectively together . . .

The girl queen took the woman's hand and
tugged, so that she walked, and they crossed the
room to the big, soft, canopied bed. They lay on
top of it, with no covering over them, and I
moved closer with my chalks and papers.

AZTEC
Gary Jennings

ARROW BOOKS

Arrow Books Limited
62–65 Chandos Place, London WC2N 4NW

An imprint of Century Hutchinson Ltd

London Melbourne Sydney Auckland
Johannesburg and agencies throughout
the world

First published in Great Britain by Macdonald 1981
Futura edition 1982
Arrow edition 1986
Reprinted 1987 and 1989

Printed and bound in Great Britain by
Cox & Wyman Ltd, Reading

ISBN 0 09 948080 8

FOR ZYANYA

You tell me then that I must perish
like the flowers that I cherish.
Nothing remaining of my name,
nothing remembered of my fame?
But the gardens I planted still are young—
the songs I sang will still be sung!

HUÉXOTZIN

Prince of Texcóco

CA. 1484

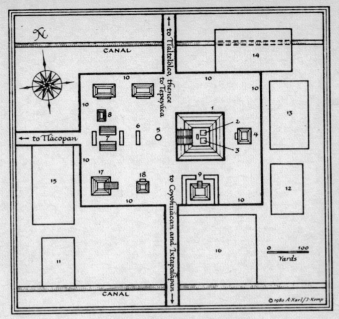

IN CEM-ANÁHUAC YOYÓTLI

THE HEART OF THE ONE WORLD

THE CENTRAL PLAZA OF TENOCHTÍTLAN, *1521*

(Only the major landmarks, and/or those mentioned in the text, are identified)

1 The Great Pyramid   2 The Temple of Tlaloc
3 The Temple of Huitzilopóchtli
4 Former Temple of Huitzilopóchtli, later (after completion of the Great Pyramid, 1487) the Coateocáli, or catch-all temple of numerous minor gods, plus gods appropriated from other nations.
5 The Stone of Tixoc   6 The Tzompántli, or skull rack
7 The Ceremonial Tlachtli Ball Court   8 The Platform of the Sun Stone
9 The Temple of Tezcatlipóca   10 The Snake Wall
11 The House of Song   12 The Menagerie
13 The Palace of Axayácatl, later of Cortés
14 The Palace of Ahuítzotl, ravaged by flood, 1499
15 The Palace of Motecuzóma I   16 The Palace of Motecuzóma II
17 The Temple of Xipe Totec   18 The Eagle Temple

COURT OF CASTILE
VALLADOLID

*To His Majesty's legate and chaplain,
Fray Don Juan de Zumárraga, lately
appointed Bishop of the See of Mexico
in New Spain, a charge upon him:*

THAT we may be better acquainted with our colony
of New Spain, of its peculiarities, its riches, the people who
possessed it, and the beliefs, rites, and ceremonies which they
heretofore held, we wish to be informed of all matters apper-
taining to the Indians during their existence in that land before
the coming of our liberating forces, ambassadors, evangels,
and colonizers.

Therefore, we order that you shall inform yourself from
ancient Indians (having first administered to them the oath, to
assure veracity) as to their country's history, their governments,
their traditions, their customs, &c. In addition to the information that you secure from witnesses, you will cause to be
brought before you any writings, tablets, or other records of
that foregone time which may substantiate what is said, and
you will cause your missionary friars to search and ask for such
records among the Indians.

Because this is a very weighty matter and very necessary

for the discharge of His Majesty's conscience, we command you to attend to the conduct of the said inquiry with all possible promptitude, care, and diligence, and that your account be set forth in much detail.

(ecce signum) CAROLUS R ✠ I

Rex et Imperator
Hispaniae Carolus Primus
Sacri Romani Imperi Carolus Quintus

IHS

✠

S.C.C.M.

Sanctified, Caesarean, Catholic Majesty,
the Emperor Don Carlos, Our Lord King:

MAY the grace, peace, and lovingkindness of Our
Lord Jesus Christ be with Your Majesty Don Carlos, by divine
mercy eternally august Emperor; and with your esteemed Queen
Mother Doña Juana, together with Your Majesty by the grace
of God rulers of Castile, of León, of Aragón, of the Two
Sicilies, of Jerusalem, of Navarre, of Granada, of Toledo, of
Valencia, of Galicia, of Mallorca, of Seville, of Sardinia, of
Córdova, of Córcega, of Murcia, of Jaén, of the Caribbees,
of Algeciras, of Gibraltar, of the Canary Isles, of the Indies,
of the islands and lands of the Ocean Sea; Counts of Flanders
and of the Tyrol, &c.

Very Fortunate and Most Excellent Prince: from this city
of Tenochtítlan-Mexíco, capital of your dominion of New
Spain, this twelfth day after the Assumption, in the Year of
Our Lord one thousand five hundred twenty and nine, greeting.

It was but eighteen months ago, Your Majesty, when we,
though the least of your vassal subjects, heeded Your Majesty's
command that we assume this trifold post as the first appointed

Bishop of México, Protector of the Indians, and Apostolic Inquisitor, all embodied in our one and own poor person. It has been but nine months since our arrival in this New World, and there was much arduous work awaiting us.

In accordance with the mandate of this appointment, we have striven zealously "to instruct the Indians in their duty to hold and worship One True God, Who is in Heaven, by Whom all creatures live and are maintained"—and likewise "to acquaint the Indians of that Most Invincible and Catholic Majesty, the Emperor Don Carlos, whom divine Providence has willed that the whole world should obey and serve."

Inculcating these lessons, Sire, has been far from easy or expeditious. There is a saying among our fellow Spaniards here, extant well before our arrival: "The Indians cannot hear except through their buttocks." But we try to bear in mind that these miserable and spiritually impoverished Indians—or Aztecs, as most Spaniards now refer to this particular tribe or nation of them hereabouts—are inferior to all the rest of mankind, and therefore, in their insignificance, deserve our tolerant indulgence.

Besides attending to the Indians' instruction—that there is only One God in Heaven, and the Emperor on earth, whose subjects they have all become and whom they must serve—and besides dealing with many other ecclesiastical and civil matters, we have attempted to comply with Your Majesty's personal adjuration to us: that we early prepare an account of the conditions of this *terra paena-incognita*, the manners and ways of life of its inhabitants, the customs, &c. formerly obtaining in this benighted land.

Your Most Lofty Majesty's royal cédula specifies that we, in providing the chronicle, shall inform ourself "from ancient Indians." This has necessitated something of a search, inasmuch as the total destruction of this city by Captain-General Hernán Cortés left us very few ancient Indians from whom to seek a credible oral history. Even the workers currently rebuilding the city consist mainly of women, children, the dolts and dotards who were unfit to fight in the siege, brute peasants conscripted from the outlying lands. Oafs, all of them.

Nevertheless, we were able to ferret out *one* ancient Indian (of some sixty and three years of age) capable of providing the desired account. This *Mexícatl*—he repudiates both the appellations Aztec and Indian—is of a high grade of intelligence (for his race), is articulate, is possessed of what education was heretofore afforded in these parts, and has been in his time a scrivener of what passes for writing among these people.

In his lifetime he has had numerous occupations besides that of scribe: as warrior, as courtier, as traveling merchant, even as a sort of emissary from the late rulers of this place to the first arriving Castilian liberators, and those envoy duties have given him a passable grasp of our language. Though his Castilian falters seldom, we of course desire precision in all details. So we have provided an interpreter, a young lad who has considerable proficiency in Náhuatl (which is what these Aztecs call their guttural language of lengthy and unlovely words). In the interrogation room, we have also seated four of our own scribes. These friars are adept in that art of swift writing by character, known as Tironian notes, which is employed at Rome for making memoranda of the Holy Father's every utterance, and even for recording the entire proceedings of many-peopled conferences.

We bade the Aztec sit down and tell us his life story. The four friars, busily flicking away at their Tironian squiggles, did not then or since lose a single word that drops from the Indian's lips. *Drops?* Better say: words that cascade in torrents alternately loathly and corrosive. You will soon see what we mean, Sire. From the very first opening of his mouth, the Aztec evinces disrespect for our person, our cloth, and our office as our Revered Majesty's personally chosen missionary, which disrespect is an implicit insult to our sovereign himself.

The first pages of the Indian's narrative follow immediately after this explanatory introduction. Sealed for your eyes only, Sire, this package of manuscript will depart Tezuítlan de la Vera Cruz the day after tomorrow in the keeping of Captain Sánchez Santoveña, master of the caravel *Gloria*.

Your Caesarean Majesty's wisdom, sagacity, and discrimination being universally known, we realize that we risk your imperial displeasure in presuming to preface the enclosed pages with a *caveat*, but, in our episcopal and apostolic capacity, we feel that obligatory upon us. We are sincerely desirous of complying with Your Majesty's cédula, of sending a true report of all there is worth knowing of this land. But others besides ourself will tell Your Majesty that the Indians are paltry beings, in whom one will scarcely find even vestiges of humanity; who do not even have a comprehensible written language; who have never had any written laws, but only barbaric customs and traditions; who have been or still are addicted to all kinds of intemperance, paganism, ferocity, and carnal lusts; who have but lately tortured and slain their own fellow beings for the sake of their misbegotten "religion."

We cannot believe that a worthwhile or edifying report can be procured from an informant like this arrogant Aztec, or from any other native, however articulate. Also, we cannot believe that our Sanctified Emperor Don Carlos can be other than scandalized by the iniquitous, salacious, and impious prattlings of this overweening specimen of a dunghill race. We have referred to the enclosure herewith as the first part of the Indian's chronicle. We fervently desire and trust that it will also, by Your Majesty's command, be the last.

May God Our Lord guard and preserve the precious life, the very royal person, and the very catholic estate of Your Majesty for uncounted years, with the enlargement of your reigns and dominions as your royal heart desires.

Of Your S.C.C.M., the ever faithful servant and chaplain,

(*ecce signum*) Fr. Juan de Zumárraga

Bishop of Mexíco
Apostolic Inquisitor
Protector of the Indians

INCIPIT:

The chronicle told by an elderly male Indian of the tribe commonly called Aztec, which narrative is addressed to His Excellency, the Most Reverend Juan de Zumárraga, Bishop of Méxíco, and recorded *verbatim ab origine* by
      Fr. Gaspar de Gayana J.
      Fr. Toribio Vega de Aranjuez
      Fr. Jerónimo Muñoz G.
      Fr. Domingo Villegas e Ybarra
      Alonso de Molina, *interpres*

DIXIT:

M<small>Y</small> LORD

Pardon me, my lord, that I do not know your formal and fitting honorific, but I trust I do not hazard my lord's taking offense. You are a man, and not one man of all the men I have met in my life has ever resented being addressed as a lord. So, my lord

Your Excellency, is it?

Ayyo, even more illustrious—what we of these lands would call an ahuaquáhuitl, a tree of great shade. Your Excellency it shall be, then. It impresses me the more that a personage of such eminent excellency should have summoned such a one as myself to speak words in Your Excellency's presence.

Ah, no, Your Excellency, do not demur if I appear to flatter Your Excellency. Common report throughout the city, and these your servitors here, have made plain to me how august a man you are, Your Excellency, while I am but a threadbare rag, a frayed raveling of what once was. Your Excellency is attired and arrayed and assured in your conspicuous excellency, and I am only I.

But Your Excellency wishes to hear of what I was. This has

also been explained to me. Your Excellency desires to learn what my people, this land, our lives were like in the years, in the sheaves of years before it pleased Your Excellency's king and his crossbearers and crossbowmen to deliver us from our bondage of barbarism.

That is correct? Then Your Excellency asks no easy thing of me. How, in this little room, out of my little intellect, in the little time the gods—the Lord God—may have vouchsafed me to finish my roads and my days, how can I evoke the vastness of what was our world, the variety of its peoples, the events of the sheaves upon sheaves of years?

Think, imagine, picture yourself, Your Excellency, as that tree of great shade. See in your mind its immensity, its mighty boughs and the birds among them, the lush foliage, the sunlight upon it, the coolness it casts upon a house, a family, the girl and boy who were my sister and myself. Could Your Excellency compress that tree of great shade back into the acorn which Your Excellency's father once thrust between your mother's legs?

Yya ayya, I have displeased Your Excellency and dismayed your scribes. Forgive me, Your Excellency. I should have guessed that the white men's private copulation with their white women must be different—of more delicacy—than I have seen them perform forcibly upon our women in public. And assuredly the Christian copulation that produced Your Excellency must have been even more

Yes, yes, Your Excellency, I desist.

But Your Excellency perceives my difficulty. How to enable Your Excellency to see at a glance the difference between our inferior *then* and your superior *now*? Perhaps one summary illustration will suffice, and you need trouble yourself with no more listening.

Look, Your Excellency, at your scribes: in our language "the word knowers." I have been a scribe myself, and I well recall how hard it was to render onto fawnskin or fiber paper or bark paper so much as the unfleshed bones of historical dates and happenings, with any degree of accuracy. Sometimes it was hard even for me to read my own pictures aloud, without stumbling, after just the few moments the colors took to dry.

But your word knowers and I have been practicing, while awaiting Your Excellency's arrival, and I am amazed, I am struck with wonder, at what any one of your reverend scribes can do. He can write and read back to me not just the substance of what I speak, but every single word, and with all the intonations and pauses and stresses of my speech. I would think it a talent of memory and mimicry—we had our word *rememberers*, too—but he tells me, shows me, proves to me, that it is all there on his page of paper. I congratulate myself, Your Excellency, that I have learned to speak your language with what proficiency my poor brain and tongue can attain, but your writing would be beyond me.

In our picture writing, the very colors spoke, the colors sang or wept, the colors were necessary. They were many: magenta-red, ocher-gold, ahuácatl-green, turquoise-blue, chocólatl, the red-yellow of the jacinth gem, clay-gray, midnight-black. And even then they were inadequate to catch every individual word, not to mention nuances and adroit turns of phrase. Yet any one of your word knowers can do just that: record every syllable forever, with a single quill instead of a handful of reeds and brushes. And, most marvelous, with *just one color,* the rusty black decoction they tell me is ink.

Very well, Your Excellency, there you have it in an acorn—the difference between us *Indians* and you white men, between our ignorance and your knowledge, between our old times and your new day. Will it satisfy Your Excellency that the mere stroke of a quill has demonstrated your people's right to rule and our people's fate to be ruled? Surely this is all that Your Excellency requires from us *Indians:* a confirmation that the victor's conquest is ordained, not by his arms and artifice, not even by his Almighty God, but by his innate superiority of nature over lesser beings like ourselves. Your Excellency can have no further need of me or words of mine.

My wife is old and infirm and unattended. I cannot pretend that she grieves at my absence from her side, but it annoys her. Ailing and irascible as she is, her annoyance is not good for her. Nor for me. Therefore, with sincere thanks to Your Excellency for Your Excellency's gracious reception of this aged wretch, I bid you

My apologies, Your Excellency. As you remark, I have not Your Excellency's permission to depart at whim. I am at Your Excellency's service for as long as

Again my apologies. I was not aware that I had repeated "Your Excellency" more than thirty times in this brief colloquy, nor that I had said it in any special tone of voice. But I cannot contradict your scribes' scrupulous account. Henceforth I will endeavor to temper my reverence and enthusiasm for your honorific, Señor Bishop, and to keep my tone of voice irreproachable. And, as you command, I will continue.

But now, what am I to say? What should I cause your ears to hear?

My life has been long, as ours is measured. I did not die in infancy, as so many of our children do. I did not die in battle or in holy sacrifice, as so many have willingly done. I did not succumb to an excess of drinking, or to the attack of a wild beast, or to the creeping decay of The Being Eaten by the Gods. I did not die by contracting one of the dread diseases that came with your ships, and of which so many thousands upon thousands have perished. I have outlived even the gods, who forever had been deathless and who forever would be immortal. I have survived for more than a full sheaf of years, to see and do and learn and remember much. But no man can know everything of even his own time, and this land's life began immeasurably long ages before my own. It is only of my own that I can speak, only my own that I can bring back to shadow life in your rusty black ink. . . .

"There was a splendor of spears, a splendor of spears!"

An old man of our island of Xaltócan used always to begin his battle tales that way. We listeners were captivated on the instant, and we remained engrossed, though it might have been a most minor battle he described and, once he had told the foregoing events and the outcome of it all, perhaps a very trivial tale hardly worth the telling. But he had the knack for blurting at once the most compelling highlight of a narrative, and then weaving backward and forward from it. Unlike him, I can but begin at the beginning and move onward through time just as I lived it.

What I now state and affirm did all occur. I only narrate what happened, without invention and without falsehood. I kiss the earth. That is to say: I swear to this.

✠

Oc ye nechca—as you would say, "Once upon a time"—ours was a land where nothing moved more rapidly than our swift-messengers could run, except when the gods moved, and there was no noise louder than our far-callers could shout, except when the gods spoke. On the day we called Seven Flower, in the month of God Ascending, in the year Thirteen Rabbit, the rain god Tlaloc was speaking his loudest, in a resounding thunderstorm. That was somewhat unusual, since the rainy season should have been then at its end. The tlalóque spirits which attend upon the god Tlaloc were striking blows with their forked sticks of lightning, cracking open the great casks of the clouds, so that they shattered with roars and rumblings and spilt their violent downpour of rain.

In the afternoon of that day, in the tumult of that storm, in a little house on the island of Xaltócan, I came forth from my mother and began my dying.

To make your chronicle clearer—you see, I took pains to learn your calendar too—I have calculated that my day of birth would have been the twentieth day of your month called September, in your year numbered one thousand four hundred sixty and six. That was during the reign of Motecuzóma Iluicamína, meaning The Wrathful Lord, He Who Shoots Arrows into the Sky. He was our Uey-Tlatoáni or Revered Speaker, our title for what you would call your king or emperor. But the name of Motecuzóma or of anybody else did not mean much to me at the time.

At the time, warm from the womb, I was doubtless more impressed by being immediately plunged into a jar of breath-taking cold water. No midwife has ever bothered to explain to me the reason for that practice, but I assume it is done on the theory that if the newborn can survive that appalling shock it can survive all the ailments which may beset it during its infancy. Anyway, I probably complained most vociferously while the midwife was swaddling me, while my mother was disentangling her hands from the knotted, roof-hung rope she had clutched as she knelt to extrude me onto the floor, and while my father was carefully wrapping my severed navel string around a little wooden war shield he had carved.

That token my father would give to the first Mexícatl warrior he chanced to encounter, and the soldier would be entrusted to plant the object somewhere on the next battlefield to which he was ordered. Thereafter, my tonáli—fate, fortune, destiny, whatever you care to call it—should have been forever urging me to go for a soldier, that most honorable of occupations for our class of people, and to fall in battle, that most honorable of deaths for such as we were. I say "should have been" because, although my tonáli has frequently beckoned or prodded me in some odd directions, even into combat, I have never really yearned either to fight or to die by violence before my time.

I might mention that, according to the custom for female babies, the navel string of my sister Nine Reed had been planted, not quite two years earlier, beneath the hearth in that room where we both were born. Her buried string was wrapped around a tiny clay spindle wheel; thus she would grow up to be a good, hard-working, and humdrum housewife. She did not. Nine Reed's tonáli was as wayward as my own.

After my immersion and swaddling, the midwife spoke most solemnly and directly to me—if I was letting her be heard at all. I scarcely need remark that I do not repeat from memory any of those doings at my birth time. But I know all the procedures. What the midwife said to me that afternoon I have since heard spoken to many a new boy baby, as it always was to all our male children. It was one of many rituals remembered and never neglected since time before time: the long-dead ancestors handing on, through the living, their wisdom to the newborn.

The midwife addressed me as Seven Flower. That day-of-birth name I would bear until I had outlived the hazards of infancy, until I was seven years old, by which age I could be presumed likely to live to grow up, and so would be given a more distinctive adult name.

She said, "Seven Flower, my very loved and tenderly delivered child, here is the word that was long ago given us by the gods. You were merely born to this mother and this father to be a warrior and a servant of the gods. This place where you have just now been born is not your true home."

And she said, "Seven Flower, you are promised to the field of battle. Your foremost duty is to give to the sun the blood of your enemies to drink, and to feed the earth with the cadavers of your opponents. If your tonáli is strong, you will be with us and in this place only a brief while. Your real home will be in the land of our sun god Tonatíu."

And she said, "Seven Flower, if you grow up to die as a xochimíqui—one of those sufficiently fortunate to merit the Flowery Death, in war or by sacrifice—you will live again in the eternally happy Tonatíucan, the afterworld of the sun, and you will serve Tonatíu forever and forever, and you will rejoice in his service."

I see you wince, Your Excellency. So should I have done, had I then comprehended that woeful welcome to this world, or the words spoken by our neighbors and kinsmen who crowded in to view the newcomer, each of them leaning over me with the traditional greeting, "You have come to suffer. Suffer and endure." If children were born able to understand such a salutation, they would all squirm back into the womb, dwindle back into the seed.

No doubt we did come into this world to suffer, to endure; what human being ever did not? But the midwife's words about soldiering and sacrifice were a mere mockingbird repetition. I have heard many other such edifying harangues, from my father, from my teachers, from our priests—and yours—all mindlessly echoing what they themselves had heard from generations long gone before. Myself, I have come to believe that the long-dead were no wiser than we, even when they were alive, and their being dead has added no luster to their wisdom. The pontifical words of the dead I have always taken—as we say, yca mapilxocóitl: with my little finger—"with a grain of salt," as your saying goes.

We grow up and look down, we grow old and look back. *Ayyo,* but what it was to be a child, to be a child! To have the roads and the days all stretching out forward and upward and away, not one of them yet missed or wasted or repented. Everything in the world a newness and a novelty, as it once was to Ometecútli and Omecíuatl, our Lord and Lady Pair, the first beings of all creation.

Without effort I remember, I recall to memory, I hear again in my age-muffled ears the sounds of dawn on our island Xaltócan. Sometimes I awoke to the call of the Early Bird, Pápan, crying his four-note "papaquíqui, papaquíqui!"—bidding the world "arise, sing, dance, be happy!" Other times I awoke to the even earlier morning sound of my mother grinding maize on the métlatl stone, or slapping and shaping the maize dough she would bake into the big, thin disks of tláxcala bread—what you now call tortillas. There were even mornings when I awoke earlier than all but the priests of the sun Tonatíu. Lying in the darkness, I could hear them, at the temple atop our island's modest pyramid, blowing the hoarse bleats of the conch trumpet, as they burned incense and ritually wrung the neck of a quail (because that bird is speckled like a starry night), and chanted to the god: "See, thus the night dies. Come now and perform your kindly labors, oh jeweled one, oh soaring eagle, come now to lighten and warm The One World. . . ."

Without effort, without striving, I remember the hot middays, when Tonatíu the sun, in all the vigor of his prime, fiercely brandished his flaming spears while he stood and stamped upon the rooftop of the universe. In that shadowless blue and gold noontime, the mountains around Lake Xaltócan seemed close enough to touch. In fact, that may be my earliest memory—I could not have been much over two years old, and I had yet no conception of distance—for the day and the world were panting all about me, and I wanted the touch of something cool. I still recall my childish surprise when I stretched out my arm and could *not* feel the blue of the forested mountain that loomed so clear and close before me.

Without effort I remember also the days' endings, when Tonatíu drew about him his sleeping mantle of brilliant feathers, and let himself down on to his soft bed of many-colored flower petals, and sank to sleep in them. He was gone from our sight to The Dark Place, Míctlan. Of the four afterworlds in which our dead might dwell, Míctlan was the nethermost, the abode of the utterly and irredeemably dead, the place where *nothing* happens, or has ever happened, or ever will. (It was compassionate of Tonatíu that for a time (a little time only, compared to what he lavished on us), he would lend his light (a little light only, dimmed by his sleeping) to The Dark Place of the hopelessly dead.

Meanwhile, in The One World—on Xaltócan, anyway, the only world I knew—the pale blue mists rose from the lake so that the blackening mountains roundabout appeared to float on them, between the red waters and the purple sky. Then, just above the horizon where Tonatíu had disappeared, there flared for a while Omexóchitl, the evening star After Blossom. That star came, After Blossom always came, she came to assure us that, though the night did darken, we need not fear *this* night's darkening to the oblivion darkness of The Dark Place. The One World lived, and would live yet a while.

Without effort I remember the nights, and one night in particular. Metztli the moon had finished his monthly meal of stars, and he was full fed, he was gorged to his roundest and brightest, so that the figure of the rabbit-in-the-moon was as clearly incised as any temple carving. That night—I suppose I was three or four years old—my father carried me on his shoulders, his hands holding tight to my ankles. His long strides bore me through cool brightness and cooler darkness: the dappled moonlight and moonshade beneath the spreading limbs and feathery leaves of the "oldest of old" trees, the ahuehuétque cypresses.

I was old enough then to have heard of the terrible things that lurked in the nighttime, just beyond the edge of a person's vision. There was Chocacíuatl, the Weeping Woman, the first of all mothers to die in childbirth, forever wandering, forever bewailing her lost baby and her own lost life. There were the nameless, headless, limbless torsos that somehow managed to moan as they writhed blind and helpless on the ground. There were the disembodied, fleshless skulls that drifted head-high through the air, chasing travelers overtaken by night upon their travels. If a mortal glimpsed any of those things, he knew it to be a sure omen of dire misfortune.

Some other denizens of the dark were not so utterly to be feared. There was, for instance, the god Yoáli Ehécatl, Night Wind, who gusted along the night roads, seeking to seize any incautious human abroad in the dark. But Night Wind was as capricious as any wind. Sometimes he seized, then let a person go free, and if that happened, the person would also be granted his heart's desire and a long life in which to enjoy it. So, in hope of keeping the god always in that indulgent mood, our people had long ago built stone benches at various of the island's crossroads, whereon Night Wind might rest in his rushings about. As I say, I was old enough to know and dread the spirits of the darkness. But that night, set on my father's broad shoulders, myself temporarily taller than a man, my hair brushed by the rustling cypress fronds, my face caressed by the dapples of moonlight, I felt not at all afraid.

Without effort I remember that night because, for the first time, I was being allowed to observe a ceremony involving human sacrifice. It was but a minor rite, for it was in homage to a very minor deity: Atláua, the god of fowlers. (In those days, Lake Xaltócan teemed with ducks and geese which, in their seasons of wandering, paused there to rest and feed—and to feed us.) So, on that night of the well-fed moon, at the start of the season of the waterfowl, just one xochimíqui, one man only, would be ritually killed to the greater glory of the god Atláua. And the man was not, for a change, a war captive going to his Flowery Death with exhilaration or resignation, but a volunteer going rather ruefully.

"I am already dead," he had told the priests. "I gasp like a fish taken from the water. My chest strains for more and more air, but the air no longer nourishes me. My limbs weaken, my sight darkens, my head whirls, I faint and fall. I had rather die all at once than flop about fishlike until I strangle at last."

The man was a slave who had come from the Chinantéca nation, far to the south. Those people were and still are prey to a curious illness which seems to run in certain of their family bloodlines. We and they called it the Painted Disease, and you Spaniards now call the Chinantéca the Pinto People, because an afflicted one's skin is blotched with livid blue. His body somehow gradually becomes unable to make use of the air it breathes, and so it dies of suffocation, exactly in the manner of a fish removed from its sustaining element.

My father and I arrived at the lakeshore, where two sturdy posts were embedded a little way apart. The surrounding night

was lighted by urn fires and made smoky by burning incense.
Through the haze danced the priests of Atláua: old men, black
all over, their robes black, their faces blackened and their long
hair matted with oxitl, which is the black pine tar our fowlers
smear on their legs and lower body to shield them from the
cold when they wade into the lake waters. Two of the priests
tweedled the ritual music on flutes made from human shin-
bones, while another thumped a drum. That was a special sort
of drum, specially suited to the occasion: a giant dried pumpkin,
partly filled with water so it floated half submerged in the lake
shallows. Beaten with thighbones, the water drum gave out a
resonant rataplan which echoed from the mountains invisible
across the lake.

The xochimíqui was led into the circle of smoky light. He
was naked, he wore not even the basic maxtlatl which customarily encircles a man's loins and private parts. Even in the
flickery firelight, I could see that his body was not of flesh
color mottled with blue, but a dead blue touched only here and
there with flesh color. He was spread-eagled between the lakeshore posts, one ankle and one wrist bound to each stake. A
priest, waving an arrow as a Song Leader waves his stick,
chanted an invocation:

"This man's life fluid we give to you, Atláua, mingled with
the life water of our beloved Lake Xaltócan. We give it to you,
Atláua, that you may in return deign to send your flocks of
precious fowl to the nets of our fowlers. . . ." And so on.

That continued long enough to bore me, if not Atláua. Then,
without any warning or ritual flourish, the priest suddenly lowered the arrow and jabbed it with all his strength upward,
twisting it, into the blue man's genital organs. The victim,
however much he might have thought he desired that release
from life, gave a scream. He howled a scream, he ululated a
scream that overrode the sound of flutes, drum, and chanting.
He screamed, but he did not scream for long.

The priest, with the bloody arrow, drew a cross on the man's
chest for a target, and all the priests pranced about him in a
circle, each carrying a bow and many arrows. As each passed
in front of the xochimíqui, he thrummed an arrow into the blue
man's heaving breast. When the prancing was done and the
arrows used up, the dead man looked like an overgrown spec-

imen of the animal we call the prickly little boar. There was not much else to the ceremony. The body was unloosed from the stakes and tied by a rope behind a fowler's acáli pulled up on the sand. The fowler rowed his canoe out into the lake, out of our view, towing the corpse until it should sink of the water that seeped in through its natural orifices and the arrow punctures. Thus Atláua received his sacrifice.

My father hoisted me to his shoulders again and started his long strides back across the island. As I bobbed along, high and safe and secure, I made a boyishly arrogant vow to myself. If ever it was my tonáli to be selected for the Flowery Death of sacrifice, even to some alien god, I would not scream, whatever was done to me, whatever pain I suffered.

Foolish child. I thought death meant only dying, and doing it badly or bravely. At that moment in my snug and unthreatened young life, being borne on strong shoulders homeward to a sweet sleep from which I would awaken to a new morning at the Early Bird's call, how could I know what death really is?

As we believed in those days, a hero slain in the service of a mighty lord or sacrificed in homage to a high god was assured of a life everlasting in the most resplendent of afterworlds, where he would be rewarded and regaled with bliss throughout eternity. And now Christianity tells us that we all may hope for an afterlife in a similarly splendid Heaven. But consider. Even the most heroic of heroes dying in the most honorable cause, even the most devout Christian martyr dying in the certainty of reaching Heaven, he will never again know the caress of *this* world's moonlight dappling his face as he walks beneath this world's rustling cypress trees. A trifling pleasure— so small, so simple, so ordinary—but never to be known again.

Your Excellency evinces impatience. Forgive me, Señor Bishop, that my old wits sometimes drift off the straight road onto meandering bypaths. I know that some things I have told, and some other things of which I shall tell, you may not regard as a strictly historical account. But I pray your forbearance, for I do not know whether I shall ever have another opportunity to say these things. And, for all I say, I do not say all that could be said. . . .

* * *

Casting my mind again backward to my childhood, I cannot claim that it was in any way extraordinary for our place and time, since I was no more or less than an ordinary boy child. The day number and year number of my birth were numbers regarded neither as fortunate nor misfortunate. I was not born during any portents in the sky—an eclipse biting at the moon, for example, which could similarly have bitten me with a harelip or permanently shadowed my face with a dark birthmark. I had none of the physical features our people regarded as unhandsome defects in a male: not curly hair nor jug-handle ears, no double chin nor any cleft in it, no protruding rabbit teeth, my nose neither flat nor too beakishly pronounced, no everted navel, no conspicuous moles. Most fortunate for me, my black hair grew straight and smooth; there were no tufts turned up or turned awry.

My boyhood comrade Chimáli had one of those unruly feathers of hair, and all his young life he prudently, even fearfully, kept that tuft clipped short and plastered down with oxitl. I remember once, in our early years, when he had to wear a pumpkin over his head for a whole day. The scribes smile; I had better explain.

The fowlers of Xaltócan caught ducks and geese, in the most practical way and in goodly numbers, by raising large nets on poles here and there in the lake's shallow red waters, then making some violent noise to startle the birds into flight, and seizing those that got entangled in the nets. But we boys of Xaltócan had our own sly method. We would cut off the top of a pumpkin or other large calabash gourd, and hollow out its inside, and cut a hole in it through which to see and breathe. We would put the pumpkin over our head, then dog-paddle out to where the ducks or geese sat placidly on the lake. Our bodies being invisible underwater, the birds never seemed to find anything alarming in the slow approach of a floating gourd or two. We could get close enough to grab a bird's legs and yank it under the surface. It was not always easy; even a small teal can put up quite a fight against a small boy; but generally we could keep the bird underwater until it drowned and went limp. The maneuver seldom even disturbed the rest of the flock afloat nearby.

Chimáli and I spent a day at that sport, and we had a respectable heap of ducks stacked onshore by the time we got tired and decided to quit. But then we discovered that all the swimming about had dissolved Chimáli's hair plaster, and his tuft was sticking up behind like the back feather worn by certain of our warriors. We were at the end of the island farthest from our village, meaning Chimáli would have to cross the whole of Xaltócan looking like that.

"Ayya, pochéoa!" he muttered. The expression refers only to the malodorous passing of gut wind, but it was a vehement enough expletive, from a boy of eight or nine years, that it would have earned him a thrashing with thorns if an adult had been there to overhear it.

"We can get back into the water," I suggested, "and swim around the island, if we stay far enough offshore."

"Maybe you could," said Chimáli. "I am so winded and waterlogged that I would sink on the instant. Suppose we wait until dark to walk back home."

I said, "In the daylight you risk running into some priest who may notice your standing tuft of hair. In the dark you risk meeting some monster even more terrible, like Night Wind. But you decide, and I am with you."

We sat and thought for a while, idly nipping at honey ants. Those were everywhere on the ground at that season, their abdomens bulging with nectar. We picked up the insects and bit their hinder ends for a sip of the sweet honey. But each droplet was minuscule and, no matter how many ants we nipped, we were getting hungry.

"I know!" Chimáli said at last. "I will wear my pumpkin all the way home."

And that is what he did. Of course he could not see too well through its eyehole, so I had to lead him, and we were both considerably encumbered by our burdens of dead, wet, heavy ducks. This meant that Chimáli quite often stumbled and fell, or walked into tree trunks, or toppled into roadside ditches. By good fortune, his pumpkin never broke to pieces. But I laughed at him all the way and dogs barked at him and, since the twilight came before we reached home, Chimáli himself may have astonished and terrified any passersby who saw him in the dusk.

But it might otherwise have been no laughing matter. There was good reason for Chimáli's being always aware and careful of his unruly hair. Any boy with such a tuft, you see, was especially preferred by the priests when they required a male youngster for sacrifice. Do not ask me why. No priest has ever told me why. But then, what priest has ever had to give us a credible reason for the unreasonable rules he makes us live by, or for the fear and guilt and shame we must endure when we sometimes circumvent them?

I do not mean to give the impression that any of us, young or old, lived lives of constant apprehension. Except for a few arbitrary vagaries like the priests' predilection for boys with disordered hair, our religion and the priests who interpreted it did not make too many or too onerous demands of us. Nor did any other authorities. We owed obedience to our rulers and governors, of course, and we had certain obligations to the pípiltin nobles, and we heeded the advice of our tlamatíntin wise men. But I was born into the middle class of our society, the macehuáltin, "the fortunate," so called because we were equally free of the upper classes' heavy responsibilities and of the lower classes' liability to being basely used.

In our time there were few laws—deliberately few, so that every man might hold them all in his head and in his heart, and have not the excuse of ignorance for flouting them. The laws were not written down, like yours, nor pasted up in public places, like yours, so that a man must forever be consulting the long lists of edicts, rules, and regulations, to measure his every last action against "you shall" and "you shall not." By your standards, our few laws may seem to have been lax or whimsical, and the penalties for their infraction unduly harsh. But our laws worked for the good of all—and all, knowing the dire consequences, obeyed them. Those who did not—they disappeared.

An example. According to the laws you brought from Spain, a thief is punished with death. So he was in our time. But, by your laws, a hungry man who steals a thing to eat is a thief. Not so in our time. One of our laws said that, in any maize field planted alongside a public road, the four rows of stalks adjacent to that road were accessible to the passerby. Any hungry warfarer could pluck as many ears of maize as his empty belly required. But a man who greedily sought to enrich himself, and plundered that maize field to collect a sackful for hoarding or trading, if he was caught, he died. Thus that one law ensured two good things: that the thieving man was permanently cured of thievery, and that the hungering man did not die of hunger.

Our lives were regulated less by laws than by long-standing customs and traditions. Most of those governed the behavior of adults or of clans or of entire communities. But, even as a child not yet grown beyond the name of Seven Flower, I was made aware of the traditional insistence on a male's being brave, strong, gallant, hard-working, and honest; of a female's being modest, chaste, gentle, hard-working, and self-effacing.

What time I did not spend at play with my toys—most of them miniature war weapons and replicas of the tools of my father's trade—and what time I did not spend at play with Chimáli and Tlatli and other boys about my own age, I spent in the company of my father, when he was not at work in the quarry. Though of course I called him Tete, as all children childishly called their fathers, his name was Tepetzálan, meaning Valley, after the low place among the mainland mountains where he had been born. Since he towered well above the average height of our men, that name, given him at the age of seven, was rather ridiculous in his adulthood. All our neighbors and his fellow quarriers called him by tall nicknames: Handful of Stars and Head Nodder and the like. Indeed, he had to nod his head far down to my level, to speak the traditional father-to-son homilies. If perhaps he caught me impudently imitating the shuffle gait of our village's hunchbacked old garbage collector, my father would tell me sternly:

"Take care that you do not mock the old, the ill, the maimed, or anyone who has fallen into some folly or transgression. Do not insult or despise them, but abase yourself before the gods, and tremble lest they bring the same misery upon you."

Or if I showed little interest in what he tried to teach me of his trade—and any macehuáli boy who did not aspire to soldiering was expected to follow in his father's footsteps—he would lean down and say earnestly:

"Flee not any labor to which the gods assign you, my son,

but be content. I pray that they may grant you merits and good fortune, but whatever they give you, take it gratefully. If it be only a small gift, do not scorn it, for the gods can take even that little away. If it be a large bestowal, perhaps some great talent, do not be proud or vainglorious, but remember that the gods must have denied that tonáli to someone else that you might have it."

Sometimes, at no discernible instigation, and with his big face reddening slightly, my father would deliver a small sermon that made no sense to me at all. Something on this order:

"Live cleanly and be not dissolute, or you will anger the gods and they will cover you with infamy. Restrain yourself, my son, until you meet the girl whom the gods destine for your wife, because the gods know how to arrange all things properly. Above all, never disport yourself with another man's wife."

It seemed an unnecessary injunction, for I did live cleanly. Like every other Mexícatl—except the priests—I bathed twice a day in hot soapy water, and swam often in the lake, and periodically sweated out my remaining bad vapors in our oven-like little steam house. I cleaned my teeth, night and morning, with a mixture of bee's honey and white ashes. As for disporting myself, I knew of no man on the island who had a wife my age, and none of us boys included girls in our games anyway.

All those father-to-son preachments were so many rote recitations, handed down through the generations word for word, like the midwife's discourse at my birth. Only on those occasions did my father Tepetzálan talk at great length; he was otherwise a taciturn man. In the noise of the quarry there was little use for talk, and at home my mother's incessant fretful chatter gave him little chance to put in a word. Tete did not mind. He always preferred action to speech, and he taught me far more by example than with the parroted harangues. If my father was at all defective in the qualities expected of our men—strength, bravery, and all that—it consisted only in his letting himself be bullied and brow-beaten by my Tene.

My mother was the most untypical female among all those of our class on Xaltócan: the least modest, least docile, least self-effacing. She was a shrill termagant, the tyrant of our little family and the bane of all our neighbors. But she preened herself on being the model of womanly perfection, so it followed that she lived in a state of perpetual and angry dissatisfaction with everything around her. If I learned anything at all useful from my Tene, it was to be sometimes dissatisfied with *myself*.

I remember being corporally punished by my father on only one occasion, when I richly deserved it. We boys were allowed, even encouraged, to kill birds like crows and grackles which pecked at our garden crops, and that we did with reed blowpipes which propelled shaped clay pellets. But one day, out of some impish perversity, I blew a pellet at the little tame quail we kept in our house. (Most houses had one of those pets, to keep down scorpions and other insect vermin.) Then, to compound my crime, I tried to blame the bird's killing on my friend Tlatli.

It took my father not long to find out the truth. While my murder of the unoffending quail might have been only moderately penalized, the strictly prohibited sin of *lying* could not. My Tete had to inflict on me the prescribed punishment for "speaking spittle and phlegm," as we called a lie. He winced himself as he did it: piercing my lower lip with a maguey thorn and leaving it there until bedtime. *Ayya ouíya*, the pain, the mortification, the pain, the tears of remorse, the pain!

The punishment left such a lasting impression on me that I have in turn left its impress upon the archives of our land. If you have seen our picture writing, then you have seen figures of persons or other creatures with a small, curly, scroll-like symbol emanating from them. That symbol represents a náhuatl, which is to say a tongue, or language, or speech, or sound. It indicates that the figure is talking or making a noise of some sort. If the náhuatl is more than ordinarily curly, and elaborated by the symbol for a butterfly or flower, then the figure is speaking poetry or singing music. When I myself became a scribe, I added another elaboration to our picture writing: the náhuatl pierced by a maguey thorn, and all our other scribes soon adopted it. When you see that symbol before a figure, you know you see a picture of someone telling a lie.

The punishments more frequently dealt out by my mother were inflicted with no hesitation, no compunction, no compassion; I suspect even with some pleasure at giving pain besides correction. They may have left no legacy to this land's pictured history, like the tongue-and-thorn symbol, but they certainly affected the life history of myself and my sister. I remember one night watching my mother ferociously beat my sister's buttocks bright red with a bundle of nettles, because the girl had been guilty of immodesty. And I should explain that immodesty did not necessarily mean to us what it evidently means to you white men: an indecent exposure of one's unclothed body.

In the matter of clothing, we children of both sexes went totally naked, weather permitting, until we were four or five years old. Then we covered our nudity with a long rectangle of rough cloth which tied at one shoulder and draped around us to mid-thigh. At the attainment of adulthood—that is, at the age of thirteen—we boys began wearing a maxtlatl loincloth under our outer mantle, which was now of finer cloth. At about the same age, depending upon when they had their first bleeding, girls donned the womanly skirt and blouse, plus an undergarment rather like what you call a diaper.

Pardon my recital of minor details, but I am trying to fix the time of that beating of my sister. Nine Reed had become Tzitzitlíni some while before—the name means "the sound of small bells ringing"—so she was past the age of seven. However, I saw her nether parts beaten nearly raw, meaning that she was wearing no undergarment, so she was not yet thirteen. All things considered, I reckon her age to have been ten or eleven. And what she had done to deserve that beating, the only thing of which she was guilty, was that she had murmured dreamily, "I hear drums and music playing. I wonder where they are dancing tonight." To our mother, that was immodesty. Tzitzi was yearning for frivolity when she should have been applying herself to a loom or something else as tedious.

You know the chili? That vegetable pod which is used in our cookery? Though the degree of piquancy varies, all the different types of chili are so hot to the tongue, so pungent, so biting, that it is no accident that their name comes from our word for "sharp" or "pointed." Like every cook, my mother used the chilis in the usual ways, but she had another use for them which I almost hesitate to mention, since your Inquisitors already have instruments enough.

One day, when I was four or five years old, I sat with Tlatli and Chimáli in our dooryard, playing the patóli bean game. This was not the grown men's gambling game, also called patóli, which on occasion has cost a family its fortune or caused a mortal family feud. No, we three boys had merely drawn a circle in the dust, and had each put a jumping bean in its center, the object being to see whose bean, warmed to activity by the sun, would be the first to hop outside the circle. My own bean tended to sluggishness, and I muttered some imprecation at it. Maybe I said "pochéoa!" or something of the sort.

Suddenly I was upside down and off the ground. My Tene had snatched me up by the ankles. I saw the inverted faces of Chimáli and Tlatli, their mouths and eyes wide with surprise, before I was whisked into the house and to the cooking hearth. My mother shifted her grip so that one of her hands was free, and with it she flung into the fire a number of dried red chilis. When they were crackling and sending up a dense yellow smoke, my Tene took me again by the ankles and suspended me head down in those acrid fumes. I leave the next little while to your imagination, but I think I nearly perished. I know that for half a month afterward my eyes watered continuously so that I could scarcely see, and I could not draw a breath without feeling as if I were inhaling flames and flints.

Yet I must count myself fortunate, for our customs did not dictate that a boy spend much time in his mother's company, and I now had every excuse not to. Thereafter, I avoided her, as my tuft-haired friend Chimáli avoided the island priests. Even when she came looking for me, to command some chore or errand, I could always retire to the safety of the hill of the lime-burning kilns. The quarriers believed that no woman should ever be allowed near the kilns, or the quality of the lime would be spoiled, and not even my mother dared to trespass on that hill.

But poor Tzitzitlíni knew no such refuge. In accordance with custom and her tonáli, a girl had to learn womanly and wifely labors—cooking, spinning, weaving, sewing, embroidering—so my sister had to spend most of every day under our mother's sharp eye and limber tongue. Her tongue neglected no opportunity to deliver one of the traditional mother-to-daughter orations. Some of those, which Tzitzi repeated to me, we agreed had been fashioned (by whatever long-ago ancestor) more for the benefit of the mother than the daughter.

"Attend always, girl, to the service of the gods and the giving of comfort to your parents. If your mother calls, do not loiter to be called twice, but come instantly. When commanded to a task, speak no insolent answer and show no reluctance to comply. Indeed, if your Tene calls another, and that other does not come quickly, come *yourself* to see what is wanted, and do it yourself, and do it well."

Other preachments were the expectable admonitions to modesty, virtue, and chastity, and even not Tzitzi or I could find fault with them. We knew that after she turned thirteen, until she was perhaps twenty and two and properly married, no man could so much as speak to her in public, nor she to him.

"If, in a public place, you meet with a likely youth, take no notice, give no sign, lest that inflame his passions. Guard against improper familiarities with men, yield not to the baser impulses of your heart, or lust will befoul your character as mud does water."

Tzitzitlíni would probably never have disobeyed that one sensible prohibition. But by the time she was twelve years old, surely she felt some sexual sensations stirring in her, and some curiosity about sex. It may have been to conceal what she considered unmaidenly and inexpressible feelings that she tried to vent them privately and alone and in secret. All I know is that one day our mother came home unexpectedly from a trip to the market and caught my sister lying on her pallet, nude from the waist down, doing an act of which I did not understand the significance for some time. She was caught playing with her tipíli parts, and using a small wooden spindle for the purpose.

You mutter under your breath, Your Excellency, and you gather the skirts of your cassock almost protectively about you. Have I somehow offended by telling frankly what occurred? I have been careful not to use the coarser words for the telling. And I must assume, since the coarser words abound in both our languages, that the acts they describe are not uncommon among either of our peoples.

* * *

To punish Tzitzitlíni's offense against her own body, our Tene seized her and seized the container of chili powder, and viciously rubbed the burning chili into those exposed, tender tipíli parts. Though she muffled her daughter's screams with the bed covers, I heard and came running, and I gasped, "Should I go to fetch the physician?"

"No! No doctor!" our mother snapped at me. "What your sister has done is too shameful to be known outside these walls!"

Tzitzi stifled her sobs and added her plea, "I am not much hurt, little brother. Summon no doctor. Mention this to no one, not even Tete. Try to pretend that even you know nothing of it. I beg you."

I might have ignored my tyrant mother, but not my beloved sister. Though I did not then know the reason for her refusal of assistance, I respected it, and I went away from there, to worry and wonder by myself.

Would that I had disregarded them both, and done *something!* I think, from what came later, that the cruelty inflicted by our mother on that occasion, intended to discourage Tzitzi's awakening sexual urges, had exactly the contrary effect. I think, from that time on, my sister's tipíli parts burned like a chili-blistered throat, hot and thirsty, clamoring to be slaked. I think it would not have been many years before dear Tzitzitlíni would have gone "astraddle the road," as we say of a depraved and promiscuous woman. That was the most sordid and squalid depth to which a decent Mexícatl maiden could sink—or so I thought, until I learned of the even worse fate that eventually did befall my sister.

How she later behaved, what she became, and what she came to be called, I will tell in its place. But I want to say here only one thing. I want to say that to me she was and always will be Tzitzitlíni: the sound of small bells ringing.

I H S

✠

S.C.C.M.

Sanctified, Caesarean, Catholic Majesty,
the Emperor Don Carlos, Our Lord King:

MAY the serene and beneficent light of Our Lord
Jesus Christ shine everlastingly upon Your Majesty Don Carlos,
divinely appointed Emperor, &c., &c.

Most August Majesty: from this City of Mexíco, capital of
New Spain, this eve of the Feast of St. Michael and All Angels,
in the Year of Our Lord one thousand five hundred twenty and
nine, greeting.

Your Majesty commands that we continue to send additional
portions of the so-called Aztec History "as quickly as the pages
are compiled." This grievously astounds and offends your well-
intentioned chaplain, Sire. We would not, for all the realms
in Your Majesty's domain, dream of disputing our sovereign's
desires and decisions. But we thought we had made plain in
our earlier letter our objections to this chronicle—which grows
daily more detestable—and we hoped that the recommendation
of Your Majesty's own delegated Bishop would not be so
casually disdained.

We are cognizant of Your Gracious Majesty's concern for

the most minute information regarding even the most remote of your subjects, that you may the more wisely and beneficently govern them. Indeed, we have respected that praiseworthy concern ever since the very first task to which Your Majesty personally set us: the extermination of the witches of Navarre. That once dissident province has been, since that sublime and prodigious purging by fire, among the most obedient and subservient of all under Your Majesty's sovereignty. Your humble servant intends equal assiduity in rooting out the age-old evils of these newer provinces—putting the curb rein to vice and the spurs to virtue—thus bringing them likewise to submission to Your Majesty and the Holy Cross.

Surely nothing can be undertaken in Your Majesty's service which will not be blessed by God. And, of a certainty, Your Most Puissant Lordship should know of matters regarding this land, for it is so limitless and marvelous that Your Majesty may well call yourself Emperor of it with no less pride than you do of Germany, which by the grace of God is now also Your Majesty's possession.

Nevertheless, in supervising the transcription of this history of what is now New Spain, only God knows how racked and outraged and nauseated we have been by the narrator's unquenchable effluxion. The Aztec is an Aeolus with an inexhaustible bag of winds. We could not complain of that if he confined himself to what we have asked: that is, an account in the manner of St. Gregory of Tours and other classical historians—names of distinguished personages, brief summaries of their careers, prominent dates, battles, &c.

But this human cataract cannot be restrained from his divagations into the most sordid and repellent aspects of his people's history and his own. Granted, this Indian was a heathen until his baptism no more than a few years ago. The infernal atrocities he committed and witnessed in his earlier life we must charitably concede were done or condoned in ignorance of Christian morality. Still, he is now at least nominally a Christian. One would expect him, if he *must* dwell on the more bestial episodes of his life and times, to manifest a decent and humble contrition befitting the horrors he describes in such lascivious detail.

He does not. He recognizes no horror in those enormities.

He does not so much as blush at the many offenses to our Lord
and to common decency which he is dinning into the ears of
our reverend friar-scribes: idolatry, pretense of magic, superstitions, bloodthirst and bloodletting, obscene and unnatural
acts, other sins so vile that we here forbear even to name them.
Except for Your Majesty's command that all "be set forth in
much detail," we would not allow our scribes to commit portions of the Aztec's narrative to the permanence of parchment.

However, Your Majesty's servant has never yet disobeyed
a royal order. We will try to regard the Indian's pernicious
maunderings merely as evidence that during his lifetime the
Adversary arranged many sorts of temptations and trials for
him, God permitting it for the stoutening of the Aztec's soul.
This, we remind ourself, is no small evidence of the greatness
of God, for He chooses not the wise and strong but the simpleminded and weak to be equally instruments and beneficiaries
of His mercy. The law of God, we remind ourself, obliges us
to extend an extra meed of tolerance to those upon whose lips
the milk of the Faith is not yet dry, rather than to those who
have already absorbed it and are accustomed to it.

So we will try to contain our disgust. We will keep the
Indian with us and let him continue to spew his sewage, at
least until we hear of Your Majesty's response to these further
pages of his story. Fortunately, we have no other urgent need
for his five attendants at this time. And the creature's only
recompense is that we allow him a share of our simple fare,
and a straw sleeping mat in an unused store closet off the
cloister for his use on those nights when he does not take our
table scraps to his apparently ailing wife, and spend the night
ministering to her.

But we are confident that we shall soon be rid of the Aztec
and the foul miasma which we feel surrounding him. We know
that when you read the following pages, Sire—indescribably
more horripilating than the previous portion—you will share
our revulsion and will cry, "No more of this filth!" much as
David cried, "Publish it not, lest the unbelievers rejoice!" We
will eagerly—nay, anxiously—await Your Esteemed Majesty's
command, by the next courier ship, that all pages compiled in
the meantime be destroyed and that we oust this reprehensible
barbarian from our precincts.

May God Our Lord watch over and preserve Your Most Excellent Majesty for many years in His holy service.

Of Your S.C.C.M., the loyal and prayerful chaplain,

(ecce signum) Zumárraga

ALTER PARS

HIS EXCELLENCY does not attend today, my lord scribes? Am I to continue, then? Ah, I see. He will read your pages of my words at his leisure.

Very well. Then let me leave, for now, my overly personal chronicle of my family and myself. Lest you get the impression that I and the few other persons I have mentioned lived in some kind of isolation, apart from the rest of humanity, let me give you a broader view. In my mind, in my recollection, I shall step back and away, so to speak, that I may better make you see our relation to our world as a whole. The world we called Cem-Anáhuac, meaning The One World.

Your explorers early discovered that it is situated between two boundless oceans east and west. The humid Hot Lands at the oceans' edges extend not far inland before they slant upward to become towering mountain ranges, and with a high plateau between those eastern and western ranges. This plateau is so near the sky that the air is thin and clean and sparkling clear. Our days here are almost always springtime mild, even during the midsummer rainy season—until the dry winter comes, when Tititl, god of the year's shortest days, chooses to make some of those days chilly or even achingly cold.

The most populous part of all The One World is this great

bowl or depression in the plateau, which you now call the Valley of México. Here are puddled the lakes that made this area so attractive to human habitation. In actuality, there is only one tremendous lake, pinched in two places by encroaching highlands, so that there are three large bodies of water connected by slightly narrower straits. The smallest and southernmost of these lakes is of fresh water, fed by clear streams melting from the snows of the mountains there. The northernmost lake, where I spent my earliest years, is of reddish and briny water, because it is surrounded by mineral lands which leach their salts into the water. The central lake, Texcóco, bigger than the other two together and composed of their mingled salty and fresh waters, is thus of a slightly brackish quality.

Despite there being only one lake—or three, if you like— we have always divided them by five names. The dun-colored Lake Texcóco alone bears a single name. The southern and most crystalline lake is called Xochimílco in its upper part: The Flower Garden, because that neighborhood is the nursery of precious plants for all the lands about. In its lower part, the lake is called Chalco, after the Chalca nation which borders it. The northernmost lake, though also a single body of water, is likewise divided. The people who live on Tzumpánco, The Skull-Shaped Island, call its upper half Lake Tzumpánco. The people of my native Xaltócan, Island of Field Mice, call their portion Lake Xaltócan.

In a sense, I might liken these lakes to our gods—our former gods. I have heard you Christians complain of our "multitudes" of gods and goddesses, who held dominion over every facet of nature and of human behavior. I have heard you complain that you never can sort out and understand the workings of our crowded pantheon. However, I have counted and compared. I do not believe that we relied on so many major and minor deities as you do—the Lord God, the Son Jesus, the Holy Ghost, the Virgin Mary—plus all those other Higher Beings you call Angels and Apostles and Saints, each of them the governing patron of some single facet of *your* world, your lives, your tónaltin, even every single day in the calendar. In truth, I believe we recognized fewer deities, but we charged each of ours with more diverse functions.

To a geographer, there is but one lake here in the valley. To a boatman laboriously paddling his acáli, there are three broad bodies of water, interconnected. To the people who live on or around the lakes, there are five, distinguished by separate names. Just so, no one of our gods and goddesses had but one face, one responsibility, one name. Like our lake of three lakes, a single god might embody a trinity of aspects. . . .

That makes you scowl, reverend friars? Very well, a god might have *two* aspects, or five. Or twenty.

Depending on the time of year: wet season or dry, long days or short, planting time or harvest time—and depending on circumstances: wartime or peacetime, feast or famine, kind rulers or cruel—a single god's duties would vary, and so would his attitude toward us, and so would our mode of worshiping or celebrating or placating him. To look at it another way, our lives and harvests and battle triumphs or failures might depend on the temperament and transient moods of the god. He could be, like the three lakes, bitter or sweet or blankly indifferent, as he chose.

Meanwhile, both the god's prevailing mood and the current happenings in our world could be differently viewed by different followers of that god. A victory for one army is a defeat for another, is that not so? Thus the god or goddess might be simultaneously regarded as rewarding and punishing, demanding and giving, doing good and evil. If you grasp all the infinite possible combinations of circumstances, you should be able to comprehend the variety of attributes we saw in every god, the variety of aspects each assumed, and the even greater variety of names we gave each of them—worshipful, respectful, grateful, fearful.

But I will not belabor this. Let me come back from the mystic to the physical. I will speak of things demonstrable to the five senses that even brute animals possess.

The island of Xaltócan is really a gigantic, almost solid rock, set well out from the mainland in the salty red lake. If it were not for three natural springs of fresh water bubbling up from the rock, the island would never have been populated, but in my time it supported perhaps two thousand people distributed among twenty villages. And the rock was our support in more than one sense, for it was tenéxtetl limestone, a valuable commodity. In its natural state, this form of limestone is quite soft and easily quarried, even with our crude tools of wood, stone, blunt copper, and brittle obsidian, so inferior to yours of iron and steel. My father was a master quarrier, one of several who directed the less expert workers. I remember one of the occasions when he took me to his quarry for instruction in his trade.

"You cannot see them," he told me, "but here—and here—run the natural fissures and striations of this particular stratum of the stone. Though they are invisible to the untrained eye, you will learn to divine them."

I never would, but he never ceased hoping. I watched while he marked the face of the stone with dabs of black oxitl. Other workers came—they were pale with sweat-caked dust—to hammer wooden wedges into the minute cracks he had marked. Then they sloshed water over the wedges. We went home and some days passed, during which the workers kept those wedges well sodden, so they would swell and exert increasing pressure inside the stone. Then my father and I went again to the quarry. We stood on the brink of it and looked down. My father said, "Watch now."

The stone might have been awaiting his presence and permission, for all of a sudden and all of its own accord, the quarry face gave a rending noise and split apart. Some of it came tumbling ponderously down in immense cubic chunks, other parts peeled off in flat square sheets, and they all fell intact into rope nets spread to receive them before they smashed on the quarry floor. We went down and my father inspected them with satisfaction.

"Only a little dressing with adzes," he said, "a little polishing with a slurry of powdered obsidian and water, and these"—he pointed to the limestone cubes—"will be perfect building blocks, while these"—the sheets as big as our house floor and as thick as my arm—"will be panels of facing."

I rubbed the surface of one of the blocks, waist high to myself. It felt both waxy and powdery.

"Oh, they are too soft for any use when they first come loose from the mother stone," said my father. He ran his thumbnail across the block and it scored a deep scratch. "After some while of exposure to the open air, they solidify, they become as strong and imperishable as granite. But our stone, while it is still malmy and workable, can be carved with any harder stone, or cut with an obsidian-grit sawing string."

Most of our island's limestone was freighted to the mainland or to the capital for use as buildings' walls and floors and ceilings. But, because of the fresh stone's easy workability, there were also sculptors busy at the quarries. Those artists chose the finest quality blocks and, while those were still soft, sculptured them into statues of our gods, rulers, and other heroes. The most perfect limestone sheets they carved into low-relief lintels and friezes with which to decorate temples and palaces. Also, using leftover chunks of stone, the artists carved the little household gods treasured by families everywhere. In our house we had small figures of Tonatíu and Tlaloc, of course, and of the maize goddess Chicomecóatl, and the hearth goddess Chántico. My sister Tzitzi even had her own private figurine of Xochiquétzal, goddess of love and flowers, to whom all young girls prayed for a suitable and loving husband.

The stone chips and other detritus from the quarries were burned in the kilns I have mentioned, from which emerged powder of lime, another valuable commodity. This is essential for the mortar used to cement a building's blocks together. It also makes a gesso for plastering and disguising buildings made of cheaper materials. Mixed with water, the lime is used for hulling the kernels of maize that our women grind into meal for tlaxcáltin tortillas and other foods. The lime was even used by a certain class of women as a cosmetic; with it they bleached their black or brown hair to an unnatural yellow hue, like that of some of your own women.

Of course the gods give nothing absolutely free of payment, and from time to time they exacted tribute from us for the wealth of limestone we dug out of Xaltócan. I happened to be at my father's quarry on a day when the gods decided to take a token sacrifice.

A number of porters were hauling a tremendous block of new-cut stone up the long incline, like a curving shelf, that spiraled from the bottom of the quarry to the top. They did it by sheer muscle power, with a tumpline around each man's forehead attached to the rope net that dragged the block. Somewhere high up on that ramp, the block slid too close to the edge, or was tilted by some irregularity in the path. Whatever happened, it slowly and implacably fell sideways. There was much shouting and, if the porters had not instantly ripped the tumplines from their heads, they would have gone over the brink with the block. But one man, far below in the noise of the quarry, did not hear the shouts. The block came down upon him, and one of its edges, like a stone adze, chopped him precisely in half at his waist.

The limestone block had gouged such a deep notch in the quarry floor that it stayed there, balanced on its angular edge. So my father and the other men who rushed to the spot were able without much difficulty to topple it to one side. They found, to their astonishment, that the victim of the gods was still alive and even conscious.

Unnoticed in the excitement, I came close and saw the man, who was now in two pieces. From the waist up, his naked and sweaty body was intact and unmarked. But his waist was pinched wide and flat, so his torso itself rather resembled an adze or a chisel. The stone had simultaneously severed him—skin, flesh, guts, spine—and neatly closed the wound so that there was not even a drop of blood spilt. He might have been a cotton doll that had been sliced across the middle, then sewn at the cut. His bottom half, still wearing its loincloth, lay separated from him, neatly pinched shut and bloodless—though the legs were twitching slightly, and that half of the body was copiously urinating and defecating.

The massive injury must have so deadened all the cut nerves that the man even felt no pain. He raised his head and looked in mild wonder at himself in two halves. To spare him the sight, the other men quickly and tenderly carried him—the upper half of him—some distance away, and leaned him against the quarry wall. He flexed his arms, opened and closed his hands, experimentally turned his head about, and said in a voice of awe:

"I still can move and talk. I see you all, my comrades. I can reach out and touch and feel you. I hear the hewing of tools. I smell the bitter dust of lime. I still live. This is a most marvelous thing."

"It is," my father said gruffly. "But it cannot be for long, Xícama. There is no use even sending for a physician. You will want a priest. Of which god, Xícama?"

The man thought for a moment. "I can soon greet all the gods, when I can no longer do anything else. But while I still can speak, I had better talk to Filth Eater."

So the call was relayed to the top of the quarry, and from there a runner sped to fetch a priest of the goddess Tlazoltéotl, or Filth Eater. Her unlovely name notwithstanding, she was a most compassionate goddess. It was to her that dying men confessed all their sins and misdeeds—quite often living men, too, when they felt particularly distressed or depressed by something they had done—so that Tlazoltéotl might swallow their sins, and those sins would disappear as if they had never been committed. Thus they did not go with a man, to count against him or to haunt his memory, in whatever afterworld he was headed for.

While we waited for the priest, Xícama kept his eyes averted from himself, where his body appeared to be squeezed into a cleft of the rock floor, and spoke calmly, almost cheerfully, to my father. He gave him messages to impart to his parents, to his widow and orphaned children, and made suggestions as to their disposition of what little property he owned, and wondered aloud what his family would do when its provider was gone.

"Do not trouble your mind," said my father. "It is your tonáli that the gods take you in exchange for the prosperity of us who remain. In thanks for your sacrifice of yourself, we and the Lord Governor will make suitable compensation to your widow."

"Then she will have a respectable inheritance," said Xícama, relieved. "And she is still a young and handsome woman. Please, Head Nodder, prevail on her to marry again."

"I will do that. Is there anything else?"

"No," said Xícama. He looked about him and smiled. "I never thought I would regret seeing the last of this dreary quarry. Do you know, Head Nodder, even this stone pit looks beautiful and inviting now? The white clouds up there, then the blue sky, then the white stone here...like clouds above and below the blue. I wish, though, I could see the green trees beyond the rim. . . ."

"You will," my father promised, "but after you have finished with the priest. We had better not chance moving you until then."

The priest came, in all his black of flaffing black robes and blood-crusted black hair and never-washed sooty face. He was the only darkness and gloom that marred the clean blue and white of which Xícama was sorry to take leave. All the other men moved away to give them privacy. (And my father espied me among them, and angrily bade me begone; that was no sight for a young boy.) While Xícama was occupied with the priest, four men picked up his stinking and still-quivering lower half, to carry it up to the top of the quarry. One of them vomited along the way.

Xícama evidently had led no very villainous life; it did not take him long to confess to Filth Eater whatever he regretted having done or left undone. When the priest had absolved him on behalf of the goddess, and had said all the ritual words and made all the ritual gestures, he stood away. Four more men carefully picked up the still-living part of Xícama and carried him, as rapidly as they could without jostling, up the incline toward the quarry rim.

It was hoped that he would go on living long enough to reach his village and say his own farewell to his family and pay his respects to whatever gods he had personally preferred. But somewhere along the upward spiraling ramp, his pinched body began to gape, to leak his blood and his breakfast and various other substances. He ceased speaking and breathing, and closed his eyes, and he never did get to see the green trees again.

Some of the limestone of Xaltócan had long ago gone into the construction of our island's icpac tlamanacáli and teocáltin— or, as you call them, our pyramid and several temples. A share of all the stone quarried was always set aside for taxes we paid to the nation's treasury, and for our annual tribute to the Revered Speaker and his Speaking Council. (The Uey-Tlatoáni Motecuzóma had died when I was three, and in that year the rule and throne had passed to his son Axayácatl, Water Face.)

Another share of the stone was reserved to the profit of our tecútli, or governor, to some other ranking nobles, and to the island's expenses: building canoes for water freighting, buying slaves to do the dirtier work, paying quarry wages, and the like. But there was still much of our mineral product left over for export and barter.

That earned for Xaltócan imported trade goods and negotiable trade currency, which our tecútli shared out among his subjects, according to their status and merit. Furthermore, he allowed all the island people—except, of course, the slaves and other low classes—to build their houses of the handy limestone. Thus Xaltócan differed from most other communities in these lands, where the houses were more often built of sun-dried mud brick or wood or cane, or where many families might be crowded into one large communal tenement building, or where folk might even live in hillside caves. Though my own family's house was of only three rooms, it was even *floored* with smooth white limestone slabs. There were not many palaces in The One World that could pride themselves on being built of finer material. Our use of our stone for building meant, also, that our island was not denuded of its trees, as were so many other peopled places in the valley.

In my time, our governor was Tlauquécholtzin, the Lord Red Heron—a man whose distant ancestors had been among the first Mexíca settlers on the island, and the man who ranked highest among our local nobility. As was customary in most districts and communities, that guaranteed his lifetime tenure as our tecútli, as representative of the Speaking Council headed by the Revered Speaker, and as ruler of the island, its quarries, its surrounding lake, and every single one of its inhabitants—except, in some measure, the priests, who maintained that they owed allegiance only to the gods.

Not every community was so fortunate in its governor as was our Xaltócan. A member of the nobility was expected to live up to his station—that is, to *be* noble—but not all of them were. And no pili born to the nobility could ever be demoted to any lower class, however ignoble his behavior. (He could, however, if his conduct was inexcusable by his pípiltin peers, be ousted from office or even put to death by them.) I might also mention that, though most nobles got that way by being born to noble parents, it was not impossible for a mere commoner to win elevation to that upper class.

I remember two Xaltócan men who were raised from the macehuáltin to the pípiltin and given an estimable lifetime income. Colótic-Miztli, an elderly onetime warrior, had lived up to his name of Fierce Mountain Lion by doing some great feat of arms in some forgotten war against some long-ago enemy. It had cost him such scars that he was gruesome to look at, but it had gained him the coveted -tzin suffix to his name: Miztzin, Lord Mountain Lion. The other man was Quali-Améyatl, or Good Fountain, a mild-mannered young architect who did no deed more notable than to design some gardens at the governor's palace. But Améyatl was as handsome as Miztzin was hideous, and during his work at the palace, he won the heart of a girl named Dewdrop, who happened to be the governor's daughter. When he married her, he became Améyatzin, the Lord Fountain.

I have tried to make clear that our Lord Red Heron was genial and generous, but above all he was a just man. When his own daughter Dewdrop tired of her lowborn Lord Fountain and was surprised in an adulterous act with a blood-born pili, Red Heron commanded that both she and the man be put to death. Many of his other nobles petitioned that the young woman be spared her life and instead be banished from the island. Even the husband swore that *he* forgave his wife's adultery, and that he and Dewdrop would remove to some far country. But the governor would not be swayed, though we all knew he loved that daughter very much.

He said, "I would be called unjust if, for my own child, I should waive a law that is enforced against my subject people." And he said to Lord Fountain, "The people would someday maintain that you forgave my daughter out of deference to my office and not of your own free will." And he commanded that every other woman and girl of Xaltócan come to his palace and witness Dewdrop's execution. "Especially all the nubile but unmarried maidens," he said, "for their juices run high, and they might be inclined to sympathize with my daughter's dalliance, or even envy it. Let them be shocked at her dying, that they may dwell instead on the severity of the consequences."

So my mother went to the execution, and took Tzitzitlíni.

On their return, my mother said the errant Dewdrop and her lover had been strangled, with cords disguised as garlands of flowers, and in full view of the populace, and that the young woman took her punishment badly, with terrors and pleas and struggling, and that her betrayed husband Good Fountain wept for her, but that the Lord Red Heron had watched without expression. Tzitzi said nothing of the spectacle. However, she told me of meeting at the palace the condemned woman's young brother, Red Heron's son Pactli.

"He looked long at me," she said with a shudder, "and he smiled and bared his teeth. Can you believe such a thing, on such a day? It was a look that gave me gooseflesh."

I would wager that Red Heron did no smiling that day. But you can understand why all the island folk so esteemed our impartially fair-minded governor. In truth, we all hoped the Lord Red Heron would live to a great age, for we regarded unhappily the prospect of being governed by that son Pactli. The name means Joy, a misgiven name if ever there was one. He was an ill-natured and despotic brat long before he even wore the loincloth of manhood. That obnoxious offspring of a courtly father did not, of course, freely associate with any middle-class boys like myself and Tlatli and Chimáli, and anyway was a year or two older. But, as my sister Tzitzi flowered into beauty, and Pactli began to manifest increased interest in her, she and I came to share a special loathing of him. However, all that was still in the future.

Meanwhile, ours was a prosperous and comfortable and untroubled community. We who had the good fortune to live there did not have to grind away our energies and spirits just for subsistence. We could look to horizons beyond our island, to heights above those to which we had been born. We could dream, as did my friends Chimáli and Tlatli. Both their fathers were sculptors at the quarries, and those two boys, unlike myself, aspired to follow their fathers' trade of art, but more ambitiously than their fathers had done.

"I want to be a *better* sculptor," said Tlatli, scraping away at a fragment of soft stone which was actually beginning to resemble a falcon, the bird for which he was named.

He went on, "The statues and friezes carved here on

Xaltócan go away in the big freighting canoes unsigned and their artists unacknowledged. Our fathers get no more credit for their work than a slave woman who weaves mats of the lake reeds. And why? Because the statues and ornaments we make here are as indistinguishable as those reed mats. Every Tlaloc, for example, looks exactly like every Tlaloc that has been sculptured on Xaltócan since our fathers' fathers' fathers were carving them."

I said, "Then they must be what the priests of Tlaloc want."

"Nínotlancuícui in tlamacázque," growled Tlatli. "I pick my teeth at the priests." He could be as stolid and immovable as any stone figure. "I intend to do sculptures different from all that have ever been done before. And no two, even of my own, will be alike. But all will be so recognizably my work that people will exclaim, 'Ayyo, a statue by Tlatli!' I will not even have to sign them with my falcon symbol."

"You want to do a work as fine as the Sun Stone," I suggested.

"Finer than the Sun Stone," he said stubbornly. "I pick my teeth at the Sun Stone." And I thought that audacity indeed, for I had seen the Sun Stone.

But our mutual friend Chimáli gazed toward even farther vistas than did Tlatli. He intended so to refine the art of painting that it would be independent of any sculpture underneath. He would be a painter of pictures on panels and murals on walls.

"Oh, I will color Tlatli's lumpy statues for him, if he likes," said Chimáli. "But sculpture requires only flat colors, since its shape and modeling gives the colors light and shade. Also, I am weary of the same old unvarying colors other painters and muralists use. I am trying to mix new kinds of my own: colors that I can modulate in tint and hue so that the colors themselves give an illusion of depth." He made excited gestures, modeling the empty air. "When you see my pictures you will think they have shape and substance, even when they have none, when they have no more dimension than the panel itself."

"But to what purpose?" I asked.

"Of what purpose is the shimmering beauty and form of a hummingbird?" he demanded. "Look. Suppose yourself to be a priest of Tlaloc. Instead of dragging a huge statue of the rain god into a small temple room, and thereby cramping the room even more, the priests of Tlaloc can simply have me paint on a wall a portrait of the god—as I imagine him to be—and with a limitless rain-swept landscape stretching away behind him. The room will seem immeasurably larger than it really is. And *there* is the advantage of thin, flat pictures over gross and bulky sculptures."

"Well," I said to Chimáli, "a shield usually *is* fairly thin and flat." I was making a joke: Chimáli means shield, and Chimáli himself was a lean and lanky boy.

At my friends' ambitious plans and grandiose boasts I smiled indulgently. Or perhaps a little enviously, for they knew what they wanted eventually to be and do, and I did not. My mind had yet conceived no notion of its own, and no god had yet seen fit to send me a sign. I knew only two things for sure. One was that I did *not* want to hew and haul stone from a noisy, dusty, god-menaced quarry. The other was that, whatever career I essayed, I did *not* intend to pursue it on Xaltócan or in any other provincial backwater.

If the gods allowed, I would take my chances in the most challenging but potentially most rewarding place in The One World—in the Uey-Tlatoáni's own capital city, where the competition among ambitious men was most merciless, and where only the worthiest could rise to distinction—in the splendid, the wondrous, the awesome city of Tenochtítlan.

✠

If I did not yet know what my life work would be, I did at least know where, and I had known since my first and only visit there, the visit having been my father's gift to me on my seventh birthday, my naming day.

Prior to that event, my parents, with me in tow, had gone to consult the island's resident tonalpóqui, or knower of the tonálmatl, the traditional naming book. After unfolding the layered pages to the book's full length—it took up most of his room's floor—the old seer gave prolonged and lip-moving scrutiny to its every mention of star patterns and godly doings relevant to the day Seven Flower and the month God Ascending and the year Thirteen Rabbit. Then he nodded, reverently re-

folded the book, accepted his fee—a bolt of fine cotton cloth—
sprinkled me with his special dedicatory water, and proclaimed
my name to be Chicóme-Xochitl Tliléctic-Mixtli, to commemorate the storm that had attended my birth. I would henceforth
formally be known as Seven Flower Dark Cloud, informally
called Mixtli.

I was sufficiently pleased with the name, a manly one, but
I was not much impressed by the ritual of selecting it. Even
at the age of seven, I, Dark Cloud, had some opinions of my
own. I said out loud that anybody could have done it, *I* could
have done it, and quicker and cheaper, at which I was sternly
shushed.

Early on the morning of the momentous birthday, I was
taken to the palace and the Lord Red Heron himself graciously
and ceremoniously received us. He patted me on the head and
said, with paternal good humor, "Another *man* grown to the
glory of Xaltócan, eh?" With his own hand, he drew my name
symbols—the seven dots, the three-petaled flower symbol, the
clay-gray puffball signifying a dark cloud—in the tocayámatl,
the official registry of all the island's inhabitants. My page
would remain there as long as I lived on Xaltócan, to be expunged only if I died or was banished for some monstrous
crime or moved permanently elsewhere. I wonder: for how
long has Seven Flower Dark Cloud's page been gone from that
book?

Ordinarily there would have been a deal of other celebration
on a naming day, as there had been on my sister's: all the
neighbors and our relatives coming with gifts, my mother cooking and serving a grand spread of special foods, the men smoking tubes of picíetl, the old folks getting drunk on octli. But
I did not mind missing all that, for my father had told me,
"A cargo of temple friezes leaves today for Tenochtítlan, and
there is room aboard for you and me. Also, word comes of a
great ceremony to be held in the capital—the celebration of
some new conquest or the like—and *that* will be your name-
day festival, Mixtli." So, after no more than a congratulatory
kiss on the cheek from my mother and my sister, I followed
my father down to the quarries' loading dock.

All our lakes bore a constant traffic of canoes, coming and
going in all directions, like hordes of water striders. Most were

the little one- and two-man acáltin of fowlers or fishermen, made from a single gutted tree trunk and shaped like a bean pod. But others ranged upward in size to the giant sixty-man war canoes, and our freight acáli consisted of eight boats nearly that big, all lashed side by side. Our cargo of the carved lime-stone panels had been carefully piled aboard, each stone wrapped in heavy fiber mats for protection.

With such a load on such an unwieldy craft, we naturally moved very slowly, though my father was one of more than twenty men paddling (or poling, where the water was shallow). Owing to the curving route—southwest through Lake Xaltócan, south into Lake Texcóco, thence southwest again to the city—we had to cover some seven of the distances we called one-long-run, each of which would be approximately equivalent to one of your Spanish leagues. Seven leagues to go, then, and our big scow seldom moved faster than a man can walk. We left the island well before midday, but it was well into the night when we tied up at Tenochtítlan.

For a while, the view was nothing out of the ordinary: the red-tinted lake I knew so well. Then the land closed in on both sides as we slipped through the southern strait, and the water around us gradually paled to a dun color as we emerged into the vast lake of Texcóco. It stretched away so far to the east and south of us that the land yonder was only a dark, toothed smudge on the horizon.

We crept southwest for a time, but Tonatíu the sun was slowly cloaking himself in the radiance of his sleeping gown by the time our oarsmen backed water to bring our clumsy craft to a halt at The Great Dike. That barrier is a double palisade of tree trunks driven into the lake bottom, the space between the parallel rows of logs packed solid with earth and rock fill. Its purpose is to prevent lake waves, whipped up by the east wind, from flooding the low-lying island-city. The Great Dike has gates set into it at intervals, and the dikemen keep those gates open in most weathers. But of course the lake traffic headed for the capital is considerable, so our freighter had to wait a while in line before it could edge through the opening.

As it did so, Tonatíu drew the dark covers of night over his bed, and the sky went purple. The mountains to the west, directly ahead of us, looked suddenly as sharply outlined and dimensionless as if they had been cut from black paper. Above them, there was a shy twinkle and then a bold spark of light: After Blossom again assuring us that this was only one more of many nights, not the last and everlasting one.

"Open wide your eyes now, son Mixtli!" called my father from his place at the oars.

As if After Blossom had been a signal fire, a second light appeared, this one low beneath the jagged line of black mountains. Then there came another point of light, and another, and twenties upon twenties more. And thus I saw Tenochtítlan for the first time in my life: not a city of stone towers, rich woodwork, and bright paint, but a city of light. As the lamps and lanterns and candles and torches were lit—in window openings, on the streets, along the canals, on building terraces and cornices and rooftops—the separate pinpoints of light became clusters, the clusters blended to form lines of light, the lines drew the outlines of the city.

The buildings themselves, from that distance, were dark and indistinct of contour, but the lights, *ayyo, the lights!* Yellow, white, red, jacinth, all the various colors of flame—here and there a green or blue one, where some temple's altar fire had been sprinkled with salt or copper filings. And every one of those shining beads and clusters and bands of light shone twice, each having its brilliant reflection in the lake. Even the stone causeways that vault from the island to the mainland, even those wore lanterns on posts at intervals along their reach across the water. From our acáli, I could see only the two causeways going north and south from the city. Each looked like a slender bright-jeweled chain across the throat of night, with the city displayed between them, a splendid bright-jeweled pendant on the night's bosom.

"Tenochtítlan, Cem-Anáhuac Tlali Yolóco," murmured my father. "It is truly The Heart and Center of the One World." I had been so transfixed with enchantment that I had not noticed him join me at the forward edge of our freighter. "Look long, son Mixtli. You may experience this wonder and many other wonders more than once. But, of first times, there is always and forever only one."

Without blinking or moving my eyes from the splendor we were all too slowly approaching, I lay prone on a fiber mat and stared and stared until, I am ashamed to say, my eyelids closed of themselves and I fell asleep. I have no recollection of what must have been considerable noise and bustle and commotion when we landed, nor of my father's carrying me to a nearby inn for boatmen, where we stayed the night.

I awoke on a pallet on the floor of an unremarkable room, where my father and a few other men lay still snoring on pallets of their own. Realizing that we were in an inn, and where that inn *was*, I leapt to lean out the window opening—and for a moment felt dizzy at seeing my altitude above the stone pavement below. It was the first time I had ever been inside a building atop a building. Or that is what I thought it was, until my father later showed me, from the outside, that our room was on the upper floor of the inn.

I lifted my eyes to the city beyond the dockside area. It shone, it pulsated, it glowed white in the early sunlight. It made me proud of my own home island, because what buildings were not constructed of white limestone were plastered white with gesso, and I knew that most of the material had come from Xaltócan. Of course the buildings were frescoed and inlaid with bands and panels of vividly colored paints and mosaics, but the dominant effect was of a city so white, so nearly silver, that it almost hurt my eyes.

The lights of the night before were all extinguished now. Only a still-smoldering temple fire somewhere sent a trail of smoke into the sky. But now I saw a new marvel: from the top of every roof, every temple, every palace in the city, from every highest eminence projected a flagpole, and from every staff flew a banner. They were not squared or triangular like battle ensigns; they were pennants many times longer than they were broad. And they were all white, except for the colored insignia they bore. Some of those I recognized—that of the city itself, of the Revered Speaker Axayácatl, of some gods— but others were unfamiliar to me: the symbols of local nobles and special city gods, I supposed.

The flags of your white men are always swatches of cloth, often impressive in their elaborate blazonings, but still mere rags which either hang limp on their staffs or flutter and snap peevishly like a country woman's washing hung to dry on cactus spines. By contrast, those incredibly long banners of Tenochtítlan were woven of feathers—feathers from which the quills had been removed and only the lightest down used for the weaving. They were not painted or dyed. The flags were intricately woven of the feathers' natural colors: egret feathers for the white grounds of the flags, and for the designs the various reds of macaws and cardinals and parakeets, the various blues of jays and herons, the yellows of toucans and tanagers. *Ayyo*, I tell you true, I kiss the earth, there were all the colors and iridescences that can come only from living nature, not from man-mixed paint pots.

But most marvelous, those banners did not sag or flap, they floated. There was no wind that morning. Just the movement of people on the streets and acáltin in the canals stirred enough air current to support those tremendous but almost weightless pennants. Like great birds unwilling to fly away, content to drift dreamily, the banners hung full-spread on the air. The thousands of feather banners undulated gently, soundlessly, magically, over all the towers and pinnacles of that magic island-city.

By daring to lean perilously far out the window opening, I could see, away to the southeast, the two volcano peaks called Popocatépetl and Ixtaccíuatl, The Incense-Burning Mountain and The White Woman. Though it was the start of the dry season and the days were warm, both the mountains were capped with white—the first snow I had ever seen—and the smoldering incense deep inside Popocatépetl wafted a blue plume of smoke that floated over him as lazily as the feather banners floated over Tenochtítlan. I hurried from the window to wake my father. He must have been weary and wanting sleep, but he arose without complaint, with a smile of understanding at my eagerness to be out and away.

The unloading and delivery of our barge's cargo being the responsibility of its freightmaster, my father and I had the day to ourselves. He had one errand—to make some purchase my mother had ordered; I forget what—so we first wended our way northward into Tlaltelólco.

As you know, reverend friars, that portion of the island— what you now call Santiago—is separated from this southern part only by a broad canal crossed by several bridges. But

Tlaltelólco was for many years an independent city, with its own ruler, and it brashly kept trying to outdo Tenochtítlan as chief city of the Mexíca. Tlaltelólco's delusions of superiority were for a long time humorously tolerated by our Revered Speakers. But when that city's late ruler Moquíhuix had the effrontery to build a temple pyramid higher than any in the four quarters of Tenochtítlan, the Uey-Tlatoáni Axayácatl was justifiably annoyed. He ordered his sorcerers to harass that now intolerable neighbor.

If the stories are true, a carved stone face on one wall of Moquíhuix's throne room suddenly spoke to him. The remark was so insulting to his manhood that Moquíhuix snatched up a war club and pulverized the carving. Then, when he went to bed with his First Lady, the lips of her tipíli parts also spoke to him, impugning his virility. Those occurrences, besides making Moquíhuix impotent even with his concubines, much affrighted him, but still he would not cede allegiance to the Revered Speaker. So, earlier in that same year in which I made my naming-day visit, Axayácatl had taken Tlaltelólco by force of arms. He himself, Axayácatl, personally threw Moquíhuix off the top of his upstart pyramid and dashed out his brains. And, just those few months later, by the time my father and I saw Tlaltelólco—though it was still a fine city of temples and palaces and pyramids—it was satisfied to be the fifth "quarter" of Tenochtítlan, the city's marketplace appendage.

Its immense open market area seemed to me to be as big as our whole island of Xaltócan, and richer, and more full of people, and far noisier. Walkway aisles separated the area into squares where the merchants laid out their wares on benches or groundcloths, and every square or a square of squares was allotted to a different kind of merchandise. There were sections for goldsmiths and silversmiths, for feather workers, for sellers of vegetables and condiments, of meat and live animals, of cloth and leather goods, of slaves and dogs, of pottery and copperware, of medicines and cosmetics, of rope and cord and thread, of raucous birds and monkeys and other pets. Ah, well, that market has been restored, and you have doubtless seen it. Though my father and I got there early in the morning, the place was already thronged with customers. Most were macehuáltin like us, but there were lords and ladies too, imperiously pointing at the wares they wanted and leaving the haggling of price to their accompanying servants.

We were fortunate in arriving early, or at least I was, for there was one stall in the market which sold a commodity so perishable that it would be gone before midmorning, the most distinctive delicacy among all the foods for sale. It was snow. It was brought the ten one-long-runs from the crest of Ixtaccíuatl, by relays of swift-messengers racing through the cool of the night, and the merchant kept it in thick clay jars under heaps of fiber mats. One serving of it cost twenty cacao beans. That was an entire day's wage for the average workman anywhere in the Mexíca nation. For four hundred beans you could buy a passably strong and healthy slave for life. So snow was more expensive, by weight, than anything else in the Tlaltelólco market, even the most costly jewelry of the goldsmiths' stalls. Few but the nobles could afford a taste of that rare refreshment. Nevertheless, said the snow man, he always sold out his morning's supply before it melted.

My father made a token grumble. "I remember the Hard Times. In the year One Rabbit, the sky snowed snow for six days in a row. Snow was not just free for the taking, it was a calamity." But of course he relented and said to the vendor, who could hardly have cared less, "Well, since it is the boy's naming day . . ."

He unslung his shoulder bag and counted out the twenty cacao beans. The merchant examined each of them to make sure it was not a carved wood counterfeit or a hollowed-out bean weighted with dirt. Then he uncovered one of his jars, scooped out a spoonful of the precious delicacy, patted it into a cone made of a curled leaf, poured over it a dollop of some sweet syrup, and handed it to me.

I took a greedy bite and nearly dropped it, so surprised was I at its coldness. It made my lower teeth and my forehead ache, but it was the most delicious thing I had eaten in my young life. I held it out for my father to taste. He lapped it once with his tongue, and obviously savored it as much as I did, but pretended he wanted no more. "Do not bite it, Mixtli," he said. "Lick it so it will last longer."

When he had bought whatever it was my mother wanted and had sent a porter carrying it to our boat, he and I went south again toward the center of the city. Although many of the ordinary buildings of Tenochtítlan were two and even three floors tall—and most of them made even taller for being set on pillars to avoid dampness—the island itself is nowhere more than two men's height above the waters of Lake Texcóco. So there were in those days almost as many canals as streets cutting up and down and across the city. In places a canal and a street ran side by side; the people walking could converse with the people afloat. At some corners we would see crowds of people bustling back and forth in front of us; at others we would see canoes gliding past. Some of those were passenger craft for hire, to whisk busy persons about the city more rapidly than they could walk. Others were the private acáltin of nobles, and those were much painted and decorated, and held awnings aloft to ward off the sun. The streets were of hard-packed smooth clay surfacing; the canals had masonry banks. In the many places where a canal's waters were almost at street level, its footbridges could be swiveled to one side while a boat passed.

Just as the network of canals made Lake Texcóco practically a part of the city, so did the three main avenues make the city part of the mainland. Where those broad streets left the island they became wide stone causeways, along which a man could walk to any of five different cities on the mainland to the north, west, and south. There was another span which was not a walkway but an aqueduct. It supported a trough of curved tiles, wider and deeper than a man's two arms could stretch, and this still brings to the city sweet water from the spring of Chapultépec on the mainland to the southwest.

Since all the roads of the land and all the water routes of the lakes converged here at Tenochtítlan, my father and I watched a constant parade of the commerce of the Mexíca nation, and of other nations as well. Everywhere about us were porters trudging under the weight of loads heaped on their backs and supported by forehead tumplines. Everywhere there were canoes of all sizes, piled high with produce going to and from the Tlaltelólco market, or the tribute from subordinate peoples going to the palaces, the treasury, the national warehouses.

Just the multicolored baskets of fruit would give an idea of the extent of the trade. There were guavas and custard apples from the Otomí lands to the north, pineapples from the Totonáca lands on the eastern sea, yellow papayas from Michihuácan to the west, red papayas from Chiapán far to the south, and from the nearer-south Tzapotéca lands the tzapótin marmalade plums which gave that region its name.

Also from the Tzapotéca country came bags of the dried little insects which yield the several brilliant red dyes. From nearby Xochimílco came flowers and plants of more kinds than I could believe existed. From the far southern jungles came cages full of colorful birds, or bales of their feathers. From the Hot Lands both east and west came bags of cacao for the making of chocolate, and the black orchid pods that make vanilla. From the southeastern coastland of the Olméca came the product which gave that people their name: óli, strips of elastic gum to be braided into the hard balls used in our game of tlachtli. Even the rival nation of Texcála, perennial enemy of us Mexíca, sent its precious copáli, the aromatic resin for making perfumes and incense.

From everywhere came packs and panniers of maize and beans and cotton; and bundles of squawking live huaxolóme (the big, black, red-wattled birds you call gallipavos) and baskets of their eggs; and cages of the barkless, hairless, edible techíchi dogs; and haunches of deer and rabbit and boar venison; and jars of the clear sweet-water sap of the maguey plant, or the thicker white fermentation of that juice, the drunk-making drink called octli. . . .

My father was pointing out to me all those things, and telling me their names, when a voice interrupted him: "For just two cacao beans, my lord, I will tell of the roads and the days that lie beyond your son Mixtli's name day."

My father turned. At his elbow, and not much taller than his elbow, stood a man who himself looked rather like a cacao bean. He wore a tattered and dirty loincloth, and his skin was the color of cacao: a brown so dark it was almost purple. His face was creased and wrinkled like the bean. He might have been much taller at some time, but he had become bent and crouched and shrunken with an age no one could have estimated. Come to think of it, he must have looked much as I do now. He held out one monkey hand, palm up, and said again, "Only two beans, my lord."

My father shook his head and said politely, "To learn of the future, I go to a far-seer."

"Did you ever visit one of those seers," the bent man asked, "and have him recognize you instantly as a master quarrier from Xaltócan?"

My father looked surprised and blurted, "You *are* a seer. You do have the vision. Then why—?"

"Why do I go about in rags with my hand out? Because I tell the truth, and people little value the truth. The seers eat the sacred mushrooms and dream dreams for you, because they can charge more for dreams. My lord, there is lime dust ingrained in your knuckles, but your palms are not callused by a laborer's hammer or a sculptor's chisel. You see? The truth is so cheap I can even give it away."

I laughed and so did my father, who said, "You are an amusing old trickster. But we have much to do elsewhere—"

"Wait," said the man insistently. He bent down to peer into my eyes, and he did not have to bend far. I stared straight back at him.

It could be assumed that the mendicant old fraud had been lurking near us when my father bought me the flavored snow, and had overheard the mention of my significant seventh birthday, and had taken us for spendthrift rustics in the big city, easily to be gulled. But much later, when events made me strain to recall the exact words he spoke...

He searched my eyes and murmured, "Any seer can look far along the roads and the days. Even if he sees something that will truly come to pass, it is safely remote in distance and time, it neither avails nor threatens the seer himself. But this boy's tanáli is to look closely at the things and doings of this world, and see them near and plain, and know them for what they signify."

He stood up. "It will seem at first a handicap, boy, but that kind of near-seeing could make you discern truths the far-seers overlook. If you were to take advantage of the talent, it could make you rich and great."

My father sighed patiently and reached into his bag.

"No, no," the man said to him. "I do not prophesy riches or fame for your son. I do not promise him the hand of a beautiful princess or the founding of a distinguished lineage.

The boy Mixtli will see the truth, yes. Unfortunately, he will also *tell* the truth he sees. And that more often brings calumny than reward. For such an ambiguous prediction, my lord, I ask no gratuity."

"Take this anyway," said my father, pressing on him a single cacao bean. "Just do not predict anything more for us, old man."

In the center of the city there was little commercial traffic, but all the citizens not occupied with urgent business were beginning to congregate in the grand plaza for the ceremony of which my father had heard. He asked some passerby what it was to be, and the man said, "Why, the dedication of the Sun Stone, of course, to celebrate the annexation of Tlaltelólco." Most of the people gathered were commoners like ourselves, but there were also enough pípiltin there to have populated a sizable city of nobody but nobles. Anyway, my father and I had arrived early on purpose. Although there were already more people in the plaza than there are hairs on a rabbit, they nowhere near filled the vast area. We had room to move about and view the various sights to be seen.

In those days, Tenochtítlan's central plaza—In Cem-Anáhuac Yoyótli, The Heart of the One World—was not of the mind-stunning splendor I would see on later visits. The Snake Wall had not yet been built to enclose the area. The Revered Speaker Axayácatl was still living in the palace of his late father Motecuzóma, while a new one was being built for him diagonally across the plaza. The new Great Pyramid, begun by that First Motecuzóma, was still unfinished. Its sloping stone walls and serpent-banistered staircases ended well above our heads, and from inside could be seen poking the top of the earlier, smaller pyramid that was being thus enclosed and enlarged.

But the plaza was already awesome enough to a country boy like me. My father told me that he had once crossed it in a straight line and paced it off, placing foot before foot, and that it measured almost exactly six hundred of his feet. That whole immense space—some six hundred man's-feet from north to south and from east to west—was paved with marble, a stone whiter even than Xaltócan's limestone, and it was polished as smooth and shiny as a tezcatl mirror. Many people there that day, if their sandals were soled with one of the more slippery kinds of leather, had to take them off and walk barefoot.

The city's three broadest avenues, each wide enough for twenty men to walk abreast, began there at the plaza and led out of it, north, west, and south, to become the three equally wide causeways going all the way to the mainland. The plaza itself was not then so full of temples and altars and monuments as it would be in later years. But there were already modest teocáltin containing statues of the chief gods. There was already the elaborate rack on which were displayed the skulls of the more distinguished xochimíque who had been sacrificed to one or another of those gods. There was the Revered Speaker's private ball court in which were played special ritual games of tlachtli.

There was also The House of Song, which contained comfortable quarters and practice studios for those foremost musicians, singers, and dancers who performed at religious festivals in the plaza. The House of Song was not, like all the other edifices on the plaza, entirely obliterated with the rest of the city. It was restored and is now, until your cathedral Church of San Francisco shall be completed, your Lord Bishop's temporary diocesan headquarters and residence. It is in one of the rooms of that House of Song that we now sit, my lord scribes.

My father correctly supposed that a seven-year-old would hardly be enraptured by religious or architectural landmarks, so he took me to the sprawling building at the southeast corner of the plaza. That housed the Uey-Tlatoáni's collection of wild animals and birds, and it too was not yet so extensive as it would be in later years. It had been begun by the late Motecuzóma, whose notion was to put on public display a specimen of the land and air creatures to be found in all the parts of all these lands. The building was divided into countless rooms— some mere cubicles, some large chambers—and troughs from a nearby canal kept a continuous flow of water flushing out the rooms' waste matter. Each room opened onto the viewers' passageway, but was separated from it by netting or in some cases stout wooden bars. There was an individual room for each creature, or for those several kinds of creatures that could live together amicably.

"Do they always make so much noise?" I shouted to my father, over the roaring and howling and screeching.

"I do not know," he said. "But right now some of them are hungry, because they have deliberately not been fed for some time. There will be sacrifices at the ceremony, and the remains will be disposed of here, as meat for the jaguar and cuguar cats, and the coyótin wolves and the tzopilótin vultures."

I was eyeing the largest animal native to our lands—the ugly and bulky and sluggish tapir; it waggled its prehensile snout at me—when a familiar voice said, "Master quarrier, why do you not show the boy the tequáni hall?"

It was the bent brown man we had earlier met in the street. My father gave him an exasperated look and demanded, "Are you following us, old nuisance?"

The man shrugged. "I merely drag my ancient bones here to see the Sun Stone dedication." Then he gestured to a closed door at the far end of the passage and said to me, "In there, my boy, are sights indeed. Human animals far more interesting than these mere brutes. A tlacaztáli woman, for instance. Do you know what a tlacaztáli is? A person dead white all over, skin and hair and all, except for her eyes, which are pink. And there is a dwarf with only half a head, who eats—"

"Hush!" my father said sternly. "This is a day for the boy to enjoy. I will not sicken him with the sight of those pitiful freaks."

"Ah, well," said the old man. "Some do enjoy viewing the deformed and the mutilated." His eyes glittered at me. "But they will still be there, young Mixtli, when you are grown mature and superior enough to mock and tease them. I daresay there will be even more curiosities in the tequáni hall by then, no doubt even more entertaining and edifying to you."

"Will you be silent?" bellowed my father.

"Pardon, my lord," said the hunched old man, hunching himself even smaller. "Let me make amends for my impertinence. It is almost midday and the ceremony will soon begin. If we go now and get good places, perhaps I can explain to you and the boy some things you might not otherwise understand."

The plaza was now full to overflowing, and the people were shoulder to shoulder. We would never have got anywhere close to the Sun Stone, except that more and more nobles were now haughtily arriving at the last moment, borne in gilded and upholstered litter chairs. The crowds of commoners and lower classes parted without a murmur to let them through, and the brown man audaciously eeled along behind them, with us behind him, until we were almost as far forward as the front ranks of real notables. I would still have been hemmed in without a view, but my father hoisted me to one shoulder. He looked down at our guide and said, "I can lift you up too, old man."

"I thank you for your thoughtfulness, my lord," said that one, half smiling, "but I am heavier than I look."

The focus of all eyes was the Sun Stone, set for the occasion on a terrace between the two broad staircases of the unfinished Great Pyramid. But it was shrouded from our sight with a mantle of shining white cotton. So I occupied myself with admiring the arriving nobles, for their litter chairs and their costumes were something to behold. The men and women alike wore mantles entirely woven of feathers, some varicolored, some of just one coruscating hue. The ladies' hair was tinted purple, as was customary on such a day, and they held their hands high to display the bangled and festooned rings on their fingers. But the lords wore many more ornaments than their ladies. All had diadems or tassels of gold and rich feathers on their heads. Some wore gold medallions on neck chains, gold bracelets and armlets and anklets. Others wore ornate plugs of gold or jewels piercing earlobes or nostrils or lower lips, or all of those.

"Here comes the High Treasurer," said our guide. "Ciuacóatl, the Snake Woman, second in command to the Revered Speaker himself."

I looked, eager to see a snake woman, which I assumed must be a creature like those "human animals" which I had not been allowed to look at. But it was just another pili, and a man at that, distinguished only for being even more gorgeously attired than most of the other nobles. The labret he wore was so heavy that it dragged his lower lip down in a pout. But it was a cunning labret: a miniature serpent of gold, so fashioned that it wriggled and flickered its tiny tongue in and out as the Lord Treasurer bobbed along in his chair.

Our guide laughed at me; he had seen my disappointment. "The Snake Woman is merely a title, boy, not a description," he said. "Every High Treasurer has always been called Ciuacóatl, though probably none of them could tell you why. My own theory is that it is because both snakes and women coil tight around any treasures they may hold."

Then the crowd in the plaza, which had been murmurous, quieted all at once; the Uey-Tlatoáni himself had appeared. He had somehow arrived unseen or had been hidden somewhere beforehand, for now he suddenly stood beside the veiled Sun Stone. Axayácatl's visage was obscured by labret, nose plug, and ear plugs, and shadowed by the sunburst crown of scarlet macaw plumes that arched completely over his head from shoulder to shoulder. Not much of the rest of his body was visible either. His mantle of gold and green parrot feathers fell all the way to his feet. His chest bore a large and intricately worked medallion, his loincloth was of rich red leather, on his feet he wore sandals apparently of solid gold, laced as high as his knees with gilded straps.

By custom, all of us in the plaza should have greeted him with the tlalqualíztli: the gesture of kneeling, touching a finger to the earth and then to our lips. But there was simply no room for that; the crowd made a sort of loud sizzle of combined kissing sounds. The Revered Speaker Axayácatl returned the greeting silently, nodding the spectacular scarlet feather crown and raising aloft his mahogany and gold staff of office.

He was surrounded by a hoard of priests who, with their filthy black garments, their dirt-encrusted black faces, and their blood-matted long hair, made a somber contrast to Axayácatl's sartorial flamboyance. The Revered Speaker explained to us the significance of the Sun Stone, while the priests chanted prayers and invocations every time he paused for breath. I cannot now remember Axayácatl's words, and probably did not understand them all at the time. But the gist was this. While the Sun Stone actually pictured the sun Tonatíu, all honor paid to it would be shared with Tenochtítlan's chief god Huitzilopóchtli, Southern Hummingbird.

I have already told how our gods could wear different aspects and names. Well, Tonatíu *was* the sun, and the sun is indispensable, since all life on earth would perish without him. We of Xaltócan and the peoples of many other communities were satisfied to worship him *as* the sun. However, it seemed obvious that the sun required nourishment to keep him strong, encouragement to keep him at his daily labors—and what could we give him more vitalizing and inspiriting than what he gave us? That is to say, human life itself. Hence the kindly sun god had the other aspect of the ferocious war god Huitzilopóchtli, who led us Mexíca in all our battle forays to procure prisoners for that necessary sacrifice. It was in the stern guise of Huitzilopóchtli that he was most revered here in Tenochtítlan, because it was here that all our wars were planned and declared and the warriors mustered. Under yet another name, Tezcatlipóca, Smoldering Mirror, the sun was the chief god of our neighbor nation of the Acólhua. And I have come to suspect that innumerable other nations I have never visited—even nations beyond the sea across which you Spaniards came—must likewise worship that selfsame sun god, only calling him by some other name, according as they see him smile or frown.

While the Uey-Tlatoáni went on speaking, and the priests kept chanting in counterpoint, and a number of musicians began to play on flutes, notched bones, and skin drums, my father and I were privately getting the history of the Sun Stone from our cacao-brown old guide.

"Southeast of here is the country of the Chalca. When the late Motecuzóma made a vassal nation of it, twenty and two years ago, the Chalca were of course obliged to make a noteworthy tribute offering to the victorious Mexíca. Two young Chalca brothers volunteered to make a monumental sculpture apiece, to be placed here at The Heart of the One World. They chose similar stones, but different subjects, and they worked apart, and no one but each brother ever saw what he carved."

"Their wives sneaked a look, surely," said my father, who had that sort of wife.

"No one ever got a look," the old man repeated, "during all those twenty and two years they worked to sculpture and paint the stones—in which time they grew middle-aged and Motecuzóma went to the afterworld. Then they muffled their finished works separately in swathings of fiber mats, and the lord of the Chalca conscripted perhaps one thousand sturdy porters to haul the stones here to the capital."

He waved toward the still-shrouded object on the terrace above us. "As you see, the Sun Stone is immense: more than twice the height of two men—and ponderously heavy: the weight of three hundred and twenty men together. The other stone was about the same. They were brought over rough trails and no trails at all. They were rolled on log rollers, dragged on wooden skids, ferried over rivers on mighty rafts. Just think of the labor and the sweat and the broken bones, and the many men who fell dead when they could no longer stand the pull or the lashing whips of the overseers."

"Where is the other stone?" I asked, but was ignored.

"At last they came to the lakes of Chalco and Xochimílco, which they crossed on rafts, to the major causeway running north to Tenochtítlan. From there it was a broad way and a straight one, no more than two one-long-runs to the plaza here. The artists sighed with relief. They had worked so hard, so many other men had worked so hard, but those monuments were within sight of their destination. . . ."

The crowd around us made a noise. The twenty or so men whose lifeblood would that day consecrate the Sun Stone were in line, and the first of them was mounting the pyramid steps. He appeared to be no captured enemy warrior, just a stocky man about my father's age, wearing only a clean white loin-cloth, looking haggard and unhappy, but he went willingly, unbound and without any guards impelling him. There on the terrace he stood and looked stolidly out over the crowd, while the priests swung their smoking censers and did ritual things with their hands and staffs. Then one priest took hold of the xochimíqui, gently turned him, and helped him lie back on a block in front of the veiled monument. The block was a single knee-high stone, shaped rather like a miniature pyramid, so, when the man lay propped on it, his body arched and his chest thrust upward as if eager for the blade.

He lay lengthwise to our view, his arms and legs held by four assistant priests, and behind him stood the chief priest, the executioner, holding the wide, almost trowel-shaped black obsidian knife. Before the priest could move, the pinioned man raised his dangling head and said something. There were other words among those on the terrace, then the priest handed his blade to Axayácatl. The crowd made noises of surprise and puzzlement. That particular victim, for some reason, was to be granted the high honor of being dispatched by the Uey-Tlatoáni himself.

Axayácatl did not hesitate or fumble. As expertly as any priest, he stabbed the knife point into the man's chest on the left side, just under the nipple and between two ribs, then made a slash with the knife edge, then rotated the wide blade sideways to separate the ribs and open the wound wider. With his other hand he reached into the wet red opening, seized the un-scratched and still-beating heart, and tore it loose from its enlacement of blood vessels. Not until then did the xochimíqui utter his first sound of pain—a blubbering sob—and the last sound of his life.

As the Revered Speaker held high the glistening, dripping, purple-red object, a priest somewhere jerked some hidden string, the shroud fell away from the Sun Stone, and the crowd gave a concerted "Ay-y-yo-o!" of admiration. Axayácatl turned, reached up, and ground the victim's heart into the very center of the circular stone, into the mouth of Tonatíu carved there. He mashed and rubbed the heart until it was only a smear on the stone and nothing was left in his hand. I have been told by priests that a heart's donor usually lived long enough to see what became of his heart. But that one could not have seen much. When Axayácatl was finished, the blood and ground meat were scarcely visible, because the carved sun face was already painted a color very like that of heart's blood.

"That was cleanly done," said the bent man at my father's side. "I have often seen a heart go on beating so vigorously that it jumps from the executioner's fingers. But I think this particular heart had already been broken."

Now the xochimíqui lay unmoving, except that his skin twitched here and there, like the skin of a dog tormented by flies. The priests rolled his carcass from the stone and let it tumble unceremoniously off the terrace, while a second victim plodded up the stair. Axayácatl honored no more of the xo-chimíque, but left the rest to the priests. As the procession went on—each man's extracted heart being used to anoint the Sun Stone—I peered closely at the massive object, so I might de-scribe it to my friend Tlatli, who, even way back then, had begun practicing to be a sculptor by whittling bits of wood into doll figures.

Yyo ayyo, reverend friars, if you could but have seen the Sun Stone! Your faces show disapproval of the dedication ceremony, but if you had ever once seen the stone, you would know it to have been worth all its cost in toil and years and human lives.

The carving alone was beyond belief, for that was porphyry, a stone as hard as granite. In the center was the face of Tonatíu, eyes staring, mouth agape, and on either side of his head were claws grasping the human hearts which were his provender. Surrounding that were the symbols of the four eras of the world which preceded the era in which we now live, and a circle comprising the symbols of our twenty day-names, and a circle of the alternating symbols of jadestone and turquoise, the gems held in highest esteem of all found in our lands. Around that, again, a circle of the day's sun rays alternating with the night's stars. And, girdling the whole, two sculptures of the Fire Serpent of Time, their tails at the top of the stone, their bodies making the round of it, and their heads meeting at the bottom. In one stone, that one artist had captured all of our universe, all of our time.

It was painted in bold colors, meticulously applied on those precise places where each color belonged. Yet the painter's real skill was most evident where no paint at all had been put on. Porphyry is a stone that holds fragments of mica, feldspar, and quartz. Wherever one of those bits of crystalline rock was embedded, the artist had left it unpainted. So, as the Sun Stone stood in the midday radiance of Tonatíu himself, those tiny clear jewels flashed at us pure sunlight from among the glowing colors. The entire great object seemed not so much colored as *lighted from within*. But I suppose you would have to have seen it in all its original glory to believe it. Or through the clearer eyes and in the clearer light I enjoyed in those days. Or perhaps with the mind of an impressionable and still-benighted little heathen boy...

Anyway, I turned my attention from the stone to our guide, who was continuing his interrupted history of the thing's painful progress hither:

"The causeway had never before known such a weight. The

two brothers' two mighty stones were moving along on their log rollers, one behind the other, when the road buckled under the leading burden, and that wrapped stone went to the bottom of Lake Texcóco. The porters rolling the second—this Sun Stone here—stopped it just short of the brink of the broken causeway. It was lowered onto a raft again and floated around the island to the plaza here. Thus it alone was saved for us to admire today."

"But the other?" asked my father. "After all that work spent, could not a little more have been expended?"

"Oh, it was, my lord. The most experienced divers went down time after time. But the floor of Lake Texcóco is a soft and maybe bottomless ooze. The divers prodded with long poles, but they never located it. The stone, whatever it was, must have gone down edge on."

"Whatever it was?" echoed my father.

"No one but its artist ever laid eyes on it. No one ever will. It may have been more magnificent even than that"—the old man indicated the Sun Stone—"but we will never know."

"Will not the artist tell?" I asked.

"He never did."

I persisted, "Well, could he not do it over again?" A task of twenty and two years seemed rather less to me then than it would now.

"Perhaps he could, but he never will. He took the disaster as evidence of his tonáli, as a sign that the gods had spurned his offering. That was he whom the Revered Speaker just now honored with the Flowery Death at his own hand. The rejected artist gave himself to be the first sacrifice to the Sun Stone."

"To his brother's work," my father murmured. "Meanwhile, what of the brother?"

"He will receive honors and rich gifts and the -tzin to his name," said our guide. "But the whole world will forever wonder, and so will he. Might there not be a work more sublime even than the Sun Stone lying unseen beneath Lake Texcóco?"

In time, indeed, the myth-enhanced unknown came to be more treasured than the tangible reality. The lost sculpture came to be called In Huehuetótetl—The Most Venerable Stone—and the Sun Stone regarded as only a middling substitute. The surviving brother never carved another work. He became an octli drunkard, a pitiful ruin, but he had enough self-respect remaining that, before he brought irredeemable shame to his new and noble title, he too volunteered to participate in a sacrificial ceremony. And when he died the Flowery Death, his heart did not, either, leap from the executioner's hand.

Ah, well, the Sun Stone too has been lost and gone these eight years now, buried under the rubble when The Heart of the One World was demolished by your war boats and cannon balls and battering beams and fire arrows. But perhaps one day your own rebuilt new City of Mexíco will be razed in its turn, and the Sun Stone will be rediscovered shining among the ruins. Even—aquin ixnéntla?—perhaps someday The Most Venerable Stone as well.

My father and I went home again that night, on our composite acáli now loaded with trade goods procured by the freightmaster. You have heard the major and most memorable events of that day, that celebration of my seventh birthday and naming day. It was, I think, the most enjoyable of all the birthdays I have passed, and I have passed more than my share.

I am glad I got to see Tenochtítlan when I did, for I never again saw it the same way. I do not mean just because the city grew and changed, or because I came back to it surfeited and no longer impressionable. I mean I literally never saw *anything* so clearly again with my own two eyes.

I have earlier spoken of my being able to discern the chiseled rabbit in the moon, and After Blossom in the twilight sky, and the details of the insignia on Tenochtítlan's feather banners, and the intricacies of the Sun Stone. Within five years after that seventh birthday, I could not have seen After Blossom if some sky god had run a surveyor's string from the star to my eye. Metztli the moon, at his fullest and brightest, became no more than a featureless yellow-white blob, his once sharp circle fuzzing indistinctly into the sky.

In brief, from about the age of seven onward, I began to lose my sight. It made me something of a rarity, and not in any enviable sense. Except for those few born blind, or those who became so from a wound or a disease, almost all our people possess the keen eyesight of eagles and vultures. My decreasingly clear vision was a condition practically unknown among us, and I was ashamed of it, and did not speak of it, and tried to keep it my own hurtful secret. When someone would point and say, "Look there!" I would exclaim, "Ah, yes!" though not knowing whether I should goggle or dodge.

The dimness did not come upon me all at once; it came gradually, but inexorably. By the time I was nine or ten, I could see as clearly as anyone, but only to a distance of perhaps two arms' length. Beyond that, the outline of things began to blur, as if I were seeing them through a transparent but distorting film of water. At a more considerable distance—say, looking from a hilltop across a landscape—all the individual outlines blurred so much that objects mingled and merged, and a landscape was to me no more than an eccentrically patterned blanket of amorphous smears of color. At least, in those years, with a clear visual field of two arms' length, I could move about without falling over things. When bidden to fetch something in one of the rooms of our house, I could find it without having to grope.

But my scope of vision continued to diminish, down to perhaps one arm's length of clarity before I reached my thirteenth birthday, and I could no longer pretend well enough for it to go unnoticed by others. For a time, I suppose my family and friends thought me merely clumsy or slipshod or maybe dimwitted. And at that time, with the perverse vanity of boyhood, I would rather have been thought a lout than a cripple. But it inevitably became obvious to everyone that I was lacking in the one most necessary of the five senses. My family and friends behaved variously toward this suddenly revealed freak among them.

My mother blamed my condition on my father's side of the family. It seems there was once an uncle who, drunk on octli, had reached for another pot of some similarly white liquid, and had swallowed it all before noticing that it was the powerful caustic xocóyatl, used for cleaning and bleaching badly begrimed limestone. He survived and never drank again, but he was blind all the rest of his life, and, according to my mother's theory, that lamentable inheritance had been handed down to me.

My father did no blaming or speculating, but consoled me rather too heartily: "Well, being a master quarrier is close-up work, Mixtli. You will have no trouble peering for the thread-like cracks and crevices."

Those of my own age—and children, like scorpions, stab instinctively, savagely—would cry out to me, "Look there!"

I would squint and say, "Ah, yes."

"That is really something to see, is it not?"

I would squint harder, desperately, and say, "It truly is."

They would burst into laughter and yell derisively, "There is nothing there to see, Tozáni!"

Others, my close friends like Chimáli and Tlatli, would also sometimes blurt out, "Look there!" but they would quickly add, "A swift-messenger comes running toward the Lord Red Heron's palace. He wears the green mantle of good news. There must have been a victorious battle somewhere."

My sister Tzitzitlíni said little, but she contrived to accompany me whenever I had to go any distance or into unfamiliar surroundings. She would take my hand, as if merely making the fond gesture of an older sister, and unobtrusively she would guide me around any obstacles in my path not readily visible.

However, the other children were so many, and they so persistently called me Tozáni, that soon their elders addressed me the same—unthinkingly, not unkindly—and eventually so did everybody but my mother, father, and sister. Even when I had adapted to my handicap, and managed no longer to be so clumsy, and other people had little cause to notice my short-sightedness, by then the sobriquet had stuck. I thought that my given name of Mixtli, meaning Cloud, ironically suited me better than before, but Tozáni I became.

The tozáni is the little animal you call the mole, which prefers to spend its life underground, in the dark. When it infrequently emerges, it is blinded by the mere light of day, and squints its tiny eyes closed. It neither sees nor cares to see.

I cared very much, and for a long time in my young life I went pitying myself. I would never become a tlachtli ball player, to hope for the high honor of someday playing in the

Revered Speaker's own court a ritual game dedicated to the gods. If I became a warrior, I could never hope to win knight-hood. Indeed, I would be god-protected if I had a life expectancy of as much as one day in combat. As for earning a living, supporting a family of my own . . . well, a quarrier I would *not* become, but of what other labor was I capable?

I toyed wistfully with the possibility of becoming some kind of traveling worker. That could take me eventually south to the far land of the Maya, and I had heard that the Maya physicians knew miraculous cures for even the most hopeless eye ailments. Perhaps there I could be healed, and could come home again in bright-eyed triumph as an unbeatable tlachtli goalsman, or a battle hero, or even a knight of one of the three orders.

But then the encroaching dimness seemed to slow its approach and stop at my arm's length. It did not, really, but after those early years its further progress was less perceptible. To-day, with the unaided eye, I cannot make out my wife's face farther than a handspan from my own. It matters little, now that I am old, but it mattered much when I was young.

Nevertheless, slowly I resigned myself and adapted myself to my limitations. That strange man in Tenochtítlan had spoken aright when he predicted that my tonáli was to look close, to see things near and plain. Of necessity I slowed my pace, I was often still, I scrutinized instead of scanning. When others hurried, I waited. When others rushed, I moved with delib-eration. I learned to differentiate between purposeful movement and mere motion, between action and mere activity. Where others, impatient, saw a village, I saw its people. Where others saw people, I saw persons. Where others glimpsed a stranger and nodded and hastened on, I made sure to see him close, and later I could draw a picture of his every lineament, so that even an accomplished artist like Chimáli would exclaim, "Why, Mole, you have caught the man, and to the life!"

I began to notice things that I think escape most people, keen-eyed though they may be. Did *you* ever notice, my lord scribes, that the maize grows faster at night than in the day? Did you ever notice that every ear of maize has an even number of rows of kernels? Or almost every ear. But to find one with an odd number of rows is a happenstance far more rare than to find a clover leaf with four petals. Did you ever notice that no two fingers—no two of your own—no two in the entire human race, if my studies are any proof—have precisely the same pattern of whorls and arches infinitesimally etched on the balls of the fingertips? If you do not believe me, compare your own. Compare each other's. I will wait.

Oh, I know there was no significance or profit in my noticing such things. They were but trivial details on which to exercise my new penchant for looking close and examining with care. But that necessity-made-virtue, combined with my aptitude for copying exactly the things I could see, finally led me to take an interest in our people's picture writing. There was no school on Xaltócan that taught such an abstruse subject, but I sought out every scrap of writing I could find, and studied it intently and struggled to read its meaning.

The numerical writing, I think, anyone could easily make out. The shell symbol for zero, the dots or fingers for ones, the flags for twenties, the little trees for hundreds. But I remember the thrill when one day I first puzzled out a pictured *word*.

My father took me along on some business visit to the governor and, to keep me occupied while they talked in some private chamber, the governor let me sit in his entry hall and look at the register of all his subjects. I turned first to my own page. Seven dots, flower symbol, gray cloud. Then I ever so carefully moved to other pages. Some of the names were as easy to comprehend as my own, simply because I was familiar with them. Not far before my page was that of Chimáli, and of course I recognized his: three fingers, the duck-billed head symbolizing the wind, the two intertwined tendrils representing smoke, rising from a feather-fringed disk—Yei-Ehécatl Pocuía-Chimáli: Three Wind Smoking Shield.

The more frequently repeated drawings were easy to espy. After all, we had only twenty day-names. But I was suddenly struck by the not so immediately evident repetition of elements from Chimáli's name and my own. One page near the back, hence recently drawn, showed six dots, then a shape like a tadpole standing on its head, then that duck-billed symbol, then the three-petaled thing. *I could read it!* I knew whose it was!

Six Rain Wind Flower, the baby sister of Tlatli, who had only last week celebrated her naming birthday.

Somewhat less gingerly now, I turned the stiff folded pages back and forth, looking at the pages on both sides of the pleats, searching for other repetitions and recognizable symbols I could piece together. The governor and my father returned just after I had laboriously worked out another name, or believed I had. With a mixture of timidity and pride I said:

"Excuse me, Lord Red Heron. Would you have the goodness to tell me, am I right, does this page record the name of some person called Two Reed Yellow Eyetooth?"

He looked and said no, it did not. He must have seen my face fall, for he patiently explained:

"It says Two Reed Yellow *Light*, the name of a laundress here in the palace. The Two Reed is obvious. And yellow, coztic, is easy to indicate simply by using that color, as you have divined. But tlanixtélotl, 'light'—or more precisely 'the eye's element'—how does one make a picture of something so insubstantial? Instead, I put a drawing of a tooth, tlanti, to represent not the meaning but the sound of the tlan at the beginning of the word, and then a picture of an eye, ixtelólotl, which serves to make clear the meaning of the whole. You grasp it now? Tlanixtélotl. Light."

I nodded, feeling rather deflated and foolish. There was more to picture writing than just recognizing the drawing of a tooth. In case I had not realized it, the governor made it plain:

"Writing and reading are for those trained in such arts, son of Tepetzálan." And he gave me a man-to-man clap on the shoulder. "They take much learning and much practice, and only the nobility have the leisure for so much study. But I admire your initiative. Whatever occupation you do undertake, young man, you ought to do it well."

I daresay the son of Tepetzálan should have complied with the Lord Red Heron's broad hint, and stuck to the trade of Tepetzálan. Weak-eyed and ill equipped as I was for any more ambitious or venturesome occupations, I could have drudged away an uneventful but never empty-bellied life as a real mole of a quarrier. A life less satisfying, perhaps, than the one I stubbornly persisted in pursuing, but it would have brought me far smoother roads and more tranquil days than I was to know when I went my own way. Right at this moment, my lords, I could be employed in helping to build your City of Mexíco. And, if Red Heron was right in his estimation of my abilities, possibly making of it a better city than your own imported architects and stonemasons are doing.

But let it pass, let it all pass, as I myself let it all pass— heedless of the Lord Red Heron's implied command, heedless of my father's genuine pride in his trade and his attempts to teach it to me, heedless of my mother's carping complaints that I was reaching above my ordained station in life.

For the governor had given me another hint, and one that I could *not* ignore. He had revealed that the picture writing did not always mean what it looked like, but what it sounded like. No more than that. But that was enlightening enough and tantalizing enough to keep me searching out bits of writing—on temple walls, on the island's tribute roll in the palace, on any paper carried by any passing tradesman—and doing my untaught, earnest best to make sense of them.

I even went to the ancient tonalpóqui who had so glibly given me my name, four years before, and asked if I might pore over his venerable naming book when it was not in use. He could not have recoiled more violently if I had asked to use one of his granddaughters as a concubine when she was not otherwise busy. He repulsed me with the information that the art of knowing the tonálmatl was reserved for the descendants of tonalpóque, not for unknown and presumptuous brats. It may have been so. But I will wager that either he remembered my declaring that I could have named myself as well as he had done, or—more likely—he was a frightened old fraud who could no more read the tonálmatl than I could at that time.

Then, one evening, I met a stranger. Chimáli and Tlatli and I and some other boys had been playing together all afternoon, so Tzitzitlíni was not along. On a shore far distant from our village we found a holed and rotting old hulk of an acáli, and got so absorbed in playing boatmen that we were taken by surprise when Tonatíu gave his red-sky warning that he was preparing for bed. We had a long way to walk home, and

Tonatíu hurried to bed faster than we could walk, so the other boys broke into a trot. In daylight I could have kept up with them, but the dusk *and* my blighted vision forced me to move more slowly and pick my way with care. Probably the others never missed me; anyway, they soon outdistanced me.

I came to a crossroads, and there was a stone ench there, I had not passed that way in some time, but now I remembered that the bench bore several incised symbols, and I forgot everything else. I forgot that it was now almost too dark for me even to see the carvings, let alone decipher tham. I forgot why the bench was there. I forgot all the lurking things that might descend on me as the night descended. I even heard an owl hoot somewhere nearby, and paid that omen of danger no attention. There was something there to read, or try to read, and I could not pass by without trying.

The bench was long enough for a man to lie upon, if he could have lain comfortably on the ridges of stone carving. I bent over the marks, and stared at them, and traced them with my fingers as well as my eyes, and moved from one to the next and the next—and nearly sprawled across the lap of a man sitting there. I sprang away as if he had been red-hot to the touch, and stammered an apology:

"M-mixpantzínco. In your august presence . . ."

Politely enough, but wearily, he made the customary reply, "Ximopanólti. At your convenience . . ."

Then we stared at each other for a space. I assume he saw only a slightly grubby, squinting boy of about twelve years old. I could not see him in detail, partly because the night was well upon us now, partly because I had leapt so far away from him. But I could make out that he was a stranger to the island, or at least to me, that his mantle was of good material though travel-stained, that his sandals were worn from long walking, and that his coppery skin was dusty from the road.

"What is your name, boy?" he asked at last.

"Well, they call me Mole—" I began.

"I can believe that, but it is not your name." Before I could put in a word, he asked another question, "What were you doing just now?"

"I was reading, Yanquícatzin." I really do not know what

there was about him, but it made me address him as Lord
Stranger. "I was reading the writing on the bench."

"Indeed?" he said, in what sounded like tired disbelief. "I
would never have taken you for an educated young noble. What
does the writing say, then?"

"It says: From the people of Xaltócan, a resting place for
the Lord Night Wind."

"Someone told you that."

"No, Lord Stranger. Excuse me, but—see?" I moved close
enough to point. "This duck-billed thing here stands for wind."

"It is not a duck bill," the man snapped. "That is the trumpet
through which the god blows the winds."

"Oh? Thank you for telling me, my lord. Anyway, it stands
for ehécatl. And this marking here—all these closed eyelids—
that means yoáli. Yoáli Ehécatl, the Night Wind."

"You really can read?"

"A very little, my lord. Not much."

"Who taught you?"

"No one, Lord Stranger. There is no one on Xaltócan to
teach the art. It is a pity, for I should like to learn more."

"Then you must go elsewhere."

"I suppose so, my lord."

"I suggest you do it now. I tire of being read to. Go elsewhere, boy called Mole."

"Oh. Yes. Of course, Lord Stranger. Mixpantzínco."

"Ximopanólti."

I turned back once for a last look at him. But he was beyond
the range of my short sight, or he was swallowed up in the
dark, or he had simply got up and gone.

I was met at home by a chorus of my father, mother, and
sister expressing a mixture of worry, relief, consternation, and
anger at my having stayed out so long alone in the perilous
dark. But even my mother quieted when I told how I had been
delayed by the inquisitive stranger. She quieted, and she and
my sister looked with wide eyes at my father. He looked with
wide eyes at me.

"You met him," my father said huskily. "You met the god
and he let you go. The god Night Wind."

All through a sleepless night I tried, without much success,
to see the dusty, weary, surly wayfarer as a god. But if he *had*

been Night Wind, then by tradition I was due to get my heart's desire. There was only one problem. Unless wanting to learn to read and write might qualify, I did not know what *was* my heart's desire. Or I did not know until I got it, if that is what I got.

It happened on a day when I was working at the first apprentice job I was given at my father's quarry. It was no onerous work; I had been appointed watchman of the big pit during the time when all the workmen downed tools and went home for their midday meal. Not that there was much risk of human thievery, but if the tools were left unguarded, small wild animals would come to gnaw the tool hafts and handles for the salt the wood had absorbed from the workers' sweat. A single prickly little boar could chew up a whole, hard ebony pry-bar during the men's absence. Fortunately, my mere presence there was sufficient to keep the salt-seeking creatures at bay, for whole swarms of them could have invaded unseen by my mole eyes.

That day, as always, Tzitzitlíni ran out from home to bring me my own midday meal. She kicked off her sandals and sat with me on the sunlit grassy rim of the quarry, chattering gaily while I ate my fare of tiny boned lake whitefish, each rolled and broiled in a tortilla. They had come wrapped in a cloth and were still hot from the fire. My sister looked warm too, I noticed, though the day was cool. Her face was flushed and she kept fanning the square-cut top of her blouse away from her breasts.

The fish rolls had a slight but unusually tart taste. I wondered if Tzitzi instead of our mother had prepared them, and whether she was chattering so volubly just to keep me from teasing her about her apparent lack of cooking skill. But the taste was not disagreeable, and I was hungry, and I felt quite replete when I had finished. Tzitzi suggested that I lie down and digest my meal in comfort; she would keep watch for any intruding prickly little boars.

I stretched out on my back and looked up at the clouds

which once I could see so clear-cut against the sky; now they were but formless white swatches among formless blue swatches. I had got accustomed to that by now. But all at once something more disturbing began to happen to my vision. The white and blue commenced swirling, slowly at first, then more rapidly, as if some god up there had begun to stir the sky with a chocolate beater. Surprised, I started to sit up, but I was suddenly so dizzy that I fell back upon the grass.

I felt uncommonly odd, and I must have made some odd noise, for Tzitzi leaned over me and looked into my face. Addled though I was, I got the impression that she had been *waiting* for something to happen to me. The tip of her tongue was caught between her brilliant white teeth, and her narrowed eyes gave me a look of seeking some sign. Then her lips smiled mischievously, her tongue's tip licked them, and her eyes widened with a light almost of triumph. She remarked on my own eyes, and her voice seemed strangely to come like an echo from far away.

"Your pupils have got so large, my brother." But she still smiled, so I felt no cause for alarm. "Your irises are scarcely brown at all, but almost entirely black. What do you see with those eyes?"

"I see you, my sister," I said, and my voice was thick. "But somehow you look different. You look..."

"Yes?" she prompted.

"You look so beautiful," I said. I could not help saying it.

Like every boy my age, I was expected to disdain and disprize girls—if I even deigned to notice them—and of course one's own sister was more to be disparaged than any other girl. But I would have known Tzitzitlíni to be beautiful even if the fact had not been remarked so often in my hearing by all the adults, women and men alike, who caught their breath at first catching sight of her. No sculptor could have captured the lissome grace of her young body, for stone or clay cannot move, and she gave the illusion of being always in flowing motion even when she was most still. No painter could have mixed the exact golden-fawn color of her skin, or the color of her eyes: doe-brown flecked with gold....

But that day something magical had been added, and that was why I could not have refused to acknowledge her beauty,

even if I had been so inclined. The magic was visible all about
her, an aura like that of the mist of water jewels in the sky
when the sun comes out immediately after a rain.

"There are colors," I said, in my curiously thickened voice.
"Bands of color, like the mist of water jewels. All around your
face, my sister. A glow of red . . . and outside that a glow of
purple . . . and . . . and . . ."

"Looking at me gives you pleasure?" she asked.

"It does. You do. Yes. Pleasure."

"Then hush, my brother, and let yourself be given pleasure."

I gasped. Her hand was underneath my mantle. And remember, I was nearly a year short of that age to wear a loincloth. I should have found my sister's bold gesture an outrageous violation of my privacy, except that somehow it did not
now seem so, and in any case I felt too numb to raise my arms
and ward her off. I could feel almost nothing except that I
seemed to be growing in a part of my body where I had never
noticeably grown before. So was Tzitzi's body changing. Her
young breasts ordinarily showed only as modest mounds beneath her blouse, but now, as she knelt over me, her nipples
were swollen; they poked like little fingertips against the thin
cloth covering them.

I managed to raise my heavy head and gazed blearily down
at my tepúli in her manipulating hand. It had never before
occurred to me that my member could be unsheathed of its skin
so far down its length. That was the first time I had ever seen
more than the tip and the pouty little mouth of what was now,
with its outer skin slid back, revealed to be a ruddy and bulbous-
ended shaft. It looked rather like a gaudy mushroom sprouting
from Tzitzi's tight grasp.

"Oéya, yoyolcatíca," she murmured, her face almost as red
as my member. "It grows, it becomes alive. See?"

"Tóton . . . tlapeztía," I said breathlessly. "It becomes glowing hot . . ."

With her free hand, Tzitzi lifted her skirt and anxiously,
fumblingly unwound her diaperlike undergarment. She had to
spread her legs to get it entirely undone, and I saw her tipíli,
close enough that it was clear even to my sight. Always before,
there had been nothing between her legs but a sort of close-
shut crease or dimple, and even that had been almost imper-

ceptible because it was blurred by a light fuzz of fine hairs.
But now her cleft was opening of itself, like

Ayya, Fray Domingo has upset and broken his inkwell. And
now he leaves us. Distressed by the accident, no doubt.

During this interruption, I might mention that some of our
men and women grow just a trace of ymáxtli, which is that
hair in that private place between the legs. But most of our race
have no hair at all there, or anywhere else on the body, except
for the luxuriant growth on the head. Even our men have only
scant facial hair, and any abundance is regarded as a disfigurement. Mothers daily bathe their boy babies' faces with scald-
ing hot lime water, and in most cases—as in my own, for
example—that treatment discourages the emergence of a beard
all through a man's life.

Fray Domingo returns not. Do I wait, my lords, or go on?

Very well. Then I return to that hilltop long ago and far
away, where I lay dazed and wondering while my sister worked
so busily to take advantage of my condition.
As I said, her tipíli cleft was opening of itself, becoming
a budding flower, showing pink petals against the flawless
fawn skin there, and the petals even glistened as if drenched
with dew. I fancied that Tzitzitlíni's new-blossomed flower
gave off a faint musky fragrance like that of the marigold. And
meanwhile, all about my sister, about her face and her body
and her now uncovered parts, there still shimmered and pulsated
those inexplicable bands and waves of various colors.
She lifted my mantle out of her way, then raised one of her
slender legs to sit astride my lower body. She moved urgently,
but with the tremor of nervousness and inexperience. With one
quivering small hand she held and aimed my tepúli. With the
other she seemed to be trying to spread farther open the petals
of her tipíli flower. As I have told earlier, Tzitzi had already
had some practice at utilizing a wooden spindle as she now
utilized me, but she was still narrowed by her chitóli membrane
and was tight within. As for me, my tepúli was of course
nowhere near man-size. (Though I know Tzitzi's ministrations

helped to hurry it toward mature dimensions—or beyond, if other women have spoken true.) Anyway, Tzitzi was still virginally pursed, and my member was at least larger than any thin spindle substitute.

So there was a moment of anguished frustration. My sister's eyes were tight shut, she was breathing like a runner in a race, she was desperate for something to happen. I would have helped, if I had known what it was supposed to be, and if I had not been so numbed in every part of my body except that one. Then, abruptly, the threshold gave way. Tzitzi and I cried out simultaneously, I in surprise, she in what might have been either pleasure or pain. To my vast amazement, and in what manner I still could not entirely comprehend, I was *inside my sister*, enveloped by her, warmed and moistened by her—and then gently massaged by her, as she began to move her body up and down in a slow rhythm.

I was overwhelmed by the sensation that spread from my warmly clenched and slowly stroked tepúli to every other part of my being. The mist of water jewels about my sister seemed to brighten and grow, to include me as well. I could feel it vibrating me and tingling me all over. My sister held more than that one small extension of myself; I felt totally absorbed into her, into Tzitzitlíni, into the sound of small bells ringing. The delight increased until I thought I could no longer tolerate it. And then it culminated in a burst even more delicious, a sort of soft explosion, like that of the milkweed pod when it splits and flings its white fluffs to the wind. At the same moment, Tzitzi breathed out a long soft moan of what even I, even in my ignorance, even half unconscious in my own sweet delirium, even I recognized as her rapturous release.

Then she collapsed limply along the length of my body, and her long soft hair billowed all about my face. We lay there for some time, both of us panting hard. I slowly became aware that the strange colors were fading and withdrawing, and that the sky above had stopped its whirling. Without raising her head to look at me, my sister said against my chest, very quietly and shyly, "Are you sorry, my brother?"

"Sorry!" I exclaimed, and frightened a quail into flying up from the grass near us.

"Then we can do it again?" she murmured, still without looking at me.

I thought about it. "*Can* it be done again?" I asked. The question was not so hilariously stupid as it sounds; I asked out of understandable ignorance. My member had slipped out of her, and was now wetly cold and as small as I had heretofore known it. I can hardly be derided for thinking that perhaps a male was allotted only one such experience in a lifetime.

"I do not mean now," said Tzitzi. "The workmen will be returning. But another day?"

"*Ayyo,* every day, if we can!"

She lifted herself on her arms and looked down at my face, her lips again mischievously smiling. "I will not have to trick you next time?"

"Trick me?"

"The colors you saw, the dizziness and numbness. I did a most sinful thing, my brother. I stole one of the mushrooms from their urn in the pyramid temple, and cooked it into your fish rolls."

She had done a daring and dangerous thing, besides a sinful one. The small black mushrooms were called teonanácatl, "flesh of the gods," which indicates how scarce and precious they were. They came, at great expense, from some holy mountain deep in the Mixtéca lands, and they were to be eaten only by certain priests and professional seers, and then only on special occasions when it was necessary to foresee the future. Tzitzi would assuredly have been killed on the spot if she had been caught filching one of the sacred things.

"No, do not ever do that again," I said. "But why did you?"

"Because I wanted to do—what we just now did—and I was afraid you might resist if you knew clearly what we were doing."

Would I have? I wonder. I did not resist then, nor any time afterward, and I found every subsequent experience just as blissful, even without the enhancement of colors and vertigo.

Yes, my sister and I coupled countless times over the next years while I still lived at home—whenever we had the opportunity—during the mealtime break at the quarry, on deserted stretches of the lakeshore, twice or thrice in our own house when both our parents were absent for what we knew would be an adequate while. We mutually learned not to be quite so awkward at the act, but of course we were both inexperienced— neither of us would have thought of trying those transports with anyone else—so there was not a great deal we could teach each other. It was a long time before we even discovered that it could be done with me on top, though after that we invented numerous variant positions.

Now my sister slid off me and stretched luxuriously. Both our bellies were wet with a small smear of blood from the rupture of her chitóli, and with another liquid, my own omícetl, white like octli but stickier. Tzitzi dipped a wad of dry grass into the small jar of water she had brought with my meal and washed us both clean, so that there should be no telltale trace on our clothes. Then she rewound her undergarment, rearranged her rumpled outer clothes, kissed me on the lips, said "Thank you"—which I should have thought of saying first— wrapped the water jar in its cloth, and ran off down the grassy slope, skipping merrily.

There and then, my lord scribes, and thus, ended the roads and the days of my childhood.

I H S
✠
S.C.C.M.

Sanctified, Caesarean, Catholic Majesty,
the Emperor Don Carlos, Our Lord King:

MOST Eminent Majesty from this City of México,
capital of New Spain, this All Souls' Day of the Year of Our
Lord one thousand five hundred twenty and nine, greeting.

In sending, at Your Majesty's behest, yet another increment
of the Aztec History, this necessarily obedient but still reluctant
servant begs leave to quote Varius Geminus, on an occasion
when he approached *his* emperor with some *vexata quaestio:*
"Whoever dares speak before thee, oh Caesar, knows not thy
greatness; whoever dares not speak before thee, knows not thy
goodness."

Though we may risk giving affront and receiving rebuke,
we beseech you, Sire, that we may be granted permission to
abandon this noxious enterprise.

Inasmuch as Your Majesty has recently read, in the previous
portion of manuscript delivered into your royal hands, the Indian's bland and almost blithe confession of having committed
the abominable sin of incest—an act proscribed throughout the
known world, civilized and savage alike; an act execrated even
by such degenerate peoples as the Basques, the Greeks, and

the English; an act forbidden even by the meager *lex non scripta* observed by the Indian's own fellow barbarians; therefore an act not to be condoned by us because it was committed before the sinner had any knowledge of Christian morality—for all these reasons, we had confidently expected that Your Pious Majesty would be sufficiently appalled to order an immediate end to the Aztec's oratory, if not to the Aztec himself.

However, Your Majesty's loyal cleric has never yet disobeyed a command from our liege. We append the further pages collected since the last were sent. And we will keep the scribes and the interpreter at their enforced and odious occupation, setting down still further pages, until such time as our Most Esteemed Emperor may see fit to give them surcease. We only beg and urge, Sire, that when you have read this next segment of the Aztec's life history—since it contains passages that would sicken Sodom—Your Majesty will reconsider your command that this chronicle be continued.

That the pure illumination of Our Lord Jesus Christ always guide the ways of Your Majesty, is the devout wish of Your S.C.C.M.'s devoted missionary legate,

(*ecce signum*) Zumárraga

TERTIA PARS

At the time of which I have been speaking, when I was given the name of Mole, I was still in school. Every sundown, when the working day was done, I and all the other boys above seven years of age, from all the villages and residences of Xaltócan, went either to The House of Building Strength, or, boys and girls together, to The House of Learning Manners.

In the former school, we boys endured rigorous physical exercises, and were taught the ball game of tlachtli and the rudiments of handling battle weapons. In the latter school, we and the girls our age were given some sketchy history of our nation and other lands, some rather more intensive instruction in the nature of our gods and the numerous festivals dedicated to them, and were taught the arts of ritual singing, dancing, and playing of musical instruments for the celebration of all those religious ceremonies.

It was only in those telpochcáltin, or lower schools, that we commoners mingled as equals with the children of the nobility, and even with a few of the demonstrably brighter and more deserving slave children. That elementary education, stressing politeness, piety, grace, and dexterity, was regarded as sufficient schooling for us middle-class youngsters, and a real honor for the handful of slave children who were deemed worthy and capable of any schooling whatever.

But none of the slave boys, and few of us middle-class boys—and *never* a girl child, even a daughter of the nobility— could look forward to any further education than that provided by The Houses of Manners and Strength. The sons of our nobles usually left the island to attend one of the calmécactin, since there was no such school on Xaltócan. Those institutions of higher learning were staffed and taught by a special order of priests, and their students learned to be priests themselves, or to be governing officials, or scribes, historians, artists, physicians, or professionals of some other calling. Entrance to a calmécac was not forbidden to any ordinary boy, but the attendance and boarding there was too costly for most middle-class families to afford, unless a boy was accepted at no cost at all, for having shown great distinction in the lower school.

And I must confess that I distinguished myself not at all in either The House of Learning Manners or that of Building Strength. I remember, on my first entering the music class at the school of manners, the Master of the Boys asked me to sing something, so that he might judge the quality of my voice. And I did, and he did, saying, "A wondrous thing to hear, but I do not believe it is singing. We will try you on an instrument."

When I proved equally incapable of wringing a tune from the four-holed flute, or any kind of harmony from the various tuned drums, the exasperated Master put me into a class which was learning one of the beginners' dances, the Thundering Serpent. Each dancer makes a small spring forward with a stamping noise, then whirls completely around, crouches on one knee and turns again in that position, then makes another stamping forward leap. When a line of boys and girls does this in progression, the sound is of a continuous rolling boom and the visual effect is that of a long snake twining its way along in sinuous curves. Or it should be.

"This is the first Thundering Serpent I ever saw with a kink in it!" shouted the Mistress of the Girls.

"Get out of that line, Malínqui!" shouted the master of the Boys.

Thereafter, to him, I was Malínqui, the Kink. And thereafter, when our school's students performed in public, at festival ceremonies in the island's pyramid plaza, my only contribution to the music and dancing was to beat a turtleshell drum with a pair of small deer antlers or to click a pair of crab claws in each hand. Fortunately, my sister maintained the honor of our family at those events, she being always the featured solo dancer. Tzitzitlíni could dance without any music at all, yet make the spectators believe they heard music all about them.

I was beginning to feel that I possessed no identity at all, or else so many that I knew not which to accept as really my own. At home I had been Mixtli, the Cloud. To the rest of Xaltócan I was becoming generally known as Tozáni, the Mole. At The House of Learning Manners I was Malínqui, the Kink. And in The House of Building Strength I soon became Poyaútla, the Fogbound.

By good fortune, I was not as lacking in muscle as in musical bent, for I had inherited my father's stature and solidity. By the time I was fourteen I was taller than schoolmates two years older. And I suppose a stone-blind man could do the stretching and leaping and weightlifting exercises. So the Master of Athletics found no fault with my performance until we began to engage in team sports.

If the game of tlachtli allowed the use of hands and feet, I might have played better, for one moves one's hands and feet almost instinctively. But the hard óli ball can be struck only with knees, hips, elbows, and buttocks, and when I could see the ball at all, it was only a dim blob further blurred by its speed. Consequently, though we players wore head protectors, hip girdles, knee and elbow sleeves of heavy leather, and thick cotton padding over the rest of our bodies, I was constantly being bruised by the blows of the ball.

Worse, I could seldom distinguish my own teammates from the opposing players. When I did infrequently knee or hip the ball, I was as likely as not to slam it through the wrong one of the squat stone arches, the knee-high goals which, according to the complicated rules of the game, are continually being lugged from place to place at the ends of the court. As for putting the ball through one of the vertical stone rings high up in the midline of the court's two enclosing walls—meaning an immediate win, no matter what the score of goals already made by either team—that is next to impossible for even the most experienced player to do even by accident; it would have been a miracle for fogbound me.

It was not long before the Master of Athletics gave up on me as a participant. I was put in charge of the players' water jar and dipper, and of the pricking thorns and sucking reeds with which, after each game, the school physician eased the stiffness of the players by drawing the turgid black blood from their bruises.

Then there were the war games and the weapons instruction, under the tutelage of an elderly and scarred cuachic, an "old eagle," the title of one whose battle valor has already been proved. His name was Extli-Quani, or Blood Glutton, and he must have been well over forty years old. For those exercises, we boys were not allowed to wear any of the plumes or paints or other array of real warriors. But we carried boy-sized shields of wood or wicker covered with leather, and we wore boy-sized suits of the soldiers' standard battle garb. Those garments were of thickly quilted cotton, toughened by having been soaked in brine, and they covered us from neck to wrists and ankles. They allowed a reasonable freedom of movement, and they were supposed to protect us from arrows—at least those arrows propelled from a distance—but *ayya!* they were hot and scratchy and sweaty things to wear for longer than a short while.

"First you will learn the battle cries," said Blood Glutton. "In combat, of course, you will be accompanied by the conch trumpeters and the beaters of the thunder drums or the groaning drums. But to those must be added your own voices shouting for slaughter, and the sound of your fists and weapons pounding upon your shields. I know from experience, my boys, that an overwhelming clamor of noise can be a weapon itself. It can shake a man's mind, water his blood, weaken his sinews, even void his bladder and bowels. But *you* must make that noise, and you will find it twice effective: it heartens your own battle resolve while it terrifies your enemy."

And so, for weeks before we had even a mock weapon, we yelled the shrieks of the eagle, the rasping grunts of the jaguar, the long-drawn hoots of the owl, the *alalalala!* of the parrot. We learned to caper in feigned eagerness for battle, to menace with broad gestures, to threaten with grimaces, to pound our shields in drumming unison until they were stained with the blood of our hands.

Some other nations had weapons different from those we Mexíca relied on, and some of our own units of warriors were equipped with arms for particular purposes, and even an individual might choose always to use whichever weapon he had become most proficient with. Those other arms included the leather sling for throwing rocks, the blunt stone ax for bludgeoning, the heavy mace whose knob was studded with jagged obsidian, the three-pointed spear of bones barbed at the ends so they inflicted a tearing wound, or the sword fashioned simply of the toothed snout of the sawfish. But the basic weapons of the Mexíca were four.

For the opening encounter with an enemy, at a long distance, there was the bow and arrow. We students practiced for a long time with arrows tipped only with soft balls of óli instead of sharp obsidian. For example, one day the Master formed twenty or so of us into a line and said:

"Suppose the enemy are in that patch of nopáli cactus." He indicated what was to my fogbound vision only a green blur some hundred strides away. "I want full pull on the bowstring and I want your arrows angled upward, exactly midway between where the sun stands and the horizon below him. Ready? Take stable stance. Now take aim at the cactus. Now let fly."

There was a swooshing noise, then the boys groaned in concert. All the arrows had arced to the ground in a respectably tight grouping and at the hundred-strides distance of the cactus patch. But that was thanks to Blood Glutton's having specified the pull and the angle. The boys groaned because they had all been equally and dismally off target; the arrows had landed far to the left of the cactus. We looked to the Master, waiting for him to tell us how we could have aimed so wrong.

He gestured at the square and rectangular battle ensigns whose staffs were stuck here and there in the ground about us. "What are these cloth flags for?" he asked.

We looked at each other. Then Pactli, son of the Lord Red Heron, replied, "They are guidons to be carried by our separate unit leaders in the field. If we get scattered during a battle, the guidons show us where to regroup."

"Correct, Pactzin," said Blood Glutton. "Now, that other flag, that long feather pennant, what is it for?"

There was another exchange of glances, and Chimáli ventured timidly, "We carry it to show pride that we are Mexíca."

"That is the wrong answer," said the Master, "but a manly one, so I will not whip you. But observe that pennon, my boys, how it floats upon the wind."

We all looked. There was not enough of a breeze that day to hold the banner straight out from its staff. It hung at an angle to the ground and—

"It is blowing to our left!" another boy shouted excitedly. "We did *not* aim wrong! The wind carried our arrows away from the target!"

"If you miss your target," the Master said drily, "you *have* aimed wrong. Blaming it on the wind god does not excuse it. To aim correctly, you must consider the force and direction in which Ehécatl is blowing his wind trumpet. That is the purpose of the feather pennon. Which way it hangs shows you which way the wind will carry your arrows. How high it hangs shows you how strongly the wind will carry them. Now, all of you march down there and retrieve your arrows. When you get there, turn about, from a line, and aim at me. The first boy who hits me will be excused for ten days from even his deserved whippings."

(We did not march, we ran for the arrows, and quite gleefully sent them back at the cuachic, but not one of us hit him.)

For fighting at a nearer range than arrow shot, there was the javelin, a narrow, pointed blade of obsidian on a short shaft. Unfeathered, it depended for accuracy and piercing power upon its being thrown with utmost strength.

"So you do not hurl the javelin unaided," said Blood Glutton, "but with this atlatl throwing-stick. It will seem a clumsy method at first, but after much practice you will feel the atlatl to be what it is: a lengthening of your arm and a doubling of your strength. At a distance of as many as thirty long strides, you can drive the javelin clear through a tree as thick as a man. So imagine, my boys, what it will do when you fling it at a *man*."

There was also the long spear, with a broader and heavier obsidian head, for jabbing, thrusting, piercing before an enemy got really close to you. But, for the inevitable hand-to-hand fighting, there was the sword called the maquáhuitl. It sounds innocent enough, "the hunting wood," but it was the most terrible and lethal weapon in our armory.

The maquáhuitl was a flat stave of the very hardest wood, a man's-arm long and a man's-hand wide, and all along both edges of its length were inset sharp flakes of obsidian. The sword's handle was long enough for wielding the weapon with one hand or with both, and it was carefully carved to fit the grip of that weapon's owner. The obsidian chips were not merely wedged into the wood; so much depended on that sword that even sorcery was added to it. The flakes were cemented solidly with a charmed glue made of liquid óli, the precious perfumed copáli resin, and fresh blood donated by the priests of the war god Huitzilopóchtli.

Obsidian makes a wicked-looking arrowhead or spear or sword edge, as shiny as quartz crystal but as black as the afterworld Míctlan. Properly flaked, the stone is so keen that it can cut as subtly as a grass-blade sometimes does, or cleave as deep as any bludgeon ax. The stone's one weakness is its brittleness; it can shatter against a foe's shield or against his opposing sword. But, in the hands of a trained fighter, the obsidian-edged maquáhuitl can slash a man's flesh and bone as cleanly as if he were a clump of weeds—and in all-out war, as Blood Glutton never ceased reminding us, the enemy are but weeds to be mowed.

Just as our practice arrows, javelins, and spears were tipped with óli gum, so were our mock maquáhuime made harmless. The stave was of light, soft wood, so the sword would break before it dealt a too punishing blow. And instead of obsidian chips, the edges were outlined only with tufts of feather down. Before any two students fought a sword duel, the Master would wet those tufts with red paint, so that every blow received would register as vividly as a real wound, and the mark would last almost as long. In a very short time, I was cross-hatched with wound marks, face and body, and I was quite embarrassed to be seen in public. Then it was that I requested a private audience with our cuachic. He was a tough old man, hard as obsidian, and probably uneducated in anything besides war, but he was no stupid clod.

I stooped to make the gesture of kissing the earth and, still kneeling, said, "Master Blood Glutton, you already know that my eyesight is poor. I fear you are wasting time and patience in trying to teach me to soldier. If these marks on my body were real wounds, I should have been dead long since."

"So?" he said coolly. Then he squatted to my level. "Fog-bound, I will tell you of a man I once met down in Quautemálan, the country of The Tangled Wood. Those people, as perhaps you know, are all timorous of death. This particular man scampered from every least suspicion of danger. He avoided the most natural risks of existence. He burrowed away in snug security. He surrounded himself with physicians and priests and sorcerers. He ate only the most nutritious foods, and he seized eagerly on every life-preserving potion he heard of. No man ever took better care of his life. He lived only to go on living."

I waited for more, but he said no more, so I asked, "What became of him, Master Cuachic?"

"He died."

"That is all?"

"What else ever becomes of any man? I no longer remember even his name. No one remembers anything at all about him, except that he lived and then he died."

After another silence, I said, "Master, I know that if I am slain in war my dying will nourish the gods, and they will amply reward me in the afterworld, and perhaps my name will not be forgotten. But might I not be of some service in *this* world for a while before I achieve my dying?"

"Strike just one telling blow in battle, my boy. Then, even if you are slain the next moment, you will have done *something* with your life. More than all those men who merely drudge to exist until the gods tire of watching their futility and sweep them off to oblivion." Blood Glutton stood up. "Here, Fog-bound, this is my own maquáhuitl. It long served me well. Just feel the heft of it."

I will admit that I experienced a thrill when for the first time I held a real sword, not a toy weapon of corkwood and feathers.

It was most atrociously heavy, but its very weight said, *"I am power."*

"I see that you lift it and swing it with one hand," observed the Master. "Not many boys your age could do that. Now step over here, Fogbound. This is a sturdy nopáli. Give it a killing stroke."

The cactus was an old one, of nearly tree size. Its spiny green lobes were like paddles, and its barked brown trunk was as thick as my waist. I swung the maquáhuitl experimentally, with my right hand only, and the obsidian edge bit into the cactus wood with a hungry *tchunk!* I wiggled the blade loose, took the handle in both hands, swung the sword far back behind me, then struck with all my force. I had expected the blade to cut rather more deeply, but I was truly surprised when it slashed cleanly all the way through the trunk, splashing its sap like colorless blood. The nopáli came crashing down, and the Master and I both had to leap nimbly away to avoid the falling mass of sharp spines.

"Ayyo, Fogbound!" Blood Glutton said admiringly. "Whatever attributes you lack, you do have the strength of a born warrior."

I flushed with pride and pleasure, but I had to say, "Yes, Master, I can strike and kill. But what of my dim vision? Suppose I were to strike the wrong man. One of our own."

"No cuachic in command of novice warriors would ever put you in a position to do so. In a War of Flowers, he might assign you to the Swaddlers who carry the ropes to bind enemy prisoners that they may be brought back for sacrifice. Or in a real war, you might be assigned to the rear-guard Swallowers whose knives give merciful release to those comrades and foes left lying wounded when the battle has swept on past them."

"Swallowers and Swaddlers," I mustered. "Hardly heroic duties to win me reward in the afterworld."

"You spoke of *this* world," the Master sternly reminded me, "and of service, not heroism. Even the humblest can serve. I remember when we marched into the insolent city of Tlaltelólco, to annex it to our Tenochtítlan. That city's warriors battled us in the streets, of course, but its women, children, and old dodderers stood upon the housetops and threw down at us large rocks, nests full of angry wasps, even handfuls of their own excrement."

Right here, my lord scribes, I had better make clear that, among the different kinds of wars we Mexíca fought, the battle for Tlaltelólco had been an exceptional case. Our Revered Speaker Axayácatl simply found it necessary to subjugate that haughty city, to deprive it of independent rule, and forcibly to make its people render allegiance to our one great island capital of Tenochtítlan. But, as a general rule, our wars against other peoples were not for conquest—at least not in the sense that your armies have conquered all of this New Spain and made it an abject colony of your Mother Spain.

No, we might defeat and humble another nation, but we would not obliterate it from the earth. We fought to prove our own might and to exact tribute from the less mighty. When a nation surrendered and acknowledged fealty to us Mexíca, it was given a tally of its native resources and products—gold, spices, óli, whatever—that henceforth it would annually deliver in specified quantities to our Revered Speaker. And it would be held subject to conscription of its fighting men, when and if they should be needed to march alongside us Mexíca.

But that nation would retain its name and sovereignty, its own ruler, its accustomed way of life, and its preferred form of religion. We would not impose on it any of our laws, customs, or gods. Our war god Huitzilopóchtli, for example, was *our* god. Under his care the Mexíca were a people set apart from others and above them, and we would not share that god or *let* him be shared. Quite the contrary. In many defeated nations we discovered new gods or novel manifestations of our known gods, and, if they appealed to us, our armies brought home copies of their statues for us to set in our own temples.

I must tell you, too, that there existed nations from which we never *were* able to wring tribute or fealty. For instance, contiguous to us in the east there was Cuautexcálan, The Land of the Eagle Crags, usually called by us simply Texcála, The Crags. For some reason, you Spaniards choose to call that land Tlaxcála, which is laughable, since that word means merely tortilla.

Texcála was completely ringed by countries all allied to us Mexíca, hence it was forced to exist like a landlocked island. But Texcála adamantly refused ever to submit in the least degree, which meant that it was cut off from importing many necessities of life. If the Texcaltéca had not, however grudgingly, traded with us the sacred copáli resin in which their forestland was rich, they would not even have had salt to flavor their food.

As it was, our Uey-Tlatoáni severely restricted the amount of trading between us and the Texcaltéca—always in expectation of bringing them to submission—so the stubborn Texcaltéca perpetually suffered humiliating deprivations. They had to eke out their meager crop of cotton, for example, meaning that even their nobles had to wear mantles woven of only a trace of cotton mixed with coarse hemp or maguey fiber; garments which, in Tenochtítlan, would have been worn only by slaves or children. You can well understand that Texcála harbored an abiding hatred for us Mexíca and, as you well know, it eventually had dire consequences for us, for the Texcaltéca, and for all of what is now New Spain.

"Meanwhile," said Master Blood Glutton to me on that day we conversed, "right now our armies are disastrously embroiled with another recalcitrant nation to the west. The Revered Speaker's attempted invasion of Michihuácan, The Land of the Fishermen, has been repulsed most ignominiously. Axayácatl expected an easy victory, since those Purémpecha have always been armed with copper blades, but they have hurled our armies backward in defeat."

"But how, Master?" I asked. "An unwarlike race wielding soft copper weapons? How could they stand against us invincible Mexíca?"

The old soldier shrugged. "Unwarlike the Purémpecha may be, but they fight fiercely enough to defend their Michihuácan homeland of lakes and rivers and well-watered farmlands. Also, it is said they have discovered some magic metal that they mix into their copper while it is still molten. When the mixture is forged into blades, it becomes a metal so hard that our obsidian crumples like bark paper against it."

"Fishermen and farmers," I murmured, "defeating the professional soldiers of Axayácatl. . . ."

"Oh, we will try again, you may wager on it," said Blood Glutton. "This time Axayácatl wanted only access to those waters rich in food fish, and those fruitful valleys. But now he will want the secret of that magic metal. He will challenge the Purémpecha again, and when he does, his armies will require every man who can march." The Master paused, then added pointedly, "Even stiff-jointed old cuáchictin like me, even those who can serve only as Swallowers and Swaddlers, even the crippled and the fogbound. It behooves us to be trained and hardened and ready, my boy."

As it happened, Axayácatl died before he could mount another invasion into Michihuácan, which is part of what you now call New Galicia. Under subsequent Revered Speakers, we Mexíca and the Purémpecha managed to live in a sort of wary mutual respect. And I hardly need remind you, reverend friars, that your own most butcherlike commander, Beltrán de Guzmán, is to this day *still* trying to crush the diehard bands of Purémpecha around Lake Chapálan and in other remote corners of New Galicia that yet refuse to surrender to your King Carlos and your Lord God.

I have been speaking of our punitive wars, such as they were. I am sure that even your bloodthirsty Guzmán can understand that kind of warfare, though I am also sure he could never conceive of a war—like most of ours—which left the defeated nation still surviving and independent. But now let me speak of our Wars of Flowers, because those seem incomprehensible to *any* of you white men. "How," I have heard you ask, "could there have been so many unprovoked and unnecessary wars between friendly nations? Wars that neither side even tried to *win?*"

I will do my best to explain.

Any kind of war was, naturally, pleasing to our gods. Each warrior, dying, spilled his lifeblood, the most precious offering a human could make. In a punitive war, a decisive victory was the objective, and so both sides fought to kill or be killed. The enemy were, as my old Master put it, weeds to be mowed. Only a comparatively few prisoners were taken and kept for later ceremonial sacrifice. But whether a warrior died on the battlefield or on a temple altar, his was accounted a Flowery Death, honorable to himself and satisfying to the gods. The only problem was—if you look at it from the gods' point of view—that punitive wars were not frequent enough. While they provided much god-nourishing blood and sent many soldiers to be afterworld servants of the gods, such wars were only sporadic. The gods might have to wait and fast and thirst for many years between. That displeased them, and in the year One Rabbit, they let us know it.

That was some twelve years before my birth, but my father remembered it vividly and often told of it with much sad shaking of his head. In that year, the gods sent to this whole plateau the harshest winter ever known. Besides freezing cold and biting winds which untimely killed many infants, sickly elders, our domestic animals, and even the animals of the wild, there was a six-day snowfall which killed every winter crop in the ground. There were mysterious lights visible in the night skies: wavering vertical bands of cold-colored lights, what my father described as "the gods striding ominously about the heavens, nothing of them visible but their mantles woven of white and green and blue heron feathers."

And that was only the beginning. The spring brought not just an end to the cold but a scorching heat; the rainy season ensued, but it brought no rain, the drought killed our crops and animals as dead as the snows had done. Nor was even that the end. The following years were equally merciless in their alternate cold and heat and dearth of rain. In the cold our lakes froze over; in the heat they shrank, they became tepid, they became bitter salt, so that the fish died and floated belly up and fouled the air with their stench.

Five or six years continued thus: what the older folk of my youth still referred to as the Hard Times. *Yya ayya*, they must have been terrible times indeed, for our people, our proud and upstanding macehuáltin, were reduced to selling themselves into slavery. You see, other nations beyond this plateau, in the southern highlands and in the coastal Hot Lands, they had not been laid waste by the climatic catastrophe. They offered shares of their own still-bounteous harvests for barter, but that was no generosity, for they knew that we had little to trade except ourselves. Those other peoples, especially those inferior to us and inimical to us, were only too pleased to buy "the swaggering Mexíca" for slaves, and to demean us further by paying only cruel and miserly prices.

The standard trade was five hundred ears of maize for a male of working age or four hundred for a female of breeding age. If a family had one sellable child, that boy or girl would be relinquished so the rest of the household might eat. If a family had only infants, the father would sell himself. But for how long could any household subsist on four or five hundred ears of maize? And when those were eaten, who or what remained to be sold? Even if the Good Times were suddenly to come again, how could a family survive without a working father? Anyway, the Good Times did not come. . . .

That was during the reign of the First Motecuzóma and, in attempting to alleviate his people's misery, he depleted both the national and his personal treasury, then emptied all the capital's storehouses and granaries. When the surplus was gone, when everything was gone except the still-grinding Hard Times, Motecuzóma and his Snake Woman convened their Speaking Council of elders, and even called in seers and sayers for advice. I cannot vouch for it, but it is said that the conference went thus:

One hoary sorcerer, who had spent months in studying the thrown bones and consulting sacred books, solemnly reported, "My Lord Speaker, the gods have made us hungry to demonstrate that *they* are hungry. There has not been a war since our last incursion into Texcála, and that was in the year Nine House. Since then, we have made only sparse blood offerings to the gods. A few prisoners kept in reserve, the occasional lawbreaker, now and then an adolescent or a maiden. The gods are quite plainly demanding more nourishment."

"Another war?" mused Motecuzóma. "Even our hardiest warriors are by now too feeble even to march to an enemy frontier, let alone breach it."

"True, Revered Speaker. But there is a way to arrange a mass sacrifice . . ."

"Slaughter our people before they starve to death?" Motecuzóma asked sardonically. "They are so gaunt and dried-up that the whole nation probably would not yield a cupful of blood."

"True, Revered Speaker. And in any case, that would be such

a mendicant gesture that the gods probably would not accept it. No, Lord Speaker, what is necessary is a war, but a different *kind* of war...."

That, or so I have been told, and so I believe, was the origin of the Flowery Wars, and this is how the first of them was arranged:

The mightiest and most centrally situated powers in this valley constituted a Triple Alliance: we the Mexíca with our capital on the island of Tenochtítlan, the Acólhua with their capital at Texcóco on the lake's eastern shore, and the Tecpanéca with their capital at Tlácopan on the western shore. There were three lesser peoples to the southeast: the Texcaltéca, of whom I have already spoken, with their capital at Texcála; the Huéxotin with their capital at Huexotzínco; and the once mighty Tya Nuü—or Mixtéca, as we called them—whose domain had shrunken until it consisted of little more than their capital city of Cholólan. The first were our enemies, as I have said; the latter two had long ago been made our tribute payers and, like it or not, our occasional allies. All three of those nations, however, like all three of ours in the Alliance, were being devastated by the Hard Times.

After Motecuzóma's conference with his Speaking Council, he conferred also with the rulers of Texcóco and Tlácopan. Those three together drafted and sent a proposal to the three rulers in the cities of Texcála, Cholólan, and Huexotzínco. In essence it said something like this:

"Let us all make war that we may all survive. We are diverse peoples, but we suffer the same Hard Times. The wise men say that we have only one hope of enduring: to sate and placate the gods with blood sacrifices. Therefore, we propose that the armies of our three nations meet in combat with the armies of your three nations, on the neutral plain of Acatzínco, safely far to the southeast of all our lands. The fighting will not be for territory, nor for rule, nor for slaughter, nor for plunder, but simply for the taking of prisoners to be granted the Flowery Death. When all participating forces have captured a sufficiency of prisoners for sacrifice to their several gods, this will be mutually made known amongst the commanders and the battle will end forthwith."

That proposal, which you Spaniards say you find incredible,

was agreeable to all concerned—including the warriors whom you have called "stupidly suicidal" because they fought for no apparent end except the extremely likely and sudden end to their own lives. Well, tell me, what professional soldier of your own would refuse any excuse for a battle, in preference to humdrum, peacetime garrison duty? At least our warriors had the stimulus of knowing that if they died in combat or on an alien altar, they earned all people's thanks for pleasing the gods, while they earned the gods' gift of life in a blissful afterworld. And, in those Hard Times, when so many died of inglorious starvation, a man had even more reason for preferring to die by the sword or the sacrificial knife.

So that first battle was planned, and it was fought as planned—though the plain of Acatzínco was a dreary long march from anywhere, so all six armies had to rest for a day or two before the signal was given to commence hostilities. Other intentions notwithstanding, a goodly number of men were killed; some inadvertently, by chance and accident; some because they or their opponents fought too exuberantly. It is difficult for a warrior, trained to kill, to refrain from killing. But most, as agreed, struck with the flat of the maquáhuitl, not with the obsidian edge. The men thus stunned were not dispatched by the Swallowers but were quickly bound by the Swaddlers. After only two days, the priest-chaplains who marched with each army decided that prisoners enough had been taken to satisfy them and their gods. One after another, the commanders unfurled the prearranged banners, the knots of men still grappling on the plain disengaged, the six armies reassembled and marched wearily home, leading their even wearier captives.

That first, tentative War of Flowers took place in midsummer, normally also mid-rainy season, but in those Hard Times just another of the interminable hot, dry spells. And one other thing had been prearranged by the six rulers of the six nations: that all of them should sacrifice all their prisoners in their six capital cities on the same day. No one remembers the exact count, but I suppose several thousand men died that day in Tenochtítlan, in Texcóco, in Tlácopan, in Texcála, in Cholólan, in Huexotzínco. Call it coincidence if you like, reverend friars, since the Lord God was of course not involved, but that day the casks of clouds at last broke their seals, and the rain poured down on all this extensive plateau, and the Hard Times came to an end.

That very day, also, many people in the six cities enjoyed full bellies for the first time in years, when they dined on the remains of the sacrificed xochimíque. The gods were satisfied to be fed merely with the ripped-out hearts heaped on their altars; they had no use for the remainder of the victims' bodies, but the gathered people did. So, as the corpse of each xochimíqui, still warm, rolled down the steep staircase of each temple pyramid, the meat cutters waiting below dissected it into its edible parts and distributed those among the eager folk crowding each plaza.

The skulls were cracked and the brains extracted, the arms and legs were cut into manageable segments, the genitals and buttocks were sliced off, the livers and kidneys were cut out. Those food portions were not just flung to a slavering mob; they were distributed with admirable practicality, and the populace waited with admirable restraint. For obvious reasons, the brains went to priests and wise men, the muscular arms and legs to warriors, the genitalia to young married couples, the less significant buttocks and tripes were presented to pregnant women, nursing mothers, and families with many children. The leftovers of heads, hands, feet, and torsos, being more bone than meat, were put aside to fertilize the croplands.

That feast of fresh meat may or may not have been an additional advantage foreseen by the planners of the Flowery War; I do not know. All the various peoples in these lands had long ago eaten every still-existing game animal, every domesticated bird and dog raised for food. They had eaten lizards and insects and cactus. But they never had eaten any of their relatives and neighbors who succumbed to the Hard Times. It might be thought an unconscionable waste of available nutriment, but in every nation the starving people had disposed of their starved fellows by burial or burning, according to their custom. Now, however, thanks to the War of Flowers, they had an abundance of bodies of unrelated enemies—even if those were enemies only by an exaggeration of definition—and so there was no compunction about making a meal of them.

In the aftermath of later wars, there was never again such an immediate butchery and gorging. Since there was never again such a massed and ravenous hunger to assuage, the priests set up rules and rituals to formalize the eating of captives' flesh. The victorious warriors of later wars took only token morsels of their dead enemies' muscular parts, and partook of them ceremoniously. The bulk of the meat was apportioned out among the really poor folk—generally meaning the slaves—or was fed to the animals in those cities which, like Tenochtítlan, maintained a public menagerie.

Human flesh, like almost any other animal flesh, when properly hung, aged, seasoned, and broiled, makes a tasty dish, and it is suitable for sustenance when there is no other meat. However, just as it can be proven that close-kinship marriage among our noble families did not result in superior offspring, but more often the contrary, I think it could be equally demonstrated that humans who feed only on humans must similarly decline. If a family's bloodline is best improved by marriage outside the line, so a man's blood must be best strengthened by the ingestion of other animals. Thus, with the passing of the Hard Times, the practice of eating the slain xochimíque became—for all but the desperate and degenerate poor—only one more religious observance, and a minor one.

But the first War of Flowers was such a success, coincidence or not, that the same six nations continued to wage others at regular intervals, for a safeguard against any future displeasure of the gods and any recurrence of the Hard Times. I daresay we Mexíca had little further need of that stratagem, for Motecuzóma and the Revered Speakers who succeeded him did not again let years elapse between *real* wars. There was seldom a time thereafter when we did not have an army in the field, extending our tributary dominion. But the Acólhua and the Tecpanéca, having few ambitions of that sort, had to depend on the Wars of Flowers to provide Flowery Deaths for their gods. So, since Tenochtítlan had been the instigator, it continued willingly to participate: The Triple Alliance versus the Texcaltéca, the Mixtéca, and the Huéxotin.

To the warriors it mattered not. Punitive war or Flowery War, a man had as much chance of dying. He had also as much opportunity of being acclaimed a hero or even awarded one of the orders of knighthood, whether he left a notable number of enemies dead on some disputed field or brought home a notable number alive from the plain of Acatzínco.

"For know this, Fogbound," said Master Blood Glutton, on that day of which I have spoken. "No warrior, in a real war or a War of Flowers, must ever expect to be counted among the fallen or the captured. He must expect to live through the war and to come out of it a hero. Oh, I will not dissemble, my boy. He may very well die, yes, while still thrilling to that expectation. But if he goes into battle *not* expecting victory for his side and glory for himself, die he *surely* will."

I tried to convey, while trying not to sound pusillanimous, that I was not afraid to die, but neither was I eager to. In whatever kind of war, I was evidently destined for no higher office than Swallower or Swaddler. Such a duty, I pointed out, could as well be assigned to women. Would I not be of more value to the Mexíca nation, to humanity as a whole, if I were allowed to exercise my other talents?

"What other talents?" grunted Blood Glutton.

That stopped me for a moment. But then I suggested that if, for example, I succeeded in mastering the picture writing, I could accompany the army as a battle historian. I could sit apart, on an overlooking hilltop perhaps, and write a description of each battle's strategy and tactics and progress, for the edification of future commanders.

The old soldier regarded me with exasperation. "First you say you cannot see to fight an opponent face to face. Now you say you will encompass the whole confused action of two entire clashing armies. Fogbound, if you are seeking exemption from this school's weapons practice, save your breath. I could not excuse you if I would. In your case, there is a charge upon me."

"A charge?" I said, nonplussed. "A charge from whom, Master?"

He frowned, annoyed, as if caught in a slip of the tongue, and growled, "A charge I impose upon myself. It is my sincere belief that every man should experience one war, or at least one battle, in his lifetime. Because, if he survives, he savors all the rest of his life the more richly and dearly. Now, enough of this. I shall expect to see you on the field as usual at to-morrow's dusk."

So I went away then, and I went on with the combat drills and lessons in the days and months that followed. I knew not what the future held for me, but I did know one thing. If I was destined for some undesirable duty, there were only two ways to evade it: either show myself incapable of it or show myself too good for it. And good scribes were at least not made weeds for the obsidian to mow. That is why, while I uncomplainingly attend both the Houses of Building Strength and Learning Manners, in private I worked ever more intensely and feverishly to puzzle out the secrets of the art of word knowing.

✠

I would make the gesture of kissing the earth, Your Excellency, if that were a custom still observed. Instead, I simply straighten my old bones upright so that I stand, like your friars, to salute your entrance.

It is an honor to have Your Excellency's presence grace our little group once again, and to hear you say that you have examined the collected pages of my story thus far. But Your Excellency asks searching questions relative to certain events therein, and I must confess that your questions make me lower my eyelids in embarrassment, even in some shame.

Yes, Your Excellency, my sister and I continued to enjoy each other at every opportunity during those growing-up years of which I have recently spoken. And yes, Your Excellency, we knew that we sinned.

Probably Tzitzitlíni knew it from the start, but I was younger, so it was only gradually that I became aware that what we were doing was wrong. Over the years I have come to realize that our females always knew more about the mysteries of sex, and knew it earlier, than any males. I suspect the same is true of the females of all races, including your own. For they seem inclined, from their youngest years, to whisper among themselves, and to trade what secrets they learn about their own bodies and the bodies of men, and to consort with old widows and crones who—perhaps because their own juices have long gone dry—are gleefully or maliciously eager to instruct young maidens in womanly wiles and snares and deceptions.

I regret that I am not, even yet, sufficiently knowledgeable of my new Christian religion to know all its rules and strictures on the subject, though I gather that it frowns on every manifestation of sexuality except an occasional copulation between Christian husband and wife for the purpose of producing a Christian child. But even we heathens observed a few laws and a great many traditions regarding accepted sexual behavior.

A maiden was to remain a virgin until she married, and she was encouraged not to marry young, for *our* religion recognized that our living room and resources would be depleted by more than a moderate harvest of children in each generation. Or a maiden might choose not to marry but to join the auyaníme, whose service to our warriors was a legitimate female occupation, if not exactly an exalted one. Or, if she was disqualified for marriage by ugliness or some other deficiency, she might become a maátitl for pay, and go astraddle the road. There were some girls who maintained their maidenhood so that they might win the honor of sacrifice in some ceremony which required a virgin; and others so that they might serve all their lives, like your nuns, as attendants to the temple priests— though there was speculation about the nature of that attendance and the duration of that virginity.

Chastity before marriage was not so demanded of our men, for they had always available the willing maátime and the slave women, willing or unwilling; and anyway, a man's virginity can hardly be proved or disproved. Neither can a woman's, I might confide—as Tzitzi confided to me—if she has time to prepare before her wedding night. There are old women who keep pigeons that they feed with the dark red seeds of some flower known to them, and they sell the eggs of those birds to would-be virgins. A pigeon's egg is small enough to be easily secreted deep inside a woman, and its shell is so fragile that an excited bridegroom will break it without feeling it, and the yolk of that specially bred egg is the exact color of blood. Also, the crones sell to women an astringent ointment made from the berry which you call the buckthorn, which will pucker the most slack and gaping orifice to adolescent tightness. . . .

As you command, Your Excellency, I shall try to refrain from giving so many specific particulars.

Rape was a crime not often heard of among our people, for three reasons. First, it was almost impossible to commit without being caught, since most of our communities were so small that everyone knew everyone else, and strangers were exceedingly noticeable. Also, it was a rather unnecessary crime, there being plenty of maátime and slave women to satisfy a man's really urgent needs. Also, rape was punished with death. So was adultery, and so was cuilónyotl, the sex act between man and man, and so was patlachúia, the sex act between woman and woman. But those crimes, while probably not rare, were rarely discovered unless the partners were caught in the act. Such sins are, like virginity, otherwise elusive of proof.

I should make it clear that I speak here only of those practices banned or shunned among us Mexíca. Except for the sexual liberties and ostentations permitted during some of our fertility ceremonies, we Mexíca were rather austere in comparison to many other peoples. I remember, when I first traveled among the Maya, far to the south of here, I was shocked by the aspect of some of their temples, which had their roof drainpipes formed in the shape of a man's tepúli. All during the rainy season they urinated unceasingly.

The Huaxtéca who live to the northeast, on the shore of the eastern sea, are exceptionally gross in matters of sex. I have seen temple friezes there carved with representations of the many positions a man and woman can assume. And any Huaxtécatl man with a tepúli larger than average would go walking about, even in public, even when visiting more civilized places, wearing no loincloth at all. That boastful strutting gave the Huaxtéca men a reputation for rampant virility, which may or may not have been deserved. However, on those occasions when captured Huaxtéca warriors have been put up for sale at the slave market, I have seen our own Mexíca noblewomen—veiled, and staying on the fringe of the crowd, but making signals for their servant to bid for this or that Huaxtécatl on the selling block.

The Purémpecha of Michihuácan to the west of here are most lax, or lenient, in matters of sex. For example, the sex act between a man and a man is not only not punished, it is condoned and accepted. It has even got into their picture writing. Perhaps you know that the symbol for a woman's tipíli is the drawing of a snail shell? Well, to write of the act between two males, the Purémpecha unashamedly would draw the picture of a nude man with a snail shell covering his real organs.

As for the act between my sister and myself—your word is incest?—yes, Your Excellency, I believe that was forbidden in every nation known. And yes, we risked death if we had been caught. The laws prescribed particularly grisly forms of execution for copulation between brother and sister, father and daughter, mother and son, uncle and niece, and so on. But such couplings were prohibited only to us macehuáltin, who constituted most of the population. As I earlier remarked, there were noble families which strove to preserve what they called the purity of their bloodlines by confining their marriages *only* to near relatives, though there was never any evidence that it improved any succeeding generations. And of course not the law nor tradition nor people in general gave much notice to what went on among the slave class: rape, incest, adultery, what have you.

But you ask how my sister and I evaded discovery during our long indulgence in our sin. Well, having been so harshly chastised by our mother for much lesser mischiefs, we had both learned to be discreet in the extreme. A time came when I was away from Xaltócan for months on end, and I ached for Tzitzitlíni, and she ached for me. But at every homecoming, I would give her only a cool brotherly kiss on the cheek and we would sit apart, concealing our inner tumult, while I recounted to our parents and other news-hungry relatives and friends all my doings in the world beyond our island. It might be a day or several days before Tzitzi and I could find or make an opportunity to be together in private and in secret and in no danger. Ah, but then, the hasty disrobing, the frantic caresses, the first release—as if we two lay on the slope of our own small, secret, and awakening volcano—then the more leisurely fondlings, the softer and more exquisite explosions. . . .

But my absences from the island came later. Meanwhile my sister and I were never once surprised in the act. Of course, we would have incurred calamity if, like Christians, we had conceived a child at every coupling, or at any of them. That possibility might never have entered my own head; what boy could imagine being a father? But Tzitzi was a female, and wiser about such things, and she had taken precautions against the contingency. Those old women of whom I have spoken, they sold secretly to unmarried maidens—as our apothecaries sold openly to married couples who did not want to make a child every time they went to bed—a powder ground from the tlatlaohuéhuetl, which is that tuber like a sweet potato, only a hundred times bigger; what you call in Spanish the barbasco. Any woman who daily takes a dose of the powdered barbasco runs no risk of conceiving an unwanted

Forgive me, Your Excellency. I had no idea I was saying anything sacrilegious. Do please be seated again.

I must report that, for a long time, I was personally running a risk, even when I was safely distant from Tzitzi. During our twilight military classes at The House of Building Strength, squads of six or eight boys together were regularly sent off to remote fields or stands of trees where we did a pretense of "standing guard against attack on the school." It was a boring duty, which we usually enlivened by playing patóli with jumping beans.

But then someone of the boys, I forget who, discovered the solitary act. He was not shy or selfish about his discovery, and immediately demonstrated the art to the rest of us. From then on, the boys no longer carried beans when they went on guard; they had their games equipment attached. For that is all it amounted to: a game. We held contests and made wagers on the amount of omícetl we could ejaculate, the number of times we could do it in succession, and the time needed in between for resurgence. It was like our even younger days, when we had competed to see who could spit or urinate farthest or most copiously. But in this new competition I was at hazard.

You see, I often came to the games not long out of the embrace of Tzitzi and, as you can imagine, my reservoir of omícetl was pretty well drained, not to mention my capacity for arousal. Hence my ejaculations were but few and feeble dribbles compared with the other boys', and often I could not get my tepúli erect at all. For a time, my comrades hooted and made fun of me, but then they began to regard me with worried and even pitying looks. Some of the more compassionate boys suggested remedies to me—eating raw meat, sweating long in the steam house, things like that. My two best friends, Chimáli and Tlatli, had discovered that they achieved vastly more thrilling sensations when each manipulated the other's tepúli rather than his own. So they suggested

Filth? Obscenity? It lacerates your ears to hear me? I am sorry if I distress Your Excellency—and you, my lord scribes—but I do not relate these events out of idle prurience. They all have a bearing on less trivial events which came later, and which came as a result of all this. If you will hear me out?

Eventually some of the older boys got the idea of putting their tepúltin where they belonged. A few of our comrades, including Pactli, the governor's son, went scouting in the village nearest our school. There they found and drafted into service a slave woman of twenty-some years, maybe even thirty. Rather fittingly, her name was Tetéo-Temacáliz, meaning Gift of the Gods. At any rate, she was a gift to the guard posts, which thereafter she visited almost daily.

Pactli had the authority to command her to that attendance, but I do not believe she had to be commanded. For she proved a willing, even vigorous participant in the sexual games. Ayya, I suppose the poor slut had reason. She had a comical bulge on her nose, and she was dumpily built, with great doughy thighs, and I imagine she had not much hope of marriage even to a man of her own tlacótli class. So she took to her new avocation of road straddler with lewd abandon.

As I have said, there might be six or eight boys camping afield at the guard posts on any given evening. When Gift of the Gods had serviced each of that number, the first would be ready for another turn, and the round would begin again. I am sure the lascivious Gift of the Gods could have gone on all night. But after a while of that activity she would get full of omícetl, slimy and slippery, and begin to give off the odor of an unhealthy fish, so the boys would stop of their own accord and send her home.

But she would be there again, the next afternoon, stripped naked, splayed wide open, and panting to commence. I had taken no part in those doings, had done no more than watch, until one evening, when Pactli finished using Gift of the Gods, he whispered something to her, and she came to where I sat.

"You are Mole," she said, leering. "And Pactzin tells me you have a difficulty." She made movements of temptation, her loose-lipped tipíli directly in front of my burning face. "Perhaps your spear would welcome being held in me and not in your fist for a change." I mumbled that I was not in any need of her at the moment, but I could not protest too much, with six or seven of my comrades standing about and grinning at my discomfiture.

"Ayyo!" she exclaimed, when with her hands she lifted my mantle and undid my loincloth. "Yours is a choice one, young Mole!" She bounced it in her palm. "Even unawakened, it is grander than the tepúli of any of the older boys. Even that of the noble Pactzin." My surrounding fellows laughed and nudged each other. I did not look up at the Lord Red Heron's son, but I knew that Gift of the Gods had just earned for me an enemy.

"Surely," she said, "a gracious macehuáli will not deny pleasure to a humble tlacótli. Let me arm my warrior with a weapon." She took my member between her big flabby breasts, squeezed them together with one arm and began to massage me with them. Nothing happened. Then she did other things to me, attentions with which she had not favored even Pactli. He turned, thunder-faced, and stalked away from us. Still nothing happened, although she even...

Yes, yes, I hasten to conclude this episode.

Gift of the Gods finally gave up in annoyance. She threw my tepúli back against my belly and said petulantly, "The conceited cub warrior saves his virginity, no doubt for a woman of his own class." She spat on the ground, abruptly left me, seized another boy, wrestled him down, and began to buck like a wasp-stung deer....

Well.

His Excellency did ask me to speak of sex and sin, did he not, reverend friars? But it seems he cannot ever listen for long without turning as purple as his cassock, and betaking himself elsewhere. I should at least like him to know what I was leading up to. But of course—I was forgetting—His Excellency can read of it when he is calmer. May I proceed then, my lords?

Chimáli came and sat beside me, and said, "I was not one of those who laughed at you, Mole. She does not excite me either."

"It is not so much that she is ugly and slovenly," I said. And I told Chimáli what my father had recently told me: of that disease nanáua which can come from unclean sexual practices, the disease which afflicts so many of your Spanish soldiers, and which they fatalistically call "the fruit of the earth."

"Women who make a decent career of their sex are not to be feared," I told Chimáli. "Our warriors' auyaníme, for instance, keep themselves clean, and they are regularly inspected by the army physicians. But the maátime who will spread themselves for just anybody, and for any number, they are best avoided. The disease comes from unclean parts, and this creature here—who knows what squalid slave men she services before she comes to us? If you ever get infected with the nanáua, there is no cure. It can rot your tepúli so it falls off, and it can rot your brain until you are a stumbling, stammering idiot."

"That is the truth, Mole?" asked Chimáli, quite ashen in the face. He looked at the sweating, heaving boy and woman on the ground. "And I was going to have her too, just so I would not be jeered at. But I had rather be unmanly than be an idiot."

He went at once and informed Tlatli. Then they must have spread the word, for the waiting line diminished after that evening, and, in the steam house, I often saw my comrades examining themselves for symptoms of rot. The woman came to be called by a variant of her name: Tetéo-Tlayo, Offal of the Gods. But some of the schoolboys continued recklessly rutting on her, and one of those was Pactli. My contempt for him must have been as obvious as his dislike of me, for he came to me one day and said menacingly:

"So the Mole is too careful of his health to soil himself with a maátitl? I know that is only your excuse for your pitiable impotence, but it implies criticism of *my* behavior, and I warn you not to slander your future brother." I gaped at him. "Yes, before I rot, as you predict, I intend to marry your sister. Even if I become a diseased and shambling idiot, she cannot refuse a nobleman. But I would prefer that she come to me willingly. So I tell you, brother-to-be. Never let Tzitzitlíni know of my sport with Offal of the Gods. Or I will kill you."

He strode away without waiting for me to reply, which, in any case, I could not have done at that moment. I was dumb with dread. It was not that I feared Pactli personally, since I was a shade the taller of us and probably the stronger. But if he had been a weakling dwarf, he was still the son of our tecútli, and now he bore me a grudge. The fact was that I had lived in trepidation ever since the boys began their games of solitary sex, and then their couplings with Offal of the Gods. My poor performance, and the derision I endured, those embarrassments did not wound my boyish vanity so much as they put fear in my vitals. I truly *had* to be thought impotent and unmanly. Pactli was as underwitted as he was overbearing, but if he ever began to suspect the real reason for my seemingly feeble sexuality—that I was lavishing it all elsewhere—he was not too stupid to wonder where. And on our small island, it would not take him long to ascertain that I could be trysting with no female except...

Tzitzitlíni had first caught Pactli's interest when she was only a bud of a girl, when she visited the palace to attend that execution of his own adulterous sister princess. More recently, at the springtime Feast of the Great Awakening, Tzitzi had led the dancers in the pyramid plaza—and Pactli had seen her dance, and he had been fully smitten. Since then, he had repeatedly managed to encounter her in public and had spoken to her, a breach of manners for any man, even a pili. He had also recently invented excuses to visit our house two or three times, "to discuss quarry affairs with Tepetzálan," and there he had to be let enter. But Tzitzi's cool reception of him and her unconcealed distaste for him would have sent any other young man slinking away for good.

And now the vile Pactli told me he was going to *marry* Tzitzi. I went home from school that night and, as we sat around our supper cloth, after our father had given thanks to the gods for the food before us, I bluntly spoke up:

"Pactli told me today that he intends to take Tzitzitlíni to wife. Not perhaps, or if she accepts him, or if the family gives consent. But that he intends it and will do it."

My sister stiffened and stared at me. She drew her hand lightly across her face, as our women always do at something unexpected. Our father looked uncomfortable. Our mother went on placidly eating, and just as placidly said, "He has spoken of it, Mixtli, yes. Pactzin will soon be out of the primary school, but he still must spend some years at the calmécac school before he can take a wife."

"He cannot take Tzitzi," I said. "Pactli is a stupid, greedy, unwholesome creature—"

Our mother leaned across the cloth and slapped my face, hard. "That is for speaking disrespectfully of our future governor. Who are you, what is your high station, that you presume to defame a noble?"

Biting back uglier words, I said, "I am not the only one of this island who knows Pactli to be a depraved and contemptible—"

She hit me again. "Tepetzálan," she said to our father. "One more word out of this unruly young man and you must attend to his correction." To me she said, "When the pili son of the Lord Red Heron marries Tzitzitlíni, all the rest of us become pípiltin as well. What are *your* great prospects, with no trade, with only your useless pretense of studying word pictures, that *you* could bring such eminence to your family?"

Our father cleared his throat and said, "I care not so much for the -tzin to our names, but I care less for discourtesy and infamy. To refuse a nobleman any request—especially to decline the honor Pactli confers by asking our daughter's hand—would be an insult to him, a disgracing of ourselves, that we could never live down. If we were let to live at all, we would have to leave Xaltócan."

"No, not the rest of you." Tzitzi spoke for the first time, and firmly. "I will leave. If that degenerate beast Pactli . . . Do not raise your hand to me, Mother. I am a woman grown, and I will strike you back."

"You are my daughter and this is my house!" shouted our mother.

"Children, what has come over you?" pleaded our father.

"I say only this," Tzitzi went on. "If Pactli demands me,

and you accede, not you or he will ever see me again. I will leave the island forever. If I cannot borrow or steal an acáli, I will swim. If I cannot reach the mainland, I will drown. Not Pactli or any other man will ever touch me, except a man I can give *myself* to."

"On all of Xaltócan—" our mother sputtered. "No other daughter so ungrateful, so disobedient and defiant, so—"

This time she was silenced by our father, who said, and said solemnly, "Tzitzitlíni, if your unfilial words had been heard outside these walls, not even I could pardon you or avert your due punishment. You would be stripped and beaten and your head shaved. Our neighbors would do it if I did not, as an example to their own children."

"I am sorry, father," she said in a level voice. "You must choose. An undutiful daughter or none."

"I thank the gods I need not choose tonight. As your mother remarked, it will be a few years yet before the young Lord Joy can marry. So let us speak of it no more now, in anger or otherwise. Many things may happen between now and then."

Our father was right: many things might happen. I did not know if Tzitzi had meant anything she said, and I had no chance to ask her that night or the next day. We dared no more than to exchange a worried and yearning glance from time to time. But, whether or not she held to her resolve, the prospect was desolating. If she fled from Pactli, I should lose her. If she succumbed and married him, I should lose her. If she went to his bed, she knew the arts of convincing him that she was virgin. But if, before then, my own behavior made Pactli suspect that another man had known her first—and *me* of all men—his rage would be monumental, his revenge inconceivable. Whatever the hideous manner he chose for slaying us, Tzitzi and I would have lost each other.

Ayya, many things *did* happen, and one of them was this. When I went to The House of Building Strength at the next day's dusk, I found my name and Pactli's on Blood Glutton's roster, as if it had been ordained by some ironic god. And when our squad got to the appointed patch of trees, Offal of the Gods was already there, already naked, sprawled, and ready. To the astonishment of Pactli and our other companions, I immediately ripped off my loincloth and flung myself upon her.

I did it as clumsily as I could, a performance calculated to make the other boys believe it was my first, and a performance that probably gave the slut as little pleasure as it gave me. When I judged it had gone on long enough, I prepared to disengage, but then the revulsion got the better of me, and I spewed vomit all over her face and naked body. The boys roared and rolled on the ground with laughter. Even the wretch Offal of the Gods was capable of recognizing the insult. She gathered up her garments, and she clutched them to her nakedness, and she ran away, and she never came back.

⳥

Not long after that incident, four other things of note occurred in rather rapid succession. At least, that is how I remember them happening.

It happened that our Uey-Tlatoáni Axayácatl died—very young, from the effects of wounds he had received in the battles against the Purémpecha—and his brother Tixoc, Other Face, assumed the throne of Tenochtítlan.

It happened that I, along with Chimáli and Tlatli, completed what schooling was afforded on Xaltócan. I was now regarded as "educated."

It happened that our island's governor sent a messenger to our house one evening to summon me immediately to his palace.

And it happened that, at last, I was parted from Tzitzitlíni, my sister and my love.

But I had best recount those occurrences in more detail, and in the order of their happening.

The change of rulers did not much affect the lives of us in the provinces. Indeed, even in Tenochtítlan, little was later remembered of Tixoc's reign except that, like his two predecessors, he continued work on the still-rising Great Pyramid in The Heart of the One World. And Tixoc added an architectural touch of his own to the plaza. He had stonemasons hew and carve the Battle Stone, a massive flat cylinder of volcanic rock which lay like a stack of immense tortillas between the unfinished pyramid and the Sun Stone's pedestal site. The Battle Stone was nearly as high as a man and about four strides across its diameter. Around the rim were low-relief carvings of Mexíca warriors. Tixoc prominent among them, engaged in combat and in subduing captives. The flat round top of the stone was the platform for a kind of public dueling, in which, a long time later, and in an unusual way, I would have occasion to participate.

Of rather more immediate concern to me, at that time, was the end of my formal schooling. Not being of the nobility, I was of course not entitled to go on to a calmécac of higher learning. And my record as Malínqui the Kink in one of our schools, and as Poyaútla the Fogbound in the other, had hardly been of a nature to make any of the higher schools on the mainland invite me to attend at no cost.

What particularly embittered me was that, while I hungered in vain for the chance to learn more than the trivial knowledge our telpochcáltin could teach, my friends Chimáli and Tlatli, who cared not a little finger for any further formal learning, *did* each get an invitation from separate calmécactin—and both of those in Tenochtítlan, my own dream destination. During their years in Xaltócan's House of Building Strength they had distinguished themselves as tlachtli players and as cub warriors. Though an elegant nobleman might have smiled at the "graces" the two boys had absorbed from The House of Learning Manners, they had nevertheless shone there too, by designing original costumes and settings for the ceremonies performed on festival days.

"It is too bad you cannot come with us, Mole," said Tlatli, sounding sincére enough but no whit less happy at his own good fortune. "You could attend all the dull schoolroom classes, and leave us free for our studio work."

Under the terms of their acceptance, both boys would, besides learning from the calmécac priests, also be apprenticed out to Tenochtítlan artists: Tlatli to a master sculptor, Chimáli to a master painter. I was sure that neither of them would pay much heed to the lessons in history, reading, writing, counting, and such, the very things I ached for most. Anyway, before they departed, Chimáli said, "Here is a good-bye gift for you, Mole. All my paints and reeds and brushes. I will have better ones in the city, and you may find them useful in your writing practice."

Yes, I was still pursuing my untutored study in the arts of reading and writing, though my ever becoming a word knower now seemed hopelessly remote, and my moving to Tenochtítlan a dream that would forever come untrue. My father had likewise despaired of my ever becoming a dedicated quarrier, and I was now too old to serve only to sit at the empty pit and shoo away animals. So, for some while past, I had been earning my keep and contributing to our family's support by working as a common farmboy.

Of course, Xaltócan has no such thing as farmland. There is not enough arable topsoil for staple crops like the maize, which requires deep earth for its nourishment. So Xaltócan, like all island communities, grows the bulk of its vegetable foods on the wide and ever spreading chinámpa which you call floating gardens. Each chinámitl is a raft of woven tree limbs and branches, moored at the lake edge, then spread with load upon load of the richest soil, freighted out from the mainland. As the crops extend their roots season by season, new roots twining down old ones, they eventually clutch the lake bottom and hold the raft firmly in place. Other gardens are built and moored alongside. Every inhabited island in all the lakes, Tenochtítlan included, wears a wide ring of fringe of these chinámpa. On some of the more fertile islands, it is difficult to discern where the god-made land leaves off and the man-made fields begin.

It takes no more than mole eyesight or mole intellect to tend such gardens, so I tended those belonging to our family and neighbors in our quarter. The work was undemanding; I had plenty of free time. I applied myself—and Chimáli's gift of paints—to the drawing of word pictures: training myself to make the most complex symbols ever simpler, more stylized, smaller in size. Unlikely as it then seemed, I still nursed the secret hope that my self-education might somehow yet improve my lot in life. I smile pityingly, now, to recall my young self sitting on a dirt raft among the sprouting maize and beans and chilis—among the reeking fertilizer of animal entrails and fish heads—while I scribbled away at my writing practice and dreamed my lofty dreams.

For example, I toyed with the ambition of becoming one of the pochtéca traveling merchants, and thus journeying to the Maya lands where some wonder-working doctor would restore my eyesight, while I should become rich from my shrewd trading along the way. Oh, I devised many a plan to turn a trifling amount of trade goods into a towering fortune, ingenious plans that I was sure no previous trader had ever thought of. The only obstacle to my assured success—as Tzitzi tactfully pointed out, when I confided some of my ideas—was that I lacked even the trifling amount of capital I reckoned I would need to begin with.

And then, one afternoon when the workday was done, one of the Lord Red Heron's messengers appeared at our house door. He wore a mantle of neutral color, signifying neither good news nor bad, and he said politely to my father, "Mixpantzínco."

"Ximopanólti," said my father, gesturing for him to enter.

The young man, about my own age, took only a single step inside and said, "The Tecútli Tlauquécholtzin, my master and yours, requires the presence of your son Chicóme-Xochitl Tliléctic-Mixtli at the palace."

My father and sister looked surprised and bewildered. I suppose I did too. My mother did not. She wailed, "Yya ayya, I knew the boy would one day offend the nobles or the gods or—" She broke off to demand of the messenger, "What mischief has Mixtli done? There is no need for the Lord Red Heron to trouble himself with whipping or whatever is decreed. We will gladly attend to the punishment."

"I do not know that anyone has done anything," said the messenger, eyeing her warily. "I merely obey my order. To bring him without delay."

And without delay I accompanied him, preferring whatever waited at the palace to whatever my mother's imagination might conceive. I was curious, yes, but I could not think of any reason to quake. If that summons had come in an earlier time, I would have worried that the malicious Pactli had contrived some charge against me. But the young Lord Joy had himself gone off, two or three years before, to a Tenochtítlan calmécac which accepted only the scions of ruling families, themselves rulers-to-be. Pactli had since come back to Xaltócan only on brief school holidays. During those visits, he had paid calls at our house, but always during the working day when I was not at home, so I had not even seen him since the days of our having briefly shared Offal of the Gods.

The messenger stayed a respectful few paces behind me as I entered the palace throne room and bent to make the gesture of kissing the earth. Beside Lord Red Heron sat a man I had never seen on the island before. Though the stranger sat on a lower chair, as was proper, he considerably diminished our governor's usual air of importance. Even my mole vision could make out that he wore a brilliant feather mantle and ornaments of a richness that no nobleman of Xaltócan could flaunt.

Red Heron said to the visitor, "The request was: make a man of him. Well, our Houses of Building Strength and Learning Manners have done their utmost. Here he is."

"I am bidden to make a test," said the stranger. He produced a small roll of bark paper and held it out to me.

"Mixpantzínco," I said to both the nobles before I unrolled the thing. It bore nothing I could recognize as a test; only a single line of word pictures, and I had seen them before.

"You can read it?" asked the stranger.

"I forgot to mention that," said Red Heron, as if he had taught me himself. "Mixtli can read some simple things with a fair measure of comprehension."

I said, "I can read this, my lords. It says—"

"Never mind," the stranger interrupted. "Just tell me: what does the duck-billed face signify?"

"Ehécatl, the wind, my lord."

"Anything else?"

"Well, my lord, with the other figure, the closed eyelids, it says Night Wind. But—"

"Yes? Speak up, young man."

"If my lord will excuse my impertinence, that one figure does not show a duck's bill. It is the wind trumpet through which the wind god—"

"Enough." The stranger turned to Red Heron. "He is the one, Lord Governor. I have your permission, then?"

"But of course, of course," said Red Heron, quite obsequiously. To me he said, "This is the Lord Strong Bone, Snake Woman to Nezahualpíli, Uey-Tlatoáni of Texcóco. Lord Strong Bone brings the Revered Speaker's personal invitation that you come to reside and study and serve at the court of Texcóco."

"Texcóco!" I exclaimed. I had never been there, or anywhere in the Acólhua country. I knew no one there, and no Acólhuatl could ever have heard of me—certainly not the Revered Speaker Nezahualpíli, who, in all these lands, was second in power and prestige only to Tixoc, the Uey-Tlatoáni of Tenochtítlan. I was so astounded that, unthinking and unmannerly, I blurted, *"Why?"*

"You are not commanded," the Texcóco Snake Woman said brusquely. "You are invited, and you may accept or decline. But you are not invited to question the offer."

I mumbled an apology, and the Lord Red Heron came to my support, saying, "Excuse the youngster, my lord. I am sure he is as perplexed as I have been these several years—that such an exalted personage as Nezahualpíli should have fixed his regard on this one of so many macehuáltin."

The Snake Woman only grunted, so Red Heron went on, "I have never been given any explanation of your master's interest in this particular commoner, and I have refrained from asking. Of course, I remember your previous ruler, that tree of great shade, the wise and kindly Fasting Coyote, and how he used to travel alone throughout The One World, his identity disguised, to seek out estimable persons deserving of his favor. Does his illustrious son Nezahualpíli carry on that same benign avocation? If so, what in the world did he see in our young subject Tliléctic-Mixtli?"

"I cannot say, Lord Governor." The haughty noble gave Red Heron almost as gruff a rebuke as he had given me. "No one questions the Revered Speaker's impulses and intentions. Not even I, his Snake Woman. And I have other duties besides waiting for an irresolute stripling to decide if he will accept a prodigious honor. I return to Texcóco, young man, at tomorrow's rising of Tezcatlipóca. Do you go with me or not?"

"I go, of course, my lord," I said. "I have only to pack

some clothes, some papers, some paints. Unless there is something in particular I should bring?" I boldly added that, in hope of prying loose a hint of *why* I was going, for *how long* I was going.

He said only, "Everything necessary will be provided."

Red Heron said, "Be here at the palace jetty, Mixtli, at the rising of Tonatíu."

Lord Strong Bone glanced coolly at the governor, then at me, and said, "Best you learn, young man, to call the sun god Tezcatlipóca from now on."

From now on *forever?* I wondered as I hastened home alone. Was I to be an adopted Acólhuatl for the rest of my life, and a convert to the Acólhua gods?

When I told my waiting family what had occurred, my father said excitedly, "Night Wind! Just as I told you, son Mixtli! It was the god Night Wind you met on the road those years ago. And it is from Night Wind that now you will get your heart's desire."

Tzitzi looked worried and said, "But suppose it is a ruse. Suppose Texcóco merely happens to need a xochimíqui of a certain age and size for some particular sacrifice..."

"No," our mother said bluntly. "Mixtli is not handsome or graceful or virtuous enough to have been specially chosen for any ceremony I know of." She sounded disgruntled at this affair's having got out of her management. "But there is certainly something suspicious in all this. Grubbing about in picture books and wallowing idly in the chinámpa, Mixtli could have done nothing to bring himself to the notice of even a slave dealer, let alone a royal court."

I said, "From the words spoken at the palace, and from the scrap of writing Lord Strong Bone carried, I think I can guess some things. That night at the crossroads I met no god, but an Acólhuatl traveler, perhaps some courtier of Nezahualpíli himself, and we have just assumed he was Night Wind. During the years since then, though I do not know why, Texcóco has kept track of me. Anyway, it now seems that I am to attend a Texcóco calmécac, where I shall be taught the art of word knowing. I will be a scribe, as I have always wanted. At least," I finished with a shrug, "that is what I surmise."

"And you call it all coincidence," my father said sternly.

"It is just as likely, son Mixtli, that you really did meet Night Wind and took him to be a mortal. Gods, like men, can travel in disguise, unrecognized. And you have profited from the encounter. It would do no harm to give thanks to Night Wind."

"You are right, father Tepetzálan. I will do so. Whether or not Night Wind was directly involved, he *is* the dispenser of hearts' desires when he chooses to be, and it is my heart's desire I am about to realize."

"But only one of my heart's desires," I said to Tzitzi, when at last we had a moment together in private. "How can I leave the sound of small bells ringing?"

"If you have good sense, you will leave here dancing and cheering," she said, with feminine practicality, but not with any perceptible cheer in her own voice. "You cannot spend your life pulling weeds, Mixtli, and inventing futile ambitions like your notion of becoming a trader. However this all happened, you now have a future, a brighter one than has ever been offered to any macehuáli of Xaltócan."

"But if Night Wind or Nezahualpíli or whoever could send one opportunity my way, there might be others, even better. I always dreamed of going to Tenochtítlan, not to Texcóco. I can still decline this offer—Lord Strong Bone said so—and I can wait. Why should I not?"

"Because you do have good sense, Mixtli. While I was still at The House of Learning Manners, the Mistress of the Girls told us that Tenochtítlan may be the strong arm of The Triple Alliance, but Texcóco is the brain. There is more than pomp and power at the court of Nezahualpíli. There is a long heritage of poetry and culture and wisdom. The Mistress also said that, of all the lands which speak Náhuatl, the people of Texcóco speak the purest form of our language. What better destination for an aspiring scholar? You must go and you will go. You will study, you will learn, you will excel. And, if you truly have won the patronage of the Revered Speaker, who knows what high plans he may have for you? When you talk of refusing his invitation, you know you talk nonsense." Her voice dropped. "And only because of me."

"Because of us."

She sighed. "We had to grow up sometime."

"I always hoped we would do it together."

"We can still and always hope. You will be coming home at festival times. We will be together then. And when your schooling is done, why, you could become rich and powerful. You could become Mixtzin, and a noble can marry whomever he chooses."

"I hope to become an accomplished word knower, Tzitzi. That is ambition enough for me. And few scribes ever do anything to get themselves entitled -tzin."

"Well... perhaps you will be sent to work in some far Acólhua province where it is not known that you have a sister. Simply send and I will come. Your chosen bride from your native island."

"That would be years from now," I protested. "And you are already approaching marriageable age. In the meantime, the accursed Pactli also comes home for holidays on Xaltócan. Long before my schooling is done, he will be back here to stay. You know what he wants, and what he wants he demands, and what he demands cannot be denied."

"Denied, no, but possibly deferred," she said. "I will do my best to discourage the Lord Joy. And he may be less insistent in his demands"—she smiled bravely up at me—"now that I shall have a relative and protector at the mightier court of Texcóco. You see? You must go." Her smile became tremulous. "The gods have arranged that we be parted for a while, so that we shall not be parted forever." The smile faltered and fell and broke, and she wept.

The Lord Strong Bone's acáli was of mahogany, richly carved, covered by a fringed awning, decorated with the jade-stone badges and feather pennons proclaiming his rank. It by-passed the lakeside city of Texcóco—what you Spaniards now call San Antonio de Padua—and proceeded about one-long-run farther south, toward a medium-sized hill which rose directly from the lake waters. "Texcotzínco," said the Snake Woman, the first word he had addressed to me during our entire morning's journey from Xaltócan. I squinted to peer at the hill, for on the other side of it was Nezahualpíli's country palace.

The big canoe slid up to a solidly built jetty, the rowers upended their oars, and the steersman jumped ashore to make the boat fast. I waited for Lord Strong Bone to be helped out by his boatmen, then myself clambered onto the pier, lugging the wicker basket in which I had packed my belongings. The laconic Snake Woman pointed to a stone staircase winding uphill from the jetty and said, "That way, young man," the only other words he spoke to me that day. I hesitated, wondering whether it would be polite to wait for him, but he was supervising his men's unloading from the acáli all the gifts Lord Red Heron had sent to the Uey-Tlatoáni Nezahualpíli. So I shouldered my basket and trudged alone up the stairs.

Some of the steps were man-laid of hewn blocks, some were carved from the living rock of the hill. At the thirteenth step I came to a broad stone landing, where there was a bench for resting and a small statue of some god I could not identify, and the next flight of stairs led off at an angle from the landing. Again thirteen steps and again a landing. I thus zigzagged up the hill and then, at the fifty-second step, I found myself on a flat terrace, a vast level place hacked out of the sloping hillside; it was riotous with the many-hued flowers of a lush garden. That fifty-second step had set me on a stone-flagged pathway, which I followed as it wound leisurely through flower beds, under splendid trees, past meandering brooks and gurgling little waterfalls, until the path again became a stairway. Again thirteen steps and a landing with a bench and statue . . .

The sky had been clouding over for some time, and now the rain came, in the usual manner of the days of our wet season—a storm like the end of the world: many-forked sticks of lightning, drum rolls of thunder, and a deluge of rain as if it would never end. But end it always did, in no longer time than a man would take for a pleasant afternoon nap; in time for Tonatíu, or Tezcatlipóca, to shine again on a wet-sparkling world, to make it steam, to make it dry and warm again before he set. When the rain came, now, I had already taken shelter on one of the stair landings which had a bench protected by a roof thatch. While I sat out the storm, I meditated on the numerical significance of the zigzagging staircase, and I smiled at the ingenuity of whoever had designed it.

Like you white men, we in these lands lived by a yearly calendar based on the sun's traversing the sky. Thus our solar year, like yours, consisted of three hundred sixty and five days, and we used that calendar for all ordinary purposes: to tell us when to plant which seeds, when to expect the rainy season, and so forth. We divided that solar year into eighteen months of twenty days apiece, plus the nemontémtin—the "lifeless days," the "hollow days"—the five days required to round out the three hundred sixty and five of the year.

However, we also observed an alternate calendar based not on the sun's daytime excursions but on the nightly appearance of the brilliant star we named for our ancient god Quetzalcóatl, or Feathered Serpent. Sometimes Quetzalcóatl served as the After Blossom which blazed immediately after sunset; at other times he moved to the other side of the sky, where he would be the last star visible as the sun rose and washed away all the others. Any of our astronomers could explain all this to you, with great diagrams, but I have never been very good at astronomy. I do know that the movements of the stars are not as random as they would seem, and that our ceremonial calendar was somehow based on the movements of the star named for Quetzalcóatl. That calendar was useful even to our ordinary folk, for naming their newborn children. Our historians and scribes used it for dating notable happenings and the length of our rulers' reigns. More important, our seers used it to divine the future, to warn against impending calamities, to select auspicious days for weighty undertakings.

In the divinatory calendar, each year contained two hundred sixty days, those days named by appending the numbers one through thirteen to each of twenty traditional signs: rabbit, reed, knife, and so on—and each solar year was itself named according to the ceremonial number and sign of its first day. As you can perceive, our solar and ritual calendars were forever overlapping each other, one lagging behind or forging ahead of the other. But, if you care to do the arithmetic involved, you will find that they balanced out at an equal number of days over a total of fifty and two of the ordinary solar years. The year of my birth was called Thirteen Rabbit, for example, and no later year bore that same name until my fifty-second came around.

So, to us, fifty and two was a significant number—a sheaf of years, we called it—since that many years were simultaneously recognized by both calendars, and since that many years were more or less what the average man could expect to live, barring accident, illness, or war. The stone staircase winding up Texcotzínco Hill, with its thirteen steps between landings, denoted the thirteen ritual numbers, and with its fifty and two steps between terraces, denoted a sheaf of years. When I eventually got to the top of the hill I had counted five hundred and twenty steps. All together, they denoted two of the ceremonial years of two hundred sixty days apiece, and likewise stood for ten sheaves of fifty and two years. Yes, most ingenious.

When the rain stopped, I continued my climb. I did not go up all the rest of those stairs in one headlong dash, though I am sure I could have, in those days of my young strength. I halted at each remaining landing only long enough to see if I could identify the god or goddess whose statue stood there. I knew perhaps half of them: Tezcatlipóca, the sun, chief god of the Acólhua; Quetzalcóatl, of whom I have spoken; Ometecútli and Omecíuatl, our Lord and Lady Pair. . . .

I stopped longer in the gardens. There on the mainland the soil was ample and the space unlimited, and Nezahualpíli was evidently a man who loved flowers, flowers everywhere. The hillside gardens were laid out in neat beds, but the terraces were not trammeled by walls. So the flowers spilled generously over the edges, and the trailing varieties dangled their brilliant blooms almost as far down the hill as the next lower terrace. I know I saw every flower I had ever previously seen in my life, besides countless kinds that I never had, and many of those must have been expensively transplanted from far countries. I also gradually realized that the numerous lily ponds, the reflecting pools, the fish ponds, the chuckling brooks and cascades were a watering system fed by the fall of gravity from some source atop the hill.

If the Lord Strong Bone was climbing behind me, I never caught sight of him. But, in one of the higher terrace gardens, I came upon another man, lolling on a stone bench. As I approached near enough to see him fairly clearly—the wrinkled cacao nut-brown skin, the ragged loincloth that was his only garment—I remembered having met him before. He stood up, at least to the extent of his hunched and shrunken stature. I had grown taller than he was.

I gave him the traditionally polite greeting, but then said, probably more rudely than I intended it to sound, "I thought you were a Tlaltelólco beggar, old man. What do you here?"

"A homeless man is at home anywhere in the world," he said, as if it were something to be proud of. "I am here to welcome you to the land of the Acólhua."

"You!" I exclaimed, for the grotesque little man was even more of an excrescence in that luxuriant garden than he had been in the motley market crowd.

"Were you expecting to be greeted by the Revered Speaker in person?" he asked, with a mocking, gap-toothed grin. "Welcome to the palace of Texcotzínco, young Mixtli. Or young Tozáni, young Malínqui, young Poyaútla, as you like."

"Long ago you knew my name. Now you know all my nicknames."

"A man with a talent for listening can hear even things not yet spoken. You will have still other names in time to come."

"Are you really a seer, then, old man?" I asked, unconsciously echoing my father's words of years before. "How did you know I was coming here?"

"Ah, your coming here," he said. "I pride myself that I had some small part in arranging that."

"Then you know a good deal more than I do. I would be grateful for a bit of explanation."

"Know, then, that I never saw you before that day in Tlaltelólco, when I overheard the mention that it was your naming day. Out of mere curiosity, I took the opportunity for a closer look at you. When I inspected your eyes, I detected their imminent and increasing loss of distant vision. That affliction is sufficiently uncommon that the distinctive shape of the afflicted eyeball affords an unmistakeable sign diagnostic. I could say with certainty that you were fated to see things close and true."

"You also said I would speak truly of such things."

He shrugged. "You seemed bright enough, for a brat, that it was safe to predict you would grow up passably intelligent. A man who is forced by weak eyesight to regard everything in this world at close range, and with good sense, is also usually inclined to describe the world as it really is."

"You are a cunning old trickster," I said, smiling. "But what has all that to do with my being summoned to Texcóco?"

"Every ruler and prince and governor is surrounded by servile attendants and self-seeking wise men who will tell him what he wants to hear, or what they want him to hear. A man who will tell only the truth is a rarity among courtiers. I believed that you would become such a rarity, and that your faculties would be better appreciated at a court rather nobler than that of Xaltócan. So I dropped a word here and there..."

"You," I said unbelievingly, "have the ear of a man like Nezahualpíli?"

He gave me a look that somehow made me feel again much smaller than he was. "I told you long ago—have I not proved it yet?—that I also speak true, and to my own detriment, when I could easily pose as an omniscient messenger of the gods. Nezahualpíli is not so cynical as you, young Mole. He will listen to the lowliest of men, if that man speaks the truth."

"I apologize," I said, after a moment. "I should be thanking you, old man, not doubting you. And I truly am grateful for—"

He waved that away. "I did not do it entirely for you. I usually get full value for my discoveries. Simply see to it that you give faithful service to the Uey-Tlatoáni, and we shall both have earned our rewards. Now go."

"But go where? No one has told me where or to whom I am to announce myself. Do I just cross over this hill and hope to be recognized?"

"Yes. The palace is on the other side, and you are expected. Whether the Speaker himself will recognize you, next time you meet, I could not say."

"We have *never* met," I complained. "We cannot possibly know each other."

"Oh? Well, I advise you to ingratiate yourself with Tolána-Tecíuapil, the Lady of Tolan, for she is the favorite of Nezahualpíli's seven wedded wives. At last count he also had forty concubines. So over there at the palace are some sixty sons and fifty daughters of the Revered Speaker. I doubt that even he knows the latest tally. He may take you to be a forgotten by-blow from one of his wanderings abroad, a son just now come home. But you will be hospitably welcomed, young Mole, never fear."

I turned, then turned back again. "Could I first be of some service to you, venerable one? Perhaps I could assist you to the top of the hill?"

He said, "I thank you for the kind offer, but I will loiter here yet a while. It is best that you climb and breast the hill alone, for all the rest of your life awaits you on the other side."

That sounded portentous, but I saw a small fallacy in it, and I smiled at my own perspicacity. "Surely my life awaits, whichever way I go from here, and whether I go alone or not."

The cacao man smiled too, but ironically. "Yes, at your age, many possible lives await. Go whichever way you choose. Go alone or in company. The companions may walk with you a long way or a little. But at the end of your life, no matter how crowded were its roads and its days, you will have learned what all must learn. And that will be too late for any starting over, too late for anything but regret. So learn it now. No man has ever yet lived out any life but one, and that one his chosen own, and most of that alone." He paused, and his eyes held mine. "Now then, Mixtli, which way do you go from here, and in what company?"

I turned and kept on up the hill, alone.

I H S
✠
S. C. C. M.

Sanctified, Caesarean, Catholic Majesty,
the Emperor Don Carlos, Our Lord King:

MOST Virtuous Majesty, our Sagacious Monarch:
from the City of Mexico, capital of New Spain, this Feast Day
of the Circumcision in the Year of Our Lord one thousand five
hundred twenty and nine, greeting.

With heavy heart but submissive hand, your chaplain again
forwards to Your Imperial Majesty, as again commanded, yet
another collection of the writings dictated to date by our still-
resident Aztec—or Asmodeus, as Your Majesty's servant is
increasingly inclined to think of him.

This humble cleric can sympathize with Your Majesty's wry
comment that the Indian's chronicle is "considerably more im-
formative than the fanfarronadas we hear incessantly from the
newly entitled Marqués, the Señor Cortés himself, who is currently favoring us with his attendance at Court." And even a
grieved and morose Bishop can perceive Your Majesty's wry
joke when you write that "the Indian's communications are the
first we have received from New Spain *not* attempting to wheedle a title, or a vast allotment of the conquered lands, or a
loan."

But, Sire, we stand aghast when you report that your royal self *and your courtiers* are "entirely rapt and enthralled at the reading aloud of these pages." We trust we do not take lightly our pledges as a subject of Your Most Eminent Majesty, but our other sacred oaths oblige us to warn most solemnly, *ex officio et de fides*, against any further indiscriminate dissemination of this foul history.

Your Astute Majesty can hardly have failed to notice that the earlier pages have treated—casually, without remorse or repentance—of such sins as homicide, prolicide, suicide, anthropophagy, incest, harlotry, torture, idolatry, and breach of the Commandment to honor father and mother. If, as it has been said, one's sins are wounds of one's soul, this Indian's soul is bleeding at every pore.

But, in the case the more sly insinuations somehow escaped Your Majesty's attention, allow us to point out that the scurrilous Aztec has dared to suggest that his people boast of some vague lineal descent from a Lord and Lady Pair, a pagan parody of Adam and Eve. He also suggests that *we Christians ourselves* are idolatrous of a whole pantheon comparable to the seething host of demons his people worshiped. With equal blasphemy, he has implied that such Holy Sacraments as Baptism, and Absolution through Confession, and even the petitioning for Grace before a meal, were observed in these lands, antedating and independent of any knowledge of Our Lord and His bestowel of the Sacraments. Perhaps his most vile sacrilege is to aver, as Your Majesty will shortly read, that one of the previous heathen rulers of these people was *born of a virgin!*

Your Majesty makes an incidental inquiry in this latest letter. Though we ourself have sat in on the Indian's storytelling sessions from time to time—and will continue to do so, time permitting, to put to him specific questions or to demand elaboration on some of his comments we have read—we must deferentially remind Your Majesty that the Bishop of Mexico has other pressing duties which preclude our personally verifying or disproving any of this prattler's boasts and asseverations.

However, Your Majesty asks information regarding one of his more outrageous assertions, and we sincerely hope that the query is merely another of our jovial sovereign's good-humored jests. In any case, we must reply: No, Sire, we know nothing of the properties the Aztec ascribes to the root called barbasco. We cannot confirm that it would be "worth its weight in gold" as a commodity of Spanish commerce. We know nothing about it that would "silence the chatter of the ladies of the Court." The very suggestion that Our Lord God could have created a vegetable efficacious in averting the conception of Christian human life is repugnant to our sensibilities and an affront to

Pardon the ink blot, Sire. Our agitation afflicts our pen hand. But *satis superque* ...

Aś Your Majesty commands, the friars and the young lay brother will continue setting down these pages until—in time, we pray—Your Majesty commands that they be relieved of their pitiable duty. Or until they themselves can no longer bear the task. We think we are not breaching the confidence of the Confessional if we merely remark that in these last months the brothers' own confessions have become phantasmatical in the extreme, and bloodcurdling to hear, and necessitating the most exigent penances for absolution.

May Our Redeemer and Master, Jesus Christ, be always Your Majesty's consolation and defense against all the wiles of our Adversary, is the constant prayer of Your S.C.C.M.'s chaplain.

(ecce signum) Zumárraga

QUARTA PARS

THE other side of the hill was even more beautiful than the side facing Lake Texcóco. The slope was gentle, the gardens undulated downward and away below me, variously formal and informal, glinting with ponds and fountains and bathing pools. There were long sweeps of green lawn, on which grazed a number of tame deer. There were shady groves of trees, and an occasional tree standing alone which had been clipped and pruned into the living statue of some animal or bird. Toward the bottom of the hill there were many buildings, large and small, but all most handsomely proportioned and set at comfortable distances from one another. I believed I could even make out richly dressed persons moving about on the walkways between the buildings—anyway, there were moving dots of brilliant colors. The Xaltócan palace of the Lord Red Heron had been a commodious building, and impressive enough, but the Texcotzínco palace of the Uey-Tlatoáni Nezahualpíli was an entire, self-contained, pastoral *city*.

The top of the hill, where I stood, was wooded with the "oldest of the old" cypress trees, some of them so big around that perhaps twelve men with arms outstretched could not have encircled their trunks, and so tall that their gray-green feathery leaves merged into the azure of the sky. I looked about and, though they were cleverly concealed by shrubbery, I espied the big clay pipes that watered those gardens and the city below. As well as I could judge, the pipes led away in the distance to an even higher mountain to the southeast, whence no doubt they brought the water from some pure spring and distributed it by letting it seek its own level.

Because I could not resist lingering to admire the various gardens and parklands through which I descended, it was getting well on toward sundown when I finally emerged among the buildings at the bottom of the hill. I wandered along the flower-bordered white gravel paths, meeting many people: richly mantled noblemen and women, knights in plumed headgear, distinguished-looking elderly gentlemen. Every one of them graciously gave me a word or a nod of greeting, as if I belonged there, but I was shy of asking any of those fine folk exactly where I did belong. Then I came upon a young man of about my own age, who seemed not to be occupied with any urgent business. He stood beside a young buck deer that was just beginning to sprout antlers, and he was idly scratching the nubs between its ears. Perhaps ungrown antlers are itchy; at any rate, the deer appeared to be enjoying the attention.

"Mixpantzínco, brother," the young man greeted me. I supposed that he was one of Nezahualpíli's offspring, and took me for another. But then he noticed the basket I carried, and said, "You are the new Mixtli."

I said I was, and returned his greeting.

"I am Huexotl," he said; the word means Willow. "We already have at least three other Mixtlis around here, so we will have to think of a different name for you."

Feeling in no great need of yet another name, I changed the subject. "I have never seen deer walk among people like this, uncaged, unafraid."

"We get them when they are fawns. The hunters find them, usually when a doe has been killed, and they bring them here. There is always a wet nurse about, with full breasts but no baby to tend at the moment, and she gives suck to the fawn. I think they will all grow up believing they *are* people. Have you just arrived, Mixtli? Would you like to eat? To rest?"

I said yes, yes, and yes. "I really do not know what I am supposed to do here. Or where to go."

"My father's First Lady will know. Come, I will take you to her."

"I thank you, Huéxotzin," I said, calling him *Lord* Willow, for I had obviously guessed right: he was a son of Nezahualpíli and therefore a prince.

As we walked through the extensive palace grounds, the deer ambling along between us, the young prince identified for me the many edifices we passed. One immense building of two floors ran around three sides of a gardened central court. The left wing, Willow told me, contained the rooms of himself and all the other royal children. In the right wing dwelt Nezahualpíli's forty concubines. The central portion contained apartments for the Revered Speaker's counselors and wise men who were always with him, whether he resided in his city or country palace; and for other tlamatíntin: philosophers, poets, men of science whose work the Speaker was encouraging. In the grounds about were dotted small, marble-pillared pavilions to which a tlamatíni could retire if he wanted to write or invent or predict or meditate in solitude.

The palace proper was a building as huge and as beautifully ornamented as any palace in Tenochtítlan. Two floors high and at least a thousand man's-feet in frontage, it contained the throne room, the Speaking Council chambers, ballrooms for court entertainments, quarters for the guardsmen, the hall of justice where the Uey-Tlatoáni regularly met with those of his people who had troubles or complaints to lay before him. There were also Nezahualpíli's own apartments and those of his seven wedded wives.

"All together, three hundred rooms," said the prince. Then he confided, with a grin, "And all sorts of concealed passages and stairways. So my father can visit one wife or another without the others' getting envious."

We dismissed the deer and entered the great central doorway, a knight-sentry on either side snapping to attention, spears vertical, as we passed them. Willow led me through a spacious hall hung with featherwork tapestries, then up a broad stone staircase and along a gallery carpeted with rushes, to the elegantly appointed chambers of his stepmother. So the second person I met was that Tolána-Tecíuapil whom the old man on the hill had mentioned, the First Lady and noblest of all the noblewomen of the Acólhua. She was conversing with a beetle-browed young man, but she turned to give us an inviting smile and a gesture to enter.

Prince Willow told her who I was, and I bent to make the motion of kissing the earth. The Lady of Tolan, with her own hand, gently lifted me from my kneeling position and, in turn, introduced me to the other young man: "My eldest son, Ixtlil-Xochitl." I immediately dropped to kiss the earth again, for this third person I had met so far was the Crown Prince Black Flower, ordained heir to Nezahualpíli's throne of Texcóco. I was beginning to feel a little giddy, and not just from bobbing up and down. Here was I, the son of a common quarrier, meeting three of the most eminent personages in The One World, and all three in a row. Black Flower nodded his black eyebrows at me, then he and his half brother departed from the room.

The First Lady looked me up and down, while I covertly studied her. I could not guess her age, though she must have been well along into middle age, at least forty, to have a son as old as the Crown Prince Black Flower, but her face was unlined and lovely and kindly.

"Mixtli, is it?" she said. "But we already have so many Mixtlis among the young folk and, oh, I *am* so bad at remembering names."

"Some call me Tozáni, my lady."

"No, you are much bigger than a mole. You are a tall young man, and you will be taller yet. I shall call you Head Nodder."

"As you will, my lady," I said, with an inward sigh of resignation. "That is also my father's nickname."

"Then we will both be able to remember it, will we not? Now, come and I will show you your quarters."

She must have pulled a bell rope or something, because when we stepped out of the room there was waiting a litter chair borne by two burly slaves. They lowered it for her to get in and sit down, then lofted her along the gallery, down the stairs (keeping the chair carefully horizontal), out of the palace, and into the deepening dusk. Another slave ran ahead carrying a pitch-pine torch, and still another ran behind, carrying the lady's banner of rank. I trotted alongside the chair. At the three-sided building that Willow had already pointed out to me, the Lady of Tolan led me inside, up the stairs and around several corners, far into the left wing.

"There you are," she said, swinging open a door made of hides stretched on a wooden frame and varnished stiff. It was not just leaned in place, but pivoted in sockets top and bottom. The slave carried the torch inside to light my way, but I stuck only my head in, saying uncertainly, "It seems to be empty, my lady."

"But of course. This is yours."

"I thought, in a calmécac, all the students were bunched together in a common sleeping room."

"I daresay, but this is an annex of the palace, and this is where you will live. My Lord Husband is contemptuous of those schools and their teacher priests. You are not here to attend a calmécac."

"Not attend—! But, my lady, I thought I came to study—!"

"And so you shall, very hard indeed, but in company with the palace children, those of Nezahualpíli and his nobles. Our children are not taught by unwashed zealot priests, but by my Lord Husband's own chosen wise men, every teacher already noted for his *own* work in whatever it is he teaches. Here you may not learn many sorceries or invocations to the gods, Head Nodder, but you will learn real, true, useful things that will make you a man of worth to the world."

If I was not already gaping at her by then, I was the next moment, when I saw the slave go about with his torch, lighting beeswax candles struck in wall sconces. I gasped, "A whole room just for myself?" Then the man went through an arch into *another* room, and I gasped, "Two of them? Why, my lady, this is almost as big as my family's whole house!"

"You will get used to comfort," she said, and smiled. She almost had to push me inside. "This is your room for studying. That one yonder is your sleeping chamber. Beyond it is the sanitary closet. I expect you will want to use that one first, to wash after your journey. Just pull the bell rope, and your servant will come to assist you. Eat well and have a good sleep, Head Nodder. I will see you soon again."

The slave followed her out of the room and shut the door. I was sorry to see such a kind lady leave, but I was also glad, for now I could scurry around my apartment, veritably like a mole, peering nearsightedly at all its furnishings and appointments. The study room had a low table and a cushioned low icpáli chair to sit on, and a wickerwork chest that I could keep my clothes and books in, and a lava-rock heating brazier already laid with mizquitl logs, and a sufficiency of candles so that I could study comfortably even after dark, and a mirror of polished tezcatl—the rare clear crystal that gave a definitive reflection, not the cheaper dark kind in which one's face was only dimly visible. There was a window opening, with a split-cane covering that could be rolled up and dropped shut by means of a string arrangement.

The sleeping chamber contained no woven reed pallet, but a raised platform, and on that some ten or twelve thick quilts apparently stuffed with down; anyway, they made a pile that felt as soft as a cloud looks. When ready to sleep, I could slide myself in between the quilts at any layer, depending on how much softness I wanted under me and how much warmth on top.

The sanitary closet, however, I could not so easily comprehend. There was a sunken tiled depression in the floor, in which to sit and bathe, but there were no water jugs anywhere about. And there was a receptacle on which to sit and perform the necessary functions, but it was solidly fixed to the floor and obviously could not be emptied after each use. Each of those, the bath and the slop jar, had a curiously shaped pipe jutting from the wall above it, but neither pipe was spouting water or doing anything else that I could ascertain. Well, I would never have thought that I should have to ask instruction in cleaning and evacuating myself, but, after studying the utilities in bafflement for a while, I went to pull the bell rope over the bed, and waited with some embarrassment for the appearance of my assigned tlacótli.

The fresh-faced little boy who came to my door said pertly, "I am Cozcatl, my lord, and I am nine years old, and I serve all the young lords in the six apartments at the end of the corridor."

Cozcatl means Jeweled Collar, rather a high-flown name for such as he, but I did not laugh at it. Since a name-giving tonalpóqui would never deign to consult his divinatory books for a slave-born child, even if the parents could afford it, no such child ever had a real and registered name. His or her parents simply picked one at whim, and it could be wildly inappropriate, as witness Gift of the Gods. Cozcatl appeared well fed and bore no marks of beatings, and he did not cringe before me, and he wore a spotlessly white short mantle in addition to the loincloth that was customarily a male slave's only apparel. So I assumed that among the Acólhua, or at least in the palace vicinity, the lower classes were fairly treated.

The boy was carrying in both hands a tremendous pottery vessel of steaming hot water, so I quickly stepped aside, and he took it to the sanitary closet and poured it into the sunken tub. He also spared me the humiliation of having to ask to be shown how the closet's facilities worked. Even if Cozcatl took me to be a legitimate noble, he could have supposed that any noble from the provinces would be unaccustomed to such luxury—and he would have been right. Without waiting to be asked, he explained:

"You can cool your bathwater to the temperature you prefer, my lord, like this." He pointed to the clay pipe jutting from the wall. It was pierced near its end by another, shorter piece of pipe stuck vertically through it. He merely twisted that short pipe and it gushed clear cold water.

"The long pipe brings water from our main supply line. The short pipe has one hole in its side, and when you twist it to make that hole face inward to the long pipe, the water can run as needed. When you are through with your bath, my lord, just remove that óli stopper in the bottom and the used water will drain away through another pipe beneath."

Next he indicated the curiously immobile slop jar and said, "The axixcáli works the same way. When you have relieved yourself in it, simply twist that short pipe above, and a gush of water will wash the wastes away through that hole in its bottom."

I had not even noticed the hole before, and I asked in ignorant horror, "The excrement falls into the room below?"

"No, no, my lord. Like the bathwater, into a pipe that carries it clear away. Into a pond from which the manure men dredge fertilizer for the farm fields. Now, I will order my lord's evening meal prepared, so it will be waiting when he has finished his bath."

* * *

It was going to take me a while to stop playing the rustic and to learn the ways of the nobility, I reflected, as I sat at my own table in my own room and dined on grilled rabbit, beans, tortillas, and batter-fried squash blossoms . . . *with chocolate to drink*. Where I came from, chocolate had been a special treat doled out once or twice a year, and only weakly flavored. Here, the foamy red drink—of precious cacao, honey, vanilla, and scarlet achíyotl seeds, all ground up and beaten together to a stiff froth—was as free for the asking as spring water. I wondered how long it would take me to lose my Xaltócan accent, to speak the precise Náhuatl of Texcóco, and gracefully to "get used to comfort," as the First Lady had phrased it.

In time I came to realize that no noble, not even an honorary or temporary one like myself, ever had to do anything for himself. When a nobleman reached one hand up to undo the shoulder clasp of his magnificent feather mantle, he simply walked away from the garment, and it never hit the floor. Some servant was always there to take it from his shoulders, *and the noble knew there would be someone there*. If a nobleman folded his legs to sit down, he never looked behind him—even if he collapsed suddenly, involuntarily, from an excess of octli drinking. But he never fell. There was always an icpáli chair slid under him, *and he knew the chair would be there*.

I wondered: were the noble folk born with such a lofty assurance, or could I possibly acquire it by practice? There was only one way to find out. At the first opportunity—I forget the occasion—I entered a room crowded with lords and ladies, made the proper salutations, sat down with assurance, and without looking behind me. The icpáli was right there. I did not even glance back to see whence it came. I knew then that a chair—or anything I wanted *and expected* from my inferiors—would always be there. That small experiment taught me a thing I never forgot. To command the respect and deference and privileges reserved for the nobility, I need only dare to *be* a noble.

On the morning after my arrival, the slave Cozcatl came with my breakfast and with an armload of new clothes for me, more clothes than I had ever worn and worn out during my whole previous life. There were loincloths and mantles of glossy white cotton, beautifully embroidered. There were sandals of rich and pliable leathers, including one gilded pair for ceremonial wear, which laced nearly to my knees. The Lady of Tolan had even sent a small gold and bloodstone clasp for my mantle, which heretofore I had worn only knotted at the shoulder.

When I had donned one of those stylish outfits, Cozcatl led me again around the palace grounds, pointing out the buildings containing schoolrooms. There were more classes available than in any calmécac. I was most interested, of course, in those dealing with work knowing, history, geography, and the like. But I could also, if I chose, attend classes in poetry, gold and silver work, feather work, gem cutting, and various other arts.

"The classes that do not require tools and benches are held indoors only in bad weather," said my little guide. "On fine days like this, the Lord Teachers and their students prefer to work outside."

I could see the groups, sitting on the lawns or gathered about the marble pavilions. The teacher of every class was an elderly man wearing a distinctive yellow mantle, but his students were an assortment: boys and men of varying sizes and ages, here and there even a girl or a woman or a slave sitting slightly apart.

"The students are not graded by age?" I asked.

"No, my lord, but by their ability. Some are much further along in one subject than in another. When you first attend, you will be interrogated by each Lord Teacher to determine in which of his classes you will fit best—for example, among the Beginners, the Learners, the Somewhat Learned, and so on. He will grade you according to what knowledge you already have and what he judges to be your capacity for learning more."

"And the females? The slaves?"

"Any daughter of a noble is allowed to attend, all the way through the highest grades, if she has the ability and the desire. The slaves are allowed to study as far as is consistent with their particular employments."

"You yourself are well spoken, for such a young tlacótli."

"Thank you, my lord. I went as far as learning good Náhuatl, deportment, and the rudiments of housekeeping. When I am older I may apply for further training, in hope of someday becoming Master of the Keys in some noble household."

I said grandly, expansively, generously, "If ever I have a noble household, Cozcatl, I promise you that position."

I did not mean "if," I meant "when." I was no longer idly wishing for a rise to eminence, I was already envisioning it. I stood there in that lovely parkland, my servant at my side, and I stood tall in my fine new clothes, and I smiled to think of the great man I would be. I sit here now, among you, my reverend masters, and I sit bent and shriveled in my rags, and I smile to think of the puffed-up young pretender I was.

The Lord Teacher of History, Neltitíca, who looked old enough to have *experienced* all of history, announced to the class, "We have with us today a new píltontli student, a Mexícatl who is to be known as Head Nodder."

I was so pleased to be introduced as a "young noble" student that I did not wince at the nickname.

"Perhaps, Head Nodder, you would be good enough to give us a brief history of your Mexíca people. . . ."

"Yes, Lord Teacher," I said confidently. I stood up, and every face in the class turned to gaze at me. I cleared my throat and said what I had been taught in Xaltócan's House of Learning Manners:

"Know, then, that my people originally dwelt in a region far to the north of these lands. It was Aztlan, The Place of Snowy Egrets, and at thát time they called themselves the Aztlantláca or the Axtéca, the Egret People. But Aztlan was a hard country, and their chief god Huitzilopóchtli told them of a sweeter land to be found to the south. He said it would be a long and difficult journey, but that they would recognize their new homeland when they reached it, for they would see there a nopáli cactus on which perched a golden eagle. So all the Aztéca abandoned their fine homes and palaces and pyramids and temples and gardens, and they set out southward."

Someone in the class snickered.

"The journey took sheaves upon sheaves of years, and they had to pass through the lands of many other peoples. Some were hostile; they fought and tried to turn the Aztéca back. Others were hospitable and let the Aztéca rest among them, sometimes for a short while, sometimes for many years, and those peoples were repaid by being taught the noble language, the arts and sciences known only to the Aztéca."

Someone in the class murmured, and someone else gave a low chuckle.

"When the Aztéca came finally into this valley, they were kindly received by the Tecpanéca people on the western shore of the lake, who gave them Chapultépec for a resting place. The Aztéca lived on that Grasshopper Hill while their priests continued to range about the valley in search of the eagle on the nopáli. Now, in the Tecpanéca dialect of our language, the nopáli cactus is called tenóchtli, so those people called the Aztéca the Tenóchca, and in time the Aztéca themselves took that name of Cactus People. Then, as Huitzilopóchtli had promised, the priests did find the sign—a golden eagle perched on a cactus—and this they found on a not-yet-peopled island in the lake. All the Tenóchca-Aztéca immediately and joyfully moved from Chapultépec to that island."

Someone in the class laughed openly.

"On the island they built two great cities, one called Tenochtítlan, Place of the Cactus People, and the other Tlatelólco, The Rocky Place. While they were building the cities, the Tenóchca noticed how every night they could see from their island the moon Metztli reflected in the lake waters. So they also referred to their new habitation as Metztli-Zíctli, In the Middle of the Moon. In time, they shortened that to Mexítli and then to Méxíco, and eventually came to call themselves the Méxíca. For their sign they adopted the symbol of the eagle perched on the cactus, and the eagle holds in its beak the ribbonlike symbol which represents war."

A number of my new classmates were laughing by now, but I persevered.

"Then the Méxíca began to extend their dominion and influence, and many peoples have benefited, either as adoptive Méxíca or as allies or as trading partners. They learned to worship our gods, or variations of them, and they let us appropriate their gods. They learned to count with our arithmetic and mark time by our calendars. They pay us tribute in goods and currency, for fear of our invincible armies. They speak our language out of deference to our superiority. The Méxíca have

built the mightiest civilization ever known in this world, and
México-Tenochtítlan stands at its center—In Cem-Anáhuac
Yoyótli, The Heart of the One World."

I kissed the earth to the aged Lord Teacher Neltitíca and sat
down. My classmates were all waving their hands for permission to speak, meanwhile making a clamor of noises ranging
from laughter to hoots of derision. The Lord Teacher gestured
imperiously, and the class sat still and silent.

"Thank you, Head Nodder," he said politely. "I had wondered what version the Méxica teachers were expounding these
days. Of history you know abysmally little, young lord, and
what little you know is wrong in almost every particular."

I stood up again, my face as hot as if I had been slapped.
"Lord Teacher, you requested a brief history. I can elaborate
in more detail."

"Kindly spare me," he said. "And in return I will do you
the kindness of correcting just one of the details already proffered. The words Méxica and México did not derive from
Metztli the moon." He waved for me to be seated, and addressed the class as a whole:

"Young lord and lady students, this illustrates what I have
often told you before now. Be skeptical of the many versions
of the world's history you are likely to hear, for some are as
full of impossible invention as they are of vanity. What is
more, I have never met a historian—I have never met *any* sort
of professional scholar who could put into his work the slightest
trace of humor or ribaldry or jollity. I have never met one who
did not consider his particular subject the most momentous and
weighty of all studies. Now, I concede the importance of schol-
arly works—but need importance always wear the long face
of stern solemnity? Historians may be serious men, and history
may sometimes be so somber that it saddens. But it is *people*
who make the history, and they often play pranks or cut capers
while they are doing it. The true story of the Méxica confirms
that."

He spoke directly to me again: "Head Nodder, your Aztéca
ancestors brought nothing to this valley: no ancient wisdom,
no arts, no sciences, no culture. They brought nothing but
themselves: a skulking, ignorant, nomad people who wore ragged animal skins crawling with vermin, and who worshiped

a loathsomely pugnacious god of slaughter and bloodshed. That rabble was despised and repulsed by every other already developed nation hereabout. Would any civilized people welcome an invasion of uncouth beggars? The Aztéca did not settle on that island in the lakeside swamp because their god gave them any sign, and they did not go there joyfully. They went because there was nowhere else to go, and because no one else had cared to claim that pimple of land surrounded by marshes."

My classmates watched me from the corners of their eyes. I tried not to flinch under Neltitíca's words.

"They did not immediately build great cities, or anything else; they had to spend all their time and energy just in finding something to eat. They were not allowed to fish, for the lake's fishing rights belonged to the nations about it. So for a long time your ancestors existed—just barely existed—by eating revolting little things like worms and water insects, and the slimy eggs of those creatures, and the only edible plant that grew in that miserable swamp. It was mexíxin, the common cress or peppergrass, a scraggly and bitter-tasting weed. But if your forebears had nothing else, Head Nodder, they had a mordant sense of humor. They began to call themselves, with wry irony, the Mexíca."

The very name evoked another knowing snicker from the class. Neltitíca went on:

"Eventually the Mexíca devised the chinámitl system of growing decent crops. But even then, they grew for themselves only a necessary minimum of staple foods like maize and beans. Their chinámpa were mainly used for growing more rare vegetables and herbs—tomatoes, sage, coriander, sweet potatoes—which their lofty neighbors could not be bothered to cultivate. And the Mexíca traded those delicacies for the necessities of life: the tools and building materials and cloth and weapons that the mainland nations would otherwise have been unwilling to give them. From then on, they made rapid progress toward civilization and culture and military might. But they never forgot that humble weed which had sustained them in the beginning, the mexíxin, and they never afterward abandoned the name they had adopted from it. Mexíca is a name now known and respected or feared throughout our world, but it means only . . ."

He paused on purpose, and he smiled, and my face flamed again, as the entire class shouted in concert:

"The Weed People!"

"I understand, young lordlet, that you have essayed some learning of reading and writing on your own," said the Lord Teacher of Word Knowing, somewhat sourly, as if he believed any such self-education impossible. "And I understand that you have brought examples of your work."

Respectfully, I handed him the long, pleated-together bark paper strip of which I was most proud. I had drawn it with extra care, and painted it in the vibrant colors Chimáli had given me. The Lord Teacher took the compacted book and began slowly to unfold its pages.

It was an account of one famous incident in the history of the Mexíca, when they first arrived in this valley, and when the most powerful nation here was that of the Culhua. The Culhua leader, Coxcox, had declared a war against the people of Xochimílco, and invited the newcome Mexíca to fight as his allies. When the war was won and the Culhua warriors brought in their Xochimílca prisoners, the Mexíca brought none at all, and Coxcox denounced them as cowards. At that, the Mexíca warriors opened the bags they carried and dumped out a mountain of ears—all left ears—which they had sliced from the multitude of Xochimílca they had vanquished. Coxcox was astounded, and glad, and from then on the Mexíca were accounted fighters to be reckoned with.

I thought I had done a very good job of picturing the incident, particularly in my meticulous rendering of the innumerable left ears and the expression of astonishment on the face of Coxcox. I waited, almost aglow with self-congratulation, for the Lord Teacher to praise my work.

But he was frowning as he flipped the book's pages apart, and he looked from one side to the other of the pleated strip, and he said at last, "In which direction am I supposed to read this?"

Puzzled, I said, "In Xaltócan, my lord, we unfold the pages leftward. That is, so we may read each panel from left to right."

"Yes, yes!" he snapped. "We *all* customarily read from left to right. But your book gives no indication that we should do so."

"Indication?" I said.

"Suppose you are bidden to write an inscription that must be read in some other direction—on a temple frieze or column, for instance, where the architecture requires that it be read from right to left, or even from top to bottom."

The possibility had never occurred to me, and I said so.

He said impatiently, "When a scribe pictures two persons or two gods conversing, naturally they must be face to face. But there is one basic rule. The majority of all the characters *must face in the direction the writing is to be read.*"

I think I gulped loudly.

"You never grasped that simplest rule of picture writing?" he asked scathingly. "And you have the effrontery to show me this?" He tossed it back to me without even refolding it. "When you attend your first class in word knowing tomorrow, join that one yonder."

He pointed across the lawn to a class assembling about one of the pavilions, and my face fell and my pride evaporated. Even from a distance, I could make out that all the students were about half my size and age.

It was mortifying to have to sit among *infants*—to begin at the very beginning in both my history and my word knowing classes—as if I had never been taught anything at all, as if I had never exerted myself to learn anything at all.

So I was cheered to discover that the study of poetry, at least, was not graded into the Beginners, the Learners, the Somewhat Learned, and so on, with me at the very bottom of the class. There was only a single gathering of aspiring poets, and they included students much older as well as much younger than myself. Among them were both the young Prince Willow and his elder half brother Crown Prince Black Flower; there were other nobles ranging even to the very old; there were both girls and women of the nobility; there were more slaves than I had seen in any other class.

It seems that it matters not who makes a poem, and it matters not what kind of poem: a tribute to some god or hero, a lengthy historical account, a love song, a lamentation, or a joking bit of banter. That poem is not judged according to the poet's age, sex, social standing, education, or experience. A poem merely is or is not. It lives or it never existed. It is made and remembered or it is forgotten so quickly that it might never have been made at all. In that class I was content to sit and listen, timorous of attempting any poetic ventures of my own. It was not until many, many years later that I happened to make a poem which I have since heard recited by strangers. So that one has lived, but it is a very small poem, and I would not call myself a poet on that account.

What I recollect most vividly about my poetry class is the first time I attended it. Some distinguished visitor had been invited by the Lord Teacher to read his works, and he was just about to begin when I arrived and sat down on a grassy bank at the rear of the crowd. I could not see him too distinctly at that distance, but I could make out that he was medium tall and well built, that he was about the age of the Lady of Tolan, that he wore a richly embroidered cotton mantle held by a gold clasp, and no other adornments to designate his office or class. So I took him to be a professional poet of sufficient talent to have been rewarded with a pension and a place at court.

He shuffled several sheets of bark paper in his hand and gave one sheet to a slave boy who sat crosslegged at his feet, holding a miniature drum on his lap. Then the visitor announced in a voice which, though soft-spoken, carried well, "With the Lord Teacher's permission, my young lord and lady students, I will not recite today from my own works, but from those of a far greater and wiser poet. My father."

"*Ayyo,* with my permission and *pleasure,*" said the Lord Teacher, nodding benignly. The class also murmured a collective *ayyo* of approval, as if everyone there already knew the works of the poet-father he had mentioned.

From what I have already told you of our picture writing, reverend friars, you will have realized that it was inadequate for setting down poetry. Our poems lived by oral repetition, or lived not at all. Anyone who heard and liked a poem would memorize it and retell it to someone else, who might in turn tell it again. To aid the hearers in that memorizing, a poem was usually constructed in such a manner that the syllables of its words had a regular rhythm, and in such a manner that the same word sounds regularly recurred at the ends of its separate lines.

The papers the visitor carried bore only enough word pictures to assure that his memory did not falter and omit a line, to remind him here and there to stress a word or a passage his poet-father had thought worthy of special note. And the papers he handed to his drummer slave were marked only with brush strokes: many small dabs of paint, some larger ones, variously commingled and variously spaced. They told the slave the rhythm to beat out with his hand on the drum as accompaniment to the poet's recital: sometimes murmurous, sometimes sharply emphasizing the words, sometimes a soft throb like a heart beating in the pauses between the lines.

The poems the visitor recited and sang and chanted that day were all felicitously worded and sweetly cadenced, but they all were slightly tinged with melancholy, as when early autumn first steals in upon the summertime. After nearly a sheaf of years, and with no word pictures to aid my recollection, no drum to mark the beats and pauses, I still can repeat one of them:

> I made a song in praise of life,
> a world as bright as quetzal feather:
> to skies of turquoise, sunlight gold,
> to streams like jadestone, gardens blooming . . .

> But gold can melt and jadestone shatter,
> leaves turn brown and trees fall down,
> our flowers fade, their petals scatter.
> The sun sets soon, the night comes looming.
> See beauty fade, our loves grow cold,
> the gods desert, their temples weather . . .

> Why does my song pierce like a knife?

When the recital was concluded, the respectfully attentive crowd of listeners stood up and broke apart. Some went strolling about by themselves, saying one or several of the poems over and over, to fix the words in their memory. I was one of those. Others milled about the visitor, kissed the earth to him, and regaled him with compliments and thanks. I was walking in circles on the grass, head bowed, repeating to myself that poem I have just repeated to you, when I was approached by young Prince Willow.

"I overheard you, Head Nodder," he said. "I too liked that poem best of all. And it made another poem waft into my own head. Would you oblige me by hearing it?"

"I should be honored to be the first," I said, and what he recited was this:

> You tell me then that I must perish
> like the flowers that I cherish.
> Nothing remaining of my name,
> nothing remembered of my fame?
> But the gardens I planted still are young—
> the songs I sang will still be sung!

I said, "I think it is a good poem, Huéxotzin, and a true one. The Lord Teacher would most certainly give you an approving nod." And I was not just slavishly flattering a prince, for you will have noticed that I have remembered that poem, too, all my life. "In fact," I went on, "it might almost have been composed by the same great poet whose works we have heard today."

"Yya, come now, Head Nodder," he chided me. "No poet of our time will ever match the incomparable Nezahualcóyotl."

"Who?"

"Did you not know? Did you not recognize my father doing the recitation? He read the works of *his* father, my grandfather, the Revered Speaker Fasting Coyote."

"What? That man who recited was Nezahualpíli?" I exclaimed. "But he wore no insignia of his office. No crown, no feather mantle, no staff or banner..."

"Oh, he has his eccentricities. Except on state occasions, my father never dresses like any other Uey-Tlatoáni. He believes that a man should display only tokens of his achievement. Medals won and scars collected, not baubles inherited or bought or married. But do you really mean you have not yet met him? Come!"

However, it seemed that Nezahualpíli was averse also to

having his people too openly manifest their regard for him. By the time the prince and I elbowed our way through the throng of students, he had already slipped away.

The Lady of Tolan had not misled me when she warned that I would work hard at that school, but I will not bore you, reverend friars, with accounts of my daily schedule, and the mundane events of my days, and the sheaves of work I took back to my chambers at the end of each day. I will tell you that I learned arithmetic, and how to keep account books, and how to calculate the exchange of the various sorts of currency in use—all facilities that would be most useful to me in years to come. I learned about the geography of these lands, though at that time not much was *known* about any of the lands beyond our immediate own, as I would later discover by exploring for myself.

I most enjoyed and profited from my studies in word knowing, getting ever more proficient at reading and writing. But I think I benefited almost as much from the classes in history, even when they refuted the Mexíca's most cherished beliefs and boasts. The Lord Teacher Neltitíca gave generously of his time, even according private sessions to some of us. I remember one, when he sat down with me and a very young boy named Poyec, son of one of Texcóco's numerous lords.

"There is a grievous gap in Mexíca history," said the teacher, "like the wide gap an earthquake can cleave in the solid earth."

He was preparing a poquíetl to smoke while he discoursed. This is a slender tube of some substance like bone or jadestone, ornamentally carved, with a mouthpiece at one end. Into the open other end is inserted a dry reed or rolled paper, firmly packed with the finely shredded dried leaves of the picíetl plant, sometimes mixed with herbs and spices for added flavor and fragrance. The user holds the tube between his fingers and sets fire to the far end of the reed or paper. It and its contents smolder slowly to ash, while the user lifts the mouthpiece at intervals to his lips to suck a breath of the smoke, inhale it, and puff it out again.

When he had lit his with a coal from a brazier, Neltitíca said, "It was just a sheaf of years ago that the Mexíca's then Revered Speaker Itzcóatl, Obsidian Snake, forged The Triple

Alliance of the Mexíca, the Acólhua, and the Tecpanéca—with the Mexíca, of course, as the dominant partner. Having secured that eminence for his people, Obsidian Snake then decreed that all the books of bygone days should be burned, and new accounts written to glorify the Mexíca past, to give the Mexíca a spurious antiquity."

I looked at the blue smoke rising from the poquíetl, and murmured, "Books... burned..." It was hard to believe that even a Uey-Tlatoáni would have the heart to burn something as precious and irreplaceable and inviolable as books.

"Obsidian Snake did it," the Lord Teacher continued, "to make his people believe that they were and always have been the true custodians of art and science, and therefore to believe that it is their duty to impose civilization on every lesser people. But even the Mexíca cannot ignore the evidence that other and finer civilizations had existed here long before their coming. So they have concocted fanciful legends to account for such evidence."

Poyec and I thought about it, and the boy suggested, "You mean things like Teotihuácan? The Place Where the Gods Gathered?"

"A good example, young Póyectzin. That city is now a tumbled and deserted and weed-grown ruin, but it obviously was once a greater and more populous city than Tenochtítlan can ever hope to be."

I said, "We were taught, Lord Teacher, that it was built by the gods when they all assembled to decide to create the earth and its people and all living things...."

"Of course you were taught that. Any grand thing not done by the Mexíca must not be credited to any other mortal men." He snorted a plume of smoke from his nostrils. "Although Obsidian Snake blotted out the Mexíca's past history, he could not burn the libraries of our Texcóco and other cities. We do still have records telling what this valley was like long before the coming of the Aztéca-Mexíca. Obsidian Snake could not change all the history of The One World."

"And those unaltered histories," I asked, "—how far back do they go?"

"Not nearly far enough. We do not pretend to have accounts dating back to the Lord and Lady Pair. You know the legends.

Those two were the very first inhabitants of this earth, and then all the other gods, and then a race of giants." Neltitíca took a few meditative puffs at his poquíetl. "That legend about the giants, you know, may be true. An old and weathered bone was dug up by a farmer and is still preserved in Texcóco—I have seen it—and the surgeons say it is most definitely a thighbone. And it is as long as I am tall."

Little Poyec laughed uneasily and said, "I should not care to meet the man whose thigh it was."

"Well," said the Lord Teacher, "gods and giants are things for the priests to ponder. My interest is the history of such men, especially the first men in this valley, the men who built such cities as Teotihuácan and Tolan. Because all we have, we inherited from them. All we know, we learned from them." He took a last puff of smoke and removed from the holder the burned-down stub of his picíetl reed. "We may never know why they disappeared, or when, though the fire-charred beams of their ruined buildings suggest that they were driven out by marauders. Probably the savage Chichiméca, the Dog People. We can read but little of the surviving wall paintings and carvings and picture writings, and none of those things tells even the name of that vanished people. But the things are so artfully executed that we respectfully refer to their makers as the Toltéca, the Master Artisans, and for sheaves of years we have been trying to equal their achievements."

"But," said Poyec, "if the Toltéca have been so long gone, I do not see how we could have learned from them."

"Because a few individuals would have survived, even when the mass of them, as a nation, disappeared. There would have been some survivors who took to the high crags or the deep forests. And those diehard Toltéca would have endured in hiding—even preserving some of their books of knowledge perhaps—hoping to hand on their culture through their children and children's children, as they intermarried with other tribes. Unfortunately, the only other peoples in this area at that time were utter primitives: the stolid Otomí, the frivolous Purémpecha, and of course the ever-present Dog People."

"Ayya," said young Poyec. "The Otomí have not yet learned even the art of writing. And the Chichiméca to this day still eat their own excrement."

"But even among barbarians there can be a handful of extraordinary specimens," said Neltitíca. "We must assume that the Toltéca chose carefully their mates, and that their children and grandchildren did likewise, and thus at least a few superior bloodlines would have been maintained. It would have been a sacred family trust, to hand down from father to son what each remembered of the ancient Toltéca knowledge. Until finally, from the north, there began to come to this valley new peoples—also primitives, but capable of recognizing and appreciating and utilizing that hoard of knowledge. New peoples with the will to fan that long-guarded ember again to flame."

The Lord Teacher paused to fit a new reed into his holder. Many men smoked the poquíetl because, they said, its fumes kept their brains clear and healthy. I took up the practice myself when I was older, and found it a great aid to cogitation. But Neltitíca smoked more than any man I ever met, and that habit may have accounted for his exceptional wisdom and long life.

He went on, "The first comers from the north were the Culhua. Then the Acólhua, my own forebears and yours, Póyectzin. Then all the other lake settlers: the Tecpanéca, the Xochimílca, and so on. Then, as now, they called themselves by different names, and only the gods know where they originally came from, but all those migrants arrived here speaking one or another dialect of the Náhuatl language. And here in this lake basin, they began to learn, from the descendants of the vanished Toltéca, what remained of the Toltéca's ancient arts and crafts."

"It could not all have been done in a day," I said. "Or in a sheaf of years."

"No, and perhaps not in many sheaves of years," said Neltitíca. "But when learning must be done largely from elusive scraps of information, and by trial and error, and by the imitation of relics—well, the more people engaged in sharing the learning, the faster it is accomplished by all. Fortunately, those Culhua and Acólhua and Tecpanéca and all the rest could communicate in a common language, and they all worked together. Meanwhile, they gradually ousted the lesser peoples from this region. The Purémpecha moved west, the Otomí and Chichiméca drifted north. The Náhuatl-speaking nations remained, and they grew in knowledge and ability at about the same pace.

It was only after those peoples had attained some measure of civilization that they ceased to be mutually supportive and began to vie for ascendancy over each other. It was then that the still-primitive Aztéca arrived."

The Lord Teacher turned his eyes on me.

"The Aztéca, or Mexíca, settled into a society that was already well developed, but a society that was beginning to separate into rival fragments. And the Mexíca managed to survive until Coxcox of the Culhua condescended to appoint one of his nobles named Acamapíchtli to be their own first Revered Speaker. Acamapíchtli introduced them to the art of word knowing, then to all the other knowledge already salvaged and shared by the longer-settled nations. The Mexíca were avid to learn, and we know what use they made of that learning. They played off the other rival factions of these lands, one against another, shifting their allegiance from one to another, until finally they themselves had achieved military supremacy over all the rest."

Little Poyec of Texcóco gave me a look as if I had been to blame for my ancestors' aggressiveness, but Neltitíca went on speaking with the dispassion of the detached historian:

"We know how the Mexíca have thrived and prospered since then. They have far surpassed, in wealth and influence, those other nations that once snubbed them as insignificant. Their Tenochtítlan is the richest and most opulent city built since the days of the Toltéca. Though there are countless languages spoken in The One World, the far-ranging Mexíca armies and traders and explorers have made our Náhuatl the second language of every people from the northern deserts to the southern jungles."

He must have seen the trace of a smug smile on my face, for the Lord Teacher concluded:

"Those accomplishments would, I think, be enough for the Mexíca to boast about, but they have insisted on even more self-glorification. They rewrote their history books, trying to persuade themselves and others that they have always been the foremost nation of this region. The Mexíca may delude themselves, and may deceive historians of generations to come. But I believe I have adequately demonstrated that the usurping Mexíca are *not* the great Toltéca reborn."

*   *   *

The Lady of Tolan invited me to take chocolate in her chambers, and I went eagerly, with a question bubbling inside me. When I arrived, her son the Crown Prince was there, and I kept silent while they discussed minor matters concerning the palace management. But when there came a lull in their colloquy, I made bold to ask the question:

"You were born in Tolan, my lady, and that was once a Toltéca city. Are you then a Toltécatl?"

Both she and Black Flower looked surprised; then she smiled. "Anyone of Tolan, Head Nodder—anyone anywhere—would be proud to claim even a drop of Toltéca blood, but in honesty, ayya, I cannot. During all of living memory, Tolan has been part of the Tecpanéca territory, so I come of Tecpanéca stock—though I suspect our family may long ago have included an Otomítl or two, before that race was ousted."

I said in disappointment, "There is *no* trace of the Toltéca in Tolan?"

"In the people, who can say for certain? In the place, yes, there are the pyramids and stone terraces and vast walled courts. The pyramids have been stunted by erosion, and the terraces are all buckled and crazed, and the walls are fallen in places. But the exquisite patterns in which their stones were set are still discernible, and the low-relief carvings, and even fragmentary paintings here and there. The most impressive and least worn objects, though, are the many statues."

"Of the gods?" I asked.

"I do not think so, for they each have the same face. They are all of the same size and shape, sculptured simply and realistically, not in the convoluted style of today. They are cylindrical columns, as if once they supported some massive roof. But the columns are carved into the form of standing humans, if you can imagine humans more then three times as tall as any human known."

"Perhaps they are portraits of the giants who lived on earth after the gods," I suggested, remembering the monstrous thighbone of which Neltitíca had told.

"No, I think they represent the Toltéca themselves, only portrayed much larger than life size. Their faces are not stern or brutal or haughty, as you would expect of gods or giants.

They wear an expression of untroubled watchfulness. Many of the columns are toppled and scattered about the low ground, but others still stand on the heights, and they look out across the countryside as if patiently, tranquilly waiting."

"Waiting for what, do you suppose, my lady?"

"Perhaps for the Toltéca to come again." It was Black Flower who answered, and he added a harsh laugh. "To emerge from wherever they have been lurking through all these sheaves of years. To come in might and fury, to conquer us interlopers, to reclaim these lands that were theirs."

"No, my son," said the First Lady. "They were never a warlike people, nor wanted to be, and that was their undoing. If they *could* ever come again, they would come in peace."

She sipped at her chocolate and made a face; it had gone flat. She took from the table at her side the beater of large and small wooden rings strung loose and jingling on a central stem, the whole instrument cunningly carved from a single stick of aromatic cedar. Putting it into her cup and holding the stem between her palms, she rubbed briskly to rotate the beater rings until the red liquid puffed up foamy and stiff again. After another sip, she licked the froth from her upper lip and said to me:

"Go sometime to the city of Teotihuácan, Head Nodder, and look at what is left of the wall paintings there. Only one of them shows a Toltécatl warrior, and he is merely playing at war. His spear has no blade, but a tuft of feathers at its point, and his arrows are tipped with óli gum, like those employed in teaching archery to boys."

"Yes, my lady, I have used such arrows in practicing the war games."

"From other murals, we can deduce that the Toltéca never gave human sacrifices to their gods, but only butterflies, flowers, quail, and such offerings. The Master Artisans were a peaceable people because their gods were gentle gods. One of them was that Quetzalcóatl still worshiped by all nations far and wide. And the Toltéca concept of that Feathered Serpent tells us much about *them*. Who but a wise and kindly people could have bequeathed to us a god that so harmoniously blends lordliness and lovingness? The most awesome but most graceful of all creatures, the snake, clad not in hard scales but in the soft and beautiful plumage of the quetzal tototl bird."

I said, "I was taught that the Feathered Serpent once really lived in these lands, and will someday come back again."

"Yes, Head Nodder, from what we can understand of the remains of Toltéca writing, Quetzalcóatl did indeed once live. He was a long-ago Uey-Tlatoáni, or whatever the Toltéca called their rulers, and he must have been a good one. It is said that he himself devised the writing, the calendars, the star charts, the numbers we use today. It is even said that he left us the recipe for ahuacamóli and all the other moli sauces, though I am sure I cannot see Quetzalcóatl doing cook's work in a kitchen."

She smiled and shook her head, then was serious again. "It is said that during his reign the farmers' fields grew not just white cotton but cotton of all colors, as if already dyed, and that a single ear of maize was as much as a man could carry. It is said that there were no deserts in his time, but fruit and flowers growing everywhere in abundance, and the air was perfumed with all their mingled fragrances. . . ."

I asked, "Is it possible that he could come again, my lady?"

"Well, according to the legends, Quetzalcóatl somehow unintentionally committed some sin so awful—or did *something* which so violated his own high standards of behavior—that he voluntarily abdicated his throne. He went to the shore of the eastern ocean and built a raft—of interwoven feathers, some say, or of intertwined live snakes. In his last words to the grieving Toltéca he vowed to return again someday. And he rowed away, and he vanished beyond the ocean's eastern horizon. Since then, the Feathered Serpent has become the one god recognized by every nation and every people known to us. But all the Toltéca have also disappeared since then, and Quetzalcóatl has yet to return."

"But he could have, he may have," I said. "The priests say that the gods often walk among us unrecognized."

"Like my Lord Father," said Black Flower, laughing. "But I believe the Feathered Serpent would be rather harder to overlook. The reappearance of such a distinctive god should certainly make a stir. Be assured, Head Nodder, if ever Quetzalcóatl comes again, with or without his retinue of Toltéca, we will know him."

* * *

I had left Xaltócan toward the close of the rainy season in the year Five Knife and, except for my frequent yearnings for the presence of Tzitzitlíni, I had been so engrossed in my studies and my enjoyments of palace life that I had scarcely noticed the swift passing of time. I was frankly surprised when my schoolmate Prince Willow informed me that the day after tomorrow would be the first of the forthcoming nemontémtin, the five lifeless days. I had to count on my fingers to believe that I had been away from home for more than the round of a whole year, and that this one was coming to a close.

"All activities are suspended during the five hollow days," said the young prince. "So this year we will take the opportunity to pack and move the entire court to our Texcóco palace, to be ready to celebrate the month of Cuáhuitl Ehua there."

That was the first month of our solar year. Its name means The Tree Is Raised and refers to the many elaborate ceremonies during which the people of all nations were accustomed to beseech the rain god Tlaloc that the forthcoming summer's wet season would be an abundantly wet one.

"And you will want to be with your family for the occasion," Willow went on. "So I ask you to accept the loan of my personal acáli to carry you thither. I will send it again at the close of Cuáhuitl Ehua, and you will rejoin the court at Texcóco."

This was all very sudden, but I accepted, expressing my gratitude for his thoughtfulness.

"Just one thing," he said. "Can you be ready to leave tomorrow morning? You understand, Head Nodder, my oarsmen will want to be safely back on their home shore before the lifeless days begin."

✠

Ah, the Señor Bishop! Once more I am pleased and honored to have Your Excellency join our little gathering. And once more, my lord, your unworthy servant makes bold to give you worshipful greeting and welcome.

... Yes, I understand, Your Excellency. You say that I have not hitherto spoken sufficiently of my people's religious rites; that you especially want to hear in person about our superstitious dread of the hollow days; that you wish to hear at first hand my account of the ensuing month's heathen rituals of petition to the rain god. I understand, my lord, and I shall cause your reverend ears to hear all. Should my old brain wander in its recollection, or should my old tongue skip too lightly over any details of relevance, please do not hesitate, Your Excellency, to interrupt with questions or demands for elucidation.

Know, then, that it was on the sixth-to-last day of the year Six House that Prince Willow's carved and bannered and canopied acáli put me ashore on a Xaltócan jetty again. My splendid borrowed craft of six oarsmen rather put to shame the uncovered, two-oared canoe of the Lord Red Heron which was, that same day, likewise bringing his son home from school for the ceremonial month of Cuáhuitl Ehua. I was even noticeably better dressed than that provincial princeling, and Pactli involuntarily gave me an ingratiating nod before he recognized me and his face froze.

At my house, I was welcomed like a hero home from some war. My father clapped his hands on my shoulders, which now nearly matched his in height and breadth. Tzitzitlíni wrapped both arms around me in a squeeze that would have looked merely sisterly to anyone who did not see her fingernails digging softly but suggestively into my back. Even my mother was admiring, if mainly of my costume. I had deliberately chosen to wear my most wonderfully embroidered mantle, with the bloodstone clasp at the shoulder, and my gilt sandals which laced almost to the knee.

Friends and relations and neighbors came crowding in to gawk at the rover returned. Among them, I was happy to see, were Chimáli and Tlatli, who had each begged a ride home from Tenochtítlan on limestone freight acáltin returning to the island to ride out the lifeless days at their moorings. My family's three rooms and dooryard, which now appeared to me to have curiously shrunken, were quite overflowing with visitors. I do not attribute that to my personal popularity, but to the fact that midnight would bring the beginning of the hollow days, during which there could be no social mingling.

Not many of the gathered people, except my father and some other quarriers, had ever been off our island, and were naturally eager to hear of the outside world. But they asked few questions; they seemed content to listen to me and Chimáli and Tlatli trading tales of our experiences in our separate schools.

"Schools!" snorted Tlatli. "It is precious little time we have for schoolwork. Every day the vile priests roust us out at dawn to sweep and clean our quarters and all the rooms of the whole building. Then we must go to the lake to tend the school's chinámpa, and pick maize and beans for the school kitchen. Or go all the way to the mainland to chop wood for the sacred fires, to cut and fetch bags full of maguey thorns."

I said, "The food and firewood I can understand, but why the thorns?"

"For penance and punishment, friend Mole," Chimáli growled. "Break the slightest rule and a priest makes you prick yourself repeatedly. In the earlobes, in the thumbs and arms, even in private places. I am punctured all over."

"But even the best-behaved suffer too," added Tlatli. "Every other day seems to be the feast day of some god or other, including many I have never heard of, and every boy must shed blood for the offering."

One of the listeners asked, "When *do* you find time for studying?"

Chimáli made a face. "What little time there is does not avail us much. The teacher priests are not learned men. They know nothing except what there is in the textbooks, and those books are old and smudged and falling apart into shreds of bark."

Tlatli said, "Chimáli and I are fortunate, though. We did not go for book learning, so the lack of it does not much trouble us. Also, we spend most of our days in the studios of our art masters, who do not waste time on religious drivel. They work us hard, so we *do* learn what *we* came to learn."

"Some other boys do, too," said Chimáli. "Those who are similarly apprenticed out—to physicians, feather workers, musicians, and the like. But I pity those who came to learn classroom subjects like the art of word knowing. When they are not engaged in rituals and bloody mortification and menial labor, they are being taught by priests as ignorant as any of the students. You can be glad, Mole, that you did not get into a calmécac. There is little to learn in one, unless you desire to be a priest yourself."

"And nobody," said Tlatli, shuddering, "would want to be a priest of any god, unless he wants never to have sex or a drink of octli or even a bath just once in his life. And unless he truly enjoys hurting himself as well as seeing other people in pain."

I had once felt envy of Tlatli and Chimáli, when they donned their best mantles and went away to their separate schools. Now here they were, still wearing the same mantles, and it was they who envied me. I did not have to say a word about the luxurious life I enjoyed at the court of Nezahualpíli. They were sufficiently impressed when I remarked that our textbooks were painted on smoked fawnskin for durability, and when I mentioned the absence of religious interruptions, the few rules and little rigidity, the willingness of the teachers to give private tutorial sessions.

"Imagine!" murmured Tlatli. "Teachers who have *worked* at what they teach."

"Fawnskin textbooks," murmured Chimáli.

There was a stir among the people nearest the door, and all of a sudden Pactli strode in, as if he had deliberately timed his arrival to display the superior product of the most select and prestigious kind of calmécac. Numerous persons dropped to kiss the earth to the son of their governor, but there was not room for all to do so.

"Mixpantzínco," my father greeted him, uncertainly.

Ignoring my father, not bothering to utter the customary response, Pactli spoke directly to me. "I came to request your aid, young Mole." He handed me a strip of folded bark paper and said, as comradely as he knew how, "I understand that your study is concentrated on the art of word knowing, and I ask that you give me your opinion of this effort of mine, before I return to school and submit it to the criticism of my Lord Teacher." But while he spoke to me, his eyes shifted to my sister. It must have cost the Lord Joy a pang, I thought, to have to use *me* as an excuse for visiting before midnight should make a visit impossible.

Though Pactli could not have cared a little finger for my opinion of his writing—he was openly leering at my sister now—I flipped through the pleated pages and said boredly, "In which direction am I supposed to read this?"

Several people looked aghast at my tone of voice, and Pactli grunted as if I had struck him. He glared at me and said, through his teeth, "From left to right, Mole, as you know very well."

"Usually from left to right, yes, but not always," I said. "The first and most basic rule of writing, which apparently you have not grapsed, is that the majority of your pictured characters must all face in the direction the writing is to be read."

I must have been feeling uncommonly inflated by the finery of my costume, by having just come from a court infinitely more cultured than Pactli's, and by being the center of attention of a houseful of friends and relations—or I should probably not have dared to flout the conventions of servility. Not troubling to scan the paper further, I refolded and handed it back to him.

Have you ever noticed, Your Excellency, how the same emotion of rage can make different persons turn different colors? Pactli's face had gone almost purple, my mother's almost white. Tzitzi lightly brushed her hand across her mouth in the gesture of surprise, but then she laughed; so did Tlatli and Chimáli. Pactli turned his baleful glare from me to them, then swept it around the entire assemblage, most of whom seemed to be wishing they could turn yet another color: the invisible color of the invisible air. Speechless with fury, the Lord Joy crushed his paper together in his fist and stalked out, rudely shouldering those who could not immediately make way for him.

Most of the rest of the company also left straightaway, as if thereby they could somehow disassociate themselves from my insubordination. They gave the excuse that their houses were more or less distant from ours, and they wanted to hurry home before darkness fell, to make sure that not a single ember in their hearths had been accidentally left smoldering alight. While that mass departure was in progress, Chimáli and Tlatli both gave me supportive grins, Tzitzi pressed my hand, my father looked stricken, and my mother looked glazed with frost. But not everyone left. Some of the guests were staunch enough not to feel trepidation at the contumacy I had displayed—and had displayed on the very eve of the lifeless days.

During those coming five days, you see, to do *anything* was regarded as rash—patently fruitless and possibly hazardous. The days were not really days; they were only a necessary gap between the year's last month of Xiutecútli and the next year's first month of Cuáhuitl Ehua; they did not exist as days. Hence we tried to keep our own existence as imperceptible as possible. That was the time of year when the gods lazed and drowsed; even the sun was pale and cool and low in the sky. No sensible person would do anything to disturb the gods' languor and risk their annoyance.

So, during the five hollow days, all worked stopped. All activities ceased, barring the most essential and unavoidable tasks. All house fires and lights were extinguished. No cooking was done and only meager cold meals were served. People did not travel or visit or mingle into crowds. Husbands and wives refrained from sexual connection. (They also refrained, or took precautions, at the proper time previous to the nemontémtin, for a child born during the lifeless days was seldom let survive them.) Throughout all our lands, then, most people stayed indoors and occupied themselves with trivial timepassers like flaking tools or mending nets, or they simply sat about and moped.

Since the hollow days themselves were so ill-omened, I suppose it was only natural that the company remaining in our house that evening conversed on the subject of omens and portents. Chimáli, Tlatli, and I sat apart and continued our comparison of our schools, but I overheard snatches of the talk of our elders:

"It was a year ago that Xopan stepped over her baby daughter who was crawling underfoot in the kitchen. I could have told Xopan what she was doing to the girl's tonáli. That child has not grown a fingerspan in the whole year since she was stepped over. She will be a dwarf, you wait and see."

"I used to scoff, but now I know that the old tales about dreams are true. One night I dreamt of a water jar being broken, and it was the very next day that my brother Xícama died. Killed in the quarry, you recall."

"Sometimes the dire results do not happen for so long that

one might forget what thoughtless action provoked them. Like the time, years ago, that I warned Teoxíhuitl to be careful with her broom, when I saw her sweep across the foot of her son playing on the floor. And sure enough, that boy grew up to marry a widow woman nearly as old as his mother Teoxíhuitl. Made himself the laughingstock of the village."

"A butterfly flew in circles about my head. It was not until a month later that I got the word. My only sister Cuepóni had died at her home in Tlácopan on that same day. But of course I should already have known, from the butterfly, for she was my nearest and dearest relation."

I could not help reflecting on two things. One was that everybody on Xaltócan really did speak a most unrefined tongue, compared with the Náhuatl of Texcóco to which I had recently become accustomed. The other was that, of all the omens of which the company spoke, not a single one ever seemed to presage anything but misfortune, deprivation, misery, or woe. Then I was diverted by Tlatli's telling me something he had learned from his Lord Teacher of Sculpture:

"Humans are the only creatures that have a nose. No, do not laugh, Mole. Of all the living creatures of which we make carvings, only men and women have a nose which is not just part of a muzzle or a beak, but sticks out from the face. So, since we elaborate our statues with so many decorative details, my master has taught me always to sculpture a human with a somewhat exaggerated nose. Thus anyone looking at the most complicated statue, even if he is ignorant of art, can tell at a glance that it represents a human and not a jaguar or a serpent or, for that matter, the frog-faced water goddess Chalchi-huítlicué."

I nodded, and tucked the idea away in my memory. Thereafter I did likewise in my picture writing, and many other scribes later imitated my practice of always limning men and women with distinctive noses. If all our people are doomed to vanish from the earth like the Toltéca—I trust that our books at least will survive. Any future readers of our picture writing may get the mistaken notion that every inhabitant of these lands had a hooked hawk beak like the Maya, but they should at least have no trouble distinguishing the human characters from the animals and the gods of animal aspect.

"Thanks to you, Mole, I have devised a unique signature for my paintings," said Chimáli, with a shy grin. "Other artists sign their works with their name symbols, but I use this." He showed me a board about the size of his sandal, embedded all over its surface with countless tiny chips of sharp obsidian. I was startled and horrified when he slapped his open left hand hard against the board, then, still grinning, held it open for me to see the blood oozing from its palm and every finger. "There may be other artists named Chimáli, but it was you, Mole, who showed me that no two hands are alike." His was now entirely covered with his blood. "Hence I have a signature which can never be imitated."

He slapped the massive household water jar nearby. On its dull brown clay surface there was now a gleaming red hand-print. Travel these lands, Your Excellency, and you will see that same signature on many a temple mural and palace paint-ing. Chimáli did a prodigious amount of work before he stopped working.

He and Tlatli were the last of the guests to leave our house that night. Those two stayed, on purpose, until we actually heard the drums and conch trumpets from the temple pyramid, announcing the start of the nemontémtin. While my mother dashed about the house to douse the lights, my friends scam-pered to get to their own homes before the beating and the bleating stopped. It was reckless of them—if the hollow days were bad, their lightless nights were far worse—but the two friends' staying saved me from chastisement for my insult to the Lord Joy. Neither my father nor mother could undertake something as serious as punishment during the ensuing days, and by the time the nemontémtin ended, the matter had been pretty well forgotten.

However, those days were not entirely uneventful for me. On one of them Tzitzi got me aside to whisper urgently, "Must I go and steal another sacred mushroom?"

"Godless sister," I hissed at her, though not angrily. "Lying together is forbidden even to husbands and wives at this time."

"*Only* to husbands and wives. To you and me, it is forbidden always, so we run no exceptional risk."

Before I could say anything else, she moved from me to

the waist-high clay jar that held our household water supply, the one that now bore Chimáli's blood-red handprint. She shoved it with all her strength; it overturned and broke, and water cascaded across the limestone floor. Our mother stormed into the room and let loose one of her tirades at Tzitzitlíni. Clumsy wench . . . jar took a whole day to fill . . . supposed to last through the nemontémtin . . . not another drop in the house and not another container that size. . . .

Unruffled, my sister said, "Mixtli and I can go to the spring with the largest other jars, and between us bring back as much in one trip."

Our mother did not think highly of that suggestion, and so she did a good deal more of her shrilling, but she really had no alternative, and finally let us go. Each of us left the house carrying a handled, big-bellied jug in either hand, but at the first opportunity we set them down.

I last described Tzitzi as she looked in early adolescence. She was now full grown and, of course, her hips and buttocks had filled out to graceful, womanly curves. Each of her breasts overflowed my cupped hand. Their nipples were more erectile, their areolas were of larger diameter and a darker russet brown against the fawn skin around them. Tzitzi was also, if possible, more quickly aroused each time than the time before, and more wanton in her responses and movements. In just the brief interval we allowed ourselves between the house and the spring, she came to culmination at least thrice. Her increased capacity for passion, and one noticeable maturation of her body, gave me the first hint of a premise, and my experiences with other women in later years served always to confirm it. So I consider it not a premise, but a proven theory, and it is this:

A woman's sexuality is in direct proportion to the diameter and darkness of her breast's areola. Never mind how beautiful her face, how shapely her form; never mind how approachable or how aloof she may seem. Those aspects can be misleading, even deliberately so on her part. But there is that one reliable indicator of the sensuality of her nature, and, to the knowing eye, no cosmetic art can hide it or counterfeit it. A woman with a large and dark area surrounding her nipple is invariably hot-blooded, even if she might wish to be otherwise. A woman with a nipple only—like the vestigial nipple of a man—is inevitably cold, although she might honestly believe herself to be otherwise, or even behave shamelessly in order to appear otherwise. And of course there are gradations of areola size and color, the gauging of which can be learned only by experience. Thus a man need contrive to get but a single glance at a woman's bare breast and, with no waste of time or chance of disappointment, he can judge how passionately she will

Your Excellency wishes me to have done with this subject. Ah, well, no doubt I dwell on it only because it is *my* theory. I have always been fond of it, and of testing it, and I never once encountered disproof. I still think the correlation of a woman's sexuality and her areola ought to have some useful application outside the bedchamber.

Yyo ayyo! Do you know, Your Excellency, it suddenly occurs to me that your Church might be interested. It could use my theory as a quick and simple test for choosing those girls best suited by nature to be nuns in your

I desist, yes, my lord.

I will just mention that, when Tzitzi and I at last returned to the house, fairly staggering with the four heavy jugs of water, we were berated by our mother for having been so long out in the open on such a day. My sister, who only a short while before had been a young wild animal—thrashing, panting, and clawing me in her ecstasy—now lied as casually and smoothly as any priest:

"You cannot scold us for loitering or dallying. There were others wanting water from the spring. Since the day forbids any congregating, Mixtli and I had to wait our turn at a distance and move nearer bit by bit. We did not waste any time."

At the end of the dreary hollow days, all The One World breathed a great sigh of relief. I do not know exactly what you mean, Your Excellency, when you mutter about "a parody of Lent," but on the first day of the month The Tree Is Raised there commenced a round of general gaiety. Throughout the following days, there were private celebrations in the bigger homes of nobles and well-to-do commoners, and in the local temples of the various villages, during which the hosts and guests, the priests and worshipers indulged in excesses of which they had been deprived during the nemontémtin.

Those preliminary festivities might have been a trifle dampened that year, for we got word of the death of our Uey-Tlatoáni Tixoc. But his reign had been the shortest in the history of Mexíca rulers, and the least noteworthy. Indeed, it was rumored that he had been quietly poisoned—either by the elders of his Speaking Council, impatient with Tixoc's uninterest in mounting new war campaigns, or by his brother Ahuítzotl, Water Monster, next in line to the throne and ambitious to show how much more brilliantly he could rule. At any rate, Tixoc had been such a colorless figure that he was not much missed or mourned. So our grand ceremony in praise and supplication of the rain god Tlaloc, held in Xaltócan's central pyramid plaza, was also dedicated to celebrating the accession of the new Revered Speaker Ahuítzotl.

The rites did not begin until Tonatíu had sunk to sleep in his western bed, lest that god of warmth should see and be jealous of the honors paid to his brother god of wetness. Then there began to gather—about the edges of the open plaza and on the slopes rising around it—every single inhabitant of the island, save those too old, too young, too ill or disabled, and those who had to remain at home to tend them. As soon as the sun set, the square and the pyramid and the temple on top were aflutter with the black-robed priests, busy at their last preparations of lighting the multitude of torches, the artificially colored urn fires, and the sweetly smoking incense burners. The sacrificial stone atop the pyramid would not be used that night. Instead, there had been brought—to the foot of the pyramid, where every spectator could see into it—an immense, hollowed-out stone tub, full of water previously sanctified by special incantations.

As the darkness deepened, the grove of trees beside and behind the pyramid also came alight: innumerable little wick lamps flickering as if the trees were nesting all the fireflies in the world. The trees' branches began to sway, swarming with children: very young and small but agile boys and girls wearing costumes lovingly fashioned by their mothers. Some of the little girls were enveloped by stiff paper globes painted to represent various fruits; others wore ruffs or skirts of paper cut and painted to represent various flowers. The boys were even more gaudily dressed, some covered in glued-on feathers to act the role of birds, others wearing translucent oiled-paper wings to play the part of bees and butterflies. All during the night's events, the boy birds and boy insects flitted acrobatically from branch to branch, pretending to "sip the nectar" of the girl fruits and girl flowers.

When the night was entirely upon us, and the island's population was assembled, the chief priest of Tlaloc appeared on the pyramid summit. He blew a blast on his conch trumpet, then raised his arms commandingly, and the hubbub of crowd noise began to subside. He held his arms aloft until the plaza hushed to absolute silence. Then he dropped his arms and, on the instant, Tlaloc himself spoke in a deafening crash of thunder—*ba-ra-ROOM!*—that kept on resounding and reverberating. The noise veritably shook the leaves on the trees, the smoke of the incense, the flames of the fires, the breath we had gasped into our lungs. It was not really Tlaloc, of course, but the mighty "thunder drum," also called "the drum that tears out the heart." Its taut and heavy snakeskin drumhead was being frenziedly hammered with óli mallets. The sound of the thunder drum can be heard two one-long-runs distant, so you can imagine its effect on us people clustered close around it.

That fearsome throbbing continued until we felt that our flesh must be about to shiver off our bones. Then it gradually diminished, quieter and quieter yet, until it merged into the pulsing of the smaller "god drum," which merely muttered while the chief priest chanted the standard greeting and invocation to Tlaloc. At intervals he paused for the crowd of us to respond in chorus—as your churchgoers say "Amen"—with a long-drawn owl cry of "Hoo-oo-ooo. . . ." At other intervals he paused while his lesser priests stepped forward, reached into their robes, plucked out small water creatures—a frog, an axólotl salamander, a snake—held them up wriggling and then swallowed them whole and alive.

The chief priest concluded his opening chant with the age-old words, as loudly as he could shout them: *"Tehuan tiez-quiáya in ahuéhuetl, in pochotl, TLÁLOCTZIN!"*—which means, "We would that we be beneath the cypress, beneath the ceiba tree, Lord Tlaloc!"—which is to say, "We would ask your protection, your dominion over us." And at that bellow, priests in every part of the plaza threw onto the urn fires clouds of finely powdered maize flour, which exploded with a sharp crack and a dazzling flash, as if a fork of lightning had stabbed down among us. Then *ba-ra-ROOM!* the thunder drum smote us again, and kept on pounding until our teeth seemed to be rattling loose in our jaws.

But again it slowly quieted, and, when our ears could hear, we were listening to music played on the clay flute shaped like a sweet potato; and on "the suspended gourds" of different sizes which give different noises when struck with sticks; and on the flute made of five reeds of different lengths fastened side by side; while, behind all of those, the rhythm was kept by "the strong bone," a deer's toothed jawbone rasped with a rod. With the music came the dancers, men and women in concentric circles doing the Reed Dance. At their ankles, knees, and elbows were fastened dried pods of seeds, which rattled, whispered, and rustled as they moved. The men, wearing costumes of water blue, each carried a length of reed about as thick as his wrist and as long as his arm. The women were dressed in blouses and skirts colored the pale green of young reeds, and Tzitzitlíni was their leader.

The male and female dancers glided through graceful interweavings in time to the happy music. The women waved their arms sinuously above their heads, and you could see the waving of reeds in a breeze. The men shook those thick canes they carried, and you could hear the dry rustling of reeds in a breeze. Then the music soared louder, and the women grouped in the center of the plaza, dancing in place, while the men formed a ring around them, and made a casting gesture with their thick reeds. At which, each of the things was revealed to be not just a single reed but a whole series of them, the thick one enclosing a less thick, which in turn enclosed a thinner, and so on.

When a man made that throwing movement, all the inner reeds slid out of the one held in his hand, to become a long, tapering, curving line whose tip met the tips of all the others thrown. The dancing women were embowered by a fragile dome of the reeds, and the watching crowd again went "Hoo-oo-ooo" in admiration. Then, with an adroit flick of their wrists, the men made all those reeds slide *back* inside each other and into their hands. The cunning trick was done again and again, in varying patterns, as when the men formed two lines and each threw his long reed to meet that of the man opposite, and the reeds made an arched tunnel through which the women danced. . . .

When the Reed Dance was done, there came a comic interlude. Into the firelit square crept and limped all those old folk who suffer from an ailment of the bones and joints. This affliction keeps them always more or less bent and crippled, but for some reason it is especially painful to them during the rainy months. So those old men and women struggled to that ceremony to dance before Tlaloc in hope that, come the wet season, he would this time take pity and ease their aching.

They were understandably serious in their intent, but the dance was bound to be grotesque, and the spectators began to titter, then to laugh aloud, until the dancers themselves recognized their ridiculousness. One after another started to play the clown, exaggerating the absurdity of his or her limp or hobble. Eventually they were hopping on all fours like frogs, or lurching sideways like crabs, or hunching their scrawny old necks at each other like cranes in the mating season—and the watching crowd roared and rocked with laughter. The aged dancers got so carried away and so prolonged their hideous, hilarious capering that the priests had to clear them almost forcibly from the scene. It may interest Your Excellency to know that those suppliant exertions never influenced Tlaloc to benefit a single cripple—quite the contrary, many of them were permanently bedridden from that night on—but those old fools still capable would keep coming back to dance again year after year.

Next came the dance of the auyaníme, those women whose bodies were reserved to the service of soldiers and knights. The dance they did was called the quequezcuícatl, "the ticklish dance," because it roused such sensations among its watchers, male and female, young and old, that they often had to be restrained from rushing in among the dancers and doing something really outrageously irreverent. The dance was so explicit in its movements that—though only the auyaníme danced, and apart even from each other—you would swear they had invisible, naked male companions with whom . . .

Yes, well, after the auyaníme had left the plaza—panting, perspiring, their hair tousled, their legs weak and wobbly—there came, to the hungry rumble of the god drum, a boy and a girl, each about four years old, in an ornate litter chair carried by priests. Because the late and unlamented Revered Speaker Tixoc had been lax in his waging of war, there had been no captive children from some other nation available for that night's sacrifice, so the priests had to buy the youngsters from two local slave families. The four parents sat well down front on the plaza and watched proudly as their babies were paraded several times past them in their several circuits of the square.

The parents and the children had reason to be proud and pleased, for the little boy and girl had been purchased long enough beforehand to have been well cared for and well fed. They were now plump and perky, waving merrily to their parents and to everyone else in the crowd who waved at them. They were better dressed than they could ever have hoped to be, for they were costumed to represent the tlalóque spirits which attend upon the rain god. Their little mantles were of the finest cotton, a blue-green color patterned with silver raindrops, and they wore on their shoulder blades cloud-white wings of paper.

As had happened at every previous ceremony in honor of Tlaloc, the children were unaware of the behaviour expected of them. They were so delighted by the excitement, the colors, the lights and music that they bounced with laughter and beamed about them as radiantly as the sun. That, of course, was just the opposite of what they were meant to do. So, as usual, the priests carrying their chair had to reach up surreptitiously and pinch their bottoms. The children were at first puzzled, then pained. The boy and girl began to complain, then to weep, then to wail, as was proper. The more bawling, the more thunderstorms to come. The more tears, the more rain.

The crowd joined in the crying, as was expected and encouraged, even for grown men and crusty warriors, until the hills roundabout echoed with the groaning and sobbing and beating of breasts. Every other drum and musical instrument now augmented the throbbing of the god drum and the ululation of the crowd, as the priests set down the litter chair on the far side of that stone tub of water by the pyramid. So unbelievably loud was the combined noise that probably not even the chief priest could hear the words he chanted over the two children when he lifted them and held them up one at a time to the sky, that Tlaloc might see and approve of them.

Then two assistant priests approached, one with a small pot, the other with a brush. The chief priest bent over the boy and girl and, though no one could hear, we all knew he was telling the children that they were now to don masks so the water would not get into their eyes while they swam in the sacred tank. They were still sniffling, not smiling, their cheeks wet with tears, but they did not protest when the priest brushed liquid óli liberally over their faces, leaving only their flower-bud lips uncoated. We could not see their expression when the priest turned from them again to chant, still unheard, the final appeal that Tlaloc accept their sacrifice, that in exchange he send a substantial rainy season, and so on.

The assistants lifted the boy and girl one last time, and the chief priest swiftly daubed the sticky liquid across their lower faces, covering mouths and nostrils, and the assistants dropped the children into the tank, where the cool water instantly congealed the gum. You see, the ceremony required that the sacrifices die *in* the water, but not *of* it. So they did not drown, they suffocated slowly behind the thick, unremovable, untearable óli masks, while they flailed desperately in the tank, and sank and rose and sank again, and the crowd wailed in mourning, and the drums and instruments continued their god-shouting cacophony. The children splashed and struggled ever more feebly, until first the girl, then the boy, ceased to move and hung only dimly visible just under the water, and on the surface their white wings floated, widespread, unmoving.

Cold-blooded murder, Your Excellency? But they were slave children. The boy and girl would otherwise have led brute lives, perhaps mated when they were grown, and begotten more brutes. When they came to die, they would have died to no purpose whatever, and they would have languished for a dreary eternity in the darkness and nothingness of Míctlan. Instead, they died to the honor of Tlaloc, and to the benefit of us who went on living, and their death earned them a happy life ever after in the lush green afterworld of Tlálocan.

Barbaric superstition, Your Excellency? But that next rainy season was as bountiful as even a Christian could have implored, and it gave us a handsome harvest.

Cruel? Heartrending? Well, yes . . . Yes, *I* at least remember it so, for that was the last happy holy day that Tzitzitlíni and I were ever to enjoy together.

✠

When Prince Willow's acáli came to fetch me again, it did not reach Xaltócan until well after midday, because it was then the season of high winds, and the oarsmen had had a turbulent crossing. It was just as rough going back—the lake was roiled into choppy waves from which the wind tore and flung a stinging spray—so we did not dock at Texcóco until the sun was halfway to bed.

Though the city's buildings and streets began there at the docks, that district was really only a fringe of lakeside industries and dwellings—boatyards; shops making nets, ropes, hooks, and the like; the houses of boatmen, fishermen, and fowlers. The city's center was perhaps half of one-long-run farther inland. Since no one from the palace had come to meet me, Willow's oarsmen volunteered to walk part of the way with me and help to carry the bundles I had brought: some additional clothes, another set of paints given me by Chimáli, a basket of sweets cooked by Tzitzi.

My companions dropped off, one by one, as we came to the neighborhoods in which they lived. But the last one told me that if I simply walked straight on, I could not fail to recognize the palace on the great central square. It was full dark by then, and there were not many other people abroad on that blustery night, but the streets were lighted. Every house seemed supplied with lamps of coconut oil or ahuácatl oil or fish oil or whatever fuel the householders could afford. Their light spilled out through the houses' window openings, even those closed by lattice shutters or cloth curtains or oiled-paper shades. In addition, there was a torchlight set at most of the street corners: high poles with copperwork baskets of blazing pine splinters on top, from which the wind blew sparks and occasional gobbets of burning pitch. Those poles were set in sockets drilled through the fists of standing or squatting stone statues of various gods.

I had not walked far before I began to tire; I was carrying so many bundles, and I was being so buffeted by the wind. It was with relief that I saw a streetside stone bench set in the darkness under a red-flowering tapachíni tree. I sank down on it gratefully, and sat for a while, enjoying being showered by the tree's scarlet petals blown loose by the wind. Then I became aware that the bench seat under me was ridged with a carved design. I had only to begin tracing it with my fingers—not even to peer at it in the dark—to know that it was picture writing, and to know what it said.

"A resting place for the Lord Night Wind," I quoted aloud, smiling to myself.

"You were reading exactly the same thing," said a voice from the darkness, "when we met at another bench some years ago."

I gave a start of surprise, then squinted to make out the figure at the other end of the seat. Again he was wearing a mantle and sandals of good quality, though travel-worn. Again he was so covered with the dust of the road that his coppery features were indistinct. But now I was probably just as dusty, and I had grown considerably, and I marveled that he could have recognized me. When I had recovered my voice, I said:

"Yes, Yanquícatzin, it is a surpassing coincidence."

"You should not address me as Lord Stranger," he growled, as surly as I remembered him. "Here *you* are the stranger."

"True, my lord," I said. "And here I have learned to read more than the simple symbols on roadside benches."

"I should hope so," he said drily.

"It is thanks to the Uey-Tlatoáni Nezahualpíli," I explained. "At his generous invitation, I have enjoyed many months of higher schooling in his court classrooms."

"And what do you do to earn such favors?"

"Well, I *would* do anything, for I am grateful to my benefactor, and eager to repay him. But I have yet to meet the Revered Speaker, and nobody else gives me anything but schoolwork to do. It makes me uncomfortable, to feel that I am only a parasite."

"Perhaps Nezahualpíli has merely been waiting. To see you prove yourself trustworthy. To hear you say you would do anything."

"I would. Anything he might ask."

"I daresay he will ask something of you eventually."

"I hope so, my lord."

We sat for some time in silence, except for the sound of the wind moaning between the buildings, like Chocacíuatl the Weeping Woman forever wandering. Finally the dusty man said sarcastically:

"You are eager to be of use at the court, but here you sit and the palace is yonder." He waved down the street. I was being dismissed as curtly as the other time.

I stood up, gathered my bundles, and said with some pique, "As my impatient lord suggests, I go. Mixpantzínco."

"Ximopanólti," he drawled indifferently.

I stopped under the torch pole at the next corner and looked back, but the light did not reach far enough to illuminate the bench. If the travel-stained stranger still sat there, I could not make out his form. All I could see was a little red whirl of tapachíni petals being danced along the street by the night wind.

I finally found the palace, and found the slave boy Cozcatl waiting to show me to my quarters. That palace at Texcóco was far larger than the one at Texcotzínco—it must have contained a thousand rooms—since there was not so much space in the central city for its necessary annexes to sprawl and spread around it. Still, the Texcóco palace grounds were extensive and, even in the middle of his capital city, Nezahualpíli evidently would not be denied his gardens and arbors and fountains and the like.

There was even a living maze, which occupied land enough for ten families to have farmed. It had been planted by some long-ago royal ancestor, and had been growing ever since, though kept neatly clipped. It was now an avenue of parallel, impenetrable thorn hedges, twice man-high, which twisted and forked and doubled upon itself. There was only a single opening in the hedge's green outer wall, and it was said that anyone entering there would, after long meandering, find his way to a little grassy glade in the center of the maze, but that the return route was impossible to retrace. Only the aged chief gardener of the palace knew the way out, a secret handed down·in his family and traditionally kept secret even from the Uey-Tlatoáni. So no one was allowed to enter there without the old gardener for a guide—except as a punishment. The occasional convicted lawbreaker was sentenced to be delivered alone and naked into the maze, at spearpoint if necessary. After a month or so, the gardener would go in and bring out whatever remained of the starved and thorn-torn and bird-pecked and worm-eaten body.

The day after my return, I was waiting for a class to begin, when young Prince Willow approached me. After welcoming me back to court, he said casually, "My father would be pleased to see you in the throne room at your convenience, Head Nodder."

At my convenience! How courteously the highest noble of the Acólhua summoned to his presence this lowly foreigner who had been battening on his hospitality. Of course I left the classroom and went immediately, almost running along the buildings' galleries, so that I was quite breathless when at last I·dropped to one knee at the threshold of the immense throne room, made the gesture of kissing the earth, and said, "In your august presence, Revered Speaker."

"Ximopanólti, Head Nodder." When I remained bowed in my position of humility, he said, "You may rise, Mole." When I stood, but stayed where I was, he said, "You may come here, Dark Cloud." As I did so, slowly and respectfully, he said, smiling, "You have as many names as a bird which flies over all the nations of The One World and which is called differently by every people." With a fly whisk he was wielding he indicated one of several icpáltin chairs ranged in a semicircle before the throne and said, "Be seated."

Nezahualpíli's own chair was no more grand or impressive than the stubby-legged one on which I sat, but it was raised on a dais so that I had to look up at him. He sat with his legs not formally crossed under him or knees up in front of him, but languidly stretched out to the front and crossed at the ankles. Though the throne room was hung with feather-work tapestries and panel paintings, there were no other furnishings except the throne, those low chairs for visitors—and, directly in front of the Uey-Tlatoáni, a low table of black onyx on which reposed, facing him, a gleaming white human skull.

"My father, Fasting Coyote, set that there," said Nezahualpíli, noticing my eyes upon it. "I do not know why. It may have been some vanquished enemy over whom he delighted to gloat. Or some lost beloved he could never stop mourning. Or he may have kept it for the same reason I do."

I asked, "And what is that, Lord Speaker?"

"There come to this room envoys bearing threats of war or offering treaties of peace. There come plaintiffs laden with grievances, petitioners asking favors. When those persons address me, their faces may contort with anger or sag with misery or smile in feigned devotion. So, while I listen to them, I look not at their faces, but at the skull."

I could only say, "Why, my lord?"

"Because *there* is the cleanest and most honest face of man. No paint or disguise, no guile or grimace, no sly wink or ingratiating smile. Only a fixed, ironic grin, a mockery of every living man's concern for urgencies. When any visitor pleads that I make a ruling here and now, I temporize, I dissimulate. I smoke a poquíetl or two, while I look long at that skull. It reminds me that the words I speak may well outlast my own flesh, may long stand as firm decrees—and to what effect on those then living? Ayyo, that skull has often served to caution me against an impatient or impulsive decision." Nezahualpíli looked from the skull to me, and laughed. "When the head lived, for all I know, it was that of a babbling idiot, but dead and silent it is a wise counselor indeed."

I said, "I think, my lord, that no counselor would be of use except to a man wise enough to heed counsel."

"I take that as a compliment, Head Nodder, and I thank you. Now, was I wise to bring you here from Xaltócan?"

"I cannot say, my lord. I do not know why you did."

"Since the time of Fasting Coyote, the city of Texcóco has been famed as a center of knowledge and culture, but such a center is not necessarily self-perpetuating. The noblest of families can breed dolts and sluggards—I could name a few of my own get—so we do not hesitate to import talent from elsewhere, and even to infuse foreign blood. You seemed a promising prospect, so here you are."

"To stay, Lord Speaker?"

"That will be up to you, or to your tonáli, or to circumstances that not you nor we can foresee. But your teachers have given good report of you, so I think it time that you became a more active participant in court life."

"I had been hoping for a means to repay your generosity, my lord. Do you mean I am to be given some useful employment?"

"If it is to your liking. During your recent absence, I took another wife. Her name is Chálchiunénetl. Jadestone Doll."

I said nothing, wondering confusedly if he had for some reason changed the subject. But he went on:

"She is the eldest daughter of Ahuítzotl. A gift from him to mark his accession as the new Uey-Tlatoáni of Tenochtítlan. She is a Mexícatl like yourself. She is fifteen years old, of an age to be your younger sister. Our ceremony of marriage has been duly celebrated, but of course the physical consummation will be postponed until Jadestone Doll is grown more mature."

I still said nothing, though I could have told even the wise Nezahualpíli something about the physical capabilities of adolescent Mexíca maidens.

He continued, "She has been given a small army of waiting women, and the entire east wing as apartments for herself, for servants' quarters, private kitchen; a private palace in miniature. So she will lack for nothing in the way of comfort, service, and female companionship. However, I wonder if you might consent, Head Nodder, to join her retinue. It would be good for her to have the company of at least one male, and he a brother Mexícatl. At the same time you would be serving me: instructing the girl in our customs, teaching her our Texcóco style of speech, preparing her to be a consort of whom I can be proud."

I said evasively, "Chálchiunénetzin might not take kindly to having me appointed her keeper, Lord Speaker. A young girl can be willful, irrepressible, jealous of her freedom. . . ."

"How well I know," sighed Nezahualpíli. "I have two or three daughters of about that same age. And Jadestone Doll, being the princess daughter of one Uey-Tlatoáni and the queen wife of another, is likely to be even more spirited. I would not condemn my worst enemy to be the keeper of a mettlesome young female. But I think, Mole, that you will find her at least pleasant to look upon."

He must have pulled a concealed bell rope some while before, for he gestured and I turned to see a slim girl in a rich ceremonial skirt, blouse, and headdress, coming slowly but regally toward the dais. Her face was perfection, her head held high, her eyes demurely lowered.

"My dear," said Nezahualpíli. "This is Mixtli, of whom I have spoken. Would you have him in your retinue, in the role of companion and protector?"

"If my Lord Husband wishes it, I comply. If the young man agrees to it, I shall be pleased to regard him as my elder brother."

The long-lashed eyelids lifted, and she looked at me, and her eyes were like unfathomably deep forest pools. I found out later that she habitually put into her eyes drops of juice from the herb camopalxíhuitl, which greatly enlarged her pupils and made her eyes lustrous as jewels. It also forced her to avoid bright lights, even the light of day, when her dilated eyes saw almost as poorly as mine.

"Well, then," said the Revered Speaker, rubbing his hands with satisfaction. I wondered, with some misgivings, just how long he had conferred with his counsel skull before deciding on this arrangement. To me he said:

"I ask only that you provide brotherly direction and advice, Head Nodder. I do not expect you to correct or chastise the Lady Jadestone Doll. It would, in any event, be a capital offense for a commoner to raise either his hand or his voice against a noblewoman. Nor do I expect you to play the jailer or the spy or the talebearer of her confidences. But I would be pleased, Mole, if you devote to your lady sister what time you can spare from your schoolwork and studies. That you serve her with the same devotion and discretion with which you serve me or the First Lady Tolána-Tecíuapil. Now go, young people, ximopanólti, and get acquainted with each other."

We made the proper obeisances and left the throne room. In the corridor, Jadestone Doll smiled sweetly at me and said, "Mole, Head Nodder, Mixtli. How many names *do* you have?"

"My lady may call me whatever she pleases."

She smiled even more sweetly, and put a delicate tapered

fingertip to her pointed little chin. "I think I shall call you . . ." She smiled still more sweetly, and said with a sweetness like the taste of sticky maguey syrup, "I will call you Qualcuíe!"

That word is the third person singular jussive of the verb "to fetch," and is always pronounced forcefully and commandingly: "Fetch!" My heart grew heavy. If my latest name was to be Fetch!, my misgivings about this arrangement seemed justified. And I was right. Though she still spoke in that maguey syrup voice, the young queen dropped all semblance of demureness, docility, and submissiveness, and said, very queenlike:

"You need not interrupt any of your daytime classwork, Fetch! However, I shall want you available in the evenings, and on call if necessary during the nights. You will please move all your effects into the apartment directly across the hall from mine." Without waiting for me to say any word of acquiescence, without herself saying any polite word of leavetaking, she turned and walked away down the hall.

Jadestone Doll. She was named for the mineral chalchíhuitl, which, though it is neither rare nor of any intrinsic value, was prized by our people because it was the color of The Center of Everything. Unlike you Spaniards, who know only the four directions of what you call the compass, we perceived five, and designated them by different colors. Like you, we had the east, north, west, and south, respectively referred to as the directions of the red, black, white, and blue. But we also had the green: to mark the center of the compass, so to speak—the place where a man *was* at any given moment, and all the space above that spot as far as the sky, and all below it as far as the Míctlan underworld. So the color green was important to us, and the green stone chalchíhuitl was precious to us, and only a child of noble lineage and high degree could appropriately have been named Jadestone Doll.

Like a jadestone, that girl queen was an object to be handled most respectfully and carefully. Like a doll, she was exquisitely fashioned, she was beautiful, she was a work of divine craftsmanship. But, like a doll, she had no human conscience or compunctions. And, though I did not immediately recognize my feeling of premonition, like a doll she was fated to be broken.

✠

I must admit that I rather reveled in the sumptuousness of my new chambers. Three rooms, and the sanitary closet contained my own private steam bath. The bed in the bedroom was an even higher than ordinary pile of quilts, over which lay an enormous coverlet made of hundreds of tiny squirrel skins bleached white and sewn together. Over the whole was suspended a fringed canopy and from that hung almost invisible, fine-meshed net curtains, which I could close around the bed to keep out mosquitoes and moths.

The one inconvenience of the apartment was that it was far distant from those others which the slave Cozcatl had in his charge. But when I mentioned that to Jadestone Doll, little Cozcatl was abruptly relieved of all his other duties, to attend solely to me. The boy was ever so proud of that promotion. Even I felt rather the pampered young lord. And later, when Jadestone Doll and I were in disgrace, I would be glad that Cozcatl had always been by me and was loyally ready to testify in my defense.

For soon I learned: if Cozcatl was my slave, I was Jadestone Doll's. On that first evening, when one of her maids admitted me to her grand suite, the young queen's first words were:

"I am glad you were given to me, Fetch!, for I was getting unutterably bored, cooped up in seclusion like some rare animal." I tried to make a demurrer regarding the word "given," but she overrode me. "I am told by Pitza"—she indicated the elderly maidservant hovering behind her cushioned bench— "that you are an expert at capturing the likeness of a person on paper."

"I flatter myself, my lady, that people have recognized themselves and each other in my drawings. But it is some while since I have practiced the craft."

"You will practice on me. Pitza, go across the corridor and have Cozcatl collect the implements Fetch! will require."

The little boy brought me some chalk sticks and several sheets of bark paper—the brown, the cheapest, uncoated with lime, which I used for rough drafts of my picture writing. At my gesture, the boy went to crouch in a corner of the big room.

I said apologetically, "You know of my poor eyesight, my lady. If I may have your permission to sit near you?"

I moved a low chair over beside the bench, and Jadestone Doll held her head still and steady, her glorious eyes on me, while I did a sketch. When I was done and handed her the paper, she did not glance at it, but held it over her shoulder to the maid.

"Pitza, is it I?"

"To the very dimple in the cheek, my lady. And no one could mistake those eyes."

At which the young queen condescended to examine it, and nodded, and smiled sweetly at me. "Yes, it is I. I am very beautiful. Thank you, Fetch! Now, can you do bodies, too?"

"Well, yes, the articulation of limbs, the folds of garments, the identifying emblems and insignia..."

"I am not interested in the outward habiliments. I mean the body. Here, do mine."

The maid Pitza gave a muted shriek and Cozcatl's mouth dropped open, as Jadestone Doll stood up and, without coyness or hesitation, stripped off all her jewelry and bangles, her sandals, her blouse, her skirt, and finally her single remaining undergarment. Pitza went away and buried her flushed face in the draperies by the window—Cozcatl seemed incapable of movement—as the young queen again reclined on the bench.

In my agitation, I dropped some of my drawing materials from my lap to the floor, but I managed to say, and in a voice of severity, "My lady, this is most unseemly."

"*Ayya*, the typical prudery of a commoner," she said, and laughed at me. "You must learn, Fetch!, that a noblewoman thinks nothing of being nude, or of bathing, or of performing any function in the presence of slaves. Male or female, they might be pet deer or quail, or a moth in the room, for all that their seeing signifies."

"I am not a slave," I said stiffly. "My seeing my lady unclad—the queen of the Uey-Tlatoáni—would be accounted a criminal liberty, a capital offense. And those who *are* slaves can talk."

"Not mine. They fear my own anger more than that of any law or any lord. Pitza, show Fetch! your back."

The maid whimpered and, without turning, slid her blouse down for me to see the raw welts inflicted by a knout of some sort. I looked at Cozcatl, to make sure that he also saw and understood.

"Now," said Jadestone Doll, smiling her maguey syrup smile. "Come as near as you please, Fetch!, and draw me entire."

So I did, though my hand trembled so that I had often to rub out and redraw a line. The tremor was not entirely because of my dismay and apprehension. The sight of Jadestone Doll stark naked would, I think, have made any man tremble. She might better have been named Golden Doll, for gold was the color of her body, and its every surface and curve and crevice and bend and hollow was as perfectly rendered as by a Toltécatl dollmaker. I might also mention that her nipples and their areolas were dark and generous in size.

I drew her in the pose she had assumed: full length on the cushioned bench, except for one leg negligently trailing onto the floor; her arms behind her head to give an even more piquant tilt to her breasts. Though I could not help viewing—I might say memorizing—certain parts of her, I confess that my prudish sense of propriety made me blur them somewhat in the drawing. And Jadestone Doll complained about that, when I gave her the finished picture:

"I am all a smudge between the legs! Are you squeamish, Fetch!, or merely ignorant of female anatomy? Surely the most sacrosanct part of my body deserves the most attention to detail."

She got up from the bench and came to stand spread-legged before me, where I sat on my low chair. With one finger she traced what she now displayed and painstakingly described. "See? How these tender pink lips come together here in front, to enfold this little xacapíli nub which is like a pink pearl and— ooh!—most responsive to the lightest touch."

I was perspiring heavily, the servant Pitza had practically enshrouded herself in the draperies, and Cozcatl appeared permanently paralyzed in his crouch in the corner.

"Now quit your prissy agonizing, Fetch!" said the girl

queen. "I did not intend to tease you; rather to test your draftmanship. I have a task for you." She turned to snap at the maid. "Pitza, stop hiding your head! Come and dress me again."

While that was being done, I said, "My lady wishes me to draw a picture of someone?"

"Yes."

"Of whom, my lady?"

"Of anyone," she said, and I blinked in puzzlement. "You see, when I walk about the palace grounds or go into the city in my chair, it would be unladylike of me to point and say *that one*. Also, my eyedrops can dazzle me so that I might overlook someone really attractive. I mean men, of course."

"Men?" I echoed stupidly.

"I want you to carry your papers and chalks wherever you go. Whenever you encounter some handsome man, put his face and figure on paper for me." She paused to giggle. "You need not undress him. I want as many different pictures of as many different men as you can provide. But no one is to know why you are doing it, or for whom. If you are questioned, say you are merely practicing your art." She tossed back to me the two drawings I had just done. "That is all. You may take your leave, Fetch!, and do not come back until you have a sheaf of pictures to show me."

I was not, even then, so dense that I did not have an inkling of what Jadestone Doll's command portended. But I put that out of my mind, to concentrate on doing the task to the best of my ability. My main problem was in trying to guess what a fifteen-year-old girl might regard as "handsome" in a man. Having been given no other criteria, I confined my surreptitious sketchings to princes and knights and warriors and athletes and other such stalwarts. But when I returned to the queen, with Cozcatl carrying my stack of bark papers, I had whimsically topped them with a drawing I had done from memory—of that bent, crooked, cacao-brown man who had so oddly kept reappearing in my life.

She sniffed, but surprised me by saying, "You think you jest in mischief, Fetch! However, I have heard whispers among women that there are special delights to be had from dwarfs and hunchbacks and even"—she glanced at Cozcatl—"a little boy with a tepúli like an earlobe. Someday, when I tire of the ordinary . . ."

She riffled through the papers, then stopped and said, "*Yyo ayyo!* This one, Fetch!, he has bold eyebrows. Who is he?"

"That is the Crown Prince Black Flower."

She frowned prettily. "No, that might cause complications." She went on, intently studying each picture, then said, "And this one?"

"I do not know his name, my lady. He is a swift-messenger whom sometimes I see running with messages."

"Ideal," she said, with that smile of hers. She pointed to the drawing and said, "Fetch!" She was not just pronouncing my name, but the verbal imperative: "Bring him!"

I had fearfully anticipated something of the sort, but I broke into a cold sweat nonetheless. With the utmost diffidence and formality, I said:

"My Lady Jadestone Doll, I have been ordered to serve you, and cautioned not to correct or criticize you. But, if I rightly perceive your intentions, I beg you to reconsider. You are the virgin princess of the greatest lord in all The One World, and the wedded virgin queen of a lord who is also great. You will be demeaning two Revered Speakers and your own noble self, if you trifle with some other man before you go to your Lord Husband's bed."

I was expecting her at any moment to produce the whip she used on her slaves, but she heard me out, still wearing her infuriating sweet smile. Then she said:

"I could tell you that your impertinence is punishable. But I will merely remark that Nezahualpíli is older than my own father, and that his virility has apparently been sapped by the Lady of Tolan, by all his other wives and concubines. He keeps me sequestered here while he is no doubt desperately trying medicines and enchantments to stiffen his limp and withered old tepúli. But why should I waste my urges and juices and the bloom of my beauty while I await his convenience or his capability? If he requires postponement of his husbandly duties, I shall arrange that they are long postponed indeed. And then, when he *and* I are ready, you may be sure I can convince

Nezahualpíli that I come to him untouched and pristine and as timorous of the experience as any maiden."

I tried again. I really did my best to dissuade her, though I do not think anyone afterward ever really believed it.

"My lady, remember who you are, and the lineage from which you descend. You are the granddaughter of the venerated Motecuzóma, and he was *born* of a virgin. His father threw a gemstone into the garden of his beloved. She tucked it into her bosom, and at that moment conceived the child Mote-cuzóma, before she ever married or coupled with his father. Thus you have a heritage of purity and virginity which you should not sully—"

She interrupted me with a laugh. "I am touched, Fetch!, by your concern. But you should have lectured me when I was nine or ten years old. When I *was* a virgin."

It belatedly occurred to me to turn to Cozcatl and say, "You had better—you may go now, boy."

Jadestone Doll said, "You know those carvings that the beastly Huaxtéca make? The wooden torsos with the oversized male member? My father Ahuítzotl keeps one hanging on the wall of a gallery in our palace as a curiosity to amuse or amaze his men friends. It interests women, too. It has been rubbed smooth and glossy by those who have handled it admiringly in passing. Noblewomen. Servant wenches. Myself."

I said, "I really do not think I care to hear . . ." But she ignored my protestation.

"I had to drag a big storage chest against the wall, on which to stand to reach the thing. And it took me many painful days, because after each of my attempts I had to wait and rest while my inadequate tipíli stopped hurting. But I persisted, and it was a day of triumph when I finally managed just the tip of the tremendous thing. Little by little, I took more of it into me. I have had perhaps a hundred men since then, but none of them has ever given me the sensation I enjoyed in those days of thumping my little belly against that crude Huaxtéca carving."

I pleaded, "I should not know these things, my lady."

She shrugged. "I make no excuses for my nature. That sort of release is something I must have, and must have often, and *will* have. I would even use you for that purpose, Fetch! You are not unappealing. And you would not inform against me, for I know you will obey Nezahualpíli's bidding that you be no talebearer. But that would not prevent your confessing your *own* guilt at our coupling, and that would be the ruin of us both. So . . ."

She handed me the picture I had drawn of the unsuspecting swift-messenger, and a ring from her finger. "Give him this. It was my Lord Husband's wedding gift to me, and there is not another like it."

The ring was of red gold, set with a huge emerald whose value was incalculable. Those jewels were only seldom brought by traders who ventured as far as the land of Quautemálan, the uttermost southern limit of our trade routes, and the emerald's origin was not even there, but in some land, its name unknown, an untold distance farther to the south of Quautemálan. The ring was one of those designed to be worn on a hand held vertically, for its circlet was hung with jadestone pendants that would show to best advantage when the wearer kept her hand uplifted. The ring had been made to the measure of Jadestone Doll's middle finger. I could barely squeeze it onto my little one.

"No, you are not to wear it," the girl warned. "Nor is he. That ring would be recognized by anyone who saw it. He is merely to carry it, hidden, and then at midnight tonight show it to the guard on the eastern gate. At sight of the ring, the guard will admit him. Pitza will be waiting just inside, to bring him here."

"Tonight?" I said. "But I must find him again, my lady. He may have been sent running on an errand to who knows where."

"Tonight," she said. "I have already been too long deprived."

I do not know what she would have done to me had I not found the man, but I did, and accosted him as if I were a young noble with a message for him to carry. I deliberately did not give him my name, but he said, "I am Yeyac-Netztlin, at my lord's service."

"At a lady's service," I corrected him. "She wishes that you attend upon her at the palace at midnight."

He looked troubled and said, "It is most difficult to run a message any distance at night, my lord—" But then his eyes fell on the ring I held in my palm, and his eyes widened, and he said, "For *that* lady, of course, not midnight nor Míctlan could prevent my doing a service."

"It is a service requiring discretion," I said, a sour taste in my mouth. "Show this ring to the guard on the east gate to be admitted."

"I hear and obey, young lord. I will be there."

And he was. I stayed awake and listened near my door until I heard Pitza lead Yeyac-Netztlin tiptoeing to the door across the corridor. After that I heard no more, so I do not know how long he stayed or how he effected his departure. And I did not listen again for his subsequent arrivals, so I do not know how often he visited. But it was a month before Jadestone Doll, yawning with boredom, asked me to start sketching prospective new consorts, so Yeyac-Netztlin apparently satisified her for that span of time. The swift-messenger's name, appropriately, meant Long Legs, and perhaps he was otherwise lengthily endowed.

Though Jadestone Doll made no demands upon my time during that month, I was not always easy in my mind. The Revered Speaker came about every eighth or ninth day to pay a courtesy call on his supposedly cosseted and patient princess-queen, and often I was present in the apartment, and I strove not to sweat visibly during those interviews. I could only wonder why, in the names of all the gods, Nezahualpíli did not recognize that he was married to a female ripe and ready for his immediate savoring. Or that of any other man.

Those jewelers who deal in jadestone say that the mineral is easily found among the commoner rocks of the field, because it proclaims its own presence and availability. Simply go into the countryside at first sunrise, they say, and you will see a rock here or there exuding a faint but unmistakable vapor which announces proudly, "There is jadestone inside me. Come and take it." Like the prized mineral for which she was named, Jadestone Doll also emanated some indefinable nimbus or essence or vibration which said to every male, "Here I am. Come and take me." Could Nezahualpíli be the only man in creation who did not sense her ardor and readiness? Could he really be impotent and uninterested, as the young queen had said?

No. When I saw and listened to them together, I realized

that he was manifesting a gentlemanly consideration and restraint. For Jadestone Doll, in her perverse reluctance to settle for just one lover, was making *him* see not a girl in the prime of nubility but a delicate and immature adolescent untimely consigned to a marriage of convenience. During his visits, she was not at all the Jadestone Doll so well known to me and her slaves—and presumably to Yeyac-Netztlin. She wore garments that concealed her provocative curves and made her look as slender and fragile as a child. Somehow she suppressed her usual aura of flagrant sexuality, not to mention her usual arrogance and irascibility. She never once used the rude name Fetch! when referring to me. Somehow she kept the real Jadestone Doll concealed—topco petlacálco, "in the bag, in the box," as we say of a secret.

In the presence of her lord, she neither lay languorously on a couch nor even sat on a chair. She knelt at his feet, her knees modestly together, her eyes demurely downcast, and she spoke in a childishly meek voice. She might have fooled even me into believing her no more than ten years old, except that I knew what she had already been even at that age.

"I hope you find your life less constricted," said Nezahualpíli, "now that you have Mixtli for a companion."

"Ayyo, yes, my lord," she said, dimpling. "He is an invaluable escort. Mixtli shows me things and explains them. Yesterday he took me to the library of your esteemed father's poetry, and recited for me some of the poems."

"And did you like them?" asked the Uey-Tlatoáni.

"Oh, I did. But I think I should like even more to hear some of your own, my Lord Husband."

Nezahualpíli accordingly recited for us some of his compositions, though with becoming modesty: "They sound better, of course, when my drummer accompanies me." One of them, praising the sunset, concluded:

> . . . Like a bright bouquet of flowers,
> our radiant god, our glowing god, the Sun
> thrusts himself into a vase
> of richest jewels, and the day is done.

"Lovely," sighed Jadestone Doll. "It makes me feel a little melancholy."

"The sunset?" asked Nezahualpíli.

"No, my lord, the mention of gods. I know that in time I shall become acquainted with all those of your people. But meanwhile, I have none of my old accustomed gods about me. Would I be forward if I asked my Revered Husband's permission to place in these rooms some statues of my family's favorites?"

"My dear Little Doll," he said indulgently, "you may do or have anything that makes you happy and less homesick. I will send Pizquitl, the resident palace sculptor, and you may instruct him to carve whatever gods your gentle heart yearns for."

When he left her rooms that time, Nezahualpíli signaled for me to accompany him. I went, still silently commanding my sweat pores to stay shut, for I fully expected to be questioned about Jadestone Doll's activities when she was not visiting libraries. Much to my relief, though, the Revered Speaker inquired about my own activities.

"Is it much of a burden on you, Mole," he asked kindly, "devoting so much time to your young lady sister?"

"No, my lord," I lied. "She is most considerate about not intruding on my school time. It is only in the evenings that we converse, or stroll about the palace, or wander about the city."

"In the conversing," he said, "I would ask that you spend some effort on trying to correct her Mexícatl accent. You yourself picked up our Texcóco speech so quickly. Do encourage her to speak more elegantly, Head Nodder."

"Yes, my lord. I will try."

He went on, "Your Lord Teacher of Word Knowing tells me that you have also made quick and admirable progress in the art of picture writing. Could you perhaps spare any other time to put that ability to a practical use?"

"To be sure, my lord!" I exclaimed eagerly, ardently. "I will *make* time."

Thus I finally began my career as a scribe, and it was thanks in large measure to Jadestone Doll's father Ahuítzotl. Immediately upon being crowned Uey-Tlatoáni of Tenochtítlan, Ahuítzotl had dramatically demonstrated his prowess as a ruler by declaring a war against the Huaxtéca of the coast to the northeast. Personally leading a combined army of Mexíca, Acólhua, and Tecpanéca, he had waged and won the war in less than a month. The armies brought back much booty, and the defeated nation was, as usual, put under annual tribute. The plunder and the yearly levy were to be divided among The Triple Alliance as was customary: two-fifths each to Tenochtítlan and Texcóco, one-fifth to Tlácopan.

The job Nezahualpíli gave me was to draw up a ledger book listing the tribute items received from the Huaxtéca, and those yet to come, and then also to enter the various items—turquoise, cacao, cotton mantles, skirts and blouses, cotton cloth in bulk— in other ledgers which kept account of the goods as they were stored in various Texcóco warehouses. It was a task that exercised my knowledge of both picture writing and arithmetic, and I threw myself into it with great pleasure, with a conscientious determination to do it well.

But, as I have said, Jadestone Doll also had use for my abilities, and called me in again to command that I renew my search for and my sketching of "handsome men." She also took that opportunity to complain about the palace sculptor's *lack* of ability.

"As my Lord Husband allowed, I ordered this statue, and I gave precise instructions to that old fool of a sculptor he sent. But look at it, Fetch! A monstrosity."

I looked at it: a life-sized male figure sculptured in clay, painted in lifelike colors and baked to hardness. It depicted no god of the Mexíca that I could recognize, but there was something familiar about it.

"The Acólhua are supposed to be so expert in the arts," the girl went on, with disdain. "Know this, Fetch! Their avowed master sculptor is woefully inept compared to some far less renowned artists whose work I have seen back home. If Pixquitl does not do my next statue better than this one, I shall send to Tenochtítlan for those Mexíca unknowns, and put him to shame. You go and tell him so!"

I rather suspected that the lady was merely preparing an excuse to import not artists but some former lovers whom she fondly remembered. Nevertheless, as commanded, I went and found the palace sculptor Pixquitl in his studio below ground level. It was clamorous with the roar of the baking kiln's fire, the stone hammering and chiseling and chipping of his students and apprentices. I had to shout to make him hear Jadestone Doll's complaint and threat.

"I did my best," said the elderly artist. "The young queen would not even tell me the name of her chosen god, so that I could refer to other statues or painted pictures of him. All that I had to work from was this."

And he showed me a chalk drawing on bark paper: my own picture of Yeyac-Netztlin. I was extremely puzzled. Why should Jadestone Doll have ordered the statue of a god—whichever god it was supposed to be—and order it made in the likeness of a mere and mortal swift-messenger? But, in expectation that she would snarl at me to mind my own business, I did not ask her.

In my next delivery of drawings, I deliberately included, and not entirely in facetious spirit, a picture of Jadestone Doll's own legitimate husband, the Revered Speaker Nezahualpíli. She gave it and me only a scornful sniff as she thrust it to one side. The picture she chose that time was one of a young under-gardener at the palace, Xali-Otli by name, and it was to him that I gave her ring and her instructions the next day. He, like his predecessor, was only a commoner, but he spoke Náhuatl with the Texcóco accent, and I hoped—since I would again be excused for a while from attendance upon the lady—that *he* would continue the refining of her speech, as Nezahualpíli desired.

When I had finished the Huaxtéca tribute entries, I delivered the ledger lists to the under-treasurer in charge of such things, who highly praised my work to his superior, the Snake Woman, and that Lord Strong Bone in turn was kind enough to give a good report of me to Nezahualpíli. Whereupon the Revered Speaker sent for me to ask if I would like to try my hand at the very same sort of work you are doing, reverend friars. That is, to take down in writing the words spoken in the chamber where the Uey-Tlatoáni met with his Speaking Council, and in the hall of justice where he gave audience to lesser Acólhua bringing requests and complaints.

Naturally I took on the job with gleeful enthusiasm and,

though at first it was not easy and I made mistakes, I eventually earned plaudits for that work too. I must say immodestly that I had already attained considerable fluency, proficiency, and accuracy in setting down my pictures. Now I had to learn to do the symbols *swiftly*, though of course I could never have become so rapid a scribe as any of you, my lords. In those council meetings and receptions of supplicants, there was seldom a moment when somebody was not speaking words to be recorded, and often there would be several persons talking at once. Fortunately for me, the system was—like yours—to have two or more experienced scribes simultaneously at work, so that what one of them missed another would probably catch.

I early learned to set down only the symbols recording the most important words of any person's discourse, and those only in sketchy outline. Afterward, at my leisure, I would strive to recall and insert the substance between, then make a clean recopying of the whole, and add the colors that made it fully comprehensible. That method not only improved my rapidity of writing, it improved my memory as well.

I also found it useful to invent a number of what I might call summary symbols, into which were compressed an entire procession of words. For example, I would put down just one little circle, representing an open mouth, for the lengthy preface with which every man or woman began every least remark to the Uey-Tlatoáni: "In your august presence, mixpantzínco, my Lord Revered Speaker Nezahualpíli . . ." If anyone talked alternately of recent and past events, I differentiated between them by drawing alternately the simple symbols that represented a baby and a vulture. The baby, you see, stood for "new" and identified the recent events. The vulture, being baldheaded, stood for "old" and identified the past events.

Ah, well. All this reminiscing may be of some professional interest to fellow scribes like yourselves, reverend friars, but in truth I speak of those things because I am loath to speak of other things—like my next summons to the chambers of the Lady Jadestone Doll.

"I require a new face," she said, though we both knew that it was not any *face* she required. "And I do not wish to wait while you collect a new series of drawings. Let me look again at those you have already done." I brought them to her and she went rapidly through the papers, giving each a mere glance, until she stopped and said, "This one. Who is he?"

"Some slave I have seen about the palace," I told her. "I believe he is employed as a litter bearer."

"Fetch!" she commanded, handing me her emerald ring.

"My lady," I protested. *A slave?*

"When I am in urgent appetite, I am not overly fastidious," she said. "Besides, slaves are often very good. The wretches dare not refuse to comply with the most debasing demands made of them." She smiled that cloyingly sweet smile of hers. "And the more spineless a man is, the more reptilian contortions he can squirm himself into."

Before I could raise any more objections, Jadestone Doll led me to a wall alcove and said, "Now look at this. The second god I have ordered from that so-called master sculptor Pixquitl."

"That is no god," I said, aghast, as I stared at the new statue. "That is the gardener Xali-Otli."

She said in a cold voice, warningly, "As far as you and everyone in Texcóco are concerned, that is an obscure god worshiped by my family in Tenochtítlan. But never mind that. You at least recognized the face. I will wager no one else would, except perhaps his mother. That old Pixquitl is hopelessly incompetent. I have sent for those Mexíca artists I spoke of. They will be here immediately after the festival of Ochpanítztli. Go and tell Pixquitl that I wish a separate and private studio prepared for them and supplied with all the materials they will require. Then find that slave. Give him the ring and the usual instructions."

When I again confronted the sculptor, he said grumpily, "I can only insist that again I did my best with the drawing given me. At least this time she also gave me a skull to work with."

"What?"

"Oh, yes, it is much easier to sculpture a good likeness when one has the actual underlying bones on which to mold the clay."

Not wanting to believe what I should have realized much

earlier, I stammered, "But—but, Master Pixquitl—no one could possibly possess the skull of a god."

He gave me a long look from his heavy-lidded old eyes. "All I know is that I was given the skull of a newly dead adult male, and that the skull's structure approximated the facial features of the drawing I was also given, and I was told that the drawing was that of some minor god. I am not a priest, to question the god's authenticity, and I am not a fool, to question an imperious queen. I do the work I am bidden to do, and so far I have kept my own skull intact. Do you understand?"

I nodded numbly. I finally did understand, and only too well.

The master went on, "I will prepare the studio for the new artists soon to arrive. But I must say, I do not envy anyone thus employed by the Lady Jadestone Doll. Not myself. Not them. Not you."

I did not envy my situation either—procurer to a murderess—but I was already far too deeply involved to see any means of extricating myself. I went and found the slave, whose name was Niez-Hueyotl, in the pathetically overweening manner of slave names: I Will Be of Greatness. Apparently he did not live up to it, for it was not long before Jadestone Doll summoned me again.

"You were right, Fetch!" she said. "A slave can be a mistake. That one actually began to fancy himself a human being." She laughed. "Well, he will be a god before long, which is more than he could ever have expected. But this makes me realize something. My Lord Husband may eventually begin to wonder why I have statues of only gods in my chambers. I should have at least one goddess. In your last showing of drawings, I saw one of a comely woman. Go and bring that picture here."

I did, though sick at heart. I was sorry I had let the young queen glimpse that sketch. I had made it for no ulterior reason, but impulsively, out of admiration for the woman, when she had attracted my own attention. Indeed, she caught many men's eyes, and lit those eyes with speculation or longing. But Nemalhuíli was already a married woman, the wife of a prosperous feather worker in the Texcóco craftsmen's market. Her beauty was not just in her lively and luminous face. Her gestures were always fluid and gentle, her carriage was proud, her lips had a smile for everyone. Nemalhuíli exuded an unquenchable happiness. And her name was apt; it meant Something Delicate.

Jadestone Doll studied her picture and, to my relief, said, "I cannot send you to her, Fetch! That would be a breach of good manners, and might cause an undesirable commotion. I will send one of my slave women."

But that did not, as I had hoped, end my involvement. The next I heard from the young queen was, "The woman Nemalhuíli will be here tonight. And this will be the first time—would you believe it?—that I have ever indulged with one of my own sex. I want you to attend, with your drawing materials, and record this adventure so that I may see later the various things we shall be doing."

Of course I was dismayed at the idea, for three reasons. First and foremost, I was angry at myself, for having inadvertently involved Something Delicate. Though I knew her only by sight and reputation, I held a high regard for her. Second, and selfishly, I could never after that night claim that I did not know *for certain* what sort of things happened in my lady's chambers. Third, I felt some revulsion at the prospect of being forced to witness an act that should be private. But there was no way I could refuse, and I must admit that among my emotions was a perverse curiosity. I had heard the word patlachúia, but I could not imagine how two females *could* perform together.

Something Delicate arrived, looking as cheerful and lightsome as ever, though understandably a bit bewildered at that clandestine midnight appointment. It was summer and the air outside was not at all chilly, but she wore a square cape over her shoulders. Perhaps she had been instructed to muffle her face in the cloak on the way to the palace.

"My lady," she said, courteously, inquiringly, glancing from the young queen to me, where I sat with a sheaf of bark papers on my lap. There had been no way for me discreetly to conceal my presence, since my eyesight required me to sit close if I was to record whatever occurred.

"Pay no attention to the scribe," said Jadestone Doll. "Pay

attention only to me. First, I must be assured that your husband knows nothing of this visit."

"Nothing, my lady. He was sleeping when I left. Your maid told me to tell him nothing, and I did not, for I thought you might somehow have need of me for—well, for something of no concern to men."

"Precisely so," said her hostess, simpering with satisfaction. When the woman's eyes again slid sideways to me, Jadestone Doll snapped, "I said ignore this one. He is furniture. He does not see or hear. He does not exist." Then she dropped her voice to a coaxing murmur. "I have been told that you are one of the most beautiful women in Texcóco. As you see, my dear, so am I. It occurred to me that we might enjoyably compare our beauties."

At that, with her own hands, she reached out and raised the cape so that its central slit lifted over Nemalhuíli's head. The visitor naturally looked surprised, at having a queen personally take her cape. But then her expression changed to shocked bafflement as Jadestone Doll next raised her long blouse and lifted it over her head, leaving her bare from the waist up.

Only her wide eyes moved. They flicked once more to me, like those of a frightened doe at bay, beseeching help from one of the hunters pressing in. But I pretended not to see, I made my face impassive, I kept my gaze apparently intent on the drawing I had just begun, and I do not think Something Delicate looked at me again. From that moment, she evidently managed to do as she had been told: to believe that I was not present or even existent. I think, if the poor woman had not been able to blot me from her consciousness, she would have died that night of shame.

While the woman stood barebreasted, as rigid as if she were already a statue, Jadestone Doll removed her own blouse—slowly, seductively—she might have been doing it to arouse an unresponsive man. Then she stepped close, until their two bodies were all but touching. Something Delicate was perhaps ten years older than the girl queen, and about a hand's breadth taller.

"Yes," said Jadestone Doll, "your breasts are beautiful. Except"—she pretended to pout—"your nipples are timid, they hold themselves folded so neatly. Can they not swell and thrust like mine?" She stood on tiptoe, leaned her upper body a little forward and exclaimed, "Why, look, they touch exactly! Our bosoms fit together so perfectly, my dear. Might not the rest of us?"

And she pressed her lips to the lips of Something Delicate. The woman did not close her eyes or change expression in the least, but Jadestone Doll's cheeks hollowed. After a moment, she drew her face back just far enough to say delightedly, "There! Your nipples *can* grow, I knew it! Do you not feel them unfolding against mine?" She leaned forward for another probing kiss, and that time Something Delicate did close her eyes, as if in fear that something unintended might show in them.

They stood like that, immobile, long enough for me to capture a picture of them: Jadestone Doll still on tiptoe, the two of them touching nowhere but at lips and breasts. Then the girl reached to the waist of the woman's skirt, and deftly undid the fastening of it, so that it dropped rustling to the floor. I was close enough to see the just perceptible ripple of the woman's muscles as she tightened her long legs protectively together. After a moment, Jadestone Doll undid her own skirt and let it fall around her feet. She had worn nothing underneath it, so she was now entirely naked except for her golden sandals. But when she pressed the entire length of her body against that of Something Delicate, she realized that the woman, like any decent woman, still wore an undergarment.

Jadestone Doll stepped away and gazed at her with mingled amusement, fondness, and mild annoyance, and she said sweetly, "I shall not remove your final modest covering, Something Delicate. I shall not even ask you to do so. I shall make you *want* to."

The girl queen took the woman's hand and tugged, so that she walked, and they crossed the room to the big, soft, canopied bed. They lay on top of it, with no covering over them, and I moved closer with my chalks and papers.

Well, yes, Fray Jerónimo, there is more. After all, I was there, I saw everything, I have forgotten nothing. But of course you may be excused from hearing of it, if that is your wish.

I might say to you remaining reverend scribes that I have seen rape in my time. I have seen soldiers, ours and yours, violently assault their women captives. But in all my life I have never seen a female so violated in her soul as well as in her sexual parts—so insidiously, thoroughly, ruinously, and horrifyingly violated—as was Something Delicate by Jadestone Doll. And what has made it remain in my memory more stark than any remembered rape of a woman by a man, is that the adolescent girl manipulated the married woman, never once by force or command, but by gentle touches and caresses that at last brought Something Delicate to a point of paroxysm after which she was no longer responsible for her behavior.

It might be appropriate here for me to mention that, in our language, when we speak of seducing a woman, we say, "I caress her with flowers. . . ."

Something Delicate lay supine and determinedly indifferent for a while, and only Jadestone Doll did anything. She used just her lips and tongue and the very tips of her fingers. She used them on the woman's closed eyelids and their lashes, on the woman's earlobes, the hollow of her throat, the cleft between her breasts, the length and breadth of her exposed body, the dimple of her navel, up and down her legs. Repeatedly she used the tip of her finger or tongue to trace slow spirals around one of the woman's breasts before at last tweaking or licking the hardened upright nipple. The girl did not again press any passionate kiss upon Something Delicate, but she kept coming back from her other activities merely to flick her tongue teasingly across the woman's closed mouth. And gradually the woman's own lips, like her teats, became swollen and ruddy. Her pale-copper skin, at first smooth, began to prickle all over with gooseflesh, and then to tremble in places.

Jadestone Doll occasionally would have to stop her fondlings and clutch tight to the woman, her body writhing. Something Delicate, even with her eyes closed, could not help feeling and knowing what was happening to the girl. Only a stone statue could have remained unaffected by it, and even the most virtuous, reluctant, frightened woman is no statue. The next time the young queen helplessly began to shudder, Something Delicate made a sort of cooing noise, as a mother might make to a distressed child. She moved her hands to lift Jadestone Doll's head from her bosom, brought it up to her own, and for the first time herself implanted a kiss. Her lips forced the girl's open, and her cheeks hollowed deeply, and a muffled whimper came from both the crushed-together mouths, and both bodies palpitated together, and the woman dropped one of her hands to rip away her undergarment from between them.

After that, Something Delicate again lay still, and closed her eyes again, and bit the back of her hand, which did not prevent a sob escaping her. Jadestone Doll, when her panting had abated, again was the only one moving on the rumpled bed. But the woman was now also naked, vulnerable in every part, and the girl had more places to which to give attention. For a while, Something Delicate kept her legs pressed tight together. But slowly, little by little, as if she had nothing to do with it, the woman let her muscles slacken and her legs relax, and they parted a little, and a little more. . . .

Jadestone Doll burrowed her head between them, seeking what she had once described to me as "the little pink pearl." That went on for some time, and the woman, as if being tortured, made many and various small noises, and finally a violent movement. When she recovered, she must have decided that, having now abandoned herself so far, no further abandonment could further abase her. Because Somthing Delicate began doing to Jadestone Doll what the girl was still doing to her. That occasioned a variety of couplings. Sometimes they would be clasped in embrace like a man and a woman, kissing mouth to mouth while their pelvises rubbed together. Sometimes they would lie reversed on the bed, each hugging the other's hips while she used her tongue as a miniature but much more nimble simulacrum of a man's member. Sometimes they would lie so that their thighs overlapped and only their lower bodies touched, straining to bring their little pink pearls into contact and mutual friction.

In that posture, they reminded me of the legend which tells how the race of humankind came into being. It was said that, after the eras when the earth was inhabited first by gods and then by giants, the gods decided to bequeath the world to human beings. Since there were then no such things, the gods had to create them, and they did: making a few men and an equal number of women. But the gods designed them badly, for those early humans had bodies that ended below the waist in a kind of smooth knob. According to the legend, the gods intended modestly to conceal the people's genitals, though that is hard to believe, since the gods and goddesses are hardly notorious for their own sexual modesty.

At any rate, those early people were able to hop about on the stumps of their bodies, and to enjoy all the beauties of the world they had inherited, but they could not enjoy each other. And they wanted to, because, concealed or no, their separate sexes mightily attracted each other. Happily for the future of mankind, those early people contrived a way to overcome their handicap. They bounded high, a man and a woman together, and in midair merged their lower bodies, the way some insects mate on the wing. Exactly how they managed that coupling, the legend does not tell, nor how the women delivered the babies thus conceived. But they did, and the next generation was complete with legs and accessible genital organs. Watching Jadestone Doll and Something Delicate in that position where they were rubbing their tipîli parts urgently together, I could not help but think of those first humans and their determination to copulate despite their having nothing to do it with.

I should mention that the woman and the girl, whatever intricate positions they assumed, and however avidly they fondled one another, did not thrash and bounce about as much as a *man* and a woman do when engaged in that act. Their movements were sinuous, not angular; graceful, not gross. Many times, however invisibly busy some parts of both of them undoubtedly were, the two appeared to me to be as still as if they slept. Then one or both would shiver, or stiffen, or jerk, or writhe. I lost count, but I know that Something Delicate and Jadestone Doll each came to many more climaxes that night than either could have achieved with the most virile and enduring man.

In between those small convulsions, though, they stayed in their several poses long enough for me to make many drawings of their bodies, separately or intertwined. If some of the pictures were smudged or drawn with a trembly line, it was not the fault of the models, except insofar as their doings agitated the artist. I was no statue, either. Several times, watching them, I was racked by sympathetic shudderings, and twice my own unruly member . . .

* * *

And now Fray Domingo leaves us, and precipitately. Odd, how one man can be adversely affected by some words, and another man by others. I think words conjure up different images in different minds. Even in the minds of impersonal scribes who are supposed to hear them only as sounds and record them only as marks on paper.

Perhaps, since that is so, I had better refrain from telling of the other things the girl and woman did during that long night. But finally they fell away from each other, exhausted, and lay breathing heavily side by side. Their lips and tipíli parts were exceedingly puffed and red; their skins shone with sweat, saliva, and other secretions; their bodies were mottled like jaguar hide with the marks of bites and kisses.

I quietly got up from my place beside the bed and, with shaking hands, gathered up the drawings scattered around my chair. When I had withdrawn to a corner of the room, Something Delicate also arose and, moving wearily, weakly, like someone just recovering from an illness, slowly put on her clothes. She avoided looking at me, but I could see that there were tears running down her face.

"You will want to rest," Jadestone Doll said to her, and pulled on the bell rope over the bed. "Pitza will show you to a private chamber." Something Delicate was still quietly weeping when the sleepy slave guided her from the room.

I said in an unsteady voice, "Suppose she tells her husband."

"She could not bear to," the young queen said with assurance. "And she will not. Let me see the drawings." I handed them over and she studied them minutely, one by one. "So that is what it looks like. Exquisite. And here I thought I had experienced every kind of . . . What a pity my Lord Nezahualpíli has provided me with only aged and plain-faced servant women. I think I will keep Something Delicate on call for quite a while."

I was glad to hear that, since I knew what the woman's fate would otherwise and quickly be. The girl gave the drawings back to me, then stretched and yawned voluptuously. "Do you know, Fetch!, I truly believe it was better than anything I have enjoyed since that old Huaxtéca object I used to employ."

It seemed reasonable, I thought, as I went to my own chambers. A woman ought to know, better than any man, how to play upon the body of another woman. Only a woman could so intimately know all the most tender, hidden, secret, responsive surfaces and recesses of her own body, hence those of any other woman's. It followed, then, that a *man* could improve his sexual talents—could enhance his own enjoyment and that of his every female partner—by knowing those same things. So I spent much time studying the drawings, and fixing in my memory the intimacies I had witnessed which the pictures could not portray.

I was not proud of the part I had played in the degradation of Something Delicate, but I have always believed that a man should try to learn and profit from his involvement in even the most lamentable occurrences.

I do not mean to say that the rape of Something Delicate was the most lamentable event I ever knew in my life. Another was awaiting me when I went home again to Xaltócan for the festival of Ochpanítztli.

That name means The Sweeping of the Road and refers to the religious rituals performed to assure that the coming harvest of maize would be a good one. The festival was celebrated in our eleventh month, about the middle of your August, and consisted of various rites all culminating in the enactment of the birth of the maize god Centéotl. That was a ceremonial time entirely given over to the women; all the men, even most of the priests, were mere spectators.

It began with Xaltócan's most venerable and virtuous wives and widows going about with brooms specially made of feathers, sweeping out all the island's temples and other holy places. Then, under the direction of our female temple attendants, women did all the singing, dancing, and music playing on the climactic night. A virgin chosen from among the island girls played the part of Teteoínan, the mother of all the gods. The high point of the night was the act she did atop our temple pyramid—all by herself, with no male partner—her pretense of being deflowered and impregnated, then going through the pains of labor and of giving birth. After that, she was put to death with arrows, by women archers, who did the job with earnest dedication but with little skill, so she usually died an untidy and prolonged death.

Of course there was always a substitution at the last moment, since we never sacrificed one of our own maidens, unless for some peculiar reason she insisted on volunteering. So it was not really the virgin portraying Teteoínan who died, but some dispensable female slave or a female prisoner captured from another people. For the simple role of dying, it was not required that she be a virgin, and sometimes it was a very old woman who was dispatched on that night.

When, after having been clumsily chipped and minced and pierced by countless arrows, the woman was finally dead, a few priests participated for the first time. They came out from the pyramid temple in which they had been hidden behind her, and, still almost invisible because of their black garb, dragged the corpse inside the temple. There they quickly flayed the skin from one of her thighs. A priest put that conical cap of flesh on his head and bounded forth from the temple to a blast of music and song. The young god of the maize, Centéotl, had been born. He skipped down the pyramid stairs, joined the women dancers, and they all danced the rest of the night away.

I tell all this now because I suppose that year's ceremony proceeded as in all the years before. I have to suppose because I did not stay to see it.

The generous Prince Willow had again lent me his acáli and oarsmen, and I arrived on Xaltócan to find that others—Pactli, Chimáli, and Tlatli—had also again come home from their distant schools for that holiday. Pactli, in fact, was home to stay, having just then completed his calmécac education. That made me worry. He would now have no occupation at all, except to wait for his father Red Heron to die and vacate the throne. Meanwhile, Pactli could concentrate all his time and energy on securing the wife he desired—my unconsenting sister—with the help of his staunchest ally, my title-hungry mother.

But I had a more immediate worry. Chimáli and Tlatli were so eager to see me that they were waiting at the jetty when my canoe made fast, and they were dancing with excitement. They both began talking, shouting, and laughing before I had even set foot on shore.

"Mole, the most wonderful thing!"

"Our first summons, Mole, to do works of art abroad!"

It took me some time, and some shouting of my own, before I could sort out and comprehend what they had to say. When I did, I was appalled. My two friends were the "Mexíca artists" of whom Jadestone Doll had spoken. They would not be returning to Tenochtítlan after the holiday. They would be accompanying me when I went back to Texcóco.

Tlatli said, "I am to do sculptures and Chimáli is to color them so they seem alive. So said the message of the Lady Jadestone Doll. Imagine! The daughter of one Uey-Tlatoáni and the wife of another. Surely no other artists our age have ever before been so honored."

Chimáli said, "We had no idea the Lady Jadestone Doll had ever even seen the work we did in Tenochtítlan!"

Tlatli said, "Seen it and admired it enough to summon us to travel so many one-long-runs. The lady must have good taste."

I said thinly, "The lady has numerous tastes."

My friends perceived that I was little infected by their excitement, and Chimáli said, almost apologetically, "This is our first real commission, Mole. The statues and paintings we did in the city were but adornments for the new palace being built by Ahuítzotl, and we were no more highly regarded or any better paid than stonemasons. Now this message says we are even to have our own private studio, all equipped and waiting. Naturally we are elated. Is there some reason why we should not be?"

Tlatli asked, "Is the lady a female tyrant who will work us to death?"

I could have said that he had put it succinctly when he spoke of being worked "to death," but I said instead, "The lady has some eccentricities. We will have plenty of time in which to talk of her. Right now, I myself am much fatigued by my own working."

"Of course," said Chimáli. "Let us carry your luggage for you, Mole. You greet your family, eat and rest. And then you must tell us everything about Texcóco and Nezahualpíli's court. We do not want to appear there as ignorant provincials."

On the way to my house, the two continued to chatter merrily of their prospects, but I was silent, thinking deeply—of their prospects. I knew very well that Jadestone Doll's crimes would eventually be exposed. When that happened, Nezahualpíli would avenge himself upon all who had aided or abetted the girl's adulteries, and the murders to hide the adulteries, and the statues to flaunt the murders. I had some slim hope that *I* might be acquitted, since I had acted strictly on the orders of her husband himself. Jadestone Doll's other servants and attendants had acted on *her* orders. They could not have disobeyed, but that fact would earn them no mercy from the dishonored Nezahualpíli. Their necks were already inside the flower-garlanded noose: the woman Pitza, and the gate guard, and perhaps Master Pixquitl, and soon Tlatli and Chimáli....

My father and sister welcomed me with warm embraces, my mother with a halfhearted one—which she excused by explaining that her arms were limp and weary from having wielded a broom all day in various temples. She went on at great length about the island women's preparations for the observance of Ochpanítztli, little of which I heard, as I was trying to think of some ruse to get away alone somewhere with Tzitzi. I was not just eager to demonstrate to her some of the things I had learned from watching Jadestone Doll and Something Delicate. I was also anxious to talk to her about my own equivocal position at the Texcóco court, and to ask her advice as to what, if anything, I should do to avert the imminent arrival there of Chimáli and Tlatli.

The opportunity never came. The night came, with our mother still complaining about the amount of work involved in The Sweeping of the Road. The black night came, and with it came the black-garbed priests. Four of them came, and they came for my sister.

Without so much as a "Mixpantzínco" to the head of the house—priests were always contemptuous of the common civilities—one of them demanded, addressing nobody in particular, "This is the residence of the maiden Chiucnáui-Acatl Tzitzitlíni?" His voice was thick and gobbly, like that of a gallipavo fowl, and the words hard to understand. That was the case with many priests, for one of their penitential diversions was to bore a hole through their tongue and, from time to time, tear the hole wider by drawing reeds or ropes or thorns through it.

"My daughter," said our mother, with a prideful gesture in her direction. "Nine Reed the Sound of Small Bells Ringing."

"Tzitzitlíni," the grubby old man said directly to her. "We come to inform you that you have been chosen for the honor of enacting the goddess Teteoínan on the final night of Ochpanítztli."

"No," said my sister, with her lips, though no sound came out. She stared at the four men in their ragged black robes, and she stroked a trembling hand across her face. Its fawn skin had gone the color of the palest amber.

"You will come with us," said another priest. "There are some preliminary formalities."

"No," said Tzitzi again, that time aloud. She turned to look at me, and I almost flinched at the impact of her eyes. They were wise, terrified, as bottomlessly black as were Jadestone Doll's when she used the pupil-dilating drug. My sister and I both knew what were the "preliminary formalities"—a physical examination conducted by the priests' female attendants to ascertain that the honored maiden was indeed a maiden. As I have said, Tzitzi knew the means to seem impeccably a virgin, and to deceive the most suspicious examiner. But she had had no warning of the sudden swoop of the raptor priests, no reason to prepare, and now there was no time to do so.

"Tzitzitlíni," our father said chidingly. "No one refuses a tlamacázqui, or the summons he brings. It would be rude to the priest, it would show disdain for the delegation of women who have accorded you this honor, and, far worse, it would insult the goddess Teteoínan herself."

"It would also annoy our esteemed governor," our mother put in. "The Lord Red Heron has already been advised of the choice of this year's virgin, and so has his son Páctlitzin."

"No one advised me!" said my sister, with one last flash of rebellion.

She and I knew now *who* had proposed her for the role of Teteoínan, without consulting her or asking her permission. We also knew *why*. It was so that our mother might take vicarious credit for the performance Tzitzi would give; so that our mother might preen in the applause of the whole island; so that her daughter's public pantomime of the sex act would further inflame the Lord Joy's lust; and so that he would be more than ever ready to elevate our whole family to the nobility in exchange for the girl.

"My Lord Priests," Tzitzi pleaded. "I am truly not suitable. I cannot act a part. Not that part. I would be awkward, and laughed at. I would shame the goddess. . . ."

"That is totally untrue," said one of the four. "We have seen you dance, girl. Come with us. Now."

"The preliminaries take only a few moments," our mother said. "Go along, Tzitzi, and when you return we will discuss the making of your costume. You will be the most brilliant Teteoínan ever to bear the infant Centéotl."

"No," my sister said again, but weakly, desperate for any excuse. "It is—it is the wrong time of the moon for me. . . ."

"There is no saying no!" barked a priest. "There are no acceptable pretexts. You come, girl, or we take you."

She and I had no chance even to say good-bye, since the presumption was that she would be gone only a brief time. As Tzitzi moved to the door, and the four malodorous old men closed about her, she flung one despairing look back at me. I almost missed seeing it, for I was looking about the room for a weapon, anything I could use for a weapon.

I swear, if I had had Blood Glutton's maquáhuitl at hand, I would have slashed our way through priests and parents— weeds to be mowed—and we two would have fled for safety somewhere, anywhere. But there was nothing sharp or heavy within reach, and it would have been futile for me to attack barehanded. I was then twenty years old, a man grown, and I could have bested all four of the priests, but my work-toughened father could have held me back without much effort. And that, for sure, would have caused suspicion, interrogation, verification, and the doom would have been upon us. . . .

I have often since then asked myself: would not that doom have been preferable to what did happen? Some such thought flickered through my mind at that moment, but I wavered, I hesitated. Was it because I knew, in a cowardly corner of my mind, that I was not involved in Tzitzi's predicament—and probably would not be—which made me waver, which made me hesitate? Was it because I held to some desperate hope that she could yet deceive the examiners—that she was not yet in danger of disgrace—which made me waver, which made me hesitate? Was it simply my immutable and inescapable tonáli— or hers—which made me waver, which made me hesitate? I will never know. All I know is that I wavered, I hesitated, and the moment for action was gone, as Tzitzi was gone, with her honor guard of vulturine priests, into the darkness.

She did not come home that night.

We sat and waited, until long past the normal bedtime, until long past the midnight trumpeting of the temple conch, and we talked not at all. My father looked worried, doubtless about his daughter and the cause for the unusual attenuation of the "preliminary formalities." My mother looked worried, doubtless about the possibility that her carefully woven scheme for self-advancement had somehow come unraveled. But at last she laughed and said, "Of course. The priests would not send Tzitzi home in the dark. The temple maidens have given her a chamber there for the night. We are foolish to wait sleepless. Let us go to bed."

I went to my pallet, but I did not sleep. I worried that if the examiners had found Tzitzi to be no virgin—and how could they find otherwise?—the priests could very well take rapacious advantage of that fact. All the priests of all our gods were ostensibly bound to an oath of celibacy, but no rational person believed that they observed it. The temple women would truthfully state that Tzitzi came to them already devoid of her chitóli membrane and virginally tight closure. That condition could only be blamed on her own prior wantonness. When she left the temple again, whatever might have happened to her in the interim, she could prove no charges against the priests.

I tossed in anguish upon my pallet, as I imagined those priests using her throughout the night, one after another, and gleefully calling in all the other priests from all the other temples on the island. Not because any of them was sexually starved; they presumably used their temple women at will. But, as you reverend friars may have observed among your own religious, the kind of women who dedicated their lives to temple service were seldom of a face or form to drive a normal man delirious with desire. The priests must have been overjoyed that night, to receive a gift of new young flesh, of the the most desirable girl on Xaltócan.

I saw them flocking to Tzitzi's defenseless body, in hordes, like vultures to an uncaring cadaver. Flapping like vultures, hissing like vultures, taloned like vultures, black like vultures. They observed another oath: never to disrobe once they had taken the priestly vow. But, even if they broke that oath, to fall' naked upon Tzitzi, their bodies would still be black and scaly and fetid, having been unwashed ever since they took to the priesthood.

I hope it was all in my fevered imagination. I hope that my beautiful and beloved sister did not spend that night as carrion for the vultures to tear at. But no priest ever afterward spoke of her stay in the temple, either to confirm or refute my imaginings, and Tzitzi did not come home in the morning.

A priest came, one of the four of the night before, and his face was blank of expression as he reported simply, "Your daughter does not qualify to represent Teteoínan in the ceremonies. She has at some time carnally known at least one man."

"Yya ouiya ayya!" my mother wailed. "This ruins everything!"

"I do not understand," my father muttered. "She was always such a good girl. I cannot believe..."

"Perhaps," the priest said blandly to them, "you would care to volunteer your daughter for the sacrifice instead."

I said to the priest, through my teeth, "Where is she?"

He said indifferently, "When the examining women found her unsatisfactory, we naturally reported to the governor's palace that another candidate must be sought. At which, the palace requested that Nine Reed Tzitzitlíni be delivered there this morning for an interview with—"

"Pactli!" I blurted.

"He will be desolated," said my father, sadly shaking his head.

"He will be infuriated, you fool!" spat my mother. "We will all suffer his wrath, because of your slut of a daughter!"

I said, "I shall go to the palace immediately."

"No," the priest said firmly. "The court no doubt appreciates your concern, but the message was most specific: that only the daughter of this family would be admitted. Two of our temple women are escorting her there. None of the rest of you is to seek audience until and unless you are summoned."

Tzitzi did not come home that day. And no one else came to call, since the whole ısland by then must have been aware of our familial disgrace. Not even the festival-organizing women came to collect my mother to do her day's sweeping. That evidence of her ostracism, by women whom she had expected soon to be looking down upon, made her even more than ordinarily vociferous and shrill. She passed the dreary day in scolding my father for his having let his daughter "run wild," and in scolding me for having doubtless introduced my sister to some "evil friends" of mine, and letting one of them debauch her. The accusation was ludicrous, but it gave me an idea.

I slipped out of the house and went to seek Chimáli and Tlatli. They received me with some embarrassment and with awkward words of commiseration.

I said, "One of you can help Tzitzitlíni, if you will."

"If there is anything we can do, of course we will," said Chimáli. "Tell us, Mole."

"You know for how many years the insufferable Pactli has been besieging my sister. Everyone knows it. Now everyone knows that Tzitzi preferred someone else over him. So the Lord Joy has been made to seem lovesick and besotted for having pursued a girl who despised him. Simply to salve his wounded pride, he will take out his humiliation on her, and he can do it in some horrible manner. One of you could prevent his doing that."

"How?" asked Tlatli.

"Marry her," I said.

No one will ever know what a heart pang it cost me to say that, for what I meant was, "I give her up. Take her away from me." My two friends reeled slightly, and looked at me with goggling astonishment.

"My sister has erred," I went on. "I cannot deny it. But you both have known her since we all were children, and you surely know that she is no promiscuous wanton. If you can forgive her misstep, and believe that she did it only to avert the unwelcome prospect of marrying the Lord Joy, then you know that you could find no more chaste and faithful and upstanding wife for yourself. I need not add that she is probably the most beautiful you would ever find."

The two exchanged an uneasy look. I could hardly blame them. That radical proposal must have hit them with the stunning abruptness of lightning thrown by Tlaloc.

"You are Tzitzi's only hope," I said urgently. "Pactli now has her in his power, as a supposed maiden suddenly found to be not so. He can accuse her of having gone astraddle the road. He can even make the lying claim that she was his betrothed and that she was deliberately unfaithful to him. That would be tantamount to adultery, and he could persuade the Lord Red Heron to condemn her to death. But he can *not* do that to a woman legitimately married or spoken for."

I looked hard into the eyes of Chimáli, then Tlatli. "If one of you were to step forward and publicly ask for her hand . . ." They dropped their eyes from mine. "Oh, I know. It would take some bravery, and it would subject you to some derision. You would be taken for the one who had despoiled her in the first place. But marriage would atone for that, and it would rescue her from anything Pactli might do. It would save her, Chimáli. It would be a noble deed, Tlatli. I beg and entreat you."

They both looked at me again, and there was now real chagrin in their faces. Tlatli spoke for them both:

"We cannot, Mole, Not either of us."

I was grievously disappointed and hurt, but, more than that, I was puzzled. "If you said you will not, I might understand. But . . . you *cannot?*"

They stood side by side before me, stocky Tlatli and reedy Chimáli. They looked pityingly at me, then turned to each other, and I could not tell what was in their mutual gaze. Tentatively, uncertainly, each reached out a hand and took the other's, their fingers intertwining. Standing there, now linked, forced by me to confess a bond I had never remotely suspected, they looked at me again. The look proclaimed a defiant pride.

"Oh," I said, demolished. After a moment, I said, "Forgive me. When you declined, I should not have persisted."

Tlatli said, "We do not mind your knowing, Mole, but we would not care to have it common gossip."

I tried again. "Then would it not be to your advantage for one of you to make a marriage? I mean simply go through the motions of the ceremony. Afterwards . . ."

"I could not," said Chimáli with quiet obstinacy, "and I would not let Tlatli. It would be a weakness, a sullying of what we feel for each other. Look at it this way, Mole. Suppose someone asked you to marry one of us."

"Well, that would be contrary to all law and custom, and scandalous. But it would be just the opposite if one of you took Tzitzi to wife. Only in *name*, Chimáli, and later—"

"No," he said, and then added, perhaps sincerely, "We are sorry, Mole."

"So am I," I sighed as I turned and left.

But I determined that I would come back to them and press my proposal. I had to convince one of them that it would be to the benefit of us all. It would deliver my sister from danger, it would quell any possible conjectures about the relationship between Tlatli and Chimáli, *and* about the relationship between Tzitzi and me. They could openly bring her with them when they came to Texcóco, and secretly bring her to me, for me. The more I thought about it, the more the plan seemed ideal for everybody concerned. Chimáli and Tlatli *could* not continue to refuse the marriage on the selfish excuse that it would somehow tarnish their own love. I would persuade them—if necessary by the brutal threat of exposing them as cuilóntin. Yes, I would come back to Tlatli and Chimáli.

But as things turned out, I did not. It was already too late.

That night, again, Tzitzi did not come home.

In spite of everything, I slept, and I did not dream of vultures, but of Tzitzi and myself and the immense jar which held the household water supply and which bore Chimáli's handprint in blood. In my dream, I was back at that time during the lifeless days when Tzitzi had sought an excuse for us to get out of the house together. She had overturned and broken the water jar. The water sluiced all about the floor, and splashed up as far as my face. I awoke in the night to find my face wet with tears.

* * *

The summons from the governor's palace came the next morning, and it was not, as one would expect, for the head of the house, my father Tepetzálan. The messenger announced that the Lords Red Heron and Joy requested the immediate presence of my mother. My father sat meek and silent, his head bowed, avoiding my eyes, the whole time we awaited her return.

When she came back, her face was pale and her hands were unsteady as they unwound the shawl from around her head and shoulders, but her manner was surprisingly inspirited. She was no longer the woman irate at having been deprived of a title, and she was not at all the bereaved mother. She told us, "It seems we have lost a daughter, but we have not lost everything."

"Lost her *how?*" I asked.

"Tzitzi never arrived at the palace," said my mother, without looking at me. "She slipped away from the temple women escorting her, and she ran away. Of course, poor Páctlitzin is nearly demented by the whole course of events. When the women reported her flight, he ordered a search of the entire island. A fowler reports his canoe missing. You remember"— she said to my father—"how your daughter once threatened to do just that. To steal an acáli and flee to the mainland."

"Yes," he said dully.

"Well, it seems she has done so. There is no telling in which direction she went, so Pactli has reluctantly given up the search. He is as heartbroken as we are." That was so patently a lie that my mother hurried on before I could speak. "We must regard the departed Tzitzitlíni as lost to us for good. She has fled as she said she would. Forever. It is no one's doing but her own. And she will not dare to show her face on Xaltócan again."

I said, "I do not believe any of this." But she ignored me and went on, addressing my father:

"Like Pactli, the governor shares our grief, but he does not hold us to blame for the misbehavior of our wayward daughter. He said to me: 'I have always respected Head Nodder.' And he said to me: 'I would like to do something to assuage his disillusions and bereavement.' And he said to me: 'Do you suppose Head Nodder would accept a promotion to become Chief Quarrier in charge of all the quarries?'"

My father's bowed head jerked up, and he exclaimed, "What?"

"Those are the words Red Heron spoke. In charge of all the quarries of Xaltócan. He said: 'It cannot make up for the shame the man has suffered, but it may demonstrate my regard for him.'"

I said again, "I do not believe any of this." The Lord Red Heron had never before spoken of my father as Head Nodder, and I doubted that he even knew of Tepetzálan's nickname.

Still ignoring my interjections, my mother said to my father, "We have been unfortunate in our daughter, but we are fortunate in having such a tecútli. Any other might have banished us all. Consider—Red Heron's own son has been mocked and insulted by our own daughter—and he offers you this token of compassion."

"Chief Quarrier . . ." my father mumbled, looking rather as if he had been hit on the head by one of his own quarry stones. "I would be the youngest ever. . . ."

"Will you accept it?" my mother asked.

My father stammered, "Why—why—it is small recompense for losing a loved daughter, however errant she . . ."

"Will you accept it?" my mother repeated, more sharply.

"It is a hand extended in friendship," my father maundered on. "To refuse that—after my lord has once been insulted—it would be another insult, and even more. . . ."

"Will you accept it?"

"Why—yes. I must. I will accept it. I could not do otherwise. Could I?"

"There!" said my mother, much pleased. She dusted her hands together as if she had just completed some disagreeably dirty task. "We may not ever be nobles, thanks to the wench whose name I will never again pronounce, but we are one step higher in the macehuáltin. And since the Lord Red Heron is willing to overlook our disgrace, so will be everyone else. We can still hold our heads high, not hang them in shame. Now," she concluded briskly, "I must go out again. The women of the delegation are waiting for me to join them in sweeping the temple pyramid."

"I will walk partway with you, my dear," said my father. "I think I will take a look at the western quarry while the workers are on holiday. I have long suspected that the Master Quarrier in charge there has overlooked a significant stratum. . . ."

As they went together out the door, my mother turned back to say, "Oh, Mixtli, will you pack your sister's belongings and stow them somewhere? Who knows, she may someday send a porter for them."

I knew she never would or could, but I did as I was bidden, and packed into baskets everything I could recognize as a possession of hers. Only one thing I did not pack and hide: her little bedside figurine of Xochiquétzal, goddess of love and flowers, the goddess to whom young girls prayed for a happy married life.

Alone in the house, alone with my thoughts, I translated my mother's story into what I was sure had happened in fact. Tzitzi had not escaped from her guardian women. They had duly delivered her to Pactli at the palace. He, in a fury—and in what manner I tried not to imagine—had put my sister to death. His father might have been fully in accord with the execution, but he was a notably fair-minded man, and he could not have condoned a killing in cold blood, done without due process of trial and condemnation. The Lord Red Heron would have had the choice, then, of bringing his own son to trial or of covering up the whole affair. So he and Pactli—and, I suspected, Pactli's long-time conspirator, my mother—had concocted the story of Tzitzi's escape and flight in a stolen canoe. And, to smooth things over even more neatly, to discourage questions or a renewed search for the girl, the governor had thrown a sop to my father.

After stowing Tzitzi's belongings, I packed those of my own which I had brought with me from Texcóco. The last thing I tucked into my portable wicker basket was the figurine of Xochiquétzal. Then I shouldered the basket and left the house, never to come back again. When I walked down toward the lakeshore, a butterfly accompanied me for a while, and several times fluttered in circles around my head.

I was fortunate enough to find a fisherman who was irreverently determined to go on working during the Ochpanítztli festival, and who was even then preparing to paddle out to await the twilight rising of the lake's whitefish. He agreed to row me all the way to Texcóco, for a payment considerably in excess of what he could have earned from a whole night's fishing.

On the way, I asked him, "Have you heard of any fisherman or fowler losing a canoe recently? Of anyone's acáli having floated away or been stolen?"

"No," he said.

I looked back at the island, sunlit and peaceful in the summer afternoon. It sprawled on the lake water as it always had and always would, except that it would never again know "the sound of small bells ringing"—or give another thought to such a small deprivation. The Lord Red Heron, the Lord Joy, my mother and father, my friends Chimáli and Tlatli, all the other inhabitants of Xaltócan, they had already agreed to forget.

I had not.

"Why, Head Nodder!" exclaimed the Lady of Tolan, the first person I encountered on my way to my apartment in the palace. "You have come back early from your holiday at home."

"Yes, my lady. Xaltócan no longer feels like home to me. And I have many things to do here."

"Do you mean you were homesick for Texcóco?" she said, smiling. "Then we must have made you learn to like us here. I am delighted to think so, Head Nodder."

"Please, my lady," I said huskily, "do not call me that anymore. I have seen enough of head nodding."

"Oh?" she said, her smile fading as she studied my face. "Whatever name you prefer, then."

I thought of the several things I had to do, and I said to her, "Tliléctic-Mixtli is the name I was given from the book of divination and prophecies. Call me what I am. Dark Cloud."

I H S
✠
S. C. C. M.

Sanctified, Caesarean, Catholic Majesty,
the Emperor Don Carlos, Our Lord King:

MOST High and Mighty Majesty, our Sovereign
Liege: from the City of Mexico, capital of New Spain, this day
of the Feast of the Dolors in the Year of Our Lord one thousand
five hundred twenty and nine, greeting.

We regret that we cannot include, with these latest collected
pages of manuscript, the pictures which Your Majesty requests
in your most recent letter: "those pictures of persons, especially
of female persons, drawn by the storyteller and referred to in
this chronicle." The aged Indian himself, when questioned as
to their whereabouts, laughs at the idea that such trivially indecent jottings should have been worth keeping all these years,
or that, even if they had been of any value, they could have
survived all these years.

We refrain from deploring the obscenities those drawings
were intended to record, since we are certain that the pictures,
even if available, would have conveyed nothing to Your Majesty. We know that our Imperial Sovereign's sense of appreciation is accustomed to works of art like those of the Master
Matsys, whose painting of Erasmus, for example, is unmis-

takably recognizable as Erasmus. The persons portrayed in the daubs made by these Indians are seldom recognizable even as human beings, except in a few of the more representational wall frescoes and reliefs.

Your Most Lofty Majesty has earlier bidden your chaplain to secure "writings, tablets, or other records" to substantiate the tales told in these pages. But we assure you, Sire, that the Aztec exaggerates wildly when he speaks of writing and reading, drawing and painting. These savages never created or possessed or preserved any mementos of their history aside from some plicate paper folders, skins and panels bearing multitudes of primitive figures such as children might scribble. These would be inscrutable to any civilized eye, and were of use to the Indians only as mnemonic aids for their "wise men," who utilized the scrawls to jog their memory as they repeated the oral history of their tribe or clan. A dubious sort of history at best.

Before your servant's arrival in this land, the Franciscan friars, sent here five years previous by His Holiness the late Pope Adrian, had already combed every part of the country adjacent to this capital city. Those good brothers had collected, from every still-standing edifice that might be considered an archival depository, many thousands of the Indian "books," but had made no disposition of them, pending higher directive.

Wherefore, as Your Majesty's delegated Bishop, we ourself examined the confiscated "libraries," and found not one item that contained anything but tawdry and grotesque figures. Most of those were nightmarish: beasts, monsters, false gods, demons, butterflies, reptiles, and other things of like vulgar nature. Some of the figures purported to represent human beings, but—as in that absurd style of art which the Bolognese call *caricatura*—the humans were indistinguishable from pigs, asses, gargoyles, or anything else the imagination might conceive.

Since there was not a single work in which there was not to be seen rank superstition and delusions inspired by the Devil, we commanded that the thousands upon thousands of volumes and scrolls be made a heap in this city's main marketplace, and there had them burned to ashes, and the ashes dispersed. We submit that such was the fitting end for those pagan mementos, and we doubt that there remain any others in all the regions of New Spain thus far explored.

Be it noted, Sire, that the Indian onlookers at the burning, though almost all of them are now *professed* Christians, unashamedly showed a disgusting degree of regret and anguish; they even wept whilst they gazed upon the pyre, as they might have been so many *real* Christians watching the desecration and destruction of so many Holy Scriptures. We take that as evidence that these creatures have not yet been so wholeheartedly converted to Christianity as we and Mother Church would wish. Hence this most humble servant of Your Very Pious and Devout Majesty still has and will have many urgent episcopal duties pertinent to the more intense propagation of the Faith.

We beg Your Majesty's understanding that such duties must take precedence over our acting as auditor and monitor of the loquacious Aztec, except in our increasingly rare spare moments. We also beg that Your Majesty will understand the necessity of our occasionally sending a package of pages without a commentary letter, and sometimes even sending it unread by us.

May Our Lord God preserve the life and expand the kingdom of Your Sacred Majesty for many years to come, is the sincere prayer of Your S.C.C.M.'s Bishop of Mexico,

(ecce signum) Zumárraga

QUINTA PARS

MY little slave boy Cozcatl welcomed me back to Texcóco with unfeigned delight and relief, because, as he told me, Jadestone Doll had been exceedingly vexed at my going on holiday, and had taken out her ill humor on him. Though she had an ample staff of serving women, she had appropriated Cozcatl as well, and had kept him drudging for her, or running at a trot, or standing still to be whipped, all the while I had been away.

He hinted at the ignobility of some of the errands and chores he had done for her, and also, at my prompting, finally disclosed that the woman named Something Delicate had drunk corrosive xocóyatl upon her next summons to the lady's chambers—and had died there, foaming at the mouth and convulsed with pain. Ever since the suicide of Something Delicate, somehow still unknown outside those precincts, Jadestone Doll had had to depend, for her clandestine entertainments, on partners procured by Cozcatl and the maids. I gathered that those partners had been less satisfactory than what I had hitherto provided. But the lady did not immediately press me into service again, or even send a slave across the corridor to convey a greeting, or give any sign that she knew or cared about my having returned. She was involved with the Ochpanítztli festivities, which of course were in progress in Texcóco as they were everywhere else.

Then, when that celebration was over, Tlatli and Chimáli arrived at the palace as scheduled, and Jadestone Doll occupied herself with getting them quartered, making sure that their studio was supplied with clay and tools and paints, and giving them detailed instructions regarding the work they were to do. I deliberately was not present at their arrival. When, a day or two later, we accidentally met in a palace garden, I gave them only a curt salute, to which they replied with a diffident mumble.

Thereafter I encountered them quite frequently, as their studio was situated in the cellars under Jadestone Doll's wing of the palace, but I merely nodded as I passed. They had by then had several interviews with their patroness, and I could see that their earlier exultation about their work had dissipated considerably. They were, in fact, now looking nervous and fearful. They obviously would have liked to discuss with me the precarious situation in which they found themselves, but I coldly discouraged any approaches.

I was busy with a job of my own: doing one particular drawing which I intended to present to Jadestone Doll when she finally should summon me to her presence, and that was a difficult project I had set myself. It was to be the most irresistibly handsome drawing of a young man I had yet done, but it also had to resemble a young man who really existed. I made and tore up many false starts and, when I at last achieved a satisfactory sketch, I spent still more time reworking and elaborating on it until I had a finished drawing that I was confident would fascinate the girl queen. And it did.

"Why, he is *beyond* handsome, he is *beautiful!*" she exclaimed when I gave it to her. She studied it some more and murmured, "If he were a woman, he would be Jadestone Doll." She could pay no higher compliment. "Who is he?"

I said, "His name is Joy."

"*Ayyo*, and it should be! Where did you find him?"

"He is the Crown Prince of my home island, my lady. Páctlitzin, son of Tlauquécholtzin, the tecútli of Xaltócan."

"And when you saw him again, you thought of me, and you drew his likeness for me. How sweet of you, Fetch! I almost forgive your deserting me for so many days. Now go and get him for me."

I said truthfully, "I fear he would not come at my behest, my lady. Pactli and I bear a mutual grudge. However—"

"Then you do not do this for his benefit," the girl interrupted. "I wonder why you should do it for mine." Her depthless eyes fixed on me suspiciously. "It is true that I have never mistreated you, but neither have you cause to feel great affection for me. Then why this sudden and unbidden generosity?"

"I try to anticipate my lady's desires and commands."

Without comment, she pulled on the bell rope and, when a maid responded, ordered that Chimáli and Tlatli be brought to join us. They came, looking trepid, and Jadestone Doll shoved the drawing at them. "You two also come from Xaltócan. Do you recognize this young man?"

Tlatli exclaimed, "Pactli!" and Chimáli said, "Yes, that is the Lord Joy, my lady, but—"

I threw him a look that shut his mouth before he could say, "But the Lord Joy never looked so noble as that." And I did not mind that Jadestone Doll intercepted my look.

"I see," she said archly, as if she had caught me out. "You two may go." When they had left the room, she said to me, "You mentioned a grudge. Some squalid romantic rivalry, I suppose, and the young noble bested you. So you cunningly arrange one last assignation for him, *knowing* it will be his last."

Pointedly looking beyond her, at Master Pixquitl's statues of the swift-messenger Yeyac-Netztlin and the gardener Xali-Otli, I put on a conspirator's smile and said, "I prefer to think that I am doing a favor for all three of us. My lady, my Lord Pactli, and myself."

She laughed gaily. "So be it, then. I daresay I owe you one favor by now. But you must get him here."

"I took the liberty of preparing a letter," I said, producing it, "and on a royally fine fawnskin. The usual instructions: midnight at the eastern gate. If my lady will put her name to it and enclose the ring, I can almost guarantee that the young prince will come in the same canoe that delivers it."

"My clever Fetch!" she said, taking the letter to a low table on which were a paint pot and a writing reed. Being a Mexícatl girl, of course she could not read or write, but, being a noble, she could at least make the symbols of her name. "You know where my private acáli is docked. Take this to the steersman and tell him to go at dawn. I want my Joy tomorrow night."

Tlatli and Chimáli had waited in the corridor outside, to waylay me, and Tlatli said in a quavering voice, "Do you know what it is you are doing, Mole?"

Chimáli said, in a slightly steadier voice, "Do you know what could be in store for the Lord Pactli? Come and look."

I followed them down the stone stair to their stone-walled studio. It was well appointed but, being underground, lighted day and night by lamps and torches, it felt very like a dungeon. The artists had been working simultaneously on several statues, two of which I recognized. The one of the slave, I Will Be of Greatness, was already sculptured full length, life size, and Chimáli had started painting the clay with his specially concocted paints.

"Very lifelike," I said, and meant it. "The Lady Jadestone Doll will approve."

"Oh, well, capturing the likeness was not difficult," Tlatli said modestly. "Not when I could work from your excellent drawing and mold the clay upon the actual skull."

"But my pictures show no colors," I said, "and even the Master Sculptor Pixquitl has been unable to recreate those. Chimáli, I applaud your talent."

I meant that, too. Pixquitl's statues had been done in the usual flat colors: a uniform pale copper for all exposed skin surfaces, an unvarying black for the hair, and so on. Chimáli's skin tones varied as do those on a living person: the nose and ears just the least bit darker than the rest of the face, the cheeks a little more pink. Even the black of the hair glinted here and there with brownish lights.

"It should look even better when it has been fired in the kiln," said Chimáli. "The colors meld more together. Oh, and look at this, Mole." He led me around to the back of the statue and pointed. At the bottom of the slave's clay mantle Tlatli had incised his falcon symbol. Under that was Chimáli's blood-red handprint.

"Yes, unmistakable," I said, without inflexion. I moved to the next statue. "And this will be Something Delicate."

Tlatli said uncomfortably, "I think, Mole, we would prefer not to know the names of the—uh—models."

"That was more than her name," I said.

Only her head and shoulders had yet been molded in clay, but they stood at the height they had stood in life, for they were supported by bones, her articulated bones, her own skeleton, held upright by a pole at the back.

"It is giving me problems," said Tlatli, as if he were speaking of a stone block in which he had found an unsuspected flaw. He showed me a picture, the one I had sketched in the marketplace, the portrait head I had first drawn of Something Delicate. "Your drawing and the skull serve me nicely for doing the head. And the colótli, the armature, gives me the body's linear proportions, but—"

"The armature?" I inquired.

"The interior support. Any sculpture of clay or wax must be supported by an armature, just as a pulpy cactus is supported by its interior woody framework. For a statue of a human figure, what better armature than its own original skeleton?"

"What indeed?" I said. "But tell me, how do you procure the original skeletons?"

Chimáli said, "The Lady Jadestone Doll provides them, from her private kitchen."

"From her *kitchen?*"

Chimáli looked away from me. "Do not ask me how she has persuaded her cooks and kitchen slaves. But they flay the skin and scoop the bowels and carve the flesh from the—from the model—without dismembering it. Then they boil the remainder in great vats of lime water. They have to stop the boiling before the ligaments and sinews of the joints are dissolved, so there are still some scraps of meat we have to scrape off. But we do get the skeleton entire. Oh, a finger bone or a rib may come loose, but . . ."

"But unfortunately," said Tlatli, "even the complete skeleton gives me no indication of how the body's exterior was padded and curved. I can guess at a man's figure, but a woman's is different. You know, the breasts and hips and buttocks."

"They were sublime," I muttered, remembering Something Delicate. "Come to my chambers. I will give you another drawing which shows your model in her entirety."

In my apartment, I ordered Cozcatl to make chocolate for us all. Tlatli and Chimáli roamed through the three rooms, uttering exclamatory noises about their finery and luxury, while I leafed through my assortment of drawings and extracted one that showed Something Delicate full length.

"Ah, completely nude," said Tlatli. "That is ideal for my purposes." He might have been passing judgment on a sample of good marl clay.

Chimáli also looked at the picture of the dead woman and said, "Truly, Mole, your drawings are skillfully detailed. If you would leave off doing only *lines*, and learn to work with the lights and shadows of paint, you could be a real artist. You too could give beauty to the world."

I laughed harshly. "Like statues built on boiled skeletons?"

Tlatli sipped at his chocolate and said defensively, "We did not kill those people, Mole. And we do not know why the young queen wants them preserved. But consider. If they were merely buried or burned, they would disintegrate into mold or ashes. We at least make them endure. And yes, we do our best to make them objects of beauty."

I said, "I am a scribe. I do not prettify the world. I only describe it."

Tlatli held up the picture of Something Delicate. "You did this, and it is quite a beautiful thing."

"From now on, I will draw nothing but word pictures. I have done the last portrait I shall ever do."

"That one of the Lord Joy," Chimáli guessed. He glanced about to make sure my slave was not within hearing. "You must know you are putting Pactli at risk of the kitchen lime vats."

"I devoutly hope so," I said. "I will not let my sister's death go unpunished." I flung Chimáli's own words back at him: "It would be a weakness, a sullying of what we felt for each other."

The two had the grace at least to lower their heads for some moments of silence before Tlatli spoke:

"You will put us all at hazard of discovery, Mole."

"You are already at hazard. I have long been. I might have told you that before you came." I gestured in the direction of their studio. "But would you have believed what is down there?"

Chimáli protested, "Those are only city commoners and slaves. They might never be missed. Pactli is a Crown Prince of a Mexíca province!"

I shook my head. "The husband of that woman in the drawing—I hear he has gone quite mad, searching to discover what became of his beloved wife. He will never be sane again. And even slaves do not just disappear. The Revered Speaker has his guardsmen already seeking and making inquiries about the several mysteriously missing persons. Discovery is only a matter of time. That time may be tomorrow night, if Pactli is prompt."

Visibly sweating, Tlatli said, "Mole, we cannot let you—"

"You cannot stop me. And if you try to flee, if you try to warn Pactli or Jadestone Doll, I will hear of it instantly, and I will go instantly to the Uey-Tlatoáni."

Chimáli said, "He will have your life along with everyone else's. Why do this to me and Tlatli, Mole? Why do it to yourself?"

"My sister's death is not upon Pactli's head alone. I was involved, you were involved. I am prepared to atone with my own life, if that is my tonáli. You two must take your chances."

"Chances!" Tlatli flung up his hands. "What chances?"

"One very good one. I suspect the lady herself has the sense not to kill a prince of the Mexíca. I suspect she will toy with him for a while, perhaps a long while, then send him home with his lips sealed by a pledge."

"Yes," Chimáli said thoughtfully. "She may court danger, but not suicide." He turned to Tlatli. "And while he is here, you and I can finish the statues already on order. Then we can plead urgent work elsewhere...."

Tlatli gulped the dregs of his chocolate. "Come! We will work night and day. We must be finished with everything on hand, we must have reason to ask leave to depart, before our lady wearies of our prince."

On that note of hope, they dashed from my chambers.

I had not lied to them, but I had neglected to mention one detail of my arrangements. I had spoken truly when I suggested that Jadestone Doll might balk at killing an invited prince. That was a very real possiblity. And for that reason, for this particular guest, I had made one small change in the usual wording of the invitation. As we say in our language, of one who deserves retribution, "he would be destroyed with flowers."

The gods supposedly know all our plans, and know their ends before their beginnings. The gods are mischievous, and they delight to potter with the plans of men. They usually prefer to complicate those plans, as they might snarl a fowler's net, or to frustrate them so the plans come to no result whatever. Very seldom do the gods intervene to any worthier purpose. But I do believe, that time, they looked at my plan and said among themselves, "This dark scheme contrived by Dark Cloud, it is so ironically good, let us make it ironically even better."

The next midnight, I kept my ear close against the inside of my door until I heard Pitza and the guest arrive and enter the apartment across the corridor. Then I cracked my door slightly to hear better. I expected some exclamation of profanity from Jadestone Doll when she first compared Pactli's brutish face with my idealized portrait. What I had not expected was what I did hear: the girls' piercing scream of real shock, and then her hysterical shrieking of my name: "Fetch! Come here at once? *Fetch!*"

That seemed rather an extreme reaction in anyone meeting even the abhorrent Lord Joy. I opened my door and stepped out, to find a spear-carrying guard stationed just outside it, and another across the hall beside my lady's door. Both of them respectfully snapped their spears to the vertical as I emerged, and neither tried to prevent my entering the other apartment.

The young queen was standing just inside. Her face was twisted and unlovely, and nearly white with shock. But it gradually went nearly purple with fury as she began screaming at me, "What kind of comedy is this, you son of a dog? Do you think you can make filthy jokes at my expense?"

She went on like that, in full voice. I turned to Pitza and the man she had brought—and, for all my mixed feelings, I could not help bursting out into loud and sustained laughter. I had forgotten about Jadestone Doll's drug-caused nearsightedness. She must have come running through all the rooms and halls of her apartment, to embrace the eagerly awaited Lord Joy, and she must have got right upon the visitor before her vision allowed her to see him clearly. That truly would have been enough of a shock to force a scream from one who had never seen him before. His presence was a staggering surprise to me too, but I laughed instead of screaming, for I had the advantage of recognizing the shriveled, hunched, cacao-brown old man.

I had worded the letter to Pactli in such a way as to assure that he could not arrive unobserved. But I had no idea how or why the old vagabond had come instead of Pactli, and it did not seem the time to ask. Besides, I could not stop laughing.

"Disloyal! Unforgivable! Despicable!" the girl was crying, over my guffaws, and Pitza was trying to fade into the nearest draperies, and the cacao man was waving my fawnskin letter and saying, "But that is your own signature, is it not, my lady?"

She broke off her vilification of me to snarl at him, "Yes! But can even you believe it was addressed to a miserable, half-naked beggar? Now shut your toothless mouth!" She whirled back to me. "It has to be a joke, since it convulses you so. Confess to it and you will merely be beaten raw. Keep on laughing like that and I swear—"

"And of course, my lady," the man persisted, "I recognize in the body of the letter the picture writing of my old friend Mole here."

"I said *be silent!* When the flower garland is around your throat, you will dearly regret every breath you have wasted. And his name is Fetch!"

"Is it, now? It fits." His slitted eyes slid to me, and the way they glittered was not at all friendly. My laughter subsided. "But the letter clearly says, my lady, for me to be here at this hour, and wearing this ring, and—"

"Not *wearing* the ring!" she shrieked, most imprudently. "You sneaking old pretender, you even pretend to read. The ring was to be carried concealed! And you must have flourished it through all Texcóco...*yya ayya!*" She ground her teeth, and swung again to me. "Do you realize what your joke may have caused, you unspeakable lout? *Yya ouiya*, but you will die in the slowest of agonies!"

"How is it a joke, my lady?" the bent man asked. "According to this invitation, you must have been expecting someone. And you came running so joyfully to greet me—"

"You! To greet *you?*" screamed the girl, throwing out her arms as if she were physically throwing away all caution. "Would the cheapest, hungriest waterfront whore in Texcóco lie with *you?*" Once more she turned on me. "Fetch! *Why did you do this?*"

"My lady," I said, speaking for the first time, and speaking the hard words gently. "I have often thought your Lord Husband did not sufficiently weigh his words, when he commanded me to serve the Lady Jadestone Doll, and to serve her without question. But I was bound to obey. As you once pointed out to me, my lady, I could not myself betray your wickedness without disobeying both you and him. I had to trick you, finally, into betraying yourself."

She took a step back from me, and her mouth worked soundlessly, while her angrily flushed face began to pale again. The words took a while to come. "You—tricked me? This—this is no joke?"

"Not his joke, at any rate, but mine," said the hunched man. "I was at the lakeside when a well-dressed and oiled and perfumed young lord debarked from your private acáli, my lady, and boldly made his way hither, with this ring highly visible and recognizable upon the little finger of his big hand. It seemed a flagrant indiscretion, if not a transgression. I summoned guards to relieve him of the ring, and then of the letter he carried. I brought the things in his stead."

"You—you—by what authority—how *dare* you meddle?" she spluttered. "Fetch! This man is a confessed thief. Kill him! I order you to kill this man, here and now, that I may see."

"No, my lady," I said, still gently, for I was almost beginning to feel sorry for her. "This one time I disobey. I think you have at last revealed your true self to another observer. I think I am released from all bonds of obedience. I think you will kill no more."

She spun swiftly and yanked open the door to the corridor. Perhaps she meant to flee, but when the sentinel outside turned to face her, blocking the doorway, she said sharply, "Guard, I have here one thief and one traitor. That beggar, see, he is wearing my stolen ring. And this commoner has disobeyed my direct command. I want you to take them both and—"

"Your pardon, my lady," the guard rumbled. "I already have my orders from the Uey-Tlatoáni. Different orders."

Her mouth fell open.

I said, "Guard, lend me your spear for one moment."

He hesitated, then handed it to me. I stepped to the nearby alcove housing the statue of the gardener Xali-Otli and, with all my strength, drove the spear point under the thing's chin. The painted head broke off, it hit the floor and rolled, its baked clay shattering and crumbling. When the head bounced to a stop against a far wall, it was a bare, white, gleaming skull, the cleanest and most honest face of man. The brown beggar watched its progress without expression. But the immense pupils of Jadestone Doll's eyes seemed now to have engulfed her eyes entirely. They were liquid black pools of terror. I gave the spear back to the guard and asked, "What are your orders, then?"

"You and your slave boy are to remain in your apartment. The lady queen and her serving women are to stay in this one. You will all remain under guard while your chambers are searched, and until further orders come from the Revered Speaker."

I said to the cacao man, "Will you join me in my captivity for a while, venerable one, to take a cup of chocolate perhaps?"

"No," he said, wrenching his gaze away from the exposed skull. "I am bidden to report on this night's events. I think the Lord Nezahualpíli will now command a more extensive search—of the sculpture studios and other places."

I made the gesture of kissing the earth. "Then I bid you good night, old man, my lady." She stared at me, but I do not think she saw me.

I returned to my own chambers to find them being ransacked by the Lord Strong Bone and some others of the Revered Speaker's confidential aides. They had already discovered my drawings of Jadestone Doll and Something Delicate in embrace.

✠

You say you attend today's sitting, my Lord Bishop, because you are interested in hearing how our judicial processes were conducted. But it is hardly necessary for me to describe the trial of Jadestone Doll. Your Excellency will find it minutely set forth in the archives of the Texcóco court, if you will trouble to examine those books. Your Excellency will also find it in the written histories of other lands, and even in the folktales of the common people, for the scandal is still remembered and related, especially by our women.

Nezahualpíli invited to the trial the rulers of every neighboring nation, and all their tlamatíntin wise men, and all their tecútlin of every least province. He even invited them to bring their wives and court ladies. He did it partly to make public demonstration that not even the highest-born of women could sin with impunity. But there was another reason. The accused was the daughter of the most powerful ruler in The One World, the ill-tempered and bellicose Revered Speaker Ahuítzotl of the Mexíca. By inviting him and every other nation's highest officials, Nezahualpíli sought also to demonstrate that the proceedings were conducted in absolute fairness. It was for that same reason that Nezahualpíli sat to one side during the trial. He delegated the questioning of defendants and witnesses to two disinterested parties: his Snake Woman, the Lord Strong Bone, and a tlamatíni judge named Tepítzic.

Texcóco's hall of justice was crowded to capacity. It may have been the greatest gathering of rulers—friendly, neutral, inimical—until then convened in one place. Ahuítzotl only was absent. He could not expose himself to the disgrace of being ogled and pitied and derided while his own daughter's shame was inexorably revealed. In his stead, he sent the Snake Woman of Tenochtítlan. Among the many other lords who did attend, however, was the governor of Xaltócan, Pactli's father, Red Heron. He sat and endured his humiliation, head bowed, throughout the entire trial. The few times he raised his sad and bleared old eyes, they fixed on me. I think he was remembering a remark he had made long ago, when he had commented on my childhood ambitions: "Whatever occupation you do undertake, young man, you ought to do it well."

The interrogation of all persons involved was lengthy and detailed and tedious and often repetitive. I recall only the more pertinent questions and replies to recount to Your Excellency.

The two foremost of the accused were, of course, Jadestone Doll and Lord Joy. He was called first, and came pale and quaking to take the oath. Among the many other words put to him by the examiners were these:

"You were seized by the palace guards, Páctlitzin, on the grounds of that wing of the palace allotted to the royal lady Chálciunenétzin. It is a capital offense for any unauthorized male to enter, for any reason or on any pretext, the premises reserved for the ladies of the court. You were aware of that?"

He gulped loudly and said feebly, "Yes," and sealed his doom.

Jadestone Doll was next called and, among the numberless questions put to her, one elicited a reply that made the audience gasp. The judge Tepítzic spoke:

"You have admitted, my lady, that it was the workers in your private kitchen who slew your lovers and prepared their skeletons for the process of preservation. We think that not even the most debased of slaves could have done such work except under extreme duress. What was the persuasion you applied?"

In the meek voice of a little girl, she said, "For a long time previous, I posted my guards in the kitchen to see that the workers got no food at all, that they did not even taste what they cooked for me. I starved them until they agreed to—do what I commanded. When they had done it once, and thereby had been full fed, they required no more persuasion or threats or watching guards. . . ."

The rest of her words were lost in the general commotion. My little slave Cozcatl was retching, and had to be taken outside the hall for a while. I knew how he felt, and my own stomach wobbled slightly. Our meals had come from that same kitchen.

As Jadestone Doll's chief accomplice, I was called next. I gave a complete account of my activities on her behalf, omitting nothing. When I came to the part about Something Delicate, I was interrupted by another uproar in the hall. The deranged widower of that woman had to be restrained by guards from rushing forward to throttle me, and he was carried out, shrieking and flailing and spraying spittle. When I came to the end of my account, the Lord Strong Bone eyed me with open contempt and said:

"A frank confession, at least. Have you anything to say in mitigation or defense?"

I said, "Nothing, my lord."

At which another voice was heard. "If the scribe Dark Cloud declines to defend himself," said Nezahualpíli, "may I, my lord justices, speak some extenuating words?" The two examiners gave reluctant permission, obviously not wanting to hear me exculpated, but not able to refuse their Uey-Tlatoáni.

Nezahualpíli said, "Throughout his attendance on the Lady Jadestone Doll, this young man was acting, however injudiciously, upon my express orders that he serve the lady without question and obey her every command. I submit that my own orders were badly expressed. It has also been shown that Dark Cloud finally seized upon the only means possible to divulge the truth about the adulterous and murderous lady. If he had not, my lord justices, we might have been trying her for the slaying of many more victims."

The judge Tepítzic grumbled, "Our Lord Nezahualpíli's words will be taken into account in our deliberations." He leveled his stern gaze on me again. "I have just one further question to ask the defendant. Did *you*, Tliléctic-Mixtli, ever lie with the Lady Jadestone Doll?"

I said, "No, my lord."

Evidently hoping they had caught me in a damning lie, the examiners called my slave Cozcatl and asked him, "Did your master ever have sexual relations with the Lady Jadestone Doll?"

He said, in a piping voice, "No, my lords."

Tepítzic persisted, "But he had every opportunity."

Cozcatl said stubbornly, "No, my lords. Whenever my master was in the lady's company for any length of time, I was always in attendance. Not my master and not any other man of the court ever lay with the lady, except one. That was during my master's absence on holiday, and one night the lady was unable to secure a partner from outside."

The judges leaned forward. "Some man of the palace? *Who?*"

Cozcatl said, "Me," and the judges rocked back again.

"*You?*" said Strong Bone. "How old are you, slave?"

"I have just turned eleven years, my lord."

"Speak more loudly, boy. Do you mean to tell us that you served the accused adulteress as a sexual partner? That you actually coupled with her? That you have a tepúli capable of—?"

"My tepúli?" squeaked Cozcatl, shocked to the impertinence of interrupting the judge. "My lords, that member is for making water with! I served my lady, as she bade me, with my mouth. I would never touch a noblewoman with something as nasty as a *tepúli*...."

If he said anything else, it was drowned out by the roar of laughter from the spectators. Even the two judges had to struggle to keep their faces impassive. It was the only mirthful moment of relief in that grim day.

Tlatli was one of the last accomplices called. I have forgotten to mention that, on the night Nezahualpíli's guards raided the studio, Chimáli was absent on some errand. There had then been no cause for Nezahualpíli or his aides to suspect the existence of another artist. Apparently no other of those accused had subsequently thought to mention Chimáli, and apparently Tlatli had since been able to pretend that he had worked alone.

Strong Bone said, "Chicuáce-Cali Ixtac-Tlatli, you admit that certain of the statues introduced in evidence were of your making."

"Yes, my lords," he said firmly. "I could hardly deny it. You see upon them my signature mark: the incised symbol of a falcon's head and beneath it the slap of my bloodied hand." His eyes sought mine and beseeched silence, as if saying, "Spare *my* woman," and I kept silent.

Eventually the two examiners retired to a private chamber for their deliberations. Everyone else in the hall of justice thankfully debouched from the big but now stuffy room to enjoy a breath of fresh air or to smoke a poquíetl in the gardens outside. We defendants remained, each with an armed guard standing alert at our side, and we carefully avoided meeting each other's eyes.

It was not long before the judges returned and the hall refilled. The Snake Woman, Lord Strong Bone, made the routine prefatory announcement: "We, the examiners, have deliberated solely upon the evidence and testimony presented here, and have come to our decisions without malice or favor, without the intervention of any other persons, with the assistance only of Tónantzin, the gentle goddess of law and mercy and justice."

He produced a sheet of the finest paper and, referring to it, pronounced first, "We find that the accused scribe, Chicóme-Xochitl Tliléctic-Mixtli, merits acquittal in that his actions, however culpable, were not ill intentioned, and furthermore were expiated by his bringing others to account. However . . ." Strong Bone threw a glance at the Revered Speaker, then glared at me. "We recommend that the acquitted one be banished from this realm as an alien who has abused its hospitality."

Well, I will not say I was pleased at that. But Nezahualpíli could easily have let the judges deal with me as severely as they dealt with the others. The Snake Woman again referred to the paper and pronounced, "The following persons we find guilty of the several crimes with which they stand charged; actions heinous, perfidious, and detestable in the sight of the gods." He read the list of names: the Lord Joy, the Lady Jadestone Doll, the sculptors Pixquitl and Tlatli, my slave Cozcatl, two guards who had alternated night duty on the palace's eastern gate, Jadestone Doll's maid Pitza and numerous other servants, all the cooks and workers of her kitchen. The judge concluded his drone, "Regarding these persons found guilty, we make no recommendations, either of severity or lenity, and their sentences will be pronounced by the Revered Speaker."

Nezahualpíli got slowly to his feet. He stood in deep study for a moment, then said, "As my lords recommend, the scribe Dark Cloud will be banished from Texcóco and all the domains of Acólhua. The convicted slave, Cozcatl, I here pardon in consideration of his tender years, but he will likewise be exiled from these lands. The nobles Páctlitzin and Chálchiunénetzin will be executed in private, and I shall leave their mode of execution to be determined by the noble ladies of the Texcóco court. All others found guilty by the lord justices are sentenced to be publicly executed by means of the icpacxóchitl, with no recourse to Tlazoltéotl beforehand. Their dead bodies, together with the remains of their victims, will be burned in a common pyre."

I rejoiced that little Cozcatl had been spared, but I felt sympathy for the other slaves and commoners. The icpacxóchitl was the flower-enlaced garroting cord, which was bad enough.

But Nezahualpíli had also denied them the solace of confessing to a priest of Tlazoltéotl. It meant that their sins would not be swallowed by the goddess Filth Eater—and, since they would then be cremated together with their victims, they would bear their guilt all the way to whichever afterworld they went to, and they would continue to suffer unbearable remorse throughout eternity.

Cozcatl and I were escorted by our guards back to my chambers, and there one of the guards growled, "What is this?" On the outside of my apartment door, at the height of my head, was a sign—the slapped print of a bloody hand—silent reminder that I was not the only culprit who had escaped alive that day, a stark warning that Chimáli did not intend to let his own bereavement go unavenged.

"Some tasteless prankster," I said, shrugging it off. "I will have my slave wash it clean."

Cozcatl took a sponge and a jar of water into the corridor while I waited, listening, just inside the door. It was not long before I heard Jadestone Doll being also returned to custody. I could not distinguish the sound of her tiny feet among the heavier tread of her escort, but when Cozcatl reentered with his jar of reddened water, he said:

"The lady came weeping, master. And with her guards came a priest of Tlazoltéotl."

I mused, "If she is already confessing her sins to be swallowed, that means she has not much time." Indeed, she had very little. It was only shortly afterward that I heard her door open again, when she was taken to the last tryst of her life.

"Master," Cozcatl said timidly, "you and I are both outcasts now."

"Yes," I sighed.

"When we are banished . . ." He wrung his work-roughened little hands. "Will you take me? As your slave and servant?"

"Yes," I said, after thinking for some moments. "You have served me loyally, and I will not abandon you. But in truth, Cozcatl, I do not have the least idea where we shall be going."

The boy and I, kept in confinement, did not witness any of the executions. But I later learned the details of the punishment inflicted on the Lord Joy and the Lady Jadestone Doll, and those details may be of interest to Your Excellency.

The priest of Filth Eater did not even give the girl the opportunity to purge herself entirely to the goddess. In a pretense of kindness, he offered her a drink of chocolate—"to calm your nerves, my daughter"—in which he had mixed an infusion of the plant toloátzin, which is a powerful sleeping drug. Jadestone Doll was probably unconscious before she had recounted even the misdeeds of her tenth year, so she went to her death still burdened with much guilt.

She was carried to the palace maze of which I have spoken, and there she was stripped of all her clothes. Then the old gardener, who alone knew the secret paths, dragged her to the very center of the maze, where Pactli's corpse already lay.

The Lord Joy had earlier been delivered to the convicted kitchen workers, and they were commanded to do one last task before their own execution. Whether they first mercifully put Pactli to death, I do not know, but I doubt it, since they had little reason to feel kindly toward him. They flayed his whole body, except for his head and genitals, and they gutted him and hacked away the other flesh on his body. When all that remained was a skeleton—not a very clean skeleton, still festooned with shreds of raw meat—they used something, perhaps an inserted rod, to stiffen his tepúli erect. That grisly cadaver was taken to the maze while Jadestone Doll was still closeted with her priest.

The girl woke in the middle of the night, at the middle of the maze, to find herself naked and her tipíli snugly impaled, as in happier times, on a tumescent male organ. But her dilated pupils must quickly have adjusted to the pale moonlight, so that she saw the ghastly thing she was embracing.

What happened after that can only be conjectured. Jadestone Doll surely leapt loose from him in horror and fled screaming from that last lover. She must have run off into the maze, again and again, the tortuous paths always bringing her back to the head and bones and upright tepúli of the late Lord Joy. And every time she came back, she would have found him in the company of more and ever more ants and flies and beetles. At last he would have been so covered by squirming scavengers that it must have looked to Jadestone Doll that the cadaver was writhing in an attempt to rise and pursue her. How many times she ran, how many times she dashed herself against the un-yielding thorn walls, how many times she found herself again stumbling onto the carrion of Lord Joy, no one will ever know.

When the gardener brought her out in the morning, she was no longer beautiful. Her face and body were gashed and blood-ied by the thorns. Her fingernails had been torn off. Patches of her scalp showed, where hanks of hair had been ripped loose. Her eye-enhancing drug had worn off, and the pupils were almost invisible points in her bulging, staring eyes. Her mouth was locked wide open in a silent scream. Jadestone Doll had always been so vain of her beauty that she would have been mortified and outraged to have been seen so ugly. But now she could not care. Somewhere in the night, somewhere in the maze, her terrified and pounding heart had finally burst.

When all was over, and Cozcatl and I were released from arrest, the guards told us we were not to go to classes, we were not to mingle or converse with any of our palace acquaintances, and I was not to go back to my writing job in the Speaking Council chamber. We were to wait, keeping ourselves as un-obtrusive as possible, for the Revered Speaker to decide how and where to send us into exile.

So I passed some days in doing nothing but wandering along the lakeshore, kicking pebbles and feeling sorry for myself and mourning the high ambitions I had entertained when I first came to that land. On one of those days, engrossed in my thoughts, I let the twilight catch me far along the shore, and I turned to hurry back to the palace before the darkness fell. Halfway to the city, I came upon a man sitting on a boulder, a man who had not been there when I had passed earlier. He looked much as he had on the two previous occasions I had encountered him: weary of traveling afoot, his skin paled and his features obscured by a coating of the lakeside's alkali dust.

When we had exchanged polite greetings, I said, "Again you come in the dusk, my lord. Do you come from afar?"

"Yes," he said somberly. "From Tenochtítlan, where a war is being prepared."

I said, "You sound as if it will be a war against Texcóco."

"It has not been declared so, but that is what it will be. The

Revered Speaker Ahuítzotl has finally finished building that Great Pyramid, and he plans a dedication ceremony more impressive than any ever known before, and for that he wants countless prisoners for the sacrifice. So he is declaring yet another war against Texcála."

That did not sound much out of the ordinary to me. I said, "Then the armies of The Triple Alliance will fight side by side once again. Why do you call it a war against Texcóco?"

The dusty man said gloomily, "Ahuítzotl claims that almost all his Mexíca forces and his Tecpanéca allies are still engaged in fighting in the west, in Michihuácan, and cannot be sent eastward against Texcála. But that is only an unconvincing pretense. Ahuítzotl was much affronted by the trial and execution of his daughter."

"He cannot deny that she deserved it."

"Which makes him the more angry and vindictive. So he has decreed that Tenochtítlan and Tlácopan will each send a mere token force against the Texcaltéca—and that Texcóco must furnish the bulk of the army." The dusty man shook his head. "Of the warriors who will fight and die to secure the prisoners for sacrifice at the Great Pyramid, perhaps ninety and nine out of each hundred will be Acólhua men. This is Ahuítzotl's way of avenging the death of Jadestone Doll."

I said, "Anyone can see that it is unfair for the Acólhua to bear the brunt. Surely Nezahualpíli could refuse."

"Yes, he could," the traveler said, in his weary voice. "But that could sunder The Triple Alliance—perhaps provoke the irascible Ahuítzotl into declaring a *real* war against Texcóco." Sounding even more melancholy, he went on, "Also, Nezahualpíli may feel that he does owe some atonement for having executed that girl."

"What?" I said indignantly. "After what she did to him?"

"Even for that, he may feel some responsibility. Through having been negligent of her, perhaps. So might some others feel some responsibility." The wayfarer's eyes were on me, and I felt suddenly uneasy. "For this war, Nezahualpíli will need every man he can get. He will doubtless look kindly on volunteers, and probably he will rescind any debts of honor they may feel they owe."

I swallowed and said, "My lord, there are some men who can be of no use in a war."

"Then they can die in it," he said flatly. "For glory, for penance, for repayment of an obligation, for a happy afterlife in the warriors' afterworld, for any other reason. I once heard you speak of your gratitude to Nezahualpíli, and your readiness to demonstrate it."

There was a long silence between us. Then, as if casually changing the subject, the dusty man said, in a conversational tone, "It is rumored that you will soon be leaving Texcóco. If you have your choice, where will you go from here?"

I thought about it for a long time, and the darkness settled all around, and the night wind began to moan across the lake, and at last I said, "To war, my lord. I will go to war."

☩

It was a sight to see: the great army forming up on the empty ground east of Texcóco. The plain bristled with spears and sparkled with bright colors and everywhere the sun glinted from obsidian points and blades. There must have been four or five thousand men all together, but, as the dusty man had foretold, the Revered Speakers Ahuítzotl of the Mexíca and Chimalpopóca of the Tecpanéca had sent only a hundred apiece, and those warriors were hardly their best, being mostly overage veterans and untried recruits.

With Nezahualpíli as battle chief, all was organization and efficiency. Huge feather banners designated the main contingents among the thousands of Acólhua and the puny hundreds from Tenochtítlan and Tlácopan. Multicolored cloth flags marked the separate companies of men under the command of various knights. Smaller guidons marked the smaller units led by the cuáchictin under-officers. There were still other flags around which mustered the noncombatant forces: those responsible for transporting food, water, armor, and spare arms; the physicians and surgeons and priests of various gods; the marching bands of drummers and trumpeters; the battlefield clean-up detachments of Swallowers and Swaddlers.

Although I told myself that I would be fighting for Nezahualpíli, and although I was ashamed at the poor participation of the Mexíca in that war, they were my countrymen, after all. So I went to volunteer my services to their leader, the one and only Mexícatl commander on the field, an Arrow Knight named Xococ. He looked me up and down and said grudgingly, "Well, inexperienced though you may be, you at least appear more physically fit than anybody in this command but me. Report to the Cuachic Extli-Quani."

Old Extli-Quani! I was so pleased to hear his name again that I fairly ran to the guidon where he stood bellowing at a group of unhappy-looking young soldiers. He wore a headdress of feathers and a splinter of bone through the septum of his nose, and held a shield painted with the symbols denoting his name and rank. I knelt and brushed the ground in a perfunctory gesture of kissing the earth, then flung an arm around him as if he had been a long-lost relative, crying delightedly, "Master Blood Glutton! I rejoice to see you again!"

The other soldiers goggled. The elderly cuachic flushed dark red and roughly thrust me away, spluttering, "Unhand me! By the stone balls of Huitzilopóchtli, but this man's army has changed since I was last afield. Doddering old growlers, pimply striplings, and now *this!* Are they enlisting cuilóntin now? To *kiss* the enemy to death?"

"It is I, Master!" I cried. "The commander Xococ told me to join your company." It took me a moment to realize that Blood Glutton must have taught hundreds of schoolboys in his time. It took him a moment to search his memory and find me in some remote corner of it.

"Fogbound, of course!" he exclaimed, though not with such glee as I had evinced. "You are in my company? Are your eyes cured, then? You can see now?"

"Well, no," I had to admit.

He stamped ferociously on a small ant. "My first active duty in ten years," he muttered, "and now this. Maybe cuilóntin would be preferable. Ah, well, Fogbound, fall in with the rest of my trash."

"Yes, Master Cuachic," I said with military crispness. Then I felt a tug at my mantle and I remembered Cozcatl, who had been at my heels all that time. "What orders have you for young Cozcatl?"

"For whom?" he said, puzzled, looking around. Not until he looked down did his gaze light on the light boy. "For *him?*" he exploded.

"He is my slave," I explained. "My body servant."

"Silence in the ranks!" Blood Glutton bawled, both to me and to his soldiers, who had begun to giggle. The old cuachic walked in a circle for a time, composing himself. Then he came and stuck his big face into mine. "Fogbound, there are a few knights and nobles who rate the services of an orderly. You are a yaoquízqui, a new recruit, the lowest rank there is. Not only do you present yourself complete with servant, but what you bring is this runt of an infant!"

"I cannot leave Cozcatl behind," I said. "But he will never be a nuisance. Cannot you assign him to the chaplains or some other rear guard where he can be useful?"

Blood Glutton growled, "And I thought I had escaped from that school to a nice restful war. All right. Runt, you report to that black and yellow guidon yonder. Tell the quartermaster that Extli-Quani ordered you to scullery duty. Now, Fogbound," he said sweetly, persuasively, "if the Mexíca army is arranged to your satisfaction, let us see if you remember anything of battle drill." I and all the other soldiers jumped when he bellowed, *"You misbegotten rabble*—FOUR ABREAST—MAKE RANKS!"

I had learned at The House of Building Strength that training to be a warrior was far different from my childhood play at being one. Now I learned that both the playing and the training were pale imitations of the real thing. To mention just one hardship that the tellers of glorious war stories omit, there is the dirt and the smell. At play or in school, after a day of hard exercise, I had always had the pleasant relief of a bath and a good sweat in the steam house. Here, there were no such facilities. At the end of a day of drilling we were filthy, and we stayed that way, and we stank. So did the open pits dug for our excretory functions. I loathed my own odor of dried sweat and unwashed garments as much as I did the ambient miasma of feet and feces. I regarded the uncleanliness and stench as the nastiest aspect of war. At that time, anyway, before I had *been* to war.

Another thing. I have heard old soldiers complain that, even

in the nominally dry season, a warrior can rely on it that Tlaloc
will mischievously make any and every battle the more difficult
and miserable, with rain drenching a man from above and mud
dragging at his feet below. Well, that was the rainy season,
and Tlaloc sent unremitting rain during the several days we
spent practicing with our weapons and rehearsing the various
maneuvers we would be expected to perform on the battlefield.
It was still raining, and our mantles were dead weights, and
our sandals were ponderous lumps of mud, and our mood was
foul, when at last we set out for Texcála.

That city was thirteen one-long-runs to the east-southeast.
In decent weather, we could have traveled there in two days
of forced march. But we would have arrived breathless and
fatigued, to face an enemy who had had nothing to do but rest
while they waited for us. So, considering the circumstances,
Nezahualpíli ordered that we make the journey more leisurely,
and stretch it over four days, so that we should arrive comparatively unwearied.

For the first two days we tramped directly east, so that we
had to climb and cross only the lower slopes of the volcanic
range which, farther south, became the steep peaks called Tlaloctépetl, Ixtaccíuatl, and Popocatépetl. Then we turned southeast and headed directly toward Texcála city. The whole way,
we went slogging through mud, except when we were slipping
and sliding on wet rock terrain. That was the farthest I had ever
been abroad, and I should have liked to see the landscape. But,
even if my circumscribed vision had not prevented that, the
perpetual veil of rain did. On that journey I saw little more
than the slowly trudging mud-caked feet of the men in front
of me.

We did not march encumbered by our battle armor. Besides
our customary garb, we carried a heavy garment called a
tlamáitl, which we wore in cold weather and rolled up in at
night. Each man also carried a pouch of pinóli, ground maize
sweetened with honey, and a leather bag of water. Each morning before starting to march, and again at the midday rest stop,
we mixed the pinóli and water to make a nourishing if not very
filling meal of atóli mush. At each night's halt, we would have
to wait for the heavier-burdened supply forces to catch up to
us. But then the commissary troops would provide every man

with a substantial meal of hot food, including a cup of thick, nutritious, spirit-lifting hot chocolate.

Whatever his other duties, Cozcatl always brought my evening meal with his own hands, and often managed to get me a larger than standard portion or to slip me a stolen fruit or sweet. Some of the other men of Blood Glutton's company grumbled or sneered at the way I was coddled, so I weakly tried to refuse the extras Cozcatl brought.

He admonished me, "Do not act noble and deny yourself, master. You are not depriving your fellows in these forward columns. Do you not know that the best-fed men are the ones who stay farthest back from the fighting? The porters and cooks and message carriers. They are also the most boastful about their service. I only wish that I could somehow sneak a pot of hot water up here. Forgive me, master, but you smell atrocious."

Late in the wet, gray afternoon of the fourth day, when we were still at least one-long-run from Texcála, our forward scouts espied the waiting Texcaltéca forces, and hurried back to report to Nezahualpíli. The enemy were waiting, in strength, on the other side of a river we should have to cross. In dry weather the river was probably no more than a shallow trickle, but after all those days of steady rain it was a formidable barrier. Though still no more than hip high at its deepest, it was swift-running and broader than arrow range from bank to bank. The enemy's plan was obvious. While we waded across the river, we should be slow-moving targets, unable either to use our weapons or to dodge the enemy's. With their arrows and atlatl-flung javelins, the Texcaltéca expected to decimate and demoralize us before we ever reached the farther side of the river.

It is told that Nezahualpíli smiled and said, "Very well. The trap has been so nicely prepared by the enemy and Tlaloc alike, we must not disappoint them. In the morning we will fall into it."

He gave orders for our army to halt for the night where it was, still well distant from the river, and for all commanding knights and under-officers to gather about him and hear their instructions. We mere soldiers sat or squatted or stretched out on the soggy ground, while the commissary workers began preparing our evening meal, an ample one, for we would have no time to eat even atóli in the morning. The armorers unpacked and laid the stacks of spare weapons handy for distribution as needed the next day. The drummers tightened their drumheads, made slack by dampness. The physicians and chaplain-priests prepared their medicines and operating instruments, their incense and books of incantations, so that they were ready either to attend tomorrow's injured or to hear, on behalf of Filth Eater, the confessions of the dying.

Blood Glutton returned from the command conference as we were being served our food and chocolate. He said, "When we have done eating, we will don our battle costume and arm ourselves. Then, when the dark has come, we will move to our assigned positions, and there we will sleep in place, for we must be early awake."

As we ate, he told us Nezahualpíli's plan. At dawn, a full third of our army, in trim formation, complete with drums and conch trumpets, would march boldly up to and into the river as if ignorant of any danger waiting on the other side. When the enemy let fly its missiles, the attackers would scatter and splash about, to give an impression of surprised confusion. When the rain of missiles got intolerable, the men would turn and flee the way they had come, in seemingly undisciplined rout. Nezahualpíli's belief was that the Texcaltéca would be deceived by that disarray and would incautiously give chase, so excited by their apparent easy triumph that they would give no thought to its possibly being a ruse.

Meanwhile, the remainder of Nezahualpíli's army would have been waiting, concealed in rocks, shrubbery, trees on both sides of the long line of march leading to the river. Not a man of them would show himself or use a weapon until our "retreating" forces had enticed the entire Texcála army across the river. The Texcaltéca would be running along a corridor between hidden walls of warriors. Then Nezahualpíli, watching from a high place, would give the nod to his drummers, and the drums would give a signal crash of noise. His men on both sides of the ambuscade would rise up, and the walls of the corridor would close together, trapping the enemy between them.

A gray-haired old soldier of our company asked, "And where will we be stationed?"

Blood Glutton grunted unhappily. "Almost as far back and safe as the cooks and priests."

"What?" exclaimed the elderly veteran. "Tramp all this way and not get close enough even to *hear* the clash of obsidian?"

Our cuáchic shrugged. "Well, you know how shamefully few we are. We can hardly blame Nezahualpíli for denying us a share of the battle, considering that he is fighting Ahuítzotl's war for him. Our Knight Xococ pleaded that we might at least march in the front, into the river, and be the bait for the Texcaltéca—we would be the likeliest to be killed—but Nezahualpíli refused us even that chance at glory."

I personally was glad enough to hear it, but the other soldier was still disgruntled. "Do we just sit here like lumps, then, and wait to escort the victorious Acólhua and their captives back to Tenochtítlan?"

"Not quite," said Blood Glutton. "We may get to take a prisoner or two ourselves. Some of the trapped Texcaltéca may break out past the closing walls of Acólhua warriors. Our Mexíca and Tecpanéca companies will be fanned out to either side, north and south, as a net to snare any who do elude the ambush."

"Be lucky if we snare so much as a rabbit," grumbled the gray-haired soldier. He stood up and said to the rest of us. "All you yaoquízque fighting for the first time, know this. Before you get into your armor, go off in the bushes and evacuate yourselves good and empty. You will have loose bowels once the drums begin, and no chance to wriggle out of that tight quilting."

He went away to take his own advice, and I followed. As I squatted, I heard him mumbling nearby, "Almost forgot this thing," and I glanced over. He took from his pouch a small object wrapped in paper. "A proud new father gave it to me to bury on the battleground," he said. "His new son's navel string and little war shield." He dropped the packet at his feet, stamped it into the mud, then squatted to urinate and defecate on it.

Well, I thought to myself, so much for that little boy's tonáli. I wondered if my own natal shield and string had been likewise disposed of.

While we lesser soldiers struggled into the quilted cotton

body armor, the knights were donning their flamboyant costumes, and they were splendid to see. There were three orders of knighthood: the Jaguar and the Eagle, to one of which a warrior might get elected for having distinguished himself in war, and the Arrow, to which belonged those who had achieved expert marksmanship and many killings with that most inaccurate of missiles.

A Jaguar Knight wore a real jaguar skin as a sort of cloak, with the big cat's head as a helmet. Its skull was removed, of course, but its front teeth were glued in place, so that its upper fangs curved down the knight's forehead and its lower hooked upward over his chin. His body armor was tinted like a jaguar's hide: tawny with dark brown markings. An Eagle Knight wore for a helmet an oversized eagle head made of wood and molded paper, covered with real eagle feathers, the open beak hooking forward above his forehead and below his chin. His body armor was also covered with eagle feathers, his sandals had artificial talons projecting beyond their toes, and his feather mantle was more or less shaped like folded wings. An Arrow Knight wore a helmet shaped like the head of whatever bird he chose—so long as it was of a lesser breed than the eagle—and his armor was covered with the same feathers that he preferred for fletching his arrows.

All the knights carried wooden, leather, or wickerwork shields covered with feathers, and those feathers were worked into colorful mosaic designs, each knight's design being his own name symbols. Many knights had become known for their bravery and prowess, so it was an act of daring for them to go into battle flaunting their symbols on their shields. They were sure to be sought out for attack by some enemy soldier, himself eager to enhance his own name as "the man who bested the great Xococ" or whomever. We yaoquízque carried unadorned shields, and our armor was uniformly white—until it got uniformly muddy. We were allowed no blazonings, but some of the older men tucked feathers into their hair or streaked their faces with paint to proclaim at least that they were not fighting their first campaign.

Once armored, I and numerous other novice soldiers went farther to the rear, to the priests, who yawned as they heard our necessarily hasty confessions to Talzoltéotl, and then gave us a medicine to prevent our showing cowardice in the coming battle. I really did not believe that anything swallowed into the stomach could quell a fear that exists in the recalcitrant head and feet, but I obediently took my sip of the potion: fresh rainwater in which was mixed white clay, powdered amethyst, leaves of the cannabis plant, flowers of the dogbane, the cacao bush, and the bell orchid. When we returned to group around Xococ's flag, the Mexícatl knight said:

"Know this. The object of tomorrow's battle is to secure prisoners for sacrifice to Huitzilopóchtli. We are to strike with the flat of our weapons, to stun, to take men alive." He paused, then said ominously, "However, while this is for us merely a War of Flowers, for the Texcaltéca it is not. They will fight for their lives, and fight to take ours. The Acólhua will suffer most—or win the most glory. But I want all of you, my men, to remember: if you should encounter a fleeing enemy, your orders are to capture him. His orders are to kill you."

With that not very inspiriting speech, he led us out into the rainy darkness—each of us armed with a spear and a maquáhuitl— northward at a right angle off the previous line of march, dropping off companies of men at intervals along the way. Blood Glutton's company was the first to be detached, and, when the other Mexíca had plodded on, the cuachic gave us one last bit of instruction:

"Those of you who have fought before, and have previously taken an enemy prisoner, you know you must take the next one unaided, or you will be accounted unmanly. However, you new yaoquízque, if you have a chance at taking your first captive, you are allowed to call for the help of as many as five of your fellow recruits, and you will all share equally in credit for the capture. Now follow me. . . . Here is a tree. You there, soldier, you climb and hide in its branches. . . . You there, crouch in that jumble of rocks. . . . Fogbound, you get behind this bush. . . ."

And so we were sown in a long line stretching northward, our separate posts a hundred strides or more apart. Even when daylight came, none of us would be within sight of the next man, but we would all be within calling distance. I doubt that many of us slept that night, except perhaps the hardened old veterans. I know I did not, for my shrub offered concealment only if I hunkered on my heels. The rain continued to drizzle down. My overmantle soaked through, and then my cotton armor, until it hung so clammy and heavy that I thought I might never be able to stand erect when the time came.

After what seemed like a sheaf of years of misery, I heard faint sounds from the southward, from my right. The main bodies of Acólhua troops would be preparing to move, some into ambuscade, some into the very teeth of the Texcaltéca. What I heard was a chaplain chanting the traditional prayer before battle, though only snatches of it were audible to me so far away:

"Oh, mighty Huitzilopóchtli, god of battles, a war is being mounted. . . . Choose now, oh great god, those who must kill, those who must be killed, those who must be taken as xochimíque that you may drink their hearts' blood. . . . Oh, lord of war, we beg you to smile upon those who will die on this field or on your altar. . . . Let them proceed straight to the house of the sun, to live again, loved and honored, among the valiants who have preceded them. . . ."

Ba-ra-ROOM! Stiff as I was, I started violently at the combined thunder of the massed "drums which tear out the heart." Not even the muffling rain all about could mute their earthquake rumble to anything less than bone-shaking. I hoped the fearsome noise would not frighten the Texcála troops into flight before they could be lured into Nezahualpíli's surprise envelopment. The roar of drums was joined by the long wails and honks and bleats of the conch trumpets, then the whole noise began slowly to diminish, as the musicians led the decoy part of the army away from me, along the line of march toward the river and the waiting enemy.

What with the rainclouds practically within arm's reach overhead, the day did not begin with anything like a sunrise, but it was by then perceptibly lighter. Light enough, anyway, for me to see that the shrub behind which I had sat hunched all night was only a wizened, nearly leafless huixáchi, which would not adequately have hidden a ground squirrel. I would have to seek a better place to lurk, and I still had plenty of time to do so. I got up creakily, carrying my maquáhuitl and dragging my spear so it was not visible above the surrounding scrub, and I moved off in a sort of crouching lope.

What I could not tell you, even to this day, reverend friars, not even if you were to put me to the Inquisitorial persuasions, is why I went in the direction I did. To find other concealment, I could have moved backward or to either side, and still have been within hailing distance of the others of my company. But where I went was forward, eastward, toward the place where the battle would soon commence. I can only presume that something inside me was telling me, "You are on the fringe of your first war, Dark Cloud, perhaps the only war you will ever be engaged in. It would be a pity to stay on the fringe, a pity not to experience as much of it as you can."

However, I did not get near the river where the Acólhua confronted the Texcaltéca. I did not even hear sounds of battle until the Acólhua, as Nezahualpíli had hoped, rushed after them in full force. Then I heard the bellow and whoop of war cries, the shrieks and curses of wounded men, and, above all, the whistling of arrows and warbling of flung javelins. All our mock weapons at school, harmlessly blunted, had made no distinctive noise. But what I heard now were real missiles, pointed and bladed with keen obsidian, and, as if they exulted in their intent and ability to deal death, they *sang* as they flew through the air. Ever afterward, whenever I drew a history that included a battle, I always pictured the arrows, spears, and javelins accompanied by the curly symbol that means singing.

I never got closer than the noise of the battle—first coming from my right front, where the armies had met at the river, then progressing farther to my right, as the Acólhua fled and the Texcaltéca gave chase. Then Nezahualpíli's signal drums abruptly boomed for the corridor to close its walls, and the tumult of battle sounds multiplied and increased in volume: the brittle clash of weapons against weapons, the thuds of jaguar grunts, eagle screams, owl hoots. I could envision the Acólhua trying to restrain their own blows and thrusts, while the Texcaltéca desperately fought with all their strength and skill, and with no compunction against killing.

I wished I could see it, for it would have been an instructive exhibition of the Acólhua's fighting skills. By the nature of the battle, theirs *had* to be the greater art. But there was rolling land between me and the battle site, and shrubbery and clumps of trees, and the gray curtain of rain, and of course my own nearsightedness. I might have tried to go nearer, but I was interrupted by a hesitant tap on my shoulder.

Still in my protective crouch, I whirled and leveled my spear, and almost skewered Cozcatl before I recognized him. The boy stood, also hunched over, with a warning finger to his lips. With the breath I had gasped in, I hissed out, "Cozcatl, curse you! What are you doing here?"

He whispered, "Following you, master. I have been near you all the night. I thought you might need a better pair of eyes."

"Impertinent pest! I have not yet—"

"No, master, not yet," he said. "But now, yes, you do. One of the enemy approaches. He would have seen you before you could see him."

"What? An enemy?" I hunkered even lower.

"Yes, master. A Jaguar Knight in full regalia. He must have fought his way out of the ambush." Cozcatl risked raising his head far enough for a quick look. "I think he hopes to circle around and fall upon our men again from an unexpected direction."

"Look again," I said urgently. "Tell me exactly where he is and where he is headed."

The little slave bobbed up and down again and said, "He is perhaps forty longpaces to your left front, master. He is moving slowly, bent over, though he does not appear to be wounded, merely cautious. If he continues as he goes, he will pass between two trees that stand ten long paces directly to your front."

With those directions, a blind man could have managed the interception. I said, "I am going to those trees. You stay here and keep a discreet eye on him. If he notices my movement, you will know it. Give me a shout and then run for the rear."

I left my spear and my overmantle lying there, and took only my maquáhuitl. Squirming almost as close to the ground as a snake does, I moved ahead until the trees loomed out of the rain. The two trees stood amid an undergrowth of high grass and low shrubs, through which an almost imperceptible deer trail had been lightly trampled. I had to assume that the fugitive Texcaltécatl was following that trail. I heard no warning call from Cozcatl, so I had got into position unobserved. I squatted on my heels at the base of one tree, keeping it between me and the man's approach. Holding my maquáhuitl with both fists, I brought it back behind my shoulder, parallel to the ground, and held it poised.

Through the drizzle sound of the rain, I heard only the faintest rustle of grass and twigs. Then a muddy foot in a muddy sandal, its sole rimmed with jaguar claws, was set down on the ground directly in front of my hiding place. A moment later, the second foot stood beside it. The man, now sheltered between the trees, must have risked standing fully upright to look about and get his bearings.

I swung the obsidian-edged sword as I had once swung at a nopáli trunk, and the knight seemed to hang in the air for an instant before he crashed full length on the ground. His feet in their sandals stayed where they were, severed above the ankles. I was on him in one bound, kicking away the maquáhuitl he still grasped, and laying the blunt point of my own against his throat, and panting the ritual words spoken by a captor to his captive. In my time, we did not say anything so crude as, "You are my prisoner." We always said courteously, as I said to the fallen knight, "You are my beloved son."

He snarled viciously, "Then bear witness! I curse all the gods and all their get!" But that outburst was understandable. After all, he was a knight of the elite Jaguar order, and he had been cut down—in his own one moment of carelessness—by a young, obviously new and untried soldier of the lowly yaoquízqui rank. I knew that, had we met face to face, he could have minced me at his leisure, sliver by sliver. He knew it too, and his face was purple and his teeth grated together. But at last his rage ebbed to resignation, and he replied with the traditional words of surrender, "You are my revered father."

I lifted my weapon from his neck and he sat up, to gaze stonily at the blood gushing from his leg stumps and at his two feet still standing patiently, almost unbloodied, side by side on the deer trail ahead of him. The knight's jaguar costume, though rain-drenched and mud-smeared, was still a handsome thing. The dappled skin which depended from the fierce helmet head was fashioned so that the animal's front legs served as sleeves, coming down the man's arms so that the claws rattled at his wrists. His fall had not broken the strap which held his brightly feathered round shield to his left forearm.

There was another rustling in the brush, and Cozcatl joined us, saying quietly but proudly, "My master has taken his first war prisoner, all unaided."

"And I do not want him to die," I said, still panting—from excitement, not exertion. "He is bleeding badly."

"Perhaps the stumps could be tied off," the man suggested, in the heavily accented Náhuatl of Texcála.

Cozcatl quickly unbound the leather thongs of his sandals and I tied one tightly around each of my prisoner's legs, just below the knee. The bleeding dwindled to an oozing. I stood up between the trees and looked and listened, as the knight had done. I was somewhat surprised at what I heard—which was not much. The uproar of battle to the south had diminished to no more than a hubbub like that of a crowded marketplace, a babble interspersed with shouted commands. Obviously, during my little skirmish, the main battle had been concluded.

I said to the glum warrior, meaning it for condolence, "You are not the only captive, my beloved son. It appears that your whole army has been defeated." He only grunted. "Now I will take you to have your wounds tended. I think I can carry you."

"Yes, I weigh less now," he said sardonically.

I bent down with my back to him and took his shortened legs under my arms. He looped his arms around my neck, and his blazoned shield covered my chest as if it had been my own. Cozcatl had already brought my mantle and spear; now he collected my wicker shield and my blood-stained maquáhuitl. Tucking those things under his arms, he picked up an amputated foot in either hand and followed me as I moved off through the rain. I trudged toward the murmurous noise to the south, where the fighting had finally wound down, and where I supposed our army would be disentangling the resultant confusion. Halfway there, I met the members of my own company, as Blood Glutton was collecting them from their various overnight stations to march them back to the main body of the army.

"Fogbound!" shouted the cuachic. "How dared you desert your post? Where have you—?" Then his roaring stopped, but his mouth stayed open, and his eyes opened almost as wide.

"May I be damned to Míctlan! Look what my most treasured student has brought! I must inform the commander Xococ!" And he dashed away.

My fellow soldiers regarded me and my trophy with awe and envy. One of them said, "I will help you carry him, Fogbound."

"No!" I gasped, the only breath I could spare. No one else would claim a share of the credit for my exploit.

And so I—bearing the sullen Jaguar Knight, trailed by the jubilant Cozcatl, escorted by Xococ and Blood Glutton proudly striding on either side of me—finally came to the main body of both armies, at the place where the battle had ended. A tall pole bore the flag of surrender which the Texcaltéca had raised: a square of wide gold mesh, like a gilded piece of fishnet.

The scene was not of celebration or even tranquil enjoyment of victory. Most of those warriors of both sides who had not been wounded, or were only trivially wounded, lay about in postures of extreme exhaustion. Others, both Acólhua and Texcaltéca, were not lying still but writhing and contorting, as they variously screamed or moaned a ragged chorus of "Yya, yyaha, yya ayya ouiya," while the physicians moved among them with their medicines and ointments, and the priests with their mumbles. A few ablebodied men were assisting the doctors, while others went about collecting scattered weapons, dead bodies, and detached parts of bodies: hands, arms, legs, even heads. It would have been difficult for a stranger to tell which of the men in that wasteland of carnage were the victors and which the vanquished. Over all hung the commingled smell of blood, sweat, body dirt, urine, and feces.

Weaving as I walked, I peered about, looking for someone in authority to whom I might deliver my captive. But the word had got there before me. I was suddenly confronted by the chief of all the chiefs. Nezahualpíli himself. He was garbed as a Uey-Tlatoáni should be—in cloak—but under that he wore the feathered and quilted armor of an Eagle Knight, and it was spattered with blood spots. He had not just stood aloof in command, but had joined in the fighting himself. Xococ and Blood Glutton respectfully dropped several steps behind me as Nezahualpíli greeted me with a raised hand.

I eased my captive down to the ground, made a tired gesture

of presentation, and said, with the last of my breath, "My lord, this—this is my—well-beloved son."

"And this," the knight said with irony, nodding up at me, "this is my revered father. Mixpantzínco, Lord Speaker."

"Well done, young Mixtli," said the commander. "Ximo-panólti, Jaguar Knight Tlaui-Colotl."

"I greet you, old enemy," said my prisoner to my lord. "This is the first time we have met outside the frenzy of battle."

"And the last time, it appears," said the Uey-Tlatoáni, kneeling down companionably beside him. "A pity. I shall miss you. Those were some wondrous duels we had, you and I. Indeed, I looked forward to the one that would not be inconclusively ended by the intervention of our underlings." He sighed. "It is sometimes as saddening to lose a worthy foe as to lose a good friend."

I listened to that exchange in some amazement. It had not earlier occurred to me to notice the device worked in feathers on my prisoner's shield: Tlaui-Colotl. The name, Armed Scorpion, meant nothing to me, but obviously it was famous in the world of professional soldiers. Tlaui-Colotl was one of those knights of whom I have spoken: a man whose renown was such that it devolved upon the man who finally bested him.

Armed Scorpion said to Nezahualpíli: "I slew four of your knights, old enemy, to fight free of your cursed ambush. Two Eagles, a Jaguar, and an Arrow. But if I had known what my tonáli had in store"—he threw me a look of amused disdain— "I would have let one of them take me."

"You will fight other knights before you die," the Revered Speaker told him, consolingly. "I will see to that. Now let us ease your injuries." He turned and shouted to a doctor working on a man nearby.

"Only a moment, my lord," said the doctor. He was bent over an Acólhuatl warrior whose nose had been sliced off, but fortunately recovered, though somewhat mashed and muddy from having been much trodden upon. The surgeon was sewing it back onto the hole in the soldier's face, using a maguey thorn for a needle and one of his own long hairs for a thread. The replacement looked more hideous than the hole. Then the doctor hastily slathered the nose with a paste of salted honey, and came scurrying to my prisoner.

"Undo those thongs on his legs," he said to a soldier assistant, and to another, "Scoop out from the fire yonder a basin of the hottest coals." Armed Scorpion's stumps began slowly to bleed again, then to spurt, and they were gushing by the time the assistant came bearing a wide, shallow bowl of white-hot embers, over which small flames flickered.

"My lord physician," Cozcatl said helpfully, "here are his feet."

The doctor grunted in exasperation. "Take them away. Feet cannot be stuck back on like blobs of noses." To the wounded man he said, "One at a time or both at once?"

"As you will," Armed Scorpion said indifferently. He had never once cried out or whimpered with pain, and he did not then, as the doctor took one of his stumps in each hand and plunged both their raw ends into the dish of glowing coals. Cozcatl turned and fled the sight. The blood sizzled and made a pink cloud of stinking steam. The flesh crackled and made a blue smoke that was less offensive. Armed Scorpion regarded the process as calmly as did the physician, who lifted the now charred and blackened leg ends out of the coals. The searing had sealed off the slashed vessels, and no more blood flowed. The doctor liberally applied to the stumps a healing salve: beeswax mixed with the yolks of birds' eggs, the juice of alder bark and of the barbasco root. Then he stood up and reported, "The man is in no danger of dying, my lord, but it will be some days before he recovers from the weakness of having lost so much blood."

Nezahualpíli said, "Let there be a noble's litter prepared for him. The eminent Armed Scorpion will lead the column of captives." Then he turned to Xococ, regarded him coldly, and said:

"We Acólhua lost many men today, and more will die of their injuries before we see home again. The enemy lost about the same, but the surviving prisoners are almost as many as our surviving warriors. To the number of thousands. Your Revered Speaker Ahuítzotl should be pleased at the work we have done for him and his god. If he and Chimalpopóca of Tlácopan had sent genuine armies of full strength, we might well have gone on to vanquish the entire land of Texcála." He shrugged. "Ah, well. How many captives did your Mexíca take?"

Knight Xococ shuffled his feet, coughed, pointed to Armed Scorpion, and mumbled, "My lord, you are looking at the only one. Perhaps the Tecpanéca took a few stragglers, I do not know yet. But of the Mexíca"—he motioned at me—"only this yaoquízqui . . ."

"No longer a yaoquízqui, as you well know," Nezahualpíli said tartly. "His first capture makes him an iyac in rank. And this single captive—you heard him say he slew four Acólhua knights today. Let me tell you: Armed Scorpion has never troubled to *count* his victims of lesser rank than knight. But he has probably accounted for hundreds of Acólhua, Mexíca, and Tecpanéca in his time."

Blood Glutton was sufficiently impressed to murmur, "Fogbound is a hero in truth."

"No," I said. "It was not really my sword stroke, but a stroke of fortune, and I could not have done it without Cozcatl, and—"

"But it happened," Nezahualpíli said, silencing me. To Xococ he continued, "Your Revered Speaker may wish to reward the young man with something higher than iyac rank. In this engagement he alone has upheld the Mexíca reputation for valor and initiative. I suggest that you present him in person to Ahuítzotl, along with a letter which I myself will write."

"As you command, my lord," said Xococ, almost literally kissing the earth. "We are very proud of our Fogbound."

"Then call him by some other name! Now, enough of this loitering about. Get your troops in order, Xococ. I appoint you and them the Swallowers and Swaddlers. Move!"

Xococ took that like a slap in the face, which it was, but he and Blood Glutton obediently went off at a trot. As I have told earlier, the Swaddlers were those who either tied or took charge of the prisoners so that none escaped. The Swallowers went about the whole area of battle and beyond, seeking out and knifing to death those of the wounded who were beyond relief. When that was done, they heaped and burned the bodies, allies and enemies together, each with a chip of jadestone in its mouth or hand.

For a few moments, Nezahualpíli and I were alone together. He said, "You have done here today a deed to be proud of— and to be ashamed of. You rendered harmless the one man most to be feared among all our opponents on this field. And you brought a noble knight to an ignoble end. Even when Armed Scorpion reaches the afterworld of heroes, his eternal bliss will have an eternally bitter taste, because all his comrades there will know that he was ludicrously brought down by a callow, shortsighted, common recruit."

"My lord," I said, "I only did what I thought was right."

"As you have done before," he said, and sighed. "Leaving for others the bitter aftertaste. I do not chide you, Mixtli. It was long ago foretold that your tonáli was to know the truth about the things of this world, and to make the truth known. I would ask only one thing."

I bowed my head and said, "My lord does not ask anything of a commoner. He commands and is obeyed."

"What I ask cannot be commanded. I entreat you, Mixtli, from now henceforward, to be prudent, even gingerly in your handling of the right and the truth. Such things can cut as cruelly as any obsidian blade. And, like the blade, they can also cut the man who wields them."

He turned abruptly away from me, called to a swift-messenger, and told him, "Put on a green mantle and braid your hair in the manner signifying good news. Take a clean new shield and maquáhuitl. Run to Tenochtítlan and, on your way to the palace, run brandishing the shield and sword through as many streets as you can, so the people may rejoice and strew flowers in your path. Let Ahuítzotl know that he has the victory and the prisoners he wanted."

The last few words Nezahualpíli did not speak to the messenger, but to himself: "That the life and the death and the very name of Jadestone Doll are now to be forgotten."

✠

Nezahualpíli and his army parted from the rest of us there, to march back the way we all had come. The Mexíca and Tecpanéca contingents, plus myself and the long column of prisoners, went directly west on a shorter route to Tenochtítlan: across the pass between the peak of Tlaloctépetl and that of Ixtaccíuatl, thence along the southern shore of Lake Texcóco.

It was a slow march, since so many of the wounded had to hobble or, like Armed Scorpion, be carried. But it was not a difficult journey. For one thing, the rain had finally stopped; we enjoyed sunny days and temperate nights. For another, once we had crossed the fairly rugged mountain pass, the march was along the level salt flats bordering the lake, with the serene, whispering waters on our right and the slopes of thick, whispering forests on our left.

That surprises you, reverend friars? To hear me speak of forests so near this city? Ah, yes, as short a time ago as that, this whole Valley of México was abundantly green with trees: the old-old cypresses, numerous kinds of oak, short- and long-leaved pines, sweet bay, acacias, laurel, mimosa. I know nothing of your country of Spain, my lords, or of your province of Castile, but they must be sere and desolate lands. I see your foresters denude one of our green hills for timbers and firewood. They strip it of all its verdure and trees that have grown for sheaves of years. Then they step back to admire the dun-gray barren that remains, and they sigh nostalgically, "Ah, Castile!"

We came at last to the promontory between the lakes Texcóco and Xochimílco, what remained of the Culhua people's once extensive lands. We smartly trimmed our formation to make a good show as we marched through the town of Ixtapalápan and, when we were past it, Blood Glutton said to me, "It has been some time since you saw Tenochtítlan, has it not?"

"Yes," I said. "Fourteen years or so."

"You will find it changed. Grander than ever. It will be visible from this next rise of the road." When we reached that eminence, he made an expansive gesture and said, "Behold!" I could, of course, see the great island-city yonder, shining white as I remembered it, but I could not make out any detail of it—except, when I squinted hard, there seemed to be an even more shining whiteness to it. "The Great Pyramid," Blood Glutton said reverently. "You should be proud that your valor has contributed to its dedication."

At the point of the promontory we came to the town of Mexicaltzínco, and from there a causeway vaulted out across the water to Tenochtítlan. The stone avenue was wide enough for twenty men to walk comfortably side by side, but we ranked our prisoners by fours, with guards walking alongside at intervals. We did not do that to stretch our parade to a more impressive length, but because the bridge was crowded on both sides with city folk come to greet our arrival. The people cheered and owl-hooted and pelted us with flowers as if our victory had been entirely the doing of us few Mexíca and Tecpanéca.

Halfway to the city, the causeway broadened out into a vast platform which supported the fort of Acachinánco, a defense against any invader's trying to take that route into Tenochtítlan. The fort, though supported entirely by pilings, was almost as big as either of the two towns we had just passed through on the mainland. Its garrison of troops also joined in welcoming us—drumming and trumpeting, shouting war cries, pounding their spears on their shields—but I could only look scornfully at them for their not having been with us in the battle.

When I and the others at the front of the column were striding into the great central plaza of Tenochtítlan, the tail of our parade of prisoners was still trooping out of Mexicaltzínco, two and a half one-long-runs behind us. In the plaza, The Heart of the One World, we Mexíca dropped out of the column and left it to the Tecpanéca soldiers. They turned the captives sharp left and marched them off along the avenue and then the causeway leading westward to Tlácopan. The prisoners would be quartered somewhere on the mainland outside that city until the day appointed for the dedication of the pyramid.

The pyramid. I turned to look at it, and I gaped as I might have done when I was a child. During my life I would see bigger icpac tlamanacáltin, but never one so luminously bright and new. It was the tallest edifice in Tenochtítlan, dominating the city. It was an awesome spectacle to those who had eyes to see it from away across the waters, for the twin temples on top of it stood proudly, arrogantly, magnificently high above every other thing visible between the city and the mainland mountains. But I had little time to look at it or at any of the other new landmarks built since I had last been in The Heart of the One World. A young page from the palace elbowed his way through the throng, asking anxiously for the Arrow Knight Xococ.

"I am he," said Xococ importantly.

The page said, "The Revered Speaker Ahuítzotl commands that you attend upon him at once, my lord, and that you bring to him the iyac named Tliléctic-Mixtli."

"Oh," said Xococ fretfully. "Very well. Where are you, Fogbound? I mean Iyac Mixtli. Come along." I privately thought we ought to bathe and steam ourselves and seek clean clothes before we presented ourselves to the Uey-Tlatoáni, but I accompanied him without protest. As the page led us through the crowd, Xococ instructed me, "Make your obeisances humbly and graciously, but then excuse yourself and retire, so that the Revered Speaker may hear my account of the victory."

Among the plaza's new features was the Snake Wall surrounding it. Built of stone, plastered smooth with white gesso, it stood twice as high as a man and its upper edge undulated like the curves of a snake. The wall, both inside and out, was studded with a pattern of projecting stones, each carved and painted to represent a serpent's head. The wall was interrupted in three places, where the three broad avenues led north, west, and south out of the plaza. And at intervals it had great wooden doorways leading to the major buildings set outside the wall.

One of those was the new palace built for Ahuítzotl, beyond the northeast corner of the Snake Wall. It was easily as big as that of any of his predecessor rulers in Tenochtítlan, as big as Nezahualpíli's palace in Texcóco, and even more elaborate and luxurious. Since it had been so recently built, it was decorated with all the latest styles of art and contained all the most modern conveniences. For example, the upper-floor rooms had ceiling lids which could be slid open to admit skylight in good weather.

Perhaps the most noticeable feature of the hollow-square-shaped palace was that it straddled one of the city's canals. Thus the building could be entered from the plaza, through its Snake Wall gate, or it could be entered by canoe. A nobleman idling in his oversized, cushioned acáli—or a common boatman paddling a freight of sweet potatoes—could take that delightfully hospitable route to wherever he was going. On his way, he would drift through a cavelike corridor of dazzling new-painted murals, then through Ahuítzotl's lushly gardened courtyard, then through another cavernous hall full of impressive new-carved statuary, before emerging into the public canal again.

The page led us, almost at a run, through the Snake Wall portal to the palace, then along galleries and around corners, to a room whose entire adornment consisted of hunting and war weapons hung upon the walls. The skins of jaguars, ocelots, cuguars, and alligators made rugs for the floor and covers for the low chairs and benches. Ahuítzotl, a man of square figure, square head, and square face, sat upon an elevated throne. It was completely covered by the thick-furred pelt of one of the giant bears of the northern mountains far beyond these lands—the fearsome beast that you Spaniards call the oso pardo, or grizzled bear. Its massive head loomed over that of the Uey-Tlatoáni, and its snarling open mouth showed teeth the size of my fingers. Ahuítzotl's face, just below it, was not much less fierce.

The page, Xococ, and I dropped to make the gesture of kissing the earth. When Ahuítzotl gruffly bade us stand, the Arrow Knight said, "As you commanded, Revered Speaker, I bring the iyac named—"

Ahuítzotl interrupted brusquely, "You also bring a letter from Nezahualpíli. Give it to us. When you return to your command quarters, Xococ, mark on your roster that the Iyac Mixtli has been elevated by our order to the rank of tequíua. You are dismissed."

"But, my lord," said Xococ, stricken. "Do you not wish my report on the Texcála battle?"

"What do you know about it? Except that you marched from here to there and home again? We will hear it from the Tequíua Mixtli, who fought in it. We said you are dismissed, Xococ. Go."

The knight gave me a hateful look and slithered backward from the room. I paid little notice, being myself in something of a daze. After having served in the army less than a month, I had already been promoted to a level that most men might have to fight many wars to attain. The rank of tequíua, which means "beast of prey," was ordinarily awarded only to those who had slain or captured at least four enemies in battle.

I had approached that interview with Ahuítzotl rather less than eagerly—not knowing what to expect—since I had been so closely associated with the Uey-Tlatoáni's late daughter and her downfall. But it seemed that he had not connected me with that scandal; there was some advantage in having a common name like Mixtli. I was relieved that he regarded me as benignly as his severe countenance would allow. Also, I was intrigued by his manner of speech. It was the first time I had ever heard a man alone refer to himself as "we" and "us."

"Nezahualpíli's letter," he said, when he had perused it, "is considerably more flattering to you, young soldier, than it is to us. He sarcastically suggests that, next time, we send him some companies of belligerent scribblers like yourself, instead of blunt arrows like Xococ." Ahuítzotl smiled as well as he could, even more resembling the bear's head over his throne. "He also suggests that, with sufficient forces, this war could finally have subdued that obstreperous land of the Texcaltéca. Do you agree?"

"I can hardly disagree, my lord, with an experienced commander like the Revered Speaker Nezahualpíli. I know only that his tactics defeated one entire army in Texcála. If we could have pushed the siege, any subsequent defenses must have been weaker and weaker."

"You are a word knower," said Ahuítzotl. "Can you write out for us a detailed account of the dispositions and movements of the various forces engaged? With comprehensible maps?"

"Yes, my Lord Speaker. I can do that."

"Do it. You have six days before the temple dedication ceremonies get under way, when all work will cease and you will have the privilege of presenting your illustrious prisoner for his Flowery Death. Page, have the palace steward provide a suitable suite of rooms for this man, and all the working materials he requires. You are dismissed, Tequíua Mixtli."

My chambers were as commodious and comfortable as those I had enjoyed at Texcóco, and, since they were on the second floor, I had the advantage of skylight for my work. The palace steward offered me a servant, but I sent the page to find Cozcatl instead, and then sent Cozcatl to find us each a change of clothes, while I bathed and steamed myself, several times over.

First I drew the map. It occupied many folded pages and opened to considerable length. I began it with the city symbol of Texcóca, then put the little black footprints showing the route of our journey eastward from there, with the stylized drawings of mountains and such to mark each of our overnight stops, and finally put the symbol for river, where the battle had been joined. There I placed the universally recognized symbol of overwhelming victory: the drawing of a burning temple— though in actuality we had not seen or destroyed any teocáli— and the symbol of our taking prisoners: a drawing of one warrior clutching another by the hair. Then I drew the footprints, alternately black and red, to indicate captors and captives, tracing our westward march to Tenochtítlan.

Never leaving my chambers, taking all my meals there, I completed the map in two days. Then I started on the more complex account of the Texcaltéca and Acólhua strategy and tactics, at least insofar as I had observed and understood them. One midday Cozcatl came into my sunny workroom and asked leave to interrupt me.

He said, "Master, a large canoe has arrived from Texcóco and is moored in the courtyard garden. The steersman says it brings belongings of yours."

I was happy to hear it. When I left Nezahualpíli's palace to join the muster of troops, I had not felt it would be right to take with me any of the fine clothes and other gifts bestowed on me in the time before my banishment. In any case, I could hardly have carried them to war. So, although Cozcatl had borrowed garments for us to wear, neither he nor I actually possessed anything but the now extremely disreputable loincloths, sandals, and heavy tlamáitin we had worn to war and back again. I told the boy:

"It is a thoughtful gesture, and we probably have the Lady of Tolan to thank for it. I hope she sent your own wardrobe as well. Get a palace tamémi to help you bring the bundle here."

When he came back upstairs, accompanied by the boat's steersman and a whole train of laboring tamémime, I was so surprised that I forgot my work utterly. I had never owned the quantity of goods that the porters brought and stacked in my chambers. One large and one small bundle, neatly bound in protective matting, were recognizable. My clothes and other belongings were in the larger, even including my memento of

my late sister, her little figurine of the goddess Xochiquétzal.
Cozcatl's clothes were in the smaller bundle. But the other
bales and packages I could not account for, and I protested that
there must have been some mistake in the delivery.

The steersman said, "My lord, every one is tagged. Is not
that your name?"

It was so. Each separate bundle carried a securely attached
piece of bark paper on which was inscribed my name. There
were many Mixtlis in these parts, and more than a few Tliléctic-
Mixtlis. But those tags bore my full name: Chicóme-Xochitl
Tliléctic-Mixtli. I asked everyone present to help open the
wrappings, so that, if the contents did prove to have been
misaddressed, the workers could help repack them for return.
And if I had been bewildered before, I was soon astounded.

One bale of fiber matting opened to reveal a neat stack of
forty men's mantles of the finest cotton, richly embroidered.
Another contained the same number of women's skirts, colored
crimson with that costly dye extracted from insects. Another
bale yielded the same number of women's blouses, intricately
hand worked in an open filigree so that they were all but
transparent. Still another bundle contained a bolt of woven
cotton which, if we had unfolded it, would have been a cloth
two-arms'-spread wide and perhaps two hundred paces long.
Though the cotton was an unadorned white, it was seamless
and therefore priceless, just for the work—possibly years of
work—some dedicated weaver had put into the weaving of it.
The heaviest bale proved to contain chunks of itztetl, rough
and unworked obsidian rocks.

The three lightest bundles were the most valuable of all, for
they contained not tradeable goods but trade currency. One was
a sack of two or three thousand cacao beans. Another was a
sack of two or three hundred of the pieces of tin and copper,
shaped like miniature hatchet blades, each of which was worth
eight hundred cacao beans. The third was a cluster of four
feather quills, each translucent quill stoppered with a dab of
óli gum and filled with gleaming pure gold dust.

I said to the boatman, "I wish it was *not* a mistake, but it
clearly is. Take it back. This fortune must belong to Nezahualpíli's treasury."

"It does not," he said stubbornly. "It was the Revered

Speaker himself who bade me bring this, and he saw it loaded in my craft. All I am to take back is a message saying it was safely delivered. With your signature symbols, my lord, if you please."

I still could not believe what my eyes beheld and my ears were told, but I could hardly protest further. Still dazed, I gave him the note, and he and the porters withdrew. Cozcatl and I stood and looked at the unwrapped riches. Finally the boy said:

"It can only be one last gift, master, from the Lord Neza-hualpíli himself."

"That may be," I conceded. "He trained me up to be a palace courtier and then had to cast me adrift, as it were. And he is a man of conscience. So he has now, perhaps, supplied me with the means to engage in some other occupation."

"Occupation!" Cozcatl squeaked. "Do you mean work, master? Why should you work? There is enough here to keep you in fair comfort all your days. You, a wife, a family, a devoted slave." He added mischievously, "You once said you would build a nobleman's mansion and make me the Master of the Keys."

"Hold your tongue," I told him. "If all I wanted was idleness, I could have let Armed Scorpion send *me* to the afterworld. I now have the means to do many things. I have only to decide what I prefer to do."

When I completed the battle report, the day before the pyramid's dedication, I took it downstairs, seeking Ahuítzotl's trophy-hung den where I had first met him. But the palace steward, looking flustered, intercepted me to accept it in his stead.

"The Revered Speaker is entertaining many notables who have come from far lands for the ceremony," said the man distractedly. "Every palace around the plaza is crammed with foreign rulers and their retinues. I do not know how or where we can accommodate many more. But I will see that Ahuítzotl gets this account of yours, when he can read it in tranquillity. He will summon you for another interview after things quiet down again." And he bustled off.

As long as I was on the ground floor, I wandered through those rooms accessible to the public, just to admire the architecture and decor. Eventually I found myself in the great hall of statues, through the middle of which the canal flowed. The walls and ceiling were spangled with light reflections from the water. Several freight boats came through while I was there, their rowers admiring—as I was doing—the several sculptures of Ahuítzotl and his wives, of the patron god Huitzilopóchtli, of numerous other gods and goddesses. They were all most excellent works, most skillfully done, as they should have been: every one of them bore the incised falcon symbol of the late sculptor Tlatli.

But, as he had boasted many years before, Tlatli's work scarcely needed a signature; his god statues were indeed very different from those which had been imitated and replicated through generations of less imaginative sculptors. His distinctive vision was perhaps most evident in his depiction of Coatlícue, the goddess mother of the god Huitzilopóchtli. The massive stone object stood nearly a third again as tall as I did, and, looking up at it, I felt my back hair prickle at the eeriness of it.

Since Coatlícue was, after all, the mother of the god of war, most earlier artists had portrayed her as grim of visage, but in form she had always been recognizable as a *woman*. Not so in Tlatli's conception. His Coatlícue had no head. Instead, above her shoulders, two great serpents' heads met, as if kissing, to compose her face: their single visible eye apiece gave Coatlícue two glaring eyes, their meeting mouths gave Coatlícue one wide mouth full of fangs and horribly grinning. She wore a necklace hung with a skull, with severed hands and torn-out human hearts. Her nether garment was entirely of writhing snakes, and her feet were the taloned paws of some immense beast. It was a unique and original image of a female deity, but a gruesome one, and I believe that only a cuilóntli man who could not love women could have carved a goddess so egregiously monstrous.

I followed the canal out of that chamber, under the weeping willows that overhung it in the courtyard garden, and into the chamber on the other side of the palace, where the walls were covered with murals. They mostly depicted the military and civic deeds done by Ahuítzotl before and since his accession to the throne: himself the most prominent participant in various battles,. himself supervising the finishing touches on the Great Pyramid. But the pictures were alive, not stiff; they teemed with detail; they were artfully colored. As I had expected, the murals were finer than any other modern paintings I had seen. Because, as I had expected, each of them was signed in its lowermost right corner with the blood-red print of Chimáli's hand.

I wondered if he was yet back in Tenochtítlan, and if we would meet, and how he would go about killing me if we did. I went in search of my little slave Cozcatl, and gave him instructions:

"You know the artist Chimáli by sight, and you know that he has reason to wish me dead. I shall have duties to perform tomorrow, so I cannot keep looking over my shoulder for an assassin. I want you to circulate among the throng and then come to warn me if you see Chimáli. In tomorrow's crowd and confusion, he may hope to knife me unobserved and slip away unsuspected."

"He cannot, if I see him first," Cozcatl said staunchly. "And I promise, if he is present, I will see him. Have I not been useful before, master, at being your eyes?"

I said, "You have indeed, young one. And your vigilance and loyalty will not go unrewarded."

✠

Yes, Your Excellency, I know that you are most particularly interested in our former religious observances, hence your attendance here today. Although I was never a priest, nor much of a friend to priests, I will explain the dedication of the Great Pyramid—the manner of it and the significance of it—as well as I can.

If that was not the most resplendent, populous, and awesome celebration ever held in the history of the Mexíca, it certainly outdid all others I beheld in my time. The Heart of the One World was a solid mass of people, of colorful fabrics, of perfumes, of feather plumes, of flesh, of gold, of body heat, of jewels, of sweat. One reason for the crowding was that lanes had to be kept open—by cordons of guards, their arms linked, struggling to contain the jostling mob—so the lines of prisoners could march to the pyramid and ascend to the sacrificial altar. But the spectator crush was also due to the fact that the standing room in the plaza had been reduced by the building of numerous new temples over the years, not to mention the gradually spreading bulk of the Great Pyramid itself.

Since Your Excellency never saw it, perhaps I had better describe that icpac tlamanacáli. Its base was square, one hundred and fifty paces from one corner to the next, the four sides sloping inward as they rose, until the pyramid's flat summit measured seventy paces to a side. The staircase ascending its front or western incline was actually two stairways, one each for those persons climbing and descending, separated by an ornamental gutter for blood to flow down. Fifty and two stairs of steep risers and narrow treads led to a terrace that encircled the pyramid a third of the way up. Then another flight of one hundred and four steps culminated in the platform on top, with its temples and their appurtenances. At either side of every thirteenth step of the staircase stood the stone image of some god, major or minor, its stone fists holding aloft a tall pole from which floated a white feather banner.

To a man standing at the very bottom of the Great Pyramid, the structures on top were invisible. From the bottom he could see only the broad dual staircase ascending, appearing to narrow, and seeming to lead even higher than it did—into the blue sky or, on other occasions, into the sunrise. A xochimíqui trudging up the stairs toward his Flowery Death must have felt that he was truly climbing toward the very heavens of the high gods.

But when he reached the top, he would find first the small, pyramidal sacrificial stone and behind that the two temples. In a sense, those teocáltin represented war and peace, for the one on the right was the abode of Huitzilopóchtli, responsible for our military prowess, and in the one on the left dwelt Tlaloc, responsible for our harvests and peacetime prosperity. Perhaps there should rightly have been a third teocáli for the sun Tonatíu, but he already had a separate sanctuary on a more modest pyramid elsewhere in the plaza, as did several other important gods. There was also in the plaza the temple in which were ranked the images of numerous gods of subordinate nations.

The new temples of Tlaloc and Huitzilopóchtli, atop the new Great Pyramid, were but square stone rooms, each containing a hollow stone statue of the god, his mouth wide open to receive nourishment. But each temple was made much taller and more impressive by a towering stone façade or roof comb: Huitzilopóchtli's indented with angular and red-painted designs, Tlaloc's indented with rounded and blue-painted designs. The body of the pyramid was predominantly a gleaming almost-silver gesso white, but the two serpentine banisters, one along each flank of the dual staircase, were painted with reptilian scales of red, blue, and green, and their big snake heads, stretching out at the ground level, were entirely covered with beaten gold.

When the ceremony began, at the first full light of day, the chief priests of Tlaloc and Huitzilopóchtli, with all their assistants, were fussing around the temples at the top of the pyramid, doing whatever it is that priests do at the last moment. On the terrace encircling the pyramid stood the more distinguished guests: Tenochtítlan's Revered Speaker Ahuítzotl, naturally, with Texcóco's Revered Speaker Nezahualpíli and Tlácopan's Revered Speaker Chimalpopóca. There were also the rulers of other cities, provinces, and nations—from far-flung Mexíca domains, from the Tzapotéca lands, from the Mixtéca, from the Totonáca, from the Huaxtéca, from nations whose names I did not then even know. Not present, of course, was that implacably inimical ruler, old Xicoténca of Texcála, but Yquíngare of Michihuácan was there.

Think of it, Your Excellency. If your Captain-General Cortés had arrived in the plaza on that day, he could have accomplished our overthrow with one swift and easy slaughter of almost all our rightful rulers. He could have proclaimed himself, there and then, the lord of practically all of what is now New Spain, and our leaderless peoples would have been hard put to dispute him. They would have been like a beheaded animal which can twitch and flail only futilely. We would have been spared, I now realize, much of the misery and suffering we later endured. But *yyo ayyo!* On that day we celebrated the might of the Mexíca, and we did not even suspect the existence of such things as white men, and we supposed that our roads and our days led ahead into a limitless future. Indeed, we did have some years of vigor and glory still before us, so I am glad—even knowing what I know—I am glad that no alien intruder spoiled that splendid day.

The morning was devoted to entertainments. There was much singing and dancing by the troupes from this very House of Song in which we now sit, Your Excellency, and they were far more professionally skilled than any performers I had seen or heard in Texcóco or Xaltócan—though to me none equaled the grace of my lost Tzitzitlíni. There were the familiar instruments: the single thunder drum, the several god drums, the water drums, the suspended gourds, the reed flutes and shinbone flutes and sweet-potato flutes. But the singers and dancers were also accompanied by other instruments of a complexity I had not seen elsewhere. One was called "the warbling waters," a flute which sent its notes bubbling through a water jug, with an echo effect. There was another flute, made of clay, shaped rather like a thick dish, and its player did not move his lips or fingers; he moved his head about while he blew into the mouthpiece, so that a small clay ball inside the flute rolled to stop one hole or another around its rim. And, of course, of every kind of instrument there were many. Their combined music must have been audible to any stay-at-homes in every community around all the five lakes.

The musicians, singers, and dancers performed on the lower steps of the pyramid and on a cleared space directly in front of it. Whenever they tired and required a rest, their place was taken by athletic performers. Strong men lifted prodigious weights of stone, or tossed nearly naked beautiful girls back and forth to each other as if the girls had been feathers. Acrobats outdid grasshoppers and rabbits with their leaping, tumbling antics. Or they stood upon each other's shoulders—ten, then twenty, then forty men at a time—to form human representations of the Great Pyramid itself. Comic dwarfs performed grotesque and indecent pantomimes. Jugglers kept incredible numbers of tlachtli balls spinning aloft, from hand to hand, in intricate looping patterns. . . .

No, Your Excellency, I do not mean to imply that the morning's entertainments were a mere diversion (as you put it) to

lighten the horror to come (as you put it), and I do not know
what you mean when you mutter of "bread and circuses." Your
Excellency must not infer that those merriments were in any
wise irreverent. Every performer dedicated his particular trick
or talent to the gods we honored that day. If the performances
were not somber but frolicsome, it was to cajole the gods into
a mood to receive with gratitude our later offerings.

Everything done that morning had some connection with
our religious beliefs or customs or traditions, though the relation
might not be immediately evident to a foreign observer like
Your Excellency. For example, there were the tocotíne, come
on invitation from the Totonáca oceanside lands where their
distinctive sport had been invented—or perhaps god-inspired.
Their performance required the erection of an exceptionally tall
tree trunk in a socket specially drilled in the plaza marble. A
live bird was placed in that hole, and mashed by the insertion
of the tree trunk, so that its blood would lend the tocotíne the
strength they would need for flying. Yes, flying.

The erected pole stood almost as tall as the Great Pyramid.
At its top was a tiny wooden platform, no bigger than a man's
circled arms. Twined all down the pole was a loose meshing
of stout ropes. Five Totonáca men climbed the pole to its top,
one carrying a flute and a small drum tied to his loincloth, the
other four unencumbered except for a profusion of bright feathers. In fact, they were totally naked except for those feathers
glued to their arms. Arriving at the platform, the four feathered
men somehow sat around the edge of the wooden piece, while
the fifth man slowly, precariously got to his feet and stood
upon it.

There on that constricted space he stood, dizzyingly high,
and then he stamped one foot and then the other, and then he
began to dance, accompanying himself with flute and drum.
The drum he patted and pounded with one hand while his other
manipulated the holes of the flute on which he blew. Though
everyone watching from the plaza below was breathlessly quiet,
the music came down to us as only the thinnest tweedling and
thumping. Meanwhile, the other four tocotíne were cautiously
knotting the pole's rope ends around their ankles, but we could
not see it, so high up they were. When they were ready, the
dancing man made some signal to the musicians in the plaza.

Ba-ra-ROOM! There was a thunderous concussion of music and drumming that made every spectator jump, and, at the same instant, the four men atop the pole also jumped—into empty air. They flung themselves outward and spread their arms, the full length of which were featherd. Each of the men was feathered like a different bird: a red macaw, a blue fisher bird, a green parrot, a yellow toucan—and his arms were his outstretched wings. That first leap carried the tocotíne a distance outward from the platform, but then the ropes around their ankles jerked them up short. They would all have fallen back against the pole, except for the ingenious way the ropes were twined. The men's initial leap outward became a slow circling around the pole, each of the men equidistant from the others, and each still in the graceful posture of a spread-winged, hovering bird.

While the man on top went on dancing and the musicians below played a trilling, lilting, pulsing accompaniment, the four bird-men continued to circle and, as the ropes gradually unwound from the pole, they circled farther out and slowly came lower. But the men, like birds, could tilt their feathered arms so that they rose and dipped and soared up and down past each other as if they too danced—but in all the dimensions of the sky.

Each man's rope was wrapped thirteen times around and down the extent of the pole. On his final circuit, when his body was swinging in its widest and swiftest circle, almost touching the plaza pavement, he arched his body and backed his wings against the air—exactly in the manner of a bird alighting—so that he skimmed to the ground feet first, and the rope came loose, and he ran to a stop. All four did that at the same moment. Then one of them held his rope taut for the fifth man to slide down to the plaza.

If Your Excellency has read some of my previous explanations of our beliefs, you will have realized that the sport of the tocotíne was not simply an acrobatic feat, but that each aspect of it had some significance. The four fliers were partly feathered, partly flesh, like Quetzalcóatl, the Feathered Serpent. The four circling men with the dancing man among them represented our five points of the compass: north, east, west, south, and center. The thirteen turns of each rope corresponded to the thirteen day and year numbers of our ritual calendar. And four times thirteen makes fifty and two, the number of years in a sheaf of years. There were more subtle relevances— the word tocotíne means "the sowers"—but I will not expatiate on those things, for I perceive that Your Excellency is more eager to hear of the sacrificial part of the dedication ceremony.

The night before, after they had all confessed to Filth Eater's priests, our Texcaltéca prisoners had been moved to the perimeter of the island and divided into three herds, so that they could move toward the Great Pyramid along the three broad avenues leading into the plaza. The first prisoner to approach, well forward of the rest, was my own: Armed Scorpion. He had haughtily declined to ride a litter chair to his Flowery Death, but came with his arms across the shoulders of two solicitous brother knights, though they were of course Mexíca. Armed Scorpion swung along between them, the remains of his legs dangling like gnawed roots. I was positioned at the base of the pyramid, where I fell in beside the three and accompanied them up the staircase to the terrace where all the nobles waited.

To my beloved son, the Revered Speaker Ahuítzotl said, "As our xochimíqui of highest rank and most distinction, Armed Scorpion, you have the honor of going first to the Flowery Death. However, as a Jaguar Knight of long and notable reputation, you may choose instead to fight for your life on the Battle Stone. What is your wish?"

The prisoner sighed. "I no longer have a life, my lord. But it would be good to fight one last time. If I may choose, then, I choose the Battle Stone."

"A decision worthy of a warrior," said Ahuítzotl. "And you will be honored with worthy opponents, our own highest-ranking knights. Guards, assist the esteemed Armed Scorpion to the stone and gird him for hand-to-hand combat."

I went along to watch. The Battle Stone, as I have earlier told, was the former Uey-Tlatoáni Tixoc's one contribution to the plaza: that broad, squat cylinder of volcanic rock situated between the Great Pyramid and the Sun Stone. It was reserved for any warrior who merited the distinction of dying as he had lived, still fighting. But a prisoner who chose to duel on the

Battle Stone was required to fight not just one opponent. If, by guile and prowess, he bested one man, another Mexícatl knight would take up the fray, and another and another—four in all. One of those was bound to kill him . . . or at least that was the way the duels had always ended before.

Armed Scorpion was dressed in full battle armor of quilted cotton, plus his knightly regalia of jaguar skin and helmet. Then he was placed upon the stone where, having no feet, he could not even stand. His opponent, armed with an obsidian-bladed maquáhuitl, had the advantage of being able to leap on and off the pedestal, and to attack from any direction. Armed Scorpion was given two weapons with which to defend himself, but they were poor things. One was simply a wooden staff for warding off his attacker's blows. The other was a maquáhuitl, but the harmless play-kind used by novice soldiers in training: its obsidian flakes removed and replaced by tufts of feathery down.

Armed Scorpion sat near one edge of the stone, in a posture almost of relaxed anticipation, the bladeless sword in his right hand, the wooden staff gripped by his left and lying across his lap. His first opponent was one of the two Jaguar Knights who had helped him into the plaza. The mexícatl leapt onto the Battle Stone at the left side of Armed Scorpion; that is, on the side away from his offensive weapon, the maquáhuitl. But Armed Scorpion surprised the man. He did not even move the weapon, he used his defensive staff instead. He swung it, hard, in an up-curving arc. The Mexícatl, who could scarcely have expected to be attacked with a mere pole, caught it under his chin. His jaw was broken and he was knocked senseless. Some of the crowd murmured in admiration and others owl-hooted in applause. Armed Scorpion simply sat, the wooden staff held languidly resting on his left shoulder.

The second duelist was Armed Scorpion's other supporting Jaguar Knight. He, naturally supposing that the prisoner's first win had been only a caprice of fortune, also bounded onto the stone at Armed Scorpion's left, his obsidian blade poised to strike, his eyes fixed on the seated man's own maquáhuitl. That time, Armed Scorpion lashed overhand with his defensive staff, over the knight's uplifted weapon hand, and brought the pole crashing down between the ears of the Mexícatl's jaguar-head helmet. The man fell backward off the Battle Stone, his skull fractured, and he was dead before he could be attended by any physician. The spectators' murmurs and hoots increased in volume.

The third opponent was an Arrow Knight, and he was justly wary of the Texcaltécatl's not at all harmless staff. He leapt onto the stone from the right, and swung his maquáhuitl in the same movement. Armed Scorpion again brought up his staff, but only to parry the swinging sword to one side. That time he also used his own maquáhuitl, though in an unusual way. He jabbed the hard blunt end of it upward, with all his strength, into the Arrow Knight's throat. It crushed that prominence of cartilage which you Spaniards call "the nut of the neck." The Mexícatl fell and writhed, and he strangled to death, right there on the Battle Stone.

As the guards removed that limp carcass, the crowd was going wild with shouts and hoots of encouragement—not for their Mexíca warriors, but for the Texcaltécatl. Even the nobles high on the pyramid were milling about and conversing excitedly. In the memory of no one present had a prisoner, even a prisoner with the use of all his limbs, ever bested as many as three opposing duelists.

But the fourth was the certain slayer, for the fourth was one of our rare left-handed fighters. Practically all warriors were naturally right-handed, had learned to fight right-handed, and had fought in that manner all their lives. So, as is well known, a right-handed warrior is perplexed and confounded when he comes up against a left-handed combatant who is, in effect, a mirror image striking him.

The left-handed man, a knight of the Eagle Order, took his time climbing onto the Battle Stone. He came leisurely to the duel, smiling cruelly and confidently. Armed Scorpion still sat, his staff in his left hand, his maquáhuitl naturally in his right. The Eagle Knight, sword in his left hand, made a distracting feint and then leapt forward. As he did so, Armed Scorpion moved as deftly as any of the morning's jugglers. He tossed his staff and maquáhuitl a little way into the air and caught them in the opposite hands. The Mexícatl knight, at that unexpected display of ambidexterity, checked his lunge as if to draw back and reconsider. He did not get the chance.

Armed Scorpion clapped his blade and staff together on the knight's left wrist, twisted them, and the man's maquáhuitl fell out of his hand. Holding the Mexícatl's wrist pinned between his wooden weapons, as in a parrot's strong beak, Armed Scorpion for the first time drew himself up from his sitting position, to kneel on his knees and stumps. With unbelievable strength, he twisted his two weapons still farther, and the Eagle Knight had to twist with them, and he fell on his back. The Texcaltécatl immediately laid the edge of his wooden blade across the supine man's throat. Placing one hand on either end of the wood, he knelt over and leaned heavily. The man thrashed under him, and Armed Scorpion lifted his head to look up at the pyramid, at the nobles.

Ahuítzotl, Nezahualpíli, Chimalpopóca, and the others on the terrace conferred, their gesticulations expressing admiration and wonderment. Then Ahuítzotl stepped to the edge of the platform and made a raising, beckoning movement with his hand. Armed Scorpion leaned back and lifted the maquáhuitl off the fallen man's neck. That one sat up, shakily, rubbing his throat, looking both unbelieving and embarrassed. He and Armed Scorpion were brought together to the terrace. I accompanied them, glowing with pride in my beloved son. Ahuítzotl said to him:

"Armed Scorpion, you have done something unheard of. You have fought for your life on the Battle Stone, under greater handicap than any previous duelist, and you have won. This swagger whom you last defeated will take your place as xochimíqui of the first sacrifice. You are free to go home to Texcála."

Armed Scorpion firmly shook his head. "Even if I could walk home, my Lord Speaker, I would not. A prisoner once taken is a man destined by his tonáli and the gods to die. I should shame my family, my fellow knights, all of Texcála, if I returned dishonorably alive. No, my lord, I have had what I requested—one last fight—and it was a good fight. Let your Eagle Knight live. A left-handed warrior is too rare and valuable to discard."

"If that is your wish," said the Uey-Tlatoáni, "then he lives. We are prepared to grant any other wish of yours. Only speak it."

"That I now be allowed to go to my Flowery Death, and to the warriors' afterworld."

"Granted," said Ahuítzotl and then, magnanimously, "The Revered Speaker Nezahualpíli and myself will be honored to bear you thither."

Armed Scorpion spoke just once more, to his captor, to me, as was customary, to ask the routine question, "Has my revered father any message he would like me to convey to the gods?"

I smiled and said, "Yes, my beloved son. Tell the gods that I wish only that you be rewarded in death as you have deserved in life. That you live the richest of afterlives, forever and forever."

He nodded, and then, with his arms across the shoulders of two Revered Speakers, he went up the remaining stairs to the stone block. The assembled priests, almost frenzied with delight at the auspicious events attendant on that first sacrifice of the day, made a great show of waving incense pots around, and throwing smoke colorings into the urn fires, and chanting invocations to the gods. The warrior Armed Scorpion was accorded two final honors. Ahuítzotl himself wielded the obsidian knife. The plucked-out heart was handed to Nezahualpíli, who took it in a ladle, carried it into the temple of Huitzilopóchtli, and fed it into the god's open mouth.

That ended my participation in the ceremonies, at least until the coming night's feasting, so I descended the pyramid and stood off to one side. After the dispatch of Armed Scorpion, all the rest was rather anticlimactic, except for the sheer magnitude of the sacrifice: the thousands of xochimíque, more than ever had before been granted the Flowery Death in one day.

Ahuítzotl ladled the second prisoner's heart into the mouth of Tlaloc's statue, then he and Nezahualpíli descended again to the pyramid terrace. They and their fellow rulers also stood off to one side, out of the way, and, when they tired of watching the proceedings, idly talked among themselves of whatever Revered Speakers talk about. Meanwhile, the three long lines of captives shuffled in single file along the avenues Tlácopan, Ixtapalápan, and Tepeyáca, and into The Heart of the One World, and between the close-pressing ranks of spectators, and one behind another up the pyramid staircase.

The hearts of the first xochimíque, perhaps the first two hundred of them, were ceremoniously ladled into the mouths of Tlaloc and Huitzilopóchtli until the statues' hollow insides could hold no more, and the stone lips of the two gods drooled and dribbled blood. Of course, those hearts crammed into the statues' cavities would in time rot down to a sludge and make room for more. But that day, since the priests had an overabundance of hearts, the ones later plucked out were tossed into waiting bowls. When the bowls were filled and heaped with hearts, still steaming, some still feebly pulsing, under-priests took them and hurried down the Great Pyramid, into the plaza and the streets of the rest of the island. They delivered the surplus bounty to every other pyramid, temple, and god statue in both Tenochtítlan and Tlaltelóco—and, as the afternoon wore on, to temples in the mainland cities as well.

The prisoners endlessly ascended the right side of the pyramid's staircase, while the gashed bodies of their predecessors tumbled and rolled down the left side, kicked along by junior priests stationed at intervals, and while the gutter between the stairs carried a continuous stream of blood which puddled out among the feet of the crowd in the plaza. After the first two hundred or so of xochimíque, the priests abandoned all effort or pretense at ceremony. They laid aside their incense pots and banners and holy wands, they ceased their chanting, while they worked as quickly and indifferently as Swallowers on a battleground—meaning that they could not work very neatly.

The hurried ladling of hearts into the statues had spattered the interior of both temples until their walls and floors and even ceilings were coated with drying blood. The excess blood ran out their doors, while still more blood poured off the sacrificial stone, until the whole platform was awash with it. Also, many prisoners, however complacently they came to their fate, involuntarily emptied their bladders or bowels at the moment of lying down under the knife. The priests—who, that morning, had been clad in their usual vulturine black of robes, lank hair, and unwashed skin—had become moving clots of red and brown, of coagulated blood, dried mucus, and a plaster of excrement.

At the base of the pyramid, the meat cutters were working just as frantically and messily. From Armed Scorpion and a number of other Texcaltéca knights they had cut the heads, to be boiled down for their skulls, which would then be mounted on the plaza skull rack reserved to commemorate xochimíque of distinction. From those same bodies they had hacked off the thighs, to be broiled for that night's feast of the victorious warriors. As more and more cadavers tumbled down to them, the meat cutters sliced off just the choicest portions, to be fed immediately to the plaza menagerie's animals, or to be salted and smoked and stored for later feeding to the beasts, or to any distressed poor folk or masterless slaves who came begging for such a dispensation.

The mutilated bodies were then hastily carried by the butchers' boys to the nearest canal, the one that flowed under the Tepeyáca avenue. There they were dumped into big freight canoes which, as each was loaded, set off for various points on the mainland: the flower nurseries of Xochimílco, the orchards and produce farms elsewhere around the lakes, where the bodies would be buried for fertilizer. A separate, smaller acáli accompanied each fleet of scows. It carried fragments and chips of jadestone—bits too small to be of any other use—one of which would be put in the mouth or the fist of each dead man before he was interred. We never denied to our vanquished enemies that talisman of green stone which was necessary for admission to the afterworld.

And still the procession of prisoners went on. From the summit of the Great Pyramid, a mixture of blood and other substances ran in such torrents that, after a while, the stairway's disposal gutter could not contain it all. It cascaded like a slow, viscous waterfall down the steep steps themselves, it surged among the dead bodies flopping down, it bathed the feet of the live men plodding up, and made many slip and fall. It ran in sheets down the smooth walls of the pyramid on all four sides. It spread out across the entire extent of The Heart of the One World. That morning the Great Pyramid had gleamed like the snow-covered conical peak of Popocatépetl. In the afternoon, it looked like a heaped platter of breast of fowl over which the cook had lavishly poured a thick red moli sauce. It looked like what it was providing: a great meal for the gods of great appetite.

*   *   *

An abomination, Your Excellency?

What horrifies and nauseates you, I think, is the number of men put to death at that one time. But how, my lord, can you set a measure to death, which is not an entity but a void? How can you multiply nothingness by any number known to arithmetic? When just one man dies, the whole living universe ends, as far as he is concerned. Every other man and woman in it likewise ceases to exist; loved ones and strangers, every creature, every flower, cloud, breeze, every sensation and emotion. Your Excellency, the world and every least thing in it dies every day, for somebody.

But what demonic gods, you ask, would countenance the obliteration of so many men in a single indiscriminate slaughter? Well, your own Lord God, for one . . .

No, Your Excellency, I do not think I blaspheme. I merely repeat what I was told by the missionary friars who instructed me in the rudiments of Christian history. If they spoke the truth, your Lord God was once displeased by the increasing corruption of the human beings He had created, so He drowned them *all* in one great deluge. He left alive only a single boatman and his family to repopulate the earth. I have always thought the Lord God preserved a rather curious selection of humans, since the boatman was prone to drunkenness, and his sons to behavior I should judge peculiar, and all their progeny to quarrelsome rivalries.

Our world too, and every human in it, was once destroyed—and also, be it noted, by a calamitous inundation of water—when the gods got dissatisfied with the men then inhabiting it. However, our histories may go back further than yours, for our priests told us that this world had been previously scoured clean of humankind on three other occasions: the first time by all-devouring jaguars, the second time by all-destroying windstorms, the third time by a rain of fire from the skies. Those cataclysms happened, of course, sheaves of sheaves of years apart, and even the most recent one, the great flood, was so long ago that not the wisest tlamatíni could precisely calculate its date.

So the gods have four times created our One World and peopled it with human beings, and four times they have declared the creation a failure, wiped it out and started again. We here, now, all of us living, constitute the fifth experiment of the gods. But, according to the priests, we live just as precariously as any of those earlier unfortunates, for the gods will someday decide to end the world and all again—the next time by means of devastating earthquakes.

There is no knowing when they may commence. We of this land always thought it possible that the earthquakes might come during the five hollow days at the end of a year, which is why we made ourselves so inconspicuous during those days. It seemed even likelier that the world would end at the end of that most significant year, the fifty-second year of a sheaf of years. So it was at those times that we abased ourselves, and prayed for survival, and sacrificed even more abundantly, and celebrated the New Fire ceremony.

Just as we did not know when to expect the world-ending earthquakes, so we did not know how the earlier men on earth had brought down the wrath of the gods in the form of jaguars, winds, fire, and flood. But it seemed a safe assumption that those men had failed sufficiently to adore and honor and make offerings of nourishment to their creators. That is why we, in our time, tried our best not to be lax in those respects.

So, yes, we slew countless xochimíque to honor Tlaloc and Huitzilopóchtli on the day of the dedication of the Great Pyramid. But try to look at it as we did, Your Excellency. Not one man gave up more than his own one life. Each man of those thousands died only the once, which he would have done anyway, in time. And dying thus, he died in the noblest way and for the noblest reason we knew. If I may quote those missionary friars again, Your Excellency, though I do not recall their exact words, it seems there is a similar belief among Christians. That no man can manifest greater love than to surrender his life for his friends.

Thanks to your instructive missionaries, we Mexíca know now that, even when we did right things, we did them for the wrong reasons. But I regret to remind Your Excellency that there are still other nations in these lands, not yet subdued and absorbed into the Christian dominion of New Spain, where the unenlightened still believe that a sacrificial victim suffers only briefly the pain of the Flowery Death before entering a delightful and eternal afterlife. Those peoples know nothing of the Christian Lord God, Who does not confine misery to our brief lives on earth, but also inflicts it in the afterworld of Hell, where the agony is everlasting.

Oh, yes, Your Excellency, I know that Hell is only for the multitude of wicked men who deserve eternal torment, and that a select few righteous men go to a sublime glory called Heaven. But your missionaries preach that, even for Christians, the felicitous Heaven is a narrow place, hard to get to, while the terrible Hell is capacious and easily entered. I have attended many church and mission services since the one that converted me, and I have come to think that Christianity would be more attractive to the heathen if Your Excellency's priests were able to describe the delights of Heaven as vividly and gloatingly as they dwell upon the horrors of Hell.

Apparently His Excellency does not care to hear my unsolicited suggestions, not even to refute or debate them, and prefers instead to take his leave. Ah, well, I am but a novice Christian, and probably presumptuous in voicing opinions still unripened. I will drop the subject of religion, to speak of other things.

The warriors' feast, held in what was then the banquet hall of this very House of Song, on the night of the Great Pyramid's dedication, did have some religious connotations, but they were minor. It was believed that, when we victors dined on the broiled hams of the sacrificed prisoners, we thereby ingested some of the dead men's strength and fighting spirit. But it was forbidden that any "revered father" eat the flesh of his own "beloved son." That is, no one could eat of any prisoner he himself had captured, because, in religious terms, that would be as unthinkable as an act of incest. So, though all the other guests scrambled to seize a slice of the incomparable Armed Scorpion, I had to be content with the thigh meat of some less esteemed enemy knight.

The meat, my lords? Why, it was nicely spiced and well cooked and served with an abundance of side dishes: beans and tortillas and stewed tomatoes and chocolate to drink and—

The meat *nauseous*, my lords? Why, quite the contrary! It was most savory and tender and pleasing to the palate. Since the subject so excites your curiosity, I will tell you that cooked human flesh tastes almost exactly like the meat you call pork, the cooked flesh of those imported animals you call swine. Indeed, it is the similarity of texture and flavor which gave rise to the rumor that you Spaniards and your swine are closely related, that both Spaniards and pigs propagate their species by mutual intercourse, if not legal intermarriage.

Yya, do not make such faces, reverend friars! I never believed the rumor, for I could see that your swine are only domesticated animals akin to the wild boars of this land, and I do not think even a Spaniard would copulate with one of those. Of course, your pig meat is much more flavorsome and tender than the gamy, sinewy meat of our untamed boars. But the coincidental similarity of pork and human flesh is probably the reason why our lower classes early took to eating pig meat with such avidity, and probably also the reason why they welcomed your introduction of swine with rather greater enthusiasm than, for instance, they welcomed your introduction of Holy Church.

As was only fair, the guests at that night's banquet consisted mostly of Acólhua warriors who had come to Tenochtítlan in Nezahualpíli's retinue. There were a token few of Chimalpopóca's knights of the Tecpanéca, and of us Mexíca there were only three: myself and my immediate superiors in the field, the Cuachic Blood Glutton and the Arrow Knight Xococ. One of the Acólhua present was that soldier who had had his nose cut off in the battle and replaced afterward, but it was gone again. He told us, sadly, that the physician's operation had not been a success; the nose had gradually turned black and finally fallen off. We all assured him that he looked not much worse without it than he had with it, but he was a mannerly man, and he sat well apart from the rest of us, not to spoil our appetites.

For each guest there was a seductively dressed auyaními woman to serve us tidbits from the platters of food, to fill the smoking tubes with picíetl and light them for us, to pour chocolate and octli for us, and, later, to retire with us to the curtained little bedrooms around the main chamber. Yes, I see the displeasure in your expressions, my lord scribes, but it is a fact. That feast of human meat and the subsequent enjoyment of casual copulation—they took place right here in this now sanctified diocesan headquarters.

I confess I do not remember everything that occurred, for I smoked my first poquíetl that night, and more than one of them, and I drank much octli. I had timidly tasted that fermented maguey juice before, but that night was the first time I indulged in enough of it to addle my senses. I remember that the gathered warriors did much boasting of their deeds in the recent war, and in wars past, and there were many toasts to my own first victory and my swift promotion upward through the ranks. At one point, our three Revered Speakers honored us with a brief appearance, and lifted a cup of octli with us. I have a vague recollection of thanking Nezahualpíli—drunkenly and fulsomely and possibly incoherently—for his gift of trade goods and trade currency, though I do not recall his reply, if he made any.

Eventually and not at all hesitantly, thanks perhaps to the octli, I retired to one of the bedrooms with one of the auyaníme. I remember that she was a most comely young woman with hair artificially colored the red-yellow of the jacinth gem. She was exceptionally accomplished at what was, after all, her life's occupation: giving pleasure to victorious warriors. So, besides the usual acts, she taught me some things quite new to me, and I must say that only a soldier in his prime of vigor and agility could have kept up his part of them for long, or endured hers. In return, "I caressed her with flowers." I mean to say, I performed upon her some of the subtle things I had witnessed during the seduction of Something Delicate. The auyaními obviously enjoyed those attentions and marveled much at them. Having coupled always and only with men, and with rather crude men, she had never before known those particular titillations—and I believe she was pleased to learn of them and add them to her own repertory.

At last, sated with sex, food, smoke, and drink, I decided I would like to be alone for a while. The banquet hall was murky with stale air and layers of smoke, with the smells of leftover food and men's sweat and burnt-out pitch torches, all of which made my stomach feel queasy. I left The House of Song and walked unsteadily toward The Heart of the One

World. There my nostrils were assailed by an even worse smell, and my stomach churned. The plaza swarmed with slaves scraping and swabbing at the blood caked everywhere. So I skirted the outside of the Snake Wall until I found myself at the door of the menagerie I had visited with my father once, long ago.

A voice said, "It is not locked. The inmates are all caged, and anyway they are now gorged and torpid. Shall we go in?"

Even at that time of night, long past midnight, I was scarcely surprised to see him: the bent and wizened cacao-brown man who had also been present at the menagerie that other time, and present at other times in my life since. I muttered some thick-tongued greeting, and he said:

"After a day spent enjoying the rites and delights of human beings, let us commune with what we call the beasts."

I followed him inside and we strolled along the walkway between the cages and cubicles. All the carnivorous animals had been well fed with the meat of the sacrifices, but the constantly running water of the drains had flushed away almost all trace and smell of it. Here and there a coyote or jaguar or one of the great constrictor snakes opened a drowsy eye at us, then closed it again. Only a few of even the nocturnal animals were awake—bats, opossums, howler monkeys—but they too were languid and made only quiet chitters and grunts.

After a while, my companion said, "You have come a long way in a short time, Fetch!"

"Mixtli," I corrected him.

"Mixtli again, then. Always I find you with a different name and pursuing a different career. You are like that quicksilver which the goldsmiths use. Adaptable to any shape, but not to be confined in any one for long. Well, you have now had your experience of war. Will you become a professional military man?"

"Of course not," I said. "You know I have not the eyesight for that. And I think I do not have the stomach for it either."

He shrugged. "Oh, a soldier acquires callosity after only a few fights, and his stomach no longer rebels."

"I did not mean a stomach for fighting, but for the celebrations afterward. Right now I feel quite—" I belched loudly.

"Your first inebriation," he said, with a laugh. "A man gets used to that, too, I assure you. Often he gets to enjoy it, even to require it."

"I think I had rather not," I said. "I have recently experienced too many firsts too rapidly. Now I should like just a little while of repose, devoid of incidents and excitements and upsets. I believe I can prevail on Ahuítzotl to engage me as a palace scribe."

"Papers and paint pots," he said disparagingly. "Mixtli, those things you can do when you are as old and decrepit as I am. Save them for when you have energy only to set down your reminiscences. Until then, collect adventures and experiences to reminisce about. I strongly recommend travel. Go to far places, meet new people, eat exotic foods, enjoy all varieties of women, look on unfamiliar landscapes, see new things. And that reminds me—the other time you were here, you did not get to view the tequántin. Come."

He opened a door and we went into the hall of the "human animals," the freaks and monstrosities. They were not caged like the real beasts. Each lived in what would have been quite a nice, small, private chamber—except that it had no fourth wall, so that spectators like us could look in and see the tequáni at whatever activity he might contrive to fill his useless life and empty days. At that time of night, all those we passed were asleep on their pallets. There were the all-white men and women—white of skin and hair—looking as impalpable as the wind. There were dwarfs and hunchbacks, and other beings twisted into even more horrid shapes.

"How do they come to be here?" I asked in a discreet murmur.

The man said, not troubling to lower his voice, "They come of their own accord, if they have been made grotesque by some accident. Or they are brought by their parents, if they were born freakish. If the tequáni sells himself, the payment is given to his parents or to whomever he designates. And the Revered Speaker pays munificently. There are parents who literally pray to beget a freak, so they may become rich. The tequáni himself, of course, has no use for riches, since he has here all necessary comforts for the rest of his life. But some of these, the most bizarre, cost riches aplenty. This dwarf, for instance."

The dwarf was asleep, and I was rather glad not to be seeing him awake, for he had only half a head. From the snaggle-toothed upper jaw to his collarbone, there was nothing—no lower mandible, no skin—nothing but an exposed white windpipe, red muscles, blood vessels and gullet, the latter opening behind his teeth and between his puffy little squirrel cheeks. He lay with that gruesome half head thrown back, breathing with a gurgling, whistling noise.

"He cannot chew or swallow," said my guide, "so his food must be poked down that upper end of his gullet. Since he has to bend his head far back to be fed, he cannot see what is given him, and many visitors here play cruel jokes on him. They may give him a prickly tonal fruit or a violent purgative or sometimes worse things. On many occasions he has nearly died, but he is so greedy and stupid that still he will throw his head back for anyone who makes an offering gesture."

I shuddered and went on to the next apartment. The tequáni there seemed not to be asleep, for its one eye was open. Where the other eye should have been was a smooth plane of skin. The head was hairless and even neckless, its skin sloping directly into its narrow shoulders and thence into a spreading, cone-shaped torso which sat on its swollen base as solidly as a pyramid, for it had no legs. Its arms were normal enough, except that the fingers of both hands were fused together, like the flippers of a green turtle.

"This one is called the tapir woman," said the brown man, and I made a motion for him to speak more softly. "Oh, we need not mind our manners," he said. "She is probably sound asleep. The one eye is permanently overgrown and the other has lost its lids. Anyway, these tequántin soon get accustomed to being publicly discussed."

I had no intention of discussing that pitiable object. I could see why it was named for the prehensile-snouted tapir: its nose was a trunklike blob that hung pendulously to hide its mouth, if it had a mouth. But I should not have recognized it for a female, had I not been told. The head was not a woman's, nor even a human's. Any breasts were indistinguishable in the doughy rolls of flesh that composed its immovable pyramid of body. It stared back at me with its one never-closable eye.

"The jawless dwarf was born in his sad condition," said my guide. "But this one was a grown woman when she was mu-

tilated in some sort of accident. It is supposed, from the lack
of legs, that the accident involved some cutting instrument,
and, from the look of the rest of her, that it also involved a
fire. Flesh does not always burn in a fire, you know. Sometimes
it merely softens, stretches, melts, so it can be shaped and
molded like—"

My sick stomach heaved, and I said, "In the name of pity.
Do not talk in front of it. In front of her."

"*Her!*" the man grunted, as if amused. "You are ever the
gallant with women, are you not?" He pointed at me almost
accusingly. "You have just come from the embrace of a beautiful *her.*" He pointed at the tapir woman. "Now how would
you like to couple with this other thing you describe as *her?*"

The very thought made my nausea uncontainable. I doubled
over, and there in front of the monstrous living heap, I vomited
up everything I had eaten and drunk that night. When I was
finally empty and had recovered my breath, I threw an apologetic glance at that staring eye. Whether the eye was awake
or merely watering, I do not know, but a single tear rolled
down from it. My guide was gone, and I did not see him again,
as I went back through the menagerie and let myself out.

But there was still another unpleasantness in store for me
that night, which by then was early morning. When I reached
the portal of Ahuítzotl's palace, the guard said, "Excuse me,
Tequíua Mixtli, but the court physician has been awaiting your
return. Will you please see him before you go to your room?"

The guard led me to the apartment of the palace doctor,
where I knocked and found him awake and fully dressed. The
guard saluted us both and went back to his post. The physician
regarded me with an expression compounded of curiosity, pity,
and professional unction. For a moment I thought he had waited
up to prescribe a remedy for the queasiness I still felt. But he
said, "The boy Cozcatl is your slave, is he not?"

I said he was, and asked if he had been taken ill.

"He has suffered an accident. Not a mortal one, I am happy
to say, but not a trivial one either. When the plaza crowd began
to disperse, he was noticed lying unconscious beside the Battle
Stone. It may be that he stood too close to the duelists."

I had not given Cozcatl a thought since I had appointed him

to keep watch for any sign of a lurking Chimáli. I said, "He was cut, then, Lord Doctor?"

"Badly cut," he said, "and oddly cut." He kept his gaze on me as he picked up a stained cloth from a table, opened its folds, and held it out for me to see what it contained: an immature male member and its sac of olóltin, pale and limp and bloodless.

"Like an earlobe," I muttered.

"What?" said the physician.

"You say it is not a mortal wound?"

"Well, you or I might consider it so," the doctor said drily. "But the boy will not die of it, no. He lost an amount of blood, and it appears from bruises and other marks on his body that he was roughly handled, perhaps by the jostling mob. But he will live, and let us hope that he will not much mourn the loss of what he never had a chance to learn the value of. The cut was a clean one. It will heal over, in no more time than it takes him to recover from the loss of blood. I have arranged that the wound, in closing, will leave a necessary small aperture. He is in your apartment now, Tequíua Mixtli, and I took the liberty of placing him in your softer bed, rather than on his pallet."

I thanked the doctor and hurried upstairs. Cozcatl was lying on his back in the middle of my thickly quilted bed, the top quilt drawn over him. His face was flushed with a slight fever and his breathing was shallow. Very gently, not to wake him, I edged the covering down off him. He was naked except for the bandage between his legs, held in place by a swathing of tape around his hips. There were bruises on his shoulder where a hand had clutched him while the knife was wielded. But the doctor had mentioned "other marks," and I saw none—until Cozcatl, probably feeling the chill of the night air, murmured in his sleep and rolled over to expose his back.

"Your vigilance and loyalty will not go unrewarded," I had told the boy, little suspecting what that reward would be. The vengeful Chimáli had indeed been in the crowd that day, but I had been almost all the time in such prominent places that he could make no sneak attack on me. So he had seen and recognized and assaulted my slave instead. But why injure such a small and comparatively valueless servant?

Then I recalled the curious expression on the doctor's face, and I realized that he had been thinking what Chimáli must also have thought. Chimáli had assumed that the boy was to me what Tlatli had been to him. He had struck at the child, not to deprive me of an expendable slave, but to mutilate my supposed cuilóntli, in the way best calculated to shock me, to mock me.

All of that went through my mind when I saw, slapped in the middle of Cozcatl's slender back, the familiar red handprint of Chimáli, only for once not in Chimáli's own blood.

Since it was then so late, or so early, that the open skylight in the ceiling was beginning to pale—and since both my head and my stomach still hurt so horrendously—I sat by Cozcatl's sickbed, not even trying to doze, trying instead to think.

I remembered the vicious Chimáli in the years before he became vicious, in the years when he was still my friend. He had himself been of just about Cozcatl's age on that memorable evening when I led him home across Xaltócan, wearing the pumpkin on his head to hide his tufted hair. I remembered how he had commiserated with me when he went off to the calmécac and I did not, and how he once had given me that gift of his specially concocted paints. . . .

Which led me to think about that other unexpected bequest I had received just a few days ago. Everything in it was of great value, except for one thing which had no apparent value whatever, at least here in Tenochtítlan. That was the bundle containing unfinished obsidian rocks, which were easily and cheaply obtainable from their nearby source, the canyon bed of The River of Knives, no long journey northeast of here. However, those rough chunks *would* be almost as prized as jadestone in the nations farther south, which had no such sources of obsidian from which to fashion their tools and weapons. That one "worthless" bundle made me recall some of the ambitions I had entertained and the ideas I had evolved in my long-ago days as an idly dreaming farm boy on the chinámpa of Xaltócan.

When the morning was full light, I quietly washed myself, cleaned my teeth, and changed into fresh garments. I went downstairs, found the palace steward, and requested an early interview with the Uey-Tlatoáni. Ahuítzotl was gracious enough to grant it, and I had not long to wait before I was ushered into his presence in that trophy-hung throne room.

The first thing he said was, "We hear that your small slave got in the way of a swinging blade yesterday."

I said, "So it seems, Revered Speaker, but he will recover."

I had no intention of denouncing Chimáli, or demanding a search for him, or even of mentioning his name. It would have necessitated some heretofore undisclosed revelations about the last days of Ahuítzotl's daughter—revelations involving Cozcatl and myself as well as Chimáli. They could rekindle Ahuítzotl's paternal anguish and anger, and he might very well execute me and the boy before he even sent soldiers looking for Chimáli.

He said, "We are sorry. Accidents are not infrequent among the spectators of the duels. We will be glad to assign you another slave while yours is incapacitated."

"Thank you, Lord Speaker, but I really require no attendant. I came to request a different sort of favor. Having come into a small inheritance, I should like to invest it all in goods, and try my success at being a merchant."

I thought I saw his lip curl. "A merchant? A stall in the Tlaltelólco market?"

"No, no, my lord. A pochtécatl, a traveling merchant."

He sat back on his bearskin and regarded me in silence. What I was asking was a promotion in civil status approximately equal to what I had been given in military rank. Though the pochtéca were all technically commoners like myself, they were of the highest class of commoners. They could, if fortunate and clever in their trading, become richer than most pípiltin nobles, and command almost as many privileges. They were exempt from many of the common laws and subject mainly to their own, enacted and enforced by themselves. They even had their own chief god, Yacatecútli, the Lord Who Guides. And they jealously restricted their numbers; they would not admit as a pochtécatl just anybody who applied to be one.

"You have been awarded a rank of command soldier," Ahuítzotl said at last, rather grumpily. "And you would neglect that to put a pack of trinkets on your back and thick-soled walking sandals on your feet? Need we remind you, young man, we Mexíca are historically a nation of valiant warriors, not wheedling tradesmen."

"Perhaps war has outlasted some of its usefulness, Lord Speaker," I said, braving his scowl. "I truly believe that our traveling merchants nowadays do more than all our armies to extend the influence of the Mexíca and to bring wealth to Tenochtítlan. They provide commerce with nations too far distant to be easily subjugated, but rich in goods and commodities they will readily barter or sell."

"You make the trade sound easy," Ahuítzotl interrupted. "Let us tell you, it has often been as hazardous as soldiering. The expeditions of pochtéca leave here laden with cargoes of considerable value. They have been raided by savages or bandits before they ever arrived at their intended destinations. When they did reach them, their wares were often simply confiscated and nothing given in return. For those reasons, we are obliged to send a sizable army troop along to protect every such expedition. Now you tell us: why should we continue to dispatch armies of nursemaids and not armies of plunderers?"

"With all respect, I believe the Revered Speaker already knows why," I said. "For a so-called nursemaid troop, Tenochtítlan supplies only the armed men themselves. The pochtéca carry, besides their trade goods, the food and provisions for each journey, or purchase them along the way. Unlike an army, they do not have to forage and pillage and make new enemies as they go. So they arrive safely at their destination, they do their profitable trading, they march themselves and your armed men home again, and they pay a lavish tax into your Snake Woman's treasury. The predators along the route learn a painful lesson and they cease to haunt the trade roads. The people of the far lands learn that a peaceable commerce is to their advantage as well as ours. Every expedition which returns makes that journey easier for the next one. In time, I think, the pochtéca will be able entirely to dispense with your supportive troops."

Ahuítzotl demanded testily, "And what then becomes of our fighting men, when Tenochtítlan ceases to extend its domain? When the Mexíca no longer strive to grow in might and power, but simply sit and grow fat on commerce? When the once respected and feared Mexíca have become a swarm of peddlers haggling over weights and measures?"

"My lord exaggerates, to put this upstart in his place," I said, purposely exaggerating my own humility. "Let your fighters fight and your traders trade. Let the armies subjugate the nations easily within their reach, like Michihuácan nearby. Let the merchants bind the farther nations to us with ties of trade. Between them, Lord Speaker, there need never be any limit set to the world won and held by the Mexíca."

Ahuítzotl regarded me again, through an even longer silence. So, it seemed, did the ferocious bear's head above his throne. Then he said, "Very well. You have told us the reasons why you admire the profession of traveling merchants. Can you tell us some reasons why the profession would benefit from your joining it?"

"The profession, no," I said frankly. "But I can suggest some reasons why the Uey-Tlatoáni and his Speaking Council might thus benefit."

He raised his bushy eyebrows. "Tell us, then."

"I am a trained scribe, which most traveling merchants are not. They know only numbers and the keeping of accounts. As the Revered Speaker has seen, I am capable of setting down accurate maps and detailed descriptions in word pictures. I can come back from my travels with entire books telling of other nations, their arsenals and storehouses, their defenses and vulnerabilities. . . ." His eyebrows had lowered again during that speech. I thought it best to trail off humbly, "Of course, I realize that I must first persuade the pochtéca themselves that I qualify for acceptance into their select society. . . ."

Ahuítzotl said drily, "We doubt that they would long remain obdurate toward a candidate proposed by their Uey-Tlatoáni. Is that all you ask, then? That we sponsor you as a pochtécatl?"

"If it pleases my lord, I should like to take two companions. I ask that I be assigned not a troop of soldiers, but the Cuachic Extli-Quani, as our military support. Just the one man, but I know him of old, and I believe he will be adequate. I ask also that I may take the boy Cozcatl. He should be ready to travel when I am."

Ahuítzotl shrugged. "The cuachic we shall order detached from active army duty. He is overage for anything more useful than nursemaiding, anyway. As for the slave, he is already yours, and yours to command."

"I would rather he were not, my lord. I should like to offer him his freedom as a small restitution for the accident he suffered yesterday. I ask that the Revered Speaker officially elevate him from the status of tlacotli to that of a free macehuáli. He will accompany me not as a slave, but with a free partner's share in the enterprise."

"We will have a scribe prepare the paper of manumission," said Ahuítzotl. "Meanwhile, we cannot refrain from remarking that this will be the most quaintly composed trading expedition ever to set out from Tenochtítlan. Whither are you bound on your first journey?"

"All the way to the Maya lands, Lord Speaker, and back again, if the gods allow. Extli-Quani has been there before, which is one reason I want him along. I hope we will return with a considerable profit to be shared with my lord's treasury. I am certain we will return with much information of interest and value to my lord."

What I did not say was that I fervently hoped also to return with my vision restored. The reputation of the Maya physicians was my overriding reason for choosing the Maya country as our destination.

"Your requests are granted," said Ahuítzotl. "You will await a summons to appear at The House of Pochtéca for examination." He stood up from his grizzled-bear throne, to indicate that the interview was terminated. "We shall be interested to talk to you again, Pochtécatl Mixtli, when you return. If you return."

I went upstairs again, to my apartment, to find Cozcatl awake, sitting up in the bed, hands over his face, crying as if his life were finished. Well, a good part of it was. But when I entered and he looked up and saw me, his face showed first bewildered shock, then delighted recognition, then a radiant smile beaming through his tears.

"I thought you were dead!" he wailed, scrambling out from the quilts and hobbling painfully toward me.

"Get back in that bed!" I commanded, scooping him up and carrying him there, while he insisted on telling me:

"Someone seized me from behind, before I could flee or cry out. When I woke later, and the doctor said you had not returned to the palace, I supposed you must be dead. I thought I had been wounded only so I could not warn you. And then, when I woke in your bed a little while ago, and you still were not here, I *knew* you must—"

"Hush, boy," I said, as I tucked him back under the quilt.

"But I failed you, master," he whimpered. "I let your enemy get past me."

"No, you did not. Chimáli was satisfied to injure you instead of me, this time. I owe you much, and I will see that the debt is paid. This I promise: when the time comes that I again have Chimáli in my power, *you* will decide the fitting punishment for him. Now," I said uncomfortably, "are you aware—in what manner he wounded you?"

"Yes," said the boy, biting his lip to stop its quivering. "When it happened, I knew only that I was in frightful pain, and I fainted. The good doctor let me stay in my faint while he—while he did what he could. But then he held something of a piercing smell under my nose, and I woke up sneezing. And I saw—where he had sewn me together."

"I am sorry," I said. It was all I could think to say.

Cozcatl ran a hand down the quilt, cautiously feeling himself, and he asked shyly, "Does this mean I am a girl now, master?"

"What a ridiculous idea!" I said. "Of course not."

"I must be," he said sniffling. "I have seen between the legs of only one female undressed, the lady who was late our mistress in Texcóco. When I saw myself—down there—before the doctor put on the bandage—it looked just the way *her* private parts looked."

"You are not a girl," I said firmly. "You are far less so than the scoundrel Chimáli, who knifes from behind, in the way only a woman would fight. Why, there have been many warriors who have suffered that same wound in combat, Cozcatl, and they have gone on being warriors of manly strength and ferocity. Some have become more mighty and famous heroes afterward than they were before."

He persisted, "Then why did the doctor—and why do you, master—look so long-faced about it?"

"Well," I said, "it does mean that you will never father any children."

"Oh?" he said, and, to my surprise, seemed to brighten. "That is no great matter. I have never liked being a child myself. I hardly care to make any others. But... does it also mean that I can never be a husband?"

"No... not necessarily," I said hesitantly. "You will just have to seek the proper sort of wife. An understanding woman. One who will accept what kind of husbandly pleasure you can give. And you did give pleasure to that unmentionable lady in Texcóco, did you not?"

"She said I did." He began to smile again. "Thank you for your reassuring me, master. Since I am a slave, and therefore cannot own a slave, I *would* like to have a wife someday."

"From this moment, Cozcatl, you are not a slave, and I am no longer your master."

The smile went, and alarm came into his face. "What has happened?"

"Nothing, except that now you are my friend and I am yours."

He said, his voice tremulous, "But a slave without a master is a poor thing, master. A rootless and a helpless thing."

I said, "Not when he has a friend whose life and fortunes he shares. I do have some small fortune now, Cozcatl. You have seen it. And I have plans for increasing it, as soon as you are fit to travel. We are going south, into the alien lands, as pochtéca. What do you think of that? We will prosper together, and you will never be poor or rootless or helpless. I have just come from asking the Revered Speaker's sanction of the enterprise. I have also asked him for the official paper which says that Cozcatl is no longer my slave but my partner and friend."

Again there were tears and a smile on his face at the same time. He laid one of his small hands on my arm, the first time he had ever touched me without command or permission, and he said, "Friends do not need papers to tell them they are friends."

Tenochtítlan's community of merchants had, not many years before, erected its own building to serve as a combined warehouse for the trading stock of all the members, as their meeting hall, accounting offices, archival libraries, and the like. The House of Pochtéca was situated not far from The Heart of the One World and, though smaller than a palace, it was quite palatial in its appointments. There was a kitchen and a dining room for the serving of refreshments to members and visiting tradesmen, and sleeping apartments upstairs for those visitors who came from afar and stayed overnight or longer. There were many servants, one of whom, rather superciliously, admitted me on the day of my appointment and led me to the luxurious chamber where three elderly pochtéca sat waiting to interview me.

I had come prepared to be properly deferential toward the august company, but not to be intimidated by them. Though I made the gesture of kissing the earth to the examiners, I then straightened and, without looking behind me, undid my mantle's clasp and sat down. Neither the mantle nor I hit the floor. The servant, however surprised he may have been by this commoner's magisterial air, somehow simultaneously caught my garment and whisked an icpáli chair under me.

One of the men returned my salute with the merest movement of a hand, and told the servant to bring chocolate for us all. Then the three sat and regarded me for some time, as if taking my measure with their eyes. The men wore the plainest of mantles, and no ornaments at all, in the pochtéca tradition of being inconspicuous, unostentatious, even secretive about their wealth and station. However, their constraint in dress was a bit belied by their all three being almost oilily fat from good eating and easy living. And two of them smoked poquíeltin in holders of chased gold.

"You come with excellent references," one of the men said acidly, as if he resented not being able to reject my candidacy forthwith.

"But you must have adequate capital," said another. "What is your worth?"

I handed over the list I had made of the various goods and currencies I possessed. As we sipped our frothy chocolate, on that occasion flavored and scented with the flower of magnolia, they passed the list from hand to hand.

"Estimable," said one.

"But not opulent," said another.

"How old are you?" the other asked me.

"Twenty and one, my lords."

"That is very young."

"But no handicap, I hope," I said. "The great Fasting Coyote was only sixteen when he became the Revered Speaker of Texcóco."

"Assuming you do not aspire to a throne, young Mixtli, what are your plans?"

"Well, my lords, I believe my richer cloth goods, the embroidered mantles and such, could hardly be afforded by any country people. I shall sell them to the nobles of the city here, who can pay the prices they are worth. Then I shall invest the proceeds in plainer and more practical fabrics, in rabbit-hair blankets, in cosmetics and medicinal preparations, in those manufactured things procurable only here. I shall carry them south and trade for things procurable only from other nations."

"That is what we have all been doing for years," said one of the men, unimpressed. "You make no mention of travel expenses. For example, a part of your investment must go to hire a train of tamémime."

"I do not intend to hire porters," I said.

"Indeed? You have a sufficient company to do all the hauling and toiling yourselves? That is a foolish economy, young man. A hired tamémi is paid a set daily wage. With companions you must share out your profits."

I said, "There will be only two others besides myself sharing in the venture."

"Three men?" the elder said scoffingly. He tapped my list. "With just the obsidian to carry, you and your two friends will collapse before you get across the southern causeway."

I patiently explained, "I do not intend to do any carrying or to hire any porters, because I will buy slaves for that work."

All three men shook their heads pityingly. "For the price of one husky slave, you could afford a whole troop of tamémime."

"And then," I pointed out, "have to keep them fed and shod and clothed. All the way south and back."

"But your slaves will go empty-bellied and barefooted? Really, young man . . ."

"As I dispose of the goods carried by the slaves, I will sell off the slaves. They should command a good price in those lands from which we have captured or conscripted so many of the native workers."

The elders looked slightly surprised, as if that was an idea new to them. But one said, "And there you are, deep in the southern wilds, with no porters *or* slaves to carry home your acquisitions."

I said, "I plan to trade only for those goods that are of great worth in little bulk or weight. I will not, as so many pochtéca do, seek jadestone or tortoiseshell or heavy animal skins. Other traders buy everything offered them, simply *because* they have the porters to pay and feed, and they might as well load them down. I will barter for nothing but items like the red dyes and the rarest feathers. It may require more circuitous traveling and more time to find such specialized things. But even I alone can carry home a bag full of the precious dye or a compacted bale of quetzal tototl plumes, and that one bundle would repay my entire investment a thousandfold."

The three men looked at me with a new if perhaps grudging respect. One of them conceded, "You have given this enterprise some thought."

I said, "Well, I am young. I have the strength for an arduous journey. And I have plenty of time."

One of the men laughed wryly. "You think, then, that we have always been old and obese and sedentary." He pulled aside his mantle to show four puckered scars in the flesh of his right side. "The arrows of the Huichol, when I ventured into their mountains of the northwest, seeking to buy their Eye-of-God talismans."

Another lifted his mantle from the floor to show that he had but one foot. "A nauyáka snake in the Chiapa jungles. The venom kills before you can take ten breaths. I had to amputate immediately, with my own maquáhuitl in my own hand."

The third man bent so that I could see the top of his head. What I had taken for a full crop of white hair was really only a fringe around a dome that was a red and crinkled scar. "I went into the northern desert, seeking the dream-giving peyotl cactus buds. I made my way through the Chichiméca dog people, through the Téochichiméca wild dog people, even through the Zácachichiméca rabid dog people. But at last I fell among the Yaki, and, compared to those barbarians, all the dog people are as rabbits. I escaped with my life, but some Yaki savage is now wearing my scalp on a belt festooned with the hair of many other men."

Chastened, I said, "My lords, I marvel at your adventures, and I am awed by your courage, and I only hope I can someday approach your stature as pochtéca of achievement. I would be honored to be counted among the least of your society, and I would be grateful to partake of your hard-won knowledge and experience."

The three men exchanged another look. One of them murmured, "What say you?" and the other two nodded. The scalped old man said to me:

"Your first trading journey will necessarily be the real test of your acceptability. For know this: not all novice pochtéca come back from even that first foray. We will do everything possible to help you prepare properly. The rest is up to you."

I said, "Thank you, my lords. I will do whatever you suggest and heed whatever you care to speak. If you disapprove of my intended plan—"

"No, no," said one of them. "It has commendable originality and audacity. Let some of the merchandise carry the rest of the merchandise. Heh heh."

"We would amend your plan only to this extent," said another. "You are right, that your luxury goods would best be sold here in Tenochtítlan. But you should not waste the time necessary to sell them piece by piece."

"No, do not waste time," said the third. "Through long experience and through counsel with the seers and sayers, we have determined that the most auspicious date to set out upon an expedition is the day One Serpent. Today is Five House, so—let me see—a One Serpent day is coming up on the calendar in just twenty and three days. It will be the only One Serpent day in this year's dry season, which—believe me—is the only season for traveling south."

The first man spoke again. "Bring to us here your stock of those rich clothes and fabrics. We will calculate their worth and give you fair exchange in more suitable trade goods. We can dispose of the luxury items locally, and in our own good time. We will deduct only a small fraction on the exchange, as your initiatory contribution to our god Yacatecútli and to the maintenance of the society's facilities."

Perhaps I hesitated for a moment. He raised his eyebrows and said, "Young Mixtli, do not distrust your colleagues. Unless each of us is scrupulously honest, none of us profits or even survives. Our philosophy is as simple as that. And know this, too: you are to deal equally honestly with even the most ignorant savages of the most backward lands. Because, wherever you travel, some other pochtécatl has gone before or will come after. Only if every one trades fairly will the next be allowed into a community—or leave it alive."

I approached old Blood Glutton with some caution, half expecting him to erupt in profanity at the proposal that he play "nursemaid" to a fogbound first-time pochtécatl and a convalescent young boy. But, to my surprise, he was more than enthusiastic.

"Me? Your only armed escort? You would trust your lives and fortune to this old bag of wind and bones?" He blinked several times, snorted, and blew his nose into his hand. "Why, how could I decline such a vote of confidence?"

I said, "I would not propose it if I did not know you to be considerably more than wind and bones."

"Well, the war god knows I want no part of another farcical campaign like that one in Texcála. And my alternative— ayya!—is to teach again in a House of Building Strength. But ayyo!—to see those far lands again . . ." He gazed off toward the southern horizon. "By the war god's granite balls, yes! I thank you for the offer and I accept with gladness, young Fog—" He coughed. "Er—master?"

"Partner," I said. "You and I and Cozcatl will share equally in whatever we bring back. And I hope you will call me Mixtli."

"Then, Mixtli, allow me to take on the first task of preparation. Let me go to Azcapotzálco and do the buying of the slaves. I am an old hand at judging man-flesh, and I have known those dealers to pull some cheating tricks. Like tamping melted beeswax under the skin of a scrawny chest."

I exclaimed, "Whatever for?"

"The wax hardens and gives a man the bulging pectoral muscles of a tocotíni flyer, or gives a woman breasts like those of the legendary pearl divers who inhabit The Islands of the Women. Of course, come a hot day, the woman's teats droop to her knees. Oh, do not worry; I will not buy any female slaves. Unless things down south have changed drastically, we will not lack for willing cooks, laundresses—bed warmers as well."

So Blood Glutton took my quills of gold dust and went off to the slave market in Azcapotzálco on the mainland and, after some days of culling and bargaining, came back with twelve good husky men. No two were of the same tribe or from the same dealer's slave pen; that was Blood Glutton's precaution against any of them being friends or cuilóntin lovers who might conspire in mutiny or escape. They came already supplied with names, but we could not trouble to memorize all of those, and simply redubbed the men Ce, Ome, Yeyi, and so on; that is, numbers One, Two, Three, through Twelve.

During those days of preparation, Ahuítzotl's palace physician was allowing Cozcatl out of bed for longer and longer periods at a time, and finally removed the stitches and bandages, and prescribed exercises for him to perform. Soon the boy was as healthy and spirited as before, and the only thing remindful of his injury was that he had to squat like a female to urinate.

I made the exchange of goods at The House of Pochtéca, turning in my high-quality wares and getting in return about sixteen times their quantity in more practical cheap trade goods. Then I had to select and purchase the equipment and provisions for our expedition, and the three elders who had conducted my examination were only too pleased to help me. I suspect they enjoyed a sense of reliving old times, in arguing over the comparative strength of maguey-fiber versus hemp-rope tumplines, in debating the respective advantages of deerskin water bags (which lose none of their contents) and clay water jars (which lose some to evaporation, but thereby keep the water cool), in acquainting me with the rather crude and imprecise maps they lent me, and in imparting all manner of old-expert advice:

"The one food that transports itself is the techíchi dog. Take along a goodly pack of them, Mixtli. They will forage for their own food and water, but they are too pudgy and timid to run wild. Dog is not the tastiest of meats, of course, but you will be glad to have it handy when wild game is scarce."

"When you do kill a wild animal, Mixtli, you need not carry and age the meat until it loses it toughness and gamy flavor. Wrap the meat in the leaves of a papaya tree and it will be rendered tender and savory overnight."

"Be wary of the women in lands where Mexíca armies have raided. Some of those women were so maltreated by our soldiers, and bear such a grudge, that they have deliberately let their parts become infected with the dread disease nanáua. Such a woman will couple with any passing Mexícatl to get her revenge, so that he will eventually suffer the rotting away of his tepúli and his brain."

"If you should run out of bark paper for keeping your accounts, simply pluck the leaves of any grapevine. Write on them with a sharp twig, and the white scratches on the green leaves are as enduring as paint on paper."

Very early in the morning of the day One Serpent, we left Tenochtítlan: Cozcatl, Blood Glutton, and I—and our twelve slaves under their tumplined burdens, and the pack of plump little dogs frisking about our feet. We set off along the causeway that leads southward across the lake. To our right, to the west, on the nearest point of the mainland, rose the mount of Chapultépec. On its rock face, the first Motecuzóma had caused his likeness to be carved in giant size, and every subsequent Uey-Tlatoáni had eumulated his example. According to report, Ahuítzotl's immense portrait there was almost finished, but we could make out no detail of any of the sculptured reliefs, because that hill was not yet in daylight. The month was our Panquetzalíztli, when the sun rises late and well to the southeast, from directly behind the peak of Popocatépetl.

When we first stepped onto the causeway, there was nothing to be seen in that direction but the usual morning fog glowing with the opal light of imminent dawn. But slowly the fog thinned, and gradually the massive but shapely volcano became discernible, as if it were moving forward from its eternal place and coming toward us. When the veil of mist all dissipated, the mountain was visible in its entirety. The snow-covered cone radiated a glorious halo from the sun behind it. Then, seemingly from the crater itself, Tonatíu bounded upward and the day came, the lake glittering, the lands all around washed with pale gold light and pale purple shadows. At the same instant, the incense-burning volcano exhaled a gout of blue smoke which rose and billowed into the form of a gigantic mushroom.

It had to be a good omen for our journey: the sun blazing on Popocatépetl's snowy crest and making it gleam like white onyx encrusted with all the jewels of the world, while the mountain itself saluted with that lazily climbing smoke, saying:

"You depart, my people, but I remain, as I always have and always will, a beacon to guide your safe return."

I H S

☩

S.C.C.M.

Sanctified, Caesarean, Catholic Majesty,
the Emperor Don Carlos, Our Lord King:

Royal and Imperial Majesty, our Revered Ruler: from the City of Mexíco, capital of New Sapin, this second day after Rogation Sunday in the year of Our Lord one thousand five hundred thirty, greeting.

Regarding the query in Your Esteemed Majesty's most recent letter, we must confess ourselves unable to report to Your Majesty the exact number of Indian prisoners sacrificed by the Aztecs on that occasion of "dedicating" their Great Pyramid, more than forty years ago. The pyramid is long gone now, and so are any records of that day's victims, if indeed any count was ever kept.

Our Aztec chronicler of that occasion, present on that occasion, is himself unable to set the number closer than "thousands"—but it is possible that the old charlatan exaggerates the figure in order to make that day (and that edifice) seem more historically important. Our precursors here, the Franciscan missionary friars, have variously estimated the number of that day's sacrifices at anywhere from four thousand to *eighty* thousand. But those good brothers, too, may have inflated the figure, perhaps unconsciously influenced by their sheer revulsion at such an occurrence, or perhaps to impress upon us, their new-come Bishop, the inherent bestiality of the native population.

We hardly require any exaggeration to persuade us of the Indians' inborn savagery and depravity. We readily believe it, for we have the daily evidence of this storyteller whose presence we endure at Your Most Magnificent Majesty's behest. Over these past months, his few utterances of any value or interest have been woefully outweighed by his vile and venereous maunderings. He has nauseated us by interrupting his accounts of solemnly intended ceremonies, significant travels, and momentous events, simply to dwell on some transient lust—his own or anybody else's—and minutely to describe the gratification of it, in all the physically possible ways, in preferably infructuous ways, in often disgusting and defiling ways, including that perversion of which St. Paul said, "Let it not so much as be named among you."

Given what we have learned from him of the Aztec character, we can readily believe that the Axtecs *would* willingly have slaughtered eighty thousand of their fellows at the Great Pyramid, and in one day, except that the feat would have been impossible. Even if the executing priests had worked unceasingly around the clock, they would have to kill fifty and five men every minute during those twenty and four hours, a rate of nearly one per second. And even the lesser estimates of the number of victims are hard to credit. Having ourself had some experience of mass executions, we find it difficult to believe that such primitive people as these could have managed the disposal of many thousands of corpses before they putrefied and engendered a citywide pestilence.

However, whether the number butchered that day had been eighty thousand, or a tenth of that figure, a hundredth, a thousandth of that figure, it still would be execrable to any Christian and a horror to any civilized person, that so many should have died in the name of a false religion and to the glory of demonic idols. Wherefore, at our instigation and command, Sire, in the seventeen months since our arrival here, there have been destroyed five hundred thirty and two temples of various sizes, from elaborate structures on high pyramids to simple altars erected inside natural caves. There have been destroyed in excess of twenty and one thousand idols of various sizes, from monstrous carved monoliths to small clay household figurines. To none of those will there ever again be a human sacrificed, and we will continue to seek out and cast down others as the borders of New Spain expand.

Even were it not the mandate and function of our office, it would still be our foremost intent: to ferret out and defeat the Devil in every guise he assumed here. In this regard, we invite Your Majesty's particular attention to our Aztec chronicler's latest claim—in the pages next following—his claim that certain of the heathens in the southern part of this New Spain had already recognized some sort of a single Almighty Lord and a seeming twin to the Holy Cross, well before the coming of any missionaries of our Mother Church. Your Majesty's chaplain is inclined to take the information with a measure of dubiety, frankly because we have such a low opinion of the informant.

In Spain, Sire, in our offices as Provincial Inquisitor of Navarre and as Guardian of the miscreants and mendicants at the Reform Institution of Abrojo, we met too many incorrigible reprobates not to recognize another, whatever the color of his skin. This one, in the rare moments when he is not obsessed by the demons of concupiscence, evinces all the other most common human faults and fallibilities—some of them, in his case, egregious—and others besides. We take him to be just as duplicitous as those despicable Marrano Jews of Spain, who have submitted to Baptism and attend our churches and even eat pig meat, but still in secreat maintain and practice their forbidden Judaic worship.

Still, our suspicions and reservations notwithstanding, we endeavor to keep an open mind. If this loathly old man is not capriciously lying or making mock of us, then that southern nation's alleged devotion to an all-highest being and to a cruciform holy symbol could be an anomaly of genuine interest to theologians. Therefore we have sent a mission of Dominican friars into that region to investigate the alleged phenomenon and we will report the results to Your Majesty in due course.

In the meantime, Sire, may Our Lord God and Jesus Christ His Son lavish blessings on Your Ineffable Majesty, that you prosper in all your undertakings, and may you look as beneficently on Your S.C.C.M.'s loyal servant,

(ecce signum) Zumárraga

SEXTA PARS

I THINK I remember every single incident of every single day of that, my first expedition, both going and returning. On later journeys I became uncaring of minor mishaps and even some major ones, of blistered feet and callused hands, of weather enervatingly hot or achingly cold, of the sometimes sickening foods I ate and waters I drank, or the not infrequent lack of any food or water at all. I learned to numb myself, like a drugged priest in trance, to endure without even noticing the many dreary days and roads on which nothing happened at all, when there was nothing to do but plod onward through country of no interest or color or variety.

But on that first journey, simply because it *was* my first, every least object and occurrence was of interest to me, even the occasional hardships and annoyances, and I conscientiously set them down in my word-picture account of the expedition. The Revered Speaker Ahuítzotl, to whom I delivered those bark papers on our return, surely found portions of them hard to decipher, owing to their having suffered the ravages of weather, and submersion in streams we forded, and their having often been blotted by my own sweat. Since Ahuítzotl was a considerably more experienced traveler than I was at that time, he also probably smiled at much in my accounts that naïvely extolled the ordinary and elucidated the obvious.

But those foreign lands and peoples were already beginning to change, even that long ago, what with the incursions of us pochtéca and other explorers bringing to them articles and customs and ideas and words they had never known before. Nowadays, with your Spanish soldiers, your settlers, your missionaries fanning out everywhere, no doubt the natives of those regions are changing beyond even their own recognition. So, whatever less lasting things I accomplished in my lifetime, I would be pleased to think that I did leave for future scholars a record of how those other lands looked, and what their people were like, in the years when they were still largely unknown to the rest of The One World.

If, as I tell you of that first journey, my lords, you should find some of my descriptions of landscapes, of persons, of events, to sound somewhat vague of detail, you must blame my limited eyesight. If, on the other hand, I vividly describe some things you would suppose I could not have seen, you may assume that I am filling in the details from my recollections of later travels along the same route, when I had the ability and opportunity to look more closely and clearly.

On a long journey, allowing for both the arduous trails and the easy, a train of laden men could count on averaging about five one-long-runs between dawn and dark. We covered only half that distance on our first day's march, merely crossing the long causeway to Coyohuácan on the southern mainland, and halting well before sundown to spend the night there, for the next day's march would be no easy one. As you know, this lake region lies in a bowl of land. To get out of it in any direction means climbing to and over its rim. And the mountains to the south, beyond Coyohuácan, are the most precipitous of all those ringing the bowl.

Some years ago, when the first Spanish soldiers came to this country, and when I had first attained some grasp of their language, one of them—watching a file of tamémime trudging along with burdens on their backs and tumplines around their foreheads—asked me, "Why in God's name did not you stupid brutes ever think to use wheels?"

I was not then very familiar with "God's name," but I knew very well what "wheels" were. When I was a small child, I had a toy armadillo made of clay, which I pulled about on a string. Since the armadillo's legs naturally could not walk, the toy was mounted on four little wooden wheels to make it mobile. I told of that to the Spaniard and he demanded, "Then why the Devil did none of you use wheels for transport, like those on our cannons and caissons?" I thought it a foolish question, and I said so, and I got a blow in the face for my insolence.

We knew the utility of round wheels, for we moved extremely heavy things like the Sun Stone by rolling them on logs placed under and ahead of them. But such rollers would have been ineffectual for lighter work, and there were in these lands no animals like your horses and mules and oxen and donkeys, to pull wheeled vehicles. Our only beasts of burden were ourselves, and a hard-muscled tamémi can carry nearly half his own weight for a long distance without strain. If he put that load on wheels, to pull or push it, he would simply be burdened by the extra weight of the wheels, and they would be even more of a hindrance in rough terrain.

Now you Spaniards have laid out many roads, and your animals do the work while your teamsters ride or walk unladen, and I grant that a procession of twenty heavy wagons drawn by forty horses is a fine spectacle. Our little train of three merchants and twelve slaves surely did not look so impressive. But we transported all our wares and most of the provisions for the journey on our own backs and legs, with at least two advantages: we had no voracious draft animals to feed and care for, and our exertions made *us* the stronger each day.

Indeed, the hard-driving Blood Glutton made us all endure more than necessary exertions. Even before we left Tenochtítlan, and at every night's halt along the way, he led the slaves—and Cozcatl and myself, when we were not otherwise occupied—in practice with the spears we all carried. (He himself carried a formidable personal armory of long spear, javelin and throwing stick, maquáhuitl and short knife, a bow and a quiver full of arrows.) It was not difficult for Blood Glutton to convince the slaves that they would be better treated by us than by any bandits who might "liberate" them, and that they had good reason to help us repel any bandits who might attack, and he showed them how.

After stopping the night in a Coyohuácan inn, we marched early again the next morning because, said Blood Glutton, "We must get across the badlands of Cuicuílco before the sun rises high." That name means The Place of Sweet Singing, and perhaps it was once such a place, but it is no longer. It is now a barren of gray-black rock, of waves and ripples and billows of pock-marked rock. From its appearance it could have been a foaming river cascade turned hard and black by the curse of some sorcerer. In actuality, it is a dried flow of lava from the volcano Xitli, which has been dead for so many sheaves of years that only the gods know when it erupted and obliterated The Place of Sweet Singing. That obviously was a city of some size, but there is no knowing what people built it and lived there. The only remaining visible edifice is a pyramid, half buried under the far edge of the lava plain. It is not square-sectioned like most in these lands. The Cuicuílco pyramid, or what can be seen of it, is a conical stack of round terraces.

The bleak black plain, whatever sweetness and song it may once have had, is now no place to linger in the daytime, for its porous lava rock sucks in the sun's heat and exhales it doubly or trebly hot. Even in the cool of that early morning long ago, that wasteland was no pleasant place to traverse. Nothing, not so much as a weed grows there, and no bird chirps, and the only sound we heard was the clangor of our footsteps, as if we walked across the great empty water jars of departed giants.

But at least, during that part of the day's journey, we walked upright. The rest of that day we all spent either hunched forward as we toiled up a mountainside, or leaning backward as we clumped down its other face, then bent forward again to climb the next mountain. And the next and the next. Of course, there was nothing perilous or even really difficult in our crossing of those first ranges, for we were in the region where all trade routes from the south converged on Tenochtítlan, and multitudes of earlier travelers had picked out the easiest paths and stamped them firm. Still, for one as inexperienced as myself, it was a sweat-wringing, back-aching, lung-straining drudgery. When we finally stopped for the night at a hostel in a high-valley village of the Xochimílca, even Blood Glutton was weary enough to make us go through only a perfunctory weapons practice. Then he and the others ate and flopped down on their pallets.

I would have, too, except that a homecoming pochtéca train was also staying the night there, and a part of its journey had bee along some of the ways I intended to take, so I held my sagging eyelids open while I conversed with the pochtécatl in charge, a middle-aged but leather-tough man. His train was one of the major companies, with perhaps a hundred porters and as many supporting Mexíca warriors, so I am sure he looked on ours with tolerant contempt. But he was kindly disposed toward a beginner. He let me unfold my crude maps, and he corrected them in numerous particulars where they were vague or in error, and he marked the location of useful watering places and the like. Then he said:

"I made a profitable trade for a quantity of the precious carmine dye of the Tzapotéca, but I heard a rumor of an even more rare coloring. A purple. Something newly discovered."

I said, "There is nothing new about purple."

"A rich and *permanent* purple," he said patiently. "One that will not fade or turn an ugly green. If such a dye really exists, it will be reserved for only the highest of the nobility. It will be more valuable than emeralds or the feathers of the quetzal tototl."

I nodded. "A really permanent purple never *has* been known before. It would indeed command any price one asked. But you did not seek to pursue the rumor?"

He shook his head. "One disadvantage of a ponderous train. It cannot feasibly be diverted from the known routes of march, or portions of it detached at random. There is too much of substance at stake to go chasing the insubstantial."

"My little troop can go where it will," I hinted.

He looked at me for a time, then shrugged. "It may be a long while before I go to those parts again." He leaned over my map and tapped a spot near the coast of the great southern ocean. "It was here, in Tecuantépec, that a Tzapotécatl merchant told me of the new dye. Not that he told me much. He mentioned a ferocious and unapproachable people called the Chóntaltin. That word means only The Strangers, and what kind of people would call themselves The Strangers? My informant also mentioned snails. Snails! I ask you: snails and strangers—does that make sense? But if you care to take your chances on such fragmentary evidence, young man, I wish you good fortune."

The next evening we came to the town which was and still is the handsomest and most hospitable in the Tlahuíca lands. It is situated on a high plateau, and its buildings are not huddled close together but set well apart and screened from each other by trees and shrubbery and other rich verdure, for which reason the town is called Surrounded by Forest, or Quaunáhuac. That melodious name your thick-tongued countrymen have contorted into the ridiculous and derogatory Cuernavaca, or Cow-Horn, and I hope they will never be forgiven for that.

The town, the surrounding mountains, the crystal air, the climate there, they are all so inviting that Quaunáhuac was always a favorite summering place for the wealthier nobles of Tenochtítlan. The first Motecuzóma built for himself a modest country palace nearby, and other Mexíca rulers afterward enlarged and added to that palace until, in size and luxury, it rivaled any in the capital, and far outdid them all in the extent of its beauteous gardens and grounds. I understand that your Captain-General Cortés has appropriated the palace for his own señorial residence. Perhaps I may be excused, my lord friars, if I remark spitefully that his having settled in Quaunáhuac would be the only legitimate reason for debasing the name of the place.

Though our little train had arrived there well before sundown, we could not resist the temptation to stay and rest the night amid Quaunáhuac's flowers and fragrances. But we rose again before the sun did, and pressed on, to put the remainder of that mountain range behind us.

In each stopping place where we lodged in a travelers' hostel, we three leaders of the train—myself, Cozcatl, and Blood Glutton—were given separate and moderately comfortable sleeping cubicles, while the slaves were squeezed into a

large dormitory room already carpeted with other snoring porters, and our bales of goods were put into guarded safe-rooms,
and our dogs were let to forage in the garbage heaps of the
kitchen yards.

During five days of travel, we were still within the area
where the southern trade routes radiated out from Tenochtítlan,
or into it, so there were many inns conveniently situated for
overnight stops. In addition to providing shelter, storage, hot
baths, and passable meals, each hostel also provided women
for hire. Not having had a woman for a month or so, I might
have been interested, except that all those maátime were extremely homely, and in any case they neglected even to flirt
with me, but concentrated their winks and suggestive gestures
on the men of homecoming trains.

Blood Glutton explained, "They hope to seduce the men
who have been long on the road, who have forgotten what a
really pretty woman looks like, and who cannot wait until they
get to the beauties of Tenochtítlan. You and I may be hungry
enough to take a maátitl on our return, but for now I suggest
we do not waste the energy and expense. There are women
where we are going, and they sell their favors for a mere trinket,
and many of them are lovely. *Ayyo,* wait until you feast your
eyes and other senses on the women of the Cloud People!"

On the sixth morning of our journey, we emerged from the
area where the trade roads converged. Sometime on that same
morning, we crossed an invisible boundary and entered the
impoverished-lands of the Mixtéca, or the Tya Nuü, as they
called themselves, Men of the Earth. While that nation was not
inimical to the Mexíca, neither was it inclined to take measures
for the protection of traveling pochtéca, nor to put up inns and
shelters for them, nor to prevent its own people from taking
what criminal advantage they could of merchant trains.

"We are now in the country where we can likeliest expect
to meet bandits," Blood Glutton warned. "They lurk hereabouts
in hope of ambushing traders either coming from or going to
Tenochtítlan."

"Why here?" I asked. "Why not farther north, where the
trade routes come together and the trains are more numerous?"

"For that precise reason. Back yonder, the trains are often

traveling in company and are too big to be attacked by anything smaller than an army. Out here, the southbound trains have parted company and the homecoming ones have not yet met and mingled. Of course, we are small game, but a bunch of robbers will not ignore us on that account."

So Blood Glutton moved out alone to march far ahead of the rest of us. Cozcatl told me he could only intermittently see the old soldier as a distant dot when we were crossing an extremely wide and flat place clear of trees or brush. But our scout shouted no warning, and the morning passed, with us marching along a still distinct but stiflingly dusty road. We tugged our mantles up to cover nose and mouth, but still the dust made our eyes water and our breathing laborious. Then the road climbed a knoll and we found Blood Glutton waiting for us, sitting halfway up it, his weapons laid neatly side by side on the dusty grass, ready for use.

"Stop here," he said quietly. "They will already know you are coming, from the dust cloud, but they cannot yet have counted you. There are eight of them, Tya Nuü, and not delicate types, crouched right in the road where it passes through a clump of trees and undergrowth. We will give them eleven of us. Any fewer would not have raised such a dust. They would suspect a trick, and be harder to handle."

"To handle how?" I asked. "What do you mean: *give* them eleven of us?"

He motioned for silence, went to the top of the rise, lay down and crawled out of sight for a moment, then crawled backward again, stood up and came to rejoin us.

"Now there are only four of them to be seen," he said, and snorted scornfully. "An old trick. It is midday, so the four are pretending to be humble Mixtéca travelers, resting in the tree shade and preparing a midday bite to eat. They will courteously invite you to partake, and when you are all friends together, sitting companionably about the fire, your weapons laid aside, the other four hidden roundabout will close in—and yya ayya!"

"What do we do, then?"

"The very same thing. We will imitate their ambush, but from a farther surround. I mean some of us will. Let me see. Four and Ten and Six, you are the biggest and the handiest with arms. Drop your packs, leave them here. Bring only your spears and come with me." Blood Glutton himself picked up his maquáhuitl and let his other weapons lie. "Mixtli, you and Cozcatl and the rest march right on into the trap, as if you had not been forewarned. Accept their invitation to stop and rest and eat. Just do not appear *too* stupid and trusting, or that too would give them cause for suspicion."

. Blood Glutton quietly gave the three armed slaves instructions I could not hear. Then he and Ten disappeared around one side of the knoll, Four and Six around the other. I looked at Cozcatl and we smiled to give each other confidence. To the remaining nine slaves I said, "You heard. Simply do what I command, and speak not a word. Let us go on."

We went in single file over the rise and down its other side. I raised an arm in greeting when we sighted the four men. They were feeding sticks to a just-kindled fire.

"Welcome, fellow travelers!" one of them called as we approached. He spoke Náhuatl and he grinned amiably. "Let me tell you, we have come many one-long-runs along this cursed road, and this is the only patch of shade. Will you share it with us? And perhaps a bite of our humble fare?" He held up two dead hares by their long ears.

"We will rest, and gladly," I said, motioning for the rest of my train to dispose themselves as they liked. "But those two scrawny animals will scarcely feed the four of you. I have others of our porters out hunting right now. Perhaps they will bring back the makings of a more sumptuous meal, and you will share with us."

The speaker changed his grin for a hurt look and said reproachfully, "You take us for bandits. So you quickly speak of your numbers. That sounds unfriendly, and it is we who should be wary: only four against your eleven. I suggest that we all put aside our weapons."

Pretending purest innocence, he unslung and tossed away from him the maquáhuitl he carried. His three companions grunted and did the same. I smiled friendlily, leaned my spear against a tree, and gestured to my men. They likewise ostentatiously put their weapons out of reach. I sat down across the fire from the four Mixtéca, two of whom were threading the long-legged carcasses onto green sticks and propping them across the flames.

"Tell me, friend," I said to the apparent leader. "What is the road like, from here southward? Is there anything we should beware of?"

"Indeed, yes!" he said, his eyes glinting. "Bandits do abound. Poor men like us have nothing to fear from them, but I daresay you are carrying goods of value. You might do well to hire us to go with you for your protection."

I said, "I thank you for the offer, but I am not rich enough to afford a retinue of guards. I will make do with my porters."

"Porters are no good as guards. And without guards you will surely be robbed." He said that flatly, stating a fact, but then spoke with a mock wheedle in his voice. "I have another suggestion. Do not risk your goods on the road. Leave them with us for safekeeping, while you go on unmolested."

I laughed.

"I think, young friend, we can persuade you that it would be in your best interest."

"And I think, friend, that now is the time for me to call in my porters from their hunting."

"Do that," he sneered. "Or allow me to call for you."

I said, "Thank you."

For an instant he looked a little puzzled. But he must have decided that I was expecting to escape his trap through sheer bluster. He gave a loud hail, and at the same moment he and his three companions lunged for their weapons. At that moment, too, Blood Glutton, Four, Six, and Ten all stepped simultaneously into the road, but from different places in the trees roundabout. The Tya Nuü froze in surprise, all on their feet, all with their maquáhuime raised, like so many statues of warriors posed in action.

"A good hunt, Master Mixtli!" boomed Blood Glutton. "And I see we have guests. Well, we bring enough and to spare." He dropped what he was carrying, and so did the slaves with him. They each threw down a severed human head.

"Come, friends, I am sure you recognize good meat when you see it," Blood Glutton said jovially to the remaining bandits. They had edged into a defensive position, all of them with their backs to the same big tree, but they looked rather shaken. "Drop the weapons, and do not be bashful. Come, eat hearty."

The four nervously looked about. All the rest of us were armed by then. They jumped when Blood Glutton raised his voice to a bellow: "*I said drop the blades!*" They did. "*I said come!*" They approached the lumps lying on the ground at his feet. "*I said eat!*" They winced as they picked up the relics of their late comrades and turned to the fire. "No, not *cook!*" roared the relentless Blood Glutton. "The fire is for the hares and the hares are for us. I said *eat!*"

So the four men squatted where they were, and began miserably to gnaw. On an uncooked head there is little that is readily chewable except the lips and cheeks and tongue.

Blood Glutton told our slaves, "Take their maquáhuime and destroy them. Go through their pouches and see if they carry anything worth our filching."

Six took the swords and, one at a time, pounded them on a rock until their obsidian edges were all smashed to powder. Ten and Four searched the bandits' belongings, even inside the loincloths they wore. They carried nothing but the barest essentials of travel: fire-drilling sticks and moss tinder, toothbrushing twigs and the like.

Blood Glutton said, "Those hares on the fire look to be ready. Start carving them, Cozcatl." He turned to bark at the Tya Nuü, "And *you!* It is unmannerly to let us eat alone. You keep feeding as long as we do."

All four of the wretches had several times regurgitated what they had already eaten, but they did as they were bidden, tearing with their teeth at the remaining gristle of what had been ears and noses. The sight was enough to spoil any appetite I might have had, or Cozcatl. But the stony old soldier and our twelve slaves fell to the broiled hare meat with alacrity.

Finally, Blood Glutton came to where Cozcatl and I sat, with our backs to the eaters, wiped his greasy mouth on his horny hand, and said, "We could take the Mixtéca along as slaves, but someone would constantly have to guard against their treachery. Not worth the trouble, in my opinion."

I said, "Then kill them, for all I care. They look very near dead right now."

"No-o," Blood Glutton said thoughtfully, sucking a back tooth. "I suggest we let them go. Bandits do not employ swift-messengers or far-callers, but they do have some method of exchanging information about troops to be avoided and traders ripe for robbery. If these four go free to spread their story around, it ought to make any other such bands think twice before attacking us."

"It certainly ought," I said to the man who had not long ago described himself as an old bag of wind and bones.

So we retrieved the packs of Four, Six, and Ten, and the spare weapons of Blood Glutton, and continued on our way. The Tya Nuü did not immediately scamper to put even more distance between us. Sick and exhausted, they simply sat where we left them, too weak even to throw away the bloody, hairy, fly-covered skulls they still held on their laps.

That day's sundown found us in the middle of a green and pleasant but totally uninhabited valley: no village, no inn, no slightest man-made shelter to be seen. Blood Glutton kept us marching until we came to a rivulet of good water, and there he showed us how to make camp. For the first time on the journey, we used our drill and tinder to kindle a fire, and on it we cooked our own evening meal—or the slaves Ten and Three did. We took our blankets from our packs to make our own beds on the ground, all of us all too conscious that there were no walls about the camp or any roof over it, that we were no multitudinous and mutually protective army, that there was only the night and the creatures of the night all around us, and that the god Night Wind that night blew chill.

After we had eaten, I stood at the edge of our circle of firelight and looked out into the darkness: so dark that, even if I could have seen, I would have seen nothing. There was no moon and, if there were stars, they were imperceptible to me.

It was not like my one military campaign, when events had taken me and many others into a foreign land. To this place I had come on my own, and in this place I felt that I was a stray, and an inconsequential one, and reckless rather than fearless. During my nights with the army, there had always been a tumult of talk and noise and commotion, there had been the realization of a crowd about. But that night, behind me in the glow of our single campfire, there was only the occasional quiet word and the subdued sound of the slaves cleaning the utensils, putting wood on the flames and dry brush under our sleeping blankets, the sound of the dogs scuffling for the leavings of our meal.

Before me, in the darkness, there was no trace of activity or humanity. I might have been looking as far as the edge of the world and seeing not another human being or any evidence of another human's ever having been there. And out of the night before me, the wind brought to my ears only one sound, perhaps the loneliest sound one can hear: the barely audible faraway ululation of a coyote wailing as if he mourned for something lost and gone.

I have seldom in my life known loneliness, even when I was most solitary. But that night I did, when I stood—deliberately, to try whether I could endure it—with my back to the world's one patch of light and warmth and my face to the black and empty and uncaring unknown.

Then I heard Blood Glutton order, "Sleep as you would at home or in any bedchamber, entirely undressed. Take off all your clothes or you will *really* feel the chill in the morning, believe me."

Cozcatl spoke up, trying but failing to sound as if he were joking, "Suppose a jaguar comes, and we have to run."

With a straight face, Blood Glutton said, "If a jaguar comes, boy, I guarantee that you will run without noticing whether you are dressed or not. Anyway, a jaguar will eat your garments with as much gusto as he eats little-boy meat." Perhaps he saw Cozcatl's lower lip tremble, for the old soldier chuckled. "Do not worry. No cat will come near a burning campfire, and I will see that it goes on burning." He sighed and added, "It is a habit left over from many campaigns. Every time the fire dims, I awaken. I will keep it fed."

I found no great discomfort in rolling myself into my two blankets, with only some brittle scrub piled between my bare body and the hard, cold ground, because for the last month in my palace chambers I had been sleeping on Cozcatl's thinly cushioned pallet. During that same time, though, Cozcatl had been sleeping in my billowy, soft, warm bed, and evidently he had got accustomed to comfort. For that night, while snores and wheezes came from the other bundled forms about the fire, I heard him restlessly shifting and turning in his place on the ground, trying to find a reposeful position, and whimpering slightly when he could not. So finally I hissed over to him, "Cozcatl, bring your blankets here."

He came, gratefully, and with his blankets and mine we arranged a double thickness of both pallet and cover. Then, the activity having chilled both our naked bodies to violent shivering, we hastened to get into the improved bed, and huddled together like two nested dishes: Cozcatl's back arched into my front, my arms around him. Gradually our shivering abated, and Cozcatl murmured, "Thank you, Mixtli," and he soon was breathing the regular soft breaths of sleep.

But then *I* could not doze off. As my body warmed against his, so did my imagination. It was not like resting alongside a man, the way we soldiers had lain in windrows to keep warm and dry in Texcála. And it was not like lying with a woman, as I had last done on the night of the warrior's banquet. No, it was like the times I had lain with my sister, in the early days of our first exploring and discovering and experimenting with each other, when she had been no bigger than the boy was. I had grown much since then, in many respects, but Cozcatl's body, so small and tender, reminded me of how Tzitzitlíni had felt, pressed against me, in the time when she too was a child. My tepúli stirred and began to push itself upward between my belly and the boy's buttocks. Sternly I reminded myself that Cozcatl *was* a boy, and only half my age.

Nevertheless, my hands also remembered Tzitzi and, without my commanding them, they moved reminiscently along the boy's body—the not yet muscular or angular shape, so much like a young girl's; the not yet toughened skin; the slight indentation of waist and the childishly pudgy abdomen; the soft, cloven backside; the slim legs. And there, between the legs, not the stiff or spongy protuberance of male parts, but a smooth, inviting inward declivity. His buttocks nestled in my groin, while my member burrowed between his thighs, against the furrow of soft scar tissue that could have been a closed tipíli, and by then I was too much aroused to refrain from doing what I did next. Hoping I might do it without waking him, I began very, very gently to move.

"Mixtli?" the boy whispered, in a wondering way.

I stopped my movement and laughed, quietly but shakily,

and whispered, "Perhaps I should have brought along a woman slave after all."

He shook his head and said sleepily, "If I can be of that use..." and he wriggled backward even more intimately against me, and he tightened his thighs about my tepúli, and I resumed my movement.

When later we were both asleep, still nestled together, I dreamt a jeweled dream of Tzitzitlíni, and I believe I did that thing once again during the night—in the dream with my sister, in reality with the little boy.

I think I can understand Fray Toribio's abrupt and flustered departure. He goes to teach a catechism class of young people, does he not?

I myself wondered if overnight I had become a cuilóntli, and whether I would henceforward yearn only for small boys, but the worry did not long persist. At the end of the next day's march we came to a village named Tlancualpícan, and it boasted a rudimentary hostel that offered meals, baths, and an adequate dormitory, but had only a single private sleeping cubicle to let.

"I will crowd in with the slaves," said Blood Glutton. "You and Cozcatl take the room."

I know my face flamed, for I realized that he must have heard something the night before: perhaps the crackling of our brush pallet. He saw my face and burst into a guffaw, then stifled it to say:

"So it was a first time on the young traveler's first long journey abroad. And now he doubts his manhood!" He shook his gray head and laughed again. "Let me tell you, Mixtli. When you truly need a woman and there is none available— or none to your taste—use whatever substitute you will. In my own experience on many military marches, the villages in our path have often sent their females fleeing into hiding. So we used for women the warriors we captured."

I know not what expression my face wore, but he laughed again at me and continued:

"Do not look so. Why, Mixtli, I have known soldiers in real

privation to utilize the animals an evacuating enemy left behind: pet does, the larger breeds of dogs. Once in the Maya lands, one of my men claimed to have enjoyed himself with a female tapir he ran down in the jungle."

I suppose I looked relieved then, if still somewhat abashed, for he concluded:

"Be glad you have your small companion, and that he is to your taste, and that he loves you enough to be compliant. I can tell you, when the next appealing female crosses your path, you will find your natural urges undiminished."

But just to be sure, I made a test. After we had bathed and dined at the inn, I wandered up and down the two or three streets of Tlancualpícan until I saw a woman seated in a window, and saw her head turn as I went by. I went back and went close enough to make out that she was smiling and that she was, if not beautiful, certainly not repugnant. She showed no signs of carrying the nanáua disease: no rash on her face; her hair abundant, not scanty; no sores about the mouth; none anywhere else, as I soon verified.

I had carried with me, on purpose, a cheap jadestone pendant. I gave that to her, and she gave me her hand to help me clamber through the window—for her husband was in the other room, laid out drunk—and we gave each other a more than generous measure of enjoyment. I returned to the inn reassured of two things. First, that I had lost none of my capacity to want and to please a woman. Second, that a capable and willing woman—in my estimation, and I had some basis for comparison—was better equipped for such enjoyments than even the prettiest and most irresistible boy.

Oh, Cozcatl and I often slept together after that first time, whenever we stayed at an inn where the accommodations were limited, or when we camped in the open and chose to bundle together for mutual comfort. But my subsequent sexual employment of him was infrequent, done only on those occasions when, as Blood Glutton had said, I really hungered for such a service and there was no other or preferable partner. Cozcatl devised various means of satisfying me, probably because he would have become bored with an always passive participation. I will not speak further of those things, and in any case we eventually ceased doing them, but he and I never ceased being the closest of friends during all the years of his life, until the day he decided to stop living.

✠

The dry-season weather remained fine for traveling, with clement days and brisk nights, though as we got farther south the nights became almost warm enough for us to sleep outdoors without blankets, and the middays became so very warm that we wished we could doff everything else we wore and carried.

It was a lovely land we crossed. Some mornings we would wake in a field of flowers on which the dew of first dawn still glittered, a field of flashing jewels extending to the horizon in all directions. The flowers might be of profuse varieties and colors, or they might be all the same: sometimes those tall ones whose big, shaggy, yellow blooms turn always to face the sun.

As the dawn gave way to day, our company might move through any kind of terrain imaginable. Sometimes it would be a forest so luxuriantly leafed as to discourage the growth of all underbrush, and its floor would be a carpet of soft grass in which the tree trunks stood as neatly spaced as in a noble-man's park planted by a master gardener. Or we might wade through cool seas of feathery fern. Or, invisible to each other, we would shoulder through banks of gold and green reeds or silver and green grasses that grew higher than our heads. Occasionally we would have to climb a mountain and, from its top, there would be a view of other and farther mountains, dimming in color from the nearby green to the hazy dove-blue of distance.

Whichever man was in the lead would often be startled by the sudden signs of unsuspected life all about us. A rabbit would crouch as still as a stump until our leader almost trod upon him, and then would break his immobility and bound away. Or the leading man might similarly stir a pheasant into booming flight, almost brushing his face. Or he would flush coveys of quail or dove, or a swift-runner bird that would dash away on foot in its peculiar stretched-out stride. Many times an armored armadillo would shuffle out of our way, or a lizard would flicker across our path—and, as we got ever farther south, the lizards became iguanas, some of them as long as Cozcatl was tall, and crested and wattled, and brilliantly colored red and green and purple.

Almost always, there was a hawk circling silently far over our heads, keeping keen watch for any small game our passage might frighten into movement and vulnerability—or a vulture circling silently, hoping we would discard something edible. In the woods, flying squirrels glided from high branches to lower ones, seeming as buoyant as the hawks and vultures, but not as silent; they chittered angrily at us. In forest or meadow, there forever fluttered or hovered about us bright parakeets and gemlike hummingbirds and the stingless black bees and multitudes of butterflies of extravagant coloring.

Ayyo, there was always color—color everywhere—and the middays were the most colorful of times, for they blazed like coffers of treasure newly opened, full of every stone and metal prized by men and gods. In the sky, which was turquoise, the sun flared like a round shield of beaten gold. Its light shone on ordinary boulders and rocks and pebbles, and transformed them into topaz or jacinths or the opals we called firefly stones; or silver or amethysts or tezcatl, the mirror stone; or pearls, which of course are not really stones but the hearts of oysters; or amber, which also is not a stone but foam made solid. All the greenery around us would turn to emerald and greenstone and jadestone. If we were in a forest, where the sunlight was dappled by the emerald foliage, we would unconsciously walk with care and delicacy, so as not to tread upon the precious golden disks and dishes and platters strewn underfoot.

At twilight the colors all began to lose their vibrancy. The hot colors cooled, even the reds and yellows subdued themselves into blue, then purple and gray. At the same time, a colorless mist would begin to rise from the clefts and hollows of the land about us, until its separate billows merged into a blanket from which we kicked tufts and fluffs as we plodded through it. The bats and night birds would begin to dart about, snatching invisible insects on the wing, and managing magically never to collide with us or any tree branches or each other. When full darkness came, we were sometimes still aware of the country's beauty, even though we could not see it. For on many nights we went to sleep inhaling the heady perfume of those moon-white blossoms that *only* at night open their petals and breathe out their sweet sighs.

If the end of a day's march coincided with our arrival at some Tya Nuü community, we would spend the night under a roof and within walls—which might be of adobe brick or wood in the more populous places, or mere reed and thatch in the smaller ones. We could usually purchase decent food, sometimes even choice delicacies peculiar to that neighborhood, and hire women to cook and serve it. We could buy hot water for baths and occasionally even rent the use of a family's steam house, where such a thing existed. In the sufficiently large communities, and for a trifling payment, Blood Glutton and I could usually find a woman apiece, and sometimes we could also procure a female slave for our men to share around among them.

On as many nights, however, the dark caught us in the empty land between populated places. Though all of us had by then got accustomed to sleeping on the ground, and had got over any uneasiness about the black void around us, those nights were naturally less enjoyable. Our evening meal might consist only of beans and atóli mush, and water to drink. But that was not so much a privation as was the lack of a bath: having to go to bed crusted with the day's dirt and itching from insect bites and stings. Sometimes, though, we were fortunate enough to camp beside a stream or pond in which we could manage at least a cold-water dip. And sometimes, too, our meal included the meat of a boar or some other wild animal, usually provided by Blood Glutton, of course.

But Cozcatl had taken to carrying the old soldier's bow and arrows and idly shooting at tress and cactus along the way, until he had become fairly proficient with the weapon. Since he was boyishly inclined to let fly at just about anything that moved, he usually brought down creatures that were too small to feed us all—a single pheasant or ground squirrel—and once he sent our entire company scattering for the several horizons when he punctured a brown-and-white-striped skunk, with consequences you can imagine. But one day, scouting out ahead of the train, he flushed a deer from its daytime bed, and put an arrow into it, and chased the wounded animal until it staggered and fell and died. He was awkwardly carving at it with his little flint knife when we caught up to him, and Blood Glutton said:

"Do not bother, boy. Let it lie for the coyotes and vultures. See, you pierced it through the guts. So the contents of its bowels spilled into the body cavity, and all the meat will have been foully tainted." Cozcatl looked crestfallen, but nodded when the old warrior instructed him, "Whatever the animal, aim to hit it here or here, in the heart or the lungs. That gives it a more merciful death and yields us a usable meat." The boy learned the lesson, and eventually did provide us with one meal of good venison from a doe he killed properly and cleanly.

At every evening's halt, whether in village or wilderness, I let Blood Glutton, Cozcatl, and the slaves make camp or make arrangements for our stay. The first thing I did was to get out my paints and bark papers and set down my account of that day's progress: a map of the route, as accurate as I could make it, with guiding landmarks, the nature of the terrain, and so on; plus a description of any extraordinary sights we had seen or any noteworthy events which had occurred. If there was not time for me to do all that before the light failed utterly, I would finish it early the next morning while the others broke camp. I always made sure to set down the chronicle as soon as possible, while I remembered every pertinent thing. The fact that, in those younger years, I so assiduously exercised my memory may account for the fact that, now in my dwindling years, I still remember so much so clearly . . . including a number of things I might wish had dimmed and disappeared.

On that journey, too, as on later ones, I added to my word knowing. I strove to learn the new words of the lands we traveled through, and the way those words were strung together by the people who spoke them. As I have said, my native Náhuatl was already the common tongue of the trade routes, and in almost every smallest village the Mexíca pochtéca could find someone who spoke it adequately. Most traveling merchants were satisfied to find such an interpreter, and to do all their dealing through him. A single trader in his career might have to barter with the speakers of every tongue spoken outside the Triple Alliance lands. That trader, occupied with all the concerns of commerce, was seldom inclined to bother learning any foreign language, let alone all of them.

I *was* so inclined, and I seemed to have a facility for picking up new languages without much difficulty. That was possibly because I had been studying words all my life, possibly because of my early exposure to the different dialects and accents of the Náhuatl spoken on Xaltócan, in Texcóco, Tenochtítlan and even, briefly, in Texcála. The twelve slaves of our train spoke their own several native tongues, in addition to the fragmentary Náhuatl they had absorbed during their captivity, so I began my learning of new words from them, by pointing at this and that object along our route of march.

I do not pretend that I became fluent and voluble in every one of the foreign languages we encountered during that expedition. Not until after many more travels could I say that. But I picked up enough of the speech of the Tya Nuü, Tzapotéca, Chiapa, and Maya that I could at least make myself understood in almost every place. That ability to communicate also enabled me to learn local customs and manners, and to conform to them, hence to be more hospitably accepted by each people. Aside from making my trip a more enjoyable experience, that mutual acceptance also secured for me some better trades than if I had been the usual "deaf and dumb" trader bargaining through an interpreter.

I offer one example. When we crossed the ridge of a minor mountain range, our ordinarily oafish slave named Four began to exhibit an uncharacteristic liveliness, even a sort of happy agitation. I questioned him in what I had learned of his language, and he told me that his natal village of Ynochíxtlan lay not far ahead of us. He had left there some years ago, to seek his fortune in the outside world, had been captured by bandits, had been sold by them to a Chalca noble, had been resold several times more, had eventually been included in an offering of tribute to The Triple Alliance, and so had ended on the block at the slave market where Blood Glutton had found him.

I would have known all that soon enough, without knowing anything of his language. For on our arrival in Ynochíxtlan we were met by Four's father, mother, and two brothers bounding out to greet the long-lost wanderer with tears and cheers. They and the village's tecútli—or chagóola, as a petty ruler is called in those parts—pleaded with me to sell the man back to them. I expressed my sympathy with their feelings, but I pointed out that Four was the biggest of all our porters and the only one who could carry our heavy sack of raw obsidian. At that, the chagóola proposed to purchase the man *and* the obsidian, undeniably of use in that country where the toolmaking rock did not exist. He suggested, as a fair trade, a quantity of the woven shawls which were the unique product of that village.

I admired the shawls shown me, for they were truly handsome and practical garments. But I had to tell the villagers that I was only a third of the way to the end of my journey, that I was not yet seeking to trade, for I did not care to acquire new goods which I should have to haul all the way south and then home again. I might have been argued out of that stand, for I had privately determined to leave Four with his family even if I had to give him away, but, to my pleased surprise, his mother and father sided with me.

"Chagóola," they said respectfully to their village chief. "Regard the young trader. He has a kindly face, and he is sympathetic. But our son is his legal property, and he surely paid a high price for such a son as ours. Would you haggle over the freedom of one of your own people?"

I hardly had to say anything more. I simply stood there, looking kindly and sympathetic, while the vociferous Four family made their own chagóola seem the hardhearted bargainer. Finally, shamefaced, he agreed to open the village treasury and to pay me in currency instead of goods. For the man and the sack, he gave me cacao beans and tin and copper bits, far less trouble to carry and much more easily negotiable than obsidian chunks. In sum, I received a fair price for the rock, plus *twice* the price I had paid for the slave. When the exchange was made, and Four was again a free citizen of Ynochíxtlan, the entire village rejoiced and declared a holiday and insisted on giving us lodging for the night, and a veritable feast, complete with chocolate and octli, and all free of charge.

The celebration was still going on when we travelers retired to our assigned huts. As he undressed for bed, Blood Glutton belched and said to me, "I always thought it demeaning even to recognize the speech of foreigners as a human language. And I thought you a witless time-waster, Mixtli, when you took pains to learn barbaric new words. But now I have to admit . . ." He gave another full-bellied belch, and fell asleep.

It may be of interest to you, young Señorito Molina, in your capacity of interpreter, to know that when you learned Náhuatl you probably learned the easiest of all our native tongues. I do not mean to scorn your achievement—you speak Náhuatl admirably, for a foreigner—but if ever you essay others of our languages, you will find them considerably more difficult.

To cite an instance, you know that our Náhuatl accents almost every word on its next to last syllable, as your Spanish seems to me to do. That may be one reason why I did not find your Spanish insuperable, though it is in other ways so different from Náhuatl. Now, our nearest neighbors of another tongue, the Purémpecha, accent almost every word on the syllable *third* from the last. You may have observed it in their still-existing place-names: Pátzkuaro and Kerétaro and the like. The Otomí's language, spoken north of here, is even more bewildering because it may accent its words *anywhere*. I would say that, of all the languages I have heard, including your own, Otomíte is the most cursedly hard to master. Just to illustrate, it has separate words for the laughter of a man and of a woman.

All my life, I had been acquiring or enduring different names. Now that I had become a traveler and was addressed in many tongues, I acquired still more names, for of course Dark Cloud was everywhere differently translated. The Tzapotéca people, for example, rendered it as Záa Nayàzú. Even after I had taught the girl Zyanya to speak Náhuatl as fluently as I, she always called me Záa. She could easily have pronounced the word Mixtli, but she invariably called me Záa, and made of its sound an endearment, and, from her lips, it was the name I most preferred of all the names I ever wore. . . .

But of that I will tell in its place.

I see you making additional little marks where you have already written, Fray Gaspar, trying to indicate the way the syllables rise and fall in that name Záa Nayàzú. Yes, they go up and down and up, almost like singing, and I do not know how that could accurately be rendered in your writing any better than in ours.

Only the Tzapotéca's language is spoken so, and it is the most melodious of all the languages in The One World, just as the Tzapotéca men are the most handsome men, and their women the most sublime women. I should also say that the commonplace word Tzapotéca is what other people call them, from the tzapóte fruit which grows so abundantly in their land. Their own name for themselves is more evocative of the heights on which most of them live: Ben Záa, the Cloud People.

They call their language Lóochi. Compared to Náhuatl, it has a stock of only a few different sounds, and the sounds are compounded into words much shorter than those of Náhuatl. But those few sounds have an infinity of meanings, according as they are spoken plain or lilted upward or pitched downward. The musical effect is not just sweet sounding; it is necessary for the words' comprehension. Indeed, the lilt is so much a working part of the language that a Tzapotécatl can dispense with the *spoken* noise and convey his meaning—to the extent of a simple message at least—by humming or whistling only the *melody* of it.

That was how we knew when we approached the lands of the Cloud People, and that was how they knew, too. We heard a shrill, piercing whistle from a mountain overlooking our path. It was a lengthy warble such as no bird would make, and, after a moment, it was repeated from somewhere ahead of us, the same in every trill. After another moment, the whistle was almost inaudibly but identically repeated from far, far ahead of us.

"The Tzapotéca lookouts," explained Blood Glutton. "They relay whistles, instead of shouting as our far-callers do."

I asked, "Why are there lookouts?"

"We are now in the land called Uaxyácac, and the ownership of this land has long been disputed by the Mixtéca and the Olméca and the Tzapotéca. In some places they mingle or live amicably side by side. In other places they harry and raid one another. So all newcomers must be identified. That whistled message has by now probably gone all the way to the palace at Záachilà, and it doubtless tells their Revered Speaker that we are Mexíca, that we are pochtéca, how many we are, and maybe even the size and shape of the bales we carry."

* * *

Perhaps one of your Spanish soldiers on horseback, traveling swiftly and far across our lands each day, would find every village in which he stopped for the night to be distinctly different from the village of the night before. But we, traveling slowly on foot, had discerned no abrupt changes from settlement to settlement. Aside from noticing that, south of the town of Quaunáhuac, everybody seemed to go barefoot except when dressed up for some local festival, we saw no great differences between one community and the next. The physical appearance of the people, their costumes, their architecture—those things all changed, yes, but the change was usually gradual and only at intervals perceptible. Oh, we might observe here and there, especially in tiny settlements where all the inhabitants had been interbreeding for generations, that one people differed slightly from others in being just a bit shorter or taller, lighter or darker of complexion, more jovial or sour of disposition. But in general the people tended to blend indistinguishably from one place to the next.

Everywhere the working men wore no garment but a white loincloth, and covered themselves with a white mantle when at leisure. The women all wore the familiar white blouse and skirt and, presumably, the standard undergarment. The people's dress-up clothes did have their whiteness enlivened by fancy embroidery, and the patterns and colors of that decoration did vary from place to place. Also, the nobles of different regions had different tastes in feather mantles and headdresses, in noseplugs and earrings and labrets, in bracelets and anklets and other adornments. But such variances were seldom remarkable by passers-through like ourselves; it would take a lifelong resident of one village to recognize, on sight, a visitor from the next village along the road.

Or such had been our experience through all our journey until we entered the land of Uaxyácac, where the first warbling whistle of the uniquely lovely language Lóochi gave notice that we were suddenly among a people unlike any we had yet encountered.

We spent our first night in Uaxyácac at a village called Texítla, and there was nothing especially noteworthy about the village itself. The houses were built, like those we had been accustomed to for some time past, of vine-tied upright saplings and roofed with straw thatch. The bath and steam huts were of baked clay, like all the others we had recently seen. The food we purchased was much the same as that which we had been served on many evenings previous. What was different was the people of Texítla. Never until then had we entered a community where the people were so uniformly good to look at, and where even their everyday garb was festive with bright colors.

"Why, they are beautiful!" Cozcatl exclaimed.

Blood Glutton said nothing, for he had of course been in those parts before. The old campaigner merely looked smug and proprietorial, as if he had personally arranged the existence of Texítla purposely to astound me and Cozcatl.

And Texítla was no isolated enclave of personable people, as we discovered when we arrived at the populous capital city of Záachilà, and as we confirmed during our passage through the rest of Uaxyácac. That was a land where *all* the people were comely, and their manner as bright as their dress. The Tzapotéca's delight in brilliant colors was understandable, for that was the country where the finest dyes were produced. It was also the northernmost range of the parrots, macaws, toucans, and other tropical birds of resplendent plumage. The reason for the Tzapotéca themselves being such remarkable specimens of humanity was less evident. So, after a day or two in Záachilà, I said to an old man of the city:

"Your people seem so superior to others I have known. What is their history? Where did they come from?"

"Come from?" he said, as if disdainful of my ignorance. He was one of the city dwellers who spoke Náhuatl, and he regularly served as an interpreter for passing pochtéca, and it was he who taught me the first words I learned of Lóochi. His name was Gíigu Nashinyá, which means Red River, and he had a face like a weathered cliff. He said:

"You Mexíca tell how your ancestors came from some place far to the north of what is now your domain. The Chiapa tell how their forebears originated somewhere far distant to the south of what is now their land. And every other people tell of their origins in some other place than where they now live. Every other people except us Ben Záa. We do not call ourselves by that name for any idle reason. We *are* the Cloud People— born of the clouds and trees and rocks and mountains of this land. We did not come here. We have always been here. Tell me, young man, have you yet seen or smelled the heart flower?"

I said I had not.

"You will. We grow it now in our dooryards. The flower is so called because its unopened bud is the shape of a human heart. The woman of a household will pluck only a single bud at a time, because that one flower, as it unfolds, will perfume the entire house. But another distinction of the heart flower is that it originally grew wild, in the mountains you see yonder, and grew nowhere else *but* in these mountains of Uaxyácac. Like us Ben Záa, it came into existence right here, and like us, it flourishes still. The heart flower is a joy to see and to smell, as it always has been. The Ben Záa are a strong and vigorous people, as they always have been."

I echoed what Cozcatl had said, "A beautiful people."

"Yes, as beautiful as they are vivacious," said the old man with no affected modesty. "The Cloud People have kept themselves so, by keeping themselves pure Cloud People. We purge any impurity which crops up or creeps in."

I said, "What? How?"

"If a child is born malformed or intolerably ugly, or gives evidence of being deficient of brain, we see that it does not live to grow up. The unfortunate infant is denied its mother's teat, and it dwindles and dies in the gods' good time. Our old people also are discarded, when they become too unsightly to be seen, or too feeble to care for themselves, or when their minds begin to decay. Of course, the old folks' immolation is generally voluntary, and done for the public good. I myself, when I feel my vigor or my senses begin to wane, I shall make my farewells and go away to the Holy Home and never be seen again."

I said, "It sounds rather an extreme measure."

"Is it extreme to weed a garden? To prune dead branches from an orchard?"

"Well . . ."

He said sardonically, "You admire the effect but you deplore the means. That we choose to discard the useless and the helpless, who would otherwise be a burden on their fellows. That we choose to let the defective die, and thus avert their begetting still more defectives. Young moralist, do you also condemn our refusal to breed mongrels?"

"Mongrels?"

"We have been repeatedly invaded by the Mixtéca and Olméca in times past, and by the Mexíca in more recent times, and we suffer creeping infiltrations from lesser tribes around our borders, but we have never mixed with any of them. Though outlanders move among us and even live among us, we will always forbid the mingling of their blood with ours."

I said, "I do not see how that could be managed. Men and women being what they are, you can hardly allow social intercourse with foreigners and hope to prevent the sexual."

"Oh, we are human," he conceded. "Our men willingly sample the women of other races, and some of our own women wantonly go astraddle the road. But any of the Cloud People who formally takes an outlander for husband or wife is, at that moment, no longer one of the Cloud People. That fact is usually enough to discourage marriage with aliens. But there is another reason why such marriages are uncommon. Surely you yourself can see it."

I shook my head uncertainly.

"You have traveled among other peoples. Now look at our men. Look at our women. In what nation outside Uaxyácac could they find partners so nearly ideal for each other?"

I already had looked, and the question was unanswerable. Granted, I had in my time known exceedingly well-favored examples of other peoples: my own beautiful sister Tzitzi, who was of the Mexíca; the Lady of Tolan, who was of the Tecpanéca; pretty little Cozcatl, who was of the Acólhua. And granted, not every single specimen of the Tzapotéca was unfaultably imposing. But I could not deny that the majority of those people were of such superb face and figure as to make the majority of other peoples seem little better than early and failed experiments of the gods.

Among the Mexíca, I was reckoned a rarity for my height and musculature; but almost every man of the Tzapotéca was as tall and strongly built as I, and had both strength and sensitivity in his face. Almost every woman was amply endowed with womanly curves, but was lithe as a willow wand; and her face was fashioned for goddesses to imitate: large and luminous eyes, straight nose, a mouth made for kissing, unblemished and almost translucent skin. Zyanya was a shapely vessel of burnished copper, brimming with honey, set in the sun. The men and women alike stood proud and moved gracefully and spoke their liquid Lóochi in soft voices. The children were exquisite and lovably well behaved. I am rather glad that I could not step outside myself to see how I compared in such company. But the other foreigners I saw in Uaxyácac—most of them immigrant Mixtéca—alongside the Cloud People looked lumpy and mud-colored and imperfectly put together.

Still, I am not entirely credulous. So, as we say, I took with my little finger the old interpreter Red River's tale of how his people had been created: spontaneously, and whole, and splendid. I could not believe that the Cloud People had sprouted from those mountains full-formed, like the heart flower. No other nation ever claimed such a nonsensically impossible origin. Every people *must* come from somewhere else, must they not?

But I could believe, from the evidence of my own eyes, that the Tzapotéca had haughtily balked at interbreeding with any outlanders, that they had preserved only their prime bloodlines, even when it meant remorselessness toward their own loved ones. Wherever and however the Cloud People truly originated, they had ever since refused to become a nation of less than the best. I could believe *that*, because there I was, walking among them: the admirable men and the desirable women. *Ayyo*, the eminently, irresistibly, excruciatingly desirable women!

✠

As is our practice here, Your Excellency, the lord scribe has just read back to me the last sentence I spoke, to remind me where we left off at our last session. Dare I suppose that Your Excellency joins us today expecting to hear how I ravished the entire female population of Záachilà?

No?

If, as you say, it would not surprise you to hear it, but you do not wish to, then let me really surprise Your Excellency. Though we spent several days in and around Záachilà, I did not once touch a woman there. Uncharacteristic of me, yes, as Your Excellency remarks. But I do not claim to have enjoyed any sudden redemption from my libertine ways. Rather, I was then afflicted by a new perversity. I did not want any of the women who could be had, because they *could* be had. Those women were adorable and seductive and doubtless skillful—Blood Glutton wallowed in lechery all the time we were there—but their very availability made me decline them. What I wanted, what I desired and lusted for was a real woman of the Cloud People: meaning some woman who would recoil in horror from a foreigner like me. It was a dilemma. I wanted what I could not possibly have, and I would settle for nothing less. So I had none, and I can tell Your Excellency nothing about the women of Záachilà.

Permit me to tell you a little about Uaxyácac instead. That land is a chaos of mountains, peaks, and crags; mountains shouldering between mountains; mountains overlaid on mountains. The Tzapotéca, content in their mountain protection and isolation, have seldom cared to venture outside those ramparts, just as they have seldom welcomed anyone else inside. To other nations, they long ago became known as "the closed people."

However, the first Uey-Tlatoáni Motecuzóma was determined to extend the Mexíca trade routes southward and ever farther southward, and he chose to do so by force, not by diplomatic negotiation. Early in the year in which I was born, he had led an army into Uaxyácac and, after causing much death and devastation, finally succeeded in taking its capital by siege. He demanded unhindered passage for the Mexíca pochtéca and, of course, laid the Cloud People under tribute to The Triple Alliance. But he lacked supply lines to support an occupying force, and so, when he marched home with the bulk of his army, he left only a token garrison in Záachilà to enforce the collection of the levy. As soon as he was out of sight, the Tzapotéca quite naturally slaughtered the garrison warriors, and resumed their former way of life, and never paid so much as a cotton rag of tribute.

That would have brought new Mexíca invasions which would have laid waste the country—Motecuzóma was not named Wrathful Lord without reason—except for two things.

The Tzapotéca were wise enough to keep their promise that Mexíca merchants could traverse their land unmolested. And in that same year Motecuzóma died. His successor, Axayácatl, was sufficiently conscious of the difficulties of defeating and holding such a faraway country, that he sent no more armies. So there was no love, but mutual truce and trade between the two nations, during the twenty years before my arrival and for some years afterward.

Uaxyácac's ceremonial center and most revered city is the ancient Lyobáan, a short journey eastward of Záachilà, which old Red River one day took me and Cozcatl to see. (Blood Glutton stayed behind to disport himself in an auyanicáli, a house of pleasure.) Lyobáan means Holy Home, but we Mexíca have long called the city Míctlan, because those Mexíca who have seen it believe it is truly the earthly entrance to that dark and dismal afterworld.

It is a sightly city, very well preserved for its great age. There are many temples of many rooms, one of those rooms being the biggest I have ever seen anywhere with a roof not supported by a forest of columns. The walls of the buildings, both inside and out, are adorned with deeply carved patterns, like petrified weaving, endlessly repeated in mosaics of white limestone intricately fitted together. As Your Excellency hardly needs to be told, those numerous temples at the Holy Home were evidence that the Cloud People, like us Mexíca and like you Christians, paid homage to a whole host of deities. There was the virgin moon goddess Béu, and the jaguar god Béezye, and the dawn goddess Tangu Yu, and I know not how many more.

But, unlike us Mexíca, the Cloud People believed, as do you Christians, that all those gods and goddesses were subordinate to one great overlord who had created the universe and who ruled everything in it. Like your angels and saints and such, those lesser gods could not exercise their several separate holy functions—indeed, they could not have existed—without the permission and supervision of that topmost god of all creation. The Tzapotéca called him Uizye Tao, which means The Almighty Breath.

The austerely grand temples are only the upper level of Lyobáan. They were specially positioned over openings in the earth which lead to natural caves and tunnels and caverns in the ground beneath, the favored burial places of the Tzapotéca for ages untold. To that city have always been brought their dead nobles, high priests, and warrior heroes, to be ceremonially interred in richly decorated and furnished rooms directly under the temples.

But there was and is room for commoners as well, in still deeper crypts. Red River told us that there was no known end to the caves, that they interconnect and run on underground for countless one-long-runs, that stone festoons hang from their ceilings and stone pedestals thrust up from their floors, that there are stone curtains and draperies of weird and wonderful but natural design: as beautiful as frozen waterfalls or as awesome as the Mexíca's imagined portals of Míctlan.

"And not only the dead come to the Holy Home," he said. "As I have already told you, when I feel my life is no longer of use, I shall walk here to disappear."

According to him, any man or woman, commoner or noble, who was crippled by old age, or weighed down by suffering or sorrow, or was tired of life for any reason, could make application to the priests of Lyobáan for voluntary *live* burial in the Holy Home. He or she, provided with a pine-splinter torch but with nothing for sustenance, would be let into one of the cave openings and it would be closed behind him. He would then wander through the maze of passages until his light or his strength gave out, or until he found a seemly cavern, or until he reached a spot where instinct told him some family ancestor had already laid himself down and found it a pleasant place to die. There the newcomer would compose himself and wait calmly for his spirit to depart for whatever other destination awaited it.

One thing about Lyobáan puzzled me: that those holiest of holy temples were set upon ground-level stone platforms and were not elevated upon high pyramids. I asked the old man why.

"The ancients built for solidity, to resist the zyuǔ," he said, using a word I did not know. But in the next moment both Cozcatl and I knew it, for we felt it, as if our guide had summoned it especially for our instruction.

"Tlalolíni," said Cozcatl, in a voice which shook like everything else around us.

We who speak Náhuatl call it tlalolíni, the Tzapotéca call it zyuüù, you call it earthquake. I had felt the land move before, on Xaltócan, but there the movement was a mild jiggling up and down, and we knew it was just the island's way of settling itself more comfortably on the unstable lake bottom. At the Holy Home the movement was different: a rolling sway from side to side, as if the mountain had been a small boat on a tossing lake. Just as I sometimes have felt on rough waters, I felt a queasiness in my stomach. Several pieces of stone dislodged themselves from high up on one building and came bouncing down to roll a little way across the ground.

Red River pointed to them and said, "The ancients built stoutly, but seldom do many days pass in Uaxyácac without a zyuüù, mild or severe. So now we generally build less ponderously. A house of saplings and thatch cannot much harm its inhabitants if it collapses upon them, and it can be easily rebuilt."

I nodded, my insides still so disquieted that I was afraid to open my mouth. The old man grinned knowingly.

"It affected your belly, yes? I will wager it has affected another organ besides."

So it had. For some reason, my tepúli was erect, engorged to such length and thickness that it actually ached.

"No one knows why," said Red River, "but the zyuüù affects all animals, most notably the human ones. Men and women get sexually aroused, and occasionally, in a turbulent quake, aroused to the extreme of doing immodest things, and in public. When the tremor is really violent or prolonged, even small boys may involuntarily ejaculate, and small girls come to a shuddering climax, as if they had been the most sensual adults, and of course they are bewildered by the occurrence. Sometimes, long before the ground moves, the dogs and coyotes start to whine or howl, the birds flit about. We have learned to judge from their behavior when a truly dangerous tremor is about to come. Our miners and quarriers run to safer ground, the nobles evacuate their stone palaces, the priests abandon their stone temples. Even when we are forewarned, though, a major convulsion can cause much damage and death." To my surprise, he grinned again. "We must nevertheless concede that the zyuùù usually gives more lives than it takes. After any severe tremor, when three-quarters of a year have passed, a great many babies are born within just a few days of each other."

I could well believe it. My rigid member felt like a club thrusting from my crotch. I envied Blood Glutton, who was probably making that a day to be forever remembered in that auyanicáli. If I had been anywhere in the city streets of Záachilà, I might have fractured the truce between the Mexíca and Tzapotéca by stripping and violating the first woman I met. . . .

No, no need to elaborate on that. But I might tell Your Excellency why I think an earth tremor arouses only fear in the lesser animals, but fear *and* sexual excitement in humans.

On the first night our company camped outdoors, at the beginning of that long journey, I had first realized and felt the fearsome impact of the darkness and emptiness and loneliness of the nighttime wilderness, and afterward I had been seized by a compelling urge to copulate. Human animals or lower animals, we feel fear when we confront any aspect of nature we can neither comprehend nor control. But the lesser creatures do not know that what they fear is death, for they do not know so well what death *is*. We humans do. A man may staunchly face an honorable death on the battlefield or the altar. A woman may risk an honorable death in childbirth. But we cannot so courageously face the death that comes as indifferently as a thumb and finger snuffing out a lamp wick. Our greatest fear is of capricious, meaningless extinction. And in the moment of our feeling that greatest fear, our instinctive impulse is to do the one most life-preserving thing we know how to do. Something deep in our brain cries to us in desperation, "Ahuilnéma! Copulate! It cannot save your life, but it may make another." And so a man's tepúli rears itself, a woman's tipíli opens invitingly, their genital juices begin to flow. . . .

Well, that is only a theory, and only my own. But you, Your Excellency, and you, reverend friars, should eventually have opportunity to verify or disprove it. This island of Tenochtítlan-Mexíco sits even more uneasily than Xaltócan upon the ooze of the lake floor, and it shifts its position now and then, sometimes violently. Soon or later, you will feel a convulsive quake of the earth. See for yourselves, then, what you feel in your reverend parts.

There was really no reason for our party to have lingered in Záachilà and its environs for as many days as we did, except that it was a most pleasant place for us to rest before we undertook the long and grueling climb through the mountains beyond—and except for the fact that Blood Glutton, belying his grizzled years, seemed determined to leave not a single one of the accessible Tzapotéca beauties neglected. I confined myself to seeing the local sights. I did not even exert myself to seek trade bargains; for one reason, the most prized local commodity, the famous dye, was out of stock.

You call that dye cochineal, and you may know that it is obtained from a certain insect, the nochéztli. The insects live in millions on immense, cultivated plantations of the one special variety of nopáli cactus on which they feed. The insects mature all at the same season, and their cultivators brush them off the cactus into bags and kill them, either by dipping the bags in boiling water or hanging them in a steam house or leaving them in the hot sun. Then the insects are dried until they are wrinkled seeds, and are sold by weight. Depending on how they were killed—boiled, steamed, or baked—they yield when crushed a dye of jacinth yellow-red or a bright scarlet or that particular luminous carmine which is obtainable from no other source. I tell all this because the Tzapotéca's latest crop had been bought in its entirety by an earlier and northbound Mexícatl trader, that one with whom I had conversed way back in the Xochimílca country, and there was no more dye to be had that year, for even the most pampered insects cannot be hurried.

I did remember what that same trader had told me: of a new and even more rare purple dye which was somehow mysteriously connected with snails and a people called The Strangers. I asked of the interpreter Red River and several of his merchant friends what they might know of the matter, but all I got from anybody was a blank look and an echo: "Purple? Snails? Strangers?" So I made only one trading transaction in Záachilà, and it was not the sort that a typically tightfisted pochtécatl would have made.

Old Red River arranged for me to pay a courtesy call on Kosi Yuela, the Bishósu Ben Záa, which means the Revered Speaker of the Cloud People, and that ruling lord kindly treated me to a tour of his palace so I might admire its luxurious furnishings. Two of those inspired my acquisitive interest. One was the Bishósu's queen, Pela Xila, a woman to make a man salivate, but I contented myself with kissing the earth to her. When I saw the other thing, however—a beautifully worked feather tapestry—I determined to have it.

"But that was made by one of your own countrymen," said my host. He sounded slightly peeved that I should stand staring at a Mexícatl artifact instead of exclaiming over the products of his own Cloud People: the interestingly mottled draperies in the throne room, for instance—colored by having been tied in knots and dyed, then retied and redyed, several times over.

Nodding at the tapestry, I said, "Let me hazard a guess, my lord. The feather-work artist was a wayfarer named Chimáli."

Kosi Yuela smiled. "You are right. He stayed in these parts for some time, making sketches of the mosaics of Lyobáan. And then he had nothing with which to pay the innkeeper, except that tapestry. The landlord accepted it, though unhappily, and later came to complain to me. So I reimbursed him, for I trust that the artist will eventually return and redeem the thing."

"I am sure he will," I said, "for I have long known Chimáli. Therefore I may see him before you do. If you would allow it, my lord, I shall be glad to pay his debt and assume the pledge myself."

"Why, that would be kind of you," said the Bishósu. "A most generous favor to your friend and to us as well."

"Not at all," I said. "I merely repay your kindness to him. And anyway"—I remembered the day I had led a frightened Chimáli home with him wearing a pumpking head—"it will not be the first time I have helped my friend out of a temporary difficulty."

Chimáli must have lived well during his stay at the hostel; it cost me quite a stack of tin and copper snippets to settle his bill. But the tapestry was easily worth ten or twenty times that much. Today it would probably be worth a hundred times as much, since almost all our feather works have been destroyed, and no more have been made in recent years. Either the feather artists were also destroyed, or they have lost all heart for the creation of beauty. So it may be that Your Excellency has never seen one of those shimmering pictures.

The work was more delicate, difficult, and time-consuming than any mode of painting, sculpture, or goldsmithery. The artist began with a cloth of the finest cotton, tightly stretched over a panel of wood. On the cloth he lightly drew the lines of the picture he envisioned. Then, painstakingly, he filled in all the spaces with colored feathers, using only the soft, plumed shaft part, the quill cut away. He attached each of the thousands and thousands of feather, one by one, with a minute dab of liquid óli. Some so-called artists were uncaring slovens who used only white birds' feathers which they tinted with paints and dyes as required, and trimmed their shapes to fit the more intricate places in the design. But a true artist used only naturally colored feathers, and carefully chose exactly the right hue from all their gradations of colors, and used large or small, straight or curved feathers as the picture demanded. I say "large," but there was seldom a feather in any of those works bigger than a violet's petal, and the smallest would be about the size of a human eyelash. An artist might have to delve and compare and select from among a stock of feathers that would fill this room we sit in.

I do not know why Chimáli had that one time forsaken his paints, but he had chosen the feather medium to do a woodland scene, and he had done it masterfully. In a sunny forest glade, a jaguar lay resting among flowers, butterflies, and birds. Every pictured bird was done in the feathers of its species, though every jay, for instance, would have required Chimáli's winnowing from the tiniest blue feathers of perhaps hundreds of real jays. The greenery was not just masses of green feathers; it seemed that every individual blade of grass and leaf of tree was a separate feather of a subtly different green. I counted more than thirty minuscule feathers composing just one small brown and yellow butterfly. Chimáli's signature was the only part of the picture done in a single unmodulated color—in the feathers of the scarlet macaw—and the handprint was modestly small, less than half life size.

I took the tapestry to our lodgings, and gave it to Cozcatl, and told him to leave just the scarlet hand affixed. When he had peeled off every other feather of the picture, I heaped them all, inextricably mixed, onto the cloth backing. I bundled and tied it tightly, and took it again to the palace. Kosi Yuela was absent, but his queen Pela Xila received me and I left the wadded parcel with her, saying:

"My lady, in case the artist Chimáli should come back this way before I meet him, have the goodness to give him this. Tell him it is a token—that all his other debts will be similarly repaid."

The only way southward out of Záachilà was up and over the mountain range called Tzempuülá, and that is the way we went, through interminable day after day. Unless you have climbed mountains, Your Excellency, I do not know how to convey to you what mountain climbing is like. I do not know how to make you feel the muscle strain and fatigue, the bruises and scrapes, the streaming sweat and the grit it collects, the giddiness of the heights and the unquenchable thirst of the hot daytimes, the ceaseless need of vigilance in placing each foot, the occasional slip and its heart-stopping instant of fright, the two backslides for every three steps upward, the almost equally arduous and perilous descent—and then no easily negotiable flat land, but another mountain. . . .

There was a trail, true, so we did not lose our way. But it had been made by and for the lean, tough men of the Cloud People, which is not to say that even they enjoyed traveling it. Nor was it any long-trodden and permanently firm path, for every mountain is continuously falling to pieces. In places the trail led across the rubble of rock slides, which shifted ominously beneath our sandals and threatened at any moment to avalanche entirely out from under us. In other places the trail was a gully worn by erosion and bottomed with an ankle-turning debris of crumbled rottenstone. In others it was cramped spiral staircase of rock, each step just big enough for one's toes to get purchase. In others it was a mere shelf slung on a mountain flank, with a sheer rock wall on one side seeming eager to push us all into the equally sheer abyss on the other side.

Many of the mountains were so high that our route took us sometimes above the timberline. Up there, except for the infrequent lichen patch on a rock, a few weeds growing from a cranny, or a stunted and wind-gnarled evergreen, there was no vegetation, and little soil for any to take root in. Those summits had been eroded down to bare rock; we might have been clambering along an exposed rib of the earth's skeleton. As we toiled up and over those peaks, we gasped as if competing with each other for what little and insubstantial air there was.

The days were still warm, too warm for such rigorous exercise. But the nights, at those heights, were cold enough to make the marrow in our bones hurt. Had it been practical, we would have traveled by night so the exertion would keep us warm, and slept by day instead of struggling along under our packs, sweating and panting and nearly fainting. But no human being could have moved among those mountains in the darkness without breaking at least a leg and probably his neck.

Only twice during that stage of our journey did we come upon communities of people. One was Xalápan, a village of the Huave tribe, who are a dull-skinned, ill-favored, and ungracious people. They received us surlily and demanded an exorbitant payment for putting us up, but we paid it. The meal they gave us was abominable: a greasy stew of suety opossum meat, but it did help piece out our own diminishing provisions. The huts they vacated for our use were smelly and verminous, but at least kept off the mountains' night wind. At the other village, Nejápa, we were much more cordially made welcome, and treated with warm hospitality, and well fed, and even were sold some eggs from the local flocks, to carry when we moved on. Unfortunately, the people there were Chinantéca, who, as I mentioned long ago, were afflicted with what you call the pinto disease. Though we knew there was no chance of an outsider's being infected—except perhaps if we lay with their women, and none of us was tempted to that—just the sight of all those blue-blotched bodies made us feel almost as itchy and uncomfortable in Nejápa as we had in Xalápan.

On the many other stretches, we tried to pace ourselves, according to the rough map I carried, so that our night's camping could be done in a hollow between two mountains. We would usually find there at least a trickle of fresh water and a growth of mexíxin cress or swamp cabbage or other edible greens. But, more important, in the lower land a slave did not have to grind the fire drill for half the night, as he did on the thin-aired heights, before he generated enough heat to ignite his tinder moss and get a campfire going. However, since none of us but Blood Glutton had ever traveled that route before, and since even he could not accurately remember all the ups and downs of it, the darkness too often caught us while we were climbing or descending a mountainside.

On one such night, Blood Glutton said, "I am sick of eating dog meat and beans, and after tonight we will have only three more dogs anyway. This is jaguar country. Mixtli, you and I will stay awake and try to spear one."

He searched the woods around our camping spot until he found a dead and hollow log, and he hacked off a piece of it, a cylinder about the length of his forearm. He appropriated the castoff skin of one of the little dogs which slave Ten was at that moment broiling over the fire, and stretched the hide over one end of the piece of log, where he tied it with a string, as if he were making a crude drum. Then he jabbed a hole in the center of the dogskin drumhead. Through that he ran a long, thin string of rawhide and knotted it so it would not slip through the skin. The rawhide hung down inside the drum, and Blood Glutton inserted his hand into the open end. When he pinched the dangling strip and ran his horny thumbnail down along it, the drumhead amplified the scratching sound into a rasping grunt exactly like that of a jaguar.

"If there is a cat anywhere about," said the old soldier, "his native curiosity will bring him to investigate our firelight. But he will approach from downwind, and not very near. So you and I will also go downwind until we find a comfortable spot in the wood. You will sit and do the thrumming, Mixtli, while I will be concealed within easy spear range. The drifting wood-smoke should sufficiently cover our scent, and your calling should make him curious enough to come right upon us."

I was not exactly rapturous at the prospect of being the bait for a jaguar, but I let Blood Glutton show me how to work his device, how to make the noises at random and irregular intervals: short grunts and longer growls. When we had finished our meal, Cozcatl and the slaves rolled into their blankets, while Blood Glutton and I went off into the night.

When the campfire was just a glimmer in the distance, but we could still faintly smell its smoke, we stopped in what Blood Glutton said was a clearing. It could have been a cavern of the Holy Home, for all I could see. I sat down on a boulder and he went crunching off somewhere behind me and, when all was quiet, I stuck my hand up inside the drum and began thumbnailing the rawhide string—a grunt, a pause, a grunt and a rumble, a pause, three gruff grunts. . . .

It sounded so very like a big cat, moodily grumbling as he prowled, that my own back hair prickled. Without really wanting to, I recalled some of the stories I had heard from experienced jaguar hunters. The jaguar, they said, never had to stalk very near its prey. It had the ability to hiccup violently, and its breath would render a victim numb and faint and helpless, even at a distance. A hunter using arrows would always have four of them in hand, because the jaguar was also notorious for being able to dodge an arrow and, insultingly, catch it in his teeth and chew it to splinters. Hence a hunter would have to discharge four arrows in a flurry, hoping that one of them would take effect, because it was a well-known fact that he could get off no *more* than four arrows before the cat's hiccups overwhelmed him.

I tried to divert my thoughts by doing some variations and improvisations in my thumb rasping—quick grunts like amused chuckles, long-drawn groans such as a yawning cat might make. I began to believe that I was getting really adept at that art, especially when I somehow produced a grunt after I had let go the rawhide, and I wondered if I might introduce the device as a new musical instrument, and myself as the world's only master of it, at some ceremonial festival. . . .

There came to my ears another grunt, and I came wide awake from my reverie, horrified, for I had not produced that grunt either. There also came to my nostrils a sort of urinous scent, and to my vision, dim though it was, a sense that a darker piece of the darkness was moving stealthily from behind me to the left side of me. The darkness grunted again, louder, and with an inquiring note. Though almost paralyzed, I thumbed the rawhide to make what I hoped was a growl of welcome. What else could I do?

From my left front there turned on me two flat, cold, yellow lights—and a sudden sharp wind sang past my cheek. I thought it was the jaguar's lethal hiccup. But the yellow lights blinked out, and there came a throat-tearing scream, like that of a female sacrifice clumsily knifed by an inept priest. The scream broke off and became a choked, bubbling noise, accompanied by the thrashing of a heavy body evidently tearing up all the shrubbery roundabout.

"I am sorry I had to let it get so close to you," said Blood Glutton at my side. "But I needed to see the gleam of its eyes to judge my aim."

"What *is* the thing?" I asked, for I could still hear in my ears that awful humanlike scream, and I feared we had got some wandering woman.

The thrashing sound ceased, and Blood Glutton went to investigate. He said triumphantly, "Right in the lung. Not bad for throwing by guess." Then he must have felt along the dead body, for I heard him mutter, "I will be damned to Míctlan," and I waited for him to confess that he had speared some poor blue Chinantécatl woman lost in the night woods. But all he said was, "Come and help me drag it up to the camp." I did, and if it was a woman she weighed as much as I did and she had a cat's hind legs.

All those in the camp, of course, had bolted up out of their blankets at the frightful noise. Blood Glutton and I let drop our prey, and I could see it for the first time: a big tawny cat, but not a spotted one.

The old soldier panted, "I must be—losing my skill. Thought I made—a jaguar caller. But that is a cuguar, a mountain lion."

"No matter," I panted. "Meat just as good. Skin make you a good mantle."

Naturally there was no more sleeping in what remained of the night. Blood Glutton and I sat and rested, and preened in the admiration of the others, and I congratulated him on his prowess, and he congratulated me on my unflinching patience. Meanwhile, the slaves skinned the animal, and some of them scraped clean the inner surface of the hide, and others cut up the carcass into pieces of convenient carrying size. Cozcatl cooked breakfast for us all: a maize atóli that would give us energy for the day, but he also provided a treat to celebrate our successful hunt. He got out the eggs we had tenderly carried and hoarded since Nejápa. With a twig he pierced each one's shell, and twirled the twig to addle the yolk and white. Then he roasted them only briefly in the outer ashes of the fire, and we sucked out the warm, rich contents through the holes.

At the next two or three nights' stops, we feasted on the rather chewy but extremely tasty cat meat. Blood Glutton gave the cuguar's hide to the burliest slave, Ten, to wear as a cape so he could continuously supple it with his hands. But we had not taken the trouble to find and rub tanbark into the skin, so it soon began to stink so rancidly that we made Ten march a good distance apart from the rest of us. Also, since mountain climbing often necessitates the use of all four limbs, Ten seldom had his hands free to work the leather to softness. The sun stiffened it until poor Ten might as well have been wearing a varnished-hide door strapped to his back. But Blood Glutton stubbornly mumbled something about making himself a shield of it, and refused to let Ten get rid of it, and so it came with us all the rest of the way through the Tzempuülá mountains.

✠

I am glad that the Señor Bishop Zumárraga is not with us today, my lord scribes, for I must tell of a sexual encounter I know His Excellency would deem sordid and repulsive. He would probably turn purple again. In truth, even though more than forty years have passed since that night, I myself am still made uneasy by the memory of it, and I would omit the episode, except that its recounting is necessary to the understanding of many and more significant incidents that later derived from it.

When the fourteen of us finally descended the last long foothills of the Tzempuülá mountains, we came down again into Tzapotéca territory at a sizable city on the bank of a wide river. You now call it the Villa de Guadalcazar, but in those days the city, the river, and all the expanse of lands about it were called in the Lóochi language Layú Béezyù, or The Place of the Jaguar God. However, since that was a busy crossroads of several trade routes, most of its people spoke Náhuatl as a second language, and as often used the name our Mexíca travelers had given the place: Tecuantépec, or simply Jaguar Hill. No one then or now, except myself, seems ever to have thought it ludicrous to apply the name of Jaguar Hill to the broad flowing river as well, and to the exceptionally unhilly lands beyond.

The city was only about five one-long-runs from where the river spills into the great southern ocean, so it had attracted immigrant settlers from several other peoples of that coastal area: Zoque, Nexítzo, some Huave, and even displaced groups of the Mixtéca. On its streets, one encountered quite a variety of complexions, physiques, costumes, and accents. But fortunately the native Cloud People predominated, so most of the city folk were as superlatively handsome and courtly as those of Záachilà.

On the afternoon we arrived, as our little company stumbled wearily but eagerly across the rope bridge spanning the river, Blood Glutton said, in a voice hoarse from dust and fatigue, "There are some excellent hostels yonder in Tecuantépec."

"The excellent ones can wait," I rasped. "We will stop at the *first* one."

And so, tired and famished, as ragged and filthy and malodorous as priests, we lurched into the dooryard of the first inn we found on the river side of the city. And from that impulsive decision of mine—just as the wisps of smoke must uncoil from the twirl of a fire-drilling stick—there inevitably unfurled all the events of all the remaining roads and days of my life, and of Zyanya's life, and the lives of persons I have already mentioned, and of other persons I shall name, and even of one person who never had a name.

Know, then, reverend friars, that it began so:

When we had all of us, the slaves included, bathed and then steamed and then bathed again and then dressed in clean garments, we called for food. The slaves ate outside in the twilit dooryard, but Cozcatl, Blood Glutton, and I had a cloth laid for us in a torch-lighted and rush-carpeted inside room. We glutted ourselves on delicacies fresh from the nearby sea: raw oysters and boiled pink shrimps and a baked red fish of great size.

My stomach's hunger assuaged, I noticed the extraordinary

beauty of the woman serving us, and I remembered that I was capable of other hungers. I also noticed something else out of the ordinary. The proprietor of the hostel was obviously of an immigrant race: a short, fat, oily-skinned man. But the serving woman to whom he brusquely snapped orders was obviously of the Ben Záa: tall and supple, with skin that glowed like amber and a face to rival that of her people's First Lady Pela Xila. It was unthinkable that she might be the landlord's wife. And, since she could hardly have been a born or bought slave in her own country, I assumed that some misfortune had forced her to indenture herself to the boorish and foreign-born innkeeper.

It was difficult to judge the age of any adult woman of the Cloud People—the years were so kind to them—especially one as sightly and graceful as that servant. If I had known that she was old enough to have a daughter of my own age, I might not have spoken to her. I might not have done it in any case, except that Blood Glutton and I were washing down our meal with copious drafts of octli. Whatever impelled me, when the woman next came near I made bold to look up at her and inquire:

"How is it that a woman of the Ben Záa labors for an uncouth inferior?"

She glanced around to make sure the innkeeper was not that moment in the room. Then she knelt to murmur in my ear, to answer my question with a question, and a most surprising question, spoken in Náhuatl:

"Young Lord Pochtécatl, will you want a woman for the night?" My eyes must have goggled, for she blushed deep marigold and lowered her own eyes. "The landlord will provide you with a common maátitl who has straddled the road from here to the fishermen's beach on the coast. Allow me, young lord, to offer myself instead. My name is Gié Bele, which in your language is Flame Flower."

I must still have gaped foolishly, for she stared straight at me and said, almost fiercely, "I *will* be a maátitl for pay, but I am not yet. This would be the first time since my husband's death that I have ever...not even with a man of my own people..."

I was so touched by her embarrassed urgency that I stammered, "I—I would be pleased."

Gié Bele glanced about again. "Do not let the innkeeper know. He exacts a part of the payment to his women, and I would be beaten for cheating him of a customer. I will be waiting outside at first dark, my lord, and we will go to my hut."

She hastily gathered up our empty dishes and left the room, as the proprietor bustled self-importantly into it. Blood Glutton, who of course had overheard our exchange, gave me a sidelong look and said sarcastically:

"The first time ever. I wish I had a cacao bean for every time a female has said that to me. And I would lop off one of my testicles for every time it proved to be the truth."

The innkeeper came over to us, smirking and rubbing his fat hands together, to ask if we would like a sweet with which to conclude our meal. "Perhaps a sweet to be enjoyed at leisure, my lords, while you rest upon your pallets in your rooms."

I said no. Blood Glutton glared at me, then bellowed at the stout man, "Yes, I will sample the fare! By Huitztli, I will have his, too!" He jerked his thumb at me. "Send them both to my room. And mind you, the two tastiest you can serve up."

The landlord murmured admiringly, "A lord of noble appetite," and scurried away. Blood Glutton still glared at me, and said in exasperation:

"You drooling imbecile. It is the *second* trick a female learns in that trade. You will arrive at her hut to find she still has her man, probably two or three of them, all strapping fishermen, and all pleased to meet this new fish she has hooked. They will rob you and stamp you flat as a tortilla."

Cozcatl said shyly, "It would be a pity if our expedition should end untimely in Tecuantépec."

I would not listen. I was besotted by more than the octli. I believed the woman to be the kind I had wanted but had been unable to approach in Záachilà: the chaste kind who would not sully herself with me. Even if, as Gié Bele had implied, I was only to be her first of many future paying lovers, I would still be the first. And yet, fuddled though I may have been by drink and desire and even imbecility, I had sense enough to wonder: why me?

"Because you are young," she said, when we met outside the inn. "You are young enough that you cannot have known many women of the kind who would make you unclean. You are not as handsome as my late husband, but you could almost pass for one of the Ben Záa. Also you are a man of property, who can afford to pay for his pleasure." When we had walked a little way in silence, she asked in a small voice, "You *will* pay me?"

"Of course," I said thickly. My tongue was as swollen by the octli as my tepúli was swollen with anticipation.

"Someone must be my first," she said, as if stating a fact of life. "I am glad it is you. I only wish they all might be like you. I am a destitute widow with two daughters, so now we are accounted no better than slaves, and my girls will never have decent husbands of the Cloud People. Had I known what their lives held in store, I would have withheld my milk when they were infants, but it is too late now to prefer them dead. If we are to survive, I must do this—and they must learn to, as well."

"Why?" I managed to ask. Because I was walking somewhat weavingly, she took my arm to guide me, and we made our way through the dark alleys of the city's poorer residential area.

Gié Bele waved her free hand back over her shoulder and said sadly, "The hostel was once ours. But my husband was bored by the life of an innkeeper and he was always going off adventuring—hoping to find a fortune that would set us free of it. He found some rare and odd things, but never anything of value, while we went ever deeper into debt to the trader who lent and exchanged currencies. On his last expedition, my husband sought a thing he was much excited about. So, to borrow the necessary funds, he put up our inn as a pledge." She shrugged. "Like a man who pursues the flicker of the Xtabai swamp ghost, he never came back. That was four years ago."

"And now that trader is the innkeeper," I muttered.

"Yes. He is a man of the Zoque, named Wáyay. But the property was not enough to redeem our entire debt. The bishósu of this city is a kindly man, but when the claim was laid before him he had no choice. I was bound over, to work from sunrise to sunset. I can be thankful that my girls were not. They earn what they can—doing sewing, embroidery, laundry—but most people who can pay for such work have daughters or slaves of their own to do it."

"For how long must you serve this Wáyay?"

She sighed. "Somehow the debt never seems to decrease. I would try to quell my revulsion and offer *him* my body, in part payment, but he is a eunuch."

I grunted in wry amusement.

"He was formerly a priest of some god of the Zoque and, as so many priest do, in a mushroom ecstasy he cut off and laid his parts on the altar. He immediately regretted that, and left the order. But he had by then set aside for himself, from the believers' offerings, enough to set himself up in business."

I grunted again.

"The girls and I live simply, but it gets harder for us every day. If we are to live at all . . ." She squared her shoulders and said firmly, "I have explained to them what we must do. Now I will show them. Here we are."

She preceded me through the tatty cloth-curtained doorway of a rickety shack of saplings and thatch. It was a single room with a pounded earth floor, lighted by one fish-oil wick lamp, and pitifully furnished. I could see only a quilt-covered pallet, a feebly glowing charcoal brazier, and a few articles of feminine apparel hung on the inside twig stumps of the sapling walls.

"My daughters," she said, indicating the two girls who stood with their backs against the far wall.

I had been expecting two small and grubby brats, who would eye with awe the stranger their mother had suddenly brought home. But the one was as old as I; she was as tall as her mother, and just as shapely and fair of face. The other was perhaps three years younger, and of equal comeliness. They both stared at me with pensive curiosity. I was surprised, to put it mildly, but I made a bravura gesture of kissing the earth to them—and would have fallen on my face, had not the younger one caught me.

She giggled despite herself, and so did I, but then I stopped in puzzlement. Few Tzapotéca females show their age until they get well along in years. But that girl was only seventeen or so, and already her black hair had one startling strand of white streaking back from her forehead, like lightning through midnight.

Gié Bele explained, "A scorpion stung her there, when she was a baby still crawling. She nearly died of it, but the only lasting effect was that one lock of hair, white ever since."

"She is—they are both as beautiful as their mother," I mumbled gallantly. But my face must have expressed my twinge of consternation at having discovered that the woman was old enough to be *my* own mother, for she gave me a worried, almost frightened look and said:

"No, please do not think of taking one of them instead of me." She whipped her blouse over her head, and instantly blushed so extensively that the blush suffused her bare breasts. "Please, young lord! I offered only myself. Not yet the girls..." She seemed to mistake my numb silence for indecision; she quickly undid both her skirt and undergarment, and let them drop to the ground, and stood naked before me and her daughters.

I glanced uneasily at them, my eyes no doubt as wide as theirs were, and it must have seemed to Gié Bele that I was comparing the available wares. Still imploring, "Please! Not my girls. Use *me!*" she forcibly dragged me down beside her on the pallet. I was too shocked to resist, and she flung my mantle to one side and tugged at my loincloth, saying breathlessly, "The innkeeper would demand five cacao beans for a maátitl, and he would keep two for himself. So I will ask only three. Is not that a fair price?"

I was too dazed to reply. The private parts of us both were exposed to the view of the girls, who stared as if they *could* not look away, and their mother was next trying to roll me on top of herself. Perhaps the girls were not unacquainted with their mother's body, and perhaps they had even seen an erect male organ before, but I was sure they had never seen the two together. Drunk though I may have been, I protested, "Woman! The lamplight, the girls! At least send them outdoors while we—"

"Let them see!" she almost screamed. "They will be lying here on other nights!" Her face was wet with tears, and I finally understood that she was not so resigned to whoredom as she had tried to pretend. I grimaced at the girls and made a violent gesture. Looking frightened, they whisked out through the door curtain. But Gié Bele did not notice, and cried again, as if demanding the utmost debasement of herself, "Let them see what they will be doing!"

"You want others to see, woman?" I growled at her. "Let them see the better, then!"

Instead of sprawling atop her, I turned onto my back, lifting her at the same time, and set her kneeling astride me, and I impaled her to the hilt of myself. After that first painful moment, Gié Bele slowly relaxed against me and lay quiescent in my embrace, though I could feel her tears continuing to trickle onto my bare chest. Well, it happened quickly and powerfully for me, and she certainly felt the spurt inside her, but she did not pull away as any other bought woman would then have done.

By then, her own body was wanting satisfaction, and I think she would not have noticed if the girls had been still in the hut, would not have given thought to the detailed demonstration provided by our position, or the damp noise of suction made by her rocking back and forth the length of my tepúli. When Gié Bele came to climax, she reared up and leaned back, her distended nipples pointing high, her long hair brushing my legs, her eyes shut tight, her mouth open in a mewing cry like that of a jaguar kitten. Then she collapsed again onto my chest, her head beside mine, and she lay so limp that I would have thought she had died, except that she breathed in short gasps.

After a little, when I had myself recovered, slightly more sober for the experience, I became aware of another head near me on my other side. I turned to see immense brown eyes, wide behind their luxuriant dark lashes: the winsome face of one of the daughters. At some point she had reentered the hut and knelt beside the pallet and was regarding me intently. I drew the quilt over the nakedness of myself and her still-motionless mother.

"Nu shishá skarú..." the girl began to whisper. Then, seeing that I did not comprehend, she spoke softly in a broken Náhuatl, and giggled when she told me guiltily, "We watched through the cracks in the wall." I groaned in shame and embarrassment; I still burn when I think of it. But then she said thoughtfully, seriously, "Always I supposed it would be a bad thing. But your faces were good, like happy."

Though I was in no philosophic mood, I told her quietly,

"I do not think it is ever really a bad thing. But it is much better when you do it with someone you love." I added, "And in private, without mice watching from the walls."

She started to say something more, but suddenly her stomach grumbled, more loudly than her voice had spoken. She looked pathetically mortified, and tried to pretend it had not happened, and drew a little away from me.

I exclaimed, "Child, you are hungry!"

"Child?" She petulantly tossed her head. "I have near your age, which is old enough for—for that. I am not a child."

I shook her drowsing mother and said, "Gié Bele, when did your daughters last eat a meal?"

She stirred and said meekly, "I am allowed to feed on the leftovers at the inn, but I cannot bring much home."

"And you asked for three cacao beans!" I said angrily.

I could have remarked that it might more rightly have been myself asking a fee, for performing to an audience, or instructing the young. But I groped for my castoff loincloth and the purse I kept sewn into it. "Here," I said to the daughter, and caught her hands and poured into them perhaps twenty or thirty beans. "You and your sister go and buy food. Buy fuel for the fire. Anything you like, and as much as you can carry."

She looked at me as if I had filled her hands with emeralds. Impulsively, she bent over and kissed my cheek, then bounded up and out of the hut again. Gié Bele raised up on one elbow to look down at my face.

"You are kind to us—and after I behaved so. Please, would you let me be kinder to *you* now?"

I said, "You gave me what I came to buy. I am not trying now to buy your affection."

"But I want to give it," she insisted, and began to give me an attention which may be exclusive to the Cloud People.

It really is much better when it is done lovingly—and in private. And she truly was so attractive that a man could hardly get enough of her. But we were up and dressed again when the girls returned, laden with comestibles: one entire and enormous plucked fowl, a basket of vegetables, many other things. Chattering cheerfully to each other, they set about building up the brazier fire, and the younger daughter courteously asked if her mother and myself would dine with them.

Gié Bele told them that we had both eaten at the inn. Now, she said, she would guide me back there and find some chore to occupy her there during what remained of the night, for if she slept she would surely oversleep the sunrise. So I bade the girls good night and we left them to what may have been, for all I knew, their first decent meal in four years. As the woman and I walked hand in hand through streets and alleys seeming darker even than before, I thought about the famished girls, their widowed and desperate mother, the greedy Zoque creditor . . . and at last I said abruptly:

"Would you sell me your house, Gié Bele?"

"What?" She started so that our hands came unlinked. "That dilapidated hut? Whatever for?"

"Oh, to rebuild into something better, of course. If I continue trading, I shall certainly pass this way again, perhaps often, and a place of my own would be preferable to a crowded inn."

She laughed at the absurdity of my lie, but pretended to take it seriously, asking, "And where in the world would *we* live?"

"In some place much finer. I would pay a good price, enough to enable you to live comfortably. And," I said firmly, "with no necessity for the girls *or* you to go astraddle the road."

"What—what would you offer to pay?"

"We will settle that right now. Here is the inn. Please to put lights in the room where we dined. And writing materials—paper and chalk will do. Meanwhile, tell me which is the room of that fat eunuch. And stop looking frightened; I am being no more imbecilic than usual."

She gave me a wavering smile and went to do my bidding, while I took a lamp to find the proprietor's room, and interrupted his snoring with a hard kick to his massive rear end.

"Get up and come with me," I said, as he spluttered with outrage and sleepy bewilderment. "We have business to transact."

"It is the middle of the night. You are drunk. Go away."

I had almost to lift him to his feet, and it took a while to convince him that I was sober, but I finally hauled him—still struggling to knot his mantle—to the room Gié Bele had lighted for us. When I half-dragged him in, she started to sidle out.

"No, stay," I said. "This concerns all three of us. Fat man, fetch out all the papers pertinent to the ownership of this hostel and the debt outstanding against it. I am here to redeem the pledge."

He and she stared at me in equal astonishment, and Wáyay, after spluttering some more, said, "This is why you rout me from my bed? You want to buy this place, you presumptuous pup? We can all go back to bed. I do not intend to sell."

"It is not yours to sell," I said. "You are not its owner, but the holder of a lien. When I pay the debt and all its accrual, you are a trespasser. Go, bring the documents."

I had the advantage of him then, when he was still befogged with sleep. But by the time we settled down to the columns of number dots and flags and little trees, he was again as acute and exacting as he had ever been in his careers of priest and currency changer. I will not regale you, my lords, with all the details of our negotiations. I will only remind you that I did know the craft of working with numbers, and I knew the craftiness possible to that craft.

What the late explorer husband had borrowed, in goods and currency, added up to an appreciable sum. However, the premium he had agreed to pay for the privilege of the loans should not have been excessive, except for the lender's cunning method of compounding it. I do not remember all the figures there involved, but I can give a simplified illustration. If I lend a man a hundred cacao beans for one month, I am entitled to the repayment of a hundred and ten. For two months, he repays a hundred and twenty beans. For three months, a hundred and thirty, and so on. But what Wáyay had done was to add the ten-bean premium at the end of the first month, and then on that *total* of a hundred and ten to calculate the next premium, so that at the end of two months he was owed a hundred twenty and *one* beans. The difference may sound trifling, but it mounts proportionately each month, and on substantial sums it can mount alarmingly.

I demanded a recalculation from the very start of Wáyay's giving credit to the inn. *Ayya,* he squawked as he must have done when he awoke from that disastrous mushroom rapture of his priesthood days. But, when I suggested that we refer the matter to Tecuantépec's bishósu for adjudication, he gritted his teeth and redid the arithmetic, with me closely monitoring. There were many other details to be argued, such as the inn's expenses and profits over the four years he had been running it. But finally, as dawn was breaking, we agreed on a lump sum due him, and I agreed to pay in currency of gold dust, copper and tin snippets, and cacao beans. Before I did so, I said:

"You have forgotten one small item. I owe you for the lodging of my own train."

"Ah, yes," said the fat old fraud. "Honest of you to remind me." And he added that to the accounting.

As if suddenly remembering, I said, "Oh, one other thing."

"Yes?" he said expectantly, his chalk poised to add it in.

"Subtract four years' wages due the woman Gié Bele."

"What?" He stared at me aghast. She stared too, but in dazzled admiration. "Wages?" he sneered. "The woman was bound over to me as a tlacótli."

"If your accounting had been honest, she would not have been. Look at your own revised arithmetic. The bishósu might have awarded you a *half* interest in this property. You have not only swindled Gié Bele, you have also enslaved a free citizen."

"All right, all right. Let me count. Two cacao beans a day—"

"Those are slave wages. You have had the services of the inn's former proprietress. Certainly worth a freeman's wage of twenty beans a day." He clutched his hair and howled. I added, "You are a barely tolerated alien in Tecuantépec. She is of the Ben Záa, and so is the bishósu. If we go to him . . ."

He immediately ceased his tantrum and began frantically to scribble, dripping sweat onto the bark paper. Then he *did* howl.

"More than twenty and nine thousand! There are not that many beans on all the cacao bushes in all the Hot Lands!"

"Translate it to gold-dust quills," I suggested. "It will not sound so big a sum."

"Will it not?" he bellowed, when he had done the figuring. "Why, if I accede to the wage demand, I have lost my very loincloth on the entire transaction. To subtract that amount means you pay me less than *half* the original amount *I* paid out as a *loan!*" His voice had gone up to a squeak and he sweated as if he were melting.

"Yes," I said. "That agrees with my own figures. How will you have it? All in gold? Or some in tin? In copper?" I had fetched my pack from the room I had not yet occupied.

"This is extortion!" he raged. "This is robbery!"

There was also a small obsidian dagger in the pack. I took it out and held its point against Wáyay's second or third chin.

"Extortion and robbery it *was*," I said in my coldest voice. "You cheated a defenseless woman of her property, then made her drudge for you during four long years, and I know to what desperate straits she had come. I hold you to the arithmetic you yourself have just now done. I will pay you the amount you last arrived at—"

"Ruination!" he bawled. "Devastation!"

"You will write me a receipt, and on it you will write that the payment voids all your claim on this property and this woman, now and forever. You will then, while I watch, tear up that old pledge signed by her husband. You will then take whatever personal possessions you have, and depart these premises."

He made one last try at defiance: "And if I refuse?"

"I march you to the bishósu at knife point. The punishment for theft is the flower-garland garrotte. I do not know what you would suffer beforehand, as a penalty for enslaving the free-born, since I do not know the refinements of torture in this nation."

Slumping in final defeat, he said, "Put away the knife. Count out the currency." He raised his head to snap at Gié Bele, "Bring me fresh paper—" then winced and made his tone unctuous, "Please, my lady, bring me paper and paints and a writing reed."

I counted quills of gold dust and stacks of tin and copper onto the cloth between us, and there was little but lint left in the pack when I was done. I said, "Make the receipt to my name. In the language of this place I am called Záa Nayàzú."

"Never was an ill-omened man better named," he muttered, as he began to make the word pictures and columns of number glyphs. And he wept as he worked at it, I swear.

I felt Gié Bele's hand on my shoulder and I looked up at her. She had labored all the day before and then had endured a sleepless night, not to mention other things, but she stood straight, and her glorious eyes shone, and her whole face glowed.

I said, "This will not take long. Why do you not go back and fetch the girls? Bring them home."

When my partners woke and came for breakfast, Cozcatl looked rested and bright again, but Blood Glutton looked somewhat drawn. He ordered a meal consisting mainly of raw eggs, then said to the woman, "Send me the landlord, too. I owe him ten cacao beans." He added, "Spendthrift lecher that I am, and at my age."

She smiled and said, "For that entertainment—for you—no charge, my lord," and went away.

"Huh?" grunted Blood Glutton, staring after her. "No inn gives *that* commodity free."

I reminded him, "Cynical old grouch, you said there are no first times. Perhaps there are."

"You may be crazy, and so may she, but the innkeeper—"

"As of last night, she *is* the innkeeper."

"Huh?" he blurted again. He said *huh?* twice more, once when his breakfast platter was brought by the surpassingly lovely girl of my own age, and again when his big cup of frothy chocolate was brought by the surpassingly lovely younger girl with the streak of pale lightning in her black hair.

"What has happened here?" Blood Glutton asked bewilderedly. "We stop at a rundown hostel, an inferior establishment of one greasy Zoque and one slave woman . . ."

"And overnight," said Cozcatl, sounding equally amazed, "Mixtli turns it into a temple full of goddesses."

Our party stayed a second night at the inn, and when all was quiet, Gié Bele stole into my room, more radiant in her newfound happiness than she had been before, and that time the lovingness of our embrace was not at all dissembled, or forced, or in any other way distinguishable from an act of true and mutual love.

When I and my troop shouldered our packs and took our leave, early the next morning, she and then each of the daughters held me tight and covered my face with tear-wet kisses and said a heartfelt thank-you. I looked back several times, until I could no longer make out the inn among the blurry jumble of other buildings.

I did not know when I would be back, but I had sown seeds there, and from that time on, however far and long I wandered, I could never again be a stranger among the Cloud People, any more than the farthest climbing tendril of a vine can detach itself from its roots in the earth. That much I knew. What I could not know, or even dream, was what fruit those seeds would bear—of glad surprise and crushing tragedy, of wealth and loss, of joy and misery. It would be a long time before I tasted the first of those fruits, and a longer time before they all ripened in their turn, and on one of those fruits I have not yet fed entirely to its bitter core.

⚜

As you know, reverend friars, this entire land of New Spain is lapped on either side by a great sea which extends from the shore to the horizon. Since the seas lie more or less directly east and west of Tenochtítlan, we Mexíca have generally referred to them as the eastern and western oceans. But, from Tecuantépec onward, the land mass itself bends eastward, so those waters are more accurately called there the northern and southern oceans, and the land is only a narrow, low-lying isthmus separating the two. I do not mean that a man can stand between the oceans and spit into whichever he chooses. The waist of the isthmus is something like fifty one-long-runs from north to south, about a ten-day journey, but an easy one, because most of the land between is so flat and featureless.

However, on that journey, we were not crossing from one coast to the other. We traveled eastward over the misnamed Jaguar Hill flat plains, with the southern oceans always somewhere not far to our right, though never within sight of the trail. We had sea gulls hovering overhead more often than vultures. Ecept for the oppressive heat of those lowlands, the marching was easy, even monotonous, with nothing to look at but tall yellow grass and low gray scrub. We made good time, and there was an abundance of easily killable game for food—rabbits, iguanas, armadillos—and the climate was comfortable for nighttime camping, so we did not sleep in any of the villages of the Mixe people whose territory we were then traversing.

I had good reason to push hard for our destination, the lands of the Maya, where I could finally start trading the goods we carried for more valuable goods to carry back to Tenochtítlan. My partners of course knew something of the extravagances in which I had lately indulged, but I did not confess to them all the details or the prices I had paid. So far, I had struck but one advantageous bargain along the way, when I sold the slave Four to his relatives, and that was a long while back. Since then I had made only two transactions, both of them costly and neither of any visible or immediate profit to us. I had bought Chimáli's feather tapestry only for the sweet revenge of destroying it. At even greater price, I had bought a hostel for the pleasure of giving it away. If I was reticent with my partners, it was from some shame at not having yet shown myself a very shrewd pochtécatl.

After several days of traveling quickly and easily across the dun-colored flats, we saw the pale blue of mountains begin to rise on our left, and gradually loom up in front of us, too, and darken to blue-green, and we were again climbing, that time into thick forests of pine and cedar and juniper. Thereabouts we began to encounter the crosses that have always been held holy by the several nations of the far south.

Yes, my lords, their cross was practically identical to your Christian cross. Like it, a trifle longer in height than in breadth, the only difference being that the top and side arms bore a bulge at their ends rather like a clover leaf. To those peoples, the religious significance of the cross resided in its symbolizing the four points and center of the compass. But it had a practical use as well. Whenever we found a waist-high wooden cross implanted in some otherwise empty wilderness, we knew that it did not demand, "Be reverent!" but invited us to "Be glad!"— for it marked the presence nearby of good, clear, fresh water.

The mountains got steeper and more rugged until they were as formidable as those back in Uaxyácac. But we were more experienced climbers by then, and we should not have found them too daunting, except that, in addition to the normal chill on the heights, we suffered a sudden attack of viciously cold weather. Well, even in those southern lands it was then mid-winter, and the short-day god Tititl was exceptionally hard on us that year.

We trudged along bundled in every kind of clothing we carried, and with our sandals tied on over swaddlings of rags around our feet and lower legs. But the obsidian winds penetrated even those coverings, and on the higher peaks the wind flung snow like tin splinters. We were glad then to have pine trees all about. We collected the sap oozing from them, and boiled it until its irritating oils were gone and it had thickened to the gummy black oxitl which repels both coldness and wetness. Then we undressed and slathered the oxitl over our entire bodies before bundling up again. Except for clear patches around our eyes and lips, we were as night-black as the blind god Itzcoliúqui is always pictured.

We were then in the country of the Chiapa and, when we began to come upon their scattered mountain villages, our grotesque appearance caused some surprise. The Chiapa do not use the black oxitl, but are accustomed to smear themselves all over with jaguar or cuguar or tapir fat, for similar protection against bad weather. However, the people themselves were almost as dark as we were; not black, of course, but the darkest cacao-brown skin I had yet seen on an entire nation of beings. It was the Chiapa tradition that their longest-ago ancestors had emigrated from some original homeland far to the south, and their complexion tended to confirm the legend. They had apparently inherited the color of forebears who had been well baked by a much fiercer sun.

We travelers would gladly have *paid* for just a touch of that sun. When we plodded through the valleys and hollows sheltered from the wind, we suffered only the numbness and lethargy of freezing cold. But when we crossed a mountain by way of a pass, the sharp wind whistled through it too, like arrows shot through a cave tunnel, none scattering, all striking. And when there was no pass, when we had to clamber all the way up and over a mountain, there would be snow or sleet pelting us at the top, or there would be old snow on the ground for us to wade and slither through. We were all miserable, but one of us was more miserable than the rest: the slave Ten had been stricken with some ailment.

He had never uttered a word of complaint and never lagged behind, so we did not even suspect that he was feeling ill until the morning his tumplined pack, like a heavy hand, simply pushed him to his knees. He tried gamely to rise but could not, and collapsed full length on the ground. When we pulled loose the tumpline and unburdened him and turned him face up, we discovered than he was so hot with fever that his plastering of oxitl had literally cooked to a dry crust all over his body. Cozcatl asked solicitously if he was especially affected in any specific part. Ten replied, in his broken Náhuatl, that his head felt cloven by a maquáhuitl and that his body felt on fire and that every one of his joints ached, but that otherwise nothing in particular was bothering him.

I asked if he had eaten of anything unusual, or if he had been bitten or stung by any venomous creature. He said he had eaten only the meals we all shared. And his only encounter with any creature had been with a notably innocuous one, seven or eight days before, when he tried to run down a rabbit for our evening stew. He would have had it, too, if it had not nipped him and bounded free. He showed me the pinch marks of the rodent teeth on his hand, then rolled away from me and vomited.

Blood Glutton, Cozcatl, and I felt sorry that, if any of us had to be taken ill, it should be Ten, for we all liked him. He was the one slave who had been the most tractable and unflagging of all our porters. He had loyally helped to save us all from the Tya Nuü bandits. It was he who had oftenest volunteered for the somewhat unmanly task of cooking. He was the strongest among the slaves, after the hulking Four we had sold, and had borne the heaviest pack from that time. He had also submissively carried the unwieldy and unwholesome cuguar pelt; indeed, he still had the thing, for Blood Glutton would not let it be discarded.

We all rested, until Ten himself was the first to get to his feet. I felt his forehead and it seemed that the fever had abated. I looked more closely at his dark brown face and said, "I have known you for more than a sheaf of days, but I only now realize. You are of this Chiapa country, are you not?"

"Yes, master," he said weakly. "From the capital city of

Chiapán. That is why I wish to press on. I hope you will be kind enough to sell me there."

So he hoisted his bundle, slipped the tumpline again around his head, and we all went on, but by twilight of that day he was staggering in a manner pitiful to behold. Still he insisted on keeping the pace, and refused all suggestions of another halt or a lightening of his load. He would not put it down until we found a valley out of the wind, with a cross marking an icy creek flowing turgidly through it, and there made camp.

"We have killed no game lately," said Blood Glutton, "and the dogs are long gone. But Ten should have some nourishing fresh food, not just atóli mush and windy beans. Have Three and Six each start twirling a drill. It should take them so long to get a fire going that I can make a catch of something."

He found a limber green withe, bent it into a hoop, tied to it a scrap of almost threadbare cloth to make a crude net, and went to try his skill in the creek. He came back after a while, saying, "Cozcatl could have done it. They were sluggish with the cold," and exhibited a mess of silvery green fish, none longer than a hand or thicker than a finger, but enough of them to fill our stew pot. Looking at them, however, I was not sure I wanted them in the pot, and I said so.

Blood Glutton waved away my objection. "Never mind that they are ugly. They are tasty."

"They are unnatural," complained Cozcatl. "Every one of them has four eyes!"

"Yes, very clever fish, these fish. They float just below the creek surface, their upper eyes watching for insects in the air, their lower eyes alert for prey under the water. Perhaps they will endow our ailing Ten with some of their own wide-awakeness."

If they did, it was only enough to prevent his getting the good night's sleep he needed. I myself woke several times to hear the sick man thrashing and coughing and hawking up phlegm and mumbling incoherently. Once or twice I did make out what sounded like a word—"binkizáka"—and in the morning I drew Blood Glutton aside to ask him if he had any idea what it meant.

"Yes, one of the few foreign words I know," he said superciliously, as if he thereby conferred a favor on it. "The binkizáka are creatures half human, half animal, which haunt the mountain heights. I am told that they are the hideous and obnoxious offspring of women who have unnaturally mated with jaguars or monkeys or whatever. When you hear a noise like thunder in the mountains, but there is no storm, you are hearing the binkizáka making mischief. Personally, I believe the sounds are of landslides and rockfalls, but you know the ignorance of foreigners. Why do you ask? Have you heard strange noises?"

"Only Ten talking in his sleep. I think he was in delirium. I think he is more ill than we supposed."

So, overriding his plaintive protests, we took Ten's load and divided it amongst the rest of us, and left him only the mountain lion's skin to carry that day. Unburdened, he walked well enough, but I could tell when he was seized by a chill, for he would bend that stiff old hide around his already thick swaddling of garments. Then the chill would pass, and the fever rack him, and he would doff the skin and even open his clothing to the cold mountain air. He also breathed with a gurgling noise, when he was not coughing, and what he coughed up was a sputum of exceptionally foul smell.

We were climbing eastward up a mountain of considerable size, and arrived at its top to find our way interrupted. We stood on the brink of a canyon running out of sight to the north and south, the steepest-sided canyon I have ever seen. It was like a gash cut through the ranges by some angry god who had slashed down from the sky with a god-sized maquáhuitl, swinging it with all his god strength. It was a sight that was breathtakingly impressive, beautiful, and deceptive, all at the same time. Though a cold wind blew where we stood, it evidently never penetrated that canyon, for the nearly perpendicular rock walls were festooned with clinging flowers of all colors. At the very bottom were forests of flowering trees, and soft-looking meadows, and a silver thread which appeared, from where we stood, to be the merest brook.

We did not try to descend into the inviting depths, but turned south and followed the canyon rim until it gradually began to slope downward. By dusk it had lowered us to the level of that "brook," which was easily a hundred man's-steps from bank to bank. I learned later that it is the River Suchiápa, the broadest, deepest, swiftest-flowing river in all of The One World. That canyon, cut by it through the Chiapa mountains, is also unique in The One World: five one-long-runs in length and, at its deepest, nearly half a one-long-run from brink to bottom.

We had come down to a plateau where the air was warmer and the wind more gentle. We also came to a village, though a poor one. It was called Toztlan, and it was scarcely big enough to support a name, and the only meal the villagers could provide us was a hash made of boiled owl, which gags me even in recollection. But Toztlan did have a hut big enough for us all to sleep under shelter for the first time in several nights, and the village population did include a physician of sorts.

"I am only an herb doctor," he said apologetically, in faltering Náhuatl, after he had examined Ten. "I have given the patient a purge, and can do no more. But tomorrow you will arrive at Chiapán, and there you will find many famous pulse doctors."

I did not know what pulse doctoring might be, but, by the next day, I could only hope it would be an improvement on herb doctoring. Before we got to Chiapán, Ten had collapsed and was being carried on the cuguar hide he had carried for so long. We took turns, by fours, bearing the improvised litter by the leg-skins at its corners, while Ten lay upon it and writhed and—between spasms of coughing—complained to us that several binkizáka were sitting on his chest and preventing him from breathing.

"One of them is gnawing on me, too. See?" And he held out his hand. What he showed was only the place where the harmless rabbit had nipped him, but, for some reason, that spot had ulcerated into an open sore. We carriers tried to tell him that we saw nothing sitting or eating upon him, and that his problem was only the thinness of the air on that high plateau. We ourselves had such difficulty in breathing that none of us could carry for long before we had to be relieved by another.

Chiapán looked nothing like a capital of anything. It was merely one more village, situated on the bank of a tributary of the Suchiápa River, and I supposed it was the capital only by virtue of its being the largest village of all the villages in the Chiapa nation. A few of its buildings, too, were of wood or adobe, instead of their all being the usual stick-and-thatch huts, and there were the crumbling remnants of two old pyramids.

Our little company came into town reeling with fatigue and calling for a doctor. A kindly passerby heeded our obviously urgent cries, and stopped to peer at the barely conscious Ten. He exclaimed, "Macoboö!" and shouted something else in his language which sent two or three other passersby off at a run. Then he made a beckoning gesture to us and trotted ahead to lead us to the abode of a physician who, we gathered from other gestures, had some command of the Náhuatl tongue.

By the time we got there, we had been joined by an excitedly jabbering crowd. It seemed that the Chiapa do not, like us Mexíca, have entirely individual names. Though each person naturally has some distinguishing name, it is attached to a family name, like those of you Spaniards, which endures unchanging through all the generations of that family. The slave we called Ten was of the Macoboö family of Chiapán, and the helpful citizen, recognizing him, had shouted for someone to run and tell his relatives of his return to town.

Ten was unhappily in no condition to recognize any of the other Macoboö who converged on us, and the doctor—though visibly gratified to find such a crowd clamoring at his door— could not let them all inside. When the four of us carrying Ten had laid him on the earthen floor, the aged physician commanded that the hut be cleared of everybody except himself, his crone of a wife who would assist him, the patient, and myself, to whom he would explain the treatment while he performed it. He introduced himself to me as Doctor Maäsh and, in not very good Náhuatl, told me the theory of pulse doctoring.

He held the wrist of Ten Macoboö while he called out the name of each god, good and bad, in whom the Chiapa believe. As he explained it, when he shouted the name of the deity who was afflicting the patient, Ten's heart would pound and his pulse quicken. Then the doctor, knowing which god was responsible for the ailment, would know exactly what sacrificial offering should be made to persuade that god to cease the molestation. He would also know the proper medicines to administer to repair whatever damage had been done by the god.

So Ten lay there on the cuguar skin, his eyes closed in the sunken hollows of their sockets, and old Doctor Maäsh held his wrist, leaned over him, and shouted into his ear:

"Kakál, the bright god!" then a pause for the pulse to respond, then, "Tótik, the dark god!" and a pause and "Téo, the love goddess!" and "Antún, the life god!" and "Hachakyúm, the mighty god!" and so on, through more Chiapa gods and goddesses than I can remember. At last he squatted back on his heels and muttered in apparent defeat, "The pulse is so feeble that I cannot be sure of the response to *any* name."

Ten suddenly croaked, without opening his eyes, "Binkizáka bit me!"

"Aha!" said Doctor Maäsh, brightening. "It would not have occurred to me to suggest the lowly binkizáka. And here indeed is a hole in his hand!"

"Excuse me, Lord Doctor," I ventured. "It was not any of the binkizáka. It was a rabbit that bit him."

The physician raised his head so he could scowl down his nose at me. "Young man, I was holding his wrist when *he* said 'binkizáka,' and I know a pulse when I feel it. Woman!" I blinked, but he was addressing his wife. He afterward explained to me that he told her, "I shall need to confer with an expert in the lesser beings. Go fetch Doctor Kamé."

The crone scuttled out of the hut, elbowing through the craning crowd, and in a few moments we were joined by another elderly man. The Doctors Kamé and Maäsh huddled and muttered, then took turns holding Ten's flaccid wrist and roaring "Binkizáka!" into his ear. Then they huddled and consulted some more, then nodded in agreement. Doctor Kamé barked another order to the old woman and she departed again in a hurry. Doctor Maäsh told me:

"It is profitless to sacrifice to the binkizáka, since they are half beasts and do not understand the rites of propitiation. This being an emergency case, my colleague and I have decided on the radical measure of burning the affliction out of the patient. We have sent for the Sun Slab, the most holy treasure of our people."

The woman came back with two men, carrying between them what looked at first glance like a simple square of rock. Then I saw that its upper surface was inlaid with jadestone in the form of a cross. Yes, very similar to your Christian cross. In the four spaces between the arms of the cross, the rock had been bored completely through, and in each of those holes was a chunk of chipílotl quartz. But—and this is important for the understanding of what followed, my lords—each of those quartz crystals had been ground and polished so it was of perfectly round circumference and smoothly convex on both its upper and lower sides. Each of those transparent panes in the Sun Slab was like a flattened ball, or an extremely symmetrical clam.

While the two men stood holding the Sun Slab over the prostrate Ten, the old woman took a broom and, with his handle, poked holes in the thatch of the roof, each hole admitting a beam of the afternoon sun, until finally she punched a hole that let a beam right down on the patient. The two doctors tugged at the cuguar pelt to adjust Ten's position relative to the sunbeam and the Sun Slab. Then occurred a thing most marvelous, and I crept closer to see better.

Under the doctors' direction, the two men holding the heavy stone slab tilted it so the sun shone through one of the shaped quartz crystals and made a round spot of light on Ten's ulcerated hand. Then, moving the stone back and forth in the sunbeam, they made that round spot of light concentrate down to one intense *dot* of light, aimed directly upon the sore. The two doctors held the limp hand steady, the two men held the dot of light steady, and—believe me or not, as you will—a wisp of smoke came from the ugly sore. In another moment, there was a sizzling noise and a small flame was there, almost invisible in the brightness of that intensified light. The doctors gently moved the hand about, so that the sun-made flame went all over the ulcer.

At last, one of them said a word. The two men carried the Sun Slab out of the hut, the old woman began trying with her broomstick to rearrange the straw of the roof, and Doctor Maäsh motioned for me to lean and look. The ulcer had been as completely and cleanly seared as if it had been done with a fire-hot copper rod. I congratulated the two physicians—sincerely, since I had never seen the like before. I also congratulated Ten on having borne the burning without a sound.

"Sad to say, he did not feel it," said Doctor Maäsh. "The

patient is dead. We might have saved him, if you had told me of the binkizáka's involvement and saved me the unnecessary routine of going through all the major gods." Even in his ragged Náhuatl, his tone came through as tartly critical. "You are all alike, when you need medical treatment. Keep a stubborn silence about the most important symptoms. Insist that a physician must first *guess* the affliction, *then* cure it, or he has not earned his fee."

"I shall be pleased to pay all fees, Lord Doctor," I said, just as tartly. "Would you be pleased to tell me what you have cured?"

We were interrupted by a small, wizened, dark-skinned woman who slipped into the hut at that moment and shyly said something in the local language. Doctor Maäsh grumpily translated:

"She offers to pay all medical expenses, if you will consent to sell her the body instead of eating it, as you Mexíca customarily do with dead slaves. She is—she was his mother."

I ground my teeth and said, "Kindly inform her that we Mexíca do no such thing. And I freely give her son back to her. I only regret that we could not have delivered him alive."

The woman's woebegone face became a little less so as the physician spoke. Then she asked another question.

"It is our custom," he translated, "to bury our dead upon the pallet on which they died. She would like to buy from you this smelly skin of a mountain lion."

"It is hers," I said, and for some reason I lied: "Her son killed the beast." I made the doctor earn his fee as an interpreter if for nothing else, for I told the whole story of the hunt, only casting Ten in Blood Glutton's role, and making it sound as if Ten had gallantly saved my life at peril of his own. By the end of the story, the woman's dark face was glowing with maternal pride.

She said something else, and the disgruntled doctor translated: "She says, if her son was so loyal to the young lord, then you must be a good and deserving man. The Macoboö are indebted to you forever."

At that, she called in four more men from outside, presumably Macoboö kinsmen, and they carried Ten away on the accursed pelt that he would not now *ever* be rid of. I emerged from the hut behind them, to find that my partners had been eavesdropping. Cozcatl was sniffling, but Blood Glutton said sarcastically:

"That was all very noble. But has it occurred to you, good young lord, that this so-called trading expedition has given away rather more of value than it has yet acquired?"

"We have just now acquired some friends," I said.

And so we had. The Macoboö family, which was a big one, insisted that we be their guest during our stay in Chiapán, and lavished on us both hospitality and adulation. There was nothing we could ask that would not be given, as freely as I had given the dead slave back to them. I believe the first thing Blood Glutton requested, after a good bath and a hearty meal, was one of the comelier female cousins; I know I was given a handsome one for my own use. But the first favor I asked was that the Macoboö find me a Chiapán resident who spoke and understood Náhuatl. And when such a man was produced, the first thing I said to him was:

"Those quartz crystals in the Sun Slab, could they not be used instead of the tedious drill and tinder for lighting fires?"

"Why, of course," he said, surprised that I should find it necessary to inquire. "We have always used them so. I do not mean the ones in the Sun Slab, for the Sun Slab is reserved for ceremonial purposes. Perhaps you noticed that its crystals are as big as a man's fist. Clear quartz of that size is so rare that naturally the priests appropriate it and proclaim it holy. But a mere fragment will serve for fire lightings, when it is properly shaped and polished."

He reached under his mantle and extracted from the waist of his loincloth a crystal of that same clamshell convexity, but not much bigger than my thumbnail.

"I need hardly remark, young lord, that it only functions as a burning instrument when the god Kakál shines his sunlight through it. But even at night it has a second use—for looking closely at small things. Let me show you."

He demonstrated how it could be held at just the proper distance between eye and object—we used the embroidery on my mantle hem for the purpose—and I almost jumped when the pattern loomed so large to my sight that I could count the colored threads of it.

"Where do you get these things?" I asked, trying to keep my voice from sounding overeager.

"Quartz is a fairly common stone in these mountains," he was frank to admit. "Whenever anybody stumbles upon a good clear bit, he saves it until it can be brought here to Chiapán. Here live the Xibalbá family, and only that family has known through all its generations the secret of fashioning the rough stone into these useful crystals."

"Oh, it is no profound secret," said the current Master Xibalbá. "Not like a knowledge of sorcery or prophecy." My interpreter had introduced us, and did the translating as the crystalsmith casually went on, "It is mainly a matter of knowing the proper curvature to impart, and then merely having the patience to grind and polish each crystal exactly so."

Hoping I sounded equally casual, I said, "They make interesting novelties. Useful, too. I wonder that I have not yet seen them copied by the craftsmen of Tenochtítlan."

My interpreter remarked that there had probably never before been any reason for the Sun Slab to have been exhibited in the presence of anyone from Tenochtítlan. Then he translated Master Xibalbá's next comment:

"I said, young lord, that there is no great secret to making the crystals. I did not say it is easy, or easily imitated. One must know, for example, how to keep the stone precisely centered for the grinding. It was my greatest-grandfather Xibalbá who first learned how."

He said that with pride. He might *seem* casual about the secrets of his craft, but I was sure that he would never reveal them to any but his own progeny. That suited me perfectly; let the Xibalbá remain the only keepers of the knowledge; let the crystals remain inimitable; let me buy up enough of them....

Pretending hesitation, I said, "I think...I believe...I might just possibly be able to sell such things for curiosities in Tenochtítlan or Texcóco. I could not quite be sure...but yes, perhaps to scribes, for greater accuracy in doing their detailed word pictures..."

The master's eyes gleamed mischievously as his comment

was relayed to me. "How many, young lord, do you think you believe you might possibly but not quite require?"

I grinned and dropped the pretense. "It would depend on how many you can provide and the price you ask."

"You see here my entire stock of working material as of this day." He waved at the one wall of his workroom which was all shelves, from thatch to ground; on every shelf, nestled in bolls of cotton, were the rough quartz stones. They were distinctive only for the angular, six-sided shapes in which they came from the earth, and they ranged in size from that of a finger joint to that of a small maize cob.

"Here is what I paid for the stock," the artisan went on, handing me a bark paper bearing numerous columns of numbers and symbols. I was mentally adding up the total when he said, "From this stock I can make six twenties of finished crystals of varying sizes."

I asked, "How long would that take?"

"One month."

"Twenty days?" I exclaimed. "I should have thought *one* crystal would take that long!"

"We Xibalbá have had sheaves of years in which to practice," he said. "And I have seven apprentice sons to help me. I also have five daughters, but of course they are not allowed to touch the rough stones, lest they ruin them, being females."

"Six twenties of crystals," I mused, repeating his provincial mode of counting. "And what would you charge for that many?"

"What you see there," he said, indicating the bark paper.

Puzzled, I spoke to the interpreter. "Did I not understand correctly? Did he not say that this is what he *paid?* For the rough rock?" The interpreter nodded, and through him I again addressed the crystalsmith:

"This makes no sense. Even a street vendor of tortillas asks more for the bread than she paid for the maize." Both he and the translator smiled indulgently and shook their heads. "Master Xibalbá," I persisted, "I came here prepared to bargain, yes, but not to steal. I tell you honestly, I would be willing to pay eight times this price, and happy to pay six, and overjoyed to pay four."

His answer came back, "And I would be obliged to refuse."

"In the name of all your gods and mine, *why?*"

"You proved yourself a friend of the Macoboö. Hence you are a friend of all the Chiapa, and we Xibalbá are Chiapa born. No, protest no more. Go. Enjoy your stay among us. Let me get to work. Return in one month for your crystals."

"Then our fortune is already made!" Blood Glutton exulted, as he played with the sample crystal the artisan had given me. "We need not travel any farther. By the great Huitztli, you can sell these things back home for any price you ask!"

"Perhaps," I said. "But we have a month to wait for them, and we have a surplus of goods we still can trade, and I have a personal reason for wanting to visit the Maya."

He grumbled, "These Chiapa women are dark of skin, but they far excel any you will find among the Maya."

"Old lecher, do you never think of anything but women?"

Cozcatl, who did not think of women at all, pleaded, "Yes, do let us go on. We cannot come this far and not see the jungle."

"I also think of eating," said Blood Glutton. "These Macoboö lay an ample dinner cloth. Besides, we lost our only capable cook when we lost Ten."

I said, "You and I will go on, Cozcatl. Let this lazy ancient stay here, if he likes, and live up to his name."

Blood Glutton groused a while longer, but, as I well knew, his appetite for wandering was as strong as any of his other appetites. He was soon off to the marketplace to procure some items he said we would need for jungle travel. Meanwhile, I went again to the Master Xibalbá and invited him to take his pick of our trade goods, as an earnest against my paying the balance of his price in harder currency. He again mentioned his numerous offspring, and was pleased to select a quantity of mantles, loincloths, blouses, and skirts. That pleased me as well, because those were the bulkiest things we carried. Their disposal unburdened two of our slaves, and I had no trouble in finding ready purchasers right there in Chiapán, and their new masters paid me in gold dust.

"Now we visit the physician again," said Blood Glutton. "I was long ago given my protection against snakebite, but you and the boy have not yet been treated."

"Thank you for your good intent," I said. "But I do not think I would trust Doctor Maäsh to treat a pimple on my bottom."

He insisted, "The jungle teems with poisonous serpents. When you step on one, you will wish you had stepped into Doctor Maäsh's hut first." He began to tick off on his fingers, "There is the yellow-chin snake, the coral snake, the nauyáka . . ."

Cozcatl paled, and I remembered the elderly trader in Tenochtítlan telling how he had been bitten by a nauyáka and had cut off his own foot to keep from dying. So Cozcatl and I went to Doctor Maäsh, who produced one fang apiece of each of the snakes Blood Glutton had mentioned, and three or four more besides. With each tooth he pricked our tongues just enough to draw blood.

"There is a tiny dried residue of venom on each of these fangs," he explained. "It will make you both break out in a mild rash. But that will vanish in a few days, and thereafter you will be safe against the bite of any snake known to exist. However, there is one further precaution you must bear in mind." He smiled wickedly and said, "From this moment for ever, *your* teeth are as lethal as any serpent's. Be careful whom you bite."

✠

So we departed from Chiapán, as soon as we could pry ourselves loose from the insistent hospitality of the Macoboö, and of those two female cousins in particular, by swearing that we would soon return and be their guests again. To continue eastward, we and our remaining slaves had to climb another mountain range, but the god Tititl had by then restored the weather to the warmth appropriate to those regions, so the climb was not too punishing, even though it took us above the timberline. On the other side, the slope swept us precipitously down and down—from the lichened rock of the heights, to the line where the trees began, then through the sharp-scented forests of pine and cedar and juniper. From there, the familiar trees gradually thinned, as they were crowded out by kinds I had never seen before, and those appeared to be fighting for their lives against the vines and lianas that climbed and curled all over them.

The first thing I discovered about the jungle was that my limited eyesight was no great handicap in there, for distances did not exist; everything was close together. Strangely contorted trees, giant-leafed green plants, towering and feathery ferns, monstrous and spongy fungus, they all stood close, they pressed in and hemmed us about, almost suffocatingly so. The canopy of foliage overhead was like a green cloud cover; on the jungle floor, even at midday we were in a green twilight. Every growing thing; even the petals of flowers, seemed to exude a warm, moist stickiness. Though that was the dry season, the air itself was dense and humid and thick to breathe, like a clear fog. The jungle smelled spicy, musky, ripe-sweet and rotten: all the odors of rampant growth rooted in old decáy.

From the treetops above us, howler and spider monkeys yelped and countless varieties of parrots screeched their indignation at our intrusion, while other birds of every conceivable color flashed back and forth like warning arrows. The air about us was hung with hummingbirds no bigger than bees and fanned by fluttering butterflies as big as bats. Around our feet the underbrush was rustled by creatures stirring or fleeing. Perhaps some were deadly snakes, but most were harmless things: the little itzam lizards which run on their hind legs; the big-fingered frogs which climb trees; the multicolored, crested, dewlapped iguanas; the glossy brown-furred jaleb, which would scamper only a short way off, then stop to peer beady-eyed at us. Even the larger and uglier animals native to those jungles are shy of humans: the lumbering tapir, the shaggy capybara, the formidably claw-footed anteater. Unless one steps incautiously into a stream where alligators or caymans lurk, even those massive armored beasts are no hazard.

We were more of a menace to the native creatures than most of them were to us. During our month in the jungle, Blood Glutton's arrows provided us with several meals of jaleb, iguana, capybara, and tapir. Edible, my lords? Oh, quite. The meat of the jaleb is indistinguishable from that of the opossum; iguana flesh is white and flaky like that of the sea crayfish you call lobster; capybara tastes like the most tender rabbit; and tapir meat is very similar to pork.

The only large animal we had to fear was the jaguar. In those southern jungles the cats are more numerous than in all the temperate lands together. Of course, only a jaguar too old or too ill to hunt more nimble prey will attack a full-grown human without provocation. But little Cozcatl might have been a temptation, so we never let him out of a protective group of us adults. And, when we marched through the jungle in single file, Blood Glutton made us all carry our spears held vertically, the blades pointing straight up above our heads, because the jungle jaguar's favored way of hunting is simply to loll on a tree branch and wait to drop on some unwary victim passing below.

Blood Glutton had bought in Chiapán two items for each of us and I do not think we could have survived in the jungle without them. One was a light and delicately woven mosquito netting which we often draped over ourselves even during the daylight marches, so pestilent were the flying insects. The other item was a kind of bed called a gíshe, simply a net of slender rope, woven in a sort of beanpod shape, which could be slung between any two close-set trees. It was so much more comfortable than a pallet that I carried a gíshe on all my later travels, for use wherever there were trees to support it.

Our elevated beds put us out of the reach of most snakes, and the mantles of netting at least discouraged things like bloodsucker bats, scorpions, and other vermin of little initiative. But nothing could keep the more ambitious creatures—ants, for instance—from using our gíshe ropes for a bridge and then tunneling under the nets. If ever you wish to know what the bite of a jungle fire ant feels like, reverend friars, hold one of Master Xibalbá's crystals between the sun and your bare skin.

And there were even worse things. One morning I awoke feeling something oppressive on my chest, and cautiously lifted my head to see a thick, hairy, black hand laid there, a hand nearly twice the span of my own. "If I am being pawed by a monkey," I thought drowsily, "it is an unheard-of new breed, bigger than any man." Then I realized that the heavy thing was a bird-eating tarantula, and that there was only flimsy mosquito cloth between me and its sickle jaws. On no other morning of my life have I ever arisen with such alacrity, getting out of my coverings and as far as the ashes of the campfire all in a single bound, trailing a yell that brought everyone else to his feet almost as urgently.

But not everything in the jungle is ugly or menacing or pestilential. For a traveler who takes reasonable precautions, the jungle can be hospitable and beautiful as well. Edible game animals are easy to secure; many of the plants make nourishing cooked greens; even some of the ghastliest fungoid growths are delicious to eat. There is one arm-thick liana that looks as crusty and dry as baked clay; but cut off an arm's-length of it and inside you find it as porous as a bees' comb; tilt it over your head and it trickles out a generous drink of the freshest, sweetest, coolest water. As for the jungle's beauty, I cannot begin to describe the brilliant flowers I saw there, except to say that, of their thousands of thousands, I remember no two of similar shape and coloring.

The most gorgeous birds we saw were the numerous varieties of the quetzal, vividly colored, distinctively crested and plumed. But only infrequently did we glimpse the most magnificent and treasured bird of all, the quetzal tototl, the one with emerald tail feathers as long as a man's legs. That bird is as proud of its plumage as any nobleman who wears it later. Or so I was told by a Maya girl named Ix Ykóki. She said that the quetzal tototl builds a globular nest unique among birds' nests because it has two doorway holes. Thus the bird can enter through one and depart through the other without having to turn around inside and risk breaking one of those splendid tail plumes. Also, said Ix Ykóki, the quetzal tototl feeds only on small fruits and berries, and it snatches those from trees and vines as it flies past, and it eats them on the wing, rather than perched comfortably on a bough, to assure that the juice does not drip and stain those pendant plumes.

Since I have mentioned the girl Ix Ykóki, I might as well remark that, in my opinion, not she nor the other resident human beings added appreciably to the beauty of those jungle lands.

According to all the legends, the Maya once had a far richer, mightier, and more resplendent civilization than we Mexíca ever approached, and the remaining ruins of their onetime cities are powerful evidence in support of those legends. There is also evidence that the Maya may have learned all their arts and skills directly from the peerless Toltéca, before those Master Artisans went away. For one thing, the Maya worship many of the same Toltéca gods that we Mexíca also later appropriated. The beneficent Feathered Serpent whom we call Quetzalcóatl they call Kukulkán. The rain god whom we call Tlaloc they call Chak.

On that expedition and later ones, I have seen the remains of many of the Maya cities, and no one could deny that they must have been overwhelming in their prime. In their empty plazas and courtyards can still be seen admirable statues and carved stone panels and richly ornamented façades and even pictures from which the lively colors have not faded in all the sheaves upon sheaves of years since they were painted. I particularly noticed one detail of the Maya buildings—door openings gracefully upward-tapered in shape—that our modern architects have never yet tried or perhaps been able to imitate.

It took countless Maya artists and artisans many generations and much labor and loving care to build and beautify those cities. Now they stand empty, forsaken, forlorn. There is no mark of their having been besieged by enemy armies, or of their having suffered even the slightest of natural disasters, yet their thousands of inhabitants for some reason abandoned every one of them. And the descendants of those inhabitants are now so ignorant and uncaring of their own history that they cannot tell—they cannot even venture a plausible guess—*why* their ancestors left those cities, why the jungle was allowed to reclaim and overthrow them. Today's Maya cannot even tell why *they*, who should have inherited all that grandeur, now live resignedly in wretched grass-shack villages on the outskirts of those ghost cities.

The once vast but unified dominion of the Maya, formerly ruled from a capital city called Mayapán, has long been fractured into geographically different northern and southern divisions. I and my companions were then traveling in the more worthwhile part: the luxuriant jungle country called Tamoán Chan, Land of the Mists, which stretches limitlessly eastward from the boundaries of the Chiapa territory. To the north, where I traveled on a later occasion, is the great peninsula jutting into the northern ocean, the first place your Spanish explorers set foot in these lands. I should have thought that, after one look at those uninviting barrens, they would have gone home and come here no more.

Instead, they gave that land a name which is even more absurd than your Cow-Horn for Quaunáhuac or Tortilla for what used to be Texcála. When those first Spaniards landed and asked, "What is this place called?" the inhabitants, never having heard Spanish before, quite naturally replied, "Yectetán," which means only "I do not understand you." Those explorers made of that the name Yucatán, and I suppose the peninsula will be called so forever. But I should not laugh. The Maya's own name for that region—Uluümil Kutz, or Land of Plenty—is just as ridiculous, or possibly ironic, since the greater part of that peninsula is pitifully unfruitful and unsuited for human habitation.

Like their divided land, the Maya themselves are no longer one people under one ruler. They have fragmented into a profusion of tribes headed by petty chiefs, and all are mutually contemptuous and disparaging, and most of them are so dispirited and sunk in lethargy that they live in what their ancestors would have considered disgusting squalor. Yet every one of those splinter tribes preens itself on being the sole and only true remnant of the master Maya race. I personally think the oldtime Maya would disavow relationship with any of them.

Why, the louts cannot even tell you the *names* of their ancestors' once great cities, but call them anything they please. One such city, though now smothered in jungle, still shows a sky-reaching pyramid and a turreted palace and numerous temples, but it is unimaginatively called Palemké, the Maya word for any trivial "holy place." In another abandoned city, the interior galleries have not yet all been invaded by destructive vines and creepers, and on those inside walls are skillfully painted murals depicting warriors at battle, court ceremonies, and the like. The descendants of those warriors and courtiers, when asked what they know of the place, shrug indifferently and speak of it as Bonampák, which means only "painted walls."

In Uluümil Kutz is a city almost unravaged by erosion, and it might well be known as The Place of Man-Made Beauty, to honor the intricate yet delicate architecture of its many buildings; but it is called only Uxmal, meaning "thrice-built." Another city is superbly situated on a hilltop overlooking a wide river, deep in the jungle. I counted the ruins or foundations of at least one hundred tremendous edifices built of green granite blocks, and I believe it must have been the most majestic of *all* the old Maya centers. But the wretches now living round-about call it merely Yaxchilán, which is to say a place where there are some "green stones."

Oh, I will grant that some of the tribes—notably the Xiu of the northern peninsula and the Tzotxil of the southern jun-gles—still manifest some intelligence and vitality and a regard for their lost heritage. They recognize classes according to birth and status: noble, middle, bonded, and slave. They still main-tain some of the arts of their ancestors: their wise men know medicine and surgery, arithmetic and calendar keeping. They carefully preserve the countless thousands of books written by their predecessors, though the fact that they know so little of their own history makes me doubt that even their best-educated priests ever take the trouble to read the old books.

But even the ancient, civilized, and cultured Maya observed some customs we moderns must regard as bizarre—and it is unfortunate that their descendants have chosen to perpetuate those eccentricities while letting so many more worthy traits wither away. To an outsider like me, the most noticeable gro-tesquery is what the Maya regard as beauty in their own ap-pearance.

From the evidence of the oldest paintings and carvings, the Maya have always had hawk-beak noses and receding chins, and they have forever striven to enhance that resemblance to birds of prey. What I mean is that the Maya, ancient and current, have deliberately deformed their children from birth. A flat board is bound to a baby's forehead and kept there throughout its infancy. When it is finally removed, the child has a forehead as steeply receding as its chin, thus making its naturally prominent nose seem still more of a beak.

That is not all. A Maya boy or girl, however otherwise naked, will always be wearing a pellet of clay or resin sus-pended by a string around the head so that it dangles right between the eyes. This is intended to make the child grow up cross-eyed, which the Maya of all lands and classes deem another mark of surpassing beauty. Some of the Maya men and women have eyes so *very* crossed that I think it is only the clifflike nose between which keeps the eyes from merging. I have said that there are many beautiful things in the jungle country of Tamoán Chan, but I would not include the human population among them.

I probably would have ignored all the unattractive, hawk-faced women, except that—in a village where we spent the night, a village of the cleanly Tzotxil—one girl seemed to gaze at me with a determined fixity, and I assumed she had been smitten with passion for me at first glance. So I introduced myself by my latest name: Dark Cloud is Ek Muyal in their language, and she shyly confided that she was Ix Ykóki, or Evening Star. Only then, standing close to her, did I discern that she was exceedingly cross-eyed, and I realized that she probably had not been looking at me at all. Even at that moment when we were face to face, she could have been staring at a tree behind my back, or her own bare foot, or maybe both at once, for all I could determine.

That somewhat disconcerted me, but curiosity impelled me to persuade Ix Ykóki to sleep that night with me. And I do not mean that I was fired by any prurient curiosity as to whether a girl with crossed eyes might be interestingly peculiar in her other organs. It was simply that I had for some time been wondering what the act of copulation, with *any* female, might be like in one of those hanging, free-swinging net beds. I am pleased to report that I found it not only possible but also delightful. Indeed, I was so transported that it was not until we lay apart in the swaying gíshe, spent and sweaty, that I realized I had given Ix Ykóki a number of love bites, and that at least one of them had drawn a bead of blood.

Of course that made me remember the warning words of Doctor Maäsh, when he had administered the snakebite treat-met, and I lay awake through most of the rest of the night, suffering an agony of apprehension. I waited for Ix Ykóki to go into convulsions, or to stiffen slowly and grow cold beside me, and I wondered what kind of punishment the Tzotxil dealt out to murderers of their women. But Ix Ykóki did nothing more alarming than to snore all night through her great nose and in the morning she bounded jauntily from the bed, her crossed eyes bright.

I was happy that I had not slain the girl, but the fact also perturbed me. If the bungling old pulse doctor who told us that our own teeth were now poisonous had merely been repeating one of his people's stupid superstitions, there was every likelihood that Cozcatl and I were not at all protected against the venomous snakes—or that Blood Glutton ever had been. I so advised my partners, and thereafter we watched even more closely where we put our feet and hands as we made our way through the jungle.

A little later, I made the acquaintance of another physician, of the kind I had wanted for so long and had come so far to see: one of those Maya doctors famed for their ability to treat ailments of the eye. His name was Ah Chel, and he was also of the Tzotxil tribe, and Tzotxil means Bat People, which I took as a good omen, since bats are the creatures which see best in the darkness. Doctor Ah Chel had two other assets which recommended him to me: he spoke an adequate Náhuatl, and he was not himself cross-eyed. I think I would have been somewhat distrustful of a cross-eyed eye doctor.

He indulged in no pulse feeling or god calling or other mystic means of diagnosis. He began straightforwardly by putting into my eyes drops of juice from the herb camopalxíhuitl, to enlarge my pupils so he could look inside them. While we waited for the drug to take effect, I talked—perhaps just to ease my own nervousness—and told him of that sham Doctor Maäsh, and the circumstances of Ten's illness and death.

"Rabbit fever," said Doctor Ah Chel, nodding. "Be glad that none of the rest of you handled that diseased rabbit. The fever does not kill of itself, but it weakens the victim so that he succumbs to another ailment which fills the lungs with a thick liquid. Your slave might still have lived if you had brought him down from the heights to a place where he could have breathed air more thick and rich. But now let us have a look at you."

And he produced a clear crystal, indubitably one of Master Xibalbá's and he peered closely into each of my eyes, then sat back and said flatly, "Young Ek Muyal, there is nothing afflicting your eyes."

"Nothing?" I exclaimed. I wondered if, after all, Ah Chel was as much a pretender as Maäsh. Between my teeth I said, "There is nothing wrong except that I can see with clarity no farther than the reach of my arm. You call that *nothing?"*

"I mean there is no disease or disturbance of your vision which I or anyone can treat."

I swore one of Blood Glutton's imprecations, and I hoped it made the great god Huitzilopóchtli wince in his private parts. Ah Chel gestured for me to hear him out.

"You see things blurred because of the *shape* of your eyes, and they were born to be that way. An uncommonly shaped eyeball distorts vision in the same way as this uncommonly shaped piece of quartz. Hold this crystal between your eye and a flower, and you see the flower plain. But hold the crystal between your eye and a distant garden, and that garden is just a blur of colors."

I said miserably, "There is no medicine, no surgery . . . ?"

"I am sorry to say there is not. If you had the blinding disease caused by the black fly, yes, I might wash that away with medications. If you were afflicted with what we call the white veil, yes, I could cut that out and give you better vision, though not perfect. But there is no operation which can make the eyeball smaller, not without destroying it entirely. We will never know a remedy for your condition, any more than any man will ever know the secret place where the aged alligators go to die."

Even more miserably, I mumbled, "Then I must live all the rest of my life in a fog, squinting like a mole?"

"Well," he said, sounding not very sympathetic to my self-pity, "you can also live the rest of your life thanking the gods that you are *not* utterly blinded by the veil or the fly or something else. You will see many who are." He paused, then said pointedly, "They will never see you."

I was so cast down by the physician's verdict that I passed the remainder of our time in Tamoán Chan in rather a glum humor, and I fear I was not very good company for my partners. When a guide from the Pokomám tribe of the far eastern jungle took us to see the marvelous lakes of Tziskáo there, I looked at them as coldly as if the Maya rain god Chak had created them to affront me personally. Those are some sixty bodies of water, ranging from small ponds to estimable lakes in size, and they have no connecting straits between them, and they have no visible inlet streams, yet they never diminish in the dry season or overflow in the wet. But the really noteworthy thing about them is that no two of all those lakes are of the same color.

From the high ground where we stood overlooking six or seven of the waters, our guide pointed and said proudly, "Behold, young traveler Ek Muyal! That one is dark green-blue, that one is the color of turquoise, that one is as bright green as an emerald, that one is dull green like jadestone, that one is the pale blue of the winter sky. . . ."

I grumbled, "They might be as red as blood, for all I could tell." And that of course was simply not true. The truth was that I was seeing everything and everybody through the dark of my own despondency.

For a brief while, I courted optimism by trying some experiments with Master Xibalbá's burning crystal I carried. I already knew that it was of use for seeing close things even closer and clearer, so I endeavored to make it help me see far things as well. I tried holding it close to my eye while I looked at a tree, then holding it at arm's length, then holding it at varying distances between. No use. When aimed at objects more than a hand span beyond it, the quartz only made them more indistinct than my unaided eye did, and the experiments only made me more depressed.

Even when dealing with the Maya buyers of our trade goods, I was sour and sullen, but fortunately there was enough demand for our wares that my unwinning demeanor was tolerated. I brusquely refused the offers of pelts of jaguar and ocelot and other animals, the feathers of macaw and toucan and other birds. What I wanted was gold dust or metal currency, but such things were not much circulated in those uncivilized lands. So I let it be known that I would trade our goods—the fabrics and garments, the jewelry and trinkets, the manufactured medicines and cosmetics—only for the plumes of the quetzal tototl.

In theory, any fowler who acquired those leg-long, emerald-green feathers was obliged, on pain of death, to present them immediately to his tribal chief, who would use them either for personal adornment or as currency in his dealing with other chiefs of the Maya and the more powerful rulers of other nations. But in practice, as I hardly need say, the fowlers gave their chiefs only a share of those rarest of feathers, and kept the rest for their own enrichment. Since I positively refused to trade for anything but the quetzal tototl plumes, the customers had to go off to do hasty trades among their fellows . . . and quetzal tototl plumes I got.

As we gradually dispensed with our goods, I sold off the slaves who had carried them. In that land of the lazy, not even the nobles had much work to which to put slaves, still less could afford to own them. But every tribal chief was eager to boast a superiority over rival chiefs, and a holding of slaves— though they might be only a drain on his treasury and his larder—constituted a legitimate boast. So, for good gold dust, I sold ours variously and impartially to the chiefs of the Tzotxil, the Quiché, and the Tzeltal, two slaves apiece, and only the remaining two accompanied our return to the Chiapa country. One carried the large but unweighty bale of feathers, the other's load consisted of those few trade items we had not yet disposed of.

As he had promised, the artisan Xibalbá had his finished crystals waiting for me when we got back to Chiapán—in all, a hundred twenty and seven of them, of varied sizes—and, thanks to my sale of the slaves, I was able to pay him in pure gold-dust currency, as I had promised. While he carefully wrapped each crystal separately in cotton, then bundled them all together in cloth to make a tidy package, I said to him, by way of the interpreter:

"Master Xibalbá, these crystals make a looked-at object look bigger. Have you ever contrived a kind of crystal that would make objects appear smaller?"

"Oh, yes," he said, smiling. "Even my greatest-grandfather probably tried his hand at fashioning other things than burning crystals. We all have. I do myself, just for amusement."

I told him how limited was my vision, and added, "A Maya doctor told me that my eyes behave as if I am always looking through one of the enlarging quartzes. I wondered, if I could find such a thing as a reducing crystal, and if I looked through it . . ."

He regarded me with interest, and rubbed his chin, and said, "Hm," and went through the back of his workshop to his house. He returned with a wooden tray of shallow compartments, each holding a crystal. They were of all different shapes; some were even miniature pyramids.

"I keep these only for curiosities," said the artisan. "They are of no practical use, but some have amusing properties. This one, for instance." He lifted out a short bar of three flat sides. "It is not quartz, but a transparent kind of limestone. And I do not grind this stone; it cleaves naturally in flat planes. Hold it yonder, in the sun, and see the light it throws on your hand."

I did, half expecting to flinch from a burn. Instead I exclaimed, "The mist of water jewels!" The sunlight passing through the crystal to my hand was transformed; it was a colored band, ranging from dark red at one extreme, through yellow and green and blue, to the deepest purple; it was a tiny simulacrum of the colored bow one sees in the sky after a rain.

"But you are not looking for playthings," said the man. "Here." And he gave me a crystal of which both surfaces were concave; that is to say, it was like two dishes with their bottoms cemented together.

I held it over the embroidered hem of my mantle, and the pattern shrank to half its width. I raised my head, still holding the crystal before me, and looked at the artisan. The man's features, blurred before, were suddenly sharp and distinct, but his face was so small that he might that instant have leapt away from me and out the door and entirely across the plaza.

"It is a marvel," I said, shaken. I put down the crystal and rubbed at my eye. "I could *see* you . . . but so far away."

"Ah, then that one diminishes too powerfully. They have different strengths. Try this one."

It was concave only on one side; the other face was perfectly flat. I raised the thing cautiously. . . .

"I can see," I said, and I said it like a prayer of thanksgiving to the most beneficent of gods. "I can see far and near. There are spots and ripples, but everything else is as clear and sharp as when I was a child. Master Xibalbá, you have done something the celebrated Maya physicians admit they cannot. You have made me *see* again!"

"And all those sheaves of years . . . we thought these things useless . . ." he murmured, sounding rather awed himself. Then he spoke briskly. "So it requires the crystal of one plane surface and an inner curve. But you cannot go about forever holding the thing out in front of you like that. It would be like peering through a knothole. Try bringing it close against your eye."

I did, and cried out, and apologized: "It hurt as if my eye was being drawn from its socket."

"Still too powerful. And there are spots and ripples, you say. So I must seek a stone more perfect and unflawed than the finest quartz." He smiled and rubbed his hands together. "You have set me the first new task the Xibalbá have had in generations. Come back tomorrow."

I was full of excitement and expectation, but I said nothing to my companions, in case that hopeful experiment too should come to nothing. They and I again resided with the Macoboö, to our great comfort and the great gratification of the two female cousins, and we stayed for six or seven days. During that time, I visited the Xibalbá workshop several times daily, while the master labored over the most scrupulously exact crystal he had ever been asked to make. He had procured a wonderfully clear chunk of jewel-grade topaz, and had begun by shaping it into a flat disk of a circumference that covered my eye from brow to cheekbone. The crystal was to remain flat on its outer side, but the inner concavity's precise thickness and curvature could be determined only by the experiment of my looking through it every time the master ground it down a little more.

"I can keep thinning it and increasing the arc of curve little by little," he said, "until we reach the exact reducing power you require. But we must know when we reach it. If ever I grind away too much, the thing is ruined."

So I kept going back for trials, and when my one eye got bloodshot from the strain, we would change to my other, and then back again. But finally, to my inexpressible joy, there came the day, and the moment in that day, when I could hold the crystal against either eye, and see through it perfectly. Everything in the world was clear and crisply outlined, from a book held in reading position to the trees on the mountain horizon beyond the city. I was in ecstasy, and Master Xibalbá was nearly so, with pride in his unprecedented creation.

He gave the crystal one final gleaming polish, with a wet paste of some fine red clay. Then he smoothed the crystal's edge and mounted it in a sturdy circlet of copper hammered to hold it securely, and that circlet had a short handle with which I could hold the crystal to either eye, and the handle was tied to a leather thong so I could keep it always about my neck, ready for use and safe from loss. I took the finished instrument to the Macoboö house, but showed it to no one, and waited for an opportunity to surprise Blood Glutton and Cozcatl.

When the twilight was turning to night, we sat in the door-yard with our hostess, the late Ten's mother, and a few others of the family, all of us elder males having a smoke after our evening meal. The Chiapa do not smoke the poquíetl. Instead, they use a clay jar punctured with several holes; this they pack with picíetl and fragrant herbs and set to smoldering; then each participant inserts a long, hollow reed into one of the jar's holes and all enjoy a community smoke.

"Yonder approaches a handsome girl," murmured Blood Glutton, pointing his reed down the street.

I could barely make out a distant suggestion of something pale moving in the dusk, but I said, "Ask me to describe her."

"Eh?" grunted the old soldier, and he lifted his eyebrows at me, and he sarcastically used my former nickname. "Very well, Fogbound, describe her—as you see her."

I put my crystal to my left eye and the girl came sharply into view, even in that poor light. Enthusiastically, like a slave trader at the block, I enumerated all the visible details of her physique—skin complexion, length of her hair plaits, the shapeliness of her bare ankles and feet, the regular features of her face, which was handsome indeed. I added that the embroidery on her blouse was of the so-called pottery pattern. "She also wears," I concluded, "a thin veil over her hair, and under it she has trapped a number of live fireflies. A most fetching adornment." Then I burst out laughing at the expression on the faces of my two partners.

Since I could use only one eye at a time, there was a certain flatness, a lack of depth to everything I looked at. Nevertheless, I could again see *almost* as clearly as I had when I was a child, and that sufficed for me. I might mention that the topaz was of the pale-yellow color; when I looked through it I saw everything seemingly sunlighted even on gray days; so perhaps I saw the world as rather prettier than others did. But, as I discovered when I looked into a mirror, the use of the crystal did not make *me* any prettier, since the eye behind it appeared much smaller than the uncovered one. Also, because it was natural for me to hold the crystal in my left hand while my right was occupied, for some time I suffered from headache. I soon learned always to hold the topaz to alternate eyes, and the headache went away.

I know, reverend scribes, that you must be amused at my fulsome babbling about an instrument that is no novelty to you. But I never saw another such device until many years later, until my first encounter with the earliest arriving Spaniards. One of the chaplain friars who came with the Captain-General Cortés wore *two* such crystals, one for each eye, held in a leather strap which was tied around his head.

But to me and the crystalsmith, my device *was* an unheard-of invention. In fact, he refused all payment for his labor and even for the topaz, which must have been most costly. He insisted that he was well repaid by his own pride in his achievement. So, since he would take nothing from me, I left with the Macoboö family a quantity of quetzal tototl plumes to be delivered to him when I was long enough gone that he could not refuse them—and I left a sufficiency to make the Master Xibalbá perhaps the richest man in Chiapán, as I felt he deserved to be.

At night I looked at stars.

From having been for so long so deeply dejected, I was suddenly and understandably buoyant of spirit, and I announced to my partners, "Now that I can see, I should like to see the ocean!"

They were so pleased with the change in me that they did not demur when we left Chiapán going southward rather than westward, and had to make our way over and through yet another jumble of rugged mountains, and mountains that were slumbering volcanoes. But we came through them without untoward incident, and came down to the oceanside Hot Land inhabited by the Mame people. That flat region is called the Xoconóchco, and the Mame occupy themselves with the production of cotton and salt for trade with other nations. The cotton is grown on the wide, fertile stretch of loam between the rocky mountains and the sandy beaches. In what was then late winter, there was nothing distinctive about those fields, but I later visited the Xoconóchco in the hottest season, when the cotton bolls are so big and profuse that even the green plants bearing them are invisible, and the whole countryside seems to be heavily blanketed by snow, even while it swelters under the sun.

The salt is made year-round, by diking the shallow lagoons along the coast and letting their waters dry, then sifting the salt from the sand. The salt, being also as white as snow, is not hard to distinguish from the sand, for all the beaches of the Xoconóchco are a dull black; they consist of the grit and dust and ashes belched by those volcanoes inland. Even the foam of the surf of that southern sea is not white, but is colored a dirty gray by the endlessly roiled dark sand.

Since the harvesting of both cotton and salt is work of the dreariest drudgery, the Mame were pleased to pay a good price in gold dust for our last two slaves, and they also bought our few remaining trade goods. That left me, Cozcatl, and Blood Glutton with no burden but our own traveling packs, the small bundle of crystals, and the bulky but not heavy bale of feathers—no great load for us to carry unaided. And, all the way home, we were not once molested by bandits, perhaps because we looked so very unlike any typical pochtéca train, or perhaps because all the existing bandits had heard of our previous encounter and its outcome.

Our route northwestward was an easy one, along the coastal flat lands all the way, with either calm lagoons or the mumbling sea surf on our left and the high mountains on our right. The weather was so balmy that we availed ourselves of overnight shelter in just two villages—Pijijía among the Mame and Tonalá among the Mixe people—and then only for the luxuries of having a freshwater bath and of dining on the delicious local sea fare: raw turtle eggs and stewed turtle meat, boiled shrimps, raw or steamed shellfish of all sorts, even broiled fillets of something called the yeyemíchi, which I was told is the biggest fish in the world, and which I can attest is one of the tastiest to eat.

We eventually found ourselves trudging directly westward, and once again on the isthmus of Tecuantépec, but we did not again go through the city of that same name. Before we got there, we met another trader, who told us that if we struck slightly to the north of our westerly route we would find an easier way through the Tzempuülá mountains than we had taken on our outbound crossing of them. I would have liked to see again the lovely Gié Bele and, not incidentally, to make more inquiries about the mysterious keepers of that purple dye. But I think that, after all our wanderings, I was being strongly pulled by the homing urge. I know my companions were, and I let them persuade me to turn as the trader had suggested. That route also had the virtue of taking us for a long way through a part of Uaxyácac we had not before traversed. We did not find ourselves retracing our outward trail until we passed again through the capital city of Záachilà.

As in setting out upon a trading expedition, certain days of the month were considered propitious for returning from one. So, as we got nearer home, we placed ourselves and even idled for one extra day in that pleasant mountain town of Quaunáhuac. When at last we breasted the final rise, and the lakes and the island of Tenochtítlan came in sight, I kept stopping to admire the view through my crystal. My one-eyed vision somewhat diminished the city's bulk to a flatness, but still it was a heart-lifting thing to see: the white buildings and palaces gleaming in the springtime sunshine, the glimpses of their many-colored roof gardens, the blue wisps of smoke from altar and hearth fires, the feather banners floating almost motionless on the soft air, the massive and twin-templed Great Pyramid dominating the whole.

With pride and gladness we finally crossed the Coyohuácan causeway and entered the mighty city, in the evening of the well-omened day One House, in the month we called The Great Awakening, in the year Nine Knife. We had been away for one hundred forty and two days, more than seven of our months, and we had known many adventures, many wondrous places and peoples, but it was good to come back to the center of Mexíca majesty, The Heart of the One World.

✠

It was forbidden that any pochtécatl bring his returning train into the city in daylight, or that he make any boastful parade of his entrance, no matter how successful and profitable his expedition might have been. Even if there had existed no such sumptuary law, every pochtécatl realized the prudence of coming home unobtrusively. Not everybody in Tenochtítlan yet recognized the prosperity of all the Mexíca depended on their intrepid traveling merchants, hence many people resented the traders' legitimately profiting from the prosperity they brought. The ruling noble classes in particular, since they derived their wealth from the tribute paid by defeated nations, insisted that any peaceful commerce detracted from their due portion of war-won plunder, and so they inveighed against "mere trade."

So every homecoming pochtécatl made sure to enter the city dressed in his plainest clothes, and to come in the concealment of dusk, and to have his treasure-laden porters follow him by ones and twos. And the home the merchant came home to would be a comparatively modest house, though in its closets and trunks and under its floors there might gradually accumulate a fortune that *could* build for him a palace rivaling that of the Uey-Tlatoáni. Not that I and my partners had to sneak into Tenochtítlan; we led no train of tamémime, and our cargo was but two dusty bales; our clothes were stained and worn, and we went to no homes of our own, but to a travelers' hostel.

The next morning, after several consecutive baths and steamings, I dressed in my best and presented myself at the palace of the Revered Speaker Ahuítzotl. Since I was no stranger to the palace steward, I had not long to wait until I was granted an audience. I kissed the earth to Ahuítzotl, but forbore from raising my crystal to see him clearly; I was not sure but that a lord might object to being viewed so. Anyway, knowing that one, I could assume that he glowered as usual, as fiercely as the grizzled bear adorning his throne.

"We are pleasantly surprised to see that you have returned

intact, Pochtécatl Mixtli," he said gruffly. "Was your expedition a success, then?"

"I believe it was profitable, Revered Speaker," I replied. "When the pochtéca elders have evaluated my cargo, you can judge for yourself from your treasury's share. Meanwhile, my lord, I hope you may find this chronicle of interest."

At which I handed to one of his attendants the travel-battered books I had so faithfully compiled. They contained much the same account I have given you, reverend friars, except that they omitted such nonessentials as my encounters with women, but included considerably more description of terrain and communities and peoples, also many maps I had drawn.

Ahuítzotl thanked me and said, "We and our Speaking Council will examine them most attentively."

I said, "In the event that some of your advisers may be old and weak of eye, Lord Speaker, they would find this helpful," and I handed over one of the crystals. "Of these I brought a number to sell, but the biggest and most brilliant I bring as a gift to the Uey-Tlatoáni."

He did not seem much impressed until I asked his permission to approach and demonstrate to him how it could be employed for close scrutiny of word pictures or of anything else. Then I led him to an open window and, using a scrap of bark paper, showed him how it could also be used for starting fires. He was enthralled and he thanked me profusely.

Long afterward, I was told that Ahuítzotl carried his fire-making stone on every war campaign in which he took part, but that he delighted more in making a less practical peacetime use of it. That Revered Speaker is remembered to this day for his irascible temper and capricious cruelties; his name has become part of our language: any troublesome person is now called an ahuítzotl. But it seems the tyrant had a streak of childish prankishness as well. In conversation with any one of his most staid and dignified wise men, he would maneuver him toward a window. Then, unnoticed, Ahuítzotl would hold his burning crystal so that it aimed the sun's painfully hot dot onto some tender place like the back of the man's bare knee—and the Revered Speaker would bellow with laughter to see the old sage leap like a young rabbit.

* * *

From the palace, I went back to the hotel to collect Cozcatl and Blood Glutton, both also newly clean and well dressed, and our two bundles of goods. Those we took to The House of Pochtéca, and we were immediately shown into the presence of the three elders who had helped send us on our way. While cups of magnolia-scented chocolate were handed around, Cozcatl unfolded our bigger bale for the inspection of its contents.

"*Ayyo!*" said one of the old men. "You have brought a respectable fortune in plumes alone. What you must do is to get the richer nobles to bid for them in gold dust, until the price is as high as it will go, and only *then* let the Revered Speaker know of the existence of this trove. Simply to maintain his own supremacy of adornment, he will pay more than the highest price bid."

"As you advise, my lords," I concurred, and motioned for Cozcatl to open the smaller bundle.

"*Ayya!*" said another of the old men. "Now here, I fear, you have been overly impetuous." He dolefully fingered two or three of the crystals. "These are nicely shaped and polished but, I regret to tell you, jewels they are not. These are bits of mere quartz, a more common stone even than jadestone, and with no religious associations to give it the adventitious worth of jadestone."

Cozcatl could not suppress a giggle, nor Blood Glutton a knowing smirk. I myself smiled as I said, "But observe, my lords," and I showed them the two properties of the crystals, and instantly they were in a ferment of excitement.

"Unbelievable!" said one of the elders. "You have brought something absolutely new to Tenochtítlan!"

"Where did you find them?" said another. "No, do not even think of answering. Forgive me for asking. A treasure unique should be the discoverer's alone."

The third said, "We will offer the bigger ones to the higher nobles and—"

I interrupted to point out that all the crystals, big and small, performed equally well as object enlargers and fire starters, but he impatiently hushed me.

"That matters not. Each pili will want a crystal of a size befitting his rank and his sense of self-importance. I suggest that you sell each by its weight, and start the bidding at eight times their weight in gold. With the pípiltin topping each other's bids, you will get considerably more."

I gasped in astonishment. "But my lords, that could earn us more than *my* weight in gold! Even after the shares paid to the Snake Woman and to this honorable society . . . and even divided three ways . . . it would put all three of us among the wealthiest men in Tenochtítlan!"

"You object to that?"

I stuttered, "It—it scarcely seems right. To profit so richly from our very first venture . . . and from common quartz, as you remark . . . and from a product I can supply in quantity. Why, I can provide a burning crystal for every humblest household in all the domains of The Triple Alliance."

One of the elders said sharply, "Perhaps you can, but if you have good sense you will not. You have said that the Revered Speaker now possesses one of these magic stones. As of now, only one hundred twenty and six other nobles can own a similar crystal. My boy, they will bid outrageously, even if these things were made of compacted mud! Later, you can go and get more, for sale to still other nobles, but never more than these few at a time."

Cozcatl was beaming happily and Blood Glutton was near to drooling. I said, "I will certainly not persist in objecting to the prospect of substantial wealth."

"Oh, you three will be spending some of it without delay," said another of the elders. "You have mentioned the shares due to the Tenochtítlan treasury and to our god Yacatecútli. Perhaps you are unaware of our tradition that every homecoming pochtécatl—if he comes home with an estimable profit—lays a banquet for all the other pochtéca who are in the city at the time."

I looked to my partners and they nodded without hesitation, so I said, "With the greatest of pleasure, my lords. But we are new to this . . ."

"Happy to be of help," said the same man. "Let us set it for the night of the day after tomorrow. We will throw open the facilities of this building for the occasion. We will also arrange for the provision of food, drink, musicians, dancers, female company, and of course we will see to the invitation of all the qualified and accessible pochtéca, while you may invite any other guests you like. Now"—he roguishly tilted his head—"this banquet can be one of modesty or extravagance, according to your taste and generosity."

I again silently consulted my partners, then said expansively, "It is our first. It should betoken our success. If you will be so kind, I should like to ask that every dish, every drink, every appointment be of the finest available, and regardless of the cost. Let this banquet be one to be remembered."

I, at least, remember it vividly.

Hosts and guests, we all were dressed in our finest. Having become full-fledged and successful pochtéca, Cozcatl, Blood Glutton, and myself were entitled to wear certain gold and jeweled ornaments to mark our new station in life. But we confined ourselves to a modest few baubles. I wore only the bloodstone mantle clasp given me by the Lady of Tolan long ago, and a single small emerald in my right nostril. But my mantle was of the finest cotton, richly embroidered; my sandals were of alligator hide, laced to the knee; my hair, which I had let grow long during the journey, was caught up at the nape with a braided circlet of red leather.

In the building's courtyard, the carcasses of three deer sizzled and turned on spits over an immense bed of coals, and all the other foods provided were of comparable quality and quantity. Musicians played, but not too loudly to overwhelm the conversation. There was a bevy of beautiful women circulating among the crowd and, every so often, one of them would perform a graceful dance to the music. Three slaves of the establishment were appointed to do nothing but serve us three partners, and, when not occupied at that, they stood and waved vast feather fans over us. We were introduced to the other arriving pochtéca, and heard accounts of their own more notable excursions and acquisitions. Blood Glutton had invited four or five of his old-soldier comrades, and he and they were soon convivially drunk. Cozcatl and I knew no one in Tenochtítlan to invite, but one unexpected guest turned out to be an old acquaintance of mine.

A voice at my side said, "Mole, you never cease to amaze me." I turned to see the shriveled, cacao-skinned, gap-toothed man who had appeared at other signal moments in my life. On that occasion he was less grubby and better dressed, at least wearing a mantle over his loincloth.

I said with a smile, "Mole no longer," and raised my topaz and took a really clear look at him. Somehow, on doing that, I sensed that there was something about him more familiar than his merely being recognizable.

He grinned almost evilly, saying, "I find you variously a nonentity, a student, a scribe, a courtier, a pardoned villain, a warrior hero. And now a prosperous merchant—gloating with a golden eye."

I said, "It was your own suggestion, venerable one, that I go and travel abroad. Why should I not enjoy my own banquet celebrating my own successful enterprise?"

"Your own?" he asked mockingly. "As all your past achievements have been your own? Unaided? Single-handed?"

"Oh, no," I said, hoping with that disclaimer to parry the darker implications of his questions. "You will meet here my partners in this endeavor."

"This endeavor. Would it have been possible without that unexpected gift of goods and capital you invested in the journey?"

"No," I said again. "And I fully intend to thank the donor, with a share of—"

"Too late," he interrupted. "She is dead."

"She?" I echoed vacantly, for I had of course been thinking of my former patron, Nezahualpíli of Texcóco.

"Your late sister," he told me. "That mysterious gift was Tzitzitlíni's bequest to you."

I shook my head. "My sister is dead, old man, as you have just remarked. And she certainly never had any such fortune to leave to me."

He went on, unheeding, "The Lord Red Heron of Xaltócan also died during your travels in the south. He called to his deathbed a priest of the goddess Tlazoltéotl, and such a sensational confession as he made could hardly be kept secret. Doubtless several of your distinguished guests here know the story, though they would be too polite to speak of it to you."

"What story? What confession?"

"How Red Heron concealed his late son Pactli's atrocity in the matter of your sister."

"It was never adequately concealed from me," I said, with a snarl. "And you of all people know how I avenged his killing of her."

"Except that Pactli did not kill Tzitzitlíni."

That staggered me; I could only gape at the man.

"The Lord Joy tortured and mutilated her, with fire and knife and vicious ingenuity, but it was not her tonáli to die of that torment. So Pactli spirited her off the island, with his father's connivance and with at least the mute acquiescence of the girl's own parents. Those things Red Heron confessed to Filth Eater, and when the priest made them publicly known they caused an uproar on Xaltócan. It grieves me to tell you also that your father's body was found on a quarry floor, where evidently he jumped from the brink. Your mother has simply and cowardly fled. No one knows where, which is fortunate for her." He started to turn away, saying indifferently, "I think that is all the news of occurrences since you left. Now shall we enjoy—?"

"You wait!" I said fiercely, clutching the shoulder knot of his mantle. "You walking fragment of Míctlan's darkness! Tell me the rest! What became of Tzitzitlíni? What did you mean about that gift having come from her?"

"She bequeathed to you the entire sum she received—and Ahuítzotl paid a handsome price—when she sold herself to his menagerie here in Tenochtítlan. She would not or could not tell whence she came or who she was, so she was popularly known as the tapir woman."

Except that I still clutched his shoulder, I might have fallen. For a moment, everything and everybody about me disappeared, and I was looking down a long tunnel of memory. I saw again the Tzitzitlíni I had so adored: she of the lovely face and shapely form and willowy movement. Then I saw that revolting immobile object in the menagerie of monstrosities, and I saw myself vomiting at the horror of it, and I saw the single sorrowful tear trickling from its one eye.

My voice sounded hollow in my ears, as if I really did stand in a long tunnel, when I said accusingly, *"You knew.* Vile old man, you knew before Red Heron ever confessed. And you made me stand before her—and you mentioned the woman I

had just lain with—and you asked me how would I like to—"
I choked, nearly vomiting again at the recollection.

"It is good that you got to see her one last time," he said,
with a sigh. "She died not long after. Mercifully, in my opinion,
though Ahuítzotl was most annoyed, having paid so prodigally. . . ."

My vision returned to me, and I found that I was violently
shaking the man and saying rather insanely, "I could never
have eaten tapir meat in the jungle if I had known. But you
knew all the time. *How did you know?*"

He did not answer. He only said blandly, "It was believed
that the tapir woman could not move that mass of bloated flesh.
But somehow she toppled over, face forward, so that her tapir
snout could not breathe, and she suffocated to death."

"Well, it is now your turn to perish, you accursed foreseer
of evils!" I think I was out of my mind with grief and revulsion
and rage. "You will go back to the Míctlan you came from!"
And I shoved into the throng of banquet guests, only dimly
hearing him say:

"The menagerie keepers still insist that the tapir woman
could not have died without assistance. She was young enough
to have lived in that cage for many, many more years. . . ."

I found Blood Glutton and rudely interrupted his conversation with his soldier friends: "I have need of a weapon, and
no time to fetch one from our lodgings. Are you carrying your
dagger?"

He reached under his mantle to the back binding of his
loincloth, and said, with a hiccup, "Are you to do the carving
of the deer meat?"

"No," I said. "I want to kill somebody."

"So early in the party?" He brought out the short obsidian
blade and squinted to see me better. "Are you killing anyone
I know?"

I said no again. "Only a nasty little man. Brown and wrinkled as a cacao bean. Small loss to anybody." I reached out
my hand. "Please, the dagger."

"Small loss!" Blood Glutton exclaimed, and withheld the
knife. "You would assassinate the Uey-Tlatoáni of Texcóco?
Mixtli, you must be as drunk as the proverbial four hundred
rabbits!"

"Assuredly somebody is!" I snapped. "Cease your babbling and give me the blade!"

"Never. I saw the brown man when he arrived, and I recognize that particular disguise." Blood Glutton tucked the knife away again. "He honors us with his presence, even if he chooses to do it in mummery. Whatever your fancied grievance, boy, I will not let you—"

"Mummery?" I said. "Disguise?" Blood Glutton had spoken coolly enough to cool me somewhat.

One of the soldier guests said, "Perhaps only we who have often campaigned with him are aware of it. Nezahualpíli likes sometimes to go about thus, so he may observe his fellows at their own level, not from the dais of a throne. Those of us who have known him long enough to recognize him do not remark on it."

"You are all lamentably sodden," I said. "I know Nezahualpíli too, and I know, for one thing, that he has all his teeth."

"A dab of oxitl to blacken two or three of them," said Blood Glutton, with another hiccup. "Lines of oxitl to feign wrinkles on a face darkened by walnut oil. And he has a talent for making his body appear crabbed and wizened, his hands gnarled like those of a very old man. . . ."

"But really he needs no masks or contortions," said the other. "He can simply sprinkle himself with dust of the road and seem a total stranger." The soldier hiccuped in his turn and suggested, "If you must slay a Revered Speaker tonight, young lord host, go after Ahuítzotl, and oblige all the rest of the world as well."

I went away from them, feeling somewhat foolish and confused, on top of all my other feelings of anguish and anger and—well, they were many and tumultuous. . . .

I went looking again for the man who was Nezahualpíli— or a sorcerer, or an evil god—no longer intending to knife him but to wring from him the answers to a great many more questions. I could not find him. He was gone, and so was my appetite for the banquet and the company and the merriment. I slipped out of The House of Pochtéca and went back to the hostel and began packing into a small bag only the essentials

I would need for traveling. Tzitzi's little figurine of the love goddess Xochiquétzal came to my hand, but my hand flinched away as if it had been red hot. I did not put it into the bag.

"I saw you leave and I followed you," said young Cozcatl from the doorway of my room. "What has happened? What are you doing?"

I said, "I have no heart to tell of all that has happened, but it seems to be common gossip. You will hear it soon enough. And because of it I am going away for a time."

"May I come with you?"

"No."

His eager face fell, so I said, "I think it best that I be alone for some while, to plan what is to become of the rest of my life. And I am not now leaving you a defenseless and masterless slave, as you once feared. You are your own master, and a rich one. You will have your share of our fortune, as soon as the elders convey it. I charge you to keep safe my share, and these other belongings of mine, until I return."

"Of course, Mixtli."

"Blood Glutton will be moving from his former barracks quarters. Perhaps you and he can buy or build a house—or a house apiece. You can resume your studies or take up some craft or set up in some business. And I will be back again, sometime. If you and our old protector still have the spirit for traveling, we can make other journeys together."

"Sometime," he said sadly, then squared his shoulders. "Well, for this abrupt departure of yours, can I help you prepare?"

"Yes, you can. In my shoulder bag and in the purse sewn into my loincloth I will carry an amount of small currency for expenses. But I also want to carry gold, in case I should come upon some exceptional find—and I wish to carry that gold dust secreted where any bandits will not easily find it."

Cozcatl thought for a moment and said, "Some travelers melt their dust into nuggets, and hide those in their rectum."

"A trick every robber knows too well. No, my hair has grown long, and I think I can make use of it. See, I have emptied all my quills of gold dust onto this cloth. Make a tidy packet of it, Cozcatl, and let us devise some way to secure it on the back of my neck, like a poultice, hidden by my hair."

While I finished packing my bag, he folded the cloth meticulously over and over. It made a pliant wad no bigger than one of his own small hands, but it was so heavy that he needed both his hands to lift it. I sat and bowed my head and he laid it across my nape.

"Now, to make it stay . . ." he muttered. "Let me see. . . ."

He fixed it in place with a stout cord tied to each end of the packet, run behind my ears and across the top of my head. That was further secured and hidden by my putting a folded cloth across my forehead, like the band of a tumpline, and tying it at the back. Many travelers wore such things to keep their hair and sweat out of their eyes.

"It is quite invisible, Mixtli, unless the wind blows. But then you can always make a cowl of your mantle."

"Yes. Thank you, Cozcatl. And"—I said it quickly; I had no wish to linger—"good-bye for now."

I had no fear of the Weeping Woman or the many other malevolent presences haunting the darkness to waylay such incautious adventurers as myself. Indeed, I snorted wrathfully when I thought of Night Wind—and the dusty stranger I had met so frequently in other nighttimes. I stepped out of the city and onto the southbound Coyohuácan causeway again. Halfway along it, at the Acachinánco fort, the sentries were more than a little surprised to see someone out walking at that time of night. However, since I was still so festively dressed, they did not detain me on suspicion of my being a thief or fugitive. They merely asked a question or two to make sure I was not drunk, that I was well aware of what I was doing, then let me proceed.

Farther on, I turned left onto the Mexicaltzínco branching of the causeway, went through that sleeping town and continued eastward, walking all night long. When the dawn began to come, and other early travelers on the road began to give me cautious greetings while eyeing me oddly, I realized that I must present an unusual spectacle: a man dressed very like a noble, with knee-laced sandals and a jeweled mantle clasp and an emerald nose ornament, but with a trader's pack and shoulder bag and a sweatband across his forehead. I removed and stowed the jewelry in my bag, then turned my mantle inside out to conceal its embroidery. The packet on the nape of my neck was an annoying encumbrance for a time, but I eventually got used to it, and took it off only when I slept or bathed in privacy.

That morning I pressed on eastward into the rising and fast-warming sun, feeling no fatigue or need to sleep, my mind still a turmoil of thoughts and recollections. (That is the most hurtful thing about sorrow: the way it invites the crowding-in of memories of happier times, for poignant comparison with one's present misery.) During most of that day I was backtracking the trail I had once marched, along the southern shore of Lake Texcóco, with the victorious army returning from the war in Texcála. But after a while that track diverged from mine, and I left the lakeside, and I was in country I had not seen before.

✠

I wandered for more than a year and a half, and through many new lands, before I reached anything like a destination. During much of that time I remained so distraught that I could not now tell you, my lord scribes, all the things I saw and did. I think, if it were not that I still remember many of the words I learned of the languages of those far places, I should find it hard to retrace in memory even the general route I followed. But a few sights and events do still stand in my recollection, much as the few volcanoes of those eastward lands stand above the lower-lying ground around them.

I strode quite boldly into Cuautexcálan, The Land of the Eagle Crags, the nation I had once entered with an invading army. No doubt, if I had announced myself as a Mexícatl, I would never have left it again. And I am just as glad not to have died in Texcála, for the people there have one religious belief so simplistic that it is ridiculous. They believe that when any noble dies, he lives a joyous afterlife; when any lesser person dies, he lives a wretched one. Dead lords and ladies merely shed their human bodies and come back as buoyant clouds or birds of radiant plumage or jewels of fabulous worth.

Dead commoners come back as dung beetles or sneaking weasels or stinking skunks.

Anyway, I did not die in Texcála, or get recognized as one of the hated Mexíca. Although the Texcaltéca people have always been our enemies, they are physically no different from us, and they speak the same language, and I was easily able to imitate their accent, to pass as one of them. The only thing that did make me somewhat conspicuous in their land was my being a young and healthy man, alive and not maimed. That battle in which I was involved had decimated the population of males between the ages of puberty and senescence. Still, there was a new generation of boys growing up. They grew up learning bitter enmity to us Mexíca, and swearing vengeance against us, and they were full grown by the time you Spaniards came, and you know what form the vengeance took.

However, at the time of my idly tramping through Texcála, all that was far in the future. My being one of the few adult and adequate males caused me no trouble. To the contrary, I was welcomed by numerous alluring Texcaltéca widows whose beds had gone long unwarmed.

From there, I drifted south to the city of Cholólan, capital of the Tya Nuü and, in fact, the largest single remaining concentration of those Men of the Earth. It was evident that the Mixtéca, as they were called by everyone but themselves, had once created and maintained an enviably refined culture. For example, there in Cholólan I saw buildings of great antiquity, lavishly adorned with mosaics like petrified weaving, and the buildings could only have been the original models for the supposedly Tzapotéca-built temples at the Cloud People's Holy Home of Lyobáan.

There is also a mountain at Cholólan, which in those days bore on its top a magnificent temple to Quetzalcóatl, a temple most artfully embellished with colored carvings of the Feathered Serpent. You Spaniards have razed that temple, but apparently you hope to borrow some of the sanctity of the site, for I hear that you are building a Christian church in its place. Let me tell you: that mountain is no mountain. It is a manmade pyramid of sun-dried mud bricks, more bricks than there are hairs on a whole herd of deer, oversilted and overgrown since time before time. We believe it to be the oldest pyramid in all these lands; we know it to be the most gigantic ever built. It may look now like any other mountain bearing trees and shrubbery, and it may serve to elevate and exalt your own new church, but I should think your Lord God would feel uncomfortable on those heights so laboriously raised for the worship of Quetzalcóatl and no other.

The city of Cholólan was ruled by not one but two men, equal in power. They were called Tlaquíach, the Lord of What Is Above, and Tlalchíac, the Lord of What Is Below, meaning that they dealt separately with spiritual and material matters. I am told that the two were often at odds, even at blows, but at the time I arrived in Cholólan they were at least temporarily united in some minor grudge against Texcála, the nation from which I had just come. I forget what the quarrel was about, but there also shortly arrived a deputation of four Texcaltéca nobles, sent by their Revered Speaker Xicoténca to discuss and resolve the dispute.

The Lords of What Is Above and What Is Below refused' even to grant audience to the envoys. Instead, they ordered their palace guards to seize and mutilate them and send them home again at spear point. The four noblemen had the skin completely flayed from their faces before they went staggering and moaning back toward Texcála, their heads raw red meat with eyeballs, their faces mere flaps hanging down on their chests. I think all the flies of Cholólan followed them northward out of the city. Since I could foresee only war resulting from that outrage, and since I did not care to be conscripted to fight in it, I also departed hastily from Cholólan, only I went to the east.

When I crossed another invisible border and was in the Totonáca country, I stopped for a day and a night in a village where the window of my inn gave me a view of the mighty volcano called Citlaltépetl, Star Mountain. I was satisfied to regard it from that respectful distance, using my topaz crystal to look upward from the green and flowered warmth of the village at that frosted and cloud-swept pinnacle.

Citlaltépetl is the highest mountain in all The One World, so high that its snowcap covers the entire upper third of it—

except when its crater overflows a gout of molten lava or burning cinders and makes the mountain for a while red-topped instead of white-topped. I am told that it is the first landmark visible to your ships coming hither from the sea. By day, their lookouts see the snowy cone or, by night, the glow of its crater, long before anything else of New Spain is to be seen. Citlaltépetl is as old as the world, but to this day, no man, native or Spaniard, has yet climbed all the way to the top of it. If anyone ever did, the passing stars would probably scrape him off his perch.

I came to the other boundary of the Totonáca lands, the shore of the eastern ocean, at a pleasant bay called Chálchihuacuécan, which means The Place of Abundant Beautiful Things. I mention that only because it constituted a small coincidence, though I could not know it then. In another springtime, other men would set foot there, and claim the land for Spain, and plant in those sands a wooden cross and a flag the colors of blood and gold, and call that the place of the True Cross: Vera Cruz.

That ocean shore was a much prettier and more welcoming one than the coast along the Xoconóchco. The beaches were not of black volcanic grit, but of powdery sands that were white or yellow, sometimes even coral pink in color. The ocean was not a green-black heaving turbulence, by a crystalline turquoise blue, gentle and murmurous. It broke upon the sands with only a whispery froth of white foam, and in many places it shelved away from the beach so shallowly that I could wade almost out of sight of the land before the water reached as high as my waist. At first the shore led me nearly directly south, but, over innumerable one-long-runs, that coast curves in a great arc. Almost imperceptibly I found that I was walking southeast, then due east, and eventually northeast. Thus, as I have said before, what we of Tenochtítlan call the eastern ocean is more properly the northern ocean.

Of course, that shore is not *all* sand beaches fringed with palm trees; I should have found it monotonous if it had been. Along my long way, I several times encountered rivers debouching into the sea, and would have to camp and wait for some fisherman or ferryman to appear and carry me across in his dugout canoe. In other places, I found the dry sands getting damp under my sandals, then wet, and turning into marshy, insect-infested swamps, where the graceful palm trees gave place to gnarled mangroves with knobby raised roots like old men's legs. To get past those swamps, I sometimes camped and waited for a passing fisher boat to take me around them offshore. But at other times I detoured inland until the swamps shallowed and dwindled into dry land on which I could circle around them.

I remember getting a fright the first time I did that. The night caught me on the soggy fringe of one of those marshes and I had a hard time finding enough dry grass and sticks to make even a small campfire. In fact, it was so small and gave so little light that, when I lifted my eyes, I could see—among the moss-hung mangroves beyond—a fire rather brighter than mine, but burning with an unnatural blue flame.

"The Xtabai!" I thought immediately, having heard many stories of the ghost woman who walks those regions, wrapped in a garment that emits an eerie light. According to the stories, any man who approaches her finds that the garment is only a hood to hide her head, and that the rest of her body is bare—and seductively beautiful. He is ineluctably tempted to come closer, but she keeps backing coyly away from him, and suddenly he discovers to his dismay that he has walked into a quicksand from which he cannot extricate himself. As he is sucked down by the sand, just before his head goes under, the Xtabai at last drops the cowl and reveals her face to be that of a wickedly grinning skull.

Using my seeing crystal, I watched that distant, flickering blue flame for a while, the skin of my spine rippling, until at last I said to myself, "Well, I will not dare sleep while that thing lurks out there. But since I am forewarned, perhaps I can get a look at her and still be on my guard against stepping into the quicksand."

Carrying my obsidian knife, I moved in a crouching walk to the tangle of trees and vines, and then in among them. The blue light waited for me. I tested each patch of ground with my foremost foot before I put my weight on it, and, though

I got wet to the knees and my mantle got much torn by the surrounding brush, I never found myself sinking. The first unusual thing I noticed was a smell. Of course, the entire swamp was fetid enough—stagnant water and decaying weeds and musty toadstools—but that new smell was awful: like rotten eggs. I thought to myself, "Why would any man pursue even the most beautiful Xtabai, if she reeks like that?" But I pressed on, and finally stood before the light, and it was no ghost woman at all. It was a smokeless blue flame, waist high, sprouting directly from the ground. I do not know what had set it alight, but it obviously fed on that noxious air seeping from a fissure in the earth.

Perhaps others *have* been lured to their deaths by the light, but the Xtabai itself is innocuous enough. I never have discovered why a noisome air should burn when ordinary air does not. But on several later occasions I again encountered the blue fire, always with the same stench, and, the last time I took the trouble to investigate, I found another material as extraordinary as the burnable air. Near the Xtabai flame I stepped into some kind of sticky muck and instantly thought, "This time the quicksand *has* got me." But it had not; I easily stepped out of it and carried a palmful of the odd substance back to my campfire.

It was black, like the oxitl we extract from pine sap, only more slimy than gummy. When I held it to my fire to examine it, a gobbet of it fell into the flames, causing them to flare higher and hotter. Rather pleased at that accidental discovery, I fed my whole handful to the fire and, without my having to add another stick, it burned brightly all night. Thereafter, whenever I had to make camp anywhere near a swamp, I did not bother to look for dry wood; I looked for the black muck oozing up from the ground, and always it made a hotter fire and a brighter light than any of the oils we are accustomed to use in our lamps.

I was then in the lands of the people we Mexíca indiscriminately called the Olméca, simply because that was the country which supplied most of our óli. The people themselves, of course, recognize various nations among them—Coátzacoáli, Coatlícamac, Cupílco, and others—but the people are all very much alike: every grown man goes about stooped under the weight of his name, and every woman and child goes about constantly chewing. I had better explain.

Of the trees native to that country, there are two kinds which, when their bark is slashed, dribble a sap that solidifies to some degree. One tree produces the óli that we use in its more liquid form for a glue, and in its harder, elastic form for our tlachtli balls. The other kind of tree produces a softer, sweet-tasting gum called tzictli. It has absolutely no use except to be chewed. I do not mean eaten; it is never swallowed. When it loses its flavor or resiliency, it is spit out and another wad thrust in the mouth, to be chewed and chewed and chewed. Only women and children do that; for a man it would be considered an effeminacy. But I thank the gods that the habit has not been introduced elsewhere, for it makes the Olméca women, who are otherwise quite attractive, look as vapid and mindless as a lumpy-faced manatee everlastingly munching river weeds.

The men may not chew tzictli, but they have developed an impediment of their own which I think just as imbecilic. At some time in the past, they started wearing name badges. On his chest a man would display a pendant of whatever material he could afford, anything from sea shell to gold, bearing his name symbols for any passerby to read. Thus a stranger asking a question of another stranger could address him by name. Unnecessary perhaps, but in those days the name badge was no worse than an encouragement to politeness.

Over the years, however, that simple pendant has been ponderously elaborated. To it now is added a symbol of the wearer's occupation: a bunch of feathers, say, if he is in that trade; and an indication of his rank in the nobility or commonalty: additional badges with the name symbols of parents and grandparents and even more distant forebears; and baubles of gold, silver, or precious stones to boast his wealth; and a tangle of colored ribbons showing that he is unmarried, married, widowed, the father of how many progeny; plus a token of his military prowess: perhaps several other disks bearing the names of communities in whose defeat he has taken part. There may be much more of that frippery, hanging from his neck nearly to his knees. So nowadays every Olmécatl man is bowed down and almost hidden by his agglomeration of precious metals, jewels, feathers, ribbons, shells, coral. And no stranger ever *has* to ask a question of another; every man wears the answer to just about everything anyone might want to know from or about him.

Those eccentricities notwithstanding, the Olméca are not all fools who have dedicated their lives to tapping the sap of trees. They are also justly acclaimed for their arts, ancient and modern. Scattered here and there along the coastal lands are the deserted old cities of their forebears, and some of the relics remaining are astonishing. I was particularly impressed by the stupendous statues carved of lava rock, now buried to their necks or chins in the ground and much overgrown. All that is visible of them is their heads. They wear most lifelike expressions of alert truculence, and all wear helmets that resemble the leather head-protectors of our tlachtli ball players, so the carvings may represent the gods who invented that game. I say gods, not men, because any one of those *heads*, not to mention the unimaginable body underground, is far too immense to fit inside the typical house of a human being.

There are also many stone friezes and columns and such, incised with naked male figures—some *very* naked and *very* male—which appear to be dancing, or drunk, or convulsed, so I assume that the Olméca's ancestors were a merry people. And there are jadestone figurines of superb finish and precise detailing, though it would be difficult to separate the older of those from the newer, for there are still many artisans among the Olméca who do incredible work in gemstone carving.

In the land called Cupílco, in its capital city of Xicalánca—beautifully situated on a long, narrow spit of land with a pale blue ocean lapping on one side and a pale green lagoon lapping at the other—I found a smith named Tuxtem whose specialty was the making of tiny birds and fishes, no bigger than a finger joint, and every infinitesimal feather or scale on those creatures was alternately of gold and silver. I later brought some of his work to Tenochtítlan, and those Spaniards who have seen and admired them—a few pieces yet remain—say that no smith anywhere in what they call the Old World has ever done anything as masterful.

* * *

I continued following the coast, which led me completely around that Maya peninsula of Uluümil Kutz. I have already described that drear land to you in brief, my lords, and I will not waste words in describing it at any greater length, except to mention that on its western coast I remember only one town of a size big enough to be called a town: Kimpéch; and on its northern coast another: Tihó; and on its eastern coast another: Chaktemál.

I had by then been gone from Tenochtítlan for more than a year. So I began, in a general way, to head homeward again. From Chaktemál I struck inland, due west, across the width of the peninsula. I carried adequate atóli and chocolate and other traveling rations, plus a quantity of water. As I have said, that is an arid land of maliferous climate, and it has no definable rainy season. I made the crossing early in what would be your month of July, which was the eighteenth month of the Maya year, the one called Kumkú—Thunderclap—not because it brought storms or the least mizzle of rainfall, but because that month is *so* dry that the already sere lands make an artificial thunder of groaning and crunching as they shrink and shrivel.

Maybe that summer was even more severely hot and parched than usual, because it provided me with a strange and, as it proved, a valuable discovery. One day I came to a small lake of what looked like that black muck I had earlier found in the Olméca swamps and utilized to fuel my campfires. But when I picked up and threw a stone into the lake, it did not go in; it bounced on the surface as if the lake had been made of congealed óli. Hesitantly, I set foot on the black stuff and found it just slightly yielding to my weight. It was chapopótli, a material like hard resin, but black. Melted, it was used to make bright-burning torches, to fill cracks in buildings, as an ingredient of various medicines, as a paint that would keep out water. But I had never seen an entire *lake* of it before.

I sat down on the bank to have a bite to eat while I contemplated that find. And, even as I sat there, the Kumkú heat—which was still making the country all about me snap and rumble—also fractured the chapopótli lake. Its surface cracked in all directions as if overlaid with a spider web, then it broke up into jagged black chunks, and those were heaved about, and among them were thrown up some lengthy brown-black things which might have been the limbs and branches of a long-buried tree.

I congratulated myself that I had not ventured out upon the lake just in time to get tossed and probably injured in its convulsions. But, by the time I had finished eating, all was quiet again. The lake was no longer flat; it was a chopped-up jumble of shiny black fragments, but it looked unlikely to be further agitated, and I was curious about those objects it had cast up. So I cautiously stepped out on the lake again and, when it did not swallow me, picked my way among the black lumps and shards, and found that the thrown-up things were bones.

Having been discolored by their interment, they were no longer white, as old bones usually are, but they were of a size inconceivable, and I was reminded that our lands were once inhabited by giants. However, though I recognized here a rib, there a thighbone, I also recognized that they were from no human giant, but from some monster animal. I could only suppose that the chapopótli had long ago been liquid, and that some creature had unwarily stepped into it and been caught and sucked down, and that over the ages the liquid had solidified to its present consistency.

I found two bones even more gigantic than the others—or at first I thought they were bones. Each was as long as I was tall, and cylindrical, but as thick as my thigh at one end, tapering to a blunt point no bigger than my thumbtip at the other end. And each would have been even longer except that it had grown in a gradual curve and recurve, like a very hesitant spiral. They, like the bones, were stained brown-black from the chapopótli in which they had been entombed. I puzzled over them for some time before I knelt and, with my knife, scraped at the surface of one until I uncovered its natural color: a shining, mellow, pearly white. Those things were teeth— long teeth like a boar's tusks. But, I thought to myself, if that trapped animal had been a boar, it had indeed been a boar fit for the age of giants.

I stoop up and considered the things. I had seen labrets and nose plugs and similar bangles carved from the teeth of bears and sharks and the tusks of ordinary-sized boars, and they sold for as much as goldwork of the same weight. What, I wondered, could a master carver like the late Tlatli do with the material of teeth such as these?

The country there was sparsely inhabited—not surprisingly, in view of its bleakness. I had to wander into the greener, sweeter land of Cupílco before I came upon a village of some obscure Olméca tribe. The men were all óli tappers by occupation, but that was not the season for collecting sap, so they were sitting about idle. I did not have to offer much in payment for four of the burliest of them to work as porters for me. I almost lost them, though, when they realized where we were headed. The black lake, they said, was both a holy and a fearsome place, and a place to be avoided; so I had to increase the promised pay before they would go on. When we got there and I pointed out the tusks, they made haste to hoist them, two men to a tooth, and then we all got away from there as quickly as possible.

I led them back through Cupílco and to the ocean shore and along that spit of land to the capital city of Xicalánca and to the workshop of that master smith Tuxtem. He looked surprised, and not much pleased, when my porters tottered in with their queer loglike burdens. "I am not a woodcarver," he said at once. But I told him what I believed the things to be, and how fortuitously I had found them, and what rarities they must be. He touched the spot I had scraped on the one tusk, and his hand lingered there, and he caressed it, and a gleam came into his eyes.

I dismissed the weary porters, with thanks and a trifle of extra payment. Then I told the artist Tuxtem that I wanted to hire his services, but that I had only the most general idea of what I wanted him to do with my find:

"I want carvings I can sell in Tenochtítlan. You may cut up the teeth as you see fit. From the larger pieces, perhaps you can carve figurines of Mexíca gods and goddesses. From the smaller pieces, perhaps you can make poquíetl tubes, combs, ornamental dagger handles. Even the tiniest fragments can make labrets and the like. But I leave it to you, Master Tuxtem, and to your artistic judgment."

"Of all the materials in which I have worked in my life," he said solemnly, "this is unique. It affords an opportunity and a challenge which I shall surely never find again. I will think long and deeply before I even abstract a small sample on which to experiment, with tools and finishing substances...." He paused, then said almost defiantly, "I had better tell you this. Of myself and my work, what I demanded is simple: only the best. This will not be the work of a day, young Lord Yellow Eye, or a month."

"Of course not," I agreed. "If you had said it was, I would have taken the trophies and gone. In any case, I do not know when I will again pass through Xicalánca, so you may take all the time you require. Now, as to your fee..."

"I am doubtless foolish to say this, but I would deem it the highest price I have ever been paid if only you promise to make it known that the pieces were sculptured by me, and tell my name."

"Foolish of your head, Master Tuxtem, though I say it with admiration of your heart's integrity. Either you set a price, or I make this offer. You take a twentieth part, by weight, of the finished works you do for me, or of the raw material to finish as you please."

"A munificent share." He bowed his head in agreement. "Had I been the most grasping of men, I should not have dared to ask such extravagant payment."

"And do not fear," I added. "I shall choose the buyers of those works as carefully as you choose your tools. They will be only persons worthy to own such things. And every one of them will be told: this was made by the Master Tuxtem of Xicalánca."

Dry though the weather had been on the peninsula of Uluúmil Kutz, it was the rainy season in Cupílco, which is an uncomfortable time to walk through those Hot Lands of almost jungle growth. So I again kept to the open beaches as I made my way west, until I came to the town of Coátzacoálcos, what you now call Espíritu Santo, which was the terminus of the north-south trade route across the narrow isthmus of Tecuantépec. I thought to myself: that isthmus is almost all level land, not heavily forested, with a good road, so it would be an easy journey even if I got frequently rained upon. And at the other side of the isthmus was a hospitable inn, and my lovely Gié Bele of the Cloud People, and the prospect of a most refreshing rest before I continued on to Tenochtítlan.

So at Coátzacoálcos I turned south. Sometimes I walked in company with pochtéca trains or with individual traders, and we passed many others going in the opposite direction. But one day I was traveling alone, and the road was empty, when I topped a rise and saw four men seated under a tree on the other side. They were ragged, brutish-looking men, and they slowly, expectantly got to their feet as I approached. I remembered the bandits I had met once before, and I put my hand to the obsidian knife in my loincloth band. There was really nothing more I could do but walk on, and *hope* to walk past them with an exchange of greetings. But those four did not put up any pretense of inviting me to partake of a meal, or ask to share my own rations, or even speak. They simply closed in on me.

☩

I came awake. Or awake enough to know that I lay unclothed on a pallet, with one quilt under me and another covering my nakedness. I was in a hut apparently empty of any other furnishings, and dark except for glints of daylight leaking through the sapling walls and the straw thatch. A middle-aged man knelt at my bedside and, from his first words, I took him to be a physician.

"The patient wakes," he said to someone behind him. "I feared he might never recover from that long stupor."

"Then he will live?" asked a female voice.

"Well, at least I can begin to treat him, which would have been impossible if he had remained insensible. I would say that he came to you barely in time."

"We almost turned him away, he looked so frightful. But then, through the blood and the dirt, we recognized him as Záa Nayàzú."

That did not sound right. At that moment, I somehow could not quite remember my name, but I believed it was something less melodious than the lilting sound spoken by that female voice.

My head hurt atrociously, and felt as if its contents had been removed and a red-hot boulder substituted, and my body was sore all over. My memory was blank of many other things besides my real name, but I was sufficiently conscious to realize that I had not just fallen ill of something; I had in some way been injured. I wanted to ask how, and where I was, and how I had come there, but I could not make my voice work.

The doctor said to the woman I could not see, "Whoever the robbers were, they intended to give him a killing blow. Had it not been for that thick bandage he already wore, his neck would have snapped or his skull shattered like a gourd. But the blow did give his brain a cruel shaking. That accounted for the copious bleeding from the nose. And now that his eyes are open—observe—the pupil of one is larger than the other."

A girl leaned over the physician's shoulder and stared down at my face. Even in my dazed condition, I took note that her own face was lovely to behold, and that the black hair framing it had one pale lock streaking back from her forehead. I had a vague remembrance of having seen her before, and, to my puzzlement, I also seemed to find something familiar even in looking up at the underside of the thatched roof.

"The unequal pupils," said the girl. "That is a bad sign?"

"Extremely so," said the doctor. "An indication that something is wrong inside the head. So, besides trying to strengthen his body and heal the cuts and bruises, we must take care that his brain rests free of exertion or excitement. Keep him warm and keep the hut dim. Give him the broth and the medicine whenever he is awake, but on no account let him sit up, and try to prevent him even from talking."

Foolishly, I attempted to tell the physician that I was quite incapable of talking. But then the hut suddenly darkened even more, and I had the sickening sensation of falling swiftly down into a deep blackness.

They told me later that I lay there for many days and nights, and that my periods of consciousness were only sporadic and brief, and that in between them I would lie in a stupor so profound that it caused the doctor much worry. Of my waking moments, I remember that sometimes the physician was at my side, but always the girl was. She would be gently spooning between my lips a warm, rich-tasting broth or a bittertasting medicine, or she would be washing with a sponge what parts of me she could reach without moving my supine body, or she would be smoothing a flower-smelling salve over it. Her face was always the same—beautiful, concerned, smiling encouragement at me—but strangely, or so it seemed to me in my daze, sometimes her black hair bore the stark white streak and sometimes it did not.

I must have wavered between life and death, and I must have chosen or been granted by the gods or been destined by my tonáli to have the former. For the day came when I awoke with my mind somewhat cleared, and I looked up at the queerly familiar roof, and I looked at the girl's face close to mine, and I looked at her hair with the white lock running through it, and I managed to croak, "Tecuantépec."

"Yáa," she said, and then said yes again, but in Náhuatl, "Quema," and she smiled. It was a weary smile, after her long vigil of night and day attendance on me. I started to ask—but she laid a cool finger across my lips.

"Do not talk. The doctor said you must not for a while." She spoke Náhuatl haltingly, but better than I remembered having heard it spoken in that hut before. "When you are well, you can tell us what you remember of what happened. For now, I will tell you what little we know."

She had, one afternoon, been feeding the fowl in the dooryard of the inn, when an apparition came staggering toward her, not along the trade road but from the north, across the empty fields bordering the river. She would have fled inside the hostel and barricaded the door, but her shocked surprise held her motionless long enough for her to see something familiar in the naked man encrusted with dirt and dried gore. Nearly dead though I had been, I must have been making deliberately for the remembered inn. My lower face was masked and my chest was coated with the blood that still trickled from my nostrils. The rest of my body was scored with red scratches from thorns, mottled with bruises from blows or falls. The soles of my bare feet were raw meat, embedded with dirt and small sharp stones. But she had recognized me as her family's benefactor, and I had been taken in. Not into the hostel, for I could not have rested quietly there. It had become a busy and thriving place, much favored by Mexíca pochtéca like myself—which, she said, accounted for her improved command of Náhuatl.

"So we brought you to our old house here, where you could be tended undisturbed by the comings and goings of guests. And, after all, the hut is *yours* now, if you remember buying it." She motioned for me not to comment, and continued, "We assume you were set upon by bandits. You arrived here wearing nothing and carrying nothing."

I was alarmed by a sudden recollection. With anxious effort, I raised an aching arm and felt about my chest until my fingers found the topaz crystal still hanging there on its thong—and I breathed a long sigh of relief. Even the most rapacious of robbers would probably have supposed that to be a god-token of some kind, and superstitiously would have refrained from seizing it.

"Yes, that much you *were* wearing," said the girl, watching my movement. "And this heavy thing, whatever it is." She slid from under my pallet the cloth wad with its strings and sweatband dangling.

"Open it," I said, my voice hoarse from having been so long unused.

"Do not talk," she repeated, but she obeyed me, carefully unfolding layer after layer of the cloth. The revealed gold dust, somewhat caked by perspiration, was so bright that it nearly lit up the hut's dark interior—and did spark golden lights in her dark eyes.

"We always supposed you were a very rich young man," she murmured. She thought for a moment and then said, "But you reached to make sure of that pendant first. Before the gold."

I did not know if I could make her comprehend my wordless explanation, but with another effort I brought the crystal up to my eye and looked at her through it for as long as I could hold it there. And then I could not have spoken, if I would. She was beautiful; more beautiful than I had once thought her, or since remembered her. Among the things I could not remember was her name.

That lightning-streak through her hair caught one's eye, but it was unnecessary to a loveliness that caught at one's heart. Her long eyelashes were like the wings of the tiniest black hummingbird. Her brows had the curve of a soaring sea gull's outflung wings. Even her lips had a winglike lift to each corner: a sort of tiny tuck, which made her appear always to be treasuring a secret smile. When she did smile, though, there was no mistaking it, for she did so then, perhaps at the wondering expression on my own face. The tucks deepened into winning dimples, and the radiance of her face was far more bright than my gold. If the hut had been full of the unhappiest of people— grieving mourners or somber-souled priests—they would have been compelled by her smile to smile in spite of themselves.

The topaz dropped from my feeble hand, and my hand dropped to my side, and I dropped not into another stupor but a healing sleep, and she told me later that I slept with a smile on my face.

I was eminently glad I had come back to Tecuantépec, and had made the acquaintance of that girl—or had made her acquaintance again—but I wished that I could have come in health and strength and in the full panoply of a successful young merchant. Instead, I was bedridden and sapless and flaccid, not very appealing to look at, covered as I was with the scabs of my numerous cuts and scratches. I was still too weak to feed myself or take my own medicines, except from her hand. And, if I was not to smell bad besides, I had to submit even to her washing me all over.

"This is not fitting," I protested. "A maiden should not be washing the naked body of a grown man."

She said calmly, "We have seen you naked before. And you must have come naked across half the extent of the isthmus. Anyway"—her smile became teasing—"even a maiden can admire the long body of a handsome young man."

I think I must have blushed the entire length of my long body, but at least my weakness spared me the mortification of having one part of that body obtrusively respond to her touch, and perhaps send her fleeing from me.

Not since the impractical dreams Tzitzitlíni and I had shared, when we were very young, had I contemplated the advantages of marriage. But it did not require much contemplation for me to decide that I would probably nowhere or never again find such a desirable bride as that girl of Tecuantépec. My head injury was still some way from full recovery; both my thinking and my memory were erratic; but I retained one recollection of the Tzapotéca traditions—that the Cloud People had little reason and less desire to marry outside the Cloud People, and that any of them who did was forever an outcast.

Nevertheless, when the doctor finally gave me leave to talk as much as I liked, I tried to speak words that would make myself attractive to the girl. Though I was only a despised Mexícatl, and at the moment a laughably poor specimen even of that breed, I exerted all the charm of which I was capable. I thanked her for her goodness to me, and complimented her on having a kindliness that equaled her loveliness, and spoke many other cajoling and persuasive words. But among my more flowery speeches, I managed to mention the considerable estate I had already amassed at a yet young age, and dwelt on my plans for enlarging it further, and made it clear that any girl who did wed me would never be in want. Though I refrained from ever blurting out a direct proposal, I did make allusive remarks like:

"I am surprised that such a beautiful girl as yourself is not married."

She would smile and say something like: "No man yet has captivated me enough to make me surrender my independence."

Another time I would say, "But certainly you are courted by many suitors."

"Oh, yes. Unfortunately, the young men of Uaxyácac have few prospects to offer. I think they yearn more to own a share of the inn than to own all of me."

On another occasion I would say, "You must meet many eligible men among the constant traffic of guests at your hostel."

"Well, they tell me they are eligible. But you know that most pochtéca are older men, too old for me, and outlanders besides. Anyway, however ardently they may pay court, I always suspect that they already have a wife at home, probably other wives at the end of every trade route they travel."

I was emboldened to say, "I am not old. I have no wife anywhere. If ever I take one, she will be the only one, and for all my life long."

She gave me a long look, and after some silence said, "Perhaps you should have married Gié Bele. My mother."

I repeat: my mind was not yet what it should have been. Until that moment, I had either somehow confused the girl with her mother, or had totally forgotten the mother. I had certainly forgotten having coupled with her mother, and—*ayya*, the shame!—in the girl's own presence. Given the circumstances, she must have thought me the most salacious of lechers, to be suddenly courting her, the daughter of that woman.

I could only mumble, in horrendous embarrassment, "Gié Bele...but I remember...old enough to be my own mother...."

At which the girl gave me another long look, and I said no more, and I pretended to fall asleep.

I reiterate, my lord scribes, that my mind had been woefully affected by my injury, and that it was excruciatingly slow to regather its wits. That is the only possible excuse for the blundering remarks I uttered. The worst blunder, the one with the saddest and longest-lasting consequences, I made when one morning I said to the girl:

"I have been wondering how you do it, and why."

"How I do what?" she asked, smiling that blithe smile.

"On some days your hair has a remarkable white streak through its whole length. On others—like today—it has not."

Involuntarily, in the feminine gesture of surprise, she passed a hand across her face, where for the first time I saw dismay. For the first time those uptilted winglike corners of her mouth drooped downward. She stood still, looking down at me. I am sure my face showed only bewilderment. What emotion she was feeling, I could not tell, but when she finally did speak there was a slight tremor in her voice.

"I am Béu Ribé," she said, and paused as if waiting for me to make some comment. "In your language, that is Waiting Moon." She paused again, and I said truthfully:

"It is a lovely name. It suits you to perfection."

Evidently she had hoped to hear something else. She said, "Thank you," but she sounded half angry, half hurt. "It is my younger sister, Zyanya, who bears the white strand in her hair."

I was struck speechless. Again, it was not until that moment that another memory came back to me: there had been not one but two daughters. During my time away, the younger and smaller had grown to be almost the identical twin of the elder. Or they *would* have been nearly identical but for the younger girl's distinctive lock of hair, the mark—I remembered that, too—of her having been stung by a scorpion when she was an infant.

I had stupidly not realized that there were two equally beautiful girls attending me alternately. I had fallen passionately in love with what, in my mind's confusion, I took to be one irresistible maiden. And I had been able to do that only because I had boorishly forgotten that I was once at least a little in love with her mother—their mother. Had I stayed longer in Tecuantépec on my first visit, that intimacy could well have culminated in my becoming the girls' stepfather. Most appalling of all, during the days of my slow convalescence, I had indiscriminately, simultaneously, with impartial ardor, been yearning for and paying court to *both* of what might have been my stepdaughters.

I wished I were dead. I wished I had died in the barrens of the isthmus. I wished I had never awakened from the stupor in which I had lain for so long. But I could only avoid the girl's eyes and say nothing more. Béu Ribé did the same. She tended my needs as deftly and tenderly as always, but with her face averted from mine, and when there was nothing further to do for me, she departed without ceremony. On her subsequent visits that day, bringing food or medicine, she remained silent and aloof.

The next day was the streak-haired younger sister's turn, and I greeted her with "Good morning, Zyanya," and I made no reference to my indiscretion of the day before, for I wistfully hoped to give the impression that I had only been playing a game, that I had all along known the difference between the two girls. But of course she and Béu Ribé must have thoroughly discussed the situation and, for all my hopefully bright banter, I fooled her no more than you would expect. She threw me sidelong glances while I babbled, though her expression seemed more amused than angry or hurt. Maybe it was only the look which both the girls ordinarily wore: that of treasuring a secret smile.

But I regret to report that I was not yet done with making blunders, or of being desolated by new revelations. At one point I asked, "Does your mother tend the inn all the time you girls are taking care of me? I should have thought Gié Bele could spare a moment to look in on—"

"Our mother is dead," she interrupted, her face going momentarily bleak.

"What?" I exclaimed. "When? How?"

"More than a year ago. In this very hut, for she could not well pass her confinement at the hostel among the guests."

"Confinement?"

"While she waited for the baby's arrival."

I said weakly, "She had a baby?"

Zyanya regarded me with some concern. "The physician said you are not to trouble your mind. I will tell you everything when you are stronger."

"May the gods damn me to Míctlan!" I erupted, with more vigor than I would have thought I could summon. "It must be *my* baby, must it not?"

"Well . . ." she said, and drew a deep breath. "You were the only man with whom she had lain since our father died. I am sure she knew how to take the proper precautions. Because, when *I* was born, she suffered extremely, and the doctor warned her that I must be the last child. Hence my name. But so many years had passed . . . she must have believed she was past the age of conceiving. Anyway"—Zyanya twisted her fingers together—"yes, she was pregnant by a Mexícatl outlander, and you know the Cloud People's feeling about such relations. She would not ask to be attended by a physician or midwife of the Ben Záa."

"She died of neglect?" I demanded. "Because your stiff-necked people refused to assist—?"

"They might have refused, I do not know, but she did not ask. A young Mexícatl traveler had been staying at the inn for a month or more. He was solicitous of her condition, and he won her confidence, and finally she told him all the circumstances, and he sympathized as wholeheartedly as any woman could have done. He said he had studied at a calmécac school, and that there had been a class in the rudimentary arts of doctoring. So when her time came, he was here to help."

"What help, if she died?" I said, silently cursing the meddler.

Zyanya shrugged in resignation. "She had been warned of the danger. It was a long labor and a difficult birth. There was a great deal of blood and, while the man tried to stanch the bleeding, the baby strangled in its navel string."

"*Both* dead?" I cried.

"I am sorry. You insisted on knowing. I hope I have not given you cause for a relapse."

I swore again, "To Míctlan with me! The child . . . what was it?"

"A boy. She planned—if they had lived—she said she would name him Záa Nayàzú, after you. But of course there was no naming ceremony."

"A boy. My son," I said, gritting my teeth.

"Please try to be calm, Záa," she said, addressing me for the first time with warm familiarity. She added, compassionately, "There is no one to blame. I doubt that any of our doctors could have done better than the kindly stranger. As I say, there was much blood. We cleaned the hut, but some traces were indelible. See?"

She swung aside the doorway's cloth curtain to admit a shaft of light. It showed, on the wooden doorpost, the ingrained stain where a man had slapped it to leave his signature of a bloody hand.

I did not suffer a relapse. I continued to mend, my brain gradually clearing of its cobwebs and my body regaining its weight and strength. Béu Ribé and Zyanya continued to wait upon me alternately, and of course I was careful nevermore to say anything to either of them that could be construed as paying court. Indeed, I marveled at their tolerance in having taken me in at all, and in lavishing so much care upon me, considering that I had been the primary cause of their mother's untimely death. As for my entertaining any hope of winning and wedding either girl—although I sincerely and perversely still loved them equally—that had become unthinkable. The possibility of their ever having been my stepdaughters was a matter of mere speculation. But that I had sired their short-lived half brother was an unalterable fact.

The day came when I felt well enough to be on my way. The physician examined me and pronounced my pupils again normal in size. But he insisted that I give my eyes some time to get used to full daylight again, and that I do so by going outdoors only a little longer each day. Béu Ribé suggested that I would be more comfortable if I passed that time of adjustment at the inn, since there happened to be a room empty there right then. So I acceded, and Zyanya brought me some of her late father's clothes. For the first time in I do not know how many days, I again donned a loincloth and mantle. The sandals provided were far too small for me, so I gave Zyanya a tiny pinch of my gold dust and she ran to the market to procure a pair of my size. And then, with faltering steps—I was really not so strong as I had thought—I left that haunted hut for the last time.

It was not hard to see why the inn had become a favored stopping place for pochtéca and other travelers. Any man with good sense and good eyesight would have pleasured in putting up there, simply for the privilege of being near the beautiful, almost twin hostesses. But the hostel also provided clean and comfortable accommodations, and meals of good quality, and a staff of attentive and courteous servants. Those improvements the girls had made deliberately; but they had also, without conscious calculation, permeated the air of the whole establishment with their own smiling good spirits. With servants enough to do the scullery and drudgery work, the girls had only supervisory duties, so they dressed always in their best and, to enhance their twin-beauty impact on the eye, always in matching colors. Though at first I resented the way the inn's guests leered at and jested with the innkeepers, I later was grateful that they were so occupied with flirtation that they did not—as I did—one day notice something even more striking about the girl's garb.

"Where did you get those blouses?" I asked the sisters, out of the hearing of the other tradesmen and travelers.

"In the market," said Béu Ribé. "But they were plain white when we bought them. We did the decoration ourselves."

The decoration consisted of a pattern bordering the blouses' bottom hems and square-cut necklines. It was what we called the pottery pattern—what I have heard some of your Spanish architects, with a seeming amazement of recognition, call the Greek fret pattern, though I do not know what a Greek fret is. And that decoration was done not in embroidery thread, but in painted-on color, and the color was a rich, deep, vibrant purple.

I asked, "Where did you get the color to do it with?"

"Ah, that," said Zyanya. "It is nice, is it not? Among our mother's effects we found a small leather flask of a dye of this color. It was given to her by our father, shortly before he disappeared. There was only enough of the dye to do these two blouses, and we could think of no other use for it." She hesitated, looked slightly chagrined, and said, "Do you think we did wrong, Záa, in appropriating it for a frivolity?"

I said, "By no means. All things beautiful should be reserved only to persons of beauty. But tell me, have you yet washed those blouses?"

The girls looked puzzled. "Why, yes, several times."

"The color does not run, then. And it does not fade."

"No, it is a very good dye," said Béu Ribé, and then she told me what I had been delicately prying to find out. "It is why we lost our father. He went to the place which is the source of this color, to buy a great quantity of it, and make a fortune from it, and he never came back."

I said, "That was some years ago. Would you have been too young to remember? Did your father mention *where* he was going?"

"To the southwest, along the coast," she said, frowning in concentration. "He spoke of the wilderness of great rocks, where the ocean crashes and thunders."

"Where there lives a hermit tribe called The Strangers," added Zyanya. "Oh, he also said—do you remember, Béu?— he promised to bring us polished snail shells and to make necklaces for us."

I asked, "Could you lead me near to where you think he went?"

"Anyone could," said the older sister, gesturing vaguely westward. "The only rocky coastline in these parts is yonder."

"But the exact place of the purple must be a well-kept secret.

No one else has found it since your father went looking. You might remember, as we went along, other hints he let drop."

"That is possible," said the younger sister. "But Záa, we have the hostel to manage."

"For a long time, while you were tending me, you alternated as innkeepers. Surely one of you can take a holiday." They exchanged a glance of uncertainty, and I persisted, "You will be following your father's dream. And he was no fool. There *is* a fortune to be made from the purple dye." I reached out to a potted plant nearby and plucked two twigs, one short, one long, and held them in my fist so that equal lengths protruded. "Here, choose. The one who picks the short twig earns herself a holiday, and earns a fortune we will all three share."

The girls hesitated only briefly, then raised their hands and picked. That was some forty years ago, my lords, and to this day I could not tell you which of the three of us won or lost in the choosing. I can only tell you that Zyanya got the shorter twig. Such a trivially tiny pivot is was, but all our lives turned on it in that instant.

✠

While the girls cooked and dried pinóli meal, and ground the mixed chocolate powder for our provisions, I went to Tecuantépec's marketplace to buy other traveling necessities. At an armorer's workshop, I hefted and swung various weapons, finally selecting a maquáhuitl and a short spear that felt best to my arm.

The smith said, "The young lord prepares to meet some hazard?"

I said, "I am going to the land of the Chóntaltin. Have you heard of them?"

"Ayya, yes. That ugly people who live up the coast. Chóntaltin is of course a Náhuatl word. We call them the Zyú, but it means the same: The Strangers. Actually, they are only Huave, one of the more squalid and bestial Huave tribes. The Huave have no real land of their own, which is why everywhere they are called The Strangers. We tolerate their living in small groups here and there, on lands fit for no other use."

I said, "Up in the mountains, I once stayed overnight in one of their villages. Not a very sociable people."

"Well, if you slept among them and woke alive, you met one of the more gracious tribes. You will not find the Zyú of the coast so hospitable. Oh, they may welcome you warmly—rather too warmly. They like to roast and eat passersby, as a change from their monotonous diet of fish."

I agreed that they sounded delightful, but asked what was the easiest and most expeditious way to reach them.

"You could go directly southwest from here, but there are mountains in the way. I suggest that you follow the river south to the ocean, then go west along the beaches. Or at our fishing port of Nozibe, you might find a boatman who will take you even more quickly by sea."

So that is what Zyanya and I did. Had I been traveling alone, I would not have been so particular about choosing an easy route. However, I was to discover that the girl was a hardy traveling companion. She never spoke a word of complaint about bad weather, about camping in the open, about eating cold food or none, about being surrounded by wilderness or wild beasts. But that first trip outbound was an agreeable and leisurely one. It was a single day's journey, a pleasant stroll, down the flat riverside plains to the port of Nozibe. That name means only Salty, and the "port" was only a scattering of palm-leaf roofs on poles, where the fishermen could sit in shade. The beach was littered with swathes of netting spread for drying or mending; there were dugout canoes coming or going through the breakers, or drawn up on the sand.

I found a fisherman who, rather reluctantly, admitted that he had occasionally visited the Zyú stretch of the coast, and had sometimes supplemented his own catch by purchasing some of theirs, and spoke a smattering of their language. "But they only grudgingly allow me to call," he warned. "A totally unknown foreigner would approach at his own peril." I had to offer an extravagant price before he would agree to paddle us along the shore to that country and back, and to interpret for me there—if I was given any chance to say anything. Meanwhile, Zyanya had found an unoccupied palm shelter and spread on the soft sand the blankets we had brought from the inn, and we slept that night chastely far apart.

We pushed off at dawn. The boat stayed close inshore, just clear of the line of breaking water, and the boatman paddled in morose silence while Zyanya and I chatted gaily, pointing out to each other the jeweled sights of the landward scenery. The stretches of beach were like powdered silver prodigally spilled between the turquoise sea and the emerald coconut palms, from which frequently burst flocks of ruby and gold birds. As we progressed westward, however, the bright sand gradually darkened through gray to black, and beyond the green palms reared a range of volcanoes. Some of them smoked sullenly. Violent eruptions and earthquakes, Zyanya said, were frequent occurrences along that coast.

In midafternoon our boatman broke his silence. "There is the Zyú village at which I call," and he waved with his oar, as our canoe turned toward a huddle of huts on the black beach.

"No!" Zyanya exclaimed, suddenly and excitedly. "You told me, Záa, that I might remember other things my father said. And I do! He mentioned the mountain that walks in the water!"

"What?"

She pointed ahead of the boat's prow. About one-long-run beyond the Zyú village, the black sands ended abruptly at a formidable crag of mountain, an outcrop of the range inland. It stood like a wall across the beach and extended far into the ocean. Even from our distance I could see, through my crystal, plumes and spouts of seawater dashing high and white against the mountain's skirts of giant boulders.

"See the great rocks the mountain has shed!" said Zyanya. "That is the place of the purple! That is where we must go!"

I corrected her, "That is where I must go, my girl."

"No," said the boatman, shaking his head. "The village is dangerous enough."

I took up my maquáhuitl and held it where he could see it, and I thumbed its edge of obsidian, and I said, "You will put the girl ashore here. Tell the villagers that she is not to be molested, that we will return for her before dark. Then you and I will make for the mountain that walks in the water."

He grumbled and predicted dire things, but he turned through the surf to the shore. I assumed that the Zyú men were out fishing, for only a few women emerged from the huts as we grounded. They were filthy creatures, bare-breasted and barefooted, wearing only ragged skirts, and they listened to what the boatman told them, and they gave ugly looks to the pretty girl being stranded among them, but they made no untoward movement as long as I had them in sight. I was not happy about leaving Zyanya there, but it was preferable to taking her farther into peril.

When the boatman and I were out from the shore again, even a landsman like myself could see that any landing on the seaward slope of the mountain was impossible. Its rubble of boulders, many of them as big as the smaller palaces of Tenochtítlan, extended forbiddingly far about it. The ocean broke among those rocks into vertical cliffs and towers and columns of white water. Those lifted incredibly high, and hung there poised, and then tumbled down with a roar like all the thunders of Tlaloc booming at once, and then slithered to sea again, making whirlpools that gulped and sucked so powerfully that even a few of the house-sized boulders could be seen to shake.

The ocean's turmoil extended so far that it took all the boatman's skill to bring us safely to the beach just east of the mountain. But he did it, and, when we had dragged the dugout up the sand out of reach of the tumultuous surf, when we had finished coughing and spitting out the salt water we had swallowed, I sincerely congratulated him:

"If you can so bravely best that vicious sea, you have little to fear from any of these contemptible Zyú."

That seemed to embolden him to some degree, so I gave him my spear to carry and motioned for him to follow me. We strode along the beach to the mountain wall and found a slope we could climb. That brought us to the ridge of the mountain about halfway between sea level and its summit, and from the ridge we could see the interrupted beach continue on the westward side. But we turned left along the ridge until we stood on the promontory above that spreading fringe of great rocks and the fury of great waters. I was at the place of which Zyanya's father had spoken, but it seemed an unlikely place to find a precious purple dye—or fragile snails, for that matter.

What I did find was a group of five men climbing the ridge toward us from the direction of the ocean. They were obviously Zyú priests, for they were as unwashed, tangle-haired, and slovenly as any Mexíca priests, with the added inelegance that they wore not ragged robes but ragged animal skins, whose rancid smell reached us before the men did. They all five looked unfriendly, and when the foremost barked something in his native language, it sounded unfriendly.

"Tell them and tell them quickly," I said to my boatman, "that I come offering gold to buy some of their purple dye."

Before he could speak, one of the men grunted, "No need him. I talk enough Lóochi. I priest of Tiat Ndik, Sea God, and this his place. You die for put foot here."

I tried to convey, in the simplest Lóochi words, that I would not have intruded on holy terrain if I could have made my proposal in any other place or manner. I begged his indulgence of my presence and his consideration of my offer. Though his four subordinates continued to glare at me murderously, the chief priest seemed slightly mollified by my obsequious approach. At any rate, his next threat on my life was not quite so blunt:

"You go away now, Yellow Eye, maybe you go alive."

I tried to suggest that, since I had already profaned those holy precincts, it would take only a little longer for us to exchange my gold for his purple.

He said, "Purple holy for Sea God. No price can buy." And he repeated, "You go away now, maybe you go alive."

"Very well. But before I go, would you at least satisfy my curiosity? What do snails have to do with the purple dye?"

"Chachi?" He echoed the Lóochi word for snails, uncomprehending, and turned for interpretation to my boatman, who was perceptibly quaking with fright.

"Ah, the ndik diok," said the priest, enlightened. He hesitated, then turned and beckoned for me to follow. The boatman and the other four Zyú stayed atop the ridge while the chief priest and I clambered down toward the sea. It was a long descent, and the thundering walls and spouts of white water broke higher and higher around us, and showered a drizzle of cold spume down upon us. But we came at last into a sheltered depression among the massive boulders, and in it was a pool where the water merely sloshed back and forth, while the rest of the ocean boomed and pounded outside.

"Holy place of Tiat Ndik," said the priest. "Where the god lets us hear his voice."

"His voice?" I said. "You mean the ocean's noise?"

"His voice!" the man insisted. "To hear, must put head under."

Not taking my eyes off him and keeping my maquáhuitl at the ready, I knelt and lowered my head until I had one ear under the sloshing water. At first I could hear my own heart making a pulse beat in my ear, and that is an eerie sound, but then there came a much stranger one, beginning softly but getting louder. It could have been someone whistling under the water—if anyone *could* whistle under water—and whistling a melody more subtle than any earthly musician could play. Even now, I cannot liken it to any other sound I ever heard in my life. I later decided it must be a wind which, following the chinks and crevices among the rocks, was simultaneously made to warble and was deflected under the water. Its telltale bubbles no doubt came up somewhere else, and the pool revealed only the unearthly music of it. But there at that moment, and in those circumstances, I was ready enough to take the priest's word that it *was* the voice of a god.

Meanwhile, he was moving around the pool and studying it from various points, and finally he bent to plunge his arm in to the shoulder. He worked for a moment, then brought up his hand and opened it for me to see, saying "Ndik diok." I daresay the creature is some relation to the familiar land snail, but Zyanya's father had been mistaken to promise her a necklace of polished shells. The slimy slug carried no shell on its back, and had no other distinction that I could see.

But then the priest bent his head close to the slug in his palm and blew hard upon it. That evidently annoyed the creature, for it either urinated or defecated into his hand: a little smear of pale yellow matter. The priest carefully replaced the sea snail on its underwater rock, then held his cupped palm out for me to observe, and I shrank from the stink of that pale yellow substance. But, to my surprise, the smear in his hand began to change color: to a yellow-green, to a green-blue, to a blue-red that deepened and intensified until it was a vibrant purple.

Grinning, the man reached out and rubbed the substance onto my mantle front. The brilliant smudge still smelled abominable, but I knew it for the dye that would never fade or wash away. He gestured again for me to follow him, and we climbed the tumbled rocks while, with a combination of hand signs and his laconic Lóochi, the priest explained about the ndik diok:

The men of the Zyú collected the snails and provoked their exudations only twice a year, on holy days selected by some complicated divination. Though there were thousands of the sea snails clinging among the rocks, each gave only a minute quantity of that substance. So the men had to go far out among those cataclysms of crashing water, and dive into them, to pry the slugs loose, make them excrete onto a hank of cotton thread or into a leather flask, then replace the creatures unharmed. The snails had to be kept alive for the next time of extraction, but the men were not so indispensable; in each of those half-yearly rituals, some four or five divers were drowned or dashed to death upon the rocks.

"But why go to all that trouble, and sacrifice so many of your people, and then refuse to profit from it?" I asked, and managed to make the priest understand. He beckoned again, and led me farther into a clammy grotto, and said proudly:

"Our Sea God whose voice you heard. Tiat Ndik."

It was a crude and lumpy statue, since it consisted only of piled round rocks: a big boulder for the abdomen, a smaller for the chest, a yet smaller one for the head. But that whole worthless heap of inanimate rock was colored the glowing purple. And all about Tiat Ndik were stacked flasks full of the dye, and hanks of yarn colored with it: a buried treasure of incalculable value.

When we had climbed as far as the ridge again, the red-hot disk of Tonatíu was just sinking into the far western ocean and boiling up a steam of clouds. Then the disk was gone, and for an instant we saw Tonatíu's light shining through the sea out there where it thins at the brink of the world—a brief, bright flash of emerald green, no more. The priest and I made our way back toward where we had left the others, while he continued explaining: that the offerings of the purple dye were essential, or Tiat Ndik would entice no more fish to the nets of the Zyú.

I argued, "For all these sacrifices and offerings, your Sea God lets you eke out a miserable fish-eating existence. Let me take your purple to market and I will bring you gold enough that you can buy a *city*. A city in a fair and pleasant country, brimming with far better foods than fish, and with slaves to serve them to you."

He remained obdurate. "The god would never allow. The purple cannot be sold." After a moment he added, "Sometimes we not eat fish, Yellow Eye."

He smiled and pointed to where the four other priests stood around a driftwood fire. It was broiling two fresh-cut human thighs, spitted on my own spear. There was no sign of the rest of the boatman. Forcing my face to give no indication of the trepidation I felt, I took from my loincloth the wadded packet of gold dust and dropped it on the ground between me and the chief priest.

"Open it carefully," I said, "lest the wind get at it." As he knelt and began to unfold the cloth, I went on, "If I were to fill my canoe with your purple, I could bring back the boat almost as full of gold. But I offer this amount of gold for only as many flasks as I can carry in my own two arms."

He had the cloth open then, and the heap of dust gleamed in the sunset light, and his four brother priests approached to ogle it over his crouching figure. He let some of the dust run through his fingers, then, holding the cloth in both hands, he bounced it gently to judge its weight. Without looking up at me, he said, "You give this much gold for the purple. How much you give for the girl?"

"What girl?" I said, though my heart lurched.

"Her behind you."

I flicked only a quick glance backward. Zyanya stood directly behind me, looking unhappy, and a little way behind her stood six or seven more men of the Zyú, eagerly craning to see around her and me, to eye the gold. The priest was still kneeling and weighing the packet between his hands when I turned again and swung my maquáhuitl. The packet and his clutching hands dropped to the ground, though the priest barely swayed, staring in shock at the blood gushing from the stumps of his wrists.

The lesser priests and the fishermen rushed to converge— whether to grab for the liberated gold or to aid their chief, I do not know—but in that same instant I whirled, seized Zyanya's hand, plunged through the closing circle of men, and dragged her after me in a headlong run along the ridge and down its eastern side. We were briefly out of sight of the milling Zyú, and I made an abrupt left swerve to dodge among some boulders higher than our heads. The Zyú would give chase, and they would expect us to bolt for our canoe. But even if we could have reached and launched it, I had no experience of rowing a seagoing craft; the pursuers could probably have caught us merely by wading after us.

Some number of them did go running and shouting past our temporary hiding place—running in the direction of the beach, as I had hoped. "Uphill now!" I said to Zyanya, and she wasted no breath in asking why, but climbed along with me. Most of that promontory was bare rock, and we had to pick our way carefully through clefts and crevices, so that we should not be visible to those below. Higher up, the mountain sprouted trees and shrubbery in which we could more effectively lose ourselves, but that green haven was still a long climb distant, and I worried that the local birds would give away our position. At every step we seemed to startle into flight a whole flock of sea gulls or pelicans or cormorants.

But then I noticed that the birds were rising not just from around us, but from all parts of the mountain—land birds as well: parakeets, doves, rock wrens—twittering and flying about aimlessly. And there were not just birds; animals normally furtive or nocturnal were also strangely in evidence: armadillos, iguanas, rock snakes—even an ocelot loped past without giving us a glance—and all the animals, like us, were moving uphill. Then, though the dusk had still a while to last before dark, I heard a coyote's mournful keening from somewhere on the heights, and not far ahead of us a sinuous skein of bats came spewing from some cranny—and I knew what was coming: one of the convulsions so common to that coast.

"Hurry," I panted to the girl. "Up there. Where the bats are coming from. Must be a cave. Dive for it."

We found it just as the last bats departed, or we might have missed it altogether: a tunnel in the rock wide enough for us to wriggle into, side by side. How deep it went, I never found out, but somewhere far within there would have been a great cavern, for the bats had been a countless multitude and, as we lay together in the rock tunnel, we could smell from the farther interior an occasional whiff of their guano droppings. Suddenly everything was quiet outside our burrow; the birds must have flown far away and the animals gone safely to ground; even the usually ever-screeching tree cicadas were silent.

The first shock was sharp but also soundless. I heard Zyanya whisper fearfully, "Zyuùù," and I clasped her protectively tight against me. Then we heard a long, low, rumbling growl from somewhere far inland. One of the volcanoes in that range was belching, if not erupting, and violently enough to quake the earth as far as the coast.

The second and third shocks, and I do not know how many more, came with such increasing rapidity that they all blended into a dizzying motion of simultaneous rocking, tilting, and bucking. The girl and I might have been wedged inside a hollow log careering down a whitewater river. The noise was so deafeningly loud and prolonged that we might equally have been inside one of the drums which tear out the heart, it being beaten by a demented priest. The noise was of our mountain falling to pieces, contributing more of itself to that rubble of immense boulders already around it in the sea.

I wondered whether Zyanya and I would be among the rubble—after all, the bats had elected not to stay—but we could not have squeezed out of the tunnel then, even if we had panicked, because it was being so fiercely shaken. Once we managed to cringe a bit farther backward inside it, when the tunnel mouth suddenly darkened; a gigantic chunk of the mountaintop had rolled right across it. Happily for us, it kept on rolling and let the twilight in again, though with a cloud of dust that set us to choking and coughing.

Then my mouth went even drier, as I heard a muted thunder from behind us, from *inside* the mountain. That vast hollow cavern of the bats was crumbling inward, its dome roof plummeting down in pieces and probably bringing with it all the weight of the mountain above it. I waited for our tunnel to be tilted backward and chute us both feet-first down into that allcrushing collapse of the immediate world. I wrapped my arms and legs around Zyanya, and held her even more tightly, in the pitiful hope that my body might give her some protection when we both slid down into the grinding bowels of the earth.

But our tunnel held firm, and that was the last alarming

shock. Slowly the upheaval and uproar quieted, until we heard no more than a few sounds outside our burrow: the trickly sounds of small stones and pebbles belatedly following the bigger rocks downhill. I stirred, intending to stick my head out and see what was left of the mountain, but Zyanya held me back.

"Do not yet," she warned. "There are often aftershocks. Or there may be a boulder still teetering right above us, ready to fall. Wait a while." Of course she was right to caution prudence, but she confessed only a little later that that was not her sole reason for holding on to me.

I have mentioned the effects of an earthquake on the human physiology and emotions. I know Zyanya could feel my bulgingly erect tepúli against her small belly. And, even with the cloth of her blouse and my mantle between us, I could feel the nuzzling of her nipples against my chest.

At first she murmured, "Oh, no, Záa, we must not..."

Then she said, "Záa, please do not. You were my mother's lover...."

And she said, "You were my little brother's father. You and I cannot..."

And, though her breathing quickened, she kept on saying, "It is not right..." until she thought to say, with the last of her breath, "But you did pay dearly to buy me from those savages..." after which she only panted silently until the whimpers and moans of pleasure began. Then, a bit later, she asked in a whisper, "Did I do it right?"

If there is anything good to be said for an earthquake, I will remark that its singular excitation enables a virgin girl to enjoy her defloration, which is not always otherwise the case. Zyanya so delighted in hers that she would not let me go until we had indulged twice more, and such was my own earthquake invigoration that we never even uncoupled. After each climax, my tepúli would naturally shrink, but each time Zyanya would tighten some little circlet of muscles down there and hold me from withdrawal, and somehow ripple those tiny muscles to tantalize my member so that it began to swell again inside her.

We might have gone on even longer without a pause, but the mouth of our tunnel had by then darkened to a queer reddish gray, and I wanted a look at our situation before it was full night, so we wriggled out and stood up. It was long after sunset, but the volcano or the earthquake had sent its cloud of dust so high into the sky that it still caught the rays of Tonatíu, from Míctlan or wherever he was by then. The sky, which should have been dark blue, was a luminous red, and it made red the streak in Zyanya's hair. It also reflected down enough light that we could see about us.

The ocean appeared to be absolutely boiling and frothing around a much greater area of rocks. The way we had come up the mountain was no longer recognizable: in places heaped with new rubble, in places cracked open into deep, wide chasms. Above and beyond where we stood, there was a sunken, shadowed hollow in the mountainside, where it had fallen inward into the bat cavern.

"It may be," I mused, "that the rockslides crushed all our pursuers, and maybe their village as well. If it did not, they are sure to blame us for this disaster, and follow us even more vengefully."

"Blame *us?*" exclaimed Zyanya.

"I defiled the holy place of their highest god. They will presume that I caused his anger." I thought about it, and wondered, and said, "Perhaps I did." Then I came back to practicality. "But if we stay and sleep in our hiding place here, and then arise early and push on before dawn, I think we can outdistance any pursuit. When we get back over the ranges to Tecuantépec—"

"Will we get back, Záa? We have no provisions, no water...."

"I still have my maquáhuitl. And I have crossed worse mountains than any between here and Tecuantépec. When we get back...Zyanya, could we be married?"

She may have been startled by the abruptness of my proposal, but not by the fact of it. She said quietly, "I would suppose that I had answered that before you asked. It may be immodest of me to say so, but I cannot entirely reproach the zyuúù for...what happened."

I said sincerely, "I *thank* the zyuúù, for making it possible. I had long wanted you, Zyanya."

"Well, then!" she said, and smiled brightly and spread her

arms in a gesture of it-is-done. I shook my head, meaning it is not so easily done, and her smile faded to some anxiety.

I said, "For me, you are a treasure greater than I could ever have hoped to find. For you, I am not." She started to speak, and I shook my head again. "If you marry me, you are forever an exile from your Cloud People. To be expelled from such a close and proud and admirable kinship, that is no small sacrifice."

She thought for a moment, then asked, "Would you believe me if I say you are worth it?"

"No," I said. "For I am better acquainted with my worth—or my unworthiness—than even you could possibly be."

She nodded as if she had expected some such answer. "Then I can only say that I love the man Záa Nayàzú more than I love the Cloud People."

"But why, Zyanya?"

"I think I have loved you ever since ... but we will not speak of yesterdays. I say only that I love you today and I will love you tomorrow. Because the yesterdays are gone. Todays and tomorrows are all the days that ever can be. And on every one of them I will say I love you. Could you believe that, Záa? Could you say the same?"

I smiled at her. "I can and I can and I do. I love you, Zyanya."

She smiled in return and said, somewhat mischievously, "I do not know why we had to argue it out. It seems we were fated anyway, by your tonáli, or mine, or both." And she pointed from her breast to mine. The dye that the priest had smeared on me had been still damp when we had lain together. We each bore an identical purple stain, she on her blouse, I on my mantle.

I laughed. Then I said, half ruefully, "I have been long in love with you, Zyanya, and now we are pledged to be man and wife, and I never yet thought to ask the meaning of your name."

When she told me, I thought she was jesting, and only her solemn insistence finally made me believe her.

As you surely have perceived by now, my lords, all our people of all nations bore names that were borrowed from some thing in nature, or some natural quality, or some combination

456

of those. It is evidenced in my own name of Dark Cloud and in others I have spoken: Something Delicate, Blood Glutton, Evening Star, Flame Flower. So it was hard for me to believe that a girl could have a name that did not signify any *thing* at all. Zyanya is only a simple and common word, and it means nothing in the world but always.

Always.

I H S

✠

S. C. C. M.

Sanctified, Caesarean, Catholic Majesty,
the Emperor Don Carlos, Our Lord King:

MOST Laudable Majesty, our Mentor and Monarch:
from this City of Mexíco, capital of New Spain, on this St.
Prosper's Day in the Year of Our Lord one thousand five
hundred thirty, greeting.

Annexed herewith as usual, Sire, is the latest outpouring
of our resident Aztec, which is also as usual: little of *vis* but
much of *vomitus*. It is evident from Your Majesty's most recent
letter that our Sovereign still finds this history sufficiently be-
guiling as to be worth five good men's continued subjection
to the hearing and transcribing of it.

Your Dedicated Majesty may also be interested to hear of
the safe return of the Dominican missionaries we sent into the
southern region called Oaxaca, to appraise our Aztec's claim
that the Indians there have for long worshiped an omnipotent
god of gods, whimsically known as the Almighty Breath, and
also that they utilized the cross as a holy symbol.
Brother Bernardino Minaya and his companion friars do
attest that they saw in that country many seemingly Christian

crosses—at any rate, crosses of the shape called in heraldry the *croix botonée*—but that they serve no religious purpose, being regarded only pragmatically, inasmuch as they mark sources of fresh water. Therefore, Your Majesty's vicar is inclined to view those crosses with Augustinian skepticism. In our appreciation, Sire, they are but one more manifestation of the Adversary's spiteful cunning. Clearly, in anticipation of our arrival in New Spain, the Devil made haste to teach some numbers of these heathens a profane imitation of various Christian beliefs and rites and sacred objects, in the hope of frustrating and confounding our later introduction of the True Faith.

Also, as well as the Dominicans could gather (they being hampered by linguistic difficulties), the Almighty Breath is not a god but a high wizard (or priest, as our chronicler would have it) who holds dominion over the subterranean crypts in the ruins of that city called Mitla, formerly considered by the natives their Holy Home. The friars, apprised by us of the pagan interments and sinfully suicidal immolations of live volunteers at that place, forced the wizard to allow them access to those crypts.

Like Theseus venturing into the Labyrinth of Daedalus, they unwound a cord behind them as they went by torchlight through the branching caves and tortuous underground passages. They were assailed by the stench of decayed flesh; they trod on the bones of countless placidly seated skeletons. Unhappily, and unlike Theseus, they lost their courage before they had gone many leagues. When they were confronted by giant, overfed rats and snakes and other such vermin, their determination dissolved in horror, and they departed in an almost undignified rout.

Once outside, they commanded, despite the Indians' lamentations and protests, that the tunnel entrances be permanently caved in and collapsed and sealed by the rolling of many boulders over them, "to wall up and hide forever that back door of Hell," as Fray Bernardino phrases it. The action was of course well warranted, and even long overdue, and not to be disparaged, since it is reminiscent of the sainted Catherine of Siena, who prayed that her own impeccable body might be splayed forever across the Pit, so that no more poor sinners would ever fall in. Nevertheless, we regret that we may now never know the full extent of that underground network of caverns, and may never recover the treasures which the ranking personages of that people no doubt took with them to their tombs. Worse, we fear that the Dominicans' impetuous action may have done little to make the Indians of that area more receptive to the Faith or more loving toward us who bring it.

We regret also to report that we ourself are not much better beloved by our own fellow Spaniards here in New Spain. Your Majesty's officers in the Crown Archive of the Indies have perhaps already received communications from persons complaining of our "interference" in secular matters. God knows they complain enough to us, particularly the landholders who employ great numbers of Indian laborers on their farms and ranches and plantations. Those lords-proprietors have even made a play upon our name, and now irreverently refer to us as Bishop Zurriago, "the Scourge." This is because, Sire, we have dared-to denounce from the pulpit their practice of working their Indians literally to death.

"And why should we not?" they demand. "There are still some fifteen thousand red men to every white one in these lands. What harm in our reducing that dangerous disparity, especially if we can wring useful work from the wretches while we do it?"

The Spaniards who hold that attitude claim that they have good religious justification for it, *viz.:* because we Christians rescued these savages from their devil worship and inevitable damnation, because we brought them hope of salvation, therefore the Indians should be eternally obligated to us their redeemers. Your Majesty's chaplain cannot deny that there is logic in the argument, but we do feel that the Indians' obligation should not require them to die indiscriminately and arbitrarily— of beatings, brandings, starvation rations, and other mistreatments—certainly not before they have been baptized and fully confirmed in the Faith.

Since the cadastral and census records of New Spain are still necessarily haphazard and incomplete, we can offer only rough calculations of the number of the native population, past and present. But there is reason to believe that approximately six million red men formerly lived within the confines of what is now New Spain. The battles of the Conquest of course took a considerable toll of them. Also, at that time and in the nine years since, an estimated two and a half million more of the Indians under Spanish authority have died of various diseases, and only God knows how many more in the yet unconquered regions, and they continue to die in great numbers everywhere.

It has apparently pleased Our Lord to make the red race peculiarly vulnerable to certain afflictions which, it seems, were not heretofore endemial in these lands. While the pestilence of the great pocks was previously known here (and not surprisingly, in view of the people's general licentiousness), it appears that the plagues of the buboes, the cholera morbus, the small pocks, the pease pocks, and the measles were not. Whether those diseases began to occur only coincidentally with the overthrow of these peoples, or are a chastisement visited upon them by God in His judgment, they ravage the Indians with far more virulence than Europeans have ever suffered.

Still, that loss of lives, while of distressing magnitude, is at any rate of natural cause, an inscrutable Act of God, and not of our countrymen's doing nor amenable to their amelioration of it. We can, however, call a halt to our countrymen's deliberate killing of the red men, and we must do so. Your Majesty gave us another office besides those of Bishop and Inquisitor, and we will uphold that title of Protector of the Indians, even if it means bearing also the hateful title of Scourge bestowed by our fellows.

That the Indians profit us, as cheap and expendable labor, must be a secondary consideration to our saving of their pagan souls. Our success in that noble task is diminished by every Indian who dies not yet a Christian. If too many should perish thus, the good name of the Church would suffer. Besides, if these Indians all die, who then would build our cathedrals and churches and chapels and monasteries and convents and cloisters and shrines and houses of retreat and other Christian edifices, and who would constitute the bulk of our congregations, and who would work and contribute and tithe to support the servants of God in New Spain?

May Our Lord God preserve Your Most Renowned Majesty, executor of so many holy works, that you may enjoy the fruits thereof in His High Glory.

(ecce signum)   Zumárraga

SEPTIMA PARS

DOES Your Excellency join us today to hear what my married life was like?

I think you will find the account rather less crowded with incident—and, I should hope, less abrasive to Your Excellency's sensibilities—than the tempestuous times of my younger manhood. Although I must regretfully report that the actual ceremony of my wedding to Zyanya was clouded by storm and tempest, I am happy to say that most of our married life afterward was sunny and calm. I do not mean that it was ever dull; with Zyanya I experienced many further adventures and excitements; indeed, her very presence brought excitement into my every day. Also, in the years following our marriage, the Mexíca were at the peak of their power and were wielding it with vigor, and I was occasionally involved in happenings that I now recognize as having been of some small importance. But at the time, they were to me and Zyanya—and doubtless to the majority of commonfolk like ourselves—only a sort of busy-figured wall painting in front of which we lived out our private lives and our own small triumphs and our inconsequential little happinesses.

Oh, not that *we* regarded any least aspect of our marriage as insignificant. Early on, I asked Zyanya how she did that twinkling contraction of her tipíli's little circlet of muscles, which made our act of love so extraordinarily exciting. She blushed with shy pleasure and murmured, "You might as well ask how I wink my eyes. It simply happens when I will it. Does it not happen with every woman?"

"I have not known every woman," I said, "and I have no wish to, now that I have the best of all."

But Your Excellency is not interested in such homely details. I think I might best make you see and appreciate Zyanya by comparing her to the plant we call the metl—though of course the metl is nothing like as beautiful as she was, and it does not love or speak or laugh.

The metl, Your Excellency, is that man-high green or blue plant you have taught us to call the maguey. Bountiful and generous and handsome to look at, the maguey must be the most useful plant that grows anywhere. Its long, curved, leathery leaves can be cut and laid overlapping to make a watertight roof for a house. Or the leaves can be crushed to a pulp, pressed, and dried into paper. Or the leaf fibers can be separated and spun into any kind of cord from rope to thread. The thread can be woven into a rough but serviceable cloth. The hard, sharp spines that outline each leaf can serve as needles, pins, or nails. They served our priests as instruments with which to torture and mutilate and mortify themselves.

The leaf shoots that grow nearest the earth are white and tender, and can be cooked to make a delicious sweet. Or they can be dried to make fuel for a long-burning, smokeless hearth fire, and the resultant clean white ash is used for everything from surfacing bark paper to making soap. Cut away the central leaves of the maguey, scoop out its heart, and in the hollow will collect the plant's clear sap. It is tasty and nutritious to drink. Smeared on the skin, it prevents wrinkles, rashes, and blemishes; our women used it extensively for that. Our men preferred to let the maguey juice sit and ferment into the drunk-making octli, or pulque, as you call it. Our children liked the clear sap boiled down to a syrup, when it is almost as thick and sweet as bees' honey.

In brief, the maguey offers every part and particle of its being for the good of us who grow and tend it. And Zyanya, besides being incomparably more, was rather like that. She

was good in every part, in every way, in every action, and not
just to me. Though of course I enjoyed the best of her, I never
knew another person who did not love and esteem and admire
her. Zyanya was not only Always, she was everything.

But I must not waste Your Excellency's time with sentimentality. Let me return to telling things in the order in which
they happened.

After our escape from the murderous Zyú and our survival
of the earthquake, it took me and Zyanya fully seven days to
return to Tecuantépec by the overland route. Whether the quake
had annihilated the savages or made them assume that it had
annihilated us, I do not know, but no one pursued us, and we
were not otherwise bothered in our crossing of the mountains,
except by occasional thirst and hunger. I had long ago lost my
burning crystal to the robbers on the isthmus, and I carried no
fire-drilling device, and we did not ever get quite hungry
enough to eat raw meat. We found sufficient wild fruits and
berries and birds' eggs, all of which we *could* eat raw, and
they also provided enough moisture to sustain us between the
infrequent mountain springs. At night, we piled up billows of
dry leaves and slept in them intertwined for mutual warmth and
other mutual comforting.

We were both perhaps a bit thinner when we arrived again
in Tecuantépec; we were certainly ragged and barefoot and
footsore, our sandals having worn out on the mountain rocks.
We trudged into the inn yard wearily and gratefully, and Béu
Ribé ran out to greet us, her face expressing a mixture of
concern, exasperation, and relief.

"I thought you had disappeared, like our father, and would
never come back!" she said, half laughing, half scolding, as
she ardently hugged first Zyanya then me. "The moment you
were out of sight, I told myself it was a foolish venture, and
a dangerous..."

Her voice faltered, as she looked from one to the other of
us, and once again I saw that smile lose its wings. She brushed
her hand lightly across her face, and repeated, "Foolish...
dangerous..." Her eyes widened when they looked more
closely at her sister, and they moistened when they looked at
me.

Though I have lived many years and known many women, I still do not know how one of them can so instantly and surely perceive when another has lain with a man for the first time, when she has made the irreversible change from maiden to woman. Waiting Moon regarded her younger sister with shock and disappointment, and me with anger and resentment.

I said hastily, "We are going to be married."

Zyanya said, "We hope you will approve, Béu. You are, after all, the head of the family."

"Then you might have said something before!" the older girl said, in a strangled voice. "Before you—" She seemed to choke on that. Then her eyes were no longer moist but blazing. "And not just *any* outlander, but a brutish Mexícatl who lusts and ruts without discrimination. If you had not been so conveniently available, Zyanya"—her voice got even louder and uglier—"he would probably have come back with a filthy Zyú female dangling from his insatiable long—"

"*Béu!*" Zyanya gasped. "I have never heard you speak so. Please! I know this seems sudden, but I assure you, Záa and I love each other."

"Sudden? Sure?" Waiting Moon said wildly, and turned to rage at me. "Are *you* sure? You have not sampled every last woman in the family!"

"*Béu!*" Zyanya begged again.

I tried to be placative, but sounded only craven. "I am not a noble of the pípiltin. I can marry only one wife." That earned me a glance from Zyanya not much more tender than her sister's glare. I quickly added, "I want Zyanya for my wife. I would be honored, Béu, if I might call you sister."

"Very well! But just to tell the sister good-bye. Then begone and take your—your *choice* with you. Thanks to you, she has here not honor, not respectability, not name, not home. No priest of the Ben Záa will marry you."

"We know that," I said. "We will go to Tenochtítlan for the ceremony." I put firmness into my voice. "But it will be no shameful or clandestine thing. We will be wed by one of the high priests of the court of the Uey-Tlatoáni of the Mexíca. Your sister has chosen an outlander, yes, but no worthless vagabond. And marry me she will, with your blessing or without it."

There was a long interval of tense silence. Tears trickled down the girls' almost identically beautiful, almost identically uneasy faces, and sweat trickled down mine. We three stood like the corners of a triangle bound by invisible straps of óli drawing more and more impossibly taut. But before anything snapped, Béu relaxed the strain. Her face wilted and her shoulders slumped and she said:

"I am sorry. Please forgive me, Zyanya. And brother Záa. Of course you have my blessing, my loving good wishes for your happiness. And I beg that you will forget the other words I spoke." She tried to laugh at herself, but the laugh cracked in the middle. "It was sudden, as you say. So unexpected. It is not every day I lose... a beloved sister. But now come inside. Get clean and fed and rested."

Waiting Moon has hated me from that day to this.

Zyanya and I stayed another ten days or so at the inn, but keeping a discreet distance between us. As before, she shared a room with her sister and I inhabited one of my own, and she and I were careful not to make any public displays of affection. While we recovered from our abortive expedition, Béu seemed to recover from the displeasure and melancholy our return had caused. She helped Zyanya choose from her personal belongings, and from their mutual possessions, the comparatively few and dear and irreplaceable things she would carry away with her.

Since I was again without so much as a cacao bean, I borrowed a small quantity of trade currency from the girls, for traveling expenses, and an additional sum which I sent by messenger to Nozibe, to be delivered to whatever family that ill-fated boatman might have left bereaved. I also reported the incident to the bishósu of Tecuantépec, who said he would in turn inform the Lord Kosi Yuela of that latest savagery committed by the despicable Zyú Huave.

On the eve of our departure, Béu surprised us with a festive party, such as she would have done to celebrate if Zyanya had been marrying a man of the Ben Záa. It was attended by all the inn's current patrons and by invited guests from among the city folk. There were hired musicians to play, and splendidly

costumed dancers doing the genda lizáa, which is the traditional
"spirit of kinship" dance of the Cloud People.

With at least a semblance of good feeling having been restored among the three of us, Zyanya and I bade farewell to
Béu the next morning, with solemn kisses. We did not go
immediately or directly toward Tenochtítlan. She and I each
carrying a pack, we headed straight north, across the flatland
isthmus, the way I had come to Tecuantépec. And, since I had
someone other than myself to think of, I was especially wary
of villains lurking on the road. I carried my maquáhuitl ready
to my hand, and kept a sharp lookout wherever the terrain
might have concealed an ambush.

We had not walked more than one-long-run when Zyanya
remarked simply, but with an excited anticipation in her voice,
"Just think. I am going farther from home than I have ever
been."

Those few words made my heart swell, and made me love
her the more. She was venturing into what was for her a vast
unknown, and doing it trustingly, because she was in my keeping. I glowed with pride, and with thankfulness that her tonáli
and mine had brought us together. All the other people in my
life were left over from yesterday or yesteryear, but Zyanya
was someone fresh and new, not made commonplace by familiarity.

"I never believed," she said, spreading wide her arms, "that
there could *be* so much land of nothing but land!"

Even viewing the lackluster vista of the isthmus, she could
thus exclaim, and make me smile and share her enthusiasm.
It was to be like that through all our todays and tomorrows
together. I would have the privilege of introducing her to things
prosaic to me but new and foreign to her. And she, in her
unjaded enjoyment of them, would make me see them, too,
as if they were sparklingly novel and exotic.

"Look at this bush, Záa. It is alive, *aware!* And it is afraid,
poor thing. See? When I touch a twig, it folds all its leaves
and flowers tight shut, and reveals thorns like white fangs."

She might have been a young goddess lately born of Teteoínan, mother of the gods, and newly sent down from the
skies to get acquainted with the earth. For she found mystery
and wonderment and delight in every least detail of the world—

including even me, even herself. She was as spirited and sportive as the never still light that lives inside an emerald. I was continually to be surprised by her unexpected attitudes toward things I took for granted.

"No, we will not undress," she said, our first night on the road. "We will make love, oh yes, but clothed, as we did in the mountains." I naturally protested, but she was firm, and she explained why. "Let me save that one last small modesty until after our wedding, Záa. And our being naked, then, for the very first time together, should make it all so new and different that we might never have done it before."

I repeat, Your Excellency, that a full account of our married life would be most undramatic, because feelings like contentment and happiness are much harder to convey in words than are mere events. I can only tell you that I was then twenty and three years old, and Zyanya was twenty, and lovers of that age are capable of the most extreme and enduring attachment they ever will know. In any event, that first love between us never diminished; it grew in depth and intensity, but I cannot tell you why.

Now that I think back, though, Zyanya may have come close to putting it into words, on that long-ago day we set out together. One of the comical swift-runner birds scampered along beside us, the first she had ever seen, and she said pensively, "Why should a bird prefer the ground to the sky? I would not, if I had wings to fly with. Would you, Záa?"

Ayyo, her spirit did have wings, and I partook of that joyous buoyancy. From the first, we were comrades who shared an ever unfolding adventure. We loved the adventure and we loved each other. No man and woman could ever have asked anything more of the gods than what they had given to me and Zyanya— except perhaps the promise of her name: that it be for always.

On the second day, we caught up to a northbound company of Tzapotéca traders, whose porters were laden with tortoise-shell of the hawkbill turtle. That would be sold to the Olméca artisans, to be heated and twisted and fashioned into various ornaments and inlays. The traders made us welcome to their company and, though Zyanya and I could have traveled faster on our own, for safety's sake we fell in with them and accom-

panied them to their destination, the crossroad trading town of
Coátzacoálcos.

We had scarcely arrived in the marketplace there—and
Zyanya had begun excitedly flitting among the goods-piled
stalls and ground cloths—when a familiar voice bawled at me,
"You are not dead, then! Did we throttle those bandits for
nothing?"

"Blood Glutton!" I exclaimed happily. "And Cozcatl! What
brings you to these far parts?"

"Oh, boredom," said the old warrior in a bored voice.

"He lies. We were worried about you," said Cozcatl, who
was no longer a little boy, but had grown to adolescence, all
knees and elbows and gawky awkwardness.

"Not worried, *bored!*" insisted Blood Glutton. "I ordered
a house built for me in Tenochtítlan, but the supervising of
stonemasons and plasterers is not the most edifying work. Also
they hinted that they could do better without my ideas. And
Cozcatl found his school studies somewhat tame after all his
adventures abroad. So the boy and I decided to track you and
find out what you have been doing for these two years."

Cozcatl said, "We could not be sure we were on the right
trail—until we first came here and found four men trying to
sell some valuables. We recognized your bloodstone mantle
clasp."

"They could not satisfactorily account for their possession
of the articles," said Blood Glutton. "So I hauled them before
the market tribunal. They were tried, convicted, and dispatched
by the flower garland. Ah, well, they doubtless deserved it for
some other misdeed. Anyway, here is your clasp, your burning
crystal, your nose trinket . . ."

"You did well," I said. "They robbed and beat me. They
thought me dead."

"So did we, but we *hoped* you were not," said Cozcatl.
"And we had no other demands on our time. So we have just
been exploring up and down this coast ever since. And you,
Mixtli, what have you been doing?"

"Also exploring," I said. "Seeking treasure, as usual."

"Find any?" growled Blood Glutton.

"Well, I found a wife."

"A wife." He hawked and spat on the ground. "And we feared you had only died."

"The same old grouch." I laughed. "But when you see her . . ."

I looked about the square and called her name and in a moment she came, looking as queenly as Pela Xila or the Lady of Tolan, but infinitely more beautiful. In just that little time, she had purchased a new blouse and skirt and sandals, and changed from her travel-stained garb, and bought what we called a living jewel—a many-colored iridescent beetle—to fix in that lightning streak of white hair. I think I gazed as admiringly as did Cozcatl and Blood Glutton.

"You were right to chide me, Mixtli," the old man conceded. "Ayyo, a maiden of the Cloud People. She is indeed a treasure beyond price."

"I recognize you, my lady," Cozcatl said gallantly to her. "You were the younger goddess at that temple disguised as an inn."

When I had made introductions all around—and my two old friends, I do believe, had fallen instantly in love with Zyanya—I said, "We are well met. I was on my way to Xicalánca, where yet another treasure waits for me. I think the four of us can transport it and I need not hire porters."

So we went on, by leisurely stages, through those lands where the women all chewed like manatees and the men all walked bent by their names, to Cupílco's capital city, and to the workshop there of the Master Tuxtem, and he brought out the items he had fashioned of the giant teeth. Since I knew something of the quality of the material I had given him to work with, I was not *quite* as taken by surprise as were Zyanya, Cozcatl, and Blood Glutton, when we saw what he had done with it.

As I had requested, there were figurine gods and goddesses of the Mexíca, some of them standing as tall as the length of my forearm, and there were engraved dagger handles and combs, which I had also suggested. But in addition there were skulls as big as those of young children, intricately etched with scenes from old legends. There were artfully worked little boxes with fitted lids, and copáli perfume vials with stoppers of the same material. There were chest medallio   and mantle clasps and whistles and brooches, in the shape of tiny jaguars and owls and exquisite little naked women and flowers and rabbits and laughing faces.

On many of those things the detail was so fine that it could be properly appreciated only by scrutiny through my close-viewing crystal. Seen thus, even the tipíli was visible on a naked-girl ornament no bigger than a maguey thorn. As instructed, Tuxtem had not wasted a fragment or sliver: there were also nose plugs and ear plugs and labrets and dainty ear picks and toothpicks. All those things, large and small, shone mellow-white, as if they possessed an interior light of their own, as if they had been carved from the moon. And they were as gratifying to touch as they were to look at, the artisan having polished their surfaces as smooth as the skin of Zyanya's breasts. Like her skin, they invited, "Touch me, caress me, fondle me."

"You promised, young Lord Yellow Eye," said Tuxtem, "that only worthy persons would ever own any of these things. Permit me the presumption of choosing the first worthy of them."

At which he stooped to kiss the earth to Zyanya, then rose and hung around her neck a delicate, sinuous chain of hundreds of links, the which must have cost him incalculable time to carve from a single length of hard tooth. Zyanya smiled radiantly and said, "The Master Tuxtem does me honor, in truth. There can never again be such works as these. They should be reserved to your gods."

"I believe only in the believable," he said. "A beautiful young woman with lightning in her hair and a Lóchi name which I know to mean Always, she is a much more credible goddess than most."

Tuxtem and I divided the articles as we had agreed, and then separated my share into four bundles. The working of the pieces had made them rather less in bulk and weight than the original tusks had been, so the resultant packages were wieldy enough that I and my three companions could carry them unaided by porters. We took them first to an inn there in Xicalánca, and engaged rooms, and rested, cleaned ourselves, and dined, and slept.

The next day, I selected one item from among our new

acquisitions: a small knife sheath, etched with the scene of Quetzalcóatl paddling away from that shore on his raft of entwined snakes. Then I dressed in my best and, while Cozcatl and Blood Glutton escorted Zyanya to show her the sights of Xicalánca, I went to the palace and requested an audience with Cupílco's ruling noble, the Tabascoöb, as he was called there. From that title—I do not know why—you Spaniards have concocted a new name for much of the land that was then Olméca country.

The lord received me graciously enough. Like most persons of other nations, he probably had no prodigious affection for us Mexíca. But his land lived by trade, and ours were the most numerous of all traders.

I said, "Lord Tabascoöb, one of your local craftsmen, the Master Tuxtem, has lately done a unique kind of artwork in which I expect to turn a profitable trade. But I thought it fitting that the very first example should be presented to the lord of these lands. Hence I offer this token as a gift in the name of my own lord, the Uey-Tlatoáni Ahuítzotl of Tenochtítlan."

"A thoughtful gesture and a generous gift," he said, examining the sheath with open admiration. "And a most beautiful work. I have never seen the like."

In return, the Tabascoöb gave me a small quill of gold dust to present to Master Tuxtem, and a boxed collection of sea creatures—starfish, sea fawns, a coral sea feather, all gold-dipped for preservation and added beauty—as a reciprocal gift for the Revered Speaker Ahuítzotl. I left the palace feeling that I had accomplished at least a little in the furtherance of good relations between Cupílco and Tenochtítlan.

I made sure to mention that to Ahuítzotl when I called on him immediately after our arrival in The Heart of the One World. I hoped the Tabascoöb's good-fellowship gift would help induce the Revered Speaker to grant my request: that Zyanya and I be married by a palace priest of impressive rank and credentials. But Ahuítzotl only gave me his most red-eyed glare and growled:

"You dare to come asking a favor of us, after having disobeyed our express instructions?"

Honestly not understanding, I said, "Disobeyed, my lord?"

"When you brought us the account of your first expedition to the south, we told you to remain available for further discussion of it. Instead you vanished, and deprived the Mexíca of a possibly valuable opportunity to make war. Now you come back, two years later, two years too late, to wheedle our sponsorship of a trifling thing like a wedding!"

Still puzzled, I said, "Assuredly, Lord Speaker, I would never have gone away if I suspected I was doing a disservice. But . . . *what* opportunity was lost?"

"Your word pictures told how your train had been beset by Mixtéca bandits." His voice rose angrily. "We have never let an attack on our traveling pochtéca go unavenged." He was obviously more angry at me than at the bandits. "Had you been available to press the grievance, we would have had good excuse to send an army against the Mixtéca. But, with no demonstrable plaintiff . . ."

I murmured apologies, and bowed my head humbly, but at the same time I made a deprecatory gesture. "The miserable Mixtéca, my lord, possess little worth the winning. However, this time I return from abroad with news of a people who do possess something well worth seizing, and they likewise deserve punishment. I was most harshly treated by them."

"By whom? How? And what do they possess? Speak! It may be that you can redeem yourself in our estimation."

I told him how I had discovered the sea-and-rock-barricaded habitat of the 'Chóntaltin, or the Zyú, or The Strangers, that viciously reclusive offshoot tribe of the Huave. I told how only that people knew when and where to dive for the sea snails, and how those unlovely slugs yield the lovely deep purple dye that never fades or discolors. I suggested that such a unique commodity would be of immeasurable market value. I told how my Tzapotécatl guide had been butchered by The Strangers, and how Zyanya and I had but narrowly escaped the same fate. During my narrative, Ahuítzotl heaved himself up from his grizzled-bear throne and strode excitedly about the room.

"Yes," he said, grinning ravenously. "The outrage against one of our pochtéca would justify a punitive invasion, and the purple alone would amply repay it. But why settle for taming just the one wretched Huave tribe? That land of Uaxyácac has many other treasures worth acquiring. Not since the long-ago days of my father's reign have the Mexíca humbled those proud Tzapotéca."

"I would remind the Revered Speaker," I said quickly, "that not even your father Motecuzóma could keep such a faraway people subject for very long. To do so would require permanent garrisons in that country. And to support the garrisons would require extended supply lines always vulnerable to disruption. Even if a military rule could be imposed and maintained, it would cost more than any expectable return in plunder and tribute."

Ahuítzotl grumbled, "You seem always to have an argument against men waging manly war."

"Not always, my lord. In this case, I would suggest that you enlist the Tzapotéca as allies. Offer them the honor of fighting alongside your own troops when you descend upon the Huave barbarians. Then put that defeated tribe under tribute, not to you, but to the Lord Kosi Yuela of Uaxyácac—to surrender to him all their purple dye from now forevermore."

"What? Fight a war and refuse the fruits of it?"

"Only hear me out, Lord Speaker. After your victory, you arrange a treaty whereby Uaxyácac sells the purple to no one but our Mexíca traders. That way both nations will profit, for of course our pochtéca will resell the dye for a much higher price. You will have bound the Tzapotéca closer to us by the bonds of increased trade—and by their having fought beside the Mexíca for the first time in a mutual military venture."

His glare at me became a gaze of speculation. "And if they fight once as our allies, they could do so again. And again." He bestowed on me a look almost kindly. "The idea is sound. We will give the order to march as soon as our seers have picked an auspicious day for it. Be ready, Tequíua Mixtli, to take command of your allotted warriors."

"But, my lord, I am to be married!"

He muttered, "Xoquíui," which is a low profanity. "You can be married any time, but a soldier is always subject to call, especially one of command rank. Also, you are again the aggrieved party in this business. You are our excuse for violating the borders of Uaxyácac."

"My physical presence will not be necessary, Lord Speaker. The excuse has already been prepared." I told him how I had

reported The Strangers' evil doings to the ruling noble of Tecuantépec, and through him to the Lord Bishósu of that land.
"None of the Tzapotéca bears any love for that squatter tribe
of Huave, so your way to them will not be impeded. Indeed,
Kosi Yuela will probably require no coaxing at all to join you
in chastising them." I paused, then said meekly, "I hope I did
right in thus presuming to ease in advance the affairs of lords
and armies and nations."

For a short while, there was no sound in the room except
that of Ahuítzotl drumming his thick fingers on a bench of
which the upholstery, I suspected, was human skin. Finally he
said:

"We are told that your intended bride is of incomparable
beauty. Very well. No man who has already done exemplary
service for his nation should be required to put the enjoyment
of war before the enjoyment of beauty. You will be married
here, in the court ballroom, which we have had newly decorated. A palace priest will officiate—our priest of the love
goddess Xochiquétzal, I think, not he of the war god Huitzilopóchtli—and our entire retinue will attend. Invite all your
fellow pochtéca, your friends, anyone else you choose. Simply
consult the palace seers, so they may set a well-omened date.
In the meantime, you and your woman go about the city and
find a home site which pleases you, one that is yet unoccupied
or is purchasable from its owner, and that will be Ahuítzotl's
wedding gift to you."

At the proper time in the afternoon of my wedding day, I
nervously approached the portal of the crowded and noisy ballroom, and I stopped there long enough to survey the gathering
through my topaz. Then, out of vanity, I let the thonged crystal
drop inside my rich new mantle before I stepped into the room.
But I had seen that the new decoration of the vast hall included
wall paintings which I would have recognized even unsigned—
and that the crowd of nobles and courtiers and privileged commoners included a tall young man who, though his back was

to me at that moment, I recognized as the artist: Yei-Ehécatl Pocuía-Chimáli.

I made my way through the throng of people, some standing, chatting and drinking from golden cups; others, mostly the court noblewomen, already kneeling or seated around the countless gold-thread-embroidered cloths spread out on the floor matting. Most of the people reached out to pat my shoulder or reached up to stroke my hand, smiling and murmuring words of congratulation. But, as tradition required, I acknowledged none of the gestures or words. I went to the front of the room, where the most elegant cloth of all was spread on a high dais, and where a number of men waited for me, among them the Uey-Tlatoáni Ahuítzotl and the priest of Xochiquétzal. As they greeted me, the performers from The House of Song began to play a muted music.

For the first part of the ceremony—that of my being given into full manhood—I had asked the three elder pochtéca to do me the honor, and they were also seated on the dais. Since the cloth was spread with platters of hot tamáltin and jugs of potent octli, and since it was prescribed that the Givers depart immediately after the first ritual, the three elderly men had already helped themselves, to the extent that they were noticeably gorged, drunk, and half asleep.

When the room had quieted and only the soft music could be heard, Ahuítzotl and the priest and I stood together. You might suppose that the priest of a goddess named Xochiquétzal would at least be cleanly in his habits, but that one was as professionally unkempt and unwashed and unsavory as any other. And, like any other, he took the occasion to make his speech a tediously long one, more full of dire warnings about the pitfalls of marriage than any mention of its pleasures. But he finally got done and Ahuítzotl spoke, to the three besotted and sentimentally smirking old men seated at his feet, just a few words and to the point:

"Lords pochtéca, your fellow trader wishes to take a wife. Regard this xelolóni I give you. It is the sign that Chicóme-Xochitl Tliléctic-Mixtli desires to sever himself from the days of his irresponsible youth. Take it and set him free to be a full-grown man."

The scalpless one of the three accepted the xelolóni, which

was a small household hatchet. Had I been an ordinary commoner getting married, the hatchet would have been a simple
utilitarian tool of wood shaft and flint head, but that one had
a solid silver haft and a blade of fine jadestone. The old fellow
brandished it, belched loudly, and said:

"We have heard, Lord Speaker, we and all present have
heard the wish of young Tliléctic-Mixtli: that henceforth he
bear all the duties, responsibilities, and privileges of manhood.
As you and he desire, so let it be."

He made a drunkenly dramatic chopping motion with the
hatchet—and very nearly chopped off the remaining foot of his
one-footed colleague. The three of them then stood and bore
away the symbolic cutting tool, the one-footed man dangling
and hopping between the other two, and all of them lurching
as they departed from the big room. The Givers were no sooner
out of sight than we heard the clamor of Zyanya's arrival at
the palace: the accumulated crowd of city commoners outside
the building calling to her: "Happy girl! Fortunate girl!"

The arrangements had been well timed, for she was coming
just at sundown, as was proper. The ballroom, which had been
getting gradually darker during the preliminary ceremony, began to glow with golden light as servants went about lighting
the pine-splint torches angled out at intervals from the painted
walls. When the hall was blazing bright, Zyanya stepped
through the entranceway, escorted by two of the palace ladies.
It was allowable for a woman at her wedding—just that one
time in her life—to beautify herself to the utmost by using all
the cosmetic arts of a courtesan auyaními: coloring her hair,
lightening her skin, reddening her lips. But Zyanya had no
need for any such artifice, and had used none. She wore a
simple blouse and skirt of virginal pale yellow and she had
selected, for the traditional festoon of feathers along her arms
and calves, the long plumes of some black-and-white bird,
obviously to repeat and accentuate the white-streaked black of
her long, flowing hair.

The two women led her to the dais, through the murmurously
admiring crowd, and she and I stood facing each other, she
looking shy, I looking solemn, as the occasion required. The
priest took from an assistant two instruments and handed one
of them to each of us: a golden chain from which depended

a perforated golden ball, inside which burned a bit of copáli incense. I raised my chain and swung the ball around Zyanya, leaving a fragrant loop of blue smoke hanging in the air about her shoulders. Then I hunched down a bit, and she stood on tiptoe to do the same to me. The priest took back the censers and bade us sit down side by side.

At that point, there should have come forward from the crowd our relatives and friends bearing presents. Neither of us had any kinfolk in attendance, so there came only Blood Glutton, Cozcatl, and a delegation from The House of Pochtéca. They all, in turn, kissed the earth to us and laid before us their varied gifts—for Zyanya items of wearing apparel: blouses, skirts, shawls, and the like, all of the finest quality; for me also an assortment of clothing, plus an estimable armory: a well-wrought maquáhuitl, a dagger, a sheaf of arrows.

When the gift bearers had retired, it was the moment for Ahuítzotl and one of Zyanya's escorting noblewomen to take turns at chanting the routine fatherly and motherly advice to the couple about to be married. In an unemotional monotone, Ahuítzotl warned me, among other things, never to be still abed when I heard the cry of the Early Bird, Pápan, but to be already up and doing. Zyanya's surrogate mother recited a long list of wifely duties—everything, it seemed to me, including the lady's favorite recipe for making tamáltin. As if that had been a signal, a servant came bearing a fresh, steaming platter of the maize-and-meat rolls, and set it before us.

The priest gestured, and Zyanya and I each picked up a tamáli and fed it to each other, which, if you have never tried it, is no easy matter. I got my chin well greased, and Zyanya her nose, but we each got at least a token bite of the other's offering. While we were doing that, the priest began another long, rote harangue, the which I will not bore you with. It concluded in his bending down, taking a corner of my mantle and a corner of Zyanya's blouse, and knotting them together.

We were married.

The quiet music suddenly boomed loud and exultant, and a shout went up from the assembled guests, as all the ceremonial stiffness relaxed into conviviality. Servants dashed about the hall, dispensing to all the separate dinner cloths platters of tamáltin and new jugs of octli and chocolate. Every guest was expected to gobble and guzzle until the torches burned out at dawn or until the males among them fell over unconscious and were borne home by their women and slaves. Zyanya and I would eat but daintily, and then would be led discreetly— everybody pretending we were invisible—to our wedding chamber, which was an upstairs suite in the palace, lent to us by Ahuítzotl. But at that point I departed from custom.

"Excuse me one moment, my dear," I whispered to Zyanya, and stepped down from the dais into the room, the Revered Speaker and the priest regarding me with puzzled eyes and open mouths showing half-chewed tamáltin.

In my long life, no doubt I have been hated by many persons; I do not know how many. I have never cared enough even to try remembering and counting them. But I had then, that night, in that room, one mortal enemy, one enemy sworn and implacable and already bloody-handed. Chimáli had mutilated and murdered others close to me. His next victim, even before myself, would be Zyanya. That he should attend our wedding was his threat of it and his defiance of my doing anything to stop it.

As I walked in search of him, winding my way among the quadrangles of seated guests, their chattering dwindled to a wondering silence. Even the musicians lowered their instruments to pay attention. The room's silence was finally broken by the crowd's collective gasp, when I swung backhanded and knocked away the golden goblet Chimáli was raising to his mouth. It rang musically as it bounced off his own wall painting.

"Do not drink too much," I said, and everyone heard. "You will want a clear head in the morning. At dawn, Chimáli, in the wood of Chapultépec. Just the two of us, but any kind and number of weapons you like. To the death."

He gave me a look compounded of loathing, contempt, and some amusement, then glanced about at his goggling neighbors. A private challenge he could have refused, or set conditions to, or even warded off by abasing himself. But that challenge had been prefaced by an insulting blow; it had been seen and heard by every leading citizen of Tenochtítlan. He shrugged, then reached for someone else's cup of octli, raised it in wry salute to me, and said clearly, "Chapultépec. At dawn. To the death." He drained the drink, stood up, and stalked out of the ballroom.

When I returned to the dais, the crowd began its buzz and chatter again behind me, though sounding somewhat subdued and aghast. Zyanya gazed at me with bewildered eyes, but to her credit she asked no question, she made no complaint about my having turned a gladsome occasion into something otherwise. The priest, however, gave me a baleful frown and began:

"Most inauspicious, young—"

"Be silent!" snarled the Revered Speaker, and the priest shut his mouth. To me, Ahuítzotl said through his teeth, "Your sudden entry into responsible manhood and espousal has deranged you."

I said, "No, my lord. I am sane and I have sound reason for—"

"Reason!" he interrupted, still without raising his voice, which made him sound more irate than any bellowing could. "Reason for making a public scandal of your own wedding feast? Reason for disrupting a ceremony arranged for you as if you were our own son? Reason for assaulting our personal courtier and invited guest?"

"I am sorry if I have offended my lord," I said, but added obdurately, "My lord would think even less of me if I pretended not to notice an enemy taunting me with his presence."

"Your enemies are your business. Our palace artist is ours. You threaten to kill him. And—look yonder—he has still one whole wall of this room to decorate."

I said, "He may well finish it yet, Lord Speaker. Chimáli was a much more accomplished fighter than I when we were together in The House of Building Strength."

"So, instead of losing our palace artist, we lose the counselor on whose advice and the plaintiff on whose behalf we are preparing to march into alien country." Still in that measured, menacing low voice, he said, "Take warning now, and a warning from the Uey-Tlatoáni named Water Monster is not to be taken lightly. If either of you dies tomorrow—our valued painter Chimáli or the Mixtli who has occasionally given us valuable counsel—it will be Mixtli who is held to blame. It will be Mixtli who pays, even if he is the dead one."

Slowly, so that I should not mistake his meaning, he turned his beetling glare from me to Zyanya.

* * *

She said in a small voice, "We should be praying, Záa."

And I said honestly, fervently, "I *am* praying."

Our chambers contained every necessary furnishing except a bed, which would not be provided until the fourth day after the ceremony. The intervening days and nights we were supposed to spend fasting—refraining both from nourishment and from consummation of our union—meanwhile praying to our various favorite gods that we would be good for each other and good to each other, that our marriage might be a happy one.

But I was silently engaged in a rather different kind of prayer. I was asking, of whatever gods there might be, only that Zyanya and I survive the morrow to *have* a marriage. I had put myself in some precarious situations before, but never one where, no matter what I did, I could not possibly triumph. If, through prowess or sheer good fortune or because my tonáli decreed it, I should succeed in killing Chimáli, then I would have two choices. I could return to the palace and let Ahuítzotl execute me for having instigated the duel. Or I could flee and leave Zyanya to take the punishment, doubtless a terrible one. The third foreseeable circumstance was that Chimáli would kill me, through his superior skill at weaponry or because I withheld my own killing blow or because his tonáli was the stronger. In which case, I would be beyond Ahuítzotl's punishment and he would exercise his wrath on my dear Zyanya. The duel must result in one of those three eventualities, and every one of them was unthinkable. But no, there was one other possibility: suppose I simply failed to appear in the wood of Chapultépec at dawn. . . .

While I thought about the unthinkable, Zyanya was quietly unpacking the little luggage we had brought. Her cry of delight roused me from my gloomy reverie. I lifted my head from my hands to see that she had found in one of my panniers the old clay figurine of Xochiquétzal, that which I had preserved ever since my sister's misfortune.

"The goddess who watched while we were married," Zyanya said, smiling.

"The goddess who fashioned you for me," I said. "She who governs all love and beauty. I meant her statuette to be a surprise gift."

"Oh, it is," she said loyally. "You are forever surprising me."

"Not all my surprises have been pleasant ones for you, I fear. Like my challenge to Chimáli tonight."

"I did not know his name, but it seems I have seen the man before. Or someone very like him."

"You saw the man himself, though I imagine he did not look quite such an elegant courtier on the earlier occasion. Let me explain, and I hope you will understand why I had to mar our wedding ceremony, why I could not postpone doing what I did—and what I must yet do."

My instant explanation of the Xochiquétzal figurine, a few moments before—that I had intended it as a memento of our wedding—was the first outright lie I had ever told Zyanya. But when I told her of my earlier life, I committed some small lies of omission. I began with Chimáli's first betrayal of me, when he and Tlatli had declined to help save Tzitzitlíni's life, and I left some gaps in my account of *why* my sister's life had been in peril. I told how Chimáli, Tlatli, and I had met again in Texcóco and, omitting some of the uglier details, how I had connived to avenge my sister's death. How, out of some mercy or some weakness, I had been satisfied to let the vengeance fall on Tlatli alone, and let Chimáli escape. How he had since repaid that favor by continuing to molest me and mine. At the last I said, "And you yourself told me how he pretended to aid your mother when—"

Zyanya gasped. "He is the traveler who attended—who *murdered* my mother and your . . ."

"He is," I said, when she paused discreetly there. "And so it happened that, when I saw him sitting arrogantly at our wedding feast, I determined that he should murder no more."

She said, almost fiercely, "Indeed you must face him. And best him, no matter what the Revered Speaker said, or what he does. But may the guards not prevent your leaving the palace at dawn?"

"No. Ahuítzotl does not know of all that I have told you, but he knows this is a matter of honor. He will not hold me back. He will hold you instead. And that is what troubles my heart—not what may happen to me, but how you may suffer for my impetuosity."

Zyanya seemed to resent that remark. "Do you think me less brave than yourself? Whatever happens on the dueling ground, and whatever comes of it afterward, I shall willingly await. There! I have said it. If you stay your hand now, Záa, you are only using me as an excuse. I could not live with you after that."

I smiled ruefully. So the fourth and final choice was closed to me. I shook my head and took her tenderly into my arms. "No," I said with a sigh. "I will not stay my hand."

"I never thought you would," she said, as matter-of-factly as if, in marrying me, she had married an Eagle Knight. "Now there remains not much time before sunrise. Lie here and let me pillow your head. Sleep while you can."

It seemed I had just laid my head on her soft breast when there was a hesitant scratching at the door and Cozcatl's voice called, "Mixtli, the sky pales. It is time."

I stood up, ducked my head in a basin of cold water, and rearranged my rumpled clothes.

"He has already departed for the acáli landing," Cozcatl told me. "Perhaps he intends to spring upon you from ambush."

"Then I will need only weapons for close fighting, not for throwing," I said. "Bring a spear, a dagger, and a maquáhuitl."

Cozcatl hurried off, and I spent a bittersweet few moments saying good-bye to Zyanya, while she spoke words meant to embolden me and reassure me that all would be well. I kissed her one last time and went downstairs to where Cozcatl waited with the arms. Blood Glutton was not present. Since he had been the Master Cuachic teaching both me and Chimáli at The House of Building Strength, it would have been unseemly for him to proffer advice or even moral support to either of us, whatever his own feelings about the duel's outcome.

The palace guards made no move to prevent our going out the gate that led through the Snake Wall into The Heart of the One World. Our sandaled footsteps on the marble paving echoed back and forth from the Great Pyramid and numerous lesser buildings. The plaza looked even more than usually immense in its early morning opal light and emptiness, there being no other people in it except a few priests shambling to their sunrise duties. We left by the opening in the western side of the Snake Wall and went through streets and over canal bridges to the edge of the island nearest the mainland, and at the boat landing I commandeered one of the canoes reserved for palace use. Cozcatl insisted on rowing me across the not very wide expanse of water, to save me tiring my muscles.

Our acáli bumped the bank at the foot of the bluff called Chapultépec, at the point where the aqueduct vaulted from the hill toward the city. High above our heads, the carved visages of the Revered Speakers Ahuítzotl, Tixoc, Axayácatl, and the first Motecuzóma stared from the otherwise rough natural rock. Another canoe was already there, its tie rope held by a palace page, who pointed to a rise of ground to one side of the cliff and said politely, "He awaits you in the wood, my lord."

I told Cozcatl, "You stay here with the other arms bearer. You will soon know whether I have further need of you or not." I stuck the obsidian dagger in the waist of my loincloth, took the obsidian-edged sword in my right hand and the obsidian-pointed spear in my left. I went to the top of the rise and looked down into the wood.

Ahuítzotl had begun to make a parkland of what had formerly been a forest wilderness. That project would not be completed for several years yet—the baths and fountains and statuary and such—but already the forest had been thinned to leave standing only the incalculably ancient, towering ahuehuétque cypresses and the carpet of grass and wild flowers growing beneath them. That carpet was quite invisible, and the mighty cypresses appeared to stand magically rootless in the pale blue ground mist rising as Tonatíu arose. Chimáli would have been equally invisible to me, had he chosen to crouch somewhere in that mist.

Instead, I saw as soon as I raised my topaz to my eye, he had elected to strip off his garments and lie naked along the length of a thick cypress limb which stretched horizontally from its tree, about half again my height above ground level. Chimáli's outstretched right arm, clutching the haft of a maquáhuitl, was also laid along the limb and pressed close to it. For a moment I was puzzled. Why such an easily seen ambuscade? Why was he unclothed?

Then I grasped his intention, and I must have grinned like a coyote. At the reception the night before, Chimáli had not seen me make that one use of my seeing crystal, and obviously no one had thought to inform him of the new and artificial improvement to my vision. He had doffed his colorful clothes so that his skin would blend with the brown of the cypress bough. He believed that there he would be invisible to his old friend Mole, his fellow student Fogbound, while I went groping and searching for him among the trees. He had only to lie there in safety until, in my halting and squinting progress, I finally passed beneath. Then he would hack downward with the maquáhuitl, a single stroke, and I would be dead.

For an instant, I felt it was almost unfair of me to have taken advantage of my crystal to descry his whereabouts. But then I thought: he must have been much pleased by my stipulation that we two meet alone. After disposing of me, he could dress and go back to the city, and tell how we had met bravely face to face, and what a savage and knightly duel we had fought, before he finally overpowered me. If I knew Chimáli, he would even inflict a few minor cuts on himself to make the story more credible. So I had no more compunction about what I was going to do. I tucked the topaz back inside my mantle, dropped my maquáhuitl to the ground and, both hands on the shaft of my leveled spear, went down into the misty wood.

I walked slowly and warily, as he would expect of the inept fighter Fogbound, my knees bent, my eyes narrowed to slits, like a mole's. Of course, I did not go directly to his tree, but began quartering the wood from well to one side of it. Every time I approached a tree, I would reach far forward and jab my spear clumsily around the opposite side of its trunk before moving farther. However, I had made mental note of Chimáli's lurking place and the position of the limb on which he lay. As I neared the spot, I began gradually to raise my spear from the horizontal until I was carrying it upright in front of me, point uppermost, as Blood Glutton had taught me to carry it in the jungle, to discourage jaguars lying in wait to pounce. With my weapon in that position, I insured that he could not slash down at me from my front; he would have to wait until the spear point and I had passed a little way under him, and then strike at the back of my head or neck.

I approached his tree as I had all the others, crouched and slowly stalking, continuously turning my frowning, peering face from side to side, keeping my squinted gaze always level, never once looking up. The moment I came under his limb, I jabbed upward two-handed, with all my strength.

I had a heart-stopping moment then. The spear point never touched him; it stopped short of meeting any flesh; it hit with a *thunk!* against the wood of the limb and sent a numbing shock through both my arms. But Chimáli must, at that same instant, have been swinging his maquáhuitl, thus simultaneously loosing his grip on the limb and putting himself off balance. For the blow I gave the limb shook him off it; he landed just behind me, flat on his back. The breath whooshed from his lungs as the maquáhuitl jumped from his hand. I whirled and clubbed him in the head with the butt end of my spear shaft, and he lay still.

I bent over him to note that he was not dead, but that he would be unconscious for some little while yet. So I simply picked up his sword and went back over the rise, retrieving my own dropped sword on the way, and rejoined the two young arms bearers. Cozcatl gave a small cheer when he saw me carrying my opponent's weapon: "I knew you would slay him, Mixtli!"

"I did not," I said. "I left him insensible, but if he wakes he will have suffered nothing worse than a bad headache. If he wakes. I told you once, long ago, that when the time came for Chimáli's execution you would decide the manner of it." I plucked my dagger from my waistband and handed it to him. The page watched us with horrified fascination. I waved Cozcatl toward the wood. "You will easily find where he lies. Go, and give him what he deserves."

Cozcatl nodded and marched over the rise and out of sight. The page and I waited. His face was discolored and contorted, and he kept swallowing in an endeavor not to be sick. When Cozcatl returned, before he got close enough to speak, we could see that his dagger was no longer a glittery black, it was a gleaming red.

But he shook his head as he approached, and said, "I let him live, Mixtli."

I exclaimed, "What? Why?"

"I overheard the Revered Speaker's threatening words last night," he said apologetically. "With Chimáli helpless before me, I was much tempted, but I did not kill him. Since he still lives, the Lord Speaker cannot vent *too* much anger on you. I took from Chimáli only these."

He held out one clenched hand and opened it so I could see the two mucously glistening globules and the flabby pink thing, raggedly cut off about halfway down its length.

I said to the miserable and retching page, "You heard. He lives. But he will require your help to return to the city. Go and stanch his bleeding and wait for him to awaken."

"So the man Chimáli lives," said Ahuítzotl frostily. "If you can call it life. So you complied with our prohibition against killing him, by not *quite* killing him entirely. So you blithely expect that we will not be outraged and vengeful as we promised." I prudently said nothing. "We grant that you obeyed our spoken word, but you understood very well our unspoken *meaning,* and what of that? What earthly use is the man to us in his present condition?"

I had by then resignedly come to expect that in any interview with the Uey-Tlatoáni I would be the focus of a bulging-eyed glare. Others quailed and quaked before that awful look, but I was beginning to take it as a matter of course.

I said, "Perhaps, if the Revered Speaker would now hear my reasons for having challenged the palace artist, my lord might be inclined to leniency regarding the tragic outcome of the duel."

He merely grunted, but I took it as permission to speak. I told him much the same history I had told Zyanya, only omitting *all* mention of the events in Texcóco, since they had so intimately involved Ahuítzotl's murder of my newborn son, hence my fears for my newly-wed wife. Ahuítzotl grunted again, then meditated on the matter—or so I assumed from his scowling silence—then finally said:

"We did not engage the artist Chimáli because of or in spite of his despicable amorality, his sexual proclivities, his vindictive nature, or his tendency to treachery. We engaged him only to paint pictures, which he did better than any other painter of these or bygone days. You may not have slain the man, but you most certainly slew the artist. Now that his eyeballs have been plucked out, he can no longer paint. Now that his tongue has been cut out, he cannot even impart to any of our other artists the secret of compounding those unique colors he invented."

I remained silent, only thinking to myself, with satisfaction, that neither could the voiceless, sightless Chimáli ever reveal to the Revered Speaker that it was I who had caused the public disgrace and execution of his eldest daughter.

He went on, as if summing up the case for and against me, "We are still wroth with you, but we must accept as mitigation the reasons you have given for your behavior. We must accept that this was an unavoidable affair of honor. We must also accept that you did take pains to obey our word, in letting the man Chimáli live; and our word we likewise keep. You are reprieved from any penalty."

I said gratefully and sincerely, "Thank you, my lord."

"However, since we made our threat in public and the whole population by now knows of it, *someone* must atone for the loss of our palace artist." I held my breath, thinking that surely he must mean Zyanya. But he said indifferently, "We will give it thought. The blame will be put upon some expendable nonentity, but all will know that our threats are not empty ones."

I let out my pent breath. Heartless though it may sound, I could not really feel much guilt or sorrow on behalf of some unknown victim, perhaps a troublesome slave, who would die at that proud tyrant's whim.

Ahuítzotl said in conclusion, "Your old enemy will be evicted from the palace as soon as the physician has finished tending his wounds. Chimáli will henceforth have to scavenge a living as a common street beggar. You have had your revenge, Mixtli. Any man would rather be dead than be what you have made of that one. Now begone from our sight, lest we have a change of heart. Go to your woman, who is probably worried about your welfare."

No doubt she was, about her own as well as mine, but Zyanya was a woman of the Cloud People; she would not have let her concern be evident to any passing palace attendant. When I entered our chambers, her placid expression did not change until I said, "It is done. He is finished. And I am pardoned." Then she wept, and then she laughed, and then she wept again, and then she plunged into my arms and held to me as if she would never let me go again.

When I had told her all that had happened, she said, "You must be near dead from fatigue. Lie down again and—"

"I will lie down," I said, "but not to sleep. I must tell you something. A narrow escape from danger seems always to have a certain effect on me."

"I know," she said, smiling. "I can feel it. But Záa, we are supposed to be praying."

I said, "There is no more sincere form of prayer than loving."

"We have no bed."

"The floor matting is softer than a mountainside. And I am eager to hold you to a promise you made."

"Ah, yes, I remember," she said. And slowly—not reluctantly, but tantalizingly—she disrobed for me, discarding everything she wore except the pearly white chain necklace the artisan Tuxtem had hung about her neck in Xicalánca.

Have I already told you, my lords, that Zyanya was like a shapely vessel of burnished copper, brimming with honey, set in the sun? The beauty of her face I had known for some time, but the beauty of her body I had known only by touch. But then I saw it and—she had been right in her promise—it might have been our first time together. I literally ached to possess her.

When she stood naked before me, all the womanly parts of her seemed to thrust forward and upward, ardently offering themselves. Her breasts were set high and tilted, and on their pale copper globes her cacao-colored areolas protruded like lesser globes, and from them her nipples extended, asking to be kissed. Her tipíli was also set high and forward so that, even though she stood with her long legs modestly pressed together, those soft lips parted just the slightest bit at their upper joining, to allow a glimpse of the pink pearl of her xacapíli, and at that moment it was moist, like a pearl just out of the sea. . . .

Enough.

Although His Excellency is not now present, and so cannot be driven out by his usual revulsion, I will not recount what happened then. I have been frankly explicit about my relations with other women, but Zyanya was my beloved wife, and I think I will miserly hoard most of my memories of her. Of all that I have possessed in my life, my memories are the only things remaining to me. Indeed, I believe that memories are the only real treasure any human can hope to hold always. That was her name. Always.

But I wander. And our delicious lovemaking was not the last event of that notably eventful day. Zyanya and I were lying in each other's arms, I just falling into sleep, when there came a scratching at the door like that of Cozcatl earlier. Foggily hoping I was not being summoned to fight another duel, I struggled to my feet, slung my mantle about me, and went to investigate. It was one of the palace under-stewards.

"Forgive the interruption of your devotions, lord scribe, but a swift-messenger brings an urgent request from your young friend Cozcatl. He asks that you make all haste to the house of your old friend Extli-Quani. It seems the man is dying."

"Nonsense," I said in a furred voice. "You must have mistaken the message."

"I hope so, my lord," he said stiffly, "but I fear I did not."

Nonsense, I said again—to myself—but I began hurriedly to dress while I explained my errand to my wife. Nonsense, I kept telling myself; Blood Glutton could not be dying. Death could not get its teeth into that leathery, sinewy old warrior. Death could not suck him dry of his still-vital juices. Old he might be, but a man still so full of manly appetites was not old enough for death. Nevertheless, I made all haste, and the steward had an acáli waiting at the courtyard bank of the canal, to take me faster than I could run to the Móyotlan quarter of the city.

Cozcatl was waiting at the door of the yet unfinished house, and he was anxiously wringing his hands. "The priest of Filth Eater is with him now, Mixtli," he said in a frightened whisper. "I hope he will have breath enough left to tell you good-bye."

"Then he *is* dying?" I moaned. "But of what? He was in the prime of health at the banquet last night. He ate like a whole flock of vultures. He kept running his hand up the skirts of the serving girls. How could something have stricken him so suddenly?"

"I suppose the soldiers of Ahuítzotl always strike suddenly."

"What?"

"Mixtli, I thought the four palace guards had come for me, because of what I did to Chimáli. But they brushed me aside and burst in upon Blood Glutton. He had his maquáhuitl handy, as he always does, so he did not succumb without a fight, and three of the four were bleeding copiously when they departed. But one sweep of a spear blade had laid the old man open."

Realization made a cold shudder rack my whole body. Ahuítzotl had promised to execute an expendable nonentity in my stead; he must have chosen even while he told me that. He had once described Blood Glutton as being overage for anything more useful than playing nursemaid to my trading expeditions. And he had said that *all* must know that his threats were not empty ones. Well, the all included me. I had congratulated myself on my reprieve from punishment, and I had celebrated it by frolicking with Zyanya, and at that very time *this* was being done. It was not meant just to horrify and grieve me. It was meant to dispel any illusions I might entertain of my own indispensability, to warn me never again to flout the wishes of the implacable despot Ahuítzotl.

"The old man bequeaths the house and all his other possessions to you, boy," said a new voice. It was the priest, materializing in the doorway, addressing Cozcatl. "I have taken down his testament and I will bear witness—"

I shoved past him and through the front rooms into the rearmost. Its still unplastered stone walls were splashed with blood and my old friend's pallet was drenched with it, though I could see no wound upon him. He wore only a loincloth, and he lay sprawled on his belly, his grizzled head turned in my direction, his eyes closed.

I threw myself down on the pallet beside him, unmindful of the gore, and said urgently, "Master Cuachic, it is your student Fogbound!"

The eyes slowly opened. Then one of them closed briefly again, in a wink accompanied by a weak smile. But the signs of death were there: his once piercing eyes gone an ashy dull color around the pupils, his once fleshy nose gone thin and sharp like a blade.

"I am sorry for this," I choked out.

"Do not be," he said faintly and in hard-forced little gasps.

"I died fighting. There are worse ways. And I am spared them. I wish you . . . as good an end. Good-bye, young Mixtli."

"Wait!" I cried, as if I could command him to. "It was Ahuítzotl who ordered this, because I vanquished Chimáli. But you had no part in the affair. You did not even take sides. Why should the Revered Speaker take vengeance on *you?*"

"Because it was I," he labored to say, "who taught you both to kill." He smiled again, as his eyes closed. "I taught well . . . did I not?"

Those were his last words, and no one could have pronounced a more appropriate epitaph. But I refused to believe he would speak no more. I thought perhaps his breathing might have been pinched off by the position in which he lay; it might resume if he reposed more comfortably on his back. Desperately, I took hold of him and lifted and turned him, and all his insides fell out.

Though I mourned Blood Glutton and seethed with anger at his assassination, I could take some consolation in a fact that Ahuítzotl would never know. In trading blow for vengeful blow, I still had precedence of him. I had deprived him of a daughter. So I made a determined effort to swallow my bile, to put the past behind me, to begin hopefully preparing for a future free of further bloodshed and heartache and rancor and risk. Zyanya and I turned our energies to the building of a home for ourselves. The site we had selected had been purchased by the Revered Speaker as his wedding present to us. I had not declined the offering at the time, and it would have been impolitic for me to spurn it even after our mutual hostilities, but in truth I had no need of gifts.

The pochtéca elders had marketed my first expedition's cargo of plumes and crystals with such profitable acumen that, even after dividing the proceeds with Cozcatl and Blood Glutton, I was affluent enough to live out a comfortable existence without ever having to engage in trade again, or lift my hand to any other kind of labor. But then my second delivery of foreign goods had astronomically increased my wealth. If the burning crystals had been a notable commercial success, the carved-tooth artifacts caused a positive sensation and a frenzy of bidding among the nobility. The prices brought by those objects could have enabled me and Cozcatl to settle down, if we had so wished, and become as bloated, complacent, and sedentary as our elders in The House of Pochtéca.

The homesite Zyanya and I had chosen was in Ixacuálco, the best residential quarter of the island, but it was occupied by only a small, drab house of mud-brick adobe. I engaged an architect, told him to pull the thing down and to construct a solid limestone edifice that would be both a fine home and a pleasurable sight for the passerby, but not ostentatious in either respect. Since the plot was, like all on the island, a narrow and constricted one, I told him to achieve commodiousness by building upward. I specified a roof garden, indoor sanitary closets with the necessary flushing arrangements, and a false wall in one room with ample hiding space behind it.

Meanwhile, without calling me in for further consultation, Ahuítzotl marched south toward Uaxyácac, leading not an immense army but a picked troop of his best warriors, at most a mere five hundred men. He left his Snake Woman as temporary occupant of the throne, but took with him as his under-commander a youth whose name is familiar to you Spaniards. He was Motecuzóma Xocóyotzin, which is to say the Younger Lord Motecuzóma; he was, in fact, about a year younger than myself. He was Ahuítzotl's nephew, a son of the earlier Uey-Tlatoáni Axayácatl, hence a grandson of the first and great Motecuzóma. He had until that time been a high priest of the war god Huitzilopóchtli, but that expedition was his first taste of actual war. He was to have many more, for he quit the priesthood to become a professional soldier and, of course, at command rank.

About a month after the troop's departure, Ahuítzotl's swift-messengers began to return at intervals to the city, and the Snake Woman made their reports publicly known. From the news of the first returning messengers, it was obvious that the Revered Speaker was following the advice I had given him. He had sent advance notice of his approach and, as I had predicted, the Bishósu of Uaxyácac had welcomed his forces and had contributed an equal number of warriors. Those combined Mexíca and Tzapotéca forces invaded the seacoast warrens of The Strangers and made short work of them—slaughtering enough that the remainder surrendered and bowed to the levy of their long-guarded purple dye.

But the later arriving messengers brought less happy news. The victorious Mexíca were quartered in Tecuantépec, while Ahuítzotl and his counterpart ruler Kosi Yuela conferred there on matters of state. Those soldiers had long been accustomed to their right to pillage whatever nation they defeated, so they were disgruntled and angered when they learned that their leader was ceding the only visible plunder—the precious purple—to the ruler of that same nation. To the Mexíca it seemed that they had waged a battle for the benefit of nobody but the very country they had invaded. Since Ahuítzotl was not the sort of man to justify his actions to his underlings and thereby quell their unrest, his Mexíca simply rebelled against all military restraint. They broke ranks and broke discipline and ran wild through Tecuantépec, looting, raping, and burning.

That mutiny could have disrupted the delicate negotiations intended to effect an alliance between our nation and Uaxyácac. But fortunately, before the rampaging Mexíca could kill anyone of importance, and before the Tzapotéca troops intervened—which would have meant a small war right there—Ahuítzotl bawled his horde to order and promised that, immediately upon their return to Tenochtítlan, he would personally pay to every least yaoquízqui of them, from his own personal treasury, a sum well in excess of what they could hope to loot from their host country. The soldiers knew Ahuítzotl for a man of his word, so that was sufficient to put down the mutiny. The Revered Speaker also paid to Kosi Yuela and the bishósu of Tecuantépec a sizable indemnity for the damage that had been done.

The reports of mayhem in Zyanya's natal city naturally worried her and me. None of the swift-messengers bearing news could tell us whether our sister Béu Ribé or her inn had been in the path of the spoilers. We waited until Ahuítzotl and his troop returned, and I made some inquiries among the officers, but still could not ascertain if anything bad had happened to Waiting Moon.

"I am most anxious about her, Záa," said my wife.

"It seems there is nothing to be discovered except in Tecuantépec itself."

She said hesitantly, "I could stay here and continue to direct our house builders, if you would consider . . ."

"You need not even ask. I had planned to revisit those parts in any case."

She blinked in surprise. "You had? Why?"

"A matter of unfinished business," I told her. "It could have waited a while, but the question of Béu's well-being means that I go now."

Zyanya was quick to understand, and she said, "You are going again to the mountain that walks in the sea! You must not, my love! Those barbarian Zyú nearly killed you last time—!"

I laid a finger gently across her lips. "I am going south to seek news of our sister, and that is the truth, and that is the only truth you will tell to anyone who inquires. Ahuítzotl must not hear any rumor that I have any other objective."

She nodded, but said unhappily, "Now I will have two loved ones to worry about."

"This one will return safe, and I will look for Béu. If she has come to harm, I will make it right. Or, if she prefers, I will bring her back here with me. And I will bring back some other precious things as well."

Of course Béu Ribé was my foremost concern and my immediate reason for going back to Uaxyácac. But you will have perceived, reverend scribes, that I was also about to consummate a plan I had carefully laid in train. When I suggested to the Revered Speaker that he raid The Strangers and make them agree to surrender all the purple dye they might forever after collect, I had *not* mentioned to him the vast treasure of that substance they had already stored in the cave of the Sea God. From my inquiries among the returned officers I knew that even in defeat The Strangers had not handed it over or volunteered any hint of its existence. But I knew of it, and I knew the grotto where it was hidden, and I had arranged that Ahuítzotl should subdue the Zyú sufficiently that it would be possible for me to go and get that fabulous hoard for myself.

I might have taken Cozcatl with me, except that he was also

busy with house building, completing the one he had inherited from Blood Glutton. So I merely asked his permission to borrow a few items from the old warrior's wardrobe there. Then I went about the city and hunted up seven of Blood Glutton's former companions-in-arms. They were younger than he had been, though some years older than myself. They were still sturdy and strong, and when, after swearing them to secrecy, I explained what I had in mind, they were keen for the adventure.

Zyanya helped spread the story that I was going out to seek the whereabouts of her sister and that, as long as I was traveling, I was making a trade expedition of it as well. So when I and the seven plodded south along the Coyohuácan causeway, we excited no comment or curiosity. Of course, had anyone looked at us very closely, he might have wondered at the incidence of scars, bent noses, and bulbous ears among the porters I had chosen. Had he inspected the men's long packs of wrapped matting, ostensibly full of goods to trade, he would have found that they contained—besides traveling rations and quills of gold dust—only leather shields, every kind of weapon more wieldy than the long spear, various colors of war paint, feathers, and other regalia of a miniature army.

We continued along the southbound trade route, but only until we were well beyond Quaunáhuac. Then we abruptly turned off to the right, along a less-used westbound route, the shortest way to the sea. Since that route led us, for most of our way, through the southernmost areas of Michihuácan, we would have been in trouble if anyone *had* challenged us and examined our packs. We would have been taken for Mexíca spies and instantly executed—or not so instantly. Though the several attempted invasions by our armies in times past had all been repulsed by the Purémpecha's superior weapons of some mysteriously hard and sharp metal, every Purémpe was still forever on guard against any Mexícatl's entering his land with dubious motive.

I might remark that Michihuácan, Land of the Fishermen, was what we Mexíca called it, as you Spaniards now call it New Galicia, whatever that means. To its natives, it has various names in various areas—Xalísco, Nauyar Ixú, Kuanáhuata, and others—but in total it is called Tzintzuntzaní, Where There Are Hummingbirds, after its capital city of the same name.

The language is called Poré and, during that journey and later ones, I learned as much as I could of it—of them, I should say, since Poré has as many variant local dialects as does Náhuatl. I know enough Poré, anyway, to wonder why you Spaniards insist on calling the Purémpecha the Tarascans. You seem to have got that name from the Poré word taráskue, which a Purémpe uses to designate himself as an aloof "distant relation" of all neighboring other peoples. But no matter; I have had more than enough different names myself. I collected yet another in that land: Dark Cloud being there rendered Anikua Pakapeti.

Michihuácan was and is a vast and rich country, as rich as the domain of the Mexíca ever was. Its Uandákuari, or Revered Speaker, reigned over—or at least collected tribute from—a region stretching from the fruit orchards of Xichú in the eastern Otomí lands to the trading port of Potámkuaro on the southern ocean. And, though the Purémpecha were constantly on guard against military encroachment by us Mexíca, they did not balk at exchanging their riches for ours. Their traders came to our Tlaltelólco market. They even sent swift-messengers daily bearing fresh fish for the delectation of our nobles. In return, our traders were allowed to travel throughout Michihuácan unmolested, as I and my seven pretended porters did.

Had we really been of a mind to barter along the way, we could have secured many valuable things: oyster-heart pearls; pottery of rich glazes; utensils and ornaments made of copper, silver, shell, and amber; the brilliant lacquerware that could be found nowhere else but in Michihuácan. Those lacquered objects, intense black etched with gold and colors, might take an artisan months or years to make, since they varied in size from simple trays to immense folding screens.

We travelers could have acquired any local product except the mystery metal of which I have spoken. No outlander was ever allowed a glimpse of that; even the weapons made of it were kept locked in armories, to be distributed to the soldiery only when they were needed. Since our Mexíca armies had never yet won a single battle against those weapons, none of our warriors had even been able to snatch from the battlefield so much as a dropped Purémpe dagger.

Well, I did no trading, but I and my men did partake of

some of the native foods new to us or seldom available to us—
the honey liquor of Tláchco, for example. The rugged mountain
country around that town literally *hummed* all day long. I could
imagine that I heard the vibration made by the men underground
digging the local silver, but aboveground I definitely could
hear the buzz of the swarms and clouds and skeins of wild bees
among the numberless flowers on those heights. And while the
men scratched for the buried silver, their women and children
worked at collecting the golden honey of those bees. Some of
it they merely strained clear and sold for sweetening. Some of
it they let dry in the sun until it became crystalline and sweeter
yet. Some of the honey they converted—by a method kept as
secret as that of making the killer metal—into a drink they
called chápari, which was far more delicious and far more
potent in its effect than the sour octli we Mexíca knew so well.

Since the chápari, like the metal, was never exported outside
Michihuácan, I and my men drank as much as we could while
we were there. We also feasted on Michihuácan's lake and
river fish, frogs' legs and eels, whenever we spent a night in
a travelers' hostel. As a matter of fact, we got rather weary of
aquatic fare after a while, but those people have peculiar strictures against killing practically every edible game animal. A
Purémpe will not hunt deer because he believes them to be
manifestations of the sun god, and that is because, to his eyes,
the male deer's antlers resemble the sun's beams. Not even
squirrels can be trapped or blowpiped, because the Purémpecha
priests, as filthy and shaggy as ours, were called tiuímencha,
and that word means "black squirrels." So most of the meals
we took at inns were, when not fish, either wild or domestic
fowl.

We were offered rather more of a choice *after* we had eaten.
I believe I have mentioned the Purémpecha's attitude regarding
sexual practices. An outlander might call it vilely loose or
tolerantly broadminded, depending on his own attitude, but it
certainly catered to every conceivable taste. Each time we finished our meal at an inn, the landlord would inquire of me and
then my bearers, "Will you have a male or female sweet?" I
did not answer for my men; I was paying them enough that
they could indulge as they chose. But, with Zyanya waiting
back home, I was not inclined to sample the offerings of every

new country I visited, as I had done in my bachelor days. I invariably replied to the innkeeper, "Neither, thank you," and the innkeeper would persist, without a blink or a blush, "Would you prefer green fruit, then?"

It may really have been necessary for a pleasure-seeking traveler to specify the precise kind of bedmate he wanted— grown woman or man, young girl or boy—for in Michihvácan it is sometimes hard for a stranger to tell which sex is which, because the Purémpecha observe another peculiar practice, or did in those days. The folk of every class higher than slaves depilated their body of every removable hair. They shaved or plucked or otherwise scoured clean all the hair from their head, the eyebrows from above their eyes, any slightest trace of fuzz from beneath their arms or between their legs. Men, women, and children, they had absolutely no hair but their eyelashes. And, in contrast to whatever lewdnesses they may have performed in the nighttime, they went about during the day modestly clothed in several layers of mantles or blouses, which was why it could be difficult to tell the females from the males.

At first, I assumed that the smooth and glossy hairlessness of the Purémpecha represented either their singular notion of beauty or a passing affectation of fashion. But there may have been an obsessively sanitary reason for it. In my study of their language I discovered that Poré has at least eight different words for dandruff and about as many more for louse.

We came to the seacoast at an immense blue harbor protected by enfolding arms of land from the battering of heavy seas and sea storms. There was situated the port village called Patámkuaro by its inhabitants and Acamepúlco by our visiting Mexíca traders, both the Poré and Náhuatl names given because of the great swales of cane and reed growing there. Acamepúlco was a fishing port in its own right, and also a market center for the peoples living along the coast to the east and west, who came in canoes to dispose of their own gleanings from the sea and land: fish, turtles, salt, cotton, cacao, vanilla, other typical products of those Hot Lands.

It was my intention that time not to hire but to buy four roomy, seagoing canoes, and for the eight of us to paddle them, so that we need have no witnesses in attendance. But that was more easily intended than accomplished. The familiar acáli of our home lake district was easily carved from the soft pine that grew there. But a sea canoe was made of the formidably heavy and hard mahogany, and it could take months to make. Almost all the canoes at Acamepúlco had been in use through generations of their owner families, and no family was inclined to sell one, since that would mean a suspension of all profitable fishing or hauling while a replacement was hacked to shape and burned hollow and rasped smooth. But I did finally acquire the four I needed, though it took frustrating days of negotiation, and a far greater outlay of gold dust than I had meant to spend.

And to row them southeastward down the coast, two of us in each, was not so easy either. We all had some experience of lake canoeing, and those big inland lakes could sometimes be roughened by the wind, but we were unaccustomed to waters roiled by currents and tidal surges even in the calm weather that—I thank the gods—attended our sea voyage. Several of those staunch old warriors, whose stomachs had never been turned by all the nauseating horrors of war, were wretchedly sick for the first two or three days. I was not, perhaps because I had been to sea before. But we early learned not to hug the shore where the water's motion was most violent and unpredictable. Though it made us all uneasy to be such a long swim from The One World, we stayed well out beyond the first billows of the breakers, only riding them in at sundown, to spend the nights gratefully on the soft and unheaving sands of the beach.

That beach, as I had seen it do before, gradually darkened from gleaming white to dull gray and then to the sullen black of volcanic sands. And then that beach was interrupted by a suddenly jutting promontory: the mountain that walks in the water. Thanks to my topaz, I espied the mountain from afar, and, it being then late afternoon, I gave the order to make landfall on the beach.

When we were seated around our campfire, I addressed my seven men, repeating the planned actions of our mission on the morrow, and adding, "Some of you may have reservations about raising your hand against a priest, even a priest of an alien god. Do not have. These priests will appear unarmed, and merely vexed at our intrusion, and helpless before our weapons. They are not. Given the least opportunity, they will slay every one of us, and carve us like boar meat, and eat us at their leisure. Tomorrow, when our work has been accomplished, we kill. We kill without mercy or we risk being killed. Remember that, and remember my signals."

When we pushed off through the combers again the next morning, we were no longer a young pochtécatl and his seven elder porters. We were a detachment of seven fearsome Mexíca warriors led by one not very old "old eagle" cuachic. We had undone the packs and donned the war regalia and armed ourselves with the weapons. I carried Blood Glutton's cuachic insignia of shield and guidon staff, and wore his cuachic headdress. The only missing insigne of that rank was a bone through my nose, but my septum had never been pierced for such a thing. The seven soldiers were, like myself, all wearing clean white quilted armor. They had stuck feathers into their hair, which was drawn up into topknots, and had painted fierce many-colored designs on their faces. We each carried a maquáhuitl, a dagger, and a javelin.

Our little fleet paddled boldly toward the mountain promontory, making no attempt at stealth, deliberately intending that the guardians there should see us come. And they did, they were waiting on the mountainside: at least twelve of the evil Zyú priests in their robes of ragged and patchy fur. We did not turn our canoes toward the beach to make an easy landing, but rowed on straight for them.

I do not know whether it was the different season of the year, or whether it was because we approached from the western side of the mountain, but the ocean was in much less turmoil than it had been that time I and the Tzapotécatl boatman came upon it from the east. Nevertheless, the sea was still agitated enough that we unpracticed seafarers might well have splintered the boats and some of ourselves against the rocks, except that a number of the priests leapt down from boulder to boulder and waded into the water and drew our canoes into protected clefts. Of course they did it only because they knew and feared our Mexíca warrior costumes—which was what I had counted on.

We wedged the craft securely there, and I left one soldier to guard them. Then I waved, the gesture including the priests as well as my men, and we all went bounding from rock to rock, through the thunders and spouts of surf, through the clouds and sheets of spray, onto the main slope of the mountain mass. The chief priest of the Sea God stood there, his arms folded across his chest to conceal the fact that he had no hands. He snarled something in his Huave dialect. When I merely raised my eyebrows, he tried Lóochi, and said with bluster:

"What more you Mexíca come for now? We only keepers of god color, and you have that."

"Not all of it," I said in the same tongue.

He seemed slightly shaken by the brusque assurance with which I spoke, but he insisted, *"We* have no more'."

"No, it is *mine* you have," I said. "Some purple for which I paid much gold. Remember? On the day I did *that."* With the flat of my maquáhuitl I slapped his arms apart so that the wrist stumps were visible. He knew me then, and his evil face became even uglier with impotent rage and hatred. The other priests on his either side spread to make a threatening ring about me and my warriors. There were two of them to each of us, but we held our javelins in a bristling circle. I said to the chief, "Lead us to the god's cave."

His mouth worked for a moment, possibly trying other lies, before he said, "Your army emptied the cave of Tiat Ndik."

I motioned to the soldier next to me. He drove his javelin's point deep into the belly of the priest standing at the chief's left. The man shrieked, fell down, and rolled on the ground, clutching his abdomen and continuing to scream.

I said, "That is to show we are in earnest. This is to show that we are in a hurry." I gestured again, and the soldier jabbed again at the fallen man, that time skewering him through the heart and abruptly stopping his cries. "Now," I said to the chief priest, "we will go to the grotto."

He swallowed and said no more; the demonstration had sufficed. With me and my javelin at his back, with my warriors prodding the remaining priests, he led the way over the jumbled rocks and down into the protected hollow and into the cave. I was much relieved to find that the god's place had not been collapsed or buried by the earthquake. When we stood before the purple-daubed heap of stones simulating a statue, I indicated the leather flasks and dyed skeins of yarn heaped all about it, and said to the chief, "Tell your attendants to start carrying all this to our canoes." He swallowed again, but said nothing.

"Tell them," I repeated, "or I cut next at your elbows, and then at your shoulders, and then elsewhere."

He hastily told them something in their language, and whatever he told them was convincing. With no words, but with many a murderous look at me, the unkempt priests began lifting and carrying the flasks and bales of yarn. My men accompanied them to the boats and back to the cave during the many trips it took them to shift the entire store of treasure. Meanwhile, I and the handless priest stayed by the statue, he immobilized by my javelin point held vertically pricking the underside of his jaw. I might have used the time to make him produce the packet of gold he had taken from me on that other occasion, but I did not. I preferred to leave the gold, wherever it was, as payment for what I was doing. It made me feel less like a plunderer and more like a trader concluding a slightly delayed but legitimate transaction.

Not until the last of the flasks were being carried out of the cave did the chief priest speak again, with loathing in his voice: "You defiled holy place before. You angered Tiat Ndik so he sent the zyuüú to punish. He will do so again, or worse. This insult and loss he will not forgive. The Sea God will not let you go free with his purple."

"Oh, perhaps he will," I said carelessly, "if I leave him a sacrifice of another color." At that, I thrust my javelin upward and the point went all the way through jaw and tongue and palate into the man's brain. He fell flat on his back, red blood fountaining from his mouth, and I had to brace my foot against his chin to yank the spear loose.

I heard a concerted shout of consternation behind me. My soldiers were just then bunching all the other priests into the grotto, and they had seen their fallen chief. But I did not have to give any command or signal to my men. Before the priests could recover from their shocked surprise, to fight or flee, they were all dead.

I said, "I promised a sacrifice to that heap of boulders there. Pile all the bodies on and around it."

When that was done, the god statue was no longer purple but shiny red, and the red was spreading over the floor of the whole cave. I do believe that Tiat Ndik must have been satisfied with the offering. We felt no earthquake on our way down to the canoes. Nothing interfered with our loading of the precious cargo or our launching of the then heavier boats. No Sea God churned up his element to prevent our paddling safely away, well out to sea and around the rock-littered waters at the tip of the promontory, out of the land of The Strangers. Without hindrance we rowed on eastward down the coast, and I never again set foot or laid eyes on the mountain that walks in the water.

However, we all eight continued to wear our Mexíca battle costumes for the next few days, while we were still in Huave and Tzapotéca waters, while we passed Nozibe and other seaside villages—and the fishing boats whose puzzled crewmen timidly waved to us—until we were well past the Tecuantépec isthmus and offshore of the Xoconóchco cotton country. There we beached at night in a secluded spot. We burned our armor and other regalia, and buried all but a necessary few of our weapons, and remade our packs, to transport the leather flasks and dyed yarn.

When we rowed away from there in the morning, we were dressed again as a pochtécatl and his porters. We landed later that day, quite openly, at the Mame village of Pijijía, and I sold our canoes—though at a pitifully low price, since the fisher folk there, as everywhere along the coast, already owned all the boats they needed. My men and I, after having been so long afloat, found that we lurched ludicrously when we tried to walk. So we spent two days in Pijijía to get reaccustomed to solid ground—and I had some interesting conversations with the Mame elders—before we took up our packs and moved on inland.

You ask, Fray Toribio, why we had taken such trouble to make that long voyage first in the guise of traders, then as warriors, then as traders again.

Well, the people of Acamepúlco knew that a trader had bought for himself and his porters four seagoing canoes, and the people of Pijijía knew that a similar group had sold similar canoes, and both peoples may have thought the circumstances odd. But those towns were so far distant from each other that they were unlikely ever to compare impressions, and they were both so far distant from the Tzapotéca and Mexíca capitals that

I had little fear of their gossip's ever reaching the ears of Kosi Yuela or Ahuítzotl.

It was inevitable that the Zyú would soon discover the mass murder of their priests and the disappearance of their hoarded purple from the god's cave. Though we had effectually silenced all the witnesses to the actual looting, there was every likelihood that other Zyú onshore had seen our approach to the sacred mountain or our departure from it. They *would* raise a clamor that would eventually be heard by the Bishósu Kosi Yuela and the Revered Speaker Ahuítzotl, and infuriate both of them. But the Zyú could only impute the atrocity to a bunch of battle-arrayed Mexíca warriors. Kosi Yuela might suspect Ahuítzotl of having played a trick to secure the treasure, but Ahuítzotl could honestly say he knew nothing of any Mexíca foragers in that area. I was wagering that the confusion would be such that the seagoing warriors could never be connected to the seagoing traders and that neither could ever be connected to me.

My plan required me to go on from Pijijía across the mountain ranges into the Chiapa country. But, since my porters were so heavily laden, I saw no necessity for them to make that climb. We arranged a day and a place to regroup in the barrens of the isthmus of Tecuantépec; it would give them plenty of time to travel there at a leisurely pace. I told them to avoid villages and encounters with other travelers on the way; a train of loaded tamémime without a leader would have provoked comment, if not their detention for investigation. So, once we were well away from Pijijía, my seven men turned west, staying in the lowlands of the Xoconóchco, while I went north into the mountains.

I came down from them finally, into the meager capital city of Chiapán, and went straight to the workshop of the Master Xibalbá.

"Ah!" said he with delight. "I thought you would be back. So I have been collecting all the quartz possible, and making of it many more burning crystals."

"Yes, they sell well," I told him. "This time I insist on paying you their full value *and* the full worth of your labors on them." I also told him how my topaz, by enhancing my vision, had much enriched my life, and how grateful I was to him.

When I had filled my pack with the cotton-wrapped crystals, I was carrying almost as much weight as each of my absent porters. But I did not stay to rest and refresh myself in Chiapán, because I could hardly have stayed anywhere but at the home of the Macoboö family, and there I should have had to fend off the advances of those two female cousins, which would hardly be polite behavior for a guest. So I paid the Master Xibalbá in gold dust, and hurried on my way.

Some days later, after only a little searching about, I found the spot, remote from any inhabited area, where my men awaited me, sitting around a campfire and a litter of picked-clean bones of armadillos and iguanas and such. There we lingered only long enough for me to get a good night's sleep, and for one of the old campaigners to cook for me my first hot meal since I had left them: a plump pheasant broiled over the fire.

When we came through the eastern reaches of the city of Tecuantépec, we could see the marks of the Mexíca's depredations, though most of the burned-over areas had already been rebuilt. In fact, the city had been rather improved thereby. There were decent and sturdy houses in the once squalid area where I had formerly seen only woebegone shanties—including the one that had been such a landmark in my life. When we made our way through the city to its western edge, however, we found that the rioting soldiers had apparently not carried their rampage that far. The familiar inn was still there. I left my men in the yard while I went in, shouting boisterously:

"Innkeeper! Have you room for a weary pochtécatl and his train?"

Béu Ribé came from some inner room, looking healthy and fit and as beautiful as ever, but her only greeting was to say:

"The Mexíca are not very popular hereabouts these days."

I said, still trying for cordiality, "Surely, Waiting Moon, you make an exception of your own brother, Dark Cloud. Your sister sent me all this way to make sure of your safety. I am happy to see you were unharmed by the troubles."

"Unharmed," she said in a flat voice. "I am happy that you are happy, since it was your doing that the Mexíca soldiers came here. Everyone knows they were sent because of your misadventures with the Zyú, and your failure to seize the purple dye."

That much was true, I admitted. "But you cannot blame me for—"

"There is blame enough for me to share it!" she said bitterly. "I am blamed that this inn ever gave you shelter in the first place!" Then she seemed suddenly to droop. "But I have long been acquainted with scorn, have I not? Yes, you may have a room, and you know where to lodge your porters. The servants will see to you."

She turned and went back to whatever she had been busy with. Hardly a tumultuous or even sisterly welcome, I thought to myself. But the servants got my men and my goods stowed away, and prepared a meal for me. When I had finished it and was smoking a poquíetl, Béu came through the room. She would have kept right on walking, but I took her wrist and stopped her and said:

"I do not deceive myself, Béu. I know you dislike me, and if the recent Mexíca riots made you love me even less—"

She interrupted me, her winglike eyebrows haughtily high. "Dislike? Love? Those are emotions. What right have I to feel *any* emotion toward you, husband of my sister?"

"All right," I said impatiently. "Despise me. Ignore me. But will you not give me some word to take back to Zyanya?"

"Yes. Tell her I was raped by a Mexícatl soldier."

Stunned, I let go of her wrist. I tried to think of something to say, but she laughed and went on:

"Oh, do not say you are sorry. I think I can still claim virginity, for he was exceptionally inept. In his attempt to debase me, he only confirmed my already abysmal opinion of the arrogant Mexíca."

I found my voice, and demanded, "His name. If he has not yet been executed, I will see to it."

"Do you suppose he introduced himself?" she said, laughing again. "I believe he was no soldier of common rank, though I do not know all your military insignia, and my room was dark. But I did recognize the costume he made *me* don for the occasion. I was forced to put soot on my face, and to put on the black, musty robes of a female temple attendant."

"What?" I said, stupefied.

"There was not much conversation, but I realized that mere virginity was not sufficient to excite him. I realized that he could only be aroused by pretending that he violated the holy and untouchable."

"I never heard of such a—"

She said, "Do not try to make excuses for your countryman. And you do not need to commiserate with me. I told you: he was quite unsuited to be a violator of women. His—I believe you call it a tepúli—his tepúli was all knobby and gnarled and bent. The act of penetration—"

"Please, Béu," I said. "This telling cannot be pleasant for you."

"Neither was the experience," she said, as coolly as if describing someone else's. "A woman who must later endure being pointed out as a victim of rape should at least have been well raped. His maimed tepúli would penetrate only as far as its head, or bulb, or whatever you call *that*. And for all his heaving and grunting, it would not stay in. When he finally emitted his juice, it merely dribbled onto my leg. I do not know if there are degrees of virginity, but I *think* I can still call myself a virgin. I also think the man felt even more shamed and mortified than I did. He could not even look me in the eye while I undressed again and he collected those awful temple garments and carried them away with him."

I said helplessly, "He certainly does not sound like—"

"Like the typical, virile Mexícatl male? Like Záa Nayàzú?" She dropped her voice to a whisper. "Tell me truly, Záa, has my little sister ever *really* been satisfied in her marriage bed?"

"Please, Béu. This is unseemly."

She said a profanity: "Gì zyabà! What can be unseemly for a woman already degraded? If you will not tell me, why not show me? Prove to me that you are a fit husband. Oh, do not blush and turn away. Remember, I saw you do it once, but my mother never said afterward whether it was *good* or not. I would be gratified to know, and from personal experience. Come to my room. Why should you have qualms about using a woman who has already been used? Not much used, of course, but—"

Firmly, I changed the subject. "I told Zyanya I would bring

you to Tenochtítlan if you were suffering or in any danger. We have a house of many rooms. I ask you now, Béu. If you find your situation here intolerable, will you come away and live with us?"

"Impossible!" she snapped. "Live under your roof? How could I there ignore you, as you have suggested?"

Unable to control myself any longer, I said loudly, "I have said and done all I know to say and do. I have spoken apology and contrition and sympathy and brotherly love. I have offered you a good home in a different city where you can hold up your head and forget what is past. But you reply only with sneers and mockery and malice. I will leave in the morning, woman, and you may come with me or not!"

She did not.

In the capital city of Záachilà, to sustain my pose as a trader, I again paid a courtesy call on the Bishósu Ben Záa, and he granted me audience, and I told my lie: how I had been roaming in the Chiapa country, how I had only recently learned of occurrences in the civilized world, and I said:

"As the Lord Kosi Yuela will have guessed, it was largely at my instigation that Ahuítzotl brought his men to Uaxyácac. So I feel I owe some apologies."

He made a casual gesture of dismissal. "Whatever intrigues were involved are of no importance. I am satisfied that your Revered Speaker came with good intentions, and I was pleased that the long animosity between our nations might finally abate, and I do not at all object to receiving the rich tribute of the purple."

I said, "But then there was the reprehensible behavior of Ahuítzotl's men in Tecuantépec. Simply as a Mexícatl, I must add my apologies for that."

"I do not blame Ahuítzotl. I do not even much blame the men."

I must have looked surprised. He explained, "Your Revered Speaker moved quickly to stop the outrages. He ordered the worst offenders garrotted, and he placated the rest of the men with promises which I am sure he has kept. Then he paid to atone for the havoc, or as much of it as *could* be paid for. Our nations would probably be now at war, if he had not acted so swiftly and honorably. No, Ahuítzotl was humbly anxious to restore good relations."

It was the first time I had ever heard the choleric Ahuítzotl, Water Monster, described as anything like humble. Kosi Yuela went on:

"But there was another man, a young man, his nephew. That one had command of the Mexíca while Ahuítzotl and I conferred, and that is when the outbreak began. The young man bears a name we Ben Záa have historical reason to detest— he is called Motecuzóma—and I believe he regarded Ahuítzotl's treaty of alliance with us as a sign of weakness. I believe he wanted the Cloud People as subjects of the Mexíca, not as equals. I strongly suspect he fomented that riot in hope of setting us at each other's throats again. If you do have Ahuítzotl's ear, young traveler, I suggest you insinuate a word of warning about his nephew. That new and upstart Mote-cuzóma, if he retains a position of any power, could undo all the good his uncle might seek to accomplish."

✠

At the causeway to Tenochtítlan, where the city loomed before us luminous white in the dove-colored dusk, I sent my men ahead of me by twos and threes. By the time I set foot on the island, the night had come down, and the city was ablaze with firelight, candlelight, and lamplight. In that inconstant illumination I could see that my house was finished, and that it was a sightly one, but I could not make out all its exterior details. Since it was set on pillars about my own height above ground level, I had to climb a short stair to the entrance. There I was admitted by a middle-aged female I had never seen before, obviously a new-bought slave. She introduced herself as Teoxíhuitl, or Turquoise, and said, "When the porters arrived, the mistress went upstairs, that you might have privacy for the business of men. She will await you in your chamber, master."

The woman showed me into the lower-floor room where my seven companions were devouring a cold meal she had hurried to lay for them. When dishes had also been provided for me, and we had all allayed our hunger, the men helped me pivot the false wall of that room and secrete their packs behind it, where some others of my goods had already been stored. Then I paid the men the homecoming share of their wages, and paid them rather more than I had promised, for they had performed admirably. They all kissed the earth to me as they departed, after making me swear that I would summon them again if I should conceive any other projects that would be to the taste of seven elder warriors otherwise consigned to peace and stagnation.

Upstairs, I found the sanitary closet exactly as I had told the architect it should be: as complete and efficiently self-emptying as those I had admired in palaces. In the adjacent steam room, the slave woman Turquoise had already heated and laid the glowing stones and, when I had finished my first bath, she poured water over them to make the clouds of steam. I sweated there for a good while, then returned to the bathing basin again, until I was satisfied that I had got all the dust and grime and smell of travel out of my pores.

When, naked, I stepped through the connecting door to the bedchamber, I found Zyanya equally naked, lying invitingly supine atop the bed stack of soft quilts. There was only a dim red light from a brazier in the room, but it glinted on the pale streak in her hair and outlined her upthrusting breasts. Each of them was a beautifully symmetrical mound, with on top of it the smaller mound of her areola, exactly like the profile of Popocatépetl as you see it through the window there, my lords friars: a cone upon a cone. No, of course there is no need for me to regale you with such details. I only explain why my breathing altered as I moved toward Zyanya, and why I spoke only a few words:

"Béu is safe. There is other news, but it can wait."

"Let it wait," she said, and she smiled, and she reached for the nearest approaching part of me.

So it was quite some time later that I told about Béu Ribé: that she was alive and safe, but dismally unhappy. I am glad that we had made love first. It gave Zyanya the usual lasting languor of pleasure and satisfaction which, I hope, softened the words I had to speak. I told of Béu's unfortunate encounter with the Mexícatl officer, and tried to make it sound—as indeed Béu had made it sound—more of a farce that a tragedy.

I concluded, "I think it is her stubborn pride that makes her stay on there, keeping the inn. She is determined to take no notice of what the townspeople may think of her, whether they think shame or sympathy. She will not leave Tecuantépec for any good reason or for any better life, because it might be taken as a sign that she had weakened at last."

"Poor Béu," Zyanya murmured. "Is there nothing we can do?"

Suppressing my own opinion of "poor Béu," I meditated and finally said, "I can think of nothing but for *you* to suffer a misfortune. If her only sister needed her desperately, I believe she would come to you. But let us not tempt or provoke the gods. Let us not discuss mischance."

The next day, when Ahuítzotl received me in his grisly throne room, I again told my confected story: that I had gone to see that my wife's sister had not suffered in the sack of Tecuantépec and, while there, had taken the opportunity to go farther south and procure more of the magical crystals. I again ceremoniously made him a present of one, and he thanked me without great enthusiasm. Then, before bringing up a subject which I expected would bulge his eyeballs and fire his irascibility, I told him something to sweeten his temper.

"My travels, Lord Speaker, took me into the coastal land of the Xoconóchco, whence comes most of our cotton and salt. I spent two days among the Mame people, in their main village of Pijijía, and there the elders called me into council. They desired me to bring a message to the Uey-Tlatoáni of the Mexíca."

He said indifferently, "Speak the message."

"Know first, my lord, that the Xoconóchco is not a nation, but a vast extent of fertile land inhabited by various peoples: the Mame, the Mixe, the Comitéca, and even smaller tribes. Their territories all overlap, and their allegiance is only to such tribal elders as those in Pijijía. The Xoconóchco has no central capital or governing body or standing army."

"Interesting," muttered Ahuítzotl. "But not very."

I went on, "To the east of the rich and fruitful Xoconóchco is the unproductive jungle country of Quautemálan, The Tangled Wood. Its natives, the Quiché and Lacandón, are degenerate remnants of the Maya. They are poor and dirty and lazy, and heretofore have been accounted beneath contempt. However, they have recently summoned the energy to emerge from Quautemálan and make raids into the Xoconóchco. Those scavengers threaten that their raids will increase in frequency, will become an unremitting war, unless the Xoconóchco peoples agree to pay them heavy tribute of cotton and salt."

"Tribute?" grunted Ahuítzotl, interested at last. *"Our* cotton and salt!"

"Yes, my lord. Now, we can hardly expect peaceable cotton farmers and sea fishers and salt panners to mount a fierce defense of their lands. But they do have spirit enough to resent those demands. They are unwilling to give to the Quiché and Lacandón what they have formerly and profitably sold to us Mexíca. They believe our Revered Speaker should be equally outraged at the idea."

"Spare us your emphasis of the obvious," growled Ahuítzotl. "What did those elders propose? That we go to war for them against Quautemálan?"

"No, my lord. They offer to give us the Xoconóchco."

"What?" He was honestly staggered.

"If the Uey-Tlatoáni will accept the Xoconóchco lands as a new province, all its petty rulers will relinquish their offices, all its separate tribes will relinquish their identities, all will swear loyalty to Tenochtítlan as voluntary Mexíca. They ask only two things: that they be allowed to go on living and working as they always have, unmolested, and that they continue to receive a living wage for their labor. The Mame speak for all their neighbor tribes in requesting that a Mexícatl noble be appointed ruler and protector of the Xoconóchco, and that a strong garrison of Mexíca troops be established and maintained there."

Looking pleased for a change, even dazzled, Ahuítzotl murmured to himself, "Incredible. A rich land, free for the taking, freely given." To me he said, more warmly than he had ever before addressed me, "You do not *always* bring annoyances and problems, young Mixtli."

I modestly said nothing.

He went on, thinking aloud, "It would be the farthest dominion of The Triple Alliance. Put an army there and we would have much of the entire One World, from sea to sea, between two jaws. The nations thus flanked would evermore hesitate to be troublesome, lest those jaws gnash together and chew them up. They would be apprehensive, biddable, servile. . . ."

I spoke up again: "If I may point out another advantage, Lord Speaker. That army will be far from here, but it need not depend on supply trains from Tenochtítlan. The Mame elders promised me that it will be supported and provisioned without stint. The soldiers will live well in the abundance of the Xoconóchco."

"By Huitztli, we will do it!" Ahuítzotl exclaimed. "We must of course present the proposition to our Speaking Council, but that will be only a formality."

I said, "My lord might care to tell the Speaking Council this, too. Once the garrison is established, the soldiers could be joined by their families. Tradesmen would follow. Still other Mexíca might wish to leave these crowded lake lands and resettle in that ample Xoconóchco. The garrison could become the seed of a colony, even a lesser Tenochtítlan, perhaps someday the second greatest city of the Mexíca."

He said, "You do not dream small, do you?"

"Perhaps I took a liberty, Revered Speaker, but I mentioned that possibility of colonization in the council of Mame elders. Far from objecting, they would be honored if their land should become the site of, so to speak, the Tenochtítlan of the south."

He looked at me approvingly, and drummed his fingers for a moment before speaking. "In civil status you are nothing but a bean-counting merchant, and in military rank a mere tequíua . . ."

"By my lord's courtesy," I said humbly.

"And yet you—a nobody—you come and give us a whole new province, more valuable than any annexed by treaty or force since the reign of our esteemed father Motecuzóma. That fact will also be brought to the attention of our Speaking Council."

I said, "The mention of Motecuzóma, my lord, reminds me." And I then told him what was harder to tell: the harsh words spoken about his nephew by the Bishósu Kosi Yuela. As I had expected, Ahuítzotl began to bulge and snort and redden conspicuously, but his anger was not directed at me. He said bluntly:

"Know, then. As a priest, young Motecuzóma paid unswerving obedience to every least and trivial and imbecilic superstition imposed by the gods. He also tried to abolish every human failing and weakness, in himself as in others. He did not froth and rage, as do so many of our priests; he was always cold and unemotional. Once, when he uttered a word that he thought might displease the gods, he pierced his tongue and dragged back and forth through it a string on which were knotted some twenty big maguey thorns. Again, when a base *thought* crossed his mind, he bored a hole through the shaft of his tepúli and did that same bloody self-punishment with the string of thorns. Well, now that he has become a military man, he seems equally fanatic on the subject of making war. It appears that, in his very first command, the coyote whelp has flexed his muscles, contrary to orders and good order. . . ."

Ahuítzotl paused. When he went on, he seemed again to be thinking aloud. "Yes, he would naturally yearn to live up to his grandfather's name of Wrathful Lord. Young Motecuzóma is not pleased to have peace between our nation and others, since that leaves him the fewer adversaries to challenge. He wants to be respected and feared as a man of hard fist and loud voice. But a man must consist of more than those things. Or he will cower when he is opposed by a harder fist, a louder voice."

I ventured to say, "My impression, my lord, is that the Bishósu of Uaxyácac dreads the possibility that your truculent nephew may someday be Uey-Tlatoáni of the Mexíca."

At that, Ahuítzotl did turn his glare on me. "Kosi Yuela will be dead long before he has to worry about his relations with some new Uey-Tlatoáni. We are but forty and three years old, and we plan to live long. Before we die or turn dotard, we will make known to the Speaking Council who our successor is to be. Offhand, we forget how many of our twenty children are male, but surely among them there is another Ahuítzotl. Bear in mind, Tequíua Mixtli, that the loudest drum is the one most hollow, and its only service or function is to stay motionless and be beaten upon. We will not set upon this throne a hollow drum like our nephew Motecuzóma. *Remember our words!*"

I did, and I do, and ruefully.

It took a while for the Revered Speaker to subdue his indignation. Then he said quietly, "We thank you, Tequíua Mixtli, for the opportunity of that garrison in the far Xoconóchco. It will be the young Wrathful Lord's next assignment. He will be ordered immediately to the south, to establish and build and command that distant post. Yes, we must keep Motecuzóma busy—and safely far from us—or we might be tempted to beat with heavy drumsticks upon our own kinsman."

Some days passed, and what time I did not spend in bed, getting reacquainted with my wife, I spent in getting accustomed to my first home of my own. Its exterior was of gleaming white Xaltócan limestone, decorated only modestly with some filigree carving, and none of that embellished with color. To the passerby, it was merely the typical home of a successful but not *too* successful pochtécatl. Inside, however, its appointments were of the finest, and it smelled throughout of newness, not of the smokes and foods and exudations and old quarrels of previous inhabitants. The doors were all of nicely carved cedar, turning in pivots in sockets top and bottom. There were windows in the outdoor-facing walls, front and back, with rollable slat blinds on all of them.

The ground floor—which, as I have said, did not rest on the ground—contained a kitchen, a separate room for dining, and another room in which we could entertain guests or I could conduct business with visiting associates. There was not space enough to make any provision for slave quarters; Turquoise simply unrolled her woven-reed pallet in the kitchen after we were abed. The upper floor of the house consisted of our bedchamber and another for guests, each with its sanitary closet and steam room; plus a third, smaller bedroom for which I could see no purpose, until Zyanya, smiling shyly, said, "Someday there may be a child, Záa. Perhaps children. It can be a room for them and their nursemaid."

The rooftop of the house was flat, surrounded by a waist-high balustrade of stones cemented in a fretwork pattern. The entire surface had already been spread with rich chinámpa loam, ready for the planting of flowers, shade shrubs, and kitchen herbs. Our house was not tall, and there were many others roundabout, so we had no view of the lake, but we could see the twin temples atop the Great Pyramid, and the peaks of the smoking volcano Popocatépetl and the sleeping volcano Ixtaccíuatl. Zyanya had furnished the rooms, upstairs and down, with only the immediately necessary items: the piled-quilt beds, some wicker storage chests, a few low chairs and benches. Otherwise the rooms were echoingly empty, the gleaming stone floors uncarpeted and the white-limed walls unadorned.

She said, "The more important furnishings, the ornaments, the wall hangings—I thought the man of the house ought to choose such things."

"We will visit the markets and the workshops together," I said. "But I will come only to agree to your choices and to pay for them."

In similar wifely restraint, she had bought just the one slave, and Turquoise had sufficed to assist Zyanya in all the work of preparing the house for habitation. But I decided that we should buy another female to share the everyday labor of cooking, cleaning, and other chores, plus a male slave to tend the rooftop garden, run my errands, and the like. So we acquired a not so young but still wiry man named, in the grandiloquent manner of the tlacótli class, Citláli-Cuicáni, or Star Singer, and a young housemaid named, quite contrary to slave custom, Que-quelmíqui, which means only Ticklish. Possibly she had got the name because she was much given to unprovoked giggling.

We immediately enrolled all three—Turquoise, Star Singer, and Ticklish—to spend their spare hours studying at the school newly founded by my young friend Cozcatl. His own highest ambition, in the days when he was himself a child slave, had been to learn the skills necessary to attain the highest domestic post in a noble household, that of Master of the Keys. But he had already risen considerably above that station, possessing an estimable house and fortune of his own. So Cozcatl had turned his residence into a school to train servants. That is, to make of them the best servants possible.

He told me, with pride, "I have of course engaged expert instructors to teach the basic employments—cookery, garden-ing, embroidery, whatever a student wishes to excel at. But I myself teach each student the elegant manners he otherwise could learn only through long experience, if at all. Since I have worked in two palaces, my students pay close heed to my teachings, even though most of them are much older than I."

"Elegant manners?" I said. "For mere menials?"

"So that they are *not* mere menials, but valuable and valued members of a household. I teach them how to comport themselves with dignity instead of the usual cringing servility. How to anticipate their employers' wants even before they are voiced. A steward, for example, learns to keep always prepared a poquíetl for his master to smoke. A housekeeper learns to advise her mistress which flowers are about to bloom in the garden, so the lady can plan in advance the floral arrangements for her rooms."

I said, "Surely no slave could afford the fee for your training."

"Well, no," he admitted. "At present all my students are already in domestic service, like those three of yours, and their fees are paid by their masters. But the schooling will so increase their ability and worth that they will earn promotions within their households—or be sold for a profit—meaning they must be replaced. I foresee a great demand for the graduates of my school. Eventually, I will be able to buy slaves from the market, train them, place them, and collect their fees from the wages they earn."

I nodded and said, "It will be a good thing for them, for their employers, and for you. An ingenious idea, Cozcatl. You have not just found your place in the world, you have carved an entirely new niche, for which no one is better fitted than yourself."

He said with humility, "I could not have done it but for you, Mixtli. Had we not adventured together, I would probably still be a drudge in some Texcóco palace. I owe all my good fortune to the tonáli, whether it was yours or mine, that linked our lives."

And I too, I thought, as I walked slowly home, was much indebted to a tonáli I had once cursed as capricious, if not malign. It had caused me grief and loss and unhappiness. But it had also made me a man of property, a man of substantial wealth, a man lofted high above the expectations of his birth, a man married to the most desirable woman among women, and a man still young enough to explore further enticing prospects.

As I strolled toward my comfortable home and the welcoming arms of Zyanya, I was moved to waft my gratitude toward the supposed sky residences of the major gods. "Gods," I said—in my mind, not aloud—"if gods there be, and you are they, I thank you. Sometimes you have taken from me with one hand while giving to me with the other. But on the whole you have given me much more than you have taken. I kiss the earth to you, gods."

And the gods must have been grateful for my gratitude. The gods wasted no time in arranging that when I entered my house, I should find a palace page waiting with a summons from Ahuítzotl. I took only time enough to give Zyanya a hurried kiss of greeting and farewell, then followed the boy through the streets to The Heart of the One World.

It was quite late that night when I came home again, and I was very differently dressed, and I was more than a little intoxicated. Our slave Turquoise, when she opened the door to me, instantly forgot any poise she might have learned at Cozcatl's school. She took one look at me and my somewhat disordered profusion of feathers, gave a piercing shriek, and fled toward the back of the house. Zyanya came, looking anxious.

She said, "Záa, you were gone so long—!" Then she too gave a squeak and recoiled from me, exclaiming, "What did that monster Ahuítzotl do to you? Why is your arm bleeding? What have you got on your feet? What is that thing on your head? Záa, *say something!*"

"Hello," I mumbled foolishly, with a hiccup in it.

"Hello?" she echoed, taken aback by the absurdity. Then she said crisply, "Whatever else, you are drunk," and went away toward the kitchen. I slumped down onto a bench, but I came energetically to my feet again—perhaps even some distance off the floor—when Zyanya poured a jar of shockingly cold water over my head.

"My helmet!" I cried, when I stopped coughing and spluttering.

"A helmet, is it?" said Zyanya, as I struggled to get it off and dry it before the wetting should damage it. "I thought you were caught in the craw of some giant bird."

"My lady wife," I said, with the stately sobriety of the half drunk, "you might have ruined this noble eagle head. Now you are standing on one of my talons. And look—just look at my poor draggled feathers."

"I am. I am looking," she said, in a strangled voice, and I perceived that she was trying mightily not to burst out laughing. "Get out of that silly costume, Záa. Go to the steam room. Sweat some of the octli out of you. Clean that blood off your arm. Then come to bed and tell me . . . tell me what on earth . . ." She could hold the laughter no longer, and it came forth in peals.

"Silly costume, indeed," I said, contriving to sound both haughty and hurt. "Only a woman could be so insensitive to the regalia of high honor. Were you a man, you would kneel in awe and admiration and congratulation. But no. I get ignominiously drenched and laughed at." With which, I turned and stalked majestically up the stairs, only stumbling occasionally in my long-taloned sandals, to go and soak and sulk in the steam room.

Thus did I behave with lugubrious bluster, thus was I received with indulgent mirth, on what should have been the most solemn evening of my life to date. Not one in ten or twenty thousand of my countrymen ever became what I had that day become—In Tlámahuichihuáni Cuaútlic: a Knight of the Eagle Order of the Mexíca.

I further humiliated myself by falling asleep in the steam room, and was quite unconscious of being moved when Zyanya and Star Singer somehow got me out of there and into the bed. So it was not until morning, when I lay late abed, sipping hot chocolate in an attempt to ease the ponderous weight of my headache, that I could coherently tell Zyanya what had happened at the palace.

Ahuítzotl had been alone in the throne room when the page and I arrived, and he said abruptly, "Our nephew Motecuzóma left Tenochtítlan this morning, leading the considerable force that will man the garrison in the Xoconóchco. As we promised, we mentioned to our Speaking Council your admirable role in negotiating the acquisition of that territory, and it was decided that you should be rewarded."

He made some signal, and the page departed, and a moment afterward the room began to fill with other men. I would have expected them to be the Snake Woman and other members of the Speaking Council. But, looking through my topaz, I was surprised to see that they were all warriors—the elite of warriors—all Eagle Knights, in full-feathered battle armor, eagle-head helmets, wing pinions fringing their arms, taloned sandals on their feet.

Ahuítzotl introduced them to me, one by one—the highest chieftains of the Eagle Order—and said, "They have voted, Mixtli, to raise you—in one vaulting bound—from the medi-ocre rank of tequíua to full knighthood in their exalted company."

There were various rituals to be performed, of course. Though I had been stricken nearly speechless, I made an effort to find my voice, so that I could swear the many and wordy oaths—that I would be faithful to and fight to the death for the Eagle Order itself, for the supremacy of Tenochtítlan, for the power and prestige of the Mexíca nation, for the preservation of The Triple Alliance. I had to gash my forearm, the knight chieftains doing likewise, so that we could rub our forearms one against another and so mingle our blood in brotherhood.

Then I donned the quilted armor with all its adornments, so that I had arms like wide wings, a body feathered all over, feet like an eagle's strong claws. The culmination of the ceremony came when I was crowned with the helmet: the eagle's head. It was made of corkwood, stiff paper, and óli-glued feathers. Its wide-open beak protruded above my forehead and under my chin, and its glaring obsidian eyes were somewhere above my ears. I was given the other emblems of my new rank: the stout leather shield with my name symbols worked in colored feathers on its front, the paints to make my face fierce, the gold nose plug to wear as soon as I felt like having my septum pierced for it. . . .

Then, rather heavily encumbered, I sat with Ahuítzotl and the other knights while the palace servants brought an opulent banquet and many jars of the best octli. I had to make a pretense of eating heartily, since by then I was so flustered and excited that I had little appetite. There was no way, though, that I could avoid drinking in response to the numerous and vociferous toasts raised—to me, to the Eagle chieftains present, to Eagle Knights who had died spectacularly in the past, to our supreme commander Ahuítzotzin, to the ever greater might of the Mexíca. . . . After a while, I lost track of the toasts. That is why, when I was finally let depart from the palace, I was more than a little addled and my splendid new uniform was in some disarray.

"I am proud of you, Záa, and happy for you," Zyanya said when I had concluded my account. "It is indeed a great honor. And now, what brave feat will you do, my warrior husband? What will be your first deed of valor as an Eagle Knight?"

I said feebly, "Were we not supposed to pick flowers today, my dear? When the freight canoe brings them from Xochimílco? Flowers to plant in our roof garden?"

My brain hurt too badly for me to strain it, so I did not even try to understand why Zyanya again, as she had done the night before, burst into peals of laughter.

✠

Our new house meant a new life for all of us who inhabited it, so we had much to occupy us. Zyanya continued to be busy with the evidently interminable task of visiting market stalls and artisans' workshops in chase of "just the right sort of matting for the nursery floor" or "a figurine of some sort for that niche at the top of the stair" or something else that seemed always to elude her.

My contributions were not always received with acclamation, as for instance when I brought home a small stone statue for that staircase niche and Zyanya pronounced it "hideous." Well, it was, but I had bought it because it looked exactly like that brown, wizened, and hunched old-man disguise in which Nezahualpíli had used to accost me. Actually, the figure represented Huehuetéotl, Oldest of Old Gods, so called because that was what he was. Though no longer widely worshiped, the aged, wrinkled, sardonically smiling Huehuetéotl was still venerated as the god first recognized in these lands and known since time before human memory, long before Quetzalcóatl or any of the later favorites. Since Zyanya refused to let me put him where guests would see him, I set The Oldest of Old Gods at my side of our bed.

Our three servants, in the free time during their first few months with us, attended their classes at Cozcatl's school, and to noticeable effect. The little maid Ticklish was cured of giggling every time she was spoken to, and gave only a modest and obliging smile. Star Singer became so attentive that he presented me with a lighted poquíetl almost every time I sat down, and—not to rebuff his solicitude—I smoked rather more than I wanted to.

My own business was that of consolidating my fortune. Trains of pochtéca had for some time been coming into Tenochtítlan from Uaxyácac, bearing flasks of purple dye and skeins of empurpled yarn which they had purhased legitimately from the collected stock of the Bishósu Kosi Yuela. They had of course paid an exorbitant price for it, and of course asked an even more extortionate price when they doled it out through the Tlaltelólco merchants. But the Mexíca nobles—their ladies especially—were so avid for that unique coloring that they paid whatever was asked. And, once the legitimately acquired purple was on the market, I was able discreetly and without detection to pour my own stock trickling into the stream.

I sold my hoard for more easily concealable currency: carved jade-stones, a few emeralds and other gems, gold jewelry, quills of gold dust. But Zyanya and I kept enough of the dye for our own use that I believe we owned more purple-embroidered garments than the Revered Speaker and all his wives. I *know* ours was the only house in Tenochtítlan with solid-purple draperies at the windows. Those were visible only to our invited guests, however; they were backed with less sumptuous stuffs on their street side.

We were most frequently visited by longtime friends: Cozcatl, lately and more properly known as Master Cozcatl; associates of mine from The House of Pochtéca; one or several of Blood Glutton's old fellows-in-arms who had helped me secure the purple. But we also made many acquaintances among our higher-class neighbors in our Ixacuálco quarter and the nobles we met at court—in particular a number of noble-women who had been captivated by Zyanya's charm. One of those was the First Lady of Tenochtítlan, which is to say Ahuítzotl's premier wife. When she came to visit, she often brought her eldest son, Cuautémoc, Swooping Eagle, the young lord who would be the likeliest successor to his father's throne. Though the Mexíca succession was not immutably patrilineal, like that of some other nations, an eldest son was the first candidate considered by the Speaking Council on the death of a Uey-Tlatoáni who left no surviving brother to succeed him. So Zyanya and I treated Cuautémoctzin and his mother with fitting deference; it does no harm to be on good terms with him whom you may someday be addressing as Revered Speaker.

From time to time during those years, a military messenger or a pochtécatl's porter coming up from the south would make a side trip past our house to bring us a message from Béu Ribé. The message was always the same: she was still unmarried, Tecuantépec was still Tecuantépec, the inn was still prospering, and even more so with the increased traffic to and from the Xoconóchco. But the very sameness of that scant news was rather depressing, since Zyanya and I could only assume that Béu remained unmarried not from inclination but from a lack of suitors.

And that always recalled the exiled Motecuzóma to my mind, for I was sure—though I never said so, even to Zyanya—that he had been the Mexícatl officer of strange proclivities who had devastated Béu's life. Just as a matter of family loyalty, I suppose I might have felt animosity toward that Motecuzóma the Younger. Just from what Béu and Ahuítzotl had told me, I might have felt contempt for a man partly crippled both in his private parts and in his appetites. But not I or anyone could deny that he did a soldierly job of holding and developing the Xoconóchco for us.

He located his army garrison practically on the border of Quautemálan, and he oversaw the design and building of a stout one, and the neighboring Quiché and Lacandón no doubt watched with dismay as its walls went up and the patrols marched about it. For those wretched people never made another foray outside their jungle, they never again threatened or blustered or, indeed, showed any other sign of ambition.

They lapsed back into being no worse than squalid and apathetic, and, as far as I am aware, they still are so.

Your own Spanish soldiers who first traveled into the Xoconóchco expressed surprise on finding there, so far distant from Tenochtítlan, so many peoples unrelated to us Mexíca—the Mame, Mixe, Comitéca, and such—who spoke our Náhuatl. Yes, that was the farthest land on which one could stand and say, "This is Mexíca soil." It was also, despite its distance from The Heart of the One World, perhaps our most loyal province, and that was due in part to the fact that many of our people moved into the Xoconóchco after its annexation.

Even before Motecuzóma's garrison was completed, other comers began to settle in the area and to build homes and market stalls and rudimentary inns and even houses of pleasure. They were Mexíca and Acólhua and Tecpanéca immigrants seeking wider horizons and opportunities than they could find in the ever more crowded lands of The Triple Alliance. By the time the garrison was fully built and armed and manned, it threw its protective shadow over a town of estimable size. The town took the Náhuatl name of Tapáchtlan, Place of Coral, and, though it never approached the size and splendor of its parent Tenochtítlan, it is still the biggest and busiest community east of the Tecuantépec isthmus.

Many of the new-come northerners, after staying a while in Tapáchtlan or elsewhere in the Xoconóchco, moved on farther yet. I have never journeyed quite so far, but I know that, east of the Quautemálan jungle, there are great fertile highlands and coast lands. And beyond them there is another isthmus, even more narrow than that of Tecuantépec, winding between the northern and southern oceans and extending no one can tell how far. Some insist that somewhere down there a river connects the two oceans. Your own Captain-General Cortés went looking for it, in vain, but some Spaniard may find it yet.

Though the onward-pressing emigrants consisted only of individual explorers, or at most of family groups, and though they settled only sparsely throughout those far lands, I am told that they have left their mark indelibly on the native peoples of those places. Tribes never originally or remotely related to any of us of The Triple Alliance now wear our faces; they speak our Náhuatl language, though in corrupt dialects; they have adopted and perpetuated many of our customs and arts and gods; they have even renamed their villages and mountains and rivers with Náhuatl names.

Several Spaniards who have traveled widely have asked me, "Was your Aztec Empire really so vast that it abutted upon the Inca Empire in the great continent to the south?" Although I do not fully comprehend the question, I always tell them, "No, my lords." I am uncertain of what an empire is, or a continent, or an Inca. But I do know that we Mexíca—Aztecs, if you must—never pushed our border beyond the Xoconóchco.

Not everybody's eyes and interests were fixed toward the south in those years. Our Uey-Tlatoáni, for one, was not ignoring the other points of the compass. I rather welcomed the interruption of my increasingly domestic daily routine when one day Ahuítzotl called me to his palace to ask if I would undertake a diplomatic mission into Michihuácan.

He said, "You did so well for us in the Xoconóchco and in Uaxyácac. Do you think you might now seek for us better relations with The Land of the Fishermen?"

I said I could try. "But why, my lord? The Purémpecha allow our travelers and merchants unhindered passage across their country. They engage freely in trade with us. What more can we ask of them in the way of relations?"

"Oh, think of something. Anything that would justify your visiting their ruling Uandákuari, old Yquíngare." I must have looked blank, for he leaned forward to explain. "Your supposedly diplomatic negotiations will be only a mask for your real mission. We want you to bring us their secret of making that superbly hard metal which defeats our obsidian weapons."

I took a long breath and, trying to sound reasonable instead of apprehensive, I said, "My lord, the artisans who know how to forge that metal are assuredly well guarded against any encounters with strangers who might tempt them to betray their secret."

"And the metal itself is kept locked away, out of sight of the inquisitive," said Ahuítzotl impatiently. "We know all that. But we also know of one exception to that policy. The Uandákuari's closest advisers and personal guards are *always* armed with weapons of that metal, to ward off any attempts on his life. Get into his palace and you have a chance of getting hold of a sword, a knife, something. That is all we need. If our own metalworkers can have but a specimen to study, they can find out the composition of it."

I sighed and said, "As my lord commands, an Eagle Knight must do." I thought over the difficulties of the task ahead and suggested, "If I am going there only to steal, I really need no complicated excuse of diplomatic negotiations. I could be merely an envoy bringing from the Revered Speaker Ahuítzotl a friendly gift for the Revered Speaker Yquíngare."

Ahuítzotl also thought about it, frowning. "But what?" he said. "There are as many precious things in Michihuácan as there are here. It would have to be something unavailable to him, something unique."

I said, "The Purémpecha are much given to strange sexual diversions. But no. The Uandákuari is an old man. Doubtless he has already sampled every sexual delight and indecency and is jaded beyond—"

"*Ayyo!*" cried Ahuítzotl exultantly. "There is one delight he cannot possibly have tried, one he cannot possibly resist. A new texquáni we have just bought for our human menagerie." I flinched, visibly I am sure, but he took no notice; he was sending a steward to bring whatever it was.

I was trying to imagine what kind of human monster could arouse the tepúli of even the most pornerastic old lecher, when Ahuítzotl said, "Look at this, Knight Mixtli. Here they are," and I raised my topaz.

The two girls were about as plain of face as any girls I had ever seen, but in simple charity I could hardly have called them monstrous. A trifle unusual, yes, in that they were identical twins. I took them to be about fourteen years old, and of some Olméca tribe, since they were both chewing tzictli, as placidly as a matched pair of manatees. They stood shoulder to shoulder, slightly turned toward each other, each with her nearmost arm thrown across the other's nearmost shoulder. They wore a single blanket wrapped around both their bodies from their chests to the floor.

"They have not yet been shown to the public," said Ahuítzotl, "because our palace seamstresses have not finished the special blouses and skirts they require. Steward, remove the blanket."

He did, and my eyes goggled when I saw the girls naked. They were not just twins; it appeared that in the womb they had somehow got melted together. From armpit to hip, the two were joined by a mutual skin, and so tightly that they could not stand, sit, walk, or lie down except half facing each other. For a moment, I thought they had only three breasts between them. But I stepped closer and saw that the middle breast was two normal breasts pressed together; I could part them with my hand. I looked the girls over: four breasts in front, two sets of buttocks in back. Except for their unlovely, unintelligent faces, I could see no deformity but that section of shared skin.

"Could they not be sliced apart?" I inquired. "They would each have a scar, but they would be separate and normal."

"Whatever for?" growled Ahuítzotl. "Of what earthly use are two more mud-faced, tzictli-chewing Olméca drabs? Together, they are novel and valuable and can enjoy the pleasurably idle life of a tequáni. At any rate, our surgeons have concluded that they cannot be separated. Inside that binding flap of skin, they share vital blood vessels. But—and this is what will beguile old Yquíngare—each girl does have her own tipíli, and both are virgins."

"It is a pity they could not be handsome," I mused. "But you are right, my lord. The sheer novelty of them should make up for that lack." I addressed the twins: "Do you have names? Can you talk?"

They said, in the Coatlícamac tongue, and almost in unison, "I am Left." "I am Right."

Ahuítzotl said, "We had planned to present them to the public as the Lady Pair. Named for the goddess Omecíuatl. A sort of joke, you see."

I said, "If an uncommon gift will make the Uandákuari more amicable toward us, the Lady Pair is that gift, and I will gladly be the bearer of it. Just one recommendation, my lord, to render them more attractive. Have them both shaved bald of hair and eyebrows. It is the Purémpe fashion."

"Singular fashion," said Ahuítzotl wonderingly. "The hair is the only thing attractive about either of these. But it will be done. Be prepared to depart as soon as their wardrobe is completed."

"At your summons, Lord Speaker. And I shall hope that the Lady Pair's presentation at that court will cause enough excitement that I can purloin one of the metal weapons unnoticed in the commotion."

"Do not just hope," said Ahuítzotl. "See to it!"

"Ah, the poor children!" Zyanya exclaimed, when I introduced her to the Lady Pair. I was surprised to hear someone express pity for them, since everyone else involved with Left and Right had either gaped or snickered, or, in the manner of Ahuítzotl, had regarded them as a marketable commodity, like the meat of some rare game animal. But Zyanya mothered them tenderly throughout the whole journey to Tzintzuntzaní, and continually kept assuring them—as if they had brains enough to care—that they were traveling toward a wondrous new life of freedom and luxury. Well, I supposed they *would* be better off in the comparative liberty of a country palace, even serving as a sort of reversible concubine, than as an object being forever pointed at and laughed at in the confines of a city menagerie.

Zyanya went with me because, when I told her of that latest and queerest embassy laid on me, she insisted on coming along. At first I said a loud no, for I knew that no one in my party would live longer than the moment in which, very likely, I would be caught trying to steal one of the sacrosanct metal weapons. But Zyanya argued persuasively that, if our host's suspicions were allayed in advance, I would have the greater opportunity of getting close to such a weapon and getting it into my possession undetected.

"And what looks less suspicious," she asked, "than a man and wife traveling together? I should *like* to see Michihuácan, Záa."

Her man-and-wife idea did have some merit, I reflected, if not exactly the merit she ascribed to it. For the lewd and licentious Purémpecha to see a man traveling with his own, everyday, commonplace female mate—in that country where, for the asking, he could have any other mate, or kind of mate, or number of mates—that would indeed dumbfound the Purémpecha. They would scornfully dismiss me as too impotent, witless, unimaginative, and lethargic to be a thief or a spy or anything else dangerous. So I said yes to Zyanya, and she immedately began packing for the journey.

Ahuítzotl sent me word, and I reported to the palace, when the twins and their wardrobe were ready to go. But *ayya*, I was horrified when I first saw the girls after they had been shorn of hair. Their naked heads looked like their naked breasts— sharply conical, tapering to a point—and I wondered if my recommendation had been an awful mistake. A bald head might be the epitome of beauty to a Purémpe, but a bald *pointed* head? Well, it was too late to remedy; bald they would have to remain.

Also, it was only then belatedly discovered that no ordinary litter chair would accommodate Left and Right, and that a special one would have to be constructed to their peculiar requirements, which delayed our departure for a few days. But Ahuítzotl was determined to spare no expense on that expedition, so, when we finally did set out, we made quite a procession.

Two palace guards strode ahead, their hands conspicuously empty of weapons, but I knew them both to be expert at hand-to-hand unarmed combat. I carried nothing but the emblazoned shield identifying me as an Eagle Knight, and the folded letter of introduction signed by the Uey-Tlatoáni Ahuítzotl. I walked beside Zyanya's four-bearer chair, and acted my role of tame husband, directing her attention to this or that landmark. Behind us came the eight-manned litter of the twins, and their spare bearers who took turn about at the heavy chair's carrying poles. That specially built litter was not just a seat, but a sort of small hut on poles, roofed above and curtained on its two open sides. The tail of the procession comprised the numerous slaves laden with our packs and panniers and provisions.

Three or four days on the westering trade road brought us to a village called Zitákuaro, where a guardpost on its outskirts marked the frontier of Michihuácan. There we halted while the Purémpecha border guards respectfully scanned the letter I presented, and then only prodded but did not open our various packs. They did look somewhat amazed when they peered into the oversized litter chair and found two identical bald girls riding side by side in what appeared to be a most uncomfortable position. But the guards did not comment. They waved courteously for me and my lady and our party to pass on through Zitákuaro.

After that, we were not again stopped or challenged, but I commanded that the curtains be kept closed on the Lady Pair's litter, so that they should not be visible to the people who eyed our passing. I knew that a swift-messenger would already have informed the Uandákuari of our approach, but I wanted to keep his gift a mystery and undescribed, insofar as, possible, until we got to his palace and surprised him with it. Zyanya thought me cruel, to make the twins ride all that way without seeing anything of the new country in which they would live. So, every time I showed *her* something of interest, she would stop our train until the road was clear of passersby, and then herself go back to lift the twins' curtain and show them whatever it was. She kept doing that all the way across Michihuácan, rather to my exasperation, since Left and Right were utterly apathetic and incurious about their surroundings.

The trip would have been tedious for me had it not been for the presence of Zyanya; I was glad she had persuaded me to let her come. She even made me forget, now and then, the hazardous task I was to undertake at our destination. Every time our train rounded a bend in the road or breasted the crown of a hill, Zyanya would see something new to her, and she would exclaim over it, and listen with childlike intensity as I explained it to her.

The first thing that excited Zyanya's attention, of course, was the preponderance of glossily hairless people. I had told her of that custom, but telling is no substitute for seeing. Until gradually she got used to it, she would stare at a passing youth and murmur, "That one is a boy. No, a girl . . ." And I must admit that her curiosity was reciprocated. The Purémpecha were accustomed to seeing other people unshorn—foreign travelers, their own lower classes, and perhaps stubborn eccentrics—but they had never seen a lovely woman with a wealth of long hair *and* a vivid white strand streaking through it. So they also stared and murmured.

There were other things to see besides the people. The part of Michihuácan which we were then traversing has mountains, as does every other land, but there they seem always to sit on the horizon as a mere frame for the level or gently rolling country they enclose. Some of that territory is forested, some is grown up in meadows of useless but lovely grass and wild flowers. But much of it consists of wide-spreading, bountifully producing farms. There are immeasurable swales of maize, beans, chilis, orchards of ahuácatin and of sweeter fruits. Here and there in the fields stand the adobe cribs in which seed and produce are stored—conical bins, rather resembling the Lady Pair's tapering heads.

In those regions, even the humblest dwellings are good to look at. All made of wood, since wood is so abundant there, they are put together without mortar or tie ropes but with ingeniously tight notches in the planks and beams. Every house has a high, peaked roof, its eaves deeply overswooping the house all around, the better to give cool shade in the hot season and to shed rain in the wet, and some of the roofs are fancifully made so that their four corners turn upward in perky ornamental points. That was the season of swallows, and there are nowhere more swallows than in Michihuácan—flitting, fluttering, flickering, gliding all about—no doubt because those capacious roof eaves make such fine nesting places for them.

With its woods and waters, Michihuácan is a hospitable home for all sorts of birds. The rivers reflect the bright flashing colors of jays and flycatchers and fisher birds. In the forests the carpenter birds make a constant tattoo of drumming and drilling. In the lake shallows stand big white and blue herons, and the even bigger kuinko. That bird has a bill shaped like a spoon, an ungainly shape, and gawky long legs. But the kuinko is superb in its sunset-colored plumage, and when a flock of them all take wing at once it is like watching the wind made pink and visible.

The single greatest concentration of Michihuácan's population lived in the multitude of villages ringing the big Lake of Rushes, Pátzkuaro, or perched on the many small islands in that lake. Although every village derived most of its sustenance from netting the waters' fish and fowl, every village was bidden by the Uandákuari to produce or provide one special, local commodity or service which it traded to all the others. One community made hammered copperware, another wove cloth, another braided rushes into matting, another made lacquerware, and so on. The village named for the lake, Pátzkuaro, was the marketplace for those various things. One island in mid-lake, Xarákuaro, was built up with temples and altars, and was the ceremonial center for the residents of every village. Tzintzuntzaní, Where There Are Hummingbirds, was the capital and heart of all that activity, so itself produced nothing but the decisions and orders and rulings that governed the whole nation. It consisted entirely of palaces and was entirely inhabited by nobles and their families, their courtiers, priests, servants, and such.

As our train approached Tzintzuntzaní, the first man-made object we could see, from several one-long-runs down the road, was the ancient iyákata, as a pyramid is called in Poré, looming on the heights east of the nobles' palaces. Old beyond imagining, not tall but extravagantly elongated, that iyákata—a curious blend of square and round edifices—was still an awe-inspiring pile of stone, though it had long ago lost all its slab sheathing and gesso and coloring, and was much crumbled and overgrown with verdure.

The numerous palaces of Where There Are Hummingbirds, being all built of wood, might have been accounted less imposing than the stone palaces of Tenochtítlan, but they had their own kind of grandeur. Under the spreading eaves of their high-peaked, curly-cornered roofs, they were all two floors high, and the upper floor was completely encircled by an outside gallery. The ponderous cedar trunks upholding those buildings, the columns and banisters, the many beams visible under the eaves, all those things were elaborately worked and carved into curls and fretwork. Wherever artists could reach, the rich lacquers had been laboriously hand-applied. Every palace was lavishly ornamented, glowing with color and gold leaf, but of course the Uandákuari's palace made all the others look trivial.

Swift-messengers had kept Yquíngare apprised of our progress, so our arrival was expected, and a crowd of nobles and their ladies waited to receive us. Our company had earlier veered off to the lakeside and, separating for privacy, we had all bathed and changed into our finest garments. We came, feeling fresh and looking proud, into the palace forecourt—a walled garden overhung by tall shade trees—where I ordered the litter chairs set down. I dismissed our guards and bearers, and they were led off to be quartered with the servants. Only Zyanya, the Lady Pair, and myself went on through the garden to the tremendous palace building. In the general confusion of the greeters milling all about us, the twins' odd way of walking went unremarked.

In a welcoming murmur and chatter, not all of which I could comprehend, we were ushered between the palace's cedar-trunk portals onto the cedar-slab terrace, then through the great open door, then through a short corridor and into Yquíngare's reception hall. It was immensely long and wide, and two floors high: like the interior court of Ahuítzotl's palace, only roofed over. Stairways on each side climbed to an encircling inside balcony off which the upper rooms opened. The Uandákuari sat on a throne that was only a low chair, but the long walk from the entrance to where he sat was clearly designed to make every visitor feel like a supplicant.

Big as it was, the hall was quite crowded with elegantly dressed ladies and gentlemen, but they all pressed back on both sides to make an aisle for us. I, then Zyanya, then the Lady Pair, in slow procession walked solemnly toward the throne, and I raised my topaz just long enough to get a good look at Yquíngare. I had seen him only once before, at the dedication of the Great Pyramid, and in those days I had not seen clearly. He had been old then, and was older now: a shriveled little wisp of a man. It might have been his hairlessness that had inspired the fashion among his people, but he did not have to use an obsidian razor to maintain his. He was as toothless as he was bald, and nearly voiceless: he bade us welcome in a faint rustle, like the sound of a small seedpod shaking. Though I was glad to be ridding myself of the lumpish Lady Pair, I felt some compunction at giving even a freak into the tendril fingers of that gnarled and withered old weed.

I handed over Ahuítzotl's letter, and the Uandákuari handed it in turn to his oldest son, peevishly commanding him to read it aloud. I had always thought of princes as being young men; that Crown Prince Tzímtzicha, if he had let his hair grow, would have been gray-headed; but his father still wheezed orders at him as if he had not yet donned a loincloth under his mantle.

"A gift for me, eh?" croaked the father, when the son had

finished reading the letter in Poré. He fixed his bleary eyes on Zyanya, standing beside me, and smacked his gums. "Ah. Could be a novelty, yes. Shave off all but that one white lock . . ."

Zyanya, horrified, took a step backward. I hastened to say, "Here is the gift, my Lord Yquíngare," and reached for the Lady Pair. I stood them directly before the throne and tore their one-piece purple garment from neck to hem. The assembled crowd gave a gasp at my destroying such a precious piece of cloth—then gave another gasp as the garment fell to the floor and the twins stood naked.

"By the feathered balls of Kurikáuri!" breathed the old man, using the Poré name for Quetzalcóatl. He went on saying something, but his voice was lost in his courtiers' hubbub of astonished exclamation, and I could only make out that he was drooling down his chin. The gift was an obvious success.

All present, including the Uandákuari's several surviving crone wives and concubines, were given an opportunity to come jostling for a close look at the Lady Pair. Some men, and a few women too, boldly reached out a hand and fondled some part of one girl or the other. When everybody's lubricious curiosity was satisfied, Yquíngare rasped a command that cleared the reception hall of all but himself, us visitors, the Crown Prince, and a few stolid guards stationed in the corners.

"Nourishment now," the old man said, rubbing his dry hands together. "Must prepare to give a good account of myself, eh?"

The prince Tzímtzicha relayed the order to one of the guards, who departed. In a moment, servants began coming in to lay a dinner cloth right there, and—when Zyanya had reclothed the twins with their torn dress—we all six sat down. I gathered that the Crown Prince would not ordinarily have been allowed to eat at the same time as his father, but he was fluent in Náhuatl and was occasionally needed as interpreter when the old man or myself mishandled one another's language. Meanwhile, Zyanya helped feed the Lady Pair with a spoon. They were otherwise inclined to eat even the foam of chocolate with their fingers, messily, and to chew with their mouths open, and generally to nauseate anyone else present.

At that, their manners were no worse than the old man's. When the rest of us had been served the delectable white fish that are found nowhere but in the Lake Pátzkuaro, he said with a toothless grin, "Eat. Enjoy. Can take nothing but milk myself."

"Milk?" Zyanya repeated, in polite inquiry. "Milk of the doe, my lord?"

Then her winglike eyebrows went up. A very large, very bald woman came in, knelt beside the Uandákuari, lifted her blouse and presented to him a very large breast which, if it had had a countenance, could have been her hairless head. During the rest of the meal, when Yquíngare was not asking for particulars of the Lady Pair's origin and acquisition, he was sucking noisily at first one noselike nipple, then the other.

Zyanya avoided looking at him again; so did the Crown Prince; and they merely pushed their food around on their gold-and-lacquer plates. The twins ate heartily, because they always did, and I ate heartily because I was paying less attention to the vulgarity of Yquíngare than I was to another thing about him. On first entering the room, I had noticed that the guards held spears whose blades were of a coppery hue, but an oddly dark-colored copper. I had then perceived that both the Uandákuari and his son wore short daggers of the same metal, hung in thong loops at their waists.

The old man was addressing to me a rambling, roundabout speech, which I suspected was going to end in his asking whether I could also procure for him a set of conjoined adolescent twin *males*, when Zyanya, as if she could listen to no more, interrupted to ask, "What *is* this delicious drink?"

The Crown Prince, appearing delighted with the interruption, leaned across the cloth to tell her that it was chápari, a product of bees' honey, a most potent product, and that she had better not drink too much of it on her first trial.

"How wonderful!" she exclaimed, draining her lacquered cup. "If honey can be so intoxicating, why are not bees always drunk?" She hiccuped and sat thinking, evidently about bees, for when the Uandákuari tried to resume his driveling inquiry, Zyanya said loudly, "Perhaps they are. Who could tell?" And she poured another cup for herself and for me, somewhat oversloshing them.

The old man sighed, took one last suck at his nurse's slobbered teat, and gave it a loud dismissing slap to signal that the dreadful meal was done. Zyanya and I hastily drank our second cups of chápari. "Now," said Yquíngare, munching his mouth so that his nose and chin several times chomped together. His son jumped around behind him to haul him to his feet.

"A moment, my lord," I said, "while I give the Lady Pair a word of instruction."

"Instruction?" he said suspiciously.

"To comply," I said, smirking like a practiced pimp. "Lest, as virgins, they be annoyingly coy."

"Ah?" he rasped, smirking back. "Virgins as well, are they? Compliance, yes, by all means compliance."

Zyanya and Tzímtzicha gave me identical looks of contempt as I led the twins aside and imparted the instructions, the urgent instructions I had just devised. It was difficult, for I had to speak fast, and in their native language of Coatlícamac, and they were so *very* stupid. But finally they both nodded a sort of dim comprehension and, with a shrug of hope and despair, I shoved them toward the Uandákuari.

Unprotesting, they accompanied him up one staircase; helped him to climb it, in fact, looking like a crab helping a toad. Just before they reached the balcony, the toad turned and called something to his son, in Poré, so hoarsely that I caught not a word. Tzímtzicha nodded obediently to his father, then turned to ask if I and my lady were ready to retire. She only hiccuped, so I said we were; it had been a long day. We followed the Crown Prince to the stairs on the other side of the hall.

Thus it happened that, there in Tzintzuntzaní, for the first and only time in our married life, Zyanya and I slept with somebody besides each other. But please to remember, reverend friars, that we were both a bit drunk on the powerful chápari. Anyway, it was not exactly what it sounds, and I will do my best to explain.

Before leaving home, I had tried to tell Zyanya about the Purémpecha's predilection for inventive, voluptuous, and even perverse sexual practices. We had agreed that we would not evince surprise or disgust, whatever hospitality of that nature our hosts might offer us, but would decline it as graciously as possible. Or we thought we had so agreed. By the time the hospitality was provided, and we recognized it for what it was, we were already partaking. And we did not then recoil because—though she and I could never afterward decide whether it was wicked or innocuous—it was undeniably delightful.

As he led us toward the upper floor, Tzímtzicha turned and gave me an imitation of my own pimplike smirk, and inquired, "Will the knight and his lady wish separate rooms? Separate beds?"

"Certainly not," I said, and I said it in a chilly voice, before he might next suggest, "Separate partners?" or some other indecency.

"A conjugal chamber then, my lord," he said, agreeably enough. "But sometimes," he went on, casually, conversationally, "after a hard day's travel, even the most devoted couple may be fatigued. The court of Tzintzuntzaní would think itself remiss if its guests should feel, ahem, too tired to indulge each other, even for a single night. Hence we offer a facility called atánatanárani. It enhances the adequacy of a man, the receptiveness of a woman, perhaps to an extreme they have never before enjoyed."

The word atánatanárani, as best I could unravel its elements, meant only "a bunching together." Before I could inquire how a bunching together could enhance anything, he had bowed us into our chambers, backed himself out, and slid shut the lacquered door.

The lamplighted room contained the biggest, deepest, softest bed of piled quilts I had ever seen. There also awaited us two elderly slaves: one male, one female. I eyed them with apprehension, but they merely asked our permission to draw our baths. Adjoining the bedroom was a separate sanitary closet for each of us, complete with its own bathing trough and already hot steam room. My servant helped me sponge myself in the bath and afterward briskly pumiced me in the steam room, but he did nothing else, nothing untoward. I assumed that the slaves, the bathing and steaming were what the Crown Prince had meant by "a facility called atánatanárani." If so, it was but a civilized amenity, nothing obscene, and it had worked well. I felt refreshed and tingly-skinned and more than "adequate," as Tzímtzicha had put it, to "indulge" my wife.

Her slave and mine bowed out, and she and I emerged from

the sanitary closets to find the main chamber dark. The windows' draperies had all been closed and the oil lamps extinguished. So it took us a moment to find each other in that big room, and another moment to find even that immense bed. It was a warm night; only the topmost quilt had been turned back; we slid under it and lay side by side, sprawled on our backs, content for the moment just to enjoy the cloud-softness under us.

Zyanya murmured sleepily, "Do you know, Záa, I still feel as drunk as a bee." Then she gave a sudden small twitch and gasped, "*Ayyo*, you are eager! You took me by surprise."

I had been about to exclaim the same thing. I reached down to where a small hand was gently touching me—*her* hand, I had supposed—and said in amazement, "Zyanya!" just as she said:

"Záa, I can feel . . . it is a *child* down there. Playing with my . . . playing with me."

"I have one, too," I said in awe. "They were waiting for us, under the quilt. What do we do?"

I expected her to say, "Kick!" or "Scream!" or to do both those things herself. Instead, she gave another small gasp, and then a honey-drugged giggle, and repeated my question: "What do we do? What is *yours* doing?"

I told her.

"So is mine."

"It is not unpleasant."

"No. Decidedly not."

"They must be trained for this."

"But not for their own satisfaction. This one, anyway, is far too young."

"No. To enhance our pleasure, as the prince said."

"They might be punished if we rebuffed them."

I make those exchanges sound cool and dispassionate. They were not. We were speaking to each other in husky voices and in phrases broken by our involuntary gasps and movements.

"Is yours a boy or a girl? I cannot reach far enough to—"

"I cannot either. Does it matter?"

"No. The head is smooth, but the face feels as if it might be beautiful. The eyelashes are long enough to—ah! yes!—with the eyelashes!"

"They are well trained."

"Oh, exquisitely. I wonder if each is trained just to . . . I mean . . ."

"Let us trade, and find out."

The two children did not object to changing places under the quilt, and their performance was not diminished by it. Perhaps my new one's mouth was a trifle more warm and wet, having just come from . . .

Well, not to linger too long on that episode, Zyanya and I were soon in a frenzy, ravenously kissing, clutching, and clawing at each other; doing other things above the waist while the children were even busier below. When I could hold back no longer, we coupled like jaguars mating, and the children, squeezed out from between us, swarmed all over our bodies, tiny fingers here, tiny tongues there.

It happened not once, but more times than I can remember. Whenever Zyanya and I paused to rest, the children would snuggle for a time against our panting and perspiring bodies. Then very delicately they would insinuate themselves again, and start to tease and fondle. They would move back and forth from her to me, sometimes individually, sometimes together, so that for a while I would be attended by both of them *and* my wife—then both they and I would concentrate on her. It did not end until she and I were simply capable of no more, and we collapsed in the slumber of surfeit. We never did find out the sex or age or appearance of our accomplices. When I was awakened very early in the morning they were gone.

What woke me was a scratching at the door. Only half conscious, I got up and opened it. I saw nothing but the predawn darkness of the balcony and the great well of the hall beyond, but then a finger scratched at my bare leg. I started and looked down, and there were the Lady Pair, as naked as myself. They were on all fours—on all eights, I should say; the crab again— and they were both grinning lasciviously up at my crotch.

"Happy thing," said Left.

"His too," said Right, jerking her pointed head—in the direction of the old man's room, I assumed.

"What are you doing here?" I demanded, as ferociously as I could in a whisper.

One of their eight extremities reached up and put Yquíngare's dagger in my hand. I peered at the dark metal, even darker in that gloom, and ran my thumb along it. Hard and sharp it was, indeed.

"You did it!" I said, feeling a rush of gratitude, almost affection, for the monster crouching at my feet.

"Easy," said Right.

"He put clothes beside bed," said Left.

"He put that in me," said Right, poking my tepúli and making me jump again. "Happy."

"I get bored," said Left. "Nothing to do. Only be jiggled. I reach to clothes, feel around, find knife."

"She hold knife while I have happy," said Right. "I hold knife while she have happy. She hold knife while—"

"And now?" I interrupted.

"Finally he snore. We bring knife. Now we go wake him. Have more happy."

As if they could hardly wait, before I could even thank them, the twins scuttled crabwise along the dark balcony. So I silently gave thanks instead to the apparently invigorating properties of mammalian milk, and went back inside the chamber to wait for sunrise.

The courtiers of Tzintzuntzaní did not appear to be early risers. Only Crown Prince Tzímtzicha joined Zyanya and me for breakfast. I told the elderly prince that I and my company might as well be on our way. It seemed obvious that his father was enjoying his gift; we would not loiter about and make him interrupt his enjoyment just to entertain uninvited guests.

The prince said blandly, "Well, if you feel you must go, we will not detain you. Except for one formality. A search of yourselves, your guards and slaves, your possessions and packs and whatever else you are taking away. No insult intended, I assure you. Even I must endure it whenever I leave here to travel anywhere."

I shrugged as indifferently as one can when a cluster of armed guards is closing in to ring one about. Discreetly and respectfully, but thoroughly, they patted the clothed parts of me and Zyanya, all over, then politely asked us to step out of our sandals for a moment. In the forecourt garden, they did the same to all our men, had all our packs emptied out, even fingered among the cushions of the litter chairs. Other people were up and about by then, most of them the children of the palace, who watched the proceedings with bright and knowing eyes. I looked at Zyanya. She was looking closely at the children, trying to see which of them... When she caught me smiling at her, she blushed darker than the small blade of metal—its wooden handle removed—which I was carrying at the back of my neck, hidden under my hair.

The guards reported to Tzímtzicha that we were taking away nothing we had not come with. His watchfulness changed abruptly to friendliness and he said, "Then of course we insist that you take *something*, as a reciprocal gift for your Uey-Tlatoáni." He handed me a small leather sack, which I later found to contain a quantity of the finest quality oyster-heart pearls. "And," he went on, "something even more precious. It will just fit in that outsized litter of yours. I do not know what my father will do without it, his most prized possession, but it is his command."

At which he gave us the tremendous, bald, and big-breasted woman who had nursed the old man at the previous night's meal.

She was at least twice as heavy as the twins together had been, and all the way home the bearers cursed their lot in life. Every one-long-run or so, the whole train had to stop and stand fidgeting while the mammal unashamedly milked herself with her fingers to relieve the pressure. Zyanya laughed the whole way back, even laughed when we presented the gift to Ahuítzotl and he ordered me garrotted on the spot. But when I hastened to tell him what that milk-animal apparently could do for the wizened old Yquíngare, Ahuítzotl looked contemplative and canceled the order that I be strangled, and Zyanya laughed the more—so that even the Revered Speaker and I joined in the laughter.

If Ahuítzotl ever did get any invigoration out of the milk woman, she was a more valuable plunder than the killer-metal dagger turned out to be. Our Mexíca metalsmiths studied it intently, and scratched deep into it, and took filings from it, and at last concluded that it was made by puddling melted copper and melted tin together. But try as they might, they never could get the proportions right, or the temperature, or something, and they never did succeed in duplicating the metal.

However, since no tin existed in these lands except for those miniature hatchet-shaped scraps we used for trade currency—and since those came up the trade routes from some unknown country far, far to the south, passed from hand to hand—Ahuítzotl was at least able to order an immediate and continuing confiscation of all of them. So the tin disappeared from circulation as currency, and since we had no other use for it, I suppose Ahuítzotl simply stacked it away somewhere out of sight.

In a way, it was a selfish gesture: if we Mexíca could not have the mystery metal, no one could. But the Purémpecha already owned enough weapons made of it to discourage Tenochtítlan's declaring war on them ever again, and the stopping of the tin supply prevented them from making enough additional weapons that they could ever be emboldened to declare war on us. So I suppose I can claim that my mission into Michihuácan was not totally without result.

✠

At the time we returned from Michihuácan, Zyanya and I had been man and wife for some seven years; and I daresay our friends looked on us as an old married couple; and she and I had come to regard our life as fixed in its course and impervious to change or disruption; and we were happy enough with each other that we were satisfied to have it so. But the gods willed otherwise, and Zyanya made it known to me in this way:

We had been one afternoon visiting the First Lady at the palace. On our way out, we saw in a hallway that milk-animal woman we had brought from Tzintzuntzaní. I suspect that Ahuítzotl simply let her live on in the palace as a general servant, but on that occasion I made some humorous remark about his "wet nurse," expecting Zyanya to laugh. Instead she said, rather sharply for her:

"Záa, you must not make vulgar jokes about milk. About mother's milk. About mothers."

I said, "Not if it gives you offense. But why should it?"

Shyly, anxiously, apprehensively, she said, "Some time

about the turn of the year, I . . . I will be . . . I will be a milk-animal myself."

I stared at her. It took me a moment to comprehend and, before I could respond, she added, "I have suspected for some little time, but two days ago the physician confirmed it. I have been trying to think of a way to tell you in soft and sweet words. And now"—she sniffled unhappily—"I just snap it at you. Záa, where are you going? *Záa, do not leave me!*"

I had gone off at an undignified run, but only to procure a palace litter chair so she would not have to walk the way back to our home. She laughed and said, "This is ridiculous," when I insisted on lifting her onto the chair cushions. "But does it mean that you are pleased, Záa?"

"Pleased?" I exclaimed. *"Pleased!"*

At our house, Turquoise looked worried to see me assisting the protesting Zyanya up the short flight of stairs. But I shouted to her, "We are going to have a baby!" and she shrieked with joy. At the noise, Ticklish came running from somewhere, and I commanded, "Ticklish, Turquoise, go this instant and give the nursery a good cleaning. Make all the necessary preparations. Run and buy whatever is lacking. A cradle. Flowers. Put flowers everywhere!"

"Záa, will you hush?" said Zyanya, half amused, half embarrassed. "It will be months yet. The room can wait."

But the two slave women had already dashed obediently, exuberantly up the stairs. And, over her protests, I helped Zyanya up there too, and insisted she lie down for a rest after her exertion of visiting the palace. I went downstairs to congratulate myself with a drink of octli and a smoke of picíetl, and to sit in the twilight and gloat in solitude.

Gradually, though, my excitement subsided into more serious meditation, and I began to perceive the several reasons why Zyanya had been somewhat hesitant about telling me of the coming event. She had said it would occur about the turn of the year. Counting backward on my fingers, I realized that our child must have been conceived during that night in old Yquíngare's palace. I chuckled at that. No doubt Zyanya was a bit discomfited by that fact. She would have preferred that the child had its beginning in more sedate circumstances. Well, I thought it far better to conceive a child in a paroxysm of rapture, as we had done, than in a torpid acquiescence to duty or conformity or inevitability, as most parents did.

But I could not chuckle at the next thought that came to me. The child could be handicapped from the moment of his birth, because it was possible that he would inherit my weakness of vision. Granted, he would not have to stumble and grope through as many years as I had done before I discovered the seeing crystal. But I pitied an infant who would have to learn how to hold a topaz to his eye even before he learned how to get a spoon to his mouth, and his being pathetically unable to toddle about on his infant excursions without it, and his being cruelly called Yellow Eye or the like by his playmates. . . .

If the child was a girl, that close-sightedness would not be such a disadvantage. Neither her childhood games nor her adult occupations would be strenuous or dependent on the keenness of her physical senses. Females were not competitive with each other until they reached the age when they vied for the most desirable husbands, and then it would be less important how my daughter saw than how she looked. But—agonizing thought—suppose she both saw *and* looked like me! A son would be pleased to inherit my head-nodder height. A girl would be desolated, and she would hate me, and I would probably be revolted by the sight of her. I imagined our daughter looking exactly like that tremendous milk woman. . . .

And that gave rise to another worry. During the many days prior to the night of the child's conception, Zyanya had been in intimate proximity to the monstrous Lady Pair! It was well attested that countless children had been born deformed or deficient when their mothers were affected by far less gruesome influences. Worse yet, Zyanya had said "some time about the turn of the year." And right then fell the five nemontémtin! A child born during those nameless and lifeless days was so ill-omened that its parents were expected, even encouraged, to let it die of malnourishment. I was not so superstitious as to do that. But then, what kind of burden or monster or evildoer might that child grow up to be . . . ?

I smoked picíetl and drank octli until Turquoise came and saw my condition and said, "For shame, my lord master!" and summoned Star Singer to help me to bed.

* * *

"I will be a shambling ruin before the time arrives," I said to Zyanya the next morning. "I wonder if all fathers have such worrisome apprehensions."

She smiled and said, "Not nearly as many as a mother does, I think. But a mother knows she can do absolutely nothing but wait."

I sighed and said, "I see no other course for me, either. I can only devote my every moment to caring for you and tending you and seeing that no slightest harm or affliction—"

"Do that and *I* will be a ruin!" she cried, as if she meant it. "Please, my darling, do find something else to occupy you."

Stung and deflated by the rejection, I slouched off to take my morning bath. But, after I had come downstairs and breakfasted, a diversion did present itself, in the person of a caller, Cozcatl.

"Ayyo, how could you have heard already?" I exclaimed. "But it was thoughtful of you to come calling so quickly."

My greeting seemed to bewilder him. He said, "Heard of what? Actually I came to—"

"Why, that we are going to have a baby!" I said.

His face went briefly bleak before he said, "I am happy for you, Mixtli, and for Zyanya. I call on the gods to bless you with a well-favored child." Then he mumbled, "It is only that the coincidence flustered me for a moment. Because I came this morning to ask your permission to marry."

"To marry? But that is news as marvelous as my own!" I shook my head. "Imagine . . . the boy Cozcatl, of an age to take a wife. Sometimes I do not notice how the years have gone. But what do you mean, ask my permission?"

"My intended wife is not free to marry. She is a slave."

"So?" I still did not comprehend. "Surely you can afford to buy her freedom."

"I can," he said. "But will you sell her? I want to marry Quequelmíqui, and she wants to marry me."

"What?"

"It was through you that I first met her, and I confess that many of my visits here have been something of a pretext, so that she and I could have a little time together. Most of our courtship has been conducted in your kitchen."

548

I was astounded. "Ticklish? Our little maid? But she is barely adolescent!"

He reminded me gently, "She was when you bought her, Mixtli. The years *have* gone."

And so they had, I thought. Ticklish could be only a year or two younger than Cozcatl, and he was—let me see—he had turned twenty and two. I said magnanimously:

"You have my permission and my congratulations and my felicitations, Cozcatl. But buy her? Most certainly not. She is but the first of our wedding gifts to you. No, no, I will hear no protest; I insist on it. Had she not been schooled by you, the girl would never have been worth consideration as a wife. I remember her when she first came here. Giggling."

"Then I thank you, Mixtli, and so will she. I also want to say"—he looked flustered again—"I have of course told her about myself. About the wound I suffered. She understands that we can never have children, like you and Zyanya."

It was then that I realized how my own abrupt announcement must have dashed his own exultation. All unknowingly and unintentionally, I had been heartless. But before I could frame words of apology, he continued:

"Quequelmíqui swears that she loves me and will accept me for what I am. But I must be sure that she fully realizes—the extent of my inadequacy. Our kitchen caresses have never got to the point of . . ."

He was floundering in embarrassment, so I tried to help. "You mean you have not yet—"

"She has never even seen me unclothed," he blurted. "And she is a virgin, innocent of all knowledge about the relations between a man and a woman."

I said, "It will be Zyanya's responsibility, as her mistress, to sit her down for a woman-to-woman talk. I am sure Zyanya will enlighten her on the more intimate aspects of marriage."

"That will be a kindness," said Cozcatl. "But after that, would you also speak to her, Mixtli? You have known me longer and—well, better than has Zyanya. You could tell Quequelmíqui more specifically of my limitations as a conjugal partner. Would you do that?"

I said, "I will do my best, Cozcatl, but I warn you. A virginally innocent girl suffers doubts and trepidations about taking even a commonplace husband of ordinary physical attributes. When I tell her bluntly what she can expect from this marriage—and what she cannot—it may further affright her."

"She loves me," Cozcatl said ringingly. "She has given her promise. I know her heart."

"Then you are unique among men," I said drily. "I know only this much. A woman thinks of marriage in terms of flowers and birdsong and butterfly flutterings. When I speak to Ticklish in terms of flesh and organs and tissues, it will at best disillusion her. At worst, she may fly in panic from ever marrying you or anybody. You would not thank me for that."

"But I would," he said. "Quequelmíqui deserves better than an appalling surprise on her wedding night. If she decides to refuse me, I had rather it be now than then. Oh, it would destroy me, yes. If the good and loving Quequelmíqui will not have me, neither will any other woman, ever. I shall enlist in some army troop and go off to war somewhere and perish in it. But whatever happens, Mixtli, I would not hold it against you. No, I plead that you do me this favor."

So, when he departed, I told Zyanya of his news and his request. She called Ticklish from the kitchen, and the girl came blushing and trembling and twisting her fingers in her blouse hem. We both embraced her and congratulated her on having captured the affection of such a fine young man. Then Zyanya put a motherly arm around her waist and led her upstairs, while I sat down with my paint pots and bark paper. When I had written the document of manumission, I nervously smoked a poquíetl—several of them, before Ticklish came downstairs again.

She had been blushing before; now she glowed like a brazier; she was quivering even more visibly. Her agitation may have made her look prettier than she usually was, but it was truly the first time I had noticed that she was in fact a most attractive girl. I suppose one never pays much attention to the familiar furnishings of one's house until someone from outside compliments a piece.

I handed her the paper and she said, "What is this, my master?"

"A document which says that the free woman Quequelmíqui must nevermore call anyone master. Try instead to think of me as a family friend, for Cozcatl has asked that I explain some things to you."

I plunged right in, with not much delicacy, I fear. "Most men, Ticklish, have a thing called a tepúli—"

She interrupted, though without raising her bowed head. "I know what that is, my lord. I had brothers in my family. My lady mistress says a man puts it inside a woman . . . here." She pointed modestly at her lap. "Or he does if he has one. Cozcatl told me how he lost his."

"And thereby lost his ability ever to make you a mother. He is also deprived of some of the pleasures of marriage. But he has not been deprived of his desire that *you* enjoy those pleasures, or his ability to give them to you. Though he has no tepúli to link you and him together, there are other means of doing the act of love."

I turned slightly away, to spare us both the unease of my seeing her blushes, and I tried to speak in the flat, bored tone of a schoolmaster. Well, the basic instructions can be told in a schoolmasterish voice, but—when I began to dwell on the numerous stimulating and satisfying things that can be done to a woman's breasts and tipíli and especially the sensitive xacapíli, by means of fingers and tongue and lips and even eyelashes—well, I could not help remembering all the nuances and refinements I myself had employed and enjoyed, in times recent and past, and my voice tended to become unsteady. So I hurried to conclude:

"A woman can find those delights nearly as satisfying as the more usual act. Many would rather be thus satisfied than merely impaled. Some even do those things with other women, and give no thought to the absence of a tepúli."

Ticklish said, "It sounds . . ." and so quaveringly that I turned to look at her. She sat with her body tensed to rigidity, her eyes and fists tight closed. "It feels . . ." Her whole body jerked. *"Won-der-ful . . . !"* The word was long-drawn, as if wrung from her. It took a while for her fists to unclench and her eyes to open. She lifted them to me, and they were like smoky lamps. "Thank you for . . . for telling me those things."

I remembered how Ticklish used to giggle without provocation. Could it be possible that she was excitable in other ways without being touched or even undressed?

I said, "I can no longer command you, and this is an impertinence you may refuse. But I should like to see your bosom."

She looked at me with wide-eyed innocence, and she hesitated, but then slowly she raised her blouse. Her breasts were not large, but they were well formed, and their nipples swelled just from the touch of my gaze upon them, and their areolas were dark and large, almost too big for a man's mouth to encompass. I sighed, and signaled that she could go. I hoped I was in error, but I very much feared that Ticklish would not *always* be satisfied with less than real copulation, and that Cozcatl risked being eventually the unhappiest kind of husband.

I went upstairs and found Zyanya standing in the doorway of the nursery, no doubt contemplating additions and improvements to its facilities. I did not say anything of my misgivings about the wisdom of Cozcatl's marriage. I merely remarked:

"When Ticklish leaves, we will be one servant short. Turquoise cannot manage the household and look after you as well. Cozcatl picked an untimely moment to declare his intentions. Most unfortunate for us."

"Misfortune!" Zyanya exclaimed brightly. "You said once, Záa, that if I needed help, we might persuade Béu to join us here. The departure of Ticklish is a very minor misfortune, thank the gods, but it provides an excuse. We *will* need another woman around the house. Oh, Záa, let us ask her!"

"An inspired notion," I said. I was not exactly palpitant at the prospect of having the embittered Béu about, especially during such a nervous time as that, but whatever Zyanya wanted I would get for her. I said, "I will send an invitation so imploring that she cannot refuse."

I sent it by the same seven soldiers who had once marched south with me, so that Waiting Moon would have a protective escort if she did agree to come to Tenochtítlan. And she did, without protest or reluctance. Nevertheless, it took her some time to make all the arrangements for leaving the inn's management to her servants and slaves. Meanwhile, Zyanya and I provided a grand wedding ceremony for Cozcatl and Ticklish, and they went off together to live in his house.

It was well into winter when the seven warriors delivered Béu Ribé to our door. By that time, I was honestly as anxious and as pleased to see her as Zyanya was. My wife had got large—alarmingly so, in my opinion—and had begun to suffer aches and irritabilities and other symptoms of distress. Although she peevishly kept assuring me that those things were quite natural, they worried me and kept me hovering about her and trying to do helpfulnesses for her, all of which made her more peevish yet.

She cried, "Oh, Béu, thank you for coming! I thank Uizye Tao and every other god that you have come!" And she fell into her sister's arms as if embracing a deliverer. "You may have saved my life! I am being *pampered* to death!"

Béu's luggage was put in the guest chamber prepared for her, but she spent most of that day with Zyanya in our room, from which I was forcibly excluded, to mope about the rest of the house and fret and feel discarded. Toward twilight, Béu came downstairs alone. While we took chocolate together, she said, almost conspiratorially:

"Zyanya will soon be at that stage of her pregnancy when you must forgo your . . . your husbandly rights. What will you do during that while?"

I nearly told her it was none of her business, but I said only, "I imagine I will survive."

She persisted, "It would be unseemly if you were to resort to a stranger."

Affronted, I stood up and said stiffly, "I may not *enjoy* enforced continence, but—"

"But you could hope to find no acceptable substitute for Zyanya?" She tilted her head as if seriously expecting an answer. "In all of Tenochtítlan you could find no one as beautiful as she is? And so you sent to faraway Tecuantépec for me?" She smiled and stood and came very close to me, her breasts brushing my front. "I look so very much like Zyanya that you might deem *me* a satisfactory substitute, am I not right?" She toyed with my mantle clasp, as if she would mischievously undo it. "But, Záa, although Zyanya and I are sisters, and physically so similar, we are not necessarily indistinguishable. In bed, you might find us very different. . . ."

Firmly I put her away from me. "I wish you a pleasant stay in this house, Béu Ribé. But, if you cannot hide your dislike of me, will you at least refrain from demonstrating it in such maliciously insincere coquetry? Cannot we both manage simply to ignore each other?"

When I strode away, her face was as flushed as if I had surprised her in some indecent act, and she was rubbing her face as if I had slapped her for it.

✠

Señor Bishop Zumárraga, it is an honor and a flattery to have you join us once again. Your Excellency is just in time to hear me announce—as proudly as I announced it those many years ago—the birth of my beloved daughter.

All my apprehensions, I am happy to say, proved unfounded. The child evinced intelligence even before she emerged into this life, for she waited prudently in the womb until after the lifeless nemontémtin days had passed, and made her appearance on the day Ce-Malináli, or One Grass, of the first month of the year Five House. I was then thirty and one years old, somewhat overage to be starting a family, but I preened and strutted just as preposterously as younger men do—as if I had alone conceived and carried and been delivered of the infant.

While Béu stayed at Zyanya's bedside, the physician and the mid-wife came to tell me that the child was a female and to answer all my anxious questions. They seemed to think me demented when I wrung my hands and said, "Speak the truth. I can bear it. Is it really two girls in one body?" No, they said, it was not any kind of twins, but a single daughter. No, she was not of extraordinarily great size. No, she was not monstrous in any respect and she appeared unmarked by any portents. When I pressed the doctor as to the acuity of her eyesight, he replied in some exasperation that newborn babies are not notable for eagle vision, or for boasting about it if they have it. I must wait until she could talk and tell me herself.

They gave me the child's navel string, then went back into the nursery to dip One Grass in cold water, to swaddle her and to subject her to the midwife's cautionary and instructive harangue. I went downstairs and, with unsteady fingers, wrapped the moist string around a ceramic spindle wheel and, mouthing a few silent prayers and thanks to the gods, buried it under the stones of the kitchen hearth. Then I hurried upstairs again to wait impatiently to be admitted for my first look at my daughter.

I kissed my wanly smiling wife and, with my topaz, examined the dwarf face cuddled in the bend of her elbow. I had seen the new offspring of other parents, so I was not shocked, but I *was* a bit disappointed to find that ours was in no way superior. She was as red and wrinkled as a chopíni chili pod, as bald and ugly as an aged Purémpe. I tried to feel a proper rush of love for her, but without success. I was assured by all present that it was indeed my daughter, a new fragment of humankind, but I would have been equally prepared to believe them if they had confessed that it was a newborn, still-hairless howler monkey. It had the howl, at any rate.

I need hardly say that the child day by day appeared more human, and that I viewed her with more appreciative and affectionate regard. I called her Cocóton, a common nickname for girl children; it means the crumb fallen from a larger piece of bread. It was not long before Cocóton began to manifest a resemblance to her mother, and necessarily her aunt, which is to say that no baby could have become more quickly more beautiful. Her hair grew in, in ringlets. Her eyelashes appeared, and they had the same abundance, in miniature, as the hummingbird-wing lashes of Zyanya and Béu. Her eyebrows grew in, and they had the same winglike uptilt as those of Zyanya and Béu. She began to smile more frequently than she howled, and her smile was that of Zyanya, compelling all about her to reflect it. Even Béu, who in recent years had been so dour, was influenced often to smile that same radiant smile again.

Zyanya was soon up and about, though her activities were for a time centered only on Cocóton, who insisted that her milk-animal be frequently available. Béu's presence made it unnecessary for me to watch over the welfare of Zyanya and our baby, and I was often ignored by both women, even by the baby, when now and then I proffered uninvited suggestions or attentions. Nevertheless, I did occasionally insist on being obeyed, simply as the man of the household. When Cocóton was nearly two months old, and was no longer so frequently needful of her milk supplier, Zyanya began to show signs of restlessness.

She had been pent in the house for months, getting no farther outdoors than our rooftop garden, to bask in the beams of Tonatíu and the breezes of Ehécatl. She would like to venture farther outside, she said, and reminded me that the ceremony honoring Xipe Totec was soon to be held in The Heart of the One World. She wanted to attend. I positively forbade it.

I said, "Cocóton was born unmarked and unmonstrous and with seemingly unimpaired eyesight, thanks to her tonáli, or ours, or the gods' good will. Let us not now put her at hazard. As long as she is nursing, we must take care that evil influences do not get into your milk, through your being frightened or upset by some shocking sight. I cannot think of anything more likely to horrify you than the Xipe Totec celebration. We will go anywhere else you ask, my love, but not to that."

Oh, yes, Your Excellency, I had often seen the honoring of Xipe Totec, for it was one of the most important religious rituals observed by us Mexíca and by many other peoples. The ceremony was impressive, I might say unforgettable, but even in those days I could scarcely believe that any participant or onlooker *enjoyed* it. Though it has now been many years since I last saw Xipe Totec die and come back to life, I still can hardly bear to describe the manner of it—and my revulsion owes nothing to my having become Christian and civilized. However, if Your Excellency is so interested and insistent...

Xipe Totec was our god of seedtime, and that came in our month of Tlacaxípe Ualíztli, which can be translated as The Gentle Flaying. It was the season when the dead stumps and stalks of last year's harvests were burned off or cleared away or turned under, so the earth was clean and ready to receive its new planting. Death making way for life, you see, as it does even for Christians, when at every seedtime the Lord Jesus dies and is reborn. Your Excellency need not make noises of protest. The impious similarity goes no further.

I will not describe all the public preliminaries and accompaniments: the flowers and music and dancing and colors and costumes and processions and the thunder of the drum which tears out the heart. I will make this as mercifully brief as I can.

Know, then, that a young man or girl was selected before-hand to act the honored role of Xipe Totec, which means The

Dear One Flayed. The personifier's sex was less important than the requirement that he or she be grown to full stature but be still a virgin. Usually it was a foreigner of noble birth, captured in some war when still a child and saved especially to represent the god when grown. Never was a slave purchased for the purpose, because Xipe Totec merited and demanded and was provided a young person of the highest available class.

For some days before the ceremony, the youth was housed in the temple of Xipe Totec and was treated with every kindness, lavished with every pleasure of food and drink and entertainment. Also, once the youth's virginity had been acceptably substantiated, it was quickly disposed of. He or she was allowed unlimited sexual license—encouraged to it, even forced to it when necessary—for it was a vital part of playing the god of springtime fertility. If the xochimíqui was a young man, he could name all the girls and women of the community whom he had ever desired, unwed or not. Assuming those women consented, as did many even of the married ones, they would be brought to him. If the xochimíqui was a girl, she could name and summon all the men she wanted, and spread herself for them.

Sometimes, however, the youth selected for the honor of godhood would be averse to that aspect of the performance. If it was a young woman, and she tried to decline the opportunity to wallow, she would be forcibly deflowered by the high priest of Xipe Totec. In the case of a determinedly chaste young man, he would be tied down and straddled by a female temple attendant. If, once introduced to the pleasure, the young person was still recalcitrant, he or she would have to endure repeated violation by the temple women or priests and, when those were sated, by any commonfolk who might desire to take a turn. There was always a sufficiency of those, the devout who slavered to couple with a god or goddess, the merely lecherous, the curious, the childless women or impotent men who hoped to be impregnated or rejuvenated by the deity. Yes, Your Excellency, there occurred every sexual excess Your Excellency's fancy can envision—except the coupling of god and man or goddess and woman. Such acts, being the very contravention of fertility, would have been repugnant to Xipe Totec.

On the day of the ceremony, after the attending crowd had

been entertained by many performances of dwarfs and jugglers and tocotíne and such, Xipe Totec made his public appearance. The young girl or man was dressed as the god, in a costume combining dry old maize husks and bright new sprigs of greenery, in a wide-spreading fan crown of the most colorful feathers, in a flowing mantle and gilded sandals. The youth was carried many times about The Heart of the One World in an elegant litter chair, with much pageantry and deafening music, while he or she scattered seeds and maize kernels over the cheering and chanting throng. Then the procession came to Xipe Totec's low pyramid in one corner of the plaza, and all the drumming and music and singing stopped, and the crowd hushed, as the young personifier of the god was set down at the foot of the temple's staircase.

There two priests helped her divest herself of the costume, piece by piece, until she stood entirely naked before all the plaza's massed eyes—some of which already knew every detail and private crevice of her body. The priests handed her a bundle of twenty small reed flutes, and she turned her back to the crowd. The two priests flanked her as she slowly climbed toward the altar stone and temple above. She played a trill on one of the flutes at each of the twenty ascending steps, then broke that flute in her hands. On the last step, she may perhaps have played a little longer and more sadly on the last flute, but the escorting priests would not let her prolong the song unduly. It was required that Xipe Totec's life end when the final flute's trilling ended.

Then she was seized by the other priests waiting at the pyramid summit, and was laid backward across the stump of stone there, and two of the priests whipped out their obsidian knives. While one rent the breast and tore out the still pulsing heart, the other sawed off the still blinking and mouthing head. In none of our other ceremonies was the sacrificial victim decapitated, and it had no religious significance even in the Xipe Totec rites, where the xochimíqui was beheaded only for a practical reason: it is easier to remove a dead person's skin when the head and body are separated.

The flaying was done out of sight of the crowd, the two pieces of the youth having been whisked inside the temple, and the priests were very deft at it. The head's skin was slit up the back, from nape to crown, the scalp and face peeled off the skull and the eyelids cut away. The body was also slit up the back, from anus to neck stump, but the skin of arms and legs was carefully loosed as untorn empty tubes. If the xochimíqui had been a young woman, the padding of soft flesh inside her breasts and buttocks was left intact to preserve their rotundity. If it had been a young man, his tepúli and olóltin were left attached and dangling.

The smallest priest of Xipe Totec—and there was always one small man among them—quickly doffed his robes and, naked, donned the two pieces of the costume. The body skin being still moist and slippery on the inside, it was not difficult for him to wriggle his own arms and legs into the corresponding tubes. The dead feet had been removed, for they would interfere with the priest's dancing, but the dead hands were left attached to wave and flap alongside his own. The torso skin of course did not meet at the back, but it was there perforated for thongs which laced it tight around his body. The priest then put on the dead youth's hair and face, positioned so that he could see through the empty eyeholes and sing through the slack lips, and it too was laced up the back. Any traces of blood on the outside of the costume were sponged off and the slit in the chest skin was sewn shut.

All that took very little longer than it takes me to tell it to Your Excellency. It seemed to the onlookers that the dead Xipe Totec had scarcely left the altar stone than he reappeared alive in the temple doorway. He stood bent, pretending to be an old man, leaning for support on two glistening thighbones, the only other parts of the xochimíqui's body utilized in the ceremony. As the drums roared to greet him, The Dear One Flayed slowly straightened up, like an old man becoming young again. He danced down the pyramid stairs and capered maniacally about the plaza, flourishing the slimy thighbones and using them to give a tap of blessing to everyone who could press close enough.

Before the ceremony, the small priest always made himself drunk and delirious by eating many of the mushrooms called the flesh of the gods. He had to, for he had the most arduous part in the remainder of the proceedings. He was required to dance frantically and unceasingly, except during those periods when he collapsed unconscious, for five days and nights thereafter. Of course, his dance gradually lost its first wild abandon, as the skin he wore began to dry and tighten on him. Toward the close of the five days, it was so shrunken and crackly as to be really constrictive, and the sun and air had turned it to a sickly yellow color—for which reason it was called the Garment of Gold—and it smelled so horrible that no one then in the plaza would come near enough for Xipe Totec to bless him with a tap of a bone. . . .

His Excellency's latest anguished departure impels me to remark—if it is not irreverent, lord scribes—that His Excellency has a remarkable faculty for joining us always to hear only those things that will most annoy or disgust him to hear.

In later years I was to say, with deep regret, that I wished I had never denied Zyanya anything; that I ought to have let her do and see and experience everything that caught her interest and dilated her eyes with wonder; that I should never even once have thwarted her blithe enthusiasm for every smallest thing in the world about her. Still, I cannot reproach myself that I kept her from ever seeing the Xipe Totec ceremony.

Whether or not I can claim any credit, no bad influences got into Zyanya's milk. The baby Cocóton thrived on it, and grew, and grew ever more pretty, a miniature of her mother and aunt. I doted on her, but I was not the only one who did. When Zyanya and Béu one day took the baby with them to market, a Totonácatl passerby saw Cocóton smiling from the shawl sling in which Béu carried her, and asked the women's permission to capture that smile in clay. He was one of those itinerant artists who turn out quantities of terra cotta figurines from molds and then tramp about the countryside to sell them cheaply to poor farm folk. On the spot, he adroitly did a little clay portrait of Cocóton, and later, after he had used it to make his mold for stamping out the duplicates, he came and presented Zyanya with the original. It was not really a perfect likeness, and he had put upon it the flared Totonáca headdress, but I instantly recognized my daughter's broad and infectious smile, complete with dimples. I do not know how many copies he made, but for a long time you could see little girls everywhere playing with that doll. Even some adults bought it under the impression that it represented the laughing young god Xochi-pîli, Lord of Flowers, or the happy goddess Xilónen, Young Maize Mother. I should not be surprised if there are still some of those figurines here and there, still unbroken, but it would lacerate my heart if I found one now and saw again that smile of my daughter and my wife.

Toward the close of the child's first year of life, when she had grown her first little maize-kernel teeth, she was weaned in the age-old manner of Mexíca mothers. When she cried to be suckled, her lips would more and more often encounter not Zyanya's sweet breast but a bitter leaf cupped over it: one of the astringent, mouth-puckering leaves of the sabila maguey. Gradually, Cocóton let herself be persuaded to take instead soft mushes like atóli, and eventually abandoned the nipple altogether. It was at that time that Béu Ribé announced that she was no longer needed by our family, that she would return to her inn, that Turquoise could easily take over the care of the infant when Zyanya was weary or occupied with other things.

I again provided an escort for Béu: the same seven soldiers whom I had come to regard as my private little army, and I walked with her and them as far as the causeway.

"We hope you will come again, sister Waiting Moon," I said, though we had already spent most of that morning saying farewells, and Béu had been given many gifts, and both women had wept a good deal.

"I will come whenever I am needed... or wanted," she said. "Getting away from Tecuantépec this first time should make it easier for me in the future. But I think I shall not often be needed or ever wanted. I would rather not admit having been wrong, Záa, but honesty compels me. You *are* a good husband to my sister."

"It takes no great effort," I said. "The best of husbands is that man who has the best of wives."

She said, with a touch of her former teasing manner, "How do you know? You have married only one. Tell me, Záa, do you never feel even a fleeting attraction to... to any other woman?"

"Oh, yes," I said, laughing at myself. "I am human, and human emotions can be unruly, and there are many other al-

luring women. Like you, Béu. I can even be attracted to women
less beautiful than Zyanya or you—merely out of curiosity
about the possible other attributes under their clothes or behind
their faces. But in nearly nine years my thoughts have never
yet progressed to the deed, and to lie beside Zyanya quickly
dispels the thoughts, so I do not blush for them."

I hasten to say, reverend friars, that my Christian catechists
taught me different: that a wanton idea can be just as sinful as
the most lascivious fornication. But I was then still a heathen;
we all were. So the whims that I did not invite and did not
commit did not trouble me any more than anybody else was
troubled by them.

Béu looked at me sidelong from her glorious eyes and said,
"You are already an Eagle Knight. It only remains for you to
be honored with the -tzin to your name. As a noble, you need
not stifle even your most secret yearnings. Zyanya could not
object to being the First Wife among your others, if she approved of the others. You could have all the women you want."

I smiled and said, "I already do. She is most aptly named
Always."

Béu nodded and turned and, without looking back, walked
out of sight along the causeway.

There were men working that day at the island end of the
causeway Béu crossed, and others working along the length
of it, as far as the midway fort of Acachinánco, and there were
other laborers at work on the mainland to the southwest. The
men were building the two ends of a new stone aqueduct to
bring an increased supply of fresh water to the city.

For a long time, the many communities and settled lands
of the lake district had been so rapidly increasing in population
that all three nations of The Triple Alliance were becoming
intolerably overcrowded. Tenochtítlan, of course, was the
worst affected, for the simple reason that it was an island
incapable of expansion. That is why, when the Xoconóchco
was annexed, so many city dwellers picked up their families
and households and moved to settle there. And that voluntary
migration gave the Uey-Tlatoáni the idea of encouraging other
removals.

By then, it had become evident that the Tapáchtlan garrison

would forever discourage any further forays of enemies into the Xoconóchco, so Motecuzóma the Younger was relieved of his command there. As I have explained, Ahuítzotl had reasons for keeping his nephew at a distance. But he was also shrewd enough to go on making use of the man's proven ability for organization and administration. He sent Motecuzóma next to Teloloápan, a flyspeck village between Tenochtítlan and the southern ocean, and commanded him to make of it another fortified and thriving community on the model of Tapáchtlan.

For that, Motecuzóma was given another sizable army troop and a sizable number of civilians. Those were families and individuals who may or may not have been dissatisfied with life in Tenochtítlan or its environs, but when the Revered Speaker said, "You will go," they went. And when Motecuzóma allotted them estimable landholdings in and around Teloloápan, they all settled down under his governorship, to make of that miserable village a respectable town.

So, as soon as Teloloápan had a garrison built and was feeding itself with its own harvests, Motecuzóma the Younger was again relieved of command and sent to do the same thing elsewhere. Ahuítzotl ordered him to one petty village after another: Oztóman, Alahuíztlan—I forget all their names, but they were all situated on the farther borders of The Triple Alliance. As those remote colonies multiplied and each of them grew, they accomplished three things pleasing to Ahuítzotl. They drained away more and more of the excess population of our lake district—from Texcóco, Tlácopan, and other lake cities as well as from Tenochtítlan. They provided us with strong frontier outposts. And the continuing process of colonization kept Motecuzóma both profitably occupied and far from any possibility of intriguing against his uncle.

But the emigrations and removals could only stop the *increase* of population in Tenochtítlan; there was never enough of an outpouring to lessen the crowding and elbowing of those who remained. The island-city's chief need was of more fresh water. A steady supply of that had been arranged by the first Motecuzóma when he built the aqueduct from the sweet springs of Chapultépec, more than a sheaf of years before, about the same time he built the Great Dike to protect the city from windblown floods. But the flow from Chapultépec could not be persuaded to increase just because more was needed. That was proved; a number of our priests and sorcerers tried all their means of suasion, and all failed.

It was then that Ahuítzotl determined to find a new source of water, and sent those same priests and sorcerers and a few of his Speaking Council wise men to scout other regions of the nearby mainland. By whatever means of divination, they did tap into a previously undiscovered spring, and the Revered Speaker at once began to plan a new aqueduct. Since that newfound stream near Coyohuácan gushed up more strongly than that of Chapultépec, Ahuítzotl even planned for it to make fountains spout in The Heart of the One World.

But not everybody was so enthusiastic, and one who advised caution was the Revered Speaker Nezahualpíli of Texcóco, when he was invited by Ahuítzotl to inspect the new spring and the work just getting under way on the new aqueduct. I did not hear their conversation with my own ears; there was no reason for me to be present on that occasion; I was probably at home playing games with my baby daughter. But I can reconstruct the consultation of the two Revered Speakers from what I was told by their attendants long after the event.

For one thing, Nezahualpíli warned, "My friend, you and your city may have to choose between having too little water and having too much of it," and he reminded Ahuítzotl of some historical facts.

This city is now and has for sheaves of years been an island surrounded by water, but it was not always so. When the earliest ancestors of us Mexíca came from the mainland to make their permanent habitation here, they *walked* here. It was no doubt a sloppy and uncomfortable march for them, but they did not have to swim. All the area that is now water between here and the mainland to the west, to the north, to the south, was in those days only a soggy swamp of mud and puddles and sawgrass, and this place was then merely the one dry and firm extrusion of land in that widespread marsh.

Over the years of building a city here, those early settlers also laid firmer paths for easier access to the mainland. Perhaps their first paths were no more than ridges of packed earth, a trifle higher than the bog. But eventually the Mexíca sank double rows of pilings and tamped rubble between them, and on top of those foundations laid the stone pavings and parapets of the three causeways that still exist. Those causeways impeded the marsh's draining its surface waters into the lake beyond, and the blocked swamp waters began perceptibly to rise.

It made a considerable improvement over previous conditions. The water covered the stinking mud and the leg-slashing sawgrass and the standing puddles from which swarms of mosquitoes were endlessly being born. Of course, if the water had continued to mount, it could eventually have covered this island, too, and flooded into the streets of Tlácopan and other mainland cities. But the causeways were built with wooden-bridged gaps in them at intervals, and the island itself was trenched with its many canals for the passage of canoes. Those spillways allowed a sufficient overflow of the waters into Lake Texcóco on the island's eastern side, so the artificially created lagoon rose only so high and no higher.

"Or it has not yet," Nezahualpíli said to Ahuítzotl. "But now you propose to pipe new water across from the mainland. It must go somewhere."

"It goes to the city for our people's consumption," Ahuítzotl said testily. "For drinking, bathing, laundering . . ."

"Very little water is ever *consumed,*" said Nezahualpíli. "Even if your people drink it all the day long, they must urinate it as well. I repeat: the water must go somewhere. And where but into this damned-in part of the lake? Its level could rise faster than it can drain out through your canals and causeway passages into Lake Texcóco beyond."

Beginning to swell and redden, Ahuítzotl demanded, "Do you suggest we ignore our newfound spring, that gift of the gods? That we do nothing to alleviate the thirst of Tenochtítlan?"

"It might be more prudent. At least, I suggest you build your aqueduct in such a way that the flow of water can be monitored and controlled—and shut off if necessary."

Ahuítzotl said in a growl, "With your increasing years, old friend, you become increasingly a fearful old woman. If we Mexíca had always listened to those who told us what could not be done, we should never have done anything."

"You asked my opinion, old friend, and I have given it," said Nezahualpíli. "But the final responsibility is yours, and"— he smiled—"your name is Water Monster."

The Aqueduct of Ahuítzotl was finished within a year or so after that, and the palace seers took great pains to choose a most auspicious day for its dedication and the first unloosing of its waters. I remember well the date of the day, Thirteen Wind, for it lived up to its name.

The crowd began to gather long before the ceremony commenced, for it was almost as much of an event as the dedication of the Great Pyramid had been, twelve years earlier. But of course all those people could not be let onto the Coyohuácan causeway where the main rituals were to be performed. The mass of commonfolk had to clump together at the southern end of the city, and jostle and lean and peer for a glimpse of Ahuítzotl, his wives, his Speaking Council, the high nobles, priests, knights, and other personages who would come by canoe from the palace to take their places on the causeway between the city and the Acachinánco fort. Unfortunately, I had to be among those dignitaries, in full uniform and in the full company of Eagle Knights. Zyanya wanted also to attend, and to bring Cocóton with her, but again I dissuaded her.

"Even if I could arrange for you to get close enough to see anything," I said, as I wriggled into my quilted and feathered armor that morning, "you would be buffeted and drenched by the lake wind and spray. Also, in that crush of people, you might fall or faint, and the child could be trampled."

"I suppose you are right," said Zyanya, sounding not much disappointed. Impulsively, she hugged the little girl to her. "And Cocóton is too pretty to be squeezed by anybody but us."

"No squeeze!" Cocóton complained, but with dignity. She slipped out of her mother's arms and toddled off to the other side of the room. At the age of two years, our daughter had a considerable store of words, but she was no chattering squirrel; she seldom exercised more than two of her words at a time.

"When Crumb was first born, I thought her hideous," I said, as I went on dressing. "Now I think her so pretty that she cannot possibly get any more so. She can only deteriorate, and it is a pity. By the time we want to marry her off, she will look like a wild sow."

* * *

"Wild sow," Cocóton agreed, from the corner.

"She will not," Zyanya said firmly. "A child, if it is pretty at all, reached its utmost infant beauty at two, and goes on being lovely—with subtle changes, of course—until it reaches its utmost childhood beauty at six. Little boys stop there, but little girls—"

I growled.

"I mean boys stop being *beautiful*. They may go on to become handsome, comely, manly, but not beautiful. Or at least they should hope not. Most women dislike pretty men as much as other men do."

I said I was glad, then, that I had grown up ugly. When she did not correct me, I assumed a look of mock melancholy.

"Then," she went on, "little girls reach another eminence of beauty at twelve or thereabouts, just before their first bleeding. During adolescence, they are usually much too gangly and moody to be admired at all. But then they begin to blossom again, and at twenty or so—yes, at twenty, I would say—a girl is more beautiful than she ever was before or ever will be again."

"I know," I said. "You were twenty when I fell in love with you and married you. And you have not aged by a day since then."

"Flatterer and liar," she said, but with a smile. "I have lines at the corners of my eyes, and my breasts are not so firm as then, and there are stretch marks on my belly, and—"

"No matter," I said. "Your beauty at twenty made such an impression on my mind that it has remained indelibly carved there. I will never see you otherwise, even when someday people tell me, 'You old fool, you are looking at an old crone.' I shall not believe them, for I cannot."

I had to pause for a moment's thought, but then I said in her native language, "Rizalazi Zyanya chuüpa chíi, chuüpa chíi Zyanya," which was a sort of playing with words, to say more or less, "Remember Always at twenty makes her twenty always."

She asked tenderly, "Zyanya?"

And I assured her, "Zyanya."

"It will be nice," she said, with a misty look about her eyes, "to think that as long as I am with you, I will forever be a girl of twenty. Or even if sometimes we must be apart. Wherever you are in the world, there I am still a girl of twenty." She blinked her lashes until her eyes were glowing again, and she smiled and said, "I should have mentioned before, Záa—you are not really ugly."

"Really ugly," said my loved and loving daughter.

It made us both laugh, and broke that enchanted moment. I took up my shield and said, "I must go." Zyanya kissed me good-bye, and I left the house.

It was still quite early in the morning. The garbage scows were plying the canal at the end of our street, collecting the night's heaps of refuse. That disposal of the city's wastes was the most menial work in Tenochtítlan, and only the most derelict of wretches were employed at it—hopeless cripples, incurable drinkers, and the like. I turned away from that depressing sight and walked in the other direction, uphill along the street toward the main plaza, and I had gone some way before I heard Zyanya call my name.

I turned and raised my topaz. She had come out of the house door to wave one more farewell and call something to me before going inside again. It could have been something womanly: "Tell me what the First Lady wore." Or something wifely: "Take care not to get too wet." Or something from the heart: "Remember that I love you." Whatever it was, I did not hear it, for a wind came up, a wind, and blew her words away.

⌘

Since the Coyohuácan spring was on a part of the mainland somewhat higher than the street level of Tenochtítlan, the aqueduct sloped downward from there. It was rather broader and deeper than a man's spread arms could reach, and it was nearly two one-long-runs in length. It met the causeway just where the Acachinánco fort stood, and there it angled left to parallel the causeway's parapet, straight into the city. Once ashore, its trough branched to feed lesser channels running throughout both Tenochtítlan and Tlaltelólco, and to fill storage basins at convenient spots in every quarter, and to spout from several newly built fountains in the main plaza.

To some degree, Ahuítzotl and his builders had heeded the caution of Nezahualpíli that the stream of water be controllable. At the angle where the aqueduct joined the causeway, and again at the point where it entered tie city, the stone trough had been notched with vertical slots, into which fitted stout boards shaped to the curvature of the trough. The boards merely had to be dropped into the slots to cut off the flow of water, should that ever be necessary.

The new structure was to be dedicated to the goddess of ponds and streams and other waters, the frog-faced Chalchi-huítlicué, and she was not so demanding of human offerings as were some other gods. So the sacrifices that day were to be only as numerous as necessary. At the far end of the aqueduct, at the spring, out of our sight, was another contingent of nobles and priests, and a number of warriors guarding a gathering of prisoners. Since we Mexíca had been lately too busy to engage even in any Flowery Wars, most of those prisoners were common bandits whom the Younger Motecuzóma had encountered in his marchings hither and yon, and captured and sent to Tenochtítlan for just such purposes.

On the causeway where Ahuítzotl stood—along with me and some hundreds of others, all of us trying to keep our various plumes and pinions from taking wing on the east wind—there were prayers and chants and invocations, during which the lesser priests swallowed a quantity of live frogs and axolóltin and other water creatures, to please Chalchihuítlicué. Then an urn fire was lighted, and some priestly secret substance sprinkled on it to make it billow a blue-colored smoke. Though the gusts of wind tore at the smoke column, it climbed high enough to signal the other ceremonial group at the Coyohuácan spring.

There the priests threw their first prisoner into the trough of that end of the aqueduct, slit his body open from throat to groin, and let his body lie there while his blood ran. Another prisoner was thrown in and the same thing done. As each earlier corpse began to run dry, it was yanked out, so that more and freshly gushing ones could be piled in. I do not know how many xochimíque were slain and drained there, before the first of their blood sluggishly oozed into view of the waiting Ahuítzotl and his priests, all of whom sent up a praiseful cheer at the sight. Another substance was sprinkled on the urn fire, producing a red smoke: the signal for the priests at the spring to cease their slaughter.

It was time for Ahuítzotl to make the most important sacrifice, and he had been provided with a uniquely suitable victim: a little girl about four years of age, dressed in a water-blue garment with green and blue gems sewn all over it. She was the daughter of a fowler who had drowned when his acáli overturned sometime before she was born, and she had been born with a face very like that of a frog—or of the goddess Chalchihuítlicué. The girl's widowed mother had taken those water-related coincidences as a sign from the goddess, and had volunteered her daughter for the ceremony.

To the accompaniment of a great deal more chanting and cawing of the priests, the Revered Speaker lifted the little girl into the trough before him. Other priests poised themselves beside the urn fire. Ahuítzotl pressed the child supine in the trough and reached for the obsidian knife at his waist. The urn fire's smoke changed to green, another signal, and the priests at the mainland end of the aqueduct let loose the spring water. Whether they did that by pulling free some kind of stopper, or breaking one last earthen dike, or rolling aside a boulder, or what, I do not know.

I do know that the water, though at first it came colored red, did not come oozing as the blood had done. With the momentum of its long slide from the mainland, it came rushing, an immense liquid spear, its point made of boiling pink foam. Where the water had to round the angle of the trough at the causeway, all of it did not; some of it reared up there and broke over the parapet like an ocean comber. Still, enough of it surged on around the bend to take Ahuítzotl by surprise. He had just slit open the child's breast and grasped her heart, but he had not had time to sever its connecting vessels, when the rush of water swept the still-writhing child away from him. She tore loose of her own little heart—Ahuítzotl stood holding it, looking stunned—and the girl shot off toward the city like a pellet through a blowpipe.

All of us on the causeway stood as if we had been sculptured there, motionless except for our wind-whipped feather headdresses and mantles and banners. Then I became aware that I was wet to the ankles. So was everybody; Ahuítzotl's women began squealing in distress. The pavement under us was awash in water that was rapidly rising. It was still leaping the parapet from the angle in the aqueduct, and the whole Acachinánco fort was shaking from the impact of it.

Nevertheless, the greater part of the water continued to race along the trough and on to the city, with such force that, when it hit the branching channels there, it broke like surf on a beach. Through my crystal I could see the tightly packed crowd of spectators milling in the splash and spray, fighting to disperse and flee. All through the city, beyond our sight, the new channels and storage basins were brimming over, wetting the streets and emptying into the canals. The new plaza fountains were spurting so exuberantly high that their water did not fall back into the drainage pools around them; it was spreading in a layer across the entire extent of The Heart of the One World.

The priests of Chalchihuítlicué broke out in a babble of prayers, beseeching the goddess to abate her abundance. Ahuítzotl roared for them to be silent, then began bellowing names—"Yolcatl! Papaquilíztli!"—the names of the men who had discovered the new spring. Those who were present obediently sloshed through the now knee-high water, and, knowing well why they had been called, one by one leaned backward across the parapet. Ahuítzotl and the priests, without any ritual words or gestures, tore open the men's chests, tore out and flung their hearts into the racing water. Eight men were sacrificed in that act of desperation, two of them ancient and august members of the Speaking Council—and it did no good whatever.

So Ahuítzotl shouted, "Drop the trough gate!" and several Arrow Knights leapt forward to the parapet. They seized the wooden panel designed to shut off the water's flow, and slid it down into the trough's slots. But, for all their combined strength and weight, the knights could push the panel only so far. As soon as its curved lower edge went into the water, the powerful current tilted it in the slot and jammed it at that point. For a moment there was silence on the causeway, except for the water's swoosh and gurgle, the sighing and hooting of the east wind, the creaking of the beleaguered wooden fort, and the muted hubbub of the fast-departing crowd at the island end. Looking at last defeated, with all his plumes drenched and drooping, the Revered Speaker said, loudly enough for us all to hear:

"We must go back to the city and see what damage has been done, and do what we can to allay the panic. Arrow and Jaguar Knights, come with us. You will commandeer all the acáltin on the island and row immediately to Coyohuácan. Those fools yonder are probably still celebrating. Do whatever you can to stop or divert the water at its source. Eagle Knights, stay here." He pointed to where the aqueduct joined the causeway. "Break it. There. *Now!*"

There was some confusion as the several designated groups disentangled. Then Ahuítzotl, his wives and his retinue, the priests and nobles, the Arrow and Jaguar Knights—all were slogging toward Tenochtítlan, as swiftly as they could with the nearly thigh-deep water dragging at them. We Eagle Knights stood contemplating the heavy stone and stout mortar of the trough. Two or three knights struck at the stone with their maquáhuime, making the rest of us dodge the flying splinters of broken obsidian. Those knights looked disgustedly at their ruined swords and threw them into the lake.

Then one elderly knight went some way down the causeway to peer over its parapet. He called to us, "How many of you can swim?" and most of us raised our hands. He pointed and said, "Right here, where the aqueduct swerves, the force of the water's changing direction is making the pilings tremble. Perhaps, if we can chop at them, we could weaken them enough that the structure will quake itself apart."

And that is what we did. I and eight other knights struggled out of our clammy and bedraggled uniforms, while unbroken maquáhuime were found for us, then we dove over the parapet into the lake on that side. As I have said, the waters west of the causeway were in those days nowhere very deep. If we had had to swim, the chopping would have been impossible, but the rising water was yet only shoulder-high at that spot. Even so, it was no trifling job. Those tree-trunk supports had been impregnated with chapopótli to resist decay, and that made them resistant to our blades as well. The night had come and gone, and the sun was up, when one of the massive pilings jerked and gave an explosive *crack!* I was underwater at that moment and the concussion nearly stunned me, but I surfaced to hear one of my fellow knights shouting for us all to climb back to the causeway.

We got there just in time. That part of the aqueduct which angled off from the causeway was quivering violently. With a grinding noise, it broke at the bend in it. Flinging water in all directions, that loose end of the structure shook like the warning tail of a coacuéchtli snake. Then a section some ten paces long slewed to one side, as the pilings we had chopped gave way under it, and broke loose with a groan and toppled with a mighty splash. The jagged end of the trough out there was still cascading water into the lake, but it was pouring no more into Tenochtítlan. Even as we stood there, the water already on the causeway began to ebb.

"Let us return home," one of my brother knights sighed, "and hope we have saved some homes to return to."

Home. Let me put off for a little while the telling of my homecoming.

The water that had poured into Tenochtítlan for the better part of a day and a whole night had inundated parts of the city as deep as the height of a man. Some houses built low, and not of stone, had crumbled in that flood; and even some houses built high had been toppled from their supports; and many people had been injured; and about twenty—mostly children—had been drowned or crushed or otherwise lost. But the damage and casualties had been limited to those parts of the city where the branch channels and storage basins had overflowed, and that water had drained away into the canals soon after we Eagle Knights severed the aqueduct.

However, before the litter of that lesser inundation could be cleared away, the second and greater flood came. We had only broken the aqueduct, not stoppered it, and the other knights whom Ahuítzotl had sent to the mainland were unable to stanch the spring there. It continued to gush its waters into the part of the lake contained and confined between our western and southern causeways. Meanwhile, the wind continued to blow from the east, preventing the excess water from draining out into the big Lake Texcóco through the causeway passages and the canals crossing our city. So the canals filled and brimmed and overflowed, and the water rose over the island, and Tenochtítlan became a great cluster of many buildings poking up not from an island but from an unbroken sheet of water.

Immediately upon his return from the aborted dedication ceremony, Ahuítzotl sent a boatman to Texcóco, and Nezahualpíli came immediately in response to the call for help. He had a force of workmen rushed straight to the unquenchable Coyohuácan spring and, as all had hoped, he did devise a means of pinching off the flow. I have never visited the site, but I know it is on a hillside, and I gather that Nezahualpíli commanded the digging of a system of trenches and earthworks which diverted part of the spring's effluence over the far side of the hill where it could run harmlessly into empty land. Once that was accomplished, and the spring tamed, and the flood all dissipated, the aqueduct could be repaired and put back into use. Nezahualpíli designed gates that would, as required by the city's needs, let much or little of the spring's water down the aqueduct. And so, to this day, we still drink those sweet waters.

But Nezahualpíli's salvage operation was no overnight accomplishment. While he and his workmen labored, that second flood stood at its crest for four entire days. Though few or no people perished in it, at least two-thirds of the city was destroyed, and the rebuilding of Tenochtítlan took some four years to complete. The flood would not have caused so much damage if the water had merely covered our streets and lain quietly there. Instead, it surged back and forth, moved one way by the force impelling it to seek a uniform level, moved the other way by the malicious east wind. Most of Tenochtítlan's buildings were held above street level by pilings or some other kind of foundation, but that was only to lift them above the ground's dampness. Their foundations had never been intended to withstand the battering currents they then endured—and most of them did not stand. Adobe houses simply dissolved in the water. Stone houses, small and large, fell when their underpinnings were gnawed away, and they broke into the blocks of which they were built.

My own house stood unharmed, probably because it was rather newer built, hence stronger than most others. In The Heart of the One World the pyramids and temples also remained standing; only the comparatively fragile skull rack came down. But just outside the plaza, one entire palace collapsed—the newest and most magnificent of all—the palace of the Uey-Tlatoáni Ahuítzotl. I have told how it straddled one of the city's main canals, so that the passing public might admire its interior. When, like all the other canals, that one overflowed, it first filled the ground floor of the palace and then bulged the lower walls outward, at which the whole great edifice came thundering down.

I did not know of those happenings, I did not even know I was fortunate enough to have still a house of my own, until after the last of the water ebbed away. In that second and worse flood, the water's rising was at least less sudden, giving time for the city to be evacuated. Except for Ahuítzotl and his other governing nobles, the palace guard, some other troops of soldiers and a number of priests stubbornly continuing to pray for godly intervention, practically everyone in Tenochtítlan fled across the northern causeway to find shelter in the mainland cities of Tepeyáca and Atzacoálco, including me, my two servants, and what remained of my family.

To go back to that earlier day, that early morning when I came home dragging my sodden Eagle Knight regalia...

It was obvious, as I approached, that my Ixacuálco quarter of the city had been among the districts hit hardest by that first spate from the aqueduct. I could see the high-water mark still wet on the buildings, as high as my head, and here and there an adobe house sat askew. The hard-packed clay of my street was slippery with a film of mud; there were puddles and rubbish and even some valuable objects apparently dropped by people in flight. There were at that moment no other people to be seen—no doubt they were indoors, unsure whether the flood wave would come again—but the street's unaccustomed emptiness made me uneasy. I was too tired to run, but I shuffled as rapidly as possible, and my heart lifted when I saw my house still standing, unmarked except for the deposit of slime on its entry stairs.

Turquoise flung open the front door, exclaiming, "Ayyo, it is our lord master! All thanks to Chalchihuítlicué for sparing you!"

Wearily but with feeling, I said I wished that particular goddess in Míctlan.

"Do not speak so!" pleaded Turquoise, tears running down the wrinkles of her face. "We feared that we had lost our master also!"

"Also?" I gasped, an invisible band tightening painfully around my chest. The elderly slave woman broke into violent weeping and could not reply. I dropped the things I was carrying and seized her by the shoulders. "The child?" I demanded. She shook her head, but whether in denial or grief I could not tell. I shook her fiercely and said, "Speak, woman!"

"It was our lady Zyanya," said another voice from behind her, that of the manservant Star Singer, who came to the doorway wringing his hands. "I saw the whole thing. I tried to stop her."

I did not let go of Turquoise or I should have fallen. I could only manage to say, "Tell me, Star Singer."

"Know then, my master. It was yesterday, at dusk, the time when the street torch lighters would ordinarily have been coming. But of course they did not; the street was a seething cataract. Only one man came—being swept along and bludgeoned against the torch poles and the house stairs. He kept trying to find his footing or to seize onto something that would stop his progress. But, even when he was still distant, I could see that he was already crippled and he could not—"

As harshly as I could, in my agony and weakness, I said, "What has all this to do with my wife? Where is she?"

"She *was* at this front window," he said, pointing, and went on with infuriating deliberation. "She had been here the whole day, worrying and waiting for your return, my lord. I was with her when the man came flailing and thrashing down the street, and she cried out that we must save him. I was naturally not eager to venture into that raging water, and I told her, 'My lady, I can recognize him from here. It is only an old derelict who sometimes of late has worked on the garbage canoes which serve this quarter. He is not worth anyone's trouble.'"

Star Singer paused, swallowed, and said huskily, "I can make no complaint if my lord beats me or sells me or slays me, for I should have gone to save the man. Because my lady gave me a look of wrath and went herself. To the door and down the stairs, while I watched from this window, and she leaned into the flood and caught him."

He paused and gulped again, and I rasped, "Well? If they were both safe...?"

Star Singer shook his head. "That is what I do not understand. Of course, my lord, the stairs were wet and slippery. But what it looked like—it looked as if my lady spoke to the man, and started to let go of him, but then...but then the waters took them. Took them both, for he was clutching to her. I could see only a tumbling bundle as they were swept together out of my sight. But at that I *did* run out, and plunged into the current after them."

"Star Singer almost drowned, my lord," said Turquoise, sniffling. "He tried, he really did."

"There was no sign of them," he resumed, miserably. "Toward the end of the street, a number of old adobe houses had fallen—perhaps on them, I thought. But it was getting too dark to see, and I was knocked nearly insensible by a floating timber. I seized the doorpost of a sturdy house and clung there all the night."

"He came home when the waters went down this morning," said Turquoise. "Then we both went out and searched."

"Nothing?" I croaked.

"We found only the man," said Star Singer. "Half buried under some fallen rubble, as I had suspected."

Turquoise said, "Cocóton has not yet been told about her mother. Will my lord go up to her now?"

"And tell her what I cannot believe myself?" I moaned. I summoned some last reserve of energy to straighten my sagging body and said, "No, I will not. Come, Star Singer. Let us search again."

Beyond my house the street gently sloped downward as it approached the canal-crossing bridge, so the houses down there had naturally been more violently struck by the wall of water. Also, they were the less impressive houses on the street, built of wood or adobe. As Star Singer had said, they were houses no longer; they were heaps of half-broken, half-dissolved bricks of mud and straw, splintered planks, and oddments of furniture. The servant pointed to a crumple of cloth among them and said:

"There lies the wretch. No loss at all. He lived by selling himself to the men of the garbage boats. Those who could not afford a woman could use him, and he charged only a single cacao bean."

He lay face down, a thing of filthy rags and mud-matted long gray hair. I used my foot to turn him over, and I looked at him for the last time. Chimáli looked back at me with empty eye sockets and gaping mouth.

Not then, but some while later, when I could think, I thought about Star Singer's words: that the man had lately been aboard the scows serving our neighborhood. I wondered: had Chimáli only recently discovered where I lived? Had he come haunting, hoping, blindly groping for one more opportunity to work mischief on me or mine? Had the flood given him the chance to inflict the most hurtful possible injury, and then to put himself beyond my vengeance forever? Or had the whole tragedy been a ghastly and gleeful contrivance of the gods? They do seem to find amusement in arranging concurrences of events that would otherwise be unlikely, inexplicable, beyond belief.

I would never know.

And at that moment I knew only that my wife was gone, that I could not accept her being gone, that I had to search. I said to Star Singer, "If the cursed man is here, so must Zyanya be. We will move every one of these millions of bricks. I will start on it, while you go for more hands to help. *Go!*"

Star Singer scampered away, and I leaned over to lift and fling aside a wooden beam, but I kept on leaning and pitched forward on my face.

It was late afternoon when I came back to consciousness, and in my own bed, with both the servants bending solicitously over me. The first thing I asked was, "Did we find her?" When both the heads shook in rueful negation, I snarled, "I told you to move every brick!"

"Master, it cannot be done," whimpered Star Singer. "The water rises again. I returned and found you just in time, or you would have been face down in it."

"We were wondering whether to rouse you," said Turquoise, in obvious anxiety. "The word has been spoken by the Revered Speaker. The whole city must be vacated before it is all under water."

And so that night I sat sleepless on a hillside among a multitude of sleeping fugitives. "Long walk," Cocóton had commented, on the way. Since only the first people to leave Tenochtítlan had found accommodations on the mainland, the later arrivals had simply stopped wherever there was room to lie down in the countryside. "Dark night," said my daughter appropriately. We four had not even a sheltering tree, but Turquoise had thought to bring blankets. She and Star Singer and Cocóton lay rolled in theirs, snugly asleep, but I sat up, with my blanket about my shoulders, and I looked down at my child, my Crumb, the precious and only remnant of my wife, and I mourned.

Some time ago, my lord friars, I tried to describe Zyanya by comparing her to the bounteous and generous maguey plant, but there is one thing I forgot to tell you about the maguey. Once in its lifetime, just once, it puts up a single spear which bears an abundance of sweet-scented yellow flowers, and then the maguey dies.

I tried hard that night to take comfort from the unctuous assurances our priests always spoke: that the dead do not repine or grieve. Death, said the priests, is merely one's awakening from a dream of having lived. Perhaps so. Your Christian priests say much the same thing. But that was small comfort to me, who had to remain behind in the dream, alive, alone, bereft. So I passed that night remembering Zyanya and the too-brief time we had together before her dream ended.

I still remember. . . .

Once, when we were on that journey into Michihuácan, she saw an unfamiliar flower growing from a cleft in a cliff, some way above our heads, and she admired it, and she said she wished she had one like it to plant at home, and I could easily have climbed up and plucked it for her. . . .

And once—oh, it was no particular occasion—she woke in love with the day, and that was not unusual for Zyanya—and she made a small song, and then a melody for it, and she went about softly singing it to fix it in her memory, and she asked me if I would buy her one of the those jug flutes called the warbling waters, upon which she could play her song. I said I would, the next time I met a musician acquaintance and could persuade him to make me one. But I forgot, and she—seeing I had other things on my mind—she never reminded me.

And once . . .

Ayya, the many times...

Oh, I know she never doubted that I loved her, but why did I let slip even the least opportunity to demonstrate it? I know she forgave my occasional thoughtless lapses and trivial neglects; she probably forgot them on the instant, which I never have been able to do. Through all the years of my life since then, I have been reminded of this or that time when I might have done such and such, and did not, and will never have the chance again. Meanwhile, the things I would prefer to remember persist in eluding me. If I could recall the words of that small song she made when she was happiest, or even just the melody of it, I could hum it sometimes to myself. Or if I knew what it was she called after me, when the wind took her words, that last time we parted....

When all of us fugitive inhabitants finally returned to the island, so much of the city was in ruins that the rubble earlier heaped along our street was indistinguishable from what had fallen afterward. Laborers and slaves were already shoving the wreckage about, salvaging the unbroken and reusable limestone blocks, leveling the rest as a foundation to rebuild upon. So Zyanya's body was never found, nor any trace of her, not so much as one of her rings or sandals. She vanished as utterly and irretrievably as that small song she once made. But, my lords, I know she is still here somewhere—though two new cities in succession have since then been built over her undiscovered grave. I know it, because she did not take with her the jadestone chip to insure her passage to the afterworld.

Many times, late at night, I have walked these streets and softly called her name. I did it in Tenochtítlan and I do it still in this City of Mexíco; an old man sleeps little at night. And I have seen many apparitions, but none of them hers.

I have encountered only unhappy or malevolent spirits, and I could not mistake any of them for Zyanya, who was happy all her life and who died while trying to do a kindness. I have seen and recognized many a dead warrior of the Mexíca; the city teems with those woebegone specters. I have seen the Weeping Woman; she is like a drifting wisp of fog, woman-shaped; and I have heard her mournful wail. But she did not frighten me; I pitied her, because I too have known deprivation;

and when she could not howl me down, she fled my words of solace. Once, it seemed to me that I met and conversed with two wandering gods, Night Wind and The Oldest of Old Gods. Anyway, that is who they claimed to be, and they did me no harm, deeming that I have had harm enough in my life.

Sometimes, on streets absolutely dark and deserted, I have heard what could have been Zyanya's merry laugh. That might be a product of my senile imagination, but the laugh has each time been accompanied by a glint of light in the darkness, very like the pale streak in her black hair. And that might be a trick of my feeble eyesight, for the vision has each time disappeared when I fumbled my topaz to my eye. Nevertheless, I know she is here, somewhere, and I need no evidence, however much I yearn for it.

I have considered the matter, and I wonder. Do I meet only the doleful and misanthropic denizens of the night because I am so like them myself? Is it possible that persons of better character and gladder heart might more readily perceive the more gentle phantasms? I beg you, my lord friars, if one of you good men should encounter Zyanya some night, would you let me know? You will recognize her at once, and you will not be affrighted by a wraith of such loveliness. She will still seem a girl of twenty, as she did then, for death at least spared her the diseases and desiccation of age. And you will know that smile, for you will be unable to resist smiling in return. If she should speak . . .

But no, you would not comprehend her speech. Just have the kindness to tell me that you saw her. For she still walks these streets. I know it. She is here and will be always.

I H S
✠
S.C.C.M.

Sanctified, Caesarean, Catholic Majesty,
the Emperor Don Carlos, Our Lord King:

ROYAL and Redoubtable Majesty, our King Paramount: from this City of Mexico, capital of New Spain, this day of St. Paphnutius, Martyr, in the year of Our Lord one thousand five hundred thirty, greeting.

It is typically thoughtful of Our Condolent Sovereign that you commiserate with Your Majesty's Protector of the Indians, and that you ask for more details of the problems and obstacles we daily confront in that office.

Heretofore, Sire, it was the practice of the Spaniards who were granted landholdings in these provinces to appropriate also the many Indians already living thereon, and to brand their cheeks with the "G" for "guerra," and to claim them as prisoners of war, and cruelly to treat and exploit them as such. That practice has at least been ameliorated to the extent that an Indian can no longer be sentenced to slave labor unless and until he is found guilty of some crime by either the secular or the ecclesiastical authorities.

Also, the law of Mother Spain is now more strictly applied

in this New Spain, so that an Indian here, like a Jew there, has the same rights as any Christian Spaniard, and cannot be condemned for a crime without due process of charge, trial, and conviction. But of course the testimony of an Indian, like that of a Jew—even of converts to Christianity—cannot be allowed equal weight against the testimony of a lifelong Christian. Hence, if a Spaniard desires to acquire as a slave some robust red man or personable red woman, all he need do, in effect, is to lodge against that Indian any accusation that he has the wit to invent.

Because we beheld the conviction of many Indians on charges that were moot at best, and because we feared for the souls of our countrymen who were apparently aggrandizing themselves and their estates by sophistical means unbecoming to Christians, we were saddened and we felt moved to action. Wielding the influence of our title as Protector of the Indians, we have succeeded in persuading the judges of the Audiencia that all Indians to be branded henceforth must be registered with our office. Therefore the branding irons are now kept locked in a box which must be opened with two keys, and one of the keys resides in our possession.

Since no convicted Indian can be branded without our co-operation, we have consistently refused to cooperate in those cases that are flagrant abuses of justice, and those Indians have perforce been reprieved. Such exercise of our office as Protector of the Indians has earned us the odium of many of our countrymen, but that we can bear with equanimity, knowing that we act for the ultimate good of all involved. However, the economic welfare of all New Spain might suffer (and the King's Fifth of its riches be diminished) if we too adamantly obstructed the recruitment of the slave labor on which depends the prosperity of these colonies. So now, when a Spaniard is desirous of acquiring some Indian for a bondsman, he does not invoke the secular arm; he charges the Indian with being a Christian convert who has committed some *lapsus fidei*. Since our prelacy as Defender of the Faith takes precedence over all our other offices and concerns, we do not in those cases withhold the brand.

Thus we simultaneously accomplish three things that we trust will find favor in Your Majesty's sight. *Primus*, we effectually prevent the misfeasance of the civil law. *Secundus*, we steadfastly uphold Church dogma as it regards lapsed converts. *Tertius*, we do not impede the maintenance of a steady and adequate labor supply.

Incidentally, Your Majesty, the brand on the convict's cheek is no longer the demeaning "G," which imputes the dishonor of defeat in war. We now apply the initials of the slave's designated owner (unless the convict is a comely woman whom the owner prefers not to deface). Besides being a mark to identify property and runaways, such a branding eventually serves also to mark those slaves who are hopelessly rebellious and unfit for work. Many such intractable malcontents, having passed through several changes of ownership, now bear numerous and overlapping initials upon their faces, as if their skin were a palimpsest manuscript.

There is touching evidence of Your Compassionate Majesty's goodness of heart, in this same latest letter, when you say of our Aztec chronicler, anent the death of his woman, "Although of inferior race, he seems a man of human emotions, capable of feeling happinesses and hurts quite as keenly as we do." Your sympathy is understandable, since Your Majesty's own abiding love for your young Queen Isabella and your baby son Felipe is a tender passion remarked and much admired by all.

However, we respectfully suggest that you expend not too much pity on persons whom Your Majesty cannot know as well as we do, and especially not on one who, over and over again, shows himself undeserving of it. This one may in his time have felt an occasional emotion or entertained an occasional human thought which would do no discredit to a white man. But Your Majesty will have noticed that, though he professes to be now a Christian, the old dotard maundered much about his dead mate's still wandering the world—and why?—because she did not have a certain green pebble by her when she died! Also, as Your Majesty will perceive, the Aztec was not long cast down by his bereavement. In these ensuing pages of the narrative, he again ramps like a colossus, and behaves in his old accustomed ways.

Sire, not long ago we heard a priest wiser than ourself say this: that *no* man should be unreservedly lauded while he still lives and still sails upon the unpredictable seas of life. Not he nor anyone can know whether he will survive all the besetting tempests and the lurking reefs and the distracting Siren songs, to make safe harbor at last. That man alone can rightly be praised whom God has guided so that he finishes his days in the port of Salvation, for the *Gloria* is sung only at the end.

May that guiding Lord God continue to smile upon and favor Your Imperial Majesty, whose royal feet are kissed by your chaplain and servant,

(ecce signum) Zumárraga

OCTAVA PARS

MY own personal tragedy naturally overshadowed everything else in the world, but I could not help being aware that the entire Mexíca nation had also suffered more of a tragedy than the demolition of its capital city. Ahuítzotl's frantic and rather uncharacteristic plea for Nezahualpíli's help in stopping the flood was the last act he ever performed as Uey-Tlatoáni. He was inside his palace when it collapsed and, though he was not killed, he would probably have preferred that he had been. For he was struck on the head by a falling beam, and thereafter—so I was told; I never saw him again alive—he was as witless as the timber that struck him. He wandered aimlessly about, talking to himself in gibberish, while an attendant followed the once great statesman and warrior everywhere he went, to keep changing the loincloth he kept soiling.

Tradition forbade that Ahuítzotl be divested of the title of Revered Speaker as long as he lived, even if his speaking was a babble and he could be revered no more than could an ambulatory vegetable. Instead, as soon as was practical, the Speaking Council convened to choose a regent to lead the nation during Ahuítzotl's incapacity. No doubt vengefully, because Ahuítzotl had slain two of their number during the panic on the causeway, those old men refused even to consider the most eligible candidate, his eldest son Cuautémoc. They chose for regent his nephew, Motecuzóma the Younger, because, they announced, "Motecuzóma Xocóyotzin has proved his ability successively as a priest, a military commander, a colonial administrator. And, having traveled so widely, he has firsthand knowledge of all the farthest Mexíca lands."

I remembered the words Ahuítzotl had thundered at me one time: "We will not set upon this throne a hollow drum!" and I decided that it was probably as well that he was out of his wits when that very thing occurred. If Ahuítzotl had been killed outright, so that he died in his right mind, he would have clambered up from the nethermost pit of Míctlan and sat his cadaver on the throne in preference to Motecuzóma. As things turned out, a dead ruler might almost have been better for the Mexíca. A corpse at least maintains a fixed position.

But at that time I was not at all interested in court intrigues; I was myself preparing to abdicate for a while, and for several reasons. For one, my home had become a place full of painful memories from which I wished to get away. I felt a pang even when I looked at my dear daughter, because I saw so much of Zyanya in her face. For another reason, I thought I had devised a way to keep Cocóton from feeling too poignantly the loss of her mother. For still another, my friend Cozcatl and his wife Quequelmíqui, when they came to comfort me with condolences, let slip the news that they were homeless, their own house having been among those toppled by the flood.

"We are not as downcast about it as we might be," Cozcatl said. "To tell the truth, we were getting rather cramped and uncomfortable, with our home and the school for servants both under one roof. Now that we are forced to rebuild, we will put up two separate buildings."

"And meanwhile," I said, "this will be your home. You will both live here. I am going away in any case, so the place and the servants will be all yours. I ask only one favor in return. Will you two be substitute mother and father to Cocóton as long as I am absent? Could you play Tene and Tete to an orphan child?"

Ticklish said, "Ayyo, what a lovely idea!"

Cozcatl said, "We will do it willingly—no, gratefully. It will be the one time we shall have had a family."

I said, "The child gives no trouble. The slave Turquoise tends to her routine needs. You will have to provide nothing but the security of your presence . . . and a show of affection from time to time."

"Of course we will!" Ticklish exclaimed, and there were tears in her eyes.

I went on, "I have already explained to Cocóton—meaning I lied to her—about her mother's absence these past several days. I said that her Tene is out marketing, buying the necessities she and I will need for a long journey we must undertake. The child only nodded and said, 'Long journey,' but it means little to her at her age. However, if you keep reminding Cocóton that her Tete and Tene are traveling in far places . . . well, I hope she will have got used to being without her mother by the time I return, so that she will not be too dismayed when I tell her that her Tene has not returned with me."

"But she would get used to being without you, too," Cozcatl warned.

"I suppose so," I said resignedly. "I can only trust that, when I do come back, she and I can get reacquainted again. In the meantime, if I know that Cocóton is well cared for, and is loved . . ."

"She will be!" Ticklish said, laying a hand on my arm. "We will live here with her for as long as need be. And we will not let her forget you, Mixtli."

They went away, to prepare for the moving in of what possessions they had saved from the ruins of their own house, and that same night I put together a light and compact traveling pack. Early the next morning I went into the nursery and woke Cocóton, and told the sleepy little girl:

"Your Tene asked me to say good-bye for us both, Small Crumb, because . . . because she cannot leave our train of porters, or they will scatter and run away like mice. But here is a good-bye kiss from her. Did not that taste exactly like her kiss?" Surprisingly, it did, to me at least. "Now, Cocóton. With your fingers, lift Tene's kiss from your lips and hold it in your hand, like that, so your Tete can kiss you, too. There. Now take mine and hers, and hold them both tight in your hand while you go to sleep again. When you get up, put them safely away and keep the kisses to return to us when we come back."

"Come back," she said drowsily, and smiled her Zyanya smile, and closed her Zyanya eyes.

Downstairs, Turquoise sniffled and Star Singer several times blew his nose as we said our good-byes, and I charged them with the management of the household and reminded them that until my return they were to obey Cozcatl and Quequelmíqui as their lord and lady. I paused once more on my way out of town, at The House of Pochtéca, and left there a message to be carried by the next merchant train going in the direction of Tecuantépec. The folded paper was to advise Béu Ribé—in the least hurtful word pictures I could compose—of her sister's death and the manner of it.

It did not occur to me that the normal flow of Mexíca commerce had been considerably disrupted, and that my message would not soon be delivered. Tenochtítlan's fringe of chinámpa had been underwater for four days, at the season when the crops of maize, beans, and other staples were just sprouting. Besides drowning those plants, the water had also invaded the warehouses kept stocked for emergencies and ruined all the dried foods stored in them. So, for many months, the Mexíca pochtéca and their porters were occupied solely with supplying the destitute city. That kept them constantly traveling, but did not take them far afield, and that is why Waiting Moon did not learn of Zyanya's death until more than a year after it happened.

I was also constantly traveling during that time, wandering like a milkweed puff wherever the winds might blow me, or wherever some scenic vista beckoned me closer, or wherever a path meandered so tantalizingly that it was forever seeming to say, "Follow me. Just around the next bend there is a land of heart's-ease and forgetfulness." There never was such a place, of course. A man can walk to the end of all the roads there are, and to the end of his days, but he can nowhere lay down his past and walk away from it and never look back.

Most of my adventures during that time were of no special account, and I sought to do no trading nor to burden myself with acquisitions, and if there were fortuitous discoveries to be made—like the giant tusks I found that other time I tried to walk away from woe—I passed them unseeing. The one rather memorable adventure that I did have, I fell into quite by accident, and it happened in this way:

I was near the west coast, in the land of Nauyar Ixú, one of the remote northwestern provinces or dependencies of Michihuácan. I had wandered up that way just to see a volcano that had been in violent eruption for almost a month and threatened never to stop. The volcano is called Tzebóruko, which means to snort with anger, but it was doing more than that: it was roaring with rage, like the overflow of a war going on down below in Míctlan. Gray-black smoke billowed from it, shot with jacinth flashes of fire, and towered up to the sky, and had been doing that for so many days that the whole sky was dirty and the whole of Nauyar Ixú in day-long twilight. From that cloud constantly rained down a soft, warm, pungent gray ash. From the crater came the incessant angry growl of the volcano goddess Chántico, and gouts of fiery-red lava, and what looked from a distance like pebbles being tossed up and out, though they were of course immense hurled boulders.

Tzebóruko sits at the head of a river valley, and its outpour found its easiest course along that riverbed. But the water was too shallow to chill and harden and stop the molten rock; the water simply shrieked to an instant boil when they met, and then steamed away before the onslaught. As each successive wave of hot, glowing lava vomited from the crater, it would surge down the mountainside and down the valley, then flow more slowly, then merely ooze as it cooled and darkened. But its hardening provided a smoother slide for the next gush, which would run farther before it stopped. So by the time I arrived to see the spectacle, the molten rock had, like a long red tongue, lapped far down the retreating river. The heat of liquefied rock and sizzling steam was so intense that I could get nowhere near the mountain itself. Nobody could, and nobody else wanted to. Most of the people living thereabouts were glumly packing their household belongings to get farther away. I was told that past eruptions had sometimes devastated the entire river valley as far as the seacoast, perhaps twenty one-long-runs away.

And so did that one. I have tried to convey the fury of the eruption, reverend scribes, just so you will believe me when I tell how it finally flung me right off The One World and out into the unknown.

Having nothing else to do, I spent some days ambling along beside the river of lava—or as close as I could walk beside its scorching heat and unbreathable fumes—while it implacably boiled away the river water and filled its bed from bank to bank. The lava moved like a wave of mud, at about the pace of a man's slow walk, so, when each night I made camp on higher ground and ate from my provisions and rolled into my blanket or hung my gíshe between two trees, I would wake in the morning to find that the moving rock had so far outdistanced me that I would have to hurry to catch up with its forward edge. But the mountain Tzebóruko, though it diminished behind me, continued to spew, so I kept on accompanying its outpour just to see how far the lava *would* go. And after some days it and I arrived at the western ocean.

The river valley there squeezes between two highlands and debouches into a long, deep crescent of beach embracing a great bay of turquoise water. There was a settlement of reed huts on the beach, but no people anywhere about; clearly the fisher folk, like those farther inland, had prudently decamped; but someone had left a small seagoing acáli drawn up on the beach, complete with its paddle. It gave me the notion of paddling out into the bay to watch, from a safe distance, when the seething rock met the sea. The shallow river had been unable to resist the lava's advance, but I knew the inexhaustible waters of the ocean would stop it. The encounter, I thought, would be something worth seeing.

It did not happen until the next day, and by then I had put my traveling pack in the canoe, and paddled out beyond the breakers, and I sat in the very middle of the bay. I could see through my topaz how the evilly smoldering lava spread and crept across the beach, advancing toward the waterline on a broad front. Not much was visible inland, except that I could just make out—through the obscuring smoke and falling ash— the pinkish flare and occasional brighter yellow twinkle of Tzebóruko still vomiting from the bowels of Míctlan.

Then the undulant, glowing-red muck on the beach seemed to hesitate and gather itself so that, instead of creeping forward, it launched itself ferociously into the ocean. During the days previous, up the river, when the hot rock and cold water had met, the sound had been an almost human screech and a hissing gasp. At the seaside, the sound was the thunderous bellow of an unexpectedly wounded god, a shocked and outraged god. It was a tumult compounded of two noises: an ocean heated to boiling so suddenly that it exploded into steam, and a lava chilled to hardness so suddenly that it exploded into fragments all along its leading edge. The steam towered up like a cliff made of cloud, and a hot spray came drizzling down on me, and my acáli jolted backward so abruptly that I nearly fell out of it. I clutched at its wooden sides, and so dropped the paddle overboard.

The canoe continued its backward swoop, as the ocean recoiled from the suddenly unfriendly land. Then the sea recovered from its apparent surprise, and sloshed toward the beach again. But the molten rock was still advancing; the thunder was uninterrupted and the cloud clawed upward as if trying to reach the sky where clouds belong; and the affronted ocean recoiled again. That whole vast bay surged seaward and landward again more times than I could count, for I was quite dizzied by the rocking and yawing of my canoe. But I was aware that each revulsion took me farther from land than each resurgence took me back. In the swirling waters about my curvetting canoe, fish and other sea creatures floated on the surface, most of them belly up.

All the rest of that day, as the twilight got ever darker, my acáli continued its progress of one wave shoreward, three waves seaward. With the very last of daylight, I saw that I was precisely between the two headlands of the bay entrance, but too far from either to swim the distance, and that beyond them was limitless empty ocean. There was nothing I could do, except two things. I leaned from the canoe and plucked out of the water every dead fish within my reach, and piled them in one end of my craft. Then I lay down with my head on my damp pack, and went to sleep.

When I woke the next morning, I might have thought I had dreamt all that turmoil, except that I was still helplessly adrift in an acáli and the shore was so far away that its only recognizable feature was the jagged profile of dim blue mountains. But the sun was rising in a clear sky, there was no pall of smoke and ash, there was no erupting Tzebóruko discernible among the distant mountains, the ocean was as calm as Lake Xaltócan on a summer day. Using my topaz, I fixed my eye on the landward horizon and attempted to imprint its profile on my vision. Then I closed my eyes for a few moments before opening them again to see any change from the remembered vision. After doing that several times, I was able to perceive that the closer mountains were moving past the farther ones, from left to right. Obviously, then, I was caught in an ocean current that was carrying me northward, but frighteningly far offshore.

I tried swerving the canoe by paddling with my hands on the side away from the land, but I quickly gave that up. There was a swirl in the formerly calm water alongside, and something struck the acáli so hard that it rocked. When I looked overside I saw a deep gouge in the hard mahogany, and an upright fin, like an oblong leather war shield, slicing through the water nearby. It circled my canoe two or three times before it disappeared with another ponderous swirl of the water, and thereafter I put not so much as a finger beyond the sheltering wood.

Well, I thought to myself, I have escaped any dangers posed by the volcano. Now I have nothing to fear except being eaten by sea monsters, or dying of hunger, or shriveling from heat and thirst, or drowning if the sea gets rough. I thought about Quetzalcóatl, the long-ago ruler of the Toltéca, who had similarly floated away alone into the other ocean to the east, and thereby had become the best beloved of all gods, the one god adored by far-apart peoples who had absolutely nothing else in common. Of course, I reminded myself, there had been a crowd of his worshipful subjects on the shore to watch his departure, and to weep when he did not turn back, and subsequently to go about informing other people that Quetzalcóatl the man was henceforth to be revered as Quetzalcóatl the god. Not a single person had seen me set off, or knew about it, or was likely— when I never came back—to start a popular demand for my elevation to godhood. So, I said to myself, if I have no hope of becoming a god, I had better do what I can to remain a man as long as possible.

I had twenty and three fish, from which I picked and laid aside ten which I recognized as being of edible species. Of those I cleaned two with my dagger and ate them raw—though not quite raw; they had been at least a little cooked in the cauldron of the bay back yonder. The thirteen questionable fish I gutted and filleted and then, getting my eating bowl from my pack, I wrung them like rags to extract every drop of their body moisture. I tucked the bowl of liquid and the eight remaining edible fish under the pack, so they were out of the sun's direct rays. Thus I was able to eat two more fish, still comparatively unspoiled, the next day. But by the third day I really had to force myself to eat two more—trying to swallow the chunks of them without chewing, they were so slimy and vile—and I threw the reeking last four over the side. For some while after that, my only sustenance—actually just a moistening of my painfully cracked lips—was a very occasional and restrained sip of the fish water from the bowl.

I think it was also on my third day at sea that the last visible mountain peak of The One World disappeared below the horizon to the east. The current had carried me entirely out of sight of land, and there was nothing firm anywhere, and that was the first such experience I had ever had in my life. I wondered if I might eventually be cast up on The Islands of the Women, of which I had heard storytellers tell, though none ever claimed to have been there in person. According to the legends, those were islands inhabited entirely by females, who spent all their time in diving for oysters and extracting the pearl hearts from those oysters which had grown hearts. Only once a year did the women ever see men, when a number of men would canoe out from the mainland to trade cloth and other such supplies for the collected pearls—and, while there, to couple with the women. Of the babies later born of the brief mating, the island women kept only the female infants and drowned the males. Or so said the stories. I meditated on what would happen if I should land on The Islands of the Women uninvited and unexpected. Would I be immediately slain or subjected to a sort of mass rape in reverse?

As it happened, I found not those mythical islands nor any others. I merely drifted miserably across those endless waters. The ocean ringed me about on every side, and I was most unhappy, feeling like an ant at the very bottom and center of a blue urn whose sides were slippery and unclimbable. The nights were not so unnerving, if I put away my topaz so I could not see the overwhelming profusion of stars. In the dark I could pretend I was somewhere safe—anywhere solid—in a mainland forest or even inside my own house. I could pretend that the rocking boat was a gíshe bed of rope-slung netting, and thus sleep soundly.

During the days, however, I could not pretend that I was anywhere but in the exact middle of that appalling blue, hot, shadeless vastness. Fortunately for my sanity, there were a few other things to see by daylight besides that unending, uncaring expanse of water. Some of those other things were not particularly comforting to contemplate either, but I forced myself to look at them with my crystal, and to examine them as closely as circumstances permitted, and to speculate on the nature of them.

A few of the things I saw, I knew what they were, though I had never seen them before. There was the blue and silver swordfish, bigger than I am, which likes to leap straight up from the water and dance for a moment on its tail. There was the even bigger sawfish, flat and brown, with elongated fins along its sides like the wavy skin flaps of a flying squirrel. I recognized both of those by their wicked beaks, which the warriors of some coastal tribes use for weapons. I dreaded the moment when one of those big fish would stave in my acáli with its sword or saw, but none ever did.

Other things I saw while adrift on that western ocean were totally unfamiliar to me. There were countless small creatures with long fins which they used like wings, to spurt from the water and glide prodigious distances. I would have thought them a kind of water insect, but one landed in my canoe, and I seized and ate him instantly, and he tasted like a fish. There were immense blue-gray fish which regarded me with intelligent eyes and a fixed grin, but they seemed more sympathetic than menacing. Numbers of them would accompany my acáli for long periods, and entertain me by doing water acrobatics in practiced unison.

But the fish that filled me with the most awe and apprehension were the biggest of all: great gray ones which came once in a while to bask on the surface of the sea—one or two or crowds of them, and they might loll roundabout me for half a day—as if they craved a breath of fresh air and a touch of sun, which is most unfishlike behavior. What was even more unfishlike about them was that they were more huge than any other living creature I have ever seen. I do not blame you, reverend friars, if you disbelieve me, but each of those monsters was long enough to span the plaza outside the window there, and each was of a breadth and bulk to match its length. Once, when I was in the Xoconóchco, years before the time of which I now speak, I was served a meal of a fish called the yeyemíchi, and the cook told me that the yeyemíchi was the most tremendous fish in the sea. If what I ate on that occasion was indeed a small slice from one of those swimming Great Pyramids I was later to meet in the western ocean, well, I am heartily sorry now that I did not seek out and meet and express my admiration for the heroic man—or the army of men—who caught and beached the thing.

Any two of those mighty yeyemíchtin, as they playfully nudged each other, could have crushed my acáli and me without even noticing. But they did not, and no other such mishap befell me, and on the sixth or seventh day of my involuntary voyage—just in time: I had licked my bowl dry of the last trace of fish water; I was gaunt and blistered and flaccid—a rain came sweeping like a gray veil across the ocean behind my craft, and caught up with me and swept over me. I was much refreshed by that, and filled my bowl and drank it empty two or three times. But then I began to worry a little, for the rain had brought with it a wind that put waves on the sea. My canoe bounced and jostled about like a mere chip of wood, and very soon I was using my bowl to bail out the water that sloshed in over the sides. But I took some heart from the fact that the rain and wind had come from behind me—from the southwest, I judged, remembering where the sun had been at the time— so at least I was not being blown farther out to sea.

Not that it mattered much where I sank at last, I thought wearily, for it appeared that I would have to sink eventually. Since the wind and rain continued without a pause, and the ocean continued to dance my acáli about, I could not sleep or even rest, but had to keep emptying out the water that slopped in. I was already so weak that my bowl felt as heavy as a great stone jar every time I dipped and filled and poured it overside.

Though I could not sleep, I gradually slipped into a sort of stupor, so I cannot now say how many days and nights passed thus, but evidently during all of them I continued the bailing as if it had become an unbreakable habit. I do recall that, toware the end, my movements dragged slower and slower, and the level of water in the boat was rising more rapidly than I could lower it. When finally I felt the canoe's bottom grate on the floor of the sea, and I knew that it had sunk at last, I could only mildly wonder at my not feeling the water close about me or the fishes playing in my hair.

I must have lost consciousness then, for when I again came to myself, the rain was gone and the sun was shining brightly, and I looked about me, marveling. I had sunk indeed, but not to any great depth. The water was only up to my waist, for the canoe had grounded just short of a gravelly beach that stretched out of sight in both directions, with no sign of human habitation. Still weak and limp and moving slowly, I stepped out of the submerged acáli, dragging my soaked pack with me, and waded ashore. There were coconut palms beyond the beach, but I was too feeble to climb or even shake one, or to look for any other sort of food. I did make the effort of emptying out the contents of my pack to dry in the sun, but then I crept to the palm shade and went unconscious again.

I awoke in darkness, and it took me a few moments to realize that I was not still bobbing about on the sea surface. Where I *was*, I had no idea, but it seemed that I was no longer alone, for all about me I heard a mysterious and unnerving noise. It was a clicking that came from nowhere and everywhere, no single click very loud, but all of them together making a crackling like an invisible brush fire advancing upon me. Or it could have been multitudes of people trying to steal upon me, but not very stealthily, for they were either trampling every loose pebble on the beach or snapping every twig among the beach litter.

I started up, and at my movement the clicking instantly ceased, but when I lay back again that sinister crepitation resumed. Every time I moved during the remainder of that night, it stopped, then started again. I had not used my burning crystal to light a fire while I was still conscious and the sun was still up, so I had no means of making a torch. I could do nothing but lie uneasily awake and wait for something to leap upon me—until the first dim light of dawn showed me the source of the noise.

At first sight, it made my flesh creep. The entire beach, except for a clearing around the spot where I lay, was covered with green-brown crabs the size of my hand, clumsily twitching and slithering over the sand and each other. They were countless, and they were of a kind that I had never seen before. Crabs are never appealingly pretty creatures, but all that I had previously seen had at least been symmetrical. Those were not; their two front claws did not match. One claw was a large, unwieldy lump, mottled brilliant red and blue; the other claw was plain crab-colored and it was narrow, like a split twig. Each crab was using its narrow claw like a drumstick to beat upon the big claw as upon a drum, tirelessly and not at all musically.

The dawn seemed to be the signal for them to cease their ridiculous ceremony; the numberless horde thinned out as the crabs scrabbled to their burrows in the sand. But I managed to catch a number of them, feeling that they owed me something for having made me quake so long awake and anxious in the dark. Their bodies were small and contained too little meat to be worth digging out of the shell, but their big drum claws, which I roasted over a fire before cracking them open, provided quite a savory breakfast.

Full fed for the first time in recent memory, and feeling a bit more alive, I stood up from my fire to take stock of my situation. I was back again on The One World, and certainly still on its western coast, but I was incalculably farther north than I had ever previously been. As always, the sea stretched to the western horizon, but it was oddly much less boisterous than the seas I had known farther south: no tumbling breakers or even a lively froth of surf, but only a gentle lapping at the shore. In the other direction, eastward, beyond the shoreline palms and other trees, there rose a range of mountains. They looked formidably high, but they were pleasantly green with forests, not like the ugly volcanic ranges of dun and black rock where I had recently been. I had no way of knowing how far I had been carried north by the ocean current and then by the rainstorm. But I did know that if I merely walked southward down the beach I would *sometime* get back to that bay near Tzebóruko, and from there I would be in familiar country. By staying on the beach, too, I would not have to worry about food and drink. I could live entirely on the drummer crabs and coconut liquid, if nothing else offered.

But the plain fact was that I had had quite enough of the cursed ocean, and I wanted to get out of sight of it. Those mountains inland were foreign to me, and possibly inhabited by savage people or wild animals of breeds I had never encountered before. Still, they were but mountains, and I had traveled in many other mountains, and I had lived well enough off the provender they offered. Most appealing to me at that moment, though, was the knowledge that the mountains would provide a variety of scenery, which no sea or seaside can ever do. So I stayed on that beach only to rest and regain my strength during two or three days. Then I repacked my pack and turned to the east, and headed for the first foothills of those mountains.

It was midsummer then, which was fortunate for me, for even at that season the nights were frigid in those heights. The few clothes and the single blanket I carried were much worn by then, and had not been improved by their long soaking in salt water. But had I ventured into those mountains in winter I would really have suffered, for I was told by the natives that the winters brought numbing cold and heavy snows that piled head-high.

Yes, I finally met some people, though not until I had been among the mountains for many days, by which time I was wondering if The One World had been totally depopulated by Tzebóruko's eruption or some other disaster while I was away at sea.

Very peculiar people they were, too, those people I met. They were called Rarámuri—I assume they still are—a word that means Fast of Feet, and with good reason, as I shall tell. I encountered the first of them when I was standing on a clifftop, resting from a breathtaking climb and admiring a breathtaking view. I was looking down into an awesomely deep chasm, its sheer sides feathered with trees. Through its bottom ran a river, and that river was fed by a waterfall that hurtled from a notched mountaintop on the other side of the canyon from where I stood. The fall must have been almost half of one-long-run— straight down—a mighty column of white water at the top, a mighty plume of white mist at the bottom. I was looking at that spectacle when I heard a hail:

"Kuira-bá!"

I started, because it was the first human voice I had heard in so long, but it sounded cheerful enough, so I took the word to be a greeting. It was a young man who had shouted, and he smiled as he came along the cliff edge toward me. He was handsome of face, in the way that a hawk is handsome, and he was well built, though shorter than myself. He was decently clad, except that he was barefoot—but so was I by that time, my sandals having long ago shredded away. Besides his clean deerskin loincloth, he wore a gaily painted deerskin mantle, of a style new to me; it had wrist-length sleeves set into it, for extra warmth.

As he came up to me, I returned his salute of "Kuira-bá." He indicated the cataract I had been admiring, and grinned as proudly as if he owned it, and said, "Basa-séachic," which I took to mean Falling Water, since a waterfall was unlikely to be named anything else. I repeated the word, and said it with feeling, to convey that I thought the water a most marvelous water, falling most impressively. The young man pointed to himself and said, "Tes-disóra," obviously his name—and meaning Maize Stalk, I later learned. I pointed to myself, said "Mixtli," and pointed to a cloud in the sky. He nodded, tapped his mantled chest, and said, "Raramuríme," then indicated me and said, "Chichimecáme."

I shook my head emphatically, slapped my bare chest and said, "Mexícatl!" at which he only nodded again, indulgently, as if I had specified one of the numberless tribes of the Chichiméca dog people. Not then, but eventually, I realized that the Rarámuri had never even heard of us Mexíca—of our civilized society, our knowledge and power and far-flung dominions—and I think they would have cared little if they had heard. The Rarámuri have a comfortable life in their mountain fastnesses—well fed and watered, content with their own company—so they seldom travel far. Hence they know no other peoples except their near neighbors, of whom the occasional raider or forager or simple wanderer happens into their country, as I had done.

To the north of their territory live the dread Yaki, and no sane people desire close acquaintance with *them*. I remembered having heard of the Yaki from that scalpless elder pochtécatl. Tes-disóra, when later I was able to understand his language, told me more: "The Yaki are wilder than the wildest beasts. For loincloths, they wear the hair of other men. They tear the scalp from a man while he yet lives, before they butcher and dismember and devour him. If they kill him first, you see, they count his hair not worth keeping and wearing. And the hair of a woman counts not at all. Any women they catch are only good for eating—after they have been raped until they split up the middle and are of no more use for raping."

In the mountains south of the Rarámuri live more peaceable tribes, related to them by fairly similar languages and customs. Along the western seacoast live tribes of fishermen, who almost never venture inland. All of those peoples are, if not what could be called civilized, at least cleanly of body and tidy of dress. The only really slovenly and squalid neighbors of the Rarámuri are the Chichiméca tribes in the deserts to the east.

I was as sunburned as any desert-dwelling Chichimécatl, and was as nearly naked. In Rarámuri eyes, I could only be one of that trash breed, though perhaps an unusually enterprising one, to have toiled my way to the mountain heights. I do think that Tes-disóra might at least have taken notice, at our first meeting, of the fact that I did not stink. Thanks to the mountains' abudance of water, I had been able to bathe every day, and, like the Rarámuri, I continued to do so. But, despite my evident gentility, despite my insistence that I was of the Mexíca, despite my reiterated glorification of that far-off nation, I never persuaded one single person of the Rarámuri that I was not just a "Chichimecáme" fugitive from the desert.

No matter. Whatever they believed me to be, or whatever they thought I was pretending to be, the Rarámuri made me welcome. And I lingered among them for a time, simply because I was intrigued by their way of life and enjoyed sharing it. I stayed with them long enough to learn their language sufficiently to be able to converse, at least with the help of many gestures on my part and theirs. Of course, during my first encounter with Tes-disóra, *all* our communication was done by gestures.

After we had exchanged names, he used his hands to indicate a shelter over his head—meaning a village, I assumed—and said, "Guagüey-bo," and pointed southward. Then he indicated Tonatíu in the sky, calling him "Ta-tevarí," or Grandfather Fire, and made me understand that we could reach the village of Guagüey-bo in a journey of three suns. I made gestures and faces of gratitude for the invitation, and we went in that direction. To my surprise, Tes-disóra set off at a lope, but, when he saw that I was winded and tired and disinclined to run, he dropped back and thereafter matched my walking pace. His lope was evidently his accustomed way of crossing mountains and canyons alike, for, even though I am long-legged, at a walk it took us five days, not three, to reach Guagüey-bo.

Early in the march, Tes-disóra gave me to understand that he was one of his village's hunters. I gestured to ask why, then, he was empty-handed. Where had he left his weapons? He grinned and motioned for me to stop walking, to crouch quietly in the underbrush. We waited there in the forest for only a little while, then Tes-disóra nudged me and pointed, and I dimly saw a dappled shape move among the trees. Before I could raise my crystal, Tes-disóra suddenly sprang from his crouch and away, as if he had been an arrow I had shot from a bow.

The wood was so dense that, even with my seeing topaz, I could not follow every movement of the "hunt," but I saw enough to make me gape in disbelief. The dappled form was that of a young doe, and she had leapt to flee in almost the same instant Tes-disóra leapt in pursuit of her. She ran fast, but the young man ran faster. She bounded and twisted this way and that, but he seemed somehow to anticipate her every desperate turn. In less time than I have been telling of it, he closed with the doe, flung himself upon her, and with his hands broke her neck.

As we made a meal of one of the animal's haunches, I made gestures of amazement at Tes-disóra's speed and agility. He made gestures of modest dismissal, informing me that he was among the least of the Fast of Feet, that other hunters were far superior at running, and that in any case a mere doe was no challenge compared to a full-grown buck deer. Then, in his turn, he gestured amazement at the burning crystal with which I had lighted our cooking fire. He conveyed that he had never seen such a wondrously useful instrument in the possession of any other barbarian.

"Mexícatl!" I repeated several times, in loud vexation. He only nodded, and we left off talking with either our hands or mouths, using them instead to feed hungrily on the tender broiled meat.

✠

Guagüey-bo was situated in another of the spectacularly vast chasms of that country, and it was a village in the sense that it housed some twenties of families—perhaps three hundred persons all together—but it contained only one visible residence, a small house neatly built of wood, in which lived the Si-ríame. That word means chief, sorcerer, physician, and judge, but it does not mean four persons; in a Rarámuri community all those offices are vested in one individual. The Si-ríame's house and various other structures—some dome-shaped clay steam houses, several open-sided storage sheds, a slate-floor platform for communal ceremonies—those sat in the canyon bottom, along the bank of the white-water river streaming through. The rest of Guagüey-bo's population lived in caves, either natural or hollowed out from the walls rising on both sides of that immense ravine.

That they inhabit caves does not mean that the Rarámuri are either primitive or lazy, merely that they are practical. If they wished, they could all have houses as neat as that one of the Si-ríame. But the caves are available or are easily dug, and their occupants make them cozily habitable. They are partitioned by interior rock walls into several rooms apiece, and every room has an opening to the outside to admit light and air. They are carpeted with spicy-smelling pine needles, swept out and renewed every day or so. Their exterior openings are curtained and their walls are decorated with deerskins painted in lively designs. The cave dwellings are rather more comfortable, commodious, and well-appointed than many a city house I have been in.

Tes-disóra and I arrived in the village moving as rapidly as we could with the burden slung on a pole we carried between us. Incredible as it may sound, in the early morning of that day he had run down and killed a buck deer, a doe, and a good-sized wild boar. We gutted and dismembered the animals, and hurried to get the meat to Guagüey-bo while the morning was still cool. The village was being plentifully stocked with food by all its hunters and gatherers because, Tes-disóra informed me, a tes-güinápuri festival was just about to begin. I silently congratulated myself on my good fortune in having encountered the Rarámuri when they were in a mood to be hospitable. But I later realized that only by ill chance could I ever have found any Rarámuri *not* enjoying some festivity, or preparing for it, or resting after it. Their religious ceremonies are not somber but frolicsome—the word tes-güinápuri can be tránslated as "Let us now get drunk"—and in total those celebrations occupy fully a third of the Rarámuri's year.

Since their forests and rivers so freely give them game and other foods, hides and skins, firewood and water, the Rarámuri do not, like most people, have to labor just to keep themselves supplied with the necessities of life. The only crop they cultivate is maize, but most of that is not for eating. It is for the making of tesgüino, a fermented beverage somewhat more drunk-making than the octli of us Mexíca and somewhat less so than the chápari honey liquor of the Purémpecha. From the lower lands east of the mountains, the Rarámuri also gather a chewable and potent little cactus which they call the jípuri—meaning "the god-light," for reasons I shall explain. What with having so little work and so much free time on their hands, those people have good cause to spend a third of the year merrily drunk on tesgüino or blissfully drugged with jípuri and joyfully thanking their gods for their bounty.

On the way to the village, I had learned from Tes-disóra some fragments of his language, and he and I were communicating more freely. So I will cease mentioning gestures and grimaces, and will report only the content of subsequent conversations. When he and I had given our load of venison to some elderly crones tending great cooking fires beside the river, he suggested that we sweat ourselves clean in one of the steam baths. He also suggested, with nice tact, that after we had bathed he could provide me with clean garments if I cared to throw my old rags into one of the fires. I was all too willing to comply.

When we undressed at the entrance to the clay steam house, I got a small surprise. Seeing Tes-disóra nude, I saw that he had small bushes of hair growing from his armpits and another between his legs, and I made some comment on that unexpected sight. Tes-disóra only shrugged, pointed to his hairiness, and said, "Raramuríme," then pointed to my hairless crotch and said, "Chichimecáme." What he meant was that he was no rarity; the Rarámuri grew abundant ymáxtli around their genitals and under their arms; the Chichiméca did not.

"I am not of the Chichiméca," I said yet again, but I said it absently, for I was thinking. Of all the peoples I had known, only the Rarámuri grew that superfluous hair. I supposed that it was induced by the extremely cold weather they endured during part of each year, though I could not see that a growth of hair in *those* places was any useful protection against the cold. Another thought occurred to me, and I asked Tes-disóra:

"Do your women grow similar little bushes?"

He laughed and said that of course they did. He explained that a sprouting of ymáxtli fuzz was one of the first signs of a child's approaching manhood or womanhood. On males and females alike, the fuzz gradually became hair—not very long hair, and no nuisance or impediment, but undeniably hair. I had already noticed, in the very brief time I had been in the village, that many of the Rarámuri women, though well muscled, were also well shaped and exceedingly fair of face. Which is to say that I found them attractive even before I knew of that distinctive peculiarity, which set me wondering: how would it feel, to couple with a woman whose tipíli was not forthrightly visible, or faintly veiled by only a fine down, but darkly and tantalizingly screened by hair like that on her head?

"You can easily find out," said Tes-disóra, as if he had divined my unspoken thought. "During the tes-güinápuri games, simply chase a woman and run her down and verify the fact."

When I had first entered Guagüey-bo, I had been the object

of some understandably wary and derisive glances from the villagers. But when I was clean, combed, and clad in loincloth and sleeved mantle of supple deerskin, I was no longer eyed with disdain. From then on, except for the occasional giggle when I made an outrageous mistake in speaking their language, the Rarámuri were courteous and friendly to me. And my exceptional size, if nothing else about me, attracted some speculative, even admiring looks from the village girls and unattached women. It seemed there were more than a few of them who would gladly run for me to chase.

They were almost always running, anyway—*all* the Rarámuri, male and female, old and young. If they were beyond the age of mere toddling and not yet at the age of doddering, they ran. At all times of day, except for those intervals of immobility when they were occupied with some task, or were sodden with tesgüino, or dazzled by the godlight jípuri, they ran. If they were not racing each other in pairs or in groups, they ran alone, back and forth along the floor of the canyon or up and down the slanting canyon walls. The men usually ran while kicking a ball ahead of them, a carved and carefully smoothed round ball of hard wood as big as a man's head. The females usually ran chasing a small hoop of woven straw, each woman carrying a little stick with which she scooped up the circlet on the run and threw it farther on, and the other women ran competing to catch up to it first and throw it next. All that frenetic and incessant commotion appeared purposeless to me, but Tes-disóra explained:

"It is partly high spirits and animal energy, but it is more than that. It is an unceasing ceremony in which, through the exertion and sweat expended, we pay homage to our gods Ta-tevarí and Ka-laumarí and Ma-tinierí."

I found it difficult to imagine any god who could be nourished by perspiration instead of blood, but the Rarámuri have those three whom Tes-disóra named: in your language their names would be Grandfather Fire, Mother Water, and Brother Deer. Perhaps the religion recognizes other gods, but those are the only three I hever heard mentioned. Considering the simple needs of the forest-dwelling Rarámuri, I suppose those three suffice.

Tes-disóra said, "Our constant running shows our creator

gods that the people they created are still alive and lively, and grateful to be so. It also keeps our men fit for the rigors of the running hunt. It is also practice for the games you will see— or join in, I hope—during this festival. And those games themselves are only practice."

"Kindly tell me," I sighed, feeling rather wearied just by the talk of so much exertion. "Practice for what?"

"For the *real* running, of course. The ra-rajípuri." He grinned at the expression on my face. "You will see. It is the grand conclusion of every celebration."

The tes-güinápuri got under way the next day, when the village's entire population gathered outside the riverside wooden house, waiting for the Si-ríame to emerge and command that the festivities begin. Everybody was dressed in his finest and most colorfully decorated garments: most of us men in deerskin mantles and loincloths, the females in deerskin skirts and blouses. Some of the villagers had painted their faces with dots and curly lines of a brilliant yellow, and many wore feathers in their hair, though the birds of that northern region do not provide very impressive plumes. Several of Guagüeybo's veteran hunters were already sweating, for they wore trophies of their prowess: ankle-length robes of cuguar hide or heavy bearskin or the thick coat of the big-horned mountain leaper.

The Si-ríame stepped out of the house, dressed entirely in shimmering jaguar hides, holding a staff topped with a knob of raw silver, and I was so astonished that I raised my topaz to make sure of what I was seeing. Having heard that the chief was also sage, sorcerer, judge, and physician, I had naturally expected to see that luminary in the person of an extremely old and solemn-faced man. But it was not a man, and not old, not solemn. She was no older than I, and pretty, and made more pretty by her warm smile.

"Your Si-ríame is a *woman?*" I exclaimed, as she began to intone the ceremonial prayers.

"Why not?" said Tes-disóra.

"I never heard of any people choosing to be governed by any but a male."

"Our last Si-ríame was a man. But when a Si-ríame dies, every other mature man and woman of the village is eligible to succeed. We all gathered together and chewed much jípuri and went into trance. We saw visions, and some of us went running wildly, and others went into convulsions. But that woman was the only one blessed by the god-light. Or at least she was the first to awaken and tell of having seen and talked with Grandfather Fire, with Mother Water and Brother Deer. She indubitably had been shone upon by the god-light, which is the supreme and sole requirement for accession to the office of Si-ríame."

The handsome woman finished her chanting, smiled again, and raised her shapely arms aloft in a general benediction, then turned and went back into the house, as the crowd gave her a cheer of affectionate respect.

"She stays in seclusion?" I asked Tes-disóra.

"During the festivals, yes," he said, and chuckled. "Sometimes our people misbehave during a tes-güinápuri. They fight among themselves, or they indulge in adulteries, or they commit other mischiefs. The Si-ríame is a wise woman. What she does not see or hear about, she does not punish."

I do not know whether it would have been regarded as a mischief, what I intended to do: to chase and catch and couple with the most delectable available sample of Rarámuri womanhood. But, as things happened, I did not exactly do that—and, far from being punished, I was rewarded in a way.

What occurred was that, first, like all the villagers, I made a glutton of myself on venison of various sorts and atóli mush of maize, and I drank heavily of tesgüino. Then, almost too heavy to stand, almost too drunk to walk, I tried to join some of the men in one of their ball-kicking runs—but I would have been outclassed by them even if I had been in perfect competing condition. I did not mind. I dropped out to watch a group of females running a hoop and stick game, and a certain nubile girl among them caught my eye. And I mean my one eye; unless I closed the other, I saw two of the same girl. I walked weaving toward her, awkwardly motioning and thickly requesting that she quit the group to essay a different game.

She smiled her acquiescence, but eluded my clutching hand. "You must catch me first," she said, and turned and ran away down the canyon.

Though I had not expected to excel as a runner among the Rarámuri men, I was sure that I could run down any female alive. But that one I could not, and I think she even slackened her pace to make it easier for me. Perhaps I would have done better if I had not been so full of food and drink, especially the drink. With one eye closed, it is hard to judge distances. Even if the girl had stood still before me, I would probably have missed when I grabbed for her. But with both eyes opened, I saw two of everything in my path—roots and rocks and such— and in trying to run between each two things I invariably tripped on one of them. After nine or ten falls, I tried to leap *over* the next doubly seen obstacle, a fairly large rock, and fell across it on my belly, so heavily that all the breath was driven from my body.

The girl had been watching me over her shoulder as she did her pretense of fleeing. When I fell, she stopped and came back to stand over my clenched body, and said in a voice of some exasperation, "Unless you catch me fairly, we cannot play any other game. If you know what I mean."

I could not even wheeze at her. I lay doubled up, painfully trying to gasp some air back into me, and I felt quite incapable of playing any further games whatever. She frowned peevishly, probably sharing my low opinion of me, but then she brightened and said:

"I did not think to ask. Have you partaken of the jípuri?"

I feebly shook my head.

"That explains it. You are not so very inferior to the other men. They have the advantage of that enhanced strength and stamina. Come! You shall chew some jípuri!"

I was still curled into a ball, but I was almost beginning to breathe again; and her imperious command allowed of no refusal. I let her take my hand and haul me upright and lead me back to the village center. I already knew what the jípuri is and does, for small quantities of it were imported even into Tenochtítlan, where it was called peyotl and where it was reserved for the exclusive use of the divinatory priests. The jípuri or peyotl is a deceptively meek-looking little cactus. Growing close against the ground, round and squat, the jípuri seldom gets larger than the palm of a hand, and it is scalloped into petals or bulges, so it resembles a very tiny, gray-green

pumpkin. For its most potent effect, it is best chewed when
fresh picked. But it can be dried for keeping indefinitely, the
wrinkled brown wads threaded on strings, and in the village
of Guagüey-bo many such strings hung from the rafters of the
several storage sheds. I reached to pluck one down, but my
companion said:

"Wait. Have you *ever* chewed jípuri?"

Again I shook my head.

"Then you will be a ma-tuáne, one who seeks the god-light
for the first time. That requires a ceremony of your purification.
No, do not groan so. It need not long delay our . . . our game."
She looked around at the villagers still eating or drinking or
dancing or running. "Everyone else is too busy to participate,
but the Si-ríame is unoccupied. She should be willing to administer the purification."

We went to the modest wooden house, and the girl jangled
a string of snail shells hung beside the door. The chief-woman,
still wearing her jaguar garments, lifted the door's deerskin
curtain and said, "Kuira-bá," and made a gracious gesture for
us to enter.

"Si-ríame," said my companion, "this is the Chichimecáme
named Mixtli who has come to visit our village. As you can
see, he is of some age, but he is a poor runner even for one
of his advanced years. He could not catch *me* when he tried.
I thought the jípuri might enliven his old limbs, but he says
he has never before sought the god-light, so . . ."

The chief-woman's eyes twinkled with amusement as she
watched me wince during that unflattering recital. I muttered,
"I am not of the Chichiméca," but she ignored me and said to
the girl:

"Of course. You are eager that he have the ma-tuáne initiation as soon as possible. I will be happy to do it." She looked
me appraisingly up and down, and the amusement in her eyes
gave place to something else. "Whatever his years, this Mixtli
seems an estimable specimen, especially considering his base
origins. And I will give you one bit of advice, my dear, which
you would not hear from any of our males. However rightly
you are expected to admire a man's racing competence, it is
his middle leg, so to speak, which better demonstrates his
manliness. That member may even dwindle from disuse when

a man devotes all his attention to developing the muscles of his other appendages. Therefore be not too quick to disdain a mediocre runner until you have examined his other attributes."

"Yes, Si-ríame," the girl said impatiently. "I intended something of the sort."

"You can do so after the ceremony. You may go now, my dear."

"Go?" the girl protested. "But there is nothing secret about the ma-tuáne initiation! The whole village always looks on!"

"We will not interrupt the celebration of the tes-güinápuri. And this Mixtli is a stranger to our customs. He might be abashed by a horde of staring onlookers."

"I am not a horde! And it was I who brought him for the purification!"

"You will have him back when it is done. Then you can judge whether he was worth your trouble. I have said you may go, my dear." Throwing a furious look at both of us, the girl went, and the Si-ríame said to me, "Sit down, guest Mixtli, while I mix you a brew of herbs to clear your brain. You should not be drunk when you chew the jípuri."

I sat down on the pounded-earth floor strewn with pine needles. She set the herbal drink to simmering on the hearth in a corner, and came to me bearing a small jar. "The juice of the sacred urá plant," she described it, and, using a small feather for a brush, she painted circles and whorls of bright yellow dots on my cheeks and forehead.

"Now," she said, when she had given me the hot beverage to drink and it was almost magically bringing me out of my fuddlement. "I do not know what the name Mixtli means, but, since you are a ma-tuáne seeking the god-light for the first time, you must choose a new name."

I nearly laughed. I had long ago lost count of all the old and new names I had worn in my time. But I said only, "Mixtli means the sky-hung thing you Rarámuri call a kurú."

"It makes a good name, but it should have a descriptive addition. We will name you Su-kurú."

I did not laugh. Su-kurú means Dark Cloud, and there was no way she could have known that that already *was* my name. But I remembered that a Si-ríame was reputedly a sorcerer, among other things, and I supposed that her god-light could show her truths hidden from other people.

"And now, Su-kurú," she said, "you must confess all the sins you have committed in your life."

"My lady Si-ríame," I said, and without sarcasm, "I probably have not iife enough left in which to recount them all."

"Indeed? So many?" She regarded me pensively, then said, "Well, since the true god-light resides exclusively in us Rarámuri, and is ours to share, we will count only your sins since you have been among us. Tell me of those."

"I have done none. Or none that I know of."

"Oh, you need not have done them. To want to do them is the same thing. To feel an anger or a hatred and a wish to avenge it. To entertain any unworthy thought or emotion. For example, you did not wreak your lust upon that girl, but you clearly chased her with lustful intent."

"Not so much lust, my lady, as curiosity."

She looked puzzled, so I explained about the ymáxtli, the body hair which I had seen on no other bodies, and the urges it had aroused in me. She burst into laughter.

"How like a barbarian, to be intrigued by what a civilized person takes for granted! I would wager it has been only a few years since you savages ceased to be mystified by fire!"

When she had done laughing and mocking me, she wiped tears from her eyes and said, more sympathetically:

"Know then, Su-kurú, that we Rarámuri are physically and morally superior to primitive peoples, and our bodies reflect our finer sensibilities, such as our high regard for modesty. So it became the nature of our bodies to grow that hair which you find so unusual. Our bodies thus insure that, even when we are unclothed, our private parts are discreetly covered."

I said, "I should think that such a growth in those parts would attract rather than distract notice. Not modest at all, but immodestly provocative."

Seated cross-legged on the ground as I was, I could not readily hide the evidence bulging my loincloth, and the Si-ríame could hardly pretend not to see it. She shook her head in wonderment and murmured, not to me but to herself:

"Mere hair between the legs . . . as common and unremarkable as weeds between the rocks . . . yet it excites an outlander.

And this talk of it makes me oddly conscious of my own..." Then she said eagerly, "We will accept your curiosity as your confessed sin. Now here, quickly, partake of the jípuri."

She produced a basket of the little cactuses, fresh and green, not dried. I selected one that had numerous lobes around its rim.

"No, take this five-petaled one," she said. "The many-scalloped jípuri is for everyday consumption, to be chewed by runners who must make a long run, or by idlers who merely wish to sit and bask in visions. But it is the five-petaled jípuri, the more rare and hard to find, that lifts one closest to the god-light."

So I bit a mouthful of the cactus she handed me—it had a slightly bitter and astringent flavor—and she selected another for herself, saying, "Do not chew as fast as I do, ma-tuáne Sukurú. You will feel the effect more quickly because it is your first time, and we should keep pace with each other."

She was right. I had swallowed very little of the juice when I was astounded to see the walls of the house dissolving from around me. They became transparent, then they were gone, and I saw all the villagers outside, variously engaged in the games and feasting of the tes-güinápuri. I could not believe that I was actually seeing through the walls, for the figures of the people were sharply defined, and I was not using my topaz; the too-clear vision had to be an illusion caused by the jípuri. But in the next moment I was not so sure. I seemed to float from where I sat, and I rose to and through the roof—or where the roof had been—and the people dropped away and became smaller as I soared toward the treetops. Involuntarily, I exclaimed, *"Ayya!"* The Si-ríame, somewhere behind or below me, called, "Not too fast! Wait for me!"

I say she called, but in fact I did not hear her. I mean to say, her words came not into my ears but somehow into my own mouth, and I tasted them—smooth, delicious, like chocolate—yet in some manner I understood them by their flavor. Indeed, all my senses seemed suddenly to be exchanging their usual functions. I *heard* the aroma of the trees and the cook fires' smoke that drifted up among the trees as I was drifting. Instead of giving off a leafy smell, the trees' foliage made a metallic ringing; the smoke made a muffled sound like a drumhead being softly stroked. I did not see, I *smelled* the colors about me. The green of the trees seemed not a color to my eyes but a cool, moist scent in my nostrils; a red-petaled flower on a branch was not red but a spicy odor; the sky was not blue bùt a clean, fleshy fragrance like that of a woman's breasts.

And then I perceived that my head was really between a woman's breasts, and ample ones. My sense of touch and feeling was unaffected by the drug. The Si-ríame had caught up to me, had thrown open her jaguar blouse, had clasped me to her bosom, and we were rising together toward the clouds. One part of me, I might say, was rising faster than the rest. My tepúli had already been earlier aroused, but it was getting even longer, thicker, harder, throbbing with urgency, as if an earthquake had occurred without my notice. The Si-ríame gave a happy laugh—I tasted her laughter, refreshing as raindrops, and her words tasted like kisses:

"That is the best blessing of the god-light, Su-kurú—the heat and glow it adds to the act of ma-rákame. Let us combine our god-given fires."

She unwound her jaguar skirt and lay naked upon it, or as naked as a woman of the Rarámuri could get, for there truly was a triangle of hair pointing from her lower abdomen down between her thighs. I could see the shape of that enticing little cushion, and the curly texture of it, but the blackness of it was, like all other colors at that moment, not a color but an aroma. I leaned close to inhale it, and it was a warm, humid, musky scent. . . .

At our first coupling, that ymáxtli felt crinkly and tickly against my bare belly, as if I were thrusting my lower body among the fronds of a luxuriant fern. But soon, so quickly did our juices flow, the hair became wet and yielding and, if I had not known it was there, I would not have known it was there. However, since I did know—that my tepúli was penetrating more than flesh, that it was held for the first time by a densely hair-tufted tipíli—the act had a new savor for me. No doubt I sound delirious in the telling of it, but delirious is what I was. I was made giddy by being at a great height, whether it was reality or illusion; by the oddity of sensing a woman's words and moans and cries in my mouth, not my ears; by the sensing of her skin's every surface and curve and gradation of color as a subtly distinct fragrance. Meanwhile, each of those sensations, as well as our every move and touch, was enriched by the effect of the jípuri.

I suppose also I felt a tinge of danger, and danger makes every human sense more acute, every emotion more vivid. Men do not ordinarily fly upward to a height, they more often fall down from one, and that is often fatal. But the Si-ríame and I stayed suspended, with no discernible floor or other support beneath us. And being unsupported we were also unencumbered by any support, so we moved as freely and weightlessly as if we had been under water but still able to breathe there. That freedom in all dimensions enabled some pleasurable positions and coilings and intertwinings that I would otherwise have thought impossible. At one point the Si-ríame gasped some words, and the words tasted like her ferned tipíli: "I believe you now. That you could have done more sins than you could tell." I have no idea how often she came to climax and how many times I ejaculated during the time the drug held us aloft and enraptured, but, for me, it was many more than I had ever enjoyed in such a short time.

The time seemed *too* short. I became aware that I was hearing, not tasting the sounds when she sighed, "Do not worry, Su-kurú, if you do not ever excel as a runner."

I was seeing colors again, not scenting them; and smelling odors, not hearing them; and I was descending from the heights of both altitude and exaltation. I did not plummet, but came down as slowly and lightly as a feather falling. The Si-ríame and I were again inside her house, side by side on our discarded and rumpled garments of jaguar and deerskin. She lay on her back, fast asleep, with a smile on her face. The hair of her head was a tumbled mass, but the ymáxtli on her lower belly was no longer crisp and curly and black; it was matted and lightened in color by the white of my omícetl. There was another dried spill in the cleft between her heavy breasts, and others elsewhere.

I felt similarly encrusted with her emanations and my own dried perspiration. I was also terribly thirsty; the inside of my mouth felt as furred as if *it* had grown ymáxtli; I later learned to expect that effect always after chewing jípuri. Moving carefully and quietly, not to disturb the sleeping Si-ríame, I got up and dressed to go and seek a drink of water outside the house. Before departing, I took one final appreciative look through my topaz at the handsome woman relaxed on the jaguar skins. It was the first time, I reflected, that I had ever had sexual relations with any sovereign ruler. I felt rather smugly pleased with myself.

But not for long. I emerged from the house to find the sun still up and the celebrations still going on. When, after drinking heartily, I raised my eyes from the dipper gourd, I looked into the accusing eyes of the girl I had earlier been chasing. I smiled as guiltlessly as I could, and said:

"Shall we run again? I can now partake at will of the jípuri. I have been properly initiated."

"You need not boast of it," she said between her teeth. "Half a day and a whole night and almost another day of initiation."

I gaped stupidly, for it was hard for me to realize that so much time had been compressed into what had seemed so little. And I blushed as the girl went on accusingly:

"She *always* gets the first and the best ma-rákame of the god-enlightened, and it is not fair! I do not care if I *am* called rebellious and irreverent. I have said before and I say again that she only *pretended* to receive the god-light from the Grandfather and the Mother and the Brother. She *lied* to be chosen as the Si-ríame, only so she can claim first right to every ma-tuáne she happens to favor."

That somewhat lessened my self-esteem in having coupled with an annointed ruler: learning that the ruler was in no way superior to any common woman gone astraddle the road. My self-esteem further suffered when, during the remainder of my stay, the Si-ríame did not again command my attendance on her. Evidently she wanted *only* "the first and the best" that a male initiate could give under the influence of the drug.

But at least I was eventually able to mollify the angry girl, after I had slept and recuperated my energies. Her name, I learned, was Vi-rikóta, meaning Holy Land, which is also the name of that country east of the mountains where the jípuri cactus is gathered. The celebration went on for many days longer, and I persuaded Vi-rikóta to let me chase her again, and since I had taken care not to overindulge in food or tesgüino, I caught her almost fairly, I believe.

We plucked some of the dried jípuri from one of the storage strings and went together to a secluded and pleasant glade in the forested canyon. We had to chew quite a lot of the less potent cactus to approximate the effects I had enjoyed in the Si-ríame's house, but after a while I felt my senses again exchanging their functions. That time the colors of butterflies and flowers around us began to *sing*.

Vi-rikóta, of course, also wore a medallion of ymáxtli between her legs—in her case a less crisp, more fluffy cushion—and that was still a novelty to me, so it again provoked me to extraordinary enterprise. But she and I never quite achieved the ecstasy I had known during my initiation. We never had the illusion of ascending skyward, and we were conscious at all times of the soft grass on which we lay. Also, Vi-rikóta was really very young, and small even for her age, and a female child simply cannot spread her thighs far enough that a man's big body can get close enough to penetrate her to the full length of his tepúli. All else aside, our coupling *had* to be less memorable than what the Si-ríame and I had done together, because Vi-rikóta and I did not have access to the fresh, green, five-petaled, *real* god-light jípuri.

Nevertheless, that young female and I suited each other well enough that we consorted with no other partners during the remainder of the festival, and we indulged many times in the ma-rákame, and I felt a genuine regret at parting from her when the tes-güinápuri concluded. We parted only because my original host Tes-disóra insisted, "It is time now for the *serious* running, Su-kurú, and you must see it. The ra-rajípuri, the race between the best runners of our village and those of Guacho-chí."

I asked, "Where are they? I have seen no strangers arriving."

"Not yet. They will arrive after we have gone, and they will arrive running. Gaucho-chí is far to the southeast of here."

He told me the distance, in the Rarámuri words for it, which I forget, but I remember that it would have translated as more than fifteen Mexíca one-long-runs or fifteen of your Spanish leagues. And he was speaking of the distance in a straight line, though in actuality any race in that rugged country has to follow a tortuous course around and between and through ravines and mountains. I calculated that in total the running distance from

Guagüey-bo to Guacho-chí must have been nearer fifty one-long-runs. Yet Tes-disóra said casually:

"To run from one village to the other, and back again, kicking the wooden ball all the way, takes a good runner one day and one night."

"Impossible!" I exclaimed. "A hundred one-long-runs? Why, it would be like a man running from the city of Te-nochtítlan to the far-off Purémpe village of Kerétaro in the same time." I shook my head emphatically. "And half of that in the darkness of night? And kicking a ball as he goes? Impossible!"

Of course Tes-disóra knew nothing of Tenochtítlan or Kerétaro, or their distance apart. He shrugged and said, "If you think it impossible, Su-kurú, you must come along and see it done."

"I? I *know* it is impossible for me!"

"Then come only part of the way and wait to accompany us home on our return. I have a pair of stout boar-hide sandals you may wear. Since you are not one of our village runners, it will not be cheating if you do not run the ra-rajípuri barefoot, as we do."

"Cheating?" I said, amused. "You mean there are rules to this running game?"

"Not many," he said, in all seriousness. "Our runners will depart from here this afternoon at the precise instant when Grandfather Fire"—he pointed—"touches his rim to the upper edge of that mountain yonder. The people of Guacho-chí have some similar means of judging that exact same instant, and their runners likewise depart. We run toward Guacho-chí, they run toward Guagüey-bo. We pass at some point between, shouting greetings and raillery and friendly insults. When the men of Guacho-chí get here, our women offer them refreshment and try all manner of wiles to detain them—and so do their women when we get there—but you may be sure we pay no heed. We turn right around and continue running, until we are back in our own respective villages. By then, Grandfather Fire will again be touching that mountain, or sinking behind it, or still some way above it, and accordingly we can determine our running time. The men of Guacho-chí do the same, and we send messengers to exchange the results, and thus we know who won the race."

I said, "For all that expenditure of time and effort, I hope the winners' prize is something worthwhile."

"Prize? There is no prize."

"What? You do all that for not even a trophy? For not even a goal to reach and hold? With no aim or end but to stagger wearily to your own same homes and women again? In the name of your three gods, *why?*"

He shrugged again. "We do it because it is what we do best."

I said no more, for I knew that it is futile to argue any matter rationally with irrational persons. However, I later gave more thought to Tes-disóra's reply on that occasion, and it is perhaps not so nonsensical as it sounded then. I suppose I could not better have defended my life-long preoccupation with the art of word knowing, if anyone had ever demanded of me to know *why*.

Only six robust males, those adjudged the best runners of Guagüey-bo, were the actual racers in the ra-rajípuri. The six, of whom Tes-disóra was one that day, were well gorged on the fatigue-averting jípuri cactus before the event began, and they each carried a small water sack and a pouch of pinóli meal, which sustenance they would snatch almost without slowing their pace. Also attached to the waists of their loincloths were some small dry gourds, each containing a pebble, whose rattling noise was intended to keep them from falling asleep on their feet.

The remainder of the ra-rajípuri runners comprised every other fit male of Guagüey-bo, from adolescents to men much older than myself, and they went along to help sustain the runners in spirit. Numerous of them had gone on ahead, as early as that morning. They were men who could run remarkably fast for a short time but tended to weaken over long distances. They posted themselves at intervals along the course between the two villages. As the chosen runners came by, those sprinters would speed alongside them, to inspire the racers to their best efforts over each of those intervals.

Others of the nonracers carried small pots of glowing coals and torches of pine splints, the latter to be fired after dark to light the racers' way throughout the night. Still other men carried spare strings of dried jípuri, spare sacks of pinóli and water. The youngest and oldest carried nothing; their task was to keep up a continuous shouting and chanting of inspiriting encouragement. All the men were painted on the face, bare chest, and back with dots and circles and spirals of the vivid yellow urá pigment. I was adorned only on my face, for, unlike the others, I was allowed to wear my sleeved mantle.

As Grandfather Fire settled toward the designated mountain in late afternoon, the Si-ríame came smiling to the door of her house, wearing her regalia of jaguar skins, holding in one hand her silver-knobbed staff and in the other the yellow-painted wooden ball the size of a man's head. She stood there, glancing sideways at the sun, while the racers and all their companions stood nearby, perceptibly leaning forward in eagerness to be off. At the moment Grandfather Fire touched the mountaintop, the Si-ríame smiled her broadest and threw the ball from her threshold among the bare feet of the waiting six racers. Every inhabitant of Guagüey-bo gave an exultant shout, and the six runners were away, playfully kicking the ball from one to another as they went. The other participants followed at a respectful distance, and so did I. The Si-ríame was still smiling when I last saw her, and little Vi-rikóta was jumping up and down as gaily as a dying candle flame.

I had fully expected the whole crowd of runners to out-distance me in a moment, but I should have guessed that they would not put all their energy into a headlong rush at the very start of the run. They set off at a moderate lope which even I could sustain. We went along the canyon riverside, and the cheering of the village women, children, and old folks faded behind us, and our own shouters began whooping and bellowing. Since the runners naturally avoided having to kick the ball uphill whenever possible, we continued along the canyon's bottom until its sides sloped and lowered sufficiently for us to climb easily out of it and into the forest to the south.

I am proud to report that I stayed with the racers for what I estimate to have been a full third of the way from Guagüey-bo to Guacho-chí. Perhaps the credit should go to the jípuri I had chewed before starting, for several times I found myself running faster than I ever have done in my life before or since that race. Those were the times when we came up to the posted sprinters and did our best to match their bursts of speed. And several times we passed the sprinters from Guacho-chí—they standing, not yet running—stationed to await the coming of their own racers from the opposite direction. Those competitors shouted cheerfully scornful names at us as we went by them— "Laggards!" and "Limpers!" and the like—especially at me, because by then I was trailing the rest of the Guagüey-bo contingent.

Running full tilt through closely spaced trees and along ravine floors strewn with ankle-twisting rocks was something to which I was unaccustomed at the best of times, but I managed well enough as long as I had light to see. When the glow of afternoon began to diminish, I had to run with my topaz held to my eye, and that forced me to slow my pace considerably. As the twilight got darker, I saw the guide lights bloom out ahead of me, where the torch bearers were firing their bundles of splints. But of course none of those men would drop back to waste his light on a nonracer, so I was left farther and farther behind the running crowd, and its cries dimmed away.

Then, as full darkness closed around me, I saw a red gleam on the ground just ahead. The kindly Rarámuri had not totally forgotten or dismissed their outlander companion Su-kurú. One of the torch bearers, after lighting his torch, had carefully set down his little clay pot of embers where I was sure to find it. So there I stopped, and laid and lit a campfire, and settled down to spend the night. I will admit that, despite my ingestion of the jípuri, I was sufficiently tired to have toppled over and slept, but I felt ashamed even to think of it, when every other male in the vicinity was exerting himself to the utmost. Also, I would have been intolerably humiliated, and so would my host village, if, when the rival runners from Guacho-chí came along that trail, they had found "a Guagüey-bo man" lying there asleep. So I ate some of my pinóli and washed it down with a drink from my water pouch and chewed on some of the jípuri I had brought, and that revived me nicely. I sat up all night, throwing an occasional stick on the fire to keep myself comfortable but not so warm that I might become drowsy.

I should be seeing the Guacho-chí runners twice before I again saw Tes-disóra and my other former companions. After the two contingents had passed each other at the midpoint of the course, the rival runners would appear from the southeast and reach my campfire at just about the exact middle moment of the night. Then they would arrive at Guagüey-bo and turn and come back from the northwest and pass me again in the morning. The returning Tes-disóra and his fellows would not reach me—so I could again join their run and go home with them—until the midday sun was overhead.

Well, my calculation of the first encounter was correct. With the aid of my topaz I kept watch of the stars and, according to them, it *was* the middle of the night when I saw bobbing blobs of firelight coming from the southeast. I decided to pretend that I was one of Guagüey-bo's posted sprinters, so I was on my feet, looking alert, before the first of the ball-kicking runners came in sight, and I began to shout, "Laggards! Limpers!" The racers and their torch bearers did not shout back; they were too busy keeping their eyes on the wooden ball, which had lost whatever paint it had worn and was looking rather splintery and shredded. But the company of other Guacho-chí runners returned my taunts, yelling, "Old woman!" and "Warm your weary bones!" and such—and I realized that my having laid a fire made me, in Rarámuri estimation, seem something less than manly. But it was too late then to douse the fire, and they all dashed past and became again just wavery red lights, dwindling to the northwestward.

After another long time, the sky in the east lightened, and finally Grandfather Fire made his reappearance, and more time passed while—as slowly as any aged human grandfather—he crept a third of the way up the sky. It was breakfast time and, by my calculations, time for the Guacho-chí men to be returning on their homeward run. I faced the northwest, where I had last seen them. Since in daylight there would be no torches to signal their coming, I strained my ears to hear them before they were in sight. I heard nothing, I saw nothing.

More time passed. In my mind I went over my reckoning, to find where I had miscalculated, but I could perceive no error. More time passed. I searched my mind, to remember whether or not Tes-disóra had ever said anything about the racers' taking different routes on their return runs. More time passed, and the sun was almost directly overhead, when I heard a hail:

"Kuira-bá!"

It was a man of the Rarámuri, wearing only a runner's loincloth and waist pouches and yellow designs on his bare skin, but he was no one I recalled ever having seen before, so I took him to be one of Guacho-chí's outpost sprinters. Evidently he took me to be a Guagüey-bo counterpart, for, when I had returned his greeting, he approached me with a friendly but anxious smile and said:

"I saw your fire last night, so I left my station and came here. Tell me confidentially, friend, how did your people arrange to detain our runners in your village? Were your women all waiting stripped naked and lying compliant?"

"It is a vision pleasant to entertain," I said. "But they were not, to my knowledge. I was wondering myself, is it possible that your men are returning by some other way?"

He started to say, "It would be the first time ever—" when he was interrupted. We both heard another shout of "Kuira-bá!" and turned to see the approach of Tes-disóra and his five fellow racers. They were lurching and reeling with fatigue, and the ball they perfunctorily kicked among them had been worn down to about the size of my fist.

"We—" said Tes-disóra to the man from Guacho-chí, and had to pause to gulp for air. Then he painfully panted, "We have not yet—met your runners. What trickery—?"

The man said, "This sprinter of yours and I were just asking each other what might have become of them."

Tes-disóra stared at the two of us, his chest heaving. Another man gasped, in a voice of disbelief, "They have—not yet—passed *here?*"

As the whole company of Guagüey-bo runners straggled up to join us, I said, "I asked the stranger if they might have taken a different course. He asked me if your women might have contrived to detain them in your village."

There was a general shaking of heads. Then the heads moved more slowly, as the men looked at one another in bewilderment.

Somebody said, softly, worriedly, "Our village."

Somebody else said, more loudly, with more anxiety, "Our women."

And the stranger said, his voice quavering, "Our best men."

Then there was realization in all their eyes, and shock and

anguish, and it was in the eyes of the Guacho-chí man as well. All those eyes turned bleakly to the northwest and, in the brief breathless moment before the men suddenly left me, all of them running harder than ever, someone among them said just one word:

"Yaki!"

No, I did not follow them to Guagüey-bo. I never went back there again. I was an outlander, and it would have been presumptuous of me to join the Rarámuri men in bewailing their bereavement. I realized what they would find: that the Yaki marauders and the Guacho-chí runners had arrived in Guagüey-bo at about the same time, and the runners would have been too tired to have put up much of a fight against the savages. The Guacho-chí men would all have suffered having the scalps torn from their heads before they died. What the Si-ríame and young Vi-rikóta and the other Guagüey-bo women would have endured before they died I did not even want to think about. I presume that the surviving Rarámuri men eventually repopulated their villages by dividing themselves and the Guacho-chí women between the two, but I will never know.

And I never saw a Yaki, not then or to this day. I would have liked to—if I could have managed it without the Yaki seeing me—for they must be the most fearsome human animals in existence, and wonderful to look upon. In all my years I have known only one man who did meet the Yaki and did live to tell of it, and he was that elder of The House of Pochtéca who had no top to his head. Nor have any of you Spaniards yet encountered a Yaki. Your explorers of these lands have not yet ventured that far north and west. I think I might almost pity even a Spaniard who goes among the Yaki.

When the stricken men went running, I stood still and watched them disappear in the forest. I stayed looking toward the northwest for a while after they were out of sight, saying a silent farewell. Then I squatted down and made a meal of my remaining pinóli and water, and chewed a jípuri to keep me awake during the rest of the day. I dumped earth on the last embers of my campfire, then stood erect, glanced at the sun for direction, and strode off to the south. I had enjoyed my stay with the Rarámuri, and I grieved at having it end so.

But I wore good clothing of deerskin and sandals of boar hide, and I had leather pouches in which to carry food and water, and I had a flint blade at my waist, and I still had my seeing crystal and my burning crystal. I had left nothing behind in Guagüey-bo, unless you count the days that I lived there. But of them I brought away and have kept the memory.

I H S

✠

S.C.C.M.

Sanctified, Caesarean, Catholic Majesty,
the Emperor Don Carlos, Our Lord King:

SUBLIME and Most August Majesty: from this City
of Mexíco, capital of New Spain, this St. Ambrose's Day in
the year of Our Lord one thousand five hundred thirty, greeting.

In our last letters, Sire, we expatiated upon our activities
as Protector of the Indians. Let us here dwell upon our primary
function as Bishop of Mexíco, and our task of propagating the
True Faith among these Indians. As Your Percipient Majesty
will discern from the next following pages of our Aztec's chronicle, his people have always been contemptibly superstitious,
seeing omens and portents not only where reasonable men see
them—in the eclipse of the sun, for example—but also in everything from simple coincidences to commonplace phenomena
of nature. That tendency to superstition and credulity has both
helped and hindered our continuing campaign to turn them from
devil-worship to Christianity.

The Spanish Conquistadores, in their first slashing sweep
through these lands, did an admirable work of casting down
the major temples and idols of the heathen deities, and putting
in their place crosses of the Christ and statues of the Virgin.

We and our colleagues of the cloth have affirmed and maintained that overthrow by erecting more permanent Christian edifices at those sites which heretofore were shrines to the demons and demonesses. Because the Indians stubbornly prefer to congregate for worship in their old accustomed places, they now find in those places not such bloodthirsty beings as their Huichilobos and Tlalóque, but the Crucified Jesus and His Blessed Mother.

To cite a few of many instances: the Bishop of Tlaxcála is building a Church of Our Lady atop that gigantic pyramid mountain in Cholula—so remindful of Shinar's overweening Tower of Babel—where formerly the Feathery Snake Quetzalcóatl was adored. Here in the capital of New Spain, our own nearly completed Cathedral Church of St. Francis is deliberately located (as nearly as Architect García Bravo can determine) on the site of what was once the Aztecs' Great Pyramid. I believe the church walls even incorporate some of the stones of that toppled monument to atrocity. On the point of land called Tepeyáca, across the lake just to the north of here, where lately the Indians worshiped one Tónantzin, a sort of Mother Goddess, we have put a shrine to the Virgin Mother instead. At the request of Captain-General Cortés, it has been given the same name as that shrine of Our Lady of Guadalupe situated in his home province of Extremadura in Spain.

To some it might appear unseemly that we should thus locate our Christian tabernacles on the ruins of heathen temples whose rubble is still blood-drenched by unholy sacrifice. But in actuality we only emulate the very earliest Christian evangels, who placed their altars where the Romans, Greeks, Saxons, &c. had been wont to worship their Jupiters and Pans and Eostras, &c.—in order that those devils might be driven away by the divine presence of Christ Sacrificed, and that the places which had been given to abomination and idolatry might become places of santification, where the people could be more readily induced by the ministers of the True God to offer the adoration due to His Divinity.

Therein, Sire, we are much abetted by the Indians' superstitions. In other undertakings we are not; for, besides being much bound by their superstitions, they are as hypocritical as Pharisees. Many of our apparent converts, even those professing themselves devout believers in our Christian Faith, yet live in superstitious dread of their old demons. They judge themselves to be only prudent in reserving *some* of their reverence for Huichilobos and the rest of that horde; doing so, they explain in all solemnity, to ward off any possibility of the demons' jealously wreaking revenge for having been supplanted.

We have mentioned our success, during our first year or so in this New Spain, at finding and destroying many thousands of idols which the Conquistadores had overlooked. When at last there were no more to be seen, and when the Indians swore to our patrolling Inquisitors that there were no more to be dug up from any hiding places, we nevertheless suspected that the Indians were still and privily venerating those proscribed old deities. So we preached most strongly, and had all our priests and missionaries do the same, commanding that *no* idol, not the least and smallest, not even an ornamental amulet, should remain in existence. Whereupon, confirming our suspicions, the Indians began to come again, meekly bringing to us and to other priests great numbers of clay and pottery figures, and in our presence renouncing them and breaking them to bits.

We took much satisfaction in that renewed discovery and destruction of so many more of the profane objects—until, after some while, we learned that the Indians were only seeking to mollify us or to make mock of us. The distinction is unimportant, since we would have been equally outraged by the imposture in either case. It seems that our stern sermons had provoked quite an industry among the Indian artisans: the hasty manufacture of those figurines for the sole purpose that they might be shown to us and broken before us in seeming submission to our admonitions.

At the same time, to our even greater distress and affront, we learned that numerous real idols—that is to say, antique statues, not counterfeits—*had* been hidden from our searching friars. And where do you suppose they had been hidden, Sire? Inside the foundations of the shrines and chapels and other Christian monuments built for us by Indian laborers! The deceitful savages, secreting their impious images in such sacrosanct places, believed them to be safe from disclosure. Worse, they believed that they could in those places go on worshiping those concealed monstrosities while they *seemed* to be paying homage to the cross or the Virgin or whatever saint was there visibly represented.

Our revulsion at those unwelcome revelations was only a little mitigated by our having the satisfaction of telling our congregations—and our taking some pleasure in seeing them cringe when they heard it—that the Devil or any other Adversary of the True God suffers untold anguish at being in proximity to a Christian cross or other embodiment of the Faith. Thereafter, without further prompting, the Indian masons who had contrived those coverts resignedly revealed the idols, and more of them than we could have found unaided.

Given so many evidences that so few of these Indians have yet entirely awakened from the sleep of their error—despite the best efforts of ourself and others—we much fear that they must be shocked awake, as was Saul outside Damascus. Or perhaps they could be more gently swayed toward a *salvatio omnibus* by some small miracle, like that one which long ago gave a Patron Saint to Your Majesty's principality of Catalonia in Aragón: the miraculous finding of the black image of the Virgin of Montserrat, not a hundred leagues from where we ourself were born. But of course we cannot pray that the Blessed Mary vouchsafe another miracle, or even a repetition of one in which She has already manifested Herself. . . .

We thank Your Generous Majesty for the gift brought by this latest arriving caravel: the many rose cuttings from the Royal Herbary to supplement those we brought originally. The cuttings will be conscientiously apportioned among the gardens of all our various Church properties. It may interest Your Majesty to know that, although there were never before any roses growing in these lands, the roses we have planted have flourished more exuberantly than we have ever seen, even in the gardens of Castile. The climate here is so salubriously like an eternal springtime that the roses bloom abundantly the year around, right through these months (it is December as we write) which according to the calendar should be midwinter. And we are fortunate in having a highly capable gardener in our faithful Juan Diego.

Despite his name, Sire, he is an Indian, like all our domestics, and, like all *our* domestics, a Christian of unimpeachable piety and conviction (unlike those we have mentioned in earlier paragraphs). The baptismal name was given to him some years ago by the chaplain accompanying the Conquistadores, Father Bartolomé de Olmedo. It was Father Bartolomé's very practical practice to baptize the Indians not individually but in populous gatherings, so that as many as possible might be granted the Sacrament as soon as possible. And of course, for convenience, he gave every Indian, of whom there were often hundreds of both sexes at each baptizing, the name of the saint whose feast day it happened to be. Owing to the multiplicity of Saints John in the Church Calendar, it now sometimes seems, to our confusion and even vexation, that every second Christian Indian in New Spain is named either Juan or Juana.

Nonetheless, we are very fond of our Juan Diego. He has a way with flowers, and a most obliging and biddable character, and a sincere devotion to Christianity and to ourself.

That the Royal Majesty whom we serve be blessed with the unceasing benignity of the Lord God Whom we both serve, is the incessant prayer of Your S.C.C.M.'s worshipful vicar and legate,

(ecce signum) Zumárraga

NONA PARS

I COME now to that time in our history when we Mexíca, having for so many sheaves of years been climbing the mountain of greatness, at last reached its pinnacle, meaning that all unwittingly we began to descend the far side.

On my way home, after a few more months of aimless wandering in the west, I stopped in Tolócan, a pleasant mountaintop town in the lands of the Matlaltzínca, one of the smaller tribes allied to The Triple Alliance. I took a room at an inn and, after bathing and dining, I went to the town's marketplace to buy new garments for my homecoming and a gift for my daughter. While I was thus engaged, a swift-messenger came trotting from the direction of Tenochtítlan, through the market square of Tolócan, and he wore two mantles. One was white, the color of mourning because it is the color denoting the west, whither the dead depart. Over that was a mantle of green, the color signifying good news. So it was no surprise to me when Tolócan's governor made the public announcement: that the Revered Speaker Ahuítzotl, who had been dead of mind for two years, had finally died in body; that the lord regent, Motecuzóma the Younger, had been officially elevated by the

Speaking Council to the exalted rank of Uey-Tlatoáni of the Mexíca.

The news put me in a mood to turn again, to set my back to Tenochtítlan and trudge off again toward the far horizons. But I did not. Many times in my life I have flouted authority and been rash in my actions, but I have not always behaved as a recreant or a fool. I was still a Mexícatl, hence subject to the Uey-Tlatoáni, whoever he might be and however far I might roam. More, I was an Eagle Knight, sworn to fealty even to a Revered Speaker whom I personally could not revere.

Without ever having met the man, I disliked and distrusted Motecuzóma Xocóyotzin—for his attempt to frustrate *his* Revered Speaker's alliance with the Tzapotéca, years before, and for the ignobly perverse manner in which he had molested Zyanya's sister Béu at that time. But Motecuzóma had probably never yet heard of me, and could not know what I knew about him, and so had no reason to reciprocate my animosity. I would be a fool to give him any such reason by making my feelings evident, or even bringing myself to his notice. If, for instance, he should take a notion to count the Eagle Knights attendant at his inauguration, he might be insulted by the inexcusable absence of one knight named Dark Cloud.

So I went on eastward from Tolócan, down the steep slopes that lead from there to the lake basin and the cities therein. Arriving at Tenochtítlan, I went directly to my house, where I was received with exultation by the slaves Turquoise and Star Singer, and by my friend Cozcatl, and with somewhat less enthusiasm by his wife, who said with tears in her eyes, "Now you will make us give up our cherished little Cocóton."

I said, "She and I will always be devoted to you, Quequelmíqui, and you may visit each other as often as you like."

"It will not be the same as *having* her."

I said to Turquoise, "Tell the child her father is home. Ask her to come to me."

They came downstairs hand in hand. At four years, Cocóton was still of an age to go about nude at home, and that made the change in her immediately evident to me. I was pleased to note that, as her mother had predicted, she was still beautiful; indeed, her facial resemblance to Zyanya was even more to be remarked. But she was no longer a formlessly pudgy infant with stubby limbs. She was recognizably a human being in miniature, with real arms and legs proportionate to her size. I had been away for two years, a span of time that a man in his middle thirties can squander unheeding. But it had been half of my daughter's lifetime, during which she had magically changed from a baby to a charming little girl. Suddenly I felt sorry not to have been present to observe her blossoming; it must have been as wonderfully perceptible, from moment to moment, as the unfolding of a water lily at twilight. I reproached myself for having deprived myself, and I made a silent vow that I would not do it again.

Turquoise made the introductions with a proud flourish: "My little mistress Ce-Malináli called Cocóton. Here is your Tete Mixtli returned at last. Greet him with respect, as you have been taught."

To my pleased surprise, Cocóton dropped gracefully to make the gesture of kissing the earth to me. She did not look up from the posture of obeisance until I called her name. Then I beckoned, and she bestowed on me her dimpled smile, and she came running into my arms, and gave me a shy, wet kiss, and said, "Tete, I am happy that you have come back from your adventures."

I said, "I am happy to find such a mannerly little lady awaiting me." To Ticklish I said, "Thank you for keeping your promise. That you would not let her forget me."

Cocóton leaned from my embrace to look around, saying, "I did not forget my Tene either. I want to greet her too."

The others in the room stopped smiling, and discreetly turned away. I drew a long breath and said:

"I must tell you with sadness, little girl, that the gods needed your mother's help in some adventures of their own. In a far place where I could not accompany her, a place from which she cannot return. And such a request from the gods cannot be refused. So she will not be coming home; you and I must make our lives without her. But still you must not forget your Tene."

"No," the child said solemnly.

"But just to make sure you remember her, Tene sent you a memento." I produced the necklace I had purchased in Tolócan, some twenty small firefly stones strung on a fine silver wire. I let Cocóton briefly handle it and coo over it, then clasped it at the nape of her slender neck. Seeing the little girl standing clad only in an opal necklace made me smile, but the women gasped with delight and Turquoise went running to bring a tezcatl mirror.

I said, "Cocóton, each of those stones sparkles as your mother did. On each of your birthdays, we will add another and a larger one. With so many fireflies twinkling all about you, their light will remind you not to forget your Tene Zyanya."

"You know she will not," said Cozcatl, and he pointed to Cocóton, who was admiring herself in the mirror held by Turquoise. "She has only to do that whenever she wishes to see her mother. And you, Mixtli, you have only to look at Cocóton." As if embarrassed by his show of sentimentality, he cleared his throat and said, with an emphasis meant for Ticklish, "I think the *temporary* parents had best be going now."

It was obvious that Cozcatl was eager to move from my house to his own rebuilt one, where he could better supervise his school for servants. But it was equally obvious that Ticklish had grown to feel for Cocóton the love of an otherwise childless mother. That day's parting entailed a struggle—almost a literal, physical struggle—to peel the young woman's arms from around my daughter. During the subsequent days, when Cozcatl and Ticklish and their porters made repeated trips to remove their possessions, it was Cozcatl who directed the removal. For his wife, each trip was an excuse to spend "one last time together" with Cocóton.

Even after Cozcatl and his wife were ensconced in their own household and she should have been helping him with the management of the school, Ticklish still contrived to invent errands which brought her to our neighborhood so that she could drop in for a visit with my daughter. I could not really complain. I understood that, while I was trying to win Cocóton's love, Ticklish was trying to relinquish it. I was making every effort to have the child accept as her Tete a man who was almost a total stranger. So I sympathized with the pain it was costing Ticklish to cease being a Tene, after two years in the role, and her need to do it gradually.

I was fortunate in that there were no other demands on me during my first several days back home, and I was free to devote that time to renewing my acquaintance with my daughter. Though the Revered Speaker Ahuítzotl had died two days before my return, his funeral—and Motecuzóma's coronation—naturally could not take place without the attendance of every other available ruler and noble and notable personage from every other nation in The One World, and many of them had to come from afar. During that time of gathering the celebrants, Ahuítzotl's body was preserved by a continuously supplied packing of snow brought by swift-messengers from the volcano peaks.

The funeral day came at last, and I, in my Eagle Knight regalia, was among the multitude filling the grand plaza, to cry the owl hoot when the litter bearers brought our late Uey-Tlatoáni on his last journey through the upper world. The whole island seemed to reverberate to our long-drawn "hoo-oo-ooo!" of lament and farewell. The dead Ahuítzotl sat upright on the litter, but hunched, knees to chest, his arms wrapped around his knees to hold them so. His First Widow and the lesser widows had washed the body in water of clover and other sweet herbs, and had perfumed it with copáli. His priests had clothed the body in seventeen mantles, but all of cotton so fine that they did not make a bulky wad. Over that ritual swathing, Ahuítzotl wore a mask and robe to give him the aspect of Huitzilopóchtli, god of war and foremost god of us Mexíca. Since Huitzilopóchtli's distinguishing color was blue, so was Ahuítzotl's garb, but not colored with mere paints or dyes. The mask over his face had its features ingeniously delineated in a mosaic of bits of turquoise set in gold, with obsidian and nacre for the eyes, and lips outlined in bloodstones. The robe was sewn all over with jadestones of that sort which tend more to blue than green.

We of the procession were formed up in order of precedence, and we several times circled The Heart of the One World, with muted drums beating a soft counterpoint to the dirge we chanted. Ahuítzotl on his litter led the way, accompanied by a continuous hoo-oo-ing of the crowd. Alongside the litter walked his successor, Motecuzóma, not triumphantly striding but dolefully shuffling, as befitted the occasion. He walked barefooted and wore nothing pretentious, only the ragged black robes of the priest he had once been. His hair hung unbound and disheveled, and he had put lime dust in his eyes to redden them and make them weep unceasingly.

Next marched all the rulers come from other nations, among them some old acquaintances of mine: Nezahualpíli of Texcóco and Kosi Yuela of Uaxyácac and Tzímtzicha of Michihuácan, who was present as the representative of his father Yquíngare, by then too old to travel. For the same reason, the aged and blind Xicoténca of Texcála had sent his son and heir, Xicoténca the Younger. Both of those latter-mentioned nations, as you know, were rivals or enemies of Tenochtítlan, but the death of any nation's ruler imposed a truce and obliged all other rulers to join in the public mourning of the departed, however much their hearts might rejoice at his departure. Anyway, they and their nobles could enter and leave the city in safety, for an assassination or other treachery would have been unthinkable at the funeral of a nation's ruler.

Behind the visiting dignitaries paraded Ahuítzotl's family: the First Lady and her children, then the lesser legitimate wives and their several children, then the more numerous concubines and their considerably more numerous children. Ahuítzotl's eldest recognized son Cuautémoc led, on a golden chain, the small dog that would accompany the dead man on his journey to the afterworld. Others of the children carried the other articles Ahuítzotl would need or want: his various banners, batons, feather headdresses, and other insignia of his office, including a great quantity of jewelry; his battle uniforms and weapons and shields; some of his other symbolic possessions which had been unofficial but dear to him—including that awesome skin and head of the grizzled bear which had adorned his throne for so many years.

Behind the family marched the old men of the Speaking Council and various others of the Revered Speaker's wise men, sorcerers, seers, and sayers. Then came all the highest nobles of his court and those noblemen who had arrived with the foreign delegations. Behind them marched the warriors of Ahuítzotl's palace guard, and old soldiers who had served with him in the days before he became Uey-Tlatoáni, and some of his favorite court servants and slaves, and of course the three companies of knights: Eagle, Jaguar, and Arrow. I had arranged for Cozcatl and Ticklish to take a front-rank position among the onlookers, and for them to bring Cocóton so she could see me parade in my uniform and in that exalted company. It made an odd note among the murmurous hoo-oo-ing and drumming and chanting of lamentation when, as I passed her, the little girl gave a squeal of glee and admiration and cried, "That is my Tete Mixtli!"

The cortege had to cross the lake, for it had been decided that Ahuítzotl would lie at the foot of the Chapultépec crag, directly under that place on it where his magnified likeness had been carved from the rock. Practically every acáli, from the elegant private craft of the court to the plain ones of freighters and fowlers and fishermen, had been commandeered to carry us of the funeral retinue, so not many citizens of Tenochtítlan were able to follow. However, when we reached the mainland, we found an almost equal crowd of people from Tlácopan, Coyohuácan, and other cities gathered to pay their final respects. We proceeded to the already dug grave at the foot of Chapultépec and there we all stood sweating and itching in our ceremonial finery, while the priests droned the lengthy instructions Ahuítzotl would need to make his way through the forbidding terrain that lies between our world and the afterworld.

In recent years, I have heard His Excellency the Bishop and quite a few other Christian fathers preach sermons inveighing against our barbaric funeral custom—when a high personage died—of slaughtering a numerous company of his wives and servants so that he might be properly attended in the other world. The criticism puzzles me. I grant that the practice should rightly be condemned, but I wonder where the Christian fathers have encountered it. I thought I was acquainted with just about every nation and people and set of customs in all The One World, and nowhere have I known such a mass burial to have occurred.

Ahuítzotl was the highest-ranking noble I ever actually saw interred, but if any other personage ever took his retinue with him in death it would have been common knowledge. And I have séen the burial places of other lands: old, uncovered tombs in the deserted cities of the Maya, the ancient crypts of the Cloud People at Lyobáan. In none of them did I ever see the remains of any but the one rightful occupant. Each had of course taken along his tokens of nobility and prestige: jeweled insignia and the like. But dead wives and slaves? No. Such a practice would have been worse than barbaric, it would have been foolish. Though a dying lord might have yearned for the company of family and servants, he would never have decreed it, for he and they and everyone else knew that such lesser persons went to an entirely different afterworld.

The only creature which died at Ahuítzotl's graveside that day was the small dog brought along by Prince Cuautémoc, and for that trivial killing there was a reason. The first obstacle to the afterworld—or so we were told—was a black river flowing through a black countryside, and the dead person always arrived there at the darkest hour of a black night. He could cross only by holding on to a dog, which could smell the far shore and swim directly to it, and that dog had to be of a medium color. If it was white, it would refuse the task, saying, "Master, I am clean from having already been in water too long, and I will not bathe again." If it was black, it would also decline, saying, "Master, you cannot see me in this darkness. If you should lose your grip on me, you would be lost." So Cuautémoc had provided a dog of a jacinth color, as red-gold as the red-gold chain by which he led it.

There were numerous other obstacles beyond the black river, but those Ahuítzotl would have to surmount on his own. He would have to pass between two huge mountains that, at unpredictable intervals, suddenly leaned and ground together. He would have to climb another mountain composed entirely of flesh-cutting obsidian chips. He would have to make his way through an almost impenetrable forest of flagpoles, where the waving banners would obscure the path and flap in his face to blind and confuse him; and then through a region of ceaseless rainfall, every raindrop an arrowhead. In between those places he would have to fight or dodge lurking snakes and alligators and jaguars, all eager to eat out his heart.

If and when he prevailed, he would come at last to Míctlan, where its ruling lord and lady awaited his arrival. There he would take from his mouth the jadestone with which he had been buried—if he had not been cowardly enough to scream and lose it somewhere along the way. When he handed the stone to Míctlantecútli and Míctlancíuatl, that lord and lady would smile in welcome and point him toward the afterworld he deserved, where he would live in luxury and bliss forever after.

It was very late in the afternoon when the priests finished their instructive and farewell prayers, and Ahuítzotl was seated in his grave with the yellow-red dog beside him, and the earth was piled in and tamped hard, and the simple stone covering was laid over it by the attending masons. It was dark when our fleet of acáltin docked again on Tenochtítlan, where we regrouped our procession as before, to march again to The Heart of the One World. The plaza was by then empty of the crowd of city folk, but we of the retinue had to stay in our respectful ranks while the priests said still more prayers from the torch-lighted top of the Great Pyramid, and burned special incense in urn fires about the plaza, and then ceremoniously escorted the rag-clad, barefooted Motecuzóma into the temple of Tez-catlipóca, Smoldering Mirror.

I should mention that the choice of that god's temple was of no special significance. Though Tezcatlipóca was regarded in Texcóco and some other places as the highest of gods, he was rather less glorified in Tenochtítlan. It simply happened that that temple was the only one in the plaza which had its own walled courtyard. As soon as Motecuzóma stepped into the yard, the priests closed its door behind him. For four nights and days, the chosen Revered Speaker would stay there alone, fasting and thirsting and meditating, being sun-burned or rain-sodden as the weather gods chose, sleeping on the courtyard's uncushioned hard stone, only at specified intervals going into the shelter of the temple to pray—to all the gods, one after another—for guidance in the office upon which he would shortly enter.

The rest of us tramped wearily off toward our several palaces or guest lodgings or homes or barracks, grateful that we would not have to dress up and endure another day-long ceremony until Motecuzóma emerged from his retreat.

I dragged my heavy, taloned sandals up my front steps and, if I had not been so fatigued, I would have evinced some surprise when Ticklish, not Turquoise, opened the door to me. A solitary wick lamp burned in the entry hall.

I said, "It is very late. Surely Cocóton has long been safely tucked in bed. Why have you and Cozcatl not gone home?"

"Cozcatl has gone to Texcóco on school business. As soon as there was an acáli free after the funeral, he engaged it to take him over there. So I was glad of the opportunity to spend the extra time with my—with your daughter. Turquoise is preparing your steam room and bath."

"Good," I said. "Well, let me call Star Singer to light your way home; and I will hurry to bed, so the servants can lay out their own pallets."

"Wait," she said nervously. "I do not want to go." Her normally light-copper face had flushed to a very ruddy copper, as if the hall's wick lamp were not behind her but inside her. "Cozcatl cannot be home again before tomorrow night at the earliest. Tonight I would like you to take me into your bed, Mixtli."

"What is this?" I said, pretending not to comprehend. "Is something wrong at home, Ticklish?"

"Yes, and you know what it is!" Her color heightened still more. "I am twenty and six years old, I have been married for more than five years, and I have yet to know a man!"

I said, "Cozcatl is as much a man as any I have ever met."

"Please, Mixtli, do not be deliberately dense," she entreated. "You know very well what it is I have not had."

I said, "If it will ease your sense of deprivation, I have reason to believe that our new Revered Speaker is almost as badly impaired in that respect as is your husband Cozcatl."

"That is hard to believe," she said. "As soon as Motecuzóma was appointed to the regency, he took *two* wives."

"Then presumably they are almost as unsatisfied as you seem to be."

Ticklish impatiently shook her head. "Obviously he is adequate enough to make his wives pregnant. They each have an infant child. And that is more than I can hope for! If I were the Revered Speaker's woman, I could at least bear a child. But I did not come here on behalf of Motecuzóma's wives. I do not give a little finger for Motecuzóma's wives!"

I snapped, "Neither do I! But I commend them for staying in their own connubial beds and not besieging mine!"

"Do not be cruel, Mixtli," she said. "If only you knew what this has cost me. *Five years, Mixtli!* Five years of submitting and pretending to be satisfied. I have prayed and made offerings to Xochiquétzal, begging that she help me to be content with the attentions of my husband. It does no good. All the time I suffer the curiosity. What is it really like, for a real man and woman? The wondering and the temptation and the indecision, and finally this abasement of asking for it."

"So you ask me, of all men, to betray my best friend. To put myself and my best friend's wife at risk of the garrotte."

"I ask you *because* you are his friend. You will never drop sly hints, as another man might do. Even if Cozcatl should somehow find out, he loves both you and me too much to denounce us." She paused, then added, "If Cozcatl's best friend will not do this, then he does Cozcatl a terrible disservice. I tell you true. If you refuse me, I will not humiliate myself further by approaching anyone else of our acquaintance. I will hire a man for a night. I will solicit some stranger in a hostel. Think what *that* would do to Cozcatl."

I thought. And I remembered his saying once that if this woman would not have him, he would somehow make an end to his own life. I believed him then, and I believed also that he would do the same if ever he learned of her betraying him.

I said, "All other considerations aside, Ticklish, I am so fatigued at this moment that I would be of no use to any woman. You have waited five years. You can wait until I have bathed and slept. And you say we have all day tomorrow. Go to your home now, and think further on this matter. If then you are still determined . . ."

"I will be, Mixtli. And I will come here again tomorrow."

I summoned Star Singer, and he lit a torch, and he and Ticklish went off into the night. I was undressed and had steamed myself and was in my bathing basin when I heard him come back to the house. I could easily have fallen asleep in the bath, but the water got so chilly as to force me out. I lurched into my chamber, fell onto the bed and dragged the top quilt over me, and fell asleep without even bothering to blow out the wick lamp Turquoise had lighted.

But, even in my heavy sleep, I must have been half anticipating and half dreading the impetuous return of the impatient Ticklish, for my eyes opened when the bedroom door did. The lamp had burned low and feeble, but there was a grayness of first dawn at the window, and what I saw made my hair prickle on my head.

I had heard no noise from downstairs to give me warning of the unexpected and unbelievable apparition—and *surely* Turquoise or Star Singer would have uttered a shriek if either of them had glimpsed that particular wraith. Though she was dressed for traveling, in a head shawl and a heavy over-mantle of rabbit skins, though the light was dim, though my hand shook when I raised the topaz to my eye . . . it was Zyanya I saw standing there!

"Záa," she breathed in a whisper but with audible delight, and it was Zyanya's voice. "You are not asleep, Záa."

But I was sure I must be. I was seeing the impossible, and I had never done that before, except in my dreams.

"I only meant to look in. I did not wish to disturb you," she said, still whispering; keeping her voice low to lessen the shock for me, I supposed.

I tried to speak and could not, an experience I had also had in dreams.

"I will go to the other chamber," she said. She began to unwind the shawl, and she did it slowly, as if she were tired from having traveled an unimaginably long, long way. I thought of the barriers—the mountains gnashing together, the black river in black night—and I shuddered.

"When you got the message of my coming," she said, "I hope you did not wait sleepless for my arrival." Her words made no sense, until the cowl of shawl came off, disclosing black hair without the distinctive white streak. Béu Ribé went on, "Of course, I would be flattered to think that the word of my coming excited you to sleeplessness. I would be pleased if you were that eager to see me."

I found my voice at last, and it was harsh. "I received no message! How dare you come stealthily into my house like this? How dare you pretend—?" But I choked there; I could not fairly accuse her of resembling her late sister on purpose.

She seemed genuinely taken aback, and she stammered as

she tried to explain. "But I sent a boy... I gave him a cacao bean to bring the word. Did he not, then? But downstairs... Star Singer greeted me cordially. And I find you awake, Záa...."

I growled, "Star Singer once before invited me to beat him. This time I shall oblige."

There was a short silence. I was waiting for my heart to abate its wild beating of mingled astonishment, alarm, and joy. Béu seemed overcome with embarrassment and self-reproach at her intrusion. At last she said, almost meekly for her, "I will go and sleep in the room I occupied before. Perhaps tomorrow... you will be less angry that I am here...." And she was gone from the room before I could say anything in rejoinder.

For a brief while in the morning, I had a respite from the feeling that I was being beleaguered by women. I was alone at breakfast, except for the two slaves serving it to me, and I began the day by snarling, "I do not much enjoy surprises in the dawn hours."

"Surprises, master?" said Turquoise, bewildered.

"The lady Béu's unannounced arrival."

She said, sounding even more nonplussed, "The lady Béu is here? In the house?"

"Yes," Star Singer put in. "It was a surprise to me too, master. But I supposed you had merely forgotten to inform us."

It transpired that Béu's messenger boy never *had* come to advise the household of her imminent arrival. The first that Star Singer had known of it was his being awakened by noises outside the street door. Turquoise had slept through that, but he had roused himself to let the visitor in, and had been told by her not to disturb me.

"Since the lady Waiting Moon arrived with a number of porters," he said, "I assumed she was expected." That explained why he had not been confronted by a seeming wraith and mistaken her for Zyanya, as I had done. "She said I was not to wake you or make any noise, that she of course knew her way about upstairs. Her porters brought quite a lot of luggage, master. I had all the packs and panniers stacked in the front room."

Well, at least I could be thankful that neither of the servants had witnessed my perturbation at Béu's sudden appearance, and that Cocóton had not been awakened and frightened, so I made no more fuss about it. I went on peaceably taking my breakfast—but not for long. Star Singer, apparently fearful of risking my anger at any new surprises, came to announce with all formality that I had another visitor and that this one he had admitted no farther than the front door. Knowing who it must be, I sighed, finished my chocolate, and went to the entrance.

"Will not anyone even invite me inside?" Ticklish said archly. "This is a very public spot, Mixtli, for what we—"

"What we must forget we ever talked about," I interrupted her. "My late wife's sister has come for a visit. You remember Béu Ribé."

Ticklish looked momentarily disconcerted. Then she said, "Well, if not here, you could come with me now to our house."

I said, "Really, my dear. It is Béu's first visit in three years. It would be exceedingly discourteous of me to leave her, and exceedingly difficult to explain."

"But Cozcatl will be home tonight!" she wailed.

"Then I fear we have lost our opportunity."

"We must make another!" she said desperately. "How can we arrange another, Mixtli, and when?"

"Probably never," I said, unsure whether to feel regretful or relieved that the delicate situation had been resolved without my having to resolve it. "From now on, there will simply be too many eyes and ears. We cannot elude them all. You had best forget—"

"You knew she was coming!" Ticklish blazed. "You only pretended weariness last night, just to put me off until you had a real excuse for refusing!"

"Believe what you will," I said, with weariness that was not at all pretended. "But I must refuse."

She seemed to slump and deflate before me. With her eyes averted she said quietly, "You were a friend to me for a long time, and to my husband even longer. But it is an unfriendly thing you do now, Mixtli. To both of us." And she walked slowly down the stairs to the street, and slowly away along the street.

Cocóton was at breakfast when I went back inside. So I found Star Singer, invented for him a totally unnecessary errand at the Tlaltelólco market, and suggested that he take the girl with him. As soon as she had finished eating, they went off together, and I waited, not very gleefully, for Béu to appear. The confrontation with Ticklish had not been easy for me, but at least it had been brief; with Waiting Moon I could not deal so summarily. She slept late and did not come downstairs until midday, her face puffy and creased from slumber. I sat across the dining cloth opposite her and, when Turquoise had served her and retired to the kitchen, I said:

"I am sorry I received you so gruffly, sister Béu. I am unaccustomed to such early visitors, and my manners are not at their best until some considerable while after dawn, and of all possible visitors I least expected you. May I inquire *why* you are here?"

She looked unbelieving, almost shocked. "You need ask, Záa? Among the Cloud People our family ties are strong and binding. I thought I could be of help, of use, even of comfort to my own sister's widower and the motherless child."

I said, "As for the widower, I have been abroad ever since Zyanya died. And so far, at least, I have survived my bereavement. As for Cocóton, she has been well tended during those same two years. My friends Cozcatl and Quequelmíqui have been a loving Tete and Tene." I added drily, "During those two years, your solicitude was nowhere in evidence."

"And whose fault is that?" she demanded hotly. "Why could you not have sent a swift-messenger to tell me of the tragedy? It was not until a year ago that your wrinkled and dirt-smudged letter was casually handed to me by a passing trader. My sister had been dead more than a year before I even knew of it! And then it took me the better part of another year to find a buyer for my inn, and to arrange all the details of its transfer, and to prepare for moving myself permanently to Tenochtítlan. Then we heard that the Revered Speaker Ahuítzotl was weakening and soon to die, meaning that our Bishósu Kosi Yuela would of course attend the ceremonies here. So I waited until I could travel in his retinue, for convenience and protection. But I stopped in Coyohuácan, not wanting to breast the crush of people here in the city during the funeral. That was where I gave the boy a bean to come and tell you I would soon be here. It was not until near dawn this morning that I could procure porters for my luggage. I apologize for the time and manner of my arrival, but..."

She had to pause for breath and I, feeling quite ashamed of myself, said sincerely, "It is I who should apologize, Béu. You have come at the best possible moment. The parents I borrowed for Cocóton have had to return to their own affairs. So the child has only me, and I am dismally inexperienced as a father. When I say you are welcome here, I am not merely mouthing a formality. As a substitute mother for my daughter, you are surely the next best to Zyanya herself."

"The next best," she said, without showing great enthusiasm for the compliment.

"For one thing," I said, "you can bring her up to speak the Lóochi language as fluently as our Náhuatl. You can bring her up to be as mannerly a child as the many I have admired among your Cloud People. Indeed, you should be the one person who can bring her up to be *all* the things Zyanya was. You will be devoting your life to a very good deed. This world will be the better when it has another Zyanya."

"Another Zyanya. Yes."

I concluded, "You are to regard this as your home from now forever, and the child your ward, and the slaves yours to command. I will give orders this moment that your room be totally emptied and scoured clean and refurnished to your taste. Whatever else you need or desire, sister Béu, you have only to speak, not ask." It seemed she was about to say something, but changed her mind. I said, "And now...here comes the Small Crumb herself, home from the market."

The little girl entered the room, radiant in a light mantle of sunshine yellow. She looked long at Béu Ribé, and tilted her head as if trying to recollect where she had seen that face before. I do not know if she realized that she had seen it often in mirrors.

"Will you not speak?" said Béu, her own voice breaking slightly. "I have waited so long...."

Cocóton said shyly, tentatively, breathlessly, "Tene...?"

"Oh, my darling!" exclaimed Waiting Moon, as her tears overflowed, as she knelt and held out her arms, as the little girl ran happily to be enfolded in them.

* * *

"Death!" roared the high priest of Huitzilopóchtli, from the top of the Great Pyramid. "It was death that laid the mantle of Revered Speaker upon your shoulders, Lord Motecuzóma Xocóyotl, and in due time your own death will come, when you must account to the gods for the manner in which you have worn that mantle and exercised that highest office."

He went on in that vein, with the usual priestly disregard for his hearers' endurance, while I and my fellow knights and the many Mexíca nobles and the visiting foreign dignitaries and their nobles all sweltered and suffered in our helmets and feathers and hides and armor and other costumes of color and splendor. The several thousand other Mexíca massed in The Heart of the One World wore nothing more cumbersome than cotton mantles, and I trust they got more enjoyment out of the ceremony of inauguration.

The priest said, "Motecuzóma Xocóyotzin, you must from this day make your heart like the heart of an old man: solemn, unfrivolous, severe. For know, my lord, that the throne of a Uey-Tlatoáni is no quilted cushion to be lolled upon in ease and pleasure. It is the seat of sorrow, labor, and pain."

I doubt that Motecuzóma sweated like the rest of us, though he wore two mantles, one black, one blue, both of them embroidered with pictures of skulls and other symbols intended to remind him that even a Revered Speaker must die someday. I doubt that Motecuzóma *ever* sweated. Of course, I never in my life put my finger to his bare skin, but it always appeared cold and dry.

And the priest said, "From this day, my lord, you must make of yourself a tree of great shade, that the multitude may take shelter under your branches and lean upon the strength of your trunk."

Though the occasion was solemn and impressive enough, it may have been a little less so than other coronations during my lifetime which I had not witnessed—those of Axayácatl and Tixoc and Ahuítzotl—since Motecuzóma was merely being confirmed in the office which he had already held unofficially for two years.

And the priest said, "Now, my lord, you must govern and defend your people, and treat them justly. You must punish the wicked and correct the disobedient. You must be diligent in the prosecution of the necessary wars. You must give special heed to the requirements of the gods and their temples and their priests, that they do not lack for offerings and sacrifices. Thus the gods will be pleased to watch over you and your people, and all the affairs of the Mexíca will prosper."

From where I stood, the softly waving feather banners that lined the staircase of the Great Pyramid appeared to converge toward the top, like an arrow pointing to the high, distant, tiny figures of our new Revered Speaker and the aged priest who just then placed the jewel-encrusted red leather crown on his head. And at last the priest was finished and Motecuzóma spoke:

"Great and respected priest, your words might have been spoken by mighty Huitzilopóchtli himself. Your words have given me much upon which to reflect. I pray that I may be worthy of the sage counsel you have dispensed. I thank you for the fervor and I cherish the love with which you have spoken. If I am to be the man my people would wish me to be, I must forever remember your words of wisdom, your warnings, your admonitions. . . ."

To be ready to shatter the very clouds in the sky at the close of Motecuzóma's acceptance speech, the ranks of priests poised their conch trumpets, the musicians raised their drumsticks and readied their flutes.

And Motecuzóma said, "I am proud to bring again to the throne the estimable name of my venerated grandfather. I am proud to be called Motecuzóma the Younger. And in honor of the nation which I am to lead—a nation even mightier than in my grandfather's day—my first decree is that the office I occupy will be no longer called Revered Speaker of the Mexíca, but that it have a more fitting title." He turned to face the crowded plaza, and he held high the gold and mahogany staff, and he shouted, "Henceforth, my people, you will be governed and defended and led to ever greater heights by Motecuzóma Xocóyotzin, Cem-Anáhuac Uey-Tlatoáni!"

Even if all of us in the plaza had been lulled to sleep by the half a day of speech making we had just endured, we would have started awake at the blast of sound that seemed to make the whole island quake. It was a simultaneous shriek of flutes and whistles, a blare of conch horns, and the incredible thunder of some twenty of the drums that tear out the heart, all massed together. But the musicians could also have been asleep, and their instruments mute, and we would all have come wide awake just from the impact of Motecuzóma's closing words.

The other Eagle Knights and I exchanged sidelong glances, and I could see the numerous foreign rulers exchanging scowls. Even the commoners must have been shocked by their new lord's announcement, and no one could have been much pleased by the audacity of it. Every previous ruler in all the history of our nation had been satisfied to call himself Uey-Tlatoáni of the Mexíca. But Motecuzóma had just extended his dominion to the farthest extent of the horizon in all directions.

He had bestowed upon himself a new title: Revered Speaker of The One World.

✠

When I dragged myself home that night, again eager to be out of my plumage and into a cleansing cloud of steam, I got only an offhand greeting from my daughter, instead of the usual scamper to fling herself upon me in a four-limbed hug. She was sitting on the floor, undressed, in an awkwardly backward-arched posture, holding a tezcatl mirror over her head as if she was trying to get a view of her bare back, and was too engrossed in the attempt to take much notice of my arrival. I found Béu in the adjoining room and asked her what Cocóton was doing.

"She is at the age of asking questions."

"About mirrors?"

"About her own body," said Béu, adding scornfully, "She was told a number of ignorant mistruths by her Tene Ticklish. Do you know that Cocóton once asked why she does not have a little dangle in front, like the boy up the street who is her favorite playmate? And do you know what that Ticklish told her? That if Cocóton is a good girl in this world, she will be rewarded in her afterlife by being reborn as a boy."

I was tired and grumpy, not too happy at that moment with my own burden of body, so I muttered, "I will never know why any woman should think it *rewarding* to be born a male."

"Exactly what I told Cocóton," Béu said smugly. "That a

female is far superior. Also much more neatly made, not having an excrescence like the dangle in front."

"Is she trying instead to grow a tail behind?" I asked, indicating the child, who was still trying with the mirror to look down her back.

"No. Today she noticed that every one of her playmates has the tlacihuítztli, and she asked me what it is, not realizing she has one herself. Now she is trying to examine it."

Perhaps, reverend scribes, like most recently arrived Spaniards, you are unfamiliar with the tlacihuítztli mark, for I understand it does not appear on any white children. If it appears on the bodies of your blackamoors, I suppose it would be unnoticeable. But all our infants are born with it: a dark spot like a bruise in the small of the back. It may be as large as a dish or as little as a thumbnail, and it seems to have no function, for it gradually diminishes and fades and, after ten years or so, entirely disappears.

"I told Cocóton," Béu went on, "that when the tlacihuítztli is all gone, she will know she has grown into a young lady."

"A lady of ten years old? Do not give her too fanciful ideas."

Béu said loftily, "Like some of the foolish notions you have given her, Záa?"

"I?" I said, astonished. "I have answered all her questions as honestly as I know how."

"Cocóton told me how one day you took her walking in the new park at Chapultépec, and she asked you why the grass was green, and you told her it was so she would not walk on the sky by mistake."

"Oh," I said. "Well, it was the most honest answer I could think of. Do you know a better one?"

"The grass is green," Béu said authoritatively, "because the gods decided it should be green."

I said, "Ayya, that never occurred to me." I said, "You are right." I nodded and said, "Beyond a doubt." She smiled, pleased with her wisdom and with my acknowledgment of it. "But tell me," I said. "Why did the gods chose *green* instead of red or yellow or some other color?"

Ah, Your Excellency arrives just in time to enlighten me. On the third day of Creation, was it? And you can recite our

Lord God's very words. "To every thing that creepeth upon the earth, I have given every green herb." One can hardly dispute it. That the grass is green is evident even to a non-Christian, and of course we Christians know that our Lord God made it so. I merely wonder, still—after all the years since my daughter inquired—why did our Lord God make it *green* instead of . . . ?

Motecuzóma? What was he like?

I understand. Your Excellency is concerned to hear matters of import; you are rightly impatient of trivial subjects like the color of the grass or the small, dear things I remember of my little family in the long-ago. Nevertheless, the great Lord Motecuzóma, in whatever forgotten place he lies now, is but a buried smudge of decomposed matter, perhaps discernible only if the grass grows a brighter green where he lies. To me, it seems that our Lord God cares more for keeping His grass green than He cares for keeping green the memory of the greatest noblemen.

Yes, yes, Your Excellency. I will cease my unprofitable musings. I will cast my mind back, that I may satisfy your curiosity about the nature of the man Motecuzóma Xocóyotzin.

And a man is all he was, a mere man. As I have said, he was about a year younger than myself, which would mean he was thirty and five when he took the throne of the Mexíca— or of the entire One World, as he would have it. He was of average height for a Mexícatl, but his body was of slender build and his head was a trifle large, and that touch of disproportion made him appear somewhat shorter than he really was. His complexion was of a fine, light copper color, his eyes were coldly bright, and he would have been handsome but for a slightly flat nose which made his nostrils spread a bit too broadly.

At his ceremony of inauguration, when Motecuzóma doffed the black and blue mantles of humility, he was draped with garments of surpassing richness, which indicated the kind of taste he would always thereafter indulge. At his every public appearance, he wore a costume that was never twice the same in every detail, but in sumptuosity was always on the order of what I now describe:

He wore either a red leather or an ornately embroidered

cotton maxtlatl, the flaps of which hung below his knees front and back. That excessively ample loincloth, I suspect, he may have adopted to prevent any accidental exposure of the genital malformation I have alluded to. His sandals were gilded and sometimes, if he was required only to appear and not do much walking, their soles were of solid gold. He might wear any number of ornaments—a golden necklace with a medallion that covered most of his chest; a labret in his lower lip, made of crystal enclosing a feather of a fisher bird; ear plugs of jadestone and a nose plug of turquoise. On his head was either a coronet or diadem of gold, tufted with tall plumes, or one of those great overarching headdresses all of arm-long quetzal tototl tail feathers.

But the most striking feature of his costume was the mantle, always of a length to hang from his shoulders to his ankles, always of the most beautiful feathers from the most rare and precious birds, always of the most painstaking feather work. He had mantles made of all scarlet feathers, or all yellow, all blue or green, or a mingling of various colors. But the one I remember best was the voluminous mantle made all of the iridescent, scintillating, varicolored feathers of none but hummingbirds. When I remind you that the largest feather on a hummingbird is scarcely bigger than the little tufty eyebrow of a moth, Your Excellency may appreciate the feathersmiths' talent and labor and ingenuity that went into the making of that mantle, and the inestimable worth of it as a true work of art.

Motecuzóma had not evinced such luxurious tastes during his two years as regent, while Ahuítzotl was still alive—or half alive. Motecuzóma and his two wives had lived simply, occupying just a few corner rooms of the old and by then rather derelict palace built by his grandfather Motecuzóma the Elder. He had dressed inconspicuously, and had eschewed pomp and ceremony, and had refrained from exercising all the powers inherent in the regency. He had promulgated no new laws, founded no new frontier settlements, instigated no new wars. He had confined his attention only to those day-to-day affairs of the Mexíca domains that required no momentous decisions or pronouncements.

However, on his installation as Revered Speaker, when Motecuzóma shed those somber blue and black robes, he threw off all humility at the same moment. I think I can best illustrate by recounting my first meeting with the man, some months after his accession, when he began calling in all his nobles and knights for interviews, one by one. His expressed intent was that he wished to become familiar with those subordinates he did not yet know except as names on a roster, but I believe his true intent was to awe and impress us all with his new air of majesty and magnificence. Anyway, when he had worked his way down through courtiers and nobles and wise men and priests and seers and sorcerers, he came eventually to the ranks of the Eagle Knights, and in due time I was summoned to present myself at court in the forenoon of a certain day. I did so, resplendent and uncomfortable again in all my feathered regalia, and the steward outside the throne room door said:

"Will my lord the Eagle Knight Mixtli divest himself of his uniform?"

"No," I said flatly. It had been trouble enough to get *into*.

"My lord," he said, seeming as nervous as a rabbit, "it is required by order of the Revered Speaker himself. If you will please to take off the eagle head and the mantle and the taloned sandals, you can cover the body armor with this."

"With *rags?*" I exclaimed, as he handed me a shapeless garment made of the maguey-fiber cloth we used for sacking. "I am no supplicant or petitioner, man! How dare you?"

"Please, my lord," he begged, wringing his hands. "You are not the first to resent it. But henceforth the custom is that *all* appearing before the Revered Speaker will come barefooted and in beggarly garb. I dare not admit you otherwise. It would cost my life."

"This is nonsense," I grumbled, but, to spare the poor rabbit, I put off my helmet, shield, and outerwear, and draped myself in the sackcloth.

"Now, when you go in—" the man started to say.

"Thank you," I said crisply, "but I know how to comport myself in the presence of high personages."

"There are some other new rules of protocol," said the wretch. "I entreat you, my lord, not to draw displeasure on yourself or on me. I merely tell you the orders given."

"Tell me," I said, through my teeth.

"There are three chalk marks on the floor between the door

and the Revered Speaker's chair. As you enter, the first mark is just beyond the threshold. There you stoop and make the gesture of tlalqualíztli—finger to floor to lips—saying, 'Lord.' Walk to the second mark, again make obeisance, and say, 'My lord.' Walk to the third mark, kiss the earth again, and say, 'My great lord.' Do not rise then until he gives you leave, and do not approach closer to his person than that third chalk mark."

"This is unbelievable," I said.

Avoiding my stare, the steward went on, "You will address the Revered Speaker only when he asks a direct question requiring your reply. Do not at any time raise your voice above a discreet murmur. The interview will be concluded when the Revered Speaker says it is. At that moment, make the tlalqualíztli where you stand. Then walk backward—"

"This is insanity."

"Walk *backward*, always keeping your face and front respectfully to the throne, dropping to kiss the earth at each chalk mark, and continue to walk backward until you are out the door and in this corridor again. Only then may you resume your garb and your rank—"

"And my human dignity," I said sourly.

"*Ayya*, I beseech you, my lord," said the terrified rabbit. "Do not essay any such jest in yonder, in the presence. You would come out not backward, but in segments."

When I had approached the throne in the prescribed humiliating manner, saying at the proper intervals, "Lord . . . my lord . . . my great lord," Motecuzóma let me remain crouched for a long moment before he condescended to drawl, "You may rise, Eagle Knight Chicóme-Xochitl Tliléctic-Mixtli."

Ranked behind his throne stood the elderly men of the Speaking Council, most of them, of course, left over from previous reigns, but there were two or three new faces. One of the new ones was the newly appointed Snake Woman, Tlácotzin. All the men were barefooted and, instead of their customary yellow mantles of distinction, wore the same drab sacking cloth that I did, and looked unhappy about it. The Revered Speaker's throne was a modestly low icpáli chair, not even raised on a dais, but the elegance of his costume—especially in contrast to the others in the room—belied any pretense of modesty. He had a number of bark papers unfolded full length across his lap and trailing to the floor on either side, and evidently he had just read from one of them my full name. Next he made a show of consulting several different panels of several different papers, and said:

"It appears that my uncle Ahuítzotl entertained the idea of someday elevating you to the Speaking Council, Knight Mixtli. I entertain no such idea."

"Thank you, Lord Speaker," I said, and meant it. "I have never aspired to—"

He interrupted, in a biting voice, "You will speak only when I indicate by a question that your reply is required."

"Yes, my lord."

"And that reply was not required. Obedience need not be expressed; it is taken for granted."

He studied the papers again, while I stood mute, hot with anger. I had once thought Ahuítzotl foolishly pompous, always speaking of himself as "we," but in retrospect he seemed warm and outgoing, compared to this icily aloof nephew of his.

"Your maps and journals of your travels are excellent, Knight Mixtli. These of Texcála will be of immediate use, for I plan a new war which will end forever the defiance of those Texcaltéca. I also have here your maps of the southern trace routes all the way into the Maya country. All superbly detailed. Very good work indeed." He paused, then flicked his cold gaze up at me. "You may say 'thank you' when your Revered Speaker compliments you."

I duly said, "Thank you," and Motecuzóma went on:

"I understand that in the years since you presented these maps to my uncle, you have made other journeys." He waited, and when I did not reply, he barked, "Speak!"

"I have not been asked a question, my lord."

Smiling without humor, he said, very precisely, "During those later journeys did you also make maps?"

"Yes, Lord Speaker, either on the road or immediately on my return home, while my memory of landmarks was still fresh."

"You will deliver those maps here to the palace. I will have use for them when eventually I make war in other places after Texcála." I said nothing; obedience was taken for granted. He continued, "I understand also that you have an admirable command of many provincial languages."

He waited again. I said, "Thank you, Lord Speaker."

He snarled, "That was not a compliment!"

"You said admirable, my lord."

Some of the Speaking Council rolled their eyes, others squeezed their eyes shut.

"Cease your insolence! Which languages do you speak?"

"Of Náhuatl, I command both the educated and the common speech used here in Tenochtítlan. Also the more refined Náhuatl of Texcóco, and the various rough dialects spoken in such foreign lands as Texcála." Motecuzóma impatiently drummed his fingers on his knee. "I am fluent in the Lóochi of the Tzapotéca, not quite so fluent in the many dialects of the Poré of Michihuácan. I can make myself understood in the language of the Mixtéca, in several of the Olméca tongues, in that of the Maya and the numerous dialects derived from Maya. I have a few words of Otomíte and—"

"Enough," Motecuzóma said sharply. "It may well be that I can give you an opportunity to practice your talents, when I make war upon some nation whose phrase for 'we surrender' I do not know. But for now, your maps will suffice. Make haste to deliver them."

I said nothing; obedience was taken for granted. Some of the old men were mouthing silently but urgently at me, and I wondered why, until Motecuzóma almost shouted, "That was *dismissal*, Knight Mixtli!"

I backed out of the throne room as required and, in the corridor as I doffed the beggar sackcloth, I said to the steward, "The man is mad. But is he tlahuéle or merely xolopítli?" Náhuatl has two words for a madman: xolopítli means one only harmlessly deranged; tlahuéle means a dangerous raving maniac. Each word made the rabbit steward flinch.

"Please, my lord, modulate your voice." Then he mumbled, "I will grant you, he has his peculiarities. Do you know? He takes only one meal a day, in the evening, but in preparation for it he orders whole twenties of dishes prepared, even hundreds, all different, so that when his mealtime comes he may call for whatever food appeals to him at that instant. Out of all those prepared, he may devour one and daintily taste of only two or three others."

"And the rest go to waste?" I asked.

"Oh, no. To every meal he invites all his favorite and highest-ranking lords, all those within the reach of his messengers. And the lords come, by twenties and even hundreds, even if it means leaving their own dinners and families, and they eat whatever foods the Uey-Tlatoáni spurns."

"Odd," I murmured. "I should not have taken Motecuzóma to be a man who liked so much company, even at mealtime."

"Actually, he does not. The other lords eat in the same great dining hall, but conversation is forbidden, and they never get the least glimpse of the Reverend Speaker. A high screen is set around the corner where he sits to dine, so he sits unseen and unmolested. The other lords might not even know he is present, except that once in a while, when Motecuzóma is particularly pleased with some one dish, he will send it around the hall, and all must taste of it."

"Then he is not mad," I said. "Remember, it has always been rumored that the Uey-Tlatoáni Tixoc died of poison. What you have just described sounds eccentric and extravagant, but it could also be Motecuzóma's shrewd way of assuring that he does not go the way his uncle Tixoc did."

Long before meeting Motecuzóma, I had conceived a considerable antipathy toward him. If I came away from the palace that day feeling any new sentiment about the man, it was only a mild stirring of pity. Yes, pity. It seemed to me that a ruler should inspire others to extol his eminence, not do it himself; that others ought to kiss the earth to him because he deserved it, not because he demanded it. To my mind, all the protocol and ritual and panoply with which Motecuzóma had surrounded himself were less majestic than pretentious, even pathetic. They were like his abundance of dress ornaments, no more than the garniture of greatness, assumed by a man uneasy, insecure, uncertain that he himself was of any greatness at all.

I got home to find that Cozcatl had come calling, and was waiting to tell me the latest news of his school. While I began to divest myself of my Eagle Knight garb for more comfortable clothes, he rubbed his hands together in great good humor and announced:

"The Revered Speaker Motecuzóma has engaged me to undertake the training of his entire palace staff of servants and slaves, from the highest stewards to the scullery help."

That was such good news that I called for Turquoise to bring us a jug of cooled octli that we might celebrate. Star Singer also came running, to bring and light for each of us a poquíetl.

"But I have just come from the palace," I said to Cozcatl. "And I got the impression that Motecuzóma's servants are already trained—or at least cowed to groveling—the same as his Speaking Council and every other person connected with his court."

"Oh, his servants *serve* well enough," said Cozcatl. He sucked on his tube and blew a smoke ring. "But he wants them polished and refined, to be the equal of Nezahualpíli's staff in Texcóco."

I said, "It appears that our Revered Speaker has feelings of envy and rivalry about more than the mannerly servants of the Texcóco court. I might even say feelings of animosity. Motecuzóma told me today that he proposes to launch a new war against Texcála, which is not surprising. What he did not say, but I have heard elsewhere, is that he tried to order Nezahualpíli to lead the assault, and with Acólhua troops forming the bulk of the army. I also hear that Nezahualpíli most firmly declined that honor, and I am glad—after all, he is no longer young. But it does seem that Motecuzóma would like to do what Ahuítzotl did in our own war days, Cozcatl. To decimate the Acólhua, or even force Nezahualpíli himself to fall in combat."

Cozcatl said, "It may be, Mixtli, that Motecuzóma has the same reason that Ahuítzotl had."

I took a bracing drink of octli and said, "Do you mean what I fear you mean?"

Cozcatl nodded. "That onetime child bride of Nezahualpíli whose name is no longer mentioned. Being Ahuítzotl's daughter, she was Motecuzóma's cousin . . . and maybe something more than cousin to him. For whatever it signifies, it was immediately after her execution that Motecuzóma took the black robes of priesthood and celibacy."

I said, "A coincidence that indeed invites speculation," and drained my cup of octli. It inspirited me enough to say, "Well, he long ago gave up the priesthood, and he now has two legal wives, and he will be taking more. Let us hope that he eventually gives up his animus toward Nezahualpíli. Let us also hope that he never learns of the part you and I played in his lady cousin's downfall."

Cozcatl said cheerfully, "Do not worry. The good Nezahualpíli has forever kept silent about our involvement. Ahuítzotl never connected us with the affair. Motecuzóma does not, either, or he would hardly be patronizing my school."

I said with relief, "You are probably right." Then I laughed and said, "You seem impervious to worry or even to pain." I pointed to his poquíetl. "Are you not likely to do yourself serious injury?"

He had apparently not noticed that the hand holding his lighted smoking tube had lowered so that the burning coal of it rested against the bare skin of his other arm. When I called it to his notice he jerked the poquíetl away and looked glumly at the angry red burn mark it had left on his skin.

"Sometimes my attention gets fixed on something," he muttered, "and I am unaware of—trifles like that."

"Trifles?" I said. "It must hurt worse than a wasp sting. I will call for Turquoise to bring an ointment."

"No, no, I do not—I hardly feel it at all," he said, and stood up. "I will see you soon again, Mixtli."

He was just leaving the house when Béu Ribé came in from some errand. Cozcatl greeted her warmly, as usual, but her smile at him seemed rather strained, and, when he was gone, she said to me:

"I met his wife on the street, and we spoke a few words. Quequelmíqui must know that I am acquainted with Cozcatl's history, and his wound, and their marriage of accommodation to it. But she seemed radiantly happy, and she looked at me with a sort of challenge, as if she dared me to make any remark."

A little drowsy from the octli, I said, "Make a remark about what?"

"About her being pregnant. It is obvious to any woman's eyes."

"You must be mistaken," I said. "You know it to be impossible."

She gave me an impatient look. "Impossible it may be, but mistaken I am not. Even a spinster recognizes that condition. It cannot be long before even her husband takes note of it. And what then?"

There was no answer to such a question, and Béu left the room without waiting for one, leaving me to sit and think. I should have realized, when Ticklish came to me pleading that I give her the one experience her husband could not, that she had really wanted me to give her something more lasting than just the experience. She wanted a child—a Cocóton of her own—and who better than the beloved Cocóton's father to provide it? More than likely, Ticklish had come to me already having eaten of fox meat or of the herb cihuapátli or one of the other specifics that supposedly assure a woman's impregnation. Well, I very nearly *had* succumbed to her blandishments. Only Béu's unexpected arrival had given me an excuse to refuse. So I was not the father, and Cozcatl could not be, but somebody was. Ticklish had made it plain that she would resort to other expedients. I said to myself, "When I sent her away from here, she had all the remainder of that day. . . ."

No doubt I should have been more concerned about the matter, but at that time I was working hard, in obedience to Motecuzóma's order that I hand over all the maps of all my travels. In doing so, I took some liberty in my interpretation of his order. I did not deliver to the palace my original maps, but took the time to make copies of them all, and submitted them one by one as they were completed. I excused the delay by explaining that many of the earlier-drawn originals were fragmentary and travel-stained, some done on poor paper or even scratched on grape leaves, and that I wanted my Lord Speaker to have fresh, clean, and durable drawings. The excuse was not entirely an untruth, but my real reason was that the original maps were precious to me as mementos of my wanderings, some of which I had made in company with my adored Zyanya, and I simply wanted to keep them.

Also, I might want to travel those roads again, and perhaps keep on going, not to return, if the reign of Motecuzóma made Tenochtítlan too uncomfortable for me. With that possible emigration in mind, I omitted some significant details from the map copies I provided to the Uey-Tlatoáni. For example, I left out any mark of the black lake where I had stumbled upon the giant boar tusks; if there was any more treasure there, I might someday have need of it.

When not working, I spent as much time as possible with my daughter. I had got into the pleasant habit of telling her a story every afternoon, and of course I told her such tales as would have most interested me when I was her age: stories replete with action and violence and high adventure. In fact, most of them were true accounts of my own experiences. Or a slightly embellished truth, or a slightly diluted truth, as the case might be. Such tales required me frequently to roar like a maddened jaguar or chatter like an angry spider monkey or howl like a melancholy coyote. When Cocóton quailed at some of the noises I produced, I prided myself on my talent for telling an adventure so vividly that a listener could almost *share* it. But one day the little girl came to me at the accustomed time for my entertaining her, and she said most solemnly:

"May we speak, Tete, as grown persons would?"

I was amused at such grave formality from a child only about six years old, but I replied just as gravely, "We may, Small Crumb. What do you have on your mind?"

"I wish to say that I do not think the stories you tell are the most fitting for a young girl to hear."

Somewhat surprised, even hurt, I said, "Do tell me your complaint about my unsuitable stories."

She said, as if soothing a petulant child even younger than herself, "I am sure they are *very good* stories. I am sure a *boy* would like very much to hear them. Boys *like* to be frightened, I think. My friend Chacálin"—she waved in the direction of a neighbor's house—"he sometimes makes animal noises and his *own* noises frighten him into crying. If you like, Tete, I will bring him each afternoon to hear your stories instead of me."

I said, perhaps a trifle peevishly, "Chacálin has his own father to tell him stories. Doubtless very exciting tales, the adventures of a pottery merchant in the Tlaltelólco market. But, Cocóton, I have never noticed you crying when I told a story."

"Oh, I would not. Not in front of you. I cry at night in bed when I am alone. For I remember the jaguars and the serpents and the bandits, and they come even more alive in the dark, and they chase me through my dreams."

"My dear child!" I exclaimed, drawing her to me. "Why did you never mention this before?"

"I am not very brave." She hid her face against my shoulder. "Not with big animals. I suppose not with big fathers either."

"From now on," I promised, "I shall try to appear smaller. And I will tell no more of fierce beasts and skulking bandits. What would you prefer that I tell about?"

She pondered, then asked in a shy voice, "Tete, did you never have any *easy* adventures?"

I could think of no immediate answer to that. I could not even imagine such a thing as an "easy adventure," unless it was something of the sort that might happen to Chacálin's father—selling a customer a jug with a hairline crack, and not being caught at it. But then I remembered something, and I said:

"I once had a *foolish* adventure. Would that be acceptable?"

She said, "Ayyo, yes, I would enjoy a foolish tale!"

I lay down on the floor on my back, and bent my knees to a peak. I pointed and said, "That is a volcano, a volcano named Tzebóruko, which means to snort with anger. But I promise, I will do no snorting. You sit up there, right on the crater of it."

When she was perched on my kneecaps, I said the traditional "Oc ye nechca," and I began to tell her how the volcano's overflow had caught me sitting stupidly in the middle of the ocean bay. During the course of the story, I refrained from making the noises of lava erupting and steam boiling, but, at the story's high point, I suddenly cried "*Uiuióni!*" and waggled my knees, then bumped them upward. "And *o-o-ómpa!* I went away with the water!" The bounce dislodged Cocóton so that, at the *ómpa*, she slid down my thighs to stop with a thump on my belly. It knocked the breath out of me and made her giggle and gurgle with delight.

It seemed I had hit on a story, and a form of story-telling, emimently suitable for a little girl. Every afternoon for a very long time thereafter, we had to play the Volcano Erupting. Even though I managed to think up other unfrightening tales,

Cocóton insisted that I also tell and demonstrate how Tzebóruko had once flung me off The One World. I told it over and over and over, always with her participation—tremulous atop my knees as I drawled and drew out ever longer the suspense of the preliminaries, then gleeful when I bounced her, squealing as she slid, then heartily laughing at my whoosh of breath when she came down with a thump. The Volcano Erupting went on erupting every day until Cocóton grew old enough that Béu began to disapprove of her "unladylike behavior," and Cocóton herself began to find it a "childish" game. I was somewhat sorry to see my daughter growing out of her childhood, but I was by then well wearied of being jolted in the belly.

Inevitably, the day came when Cozcatl called on me again—in a pitiable state: his eyes red-rimmed, his voice hoarse, his hands interlaced and twisting as if they fought each other.

I asked him gently, "Have you been crying, my friend?"

"Doubtless I have reason to," he said in that gravelly voice. "But no, I have not. What it is . . ." He unlaced his knotted fingers to gesture distractedly. "For a while past, my eyes and my tongue both seem somehow to have been—thickening—filming over."

"I am sorry," I said. "Have you consulted a physician?"

"No, and I did not come to speak of that. Mixtli, was it you who did it?"

I made no hypocritical pretense of ignorance. I said, "I know what you mean. Béu remarked on it some time ago. But no, it was not my doing."

He nodded and said miserably, "I believe you. But that only makes it harder to bear. I will never know who it was. Even if I beat her half to death, I do not think she would tell. And I could not beat Quequelmíqui."

I consider for a moment, then said, "I will tell you this. She *wanted* me to be the father."

He nodded again, like a palsied old man. "I had supposed so. She would have wanted a child as much like your daughter as possible." After a pause, he said, "If you had done it, I would have been hurt, but I could have borne it. . . ."

With one hand he stroked a curiously pale patch on his cheek, almost silver in color. I wondered if he had again absentmindedly burned himself. Then I noticed that the fingers of his stroking hand were almost colorless at the tips. He went on, "My poor Quequelmíqui. She could have endured a marriage to a sexless man, I think. But after she came to have such a mother love for your daughter, she could not endure an unfruitful marriage."

He looked out the window, and he looked unhappy. My little girl was playing with some of her friends in the street outside.

"I hoped—I tried to provide a substitute satisfaction for her. I started a special class for the children of the servants already in my charge, preparing them to follow their parents into domestic service. My real reason was that I hoped they would divert my wife's yearning, that she could learn to love them. But they were other people's children . . . and she had not been acquainted with them from infancy, as with Cocóton. . . ."

"Look, Cozcatl," I said. "This child in her womb is not yours. It never could have been. But, except for the seed, the child is *hers*. And she is your beloved wife. Suppose it had happened that you married a widow already the mother of a young child. Would you suffer torments if that had been the case?"

"She has already tried that argument on me," he said gruffly. "But that, you see, would not have been a betrayal. After all these years of a happy marriage. Happy for me, at least."

I recalled the years during which Zyanya and I had been all in all to each other, and I tried to imagine how I would have felt if she had ever been unfaithful, and finally I said, "I sympathize sincerely, my friend. But it *will* be your wife's issue. She is a handsome woman, and the child is bound to be a comely one. I can almost promise that you will soon find yourself accepting it, taking it to your heart. I know your kind nature, and I know you can love a fatherless child as deeply as I love my motherless daughter."

"Not exactly fatherless," he growled.

"It is your wife's child," I persisted. "You are her husband. You are its father. If she will not name a name even to you, she will hardly tell another. And of the physical circumstances, who else is there who knows? Béu and myself, yes, but you can be certain that we would never tell. Blood Glutton is long dead, and so is that old palace doctor who tended you after your injury. I can think of no one else who—"

"I can!" he interrupted grimly. "The man who *is* the father. He may be an octli drunkard who has been boasting of his conquest in every lakefront drinking house for months past. He may even appear at our house someday and demand—"

I said, "One would suppose that Ticklish exercised discretion and discrimination," though privately I could not be too sure of that.

"There is another thing," Cozcatl continued. "She has now enjoyed a—a natural kind of sex. Can she ever really be satisfied any longer with... with my kind? Might she not go seeking a *man* again?"

I said sternly, "You are agonizing over possibilities that probably will never come to pass. She wanted a child, that is all, and now she will have a child. I can tell you that new mothers have little leisure for promiscuity."

"Yya ouiya," he sighed huskily. "I wish you *were* the father, Mixtli. If I knew it was the doing of my oldest friend... oh, it would have taken a while, but I could have made my peace with it...."

"Stop this, Cozcatl!" He was making me feel twice guilty— that I very nearly *had* coupled with his wife—and that I had *not*.

But he would not be silenced. "There are other considerations," he said vaguely. "But no matter. If it were your child inside her, I could make myself wait... could have been a father for a time, at least..."

He seemed to have drifted into senseless rambling. I sought desperately for words that would bring him back to sobriety. But he suddenly burst out weeping—the harsh, rasping, dry sobs with which a man cries; nothing like the gentle, melting, almost musical weeping of a woman—and he ran from the house.

I never saw him again. And the rest is ugly, so I will tell it quickly. That same afternoon, Cozcatl marched away from his home and school and students—including all the palace servants in his charge—marched off to enlist in the forces of

The Triple Alliance fighting in Texcála, and marched onto the point of any enemy spear.

His abrupt departure and sudden death occasioned as much puzzlement as grief among Cozcatl's many friends and associates, but his motive was generally assumed to have been a rather too reckless loyalty to his patron, the Revered Speaker. Not Ticklish nor Béu nor I ever said anything to cast doubt on that theory, or on the equally accepted assumption that the bulge under his wife's skirt had been put there by Cozcatl before he so rashly went off to war.

For my part I never said anything to any of our acquaintances, not even to Béu, about a suspicion of my own. I remembered Cozcatl's unfinished fragments of sentences: "I could make myself wait . . . could have been a father for a time, at least . . ." And I remembered the poquíetl burn he had not felt, the thickened voice and gummy eyes, the silvery stain on his face. . . .

The funeral services were held over his maquáhuitl and shield, brought home from the battlefield. On that occasion, in the company of countless other mourners, I coldly proffered formal condolences to the widow, after which I deliberately avoided seeing her again. Instead, I sought out the Mexícatl warrior who had brought Cozcatl's relics and was present at their interment. I put to him a blunt question and, after some hesitant shuffling of his feet, he answered:

"Yes, my lord. When the physician of our troop tore open the armor from around this man's wound, he found lumps and scaly patches of skin over much of the man's body. You have guessed right, my lord. He was afflicted with the téococolíztli."

The word means The Being Eaten by the Gods. Clearly, the disease is also known in the Old World you came from, for the first arriving Spaniards said, "Leprosy!" when they encountered here certain men and women lacking fingers, toes, nose or—in the final stages—much of a face at all.

The gods may begin eating their chosen teocócox abruptly or gradually, and they may do the eating slowly or voraciously, or in various different ways, but none of the God-Eaten has ever felt honored to be thus chosen. At first there may be only a numbness in parts of the body, as in the case of Cozcatl, who failed to feel that burn on his forearm. There can be a thickening of the tissues inside the eyelids, nose, and throat, so that the sufferer's sight is affected, his voice coarsened, his swallowing and breathing made difficult. The body's skin may dry and slough off in tatters, or it may bulge with numberless nodules that break into suppurant sores. The disease is invariably fatal, but the most horrible thing about it is that it usually takes so long to eat its victim entirely. The smaller extremities of the body—fingers, nose, ears, tepúli, toes—are gnawed away first, leaving only holes or slimy stumps. The skin of the face grows leathery, silvery-gray, and loose, and it sags, so that a person's forehead may droop down over the aperture where his nose used to be. His lips may bloat, the lower one so heavy and pendulous that his mouth hangs open ever after.

But even then the gods continue leisurely with their meal. It may be a matter of months or years before the teocócox is unable to see or talk or walk or make any use of his fingerless hand stumps. And still he may go on existing—bedridden, helpless, stinking of decay, suffering that ghastly misery—for many more years before he finally suffocates or strangles. But not many men or women choose to endure that half-life. Even if they themselves could bear it, their most loving loved ones cannot long endure the stomach-turning horror of tending their needs and bodily functions. Most of the God-Eaten choose to live only so long as they are still human beings, then they take their own life with a draft of poison or an improvised garrotte or a dagger thrust—or by finding some way to achieve the more honorable Flowery Death, as Cozcatl did.

He had known what awaited him, but he loved his Que-quelmíqui so much that he would have endured and defied the God-Eating as long as he could—or as long as *she* could, without recoiling at the sight of him. Even when he realized that his wife had betrayed him, Cozcatl might have stayed to see the child—to be a father for a time, at least, as he told me—if the child had been mine. But it was not; his wife had betrayed him with a stranger. He had no wish or reason to postpone the inevitable; he went and impaled himself on a Texcaltéca spear.

I felt more than the simple grief of bereavement at losing my friend Cozcatl. After all, I had been responsible for him during much of his life, ever since he was my nine-year-old slave in Texcóco. Even that long ago, I had almost caused his execution by involving him in my campaign of revenge against the Lord Joy. Later he had lost his manhood while trying to protect me from Chimáli. It was my asking Ticklish to be mother to Cocóton that had made her so avidly desire real motherhood. My near involvement in her adultery had been only narrowly averted by circumstances, not by my rectitude or my fidelity to Cozcatl. And even there I had done him a disservice. If I *had* bedded and impregnated Ticklish, Cozcatl might yet have lived a while, and even happily, before the God-Eating took him. . . .

Thinking on it, I have often wondered why Cozcatl ever called me friend.

Cozcatl's widow served as sole director of their school and staff and students for some few months longer. Then she came to term and was delivered of her accursed bastard. And cursed it was; it was born dead; I do not recall even hearing what sex it would have been. When Ticklish was able to walk, she also, like Cozcatl, went walking away from Tenochtítlan, and never came back. The school was left in confusion, with the unpaid teachers threatening to leave too. So Motecuzóma, vexed by the prospect of having his servants return to him only half polished, ordered that the abandoned property be confiscated. He put it in the charge of teacher-priests recruited from a calmécac, and the school continued in existence as long as the city did.

✠

It was about that time that my daughter Cocóton passed her seventh birthday, and we all of course ceased to call her Small Crumb. After much deliberation and choosing and discarding, I decided to add to her birth-date name of One Grass the adult name of Zyanya-Nochípa, which means Always Always, said first in her mother's language of Lóochi and repeated in Náhuatl. I thought the name, besides being a memorial of her mother, was also an adroit employment of the words. Zyanya-Nochípa could be taken to mean "always and forever," an enhancement of her mother's already lovely name. Or it could be rendered *"always* Always," to signify that the mother lived on in the person of her daughter.

With Béu's help, I arranged a grand feast of celebration for the day, to be attended by the little neighbor Chacálin and all my daughter's other playmates and all their parents. Beforehand, however, Béu and I escorted the birthday girl to have her new name inscribed in the register of citizens just come of that age. We did not go to the man who was in charge of keeping track of the general population. Since Zyanya-Nochípa was the daughter of an Eagle Knight, we went to the palace tonalpóqui, who kept the register of the more elite citizens.

The old archivist grumbled, "It is my duty and my privilege to use the divinatory tonálmatl book and my interpretive talents to select the child's name. Things have come to a grievous pass when parents can simply come and *tell* me what the new citizen is to be named. That is unseemly enough, Lord Knight, but you are also naming the poor young one with two words exactly alike, though in two different languages, and neither word means any *thing*. Could you not at least call her Always Bejeweled or something comprehensible like that?"

"No," I said firmly. "It is to be Always Always."

He said in exasperation, "Why not Never Never? How do you expect me to draw upon her page in the registry a name symbol of abstract words? How do I make a picture of meaningless noises?"

"They are not at all meaningless," I said with feeling. "However, Lord Tonalpóqui, I anticipated such an objection, so I presumed to work out the word pictures myself. You see, I have been a scribe in my time." I gave him the drawing I had made, which showed a hand gripping an arrow on which was perched a butterfly.

He read aloud the words for hand, arrow, and butterfly, "Noma, chichiquíli, papálotl. Ah, I see you are acquainted with the useful mode of picturing a thing for its sound alone. Yes, indeed, the first sounds of the three words do make no-chí-pa. Always."

He said it with admiration, but it appeared to cost him some effort. I finally grasped that the old sage was afraid of being cheated of his full fee, since I had left him nothing but copywork to do. So I paid him an amount of gold dust that would amply have reimbursed him for several days' and nights' study of his divinatory books. At that, he ceased grumbling and set to work most eagerly. With the proper ceremony and care, and the use of rather more brushes and reeds than were really necessary, he painted on a panel page of his register the symbols: the One single dot and the tufty Grass and then my concocted symbols for Always, twice repeated. My daughter was formally named: Ce-Malináli Zyanya-Nochípa, to be familiarly called Nochípa.

At the time Motecuzóma acceded to the throne, his capital of Tenochtítlan had only half recovered from the devastation of the great flood. Thousands of its inhabitants were still living crowded together with those of their relations fortunate enough to have a roof, or were living in shanties heaped up of the flood's rubble or of maguey leaves brought from the mainland, or were living even more wretchedly in canoes moored under the city causeways. It took two more years before Tenochtítlan's reconstruction, with adequate buildings for tenement dwelling, was completed under Motecuzóma's direction.

And while he was at it, he built a fine new palace for himself, on the bank of the canal at the southern side of The Heart of the One World. It was the most immense, most luxurious, most elaborately decorated and furnished palace ever built anywhere in these lands, far grander even than Nezahualpíli's city and country estates combined. As a matter of fact, Motecuzóma, determined to outdo Nezahualpíli, built himself an elegant country palace as well, on the outskirts of that lovely mountain town of Quaunáhuac which I have several times admiringly mentioned. As you may know, my lord friars, if any of you have visited there since your Captain-General Cortés appropriated that palace for his residence, its gardens must be the most vast, the most magnificent and variously planted of any you have ever seen anywhere.

The reconstruction of Tenochtítlan might have proceeded more rapidly—the whole of the Mexíca domain might have been better assured of prosperity—had not Motecuzóma been engaged, almost from the moment he took the throne, in supervising one war after another, and sometimes two wars at once. As I have told, he immediately launched a new assault on the oft-beset but always obdurate land of Texcála. But that was only to be expected. A newly installed Uey-Tlatoáni almost always began his reign by flexing his muscles, and that land was, by virtue of its propinquity and stolid enmity, the most natural victim, however little value it would have been to us if we ever *had* conquered it.

But at the same time, Motecuzóma was first beginning to lay out the gardens of his country estate, and he heard from some traveler about a distinctive tree which grew only in one small region of northern Uaxyácac. The traveler rather unimaginatively called it just "the red-painted-flower tree," but his description of it intrigued the Revered Speaker. That tree's blossoms, said the man, were so constructed that they looked exactly like miniature human hands, their red petals or lobes making fingers with an apposed thumb. Unfortunately, said the traveler, the sole habitat of that tree was also the home ground of one paltry tribe of the Mixtéca. Its chief or elder, an old man named Suchix, had reserved the red-painted-flower tree to himself—three or four big ones growing about his squalid hut—and kept his tribesmen forever searching for and uprooting any new sprouts that might dare to spring up elsewhere.

"He does not just have a passion for exclusive possession," the traveler is reported to have said. "The hand-shaped flower makes a medicine that cures heart ailments which resist any other treatment. Old Suchix heals sufferers from all the lands about, and charges them extravagantly. That is why he is anxious that the tree remain a rarity, and his alone."

Motecuzóma is said to have smiled indulgently. "Ah, if it is a mere matter of greed, I shall simply offer him more gold than he and his trees can earn in his lifetime."

And he sent a Mixtéca-speaking swift-messenger trotting toward Uaxyácac, carrying a fortune in gold, with instructions to buy one of the trees and pay any price Suchix asked. But there must have been more than miserliness about that old Mixtécatl chief; there must have been some trace of pride or integrity in his nature. The messenger returned to Tenochtítlan with the fortune undiminished by a single grain of gold dust, and with the news that Suchix had haughtily declined to part with so much as a twig. So Motecuzóma next sent a troop of warriors, carrying only obsidian, and Suchix and his whole tribe were exterminated, and you can now see the tree of the handlike blossoms growing in those gardens outside Quaunáhuac.

But the Revered Speaker's concern was not entirely for events abroad. When he was not plotting or trying to provoke a new war, or directing its prosecution from one of his palaces, or personally enjoying it by leading an army into combat himself, he stayed at home and worried about the Great Pyramid. If that seems inexplicably eccentric to you, reverend scribes, so did it seem to many of us, his subjects, when Motecuzóma conceived a peculiar preoccupation with what he had decided was the structure's "misplacement." It seems that what was wrong was that on the two days of the year, in spring and autumn, when the length of day and night are precisely equal, the pyramid threw a small but perceptible shadow to one side at high midday. According to Motecuzóma, the temple should not have cast any shadow at all at those two instants of the year. That it did, he said, meant that the Great Pyramid had been built just slightly—perhaps only the breadth of a finger or two—skewed from its proper position in relation to Tonatíu's course across the sky.

Well, the Great Pyramid had placidly sat so for some nineteen years since its completion and dedication—for more than a hundred years since Motecuzóma the Elder first started its construction—and during all that time not the sun god nor any other had given any sign of being displeased with it. Only Motecuzóma the Younger was troubled by its being that tiny bit off axis. He could often be seen standing and regarding the mighty edifice, looking morose, as if he might have been about to give a vexed and corrective kick at one of its misplaced corners. Of course, the only possible rectification of the original architect's error would have been to tear down the Great Pyramid entirely and rebuild it from the ground up, a daunting project to contemplate. Nevertheless, I believe that Motecuzóma might have got around to doing just that, except that his attention was forcibly diverted to other problems.

For it was about that time that a series of alarming omens began to occur: the strange happenings that, everyone is now firmly convinced, presaged the overthrow of the Mexíca, the downfall of all the civilizations flourishing in these lands, the death of all our gods, the end of The One World.

One day toward the close of the year One Rabbit, a palace page came hurrying to summon me to an immediate appearance before the Uey-Tlatoáni. I mention the year because it had an ominous significance of its own, as I shall explain later. Motecuzóma did not bid me omit the ritual of repeatedly kissing the earth as I entered and crossed the throne room, but he impatiently drummed his fingers upon his knee, as if wishing I would hasten the approach.

The Revered Speaker was unattended on that occasion, but I noticed two new additions to the room. On each side of his icpáli throne a great metal wheel hung by chains in a carved wooden frame. One was of gold, the other of silver; each disk was three times the diameter of a war shield; both were intricately embossed and etched with scenes of Motecuzóma's triumphs and with word-pictures explaining them. The two wheels were of incalculable worth just for their weight of precious metal, but they were made vastly more valuable by the artistry lavished upon them. It was not until a later time that I learned they were more than ornaments. Motecuzóma could reach out and pound a fist upon either of them, which sent a hollow boom resounding throughout the palace. Since each made a slightly different booming note, his hammering on the silver disk would bring the chief steward hurrying to him, and a blow upon the gold would bring a whole troop of armed guards on the run.

Without any formal greeting, without any withering sarcasm, with considerably less than his customary icy calm, Motecuzóma said, "Knight Mixtli, you are familiar with the Maya lands and peoples."

"I said, "Yes, Lord Speaker."

"Would you consider those people unusually excitable or unstable?"

"Not at all, my lord. To the contrary, most of them are nowadays about as phlegmatic as so many tapirs or manatees."

He said, "So are many priests, but that does not hinder their seeing portentous visions. What of the Maya in that respect?"

"Seeing visions? Well, my lord, I daresay the gods might vouchsafe a vision to even the most torpid of mortals. Especially if he has intoxicated himself with something like the god-flesh mushrooms. But the pathetic remnants of the Maya scarcely take note of the real world around them, let alone anything extraordinary. Perhaps if my lord would further enlighten me as to exactly what we are discussing..."

He said, "A Maya swift-messenger came, from what nation or tribe I do not know. He came rushing through the city—not at all torpidly—and paused only long enough to gasp a message to the guard at my palace gate. Then he ran on in the direction of Tlácopan before I could be told the message, or I would have ordered him held for questioning. It appears that the Maya are sending such men pelting through all lands to tell of a marvel which has been seen in the south. There is a peninsula there called Uluúmil Kutz, which juts into the northern ocean. You know it? Very well, the Maya inhabitants of that coast have recently been amazed and affrighted by the appearance offshore of two objects never seen by them before." He could not resist keeping me in suspense for a moment's pause. "Something like a giant house floating upon the sea. Something gliding along with the aid of widespread wings." I smiled in spite of myself, and he scowled, saying, "Are you now about to tell me that the Maya *do* have demented visions?"

"No, my lord," I said, still smiling. "But I believe I know what it was they saw. May I ask a question?" He gave me a curt nod. "Those things mentioned—floating house, winged object—were they the same things, or separate?"

Motecuzóma scowled more darkly. "The messenger was gone before any more details could be elicited. He did say that two things had been sighted. I suppose one could have been a floating house and the other an object with wings. Whatever they were, they reportedly stayed well offshore, so it is likely that no observer could give any very accurate description. Why do you maintain that cursed grin?"

I tried to repress it, and said, "Those people did not imagine those things, Lord Speaker. They are merely too lazy to have investigated them. If any observer had had the initiative and courage to swim close, he would have recognized them as sea creatures—wonderful ones, and perhaps not a common sight, but no profound mystery—and the Maya messengers would not now be spreading unwarranted alarm."

"Do you mean *you* have seen such things?" said Mote-cuzóma, regarding me almost with awe. "A floating house?"

"Not a house, my lord, but a fish literally and honestly *bigger* than any house. The ocean fishermen call it the yeye-míchi." I told of how I had once been helplessly adrift in a canoe upon the sea, when whole hosts of the monsters had floated close enough to endanger my frail craft. "The Revered Speaker may find it hard to credit, but if a yeyemíchi had its head butting the wall outside my lord's window yonder, its tail would be flapping among the remains of the late Speaker Ahuítzotl's palace, clear on the other side of the great plaza."

"Say you so?" Motecuzóma murmured wonderingly, look-ing out the window. Then he turned again to me to ask, "And during your sojourn at sea, did you also encounter water crea-tures with wings?"

"I did, my lord. They flew in swarms about me, and at first I took them to be ocean insects of immense size. But one of them actually glided into my canoe, and I seized and ate it. Indisputably it was a fish, but just as indisputably it had wings with which it flew."

Motecuzóma's rigid posture relaxed a little, clearly in relief. "Only fish," he muttered. "May the doltish Maya be damned to Míctlan! They could panic entire populations with their wild tales. I will see that the truth is instantly and widely told. Thank you, Knight Mixtli. Your explanation has served a most useful purpose. You deserve a reward. Let it be this. I invite you and your family to be among the select few who, with me, will ascend Huixáchi Hill for the New Fire ceremony next month."

"I shall be honored, my lord," I said, and I meant it. The New Fire was lighted only once in the average man's lifetime, and the average man never got a close look at the ceremony, for Huixáchi Hill could accommodate only a comparatively few spectators in addition to the officiating priests.

"Fish," Motecuzóma said again. "But you saw them far at sea. If they have only now come close enough inshore for the Maya to see them for the first time, they still could constitute an omen of some significance. . . ."

I need not stress the obvious, reverend friars; I can only blush at the recollection of my brash skepticism. The two ob-jects glimpsed by the Maya coast dwellers—what I so fatuously dismissed as one giant fish and one winged fish—were of course Spanish seagoing vessels under sail. Now that I know the sequence of long-ago events, I know that they were the two ships of your explorers de Solís and Pinzón, who surveyed but did not land upon the shore of Uluúmil Kutz.

I was wrong, and an omen it was.

That interview with Motecuzóma took place toward the end of the year, when the nemontémtin hollow days were approaching. And, I repeat, that was the year One Rabbit—by your count, the year one thousand five hundred and six.

During the unnamed empty days at the close of every solar year, as I have told you, our people lived in apprehension of the gods' smiting them with some disaster, but never did our people live in such morbid apprehension as then. For One Rabbit was the last year of the fifty and two composing a xiumolpíli, or sheaf of years, which caused us to dread the worst disaster imaginable: the complete obliteration of mankind. According to our priests and our beliefs and our traditions, the gods had four times previously purged the world clean of men, and would do it again whenever they chose. Quite naturally, we assumed that the gods—if they did decide to exterminate us—would pick a fitting time, like those last days of the last year binding up a sheaf of years.

And so, during the five days between the end of the year One Rabbit and the beginning of its successor Two Reed—which, assuming Two Reed arrived and we survived to know it, would start the next sheaf of fifty and two years—it was fear as much as religious obedience which made most people behave in the approved meek and muted manner. People almost literally walked on tiptoe. All noise was hushed, all talking done in whispers, all laughter forbidden. Barking dogs, gobbling fowl, wailing babies were silenced insofar as possible. All household fires and lights were put out, as in the empty days that terminated every ordinary solar year, and all *other* fires were extinguished as well, including those in temples, on altars, in the urns set before the statues of the gods. Even the fire atop Huixáchi Hill, the one fire that had been kept ever burning for the past fifty and two years, even that was put out.

In all the land there was not a glimmer of light during those five nights.

Every family, noble or humble, smashed all their clay vessels used for cooking and storage and dining; they buried or threw into the lake their maize-grinding metlátin stones and other utensils of stone or copper or even precious metals; they burned their wooden spoons and platters and chocolate beaters and other such implements. During those five days they did no cooking, anyway, and ate only scantily, and used segments of maguey leaves for dishes, and used their fingers to scoop and eat the cold baked camótin or congealed atóli mush or whatever else they had prepared in advance. There was no traveling, no trading or other business conducted, no social mingling, no wearing of jewelry or plumes or any but the plainest garments. No one, from the Uey-Tlatoáni to the lowliest tlacótli slave, did anything but wait, and remain as inconspicuous as possible while he waited.

Though nothing noteworthy happened during those somber days, our tension and apprehension understandably increased, reaching its height when Tonatíu went to his bed on the fifth evening. We could only wonder: would he rise once more and bring another day, another year, another sheaf of years? I should say that the common folk could only wonder; it was the task of the priests to try what persuasion was in their power. Shortly after that sundown, when the night was full dark, a whole procession of them—the chief priest of every god and goddess, major and minor, each priest costumed and masked and painted to the semblance of his particular deity—marched from Tenochtítlan and along the southern causeway toward Huixáchi Hill. They were trailed by the Revered Speaker and his invited companions, all dressed in such humbly shapeless garments of sacking that they were unrecognizable as lords of high degree, wise men, sorcerers, whatever. Among them was myself, leading my daughter Nochípa by the hand.

"You are only nine years old now," I had told her, "and there is a very good chance that you will still be here to see the *next* New Fire, but you might not be invited to see that ceremony up close. You are fortunate to be able to observe this one."

She was thrilled by the prospect, for it was the first major

religious celebration to which I had yet escorted her. Had it
not been such a solemn occasion, she would have skipped
merrily along at my side. Instead, she paced slowly, as was
proper, wearing drab raiment and a mask fashioned by me from
a piece of a maguey leaf. As we followed the rest of the
procession through a darkness relieved only by the dim light
of a sliver of moon, I was reminded of the time so long ago
when I had been thrilled to accompany my own father across
Xaltócan to see the ceremony honoring the fowler-god Atláua.

Nochípa wore a mask concealing her whole face because,
on that most precarious night of all nights, every child did. The
belief—or the hope—was that the gods, if they did decide to
expunge mankind from the earth, might mistake the disguised
young folk for creatures other than human, and might spare
them, and so there would be at least some seedling survivors
to perpetuate our race. The adults did not try any such feeble
dissimulation, but neither did they go to sleep resigned to the
inevitable. Everywhere in the lightless land, our people spent
that night upon their rooftops, nudging and pinching each other
to keep awake, their gaze fixed in the direction of Huixáchi
Hill, praying for the blaze of the New Fire to tell them that the
gods had once again deferred the ultimate disaster.

The hill called in our language Huixáchtlan is situated on
the promontory between lakes Texcóco and Xochimílco, just
south of the town of Ixtapalápan. Its name came from its thickets of huixáchi shrub which, at that season of the turning of
the year, were just beginning to open their tiny yellow flowers
of disproportionately great and sweet fragrance. The hill had
little other distinction, since it was a mere pimple in comparison
to the mountains farther distant. But, jutting up abruptly from
the flat terrain around the lakes, it was the one eminence sufficiently high and near enough to all the lake communities to
be visible to the inhabitants of them all—as far away as Texcóco
to the east and Xaltócan to the north—and that was the reason
for its having been selected, sometime far back in our history,
as the site of the New Fire ceremony.

As we mounted the path that spirals gently upward to the
hilltop, I was close enough to Motecuzóma to hear him murmur
worriedly to one of his counselors, "The chiquacéntetl *will rise*
tonight, will they not?"

The wise man, an elderly but still-keen-eyed astronomer, shrugged and said, "They always have, my lord. Nothing in my studies indicates that they will not always do so."

Chiquacéntetl means a group of six. Motecuzóma was referring to the tight little cluster of six faint stars whose ascent in the sky we had come to see—or hoping to see. The astronomer, whose function was to calculate and predict such things as star movements, sounded sufficiently confident to dispel anybody's qualms. On the other hand, the old man was notoriously irreligious and outspoken in his opinions. He had infuriated many a priest by saying flatly, as he did just then, "No god, of all the gods we know, has ever shown any power to disrupt the orderly progress of the heavenly bodies."

"If the gods put them there, old unbeliever," snapped a seer, "the gods can shift them at will. They simply have not, in our lifetime of watching the skies, been so inclined. Anyway, the question is not so much whether the chiquacéntetl will rise, but will the group of six be at the exact proper point of ascent in the sky at the exact middle point of the night?"

"Which is not so much up to the gods," the astronomer said drily, "as to the time sense of the priest blowing the midnight trumpet, and I will wager he is drunk long before then. But, by the way, friend sorcerer, if you are still basing any of your prophecies on the so-called group of six stars, I am not surprised that you are so often wrong. We astronomers have long known them to be chicóntetl, a group of seven."

"You dare to refute the books of divination?" sputtered the seer. "They all say and always have said chiquacéntetl."

"So do most people speak of a group of six. It takes a clear sky and clear eyes to see it, but there is indeed a seventh pale star in that cluster."

"Will you never cease your irreverent aspersions?" snarled the other. "You are simply trying to confound me, to cast doubt on my predictions, to defame my venerable profession!"

"Only with facts, venerable sorcerer," said the astronomer. "Only with facts."

Motecuzóma chuckled at the exchange, sounding no longer worried about the outcome of the night, and then the three men moved out of my hearing as we reached the summit of Huixáchi Hill.

A number of junior priests had preceded us there, and they had everything in readiness. There was a neat stack of unlighted pine-splint torches and a towering pyramid of kindling and logs which would be the signal fire. There were other combustibles: a fire-drilling stick and its block and scorched-thread tinder, finely shredded bark, wads of oil-soaked cotton. The night's chosen xochimíqui, a clean-limbed young warrior recently captured from Texcála, already lay arched naked across the sacrificial stone. Since it was essential that he lie still throughout the ceremony, he had been given a drink containing some priestly drug. So he lay quite relaxed, his eyes closed, his limbs loose, even his breathing barely perceptible.

The only light was from the stars and bit of moon overhead, and the reflected moonlight made the lake shine below us. But our eyes had by then become adjusted to the darkness, and we could make out the folds and contours of the land around the hill, the cities and towns looking dead and deserted, but really waiting wide awake and almost audibly pulsing with apprehension. There was a cloud bank on the horizon to the east, so it was some while before the awaited and prayed-for stars climbed above it into visibility. But finally they came: the pale cluster and, after them, the bright red star that always follows. We waited while they made their slow way up the sky, and we waited breathlessly, but they did not vanish on the way, or fly asunder, or veer from their accustomed course. At last, a collective sigh of relief went up from the crowded hill when the time-counting priest blew a bleat on his conch shell to mark the night's mid-moment. Several people breathed, "They are right in place, right on time," and the chief priest of all the priests present, the high priest of Huitzilopóchtli, commanded in a mighty roar, *"Let the New Fire be lighted!"*

A priest placed the fire block on the chest of the prostrate xochimíqui, and carefully fluffed the threads of tinder upon it. A second priest, on the other side of the stone, leaned over with the drilling stick and began to twirl it between his palms. All of us spectators waited anxiously; the gods could still deny us the spark of life. But then a wisp of smoke rose from the tinder. In another moment there was a glow of tentative smoldering. The priest holding the block steady with his one hand used his other to feed and coax the firefly spark: tufts of oily cotton, shreds of dry bark—and achieved a small, flickering, but definite flame. It seemed to wake the xochimíqui slightly; his eyes opened enough to look down at the awakening New Fire on his breast. But he did not look for long.

One of the attending priests gingerly moved the fire-bearing block aside. The other produced a knife, and made his slash so deftly that the young man scarcely twitched. When the chest was laid open, the one priest reached in, plucked loose the throbbing heart, and lifted it out, while the other set the blazing block in its place in the gaping wound, then quickly but expertly laid upon it still more and bigger bits of cotton and bark. When there was a sizable flag of flame rising from the chest of the feebly stirring victim, the other priest laid the heart gently in the middle of the fire. The flames subsided momentarily, dampened by the heart's blood, but they rose again with vigor and the frying heart sizzled loudly.

A cry went up from all present, *"The New Fire is lighted!"* and the crowd, immobile until then, commenced a bustle of movement. One after another, in order of rank, the priests seized torches from the stack and touched them to the xochimíqui's fast-crisping breast to light them in the New Fire, then bore them away at a run. The first one used his torch to ignite the waiting pyramid of wood, so that every distant eye fixed on Huixáchi Hill should see the great blaze and know that all danger was past, that all was still well with The One World. I fancied I could hear the cheers and laughs and happy sobs that went up from the rooftop watchers all around the lakes. Then the priests ran down the hill's pathway, their torch fires fluttering behind them like hair aflame. At the base of the hill waited still other priests, gathered from communities near and far. They seized the torches and scattered to bear the precious fragments of the New Fire to the temples of the various cities and towns and villages.

"Take off your mask, Nochípa," I told my daughter. "It is safe now to do so. Take it off so you may see better."

She and I stood on the north side of the hilltop, watching the tiny flares and sparks of light explode away from beneath us, streaking off in all directions. Then there were other silent explosions. The nearest town, Ixtapalápan, was the first to have its main temple fire relighted, then the next-nearest town of

Mexicaltzínco. And at each temple were waiting numbers of the town's inhabitants, to plunge their own torches into the temple fires and run to relight the long-cold hearth fires of their families and neighbors. So each torch that streaked away from Huixáchi Hill first dwindled to a mere bright dot in the distance, then blossomed into a temple fire, then that exploded into an outflung burst of sparks, and each darting spark left a trail of motionless sparks behind it. The sequence was repeated over and over, in Coyohuácan, in great Tenochtítlan, in communities farther away and farther apart, until the whole vast bowl of the lake lands was fast coming again to light and life. It was a cheering, thrilling, exhilarating sight to see—and I tried hard to imprint it among my happier memories, because I could not hope to see such a sight ever again.

As if reading my thoughts, my daughter said quietly, "Oh, I do hope I live to be an old woman. I should so like to see this wonder the next time, Father."

When Nochípa and I finally turned back to the big fire, four men were crouched near it in earnest consultation: the Revered Speaker Motecuzóma, the chief priest of Huitzilopóchtli, the seer, and the astronomer of whom I earlier spoke. They were discussing what words the Uey-Tlatoáni would speak, the next day, to proclaim what the New Fire had promised for the years to come. The seer, squatting over some diagrams he had drawn in the earth with a stick, had evidently just delivered himself of a prophecy to which the astronomer took exception, for the latter was saying mockingly:

"No more droughts, no more miseries, a fruitful sheaf of years in the offing. Very consoling, friend sorcerer. But you see no imminent omens appearing in the skies?"

The seer snapped at him, "The skies are your affair. You make the maps of them and I will attend to reading what the maps have to tell."

The astronomer snorted. "You might find more inspiration if once in a while *you* looked at the stars instead of the foolish circles and angles you draw." He pointed at the scratches in the dirt. "You read of no impending yqualóca, then?"

The word means an eclipse. The seer, the priest, the Revered Speaker, all three repeated together, and unsteadily, "Eclipse?"

"Of the sun," said the astronomer. "Even this old fraud

could foresee it, if he once looked at past history instead of pretending to know the future."

The seer sat gulping, speechless, Motecuzóma glared at him. The astronomer went on:

"It is on record, Lord Speaker, that the Maya of the south saw an yqualóca take a hungry bite at Tonatíu the sun in the year Ten House. Next month, on the day Seven Lizard, it will have been exactly eighteen solar years and eleven days since that occurred. And according to the records collected by me and my predecessors, from lands north and south, such a darkening of the sun regularly happens *somewhere* in The One World at intervals of that duration. I can confidently predict that Tonatíu will again be eclipsed by a shadow on the day Seven Lizard. Unfortunately, not being a sorcerer, I cannot tell you how severe will be that yqualóca, nor in which lands it will be visible. But those who see it may take it for a most maleficent omen, coming so soon after the New Fire. I would suggest, my lord, that all peoples ought to be informed and forewarned, to make their fright the less."

"You are right," said Motecuzóma. "I will send swift-messengers into all lands. Even those of our enemies, lest they interpret the omen to mean that our power is weakening. Thank you, Lord Astronomer. As for you . . ." He turned coldly to the trembling seer. "The most wise and expert of diviners is liable to error, and that is forgivable. But a totally inept one is a real hazard to the nation, and that is intolerable. On our return to the city, report to my palace guard for your execution."

In the morning of the next day, Two Reed, first day of the new year Two Reed, the big market of Tlaltelólco, like every other market in The One World, was crowded with people buying new household implements and utensils to replace the old ones they had destroyed. Though the people could have had but little sleep after the lighting of the New Fire, they were all cheerful and vocal, refreshed as much by the fact that they had resumed their best garments and jewelry as by the fact that the gods had seen fit to let them go on living.

At midday, from the top of the Great Pyramid, the Uey-Tlatoáni Motecuzóma made the traditional address to his people. In part, he related what the late seer had predicted—good weather, good harvests, and so on—but he prudently diluted that oversweet honey with warnings that the gods would continue their benefices only so long as the gods were pleased with the Mexíca. Therefore, said Motecuzóma, all men must work hard, all women be thrifty, all wars be fought with vigor, all the proper offerings and sacrifices be made on ceremonial occasions. In essence, the people were told that life would go on as it always had. There was nothing novel or revelatory in Motecuzóma's address, except that he did announce—as casually as if he had arranged it for a public entertainment—the forthcoming eclipse of the sun.

While he was orating from the pyramid summit, his swift-messengers were already trotting out from Tenochtítlan to all points of the horizon. They carried to rulers and governors and community elders everywhere the news of the imminent eclipse, and they stressed the fact that the gods had given our astronomers prior notice of the event, hence it would bring no tidings, good or bad, and should cause no unease. But it is one thing when people are told to pay no attention to a fearsome phenomenon; it is quite another thing when those people are exposed to it.

Even I, who had been one of the first to hear of the impending yqualóca, could not regard it with yawning composure when it did take place. But I had to pretend to view it with calm and scientific disinterest, for Nochípa and Béu Ribé and both the servants were with me in our rooftop garden that day of Seven Lizard, and I had to set them all an example of fearlessness.

I do not know how it appeared in other parts of The One World, but here in Tenochtítlan it seemed that Tonatíu was totally swallowed. And it was probably only for a brief while, but to us it was an eternity. That day was heavily overcast, so the sun was only a pale and moonlike disk at his brightest, and we could look directly at him. We could see the first bite taken from his rim, as it were from a tortilla, and then see the munching proceed right across his face. The day darkened and the springtime warmth fled away and a winter chill blew across the world. Birds flew about our rooftop, all confused, and we could hear the howling of neighbors' dogs.

The crescent bitten out of Tonatíu got bigger and bigger,

until at last his whole face was swallowed and it became as dark a brown as the face of a Chiapa native. For an instant, the sun was even darker than the clouds around it, as if we looked through a small hole in the day and into the night. Then the clouds, the sky, all the world darkened to that same night darkness, and Tonatíu was gone entirely from our sight.

The only comforting lights to be seen from our roof were the few flickers of fires burning outside temples and a pink tinge on the underside of the smoke hanging over Popocatépetl. The birds ceased to fly about, except that one scarlet-headed flycatcher fluttered down between me and Béu and perched in one of our garden shrubs, tucked its head under its wing and apparently went to sleep. For those long moments while the day was night, I almost wished I could hide my own head. From other houses on the street, I could hear shrieks and moans and prayers. But Béu and Nochípa stood silent, and Star Singer and Turquoise were only quietly whimpering, so I suppose my attitude of staunchness had some reassuring effect.

Then a slender crescent of light showed again in the sky, and slowly broadened and brightened. The arc of the swallowing yqualóca slid reluctantly away, letting Tonatíu emerge from its lips. The crescent grew, the bitten segment diminished, until Tonatíu was a disk again, and entire, and the world was again in daylight. The bird on the branch beside me raised its head, looked about in almost comical puzzlement, and flew away. My women and servants turned pale faces and tremulous smiles on me.

"That is all," I said authoritatively. "It is over." And we trooped downstairs to resume our own several activities.

Rightly or wrongly, many people later claimed that the Revered Speaker had deliberately told an untruth when he said that the eclipse would be a matter of no ill omen. Because, only a few days later, the entire lake district was shaken by an earthquake. It was a mere tremor compared to the zyuüù which Zyanya and I had once lived through, and, though my house shook as others did, it stood as sturdily as it had during the great flood. But, trivial though I accounted it, the quake was one of the worst ever felt in these parts, and many buildings did fall in Tenochtítlan, in Tlácopan, in Texcóco, and in smaller communities, and in their falling crushed their occupants to death. I believe some two thousand people died, and the survivors' wrath against Motecuzóma was so loud that he had to pay heed to it. I do not mean he paid any reparations. What he did was to invite all people to The Heart of the One World to see the public garrotting of that astronomer who had predicted the eclipse.

But that did not end the omens, if omens they were. And some of them I say flatly were not. For example, in that single year Two Reed, more stars were seen to fall from the night sky than had been reported in *all* the years, all of them together, during which our astronomers had been keeping count of such things. Throughout those eighteen months, every time a star fell, everyone who saw it would come or send a message to the palace to report it. Motecuzóma did not himself see the obviously erroneous arithmetic involved and, since his pride would not let him risk another accusation of having misled his subjects, he made public announcements of that seeming deluge of stars, as the count mounted alarmingly.

To me and others, the reason for the unprecedented total of dying stars was evident: ever since the eclipse, more people were watching the skies, and more apprehensively, and every single one of them was eager to announce anything unnatural that he saw there. On any night of any year, a man standing outdoors with his eyes on the sky, for only the time it takes to smoke a poquíetl, will see two or three of the more fragile stars lose their feeble grip on the sky and fall dying to earth, trailing a shroud of sparks. But, if great numbers of watchers see and report just those two or three, the combined reports must make it seem as if every night is constantly and ominously raining down stars. And that is what our people remember of that year Two Reed. Had it truly been so, the sky would have been blackly empty of all its stars by year's end, and ever since.

That unprofitable game of collecting fallen stars might have gone on unabated, except that in the following year, Three Knife, our people were diverted by a different sort of omen, and one that more directly involved Motecuzóma. His unmarried sister Pápantzin, the Lady Early Bird, chose that time to die. There was nothing remarkable about her death, except that she died rather young, for she supposedly died of some typical and unremarkable female ailment. What was ominous was that, only two or three days after her burial, numerous citizens of Tenochtítlan claimed to have met the lady walking about by night, wringing her hands and wailing a warning. According to the report of those who encountered her—and those multiplied nightly—the Lady Pápan had left her grave to bring a message. And her message was that, from the afterworld, she had seen great conquering armies advancing upon Tenochtítlan from the south.

I privately concluded that the rumormongers had seen only the familiar and tiresome old spirit of the Weeping Woman, who was *forever* wailing and wringing her hands, and that they had either wrongly or willfully misinterpreted her weary old complaint. But Motecuzóma could not so easily disown the purported phantasm of his own sister. He could quell the rising gossip only by ordering that Pápan's grave be opened, and at night, to prove that she lay quiet therein and was not wandering about the city.

I was not among those who made the midnight excursion, but the lurid story of what happened on that occasion became well known to all in these lands. Motecuzóma went in company with a number of priests, and some of his courtiers for witnesses. The priests dug away the covering earth and lifted the splendidly shrouded body to the surface of the ground, while Motecuzóma stood fidgeting nervously nearby. The priests unwound the swathings of the dead woman's head to make positive her identification. They found her not yet much decayed, and they found her to be certainly the Lady Early Bird and certainly dead.

Then, it is said, Motecuzóma gave a terrified shriek, and even the impassive priests recoiled, when the lady's eyelids slowly opened and an unearthly green-white light shone from where her eyeballs had been. According to the story, that glare fixed directly upon her brother, and he, in the grip of horror, addressed to her a long but incoherent speech. Some said it was an apology for disturbing her rest. Some said it was a guilty confession, and they also later said that the illness of which Motecuzóma's supposedly maiden sister had died was in fact a fatally miscarried pregnancy.

Gossip aside, it was attested by all the witnesses present

that the Revered Speaker finally turned and fled from the open grave. He fled too soon to see one of the glowing green-white eyes of the corpse begin to move, to uncoil and to ooze down her shrunken cheek. It was nothing unnatural, only a petlazolcóatl, one of those long, leg-fringed, nasty-looking centipedes that, like the glowworms, are peculiarly and brightly luminous in the dark. Two of the creatures had evidently burrowed into the cadaver through the portals most easily chewed, and had curled up, one in each eye socket, to live comfortably and dine leisurely inside the lady's head. That night, disturbed by the commotion, they slowly, blindly crawled out from where the eyes had been, and, squirming between her lips, disappeared again.

Pápantzin made no more recorded public appearances, but other strange events were noised about, causing so much trepidation that the Speaking Council appointed special investigators to seek the truth of them. But, as I remember, none could be corroborated, and most were dismissed as the fabrications of attention seekers or the hallucinations of heavy drinkers.

Then, when that hectic year had ended, and its hollow days were over, and the succeeding year of Four House began, the Revered Speaker Nezahualpíli unexpectedly arrived from Texcóco. It was told that he had come to Tenochtítlan merely to enjoy our celebration of The Tree Is Raised, he having seen his native Texcóco's version so often over the years. The truth is that he had come for a secret consultation with Motecuzóma. But the two rulers had been closeted together for no longer than a small part of a morning before they sent to command a third consultant to join them. To my surprise, it was me they sent for.

In the prescribed robe of sacking, I made my entrance into the throne room, and made it even more humbly than was demanded by protocol, since the room contained two Revered Speakers that morning. I was slightly shocked to see that Nezahualpíli had gone nearly bald of head and that his remaining hair was gray. When I at last stood upright before the dais and the two icpáltin thrones side by side between the gold and silver gongs, the Uey-Tlatoáni of Texcóco recognized me for the first time. He said, almost with glee:

"My former courtier Head Nodder! My onetime scribe and picture maker Mole! My once-heroic soldier Dark Cloud!"

"Dark Cloud indeed," growled Motecuzóma. That was his only greeting to me, and he gave it with a glower. "You know this wretch, then, my lord friend?"

"Ayyo, there was a time we were very close," said Nezahualpíli, smiling broadly. "When you spoke of an Eagle Knight named Mixtli, I did not make the connection, but I should have known he would rise from title to title." To me he said, "I greet you and congratulate you, Knight of the Eagle Order."

I hope I mumbled the proper response. I was occupied with being glad that I wore the long-skirted sack, for my knees were slightly knocking together.

Motecuzóma asked Nezahualpíli, "Was this Mixtli *always* a liar?"

"Not *ever* a liar, lord friend, my pledge on that. Mixtli has always told the truth as he saw it. Unfortunately, his vision has not always accorded comfortably with that of other people."

"Neither does that of a liar," said Motecuzóma through his teeth. To me he said, almost shouting, "You made us all believe that there was nothing to be feared from—"

Nezahualpíli interrupted, saying soothingly, "Permit me, lord friend. Mixtli?"

"Yes, Lord Speaker?" I asked huskily, still unaware of what trouble I was in, but all too aware that I was in it.

"A little more than two years ago, the Maya sent swift-messengers through all these lands, to give notice of strange objects—floating houses, they said—sighted off the shores of the peninsula called Uluümil Kutz. You recall the occasion?"

"Vividly, my lord," I said. "As I interpreted the message, they had but seen a certain great fish and a certain flying fish."

"Yes, that was the reassuring explanation put abroad by your Revered Speaker Motecuzóma, and believed by all people, to their considerable relief."

"To *my* considerable embarrassment," Motecuzóma said grimly.

Nezahualpíli made a placative gesture in his direction, and continued speaking to me. "It transpires that some of the Maya who saw that apparition made pictures, young Mixtli, but it is only now that one of them has come into my possession. Would you still say that this pictured object is a fish?"

He handed down to me a small square of tattered bark paper, and I scrutinized it. It bore a typically Maya drawing, so small and crabbed of style that I could not do more than guess at what it was meant to represent in fact. But I had to say, "I confess, my lords, that it more resembles a house than it does the mighty fish with which I confused it."

"Or the flying fish?" asked Nezahualpíli.

"No, my lord. The wings of that fish spread sideways. As well as I can tell, this object appears to wear its wings sticking straight upward from its back. Or its roof."

He pointed. "And those round dots in a row between the wings above and the roof below them. What do you make of those?"

I said uncomfortably, "It is impossible to be certain from this crude drawing, but I venture the guess that the dots are meant to show the heads of men."

Miserably, I raised my eyes from the paper, to look straight at each Speaker in turn. "My lords, I recant my former interpretation. I can only plead that I was inadequately informed. Had I seen this picture at that time, I would have said that the Maya were rightly frightened, and right to warn the rest of us. I would have said that Uluúmil Kutz had been visited by immense canoes somehow moved by wings and filled with men. I could not say of what people the men are or whence they come, except that they are strangers and obviously have much knowledge. If they can build such war canoes, they can wage war—and perhaps a war more fearsome than we have ever known."

"There!" said Nezahualpíli, with satisfaction. "Even at the risk of displeasing his Lord Speaker, Mixtli flinches not from telling the truth as he sees it—when he sees it. My own seers and sayers read the same portent when they saw that Maya drawing."

"Had the omens been read correctly and sooner," muttered Motecuzóma, "I would have had more than two years in which to fortify and man the coasts of Uluúmil Kutz."

"To what purpose?" Nezahualpíli asked. "If the strangers do choose to strike there, let the expendable Maya bear the brunt. But if, as it seems, they can invade from the limitless sea, there are limitless coasts on which they might land, east or north, west or south. Not all the warriors of all nations could adequately man every vulnerable shore. You had better concentrate your defenses in a tighter ring and closer to home."

"I?" Motecuzóma exclaimed. "What of you?"

"Ah, I will be dead," said Nezahualpíli, yawning and stretching luxuriously. "The seers assure me of that, and I am glad, for it gives me reason to spend my last years in peace and repose. From now until my death I shall make war no more. And neither will my son Black Flower when he succeeds to my throne."

I stood before the dais uncomfortably, but apparently unnoticed and forgotten; I was given no signal of dismissal.

Motecuzóma stared at Nezahualpíli and his face darkened. "You are removing Texcóco and your Acólhua nation from The Triple Alliance? Lord friend, I should hate to speak the words betrayal and cowardice."

"Then do not," snapped Nezahualpíli. "I mean that we will—we *must*—reserve our warring for the invasion foretold. And when I say we, I mean *all* nations of these lands. We must no longer waste our warriors and our resources in fighting each other. The feuds and rivalries must be suspended, and all our energies, all our armies pooled together to repel the invader. That is how I see it, in the light of the omens and my wise men's interpretation of them. That is how I shall spend my remaining days, and Black Flower will do the same after me— working for a truce and solidarity among all nations, so that all may present a united front when the outlanders come."

"All very well for you and your tamely disciplined Crown Prince," said Motecuzóma insultingly. "But we are the Mexíca! Ever since we attained our supremacy in The One World, no outsider has set foot inside this dominion without our permission. So it shall ever be, if we must fight alone against all nations known or unknown, if *all* our allies desert us or turn against us."

I was a little sorry to see the Lord Nezahualpíli take no umbrage at that outright expression of contempt. He said, almost sadly:

"Then I will tell you of a legend, lord friend. Perhaps it has been forgotten by you Mexíca, but it still can be read in our Texcóco archives. According to that legend, when your Aztéca ancestors first ventured out of their northern homeland of Aztlan and made their years-long march which ended here, they knew not what obstacles they might encounter on the way. For all they knew, they might find lands so forbidding or peoples so unfriendly that they would deem it preferable to retrace their road and return to Aztlan. Against that contingency, they arranged for a swift and safe withdrawal. At eight or nine of the places they stopped between Aztlan and this lake district, they collected and hid ample stocks of weapons and provender. If they were forced to retreat homeward again, they could do it at their own pace, well nourished and well armed. Or they could turn and make a stand at any of those prepared positions."

Motecuzóma gaped; clearly he had *not* heard that tale before. Well, neither had I. Nezahualpíli concluded:

"At least, so says the legend. Unhappily, it does not say where those eight or nine places are. I respectfully suggest, lord friend, that you send explorers northward through the desert lands to seek them out. Either that or lay out another line of stores. If you choose not to make every neighbor nation your ally now, the time will come when none will be, and you may have need of that escape route. We of the Acólhua prefer to gird ourselves with friends."

Motecuzóma sat silent for a long while, hunched on his chair as if huddled against an approaching storm. Then he sat up straight, squared his shoulders, and said, "Suppose the outlanders never come. You will have lain supine to no purpose but to be trampled by whichever *friend* first feels strong enough."

Nezahualpíli shook his head and said, "The outlanders will come."

"You seem very sure."

"Sure enough to make a wager of it," said Nezahualpíli, suddenly jovial. "I challenge you, lord friend. Let us play at tlachtli in the ceremonial court. No teams, just you against me. The best of three games, say. If I lose, I will take it as an omen contradicting every other. I will retract all my gloomy warnings and put all the Acólhua arms and armies and resources at your command. If you lose . . ."

"Well?"

"Concede only this. You will leave me and my Acólhua free from all your future entanglements, so that we may pass our last days in more peaceful and pleasant pursuits."

Motecuzóma instantly said, "Agreed. The best of three games," and he smiled wickedly.

He might well have smiled so, for he was not alone in thinking Nezahualpíli mad to have challenged him to the games. Of course, no one else except myself—and I had been sworn to secrecy—knew at that time what the Revered Speaker of Texcóco had wagered on the outcome. So far as Tenochtítlan's citizens and visitors were concerned, the contest would be simply another entertainment for them, or an extra honor paid to Tlaloc, during the city's celebration of The Tree Is Raised. But it was no secret that Motecuzóma was at least twenty years younger than Nezahualpíli, nor that tlachtli is a brutal game best played by the young, strong, and sturdy.

All around and beyond the ball court's outer walls, The Heart of the One World was packed with people, nobles as well as commoners, squeezed shoulder to shoulder, though not one in a hundred of them could have hoped to see even a glimpse of the games. But when some bit of play made the favored spectators inside the court cry a praiseful "ayyo!" or groan "ayya!" or breathe a prayerful "hoo-oo-ooo," all the people in the plaza outside echoed and amplified the cheer or the lament or the owl hoot, without even knowing why.

The steplike tiers of stone slanting upward from the court's marble inner walls were crowded with the very highest nobles of Tenochtítlan and those of Texcóco who had come with Nezahualpíli. Possibly in compensation or bribe for my keeping their secret, the two Revered Speakers had allotted me one of the precious seats there. Though an Eagle Knight, I was the lowest-ranking person in that august company—excepting Nochípa, for whom I had arranged a place by perching her on my lap.

"Watch and remember, Daughter," I said into her ear. "This is something never seen before. The two most notable and lordly men in all The One World, pitted one against the other, and in public show. Watch it and remember it all your life. You will never see such a spectacle again."

"But, Father," she said, "that player wearing the blue helmet is an *old man.*" She used her chin to point discreetly at Nezahualpíli, who stood at center court, a little apart from Motecuzóma and the high priest of Tlaloc, the priest in charge of all that month's-ceremonies.

I said, "Well, the player in the green head-protector is about my own age, so he is no spry juvenile either."

"You sound as if you favor the old man."

"I hope you will cheer for him when I do. I have wagered a small fortune on his winning."

Nochípa swung sideways on my lap and leaned back to stare into my face. "Oh, you foolish Father. Why?"

I said, "I do not really know." And I did not. "Now sit still. You are heavy enough without wriggling."

Though my daughter had just then turned twelve years of age and had had her first bleeding, hence wore the garb of a woman, and was beginning to swell and curve prettily into woman's shape, she had not—I thanked the gods—inherited her father's size, or I could not have endured sitting between her and the hard stone seat.

The priest of Tlaloc made special prayers and invocations and incense burnings—at tedious length—before he threw high the ball to declare the first game under way. I will not attempt, my lord scribes, to tell of the ball's every bound and bounce and rebound, for I know you are ignorant of the complex rules of tlachtli and could not begin to appreciate the finer points of the game. The priest scuttled from the court like a black beetle, leaving only Nezahualpíli and Motecuzóma—and the two goal-keepers at either end of the court, but those men stayed immobile and unnoticed except when the progress of the game required them to move one goal yoke or another.

Those things, the movable low arches through which the players had to try to put the ball, were not the simple half-circles of stone provided on ordinary courts. The goal yokes, like the court's vertical walls, were of finest marble and, like the winning-goal rings set high in the walls' center points, they were elaborately carved and polished and brilliantly colored. Even the ball had been specially braided for that contest, of strips of the liveliest óli, the overlapping strips colored alternately blue and green.

Each of the Revered Speakers wore a padded leather band around his head and ears, secured by straps crossing the top of his head and under his chin; and heavy leather disks at elbows and knees; and a tightly wound, bulkily quilted loincloth, over which was belted a leather hip girdle. The head protectors were, as I have mentioned, of the two colors of Tlaloc—blue for Nezahualpíli and green for Motecuzóma—but, even without that differentiation, even without my topaz, even I would have had no trouble distinguishing the two opponents. Between the paddings and quiltings, Motecuzóma's body showed firm and smooth and muscular. Nezahualpíli's was gaunt and ribby and stringy. Motecuzóma moved easily, springingly, lithe as óli himself, and the ball was his from the moment the priest tossed it up. Nezahualpíli moved stiffly and awkwardly; it was pitiful to see him chase his fleet adversary, like Motecuzóma's shadow detached and trying to catch him up. A sharp elbow nudged my back; I turned to see the Lord Cuitláhuac, Motecuzóma's younger brother and commander of all the Mexíca armies. He grinned tauntingly at me; he was one of the several men with whom I had laid a sizable wager in gold.

Motecuzóma ran, he leapt, he floated, he flew. Nezahualpíli plodded and panted, his bald head gleaming with sweat under the straps of his headgear. The ball hurtled, it bounced, it flickered back and forth—but always from Motecuzóma to Motecuzóma. From one end of the court, he would hip it hard toward the wall where Nezahualpíli stood indecisive, and Nezahualpíli was never quick enough to intercept it, and the ball would angle off that wall toward the farther end of the court, and somehow, impossibly, Motecuzóma would be there to strike it again with elbow or knee or buttock. He sent the ball like an arrow through this goal yoke, like a javelin through that one, like a blowpipe pellet through the next, the ball going through every low arch without ever touching either side of the stone, every time scoring a goal against Nezahualpíli, every time raising an ovation from every spectator except me, Nochípa, and Nezahualpíli's courtiers.

The first game to Motecuzóma. He bounded off the court

like a young buck deer, untired, unwinded, to the handlers who rubbed him down and gave him a refreshing sip of chocolate, and he was standing, haughty, ready for the next game, when the trudging, sweat-dripping Nezahualpíli had barely reached his resting seat among his own handlers. Nochípa turned and asked me, "Will we be poor, Father?" And the Lord Cuitláhuac overheard, and gave a great guffaw, but he laughed no more when the play resumed.

Long afterward, veteran tlachtli players were still arguing various and contradictory explanations for what subsequently occurred. Some said it had simply taken the playing of the first game to limber Nezahaulpíli's joints and reflexes. Some said that Motecuzóma had rashly played the first game so strenuously that he prematurely tired himself. And there were many other theories, but I had my own. I knew Nezahualpíli of old, and I had too often seen a similar rickety, hobbling, pathetic old man, a man the color of a cacao bean. I believe I saw, that day of the tlachtli contest, Nezahualpíli's last pretense at that decrepitude when he mockingly gave away the first game to Motecuzóma.

But no theory, including mine, can really account for the marvel that then occurred. Motecuzóma and Nezahualpíli faced off for the second game, and Motecuzóma, having won the previous one, threw the ball into play. With his knee he lobbed it high in the air. It was the last time he ever touched that ball.

Naturally, after what had gone before, almost everyone's eyes were on Motecuzóma, expecting him to flicker away that instant and be under the ball before his aged opponent could creak into motion. But Nochípa, for some reason, watched Nezahualpíli, and it was her squeal of delight that brought every other spectator to his feet, everybody roaring together like a volcano in eruption. The ball was jiggling merrily inside the marble ring high in the north wall of the court, as if pausing there long enough to be admired, and then it fell through on the side away from Nezahualpíli, who had elbowed it up there.

There was an uproar of exultation on the court and in the tiers, and it went on and on. Motecuzóma rushed to embrace his opponent in congratulation, and the goalkeepers and handlers milled about in a frenzy. The priest of Tlaloc came dancing and flaffing onto the court, waving his arms and raving, unheard in the din, probably proclaiming that to have been an augury of favor from Tlaloc. The cheering spectators jumped up and down in place. The bellow of "AYYO!" got even louder, ear-breakingly louder, when the crowd in the great plaza beyond the court heard the word of what had occurred. You will have gathered, reverend friars, that Nezahualpíli had won that second game. Placing the ball through that vertical ring on the wall would have won it for him even if Motecuzóma had already been many goals ahead.

But you must understand that such a ringed ball was almost as much of a thrill for the onlookers as for the man who ringed it. That was so rare an occurrence, so unbelievably rare, that I do not know how to tell you *how* rare it was. Imagine that you have a hard óli ball the size of your head, and a stone ring, its aperture of just slightly larger diameter than that of the ball, poised vertically and twice your height above you. Try putting that ball through that hole, using not your hands, using only your hips, knees, elbows, or buttocks. A man might stand for days, doing nothing else, uninterrupted and undistracted, and never do it. In the swift movement and confusion of a real game, its doing was a thing miraculous.

While the crowd inside and outside the court continued its wild applause, Nezahualpíli sipped at chocolate and smiled modestly, and Motecuzóma smiled approvingly. He could afford to smile, for he had only to take the remaining game to win the contest, and the ringed ball—albeit his opponent's doing—would ensure that the day of his victory would be remembered for all time, both in the archives of the sport and in the history of Tenochtítlan.

It was remembered, the day is still remembered, but not joyously. When the tumult finally quieted, the two players faced off again, the throw to be Nezahualpíli's. He kneed the ball into the air at an angle and, in the same movement, dashed away to where he knew it would descend, and there kneed the ball again, and again with precision, up to and through the stone ring above. It happened so swiftly that I think Motecuzóma had no time to move at all. Even Nezahualpíli appeared unbelieving of what he had done. That ringing of the ball twice in a row was more than a marvel, more than a record never to be matched in all the annals of the game, it was an accomplishment veritably stunning.

Not a sound went up from the ranks of spectators. We scarcely moved, not even our eyes, which were fixed wonderingly on that Revered Speaker. Then, a cautious murmuring began among the onlookers. Some of the nobles mumbled hopeful things: that Tlaloc had shown himself so mightily pleased with us as to have taken a hand in the games himself. Others growled suspicions: that Nezahualpíli had ensorcelled the games by devious magic. The nobles from Texcóco disputed that accusation, but not loudly. No one seemed to care to speak in a loud voice. Even Cuitláhuac did not grumble audibly when he handed me a leather pouch heavy with gold dust. Nochípa regarded me solemnly, as if she suspected me of being secretly a seer of the outcome of things.

Yes, I won a great deal of gold that day, through my intuition, or a trace of loyalty, or whatever undefinable motive had made me put my wagers on my onetime lord. But I would give all that gold, if I had it now—I would give more than that, *ayya,* a thousand of thousand times more than that, if I had it—*not* to have won that day.

Oh, no, lord scribes, not just because Nezahualpíli's victory validated his predictions of an invasion sometime to come from the sea. I already believed in the likelihood of that; the Maya's crude drawing had convinced me. No, the reason I so bitterly regret Nezahualpíli's having won the contest is that it brought a more immediate tragedy, and upon no one but me and mine.

I was in trouble again almost as soon as Motecuzóma, in a furious temper, stalked off the court. For somehow, by the time the people had emptied out of the seats and the plaza that day, they had all learned that the contest had involved more than the two Revered Speakers—that it had been a trial of strength between their respective seers and sayers. All realized that Nezahualpíli's victory lent credence to his doomful prophecies, and knew what those prophecies were. Probably one of Nezahualpíli's courtiers made those things known, while trying to quell the rumors that his lord had won the games by sorcery. All I know for certain, though, is that the truth got out, and it was not my doing.

* * *

"If it was not your doing," said the icily irate Motecuzóma, "if you have done nothing to deserve punishment, then clearly I am not punishing you."

Nezahualpíli had just left Tenochtítlan, and two palace guards had almost forcibly brought me before the throne, and the Revered Speaker had just told me what was in store for me.

"But my lord commands me to lead a military expedition," I protested, flouting all the established throne-room protocol. "If that is not punishment, it is banishment, and I have done nothing—"

He interrupted, "The command I give you, Eagle Knight Mixtli, is in the nature of an experiment. All the omens indicate that any invading hordes, if they come at all, will come from the south. It behooves us to strengthen our southern defenses. If your expedition is a success, I will send other knights leading other emigrant trains into those areas."

"But, my lord," I persisted, "I know nothing at all about founding and fortifying a colony."

He said, "Neither did I, until I was bidden to do exactly that, in the Xoconóchco, many years ago." I could not gainsay it; I had been somewhat responsible for it. He went on, "You will take some forty families, approximately two hundred men, women, and children. They are farm people for whom there is simply no available land to farm here in the middle of The One World. You will establish your emigrants on new land to the south, and see that they build a decent village, and arrange its defenses. Here is the place I have chosen."

The map he showed me was one I had drawn for him myself, but the area to which he pointed was empty of detail, for I had never yet visited there.

I said, "My Lord Speaker, that spot is within the lands of the Teohuacána people. They also may resent being invaded by a horde of foreigners."

With a humorless smile he said, "Your old friend Nezahualpíli advised us to make friends of all our neighbors, did he not? One of your jobs will be to convince the Teohuacána that you come as a good friend and staunch defender of their country as well as ours."

"Yes, my lord," I said unhappily.

"The Revered Speaker Chimalpopóca of Tlácopan is kindly providing your military escort. You will command a detachment of forty of his Tecpanéca soldiers."

"Not even Mexíca?" I blurted in dismay. "My Lord Motecuzóma, a troop of Tecpanéca are sure to be unruly under the command of one Mexícatl knight!"

He knew it as well as I; it was part of his malice, part of my punishment for having been a friend of Nezahualpíli. Blandly, he went on:

"The warriors will provide protection on the journey into Teohuacán, and will stay to man the stronghold you are to build there. You will also stay, Knight Mixtli, until all the families are well settled and self-supporting. That settlement you will name simply Yanquítlan, The New Place."

I ventured to ask, "May I at least recruit a few good Mexíca veterans, my lord, to be my under-officers?" He would probably have said an immediate no, but I added, "Some old men I know, who were long ago discharged as over-age."

He sniffed contemptuously and said, "If it will make you feel *safer* to recruit additional warriors, you will pay them yourself."

"Agreed, my lord," I said quickly. Eager to get away before he could change his mind, I dropped to kiss the earth, murmuring as I did so, "Has the Lord Speaker anything else to command?"

"That you depart immediately and make all haste southward. The Tecpanéca warriors and the families of your train are being mustered now at Ixtapalápan. I want them in your new community of Yanquítlan in time to get their spring seeding in the ground. Be it done."

"I go at once," I said, and shuffled on bare feet backward to the door.

⌘

Even though it was pure vindictiveness that made Motecuzóma fix on me as his pioneer colonizer, I could not complain overmuch, since it was I who had first urged the idea of such colonization—to Ahuítzotl, those many years earlier. Besides, to be honest, I had lately become rather bored with being the idle rich man; I had been haunting The House of Pochtéca, hoping to hear of some rare trading opportunity that would take me abroad. So I would have welcomed my assignment to lead the emigrant train, except that Motecuzóma insisted I *stay* with the new settlement until it was firmly rooted. As well as I could estimate, I would be immured in Yanquítlan for a full year, if not for two or more. When I was younger, when my roads and my days seemed limitless and countless, I would not have missed that much time subtracted from my life. But I was forty and two, and I begrudged the spending of even one of my remaining years tied to a dull job in a dull farm village, while perhaps brighter horizons beckoned all about.

Nevertheless, I prepared for the expedition with all possible enthusiasm and organization. First I called together the women and servants of my household, and told them of the mission.

"I am selfish enough not to want to be without my family during that year or more, and also I think the time can be used to advantage. Nochípa my daughter, you have never traveled farther from Tenochtítlan than the mainland beyond the causeways, and then only seldom. This journey may be rigorous but, if you would care to accompany me, I believe you would benefit by seeing and knowing more of these lands."

"And you think I must be *asked?*" she exclaimed with delight, and clapped her hands. Then she sobered to say, "But what of my schooling, Father, at The House of Learning Manners?"

"Simply tell your Mistress Teachers that you are going abroad. That your father guarantees you will learn more on the open road than inside any four walls." I turned to Béu Ribé. "I should like you to come too, Waiting Moon, if you would."

"Yes," she said at once, her eyes bright. "I am glad, Záa, that you no longer wish to walk alone. If I can be—"

"You can. A maiden of Nochípa's age should not go unattended by an older woman."

"Oh," she said, the brightness leaving her eyes.

"A company of soldiers and lower-class farm folk may be rude company. I should like you to stay always at Nochípa's side, and share her pallet every night."

"Her pallet," Béu repeated.

I said to the servants, "That will leave you, Turquoise and Star Singer, to occupy and care for the house and safeguard our belongings." They said they could and would, and promised that we would find everything in perfect order when we came back, however long we might be gone. I said I had no doubt of it. "And right now I have one errand for you, Star Singer."

I sent him to summon the seven old warriors who had been my own small army on other expeditions. I was saddened but not much surprised when he returned to report that three of them had died since last I had required their services.

The surviving four who did come had been fairly along in years when I first knew them as friends of Blood Glutton; they had not grown younger, but they came without hesitation. They came into my presence bravely, forcing themselves to walk with upright posture and sturdy tread, to divert my attention from their ropy musculature and knobby joints. They came booming with loud voices and laughs of anticipation, so the wrinkles and folds of their faces might have been taken to be only the lines of good humor. I did not insult them by remarking on their pretense at youth and vigor; their having come so gladly was proof enough to me that they were still capable men; I would have enlisted them even if they had arrived limping on sticks. I explained the mission to them all, then spoke directly to the oldest, Qualánqui, whose name meant Angry at Everybody:

"Our Tecpanéca soldiers and the two hundred civilians are waiting at Ixtapalápan. Go there, friend Angry, and make sure they will be ready to march when we are. I suspect you will find them unprepared in many respects; they are not seasoned travelers. The rest of you men, go and purchase all the equipment and provisions *we* will need—the four of you, myself, my daughter, and my lady sister."

I was more concerned with my emigrants' completing the long march than with any unfriendly reception we might meet in Teohuacán. Like the farm folk I was escorting, the Teohuacána were an agricultural people, and few in number, and not known for pugnacity. I fully expected that they would even welcome my settlers, as new people to mingle with and marry their offspring to.

When I speak of Teohuacán and the Teohuacána, I am of

course using the Náhuatl names bestowed on them. The Teohuacána were actually some branch of the Mixtéca, or Tya Nuü, and called themselves and their country Tya Nya. The land had never been besieged by us Mexíca or put under tribute to us because, except for farm products, its treasures were few. They consisted of hot mineral springs, not resources easily confiscated, and anyway the Tya Nya freely traded to us pots and flasks of the water from those springs. The water tasted and smelled awful, but it was much in demand as a tonic. And since physicians often ordered their patients to go to Tya Nya and bathe in those hot, stinking waters, the natives had also profited by building some rather luxurious inns adjacent to the springs. In sum, I did not expect much trouble from a nation of farmers and innkeepers.

Angry at Everybody returned to me the next day to report, "You were right, Knight Mixtli. That band of rustic louts had brought all their kitchen grinding stones and images of all their favorite gods, instead of an equal weight of seed for planting and pinóli powder for traveling rations. There was much grumbling, but I made them discard every replaceable encumbrance."

"And the people themselves, Qualánqui? Will they constitute a self-supporting community?"

"I believe so. They are all farmers, but there are men among them who have also the skills of masons and brickmakers and carpenters and such. They complain of only one trade lacking. They are not provided with priests."

I said sourly, "I never heard of a community which settled or grew anywhere, but that a plenitude of priests seemed to sprout from the ground, demanding to be fed and feared and revered." Nevertheless, I passed the word on to the palace, and our company was supplied with six or seven novice tlamacázque of various minor gods, priests so young and new that their black robes had hardly yet begun to be encrusted with blood and grime.

Nochípa, Béu, and I crossed the causeway on the eve of our planned departure day, and spent the night in Ixtapalápan, so that I could call the train to order at first light, and introduce myself, and see that the tumplined loads were equitably divided among all the able-bodied men, women, and older children, and get us all early on the road. My four under-officers bawled the Tecpanéca troops to attention, and I closely inspected them, using my topaz. That caused some covert snickering in the ranks, and the soldiers thereafter referred to me among themselves—I was not supposed to be aware of it—as Mixteloxíxtli, a rather clever blending of my name with other words. It would translate roughly as Urine Eye Mixtli.

The civilians of the train probably called me by even less flattering names, for they had numerous grievances, of which the main one was that they had never intended or wanted to be emigrants at all. Motecuzóma had omitted to tell me that they had not volunteered for removal, but were "surplus population" rounded up by his troops. So they felt, with some justification, that they were being unfairly banished to the wilderness. And the soldiers were almost equally unhappy. They disliked their role of nursemaid escort, and the making of a long march from their Tlácopan home, with their destination no honorable battlefield but an indefinite garrison duty. Had I not brought my four veterans to keep the troops in order, I fear that Commander Urine Eye would have had to cope with mutiny or desertion.

Ah, well. Much of the time I was wishing *I* could desert. The soldiers at least knew how to march. The civilians lagged, they strayed, they got sorefooted and lame, they grumbled and whimpered. No two of them could ever pause to relieve themselves at the same time; the women demanded halts to breast feed their infants; the priest of this or that god had to stop at specified times of day to offer up a ritual prayer. If I set a smart marching pace, the lazier people complained that I was running them to death. If I slowed to accommodate the laggards, the others complained that they would die of old age before journey's end.

The one thing that made the march pleasurable for me was my daughter Nochípa. Like her mother Zyanya, on *her* first trip far from home, Nochípa exclaimed joyously at each new vista revealed by each new turn in the road. There was no landscape so ordinary but that something in it gladdened her eye and heart. We were following the main trade road southeastward, and it *is* a route of much scenic beauty, but it was somewhat over-familiar to me and Béu and my under-officers—and the emigrants were incapable of exclaiming over anything but their miseries. But we could have been crossing the dead wastes of Míctlan, and Nochípa would have found it all new and wonderful.

She sometimes would break into song, as birds do, for no seeming reason except that they are winged creatures, and happy to be so. (Like my sister Tzitzitlíni, Nochípa had won many honors at her school for her talent at singing and dancing.) When she sang, even the most hateful malcontents among our company would cease their grumbling for a while, to listen. Also, when she was not too tired from the day's walking, Nochípa would lighten the dark nights by dancing for us after our evening meal. One of my old men knew how to play a clay flute, and had brought it along. On those nights Nochípa danced, the company would bend down on the hard ground with less lamentation than usual.

Apart from Nochípa's brightening of the long and tiresome journey, I remember only one incident along the way that struck me as out of the ordinary. At one night's camping place, I walked some distance out of the firelight to relieve myself against a tree. Chancing to pass the tree again some while later, I saw Béu—she did not see me—and she was doing a singular thing. She was kneeling at the base of that same tree and scooping up the bit of mud made by my urination. I thought that perhaps she was preparing a soothing poultice for some marcher's blistered foot or sprained ankle. I did not interrupt her or later remark on the occurrence.

But I should tell you, lord scribes, that among our people there were certain women, usually very old women—you call them witches—who had knowledge of certain secret arts. One of their capabilities was to make a crude little image of a man, using the mud from a place where he had recently urinated, and then, by subjecting that doll to certain indignities, to make the man himself suffer an unexplainable pain or illness or madness or lust or loss of memory or even loss of his possessions until he became impoverished. But I had no reason to suspect Waiting Moon of having been a witch all her life without my ever realizing it. I dismissed her collection of the mud that night as a mere coincidence, and forgot all about it until much later.

Some twenty days' march out of Tenochtítlan—it would

have been only twelve days for an experienced and unencumbered traveler—we came to the village of Huajuápan, which I knew of old. And, after spending the night there, we turned sharply northeastward on a lesser trade road that was new to all of us. The path led through pleasant valleys green with early spring verdure winding among low and lovely blue mountains, toward Tya Nya's capital town, which was also called Tya Nya, or Teohuacán. But I did not take the entire train that far. After some four days along that route, we found ourselves in an extensive valley, at the ford of a wide but shallow stream. I knelt and took up a palmful of the water. I smelled it, then tasted it.

Angry at Everybody came to stand beside me, and asked, "What do you think?"

"Well, it does not spout from one of the typical Teohuacán springs," I said. "The water is not bitter or malodorous or hot. It will be good for drinking and for irrigation. The land looks to be good earth, and I see no other habitations or plantations. I think this is the place for our Yanquítlan. Tell them so."

Qualánqui turned and bellowed for everyone to hear, "Set down your packs! We have arrived!"

I said, "Let them rest for the remainder of today. Tomorrow we will begin—"

"Tomorrow," interrupted one of the priests, suddenly at my elbow, "and the day after that, and the day after that, we will devote to the consecration of this ground. With your permission, of course."

I said, "This is the first community I ever founded, young Lord Priest, and I am unacquainted with the formalities. By all means, do everything that is required by the gods."

Yes, I said those very words, not realizing how the words could be taken as my bestowal of unlimited religious license; not foreseeing the manner in which the words might eventually be interpreted by the priests and people; not remotely suspecting that I would, all my life long, regret that casual utterance.

The initial ritual, the consecration of the local terrain, took three entire days of prayer and invocation and incense burning and the like. Some of the rites occupied only the priests, but others required the participation of all of us. I did not mind, for the soldiers and settlers alike were enlivened by the days of rest and diversion. Even Nochípa and Béu were obviously glad that the ceremonies gave them reason to dress in clothes more rich and feminine and ornamental than the traveling garb they had worn for so long.

And that gave some of the colonists another diversion—me too, since it amused me to watch it. Most of the men of the train had wives and families, but there were three or four widowers with children but no wives, and those took the opportunity of the consecration days to pay court to Béu, one after another. There were also, among the males of the train, boys and young men of an age to make awkward approaches to Nochípa. I could not blame them, young men or older ones, for Nochípa and Béu were infinitely more beautiful and refined and desirable than the squatly built, coarse-featured, paddle-footed farm women and girls of the company.

Béu Ribé, when she thought I was not watching, would haughtily repulse the men who came asking that she be their partner in one of the ceremonial dances, or inventing any other excuse to be near her. But sometimes, when she knew I was nearby, she would let the oaf stand there while she flirted and teased outrageously, her smile and eyes so warm that they made the wretch begin to sweat. She was clearly trying just to taunt me by making me realize anew that she was still an attractive woman. I did not have to be reminded; Waiting Moon was indeed as lovely of face and body as Zyanya had been; but I, unlike the farmers fawning on her, had long been inured to her spiteful wiles of first temptation then rejection. I merely beamed and nodded, like a benevolently approving brother, and her eyes would go from warm to cold, her voice from sweet to corrosive, and the suddenly spurned suitor would retreat in confusion.

Nochípa played no such games; she was as chaste as all her dances had been. To every young man who approached, she turned a look of such wonderment, almost astonishment, that he very soon—after mumbling only a few shy words—quailed before her gaze and slunk away, red-faced, kicking the ground. Hers was an innocence that proclaimed itself inviolable, an innocence that apparently made every supplicant feel as embarrassed and ashamed as if he had lewdly exposed himself. I stood apart, feeling two kinds of pride in my daughter: pride in seeing that she was lovely enough to attract many men; pride in knowing that she would wait for the one man she wanted. Many times since then, I have wished that the gods had struck me down in that instant, in punishment for my complacent pride. But the gods know crueler punishments.

On the third night, when the exhausted priests announced that all the consecration was accomplished, that we could begin the mundane work of locating a new community on ground presumably made hospitable and safe, I said to Angry at Everybody:

"Tomorrow we will have the farm women start cutting branches for huts, and grass for thatching them, while their men start clearing the riverside for planting. It was Montecuzóma's command that they get seed in the earth as soon as possible, and the people will need only the flimsiest of houses while they work at that. Later, but before the rains start, we will lay out streets and plots for their permanent dwellings. But in the meantime the soldiers have nothing to occupy them. Also, by now, the news of our coming must have reached the capital. I think we should hasten to visit the Uey-Tlatoáni, or whatever the Teohuacána call their ruling lord, and make our intentions known. We will take the soldiers along. They are numerous enough to prevent our being summarily seized or repelled, yet not such a large force as to imply that we come in belligerence."

Qualánqui nodded and said, "I will inform the farm families that their holiday ends tomorrow, and I will have the Tecpanéca ready to march."

As he went off, I turned to Béu Ribé and said, "Your sister my wife once lent her charm to help me sway another foreign ruler, a man far more formidable than any in these lands. If I arrive at the court of Teohuacán similarly accompanied by a beautiful woman, it might make this mission, too, appear more friendly than audacious. Could I ask you, Waiting Moon . . . ?"

"To go with you, Záa?" she said eagerly. "As your consort?"

"To all appearances. We need not reveal that you are merely my lady sister. Considering our age, it should excite no comment when we request separate accommodations."

She surprised me by flaring angrily, "Our age!" But she

calmed just as quickly, and murmured, "Of course. Reveal nothing. Your mere sister is yours to command."

I said, "Thank you."

"However, lord brother, your earlier command was that I stay at Nochípa's side to protect her from this rude company. If I go with you, what of Nochípa?"

"Yes, what of me?" asked my daughter, plucking at my mantle on the other side. "Do I go too, Father?"

"No, you stay here, child," I said. "I do not really expect to meet trouble on the road or in the capital, but there is always that risk. Here you will be safe among the numbers. And safe in the presence of the priests, whom any hostiles would hesitate to attack, out of religious awe. These farmer louts will be toiling so hard that they will have no time to molest you, and they will be too tired at night for the eligible males even to attempt flirting with you. In any case, Daughter, I have observed that you can discourage them capably enough. You will be safer here, Nochípa, than on the open road, and we will not be gone for long."

But she looked so downcast that I added, "When I return, we will have ample leisure time and the freedom of all this country. I promise you that we will see more of it. Just you and me, Nochípa, traveling light and far."

She brightened and said, "Yes, that will be even better. Just you and me. I will stay here willingly, Father. And at night, when the people are tired from their labors, perhaps I can make them forget their weariness. I can dance for them."

Even without the dragging train of colonists, it took another five days for me and Béu and our escort of forty and four to reach the town of Teohuacán, or Tya Nya. I remember that much, and I remember that we were most graciously received by the lord ruler, though I no longer remember his name or his lady's, or how many days we stayed as their guests in the rather ramshackle edifice they called a palace. I do remember his saying:

"That land you have occupied, Eagle Knight Mixtli, is one of our most pleasant and fertile stretches of terrain." To which he hastily added, "But we have not people to spare from other farms and other occupations to go and work it. Your colonists are welcome to it, and we welcome their presence. Any nation profits from new blood in its body."

He said much more, of the same import, and he gave me gifts in exchange for those I had brought him from Motecuzóma. And I remember that we were often and bountifully feasted—my men as well as Béu and myself—and we forced ourselves to drink that nasty mineral water of which the Teohuacána are so proud; we even smacked our lips in a pretense of savoring it. And I remember that there were no noticeably raised eyebrows when I asked for separate rooms for Béu and myself, though I have a vague recollection of her coming into my room during one of the nights there. She said something, she begged something—and I replied harshly—and she pleaded. I think I slapped her face . . . but now I cannot recall. . . .

No, my lord scribes, do not look at me so. It is not that my memory has begun *now* suddenly to fail. All those things have been unclear to me during all the years since they happened. It is because something else happened soon afterward, and that thing so seared itself into my brain that it burned out my remembrance of the events preceding. I remember that we parted from our Tya Nya hosts with many mutual expressions of cordiality, and the townspeople lined the streets to cheer us on our way, and only Béu seemed less than happy at the success of our embassy. And I suppose it took us another five days to retrace our route. . . .

It was twilight when we came to the river, at the bank opposite Yanquítlan. There did not seem to have been much building done during our absence. Even using my seeing crystal, I could make out only a few huts erected on the village site. But there was some sort of celebration again in progress, and many fires burned high and bright, though the night was not yet fallen. We did not immediately start to ford the river, but stood listening to the shouts and laughter from the other side of the water, because it was the happiest sound we had ever heard from that uncouth company. Then a man, one of the older farmers, unexpectedly emerged from the river before us. He saw our troop halted there, and came splashing through the shallows, hailing me respectfully:

"Mixpantzínco! In your august presence, Eagle Knight, and welcome back. We feared you might miss *all* of the ceremony."

"What ceremony?" I asked. "I know of no ceremony in which the celebrants are bidden to go swimming."

He laughed and said, "Oh, that was my own notion. I was so warm from the dancing and merrymaking that I had to cool off. But I have already had my share of blessings with the bone." I could not speak. He must have taken my silence for incomprehension; he explained, "You yourself told the priests to do all things required by the gods. Surely you realize that the month of Tlacaxípe Ualíztli was already well along when you left us, and the god not yet invoked to bless the clearing of the land for planting."

"No," I said, or groaned. I did not disbelieve his word; I knew the date. I was only trying to reject the thought that made my heart clench like a fist closing. The man went on, as if he was proud to be the first to tell me:

"Some wanted to await your return, Lord Knight, but the priests had to hurry the preparations and the preliminary activities. You know that we had no delicacies for feasting the chosen one, or instruments for making the proper music. But we have sung loudly and burned much copáli. Also, since there is no temple for the requisite coupling, the priests sanctified a patch of soft grass screened by bushes, and there has been no lack of volunteer mates, many of them several times over. Since all agreed that our commander should be honored, even in his absence, all were unanimous in the choice of the symbolic one. And now you have returned in time to see the god represented in the person of—"

He stopped abruptly there, for I had swung my maquáhuitl through his neck, cleaving it clear to the bone at the back. Béu gave a small scream, and the soldiers behind her goggled and craned. The man stood wavering for a moment, looking bewildered, nodding slightly, soundlessly opening and shutting his mouth and the wider red lips below his chin. Then his head flopped backward, the wound yawned open, blood spouted, and he fell at my feet.

Béu said, aghast, "Záa, *why?* What made you do that?"

"Be silent, woman!" snapped Angry at Everybody. Then he gripped my upper arm, which perhaps stopped me from falling too, and said, "Mixtli, we may yet be in time to prevent the final proceeding. . . ."

I shook my head. "You heard him. He had been blessed with the bone. *All* has been done as that god requires."

Qualánqui sighed and said hoarsely, "I am sorry."

One of his ancient comrades took my other arm and said, "We are all sorry, young Mixtli. Would you prefer to wait here while we—while we go across the river?"

I said, "No. I am still in command. I will command what is to be done in Yanquítlan."

The old man nodded, then raised his voice and shouted to the soldiers bunched on the path, "You men! Break ranks and spread out. Make a skirmish line up and down the riverbank. Move!"

"Tell me what has happened!" cried Béu, wringing her hands. "Tell me what we are about to do!"

"Nothing," I said, my voice a croak. "You do nothing, Béu." I swallowed the impediment in my throat, and I blinked my eyes clear of tears, and I did my best to stand up straight and strong. "You do nothing but stay here, on this side of the water. Whatever you hear from over here, and however long it goes on, do not move from this spot until I come for you."

"Stay here alone? With that?" She pointed at the corpse.

I said, "Do not fear that one. Be happy for that one. In my first rage I was too hasty. I gave that one an easy release."

Angry at Everybody shouted, "You men! Advance in skirmish line across the river. Make no sound from here on. Encircle the village area. Let no least person escape, but surround them all and then wait for orders. Come, Mixtli, if you think you must."

"I know I must," I said, and I was the first to wade into the water.

Nochípa had spoken of dancing for the people of Yanquítlan, and so she was doing. But it was not the restrained and modest dancing which I had always seen her do. In the purple dusk, in the mixture of twilight and firelight, I could see that she was totally unclothed, that she danced with no grace, but with grossly indecent sprawlings of her legs, while she waved two white wands above her head, occasionally reaching one of them out to tap some person who pranced near.

Though I did not want to, I raised my topaz to see her more clearly. The only thing she wore was the necklace of opals I had given her when she was four years old, and to which I had added a new firefly stone on each of the eight birthdays—the so very few birthdays—she had had since. Her usually braided hair hung loose and tangled. Her breasts were still firm little mounds, and her buttocks still shapely, but between her thighs, where her maiden tipíli should have been almost invisible, there was a rent in her skin, and through it protruded a flopping male tepúli and jiggling sac of olóltin. The white things she waved were her own thigh bones, but the hands that waved them were a man's, and her own half-severed hands dangled limply from his wrists.

A cheer went up from the people as I stepped inside the circle of them dancing around the dancing thing that had been my daughter. She had been a child, and a shining, and they had made carrion of her. That effigy of Nochípa came dancing toward me, one glistening bone extended, as if she would give me a blessing tap before I hugged her in a father's loving embrace. The obscene thing came close enough for me to look into the eyes that were not Nochípa's eyes. Then its dancing feet faltered, it ceased to dance, it stopped just out of my reach, stopped by my look of loathing and revulsion. And when it stopped, so did the gleeful crowd stop its milling and its prancing and its joyful noise, and the people stood looking uneasily at me and at the soldiers who had ringed the site. I waited until nothing could be heard but the crackling of the celebration fires. Then I said, addressing nobody in particular:

"Seize this foul creature—but seize him gently, for he is all that remains of a girl who once was alive."

The small priest in Nochípa's skin stood blinking in unbelief, and then two of my warriors had him. The other five or six priests of the train came shouldering through the crowd, angrily protesting my interruption of the ceremony. I ignored them and said to the men holding the god-impersonator:

"Her face is separate from her body. Remove the face from him—with the greatest care—and bear it reverently to that fire yonder, and say some small prayer for her who gave it beauty, and burn it. Bring me the opals she wore at her throat."

I averted my own face while that was done. The other priests began to rage even more indignantly, until Angry at Everybody gave such a fearsome snarl that the priests became as quiet and meek as the motionless crowd.

"It is done, Knight Mixtli," said one of my men. He handed me the necklace; some of the firefly stones were red with Nochípa's blood. I turned again to the captive priest. He no longer wore my daughter's hair and features, but his own face, and it twitched with fright.

I said, "Lay him supine on the ground, right here, being very careful not to lay rough hands on my daughter's flesh. Peg his hands and feet to the ground."

He was, like all the priests of the train, a young man. And he screamed like a boy when the first sharp stake was hammered through his left palm. He screamed four times altogether. The other priests and people of Yanquítlan moved and murmured, rightly apprehensive of their own fate, but all my soldiers held their weapons at the ready, and no one dared be the first to try to run. I looked down at the grotesque figure on the ground, writhing against the four stakes that fixed its spraddled extremities. Nochípa's youthful breasts proudly pointed their russet nipples toward the sky, but the male genitals protruding from between her spread legs had gone flaccid and shrunken.

"Prepare lime water," I said. "Use much lime in the concentration, and drench the skin with it. Keep on wetting the skin all night long, until it has become well sodden. Then we will wait for the sun to come up."

Angry at Everybody nodded approvingly. "And the others? We await your command, Knight Mixtli."

One of the priests, impelled by terror, lunged between us and knelt before me, his bloodstained hands clutching the hem of my mantle, and he said, "Knight Commander, it was by your leave that we conducted this ceremony. Any other man here would have rejoiced to see his son or daughter chosen for the personation, but it was yours who best met all the qualifications. Once she had been chosen by the populace, and that choice approved by the people's priests, *you could not have refused* to relinquish her for the ceremony."

I gave him a look. He dropped his gaze, then stammered, "At least—in Tenochtítlan—you could not have refused." He tugged at my mantle again and said imploringly, "She was a virgin, as required, but she was mature enough to function as a woman, which she did. You told me yourself, Knight Commander: do all things required by the gods. So now the girl's Flowery Death has blessed your people and their new colony, and assured the fertility of this ground. You could not have withheld that blessing. Believe me, Knight Commander, we intended only *honor* . . . to Xipe Totec and to your daughter . . . and to you!"

I gave him a blow that toppled him to one side, and I said to Qualánqui, "You-are familiar with the *honors* traditionally accorded to the chosen Xipe Totec?"

"I am, friend Mixtli."

"Then you know the things that were done to the innocent and unblemished Nochípa. Do all the same things to all this filth. Do it in whatever manner you please. You have sufficient soldiers. Let them indulge themselves, and they need not hurry. Let them be inventive, and leisurely at it. But when all that is done, I want nobody—*nothing*—left alive in Yanquítlan."

It was the last command I gave there. Angry at Everybody took charge then. He turned and barked more specific orders, and the crowd howled as if already in agony. But the soldiers moved eagerly to comply with their instructions. Some of them swept all the adult men into a separate group, and held them there with their weapons. The other soldiers put down their arms and took off their clothes and went to work—or to play— and when any one of them tired, he would change places with one of those standing guard.

I watched, all through the night, for the great fires kept the night alight until dawn. But I did not really see, or gloat at what happened before my eyes, or take any satisfaction in the reprisal. I paid no heed to the screams and bellows and wails and other, more liquid noises occasioned by the mass rape and carnage. I could see and hear only Nochípa dancing gracefully in the firelight, singing melodiously as she did so, to a single flute's accompaniment.

What Qualánqui had ordered, what actually occurred, was this. All the smallest children, the babes in arms and toddling infants, were snatched by the soldiers and cut to pieces—not quickly, but as one would slowly peel and slice a fruit for the eating of it—while their parents watched and wept and threatened and cursed. Then the remaining children, all those judged old enough to be sexually used, the males as well as females, were used by the Tecpanéca, while their older sisters and brothers, mothers and fathers were forced to look on.

When those children had been so riven that they no longer afforded pleasure, the soldiers flung them aside to die. They next seized the bigger children, and the adolescent girls and boys, and finally the younger women and men—I have mentioned that the priests were all young men—and similarly served them. The one priest staked to the ground watched and whimpered, and looked fearfully down toward his own vulnerably exposed parts. But even in this slavering rampage, the Tecpanéca realized that that one was not to be touched, and he was not.

From time to time, the older men penned at one side tried frantically to break loose, when they saw wives, sisters, brothers, sons, daughters being despoiled. But the ring of guards stolidly held the men captive, and would not even let them turn away from watching the spectacle. Finally, when every other usable piece of flesh had been used until it was no longer usable, when it lay dead or lay wishing and trying to die, the Tecpanéca turned to the older folk. Though by then somewhat depleted of both appetite and ability, the soldiers managed adequately to ravish all the mature women, and even the two or three elderly grandmothers who had made the journey.

The next day's sun was high when all that was over, and Angry at Everybody ordered the penned men let loose. They, the husbands and fathers and uncles of the ruined, went about the littered ground, flinging themselves weeping on this and that limp, broken, naked body besmeared with blood and drool and omícetl. Some of the used bodies were still alive, and they lived to see the soldiers—at Qualánqui's next command—seize their husbands and fathers and uncles. What the Tecpanéca did to those men with their obsidian knives, and with the things they amputated, made each man sexually abuse himself while he lay bleeding to death.

Meanwhile, the staked-down priest had been keeping quiet, perhaps hoping he had been forgotten. But as the sun rose higher, he realized that he was to die more hideously than all the others, for what was left of Nochípa began to exact its own revenge. The skin, saturated with lime water, slowly and excruciatingly contracted as it dried. What had been Nochípa's breasts gradually flattened as the skin tightened its embrace around the priest's chest. He began to gasp and wheeze. He might have wished to express his terror in a scream, but he had to hoard what air he could inhale, just to live a little longer.

And the skin continued inexorably to contract, and began to impede the movement of the blood in his body. What had been Nochípa's neck and wrists and ankles shrank their openings like slow garrottes. The man's face and hands and feet began to bloat and darken to an ugly purple color. Through his distended lips came the sound "ugh . . . ugh . . . ugh . . ." but that gradually was choked off. Meanwhile, what had been Nochípa's little tipíli shut ever more virginally tight around the roots of the priest's genitals. His olóltin sac swelled to the size and tautness of a tlachtli ball, and his engorged tepúli bulged to a length and thickness bigger than my forearm.

The soldiers wandered about the area, inspecting every body lying about, to ascertain that each was surely dead or dying. The Tecpanéca did not mercifully dispatch the ones still alive, but only verified that they would die in the gods' good time— to leave, as I had commanded, no living thing in Yanquítlan. There was nothing more to keep us there, except to view the dying of that one remaining priest.

So I and my four old comrades stood over him and watched his agonized, slight stirring and the shallow movement of his chest, while the ever constricting skin made his torso and limbs get thinner and his visible extremities get larger. His hands and feet were like black breasts with many black teats, his head was a featureless black pumpkin. He found breath enough to give one last loud cry when his rigid tepúli could no longer contain the pressure, and split its skin, and exploded black blood, and fell in tattered shreds.

He was still dimly alive, but he was finished, and our vengeance was done. Angry at Everybody ordered the Tecpanéca to pack in preparation to march, while the other three old men forded with me back across the river to where Béu Ribé waited. Silently, I showed her the bloodstained opals. I do not know how much else she had seen or heard or guessed, and I do not know how I looked at that moment. But she regarded me with eyes full of horror and pity and reproach and sorrow—the horror uppermost—and for an instant she shrank from the hand I reached out to her.

"Come, Waiting Moon," I said stonily. "I will take you home."

IHS

☩

S.C.C.M.

Sanctified, Caesarean, Catholic Majesty,
the Emperor Don Carlos, Our Lord King:

MOST Perspicacious and Oracular Prince: from the City of México, capital of New Spain, two days after the Feast of the Purification, in this Year of Our Lord one Thousand five hundred thirty, greeting.

Sovereign Sire, we can only express our admiration at the depth and daring of our Liege's cogitations in the field of speculative hagiology, and our genuine awe at the brilliant conjecture propounded in Your Majesty's latest letter. *Viz.*, that the Indian's best-beloved deity, Quetzalcóatl, so frequently alluded to in our Aztec's narrative, could have been in actuality *the Apostle Thomas*, visiting these lands fifteen centuries ago for the purpose of bringing the Gospel to these heathens.

Of course, even as Bishop of México, we cannot give the episcopal imprimatur to such a strikingly bold hypothesis, Sire, prior to its consideration among higher ranks of the Church hierarchy. We can, however, attest that there exists a body of circumstantial evidence to support Your Majesty's innovative theory:

Primus. The so-called Feathery Snake was the one supernatural being recognized by every separate nation and variant religion so far known to have existed in all of New Spain, his name being severally rendered as Quetzalcóatl among the Náhuatl-speakers, Kukulkán among the Maya-speakers, Gukumatz among peoples even farther south, &c.

Secundus. All these peoples agree in the tradition that Quetzalcóatl was first a human, mortal, incarnate king or emperor who lived and walked on earth during the span of a lifetime, before his transmutation into an insubstantial and immortal deity. Since the Indians' calendar is exasperatingly inutile, and since there no longer exist the books of even mythical history, it may never be possible to date the alleged earthly reign of Quetzalcóatl. Therefore, he *could* very well have been coeval with St. Thomas.

Tertius. All these peoples likewise agree that Quetzalcóatl was not so much a ruler—or tyrant, as most of their rulers have been—but a teacher and a preacher and, not incidentally, a celibate by religious conviction. To him are attributed the invention or introduction of numerous things, customs, beliefs, &c., which have endured to this day.

Quartus. Among the numberless deities of these lands, Quetzalcóatl was one of the very few that never demanded or countenanced human sacrifice. The offerings made to him were always innocuous: birds, butterflies, flowers, and the like.

Quintus. The Church holds it to be historical fact that St. Thomas did travel to the land of India in the East, and did there convert many pagan peoples to Christianity. So, as Your Majesty suggests, "May it not be a reasonable supposition that the Apostle should also have done so in the then-unknown Indies of the West?" A reprobate materialist might remark that the sainted Thomas had the advantage of an overland route from the Holy Land to the East Indies, whereas he would have found some difficulty in crossing the Ocean Sea fifteen centuries before the development of the vessels and navigational facilities available to modern-day explorers. However, any cavil at the abilities of one of the Twelve Disciples would be as injudicious as was the doubt once voiced by Thomas himself and rebuked by the risen Christ.

Sextus et mirabile dictu. A common Spanish soldier named Díaz, who occupies his off-duty hours in idly exploring the old ruins of this area, recently visited the abandoned city of Tolan, or Tula. This is revered by the Aztecs as having been once the seat of the legendary people called the Toltecs—and of their ruler, the king later to become deity, Quetzalcóatl. Among the roots of a tree sprung from a crack in one of the old stone walls, Díaz found a carved onyx box, of native manufacture but of indeterminate age, and in this box he found a number of white wafers of delicate bread, quite unlike anything baked by these Indians. Díaz at once recognized them, and we, when they were brought to us, verified them as the Host. How these sacramental wafers came to be in that place and in a native-made pyx, how many centuries they may have been secreted there, and how it is that they did not long ago dry and crumble and perish, no one can guess. Could it be that Your Erudite Majesty has supplied the answer? Could the Communion wafers have been left as a token by the evangelist St. Thomas?

We are this day relating all these data in a communication to the Congregatio de Propaganda Fide, giving due credit to Your Majesty's inspired contribution, and will eagerly await the opinion of those theologians at Rome, far more sapient than ourself.

May Our Lord God continue to smile upon and favor the enterprises of Your Imperial Majesty, to whom unbound admiration is due and professed by all your subjects, not least by your S. C. C. M.'s chaplain and servant,

(ecce signum) Zumárraga

DECIMA PARS

FOR the same reason that I do not have much recollection of the events just prior to the obliteration of Yanquítlan, I do not clearly remember the things that happened immediately afterward. I and Béu and our escort marched north again toward Tenochtítlan, and I suppose the journey was unremarkable, for I recall little of it except two brief conversations.

The first was with Béu Ribé. She had been weeping as she walked, weeping almost constantly, ever since I told her of Nochípa's death. But one day, somewhere on the return route, she suddenly stopped both weeping and walking, and looked about her, like someone roused from sleep, and she said to me:

"You told me you would take me home. But we are going north."

I said, "Of course. Where else?"

"Why not south? South to Tecuantépec?"

"You have no home there," I said. "No family, probably no friends. It has been—what?—eight years since you left there."

"And what have I in Tenochtítlan?"

A roof under which to sleep, I might have remarked, but I knew what she really meant. So I said simply, "You have as much as I have, Waiting Moon. Memories."

"Not very pleasant ones, Záa."

"I know that too well," I said, without sympathy. "They are the same ones I have. And we will have them wherever we wander, or wherever we call home. At least you can grieve and mourn in comfort in Tenochtítlan, but no one is dragging you there. Come with us or go your own way, as you choose."

I walked on and did not look back, so I do not know how long it took her to decide. But the next time I lifted my gaze from my own inward visions, Béu was again walking at my side.

The other conversation was with Angry at Everybody. For many days the men had respectfully left me to my brooding silence, but one day he strode along with me and said:

"Forgive my intrusion on your sorrow, friend Mixtli. But we are getting near home, and there are things you should know. They are some things which we four elders have discussed and presumed to settle among ourselves. We have made up a story, and we have instructed the Tecpanéca troops to tell the same. It is this. While all of us—you and we and the soldiers—were making that embassy to the court of Teohuacán, while we were necessarily absent with good reason, the colony was set upon by bandits, and looted and massacred. On our return to Yanquítlan, we naturally went raging and searching for the marauders, but found no trace of them. Not so much as one of their arrows, whose feathering would have told us from what nation they came. That uncertainty of the bandits' identity will prevent Motecuzóma from instantly declaring a war upon the innocent Teohuacána."

I nodded and said, "I will tell it exactly so. It is a good story, Qualánqui."

He coughed and said, "Unfortunately, not good enough for *you* to tell, Mixtli. Not to Motecuzóma's face. Even if he believed every word of it, he would not hold you blameless for the failure of that mission. He would either order you throttled by the flower garland or, if he happened to be feeling kindly, he would give you another chance. Meaning you would be commanded to lead another train of colonists, and probably to the same unspeakable place."

I shook my head. "I could not and would not."

"I know," said Angry at Everybody. "And besides, the truth is bound to leak out, soon or later. One of those Tecpanéca soldiers, when he gets home safe to Tlácopan, is sure to boast of his part in the massacre. How he raped and slew six children and a priest, or whatever. It would get back to Motecuzóma; you would be caught in a lie; and you would certainly get the garrotte, if not worse. I think it better that you leave the lying to us old men, who are only hirelings, beneath Motecuzóma's notice, hence in less danger. I also think you might consider not returning to Tenochtítlan at all—not for some time, anyway—since your future there seems to offer only a choice of capital punishment or renewed banishment to Yanquítlan."

I nodded again. "You are right. I have been mourning the dark days and roads behind me, not looking toward those ahead. It is an old saying, is it not, that we are born to suffer and endure? And a man must give thought to his enduring, must he not? Thank you, Qualánqui, good friend and wise adviser. I will meditate upon your counsel."

When we came to Quaunáhuac, and that night took lodgings at an inn, I had a dining cloth set apart for me and Béu and my four old comrades. When we had done eating, I took from my waistband my leather sack of gold dust and dropped it on the cloth, and said:

"There is your pay for your services, my friends."

"It is far too much," said Angry at Everybody.

"For what you have done, it could not possibly be. I have this other purse of copper bits and cacao beans, sufficient for what I will do now."

"Do now?" echoed one of the old men.

"Tonight I abdicate command, and these are my last instructions to you. Friend officers, you will proceed from here around the western border of the lakes, to deliver the Tecpanéca troops to Tlácopan. From there you will cross the causeway to Tenochtítlan and escort the lady Béu to my house, before you report to the Revered Speaker. Tell him your nicely concocted story, but add that I have inflicted on myself a punishment for the failure of this expedition. Tell him that I have voluntarily gone into exile."

"It will be done so, Commander Mixtli," said Angry at Everybody, and the other three men murmured agreement.

Only Béu asked the question: "Where are you going, Záa?"

"In search of a legend," I said, and I told them the story

that Nezahualpíli had not long ago told to Motecuzóma in my hearing, and I concluded, "I will retrace that long march our forefathers made in the time when they still called themselves the Aztéca. I will go northward, following their route as nearly as I can construe it and as far as I can trace it... all the way to their homeland of Aztlan, if such a place still exists or ever did. And if those wanderers truly did bury armories of weapons and stores at intervals, I will find them too, and map their locations. Such a map could be of great military value to Motecuzóma. Try to impress that upon him when you report to him, Qualánqui." I smiled ruefully. "He may welcome me with flowers instead of a flower garland when I return."

"If you return," said Béu.

I could not smile at that. I said, "It seems my tonáli forces me always to return, but every time a little more alone." I paused, then said between my teeth, "Someday, somewhere, I will meet a god and I will ask him: Why do the gods never strike me down, when I have done so much to deserve their anger? Why do they instead strike down every undeserving one who has ever stood close to me?"

The four elderly men appeared slightly uneasy at having to hear my bitter lament, and they seemed relieved when Béu said, "Old friends, would you be kind enough to take your leave, that Záa and I may exchange a few private words?"

They got up, making a cursory gesture of kissing the earth to us, and, when they went off toward their quarters, I said brusquely, "If you are going to ask to accompany me, Béu, do not ask."

She did not. She was silent for a considerable time, her eyes downcast to her nervously twining fingers. Finally she said, and her first words seemed totally irrelevant, "On my seventh birthday I was named Waiting Moon. I used to wonder why. But then I knew, and I have known for years now, and I think Waiting Moon has waited long enough." She raised her beautiful eyes to mine, and somehow she had made them entreating instead of mocking for a change, and somehow she even managed a maidenly blush. "Let us now at last be married, Záa."

So *that* was it, I said to myself, remembering again how she had surreptitiously collected that mud I had made. Earlier, and for only a brief time, I had wondered if she fashioned an image of me in order to curse it with misfortune, and if that was what had deprived me of Nochípa. But that suspicion had been a fleeting one, shaming me even to think of it. I knew Béu had loved my daughter dearly, and her weeping had demonstrated a sorrow as genuine as my tearless own. So I had forgotten the mud doll—until her own words revealed that she *had* made it, and why. Not to blight my life but merely to weaken my will, so that I could not reject her pretendedly impulsive but transparently long-planned proposal. I did not immediately reply; I waited while she proffered her carefully marshaled arguments. She said first:

"A moment ago, Záa, you remarked that you are ever more and more alone. So am I, you know. We both are, now. We have no one left but each other."

And she said, "It was acceptable that I should live with you while I was known to be the guardian and companion of your motherless daughter. But now that Nochípa . . . now that I am no longer the resident aunt, it would be unseemly for an unmarried man and woman to share the same house."

And she said, with another blush, "I know there could never be a replacement for our beloved Nochípa. But there could be . . . I am not too old . . ."

And there she let her voice fade away, in a very good simulation of modesty and inability to say more. I waited, and held her eyes, until her blushing face glowed like copper being heated, and then I said:

"You need not have troubled with conjuration and cajolery, Béu. I intended to ask you the same thing this very night. Since you seem agreeable, we will be married tomorrow, as early as I can awaken a priest."

"What?" she said faintly.

"As you remind me, I am now most utterly alone. I am also a man of estimable estate and, if I die without an heir, my property is forfeit to the nation's treasury. I should prefer that it not go to Motecuzóma. So tomorrow the priest will draw a document affirming your inheritance as well as the paper attesting our marriage."

Béu slowly got to her feet and looked down at me, and she stammered, "That is not what . . . I never gave a thought to . . . Záa, I was trying to say . . ."

"And I have spoiled the performance," I said, smiling up at her. "All the blandishments and persuasions were unnecessary. But you need not count them wasted, Béu. Tonight may have been good practice for some future use, when perhaps you are a wealthy but lonely widow."

"Stop it, Záa!" she exclaimed. "You refuse to hear what I am earnestly trying to tell you. It is hard enough for me, because it is not a woman's place to say such things...."

"Please, Béu, no more," I said, wincing. "We have lived too long together, too long accustomed to our mutual dislike. Saying sweet words at this late date would strain either of us, and probably astound all the gods. But at least, from tomorrow on, our detestation of each other can be formally consecrated and indistinguishable from that of most other married—"

"You are cruel!" she interrupted. "You are immune to any tender sentiment, and heedless of a hand reaching out to you."

"I have too often felt the hard back of your tender hand, Béu. And am I not about to feel it again? Are you not going to laugh now and tell me that your talk of marriage was just another derisive prank?"

"No," she said. "I meant it seriously. Did you?"

"Yes," I said, and raised high my cup of octli. "May the gods take pity on us both."

"An eloquent proposal," she said. "But I accept it, Záa. I will marry you tomorrow." And she ran for her room.

I sat on, moodily sipping my octli and eyeing the inn's other patrons, most of them pochtéca on their way home to Tenochtítlan, celebrating their profitable journeys and safe return by getting eminently drunk, in which pursuit they were being encouraged by the hostel's numerous available women. The innkeeper, already aware that I had engaged a separate room for Béu, and seeing her depart alone, came sidling to where I sat, and inquired:

"Would the Lord Knight care for a sweet with which to conclude his meal? One of our charming maátime?"

I grunted, "Few of them look exceptionally charming."

"Ah, but looks are not everything. My lord must know that, since his own beautiful companion seems cool toward him. Charm can reside in other attributes than face and figure. For example, regard that woman yonder."

He pointed to what must surely have been the least appealing female in the establishment. Her features and her breasts sagged like moist clay. Her hair, from having been so often bleached and recolored, was like wire grass dried to kinky hay. I grimaced, but the innkeeper laughed and said:

"I know, I know. To contemplate that woman is to yearn for a boy instead. At a glance, you would take her for a grandmother, but I know for a fact that she is scarcely thirty. And would you believe this, Lord Knight? *Every man* who has ever once tried Quequelyéhua always *demands* her on his next visit here. Her every patron becomes a regular, and will accept no other maátitl. I do not indulge, myself, but I have it on good authority that she knows some extraordinary ways to delight a man."

I raised my topaz and took another, more searching look at the draggle-haired, bleary-eyed sloven. I would have wagered that she was a walking pustule of the nanáua disease, and that the effeminate innkeeper knew it, and that he took malicious pleasure in trying to peddle her to the unsuspecting.

"In the dark, my lord, all women look alike, no? Well, boys do too, of course. So it is other considerations that matter, no? The highly accomplished Quequelyéhua probably already has a waiting line for tonight, but an Eagle Knight can demand precedence over mere pochtéca. Shall I summon Quequelyéhua for you, my lord?"

"Quequelyéhua," I repeated, as the name evoked a memory. "I once knew a most beautiful girl named Quequelmíqui."

"Ticklish?" said the innkeeper, and giggled. "From her name, she must have been a diverting consort too. But this one should be far more so. Quequelyéhua, the Tickler."

Feeling rather sick at heart, I said, "Thank you for the recommendation, but no, thank you." I took a large drink of my octli. "That thin girl sitting quietly in the corner, what of her?"

"Misty Rain?" said the innkeeper, indifferently. "They call her that because she weeps all the time she is, er, functioning. A newcomer, but competent enough, I am told."

I said, "Send that one to my room. As soon as I am drunk enough to go there myself."

"At your command, Lord Eagle Knight. I am impartial in the matter of other people's preferences, but sometimes I am mildly curious. May I ask why my lord chooses Misty Rain?"

I said, "Simply because she does not remind me of any other woman I have known."

The marriage ceremony was plain and simple and quiet, at least until its conclusion. My four old stalwarts stood as our witnesses. The innkeeper prepared tamáltin for the ritual meal. Some of the inn's earlier-rising patrons served as our wedding guests. Since Quaunáhuac is the chief community of the Tlahuíca people, I had procured a priest of the Tlahuíca's principal deity, the good god Quetzalcóatl. And the priest, observing that the couple standing before him were somewhat past the first greening of youth, tactfully omitted from his service the usual doleful warnings to the presumably innocent female, and the usual cautionary exhortations to the presumably lusting male. So his harangue was mercifully brief and bland.

But even that perfunctory ritual elicited some emotion from Béu Ribé, or she pretended it did. She wept a few maidenly tears and, through the tears, smiled tremulous smiles. I must admit that her performance enhanced her already striking beauty; which, as I have never denied, was equal to and almost indistinguishable from the sublime loveliness of her late sister. Béu was dressed most enticingly and, when I looked at her without the clarification of my crystal, she appeared still as youthful as my forever twenty-year-old Zyanya. It was for that reason that I had made repeated use of the girl Misty Rain throughout the night. I would not risk Béu's making me want her, even physically, so I drained myself of any possibility of becoming aroused against my will.

The priest finally swung his smoking censer of copáli around us for the last time. Then he watched while we fed each other a bite of steaming tamáli, then he knotted the corner of my mantle to a corner of Waiting Moon's skirt hem, then he wished us the best of fortune in our new life.

"Thank you, Lord Priest," I said, handing him his fee. "Thank you especially for the good wishes." I undid the knot that tied me to Béu. "I may need the gods' help where I am now going." I slung my traveling pack on my shoulder and told Béu good-bye.

"Good-bye?" she repeated, in a sort of squeak. "But Záa, this is our wedding day."

I said, "I told you I would be leaving. My men will see you safely home."

"But—but I thought—I thought surely we would stay here at least another night. For the . . ." She glanced about, at the watching and listening guests. She blushed hotly and her voice rose, "Záa, I am now your wife!"

I corrected her, "You are married to me, as you requested, and you will be my widow and my heiress. Zyanya was my wife."

"Zyanya has been ten years dead!"

"Her dying did not sever our bond. I can have no other wife."

"Hypocrite!" she raged at me. "You have not been celibate for these ten years. You have had other women. Why will you not have the one you just now wed? Why will you not have me?"

Except for the innkeeper, who was smirking lewdly, most of the people in the room stood fidgeting and looking uncomfortable. So did even the priest, who nerved himself to say, "My lord, it is customary, after all, to seal the vows with an act of . . . well, to know each other intimately. . . ."

I said, "Your concern does you credit, Lord Priest. But I already know this woman far too intimately."

Béu gasped. "What a horrid lie to tell! We have never once—"

"And we never will. Waiting Moon, I know you too well in other ways. I also know that the most vulnerable moment in a man's life occurs when he couples with a woman. I will not chance arriving at that moment to have you disdainfully reject me, or break into your mocking laughter, or diminish me by any other of the means you have been so long practicing and perfecting."

She cried, "And what are you doing to me this moment?"

"The very same," I agreed. "But this once, my dear, I have done it first. Now the day latens, and I must be on my way."

When I left, Béu was dabbing at her eyes with the crumpled corner of her skirt that had been our marriage knot.

✠

It was not necessary for me to begin retracing my ancestors' long-ago long march from its terminus in Tenochtítlan, nor

from any of the places they had earlier inhabited in the lake
district, since those sites could hold no undiscovered secrets
of the Aztéca. But, according to the old tales, one of the
Aztéca's next-earlier habitations, before they found the lake
basin, had been somewhere to the north of the lakes: a place
called Atlitalácan. So, from Quaunáhuac, I traveled northwest,
then north, then northeast, circling around and staying well
outside the domains of The Triple Alliance, until I was in the
sparsely settled country beyond Oxitípan, the northernmost
frontier town garrisoned by Mexíca soldiers. In that unfamiliar
territory of infrequent small villages and infrequent travelers
between them, I began inquiring the way to Atlitalácan. But
the only replies I got were blank looks and indifferent shrugs,
because I was laboring under two difficulties.

One was that I had no idea what Atlitalácan *was*, or what
it had been. It could have been an established community at
the time the Aztéca stayed there, but which had since ceased
to exist. It could have been merely a hospitable place for camping—a grove or meadow—to which the Aztéca had given that
name only temporarily. My other difficulty was that I had
entered the southern part of the Otomí country, or, to be accurate, the country to which the Otomí peoples had grudgingly
removed when they were gradually ousted from the lake lands
by the successively arriving waves of Culhua, Acólhua, Aztéca,
and other Náhuatl-speaking invaders. So, in that amorphous
border country, I had a language problem. Some of the folk
I accosted spoke a passable Náhuatl, or the Poré of their other
neighbors to the west. But some spoke only Otomíte, in which
I was by no means fluent, and many spoke a bastard patchwork
of the three languages. Although my persistent questioning of
villagers and farmers and wayfarers enabled me eventually to
acquire a working vocabulary of Otomíte words, and to explain
my quest, I still could find no native who could direct me to
the lost Atlitalácan.

I had to find it myself, and I did. Fortunately, the place-
name itself was a clue—Atlitalácan means "where the water
gushes"—and I came one day to a neat and cleanly little village
named D'ntado Dehé, which in Otomíte means approximately
the same thing. The village was built where it was because a
sweet-water spring bubbled from the rocks there, and it was

the only spring within a considerably extensive arid area. It seemed a likely place for the Aztéca to have stopped, since an old road came into the village from the north and proceeded southward from it in the general direction of Lake Tzumpánco.

The meager population of D'ntado Dehé naturally regarded me askance, but one elderly widow was too poor to indulge too many misgivings, and she rented me a few days' lodging in the nearly empty food-storage loft under the roof of her one-room mud hut. During those days I tried smilingly to ingratiate myself with the taciturn Otomí, and to coax them into conversation. Failing in that, I prowled the outskirts of the village in a widening spiral, seeking whatever supplies my forefathers might have secreted there, even though I suspected that any such random search would be futile. If the Aztéca *had* hidden stores and arms along their line of march, they must have made sure the deposits could not be dug up by the local residents or any later passersby. They must have marked the caches with some obscure sign recognizable only by themselves. And none of their Mexíca descendants, including me, had any notion of what that sign might have been.

But I cut a long, stout pole, and sharpened the end of it, and with it I prodded deep into every feature of the local terrain that might conceivably *not* have been there since the world was first created: suspiciously isolated hills of earth, oddly uncleared thickets of scrub growth, the fallen-in remains of ancient buildings. I do not know whether my behavior moved the villagers to amusement or to pity of the alien madman or to simple curiosity, but at last they invited me to sit down and explain myself to their two most venerable elders.

Those old men answered my questions in as few and simple words as possible. No, they said, they had never heard of any such place as Atlitalácan, but if the name meant the same as D'ntado Dehé, then D'ntado Dehé was doubtless the same place. Because yes, according to their fathers' fathers' fathers, a long time ago a rough, ragged, and verminous tribe of outlanders had settled at the spring—for some years of residence—before moving on again and disappearing to the southward. When I delicately inquired about possible diggings and deposits therein, the two aged men shook their heads. They said n'yéhina, which means no, and they said a sentence that they had to repeat several times before I laboriously made sense of it:

"The Aztéca were here, but they brought nothing with them, and they left nothing when they went."

Within not many days, I had left the regions where the last vestiges of even mongrel Náhuatl or Poré were spoken, and was well into the territory inhabited solely by Otomí speaking only Otomíte. I did not travel an unswervingly fixed course, for that would have required me to climb trackless hills and scale formidable cliffs and fight my way through many cactus thickets, which I was sure the migrant Aztéca had not done. Instead, as they surely had done, I followed the roads, where there were any, and the more numerous well-trodden footpaths. That made my journey a meandering one, but always I bore generally northward.

I was still on the high plateau between the mighty mountain ranges invisibly far to the east and west, but as I progressed the plateau perceptibly sloped downward before me. Each day I descended a little farther from the highlands of crisp, cool air, and those days of late springtime got warmer, sometimes uncomfortably warm, but the nights were gentle and balmy. That was a good thing, for there were no wayside inns in the Otomí country, and the villages or farmsteads where I could request lodging were often far between. So most nights I slept on the open ground, and even without my seeing crystal I could make out the fixed star Tlacpac hung high above the northern horizon toward which I would plod again at dawn.

The lack of inns and other eating places did not work much hardship on me. The paucity of people in that region made the wild creatures less timid than they were in more populous places; rabbits and ground squirrels would sit up boldly from the grass to watch me pass; an occasional swift-runner bird would companionably pace at my very side; and at night an armadillo or opossum might even come to investigate my camp-fire. Although I carried no weapon but my maquáhuitl, scarcely designed for hunting small game, I usually had to do no more than make a swipe with it to secure for myself a meal of fresh meat or fowl. For variety or for side dishes, there was a plenty of growing things.

The name of that northern nation, Otomí, is a shortened rendition of a much longer and less pronounceable term meaning something like "the men whose arrows bring down birds on the wing," though I think it must have been a very long time since hunting was their chief occupation. There are numerous tribes of the Otomí, but they all live by pastoral pursuits: farming tidy fields of maize, xitómatin, and other vegetables; or gathering fruit from trees and cactus; or collecting the sweetwater sap of the maguey plants. Their fields and orchards were so productive that they had a great surplus of fresh foods to send to Tlaltelólco and other foreign markets, and we Mexíca called their country Atóctli, The Fertile Land. However, as an indication of how lowly we regarded those people themselves: we ranked our octli liquor according to three grades of quality, respectively called fine, ordinary, and Otomí.

The Otomí villages all have nearly unpronounceable names—like the largest of them all, N't Tahí, the one your explorers of the northern regions now refer to as Zelalla. And in none of those mumble-named communities did I find a hidden supply store or any other trace of the Aztéca's ever having passed. In only an infrequent village could the aged local storyteller strain his memory backward to recall a tradition that yes, untold sheaves of years ago, a vagrant train of footsore nomads had slouched through the neighborhood, or stopped to rest for a time. And every such elder told me, "They brought nothing with them, and they left nothing when they went." It was discouraging. But then, I was a direct descendant of those vagabonds and I likewise brought nothing. Just once during my journey through those Otomí lands, I may have *left* a little something. . . .

The Otomí men are short, squat, dumpy, and, like most farm folk, sullen and surly of disposition. The Otomí women are also small, but slim of body, and far more vivacious than their glum men. I will even say the women are pretty—from the knees upward—which I realize is a curious kind of compliment. What I mean is that they have fetching faces, nicely molded shoulders and arms and breasts and waists and hips and buttocks and thighs, but, below the knees, their calves are disappointingly straight and skinny. They dwindle tapering down to their tiny feet, giving the women somewhat the look of tadpoles balancing on their tails.

Another peculiarity of the Otomí is that they enhance their appearance—or so they believe—by the art they call n'detade, which means coloring themselves with *permanent* colors. They dye their teeth black or red, or alternately black and red. They adorn their bodies with designs of a blue color, pricked into the skin with thorns so the designs remain forever. Some make only a small decoration on the forehead or on a cheek, but others continue doing the n'detade, as frequently as they can stand the pain of it, over the skin of their entire body. They appear always to be standing behind the web of some extraordinary spider that spins blue.

The Otomí men, as far as I am concerned, are neither improved nor impaired by their adornment. For a while, I did think it a shame that so many otherwise handsome women should obscure their beauty behind those webs and whorls and patterns they could never remove. However, as I became more accustomed to seeing the n'detade, I must confess that I began to regard it as a subtle beguilement. The very veiling made the females seem in a measure unapproachable, and therefore challenging, and therefore tantalizing. . . .

At the farthest northern extent of the Otomí lands was a riverside village called M'boshte, and one of the villagers was a young woman named R'zoöno H'donwe, which means Flower of the Moon. And flowery she was: every visible part of her blossoming with blue-drawn petals and leaves and fronds. Behind that artificial garden, she was fair of face and figure, excepting of course those disappointing calves. At first sight of her, I felt an urge to part her clothes and see how much of her was flower-petaled, then to make my way through the petals to the woman underneath.

Flower of the Moon was attracted to me, too, and I suspect in much the same way: an urge to enjoy an oddity, since my height and breadth, oversized even among the Mexíca, made me rather a giant among the Otomí. She conveyed to me that she was at the time unattached to any other male; she had been recently widowed, when her husband died in the R'donte Sh'mboi, the River Slate, which trickled past the village. Since that water was only about a hand span deep and almost narrow enough for me to jump across, I suggested that her husband must have been a *very* small man to have drowned in it. She laughed at that, and made me understand that he had fallen and cracked his skull on the river's slate bed.

So the one night which I spent in M'boshte I spent with Flower of the Moon. I cannot speak of other Otomí females, but that one was decorated on every exposable surface of her skin, everywhere but on her lips, her eyelids, her fingertips, and the nipples of her breasts. I remember thinking that she must have suffered excruciatingly when the local artist pricked the flower designs right to the margins of her tender tipíli membranes. For, in the course of that night, I got to see every blossom she wore. The act of copulation is called in Otomíte agui n'degue, and it began—or at least Flower of the Moon preferred that I begin—by examining and tracing and fondling and, well, tasting every last petal of every single flower of her whole body's garden. I felt rather like a deer browsing through a sweet and abundant meadow, and I decided that deer must be happy animals indeed.

When I prepared to depart in the morning, Flower of the Moon gave me to understand that she hoped I had made her pregnant, which her late husband had never done. I smiled, thinking she paid me a compliment. But then she conveyed her reason for hoping to bear my son or daughter. I was a big man, so the child should also grow to goodly size, so it would have an exceptional expanse of skin to be embellished with a prodigious number of n'detade drawings, so it would be a rarity that would make M'boshte the envy of every other Otomí community. I sighed, and went on my way.

As long as my course lay beside the waters of the R'donte Sh'mboi, the land about was green with grass and leaves, dotted with the red and yellow and blue of many blossoms. However, three or four days later, the River Slate bent westward, away from my northering course, and took all the cool and colorful verdure with it. Ahead of me were still some gray-green mízquitin trees and silver-green clumps of yuca and a heavy undergrowth of various dusty-green bushes. But I knew that the trees and shrubs would gradually thin out and move farther apart as I moved on, until they would give way to the open and sun-baked and almost barren desert.

For a moment I paused, tempted to turn with the river and stay in the temperate Otomí country, but I had no excuse for doing so. The only reason for my journey was to backtrack the Aztéca, and, as well as I knew, they had come from somewhere yonder—from that desert—or beyond, if there was anything beyond, So I filled my water bag from the river, and I inhaled a last deep breath of the river-cooled air, and I walked on northward. I turned my back on the living lands. I walked into the empty lands, into the burned lands, into the dead-bone lands.

The desert is a wilderness which the gods torment, when they are not ignoring it utterly.

The earth goddess Coatlícue and her family do nothing to add interest to the monotonous and almost uniformly level terrain of gray-yellow sand, gray-brown gravel, and gray-black boulders. Coatlícue does not deign to disturb that land with earthquakes. Chántico does not spurt volcanoes through it, nor Temazcaltóci spit any spouts of hot water and steam. The mountain god Tepeyólotl stays aloofly far away. I could, with the aid of my topaz, just make out the low profiles of mountains far to east and west, jagged mountains colored the gray-white of granite. But they remained always infinitely distant; they never came nearer to me nor I to them.

Each morning, the sun god Tonatíu sprang angrily from his bed, without his accustomed dawn ceremony of selecting his bright spears and arrows for the day. Each evening, he plummeted into bed without donning his lustrous feather mantle or spreading wide his colorful flower quilts. In between the abrupt lifting and dropping of the nights' blessedly cool darkness, Tonatíu was merely a brighter yellow-white spot in the yellow-white sky—sultry, sullen, sucking all the breath from that land—burning his way across the parched sky as slowly and laboriously as I crept across the parched sands below.

The rain god Tlaloc paid even less attention to the desert, though it was by then the season of rains. His casks of clouds often piled up, but only over the granite mountains far away to east and west. The clouds would belly and billow and tower high over the horizon, then darken with storm, and the tlalóque spirits would flail their blazing forked sticks, making a drumming that came to me as a faint mutter. But the sky above me and ahead of me remained forever that unrelieved yellow-white. Neither the clouds nor the tlalóque ventured into the oven heat of the desert. They let their rain spill only as distant gray-blue veils onto those distant gray-white mountains. And the goddess of running water, Chalchihuítlicué, was nowhere in evidence, never.

The wind god Ehécatl blew now and then, but his lips were as parched as the desert earth, his breath as hot and dry, and he seldom made a sound, since he had practically nothing to blow against. Sometimes, though, he blew so hard that he whistled. Then the sand stirred and lifted and drove across the land in clouds as abrasive as the obsidian dust that sculptors use to wear away solid rock.

The gods of living creatures have little to do in that hot, harsh, arid land; least of all Mixcóatl, the god of hunters. Of course I saw or heard the occasional coyote, because that beast seems able to forage a living anywhere. And there were some rabbits, probably put there only for the coyotes to live on. There were wrens, and owls not much bigger than the wrens, living in holes gouged in the cactuses, and always a scavenger vulture or two soaring in circles high above me. But every other desert inhabitant seemed to be of the vermin variety, living underground or under rocks—the venomous rattle-tailed snakes, lizards like whips, other lizards all warts and horns, scorpions almost as long as my hand.

The desert likewise contains little to have interested our gods of growing things. I grant that even there, in the autumn, the nopáli cactus puts forth its sweet red tónaltin fruits, and the gigantic quinámetl cactus offers sweet purplish pitaáya fruits at the ends of its uplifted arms, but most of the desert cactuses grow only spikes and spines and hooks and barbs. Of trees there is only an occasional gnarled mizquitl, and the yuca of spearlike leaves, and the quaumátlatl which is curiously colored a light, bright green in its every part: leaves, twigs, branches, and even its trunk. The smaller shrubs include the useful chiyáctic, whose sap is so like an oil that it makes an easily lighted campfire, and the quauxelolóni, whose wood is harder than copper, almost impossible to cut, so heavy that it would sink in water, if there were any water about.

Only one kindly goddess dares to stroll through that forbidding desert, to reach among the fangs and talons of those touch-me-not plants, to sweeten their ill nature with her caress. That is Xochiquétzal, goddess of love and flowers, the goddess best loved by my long-gone sister Tzitzitlíni. Each spring, for a little while, the goddess beautifies every meanest shrub and cactus. During the rest of the year, it might seem to an ordinary traveler that Xochiquétzal has abandoned the desert to unenlivened ugliness. But I still, as I had done in my short-sighted childhood, looked closely at things that would not catch the eye of people with normal vision. And I found flowers in the desert in every season, on the long, thready vines that crept along the surface of the ground. They were miniature flowers, almost invisible unless they were sought, but they were flowers, and I knew that Xochiquétzal was there.

Though a goddess may frequent the desert with ease and impunity, it is no comfortable environment for a human being. Everything that makes human life livable is either scarce or absent. A man trying to cross the desert, ignorant of its nature and unprepared for it, would soon come to his death—and not a quick or an easy one. But I, though I was making my first venture into that wasteland, was not entirely ignorant or unprepared. During my schooldays, when we boys were taught to soldier, the Cuachic Blood Glutton had insisted on including some instruction in how to survive in the desert.

For example, I never lacked for water, thanks to his teachings. The most convenient source is the comitl cactus, which is why it is called the comitl, or jar. I would select a sizable one and lay a ring of twigs around it, and set them afire, and wait until the heat drove the comitl's moisture toward its interior. I then had only to slice off the top of the cactus, mash its inner pulp and squeeze the water from that into my leather bag. Also, each night, I cut down one of the tall, straight-trunked cactuses and laid it with its ends propped on rocks so that it sagged in the middle. By the morning, all its moisture would have collected in that middle, where I had only to cut out a plug and let the water trickle into my bag.

I seldom had any meat to cook over my evening campfire, except an occasional lizard, sufficient for about two mouthfuls—and once a rabbit which had still been kicking when I drove off the vulture tearing at it. But meat is not indispensable to the sustenance of life. Throughout the year, the mizquitl tree is festooned with seed pods, new green ones as well as the withered brown ones left from the year before. The green pods can be cooked to tenderness in hot water and then mashed into an edible pulp. The dry seeds inside the old pods can be crushed between two rocks to the consistency of meal. That coarse powder can be carried like pinóli and, when no fresher food is available, mixed with water and boiled.

Well, I survived, and I traveled in that dreadful desert for a whole year. But I need describe it no more, since every one-long-run was indistinguishable from every other. I will only add—in case you reverend friars cannot yet envision its vastness and emptiness—that I had been trudging through it for at least a month before I encountered another human being.

From a distance, because it was dust-colored like the desert, I took it to be just a strangely shaped hummock of sand, but as I got closer I saw it was a seated human figure. Rather joyfully, since I had been so long alone, I gave a hail, but I heard no reply. As I continued to approach I called again, and still I got no answer, though by then I was close enough to see that the stranger's mouth was open wide enough to be scream-ing.

Then I stood over the figure, a naked woman sitting on the sand and wearing a light powdering of it. If she had once been screaming, she was no more, for she was dead, with eyes and mouth wide. She sat with her legs out before her and parted, with her hands pressed flat on the ground as if she had died while trying strenuously to push herself erect. I touched her dusty shoulder; the flesh was yielding and not yet chill; she had not been dead for long. She stank of being unwashed, as no doubt I did too, and her long hair was so full of sand fleas that it might have writhed had it not been so matted. Never-theless, given a good bath, she would have been handsome of face and figure, and she was younger than I was, with no marks of disease or injury, so I was puzzled as to the cause of her death.

During the past month, I had got into the habit of talking to myself, for lack of anyone else, so then I said to myself, forlornly, "This desert is surely abandoned by the gods—or I am. I have the good fortune to meet what is perhaps the only other person in all this wasteland, and by good fortune it is a woman, who would have been ideal for a traveling companion, but by ill fortune she is a corpse. Had I come a day earlier, she might have been pleased to share my journey and my blanket and my attentions. Since she is dead, the only attention I can pay is to bury her before the vultures come flocking."

I shed my pack and my water bag and began to scrape with my maquáhuitl in the sand nearby. But I seemed to feel her eyes reproachfully on me, so I decided she might as well lie down restfully while I dug the grave. I dropped my blade and took the woman by her shoulders to ease her onto her back— and I got a surprise. She resisted my hands' pressure, she insisted on remaining in a sitting position, as if she had been a stuffed doll sewn to stay bent in the middle. I could not understand the body's reluctance; its muscles had not yet been stiffened, as I proved by lifting one of her arms and finding it quite limber. I tried again to move her, and her head lolled onto her shoulder, but her torso would not be budged. A mad thought came into my mind. Did desert people, when they died, perhaps grow roots that fixed them in place? Did they perhaps gradually turn into those giant but often very human-shaped quinámetin cactuses?

I stepped back to consider the incomprehensibly stubborn cadaver—and was surprised again when I felt a sharp stab between my shoulderblades. I whirled around to find myself in a half circle of arrows, all pointed at me. Each was poised on the taut string of a bow, and every bow was held by an angrily frowing man, and every man was clad in nothing but a greasy loincloth of ragged leather, a crust of body dirt, and some feathers in his lank hair. There were nine of the men. Admittedly, I had been preoccupied with my peculiar find, and they had taken pains to come noiselessly, but I should have smelled them long before they were upon me, for their stink was that of the dead woman multiplied by nine.

"The Chichiméca!" I said to myself, or perhaps I said it aloud. I did say to them, "I just now happened upon this unfortunate woman. I was trying to be of help."

Since I blurted that out in a hurry, hoping it would hold

back their arrows, I spoke in my native tongue of Náhuatl. But I accompanied the words with gestures intended to be understandable even by savages, and even in that tense moment I was thinking that, if I lived long enough to say anything else, I should have the task of learning yet another foreign language. But, to my surprise, one of the men—the one who had jabbed me with his arrow point, a man about my own age and nearly of my height—said in easily understandable Náhuatl:

"The woman is my wife."

I cleared my throat and said condolingly, as one does when imparting bad news, "I regret to say she *was* your wife. She appears to have died a short while ago." The Chichimécatl's arrow—all nine arrows—stayed aimed at my middle. I hastened to add, "I did not cause her death. I found her thus. And I had no thought of molesting her, even if I had found her alive."

The man laughed harshly, without humor.

"In fact," I went on, "I was about to do her the favor of burying her, before the scavengers should get at her." I indicated the place where my maquáhuitl lay.

The man looked at the furrow I had begun, then up at a vulture already hovering overhead, then at me again, and his stern face softened somewhat. He said, "That was kindly of you, stranger," and he lowered his arrow and relaxed the bowstring.

The other eight Chiciméca did likewise, and tucked their arrows into their tangled hair. One of the men went to pick up my maquáhuitl and examine it appraisingly; another began to poke through the contents of my pack. Maybe I was about to be robbed of what little I carried, but at least it seemed that I would not immediately be killed as a trespasser. To maintain the mood of amiability, I said to the just-widowed husband:

"I sympathize in your bereavement. Your wife was young and comely. Of what did she die?"

"Of being a bad wife," he said glumly. Then he said, "She was bitten by a rattle-tailed snake."

I could make no connection between his two statements. I could only say, "Strange. She does not at all appear to have been ill."

"No, she recovered from the venom," he growled, "but not before she had made her confession to Filth Eater, and with me at her side. The only bad deed she confessed to Tlazoltéotl was her having lain with a man of another tribe. Then she had the misfortune not to die of the snakebite."

He shook his head somberly. So did I. He continued:

"We waited for her to recover her health, for it would be unseemly to execute an ailing woman. When she was well and strong again, we brought her here. This morning. To die."

I gazed at the remains, wondering what mode of execution could have left the victim without any mark but staring eyes and silently screaming mouth.

"Now we come to remove her," the widower concluded. "A good place of execution is not easy to find in the desert, so we do not desecrate this one by leaving our carrion to attract the vultures and coyotes. It was thoughtful of you, stranger, to have appreciated that fact." He laid a hand companionably on my shoulder. "But we will attend to the disposal, and then perhaps you will share our night's meal at our camp."

"Gladly," I said, and my empty stomach rumbled. But what happened next nearly spoiled my appetite.

The man went to where his wife sat, and he moved her in a way that had not occurred to me. I had tried laying her down. He gripped her under her armpits and lifted. Even so, she still moved reluctantly, and he visibly had to exert some strength. There was a horrid sucking and tearing sound, rather as if the dead woman's bottom *had* put down roots in the earth. Then she came up off the stake on which she had been impaled.

I knew then why the man had said that a good place of execution was not easy to find. It had to provide a tree of just the right size, one growing straight from the ground without obstructive roots. That stake had been a mizquitl sapling as big around as my forearm, severed at knee height, then sharped to a point at the top, but the coarse bark left on the rest of it. I wondered whether the betrayed husband had sat his wife delicately on the stake point and only slowly let her down its cruelly barked length, or whether he had given her a slightly more merciful quick downward shove. I wondered, but I did not inquire.

When the nine men led me to their camp, they made me welcome there, and they treated me courteously as long as I

stayed with them. They had thoroughly inspected the belongings I carried, but they stole nothing, not even my small store
of copper trade currency. However I think I might have been
treated otherwise if I had been carrying anything of value or
leading a train of laden porters. Those men were, after all, the
Chichiméca.

The name was always spoken among us Mexíca with contempt or derision or loathing, as you Spaniards speak of "barbarians" and "savages." We derived the name from chichíne,
one of our words meaning dog. When we said Chichiméca, we
generally referred to those dog people among whom I had then
arrived; the homeless, unwashed, forever wandering tribes of
the desert not far north of the Otomí lands. (Which is why,
some ten years earlier, I had been so indignant when the Fast
of Feet Rarámuri mistook *me* for a Chichimécatl.) Those of the
near north were sufficiently despied by us Mexíca, but it was
widely believed that there were others of even lower degree.
Farther north of the dog people supposedly lived still fiercer
desert tribes, which we designated the Téochichiméca—as one
might say, "the even more awful dog people." And in the
desert's farthest northernmost regions supposedly lived even
more fearsome tribes, which we called the Zácachichiméca,
much as to say, "the most depraved of all the dog people."

But I must report, after having traveled through almost the
whole extent of those desert lands, that I found none of those
tribes inferior or superior to another. They were all ignorant,
insensitive, and often inhumanly cruel, but it was that cruel
desert which had made them so. They all lived in a squalor
that would disgust a civilized man or a Christian, and they
lived on foods that would nauseate a city man's stomach. They
had no houses or trades or arts, because they had to keep
ceaselessly roaming to forage for the scant sustenance they
could wring from the desert. Though the Chichiméca tribes
among which I sojourned all spoke a coherent Náhuatl, or some
dialect of it, they had no word knowing or other education,
and some of their habits and customs were veritably repulsive.
But, while they would have horrified any civilized community
that they might ever try to visit, I have to say that the Chichiméca had admirably adapted themselves to life in the pitiless

desert, and I know few civilized men who could have done the same.

That first camp I visited, the only home its people knew, was just one more piece of the desert, on which they had elected to squat because they knew there was a seepage of underground water accessible by digging some way down in that particular patch of sand. The camp's only homelike aspect was the cooking fires of the tribe's sixteen or eighteen families. Except for the rudimentary cooking pots and utensils, there was no furniture. Near each fire was stacked each family's armory of hunting weapons and tools: a bow and some arrows, a javelin and its atlatl, a skinning knife, a meat-cutting ax, and the like. Only a few of those things were tipped or bladed with obsidian, that rock being a rare commodity in those regions. The majority of weapons were made of the copper-hard quauxelolóni wood, cunningly shaped and sharpened by fire.

Of course there were no solid-built houses, and only two temporary ones: crude little huts constructed by leaning deadwood sticks haphazardly together. In each hut, I was told, lay a pregnant woman awaiting childbirth, for which reason that camp was more permanent than most, meaning it might exist for several days instead of being merely the usual overnight stop for sleep. The rest of the tribe scorned any shelter. Men, women, and the smallest infant children slept on the ground, as I had lately been doing, but instead of a ground-softening blanket, like mine of felted rabbit hair, they used only old and dirty and tattered deerskins. Equally bedraggled animal skins also composed what sketchy clothing they wore: loinclothes for the men; sleeveless, shapeless, knee-length blouses for the women; nothing at all for the children, even those almost full grown.

But the vilest thing about the camp was its odor, which even the surrounding vastness of open air failed to dispel, and the odor was that of the dog people, every one of them far dirtier than any dog. It might be doubted that a person could get soiled in the desert, for sand is as clean as snow. But those people were mainly befouled with their own dirt, their own secretions, their own negligence. They let their sweat cake on their bodies, so it encrusted the other oils and scurfs that the body normally sheds in unnoticeable flakes. Every wrinkle and fold of their bodies was a tracery of dark grime: knuckles, wrists, throats, inner elbows, backs of knees. Their hair flapped in mats, not strands, and lice and fleas crawled among that greasy matting. Their skin garments, as well as their own skins, were permeated with the additional odors of wood smoke, dried blood, and rancid animal fats. The total stench was staggering, and, although I eventually ceased to notice it, I long thought the Chichiméca the filthiest people I had ever encountered, and the people most *uncaring* about their filthiness.

They all had extremely simple names—such as Zoquitl and Nacatl and Chachápa, which mean Mud and Meat and Cloudburst—names rather pitiably unsuited to their blighted and starved habitat; but then, maybe they chose such names in a spirit of wishfulness. Meat was the name of the newly made widower who had invited me to visit the camp. He and I sat down at the cooking fire built by a number of other unattached males, apart from the fires of the family groups. Meat and his fellows already knew that I was a Mexícatl, but I was uncomfortably uncertain how to refer to their nationality. So, while one of the men used a yuca-leaf ladle to serve each of us some unidentifiable stew on a curved segment of maguey leaf, I said:

"As you probably know, Meat, we Mexíca are accustomed to speak of all desert inhabitants as the Chichiméca. But no doubt you have another name for yourselves."

He indicated the scattering of campfires and said, "We here are the Tecuéxe tribe. There are many others in the desert—Pame, Janámbre, Hualahuíse, many others—but yes, we are all Chichiméca, since we are all red-skinned people." I privately thought that he and his tribesmen were more the gray color of grime. Meat swallowed a mouthful of stew and added, "You too are a Chichimécatl. No different from us."

I had resented the Rarámuri's calling me that. It was even more outrageous that a desert savage himself should claim kinship with a civilized Mexícatl. But he said it so casually that I realized he meant no presumption. It was true that, underneath their dirt, Meat and the other Tecuéxe were of a coppery complexion similar to my own and that of every other person I knew. Tribes and individuals of our race might vary, from palest red-gold to the ruddy brown of cacao, but, generally speaking, red-skinned was the most inclusive description. And so I understood: those scruffy, half-naked, ignorant nomads obviously believed that the name Chichiméca derived not from the chichíne, dog, but from the word chichíltic, meaning red. To anyone who chose to believe *that*, Chichiméca was no contemptuous name; it described every human being in every desert, every jungle, every civilized city of The One World.

I went on feeding my grateful belly—the stew was gritty with sand, but tasty nonetheless—and I meditated on the ties between diverse peoples. Clearly the Chichiméca must once have had some improving contact with civilization. Meat had mentioned his wife's imprudent sickbed confession to Tlazoltéotl, so I already knew of the Chiciméca's acquaintance with that goddess. I later learned that they worshiped most of our other gods as well. But, in their isolation and ignorance, they had invented a new one just for themselves. They held the laughable belief that the stars are butterflies made of obsidian, and that the stars' twinkling light is only a reflection of moonlight from those fluttering wings of shiny stone. So they had conceived a goddess—Itzpapálotl, Obsidian Butterfly—whom they regarded as the highest of all gods. Well, in the desert night, the stars *are* spectacularly bright, and they do seem to hover, like butterflies, just beyond one's reach.

But even if the Chiciméca have some things in common with more civilized peoples, and even if they interpret the very name Chiciméca to imply that all red-skinned peoples are somehow distantly related, they have no compunction about living at the expense of those relatives, distant or near. On that first night I dined with the Tecuéxe tribe, the mealtime stew contained bits of tender white meat flaking off delicate bones which I could not recognize as being the bones of lizards or rabbits or any other creatures I had seen in the desert. So I inquired:

"Meat, what is this meat we are eating?"

He grunted, "Baby."

"Baby what?"

He said again, "Baby," and shrugged. "Food for the hard times." He saw that I still did not comprehend, so he explained, "We sometimes leave the desert to pillage an Otomí village and we take, among other things, their infant children. Or we might fight with another Chichiméca tribe in the open desert. When the defeated tribe withdraws, it must leave those of its children too small to run. Since such tiny captives would be of no other use to their captors, they are gutted and cured in the sun, or smoked over a mizquitl fire, so they last a long time without spoiling. They weigh little, so each of our women can easily carry three or four of them dangling from a cord around her waist. They are carried to be cooked and eaten when—as happened today—Obsidian Butterfly neglects to send game for our arrows."

I can see from your faces, reverend scribes, that you deem that practice reprehensible. But I must confess that I learned to eat *almost* anything edible, with as much satisfaction and as little repugnance as any Chichimécatl, for during that desert journey I knew no laws more peremptory than those of hunger and thirst. Nevertheless, I did not totally discard the manners and discriminations of civilization. There were other dietary eccentricities of the Chichiméca in which not even the direst deprivations could make me participate.

I accompanied Meat and his fellows as long as their wanderings tended more or less northward, in the way I was going. Then, when the Tecuéxe decided to veer off to the east, Meat kindly escorted me to the camp of another tribe, the Tzacatéca, and introduced me to a friend there with whom he had often done battle, a man named Greenery. So I went along with the Tzacatéca as long as they drifted northward, and, when our paths diverged, Greenery in turn introduced me to another friend, by the name of Banquet, of the Hua tribe. Thus I was handed on from one band of Chichiméca to another—to the Tobóso, the Iritíla, the Mapimí—and thus it was that I lived in the desert through all the seasons of an entire year, and thus it was that I observed some really disgusting customs of the Chichiméca.

In the late summer and early autumn of the year, the various desert cactuses put out their fruit. I have mentioned the towering quinámetl cactus, which resembles an immense green man with many uplifted arms. It bears the fruit called the pitaáya, which is admittedly tasty and nourishing, but I think it is most prized because it is so difficult of acquisition. Since no man can climb a spine-clothed quinámetl, the fruit can be coaxed loose only with the aid of long poles or thrown rocks. Anyway, the pitaáya is a favorite delicacy of the desert dwellers—such a luxury that they eat each fruit *twice*.

A Chichimécatl man or woman will gobble one of the purplish globes entire, pulp and juice and black seeds together, and then wait for what those people call the ynic ome pixquitl, or "second harvest." That means only that the eaters digest the fruit and excrete the residue, among which are the undigested pitaáya seeds. As soon as a person has voided his bowels, he examines his excrement, he fingers through it and picks out those nutlike seeds and then eats them again, voluptuously crunching and chewing them to extract their full flavor and measure of nourishment. If a man or woman finds a trace of other excrement anywhere in the desert in that season—whether it be the droppings of an animal or vulture or another human—he or she will leap to examine it and paw through it, in hope of finding overlooked pitaáya seeds to appropriate and eat.

There is another practice of those people which I found even more repellent, but to describe it I must explain something. When I had been traveling in the desert for almost a year, and the springtime came—I was at that time in the company of the Iritíla tribe—I saw that Tlaloc *does* condescend to spill some of his rain upon the desert. For about a month of twenty days, he rains. On some of those days he storms so liberally that the desert's long-dry gullies become raging, frothing torrents. But Tlaloc's dispensation continues for no longer than that one month, and the water soon is sucked into the sands. So it is only during those twenty or so days of rain that the desert becomes briefly colorful, with flowers on the cactuses and the otherwise sere scrub bushes. At that time, too, in places where the ground stays soggy long enough, the desert sprouts a growth I had not seen before: a mushroom called the chichinanácatl. It consists of a skinny stem topped by a blood-red cap which is disfigured by white warts.

The Iritíla women eagerly gathered those mushrooms, but they never served any of them in the meals they prepared, and I thought that odd. During that same short, moist springtime, the chief of the Iritíla ceased to urinate on the ground like other men. During that time, one of his wives carried always and everywhere a special clay bowl. Whenever the chief felt the urge to relieve himself, she held the bowl and he urinated into it. And there was one other odd circumstance during that season: each day, various of the Iritíla males would be too drunk to go out hunting or foraging, and I could not imagine how they could have found or concocted a drunk-making drink. It was a while before I discerned the connection among those various odd things and events.

There was really no great mystery. The mushrooms were reserved to be eaten only by the chief of the tribe. The eating of them gives the eater a sort of combined drunkenness and delicious hallucination, rather like the effect of chewing peyotl. And the inebriating effect of the chichinanácatl is only a little diminished by its being eaten and digested; whatever magical substance it contains goes right through the human body and out by way of the bladder. While the chief was in a constant state of happy stupefaction, he was also frequently urinating into his bowl, and his urine was almost as potent an intoxicant as the original mushrooms.

The first full bowl was passed among his wise men and sorcerers. Each of them swigged greedily from it, and soon was staggering about or lying sodden in bliss. The next full bowl went to the chief's closest friends, the next to the tribe's more stalwart warriors, and so on. Before many days had passed, the bowl was circulating among the tribe's lesser men and oldsters, and finally even among the females. Eventually all the Iritíla enjoyed at least one brief respite from the lackluster existence they endured during the rest of the year. The bowl was even hospitably proffered to the stranger among them, but I respectfully declined the treat, and no one seemed insulted or sorry that I did not take a portion of the precious urine.

Despite the Chichiméca's numerous and flagrant depravities, I ought in fairness to say that those desert people are not entirely degraded and detestable. For one thing, I gradually realized that they are not unclean of body and verminous and smelly because they *want* to be. During seventeen months of the year, every drop of water that can be wrung from the desert—if it is not immediately and avidly lapped up by a thirsty tongue—must be hoarded against the day when there is not even a meagerly moist cactus within reach, and there are many such days. During seventeen months of the year, water is for the inside of the body, not the outside. The short and fleeting season of early spring is the only time when the desert provides water to spare for the luxury of bathing. Like me, every member of the Iritíla tribe took advantage of that opportunity to bathe as thoroughly and as often as possible. And, disencumbered of filth, a Chichimécatl looks as human as any civilized person.

I remember one lovely sight I saw. It was late one afternoon, and I had wandered idly some distance from the place where the Iritíla had just made camp for the night, and I came upon a young woman taking what was obviously her first bath of the year. She stood in the middle of a small and shallow rain pool caught in a rock basin, and she was alone, no doubt wanting to enjoy the pure water before others also found it and came jostling to share and dirty it. I did not make my presence known, but watched through my seeing crystal, while she lathered herself with the soaplike root of an amóli plant and then rinsed repeatedly—but slowly, leisurely, savoring the unaccustomed pleasure of the occasion.

Tlaloc was preparing a storm in the east, behind her, erecting a wall of clouds as dark as a wall of slate. At first, the girl was almost indistinguishable against it, she was so discolored by her year's accumulation of dirt. But as she lathered and rinsed away layer after layer, her normal skin color came clearer and clearer. Tonatíu was setting in the west, and his beams accentuated the copper-gold of her. In that vast landscape, stretching flat and empty all the way to the dark cloud wall at the horizon, the young woman was the only bright thing. The curves of her naked body were outlined by their gleam of wetness, her clean hair glistened, the water she splashed upon herself broke into drops that glittered like jewels. Against the menacing storm sky behind her, she shone in the last sunlight as prettily as a small piece of glowing amber laid on a great dull slab of slate.

It had been a long time since I had lain with a woman, and that one, clean and comely, was a powerful temptation. But I remembered another woman—impaled on a stake—and I did not go near the pool until the girl finally, reluctantly left it.

During all my wanderings with the various Chichiméca tribes, I took care not to trifle with their women or to disobey any of their few laws or to offend them in any other manner. So I was treated by every tribe as a fellow wanderer and an equal. I was never robbed or mistreated, I was given my share of whatever pitiful fare and comfort they themselves could wrest from the desert—except for the occasional treats I declined, like the bliss-giving urine. The only favor I asked of any of them was information: what they might know of the long-ago Aztéca and their long-ago journey and the rumor that they had buried stores of supplies along their route.

I was told by Meat of the Tecuéxe, and by Greenery of the Tzacatéca, and by Banquet of the Hua, "Yes, it is known that such a tribe once came through some of these lands. We know nothing else of them except that, like us, like all Chichiméca, they carried little with them and they left nothing of it behind."

It was the same discouraging reply I had kept hearing from the very beginning of my quest, and I continued to hear that same discouraging reply when I put my query to the Tobóso, to the Iritíla, and to every other tribe with which I traveled for even the briefest time or the shortest distance. Not until my second summer in that accursed desert, by which time I was unutterably sick of it and of my Aztéca ancestors as well, did my question elicit a slightly different response.

I had attached myself to the tribe called Mapimí, and its habitat was the hottest, driest, most dismal desert region of all those I had yet crossed. It was so incalculably far north of the living lands that I would have sworn there could *be* no more desert beyond. But indeed there was, said the Mapimí, illimitable expanses of it, and even more terrible terrain than any I had seen. That information was naturally distressing to my ears, and so were the opening words of the man to whom I wearily put my stale old question about the Aztéca.

"Yes, Mixtli," he said. "There was once such a tribe, and they made such a journey as you describe. But they brought nothing with them . . ."

"And," I finished for him, my voice bitter, "they left nothing when they were gone."

"Except us," he said.

It took a moment for those words to penetrate my dejectedness, but then I gaped at him, struck dumb.

He smiled a toothless smile. He was Patzcatl, chief of the Mapimí, a very old man, shrunken and shriveled dry by the sun, and he was even more incongruously named than most other Chichiméca, since Patzcatl means Juice. He said:

"You spoke of the Aztéca's journey, from some unknown homeland called Aztlan. And you spoke of their ultimate destination, the great city they founded far to the south of here. We Mapimí and other Chichiméca, during all the sheaves of years we have inhabited these deserts, we have heard rumors of that city and its grandeur, but none of us has ever approached anywhere near enough to glimpse it. So think, Mixtli. Does it not strike you as remarkable that we barbarians, so distant from your Tenochtítlan and so ignorant of it, should nevertheless speak the same Náhuatl you speak there?"

I considered and said, "Yes, Chief Juice. I was surprised and pleased to find that I could converse with so many different tribes, but I did not pause to wonder why that should be possible. Have you a theory to account for it?"

"More than a theory," he said, with some pride. "I am an old man, and I come from a long line of fathers, all of whom lived to a great age. But I and they were not always old, and in our youth we were inquisitive. Each asked questions and remembered the answers. So each learned and repeated to his sons what knowledge had been preserved of our people's origins."

"I should be grateful for a sharing of your knowledge, venerable chief."

"Know then," said old Juice. "The legends tell that *seven* different tribes—among them your Aztéca—departed long ago from that Aztlan, The Place of Snowy Egrets, in search of a more pleasant place to live. The tribes were all related, they spoke the same language and recognized the same gods and observed the same customs, and for a long while that mixed company traveled amicably. But, as you might expect, among so many persons on such a long journey, there arose frictions and dissensions. Along the way, various of them dropped out of the march—families, whole calpúli clans, even entire tribes. Some quarreled and left, some stopped from sheer fatigue, some took a liking to a place in which they found themselves and decided to go no farther. It is impossible now to say which of them went where. Over the sheaves of years since then, those truant tribes themselves have often fragmented and moved apart. It is known that your Aztéca continued all the way to wherever your Tenochtítlan now stands, and perhaps others also traveled that far. But we were not among them, we who are now the Chichiméca. That is why I say this. When your Aztéca crossed the desert lands, they left no stores for future use, they left no trace, they left nothing behind them but us."

His account sounded all too believable, and it was as disconcerting as the assertion of my earlier companion Meat: that the term Chichiméca embraced all peoples of our skin color. The implication was that, instead of finding anything of possible value, like the allegedly hidden hoards of stores, I had found only a horrid rabble eager to claim kinship as my cousins. Quickly putting that ghastly possibility out of my mind, I said with a sigh:

"I still would like to discover the whereabouts of Aztlan."

Chief Juice nodded, but said, "It is far from here. As I told you, the seven tribes came a long way from their homeland before they began to separate."

I looked northward, into what I had been told was an even more awful and limitless desert, and I groaned. *"Ayya, then I must keep on through this blighted and accursed wasteland. . . ."*

The old man glanced in that direction. He looked mildly puzzled and he asked, "Why?"

Probably I also looked puzzled, at such a foolish question from a man I had thought fairly intelligent. I said, "The Aztéca came from the north. Where else should I be going?"

"North is not a *place,"* he explained, as if I were the dullard. "It is a direction, and an imprecise direction at that. You have already come too far north."

I cried, "Aztlan is *behind* me?"

He chuckled at my dismay. "Behind, beside, and beyond."

I said impatiently, "And you speak of imprecise directions!"

Still laughing, he went on, "By keeping to the desert all the way, you moved always in a direction west and north, but not enough to the west. Had you not been misled by the notion of *north,* you might have found Aztlan long ago, without ever braving the desert, without ever leaving the living lands."

I made some sort of strangled noise. The chief continued:

"According to my fathers' fathers, *our* Aztlan was somewhere southwest of this desert, on the seashore, on the coast of the great sea, and surely there was never more than one Aztlan. But from there, our ancestors—and yours—did much circuitous wandering in those sheaves of years. Quite possibly the Aztéca's last march, as remembered in your Mexíca legends, *did* bring them directly from the north into what is now Tenochtítlan. Nevertheless, Aztlan should lie almost directly northwest of there."

"So I must go back again . . . southwest from here . . ." I muttered, regretting all the dreary months and tedious one-long-runs and dirt and misery I had needlessly endured.

Old Juice shrugged. "I do not say you must. But if you *will* go on, I advise against your going farther north. Aztlan is not there. Northward is only more desert, more terrible desert, merciless desert in which even we hardy Mapimí cannot live. Only the Yaki can make even brief forays into that desert, and they only because they are more cruel than the desert itself."

I said, with sadness at the recollection, "I know what the Yaki are like. I will turn back, Chief Juice, as you advise."

"Go yonder." He gestured to the southward of where Tonatíu was dropping ungowned into an unquilted bed behind the indistinct gray-white mountains which had kept pace with me—but kept their distance—all the way I had come through the desert. "If you would find Aztlan, you must go to those mountains, over those mountains, through those mountains. Beyond those mountains you must go."

⌘

And that is what I did: I went southwest, to and over and through and beyond the mountains. I had been seeing that remote, pale range for more than a year, and I fully expected to have to scale walls of sheer granite. But as I neared them, I saw that it had been only their distance that had made them appear so. The foothills rising from the desert were sparsely covered with typical dusty desert scrub, but the growth got denser and greener as I progressed. The genuine high mountains, when I reached them, I found to be as verdantly forested and hospitable as those of the Rarámuri country. Indeed, as I made my way through those mountains, I found cave villages where the inhabitants resembled the Rarámuri—even in the matter of bodily hair—and spoke very similar languages, and told me that they were in fact relatives of the Rarámuri, whose country, they said, was considerably farther north in that same mountain range.

So, when I came down from those heights at last, on the other side of the ranges, I came down to a beach somewhere south of the beach where I had landed after my involuntary sea voyage, more than ten years before. That coast is called the Sinalobóla, I learned from the fisher tribes whose villages I found dotted along it. Those people, the Kaíta, were not hostile to my traveling along their beaches, but neither were they inviting, they were simply indifferent; and their women smelled of fish. So I did not linger long in any of their villages as I went south along the Sinalobóla, trusting in old Chief Juice's assertion that Aztlan was somewhere on that "coast of the great sea."

For most of my way, I kept to the level sands of the shore, with the ocean on my right hand. Sometimes I had to turn far inland to skirt a sizable lagoon or a coastal swamp or an impenetrable tangle of the stringy mangrove trees, and sometimes I had to wait on the bank of a river full of alligators until a Kaíta boatman came by who would grudgingly ferry me to the other side. But my progress was more often rapid, unhindered, and uneventful. A cool breeze from off the ocean tempered the heat of the daytime sun, and after sundown the beach sands retained that same heat, so they were most comfortable to sleep on.

Long after I had left the Kaíta lands and found no more villages where I could buy a meal of fish, I was able to dine well on those same odd drumming crabs that had frightened me when I first encountered them, years before. Also, the ocean's tidal movement led me to discover another seafood which I commend as a superbly tasty dish. I noticed that, whenever the waters receded, the flats of mud or sand were not entirely quiescent. Here and there, little spouts and plumes of water quirted upward from the exposed sea bed. Impelled by curiosity, I sloshed out across the flats, waited for one of the little wisps to squirt nearby, and dug down with my hands to find what had caused it. I came up with an ovoid, smooth blue shell, a clam as big as my palm. I suppose the spurt of water was its way of coughing sand out of its throat, or whatever a clam uses for a throat. Anyway, I splashed about the flats and collected an armload of the shellfish and took them ashore, intending to eat them raw.

But then I had a notion. I dug a shallow pit in the dry beach sand and laid the clams in it, first wrapping each shell in damp seaweed to prevent any grit from getting inside, then I piled a layer of sand over them. On top of that I laid a fire of hot-burning dead palm fronds, and let it blaze for a time, then scraped its ashes aside and disinterred my clams. Their shells had acted as miniature steam-bath houses, cooking them in their own salty juices. I pried off their upper shells and ate them—hot, tender, delicious—and I slurped the liquid from their nether shells, and I tell you: I have seldom enjoyed a better meal served up by even a palace kitchen.

As I continued on down the interminable coast, however, the tides no longer uncovered smooth and accessible flats onto which I could stroll to gather clams. The tides simply raised or lowered the level of the water standing in the boundless marshes which I found in my path. Those were thickets of almost junglelike undergrowth tangled among moss-hung mangroves which stood fastidiously high upon their multiple roots. At low tide, the swamp ground was a morass of slimy mud and stagnant puddles. At high tide, it was covered by great sheets of sullen salt water. At all times, the marshes were hot, damp, sticky, stinking, and infested with voracious mosquitoes. I tried to go eastward and find a way around them, but the swamps appeared to extend inland as far as the mountain ranges. So I made my way through them as best I could, wherever possible leaping from one to the next of the drier hummocks of land, the rest of the time wading in wretched discomfort through the fetid water and mud.

I do not remember how many days I struggled slowly through that ugliest, nastiest, and most disagreeable piece of country I had ever encountered. I lived mainly on palm sprouts and mexíxin cress and other such greens that I recognized as edible. I slept each night by choosing a tree with a crotch high out of the reach of any passing alligator and the crawling night mists. I would pad that with as much gray paxtli moss as I could gather, and then wedge myself in it. I was not much surprised that I met no other human being, for none but the most torpid and spiritless of humans would have lived in that noxious wilderness. I had no idea what nation it belonged to, or if any had ever bothered to lay claim to it. I knew I was by then far south of the Sinalobóla of the Kaíta, and I guessed that I must be nearing the land of Nauyar Ixú, but I could not be sure until I heard somebody speak some word of some language.

And then, one afternoon, in the depths of that miserable swamp, I did come upon another human being. A loinclothed young man stood beside a scummy pool of water, peering down into it, holding poised over it a crude spear of three bone points. I was so surprised to see anybody, and so glad, that I did an inexcusable thing. I hailed him in a loud voice—at the very moment he struck his spear down into the water. He snapped his head up, glared at me, and replied in a snarl:

"You made me miss!"

I stood amazed—not by his rude words, for he had reason to resent my having spoiled his aim—but by his not having spoken, as I would have expected, in some dialect of Poré.

"I am sorry," I called, less loudly. He merely dropped his gaze to the water again, wrenching his spear loose from the muck at the bottom, while I approached him quietly and unobtrusively. As I reached his side, he jabbed down with the spear once more, and that time brought it up with a frog wriggling impaled on one of its tines.

"You speak Náhuatl," I said. He grunted and dropped the frog onto a pile of others in a lopsided basket of woven vines. Wondering if I had found a descendant of some stay-at-home ancestor of old Chief Juice, I asked, "Are you a Chichimécatl?" I would of course have been surprised if he had said he was, but what he did say was even more astounding:

"I am an Aztécatl." He leaned over the scummy pool again and slanted his spear and added, "And I am busy."

"And you have a most discourteous way of greeting a stranger," I said. His surliness dispelled whatever awe and stupefaction I might otherwise have been feeling at the discovery of an apparently actual, living, breathing remnant of the Aztéca.

"Courtesy would be wasted on any stranger so misguided as to come here," he growled, not even looking at me. The dirty water splashed as he skewered another frog. "Would any but a fool be visiting this stinking sink of the world?"

I remarked, "Any fool living in it has little cause to insult one who merely visits."

"You are right," he said indifferently, dropping the frog in his basket. "Why do you stand here being insulted by another fool? Go away."

I said tightly, "I have traveled for two years and thousands of one-long-runs, in search of a place called Aztlan. Perhaps you can tell me—"

"You have found it," he interrupted, in an uncaring voice.

"Here?" I exclaimed, in utter astonishment.

"Just yonder," he grunted, jerking a thumb over his shoulder, still not troubling to lift his eyes from his putrid frog pond. "Follow the path to the lagoon, then shout for a boat to take you across."

I turned away from him and looked, and there *was* a path leading off through the rank undergrowth, and I started along it, hardly daring to believe. . . .

But then I remembered that I had not thanked the young man. I turned again and walked back to where he stood aiming his spear at the pond. "Thank you," I said, and I kicked his legs out from under him, so he fell with a mighty splash into the foul water. When his head broke the surface, festooned with slimy weeds, I dumped the basket of dead frogs onto him. Leaving him spluttering and cursing and clawing for a hold on the slippery bank, I turned yet again and walked toward The Place of the Snowy Egrets, the long-lost, the legendary Aztlan.

I do not really know what I expected or hoped to find. Perhaps an early, less elaborate version of Tenochtítlan? A city of pyramids and temples and towers, only not so modern of design? I do not really know. But what I did find was pitiful.

I followed the dry path winding through the marsh, and the trees around me grew farther and farther apart, the mud on either side of me became more wet and watery. At last the downward-dangling mangrove roots gave place to reeds growing upward through a sheet of water. There the path ended and

I was standing on the shore of a lake stained blood-red by the setting sun. It was a great expanse of brackish water, but not a very deep one, to judge from the reeds and canes piercing its surface and the white egrets standing everywhere. Directly in front of me was an island, perhaps two arrow shots distant across the water, and I raised my crystal for a clear look at the place to which those egrets had given the name.

Aztlan was an island in a lake, as is Mexíco-Tenochtítlan, but there, it seemed, the resemblance ended. It was a low hump of dry land made not much higher by the city erected upon it, for there was not a building visible that was of more than one floor. There was not a single upthrusting pyramid, not even a temple tall enough to be seen. The island's sunset redness was overlaid with the blue smoke of evening hearth fires. From the lake around, numerous dugout canoes moved homeward toward the island, and I shouted to the nearest of them.

The man aboard was propelling it with a pole, the lake being too shallow to require the use of a paddle. He slid the canoe through the reeds to where I stood, then peered suspiciously at me and grunted a profanity and said, "You are not the—you are a stranger."

And you are another ill-bred Aztécatl, I thought, but did not say aloud. I stepped into the boat before he could move it away, and said, "If you came for the frog sticker, he claims to be busy, and I believe he is. You will please convey me to the island."

Except for a repetition of the profanity, he made no protest and evinced no curiosity and said not another word as he poled me across the water. He let me step ashore on the edge of the island, then went away—through one of what I then discovered were several canals cut through the island, its only other resemblance to Tenochtítlan. I strolled along the streets for a while. Besides a wide one circling the island's rim, there were only four others, two running the length of the island, two crossing it, all of them primitively paved with crushed oyster and clam shells. The houses and huts that crowded wall to wall along the streets and canals, though I suppose they had wooden frameworks, were plastered with a white surfacing also made of powdered shells.

The island was oval-shaped and quite large, about the size

of Tenochtítlan without its northern district of Tlaltelólco. It probably had as many buildings too, but, since they were only of one level, they did not contain anything like the teeming population of Tenochtítlan. From the center of the island I could see the rest of the surrounding lake, and could see that the lake was also surrounded in all directions by the same feculent marsh through which I had come. The Aztéca at least were not so degraded as to live *in* that dismal swamp, but they might as well have done. The intervening lake waters did not prevent the swamp's night mists and miasmas and mosquitoes from invading the island. Aztlan was a thoroughly unwholesome habitat, and I was glad that my ancestors had had the good sense to abandon it.

I took the current inhabitants to be the descendants of those who had been too dull and listless to have left it in search of a better place to live. And, so far as I could tell, the descendants of the stay-behinds had not acquired any more initiative or enterprise in all the generations since. They seemed defeated and beaten down by their wretched surroundings, and resentful of them, but drearily resigned to them. The people on the streets gave me a glance of knowing me for a newcomer, and a newcomer certainly must have been a rarity there, but not one of them commented to another on my presence. Not one gave me greeting, or kindly inquired if I was as hungry as I doubtless looked, or even sneered at me for an unwelcome intruder.

The night came on, and the streets began to empty of people, and the darkness was relieved only by the fitful gleams of hearth fires and coconut-oil lamps leaking out from the houses. I had seen enough of the city, and in any case could then see very little, which meant I was likely at any moment to walk off the verge of a canal. So I intercepted a latecomer trying to hurry by me unnoticed, and asked him where I could find the palace of the city's Revered Speaker.

"Palace?" he repeated vacantly. "Revered Speaker?"

I should have known that anything like a palace would be inconceivable to those hut dwellers. And I should have remembered that no Revered Speaker of the Aztéca had adopted that title until long after they had become the Mexíca. I amended my question:

"I seek your ruler. Where does he reside?"

"Ah, the Tlatocapíli," said the man, and Tlatocapíli means nothing more eminent than a tribal chief, like the leader of any barbarian desert rabble. The man gave me hurried directions, then said, "Now I am late for my meal," and vanished in the night. For a people marooned in the middle of nowhere, with so little of *anything* to occupy them, they seemed foolishly fond of pretending urgency and activity.

Though the Aztéca of Aztlan spoke Náhuatl, they used many words that I suppose we Mexíca long ago discarded, and others that they obviously had adopted from neighbor tribes, for I recognized some of them as Kaíta and corrupt Poré. On the other hand, the Aztéca were uncomprehending of many Náhuatl words I used—words that I suppose had come into the language after the migration, inspired by things and circumstances in the outside world of which those stay-at-homes knew nothing. After all, our language still changes to accommodate itself to new situations. Just in recent years, for example, it has added such words as cahuáyo for horse, Crixtanóyotl for Christianity, Caxtiltéca for Castilians and Spaniards in general, pitzóme for pigs. . . .

The city's "palace" was at least a decently constructed house, faced with shining shell plaster, and of several rooms. I was met at the entrance by a young woman who said she was the wife of the Tlatocapíli. She did not bid me enter, but nervously asked what I wanted.

"I want to see the Tlatocapíli," I said, with the last of my patience. "I have come a long way, especially to see him."

"You have?" she said, biting her lip. "Few come to see him, and he cares to see even fewer. Anyway, he is not home yet."

"May I come in and wait?" I asked testily.

She thought it over, then stood aside, saying indecisively, "I suppose you may. But he will be hungry, and wanting to eat before anything else." I started to remark that I would not mind something of that sort myself, but she went on, "He desired to eat frogs' legs tonight, so he had to go to the mainland, since the lake is too salty for them. And the catch must have been scant, for he is very late coming home."

I nearly backed out of the house again. But then I thought: can the punishment for ducking the Tlatocapíli be any worse than spending the night trying to avoid him by wandering this vile island among the pestilent mosquitoes? I followed her through a room where a number of young children and very old folks sat eating a meal of swamp greens. They all goggled at me, but said nothing, and offered me no place at the cloth. She led me to an empty room, where I gratefully sat down on a rough icpáli chair. I asked her:

"How does one address the Tlatocapíli?"

"His name is Tliléctic-Mixtli."

I almost fell off the low chair, the coincidence was so startling. If he was also Dark Cloud, what should I call myself? Certainly a man whom I had kicked into a pond would take me for an impudent mocker if I introduced myself with *his* name. Just then, from the outer room, came the noise of his arrival, and his timorous wife ran to welcome her lord and master. I slid my knife around to the back of my waistband, out of sight, and kept my right hand near it.

I heard the murmur of the woman's voice, then the roar of the husband's: "A visitor to see me? To Míctlan with him! I am starving! Prepare these frogs, woman! I had to catch the cursed things twice!" His wife murmured meekly again, and he roared more loudly, "What? *A stranger?*"

With a savage jerk, he tore aside the curtain at the doorway of the room where I sat. It was indeed the same young man; he still had some of the pond weeds in his hair and he was clotted with mud from his waist down. He glared for an instant, then bellowed, *"You!"*

I bent from my chair to kiss the earth, but I made the gesture using my left hand, and I still had my right on the haft of my knife when I politely got to my feet. Then, to my great surprise, the young man burst into a peal of hearty laughter and leapt forward to fling his arms around me in a brotherly hug. His wife and several of the younger and older relatives peeked around the door frame, their eyes wide with wonder.

"Welcome, stranger!" he shouted, and laughed some more. "By the splayed legs of the goddess Coyolxaúqui, I am pleased to see you again. Just look what you did to me, man! When I finally got out of that sump, all the canoes had gone for the night. I had to wade home across the lake."

I asked cautiously, "You found that amusing?"

He laughed some more. "By the cold hole of the moon

goddess's dry tipíli, yes! Yes, I did! In all my lifetime in this weary and wearisome backwater, it was the first occurrence not ordinary and expectable. I thank you for making one unusual thing happen at last in this abyss of monotony. How are you called, stranger?"

I said, "My name is, er, Tepetzálan," taking that of my father for the occasion.

"Valley?" he said. "Tallest valley I ever saw. Well, Tepetzálan, do not fear any retaliation for your treatment of me. By the flabby teats of the goddess, it is a pleasure finally to meet a man with testicles under his loincloth. If my tribesmen have any, they display them only to their women." He turned to bark at his own woman, "There are frogs enough for my friend and myself. Prepare them while I steam away some of this muck. Friend Tepetzálan, perhaps you would also like a refreshing bath?"

As we stripped at the steam house behind the residence—and I took note that his torso was as hairless as mine—the Tlatocapíli said, "I presume you are one of our cousins from the far desert. No nearer neighbors speak our language."

"One of your cousins, I think," I said. "But not from the desert. Do you know of the Mexíca nation? Of the great city Tenochtítlan?"

"No," he said carelessly, as if his ignorance was nothing to be ashamed of. He even said, "Among the various miserable villages in these parts, Aztlan is the only city." I did not laugh, and he went on, "We pride ourselves on our self-sufficiency here, so we seldom go traveling or engage in traffic with any other tribes. We know only our closest neighbors, though we care not to mingle with them. To the north of these swamps, for instance, are the Kaíta. Since you came from that direction, you must have recognized them as a paltry people. In the swamps south of here, there is only the single insignificant village of Yakóreke."

I was pleased to hear that. If Yakóreke was the nearest community to the southward, then I was closer to home than I had reckoned. Yakóreke was an outpost village of the Nauyar Ixú lands subject to the Purémpecha nation. From anywhere in Nauyar Ixú it was not an impossibly long journey to Michihuácan, and beyond that country lay the lands of The Triple Alliance.

The young man continued, "Eastward of these swamps are the high mountains, in which dwell peoples called the Cora and the Huichol. Beyond those mountains lies a desert wasteland where some of our poor relations have long lived in exile. Only once in a great while does one of them find his way here to the home of his forefathers."

I said, "I know of your poor relations in the desert. But I repeat, I am not one of them. And I also know that not all of your distant relations are poor. Of those who left here so long ago to seek their fortune in the outside world, some of them did find a fortune, a fortune beyond your imagining."

"I rejoice to hear it," he said indifferently. "My wife's grandfather will be even more pleased. He is Aztlan's Rememberer of History."

That remark made me realize that, of course, the Aztéca could have no knowledge of picture writing. We Mexíca had attained it only long after the migration. So they could not possess any history books or other archives. If they relied on an old man to be the repository of their history, then he would be only the latest in a long line of old men who had handed that history down through the ages, one to another.

The other Mixtli went on, "The gods know that this crack in the buttocks of the world is no joyous place to live. But we live here because it has everything we need for life. The tides bring us seafood to eat, without our even having to seek it. The coconut gives us sweets, and oil for our lamps, and its liquid is fermented into a most enjoyably intoxicating drink. Another kind of palm gives us fiber from which to weave cloth, another yields flour, another bears the coyacapúli fruit. We need not trade for any resource with any other tribes, and the swamps protect us from molestation by them...."

He went on with his unenthusiastic listing of the awful Aztlan's natural advantages, but I had ceased listening. I felt slightly dazed, realizing how *very* remotely related I was to my "cousin" of the same name. It is possible that we two Mixtlis could have sat down and traced our lineage back to a common ancestor, but our divergent development had moved us far apart in more than distance. We were separated by an immeasurable disparity of education and outlook. That cousin Mixtli might as well have been living in the Aztlan of antiquity from which his ancestors had refused to stir, for Aztlan was still what it had been then: the abode of unadventurous sluggards. Ignorant of picture writing, they were equally ignorant of all it could teach: arithmetic, geography, architecture, commerce, conquest. They knew even less than the barbarian cousins they despised, the desert Chichiméca, who had at least ventured *some* way beyond Aztlan's constricted horizons.

Because my forebears had left that hind end of nowhere and had found a place where the art of word knowing flourished, I had had access to the libraries of the knowledge and experience accumulated by the Aztéca-Mexíca in all the subsequent sheaves of years, not to mention the finer arts and sciences of even older civilizations. Culturally and intellectually, I was as superior to my cousin Mixtli as a god might be to me. But I decided I would refrain from flaunting that superiority. It was not his fault that he had been deprived of my advantages through the lethargy of his ancestors. I felt sorry for that cousin Mixtli. I would do what I could to coax him out of his benighted Aztlan into the enlightened modern world.

His wife's grandfather, Canaútli, the aged historian, sat with us while we dined. The old man was one of the persons I had earlier seen eating the unlovely swamp greens, and he watched rather wistfully as we two Mixtlis savored our dish of delicate frogs' legs. I think old Canaútli paid more attention to our lip smacking and chop licking than he did to my discourse. Hungry though I was, I managed, between mouthfuls, to tell briefly what had become of the Aztéca who had departed Aztlan: how they had become known as the Tenóchca, then as the Mexíca, then as the foremost lords of The One World. The old man and the young one occasionally shook their heads in mute admiration—or maybe disbelief—as I recounted one achievement and advancement and war triumph after another.

The Tlatocapíli interrupted once to murmur, "By the six fragments of the goddess, if the Mexíca have become all that grand, perhaps we ought to change the name of Aztlan." Meditatively, he tried two or three new names: "Place of the Mexíca. First Homeland of the Mexíca..."

I went on to give a brief biography of the Mexíca's current

Uey-Tlatoáni, Motecuzóma, then a lyrical description of his capital city of Tenochtítlan. The old grandfather sighed and closed his eyes, as if to see it better in his imagination.

I said, "The Mexíca could not have progressed so far and so fast if they had not availed themselves of the art of word knowing." Then I hinted heavily, "You too, Tlatocapíli Mixtli, might make of Aztlan a grander city—make your people the equals of their Mexíca cousins—if you learned how to preserve the spoken word in lasting pictures."

He shrugged and said, "We have not yet suffered by not knowing."

Nevertheless, his interest seemed to quicken when I showed him—using a slender frog bone to scratch the hard earth of the floor—how simply his own name could be permanently graven.

"Yes, that is a cloud shape," he conceded. "But how could it say *Dark* Cloud?"

"Merely color it with a dark paint, gray or black. A single picture is capable of infinite useful variations. Paint that figure blue-green, for example, and you have the name Jadestone Cloud."

"Is that so?" he said, and then, "What is jadestone?" And the gulf gaped again between us. He had never seen or even heard of the mineral held sacred by all civilized peoples.

I muttered something about the night getting late, that I would tell more on the morrow. My cousin offered me a pallet for the night, if I did not object to sleeping in a room full of some other probable male relations of mine. I thanked him and accepted, and concluded my evening's discourse by explaining how I had come to Aztlan: tracking backward along my ancestors' route of march, trying to verify a legend. I turned to old Canaútli and said:

"Perhaps you would know, venerable Rememberer of History. When they left here, did they carry a sufficiency of supplies that they could have made provision for a necessary return?"

He did not reply. The venerable Rememberer had fallen asleep.

But the next day he said, "Your ancestors took almost nothing with them when they left here."

I had breakfasted together with the whole "palace family," on tiny fish and mushrooms grilled together, and some kind of hot herb drink. Then my namesake had gone out on some civic business, leaving me to converse with the aged historian. But that day, unlike the night before, it was Canaútli who did most of the talking.

"If all our Rememberers have spoken truly, those people who departed took only what belongings they could pack in a hurry, and only meager rations for the march. And they took the image of their villainous new god: a wooden image newly and roughly and hastily made, because of the urgency of their going. But that was untold sheaves of years ago. I daresay your people have built many finer statues to replace it since then. We of Aztlan have a different high deity, and only the one image of it. Oh, of course we recognize all the other gods, and have recourse to them when necessary. Tlazoltéotl, for instance, cleanses us of our sins; Atláua fills our fowlers' nets, and so on. But only one reigns supreme. Come, cousin, let me show you."

He took me out of the house and along the city's shell streets. As we walked, his birdlike little black eyes flung an occasional look sideways from their nests of wrinkles, a shrewd and humorous glance at me, and he said:

"Tepetzálan, you have been courteous, or at least discreet. You have not spoken your opinion of us, the remaining Aztéca. But permit me to guess. I would wager that you consider us the dregs that were left in Aztlan when the more worthy ones went away."

True, that was my opinion. I might have said something to put a slightly better face on it, but he went on:

"You believe that our forefathers were too lazy or listless or timid to raise their eyes to some beckoning vision of glory. That they feared the risk and so lost the opportunity. That your own ancestors, by contrast, ventured boldly forth from here in the certain knowledge that they were destined to be exalted above all other peoples of the world."

"Well . . ." I said.

"Here is our temple." Canaútli stopped at the entrance to a low building of the customary crushed-shell plastering, but with many fine shells of conch and other sea creatures inset entire. "Our only temple, and a humble one, but if you will enter..."

I did, and with my topaz I looked at what stood there, and I said, "That is Coyolxaúqui," and I said truthfully, admiringly, "That is a superb work of art."

"You recognize her?" The old man sounded a trifle surprised. "I should have thought that your people would have forgotten her by now."

"I confess, venerable one, that she is now regarded only as a minor goddess among our many gods. But the legend is one of our oldest, and it is still remembered."

To tell it briefly, reverend friars, the legend was this. Coyolxaúqui, whose name means Adorned with Bells, was one of the godling children of the high goddess Coatlícue. And that goddess Coatlícue, though already a mother many times over, became gravid again when one day a feather floated down upon her from the skies. (How that could impregnate any female, I do not know, but such things happened in many old stories. And it would seem that the daughter-goddess Coyolxaúqui was also skeptical when her mother told of it.) Coyolxaúqui gathered her brothers and sisters and said, "Our mother has brought shame upon herself and us her children. We must put her to death for it."

However, the child in Coatlícue's womb was the war god Huitzilopóchtli. He heard those words and he sprang instantly out of his mother, full grown and already armed with an obsidian maquáhuitl. He slew his scheming sister Coyolxaúqui and cut her in pieces and flung those dismembered parts to the sky, where their blood stuck them to the moon. He likewise threw all his other sisters and brothers to the sky, where they have since been stars indistinguishable from the older stars. That newborn war god Huitzilopóchtli, of course, was ever afterward the chief god of us Mexíca, and we accorded to Coyolxaúqui no importance whatever. We erected no statues of her or temples for her, and we dedicated no feast days to her.

"To us," said the old historian of Aztlan, "Coyolxaúqui has always been the goddess of the moon, and always will be, and we worship her in that guise."

I did not understand, and I said so. "Why worship the moon,

venerable Canaútli? I ask in all respect. But the moon is of no benefit to mankind, except for its night light, and that is dim at its brightest."

"Because of the sea tides," said the old man, "and those *are* of benefit to us. This lake of ours, at its western end, is separated from the ocean by only a low rock barrier. When the tide rises, it spills fish and crabs and shellfish into our lake, and they stay here when the tide waters recede. Catching those creatures for our food is much easier in this shallow lake than it would be in the deep sea outside. We are grateful to be so lavishly and punctiliously supplied."

"But the moon?" I said, perplexed. "Do you believe that the *moon* somehow causes the *tides?*"

"Causes? I do not know. But the moon certainly gives notice of them. When the moon is at its thinnest, and again when it is at its full round, we know that at a determinable later time the tide will be at its highest, and its spill of provender the most bountiful. Clearly the moon goddess has *something* to do with it."

"So it would seem," I said, and regarded the image of Coyolxaúqui more respectfully.

It was not a statue. It was a disk of stone as perfectly round as the full moon and nearly as immense as the great Sun Stone of Tenochtítlan. Coyolxaúqui was sculptured in high relief, as she looked after her dismemberment by Huitzilopóchtli. Her torso occupied the center of the stone—of the moon—her breasts bared to view and hanging slackly. Her decapitated head was in profile at the top center of the moon; it wore a feather headdress, and on the visible cheek was incised the bell symbol from which she took her name. Her severed arms and legs were distributed around her, adorned with bracelets and anklets. There was no picture writing anywhere on the stone, or course, but it still bore traces of its original paint: a pale blue on the stone background, a pale yellow on the goddess's various parts. I asked how old it was.

"Only the goddess knows," said Canaútli. "It has been here since long before your forebears went away, since time past all remembering."

"How do you pay homage to her?" I asked, looking around

the room, which was otherwise empty except for a strong smell of fish. "I see no signs of sacrifice."

"You mean you see no blood," he said. "Your forefathers also sought blood, and that is why they left here. Coyolxaúqui has never demanded any such thing as a human sacrifice. We offer to her only lesser creatures, things of the sea and things of the night. Owls and the nightflying herons and the great green moon moths. Also there is a small fish, so oily of flesh that it can be dried and burned like a candle. Worshipers light them here when they feel the need of communing with the goddess."

As we stepped out of the fishy-smelling temple into the street again, the old man resumed, "Know now, cousin Tepetzálan, what we Rememberers have remembered. In a time long past, we Aztéca were not confined to this single city. This was the capital of a considerable domain, stretching from this coast high into the mountains. The Aztéca comprised numerous tribes, each of many calpúltin clans, and they were all under the rule of a single Tlatocapíli who was not—like my grandson-by-marriage—a chief in name only. They were a strong people, but they were a peaceable people, satisfied with what they had, and they deemed themselves well cared for by the goddess."

"Until some of those people showed more ambition," I suggested.

"Until some showed weakness!" he said sharply. "The tales tell how some of them, hunting in the high mountains, one day met a stranger from a far land. That one laughed in scorn to hear of our people's simple way of life and their undemanding religion. The stranger said, 'Of all the numberless gods there are, why do you choose to worship the one most feeble, the goddess who was so deservedly humiliated and slain? Why do you not worship the one who overthrew her, the strong and fierce and virile god Huitzilopóchtli?'"

I wondered: who could that outlander have been? Perhaps one of the Toltéca of olden times? No, if a Toltécatl had wished to wean the Aztéca from their worship of Coyolxaúqui, he would have proposed the beneficent god Quetzalcóatl as the substitute.

Canaútli went on, "Those were the first of our people to be evilly influenced by the stranger, and they began to change.

The stranger said, 'Worship Huitzilopóchtli,' and they did. The stranger said, 'Give blood to feed Huitzilopóchtli,' and they did. According to our Rememberers, those were the first human sacrifices ever made by any people who were not outright savages. They held their ceremonies secretly, in the seven great caves in the mountains, and they took care to spill only the blood of expendable orphans and old people. The stranger said, 'Huitzilopóchtli is the god of war. Let him lead you to conquer richer lands.' And more and more of our people listened and heeded, and they offered up more and more sacrifices. The stranger urged, 'Nourish Huitzilopóchtli, make him stronger yet, and he will win for you a life better than you could ever have dreamed.' And the misbelievers grew more numerous, more dissatisfied with their old ways of life, more ready and avid for bloodshed. . . ."

He stopped talking and stood silent for a moment. I looked about us, at the men and women passing by on the street. The residue of the Aztéca. Dress them a little better, I thought, and they could be the Mexíca citizens on any street in Tenochtítlan. No, dress them a little better *and* put a stiffer backbone into them.

Canaútli resumed, "When the Tlatocapíli learned what was happening in those fringe regions of his lands, he realized *who* would be the first victims of the new war god. It would be the Aztéca still peaceable and content with their unwarlike goddess Coyolxaúqui. And why not? What more available and easy first conquest for the followers of Huitzilopóchtli? Well, the Tlatocapíli had no army, but he did have a staunch and loyal body of city guardsmen. He and they went to the mountains and swooped down on the misbelievers, and took them by surprise, and slew many of them. All the rest he disarmed of every weapon they possessed. And he put the curse of banishment on all those traitor men and women. He said, 'So you wish to follow your foul new god? Then take him and take your families and your children and follow your god far away from here. You have until tomorrow to be gone or to be executed.' And by the dawn they had departed, in numbers not now remembered."

After a pause, he added: "I am glad to hear from you that they no longer claim the name of Aztéca."

I stood silent, stunned, until I thought to ask, "And what of the stranger who brought that banishment upon them?"

"Oh, she was among the first slain, naturally."

"*She!*"

"Did I not mention that the stranger was a woman? Yes, all our Rememberers have remembered that she was a runaway Yaki."

"But that is incredible!" I exclaimed. "What would a Yaki woman know of Huitzilopóchtli or Coyolxaúqui or any other Aztéca gods?"

"By the time she got here she had traveled far, and no doubt had heard much. Of a certainty she had learned our language. Some of our Rememberers have suggested that she could have been a sorceress, as well."

"Even so," I persisted, "why should she preach the worship of Huitzilopóchtli, who was no god of hers?"

"Ah, there we can only conjecture. But it is known that the Yaki live mainly by hunting deer, and their chief god is the god who provides those deer, the god *we* call Mixcóatl. Whenever the Yaki hunters find that the herds are thinning out, they perform a particular ceremony. They seize one of their more dispensable females and truss her as they would truss a deer caught alive, and they dance as they would dance after a successful hunt. Then they gut and disjoint and eat the woman, as they would eat a deer. In their simpleminded, savage belief, that ceremony persuades their god of hunting to replenish the deer herds. Anyway, it is known that the Yaki behaved so in the olden time. Perhaps they are not quite so ferocious nowadays."

"I believe they are," I said. "But I do not see how it could have caused what happened here."

"The Yaki woman had run away from her people to escape that fate reserved for women. I repeat, it is only conjecture, but our Rememberers have always supposed that the woman burned with a desire to see men suffer the same way. Any men. Her hatred of them was indiscriminate. And she found her opportunity here. Our own beliefs may have given her the idea, for do not forget: Huitzilopóchtli had slain and dismembered Coyolxaúqui with no more remorse than a Yaki would have shown. So that woman, by pretending to admire and exalt

Huitzilopóchtli, hoped to set our men fighting against each other, killing and spilling each other's blood and entrails, as hers might have been spilled."

I was so appalled that I could only whisper, "A woman? It was some unimportant and nameless *female* who conceived the idea of human sacrifice? The ceremony that is now practiced everywhere?"

"It is not practiced here," Canaútli reminded me. "And our supposition may be a total misjudgment. After all, that was long, long ago. But it sounds a typically feminine notion of vengeance, does it not? And evidently it succeeded, for *you* have mentioned that, in the world outside, men have not ceased slaughtering their fellow men, in the name of one god or another, during all the sheaves of years since."

I said nothing. I could not think what to say.

"So you see," the old man continued, "those Aztéca who left Aztlan were not the best and the bravest. They were the worst and the unwanted, and they went because they were forcibly expelled."

I still said nothing, and he concluded:

"You say you search for the stores your ancestors might have secreted along their route from here. Give up the search, cousin. It is futile. Even if those people had been allowed to leave here with any possessions of use or value, they would not have stored them for a possible retreat along that route. They knew they could never come back."

I stayed not many more days in Aztlan, though my cousin the other Mixtli would have had me stay for months, I believe. He had decided that he wished to learn word knowing and picture writing, and he bribed me to teach him, by giving me a private hut and one of his younger sisters to keep me company in it. She was in no way comparable to a sister once known as Tzitzitlíni, but she was a pretty girl, a sufficiently obliging and enjoyable companion. Nevertheless, I had to tell her brother that word knowing could not be learned as quickly as, say, the art of frog spearing. I taught him how to represent physical things by drawing simplified pictures of them, and then I said:

"To learn how to utilize those pictures to build written language, you will require a teacher dedicated to such teaching, which I am not. Some of the best are in Tenochtítlan, and I advise you to go there. I have told you where it lies."

He growled, with some of his earlier surliness, "By the stiff limbs of the goddess, you simply want to get away. And I cannot. I cannot leave my people leaderless, with no excuse except my sudden whim to have a bit of education."

"There is a much better excuse," I said. "The Mexíca have extended their dominions far and wide, but they have yet no colony on this northern shore of the western ocean. The Uey-Tlatoáni would be delighted to learn that he has cousins already established here. If you were to present yourself to Mote-cuzóma, bearing a suitable gift of introduction, you might very well find yourself appointed the ruler of an important new province of The Triple Alliance, a province much more worth ruling than it is now."

"What suitable gift?" he said sardonically. "Some fish? Some frogs? One of my other sisters?"

Pretending I had only that moment thought of it, I said, "Why not the stone of Coyolxaúqui?"

He reeled in shock. "Our one and only sacred image?"

"Motecuzóma may not esteem the goddess, but he does appreciate fine works of art."

He gasped, "Give away the Moon Stone? Why, I would be worse hated and reviled than that cursed Yaki sorceress of whom the grandfather Canaútli tells!"

"Quite the contrary," I said. "She caused the dissolution of the Aztéca. You would be effecting their reconciliation—and much more. I should sày that the sculpture would be a small price to pay for all the advantages of reuniting again with the mightiest nation in all the known lands. But think about it."

And so it was that, when I took my leave of my cousin Mixtli and his pretty sister and the others of his family, he was mumbling, "I could not roll the Moon Stone all that way by myself alone. I must convince others. . . ."

I no longer had any valid reason for exploring; I would be wandering only for the sake of wandering. It was time I went home again; and Canaútli told me I would make best time by going straight inland, where the swamps eventually ended, and then over the mountains of the Cora and Huichol. But I will not tell of my progress through those mountains; they were merely more mountains—or of the various peoples I encountered there; they were merely more mountain people. And in truth I have little recollection of that part of my homeward journey, for I was too deeply occupied with my thoughts of all the many things I had already seen and learned . . . and unlearned. For example:

The word Chichiméca did not necessarily mean "barbarians," though that is what they are. The word could as well mean "red people," the whole race of mankind to which I and every other human belonged. We Mexíca might boast of our accumulated years and layers of civilization and culture, but we were not otherwise superior to those barbarians. The Chichiméca were indisputably cousins of ours. And we too—we proud and haughty Mexíca—we too had once been drinkers of our own urine, eaters of our own excrement.

Our vaunted histories of our peerless lineage were sadly or laughably in error. Our ancestors had not left Aztlan in any daringly heroic bid for greatness. They had been mere dupes, deluded by a woman either mad or magical or simply spiteful. And she a specimen of the most inhuman humans known to exist! But even if that legendary Yaki woman had never really existed, the fact remained that our ancestors had become so bestial and obnoxious that their own people could no longer abide their presence. Our ancestors had left Aztlan at the point of a spear, slinking away under cover of night, in shame and ignominy. Most of them were still outcasts from every decent society, resigned to their perpetual exile in the empty desert. Only a few had somehow wandered into the civilized region of the lakes, and had been let stay there long enough to learn and grow and prosper and themselves appropriate the blessings of civilization. It was only because of that good fortune that they . . . that we . . . that *I* . . . and all the other Mexíca were not still living an aimless existence, roaming the wilderness, clad in stinking skin garments, keeping alive by eating sun-dried child meat, or worse.

For a long time, as I slouched slowly eastward, I mused on those demeaning and disturbing realizations. For much of that time, I could only gloomily regard us Mexíca as the fruit of a tree rooted in swamp ooze and fed by human manure. But gradually I came to a new realization. People are not plants. They are not fixed to any roots or dependent on them. People are mobile and free to move far from their beginnings—far away, if that satisfies them—far upward, if they have the ambition and ability. The Mexíca had long been vain of their ancestry, and I had suddenly been made ashamed of it. But both attitudes were equally foolish: our ancestors merited neither blame nor credit that we were what we were.

We *had* aspired to something better than a swamp life, and we had achieved it. We had moved from the island of Aztlan to another island no more promising, and we had made of it the most resplendent city ever seen, the capital of a dominion unsurpassed, the center of a civilization ever broadening outward into lands that would still be mean and poor but for our influence. Whatever our origins or the forces that had impelled us, we *had* climbed to a height never reached by any other people. And we needed not to argue or explain or excuse our beginnings, our arduous journey through the generations, our arrival at the pinnacle we finally occupied. To command the respect of every other people, we needed to say only that *we were the Mexíca!*

I straightened my back and squared my shoulders and lifted my head and proudly faced in the direction of The Heart and Center of the One World.

✠

But I found that I could not long maintain that firm and prideful stride. During all of that journey I had been retracing and unearthing and piecing together the past history of ancient lands and peoples. The nearer I got to home, the more it seemed that all that collected antiquity had permeated my mind, my muscles, and my bones. I felt that I was carrying every sheaf of the years gone by since history began, and I do not think I was simply imagining that burden. There was evidence that it really weighed on me. I walked more slowly and less erectly than I had used to do, and on breasting the higher hills I breathed hard, and when I labored up some very steep slopes my heart pounded on my ribs in angry complaint.

Because of my feeling that I had become weighted with all the ages of the world, I swerved aside as I approached Tenochtítlan. It was too modern for my mood. I decided to go first to an older place, a place I had never yet visited, though it lies not far to the east of where I was born. I wanted to see the place first inhabited in all this area, the site of the earliest civilization ever to flourish here. I circled around the lake basin—north, then southeastward, staying on the mainland—and I came at last to the ages-remembering city of Teotihuácan, The Place Where the Gods Gathered.

There is no knowing how many sheaves of sheaves of years it remembers in its dreaming silence. Teotihuácan is a ruin now, though a majestic ruin, and it has been a ruin during all the recorded history of all the peoples now living in this region. The pavement of its broad avenues was long ago buried under windblown silt and overgrowing weeds. Its ranks of temples are no more than rubble outlines of their former foundations. Its pyramids still tower over the plain, but their topmost points are blunted, their straight lines and sharp angles have softened and crumbled under the battering of years and weathers beyond reckoning. The colors with which the city would once have blazed are worn away—the radiance of its white lime gesso, the gleam of beaten gold, the brilliance of many different paints—and the whole city is now the drab dun and gray of its underlying rock construction. According to Mexíca tradition, the city was built by the gods, to be the place in which they convened while they made their plans for creating the rest of the world. Hence the name we gave it. But according to my old Lord Teacher of History, that legend is only a romantically mistaken notion; the city was actually built by men. Still, that would hardly lessen the wondrousness of it, for those men must have been the long-vanished Toltéca, and those Master Artisans built magnificently.

To see Teotihuácan as I first saw it—in an extravagantly colorful sunset, its pyramids looming up from the flatland and looking in that light as if newly sheathed in the richest red gold, luminous against the background of distant purple mountains and deep blue sky—that is a sight so overwhelming as to make one believe that the city was the work of the gods, or, if it was made by men, that they were a godlike race of men.

I entered the city at its northern end and picked my way through the litter of fallen stone blocks around the base of the pyramid that our Mexíca wise men supposed had been dedicated to the moon. That pyramid had lost at least a third of its height, where its top has been worn away, and its staircase ascends to a welter of loose rocks up there. The Pyramid of the Moon is surrounded by the standing or toppled columns and walls of buildings that must once have been two or three floors high. One edifice we called The Palace of the Butterflies, because of the abundance of those blithe creatures pictured in the murals still visible on its interior walls.

But I did not loiter there. I walked south along the city's central avenue, which is as long and broad as the floor of a good-sized valley, but much more level. We called it In Micaótli, The Avenue of the Dead, and, although it is thick with brush through which snakes slither and rabbits bounce, it still affords a pleasant stroll. More than a one-long-run in length, it is bordered by the ruins of temples on either side—until you are halfway along it. There the left-hand row of temples is interrupted for the unbelievably immense bulk of the icpac tlamanacáli that our wise men had decided was The Pyramid of the Sun.

If I say that the whole city of Teotihuácan is impressive, but that The Pyramid of the Sun makes all the rest look trivial, perhaps that will give you some idea of its size and majesty. It is easily half again as big in every dimension as was the Great Pyramid of Tenochtítlan, and that was the grandest I had ever seen before. In fact, no one can say how big The Pyramid of the Sun really is, because much of its base is under the earth deposited there by wind and rain during the ages since Teotihuácan was abandoned. But what remains visible and measurable is awesome. At ground level, each of the four sides is two hundred and thirty paces from corner to corner, and the structure soars as high as twenty ordinary houses piled up on top of each other.

The pyramid's entire surface is rough and jagged, because the smooth slabs of slate with which it was once clad have all come loose from the jutting rock studs that held them. And long before those slates slid down to become a jumble of shards on the ground, I imagine they had already shed their original coating of white lime gesso and colored paints. The structure rises in four tiers, and each one slopes upward at a slightly different angle, for no reason except that that refinement of design deceives the eye and makes the entire edifice somehow appear even bigger than it is. So there are three wide terraces around the four sides and, at the very top, a square platform on which a temple must once have stood. But it would have had to be a very small temple, and quite inadequate for ceremonies of human sacrifice. The staircase ascending the pyramid's front is now so broken and crumbled that the individual steps are barely discernible.

The Pyramid of the Sun faces westward, toward the setting sun, and its front was still colored flame and gold when I reached it. But at that moment the lengthening shadows of the ruined temples on the other side of the avenue began to creep up the pyramid's front, like jagged teeth biting at it. I quickly began to scramble up what remained of the staircase, keeping in the jacinth sunlight all the way, just above and ahead of the encroaching shadow teeth.

I attained the platform at the summit at the same time the last sunlight lifted from the pyramid, and I sat down heavily, wheezing for breath. A late-flying butterfly came fluttering up from somewhere and perched on the platform companionably near me. It was a very large and entirely black butterfly, and it gently waggled its wings as if it too were panting from the climb. All of Teotihuácan was by then in twilight, and before long a pale mist began to rise from the ground. The pyramid on which I sat, for all its massiveness, seemed to be floating unattached to the earth. The city, which had been flamboyantly red and yellow, had become muted blue and silver. It looked peaceful and drowsy. It looked its great age. It looked older than time, but so steadfast that it would still endure when all of time had passed away.

I scanned the city from end to end—at that height it was possible—and, using my topaz, I could see the innumerable pits and dimples in the weed-grown land stretching far on both sides of The Avenue of the Dead: the places where had stood more habitations than there were in Tenochtítlan. Then I saw something else, and it startled me: distant small fires taking bloom. Was the dead city coming to life again? But then I perceived that they were torch lights, a long double line of them, approaching from the south. I was briefly annoyed that I no longer had the city to myself. But I knew that pilgrims often came there, singly or in crowds—from Tenochtítlan, from Texcóco and other parts—to make offerings or prayers in that place where the gods once had gathered. There was even a campground to accommodate such visitors: a vast, rectangular, sunken meadow at the southern extremity of the main avenue. It was believed that it had originally been Teotihuácan's marketplace, and that under the grass must be enclosing walls and a stone-paved plaza.

The night was full dark by the time the torchlight procession reached that place, and for a time I watched, as some of the torches stopped and stayed in a circle, while others moved here and there, their carriers busy with the activity of making camp. Then, being sure that none of the pilgrims would venture farther into the city before morning, I swung around on the platform to face eastward and watch the early rising moon. It was full, as perfectly round and benignly beautiful as Aztlan's stone of Coyolxaúqui. When it was well up above the undulant profile of the far-off mountains, I turned yet again to look at Teotihuácan by its light. A gentle night breeze had dispelled the ground mist, and the many edifices were sharply outlined in every detail by the blue-white moonlight, and they threw stark black shadows across the blue ground.

Almost all the roads and the days of my life had been hectic and eventful, with not many leisurely intervals, and I expected that they would continue to be so to their end. But I sat in serenity there for a little time, and I treasured it. I was even moved to make the one poem I ever made in my life. It had little regard for facts or history; it was inspired purely by the moonlight loveliness and silence and tranquillity of that place and that time. When I had made the poem in my head, I stood erect atop that towering Pyramid of the Sun, and I said the poem aloud to the empty city:

> Once, when nothing was but night,
> they gathered, in a time forgotten—
> all the gods of greatest might—

to plan the dawn of day and light.
Here...
at Teotihuácan.

"Very nice," said a voice not my own, and I started so that
I nearly leapt off the pyramid. The voice recited the poem back
to me, word for word, slowly and savoringly, and I recognized
the voice. I have heard my small effort recited by other people
on later occasions, and even in recent times, but never again
by the Lord Motecuzóma Xocóyotl, Cem-Anáhuac Uey-Tlatoáni, Revered Speaker of the One World.

"Very nice," he said again. "Especially since Eagle Knights
are not noted for their poetic turn of mind."

"Nor even sometimes for their knightliness," I said ruefully,
knowing that he had recognized me too.

"No need for apprehension, Knight Mixtli," he said, without
any audible emotion. "Your elderly under-chiefs took all blame
for the failure of the Yanquítlan colony. They were duly executed. There remains no debt outstanding. And before they
went to the flower garland they told me of your intended ex-
ploration. How did you fare?"

"No better than at Yanquítlan, my lord," I said, suppressing
a sigh for the friends who had died on my behalf. "I merely
proved that the fabled Aztéca stores do not exist and never
did." I gave him a much abbreviated account of my journey,
and of my finding the legendary Aztlan, and I concluded with
the words I had heard in various languages everywhere. Motecuzóma nodded somberly and repeated the words, staring out
into the night as if he could see before him all the lands of his
domains, and he made the words sound ominously like an
epitaph:

"The Aztéca were here, but they brought nothing with them,
and they left nothing when they went."

After a while of rather uncomfortable silence, I said, "For
more than two years I have had no news of Tenochtítlan or
The Triple Alliance. How fare things there, Lord Speaker?"

"About as dismally as you describe the affairs of the dreary
Aztlan. Our wars win us nothing. Our territories have not grown
by a hand span since you last knew them. Meanwhile the omens

multiply, ever more mysterious and threatening of future disaster."

He favored me with a short history of recent events. He had never ceased harrying and trying to subdue the stubbornly independent neighbor nation of Texcála, but with notable lack of success. The Texcaltéca were still independent, and more inimical than ever toward Tenochtítlan. The only recent fighting that Motecuzóma could call even moderately successful had been a mere raid of reprisal. The inhabitants of a town called Tlaxiáco, somewhere in the Mixtéca country, had been intercepting and keeping for themselves the rich goods of tribute intended for Tenochtítlan, sent by cities farther south. Motecuzóma had personally led his troops there and turned the town of Tlaxiáco to a puddle of blood.

"But the affairs of state have not been so disheartening as the doings of nature," he went on. "One morning about a year and a half ago, the entire lake of Texcóco suddenly became as turbulent as a stormy sea. For a day and a night, it tossed and foamed and flooded some low-lying areas. And for no reason: there was no storm, no wind, no earthquake to account for the water's upheaval. Then, last year, and just as inexplicably, the temple of Huitzilopóchtli caught fire and burned until it was completely ruined. It has since been restored, and the god has evinced no sign of outrage. But that fire on top of the Great Pyramid was visible everywhere around the lake, and it struck terror into the hearts of all who saw."

"Most strange," I agreed. "How could a temple of stone catch fire, even if some madman held a torch to it? Stone does not burn."

"Coagulated blood does," said Motecuzóma, "and the temple's interior was thickly caked with it. The stench hung over the city for days afterward. But those occurrences, whatever they might have portended, were in the past. Now comes *this* accursed thing."

He pointed to the sky, and I raised my crystal to peer upward, and I grunted involuntarily when I saw the thing. I had never seen one before; I probably would never have noticed that one if my weak eyes had not been directed to it; but I recognized it as what we called a smoking star. You Spaniards call it a hairy star, or a comet. It was really quite pretty—like a luminous little tuft of down snagged among the ordinary stars—but of course I knew it was to be regarded with dread, as a sure precursor of evil.

"The court astronomers first espied it a month ago," said Motecuzóma, "when it was too small to have been seen by an untrained eye. It has appeared in the same place in the sky every night since, but ever growing larger and brighter. Many of our people will not venture out of their houses at night, and even the boldest make sure their children stay indoors, safe from its baleful light."

I said, "So the smoking star impels my lord to seek communion with the gods of this sacred city?"

He sighed and said, "No. Or not entirely. That apparition is troubling enough, but I have not yet spoken of the even more recent and more dire omen. You know, of course, that the chief god of this city Teotihuácan was the Feathered Serpent, and that it has long been believed that he and his Toltéca would eventually come back to reclaim these lands."

"I know the old tales, Lord Speaker. Quetzalcóatl built some sort of magical raft, and drifted away across the eastern sea, vowing to return some day."

"And do you remember, Knight Mixtli, some three years ago, when you and I and the Lord Speaker Nezahualpíli of Texcóco discussed a drawing on a piece of paper brought from the Maya lands?"

"Yes, my lord," I said uneasily, not much liking to be reminded of it. "A house of great size floating upon the sea."

"Upon the *eastern* sea," he stressed. "In the drawing, the floating house appeared to have occupants. You and Nezahualpíli called them men. Strangers. Outlanders."

"I remember, my lord. Were we mistaken in calling them strangers? Do you mean the drawing represented the returning Quetzalcóatl? Bringing his Toltéca back from the dead?"

"I do not know," he said, with uncommon humility. "But I have just had report that one of those floating houses appeared again off the Maya coast, and it turned over in the sea, like a house toppling sideways in an earthquake, and two of its occupants were washed ashore, nearly dead. If there were others in that house, they must have drowned. But those two survivors came alive after a while, and are now living in some village called Tihó. Its chief, a man named Ah Tutál, sent a swift-messenger to ask of me what to do with them, for he asserts that they are gods, and he is unaccustomed to entertaining gods. At any rate, not living and visible and palpable gods."

I had listened in growing astonishment. I blurted, "Well, my lord? *Are* they gods?"

"I do not know," he said again. "The message was typical of Maya ineptitude—so hysterical and incoherent that I cannot tell even whether those two are male or female—or one of each, like the Lord and Lady Pair. But the description, such as it is, described no man or woman of my experience. Inhumanly white of skin, exceedingly hairy of face and body, speaking a language incomprehensible even to the wisest of the wise men thereabouts. Surely gods *would* look and talk differently than we do, would they not?"

I thought about it and finally said, "I should suppose that gods can assume any appearance they choose. And speak any human tongue, if they really wish to communicate. One thing I find hard to believe is that gods could capsize their traveling house and half drown themselves, like any clumsy boatmen. But what have you advised that chief, Lord Speaker?"

"First, to remain silent until we can ascertain what sort of beings they are. Second, to ply them with the best food and drink, with all manner of comforts, with companionship of the opposite sex if they desire it, so that they may rest content in Tihó. Third, and most important, to *keep* them there, well enclosed, unseen by more eyes than have seen them already, to keep their existence as little known as possible. The apathetic Maya may not be unduly excited by this occurrence. But if the news gets out among more discerning and sensitive peoples, it could cause turmoil, and I do not want that."

"I have visited Tihó," I said. "It is more than a village, quite a respectable town in size, and its inhabitants are the Xiu people, considerably superior to most other remnants of the Maya. I expect they will comply, Lord Speaker. That they will keep the matter secret."

In the moonlight I could see Motecuzóma turn in my direction, and his head inclined sharply toward me as he said, "You speak the Maya languages."

"That Xiu dialect, yes, my lord. Passably."

"And you are quick with other exotic languages." He went on before I could comment, but he seemed to speak to himself. "I came to Teotihuácan, the city of Quetzalcóatl, hoping that he or some other god might give me a sign. Some indication of how I should best contend with this situation. And what do I find at Teotihuácan?" He laughed, though the laughter sounded strained, and he addressed me again. "You could atone for many past derelictions, Knight Mixtli, if you were to volunteer to do a thing beyond the capabilities of other men, even the highest priests of men. If you were to be the emissary of the Mexíca—of all mankind—our emissary to the gods."

He said the last words facetiously, as if of course he disbelieved them, though we were both aware that they were not entirely beyond belief. The idea was breathtaking: that I might be the first man ever to talk—not harangue, as the priests did, or confer by some mystic means—but really *talk* with beings who perhaps were not human, who perhaps were something eminently greater than human. That I might speak words to and hear words spoken by ... yes ... *the gods*. ...

But at that moment I could not speak at all, and Motecuzóma laughed again, at my speechlessness. He got to his feet, upright on the pyramid summit, and he leaned down to clap me on the shoulder, and he said cheerfully, "Too weak to say yes or no, Knight Mixtli? Well, my servants should have a hearty meal ready by now. Come be my guest and let me feed your resolve."

So we cautiously picked our way down a moonlit side of The Pyramid of the Sun, a descent almost as difficult as the climb, and we walked south along The Avenue of the Dead to the campground—overlooked by the third and least of Teotihuácan's pyramids—where fires were burning, cooking was being done, and mosquito-netted pallets were being laid out by the hundred or so servants, priests, knights, and other courtiers who had accompanied Motecuzóma. We were met there by the high priest whom I remembered as having officiated at the New Fire ceremony some five years before. He gave me only a passing glance, and started to say, with pompous importance:

"Lord Speaker, for tomorrow's petitions to the old gods of this place, I suggest first a ritual of—"

"Do not bother," Motecuzóma interrupted him. "There is now no need for pretentious petitions. We will return to Tenochtítlan as soon as we wake tomorrow."

"But, my lord," the priest protested. "After coming all the way out here, with all your retinue and august guests..."

"Sometimes the gods volunteer their blessing before it is even asked," said Motecuzóma, and he threw an equivocal look at me. "Of course, we may never be sure if it is given seriously or only in mocking jest."

So he and I sat down to eat, among a circle of his palace guardsmen and other knights, many of whom recognized and greeted me. Although I was disreputably ragged, dirty, and out of place in that gaudily feathered and jeweled assemblage, the Uey-Tlatoáni directed me to the pillowed seat of honor on the ground at his right. While we ate, and while I tried heroically to moderate my voracity, the Lord Speaker spoke at some length about my forthcoming "mission to the gods." He suggested questions I should ask of them, when I had mastered their language, and what questions of theirs I might prudently avoid answering. I waited for him to be silenced by a mouthful of grilled quail, and then I ventured to say:

"My lord, I would make one request. May I rest at home for at least a short time before I set out traveling again? I started this last journey in all the vigor of my manhood's prime, but I confess that I feel as if I have come home in the age of never."

"Ah, yes," the Lord Speaker said understandingly. "No need to apologize; it is the common fate of man. We all come at last to the ueyquin ayquic."

From your expressions, reverend scribes, I take it that you do not comprehend the meaning of the ueyquin ayquic, "the age of never." No, no, my lords, it does not signify an age of any specific number of years. It comes early to some people, later to others. Considering that I was then forty and five years old, well into my middle years, I had eluded its clutch for longer than most men. The ueyquin ayquic is the age when a man beings to mutter to himself, "Ayya, the hills never seemed so steep before..." or "Ayya, my back never used to give me these twinges of pain..." or "Ayya, I never found a gray hair in my head before now...."

That is the age of never.

Motecuzóma went on, "By all means, Knight Mixtli, take time to recover your strength before you go south. And this time you will not go afoot or alone. An appointed emissary of the Mexíca must go in pomp, especially when he is to confer with gods. I will provide for you a stately litter and strong bearers and an armed escort, and you will wear your richest Eagle Knight regalia."

As we prepared to bed down, by the combined light of the setting moon and the dying campfires, Motecuzóma called for one of his swift-messengers. He gave instructions to the man, and the runner immediately set off for Tenochtítlan, to take word to my household of my impending return. It was thoughtful of the Speaker to do that, and it was well intentioned, so that my servants and my wife Béu Ribé should have time to prepare a fitting reception for my homecoming. But the actual effect of that reception was nearly to kill me, and then to make me nearly kill Béu.

I made my way through the streets of Tenochtítlan at the next midday. Because I was as unprepossessing as any beggar leper, and almost as immodestly exposed as a genital-proud Huaxtécatl, the passing people either made a wide circuit around me or ostentatiously drew their mantles close to avoid brushing against me. But when I reached my home quarter of Ixacuálco I began to meet remembered neighbors, and they greeted me civilly enough. Then I saw my own house, and its mistress standing in the open door at the top of the street stairs, and I raised my topaz for a look at her, and I almost fell at that moment, right there in the street. It was Zyanya waiting for me.

She stood in the bright light of day, dressed only in blouse and skirt, her lovely head bare—and the unique, the beautiful white streak was clearly visible in her flowing black hair. The shock of the illusion was like the shock of a blow that deranged all my body's senses and organs. I suddenly seemed to be looking out from underwater, from inside a whirlpool; the street's houses and people moved in circles about me. My throat constricted, and my breath would go neither in nor out. My heart bounded first in joy, then in frenzied protest at the strain; it hammered even harder than it had lately done during strenuous hill climbs. I tottered and groped for the support of a nearby torch-lamp post.

"Záa!" she cried, catching hold of me. I had not seen her come running. "Are you wounded? Are you ill?"

"Are you really Zyanya?" I managed to say, in a thin voice squeezed out through my tightened throat. The street had darkened in my sight, but I could still see the gleam of that strand of her hair.

"My dear!" was all she replied. "My dear...old... Záa..." and she held me close against her soft, warm bosom.

I said what seemed obvious to my addled mind, "Then you are not here. I am there." I laughed for sheer happiness at being dead. "You have waited for me all this time . . . on the nearmost border of the far country. . . ."

"No, no, you are not dead," she crooned. "You are only weary. And I was thoughtless. I should have saved the surprise."

"Surprise?" I said. My vision was clearing and steadying, and I lifted my eyes from her breast to her face. It was Zyanya's face, and it was beautiful beyond the beauty of all other women, but it was not my remembered Zyanya at twenty. The face was as old as mine, and the dead do not age. Somewhere Zyanya was still young, and Cozcatl was younger yet, and old Blood Glutton was still lustily ageless, and my daughter Nochípa would forever be a child of twelve. Only I, Dark Cloud, was left in this world, to endure the ever darker and cloudier age of never.

Béu Ribé must have seen something frightful in my eyes. She let go of me and warily stepped backward. My heart's wildness and the other symptoms of shock had ceased; I merely felt cold all over. I stood erect and I said grimly:

"This time you deliberately pretended. This time you did it on purpose."

Continuing slowly to edge away from me, she said in a quaver, "I thought—I hoped it would please you. I thought, if your wife again looked the way you had loved her . . ." When her voice trailed away in a whisper, she cleared her throat to say, "Záa, you know the one and only visible difference between us was her hair."

I said through my teeth, "The only difference!" and I took from my shoulder my empty leather water bag.

Béu went on desperately, "So last night, when the messenger told of your return, I made lime water and I bleached just this one lock. I thought you might . . . accept me . . . for a while at least. . . ."

"I could have died!" I gritted. "And I gladly would have done. But not for you! I promise, this will be the last of your cursed trickeries and sorceries and indignities heaped upon me."

I had the straps of the leather bag in my right hand. With my left, I lunged to seize her wrist, and I twisted it so she sprawled on the earth.

Absurdly, she cried, "Záa, there is white in your own hair now!"

Our neighbors and some other folk were standing along the street, and they had been simpering to see my wife run to embrace the traveler come home. They stopped that fond smiling when I began to beat her. I truly do think I would have done her to death if I had had the strength and the endurance. But I was weary, as she had remarked, and I was not young, as she had also remarked.

Even so, the flailing leather ripped her light clothing to ribbons, and then scattered the scraps, so that she lay there naked except for a few remaining rags around her neck. Her body of honeyed copper, which could have been Zyanya's body, was striped with vivid red welts, but my strength had not been sufficient to break her skin and draw blood. When I could whip no more, she had fainted from the pain. I left her lying there naked to the gaze of all who cared to look, and I staggered to my house stairs, myself half dead again.

The old woman Turquoise, older yet, was peeking fearfully from the door. I had no voice to speak; I could only gesture for her to see to her mistress. Somehow I made my way up the stairs to the upper floor of the house. Only one bedchamber had been made ready: the one that had been mine and Zyanya's. Its bed was piled high with soft quilts, the top one invitingly turned down on both sides. I cursed, and lurched into the spare chamber, and with great effort unrolled the quilts stored there, and let myself fall limply face forward onto them. I fell into sleep as sometime I will fall into death and into Zyanya's arms.

I slept until the middle of the next day, and old Turquoise was hovering anxiously outside my door when I awoke. The door to the main bedchamber was closed, and no sound came from beyond it. I did not inquire into Béu's condition. I commanded Turquoise to heat water for my bath trough and stones for my steam closet, and to lay out clean clothes for me, and then to start cooking and not to stop until I gave the order. When I had finally had enough of alternate steaming and soaking, and had dressed, I went downstairs and all by myself ate and drank enough for three men.

As the servant was setting down the second platter and perhaps the third jug of chocolate, I told her, "I shall be wanting all the apparel and armor and other accessories of my Eagle Knight garb. When you are finished serving, please get them from wherever they are stored, and see that they are freshly aired, that all the feathers are preened, that all is in perfect order. But right now, send Star Singer to me."

In a tremulous old voice, she said, "I regret to tell you, master, but Star Singer died of the cold of last winter."

I said I was sorry to hear that. "Then you must do the errand, Turquoise, before you attend to my wardrobe and regalia. You will go to the palace—"

She recoiled and gasped, "I, master? To the palace? Why, the guards would not let me near the great door!"

"Tell them you come from me and they will," I said impatiently. "You are to speak a message to the Uey-Tlatoáni and to no one else."

She gasped again, "To the Uey—!"

"Hush, woman! You are to tell him this. Memorize it. Just this. 'The Lord Speaker's emissary requires no more rest. Dark Cloud is prepared to start upon his mission as soon as the Lord Speaker can make ready the escort.'"

And so, without seeing Waiting Moon again, I went off to meet the waiting gods.

I H S

✠

S.C.C.M.

Sanctified, Caesarean, Catholic Majesty,
the Emperor Don Carlos, Our Lord King:

MOST High Majesty, Preëminent among Princes: from this City of Mexíco, capital of New Spain, this eve of Corpus Christi in the year of Our Lord one thousand five hundred thirty and one, greeting.

We write this with woe and anger and contrition. In our last letter, we expressed our elation at our Sovereign's sage observation regarding the possible—nay, the seemingly irrefutable—resemblance between the Indians' deity called Quetzalcóatl and our Christian St. Thomas. Alas, we must now, with chagrin and embarrassment, impart some bad news.

We hasten to say that no doubt has been cast upon Your Most Benevolent Majesty's brilliant theory *per se*. But we must tell you that your devoted chaplain was overly impetuous in adducing evidence to support that hypothesis.

What seemed to us *certain* proof of our Sovereign's supposition was the otherwise unaccountable presence here of the Host, secreted in that native-made pyx at the ancient city of Tula. We have but recently learned, from listening to our resident Aztec's narrative—as Your Majesty will learn from reading the transcribed pages herewith—that we were deceived by what was no more than a superstitious act of the Indians, committed only a comparatively few years ago. And they were abetted in that by an evidently failed or apostate Spanish priest who had earlier dared an unspeakably profane act of larceny. Wherefore, we have regretfully written to the Congregatio de Propaganda Fide, confessing our gullibility and requesting that they ignore that false item of evidence. Since all the other apparent links between St. Thomas and the mythical Feathery Snake are purely circumstantial, it is to be expected that the Congregatio will, at least until more tenable proofs are forthcoming, dismiss Your Majesty's suggestion that the Indian deity could in reality have been the Apostle Thomas making an evangelical sojourn in this New World.

It grieves us to make such a disheartening report, but we maintain that it was not the fault of our eagerness to make even more evident the astuteness of our Most Admired Majesty. *It was entirely the fault of this ape of an Aztec!*

He was aware that we had come into possession of that pyx containing the Sacrament, preserved fresh and intact and, as we judged, for perhaps fifteen centuries. He was aware of the marveling excitement which it engendered in us and in every other Christian in these lands. The Indian could at that time have told us how that object came to be where it was found. He could have averted our premature exclamations over that discovery, and the many church services held to celebrate it, and the high reverence in which we held that apparently divine relic. Above all, he could have prevented our making a fool of ourself by so hurriedly and mistakenly reporting the matter to Rome.

But no. The despicable Aztec watched all the excitement and jubilation, no doubt with concealed and malicious merriment, and said not a word to disabuse us of our joyous misapprehensions. Not until too late, and in the chronological course of his narrative, and only casually, does he make mention of the true origin of those Communion wafers and the manner of their having been secreted at Tula! We ourself feel sufficiently humiliated, knowing how our superiors at Rome will be amused by or disparaging of our having been victimized by a hoax. But we feel immeasurably more contrite because, in our haste to inform the Congregatio, we seemed to impute a similar gullibility to our Most Respected Emperor and King, albeit the deed was done with all good intent of giving Your Majesty due credit for what *should* have been a reason for rejoicing among Christians everywhere.

We beg and trust that you will see fit to put the blame for our mutual embarrassment where it belongs: on the tricksome and treacherous Indian, whose silence, it is now evident, can be almost as outrageous as some of his utterances. (In the next pages, if you can believe it even when you read it, Sire, he uses the noble Castilian language as an excuse to speak words which surely have never before been deliberatly inflicted on the ears of any other Bishop anywhere!) Perhaps our Liege will now take cognizance that, when this creature so brazenly makes jape of Your Majesty's vicar, there can be no question but that, by extension, he makes jape of Your Majesty as well, and not at all unintentionally. Perhaps, Sire, you will at last agree that the day is considerably overdue when we might dispense with the employment of this depraved old barbarian whose unwelcome presence and unwholesome disclosures we have now endured for more than a year and a half.

Please to forgive the brevity and acrimony and unmannerly curtness of this communication, Your Majesty. We are at present too vexed and discomposed to write at greater length or with the mansuetude fitting to our holy office.

May all the goodness and virtue that shine from Your Radiant Majesty continue to illumine the world. Such is the prayer of Your S.C.C.M.'s devoted (if chastened) chaplain,

(ecce signum) Zumárraga

UNDECIMA PARS

AYYO! After so long neglect, Your Excellency joins us once again. But I believe I can divine the reason. I am now about to speak of those new-come gods, and gods clearly are of interest to a man of God. We are honored by your presence, my Lord Bishop. And not to demand too much of Your Excellency's valuable time, I will hasten my tale to that encounter with those gods. I will only digress to tell of a meeting with one small and lesser being on the road, for that being was later to prove not small at all.

I left Tenochtítlan on the day after the day I had returned to it, and I left in style. Since the fearsome smoking star was not in evidence in the daytime, the streets were crowded with people, and they ogled my parade of departure. I wore my ferociously beaked helmet and feathered armor of an Eagle Knight, and I carried my shield bearing the feather-worked symbols of my name. However, as soon as I had crossed the causeway, I entrusted those things to the slave who carried my flag of rank and my other regalia. I put on more comfortable clothing for the journey, and did not again dress in all my finery except when we came to one or another important community along the way, where I wished to impress the local ruler with my own importance.

The Uey-Tlatoáni had provided a gilded and bejeweled litter in which I rode whenever I tired of walking, and another litter full of gifts for me to present to the Xiu chief Ah Tutál, besides other gifts which I was to present to the gods—if gods they proved to be, and if they did not scorn such offerings. In addition to my litter bearers and the porters carrying our travel provisions, I was accompanied by a troop of Motecuzóma's tallest, most robust and imposing palace guards, all of them formidably armed and magnificently garbed.

I need hardly say that no bandits or other villains dared to attack such a train. I need hardly describe the hospitality with which we were received and regaled at every stop along our route. I will recount only what happened when we spent one night at Coátzacoálcos, that market town on the northern coast of the narrowest land between the two great seas.

I and my party arrived near sunset on one of the town's apparently busiest market days, so we did not push into its center to be quartered as distinguished visitors. We merely made camp in a field outside the town, where other late-arriving trains were doing the same. The one that settled nearest ours was the train of a slave trader herding to market a considerable number of men, women, and children. After our company had eaten, I sauntered over to the slave camp, half thinking that I might find a suitable replacement for my late servant Star Singer, and that I might strike a good bargain if I bought one of the men before they went up for bidding in the town market on the morrow.

The pochtécatl told me he had acquired his human herd, by ones and twos, from such inland Olméca tribes as the Coatlícamac and Cupílco. His string of male slaves was literally a string: they traveled and rested and ate and even slept all linked together by a long rope threaded through each man's pierced nose septum. The women and girls, however, were left free to do the work of making the camp, laying the fires, doing the cooking, fetching water and wood and such. As I strolled about, idly eyeing the wares, one young girl carrying a jug and a gourd dipper shyly approached me and sweetly asked:

"Would my Lord Eagle Knight care for a refreshing drink of cool water? At the far side of the field, there is a clear river running to the sea, and I dipped this long enough ago that all the impurities have settled."

I looked at her across the gourd as I sipped. She was plainly a back-country girl, short and slender, not very clean, dressed in a knee-length blouse of cheap sackcloth. But she was not coarse or dark of complexion; in a soft and unformed adolescent way, she was quite pretty. She was not, like every other female in the neighborhood, chewing tzictle, and she was obviously not as ignorant as might have been expected.

"You addressed me in Náhuatl," I said. "How do you come to speak it?"

The girl put on a woebegone expression and murmured, "One does much traveling, being repeatedly bought and sold. It is at least an education of sorts. I was born to the Coatlícamac tongue, my lord, but I have learned some of the Maya dialects and the trade language of Náhuatl."

I asked her name. She said, "Ce-Malináli."

"One Grass?" I said. "That is only a calendar date, and only half a name."

"Yes," she sighed tragically. "Even the slave children of slave parents receive a seventh-birthday name, but I never did. I am less than a slave born of slaves, Lord Knight. I have been an orphan since my birth."

She explained. Her unknown mother was some Coatlícamatl drab, made pregnant by some unknown one of the many men who had straddled her. The woman had given birth in a farm furrow one day while working in the fields, as casually as she would have defecated, and had left the newborn infant there, as uncaringly as she would have left her excrement. Some other woman, less heartless, or perhaps herself childless, had found the abandoned baby before it perished, and had taken it home and given it succor.

"But who that kindly rescuer was, I no longer remember," said Ce-Malináli. "I was still a child when she sold me—for maize to eat—and I have been passed from owner to owner since then." She put on the look of one who has suffered long but persevered. "I know only that I was born on the day One Grass in the year Five House."

I exclaimed, "Why, that was the very day and year of my own daughter's birth in Tenochtítlan. She too was Ce-Malináli until she became Zyanya-Nochípa at the age of seven. You are small for your age, child, but you are precisely the age she—"

The girl interrupted excitedly, "Then perhaps you would buy me, Lord Knight, to be personal maid and companion to your young lady daughter!"

"Ayya," I mourned. "That other Ce-Malináli . . . she died . . . nearly three years ago. . . ."

"Then buy me to be your house servant," she urged. "Or to wait upon you as your daughter would have done. Take me with you when you return to Tenochtítlan. I will do any kind of work or"—she demurely lowered her eyelashes—"any *not* daughterly service my lord might crave." I was drinking again from the dipper at that moment, and I spluttered the water. She said hastily, "Or you can sell me in Tenochtítlan, if my lord is perhaps beyond the age of such cravings."

I snapped, "Impudent little vixen, the women I crave I do not have to buy!"

She did not cringe at my words; she said boldly, "And I do not wish to be bought just for my body. Lord Knight, I have other qualities—I know it—and I yearn for the opportunity to make use of those qualities." She grasped my arm to emphasize her pleading. "I want to go where I will be appreciated for more than just my being a young female. I want to try my fortunes in some great city. I have ambitions, my lord, I have dreams. But they are vain if I am condemned to be forever a slave in these dreary provinces."

I said, "A slave is a slave, even in Tenochtítlan."

"Not always, not necessarily forever," she insisted. "In a city of civilized men, my worth and intelligence and aspirations could perhaps be recognized. A lord might elevate me to the status of concubine, and then even make me a free woman. Do not some lords free their slaves, when they prove deserving?"

I said they did; even I had once done so.

"Yes," she said, as if she had wrung some concession from me. She squeezed my arm, and her voice became wheedling. "You do not require a concubine, Lord Knight. You are a man stalwart and handsome enough that you need not buy your women. But there are others—old or ugly men—who must and

do. You could sell me at a profit to one of those in Tenochtítlan."

I suppose I should have sympathized with the child. I too
had once been young, and brimming with ambition, and I had
yearned to try the challenge of the greatest city of them all.
But there was something so hard and intense about the way in
which Ce-Malináli tried to ingratiate herself that I found her
less than appealing. I said, "You seem to have a very high
opinion of yourself, girl, and a very low opinion of men."

She shrugged. "Men have always used women for their
pleasure. Why should not one woman use men for her advancement? Although I do not like the act of sex, I can pretend
to. Although I have not yet been often used, I have become
quite good at it. If that talent can help lift me from slavery . . . well . . . I have heard that a concubine of a high lord
may enjoy more privilege and power than his legitimate first
lady. And even the Revered Speaker of the Mexíca collects
concubines, does he not?"

I laughed. "Little bitch, you have high ambitions indeed."

She said tartly, "I know I have more to offer than a hole
between my legs that is still invitingly tight and tender. A man
can buy a techíchi bitch and get that!"

I disengaged her grip on my arm. "Know this, girl. Sometimes a man may keep a dog just to have an affectionate companion. I discern no capacity for affection in you. A techíchi
can also be a nourishing meal. You are not clean or appetizing
enough to be cooked. You are articulate for one of your age
and low origins. But you are only a backwoods brat with
nothing to offer except windy boasts and ill-concealed greed
and a pathetic notion of your own importance. You admit that
you do not even *like* to employ that vaunted tight hole of yours,
which is your only worth. If you exceed any of your sister
slaves in any respect, it is merely in vainglorious presumption."

She raged at me. "I can go yonder to the river and wash
myself clean—make myself appetizing—and you would not
reject me! In fine clothes I can pass for a fine lady! I can
pretend affection, and make even you believe it genuine!" She
paused, then sneered, "What other woman has ever done otherwise with you, my lord, when she aspired to be something
more than a receptacle for your tepúli?"

My fingers twitched to punish her impertinence, but the grubby slave was too nearly grown to be spanked like a child, and too young to be whipped like an adult. So I only put my hands on her shoulders, but I held her hard enough to hurt, and I said between my teeth:

"It is true that I have known other females like you: venal and deceitful and perfidious. But I have known others who were not. One of them was my daughter, born to the same name you wear, and had she lived she would have made it a name to be proud of." I could not suppress my rising anger, and my voice rose with it: "Why did she die, and you live?"

I shook that Ce-Malináli so fiercely that she dropped the water jar. It broke with a crash and a splash, but I paid no heed to that portent of misfortune. I shouted so loudly that heads turned throughout the camp, and the slave trader came running to beg that I not mishandle his merchandise. I think, in that moment, I had been briefly granted the vision of a far-seer, and it had shown me a glimpse of the future, because what I shouted was this:

"You will make that name vile and filthy and contemptible, and all people will spit when they speak it!"

I note Your Excellency's impatience at my dwelling on an encounter that must seem meaningless. But the episode, though brief, was not trivial. Who that girl was, and who she became in womanhood, and what was the ultimate outcome of her precocious ambitions—all those things are of utmost significance. But for that child, Your Excellency might not now be our excellent Bishop of Mexíco.

I had forgotten her myself by the time I fell asleep that night, under the ill-omened smoking star that hung in the black sky above. The next day I and my company moved on, beyond Coátzacoálcos, and kept to the coast, passing through the cities of Xicalánca and Kimpéch, and at last we came to the place where the presumed gods waited, in the town called Tihó, capital of the Xiu branch of the Maya people, at the northern extremity of the Uluúmil Kutz peninsula. On arrival, I was attired in all the splendor of my Eagle Knight regalia, and of course were were respectfully received by the personal guard troops of the Xiu chief Ah Tutál, and we were conducted through the streets of the all-white city in solemn procession to his palace. It was not much of a palace; one does not expect much grandeur among any of the remnant Maya. But its one-floor, thatched-roof buildings of adobe brick were, like the rest of the town, brightly whitewashed with lime, and the palace buildings were arranged in a square around a commodious inner court.

Ah Tutál, a superbly cross-eyed gentleman of about my age, was properly impressed by the magnificence of the gifts sent him by Motecuzóma, and I was properly feasted with a welcoming banquet, and while we ate he and I conversed on matters like his health and mine and that of all our various living friends and relations. We could not have cared a little finger for such trivial exchanges; the purpose was to measure my grasp of the local dialect of the Maya tongue. When we had more or less determined the extent of my Xiu vocabulary, we got to the reason for my visit.

"Lord Mother," I said to him, for that ludicrous title is the proper way of addressing the chief of any community in those parts. "Tell me. Are they gods, these new-come strangers?"

"Knight Ek Muyal," said the Mother, using the Maya version of my name, "when I sent word to your Revered Speaker, I was sure they must be. But now . . ." He made a face of uncertainty.

I asked, "Could either of them be the long-gone god Quetzalcóatl who promised to return, the god you call in these lands Kukulkán?"

"No. At any rate, neither of the outlanders has the form of a feathered serpent." Then he sighed and shrugged and said, "In the absence of any marvelous aspect, how does one recognize a god? These two are passably human in appearance, though much hairier and larger than normal. They are bigger than you are."

I said, "According to tradition, other gods have adopted human bodies for a visit to the mortal world. They might understandably choose bodies of intimidating appearance."

Ah Tutál went on, "There were four in the strangely built canoe that was washed ashore on the beach north of here. But when they were brought in litters to Tihó, we discovered that two of them were dead. Can gods be dead?"

"Dead . . ." I mused. "Could it be that they were *not yet alive?* Perhaps they were spare bodies the two live ones like to carry about with them, to slip into when they desire a change."

"That never occurred to me," Ah Tutál said uncomfortably. "Certainly their other habits and appetites are most peculiar, and their language is beyond our understanding. Would not gods who take the trouble to appear human also take the trouble to speak human language?"

"There are many human languages, Lord Mother. They may have chosen to speak one that is not comprehensible in this region, but I may recognize it from my travels elsewhere."

"Lord Knight," the chief said, a trifle peevishly, "you have as many arguments as any priest. But can you argue any reason why the two beings refuse to *bathe?"*

I thought about it. "In water, you mean?"

He gave me a look of wondering if Motecuzóma had sent his court fool as his emissary. He said, enunciating with careful precision, "Yes, in water. What else would I mean by bathing?"

I gave a polite cough and said, "How do you know the gods are not accustomed to bathing in pure air? Or in even purer sunlight?"

"Because they *stink!"* said Ah Tutál, triumphantly and disgustedly at the same time. "Their bodies smell of old odors and sweats and rancid breath and encrusted dirt. If that were not bad enough, they seem content to empty their bladders and bowels out the back window of their rooms, and content to let that ordure pile up out there, and content to live with the appalling stench of it. The two seem as unacquainted with cleanliness as they are unacquainted with freedom and the good foods we provide."

I said, "What do you mean: unacquainted with freedom?"

Ah Tutál pointed through one of the lopsided windows of his throne room, indicating another low building on the opposite side of the court. "They are in there. They stay in there."

I exclaimed, "Surely you do not keep *gods* in captivity?"

"No, no, no! It is their own choice. I told you they behave

most eccentrically. They have not emerged since their first arrival here, when they were allotted those quarters."

I said, "Forgive the question, Lord Mother. But were they perhaps rudely treated when they first came?"

Ah Tutál looked offended and said icily, "From the very first, they have been treated with cordiality, consideration, even reverence. As I said, two were dead when they got here—or convinced our best physicians that they were dead. So naturally, in accordance with civilized custom, we paid the dead every funeral honor and devotion, including the ceremonial cooking and eating of their most estimable parts and organs. It was at that time that the two live gods scuttled to their quarters, and they have sullenly stayed in there ever since."

I hazarded a guess. "Perhaps they were annoyed that you so hastily disposed of what might have been their extra bodies."

Ah Tutál threw up his hands in exasperation and said, "Well, their self-imposed seclusion would by now have starved the bodies they *are* wearing, if I did not regularly send to them servants bearing food and drink. Even so, the two eat only sparingly—of the fruits and vegetables and grains, not of any meat, not even delicacies like tapir and manatee. Knight Ek Muyal, I have tried assiduously to ascertain their preferences in all things, but I confess I am baffled. Take the matter of women—"

I interrupted, "Then they use women as mortal men do?"

"Yes, yes, yes," he said impatiently. "According to the women, they are human and male in every particular except their excessive hairiness. And I daresay any god equipped like a man is going to employ that equipment as a man does. If you think about it, Lord Knight, there are not a great many other ways for even a god *to* use it."

"You are right, of course, Lord Mother. Do go on."

"I have kept sending in women and girls, two at a time, but the outlanders have retained none of them for more than two or three consecutive nights. They keep putting them out again— for me to send others in, I suppose, so I do. None of our women seems to satisfy either of them for long. If they are hoping and hinting for some particular or peculiar *kind* of woman, I have no way of knowing what it would be or where to get it. I tried sending in two pretty boys one night, and the guests made a frightful commotion and beat the boys and threw them out. By now, there are not many dispensable women left in Tihó or the surrounding countryside for me to try on them. They have already had the wives and daughters of just about every Xiu except myself and others of the nobility. Furthermore, I am risking a rebellion of *all* our women, since I must use brute force to propel even the lowliest female slave into that fetid den. The women say that the most unnatural and the worst thing about the strangers is that even their *private parts* are overgrown with hair, and that the outlanders smell even more awful in that crotch of their bodies than in the reek of their breath or their armpits. Oh, I know that your Revered Speaker claims to consider me highly favored and honored to be the host of two gods, or whatever they are. But I wish Motecuzóma were here, so he could try his own skill at being custodian of two such pestiferous guests. I tell you, Knight Ek Muyal, I am beginning to find the honor more of a trial and a nuisance! And how long is it to go on? I no longer want them here, but I dare not turn them out. I thank all the other gods that I chose to house those two clear across the palace square, but even so, at the wind god's caprice, I get a whiff of those unwelcome beings and it nearly knocks me to the ground. In another day or so, the stink will need no wind to help it crawl this far. Right now, some of my courtiers are dreadfully ill of a disease the physicians say they have never encountered before. I personally think we are all beginning to be poisoned by smelling those unclean strangers. And I strongly suspect the reason for Motecuzóma's having sent me so many rich gifts. He hopes to bribe me to *keep* those two, and to keep them well downwind of his clean city. And I will say moreover—"

"You have been tried indeed, Lord Mother," I put in hastily, to stop his recital of his woes. "It is to your credit that you have borne this responsibility this long. But now that I am here, I may be able to make some helpful suggestions. First of all, before I am formally presented to those beings, I should like an opportunity of hearing their speech, without their knowing that I hear."

"That is easy," Ah Tutál said grumily. "Just walk across the court and stand to one side of their window, where they cannot see you. During the day, they do nothing in there *but* jabber as incessantly as monkeys. Only I warn you: hold your nose."

I smiled indulgently as I excused myself from his presence, for I assumed the Mother was exaggerating in that respect, as in some of his other testy attitudes toward the outlanders. But I was wrong. When I approached their quarters, the nauseating stench almost made me bring up the meal I had just eaten. I snorted to clear my nose, and then I did hold it pinched in my fingers as I hurried to flatten myself against the building's wall. There were voices murmuring within, and I sidled closer to the door opening, where I might be able to distinguish intelligible words. Of course, Your Excellency, at that time the sounds of the Spanish language meant nothing to me, as I soon verified by listening. But I knew that moment to be a historic moment, and I stood transfixed in a sort of awe, to hear and remember, as I do to this day, the emphatic words of a strange new being who might very well be a god:

"I swear by Santiago, I am sick of fucking bald cunts!"

And the other voice said

Ayya!

You startled me, Your Excellency. You leap with such agility for a man well into his age of never. I frankly envy your

With all respect, Your Excellency, I regret that I cannot retract the words or apologize for them, since they were not my words. I memorized them that day only in the way a parrot does: by repeating the sounds of them. A parrot might innocently caw such sounds even in your cathedral church, Your Excellency, because a parrot cannot know what they signify. The most intelligent parrot could not possibly know, because a female parrot does not possess what you could properly call a

Very well, Your Excellency, I will belabor the matter no further, and I will refrain from repeating the exact sounds made by the other outlander. But he said, in effect, that he likewise missed and longed for the services of a good Castilian whore, abundantly hairy in her nether parts. And that was all I could stay to overhear, without being sick from the smell and making my presence known. I hastened back to the throne room, gulping fresh air as I went, and there I told the chief Ah Tutál:

"You assuredly did not overstate the fact of their fragrance, Lord Mother. I must see them and try to speak with them, but I should definitely prefer to do that in the open."

He said, "I can have their next meal drugged, and extract them from their den while they sleep."

"No need," I said. "My guardsmen can drag them out right now."

"You would lay hands on the gods?"

"If they summon the lightning and strike us all dead," I said, "we will at least know they *are* gods."

They did nothing of the sort. Though they struggled and squealed as they were forcibly brought from their quarters into the open courtyard, the two outlanders were not nearly so displeased as were my guardsmen, who could scarcely suppress their retching and gagging. And when the brawny captors released their grip, the two did not leap angrily about or make threatening noises or perform any recognizable sorceries. They fell to their knees before me, and they began to babble piteously, and they made strange gestures with their hands, first clasping them before their faces, then moving them in a repeated pattern. Of course I know now that they were reciting over their clenched hands a prayer in the Christian Latin language, and that they were frantically sketching the sign of the Christian cross from forehead to heart to shoulders.

Also, it did not take me long to divine that they had stayed hidden in the safety of their quarters because they had been affrighted by the Xiu's well-intentioned disposition of their two dead companions. If the outlanders had been terrified by the Xiu, who are a people of gentle mien and simple costume, I could understand their being scared half to death when suddenly confronted by me and my Mexíca—grim-faced big men, clearly warriors, fearsomely arrayed in our battle dress of helmets and plumes and obsidian weapons.

For a time, I only stared at them through my seeing crystal, which made them quail even more abjectly. Though I am now well accustomed and resigned to the unappealing appearance of white men, I was not at that time, and I was both intrigued and repelled by the lime-whiteness of their facial skin—because in our One World white was the color of death and mourning. No human being *was* that color, except the infrequent tlacaztáli freak. Those two at least had humanly brown eyes and black or dark brown hair, but it was uncommonly curly, and the hair atop their heads merged into equally dense growths on their cheeks, upper lips, chins, and throats. The rest of them was concealed by what seemed an inordinate amount of clothing. I am now acquainted with shirts and doublets and pantaloons and gauntlets and jackboots and such things, but I still regard them as excessively clumsy, restrictive, and probably uncomfortable, in comparison with our men's simple and unencumbering everyday costume of loincloth and mantle.

"Undress them," I commanded my guards, who grumbled and glared at me before they complied. The two outlanders again struggled and squealed, and even more loudly, as if they were being flayed of their skin instead of cloth and leather. It was we watchers who might better have complained, since each layer that was removed let free a new and more ghastly wave of fetor. And when their boots were pulled off—*yya ayya!*—when their boots came off, everyone else in the palace yard, myself included, retreated so hastily and so far that the two outlanders stood cringing naked at the center of an extremely wide and distant circle of onlookers.

I have earlier spoken superciliously of the filth and squalor of the Chichiméca desert dwellers, but I have explained that their dirtiness was a result of the circumstances in which they lived, and that they *did* bathe and comb and delouse themselves whenever they were able. The Chichiméca were garden flowers by comparison with the white men, who seemed to *prefer* their repulsiveness and to *fear* cleanliness as a mark of weakness or effeminacy. Of course, I speak of the white soldiers only, Your Excellency, all of whom, from the lowliest troopers to their Commander Cortés, shared that gross eccentricity. I am not so well acquainted with the bathing habits of the better-bred later arrivals, such as Your Excellency, but I early noticed that all such gentlemen liberally employ perfumes and pomades to give the sweet-smelling *impression* of being frequent bathers.

The two outlanders were not giants, as Ah Tutál's description might have led me to expect. Only one of them was actually bigger than I was, though the other was about my own size, meaning that they were indeed larger than the average male of these lands. But they stood hunched and quivering as if awaiting the lash of a whip, and they cupped their hands over their genitals like a pair of maiden's dreading ravishment, so the bigness of their bodies was less than impressive. Rather, they looked pitifully flimsy, for their body skin was even whiter than that of their faces.

I said to Ah Tutál, "I shall never be able to get close enough to interrogate them, Lord Mother, until they are washed. If they will not do it, it must be done to them."

He said, "Having now smelled them undressed, Knight Ek Muyal, I must decline the loan of my bathing troughs or steam houses. I should have to destroy and rebuild them."

"I quite agree," I said. "Simply bid your slaves bring water and soap and do it right here."

Although the chief's slaves used tepid water, smooth ash soap, and soft bathing sponges, the objects of their attention fought and screeched as if they were being greased for the cooking spit, or scalded in the way boars are made tender for the scraping off of their bristles. While that uproar was going on, I spoke to a number of the Tihó girls and women who had spent a night or more with the outlanders. The females had learned a few words of their language, and told them to me, but they were only new words for the tepúli, the sexual act—words not very useful for a formal interrogation. The women also confided to me that the strangers' members were of a size proportionate to their big bodies, hence were admirably immense in erection, compared to the more familiar organs of the Xiu men. Any woman would delight in having such a massive tepúli at her service, they said, were it not so rancid with a lifetime's accumulation of curds that a woman might vomit at sight or scent of it. As one girl remarked, "Only a female vulture could really *enjoy* coupling with such creatures."

Nevertheless, the women averred, they had dutifully done their best to extend every sort of feminine hospitality—and they professed to be puzzled by the outlanders' prim and disapproving rejection of some of their proferred intimacies. Clearly, said the women, the strangers knew only one mode and one position of taking or giving pleasure, and, as bashfully and stubbornly as boys, refused to essay any variations.

Even if all other evidence had proclaimed the outlanders to be gods, the testimony of the Xiu women would have made me doubt. From what I knew of Gods, they were not at all prudish about the manner of satisfying their lusts. So I early suspected that the strangers were something other than gods, though it was not until much later that I learned they were merely good Christians. Their ignorance and inexperience of sexual variety only reflected on their adherence to Christian morality and normality, and I never knew any Spaniard to deviate from those strict standards even during the boisterous act of committing rape. I can truthfully say that I never saw a single Spanish soldier rape one of our women except in the one orifice and one position permissible to Christians.

Even when the two outlanders were adjudged as clean as they could be made, short of their being boiled for a day or two, they still were not exactly pleasant company. The slaves could do little with soap and water to improve their green mossy teeth and bad breath, for instance. But they were given clean mantles, and their own miasmic, almost crawling clothes were taken away to be burned. My guards brought the two to the corner of the courtyard where Ah Tutál and I sat on low chairs, and pushed them down to sit on the ground facing us.

Ah Tutál had thoughtfully prepared one of those perforated smoking pots, filling it with his richest picíetl and various other pungent herbs. He lighted the mixture and we each pushed a reed through one of the pot's holes and puffed great clouds of aromatic smoke to make an olfactory screen between us and the subjects of our interview. When I saw that they were trembling, I supposed it was from the chill of their drying bodies, or perhaps the intolerable shock of being clean. I later learned that they quaked because they were terrified to see, for the first time, "men breathing fire."

Well, if they did not like the look of us, I did not much like the look of them. Their faces were even paler since they had lost several layers of ingrained dirt, and what skin was visible above their beards had not the smooth complexion of ours. One man's face was pitted all over like a chunk of lava rock. The other's face was pebbly with pimples and boils and open pustules. When I had enough command of their language to frame a delicate question on that subject, they only shrugged indifferently and said that almost all of their race, male and female, at some time in their lives indured the "small pocks." Some died of the affliction, they said, but most suffered no worse than facial disfigurement. And, since so many were similarly blemished, they did not feel that it detracted from their beauty. Maybe they did not; I thought it a most unsightly mutilation. Or I did then. Nowadays, when so many of my own people have faces pitted like lava rock, I try not to wince when I look at them.

I usually began learning a foreigner's language by pointing to nearby objects and encouraging him to speak the names by which he knew those objects. A slave girl had just then served cups of chocolate to me and Ah Tutál, so I stopped her and held her, and I flipped up her skirt to expose her feminine parts. I pointed a finger there and I said—I said what I now know is a most improper Spanish word. The two outlanders looked very much surprised and a little embarrassed. I pointed toward my own crotch and said another word which I now know better than to say in public.

It was my turn to be surprised. The two bounded to their feet, wild-eyed with distress. Then I understood their panic, and I could not help laughing. They obviously thought that, if I could order them summarily scoured, I could as easily order them castrated for having taken advantage of the local women. Still laughing, I shook my head and made other placative gestures. I pointed again to the girl's crotch and my own, saying "tipíli" and "tepúli." Then I pointed to my nose and said "yacatl." The two heaved sighs of relief and nodded to each other in comprehension. One of them pointed a shaking finger to his own nose and said "nariz." They sat down again and I began to learn the last new language I would ever need to know.

That first session did not end until well after dark, when they began to doze between words. No doubt their vigor had been sapped by their bath, perhaps the first bath in their lives, so I let them stumble to their quarters and to sleep. But I had them up early the next morning and, after one whiff of them, gave them the choice of washing themselves or again being forcibly scrubbed. Though they looked amazed and displeased that anybody should have to suffer such a thing *twice* in his lifetime, they chose to do it themselves. They did it every morning thereafter, and learned to do it sufficiently well that I could bear to sit with them all day long without too much discomfort. So our sessions lasted from morning to night; we even traded words while we ate the meals brought to us by the palace servants. I might also mention that the guests eventually began to eat the meat dishes, once I was able to explain from what animals they came.

Sometimes to reward my instructors' cooperation, sometimes to bolster them when they got tired and querulous, I would give them a refreshing cup or two of octli. I had brought, among Motecuzóma's "gifts for the gods," several jars of the finest grade of octli, and it was the only one of his many gifts I ever presented to them. On first tasting it, they made faces and called it "sour beer," whatever that might be. But they soon acquired a liking for it, and one night I deliberately made the experiment of letting them drink as much as they wanted. I was interested to note that they got as disgustingly drunk as any of our own people could do.

As the days passed and my vocabulary enlarged, I learned numerous things, and the most important was this. The outlanders were not gods but men, ordinary men, however extraordinary in appearance. They did not pretend to be gods, nor even any kind of spirit attendants preparing the way for the arrival of godly masters. They seemed honestly bewildered and mildly shocked when I made guarded mention of our people's expectation of gods someday returning to The One World. They earnestly assured me that no god had walked this world in more than one thousand and five hundred years, and they spoke of that one as if he were the *only* god. They themselves, they said, were only mortal men who, in this life and afterward, were sworn devotees of that god. While they lived in this world, they said, they were also obedient subjects of a King, who was likewise a man but a most exalted man, clearly their equivalent of a Revered Speaker.

As I shall later tell, Your Excellency, not all of our people were disposed to accept the outlanders' assertion—or mine— that they were mere men. But after my earliest association with them I never doubted that, and in time I was of course proved right. So, Your Excellency, I will henceforth speak of them not as outlanders or aliens or strangers of mysterious beings, but as men.

The man with the pimples and sores was Gonzalo Guerrero, a carpenter by trade. The man with the pitted face was Jerónimo de Aguilar, a professional scribe like the reverend friars here. It may even be that some of you could have known him at some time, for he told me that his earliest ambition had been to be a priest of his god, and that he had studied for some time in a calmécac or whatever you call your schools for priests.

The two had come, they said, from a land to the eastward, well out of sight beyond the ocean horizon. I had of course already surmised that, and I was not much further enlightened when they told me the land was called Cuba, and that Cuba was only one colony of a much greater and still more distant eastern land called Spain or Castile, from which seat of power their King ruled all his far-flung Spanish dominions. That Spain or Castile, they said, was a land in which all men and women were white of skin, except for a few inferior persons called Moors, whose skins were totally black. I might have found that last statement so incredible as to make me suspicious of everything else the men told me. But I reflected that in these lands there was born the occasional freakish white tlacaztáli. In a land of all white people, why should not the freaks be black?

Aguilar and Guerrero explained that they had come to our shores purely by misadventure. They had been among some hundreds of men and women who had left Cuba in twelve of the big floating houses—ships, they called them—under the command of a Captain Diego de Nicuesa, who was taking them to populate another Spanish colony of which he was to be governor, some place called Castilla de Oro, somewhere far to the southeast of here. But the expedition had run into misfortune, which they were inclined to blame on the coming of the ill-omened "hairy comet."

A fierce storm had scattered the ships, and the one carrying them was finally blown onto sharp rocks which punctured and overturned and sank it. Only Aguilar and Guerrero and two other men had managed to flee the flooding vessel in a sort of large canoe carried upon the ship for such emergencies. To their surprise, the canoe had not been long afloat when the ocean threw it upon the beach of this land. The other two occupants of the canoe drowned in the turbulent breakers, and Aguilar and Guerrero might have died too, had not "the red men" come running to help them to safety.

Aguilar and Guerrero expressed gratitude for their having been rescued, and hospitably received, and well fed and entertained. But they would be even more grateful, they said, if we red men would guide them back to the beach and their canoe. Guerrero the carpenter was sure he could repair any damage it had sustained, and make oars to propel it with. He and Aguilar were both sure that, if their god gave them fair weather, they could row eastward and find Cuba once more.

"Shall I let them go?" asked Ah Tutál, to whom I was translating as the interviews progressed.

I said, "If they can find the place called Cuba from here, then they should have no trouble finding Uluümil Kutz again from there. And you have heard: their Cuba seems to be teeming with white men eager to plant new colonies everywhere they can reach. Do you want them swarming here, Lord Mother?"

"No," he said worriedly. "But they might bring a physician who could cure the strange disease that is spreading among us. Our own have tried every remedy they know, but daily more persons fall ill and already three have died."

"Perhaps these men themselves would know something about it," I suggested. "Let us look at one of the sufferers."

So Ah Tutál led me and Aguilar to a hut in the town, and inside, where a doctor stood muttering and rubbing his chin and frowning down at a pallet where a young girl lay tossing in fever, her face shiny with sweat, her eyes glazed and unseeing. Aguilar's whiteness went rather pink when he recognized her as one of the females who had visited his and Guerrero's quarters.

He said slowly, so that I should understand, "I am sorry to tell you that she has the small pocks. You see? The eruptions are beginning to grow on her forehead."

I translated that to the physician, who looked professionally mistrustful, but said, "Ask him what his people do to treat it."

I did, and Aguilar shrugged and said, "They pray."

"Evidently a backward people," grunted the doctor, but added, "Ask him to which god."

Aguilar said, "Why, they pray to *the* Lord God!"

That was of no help, but I thought to ask, "Do you pray to that god in some manner which we might imitate?"

He tried to explain, but the explanation was of a complexity beyond my grasp of the language. So he indicated that it could more easily be demonstrated, and the three of us—Ah Tutál, the physician, and I—hurried after him back to the palace courtyard. He ran to his quarters while we stayed at a distance, and he came back to us with something in each hand.

One of the things was a small box with a tight-fitting cover. Aguilar opened it to show its contents: a considerable number of small disks that appeared to have been cut from heavy white paper. He attempted another explanation, from which I gathered that he had illicitly kept or stolen the box as a memento of his days in the priest school. And I further understood that the disks were a special sort of bread, the most holy and potent of all foods, because a person who ate one of them partook of the strength of that almighty Lord God.

The other object was a string of many small beads irregularly interspersed among numerous larger ones. All the beads were of a blue substance that I had never seen before: as blue and hard as turquoise but as transparent as blue water. Aguilar started another complex explanation, of which I heard only the information that each bead represented a prayer. Naturally I was reminded of the practice of placing a jadestone chip in the mouth of someone dead, and I thought the prayer beads might be similarly and beneficially employed by the not yet dead. So I interrupted Aguilar to ask urgently:

"Do you put the prayers in the mouth, then?"

"No, no," he said. "They are held in the hands." Then he gave a cry of protest as I snatched the box and beads from him.

"Here, Lord Physician," I said to the doctor. I broke the string and gave him two of the beads, and I translated what little I had comprehended of Aguilar's instructions: "Take the girl's hands and clench each hand around one of these prayers. . . ."

"No, no!" Aguilar wailed. "Whatever you are doing, it is wrong! There is more to prayer than just—"

"Be quiet!" I snapped, in his language. "We have not time for more!"

I fumbled some of the papery little bits of bread from the box and put one in my mouth. It *tasted* like paper, and it dissolved on my tongue without my having to chew it. I felt no instant surge of god strength, but at least I realized the bread could be fed to the girl even in her half-conscious condition.

"No, no!" Aguilar shouted yet again, when I ate the thing. "This is unthinkable! *You* cannot receive the Sacrament!

He regarded me with the same expression of horror that I see right now on Your Excellency's face. I am sorry for my impulsive and shocking behavior. But you must remember that I was only an ignorant pagan then, and I was concerned with hurrying to save a girl's life. I pressed some of the little disks into the doctor's hand and told him:

"This is god food, magic food, and easy to eat. You can force them into her mouth without the risk of choking her."

He went off at a run, or as much of a run as his dignity would permit. . . .

In much the way that His Excellency has just now done.

I clapped Aguilar companionably on the shoulder and said, "Forgive me for taking the matter out of your hands. But if the girl is cured, you will get the credit, and you will be much honored by these people. Now let us find Guerrero and sit and talk some more about *your* people."

There were still many things I wished to learn from Jerónimo de Aguilar and Gonzalo Guerrero. And, since by then we could converse with fair comprehension, albeit haltingly, they were equally curious about things in these lands. They asked some questions that I pretended not to understand: "Who is your King? Does he command great armies? Does he possess great riches of gold?" And some questions that I truly did not understand: "Who are your Dukes and Counts and Marquises? Who is the Pope of your Church?" And some questions that I daresay no one could answer: "Why do your women have no hair down there?" So I warded off their questions by asking my own, and they answered all of them with no perceptible hesitation or suspicion or guile.

I could have stayed with them for at least a year, improving my grasp of their language and constantly thinking of new things to ask. But I made the precipitate decision to leave their company when, two or three days after our visit to the ailing girl, the physician came to me and silently beckoned. I followed him to that same hut, and looked down at the girl's dead face, hideously bloated beyond recognition and flushed to a gruesome purple color.

"All her blood vessels burst and her tissues swelled," said the doctor "including those inside her nose and mouth. She died in an agony of simply trying to breathe." He added disparagingly, "The god food you gave me worked no magic."

I asked, "And how many sufferers have you cured, Lord Physician, without recourse to that magic?"

"None," he sighed, and his pomposity deflated. "Nor have any of my colleagues saved a single patient. Some die like this, of strangulation. Some die with a gush of blood from the nose and mouth. Some die in raving delirium. I fear that all will die, and die miserably."

Looking at the ruin of what had been quite a pretty child, I said, "She told me, this very girl, that only a vulture could take pleasure from the white men. She must have had a true premonition. The vultures will now be pleased to gorge on her carrion, and her dying was somehow the doing of the white men."

When I returned to the palace and reported to Ah Tutál, he said emphatically, "I will no longer have the diseased and unclean strangers here!" I could not make out whether his crossed eyes glared at me or past me, but they were undeniably angry. "Do I let them go away in their canoe, or do you take them to Tenochtítlan?"

"Neither," I said. "And do not kill them either, Lord Mother, at least until you receive permission from Motecuzóma. I would suggest that you get rid of them by giving them into slavery. Give them to the chiefs of tribes well distant from here. The chiefs should feel flattered and honored by such gifts. Not even the Revered Speaker of the Mexíca has a white slave."

"Um . . . yes . . ." Ah Tutál said thoughtfully. "There are two chiefs I particularly dislike and distrust. It would not grieve me should the white men bring misery on them." He regarded me more kindly. "But you were sent all this way, Knight Ek Muyal, to find the outlanders. What will Motecuzóma say when you return empty-handed?"

"Not quite empty-handed," I said. "I will take back at least the box of god food and the little blue prayers, and I have learned many things to tell to Motecuzóma." A sudden thought struck me. "Oh, yes, Lord Mother, there could be one other thing to show him. If any of your females who lay with the white men should prove pregnant, and if they do not fall victim to the small pocks—well, if there are offspring, send *them* to Tenochtítlan. The Revered Speaker can put them on display in the city menagerie. They ought to be monsters unique among monsters."

Word of my returning to Tenochtítlan must have preceded me by several days, and Motecuzóma must certainly have been simmering with impatience to know what news—or what visitors—I might be bringing. But he was the same old Motecuzóma, and I was not ushered immediately into his presence. I had to stop in the corridor outside his throne room, and change from my Eagle Knight costume into the sackcloth of a suppliant, and then do the ordained adulatory ritual of kissing the earth all the way across the chamber to where he sat between the gold and silver gongs. Despite his cool and unhurried reception of me, though, he was obviously determined to be the first to hear my report—perhaps the only one to hear—for the other members of his Speaking Council were not present. He did allow me to dispense with the formality of speaking only when queried, and I told him all that I have thus far told you, reverend friars, and a few other things I had learned from your two countrymen:

"As best I can calculate, Lord Speaker, it was about twenty years ago that the first floating houses, called ships, set out from that distant land of Spain to explore the ocean to the west of it. They did not then reach our coast because it seems there are a great many islands, large and small, between here and Spain. There were people already resident on those islands and, from the description, I take them to have been something like the barbaric Chichiméca of our northern lands. Some of those islanders fought to repel the white men, some of them meekly allowed the incursion, but all by now have been made subject to those Spaniards and their King. During the past twenty years, then, the white men have been occupied with settling colonies on those islands, and plundering their resources, and trading between the islands and their Spanish homeland. Only a few of their ships, moving from one island to another, or idly exploring, or blown astray by the wind, have until now even glimpsed these lands. We might hope that the islands will keep the white men busy for many more years, but I beg leave to doubt it. Even the biggest island is only an island, therefore limited in riches worth taking and land worth populating. Also, the Spaniards seem insatiable both in their curiosity and in their rapacity. They are already seeking beyond the islands for new discoveries and new opportunities. Soon or later, their seeking will bring them to these lands. It will be as the Revered Speaker Nezahualpíli foretold: an invasion, for which we had best prepare."

"Prepare!" snorted Motecuzóma, probably stung by the memory of Nezahualpíli's having supported that prophecy by winning the tlachtli contest. "That aged fool *prepares* by sitting down and sitting still. He will not even help me war against the insufferable Texcaltéca."

I did not remind him of what else Nezahualpíli had said: that all our peoples should cease the perpetuation of old enmities and unite against that impending invasion.

"Invasion, you said," Motecuzóma went on. "You also said that those two outlanders came without weapons and totally defenseless. It would imply an unusually peaceable invasion, if any."

I said, "What weapons might have gone down with their flooded ship, they did not confide. They may need no weapons at all—not weapons of the sort we know—if they can inflict a killing disease to which they themselves are casually indifferent."

"Yes, that would be a potent weapon indeed," Motecuzóma said. "A weapon heretofore reserved to the gods. And yet you insist they are not gods." Meditatively he regarded the little box and its contents. "They carry with them a god-given food." He fingered some of the blue beads. "They carry with them prayers made palpable, and made of a mysterious stone. Yet you insist they are not gods."

"I do, my lord. They get drunk as men do, they lie with women as men do—"

"*Ayyo!*" he interrupted triumphantly. "Exactly the reasons why the god Quetzalcóatl went away from here where he did. According to all the tales, he once succumbed to intoxication and committed some sexual misdeed, and in shame he abdicated his rule of the Toltéca."

"Also according to all the tales," I said drily, "in the days of Quetzalcóatl these lands were everywhere perfumed by flowers, and every wind blew a sweet fragrance. The aroma of the two men I met would suffocate the wind god." I patiently insisted, "The Spaniards are but men, my lord. They differ from us only in being white of skin, and hairy, and perhaps larger in their average size."

"The statues of the Toltéca at Tolan are *much* larger than any of us," Motecuzóma said stubbornly, "and whatever colors they were painted are no longer perceptible. For all we know, the Toltéca were white of skin." I exhaled a sigh of exasperation, but he paid it no heed. "I will set our historians to a close scrutiny of every ancient archive. We will find out what the Toltéca *did* look like. Meanwhile, I will have our highest priests put this god food in a finely made container and bear it reverently to Tolan and set it within reach of those sculptured Toltéca. . . ."

"Lord Speaker," I said. "In conversation with those two white men, I several times mentioned the name of the Toltéca. It meant nothing at all to them."

He snapped his gaze up from the god bread and the beads, and he smiled a really victorious smile. "There you are, then! The name would *not* mean anything to a genuine Toltécatl. We call them the Master Artisans *because we do not know what they called themselves!*"

He was right, of course, and I was embarrassed. I could think of no retort except to mumble, "I doubt that they called themselves Spaniards. That word—their whole language—has no relation to any languages I have encountered anywhere in these lands."

"Eagle Knight Mixtli," he said, "those white men could be as you say—human beings, mere men—*and still be Toltéca*, descendants of those who vanished so long ago. That King of whom they told you could be the self-exiled god Quetzalcóatl. He could be ready now to return as he promised, waiting beyond the sea only until his Toltéca subjects tell him that we are amenable to his return."

"*Are* we amenable, my lord?" I asked impudently. "Are you amenable? The return of Quetzalcóatl would unseat every ruler now ruling, from Revered Speakers to the lowliest tribal chiefs. He would rule supreme."

Motecuzóma put on an expression of pious humility. "A returned god will no doubt be grateful to those who have preserved and even improved his dominions, and he will no doubt make evident his gratitude. If he should grant only that I be a voice among his Speaking Council, I would be more highly honored than any other mortal ever has been."

I said, "Lord Speaker, I have erred before. I may err now in supposing the white men to be no gods or forerunners of any god. But might you not err more gravely in supposing that they are?"

"Suppose? I do not suppose!" he said sternly. "I do not say yes a god comes, or no he does not, as you so impertinently presume to do!" He stood erect and almost shouted, "I am the Revered Speaker of the One World, and I do not say this or that, yes or no, gods or men, until I have pondered and observed and waited to make *certain!*"

I took his standing up as my dismissal. I backed away from the throne, repeatedly kissing the earth as prescribed, and I left the chamber, and I tore off the sackcloth robe, and I went home.

As to the question—gods or men?—Motecuzóma had said he would wait until he was certain, and that is what he did. He waited, and he waited too long, and even when it could no longer matter, he was still not really certain. And because he waited in uncertainty, he died at last in disgrace, and the last command he tried to give his people began uncertainly, "Mixchía—!" I know; I was there; and I heard that last word Motecuzóma ever spoke in his life: "Wait—!"

✠

Waiting Moon did nothing to spoil my homecoming that time. There was by then some natural gray in her hair, but she had dyed or cut whatever remained of that offending strand of bleached white. And although Béu had ceased trying to make herself into a simulacrum of her dead sister, she had nevertheless made herself into quite a different person from the one I had known for nearly half a sheaf of years, ever since we first met in her mother's Tecuantépec hut. During all those years, every time we had been in each other's company, it seemed we had quarreled or fought or at best maintained only an uneasy truce. But she seemed to have decided that henceforth we would act the roles of an ageing couple, long and amicably married. I do not know whether it was a result of my having so thoroughly chastised her, or whether it was meant for the admiration of our neighbors, or whether Béu Ribé had resigned herself to the age of never and had said to herself, "Never any more open animosities between us."

Anyway, her new attitude made it easier for me to settle down and adapt to living in a house and a city again. Always before, even in the days when my wife Zyanya or my daughter Nochípa still lived, every time I had come home it was with the expectation of sometime leaving again on a new adventure. But the latest homecoming made me feel that I had come home to stay for the remainder of my life. Had I been younger, I should have rebelled at that prospect, and soon have found some reason to depart, to travel, to explore. Or had I been a poorer man, I should have *had* to bestir myself, just to earn a living. Or had Béu been her former harridan self, I should have seized *any* excuse to get away—even leading a troop to war somewhere. But, for the first time, I had no reason or necessity to go on running and seeking down all the roads and all the days. I could even persuade myself that I *deserved* the long rest and the easy life that my wealth and my wife could provide. So I gradually eased into a routine which, while neither demanding nor rewarding, at least kept me occupied and not too bored. I could not have done that, but for the change in Béu.

When I say she had changed, I mean only that she had succeeded in concealing her lifelong dislike and contempt of me. She has never yet given me reason to think that those feelings ever abated, but she did stop letting them show, and that small sham has been enough for me. She ceased being proud and assertive, she became bland and docile in the manner of most other wives. In a way, I rather missed the high-spirited woman she had been, but that twinge of regret was outweighed by my relief at not having to contend with her former willful self. When Béu submerged her once distinctive personality and assumed the near invisibility of a woman all deference and solicitude, I was enabled to treat her with equal civility.

Her dedication to wifeliness did not include the slightest hint that I might finally use her for the one wifely service of which I had refrained from availing myself. She never suggested that we consummate our marriage in the accepted way; she never again flaunted her womanhood or taunted me to try it; she never complained of our sleeping in separate chambers. And I am glad she did not. My refusing any such advances would have disturbed the new equanimity of our life together, but I simply could not have made myself embrace her as a wife. The sad fact was that Waiting Moon was as old as I, and she looked her age. Of the beauty that had once been equal to Zyanya's, little remained except the beautiful eyes, and those I seldom saw. In her new role of subservience, Béu tried always to keep them modestly downcast, in the same way that she kept her voice down.

Her eyes had used to flash brilliantly at me, and her voice had used to be tart or mocking or spiteful. But in her new guise she spoke only quietly and infrequently. As I left the house of a morning, she might ask, "When would you like your meal waiting, my lord, and what would it please you to eat?" When I left the house in the evening, she might caution me, "The night grows chill, my lord, and you risk catching cold if you do not wear a heavier mantle."

I have mentioned my daily routine. That was it: I left my house at morning and evening, to pass the time in the only two ways I could think of.

Each morning I went to The House of Pochtéca and spent the greater part of the day there, talking and listening and sipping the rich chocolate handed around by the servants. The three elders who had interviewed me in those rooms, half a sheaf of years before, were of course long dead and gone. But they had been replaced by numerous other men just like them: old, fat, bald, complacent and assured in their importance as fixtures of the establishment. Except that I was not yet either bald or fat and did not *feel* like an elder, I suppose I could have passed for one of them, doing little but basking in remembered adventures and present affluence.

Occasionally the arrival of a merchant train afforded me the opportunity to make a bid for its cargo, or for whatever part of it I fancied. And before the day was out I could usually engage another pochtécatl in a round of bargaining, and end by selling him my merchandise at a profit. I could do that without ever setting down my cup of chocolate, without ever seeing what it was I had bought and sold. Occasionally there would be a young and newly aspiring trader in the building, making preparations to set out on his first journey somewhere. I would detain him for as long as it might take to give him the benefit of all my experience on that particular route, or for as long as he would listen without fidgeting and pleading urgent errands.

But on most days there were few persons present except myself and various retired pochtéca who had no place they would rather be. So we sat together and traded stories instead of merchandise. I listened to them tell tales of the days when they had fewer years and less wealth, but ambitions illimitable; the days when they themselves did the traveling, when they did the daring of risks and dangers. Our stories would have been interesting enough, even unadorned—and I had no need to exaggerate mine—but since the old men all tried to outdo each other in the uniqueness and variety of their experiences, in the hazards they had faced and bested, the narrow escapes they had enjoyed, the notable acquisitions they had so cunningly made . . . well, I noticed that some of the men present began to embroider their adventures after the tenth or twelfth telling. . . .

In the evenings I left my house to seek not company but solitude, in which I could reminisce and repine and yearn unobserved. Of course, I would not have objected if that solitude had been interrupted by one longed-for encounter. However, as I have told, that has never happened yet. So it was only with wistful hope, not with expectation, that I walked the nearly empty night streets of Tenochtítlan, from end to end of the island, remembering how here had occurred a certain thing and there another.

In the north was the causeway to Tepeyáca, across which I had carried my baby daughter when we fled from the flooding city to safety on the mainland. At that time Nochípa could speak only two-word sentences, but some of them had said much. And on that occasion she had murmured, "Dark night."

In the south was the causeway to Coyohuácan and all the lands beyond, the causeway I had crossed with Cozcatl and Blood Glutton on my very first trading expedition. In the splendor of that day's dawn the mighty volcano Popocatépetl had watched us go, and had seemed to say, "You depart, my people, but I remain. . . ."

In between were the island's two vast plazas. In the more southerly one, The Heart of the One World, stood the Great Pyramid, so massive and solid and eternal of aspect that a viewer might assume it had towered there for as long as Popocatépetl had towered on the distant horizon. It was difficult for even me to believe that I was older than the completed pyramid, that it had been only an unfinished stump the first time I saw it.

In the more northerly plaza, Tlaltelólco's wide-spreading market area, I had walked for the first time holding tightly to my father's hand. There he had generously paid the extravagant price to buy me my first taste of flavored snow, while he told the vendor, "I remember the Hard Times. . . ." It was then that I had first met the cacao-colored man, he who so accurately foretold my life to come.

That recollection was slightly disturbing, for it reminded me that all the future he had foreseen for me was in my past. Things I had once looked forward to had become memories. I was nearing the full sheaf of my years, and not many men lived more than those fifty and two. Then was there to *be* no more future for me? When I told myself that I was at last rightfully enjoying the idle life I had labored so long to earn, perhaps I was just refusing to confess that I had outlived my usefulness, that I had outlived every person I ever loved or who ever loved me. Was I only taking up space in this world until I should be summoned to some other one?

No! I refused to believe that, and for confirmation I looked up to the night sky. Again a smoking star hung there, as a smoking star had hung over my reunion with Motecuzóma at Teotihuácan, and then over my meeting with the girl Ce-Ma-lináli, and then over my meeting with the white visitors from Spain. Our astronomers could not agree: whether it was the same comet returning in a different shape and brightness and in a different corner of the sky, or whether it was a new comet each time. But, after the one that accompanied me on my last journey southward, *some* smoking star appeared in the night sky again in both of the two subsequent years, and each time was visible for nearly a month of nights. Even the usually imperturbable astronomers had to agree that it was an omen, that three comets in three years defied any other explanation. So something was going to happen in this world and, good or bad, it ought to be worth waiting for. I might or might not have any part to play in the event, but I would not resign from this world just yet.

Various things did happen during those years, and each time I wondered: is this what the smoking stars portended? The happenings were all remarkable in one respect or another, and some of them were lamentable, but none seemed *quite* momentous enough to have justified the gods' sending us such ominous warnings.

For example, I had been only a few months returned from my meeting with the Spaniards, when word came from Uluúmil Kutz that the mysterious disease of the small pocks had swept like an ocean wave over the entire peninsula. Among the Xiu, the Tzotxil, the Quiché, and all the other Maya-descendant tribes, something like three of every ten persons had died— among them my host, the Lord Mother Ah Tutál—and almost every survivor would live the rest of his or her life disfigured by the pock marks.

However uncertain Motecuzóma was about the nature and intention of those god-or-men visitors from Spain, he was not eager to expose himself to any god disease. For once, he acted promptly and decisively, putting a strict prohibition on any trade with the Maya lands. Our pochtéca were forbidden to go there, and our southern frontier guards were instructed to turn back all produce and merchandise coming from there. Then the rest of The One World waited in apprehension for some months longer. But the small pocks were successfully contained within the unfortunate Maya tribes and did not—not then—afflict any other peoples.

Some more months passed, and one day Motecuzóma sent a messenger to fetch me to the palace, and again I wondered: does *this* mean that the smoking stars' prophecy has been fulfilled? But, when I made the customary supplicant-in-sackcloth entrance to the throne room, the Revered Speaker looked only annoyed, not stricken with fear or wonder or any of the other larger emotions. Several of his Speaking Council, standing about the room, appeared rather amused. I myself must have looked puzzled when he said:

"This madman calls himself Tliléctic-Mixtli."

Then I realized that he was not speaking *of* me, but to me, and was pointing at a glum-faced, shabbily dressed stranger held firm in the grip of two palace guards. I raised my seeing crystal for a look, and recognized the man as no stranger, and I smiled first at him, then at Motecuzóma, and I said:

"Tliléctic-Mixtli is his name, my lord. The name Dark Cloud is not at all uncommon among—"

"You know him!" Motecuzóma interrupted, or accused. "Some relative of yours, perhaps?"

"Perhaps of yours as well, Lord Speaker, and perhaps of equal nobility."

He blazed, "You dare compare me to this filthy and witless beggar? When the court guards apprehended him, he was demanding audience with me by reason of his being a visiting dignitary. But look at him! The man is mad!"

I said, "No, my lord. Where he comes from, he is indeed the equivalent of yourself, except that the Aztéca do not use the title Uey-Tlatoáni."

"What?" said Motecuzóma, surprised.

"This is the Tlatocapíli Tliléctic-Mixtli of Aztlan."

"Of where?" cried Motecuzóma, astounded.

I turned my smile again to my namesake. "Did you bring the Moon Stone, then?"

He gave an abrupt, angry nod and said, "I begin to wish I had not. But the Stone of Coyolxaúqui lies yonder in the plaza, watched by the men who survived the labor of helping me roll it and raft it and drag it. . . ."

One of the guards holding him murmured audibly, "That cursed great rock has torn up half the paving of the city between here and the Tepeyáca causeway."

The newcomer resumed, "Those remaining men and I are near dead of fatigue and hunger. We hoped for a welcome here. We would have been satisfied with common hospitality. But I have been called a liar for speaking only *my own name!*"

I turned back to Motecuzóma, who was still staring in unbelief. I said, "As you perceive, Lord Speaker, the Lord of Aztlan is himself capable of explaining his name. Also his rank and his origin and anything else you might wish to know about him. You will find the Aztéca Náhuatl a trifle antiquated, but easily comprehensible.

Motecuzóma came alert with a start, and expressed apologies and greetings—"We will converse at your convenience, Lord of Aztlan, after you have dined and rested"—and gave orders to the guards and counselors that the visitors be fed and clothed and quartered as befitted dignitaries. He motioned for me to stay when the crowd left the throne room, then said:

"I can hardly believe it. An experience as unsettling as meeting my own legendary Grandfather Motecuzóma. Or like seeing a stone figure step down from a temple frieze. Imagine! A genuine Aztécatl, come to life." However, his natural suspicion quickly asserted itself, and he asked, "But what is he doing *here?*"

"He brings a gift, my lord, as I suggested to him when I rediscovered Aztlan. If you will go down to the plaza and look at it, I think you will find it worth many broken paving stones."

"I will do so," he said, but added, still suspiciously, "He must want something in return."

I said, "I think also that the Moon Stone is worth the bestowal of some high-sounding titles on its giver. And some feathered mantles, some jeweled ornaments, that he may be dressed according to his new station. And perhaps the bestowal of some Mexíca warriors as well."

"Warriors?"

I told Motecuzóma the idea I had earlier expounded to that ruler of Aztlan: that a renewed family tie between us Mexíca and those Aztéca would give The Triple Alliance what it did not currently have, a strong garrison on the northwestern coast.

He said cautiously, "Bearing in mind all the omens, this may not be the time to disperse any of our forces, but I will consider the notion. And one thing is certain. Even if he is younger than you and I, our ancestor deserves a better title than that of Tlatocapíli. I will at least put the -tzin to his name."

So I left the palace that day feeling rather pleased that a Mixtli, even if it was not myself, had achieved the noble name of Mixtzin. As things turned out, Motecuzóma complied in full with my suggestions. The visitor left our city bearing the resounding title of Aztéca Tlani-Tlatoáni, or Lesser Speaker of the Aztéca. He also took with him a considerable troop of armed soldiers and a number of colonist families selected for their skill at building and fortifying.

I had the opportunity for only one brief conversation with my namesake while he was in Tenochtítlan. He thanked me effusively for my part in his having been welcomed and ennobled and made a partner in The Triple Alliance, and he added:

"Having the -tzin suffixed to my name puts it also on the names of all my family and descendants, even those of slightly indirect descent and divergent lineage. You must come again to Aztlan, Brother, for a small surprise. You will find more than a new and improved city."

At the time, I supposed he meant that he would arrange a ceremony to make me some sort of honorary lord of the Aztéca. But I have never been again to Aztlan, and I do not know what it became in the years after Mixtzin's return there. As for the magnificent Moon Stone, Motecuzóma dithered as usual, unable to decide where in The Heart of the One World it might best be displayed. So the last time I remember seeing it, the Moon Stone was still lying flat on the plaza pavement, and it is now as buried and lost as the Sun Stone.

The fact is that something else happened, to make me and most other people speedily forget the visit of the Aztéca, their bringing of the Moon Stone, and their plans for making Aztlan into a great seaside city. What happened was that a messenger came across the lake from Texcóco, wearing the white mantle of mourning. The news was not shockingly unexpected, since the Revered Speaker Nezahualpíli was by then a very old man, but it desolated me to hear that my earliest patron and protector was dead.

I could have gone to Texcóco with the rest of the Eagle Knights, in the company of all the other Mexíca nobles and courtiers who crossed the lake to attend the funeral of Nezahualpíli, and who would either stay there or cross the lake again, some while later, to attend the coronation of the Crown Prince Ixtlil-Xochitl as new Revered Speaker of the Acólhua nation. But I chose to go without pomp and ceremony, in plain mourning dress, as a private citizen. I went as a friend of the family, and I was received by my old schoolmate, the Prince Huexotl, who greeted me as cordially as he had first done thirty and three years before, and greeted me with the name I had worn then: "Welcome, Head Nodder!" I could not help noticing that my old schoolmate Willow *was* old; I tried not to let my expression show what I felt when I saw his graying hair and lined visage; I had remembered his as a lithe young prince strolling with his pet deer in a verdant garden. But then I thought, uncomfortably: he is no older than *I* am.

The Uey-Tlatoáni Nezahualpíli was buried in the grounds of his city palace, not at the more expansive country extate near Texcotzínco Hill. So the smaller palace's lawns fairly overflowed with those come to say farewell to that much loved and respected man. There were rulers and lords and ladies from the nations of The Triple Alliance, and from other lands both friendly and not so. Those emissaries of farther countries who could not arrive in time for Nezahualpíli's funeral were nevertheless on their way to Texcóco at that moment, hurrying to be in time to salute his son as the new ruler. Of all who *should* have been at the graveside, the most conspicuously absent was Motecuzóma, who had sent in his place his Snake Woman Tlácotzin and his brother Cuitláhuac, chief commander of the Mexíca armies.

Prince Willow and I stood side by side at the grave, and we stood not far from his half brother, Ixtlil-Xochitl, heir to the Acólhua throne. He still somewhat resembled his name of Black Flower, since he still had the merged black eyebrows that made him appear always to be scowling. But he had lost most of what other hair he had had, and I thought: he must be ten years older than his father was when I first came to school in Texcóco. After the interment, the crown repaired to the palace ballrooms, to feast and chant and grieve aloud and loudly recount the deeds and merits of the late Nezahualpíli. But Willow and I secured several jars of prime octli, and we went to the privacy of his chambers, and we gradually got very drunk as we relived the old days and contemplated the days to come.

I remember saying at one point, "I heard much muttering about Motecuzóma's rude absence today. He has never forgiven your father's aloofness in these past years, particularly his refusal to help in fighting petty wars."

The prince shrugged. "Motecuzóma's bad manners will win him no concessions from my half brother. Black Flower is our father's son, and believes as he did—that The One World will someday soon be invaded by outlanders, and that our only security is in unity. He will continue our father's policy; that we Acólhua must conserve our energies for a war that will be anything but petty."

"The right course, perhaps," I said, "But Motecuzóma will love your brother no better than he loved your father."

The next thing I remember was looking at the window and exclaiming, "Where has the time gone? It is late at night—and I am woefully inebriated."

"Take the guest chamber yonder," said the prince. "We must be up tomorrow to hear all the palace poets read their eulogies."

"If I sleep now I shall have a horrendous head in the morning," I said. "With your leave, I will first go for a walk in the city and let Night Wind blow some of the vapors from my brain."

My mode of walking was probably a sight to see, but there was nobody to see it. The night streets were even emptier than usual, for every resident of Texcóco was in mourning and indoors. And the priests had evidently sprinkled copper filings in the pine-splint torches on the street corner poles, for their flames burned blue, and the light they cast was dim and somber. In my muddled state, I somehow got the impression that I was repeating a walk I had walked once before, long ago. The impression was heightened when I saw ahead of me a stone bench under a red-flowering tapachíni tree. I sank down on it gratefully, and sat for a while, enjoying being showered by the tree's scarlet petals blown loose by the wind. Then I became aware that on either side of me was seated another man.

I turned left and squinted through my topaz, and saw the same shriveled, ragged, cacao-colored man I had seen so often in my life. I turned to my right, and saw the better-dressed but dusty and weary man I had seen not quite so often before. I suppose I should have started up with a loud cry, but I only chuckled drunkenly, aware that they were illusions induced by all the octli I had imbibed. Still chuckling, I addressed them both:

"Venerable lords, should you not have gone underground with your impersonator?"

The cacao man grinned, showing the few teeth he had. "There was a time when you believed us to be gods. You supposed that I was Huehuetéotl, Oldest of Old Gods, he who was venerated in these lands long before all others."

"And that I was the god Yoáli Ehécatl," said the dusty man. "The Night Wind, who can abduct unwary walkers by night, or reward them, according to his whim."

I nodded, deciding to humor them even if they were only hallucinations. "It is true, my lords, I was once young and credulous. But then I learned of Nezahualpíli's pastime of wandering the world in disguise."

"And that made you disbelieve in the gods?" asked the cacao man.

I hiccuped and said, "Let me put it this way. I have never met any others except you two."

The dusty man murmured obscurely, "It may be that the real gods appear only when they are about to disappear."

I said, "You had better disappear, then, to where you belong. Nezahualpíli cannot be very happy, walking the dismal road to Míctlan while two embodiments of himself are still above-ground."

The cacao man laughed. "Perhaps we cannot bear to leave *you*, old friend. We have so long followed your fortunes in *your* various embodiments: as Mixtli, as Mole, as Head Nodder, as Fetch!, as Záa Nayàzú, as Ek Muyal, as Su-kurú—"

I interrupted, "You remember my names better than I do."

"Then remember ours!" he said, rather sharply. "I am Huehuetéotl and this is Yoáli Ehécatl."

"For mere apparitions," I grumbled, "you are cursedly persistent and insistent. I have not been this drunk for a long time. It must have been seven or eight years ago. And I remember... I said then that someday, somewhere I would meet a god, and I would ask him. I would ask him this. Why have the gods let me live so long, while they have struck down every other person who ever stood close to me? My dear sister, my beloved wife, my infant son and treasured daughter, so many close friends, even transient loves..."

"That is easily answered," said the ragged apparition who called himself The Oldest of Old Gods. "Those persons were, so to speak, the hammers and chisels used for the sculpturing of you, and they got broken or discarded. You did not. You have weathered all the blows and the chipping and the abrasion."

I nodded with the solemnity of inebriation and said, "That is a drunken answer, if ever I heard one."

The dusty apparition who called himself Night Wind said, "You of all people, Mixtli, know that a statue or monument does not come already shaped from the limestone quarry. It must be hewn with adzes and ground with obsidian grit and hardened by exposure to the elements. Not until it is carved and toughened and polished is it fit for use."

"Use?" I said harshly. "At this dwindling end of my roads and my days, of what use could I possibly be?"

Night Wind said, "I mentioned a monument. All it does is stand upright, but that is not always an easy thing to do."

"And it will not get easier," said The Oldest of Old Gods. "This very night, your Revered Speaker Motecuzóma has made one irreparable mistake, and he will make others. There is coming a storm of fire and blood, Mixtli. You were shaped and hardened for only one purpose. To survive it."

I hiccuped again and asked, "Why me?"

The Oldest said, "A long time ago, you stood one day on a hillside not far from here, undecided whether to climb. I told you then that no man has ever yet lived out any life except his one chosen own. You chose to climb. The gods chose to help you."

I laughed a horrible laugh.

"Oh, you could not have appreciated their attentions," he admitted, "any more than the stone recognizes the benefits conferred by hammer and chisel. But help you they did. And you will now requite their favors."

"You will survive the storm," said Night Wind.

The Oldest went on, "The gods have helped you to become a knower of words. Then they helped you to travel in many places and to see and learn and experience much. That is why, more than any other man, you know what The One World was like."

"Was?" I echoed.

The Oldest made a sweeping gesture with his skinny arm. "All this will disappear from sight and touch and every other human sense. It will exist only in memory. You have been charged with remembering."

"You will endure," said Night Wind.

The Oldest gripped my shoulder and said, with infinite melancholy, "Someday, when all that was is gone . . . never to be seen again . . . men will sift the ashes of these lands, and they will wonder. You have the memories and the words to tell of The One World's magnificence, so it will not be forgotten. You, Mixtli! When all the other monuments of all these lands have fallen, when even the Great Pyramid falls, you will not."

"You will stand," said Night Wind.

I laughed again, scoffing at the absurd idea of the ponderous Great Pyramid ever falling down. Still trying to humor the two admonitory phantasms, I said, "My lords, I am not made of stone. I am only a man, and a man is the frailest of monuments."

But I heard no reply or reproof. The apparitions had gone as quickly as they had come, and I was talking to myself.

From some distance behind my bench, the street lamp flickered its moody blue flames. In that mournful lighting, the red tapachíni blossoms that fluttered down onto me were dark, a crimson color, like a drizzle of drops of blood. I shuddered, for I felt a feeling I had experienced only once before—when for the first time I had stood at the edge of the night and the edge of the darkness—the feeling of being utterly alone in the world, and desolate, and forlorn. The place where I sat was only a tiny island of dim blue light, and all about that place there was nothing but darkness and emptiness and the low moaning of the night wind, and the wind moaned, "Remember. . . ."

When I was awakened by a street-lamp tender making his rounds at dawn, I laughed at my unbecomingly drunken behavior and my even more foolish dream. I limped back to the palace, stiff from having slept on the cold stone bench, expecting to find the whole court still asleep. But there was great excitement there, everyone up and dashing frantically about, and a number of armed Mexíca soldiers inexplicably posted at the building's various portals. When I found Prince Willow and he glumly told me the news, I began to wonder if my nighttime encounter really had been a dream. For the news was that Motecuzóma had done a base and unheard-of thing.

As I have said, it was an inviolable tradition that solemn ceremonies like the funeral of a high ruler would not be marred by assassination or other such treacheries. As I have also said, the Acólhua army had been all but disbanded by the late Nezahualpíli, and the token few troops still under arms were in no state of readiness to repel invaders. As I have also said, Motecuzóma had sent to the funeral his Snake Woman Tlácotzin and his army commander Cuitláhuac. But I have not said, because I did not know, that Cuitláhuac had brought with him a war acáli carrying sixty hand-picked Mexíca warriors, who he had secretly debarked outside Texcóco.

During that night, while in my drunken confusion I was conversing with my hallucinations or with myself, Cuitláhuac and his troops had routed the palace guards, had taken over the building, and the Snake Woman had summoned all its occupants to hear a proclamation. The Crown Prince Black Flower would *not* be crowned his father's successor. Motecuzóma, as chief ruler of The Triple Alliance, had decreed that the crown of Texcóco would go instead to the lesser prince Cacáma, Maize Cob, the twenty-year-old son of one of Nezahualpíli's concubines who, not incidentally, was Mote-cuzóma's youngest sister.

Such a display of duress was unprecedented, and it was reprehensible, but it was incontestable. However admirable Nezahualpíli's pacificatory policy might have been in principle, it had left his people sadly unprepared to resist the Mexíca's meddling in their affairs. Crown Prince Black Flower put up a furious show of black indignation, but that was all he could do. Commander Cuitláhuac was not a bad man, despite his being Motecuzóma's brother and his following Motecuzóma's orders. He expressed his condolences to the deposed prince, and advised him to go quietly away somewhere, before Motecuzóma should get the very practical notion of ordering him imprisoned or eliminated.

So Black Flower departed that same day, accompanied by his personal courtiers and servants and guards and quite a number of other nobles equally infuriated by the turn of events, all of them loudly vowing revenge for having been betrayed by their longtime ally. The rest of Texcóco could only seethe in impotent outrage, and prepare to witness the coronation of Motecuzóma's nephew as Cacámatzin, Uey-Tlatoáni of the Acólhua.

I did not stay for that ceremony. I was a Mexícatl, and no Mexícatl was very popular in Texcóco right then, and indeed I was not very proud of being a Mexícatl. Even my old school-mate Willow was eyeing me pensively, probably wondering if I had spoken a veiled threat when I told him, "Motecuzóma will love your brother no better than he loved your father." So I left there and returned to Tenochtítlan, where the priests were jubilantly arranging special rites in almost every temple to celebrate "our Revered Speaker's clever stratagem." And Cacámatzin's buttocks had barely warmed the Texcóco throne before he was announcing a reversal of his father's policy: calling a new muster of Acólhua troops to help his uncle Motecuzóma mount still another offensive against the eternally beleaguered nation of Texcála.

And that war too was unsuccessful, mainly because Motecuzóma's new and young and bellicose ally, though personally selected by him and related by blood to him, was not of much help to him. Cacáma was neither loved nor feared by his subjects, and his call for volunteer soldiers went absolutely ignored. Even when he followed his call with a stern order of conscription, only a comparatively few men responded, and did so reluctantly, and proved remarkably listless in battle. Others of the Acólhua, who would otherwise eagerly have taken up arms, pleaded that they had grown old or ill during Nezahualpíli's years of peace, or that they had fathered large families they could not leave. The truth was that they were still loyal to the Crown Prince who should have been their Revered Speaker.

On leaving Texcóco, Black Flower had removed to another of the royal family's country residences, somewhere in the mountains well to the northeast, and had begun making of it a fortified garrison. Besides the nobles and their families who had voluntarily gone into exile with him, many other Acólhua joined that company: knights and warriors who had formerly served under his father. Still other men, who could not permanently leave their homes or occupations in the domains of Cacáma, did slip away at intervals to Black Flower's mountain redoubt, for training and practice with the other troops. All those facts were unknown to me at the time, as they were unknown to most people. It was a well-kept secret that Black Flower was preparing, slowly but carefully, to wrest his throne from the usurper, even if that should mean his having to fight the entire Triple Alliance.

Meanwhile, Motecuzóma's disposition, poisonous at the best of times, was not being improved. He suspected that he had fallen much in the esteem of other rulers by his domineering intervention in the affairs of Texcóco. He felt humiliated by his latest failure to humble Texcála. He was not much pleased with his nephew Cacáma. Then, as if he had not enough to worry and annoy him, even more troublesome things began to occur.

Nezahualpíli's death might almost have been the signal for the fulfillment of his gloomiest predictions. In the month of The Tree is Raised next following his funeral, a swift-messenger from the Maya lands arrived with the disturbing news that the strange white men had come again to Uluúmil Kutz, and not two of them that time, but a hundred. They had come in three ships, and moored off the port town of Kimpéch on the western shore of the peninsula, and rowed to the beach in their big canoes. The people of Kimpéch, those who had survived the decimation of the small pocks, resignedly let them land without fuss or opposition. But the white men boldly entered a temple and, without even gestures of requesting permission, began to strip the temple of its golden ornamentation. At that, the local populace put up a fight.

Or they tried to, said the messenger, for the weapons of the Kimpéch warriors shattered on the white men's *metal bodies*, and the white men shouted a war cry, "Santiago!" and they fought back with the sticks they carried, which were not mere staves or clubs. The sticks spat thunder and lightning like the god Chak at his angriest, and many Maya fell dead at a great distance from the spitting sticks. Of course, we all know now that the messenger was trying to describe your soldiers' steel armor and far-killing harquebuses, but at the time his story sounded demented.

However, he brought two articles to substantiate his wild tale. One was a bark paper tally of the dead: more than a hundred of the Kimpéch men, women, and children; forty and two of the outlanders—an indication that Kimpéch had put up a brave fight against those terrible new weapons. At any rate, the defense had repelled the invaders. The white men had retreated to their canoes, thence to their ships, which had spread their wings and disappeared again beyond the horizon. The other article brought by the messenger was the face of one of the dead white men, flayed from its head, complete with hair and beard, and dried taut on a willow hoop. I later had an opportunity to see it myself, and it much resembled the faces of the men I had met—in its limelike skin, at least—but the hair of scalp and face was of an even more odd color: as yellow as gold.

Motecuzóma rewarded the messenger for bringing him that trophy, but, after the man had gone, he reportedly did much cursing about what fools the Maya were—"Imagine, attacking visitors who might be gods!"—and in great agitation he closeted himself with his Speaking Council and his priests and his seers and sorcerers. But I was not summoned to join the conference and, if it came to any conclusions, I did not hear of them.

However, a little more than a year later, in the year Thirteen Rabbit, the year when I turned my sheaf of years, the white men came again from beyond the horizon, and that time Motecuzóma did call me to a private audience.

"For a change," he said, "this report was not brought by a Maya of sloping forehead and constricted brain. It was brought by a group of our own pochtéca who happened to be trading along the coast of the eastern sea. They were in Xicalánca when six of the ships came, and they had the good sense not to panic nor to let the townsfolk panic."

I remembered Xicalánca well: that town so beautifully situated between blue ocean and green lagoon, the the Olméca country.

"So there was no fighting," Motecuzóma went on, "although the white men this time numbered two hundred and forty, and the natives were much affrighted. Our staunch pochtéca took command of the situation, and kept everyone calm, and even persuaded the ruling Tabascoöb to greet the newcomers. So the white men made no trouble, they ravaged no temples, they stole nothing, they did not even molest any women, and they went away again after spending the day admiring the town and sampling the native foods. Of course, nobody could communicate in their language, but our merchants managed with signs to suggest some bartering. The white men had come ashore with not much to trade. But they did, in exchange for some quills of gold dust, give *these!*"

And Motecuzóma, with the gesture of a street sorcerer magically producing sweets for a crowd of children, whipped from under his mantle several strings of beads. Though they were made of various materials in various colors, they were identical in the numbers of small beads separated at intervals by larger beads. They were strings of prayers like the string I had acquired from Jerónimo de Aguilar seven years earlier. Motecuzóma smiled a smile of vindication, as if he expected me suddenly to grovel and concede, "You were right, my lord, the strangers *are* gods."

Instead, I said, "Clearly, Lord Speaker, the white men all worship in the same manner, which indicates that they all come from the same place of origin. But we already supposed that much. This tells us no new thing about them."

"Then what about *this?*" And from behind his throne, with that same air of triumph, he brought out what looked like a tarnished silver pot. "One of the visitors took that from off his own head and traded it for gold."

I examined the thing. It was no pot, for its rounded shape would have prevented its standing upright. It was of metal, but of a kind grayer than silver and not so shiny—it was steel, of course—and at its open side were affixed some leather straps, evidently to be secured beneath the wearer's chin.

I said, "It is a helmet, as I am sure the Revered Speaker has already ascertained. And a most practical sort of helmet. No maquáhuitl could split the head of a man wearing one of these. It would be a good thing if our own warriors could be equipped with—"

"You miss the important point!" he interrupted impatiently. "That thing is of the exact same shape as what the god Quetzalcóatl habitually wore on *his* revered head."

I said, skeptically but respectfully, "How can we possibly know that, my lord?"

With another swoop of movement, he produced the last of his triumphant surprises. "There! Look at that, you stubborn old disbeliever. My own nephew Cacáma sent it from the archives of Texcóco."

It was a history text on fawnskin, recounting the abdication and departure of the Toltéca ruler Feathered Serpent. Motecuzóma pointed, with a slightly trembling finger, to one of the pictures. It showed Quetzalcóatl waving good-bye as he stood on his raft, floating out to sea.

"He is dressed as we dress," said Motecuzóma, his voice also a little tremulous. "But he wears on his head a thing which must have been the crown of the Toltéca. Compare it with the helmet you hold at this moment!"

"There is no disputing the resemblance between the two objects," I said, and he gave a grunt of satisfaction. But I went on, cautiously, "Still, my lord, we must bear in mind that all the Toltéca were long gone before any of the Acólhua learned to draw. Therefore the artist who did this could never have *seen* how any Toltécatl dressed, let alone Quetzalcóatl. I grant that the appearance of his pictured headgear is of marvelous likeness to the white man's helmet. But I know well how storytelling scribes can indulge their imagination in their work, and I remind my lord that there is such a thing as coincidence."

"*Yya!*" Motecuzóma made the exclamation sound rather like a retch of nausea. "Will *nothing* convince you? Listen, there is even more proof. As I long ago promised, I set all the historians of all The Triple Alliance to the task of learning all they could about the vanished Toltéca. To their own surprise— they confess it—they have unearthed many old legends, hitherto mislaid or forgotten. And hear this: according to those rediscovered legends, the Toltéca were of uncommonly pale complexion and of uncommon hairiness, and their men accounted it a sign of manliness to encourage the growth of hair on their faces." He leaned forward, the better to glare at me. "In simple words, Knight Mixtli, the Toltéca were white and bearded men, exactly like the outlanders making their ever more frequent visits. *What do you say to that?*"

I could have said that our histories were so full of legends and variant legends and elaborations on legends that any child could find *some* one of them that would support any wildest belief or new theory. I could have said that the most dedicated historian was not likely to disappoint a Revered Speaker who was infatuated with an irrational idea and demanding substantiation of it. I did not say those things. I said circumspectly:

"Whoever the white men may be, my lord, you rightly remark that their visits are becoming ever more frequent. Also, they are coming in greater numbers each time. Also, each landing has been more westerly—Tihó, then Kimpéch, now Xicalánca—ever closer to these lands of ours. What does my lord make of that?"

He shifted on his throne, as if unconsciously suspecting that he sat only precariously there, and after a few moments of cogitation he said:

"When they have not been opposed, they have done no harm or damage. It is obvious from their always traveling in ships that they prefer to be on or near the sea. You yourself told that they come from islands. Whoever they are—the returning Toltéca or the veritable gods of the Toltéca—they show no inclination to press on inland toward this region which once was theirs." He shrugged. "If they wish to return to The One World, but wish only to settle in the coastlands ... well ..." He shrugged again. "Why should we and they not be able to live as friendly neighbors?" He paused, and I said nothing, and he asked with asperity, "Do you not agree?"

I said, "In my experience, Lord Speaker, one never really knows whether a prospective neighbor will be a treasure or a trial, until that neighbor has moved in to stay, and then it is too late to have regrets. I might liken it to an impetuous marriage. One can only hope."

Less than a year later, the neighbors moved in to stay. It was in the springtime of the year One Reed that another swift-messenger came, and again from the Olméca country, but that time bringing a most alarming report, and Motecuzóma sent for me at the same time he convened his Speaking Council to hear the news. The Cupílcatl messenger had brought bark papers documenting the sad story in word pictures. But, while we examined them, he also told us what had happened, in his own breathless and anguished words. On the day Six Flower, the ships had again floated on their wide wings to that coast, and not a few but a frightening *fleet* of them, *eleven* of them. By your calendar, reverend scribes, that would have been the twenty-fifth day of March, or your New Year's Day of the year one thousand five hundred and nineteen.

The eleven ships had moored off the mouth of The River of the Tabascoöb, farther to the west than on the earlier visit, and they had disgorged onto the beaches uncountable *hundreds* of white men. All armed and sheathed with metal, those men had swarmed ashore—shouting "Santiago!," apparently the name of their war god—coming with the clear intent of doing more than admiring the local landscape and savoring the local foods. So the populace had immediately mustered their warriors—the Cupílco, the Coatzacuáli, the Coatlícamac, and others of that region—some five thousand men altogether. Many battles had been fought in the space of ten days, and the people had fought bravely, but to no avail, for the white men's weapons were invincible.

They had spears and swords and shields and body coverings of metal, against which the obsidian maquáhuime shattered at first blow. They had bows that were contemptibly small and held awkwardly crossways, but which somehow propelled short arrows with incredible accuracy. They had the sticks that spat lightning and thunder and put an almost trifling but death-dealing hole in their victims. They had metal tubes on large wheels, which even more resembled a furious storm god, for they belched still brighter lightning, louder thunder, and a spray of jagged metal bits that could mow down many men at once, like maize stalks beaten down by a hailstorm. Most wondrous and unbelievable and terrifying of all, said the messenger, some of the white warriors were beast-men: they had bodies like giant, hornless deer, with four hoofed legs on which they could gallop as fleetly as deer, while their two human arms wielded sword or spear to lethal effect, and while the very sight of them sent brave men scattering in fear.

You smile, reverend friars. But at that time, neither the messenger's tumbling words nor the crude Cupílco drawings conveyed to us any coherent idea of soldiers mounted on animals larger than any animal in these lands. We were equally uncomprehending of what the messenger called lion-dogs, which could run down a running man, or sniff him out of hiding, and rend him as terribly as a sword or jaguar could do. Now, of course, we have all become intimately acquainted with your horses and staghounds, and their utility in hunting or in battle.

When the combined Olméca forces had lost eight hundred men to death and about an equal number to severe wounds, said the messenger, and had in the meantime killed only fourteen of the white invaders, the Tabascoöb called them all to retreat from the engagement. He sent emissary nobles carrying the gilt mesh flags of truce, and they approached the houses of cloth which the white men had erected upon the ocean beach. The nobles were surprised to find that they could communicate without having to use gestures, for they found that one of the white men spoke an understandable dialect of the Maya language. The envoys asked what terms of surrender the white men would demand, that a peace might be declared. One of the white men, evidently their chief, spoke some unintelligible words, and the Maya-speaking one translated.

Reverend scribes, I cannot testify to the exactitude of those words, since I repeat to you only what the Cupílcatl messenger said that day, and he of course had heard them only after their passing through several mouths and the several languages spoken by the several parties. But the words were these:

"Tell your people that we did not come to make war. We came seeking a cure for our ailment. We white men suffer from a disease of the heart, for which the only remedy is gold."

At that, the Snake Woman Tlácotzin looked up at Motecuzóma and said, in a voice meant to be encouraging, "That could be a valuable thing to know, Lord Speaker. The outlanders are not invulnerable to *everything*. They are afflicted with a curious disease which has never troubled any of the peoples in these lands."

Motecuzóma nodded hesitantly, uncertainly. All the old men of his Speaking Council followed his lead and likewise nodded as if reserving judgment. Only one old man in the room was rude enough to speak an opinion, and that of course was myself.

"I beg to differ, Lord Snake Woman," I said. "I have known numerous of our own people to show symptoms of that affliction. It is called greed."

Both Tlácotzin and Motecuzóma threw me peevish glances, and I said nothing else. The messenger was told to proceed with his story, of which there was not much more.

The Tabascoöb, he said, had bought peace by heaping upon the sands every fragment of gold he could immediately order brought to that place: vessels and chains and god images and jewels and ornaments of wrought gold, even dust and nuggets and chunks of the raw metal yet unworked. The obviously commanding white man asked, almost off-handedly, where the people acquired that heart-soothing gold. The Tabascoöb replied that it was found in many places in The One World, but that most of it was pledged to the ruler Motecuzóma of the Mexíca, hence the greatest store of it was to be found in his capital city. The white men had seemed much beguiled by that remark, and inquired where that city might be. The Tabascoöb told them that their floating houses could get near to it by floating farther along the coast, west, then northwest.

Motecuzóma growled, "Nice helpful neighbors we already have."

The Tabascoöb had also given the white commander a gift

of twenty beautiful young women to be divided among himself
and his ranking under-chiefs. Nineteen of the girls has been
selected, by the Tabascoöb himself, as the most desirable of
all the virgins in that immediate region. They did not go too
happily into the camp of the outlanders. But the twentieth girl
had unselfishly volunteered herself to make the gift total
twenty, which ritual number might influence the gods to send
the Olméca no more such visitations. So, the Cupílcatl concluded, the white men had loaded their plunder of gold and
young womanhood into their big canoes, then into their immeasurably bigger floating houses and, as all the people had
fervently hoped, the houses had unfurled their wings and set
off westward, on the day Thirteen Flower, keeping close along
the shoreline.

Motecuzóma growled some more, while the elders of his
Speaking Council huddled in a muttering conference, and while
the palace steward ushered the messenger from the room.

"My Lord Speaker," one of the elders said with diffidence,
"this is the year One Reed."

"Thank you," Motecuzóma said sourly. "That is one thing
which I already knew."

Another old man said, "But perhaps the possible significance of it has escaped my lord's attention. According to at
least one legend, One Reed was the year in which Quetzalcóatl
was born in his human form, to become the Uey-Tlatoáni of
the Toltéca."

And another said, "One Reed would also, of course, have
been the designation of the succeeding year in which Quetzalcóatl attained his sheaf of fifty and two years. And, again
according to legend, it was in *that* year One Reed that his
enemy the god Tezcatlipóca tricked him into becoming drunk,
so that without intent he sinned abominably."

And another said, "The great sin he committed, while inebriated, was to couple with his own daughter. When he awoke
beside her in the morning, his remorse made him abdicate his
throne and go away alone upon his raft, beyond the eastern
sea."

And another said, "But even as he went away, he vowed
to return. You see, my lord? The Feathered Serpent was born
in the year One Reed, and he vanished in the next year known

as One Reed. Admittedly, that is only a legend, and other legends about Quetzalcóatl cite different dates, and all of them were countless sheaves of years ago. But, since this *is* another One Reed year, might it not be likely to wonder . . . ?"

That one let his question trail off into silence, because Motecuzóma's face had gone almost as pale as that of any white man. He was shocked to speechlessness. It may have been because the reminder of the coincidental dates had followed so closely upon what the messenger had told: that the men from beyond the eastern sea were apparently intent on seeking his own city. Or he may have paled at the suggestive hint of a resemblance between himself and the Quetzalcóatl dethroned by shame at his own sin. Motecuzóma by then had numerous children of varying ages, by his various wives and concubines, and for some time there had been scurrilous gossip regarding his rumored relationship with two of three of his own daughters. The Revered Speaker had a sufficiency of things to ponder upon at that moment, but the palace steward came in again, kissing the earth and begging permission to announce the arrival of more messengers.

It was a delegation of four men from the Totonáca country on the eastern coast, come to report the appearance *there* of those eleven ships full of white men. The entry of the Totonáca messengers so immediately after the Cupílcatl messenger was yet another unsettling coincidence, but it was not an inexplicable one. Some twenty days had elapsed between the ships' leaving the Olméca lands and appearing on the Totonáca coast, but the latter country was almost directly east of Tenochtítlan and there were well-trodden trade routes between. The man from the Olméca country had had to come by a much longer and more arduous route. So the nearly simultaneous arrival of the separate reports was not remarkable, but neither did it make any of us in the throne room feel any easier.

The Totonáca were an ignorant people, and had not the art of word knowing, so they had sent no word-picture documentation of events. The four messengers were word *rememberers*, delivering a memorized report from their ruler, the Lord Patzínca, as he had spoken it to them, word for word. I should here remark that word rememberers were almost as useful as written accounts, in one respect: they could repeat whatever they had memorized, over and over again, as many times as necessary, and not omit or misplace a word of it. But they had their limitations, being impervious to questioning. When asked to clarify some obscure point in their message, they could not, They could only repeat the obscurity. The could not even elaborate a message by adding opinions or impressions of their own, for their single-mindedness precluded their having any such things.

"On the day Eight Alligator, my Lord Speaker," began one of the Totanáca, and went on to recite the message sent by Patzínca. On the day Eight Alligator, the eleven ships had suddenly materialized on the ocean and had come to a halt outside the bay of Chálchihuacuécan. It was a place I had once visited myself, The Place of Abundant Beautiful Things, but I made no comment, knowing better than to interrupt a word rememberer. The man went on to report that, on the following day, the day Nine Wind, the white and bearded strangers had begun to come ashore and build themselves little houses of cloth on the beach, and to erect large wooden crosses in the sand, also large banners, and to enact what appeared to be some sort of ceremony, since it included much chanting and gesticulation and kneeling down and standing up, and there were several priests, unmistakably priests, for they dressed all in black, just like those of these lands. Such were the occurrences of the day Nine Wind. On the next day...

One of the old men of the Speaking Council said pensively, "Nine Wind. According to at least one legend, Quetzalcóatl's full name was Nine Wind Feathered Serpent. That is to say, he was born on the day Nine Wind."

Motecuzóma flinched slightly, perhaps because that information struck him as portentous, perhaps because the informant should have known that it was a mistake ever to interrupt a word rememberer. A word rememberer could not just pick up his recitation where it was broken off; he had to back up and start from the beginning again.

"On the day Eight Alligator..."

He droned along to the point he had reached before, and went on, to report that there had been no battles on the beach, or anywhere else as yet. That was understandable. The Totonáca, besides being ignorant, were a servile and whining people. For years they had been subordinate to the Triple Alliance, and they regularly, though with querulous complaints, had paid us their annual tribute of fruits, fine woods, vanilla and cacao for making chocolate, picíetl for smoking, and other such products of the Hot Lands.

The residents of that Place of Abundant Beautiful Things, said the messenger, had not opposed the outlanders' arrival, but had sent word of it to their Lord Patzínca in the capital city of Tzempoálan. Patzínca in turn sent nobles bearing many gifts to the bearded white strangers, and also an invitation that they come to visit his court. So five of their presumably highest-ranking personages went to be his guests, taking with them one woman who had come ashore with them. She was neither white nor bearded, said the messenger, but was a female of some nation of the Olméca lands. At the Tzempoálan palace, the visitors presented gifts to Patzínca: a chair of curious construction, many beads of many colors, a hat made of some heavy, fuzzy red cloth. The visitors then announced that they came as envoys of a ruler called Kinkárlos and of a god called Our Lord and a goddess called Our Lady.

Yes, reverend scribes, I know, I know. I merely repeat it as the Totonácatl ignorantly repeated it.

Then the visitors intensely questioned Patzínca as to the circumstances obtaining in his land. To what god did he and his people pay homage? Was there much gold in this place? Was he himself an emperor or a king or merely a viceroy? Patzínca, though considerably perplexed by the many unfamiliar terms employed in the interrogation, replied as best he could. Of the multitudinous gods in existence, he and his people recognized Tezcatlipóca as the highest. He himself was ruler of all the Totonáca, but was subservient to three mightier nations farther inland, the mightiest of which was the nation of the Mexíca, ruled by the Revered Speaker Motecuzóma. At that very moment, confided Patzínca, five registrars of the Mexíca treasury were in Tzempoálan to review this year's list of the items the Totonáca were to yield in tribute. . . .

"I should like to know," a Council elder suddenly said, "how was this interrogation conducted? We have heard that one of the white men speaks the Maya tongue. But none of the Totonáca speaks anything but his own language and our Náhuatl."

The word rememberer looked momentarily flustered. He cleared his throat and went all the way back to: "On the day Eight Alligator, my Lord Speaker..."

Motecuzóma glared with exasperation at the hapless elder who had interrupted, and said between his teeth, "Now you may perish of old age before the lout ever gets around to explaining that."

The Totonácatl cleared his throat again. "On the day Eight Alligator..." and we all sat fidgeting until he worked his way through his recital and arrived again at new information. When he did, it was of sufficient interest to have been almost worth the wait.

The five haughty Mexíca tribute registrars, Patzínca told the white men, were exceedingly angry at him because he had made those strangers welcome without first asking the permission of their Revered Speaker Motecuzóma. In consequence, they had added to their tribute demand ten adolescent Totonáca boys and ten virgin Totonáca maidens, to be sent with the vanilla and cacao and other items to Tenochtítlan, to be sacrificed when such victims should be required by the Mexíca gods.

On hearing that, the chief of the white men made noises of great revulsion, and stormed at Patzínca that he should do no such thing, that he should instead have the five Mexíca officials seized and imprisoned. When the Lord Patzínca expressed a horrified reluctance to lay hands on Motecuzóma's functionaries, the white chief promised that his white soldiers would defend the Totonáca against any retaliation. So Patzínca, though sweating in apprehension, had given the order, and the five registrars were last seen——by the word rememberers, before they departed for Tenochtítlan——caged in a small cage of vine-tied wooden bars, all five stuffed in together like fowl going to market, their feather mantles lamentably ruffled, to say nothing of their state of mind.

"This is outrageous!" cried Motecuzóma, forgetting himself. "The outlanders may be excused for not knowing out tributary laws. But that witless Patzínca——!" He stood up from his throne and shook a clenched fist at the Totonácatl who had been speaking. "Five of my treasury officials treated so, and you dare to come and *tell* me! By the gods, I will have you thrown alive to the great cats in the menagerie unless your next words explain and excuse Patzínca's insane act of treason!"

The man gulped and his eyes bulged, but what he said was, "On the day Eight Alligator, my Lord Speaker . . ."

"*Ayya ouiya*, BE STILL!" roared Motecuzóma. He sank back onto his throne and despairingly covered his face with his hands. "I retract the threat. Any cat would be too proud to eat such trash."

One of the Council elders diplomatically supplied a diversion by signaling for one of the other messengers to speak. That one immediately began to babble rapidly, and in a mixture of languages. It was evident that he had been present during at least one of the conferences between his ruler and the visitors, and was repeating every single word that had passed among them. It was also evident that the white chief spoke in Spanish, after which another visitor translated that into Maya, after which still another translated *that* into Náhuatl for Patzínca's comprehension, after which Patzínca's replies were relayed back to the white chief along that same chain of interpretation.

"It is good that you are here, Mixtli," Motecuzóma said to me. "The Náhuatl is poorly spoken but, with enough repetitions, we may be able to make sense of it. Meanwhile, the other tongues—can you tell us what they say?"

I would have liked to show off with an immediate and glib translation but, in truth, I understood little more of the welter of words than did anyone else there. The messenger's Totonácatl accent was enough of an impediment. But also his ruler did not speak Náhuatl very well, since it was for him a language acquired only for conversing with his betters. Also, the Maya dialect being spoken as an intermediate translation was that of the Xiu tribe and, while I was competent enough in that tongue, the presumably white interpreter was not. Also, I was of course far from fluent in Spanish at that time. Also, there were many Spanish words used—such as "emperadore" and "virrey"—for which there were then no substitutes in any of our languages, so they were merely and badly parroted without translation in both the Xiu and Náhuatl the messenger recited. Somewhat abashedly, I had to confess to Motecuzóma:

"Perhaps I too, my lord, hearing enough repetitions, might be able to extract some pertinence. But at this moment I can only tell you that the word most often spoken by the white men in their own tongue is 'cortés.'"

Motecuzóma said gloomily, "One word."

"It means courteous, Lord Speaker, or gentle, mannerly, kindly."

Motecuzóma brightened a little and said, "Well, at least it does not bode too ill if the outlanders are speaking of gentleness and kindliness." I refrained from remarking that they had hardly behaved gently in their assault upon the Olméca lands.

After some moody cogitation, Motecuzóma told me and his brother, the war chief Cuitláhuac, to take the messengers elsewhere, to listen to what they had to say, as often as necessary, until we could reduce their effusions to a coherent report of the occurrences in the Totonáca country. So we took them to my house, where Béu kept us all supplied with food and drink while we devoted several whole days to listening to them. The one messenger recited, over and over, the message he had been given by the Lord Patzínca; the other three repeated, over and over, the garble of words they had memorized at the many-voiced conferences between Patzínca and the visitors. Cuitláhuac concentrated on the Náhuatl portions of the recitals, I on the Xiu and Spanish, until our ears and brains were all but benumbed. However, from the flux of words, we at last got a sort of essence, which I put into word pictures.

Cuitláhuac and I perceived the situation thus. The white men professed to be scandalized that the Totonáca or any other people should be fearful of or subject to the domination of a "foreign" ruler called Motecuzóma. They offered to lend their unique weapons and their invincible white warriors, to "liberate" the Totonáca and any others who wished to be free of Motecuzóma's despotism—on condition that those peoples would instead give their allegiance to an even more foreign King Carlos of Spain. We knew that some nations might be willing to join in an overthrow of the Mexíca, for none had ever been *pleased* to pay tribute to Tenochtítlan, and Motecuzóma had lately made the Mexíca even less popular throughout The One World. However, the white men attached one other condition to their offer of liberation, and any ally's acceptance of it would commit that ally to another act of rebellion that was appalling to contemplate.

Our Lord and Our Lady, said the white men, were jealous of all rival deities, and were revolted by the practice of human sacrifice. All the peoples desirous of becoming free of Mexíca domination would also have to become worshipers of the new god and goddess. They would eschew blood offerings, they would topple all the statues and temples of their old deities, they would instead set up crosses representing Our Lord and images of Our Lady—which objects the white men were conveniently ready to supply. Cuitláhuac and I agreed that the Totonáca or any other disaffected people might see much advantage in deposing Motecuzóma and his everywhere pervasive Mexíca, in favor of a faraway and invisible King Carlos. But we were also sure that no people would be so ready to disavow the old gods, immeasurably more fearsome than *any* earthly ruler, and thereby risk an immediate earthquake destruction of themselves and the entire One World. Even the easily swayed Patzínca of the Totonáca, we gathered from his messengers, was aghast at that suggestion.

So that was the account, and the conclusions we had drawn from it, which Cuitláhuac and I took to the palace. Motecuzóma laid my book of bark paper across his lap and began reading it, cheerlessly unfolding pleat after pleat, while I told its content aloud for the benefit of the Speaking Council elders also convened in the room. But that meeting, like an earlier one, was interrupted by the palace steward's announcement of new arrivals imploring immediate audience.

They were the five treasury registrars who had been in Tzempoálan when the white men arrived there. Like all such officials traveling in tributary lands, they wore their richest mantles and feather headdresses and insignia of office—to impress and awe the tribute payers—but they entered the throne room looking like birds that had been blown by a storm through several thorny thickets. They were disheveled and dirty and haggard and breathless, partly because, they said, they had come from Tzempoálan at their fastest pace, but mainly because they had spent many days and nights confined in Patzínca's accursed prison cage, where there was no room to lie down and no sanitary facilities.

"What madness is going on over there?" Motecuzóma demanded.

One of them sighed wearily and said, "Ayya, my lord, it is indescribable."

"Nonsense!" snapped Motecuzóma. "Anything survivable is describable. How did you manage to escape?"

"We did not, Lord Speaker. The leader of the white strangers secretly opened the cage for us."

We all blinked and Motecuzóma exclaimed, *"Secretly?"*

"Yes, my lord. The white man, whose name is Cortés—"

"His *name* is Cortés?" Motecuzóma followed that exclamation with a piercing look at me, but I could only shrug helplessly, being as mystified as he. The word rememberers' memorized conversations had given me no hint that the word was a name.

The newcomer went on patiently, wearily. "The white man Cortés came to our cage secretly, in the night, when there were no Totonáca about, and he was accompanied only by two interpreters. He opened the cage door with his own hands. Through his interpreters, he told us that his name is Cortés, and he told us to flee for our lives, and he asked that we convey his respects to our Revered Speaker. The white man Cortés wishes you to know, my lord, that the Totonáca are in a rebellious mood, that Patzínca imprisoned us despite the urgent cautioning of Cortés that the envoys of the mighty Motecuzóma should not be so rashly manhandled. Cortés wishes you to know, my lord, that he has heard much of the mighty Motecuzóma, that he is a devoted admirer of the mighty Motecuzóma, and that he willingly risks the fury of the treasonous Patzínca in thus sending us back to you unharmed, as a token of his regard. He wishes you also to know that he will exert all his persuasion to prevent an uprising of the Totonáca against you. In exchange for his keeping the peace, Lord Speaker, the white man Cortés asks only that you invite him to Tenochtítlan, so that he may pay his homage in person to the greatest ruler in all these lands."

"Well," said Motecuzóma, smiling and sitting straighter on

his throne, unconsciously preening in that spate of adulation.
"The white outlander is aptly named Courteous."

But his Snake Woman, Tlácotzin, addressed the man who
had just spoken: "Do you *believe* what that white stranger told
you?"

"Lord Snake Woman, I can recount only what I know. We
were imprisoned by Totonáca guards and we were freed by the
man Cortés."

Tlácotzin turned again to Motecuzóma. "We were told by
Patzínca's own messengers that he laid hands on these officials
only after being commanded to do so by that same chief of the
white men."

Motecuzóma said uncertainly, "Patzínca could have lied,
for some devious reason."

"I know the Totonáca," Tlácotzin said contemptuously.
"None of them, including Patzínca, has the courage to rebel
or the wit to dissemble. Not without assistance."

"If I may speak, Lord Brother," said Cuitláhuac. "You had
not yet finished reading the account prepared by the Knight
Mixtli and myself. The words repeated therein are the actual
words spoken between the Lord Patzínca and the man Cortés.
They do not at all accord with the message just received from
that Cortés. There can be no doubt that he has artfully tricked
Patzínca into treason, and that he has shamelessly lied to these
registrars."

"It does not make sense," Motecuzóma objected. "Why
should he incite Patzínca to the treachery of seizing these men,
and then negate that by setting them loose himself?"

"He hoped to make sure that we blamed the Totonáca for
the treason," resumed the Snake Woman. "Now that the officials have returned to us, Patzínca must be in a frenzy of fear,
and mustering his army against our reprisal. When that army
is gathered to mount a defense, the man Cortés may just as
easily incite Patzínca to use them for attack instead."

Cuitláhuac added, "And that *does* accord with our conclusions, Mixtli. Does it not?"

"Yes, my lords," I said, addressing them all. "The white
chief Cortés clearly wants *something* from us Mexíca, and he
will use force to get it, if necessary. The threat is implicit in
the message brought by these registrars he so cunningly freed.

His price for keeping the Totonáca in check is that he be invited here. If the invitation is withheld, he will use the Totonáca—and perhaps others—to help him fight his way here."

"Then we can easily forestall that," said Motecuzóma, "by extending the invitation he requests. After all, he says he merely wishes to pay his respects, and it is proper that he should. If he comes with no armies, with just an escort of his ranking subordinates, he can certainly work no harm here. My belief is that he wishes to ask our permission to settle a colony of his people on the coast. We already know that these strangers are by nature island dwellers and seafarers. If they wish only an allotment of some seaside land . . ."

"I hesitate to contradict my Revered Speaker," said a hoarse voice. "But the white men want more than a foothold on the beach." The speaker was another of the returned registrars. "Before we were freed from Tzempoálan, we saw the glow of great fires in the direction of the ocean, and a messenger came running from the bay where the white men had moored their eleven ships, and eventually we heard what had happened. At the order of the man Cortés, his soldiers stripped and gutted every useful item from ten of those ships, and the ten were burned to ashes. Only one ship is left, apparently to serve as a courier craft between here and wherever the white men come from."

Motecuzóma said irritably, "This makes less and less sense. Why should they deliberately destroy their only means of transport? Are you trying to tell me that the outlanders are all madmen?"

"I do not know, Lord Speaker," said the hoarse-voiced man. "I know only this. The hundreds of white warriors are now aground on that coast, with no means of returning whence they came. The chief Cortés will not now be persuaded or forced to go away, because, by his own action, he cannot. His back is to the sea, and I do not believe he will simply stand there. His only alternative is to march forward, inland from the ocean. I believe the Eagle Knight Mixtli has predicted correctly: that he will march this way. Toward Tenochtítlan."

Seeming as troubled and unsure of himself as the unhappy Patzínca of Tzempoálan, our Revered Speaker refused to make any immediate decision or to order any immediate action. He commanded that the throne room be cleared and that he be left alone. "I must give these matters deep thought," he said, "and closely study this account compiled by my brother and the Knight Mixtli. I will commune with the gods. When I have determined what should be done next, I will communicate my decisions. For now, I require solitude."

So the five bedraggled registrars went away to refresh themselves, and the Speaking Council dispersed, and I went home. Although Waiting Moon and I seldom exchanged many words, and then only regarding trivial household matters, on that occasion I felt the need of someone to talk to. I related to her all the things that had been happening on the coast and at the court, and the troublous apprehensions they were causing.

She said softly, "Motecuzóma fears that it is the end of our world. Do you, Záa?"

I shook my head noncommittally. "I am no far-seer. Quite the contrary. But the end of The One World has been often predicted. So has the return of Quetzalcóatl, with or without his Toltéca attendants. If this Cortés is only a new and different sort of marauder, we can fight him and probably vanquish him. But if his coming is somehow a fulfillment of all those old prophecies . . . well, it will be like the coming of the great flood twenty years ago, against which none of us could stand. I could not, and I was then in my prime of manhood. Even the strong and fearless Speaker Ahuítzotl could not. Now I am old, and I have little confidence in the Speaker Motecuzóma."

Béu regarded me pensively, then said, "Are you thinking that perhaps we should take our belongings and flee to some safer haven? Even if there is calamity here in the north, my old home city of Tecuantépec should be out of danger."

"I *had* thought of that," I said. "But I have for so long been involved in the fortunes of the Mexíca that I should feel like a deserter if I departed at this juncture. And it may be perverse of me, but if this *is* some kind of ending, I should like to be able to say, when I get to Míctlan, that I saw it all."

Motecuzóma might have gone on vacillating and temporizing for a long time, except for what occurred that very night. It was yet another omen, and a sufficiently alarming one that he bestirred himself at least to send for me. A palace page came, himself much perturbed, and roused me from my bed to accompany him at once to the palace.

As I dressed, I could hear a subdued hubbub from the street outside, and I grumbled, "What has happened now?"

"I will show you, Knight Mixtli," said the young messenger, "as soon as we are outdoors."

When we were, he pointed to the sky and said in a hushed voice, "Look there." Late though it was, well after midnight, we were not the only ones watching the apparition. The street was full of people from the neighboring houses, scantily clad in whatever garments they had snatched up, all of them with their faces upturned, all of them murmuring uneasily except when they were calling for other neighbors to wake up. I raised my crystal and looked at the sky, at first as wonderingly as everyone else. But then a memory came to my mind from long ago, and it somewhat diminished the dreadfulness of the spectacle, at least for me. The page glanced sideways at me, perhaps waiting for me to utter some exclamation of dismay, but I only sighed and said:

"This is all we lacked."

At the palace, a half-dressed steward hurried me up the stairs to the upper floor, then up another staircase to the roof of the great building. Motecuzóma sat on a bench in his roof garden, and I think he was shivering, though the spring night was not cold and he was swathed in several mantles hastily flung around him. Without shifting his gaze from the sky, he said to me:

"After the New Fire ceremony came the eclipse of the sun. Then the falling stars. Then the smoking stars. All those things of the past years were omens evil enough, but at least we knew them for what they were. *This* is an apparition never seen before."

I said, "I beg to correct you, Lord Speaker—only that I may relieve your apprehensions to some degree. If you will wake your historians, my lord, and set them to searching the archives, they can ascertain that this *has* occurred before. In the year One Rabbit of the last preceding sheaf of years, during the reign of your namesake grandfather."

He stared at me as if I had suddenly confessed to being

some kind of sorcerer. "Sixty and six years ago? Long before you were born. How could you know of it?"

"I remember my father telling of lights like these, my lord. He claimed it was the gods striding about the skies, but with only their mantles visible, all tinted in the same cold colors."

And that *is* what the lights looked like that night: like filmy cloth draperies depending from a point at the top of the sky and hanging all the way down to the mountain horizon, and swaying and stirring as if in a light breeze. But there was no noticeable breeze, and the long curtains of light made no swishing sound as they swung. They merely glowed coldly, in colors of white and pale green and pale blue. As the draperies softly undulated, those colors subtly changed places and sometimes merged. It was a beautiful sight, but a sight to make one's hair similarly stir.

Much later, I chanced to mention that night's spectacle to one of the Spanish boatmen, and told him how we Mexíca had interpreted it as a warning of dire things coming. He laughed and called me a superstitious savage. "We too saw the light that night," he said, "and we were mildly surprised to see it this far south. But I know it signifies nothing, for I have seen it on many nights when sailing in the cold northern oceans. It is a commonplace sight there in those seas chilled by Boreas, the north wind. Hence the name we call it, the Boreal Lights."

But that night I knew only that the pale and lovely and fearsome lights were being seen in The One World for the first time in sixty and six years, and I told Motecuzóma, "According to my father, they were the omen that presaged the Hard Times back then."

"Ah, yes." He nodded somberly. "The history of those starvation years I have read. But I think any bygone Hard Times will prove to have been negligible in comparison to what is now in store." He sat silent for a time, and I thought he was only moping, but suddenly he said, "Knight Mixtli, I wish you to undertake another journey."

I protested as politely as I could, "My lord, I am an ageing man."

"I will again provide carriers and escorts, and it is no rigorous trail from here to the Totonáca coast."

I protested more strongly, "The first formal meeting between the Mexíca and the white Spaniards, my lord, should be entrusted to no lesser personages than the nobles of your Speaking Council."

"Most of them are older than you are, and less fit for traveling. None of them has your facility at word picture accounts, or your knowledge of the strangers' tongue. Most important, Mixtli, you have some skill at picturing people as they really look. That is something we have not yet had, not since the outlanders first arrived in the Maya country—a good picture of them."

I said, "If that is all my lord requires, I can still draw from memory the faces of those two I visited in Tihó, and do a passably recognizable portrayal."

"No," said Motecuzóma. "You said yourself that they were only artisan commoners. I wish to see the face of their leader, the man Cortés."

I ventured to say, "Has my lord then concluded that Cortés *is* a man?"

He smiled wryly. "You have always disdained the notion that he might be a god. But there have been so many omens, so many coincidences. If he is not Quetzalcóatl, if his warriors are not the Toltéca returning, they could still have been sent by the gods. Perhaps as a retribution of some sort." I studied his face, rather corpse-looking in the greenish glow from above. I wondered if, when he spoke of retribution, he was thinking of his having snatched the throne of Texcóco from the Crown Prince Black Flower, or if he had other, private, secret sins in mind.

But he suddenly drew himself up and said in his more usual tart manner, "That aspect of the matter need not concern you. Only bring me a portrait of Cortés, and word pictures numbering his forces, describing their mysterious weapons, showing the manner in which they fight, anything else that will help us know them better."

I tried one last demurrer. "Whatever the man Cortés may be or may represent, my lord, I judge that he is no fool. He is not likely to let a spying scribe wander at will about his encampment, counting his warriors and their armory."

"You will not go alone, but with many nobles, richly accoutered according to their station, and all of you will address the man Cortés as an equal noble. That will flatter him. And you will take a train of porters bearing rich gifts. That will allay his suspicions as to your real intent. You will be high emissaries from the Revered Speaker of the Mexíca and The One World, fitly greeting the emissaries of that King Carlos of Spain." He paused and gave me a look. "Every man of you will be an authentic and fully accredited lord of the Mexíca nobility."

When I got home again, I found Béu also awake. After having watched the night sky's lights for some time, she was brewing chocolate for my return. I greeted her considerably more exuberantly than usual, "It has been quite a night, my Lady Waiting Moon."

She obviously took that for an endearment, and looked both startled and delighted, for I do not believe I had ever in our married life spoken an endearment to her.

"Why, Záa," she said, and blushed with pleasure. "If you were merely to call me 'wife' it would lift my heart. But—*my lady*? Why this sudden affection? Has something—?"

"No, no, no," I interrupted. I had for too many years been satisfied with Béu's closed and contained demeanor; I did not want her suddenly gushing sentimentality. "I spoke with the prescribed formality. 'Lady' is now your entitled mode of address. This night the Revered Speaker awarded me the -tzin to my name, which confers it upon you as well."

"Oh," she said, as if she would have preferred some other sort of benefaction. But she quickly reverted to her cool and unemotional former self. "I take it you are pleased, Záa."

I laughed, somewhat ironically. "When I was young I dreamt of doing great deeds and earning great wealth and becoming a noble. Not until now, past my sheaf of years, am I Mixtzin, the Lord Mixtli of the Mexíca, and perhaps only briefly, Béu.... Perhaps only as long as there *are* lords, only as long as there are Mexíca...."

There were four other nobles besides myself, and, since they had been born to their titles, they were not much pleased that Motecuzóma had set an upstart like me in command of the expedition and the mission we were charged to accomplish.

"You are to lavish esteem, attention, and flattery on the man Cortés," said the Revered Speaker, giving us our instructions, "and on any others of his company you perceive to be of high rank. At every opportunity you will lay a feast for them. Your porters include capable cooks, and they carry ample supplies of our tastiest delicacies. The porters also carry many gifts, which you are to present with pomp and gravity, and say that Motecuzóma sends these things as a token of friendship and peace between our peoples." He paused to mutter, "Besides the other valuables, there should be enough gold there to assuage all their heart ailments."

There certainly should, I thought. In addition to medallions and diadems and masks and costume adornments of solid gold—the most beautifully worked pieces from the personal collection of himself and prior Revered Speakers, many of them pieces of great antiquity and inimitable craftsmanship— Motecuzóma was even sending the massive disks, one of gold, one of silver, that had flanked his throne and served him for gongs of summons. There were also splendid feather mantles and headdresses, exquisitely carved emeralds, amber, turquoises, and other jewels, including an extravagant quantity of our holy jadestones.

"But, above all things, do this," said Motecuzóma. "Discourage the white men from coming here, or even wanting to come here. If they seek only treasure, your gift of it may be sufficient to send them seeking in other nations there along the coast. If not, tell them the road to Tenochtítlan is hard and perilous, that they could never make the journey alive. If that fails, then tell them that your Uey-Tlatoáni is too busy to receive them—or too aged or ill—or too unworthy to merit a visit by such distinguished personages. Tell them *anything* that will make them lose interest in Tenochtítlan."

When we crossed the southern causeway and then turned east, I was leading a longer and richer and more heavily laden train than any pochtécatl ever had done. We skirted south of the unfriendly land of Texcála, and went by way of Cholólan. There and in other cities, towns, and villages along the rest of our route, the anxious inhabitants pestered us with questions about the "white monsters" whom they knew to be disturbingly nearby, and about our plans for keeping them at a distance.

When we rounded the base of the mighty volcano Citlaltépetl, we began to descend through the last of the mountainous country into the Hot Lands. On the morning of the day that would bring us clear to the coast, my fellow lords donned their splendiferous regalia of feather headdresses, mantles, and such, but I did not.

I had decided to add a few refinements to our plans and instructions. For one reason, it had been eight years since I had learned what Spanish I knew, and that had hardly improved with disuse. I wanted to mingle with the Spaniards unobserved, and hear them talk their language, and absorb it, and possibly gain a bit more fluency before I attended any of the formal meetings between our lords and theirs. Also, I had spying and note taking to do, and I could do those tasks better if I was invisible.

"So," I told the other nobles, "from here to the meeting ground I will go barefoot, and wear only a loincloth, and carry one of the lighter packs. You will lead the train, you will greet the outlanders, and when you make camp you will let our porters disperse and relax as they like. For one of them will be me, and I want freedom to wander. You will do the feasting and consultation with the white men. From time to time I will confer with you, privately, after dark. When we have jointly collected all the information the Revered Speaker requested, I will give the word and we will take our leave."

✠

I am glad that you again join us, Lord Bishop, for I know you will wish to hear of the first real confrontation between your civilization and ours. Of course, Your Excellency will appreciate that many of the things I saw at that time were so new and exotic as to be baffling to me, and many of the things I heard sounded like monkey gibberish. But I will not prolong this account by repeating my ingenuous and often erroneous first impressions. I will not, as our earlier observers had done, speak foolishly of such things as the Spanish soldiers wearing the four legs of animals. The things I saw I will report in the light of my later and clearer understanding of them. The things

I heard I will recount as I later construed them when I had a more perfect knowledge of your language.

As a pretended porter, I could only infrequently and surreptitiously use my topaz for looking at things, but these were the things I saw first. As we had been told to expect, there was in the bay only one ship. It was some distance from shore, but it *was* obviously as big as a goodly house. Its wings were apparently furled, for there extended upward from its roof only some tall poles and a tangle of ropes. Here and there about the bay, similar poles stuck up from the water, where the other ships had sunk as they burned. On the beach of the bay, the white men had erected three markers to commemorate the spot where they had first stepped ashore. There was a very large cross made of heavy wooden timbers from one of the destroyed ships. There was a high flagstaff flying a tremendous banner, the colors of blood and gold, the colors of Spain. And there was a shorter flagstaff bearing a smaller flag, the personal ensign of Cortés, blue and white with a red cross in the center.

The Place of Abundant Beautiful Things, which the white men had named the Villa Rica de la Vera Cruz, had sprouted quite a village. Some of the dwellings were only of cloth supported on sticks, but others were the typical coastal huts of cane walls and palm-leaf thatch, built for the visitors by their submissive Totonáca hosts. But that day there were not many white men in evidence—or their animals or their conscripted Totonáca laborers—for most of them, we learned, were working in a place some way farther north, where Cortés had decreed the construction of a more permanent Villa Rica de la Vera Cruz, with solid houses of wood and stone and adobe.

Our train's approach had of course been noted by sentries and reported to the Spaniards. So there was a small group of them waiting to greet us. Our party halted at a respectful distance and our four lords, as I had privately recommended to them, lighted censers of copáli incense and began swinging them on their chains, making coils of blue smoke in the air about them. The white men assumed, then and long afterward— to this day, as far as I know—that the wafting of perfumed smoke was our traditional way of saluting distinguished strangers. It was really only our attempt to draw a defensive veil between us and the intolerable smell of those ever-un-washed strangers.

Two of them came forward to meet our lords. I estimated them both to be of about thirty and five years of age. They were well dressed, in what I know now to have been velvet hats and cloaks, long-sleeved doublets and bulbous breeches made of merino, with thigh-high boots of leather. One of the men was taller than I, and broad and muscular, and most striking of appearance. He had a wealth of gold-colored hair and beard which flamed in the sunlight. He had bright blue eyes and, though his skin was of course pallid, his features were strong. The local Totonáca had already given him the name of their sun god, Tezcatlipóca, for his sunny appearance. We new arrivals naturally took him to be the white men's leader, but soon learned that he was only second in command, Pedro de Alvarado by name.

The other man was rather shorter and much less prepossessing, with bandy legs and a pigeon chest like the prow of a canoe. His skin was even whiter than the other's, though he had black hair and beard. His eyes were as colorless and cold and distant as a winter sky of gray cloud. That unimpressive person was, he told us pompously, the Captain Don Hernán Cortés of Medellín in the Extremadura, more recently of Santiago de Cuba, and he was come here as representative of His Majesty Don Carlos, Emperor of the Holy Roman Empire and King of Spain.

At the time, as I have said, we could understand little of that lengthy title and introduction, although it was repeated for us in Xiu and Náhuatl by the two interpreters. They also had come toward us, walking a few paces behind Cortés and Alvarado. One was a white man, with a pockmarked face, dressed in the manner of their common soldiers. The other was a young woman of one of our own nations, clad in a maidenly yellow blouse and skirt, but her hair was an unnaturally reddish brown, almost as gaudy as Alvarado's. Of all the numerous native females presented to the Spaniards by the Tabascoöb of Cupílco and more recently by Patzínca of the Totonáca, that one was the most admired by the Spanish soldiers, because her red hair was, they said, "like that of the whores of Santiago de Cuba." But I could recognize hair artificially reddened by a brew of achíyotl seeds, just as I could recognize both the man and the girl. He was that Jerónimo de Aguilar who had been a reluctant guest of the Xiu for the past eight years. Before touching at the Olméca lands and then here, Cortés had paused at Tihó and found and rescued the man. Aguilar's fellow castaway, Guerrero, after having infected all that Maya country with his small pocks, had died of them himself. The red-haired girl, though by then about twenty and three years old, was still small, still pretty, still the slave Ce-Malináli whom I had met in Coátzacoálcos on my own way to Tihó, those eight years before.

When Cortés spoke in Spanish, it was Aguilar who rendered the words into the labored Xiu he had learned during his captivity, and it was Ce-Malináli who translated that into our Náhuatl, and, when our emissary lords spoke, the process was reversed. It did not take me long to realize that the words of both the Mexíca and Spanish dignitaries were often being imperfectly rendered, and not always because of the cumbersome three-language system. However, I said nothing, and neither of the interpreters took notice of me among the porters, and I determined that they should not for a while yet.

I stayed in attendance while the Mexíca lords ceremoniously presented the gifts we had brought from Motecuzóma. A gleam of avarice enlivened even the flat eyes of Cortés, as one porter after another laid down his burden and undid its wrappings—the great gold gong and the silver gong, the feather-work articles, the gems and jewelry. Cortés said to Alvarado, "Call the Flemish lapidary," and they were joined by another white man who evidently had come with the Spaniards for the sole purpose of evaluating the treasures that they might find in these lands. Whatever a Flemish is, he spoke Spanish, and, though his words were not translated for us, I caught the sense of most of them.

He pronounced the gold and silver items to be of great worth, and likewise the pearls and opals and turquoise. The emeralds and jacinths and topazes and amethysts, he said, were even more valuable—above all, the emeralds—though he would have preferred them cut in facets instead of sculptured into miniature flowers and animals and such. The feather-work headdresses and mantles, he suggested, might have some curiosity value as museum pieces. The many gem-worked jade-stones he contemptuously swept to one side, though Ce-Ma-lináli tried to explain that their religious aspect made them the gifts most to be respected.

The lapidary shrugged her off and said to Cortés, "They are not the jade of Cathay, nor even a passable false jade. They are only carved pebbles of green serpentine, Captain, worth hardly more than our glass trade beads."

I did not then know what glass is, and I still do not know what jade of Cathay is, but I had always known that our jade-stones possessed only ritualistic value. Nowadays, of course, they have not even that; they are playthings for children and teething stones for infants. But at that time they still meant something to us, and I was angered by the way in which the white men received our gifts, putting a price on everything, as if we had been no more than importunate merchants trying to foist upon them spurious merchandise.

What was even more distressing: although the Spaniards so superciliously set values to everything we gave them, they clearly had no appreciation of works of art, but only of their worth as bulk metal. For they pried all the gems from their gold and silver settings, and put the stones aside in sacks, while they broke and bent and mashed the residue of finely wrought gold and silver into great stone vessels, and set fires under them, and by squeezing leather devices pumped those fires to fierce heat, so that the metals melted. Meanwhile, the lapidary and his assistants scooped rectangular depressions in the damp sand of the shore, and into those they poured the molten metals to cool and harden. So what remained of the treasures we had brought—even those huge and irreplaceably beautiful gold and silver disks which had served Motecuzóma for gongs—became only solid ingots of gold and silver as featureless and unlovely as adobe bricks.

Leaving my fellow lords to act their lordliest, I spent the next several days drifting to and fro among the mass of common soldiers. I counted them and their weapons and their tethered horses and staghounds, and other appurtenances of which I could not then divine the purpose: such things as stores of heavy metal balls and strangely curved low chairs made of leather. I took care not to attract attention as a mere idler. Like the Totonáca men whom the Spaniards had put to forced labor, I made sure to be always carrying something like a plank of wood or a water skin, and to look as if I were taking it to some destination. Since there was a constant traffic of Spanish soldiers and Totonáca porters between the camp of Vera Cruz and the rising town of Vera Cruz, and since the Spaniards then (as they still do) claimed that they "could not tell the damned Indians apart," I went as unnoticed as any single blade of the dune grasses growing along that shore. Whatever pretended freight I carried did not interfere with my subtly using my topaz, and making notes of the things and persons I counted, and quickly jotting down word picture descriptions of them.

I could have wished that I was carrying a censer of incense, instead of a plank or whatever, when I was among the Spaniards. But I must concede that they did not all smell quite so bad as I remembered. While they still showed no inclination to wash or steam themselves, they did—after a day of hard work—strip down to their startlingly pale skin, only leaving on their filthy underclothes, and wade out into the sea surf. None of them could swim, I gathered, but they splashed about sufficiently to rinse the day's sweat from their bodies. That did not make them smell like flowers, particularly since they climbed right back into their crusty and rancid outer clothes, but the rinsing at least made them slightly less fetid than a vulture's breath.

As I rambled up and down the coast, and spent the nights in either the Vera Cruz camp or the Vera Cruz town, I kept my ears as wide open as my eyes. Though I seldom heard anything rousingly informative—the soldiers spent a good deal of their talk in grumbling about the unfamiliar baldness of the "Indian" women's torsos, as compared to the comfortably hairy crotches and armpits of their women across the water—I did recover and improve my understanding of the Spanish language. Still, I took care not to be overheard by any of the soldiers when I practiced repeating their words and phrases to myself.

As a further safeguard against exposure as an imposter, I did not converse with the Totonáca either, so I could not ask anyone to explain a curious thing which I saw repeatedly, and was puzzled by. Along the coast, and especially in the capital city of Tzempoálan, there are many pyramids erected to Tez-catlipóca and other gods. There is even one pyramid that is not square but a conical tower of diminishing round terraces; it is dedicated to the wind god Ehécatl, and was constructed so that his winds might blow freely about it without having to angle around corners.

Every one of the Totonáca pyramids has a temple on top, but all those temples had been shockingly changed. Not a single one any longer contained the statue of Tezcatlipóca or Ehécatl or any other god. All of them had been scraped and scrubbed of their accumulation of coagulated blood. All of them had been refinished on the inside with a clean wash of white lime. And in every one stood only a stark wooden cross and a single small figure, also made of wood, rather crudely carved. It represented a young woman, her right hand raised in a vaguely admonitory gesture. Her hair was painted flat black, her robe a flat blue and her eyes the same, her skin a pinkish-white like that of the Spaniards. Most queer, the woman wore a gilded circular crown that was so much too large for her that it no-where rested on her head but was attached at the back of her hair.

It was clear to me that, although the Spaniards had not sought or provoked any battle with the Totonáca, they *had* threatened and bullied and frightened those people into replac-ing all their mighty and ancient gods with the single pallid and placid female. I took her to be the goddess Our Lady of whom I had heard, but I could not see what made the Totonáca accept her as in any way superior to the old gods. In truth, from the vapid look of her, I could not understand why even the Span-iards saw in Our Lady any godlike attributes worth their own veneration.

But then my wanderings brought me one day to a grassy hollow some way inshore, and it was full of Totonáca who were standing and listening, with an appearance of attentive stupidity, while they were harangued by one of the Spanish priests who had come with the military men. Those priests, I might remark, seemed not so alien and unnatural as did the soldiers. Only the cut of their hair was different; otherwise their black garments much resembled those of our own priests, and smelled very like them, too. The one preaching to that assemblage was doing so with the help of the two interpreters, Aguilar and Ce-Malináli, whom evidently he borrowed whenever they were not required by Cortés. The Totonáca appeared to listen stolidly to his speech, though I knew they could not understand two words in ten of even Ce-Malináli's Náhuatl translation.

Among many other things, the priest explained that Our Lady was not exactly a goddess, that she was a female human being called Virgin Mary who had somehow remained a virgin even while copulating with the Holy Spirit of the Lord God, who *was* a god, and that thereby she had given birth to the Lord Jesus Christ, who was the Son of God thus enabled to walk the world in human form. Well, none of that was too hard to comprehend. Our own religion contained many gods who had coupled with human women, and many goddesses who had been exceedingly promiscuous with both gods and men—and prolific of godling children—while somehow retaining unsmirched their reputation and appellation of Virgin.

Please, Your Excellency, I am recounting the way things seemed *then* to my still untutored mind.

I also followed the priest's explanation of the act of baptism, and how we could all, that very day, partake of it—although it was normally inflicted on children soon after their birth: an immersion in water which forever bound them to adore and serve the Lord God in exchange for bounties to be granted during this life and in an afterlife. I could perceive very little difference from the belief and practice of most of our own peoples, thought they did the immersing with different gods in mind.

Of course, the priest did not try in that one speech to tell us every detail of the Christian Faith, with all its complications and contradictions. And although I, of all his audience that day, could best understand the words spoken in Spanish, Xiu, and Náhuatl, even I was mistaken in many of the things I thought I understood. For example, because the priest spoke so familiarly of Virgin Mary, and because I had already seen the fair-skinned, blue-eyed statues of her, I assumed Our Lady to be a Spanish woman, who might soon come across the ocean to visit us in person and perhaps bring her little boy Jesus. I also took the priest to be speaking of a countryman when he said that that day was the day of San Juan de Damasco, and that we would all be honored by being given the name of that saint when we were baptized.

With that, he and his interpreters called for all who wished to embrace Christianity to kneel down, and practically every Totonácatl present did so, though surely most of those dull-witted folk had no least idea of what was occurring, and may even have thought that they were about to be ritually slaughtered. Only a few old men and some small children took their departure. The old men, if they had understood anything at all, probably saw no benefit in burdening themselves with yet another god at their time of life. And the children probably had more enjoyable games they preferred to play.

The sea was not far distant, but the priest did not take all those people there for a ceremonial immersion. He simply walked up and down the rows of kneeling Totonáca, sprinkling them with water from a little wand in one hand and giving them a taste of something from the other hand. I watched, and when none of the baptized fell dead or showed any other dire effect, I decided to stay and partake myself. Apparently it would do me no harm and it might even give me some obscure advantage in later dealings with the white men. So I got a few drops of water on my head, and on my tongue a few grains of the salt from the priest's palm—that is all it was: common salt—and some words mumbled over me in what I know now is your religious language of Latin.

To conclude, the priest chanted over all of us another short speech in that Latin, and told us that henceforth all of us males were named Juan Damasceno and all the women Juana Damascena, and the ceremony was over. As best I can recollect, it was the first new name I had acquired since that of Urine Eye, and the last new name I have acquired to this day. I daresay it is a better name than Urine Eye, but I must confess that I have seldom thought of myself as Juan Damasceno. However, I suppose the name will endure longer than I do, because I have been thus inscribed on all the head-count rolls and other official papers of all the government departments of New Spain, and the last entry of all will no doubt say Juan Damasceno, deceased.

During one of my secret nighttime conferences with the other Mexíca lords, in the flapping cloth house that had been erected for their quarters, they told me:

"Motecuzóma has wondered much, whether these white men might be gods or the Toltéca followers of gods, so we decided to make a test. We offered to sacrifice to the leader Cortés, to slay for him a xochimíqui, perhaps some available lord of the Totonáca. He was highly insulted at the suggestion. He said, 'You know very well that the benevolent Quetzalcóatl never required or allowed human sacrifices to him. Why should I?' So now we do not know what to think. How could this outlander know such things about the Feathered Serpent, unless—?"

I snorted. "The girl Ce-Malináli could have told him all the legends of Quetzalcóatl. After all, she was born somewhere along this coast from which the god made his departure."

"Please, Mixtzin, do not call her by that common name," said one of the lords, seeming nervous. "She is most insistent that she be addressed as Malíntzin."

I said, amused, "She has risen far, then, since I first met her in a slave market."

"No," said my fellow envoy. "Actually, she was a noble before she was a slave. She was the daughter of a lord and lady of the Coatlícamac. When her father died and her mother remarried, the new husband jealously and treacherously sold her into slavery."

"Indeed," I said drily. "Even her imagination has improved since I first met her. But she did say that she would do anything to realize her ambitions. I suggest to all of you that you be most guarded in the words you speak within hearing of the Lady Malináli."

I think it was on the next day that Cortés arranged for the lords a demonstration of his marvelous weapons and his men's military prowess, and of course I was present, among the crowd of our porters and the local Totonáca who also gathered to watch. Those commoners were awe-stricken by what they saw; they gasped at intervals and murmured "Ayya!" and called often upon their gods. The Mexíca envoys kept they faces impassive, as if they were unimpressed, and I was too busy memorizing the various events to make any exclamations myself. Nevertheless, the lords and I several times flinched at the sudden claps of noise, as startled as any commoners.

Cortés had had his men build a little mock house of driftwood and some leftover ship's timbers, so far up the beach that it was only just visible from where we stood. On the beach before us, he had positioned one of the heavy yellow-metal tubes on high wheels. . . .

No, I will call things by their proper names. The wheel-mounted tube was a brass cannon whose muzzle pointed toward the distant wooden house. Ten or twelve soldiers led horses into a row on the hard-packed damp sand between the cannon and shoreline. The horses wore some of that equipment I had earlier been unable to comprehend: the leather chairs which were saddles for sitting on, leather reins for the animals' guidance, skirts of quilted material very like our people's fighting armor. Other men stood behind the horses, with the giant staghounds straining against the leather straps that held them in check.

All the soldiers were in full fighting garb, and very warlike they looked, with shining steel helmets on their heads and shining steel corselets over leather doublets. They carried swords sheathed at their sides, but when they mounted to their saddles, they were handed long weapons resembling our spears, except that their steel blades, besides being pointed, had protrusions at either side to deflect the blows of any enemies they rode against.

Cortés smiled with proprietorial pride as his warriors got into position. He was flanked by his two interpreters, and Ce-Malináli was also smiling, with the mildly bored superiority of having seen the performance before. Through her and Aguilar, Cortés said to our Mexíca lords, "Your own armies are fond of drums. I have heard their drums. Shall we commence this spectacle with a drum beat?"

Before anyone could answer, he shouted, "For Santiago—*now!*" The three soldiers tending the cannon did something that flashed a small flame at the rear of the tube, and there came a single drumbeat, as loud as any noise ever made by our drum which tears out the heart. The brass cannon jumped—and so did I—and from its mouth came a smoke like stormclouds, and a thunder to rival Tlaloc's, and a lightning brighter than any of the forked sticks of the tlalóque. Then, after my blink of surprise, I saw a small object hurtling away through the air. It was of course an iron cannon ball, and it hit the faraway house and smashed it into its separate pieces of wood.

The cannon's sudden crash of thunder was prolonged, as Tlaloc's often is, into a rumble of lesser thunder. That was the sound the horses' iron-shod feet made, pounding on the sand flats, for the riders had put their mounts to a full gallop at the moment the cannon had bellowed. They went off along the beach, side by side, as fast as any unencumbered deer could run, and the great dogs, let loose at the same time, easily kept up with them. The horsemen converged on the ruins of the house, and we could see the glint of their flourished spears, as they pretended to cut down any survivors of the demolition. Then they all turned their mounts and came pounding back down the beach toward us again. The dogs did not immediately accompany them, and, although my ears were ringing, I could distantly hear the staghounds making ravenous roaring noises, and I thought I heard men shrieking. When the dogs did return, their fearsome jaws were smeared with blood. Either some of the Totonáca had chosen to hide near that mock house to watch the proceedings, or Cortés had deliberately and callously arranged for them to be there.

Meanwhile, the approaching horsemen were no longer keeping in a line abreast. They were weaving their horses back and forth among each other, in intricate movements and crossings and patterns, to show us what perfect control they could maintain even at that headlong speed. Also, the big red-bearded man, Alvarado, did an even more amazing performance all his own. At full gallop, he swung off his saddle and, holding to it with just one hand, *ran* alongside his thundering animal, easily keeping pace with it, and then somehow, without slowing speed, vaulted from the ground back onto the leather seat. It would have been an exploit of admirable agility even for one of the Fast of Feet Rarámuri, but Alvarado did it while wearing a costume of steel and leather that must have weighed as much as he did.

When the horsemen had finished displaying the speed and

surefootedness of their massive animals, a number of foot soldiers deployed on the beach. Some carried the metal harquebuses as long as the men were tall, and the metal rods upon
which those things must be rested for taking aim. Some carried
the short bows mounted crossways on heavy stocks which are
held braced against the shoulder. A number of adobe bricks
were brought by some Totonáca laborers and stood on end a
good arrow's flight distant from the soldiers. Then the white
men knelt and alternately discharged the bows and the harquebuses. The bowmen's accuracy was commendable, hitting
perhaps two of every five bricks, but they were not very quick
with their weapons. After propelling an arrow, they could not
just pull the bowstring back again by hand, but had to draw
it taut along the stock by means of a small turning tool.

The harquebuses were more formidable weapons; just the
crash of noise and the billows of smoke and the flashes of fire
they made were enough to daunt any enemy facing them for
the first time. But they threw more than fear; they threw small
metal pellets, flying so fast that they were invisible. Where the
short arrows of the crossbows merely stuck in the bricks they
hit, the metal pellets of the harquebuses struck the bricks
so hard that they blew apart into fragments and dust. Nevertheless, I took note that the pellets really flew no farther than
one of our arrows could fly, and a man using the harquebus
took so long to prepare it for its next discharge that any of our
bowmen could have sent six or seven arrows at him in the interval.

By the time the demonstration was over, I had still more
bark paper drawings to show to Motecuzóma, and much to tell
him besides. I lacked only the pictured face of Cortés he had
requested. Many years before, in Texcóco, I had sworn never
to draw any more portraits, for they seemed always to visit
some disaster upon the person I portrayed, but I had no compunction about bringing trouble to any of the white men. So
the next evening, when the Mexíca lords sat down for their
final meeting with Cortés and his under-chiefs and his priests,
there were five of us lords. None of the Spaniards seemed to
notice or to care that our number had been increased by a
newcomer, and neither Aguilar nor Ce-Malináli recognized me

in my lordly vestments any more than they had when I was posing as a porter.

We all sat and dined together, and I will refrain from comment on the eating manners of the white men. The food had been provided by us, so it was all of the best quality. The Spaniards had contributed a beverage called wine, poured from large leather bags. Some of it was pale and sour, some dark and sweet, and I drank only sparingly, for it was quite as intoxicating as octli. While my four companion envoys carried the burden of what conversation there was, I sat silent, trying as unobtrusively as possible to capture Cortés's likeness with my chalk and bark paper. Seeing him close for the first time, I could discern that the hair of his beard was rather more sparse than that of his fellows. It could not adequately conceal an ugly puckered scar under his lower lip, and a chin that receded almost like a Maya chin, and I put those details into my portrait. Then I became aware that the whole circle of men had fallen silent, and I looked up to find Cortés's gray eyes fixed on me.

He said, "So I am being recorded for posterity? Let me see it." He spoke in Spanish, of course, but his extended hand would have conveyed the same command, so I gave him the paper.

"Well, I would not call it flattering," he said, "but it is recognizable." He showed it to Alvarado and the other Spaniards, and they severally chuckled and nodded. "As for the artist," said Cortés, still staring at me, "regard the face on *him*, comrades. Why, if he were plucked of all those feathers he wears, and powdered a little paler of complexion, he could pass for an hijodalgo, even a grandee. Were you to meet him at the Court of Castile—a man of that stature and that craggy face—you would doff your hats in a sweeping bow." He gave the picture back to me, and his interpreters translated the next remark, "Why am I being thus portrayed?"

One of my companion lords, thinking quickly, said, "Since our Revered Speaker Motecuzóma will unfortunately not have the opportunity of meeting you, my Lord Captain, he asked that we bring him your likeness as a memento of your short stay in these lands."

Cortés smiled with his lips, not with his flat eyes, and said, "But I *will* meet your emperor. I am determined on it. All of us so admired the treasures he sent as gifts that we are all most eager to see the other wonders that must reside in his capital city. I would not think of departing before I and my men feast our eyes of what we have been told is the richest city in these lands."

When that exchange had been translated back and forth, another of my companions put on a mournful face and said, "Ayya, that the white lord should travel such a long and hazardous way to find only disappointment. We had not wanted to confess it, but the Revered Speaker stripped and despoiled his city to provide those gifts. He had heard that the white visitors prized gold, so he sent all the gold he possessed. Also all his other trinkets of any value. The city is now poor and bleak. It is not worth the visitors' even looking at it."

When Ce-Malináli translated that speech to Aguilar in the Xiu language, whe translated it thus: "The Revered Speaker Motecuzóma sent those trifling gifts in hope that the Captain Cortés would be satisfied with them and would immediately go away. But in fact they represented only the merest skimming of the inestimable treasures in Tenochtítlan. Motecuzóma wishes to discourage the Captain from seeing the *real* wealth that abounds in his capital city."

While Aguilar was putting that into Spanish for Cortés, I spoke for the first time, and quietly, and to Ce-Malináli, and in her native tongue of Coatlícamac, so that only she and I would understand:

"Your job is to speak what is spoken, not to invent lies."

"But *he* lied!" she blurted, pointing to my companion. Then she blushed, realizing that she had been caught in her duplicity and that she had confessed to having been caught.

I said, "I know his motive for lying. I should be interested to know yours."

She stared at me, and her eyes widened in recognition. "*You!*" she breathed, mingling fright, loathing, and dismay in that one word.

Our brief colloquy had gone unnoticed by the others, and Aguilar still had not recognized me. When Cortés spoke again, and Ce-Malináli translated it, her voice was only a little unsteady:

"We would be gratified if your emperor were to extend to us his formal invitation to visit his magnificent city. But tell him, my lords ambassadors, that we do not insist upon any official welcome. We will come there, with or without an invitation. *Assure* him that we will come."

My four companions all began at once to expostulate, but Cortés cut them short, saying:

"Now, we have carefully explained to you the nature of our mission, how our emperor the King Carlos sent us with most particular instructions to pay our respects to your ruler, and to ask his permission to introduce the Holy Christian Faith into these lands. And we have carefully explained the nature of that Faith, of the Lord God, the Christ Jesus, and the Virgin Mary, who wish only that all peoples live in brotherly love. We have also taken the trouble to demonstrate to you the insuperable weapons we possess. I cannot think of anything we have neglected to make clear to you. But before you depart, is there anything else you would know of us? Any questions you care to ask?"

My four companions looked bothered and indignant, but they said nothing. So I cleared my throat, and spoke directly to Cortés, and in his own language: "I have one question, my lord."

The white men all looked surprised at being addressed in Spanish, and Ce-Malináli stiffened, no doubt fearing that I was about to denounce her—or perhaps apply to take her place as interpreter.

"I am curious to know..." I began, pretending humility and uncertainty. "Could you tell me...?"

"Yes?" prompted Cortés.

Still seeming shy and hesitant, I said, "I have heard your men—so many of your men—speak of our women as, well, incomplete in a certain respect...."

There was a clanking of metal and a squeaking of leather as all the white men bent closer their attention to me. "Yes? Yes?"

I asked as if I really wanted to know, and asked politely, solemnly, with no hint of scurrility or mockery. "Do your women . . . does your Virgin Mary have hair covering her private parts?"

There was another clank and squeak of their armor; I think their opening mouths and eyelids almost squeaked too, as they all sat back and gaped at me—rather as Your Excellency is doing at this moment. There were shocked mutters of "Locura!" and "Blasfemia!" and "Ultraje!"

Only one of them, the big flame-bearded Alvarado, laughed uproariously. He turned to the priests dining with us and pounded his big hands on the shoulders of two of them and, between his gusts of laughter, asked, "Padre Bartolomé, Padre Merced, have you ever been asked *that* before? Did the seminary teach you a suitable answer to that question? Have you ever even *thought* of it before? Eh?"

The priests made no comment, except to glare at me and grind their teeth and make the cross sign to ward off evil. Cortés had not taken his eyes off me. Still skewering me with his falcon gaze, he said, "No, you are no hijodalgo or grandee, or any other sort of courtly gentleman. But you will bear remembering. Yes, I will remember you."

Next morning, while our party was packing to depart, Ce-Malináli came and imperiously beckoned to me, indicating that she wished a private discussion. I took my time about joining her. When I did, I said:

"This should be interesting. Speak, One Grass."

"Kindly do not address me by my discarded slave name. You will call me Malíntzin or Doña Marina." She explained, "I was christened with the name of the Santa Margarita Marina. That means nothing to you, of course, but I suggest that you show me the proper respect, for the Captain Cortés regards me highly, and he is quick to punish insolence."

I said coldly, "Then *I* suggest that you sleep very close against your Captain Cortés, for at a word from me any of these Totonáca hereabout will gladly slip a blade between your ribs the first time you are off guard. You are talking insolently now to the Lord Mixtli, who *earned* the -tzin to his name. Slave girl, you may fool the white men with your pretensions to nobility. You may endear yourself to them by coloring your hair like a maátitl. But your own people see exactly that: a red-haired slut who has sold more than just her own body to the invader Cortés."

That shook her, and she said defensively, "I do not sleep with the Captain Cortés. I serve only as his interpreter. When the Tabascoöb presented us, we twenty women were shared out among the white men. I was given to that man." She indicated one of the under-chiefs who had dined with us. "His name is Alonso."

"Are you enjoying him?" I asked drily. "As I recall from our earlier meeting, you expressed a hatred of men and the use they make of women."

"I can pretend *anything*," she said. "Anything that serves my purpose."

"And what is your purpose? I am sure the mistranslation I overheard was not your first. Why do you goad Cortés to press on to Tenochtítlan?"

"Because *I* wish to go there. I told you so, years ago, when we first met. Once I get to Tenochtítlan, I care not what happens to the white men. Perhaps I will be rewarded for having brought them to where Motecuzóma can squash them like bugs. Anyway, I will be where I have always wanted to be, and I will be noticed and known, and it will not take me long to become a noblewoman in fact as well as in name."

"On the other hand," I suggested, "if by some quirk of chance the white men are *not* squashed, you would be even better rewarded."

She made a gesture of indifference. "I only wish to ask . . . to beg if you like, Lord Mixtli . . . that you do nothing to imperil my opportunity. Only give me time to prove my usefulness to Cortés, so that he cannot dispense with my help and advice. Only let me get to Tenochtítlan. It can matter little to you or to your Revered Speaker or to anyone else, but it matters much to me."

I shrugged and said, "I do not step out of my way just to squash bugs. I will not impede your ambitions, slave girl, unless and until they conflict with the interests I serve."

While Motecuzóma studied the portrait of Cortés and the other drawings I had given him, I enumerated the persons and things I had counted:

"Including the leader and his several officers, there are five hundred and eight fighting men. Most of them carry the metal swords and spears, but thirteen of them have also the fire-stick harquebuses, thirty and two have the crossbows, and I venture to suppose that all the other men are equally capable of using those special weapons. There are, in addition, one hundred men who were evidently the boatmen of the ten ships that were burned."

Motecuzóma handed the sheaf of bark papers over his shoulder. The elders of the Speaking Council, ranged behind him, began to pass them back and forth.

I went on, "There are four white priests. There are numerous women of our own race, given to the white men by the Tabascoöb of Cupílco and by Patzínca of the Totonáca. There are sixteen of the riding horses and twelve of the giant hunting dogs. There are ten of the far-throwing cannons and four smaller cannons. As we were told, Lord Speaker, there remains only one ship still floating in the bay, and there are boatmen aboard, but I could not count them."

Two of the Council, two physicians, were solemnly scrutinizing my drawings of Cortés and conferring in professional mumbles.

I concluded, "Besides the persons I have mentioned, practically the entire Totonáca population appears to be at Cortés's command, working as porters and carpenters and masons and such... when they are not being taught by the white priests how to worship before the cross and the lady image."

One of the two doctors said, "Lord Speaker, if I may make a comment..." Motecuzóma nodded permission. "My colleague and I have looked hard at this drawing of the face of the man Cortés, and at the other drawings which show him entire."

Motecuzóma said impatiently, "And I suppose, as physicians, you officially declare him to be a man."

"Not just that, my lord. There are other signs diagnostic. It is impossible to say with certainty, unless we should sometime have a chance to examine him in person. But it very much appears, from his weak features and sparse hair and the ill proportioning of his body, that he was born of a mother afflicted with the shameful disease nanáua. We have seen the same characteristics often in the offspring of the lowest class of maátime."

"Indeed?" said Motecuzóma, visibly brightening. "If this is true, and the nanáua has affected his brain, it would explain some of his actions. Only a madman would have burned those vessels and destroyed his only means of retreat to safety. And if a man consumed by the nanáua is the *leader* of the outlanders, the others must be vermin of even feebler intellect. And you, Mixtzin, tell us that their weapons are not so invincibly terrible as others have described them. Do you know, I begin to think that we may have much exaggerated the peril posed by these visitors."

Motecuzóma was suddenly more cheerful than I had seen him in a long time, but his swift rebound from gloom to jauntiness did not dispose me to imitate it. He had until then held the white men in awe, as gods or messengers of gods, requiring our respect and propitiation and perhaps our utter submission. But, on hearing my report and the doctors' opinion, he was just as ready to dismiss the white men as undeserving of our attention or concern. One attitude seemed to me as dangerous as the other, but I could not say that in so many words. Instead I said:

"Perhaps Cortés is diseased to the point of madness, Lord Speaker, but a madman can be even more fearsome than a sane one. It was only months ago that these same vermin easily vanquished some five thousand warriors in the Olméca lands."

"But the Olméca defenders did not have our advantage." It was not Motecuzóma who spoke, but his brother, the war chief Cuitláhuac. "They went against the white men in the age-old tactic of close combat. But thanks to you, Lord Mixtli, we now know something of the enemy's capabilities. I will equip the majority of my troops with bows and arrows. We can stay out of range of their metal weapons, we can dodge the discharges of their unwieldy fire weapons, and we can deluge them with arrows faster than they can send projectiles in return."

Motecuzóma said indulgently, "It is expectable that a war chief speaks of war. But I see no need for fighting at all. We simply send a command to the Lord Patzínca that the Totonáca cease all aid to the white men, and all supplying of food and women and other comforts. The intruders should soon tire of eating only what fish they can catch, and drinking only coconut juice, and enduring high summer in the Hot Lands."

It was his Snake Woman, Tlácotzin, who disputed that. "Patzínca seems disinclined to refuse anything to the white men, Revered Speaker. The Totonáca have never rejoiced at being our tributary subjects. They may prefer this change of overlords."

One of the envoys who had gone with me to the coast said, "Also, the white men speak of other white men, countless numbers more, living wherever it is that these came from. If we fight and vanquish this company, or starve them into surrender, how can we know when the next will come, or how many they will be, or what more powerful weapons they may bring?"

Motecuzóma's new cheerfulness had rather dissipated. His eyes darted restlessly about, as if he were unconsciously seeking an escape—whether from the white men or from the necessity of making a firm decision, I do not know. But his gaze eventually touched me, and stayed on me, and he said, "Mixtzin, your fidgeting speaks of impatience. What is it you would say?"

I said without hesitation, "Burn the white men's one remaining ship."

Some of the men in the throne room blurted, "What?" or "Shame!" Others said things like, "Attack the visitors without provocation?" and "Open war without sending the tokens of declaration?" Motecuzóma silenced them all with a slashing gesture and said to me only, "Why?"

"Before we left the coast, my lord, that ship was being loaded with the melted-down gold and the other gifts you sent. It will soon wing away to the place called Cuba or the place called Spain, or perhaps directly to report to that King Carlos. The white men were hungry for gold, and my lord's gifts have not sated them, but only whetted their appetite for more. If that ship is allowed to depart, with proof that there is gold here, nothing can save us from an inundation of more and more white men hungry for gold. But the ship is made of wood. Send only a few good Mexíca warriors out upon that bay, my lord, by night and in canoes. While pretending to fish by torchlight, they can approach near enough to fire that ship."

"And then?" Motecuzóma chewed his lip. "Cortés and his company would be entirely cut off from their homeland. They would *certainly* march this way—and certainly with no friendly intent, not after such a hostile action on our part."

"Revered Speaker," I said wearily, "they will come anyway, whatever we do or refrain from doing. And they will come with their tame Totonáca to show them the way, to carry supplies for the journey, to make sure they survive the mountain crossings and their encounters with other people on the way. But we can prevent that, too. I have made careful note of the terrain. There are only so many ways to ascend from the coast to the higher lands, and they all lead through steep and narrow defiles. In those tight places, the white men's horses and harquebuses and cannons will be all but useless, their metal armor no defense. A few good Mexíca warriors posted in those passes, with nothing but boulders for weapons, could mash every man of them to pulp."

There was another chorus of horrified exclamation, at my suggestion that the Mexíca attack by stealth, like savages. But I went on, more loudly:

"We must stop this invasion by whatever ugly means is most expedient, or we have no hope of averting further invasions. The man Cortés, perhaps being mad, has made it easier for us. He has already burned ten of his ships, leaving us only the one to destroy. If that messenger ship never returns to the King Carlos, if not one white man is left alive and capable of making even a raft for his escape, the King Carlos will never know what became of this expedition. He may believe it traveled on forever without finding land, or that it disappeared in some sea of perpetual storm, or that it was obliterated by a formidably powerful people. We can hope that he will never risk sending another expedition."

There was a long silence in the throne room. No one wanted to be the first to comment, and I tried not to fidget. Finally it was Cuitláhuac who said, "It sounds practical advice, Lord Brother."

"It sounds monstrous," grumbled Motecuzóma. "First to destroy the outlander's ship, and thereby prod them into advancing inland, and then to catch them defenseless in a sneak attack. This will require much meditation, much consultation with the gods."

"Lord Speaker!" I said urgently, desperately. "That messenger ship may be spreading its wings at this very moment!"

"Which would indicate," he said, impervious, "that the gods meant for it to go. Kindly do not flap your hands at me like that."

My hands actually wanted to strangle him, but I constrained them to a gesture of no more than resigned relinquishment of my proposal.

He mused aloud, "If the King Carlos hears no more of his company and assumes them to be in trouble, that King may not hesitate to send rescuers or reinforcements. Perhaps uncountable ships bringing uncountable white men. From the casual way in which Cortés burned his ten ships, it is apparent that the King Carlos has plenty in reserve. It may be that Cortés is only the merest point of a spearhead already launched. It may be our wisest course to treat warily and peaceably with Cortés, at least until we can determine how heavy is the spear behind him." Motecuzóma stood up, to signal our dismissal, and said in parting, "I will think on all that has been said. Meanwhile, I will send quimíchime to the Totonáca lands, and to all lands between here and there, to keep me advised of the white men's doings."

Quimíchime means mice, but the word was also used to mean spies. Motecuzóma's retinue of slaves included men from every nation in The One World, and the more trusty of them he employed often to spy for him in their native lands, for they could infiltrate their own people and move among them with perfect anonymity. Of course, I myself had recently played the spy in the Totonáca country, and I had done similar work on other occasions—even in places where I could not pass for a native—but I was only one man. Whole flocks of mice, such as Motecuzóma then sent, could cover much more ground and bring back much more information.

Motecuzóma again called for the presence of the Speaking Council and myself, when the first quimíchi returned—to report that the white men's one floating house had indeed unfurled large wings and gone eastward out of sight across the sea.

Dismayed though I was at hearing that, I nevertheless listened to the rest of the report, for the mouse had done a good job of looking and listening, even overhearing several translated conversations.

The messenger ship had departed with however many boatmen it required, plus one man detached from Cortés's military force, presumably entrusted to deliver the gold and other gifts, and to make Cortés's official report to his King Carlos. That man was the officer Alonso, who had had the keeping of Ce-Malináli, but of course he had not taken that valuable young woman with him when he left. The not noticeably bereaved Malíntzin—as everyone was increasingly calling her—had immediately become concubine as well as interpreter to Cortés.

With her help, Cortés had made a speech to the Totonáca. He told them that the messenger ship would return with his King's commission elevating him in rank. He would anticipate that promotion, and henceforth be entitled not mere Captain but Captain-General. Further anticipating his King's commands, he was giving a new name to Cem-Anáhuac, The One World. The coastal land which he already held, he said, and all the lands he would in future discover, would henceforth be known as the Captaincy General of New Spain. Of course, those Spanish words meant little to us then, especially as the quimíchi relayed them to us in his Totonácatl accent. But it was clear enough that Cortés—whether pitiably mad or incredibly bold or, as I suspected, acting on the prompting of his ambitious consort—was arrogating to himself limitless lands and numberless peoples he had not yet even seen, let alone conquered by combat or other means. The lands over which he claimed dominion included *ours,* and the peoples over whom he claimed sovereignty included *us,* the Mexíca.

Almost frothing with outrage, Cuitláhuac said, "If that is not a declaration of war, Revered Brother, I have never heard one."

Motecuzóma said uncertainly, "He has not yet sent any war gifts or other tokens of such intention."

"Will you wait until he discharges one of those thunder cannons into your ear?" Cuitláhuac impertinently demanded. "Obviously he is ignorant of our custom of giving due advisement. Perhaps the white men do it only with words of challenge and presumption, as he has done. So let us teach the upstart some good manners. Let us send *him* our war gifts of token weapons and banners. Then let us go down to the coast and push the insufferable braggart into the sea!"

"Calm yourself, Brother," said Motecuzóma. "As yet, he had bothered nobody in these parts except the paltry Totonáca, and even at them he has only made noise. So far as I am concerned, Cortés can stand on that beach forever, and preen and posture and break wind from both ends. Meanwhile, until he actually *does* something, we will wait."

IHS

✠

S.C.C.M.

Sanctified, Caesarean, Catholic Majesty,
the Emperor Don Carlos, Our Lord King:

ESTEEMED Majesty, our Royal Patron: from this City of Méxíco, capital of New Spain, this eve of the Feast of the Transfiguration in the year of Our Lord one thousand five hundred thirty and one, greeting.

Since we have received from Your Transcendent Majesty no order to desist in the compilation of this chronicle, and since with the following pages it now at last seems to us complete, and since even the narrating Aztec himself declares that he has no more to say, we herewith annex the final and concluding segment.

Much of the Indian's relation of the Conquest and its aftermath will already be familiar to Your Omnilegent Majesty, from the accounts sent during those years by Captain-General Cortés and other officers chronicling the events in which they took part. However, if nothing else, our Aztec's account rather repudiates the Captain-General's tediously repeated boast that only "he and a handful of stout Castilian soldiers" conquered this whole continent unaided.

Beyond any doubt, now that we and you, Sire, can contemplate this history entire, it is nothing like what Your Majesty must have envisioned when your royal cédula commanded its commencement. And we hardly need reiterate our own dissatisfaction with what it proved to be. Nevertheless, if it has been in the least informative to our Sovereign, or to any extent edifying in its plethora of bizarre minutiae and arcana, we will try to persuade ourself that our patience and forbearance and the drudging labors of our friar scribes have not entirely been a waste. We pray that Your Majesty, imitating the benign King of Heaven, will consider not the trivial value of the accumulated volumes, but the sincerity with which we undertook the work and the spirit in which we offer it, and that you will regard it and us with an indulgent aspect.

Also, we would inquire, before we terminate the Aztec's employement here, might Your Majesty desire that we demand of him any further information or any addenda to his already voluminous account? In such case, we shall take care to see to his continued availability. But if you have no further use for the Indian, Sire, might it be your pleasure to dictate the disposition now to be made of him, or would Your Majesty prefer that we simply relinquish him to God for the determination of his due?

Meantime, and at all times, that God's holy grace may dwell continuously in the soul of our Praiseworthy Majesty, is the uninterrupted prayer of Your S.C.C.M.'s devoted servant,

(*ecce signum*) Zumárraga

ULTIMA PARS

AS I have told you, reverend scribes, the name of our eleventh month, Ochpaníztli, meant The Sweeping of the Road. That year, the name took on a new and sinister import, for it was then, toward the close of that month, when the rains of the rainy season began to abate that Cortés began his threatened march inland. Leaving his boatmen and some of his soldiers to garrison his town of Villa Rica de la Vera Cruz, Cortés headed westward to the mountains, with about four hundred fifty white troops and about one thousand three hundred Totonáca warriors, all armed and wearing fighting garb. There were another thousand Totonáca men serving as tamémime to carry spare arms, the dismantled cannons and their heavy projectiles, traveling rations, and the like. Among those porters were several of Motecuzóma's mice, who communicated with other quimíchime posted along the route, thereby keeping us in Tenochtítlan informed of the procession's composition and its progress.

Cortés led the march, they said, wearing his shining metal armor and riding the horse he derisively but affectionately called She-Mule. His other female possession, Malíntzin, carried his banner and walked proudly beside his saddle at the head of the company. Only a few of the other officers had brought their women, for even the lowest-ranking white soldiers expected to be given or to take other women along the way. But all the horses and dogs had been brought, though the quimíchime reported that the mounts became slow and clumsy and troublesome when they were on the mountain trails. Also, in those heights Tlaloc was prolonging his rainy season, and the rain was cold, windblown, often mixed with sleet. The travelers, soaked and chilled, their armor a clammy weight on them, were hardly enjoying the journey.

"*Ayyo!*" said Motecuzóma, much pleased. "They find the interior country not so hospitable as the Hot Lands. I will now send my sorcerers to make life even more uncomfortable for them."

Cuitláhuac said grimly, "Better you let me take warriors and make life *impossible* for them."

Motecuzóma still said no. "I prefer to preserve an illusion of amiability as long as the pretense may serve our purpose. Let the sorcerers curse and afflict that company until they turn back of their own accord, not knowing it was our doing. Let them report to their King that the land is unhealthy and impenetrable, but give no bad report of us."

So the court sorcerers went scurrying eastward, disguised as common travelers. Now, sorcerers may be capable of doing many strange and wonderful things beyond the power of ordinary folk, but the impediments they put in the way of Cortés proved pitifully ineffectual. First, in the trail ahead of the marching company, they stretched between trees some thin threads on which hung blue papers marked with mysterious designs. Although those barriers were supposed to be impassable by any but sorcerers, the horse She-Mule, leading the train, unconcernedly broke through them, and probably not its rider Cortés nor anyone else even noticed the things. The sorcerers sent word back to Motecuzóma, not that they had failed, but that the *horses* possessed some sorcery which defeated that particular stratagem.

What they did next was secretly to meet with the quimíchime traveling unsuspected with the train, and arrange to have those mice insinuate into the white men's rations some ceiba sap and tónaltin fruits. The sap of the ceiba tree, when ingested by a person, makes that person so hungry that he eats voraciously of everything on which he can get his hands and teeth, until, in only a matter of days, he becomes so fat that he cannot move. At least, so say the sorcerers; I have never witnessed the phenomenon. But the tonal fruit demonstrably does work mischief, though of a less spectacular nature. The tonal is what you call the prickly pear, the fruit of the nopáli cactus, and the early-arriving Spaniards did not know to peel it carefully before biting into it. So it was the expectation of the sorcerers that the white men would be intolerably tormented when the tiny, invisible but painful prickles got irremovably into their fingers and lips and tongues. The tonal does something else besides. Anyone who eats its red pulp urinates an even brighter red urine, and a man passing what looks like blood may be terrified by the certainty that he is mortally ill.

If the ceiba sap made any of the white men fat, none of them got so fat as to be immobilized. If the white men cursed the tónaltin needles, or were dismayed when they apparently leaked blood, that did not stop them either. Perhaps their beards gave them some protection against the prickles and, for all I know, they *always* urinated red. But it is more likely that the woman Malíntzin, knowing how easily her new comrades *could* be poisoned, paid close attention to what they ate, and showed them now to eat tónaltin, and told them what to expect afterward. At any rate, the white men kept moving inexorably westward.

When Motecuzóma's mice brought him word of his sorcerers' futility, they brought another and even more worrisome report. Cortés's company was passing through the lands of many minor tribes resident in those mountains, tribes like the Tepeyahuáca, the Xica, and others who had never been very amenable to paying tribute to our Triple Alliance. At each village, the marching Totonáca soldiers would call out, "Come! Join us! Rally to Cortés! He leads us to free ourselves from the detested Motecuzóma!" And those tribes did willingly contribute many warriors. So, although by then several white men were being carried in litters because they had injured themselves by falling off their stumbling horses, and although numbers of the lowland Totonáca had dropped by the wayside when they were made ill by the thin air of those heights, Cortés's company did not dwindle but increased in strength.

"You hear, Revered Brother!" Cuitláhuac stormed at Motecuzóma. "The creatures even dare to boast that they are coming to confront *you personally!* We have every excuse to swoop upon them, and now is the time to do it. As the Lord Mixtli predicted, they are nearly helpless in those mountains. We need not fear their animals or weapons. You can no longer say *wait!*"

"I say wait," Motecuzóma replied, imperturbable. "And I have good reason. Waiting will save many lives."

Cuitláhuac literally snarled, "Tell me: *when* in all of history has any single life ever been *saved?*"

Motecuzóma looked annoyed and said, "Very well, then, I speak of not cutting unnecessarily short the life of any Mexícatl soldier. Know this, Brother. Those outlanders are now approaching the eastern border of Texcála, the nation that has for so long repelled the fiercest assaults of even us Mexíca. That land will not be any more ready to welcome another enemy of a different color coming from a different direction. Let the *Texcaltéca* fight the invaders, and we Mexíca will profit in at least two respects. The white men and their Totonáca will most surely be vanquished,.but I also trust that the Texcaltéca will suffer sufficient losses that we can strike them immediately afterward and, at last, defeat them utterly. If in the process we should find any white men still surviving, we will give them succor and shelter. It will appear to them that we have fought solely to rescue them. We will have won their gratitude and that of their King Carlos. Who can say what further benefits may accrue to us? So we will continue to wait."

If Motecuzóma had confided to Texcála's ruler Xicoténca what we had learned of the white men's fighting capabilities and limitations, the Texcaltéca would wisely have pounced upon the white men somewhere in the steep mountains of which their nation has an abundance. Instead, Xicoténca's son and war chief, Xicoténca the Younger, chose to make his stand on one of Texcála's few level grounds of great expanse. In the traditional manner, he arrayed his troops in preparation for fighting one of the traditional battles—in which both opponents poised their forces, exchanged the traditional formalities, and then rushed together to pit human strength against human strength. Xicoténca may have heard rumors that the new enemy possessed more than human strength, but he had no way of knowing that the new enemy cared not a little finger for our world's traditions and our established rules of war.

As we in Tenochtítlan heard later, Cortés walked out of a wood on the edge of that plain, leading his four hundred fifty white soldiers and by then about three thousand warriors of the Totonáca and other tribes, to find himself facing, on the other side of that ground, a solid wall of Texcaltéca, at least ten thousand of them; some reports said as many as thirty thousand. Even if Cortés had been deranged by disease, as alleged, he would have recognized the formidability of his opponents. They were garbed in their quilted armor of yellow and white. They bore their many great feather banners, variously worked with the wide-winged golden eagle of Texcála and the white heron symbol of Xicoténca. They threateningly thumped their war drums and played the shrill war whistle on their flutes. Their spears and maquáhuime flashed brilliant lights from the clean black obsidian that thirsted to be reddened.

Cortés must have wished then that he had better allies than his Totonáca, with their weapons made mostly of sawfish snouts and sharpened bones, their unwieldy shields which were nothing but the carapaces of sea turtles. But if Cortés was at all worried, he remained calm enough to keep his most out-landish weapon concealed. The Texcaltéca saw only him and those of his army who were afoot. All the horses, including his own, were still in the wood, and at his command they stayed there, out of sight of the defenders of Texcála.

As tradition dictated, several Texcaltéca lords stepped forward from their ranks and crossed the green plain between the two armies, and ceremoniously presented the symbolic weapons, the feather mantles and shields, to declare that a state of hostility existed. Cortés deliberately lengthened that ceremony by asking that the meaning of it be explained to him. And I should remark that Aguilar was by then seldom needed as an intermediate interpreter; the woman Malíntzin had exerted herself to learn Spanish, and she had progressed rapidly; after all, bed is the best place to learn any language. So, after acknowl-edging the Texcaltéca's declaration, Cortés made one of his own, unrolling a scroll and reading from it while Malíntzin translated to the waiting lords. I can repeat it from memory, for he made the same proclamation outside every village, town, city and nation that shut itself against his approach. He first demanded that he be let enter without hindrance, and then he said:

"But if you will not comply, then, with the help of God, I will enter by force. I will make war against you with the utmost violence. I will bind you to the yoke of obedience to our Holy Church and our King Carlos. I will take your wives and children, and make them slaves, or sell them, according to His Majesty's pleasure. I will seize your belongings, and do you all the mischief in my power, regarding you as rebellious subjects who maliciously refuse to submit to their lawful sovereign. Therefore, all ensuing bloodshed and calamity are to be imputed to you, and not to His Majesty or to me or to the gentlemen who serve under me."

It can be imagined that the Texcaltéca lords were not much pleased to be called subjects of any alien, or to be told that they were disobeying any alien in defending their own frontier. If anything, those haughty words only heightened their desire for bloody battle, and the bloodier the better. So they made no reply, but turned and stalked back the long distance to where their warriors were more and more loudly whooping and making their flutes shriek and their drums throb.

But that exchange of formalities had given Cortés's men ample time to assemble and position their ten big-mouthed cannons and the four smaller ones, and to charge them not with house-battering balls but with scraps of jagged metal, broken glass, rough gravel, and the like. The harquebuses were prepared and set upon their supports and aimed, and the crossbows were readied. Cortés quickly gave commands, and Malíntzin repeated them to the allied warriors, and then she hurried to safety, back the way they had come. Cortés and his men stood or knelt while others, staying in the woods, sat upon their horses. And they all waited patiently, while the great wall of yellow and white suddenly surged forward, and a rain of arrows arced from it across the field between, and the wall resolved itself into a rush of thousands of warriors, beating their shields, roaring like jaguars, screaming like eagles.

Not Cortés nor any of his men moved to meet them in the traditional manner. He merely shouted, *"For Santiago!"* and the bellow of the cannons made the Texcaltéca's war noises sound like the creaking of crickets in a thunderstorm. All the warriors in the first onrushing rank tore apart in bits of bone and blobs of flesh and spatters of blood. The men in the following rank simply fell, but fell dead, and for no immediately apparent reason, since the harquebuses' pellets and the crossbow's short arrows disappeared inside their thick quilted armor. Then there was a different kind of thunder, as the horsemen came at full gallop out of the wood, the staghounds running with them. The white soliders rode with their spears leveled, and they skewered their quarry in the way that chilis are strung on a string, and when their spears could collect no more bodies, the riders dropped the spears and unsheathed their steel swords and rode flailing them so that amputated hands and arms and even heads flew in the air. And the dogs lunged and ripped and tore, and cotton armor was no protection against their fangs. The Texcaltéca were understandably taken by surprise. Shocked, dismayed, and terrified, they lost their impetus and will to win; they scattered and milled about and wielded their inferior weapons desperately but to little use. Several times their knights and cuáchictin rallied and regrouped them and led them in renewed charges. But each time the cannons and harquebuses and crossbows had again been prepared, and they let loose their terrible shredding and piercing projectiles again and again into the Texcaltéca ranks, causing unspeakable devastation. . . .

Well, I need not tell every detail of the one-sided battle; what happened that day is well known. In any case, I can describe it only from what was later told by the day's survivors, though I myself eventually saw occasions of similar slaughter. The Texcaltéca fled from the field, pursued by Cortés's native Totonáca warriors, who loudly and cowardly exulted in the opportunity to participate in a battle that required them only to harry the retreating warriors from behind. The Texcaltéca left perhaps one-third of their entire force lying on the field that day, and they had inflicted only trivial casualties on the enemy. One horse downed, I think, and a few Spaniards pricked by the first arrows, and some others more badly injured by fortunate strokes of maquáhuime, but none killed or put out of action for long. When the Texcaltéca had fled beyond range of pursuit, Cortés and his men made camp right there on the battlefield, to bind up their few wounds and to celebrate their victory.

Considering the awful losses it had suffered, it is to the credit of Texcála that the nation did not surrender itself to Cortés forthwith. But the Texcaltéca were a brave and proud and defiant people. Unfortunately, they had an unshakable faith in the infallibility of their seers and sorcerers. So it was to those wise men that the war chief Xicoténca resorted, in the very evening of that day of defeat, and asked of them:

"Are these outlanders really gods, as rumored? Are they truly invincible? Is there any way to overcome their flame-spouting weapons? Should I waste still more good men by fighting any longer?"

The seers, after deliberating by whatever magical means they employed, said this:

"No, they are not gods. They are men. But the evidence of their weapons' discharging flame suggests that they have some-how learned to employ the hot power of the sun. As long as the sun shines, they have the superiority of their fire-spitting weapons. But when the sun goes down, so will their sun-given strength. By night, they will be only ordinary men, able to use only ordinary weapons. They will be as vunerable an any other men, and as weary from the day's exertions. If you would vanquish them, you must attack by night. Tonight. This very night. Or at sunrise, they will rise also, and they will sweep your army from the field as weeds are mowed."

"Attack at night?" Xicoténca murmured. "It is against all custom. It violates all the traditions of fair combat. Except in siege situations, no armies have ever done battle by night."

The sages nodded. "Exactly. The white outlanders will be off guard and not expecting any such assault. Do the unex-pected."

The Texcaltéca seers were as calamitously in error as seers everywhere so often are. For white armies in their own lands evidently *do* fight often by night among themselves, and are accustomed to taking precautions against any such surprises. Cortés had posted sentries at a distance all around his camp, men who stayed awake and alert while all their fellows slept in full battle garb and armor, with their weapons already charged and near to their hands. Even in the darkness, Cortés's sentries easily descried the first advance Texcaltéca scouts creeping on their bellies across the open ground.

The guards raised no cry of alarm, but slipped back to camp and quietly woke Cortés and the rest of his army. No soldier stood up in profile against the sky; no man raised himself higher than a sitting or kneeling position; none made a noise. So Xicoténca's scouts returned to report to him that the whole camp seemed to be defenselessly asleep and unaware. What remained of the Texcaltéca army moved in mass, on hands and knees, until they were right upon the camp's perimeter. Then they rose up to leap upon the sleeping enemy, but they had no chance to give even a war cry. As soon as they were upright, and easy targets, the night exploded in lightning and thunder and the whistle of projectiles... and Xicoténca's army was swept from the field as weeds are mowed.

The next morning, though his blind old eyes wept, Xicoténca the Elder sent an embassy of his highest nobles, carrying the square gold-mesh flags of truce, to negotiate with Cortés the terms of Texcála's surrender to him. Much to the envoys' surprise, Cortés evinced none of the demeanor of a conqueror; he welcomed them with great warmth and apparent affection. Through his Malíntzin, he praised the valor of the Texcaltéca warriors. He regretted that their having mistaken his intentions had necessitated his having to defend himself. Because, he said, he did not want surrender from Texcála, and would not accept it. He had come to that country hoping only to befriend and help it.

"I know," he said, no doubt having been well informed by Malíntzin, "that you have for ages suffered the tyranny of Motecuzóma's Mexíca. I have liberated the Totonáca and some other tribes from that bondage. Now I would free you from the constant threat of it. I ask only that your people join me in this holy and praiseworthy crusade, that you provide as many warriors as possible to augment my forces."

"But," said the bewildered nobles, "we heard that you demand of all peoples that they vow submission to your alien ruler and religion, that all our venerable gods be overthrown and new ones worshiped."

Cortés made an airy gesture of dismissing all that. The

Texcaltéca's resistance had at least taught him to treat them with some shrewd circumspection.

"I ask alliance, not submission," he said. "When these lands have all been purged of the Mexíca's malign influence, we will be glad to expound to you the blessings of Christianity and the advantages of an accord with our King Carlos. Then you can judge for yourselves whether you wish to accept those benefits. But first things first. Ask your esteemed ruler if he will do us the honor of taking our hand in friendship and making common cause with us."

Old Xicoténca had hardly heard that message from his nobles before we in Tenochtítlan had it from our mice. It was obvious to all of us gathered in the palace that Motecuzóma was shaken, he was appalled, he was enraged by the way his confident predictions had turned out, and he was agitated near to panic by the realization of what could come of his having been so irredeemably wrong. It was bad enough that the Texcaltéca had *not* stopped the white invaders for us, or even proved a hindrance to them. It was bad enough that Texcála was not laid open for *our* vanquishing. Worse, the outlanders were not at all discouraged or weakened; they were still coming, still uttering threats against us. Worst of all, the white men would now come reinforced by the strength and hatred of our oldest, fiercest, most unforgiving enemies.

Recovering himself, Motecuzóma made a decision that was at least a bit more forceful than "wait." He called for his most intelligent swift-messenger and dictated to him a message and sent him running immediately to repeat it to Cortés. Of course, the message was lengthy and fulsome with complimentary language, but in essence it said:

"Esteemed Captain-General Cortés, do not put your trust in the disloyal Texcaltéca, who will tell you any lies to win your confidence and then will treacherously betray you. As you can easily discover by inquiry, the nation of Texcála is an island completely surrounded and blockaded by those neighbor nations of which it has made enemies. If you befriend the Texcaltéca you will be, like them, despised and shunned and repelled by all other nations. Heed our advice. Abandon the unworthy Texcaltéca and unite yourself instead with the mighty

Triple Alliance of the Mexíca, the Acólhua, and the Tecpanéca. We invite you to visit our allied city of Cholólan, an easy march south of where you are. There you will be received with a great ceremony of welcome befitting so distinguished a visitor. When you have rested, you will be escorted to Tenochtítlan, as you have desired, where I, the Uey-Tlatoáni Motecuzóma Xocóyotzin, wait eagerly to embrace my friend and do him all honor."

It may be that Motecuzóma meant exactly what he said, that he was willing to capitulate to the extent of granting audience to the white men while he pondered what to do next. I do not know. He did not then confide his plans to me or to any of his Speaking Council. But this I do know. If I had been Cortés, I should have laughed at such an invitation, especially with the sly Malíntzin standing by to interpret it more plainly and succinctly:

"Detested enemy: Please to dismiss your new-won allies, throw away the additional forces you have acquired, and do Motecuzóma the favor of walking stupidly into a trap you will never walk out of."

But to my surprise, since I did not then know the man's audacity, Cortés sent the messenger back with an acceptance of the invitation, and he *did* march south to pay a courtesy call on Cholólan, and he *was* received there like a notable and welcome guest. He was met on the city's outskirts by its joint rulers, the Lord of What Is Above and the Lord of What Is Below, and by most of the civilian population, and by no armed men. Those lords Tlaquíach and Tlalchíac had mustered none of their warriors, and no weapons were in evidence; all appeared as Motecuzóma had promised, peaceable and hospitable.

Nevertheless, Cortés had naturally not complied with all of Motecuzóma's suggestions; he had not divested himself of his allies before coming to Cholólan. In the interim, old Xicoténca of the defeated Texcála had accepted Cortés's offer of making common cause, and had given into his command fully ten thousand Texcaltéca warriors—not to mention many other things: a number of the most comely and noble Texcaltéca females to be divided among Cortés's officers, and even a numerous retinue of maids to be the personal serving women of the *Lady* One Grass, or Malíntzin, or Doña Marina. So Cortés arrived at Chololán leading that army of Texcaltéca, plus his three thousand men recruited from the Totonáca and other tribes, plus of course his own hundreds of white soldiers, his horses and dogs, his Malíntzin and the other women traveling with the company.

After properly saluting Cortés, the two lords of Chololán looked fearfully at that multitude of his companions and meekly told him, through Malíntzin, "By command of the Revered Speaker Motecuzóma, our city is unarmed and undefended by any warriors. It can accommodate your lordly self and your personal troops and attendants, and we have made arrangements to accommodate all of you in comfort, but there is simply no room for your countless allies. Also, if you will excuse our mentioning it, the Texcaltéca are our sworn enemies, and we should be most uneasy if they were let to enter our city. . . ."

So Cortés obligingly gave orders that his greater force of native warriors stay outside the city, but camping in a circle that would entirely surround it. Cortés surely felt secure enough, with all those thousands so near and on call if he should need help. And only he and the other white men entered Chololán, striding as proudly as nobles or riding their horses in towering majesty, while the gathered populace cheered and tossed flowers in their path.

As had been promised, the white men were given luxurious lodgings—every least soldier being treated as obsequiously as if he were a knight—and they were provided with servants and attendants, and women for their beds at night. Chololán had been forewarned of the men's personal habits, so no one—not even the women commanded to couple with them—ever commented on the dreadful smell of them, or their vulturine manner of eating, or their never taking off their filthy clothes and boots, or their refusal to bathe, or their neglect even to clean their hands between performing excretory functions and sitting down to dine. For fourteen days, the white men lived the kind of life that heroic warriors might hope for in the best of afterworlds. They were feasted, and plied with octli, and let to get as drunk and disorderly as they pleased, and they made free with the women assigned to them, and they were entertained with music and song and dancing. And after those fourteen days, the white men rose up and massacred every man, woman, and child in Cholólan.

We got the news in Tenochtítlan, probably before the harquebus smoke had cleared from the city, by way of our mice who flitted in and out of Cortés's own ranks. According to them, the slaughter was done at the instigation of the woman Malíntzin. She came one night to her master's room in the Cholólan palace, where he was swilling octli and disporting himself with several women. She snapped at the women to begone and then warned Cortés of a plot in progress. She had learned of it, she said, by mingling and conversing with the local market women, who innocently supposed her to be a war captive eager for liberation from her white captors. The whole purpose of the visitors' being so lavishly entertained, said Malíntzin, was to lull and weaken them while Motecuzóma secretly sent a force of twenty thousand Mexíca warriors to encircle Cholólan. At a certain signal, she said, the Mexíca forces would fall upon the native troops camped outside, while the city men inside would arm themselves and turn on the unready white men. And, she said, on her way to expose the scheme, she had seen the city folk already grouping under banners in the central square.

Cortés burst from the palace, with his under-officers who had also been lodged there, and their shouts of "Santiago!" brought their troops converging from other lodgings in the city, throwing aside their women and their cups and seizing up their weapons. As Malíntzin had warned, they found the plaza packed with people, many of them bearing feather banners, all of them wearing ceremonial garments which perhaps did look like battle garb. Those gathered people were given no time to raise a war cry or issue a challenge to combat—or otherwise to explain their presence there—for the white men instantly discharged their weapons and, so dense was the crowd, the first volley of pellets and arrows and other projectiles mowed them down like weeds.

When the smoke cleared a bit, perhaps the white men saw that the plaza contained women and children as well as men, and they may even have wondered if their precipitate action had been warranted. But the noise of it brought their Texcaltéca and other allies swarming from their camps into the city. It was they who, more wantonly than the white men, laid waste the city and slew its populace without mercy or discrimination, killing even the lords Tlaquíach and Tlalchíac. Some of the men of Cholólan did run to get weapons with which to fight back, but they were so outnumbered and encircled that they could only fight a delaying action as they retreated upward along the slopes of Cholólan's mountain-sized pyramid. They made their last stand at the very top of it, and at the end were penned inside the great temple of Quetzalcóatl there. So their besiegers simply piled wood about the temple and set it afire and incinerated the defenders alive.

That was nearly twelve years ago, reverend friars, when that temple was burned and leveled and its rubble scattered. There remained nothing but trees and shrubs to be seen, which is why so many of your people have since been unable to believe that the mountain is *not* a mountain but a pyramid long ago erected by men. Of course, I know that it now bears something more than greenery. The summit where Quetzalcóatl and his worshipers were that night overthrown has lately been crowned with a Christian church.

When Cortés arrived at Cholólan, it was inhabited by some eight thousand people. When he departed, it was empty. I say again that Motecuzóma had confided to me none of his plans. For all I know, he *did* have Mexíca troops moving stealthily toward that city, and he *had* instructed the people to rise up when the trap was sprung. But I beg leave to doubt it. The massacre occurred on the first day of our fifteenth month, called Panquétzalíztli, which means The Flourishing of the Feather Banners, and was everywhere celebrated with ceremonies in which the people did just that.

It may be that the woman Malíntzin had never before attended an observance of that festival. She may genuinely have believed, or mistakenly assumed, that the people were massing with battle flags. Or she could have invented the "plot," perhaps from her jealous resentment of Cortés's attentions to the local women. Whether she was moved by misunderstanding or malice, she effectually moved Cortés to make a desert of Cholólan. And if he regretted that at all, he did not regret it for long, because it advanced his fortunes more than even his defeat of the Texcaltéca had done. I have mentioned that I have visited

Cholólan, and found the people there to be rather less than
lovable. I had no reason to care if the city went on existing,
and its abrupt depopulation caused me no grief, except insofar
as that added to Cortés's increasingly fearsome reputation.
Because, when the news of the Cholólan massacre spread by
swift-messenger throughout The One World, the rulers and war
chiefs of many other communities began to consider the course
of events to date, no doubt in some such words as these:

"First the white men took the Totonáca away from Motecuzóma. Then they conquered Texcála, which not Motecuzóma
nor any of his predecessors ever could do. Then they obliterated
Motecuzóma's allies in Cholólan, caring not a little finger for
Motecuzóma's anger or vindictiveness. It begins to appear that
the white men are mightier even than the long-mightiest
Mexíca. It may be wise for us to side with the superior
force ... while we still can do so of our own volition."

One powerful noble did so without hesitation: the Crown
Prince Ixtlil-Xochitl, rightful ruler of the Acólhua. Motecuzóma must have bitterly regretted his ouster of that prince,
three years before, when he realized that Black Flower had not
just spent those years sulking in his mountain retreat, that he
had been collecting warriors in preparation for reclaiming his
Texcóco throne. To Black Flower, the coming of Cortés must
have seemed a god-sent and timely help to his cause. He came
down from his redoubt to the devastated city of Cholólan,
where Cortés was regrouping his multitude in preparation for
continuing their march westward. At their meeting, Black
Flower surely told Cortés of the mistreatment he had suffered
at Motecuzóma's hands, and Cortés presumably promised to
help him redress it. Anyway, the next piece of bad news we
heard in Tenochtítlan was that Cortés's company had been
augmented by the addition of the vengeful Prince Black Flower
and his several thousand superbly trained Acólhua warriors.

Clearly, the impulsive and perhaps unnecessary massacre
in Cholólan had proved a master stroke for Cortés, and he had
his woman Malíntzin to thank, whatever had been her reason
for provoking it. She had demonstrated her wholehearted dedication to his cause, her eagerness to help him achieve his
destiny, even if it meant trampling the dead bodies of men,
women, and children of her own race. From then on, though

Cortés still relied on her as an interpreter, he valued her even more as his chief strategic adviser, his most trusted under-officer, his staunchest of all his allies. He may even have come to love the woman; no one ever knew. Malíntzin had achieved her two ambitions: she had made herself indispensable to her lord; and she was going to Tenochtítlan, her long-dreamed-of destination, with the title and perquisites of a lady.

Now, it may be that all the events I have recounted would have come to pass even if the orphan brat Ce-Malináli had never been born to that slave slut of the Coatlícamac. And I may have a personal motive in so contemptuously reviling her groveling devotion to her master, her shameful disloyalty to her own kind. It may be that I nursed a special loathing of her, simply because I could not forget that she had the same birth-name as my dead daughter, that she was the same age Nochípa would have been, that her despicable actions seemed, to my mind, to cast obloquy on my own Ce-Malináli, blameless and defenseless.

But, my personal feelings aside, I *had* twice encountered Malíntzin before she became Cortés's most wicked weapon, and either time I could have prevented her becoming that. When we first met at the slave market, I could have bought her, and she would have been content to spend her life in the great city of Tenochtítlan as a member of the household of an Eagle Knight of the Mexíca. When we met again in the To-tonáca country, she was still a slave, and the property of an officer of no consequence, and a mere link in the chain of interpreting of conversations. Her disappearance then would have occasioned only a minimum of fuss, and I could easily have arranged her disappearance. So twice I might have changed the course of her life, I might perhaps have changed the course of history, and I had not. But her instigation of the Cholólan butchery made me recognize the menace of her, and I knew that I would eventually see her again—in Tenochtítlan, whither she had been traveling all her life—and I swore to myself that I would arrange for her life to end there.

Meanwhile, immediately after receiving news of the mas-sacre at Cholólan, Motecuzóma had made another of his ir-resolute shows of resolute action, by sending there another delegation of nobles, and that embassy was headed by his Snake

Woman Tlácotzin, High Treasurer of the Mexíca, second in command only to Motecuzóma himself. Tlácotzin and his companion nobles led a train of porters again laden with gold and many other riches—not intended to provide for a repopulation of the unfortunate city, but for the cajoling of Cortés.

In that one move, I believe, Motecuzóma revealed the ultimate hypocrisy of which he was capable. The people of Cholólan had either been totally innocent and undeserving of their annihilation, or, if they *had* been planning to rise up against Cortés, they could only have been obeying secret orders from Motecuzóma. However, the Revered Speaker, in the message conveyed to Cortés by Tlácotzin, blamed his Cholólan allies for having contrived the dubious "plot" entirely on their own; he claimed to have had no knowledge of it; he described them as "traitors to both of us"; he praised Cortés for his swift and complete extinction of the rebels; and he hoped the unhappy occurrence would not imperil the anticipated friendship between the white men and The Triple Alliance.

I think it was fitting that Motecuzóma's message was delivered by his Snake Woman, since it was a masterpiece of reptilian squirming. It went on, "Nevertheless, if Cholólan's perfidy has discouraged the Captain-General and his company from venturing any farther through such hazardous lands and unpredictable people, we will understand his decision to turn and go homeward, though we will sincerely regret having missed the opportunity of meeting the valiant Captain-General Cortés face to face. Therefore, since you will not be visiting us in our capital city, we of the Mexíca ask that you accept these gifts as a small substitute for our friendly embrace, and that you share them with your King Carlos when you have returned to your native country."

I heard later that Cortés could hardly contain his mirth when that transparently devious and wishful message was translated to him by Malíntzin, and that he mused aloud, "I do look forward to meeting, face to face, a man with two faces." But he then made reply to Tlácotzin:

"I thank your master for his concern, and for these gifts of amends, which I gratefully accept in the name of His Majesty King Carlos. However"—and here he yawned, Tlácotzin reported—"the recent trouble here at Cholólan was no trouble at all." And here he laughed. "As we Spanish fighting men account trouble, this was no more than a fleabite to be scratched. Your lord need not worry that it has lessened our determination to continue our explorations. We will keep on traveling westward. Oh, we may digress here and there, to visit other cities and nations which may wish to contribute forces to our retinue. But eventually, assuredly, our journey will bring us to Tenochtítlan. You may give your ruler our solemn promise that we will meet." He laughed again. "Face to face to face."

Naturally, Motecuzóma had foreseen that the invaders might still resist dissuasion, so he had provided his Snake Woman with one more squirm.

"In that case," said Tlácotzin, "it would please our Revered Speaker to have the Captain-General no longer delay his arrival." Meaning that Motecuzóma did not *want* him wandering at will among the malcontent tributary peoples, and probably enlisting them. "The Revered Speaker suggests that in these uncomfortable and primitive outer provinces you can get the impression only that our people are barbarous and uncivilized. He is desirous that you see his capital city's splendor and magnificence, so you may realize our people's real worth and ability. He urges that you come now and directly to Tenochtítlan. I will guide you there, my lord. And since I am Tlácotzin, second to the ruler of the Mexíca, my presence will be proof against any other people's trickery or ambush."

Cortés swept his arm in a gesture encompassing the troops ranked and waiting all about Cholólan. "I do not fret overmuch about trickery and ambush, friend Tlácotzin," he said pointedly. "But I accept your lord's invitation to the capital, and your kind offer to guide. We are ready to march when you are."

It was true that Cortés had little to fear from either open or sneak attack, or that he had any real need to continue collecting new warriors. Our mice estimated that, when he departed Cholólan, his combined forces numbered about twenty thousand, and there were in addition some eight thousand porters carrying the army's equipment and provisions. The company stretched over two one-long-runs in length, and required a quarter of a day to march past any given point. Incidentally, by then, every warrior and porter wore an insigne that proclaimed him a man of Cortés's army. Since the Spaniards still complained that they "could not tell the damned Indians apart," and could not in the confusion of battle distinguish friend from enemy, Cortés had ordered all his native troops to adopt a uniform style of headdress: a high crown of mazátla grass. When that army of twenty and eight thousand advanced toward Tenochtítlan, said the mice, it resembled from a distance a great, undulating, grass-grown field magically on the move.

Motecuzóma had probably considered telling his Snake Woman to lead Cortés aimlessly around and about the mountain country until the invaders were either desperately fatigued or hopelessly lost, and could be abandoned there; but of course there were many men among the Acólhua and Texcaltéca and other accompanying troops who would soon have divined that trick. However, Motecuzóma apparently *did* instruct Tlácotzin to make it no easy journey, no doubt still wistfully hoping that Cortés would give up the expedition in discouragement. At any rate, Tlácotzin brought them westward along none of the easier trade routes through the lower valleys; he led them up and over the high pass between the volcanoes Ixtaccíuatl and Popocatépetl.

As I have said, there is snow on those heights even in the hottest days of summer. By the time that company came across, the winter was beginning. If anything *was* likely to dishearten the white men, it would have been the numbing chill and fierce winds and great drifts of snow they had to make their way through. To this day, I do not know what the climate of your native Spain is like, but Cortés and his soldiers had all spent years in Cuba, which I understand is as torrid and humid as any of our coastal Hot Lands. So the white men, like their allies the Totonáca, were unprepared and unclothed to withstand the piercing cold of the frozen route Tlácotzin chose. He later reported with satisfaction that the white men had suffered terribly.

Yes, they suffered and they complained, and four white men died, and so did two of their horses and several of their staghounds, and so did perhaps a hundred of their Totonáca, but the remainder of the train persevered. In fact, ten of the Spaniards, to show off their stamina and prowess, briefly digressed from the route of march, with the declared intention of climbing all the way to the top of Popocatépetl to look down into his incense-smoking crater. They did not get that far; but then, not many of our own people have ever done so, or have cared to try. The climbers rejoined their company, blue and stiff with cold, and some of them later had a number of their fingers and toes fall off. But they were much admired by their comrades for having made the attempt, and even the Snake Woman grudgingly had to admit that the white men, however foolhardy, were men of dauntless courage and energy.

Tlácotzin also reported to us the white men's very human expressions of astonishment and awe and gladness when at last they came out from the western end of the pass, and they stood on the mountain slopes overlooking the immense lake basin, and the falling snow briefly parted its curtain to give them an unimpeded view. Below and beyond them lay the interconnected and varicolored bodies of water, set in their vast bowl of luxuriant foliage and tidy towns and straight roads between. So suddenly seen, after the unappealing heights they had just crossed, the sweep of land below would have appeared like a garden: pleasant and green, all shades of green, thick green forests and neat green orchards and variously green chinámpa and farm plots. They could have seen, though only in miniature, the numerous cities and towns bordering the several lakes, and the lesser island communities set in the very waters. They were then still at least twenty one-long-runs from Tenochtítlan, but the silvery-white city would have shone like a star. They had journeyed for months, from the featureless seacoast beaches, over and around numberless mountains, through rocky ravines and rough valleys, meanwhile seeing only towns and villages of no particular distinction, finally breasting the formidably bleak pass between the volcanoes. Then, suddenly, the travelers looked down on a scene that—they said it themselves—"seemed like a dream . . . like a marvel from the old books of fables. . . ."

Coming down from the volcanoes, the travelers of course entered the domains of The Triple Alliance by way of the Acólhua lands, where they were met and greeted by the Uey-Tlatoáni Cacámatzin, come out from Texcóco with an impressive assembly of his lords and nobles and courtiers and guards. Though Cacáma, as instructed by his uncle, made a warm speech of welcome to the newcomers, I daresay he must have felt uneasy, being glared at by his dethroned half brother Black Flower, who at that moment stood before him with a powerful force of disaffected Acólhua warriors at his command. The confrontation between those two might have erupted into battle right there, except that both Motecuzóma and Cortés had strictly forbidden any strife that might mar their own momentous meeting. So, for the time being, all was outwardly amicable, and Cacáma led the whole train into Texcóco for lodging and refreshment and entertainment before it continued on to Tenochtítlan.

However, there is no doubt that Cacáma was embarrassed and enraged when his own subjects crowded the streets of Texcóco to receive the returning Black Flower with cheers of rejoicing. That was insult enough, but it was not long before Cacáma had to endure the even worse insult of mass desertion. During the day or two that the travelers spent in that city, perhaps two thousand of the men of Texcóco dug out their long unused battle armor and weapons, and when the visitors moved on, those men marched with them as volunteer additions to Black Flower's troop. From that day on, the Acólhua nation was disastrously divided. Half of its population remained submissive to Cacáma, who *was* their Revered Speaker and was so recognized by his fellow rulers of The Triple Alliance. The other half gave their loyalty to the Black Flower who *should* have been their Revered Speaker, however much they may have deplored his having cast his lot with the alien whites.

From Texcóco, the Snake Woman Tlácotzin conducted Cortés and his multitude around the southern margin of the lake. The white men marveled at the "great inland sea," and marveled even more at the increasingly evident splendor of Tenochtítlan, which was visible from several points along their route, and which seemed to grow in size and magnificence as they neared it. Tlácotzin took the entire company to his own sizable palace at the promontory town of Ixtapalápan, where they lodged while they polished their blades and armor and cannons, while they groomed their horses, while they furbished their shabby uniforms insofar as possible, that they might look suitably imposing when they made the last march across the causeway into the capital.

While that was going on, Tlácotzin informed Cortés that the city, being an island and already densely populated, had no room for quartering even the smallest part of his thousands of allies. The Snake Woman also made it plain that Cortés should not tactlessly take with him to the city such an unwelcome guest as Black Flower, or a horde of troops which, although of our own race, were from notably unfriendly nations.

Cortés, having already seen the city, at least from a distance, could hardly dispute its limitations of accommodation, and he was willing enough to be diplomatic in his choice of those who would accompany him there. But he set some conditions. Tlácotzin must arrange for his forces to be distributed and quartered along the mainland shore, in an arc extending from the southern causeway to the most northern—in effect, covering every approach to and egress from the island-city. Cortés would take with him into Tenochtítlan, besides most of his Spaniards, only a token number of warriors from the Acólhua, Texcaltéca, and Totonáca tribes. And he must be promised that those warriors would have unhindered passage on and off the island, at all times, so he could use them as couriers to maintain contact with his mainland forces.

Tlácotzin agreed to those conditions. He suggested that some of the native troops could remain where they were, in Ixtapalápan, convenient to the southern causeway; others could be camped about Tlácopan near the western causeway; others in Tepeyáca near the northern causeway. So Cortés selected the warriors he would keep with him for couriers, and he sent the remaining thousands marching off with the guides Tlácotzin provided, and he ordered various of his white officers and soldiers to go in command of each of the detached forces. When runners came back from each of the detachments to report that they were in position and making camp to stay on call as long as necessary, Cortés told Tlácotzin, and the Snake Woman sent the word to Motecuzóma: the emissaries of King Carlos and the Lord God would enter Tenochtítlan the next day.

✠

That was the day Two House in our year of One Reed, which is to say, early in your month of November, in your year counted as one thousand five hundred and nineteen.

The southern causeway had known many processions in its time, but never one that made such an unaccustomed noise. The Spaniards carried no musical instruments, and they did not sing or chant or make any other sort of music to accompany their pacing. But there was a jingling and clashing and clanging of all the weapons they carried and the steel armor they wore and the harness of their horses. Though the procession moved at a ceremonially slow walk, the horses' hooves struck heavily on the paving stones and the big wheels of the cannons rumbled ponderously; so the whole length of the causeway vibrated; and the whole lake surface, like a drumhead, amplified the noise; and the clamor echoed back from all the distant mountains.

Cortés led, of course, mounted on his She-Mule, carrying on a tall staff the blood-and-gold banner of Spain, and Malíntzin proudly paced beside the horse, carrying her master's personal flag. Behind them came the Snake Woman and the other Mexíca lords who had gone to Cholólan and back. Behind them came the mounted Spanish soldiers, their upright spears bearing pennons at their points. Then came the fifty or so selected warriors of our own race. Behind them came the Spanish foot soldiers, their crossbows and harquebuses held at parade position, their swords sheathed and their spears casually leaned back upon their shoulders. Trailing that neatly ranked and professionally marching company came a jostling crowd of citizens from Ixtapalápan and the other promontory towns, merely curious to see the unprecedented sight of warlike foreigners walking unopposed into the hitherto unassailable city of Tenochtítlan.

Halfway along the causeway, at the Acachinánco fort, the procession was met by its first official greeters: the Revered Speaker Cacámatzin of Texcóco and many Acólhua nobles, who had come by canoe across the lake, also Tecpanéca nobles from .Tlácopan, the third city of The Triple Alliance. Those magnificently garbed lords led the way, as humbly as slaves, sweeping the causeway with brooms and strewing it with flower petals in advance of the parade, all the way to where the causeway joined the island. Meanwhile, Motecuzóma had been carried from his palace in his most elegant litter. He was accompanied by a numerous and impressive company of his Eagle, Jaguar, and Arrow Knights, and all the lords and ladies of his court, including this Lord Mixtli and my Lady Béu.

The timing had been arranged so that our procession arrived at the island's edge—at the entrance to the city—just as the incoming procession did. The two trains stopped, some twenty paces apart, and Cortés swung down from his horse, handing his banner to Malíntzin. At the same moment, Motecuzóma's canopied litter was set by its bearers on the ground. When he stepped out from its embroidered curtains, we were all surprised by his dress. Of course, he wore his most flamboyant long mantle, the one made all of shimmering hummingbird feathers, and a fan crown of quetzal tototl plumes, and many medallions and other adornments of the utmost richness. But he did not wear his golden sandals; he was barefoot—and none of us Mexíca was much pleased to see our Revered Speaker of the One World manifest even that token humility.

He and Cortés stepped forward from their separate companies and slowly walked toward each other across the open space between. Motecuzóma made the deep bow of kissing the earth, and Cortés responded with what I know now is the Spanish military hand salute. As was fitting, Cortés presented the first gift, leaning forward to drape around the Speaker's neck a perfumed strand of what appeared to be alternate pearls and flashing gems—a cheap thing of nacre and glass, it later proved to be. Motecuzóma in turn looped over Cortés's head a double necklace made of the rarest sea shells and festooned with some hundred finely wrought solid-gold bangles in the shapes of various animals. The Revered Speaker then made a lengthy and flowery speech of welcome. Malíntzin, holding an alien flag in either hand, boldly stepped forward to stand beside her master, to translate Motecuzóma's words, and then those of Cortés, which were somewhat fewer.

Motecuzóma returned to his litter chair, Cortés remounted his horse, and the procession of us Mexíca led the procession of Spaniards through the city. The marching men began to march a little less orderly, bumping into each other and treading on each other's heels, as they gawked about—at the well-dressed people lining the streets, at the fine buildings, at the hanging rooftop gardens. In The Heart of the One World, the horses had trouble keeping their footing on the sleek marble paving of that immense plaza; Cortés and the other riders had to dismount and lead them. We went past the Great Pyramid and turned right, to the old palace of Axayácatl, where a sumptuous banquet was spread for all those hundreds of visitors and all us hundreds who had received them. There must have been equally as many hundreds of different foods, served on thousands of platters of gold-inlaid lacquerware. As we took our places at the dining cloths, Motecuzóma led Cortés to the dais set for them, saying meanwhile:

"This was the palace of my father, who was one of my predecessors as Uey-Tlatoáni. It has been scrupulously cleaned and furnished and decorated to be worthy of such distinguished guests. It contains suites of chambers for yourself, for your lady"—he said that with some distaste—"and for your chief officers. There are ample and suitable quarters for all the rest of your company. There is a complete staff of slaves to serve you and cook for you and attend to your needs. The palace will be your residence for as long as you stay in these lands."

I think any other man but Cortés, in his equivocal situation, would have declined that offer. Cortés knew that he was a guest only by self-invitation, and was more likely regarded as an unwelcome aggressor. By taking up residence in the palace, even with some three hundred of his own soldiers under the same roof, the Captain-General would be in a position far more dangerous than when he had stayed in the palace of Cholólan. Here, he would be at all times under Motecuzóma's eye, and within Motecuzóma's reach, should his host's unwillingly extended hand of friendship suddenly decide to clutch or clench. The Spaniards would be captives—unfettered, but captives— in Motecuzóma's own stronghold city, the city perched on an island, the island encircled by a lake, the lake surrounded by all the cities and peoples and armies of The Triple Alliance. While Cortés stayed in the city, his own allies would not be within easy call, and, even if he did call, those reinforcements might have trouble getting to his side. For Cortés would have noticed, as he came along the southern causeway, that its several bridged canoe passages could easily be unbridged to prevent its being crossed. He must have guessed that the city's other causeways were similarly constructed, as of course they were.

The Captain-General could tactfully have told Motecuzóma that he preferred to make his residence on the mainland, and from there to visit the city as their intermittent conferences might require. But he said no such thing. He thanked Motecuzóma for the hospitable offer, and accepted it, as if a palace were no more than his due, and as if he scorned even to consider any danger in occupying it. Though I bear no love for Cortés, and no admiration for his guile and his deceits, I must grant that in the face of danger he always acted without hesitation, with a daring that defied what other men call common sense. Perhaps I felt that he and I had temperaments much alike, because in my lifetime I also often took audacious risks that "sensible" men would have shunned as insane.

Still, Cortés did not trust his survival entirely to chance. Before he and his men spent their first night in the palace, he had them use heavy ropes and great effort to hoist four of his cannons to the roof—uncaring that the process rather thoroughly destroyed the flower garden newly planted up there for his delectation—and positioned the cannons so they could cover every approach to the building. Also, on that night and every night, soldiers carrying charged harquebuses paced all night long around the rooftop and around the palace's exterior at ground level.

During the following days, Motecuzóma personally conducted his guests on tours of the city, accompanied by the Snake Woman or others of his Speaking Council, and by a number of his court priests, who wore faces of extreme disapproval, and by me. I was always in the company, at Motecuzóma's insistence, because I had warned him of Malíntzin's cunning aptitude for mistranslating. Cortés remembered me, as he had said he would, but apparently without any rancor. He smiled his thin smile when we were introduced by name, and he accepted my company amiably enough, and he spoke his words as often through my translation as through that of his woman. She also recognized me, of course, and with obvious odium, and she addressed me not at all. When her master chose to speak through me, she glared as if she were awaiting only a propitious moment to have me put to death. Well, fair enough, I thought. It was what I planned for her.

On those walks about the city, Cortés was always accompanied by his second in command, the big, flame-haired Pedro de Alvarado, and by most of his other officers, and naturally by Malíntzin, and by two or three of his own priests, who looked about as sour as ours. We would also usually be followed by a straggle of the common soldiers, though other groups of them might wander about the island on their own, while the native warriors of their company tended not to stray far from the security of their barracks at the palace.

As I have said, those warriors wore the new headdress ordained by Cortés: it looked like a clump of high, pliant grass growing from the tops of their heads. But the Spanish soldiers too, since I had seen them last, had added to their military headgear a distinctive adornment. Each of them wore a curious, pale-leather band encircling the crown of his steel helmet, just above its flanged brim. It was not particularly decorative, and served no apparent purpose, so eventually I inquired about it and one of the Spaniards, laughing, told me what it was.

During the affray at Cholólan, while the Texcaltéca were indiscriminately butchering the mass of the city's inhabitants, the Spaniards had gone looking specifically for the females with whom they had disported themselves during their fourteen days of revel, and they found most of those women and girls still in their quarters, trembling with fear. Convinced that the females had coupled with them only to sap their strength, the Spaniards exacted a unique revenge. They seized the women and girls, stripped them naked, and used some of them a last time or two. Then, though the females screamed and pleaded, the soldiers held them down and, with their sharp steel knives, they cut away from each female's crotch a hand-sized flap of skin containing the oval opening of her tipíli. They left the mutilated and sexless women to bleed to death, and went away. They took the warm, purselike pouches of skin and stretched the lips of them around the pommels of their horses' saddles. When the flesh had dried but was still pliable, they slipped the resultant circlets over their helmets, each with its little xacapíli pearl facing front—that is, the shriveled, beanlike gristle that *had been* a tender xacapíli. I do not know whether the soldiers wore those trophies as a grisly joke or as a warning to other scheming females.

All the Spaniards remarked approvingly on the size and population and splendor and cleanliness of Tenochtítlan, and compared it to other cities they had visited. The names of those other cities mean nothing to me, but you reverend friars may know them. The guests said our city was bigger in extent than Valladolid, that it was more populous than Seville, that its buildings were *almost* as magnificent as those of Holy Rome, that its canals made it resemble Amsterdam or Venice, that its streets and airs and waters were cleaner than in *any* of those places. We guides refrained from remarking that the effluvium of the Spaniards was noticeably diminishing that cleanliness. Yes, the newcomers were much impressed by our city's architecture and ornamentation and orderliness, but do you know what most impressed them? What moved them to their loudest exclamations of wonder and amazement?

Our sanitary closets.

It was clear that many of those men had traveled widely in your Old World, but it was equally clear that nowhere had they encountered an indoor facility for performing one's necessary functions. They were amazed enough to find such closets in the palace they occupied; they were astonished beyond words when we took them to visit the market square of Tlaltelólco and they found *public conveniences* provided for even the common folk: the vendors and the marketers there. When the Spaniards first noticed the things, every single man of them, Cortés included, just *had* to go inside and void himself. So did Malíntzin, since such conveniences were as unknown in her native backcountry of the uncivilized Coatlícamac as they evidently are in Spain's Holy Rome. As long as Cortés and his company stayed on the island, and as long as the marketplace existed, those public closets were the most popular and most often visited attractions of all that Tenochtítlan had to offer.

While the Spaniards were enchanted by the closets of continually flushing water, our Mexíca physicians were cursing those same conveniences, for they avidly wished to get a sample of Cortés's bodily wastes. And if the Spaniards were behaving like children with a new toy, those doctors were behaving like quimíchime mice, forever following Cortés about or popping their heads suddenly from around corners. Cortés could not help noticing those various elderly strangers peeking and peering at him everywhere he went in public. He finally asked about them, and Motecuzóma, secretly amused by their antics, replied only that they were doctors watching over the health of their most honored guest. Cortés shrugged and said no more, though I suspect he formed the opinion that all our physicians were more pathetically ill than any patients they might attend. Of course, what the doctors were doing, and not doing very subtly, was trying to verify their earlier conclusion that the white man Cortés was indeed afflicted with the nanáua disease. They were trying to measure with their eyes the significant curvature of his thighbones, trying to get close enough to hear if he breathed with the characteristic snuffling noise, or to see if his incisor teeth had the telltale notches.

Even I began to find them an embarrassment and an annoyance, always lurking in the way of our walks about the city and abruptly pouncing from unexpected places. When one day I literally tripped over an old doctor who was crouching for a leg-level view of Cortés, I angrily took him aside and demanded, "If you dare not ask for permission to examine the exalted white man, surely you can invent some excuse for examining his woman, who is merely one of us."

"It would not serve, Mixtzin," said the physician unhappily. "She will not have been infected by their connection. The nanáua can be transmitted to a sexual partner only in its early and flagrantly evident stages. If, as we suspect, the man was born of a diseased mother, then he is long past being a hazard to any other woman, though he could give *her* a diseased child. We are all naturally eager to know if we rightly divined his condition, but we cannot be sure. If only he were not so fascinated by the sanitary facilities, if we could examine his urine for traces of chiatóztli . . ."

I said in exasperation, "I keep finding you everywhere *except* squatting under him in the closets. I suggest, Lord Physician, that you go and instruct their palace steward to have slaves dismantle the man's closet there, and explain that it is clogged, and provide a pot for him to use in the meantime, and instruct his chambermaid to bring the pot—"

"*Ayyo,* a brilliant idea," said the physician, and he went hurrying off. We were molested no more during our excursions, but I never did hear whether the doctors found any definite evidence of Cortés's being a sufferer of the shameful disease.

I must report that those first Spaniards did not admire *everything* in Tenochtítlan. Some of the sights we showed them they disliked and even deplored. For example, they recoiled violently at sight of the skull rack in The Heart of the One World. They seemed to find it digusting that we should wish to keep those relics of so many persons of renown who had gone to their Flowery Deaths in that plaza. But I have heard your Spanish storytellers tell of your own long-ago hero, El Cid, whose death was kept secret from his enemies, while his stiff body was bent to a shape that could be mounted on a horse, and thus he led his army to win its last battle. Since you Spaniards so treasure that tale, I do not know why Cortés and his company thought our display of notable persons' skulls any more gruesome than El Cid's preservation after death.

But the things that most repelled the white men were our temples, with their evidence of many sacrifices, both recent and long past. To give his visitors the best possible view of his city, Motecuzóma took them to the summit of the Great Pyramid, which, except during sacrificial ceremonies, was always kept scrubbed and gleaming on its outside. The guests climbed the banner-bordered stairs, admiring the grace and immensity of the edifice, the vividness of its painted and beaten-gold decoration, and they looked all about them at the vista of city and lake which broadened as they climbed. The two temples atop the pyramid were also bright on the outside, but the interiors were never cleaned. Since an accumulation of blood signified an accumulation of veneration, the temples' statues and walls and ceilings and floors were thick with coagulated blood.

The Spaniards entered the temple of Tlaloc, and instantly lunged out again, with retching exclamations and faces expressive of nausea. It was the first and only time I ever knew the white men to back away from a smell, or even acknowledge one, but in truth the stench of that place *was* worse than their own. When they could control their heaving stomachs, Cortés and Alvarado and the priest Bartolomé went inside again, and went into spasms of rage when they discovered Tlaloc's hollow statue to be filled, right up to the level of his gaping square mouth, with the decaying human hearts on which he had been fed. Cortés was so infuriated that he whipped out his sword and gave the statue a mighty blow. It only chipped away a fragment of dried blood from Tlaloc's stone face, but it was an insult that made Motecuzóma and *his* priests gasp with consternation. However, Tlaloc did not respond with any devastating blast of lightning, and Cortés caught hold of his temper. He said to Motecuzóma:

"This idol of yours is not god. It is an evil thing which we call a devil. It must be cast down and out and into eternal darkness. Let me set here in its place the cross of Our Lord and an image of Our Lady. You will see that this demon dares not object, and from that you will realize that it is inferior, that it fears the True Faith, and that you will be well advised to abjure such wicked beings and embrace our kindly ones."

Motecuzóma said stiffly that the idea was unthinkable, but the Spaniards went into convulsions again when they entered the adjacent temple of Huitzilopóchtli, and yet again when they beheld the similar temples atop the lesser pyramid at Tlaltelólco, and each time Cortés expressed his repugnance more strongly and in more intemperate words.

"The Totonáca," he said, "have swept their country clean of these foul idols, and have given their allegiance to Our Lord and His Virgin Mother. The monstrous mountain temple at Cholólan has been leveled. At this moment, some of my friars are instructing King Xicoténca and his court in the blessings of Christianity. I tell you, in none of those places have the old devil-deities so much as whimpered. And I swear on my oath, neither will they when *you* cast them out!"

Motecuzóma replied, and I translated, doing my best to convey the iciness of his words, "Captain-General, you are here as my guest, and a mannerly guest does not deride his host's beliefs any more than he would mock his host's taste in dress or wives. Also, although you are my guest, a majority of my people resent that they too must be hospitable to you. If you try to tamper with their gods, the priests will raise an outcry against you, and in matters of religion the priests can overrule my mandates. The people will heed the priests, not me, and you will be fortunate if you and your men are only evicted alive from Tenochtítlan."

Even the brash Cortés understood that he was being sharply reminded of his tenuous position, and he withdrew from pressing the topic further, and he muttered words of apology. At which Motecuzóma likewise thawed a little, and said:

"However, I try to be a fair man and a generous host. I realize that you Christians have no place here in which to worship your own gods, and I have no objection to your doing that. I will order that the small Eagle Temple in the grand plaza be cleared of its statues and altar stones and anything else offensive to your faith. Your priests may put in whatever furnishings they require, and the temple is *your* temple for as long as you want it."

Our own priests naturally were not pleased at even that minor concession to the aliens, but they did no more than grumble when the white priests took over the little temple. Thereafter, in fact, the place was more frequented than it had ever been. The Christian priests seemed to hold their Masses and other services continuously from morning to night, whether the white soldiers attended or not—because numbers of our own people, drawn by simple curiosity, began to drift in to those services. I say our own people; in actuality, they were mainly the white men's female consorts and allied warriors from other nations. But the priests employed Malíntzin to translate their sermons, and were delighted when many of those heathen participants submitted—still no more than curious about the novelty of it—to take the salt and sprinkling and new-naming of baptism. Anyway, Motecuzóma's granting of that temple temporarily diverted Cortés from laying violent hands on our ancient gods, as he had done in other places.

The Spaniards had been in Tenochtítlan for little more than a month when something happened that could have expunged them forever from Tenochtítlan, probably from the entire One World. A swift-messenger came from Lord Patzínca of the Totonáca and, if he had reported to Motecuzóma, as formerly he would have done, the white men's sojourn might have ended then and there. However, the messenger made his report to the Totonáca army camped on the mainland, and he was brought by one of that company into the city to repeat it privily to Cortés. His news was that a serious commotion had occurred on the coast.

What had happened was this. A Mexícatl tribute collector named Cuaupopóca, making his accustomed annual round of various tributary nations, accompanied by a troop of Mexíca warriors, had collected the year's levy from the Huaxtéca, who also live on the seacoast, but to the north of the Totonáca. Then, leading a train of Huaxtéca porters, conscripted to carry their own tribute goods to Tenochtítlan, Cuaupopóca had moved on south into the Totonáca country, as he had been doing every year for years. But on reaching the capital city of Tzempoálan, he was shocked and indignant to find that the Totonáca were unprepared for his arrival. There was no stock of goods ready to go; there were no local men waiting to serve as porters; the ruling Lord Patzínca had not even the usual list compiled for Cuaupopóca to know what the tribute was supposed to consist of.

Having come from the northern hinterlands, Cuaupopóca had heard nothing of the misadventure that had befallen the Mexíca registrars who always went ahead of him, and he knew nothing of all the occurrences since then. Motecuzóma could easily have sent word to him, but had not. And I will never know whether the Revered Speaker simply forgot, in the press of so many other events, or whether he deliberately chose to let the tribute collection proceed as usual, just to see what *would* happen. Well, Cuaupopóca tried to do his duty. He demanded the tribute from Patzínca, who did his customary cringing but refused to comply, on the ground that he was no longer subordinate to The Triple Alliance. He had new masters, white ones, who lived in a fortified village farther down the beach. Patzínca whiningly suggested that Cuaupopóca apply to the white officer in charge there, a certain Juan de Escalante.

Angry and mystified, but determined, Cuaupopóca led his men to the Villa Rica de la Vera Cruz, to be received only with jeers in a language that was incomprehensible but recognizably insulting. So he, a mere tribute collector, did what the mighty Motecuzóma never had done yet; he objected to being thus disdainfully treated, and he objected strenuously, violently, decisively. In so doing, Cuaupopóca may have made a mistake, but he made it in the grand manner, in the lordly manner to be expected of the Mexíca. Patzínca and Escalante made a worse mistake in provoking him to it, for they should have been aware of their vulnerability. Practically the entire Totonáca army had marched away with Cortés, along with practically all of his own. Tzempoálan had few men left to defend it, and Vera Cruz was not much better manned, since most of its garrison consisted of the boatmen left there simply because they had no ships to require their employment.

Cuaupopóca, I repeat, was only a minor Mexícatl official. I may be the only person who even remembers his name, though many still remember the fate to which his tonáli brought him. The man was diligent in his duty of collecting levies, and that was the first time in his career that he had ever met defiance from a tributary nation, and he must have been as fiery-tempered as his name implied—it meant Smoldering Eagle—and he would not be balked in accomplishing his mission. He snapped an order to his force of Mexíca warriors and they leapt eagerly into action, because they were fighting men, bored by an undemanding journey of escort duty. They happily seized the opportunity for combat, and they were not long deterred by the few harquebuses and crossbows discharged at them from the stockade walls of the white men's village.

They killed Escalante and what few professional soldiers Cortés had detached to his command. The remaining population of unwarlike boatmen immediately surrendered. Cuaupopóca set guards there and around the Tzempoálan palace, then ordered the rest of his men to strip clean the entire surrounding country. This year, he proclaimed to the terrorized Totonáca, their levy would comprise no fraction of their goods and produce, but *all* of it. So it had been something of a feat for Patzínca's messenger to escape from the cordoned palace, and to slip past the scourging warriors of Cuaupopóca, and to bring Cortés the bad news.

Surely Cortés perceived how much more perilous his own position had suddenly become, and how uncertain his future, but he wasted no time in brooding. He went immediately to Motecuzóma's palace, and in no subdued or fearful mood. He took with him the red giant Alvarado and Malíntzin and a number of heavily armed men, and all of them stormed past the palace stewards and, without ceremony, directly into Motecuzóma's throne room. Cortés raged, or pretended to rage, as he regaled the Revered Speaker with an amended version of the report he had received. As he told it, a roving band of Mexíca bandits had without provocation attacked his few men peaceably living on the beach, and had slaughtered them. It was a grave breach of the truce and friendship Motecuzóma had promised, and what did Motecuzóma intend to do about it?

The Revered Speaker knew of the tribute train's presence in that general area, so, from hearing Cortés's account, he would have supposed that it had got involved in a skirmish there and *had* done some damage among the white men. But he need not have hastened to conciliate Cortés; he could have temporized long enough to find out the true state of affairs. And the truth was this: the white men's one and only established settlement in these lands had surrendered itself to Cuaupopóca's Mexíca troops; the white men's one most biddable ally, Lord Patzínca, was cowering inside his palace, a prisoner of the Mexíca. Meanwhile, Motecuzóma had almost all the rest of the white men contained on his island, easy prey for elimination; and Cortés's other white and native troops could easily have been held off the island while the mainland armies of The Triple Alliance gathered to pulverize them. Thanks to Cuaupopóca, Motecuzóma held the Spaniards and all their supporters helpless in his hand. He had only to close that hand into a fist and squeeze until the blood ran out between his fingers.

He did not. He expressed to Cortés his dismay and condolence. He sent a force of his palace guard to make apologies in Tzempoálan and Vera Cruz, to relieve Cuaupopóca of his authority, to bring him and his chief military officers under arrest to Tenochtítlan.

What was worse, when the praiseworthy Cuaupopóca and his four commendable cuáchictin "old eagles" of the Mexíca army knelt in obeisance before the throne, Motecuzóma sat flaccidly slumped on that throne, flanked by the sternly erect Cortés and Alvarado, and in a not at all lordly voice he said to the prisoners:

"You have exceeded the authority of your mission. You have seriously embarrassed your Lord Speaker and compromised the honor of the Mexíca nation. You have broken the promise of truce I granted to these esteemed visitors and all their subordinates. Have you anything to say for yourselves?"

Cuaupopóca was dutiful to the end, though he was recognizably more of a man, more of a noble, more of a Mexícatl, than the creature on the throne to whom he said respectfully, "It was all my doing, Lord Speaker. And I did what I thought best to do. No man can do more."

Motecuzóma said dully, "You have caused me grievous hurt. But the death and damage you caused have more grievously hurt these our guests. Therefore ..." And incredibly the Revered Speaker of the One World said, "Therefore, I will defer judgment to the Captain-General Cortés, and let him determine what punishment you deserve."

Cortés had evidently given prior thought to that matter, for he decreed a punishment that he must have been sure would deter any other individuals trying to oppose him, and it was at the same time a punishment intended to flout our traditions and spite our gods. He commanded that the five should be put to death, but not to any Flowery Death. No heart would be fed to any god, no blood would be spilled to the honor of any god, no flesh or organ of the men would remain to be used as any least sacrificial offering.

Cortés had his soldiers bring a length of chain; it was the thickest chain I ever saw, like looped constrictor snakes made of iron; I learned later that it was a segment of what is called an anchor chain, used for mooring the heavy ships. It took considerable effort on the part of the soldiers, and surely caused considerable pain to Cuaupopóca and his four officers, but the giant links of that chain were forced over the heads of the condemned men, so a link hung around each man's neck. They were taken into The Heart of the One World, where a great log had been fixed upright in the square ... just yonder, in front of where the cathedral now stands, where the Señor Bishop now has his pillory for the exposure of sinners to public vilification. The chain was fastened around the top of that heavy post, so the five men stood in a circle, their backs to the log, pinioned by their necks. Then a pile of wood, previously soaked in chapopótli, was heaped around their feet and as high as their knees, and it was set afire.

Such a novel punishment—a deliberately bloodless execution—had never been known in these lands before, so almost everyone in Tenochtítlan came to see it. But I watched it while standing beside the priest Bartolomé, and he confided to me that such burnings are quite common in Spain, that they are especially suited to the execution of enemies of Holy Church, because the Church has always forbidden its clerics to shed the blood of even the worst sinners. It is a pity, reverend scribes, that your Church is thereby enjoined from employing more merciful methods of execution. For I have seen many kinds of killing and dying in my time, but none more hideous, I think, than what Cuaupopóca and his officers suffered that day.

They bore it staunchly for a while, as the flames first licked up along their legs. Above the heavy iron collars of the chain links, their faces were calm and resigned. They were not otherwise bound to the post, but they did not kick their legs or flail their arms or struggle in any unseemly manner. However, when the flames reached their groins and burned away their loincloths and began to burn what was underneath, their faces became agonized. Then the fire needed no longer to be fed by the wood and chapopótli; it caught the natural oils of their skin and the fatty tissue just under the skin. The men, instead of being burned, began to burn of themselves, and the flames rose so high that we could barely see their faces. But we saw the brighter flash of their hair going in one blaze, and we could hear the men begin to scream.

After a while, the screams faded to a thin, high shrilling, just audible above the crackling of the flames, and more unpleasant to hear than the screaming had been. When we onlookers got a glimpse of the men inside the blaze, they were black and crinkled all over, but somewhere inside that char they still lived and one or more of them kept up that inhuman keening. The flames eventually ate under their skin and flesh, to gnaw on their muscles, and that made the muscles tighten in odd ways, so that the men's bodies began to contort. Their arms bent at the elbows; their hands of fused fingers came up before their faces, or where their faces had been. What was left of their legs slowly bent at the knees and hips; they lifted off the ground and bunched up against the men's bellies.

As they hung there and fried, they also shrank, until they

ceased to resemble men, in size as well as appearance. Only their crusted and featureless heads were still of adult size. Otherwise they looked like five children, charred black, tucked into the position in which young children so often sleep. And still, though it was hard to believe that life still existed inside those pitiful objects, that shrill noise went on. It went on until their heads burst. Wood soaked in chapopótli gives a hot fire, and such heat must make the brain boil and froth and steam until the skull can no longer contain it. There was a sudden noise like a clay pot shattering, and it sounded four times more, and then there was no noise except the sizzle of some last droplets from the bodies falling into the fire, and the soft crunch of the wood relaxing into a bed of embers.

It was a long time before the anchor chain was cool enough for Cortés's soldiers to undo it from the blackened post, and let the five small things drop into the embers to burn entirely to ash, and they took the chain away to be saved for future use, though no other such execution has taken place since then. That was eleven years ago. But just last year, when Cortés returned from his visit to Spain, where your King Carlos raised him from his rank of Captain-General and ennobled him as the Marqués del Valle, Cortés himself designed the emblem of his new nobility. What you call his coat of arms is now to be seen everywhere: it is a shield marked with various symbols, and the shield is encircled by a chain, and in the links of that chain are collared five human heads. Cortés might have chosen to commemorate others of his triumphs, but he knows well that the end of the brave Cuaupopóca marked the beginning of the Conquest of The One World.

Since the execution had been decreed and directed by the white strangers who should have had no such authority, it caused much trepidation and unrest among our people. But the next occurrence was even more unexpected and unbelievable and mystifying: Motecuzóma's public announcement that he was moving out of his own palace to go and live for a while among the white men.

The citizens of Tenochtítlan crowded The Heart of the One World, watching with stony faces, on the day their Revered Speaker strolled leisurely across the plaza, arm in arm with

Cortés, under no restraint or any visible compulsion, and entered the palace of his father Axayácatl, the palace occupied by the visiting aliens. During the days following, there was a constant traffic back and forth across the square, as Spanish soldiers helped Motecuzóma's porters and slaves to move his entire court from the one palace to the other: Motecuzóma's wives and children and servants, their wardrobes and the furnishings of all their chambers, the contents of the throne room, libraries of books and treasury accounts, all the appurtenances necessary to conducting court business.

Our people could not understand *why* their Revered Speaker would become a guest of his own guests, or, in effect, a prisoner of his own prisoners. But I think I know why. I long ago heard Motecuzóma described as a "hollow drum," and over the years I heard that drum make loud noises, and on most of those occasions I knew those noises to be produced by the thumping of hands and events and circumstances over which Motecuzóma had no control... or things which he could only pretend he controlled... or which he only halfheartedly tried to control. If there had ever been any hope that he might someday wield his own drumsticks, so to speak, that hope vanished when he relinquished to Cortés the resolution of the Cuaupopóca affair.

For our war chief Cuitláhuac soon afterward ascertained what Cuaupopóca had in fact achieved—an advantage that could have put the white men and all their allies at our mercy— and Cuitláhuac used no brotherly words in telling how Motecuzóma had so hastily and weakly and disgracefully thrown away the one best chance for saving The One World. That revelation of his latest and worst mistake drained away any strength or will or lordliness still inherent in the Revered Speaker. He became a hollow drum indeed, too flabby even to make a noise when beaten. Meanwhile, as Motecuzóma dwindled into lethargy and enfeeblement, Cortés stood taller and bolder. After all, he had demonstrated that he held a power of life and death, even inside the stronghold of the Mexíca. He had snatched from near-extinction his Vera Cruz settlement and his ally Patzínca, not to mention himself and all the men with him. So he did not hesitate to make of Motecuzóma the outrageous demand that he voluntarily submit to his own abduction.

"I am not a prisoner. You can see that," said Motecuzóma, the first time he summoned the Speaking Council and me and some other lords to call upon him in his displaced throne room. "There is ample space here for my whole court, and comfortable chambers for us all, and ample facilities for me to continue conducting the affairs of the nation—in which, I assure you, the white men have no voice. Your own presence at this moment is evidence that my counselors and priests and messengers have free access to me and I to them, without any of the outlanders present. Neither will they interfere with our religious observances, even those requiring sacrifices. In brief, our lives will go on exactly as always. I made the Captain-General give me those guarantees before I agreed to the change of residence."

"But why agree at all?" asked the Snake Woman, in an anguished voice. "It was not seemly, my lord. It was not necessary."

"Not necessary, perhaps, but expedient," said Motecuzóma. "Since the white men entered my domains, my own people or allies have twice made attempts on their lives and property—first at Chololán, more recently on the coast. Cortés does not hold me to blame, since those attempts were made either in defiance or in ignorance of my promise of truce. But such things could happen again. I myself have warned Cortés that many of our people resent the white men's presence. Any aggravation of that resentment might make our people forget their obedience to me, and rise up again in troublesome disorder."

"If Cortés is concerned about our people's resentment of him," said a Council elder, "he can easily allay it. He can go home."

Motecuzóma said, "I told him exactly that, but of course it is impossible. He has no means of doing so until, as he expects, his King Carlos sends more ships. In the meantime, if he and I are resident in the same palace, it demonstrates two things: that I trust Cortés to do me no harm, and that I trust my people not to provoke him into doing harm to anybody. So those people should be less inclined to cause any further contention. It was for that reason that Cortés requested my being his guest here."

"His prisoner," said Cuitláhuac, almost sneering.

"I am *not* a prisoner," Motecuzóma insisted again. "I am still your Uey-Tlatoáni, still the ruler of this nation, still the chief partner in The Triple Alliance. I have made only this minor accommodation to insure the keeping of peace between us and the white men until they depart."

I said, "Excuse me, Revered Speaker. You seem confident that they will go. How do you know? When will it be?"

He gave me a look of wishing I had not asked. "They will go when they have the ships to take them. And I know they will go because I have promised that they can take with them what they came for."

There was a short silence; then someone said, "Gold."

"Yes. Much gold. When the white soldiers were assisting in my change of residence, they searched my palace with great thoroughness. They discovered the treasury chambers, although I had taken the precaution of walling over the doors of them, and—"

He was interrupted by cries of chagrin from most of the men present, and Cuitláhuac demanded, "You will give them the nation's treasury?"

"Only the gold," said Motecuzóma defensively. "And the more valuable gems. It is all they are interested in. They care nothing for plumes and dyes and jadestones and rare flower seeds and the like. Those stores we will keep, and those riches will adequately sustain the nation while we work and fight and increase our tribute demands to make up the treasury's depletion."

"But to *give* it away!" someone wailed.

"Know this," Motecuzóma went on. "The white men could demand that, and the wealth of every single noble besides, as the price of their departure. They could make it a cause of war, and call for their mainland allies to help them take it from us. I prefer to avert any such ugliness by offering the gold and jewels as a seeming gesture of generosity."

The Snake Woman said between his teeth, "Even as High Treasurer of the nation, *ostensibly* the keeper of the treasure my lord is giving away, I must concede that it would be a small price to pay for the expulsion of the outlanders. But I remind my lord: every other time they have been given gold, they have only been stimulated to want more."

"I have no more to give, and I believe I have convinced them of that truth. Except for what gold is in circulation as trade currency, or in the keeping of private individuals, there *is* no more in the Mexíca lands. Our treasury of gold represents the collection of sheaves and sheaves of years. It is the hoard of all our past Revered Speakers. It would take lifetimes to scratch even a fraction more from the earth of our lands. I have also made the gift conditional. They do not take it until they depart from here, and they are to take it directly to their King Carlos, as a personal gift from me to him—a gift of *all the treasure we have*. Cortés is satisfied, and so am I, and so will their King Carlos be. When the white men leave, they will not come back."

None of us said anything to dispute that—until after we had been dismissed and had passed through the palace gate in the Snake Wall and were making across the plaza.

Someone said, "This is intolerable. The Cem-Anáhuac Uey-Tlatoáni being held prisoner by those filthy and stinking barbarians."

Someone else said, "No. Motecuzóma is right. *He* is not a prisoner. All the rest of us are. As long as he meekly sits hostage, no other Mexícatl dares even to spit on a white man."

Someone else said, "Motecuzóma has surrendered himself and the proud independence of the Mexíca and the bulk of our treasury. If the white men's ships are long in coming, who can say what he will surrender next?"

And then someone said what was in all our minds: "In the entire history of the Mexíca, no Uey-Tlatoáni has ever been deposed while he still lives. Not even Ahuítzotl, when he was totally incapable of ruling."

"But a regency was appointed to act in his name, and it worked well enough while it bridged the succession."

"Cortés might take it into his head to kill Motecuzóma at any time. Who knows the white men's whims? Or Motecuzóma might die of his own self-loathing. He looks ready to."

"Yes, the throne might suddenly be left vacant. If we make provision for that eventuality, we would also have a provisional ruler standing ready . . . in case Motecuzóma's behavior becomes such that we *must* depose him by order of the Speaking Council."

"It should be decided and arranged in secret. Let us spare Motecuzóma the humiliation until and unless there is no choice. Also, Cortés must not be given any least reason to suspect that his precious hostage can suddenly be rendered worthless to him."

The Snake Woman turned to Cuitláhuac, who had until then made no remark at all, and said, using his lordly title, "Cuitláhuatzin, as the Speaker's brother you would normally be the first candidate considered as his successor on his death. Would you accept the title and responsibility of regent if, in formal conclave, we determine that such a post should be created?"

Cuitláhuac walked on some paces farther, frowning in meditation. At last he said, "It would grieve me to usurp the power of my own brother while he lives. But in truth, my lords, I fear he now only *half* lives, and has already abdicated most of his power. Yes, if and when the Speaking Council may decide that our nation's survival depends on it, I will rule in whatever capacity is asked of me."

As it happened, there was no immediate need for an overthrow of Motecuzóma, or any other such drastic action. Indeed, for a considerable while, it seemed that Motecuzóma had been right to counsel that we all simply be calm and wait. For the Spaniards stayed in Tenochtítlan throughout that winter and, if they had not been so obviously white, we might hardly have noticed their presence. They could have been country folk of our own race, come to the big city for a holiday, to see the sights and peaceably enjoy themselves. They even behaved irreproachably during our religious ceremonies. Some of those, the celebrations involving only music, singing, and dancing, the Spaniards watched with interest and sometimes amusement. When the rites involved the sacrifice of xochimíque, the Spaniards discreetly stayed inside their palace. We city folk, for our part, tolerated the white men, treating them politely but distantly. So, all during that winter, there were no frictions between us and them, no untoward incidents, not even any more omens seen or reported.

Motecuzóma and his courtiers and counselors seemed to adapt easily to their change of residence, and his governing of the nation's affairs appeared unaffected by the dislocation of the center of government. As he and every other Uey-Tlatoáni had always done, he regularly met with his Speaking Council; he received emissaries from outlying Mexíca provinces, from the other countries of The Triple Alliance, and from foreign nations; he gave audience to private supplicants bringing pleas and plaintiffs bringing grievances. One of his most frequent visitors was his nephew Cacáma, no doubt nervous, and rightly so, about the shakiness of his throne in Texcóco. But perhaps Cortés too was bidding his allies and subordinates to "be calm and wait." At any rate, none of them—not even Prince Black Flower, impatient to take that throne of the Acólhua—did anything rash or unruly. Throughout that winter, our world's life seemed to go on, as Motecuzóma had promised, exactly as always.

I say "seemed," because I personally had less and less to do with matters of state. My attendance at court was seldom required, except when some question arose on which Motecuzóma desired the opinions of all his lords resident in the city. My less lordly job as interpreter also became less often necessary and finally ended altogether, for Motecuzóma apparently decided that, if he was going to trust the man Cortés, he might as well trust the woman Malíntzin as well. The three of them were seen to spend much time together. That could hardly have been avoided, with them all under the same roof, big though that palace was. But in fact Cortés and Motecuzóma came to enjoy each other's company. They conversed often on the history and current estate of their separate countries and religions and ways of life. For a less solemn diversion, Motecuzóma taught Cortés how to play the gambling bean game of patóli—and I, for one, hoped that the Revered Speaker was playing for high wagers, and that he was winning, so that he would get to keep part of that treasury he had promised to the white men.

In his turn, Cortés introduced Motecuzóma to a different diversion. He sent to the coast for a number of his boatmen—the artisans you call shipwrights—and they brought with them the necessary metal tools and equipment and fittings, and they had woodsmen cut down for them some good straight trees, and they almost magically shaped those logs into planks and beams and ribs and poles. Within a surprisingly short time, they had built a half-size replica of one of their oceangoing ships and launched it on Lake Texcóco: the first boat ever seen on our waters wearing the wings called sails. With the boatmen to do the complicated business of steering it, Cortés took Motecuzóma—sometimes accompanied by members of his family and court—on frequent outings over and among all the five interconnected lakes.

I did not at all regret my gradual relief from close attendance at the court or on the white men. I was pleased to resume my former life of idle retirement, even again spending some time at The House of Pochtéca, though not so much time as I had used to spend there. My wife did not ask, but I felt that I ought to be oftener around the house and in her company, for she seemed weak and inclined to tire easily. Waiting Moon had always occupied her empty time with womanly little crafts like embroidery work, but I noticed that she had taken to holding the work very close to her eyes. Also, she would sometimes pick up a kitchen pot or some other thing, only to drop and break it. When I made solicitous inquiry, she said simply:

"I grow old, Záa."

"We are almost exactly the same age," I reminded her.

That remark seemed to give offense, as if I had abruptly begun frisking and dancing to show my comparative vivacity. Béu said rather sharply, for her, "It is one of the curses of women. At every age, they are older than the male." Then she softened, and smiled, and made a pallid joke of it. "That is why women treat their men like children. Because they never seem to grow old . . . or even to grow up."

So she lightly dismissed the matter, and it was a long time before I realized that she was in fact showing the first symptoms of the ailment that would gradually bring her to the sickbed she now has occupied for years. Béu never complained of feeling bad, she never requested any attention from me, but I gave it anyway, and, although we spoke so little, I could tell that she was grateful. When our aged servant Turquoise died, I bought two younger women—one to do the housekeeping, one to devote herself entirely to Béu's needs and wishes. Because for so many years I had been accustomed to calling for Turquoise whenever I had any household orders to give, I could not break myself of the habit. I called the two women interchangeably Turquoise, and they got used to it, and to this day I cannot remember what their real names were.

Perhaps I had unconsciously adopted the white men's disregard for proper names and correct speech. During that nearly half a year of the Spaniards' residence in Tenochtítlan, none of them made any effort to learn our Náhuatl tongue, or the rudiments of its pronunciation. The one person of our race with whom they were most closely associated was the woman who called herself Malíntzin, but even her consort Cortés invariably mispronounced that assumed name as Malinche. In time, so did all our own people, either in polite emulation of the Spaniards or mischievously to spite the woman. For it always made Malíntzin grind her teeth when she was called Malinche—it denied her the -tzin of nobility—but she could hardly complain of the disrespect without seeming to criticize her master's own slovenly speech.

Anyway, Cortés and the other men were impartial; they misnamed everybody else as well. Since Náhuatl's soft sound of "sh" does not exist in your Spanish language, we Mexíca were for a long time called either Mes-síca or Mec-síca. But you Spaniards have lately preferred to bestow on us our older name, finding it easier to call us Aztecs. Because Cortés and his men found the name Motecuzóma unwieldy, they made of it Montezuma, and I think they honestly believed they were doing no discourtesy, since the new name's inclusion of their word for "mountain" could still be taken to imply greatness and importance. The war god's name Huitzilopóchtli likewise defeated them, and they loathed that god anyway, so they made his name Huichilobos, incorporating their word for the beasts called "wolves."

✠

Well, the winter passed, and the springtime came, and with it came more white men. Motecuzóma heard the news before Cortés did, but only barely and only by chance. One of his quimíchime mice still stationed in the Totonáca country, having got bored and restless, wandered a good way south of where he should have been. So it was that the mouse saw a fleet of the wide-winged ships, only a little distance offshore and moving only slowly northward along the coast, pausing at bays and inlets and river mouths—"as if they were searching for sight of their fellows," said the quimíchi, when he came scuttling to Tenochtítlan, bearing a bark paper on which he had drawn a picture enumerating the fleet.

I and other lords and the entire Speaking Council were present in the throne room when Motecuzóma sent a page to bring the still uninformed Cortés. The Revered Speaker, taking the opportunity to pretend that he knew all things happening everywhere, broached the news, through my translation, in this fashion:

"Captain-General, your King Carlos has received your messenger ship and your first report of these lands and our first gifts which you sent to him, and he is much pleased with you."

Cortés looked properly impressed and surprised. "How can the Don Señor Montezuma know that?" he asked.

Still feigning omniscience, Motecuzóma said, "Because your King Carlos is sending a fleet twice the size of yours— a full *twenty* ships to carry you and your men home."

"Indeed?" said Cortés, politely not showing skepticism. "And where might they be?"

"Approaching," said Motecuzóma mysteriously. "Perhaps you are unaware that my far-seers can see both into the future and beyond the horizon. They drew for me this picture while the ships were still in mid-ocean." He handed the paper to Cortés. "I show it to you now because the ships should soon be in sight of your own garrison."

"Amazing," said Cortés, examining the paper. He muttered to himself, "Yes . . . galleons, transports, victuallers . . . if the damned drawing is anywhere near correct." He frowned. "But . . . *twenty* of them?"

Motecuzóma said smoothly, "Although we have all been honored by your visit, and I personally have enjoyed your companionship, I am pleased that your brothers have come and that you are no longer isolated in an alien land." He added, somewhat insistently, "They *have* come to bear you home, have they not?"

"So it would appear," said Cortés, though looking a trifle bemused.

"I will now order the treasury chambers in my palace unsealed," said Motecuzóma, sounding almost happy at the imminence of his nation's impoverishment.

But at that moment the palace steward and some other men came kissing the earth at the throne room door. When I said that Motecuzóma had barely got the news of the ships before Cortés did, I spoke literally. For the newcomers were two swift-messengers sent by Lord Patzínca, and they had been hurriedly brought from the mainland by the Totonáca knights to whom they had reported. Cortés glanced uncomfortably about the room; it was plain that he would have liked to take the men away and interrogate them in private; but he asked me if I would convey to all present whatever the messengers had to say.

The one who spoke first brought a message dictated by Patzínca: "Twenty of the winged ships, the biggest yet seen, have arrived in the bay of the lesser Villa Rica de la Vera Cruz. From those ships have come ashore one thousand three hundred white soldiers, armed and armored. Eighty of them bear harquebuses and one hundred twenty bear crossbows, in addition to their swords and spears. Also there are ninety and six horses and twenty cannons."

Motecuzóma looked suspiciously at Cortés and said, "It seems quite a warlike force, my friend, just to escort you home."

"Yes, it does," said Cortés, himself looking less than delighted at the news. He turned to me. "Have they anything else to report?"

The other messenger spoke then, and revealed himself to be one of those tedious word rememberers. He rattled off every word overheard from Patzínca's first meeting with the new white men, but it was a monkeylike babble of the Totonáca and Spanish languages, quite incomprehensible, owing to there having been no interpreters present to sort out the speeches. I shrugged and said, "Captain-General, I can catch nothing but two names frequently repeated. Your own and another which sounds like Narváez."

"Narváez here?" blurted Cortés, and he added a very coarse Spanish expletive.

Motecuzóma began again, "I will have the gold and gems brought from the treasury, as soon as your train of porters—"

"Pardon me," said Cortés, recovering from his evident surprise. "I suggest that you keep the treasure hidden and safe, until I can verify the intentions of these new arrivals."

Motecuzóma said, "Surely they are your own countrymen."

"Yes, Don Montezuma. But you have told me how your own countrymen sometimes turn bandit. Just so, we Spaniards must be chary of some of our fellow seafarers. You are commissioning me to carry to King Carlos the richest gift ever sent by a foreign monarch. I should not like to risk losing it to the sea bandits we call pirates. With your leave, I will go immediately to the coast and investigate these men."

"By all means," said the Revered Speaker, who could not have been more overjoyed if the separate groups of white men decided to go for each other's throats in mutual annihilation.

"I must move rapidly, by forced march," Cortés went on, making his plans aloud. "I will take only my Spanish soldiers and the pick of our allied warriors. Prince Black Flower's are the best. . . ."

"Yes," said Motecuzóma approvingly. "Good. Very good." But he lost his smile at the Captain-General's next words:

"I will leave Pedro de Alvarado, the red-bearded man your people call Tonatíu, to safeguard my interests here." He quickly amended that statement. "I mean, of course, to help defend your city in case the pirates should overcome me and fight their way here. Since I can leave with Pedro only a small reserve of our comrades, I must reinforce them by bringing native troops from the mainland. . . ."

And so it was that, when Cortés marched away eastward with the bulk of the white force and all of Black Flower's Acólhua, Alvarado was left in command of about eighty white men and four hundred Texcaltéca, all quartered in the palace. It was the ultimate insult. During his winter-long residence there, Motecuzóma had been in a situation that was peculiar enough. But spring found him in the even more degrading position of living not just with the alien whites, but also with that horde of surly, glowering, not at all respectful warriors who were veritable invaders. If the Revered Speaker had seemed briefly to come alive and alert at the prospect of being rid of the Spaniards, he was again dashed down to morose and impotent despair when he became both host and captive of his lifelong, most abhorrent, most abhorred enemies. There was only one mitigating circumstance, though I doubt that Motecuzóma found much comfort in the fact: the Texcaltéca were notably cleanlier in their habits and much better smelling than an equal number of white men.

The Snake Woman said, "This is intolerable!"—words I was hearing more and more frequently from more and more of Motecuzóma's disgruntled subjects.

The occasion was a secret meeting of the Speaking Council, to which had been summoned many other Mexíca knights and priests and wise men and nobles, among them myself. Motecuzóma was not there, and knew nothing of it.

The war chief Cuitláhuac said angrily, "We Mexíca have only rarely been able to penetrate the borders of Texcála. We have *never* fought our way as far as its capital." His voice rose during the next words, until at the last he was fairly shouting. "And now the detestable Texcaltéca are *here*—in the impregnable city of Tenochtítlan, Heart of the One World—in the palace of the warrior ruler Axayácatl, who surely must be trying right now to claw his way out of the afterworld and back to this one, to redress the insult. The Texcaltéca did not invade us by force—they are here by *invitation*, but not *our* invitation—and in that palace they live side by side, on an equal standing, *with our* REVERED SPEAKER!"

"Revered Speaker in name only," growled the chief priest of Huitzilopóchtli. "I tell you, our war god disowns him."

"It is time we all did," said the Lord Cuautémoc, son of the late Ahuítzotl. "And if we dally now, there may never be another time. The man Alvarado shines like Tonatíu, perhaps, but he is less brilliant as a surrogate Cortés. We must strike against him, before the stronger Cortés comes back."

"You are sure, then, that Cortés will come back?" I asked, because I had attended no Council meetings, open or secret, since the Captain-General's departure some ten days before, and I was not privy to the latest news. Cuautémoc told me:

"It is all most strange, what we hear from our quimíchime on the coast. Cortés did not exactly greet his newly arrived brothers like brothers. He fell upon them, made a night attack upon them, and took them unprepared. Though outnumbered by perhaps three to one, his forces prevailed over them. Curiously, there were few casualties on either side, for Cortés had ordered that there be no more killing than necessary, that the newcomers be only captured and disarmed, as if he were fighting a Flowery War. And since then, he and the new expedition's chief white man have been engaged in much argument and negotiation. We are at a loss to understand all these occurrences. But we must assume that Cortés is arranging the surrender of that force to his command, and that he will return here leading all those additional men and weapons."

You can understand, lord scribes, why all of us were bewildered by the quick turns of events in those days. We had supposed that the new arrivals came from the King Carlos, at the request of Cortés himself; thus his attacking them without provocation was a mystery we could not plumb. It was not until long afterward that I gathered enough fragments of information, and pieced them together, to realize the true extent of Cortés's deception—both of my people and of yours.

From the moment of his arrival in these lands, Cortés represented himself as the envoy of your King Carlos, and I know now that he was no such thing. Your King Carlos never sent Cortés questing here—not for the enhancement of His Majesty, not for the aggrandizement of Spain, not for the propagation of the Christian Faith, not for any other reason. When Hernán Cortés first set foot on The One World, your King Carlos had never *heard* of Hernán Cortés!

To this day, even His Excellency the Bishop speaks with contempt of "that pretender Cortés" and his lowly origins and his upstart rank and his presumptuous ambitions. From the remarks of Bishop Zumárraga and others, I now understand that Cortés was orginally sent here, not by his King or his Church, but by a far less exalted authority, the governor of that island colony called Cuba. And Cortés was sent with instructions to do nothing more venturesome than to explore our coasts, to make maps of them, perhaps to do a little profitable trading with his glass beads and other trinkets.

But even I can comprehend how Cortés came to see far greater opportunities, after he so easily defeated the Olméca forces of the Tabascoöb, and more especially after the weakling Totonáca people submitted to him without even a fight. It must have been then that Cortés determined to become the Conquistador en Jefe, the conqueror of all The One World. I have heard that some of his under-officers, fearful of their governor's anger, opposed his grandiose plans, and it was for that reason that he ordered his less timid followers to burn their ships of transport. Stranded on these shores, even the objectors had little choice but to fall in with Cortés's scheme.

As I have heard the story, only one misfortune briefly threatened to impede Cortés's success. He sent his one remaining ship and his officer Alonso—that man who had first owned Malíntzin—to deliver the first load of treasure extorted from our lands. Alonso was supposed to steal past Cuba and go straight across the ocean to Spain, there to dazzle King Carlos with the rich gifts, that the King might give his royal blessing to Cortés's enterprise, along with a grant of high rank to make legitimate his foray of conquest. But somehow, I do not know how, the governor got word of the ship's secretive passing of his island, and guessed that Cortés was doing *something* in defiance of his orders. So the governor mustered the twenty ships and the multitude of men and set Pámfilo de Narváez in command of them—to chase and catch the outlaw Cortés, to strip him of all authority, to make peace with any peoples he had offended or abused, and to bring Cortés back to Cuba in chains.

However, according to our watching mice, the outlaw had bested the outlaw hunter. So, while Alonso was presumably laying golden gifts and golden prospects before your King Carlos in Spain, Cortés was doing the same at Vera Cruz—showing Narváez samples of the riches of these lands, persuading him that the lands were all but won, convincing Narváez to join him in concluding the conquest, assuring him that they had no reason to fear the wrath of any mere colonial governor. For they would soon deliver—not to their insignificant immediate superior, but to the all-powerful King Carlos—a whole new colony greater in size and wealth than Mother Spain and all its other colonies put together.

Even if we leaders and elders of the Mexíca had known all those things on that day we met in secret, I do not suppose we could have done more than what we did. And that was, by formal vote, to declare Motecuzóma Xocóyotzin "temporarily incapacitated," and to appoint his brother Cuitláhuatzin as regent to rule instead, and to approve his first decision in that office: that we swiftly eliminate all the aliens then infesting Tenochtítlan.

"Two days from now," he said, "occurs the ceremony in honor of the rain god's sister, Iztocfuatl. Since she is only the goddess of salt, it would normally be a minor event involving only a few priests, but the white men cannot know that. Neither can the Texcaltéca, who have never before attended any religious observances in this city." He gave a small, wry laugh. "For that reason, we can be glad that Cortés chose to leave our old enemies here, and not the Acólhua, who are well acquainted with our festivals. Because I will go now to the palace and, bidding my brother show no surprise, I will tell that officer Tonatíu Alvarado a blatant lie. I will stress to him the *importance* of our Iztocfuatl ceremony, and ask his permission that all our people be allowed to gather in the grand plaza during that day and night, to make worship and merriment."

"Yes!" said the Snake Woman. "Meanwhile, the rest of you will alert every ablebodied knight and warrior within call, every least yaoquízqui who can bear arms. When the outlanders see a crowd of people harmlessly flourishing weapons in what appears to be only a ritual dance, accompanied by music and singing, they will merely look on with their usual tolerant amusement. But, at a signal—"

"Wait," said Cuautémoc. "My cousin Motecuzóma will not give away the deception, since he will divine our good reason for it. But we are forgetting that cursed woman Malíntzin. Cortés left her to be the officer Tonatíu's interpreter during his absence. And she has made it her business to learn much about our customs. When she sees the plaza full of people other than priests, she will know that it is not the customary homage to the salt goddess. She is certain to cry the alarm to her white masters."

"Leave the woman to me," I said. It was the opportunity I had waited for, and it would effect more than just my personal satisfaction. "I regret that I am a bit too old to fight in the plaza, but I *can* remove our one most dangerous enemy. Proceed with your plans, Lord Regent. Malíntzin will not see the ceremony, or suspect anything, or disclose anything. She will be dead."

The plan for the night of Iztocíuatl was this. It would be preceded by day-long singing and dancing and mock combat in The Heart of the One World, all performed by the city's women, girls, and children. Only when the twilight began to come down would the men begin to drift in by twos and threes and take the places of the women and children dancing out of the plaza by twos and threes. By the time it was full dark, and the scene was illuminated by torches and urn fires, most of the watching outlanders might well have tired of it and gone to their quarters, or at least, in the fitful firelight, might not observe that all the performers had become large and male. Those chanting, gesticulating dancers would gradually form lines and columns that would twine and weave their way from the center of the plaza toward the Snake Wall entrance to the palace of Axayácatl.

The strongest deterrent to their assault was the menace of the four cannons on the roof of that palace. One or more of them could rake almost all of the open plaza with their terrible shards, but they could not so easily be aimed directly downward. So it was Cuitláhuac's intention to get all his men crowded as closely as possible against the very walls of that palace before the white men realized that they were under attack. Then, at his signal, the entire Mexíca force would burst in past the doorway guards and do their fighting in the rooms and courts and halls and chambers inside, where the greater numbers of their obsidian maquáhuime should overwhelm their opponents' stronger but fewer steel swords and more unwieldly harquebuses. Meanwhile, other Mexíca would have lifted and removed the wooden bridges spanning the canoe passages of the three island causeways, and, with bows and arrows, those men would repel any attempt by Alvarado's mainland troops to swim or otherwise cross those gaps.

I made my own plans just as carefully. I visited the physician who had for long attended my household, a man I could trust, and without flinching at my request he gave me a potion on which he swore I could rely. I was of course well known to the servants of Motecuzóma's court and the workers in the kitchens, and they were unhappy enough in their current service that I had no trouble in getting their agreement to employ the potion in the exact manner and at the exact time I specified. Then I told Béu that I wanted her out of town during the Iztocíuatl ceremony, though I did not tell her why: that there was to be an uprising, and I feared the fighting might spread over the whole island, and I fully expected—because of my singular part in the affair—that the white men, if they had the chance, might wreak their most vengeful fury on me and mine.

Béu was, as I have said, frail and unwell, and she was clearly less than enthusiastic about leaving our house. But she was not unaware of the secret meetings I had attended, so she knew *something* was going to happen, and she complied without protest. She would visit a woman friend who lived in Tepeyáca on the mainland. As a concession to her weakened condition, I let her stay at home, resting, until shortly before the causeway bridges should be lifted. It was in the afternoon that I sent her off in a little chair, the two Turquoises walking alongside.

I remained in the house, alone. It was far enough from The Heart of the One World that I could not hear the music or other sounds of the feigned revelry, but I could imagine the plan unfolding as the twilight deepened: the causeways being sundered, the armed warriors beginning to replace the female celebrants. I was not particularly elated by my imaginings, since my own contribution had been to kill by stealth for the first time in my life. I got a jug of octli and a cup from the kitchen, hoping the strong beverage would dull the twinges of my conscience. Then I sat in the gathering dusk of my downstairs front room, not lighting any lamps, trying to drink to numbness, waiting for whatever might happen next.

I heard the tramp of many feet in the street outside, and then a heavy banging upon my house door. When I opened it, there stood four palace guards, holding the four corners of a plaited-reed pallet on which lay a slender body covered by a fine white cotton cloth.

"Forgive the intrusion, Lord Mixtli," said one of the guards, sounding not at all anxious for forgiveness. "We are bidden to ask you to look upon the face of this dead woman."

"No need," I said, rather surprised that Alvarado or Motecuzóma had so quickly guessed the perpetrator of the murder. "I can identify the bitch coyote without looking."

"You will regard her face," the guard sternly insisted.

I lifted the sheet from her face, lifting my topaz to my eye at the same time, and I may have made some involuntary noise, for it was a young girl I could not recognize as anyone I had seen before.

"Her name is Laurel," said Malíntzin, "or it was." I had not noticed that a litter chair was at the foot of my stairs. Its bearers set it down, and Malíntzin stepped from it, and the guards bearing the pallet edged aside to make room for her to come up to me. She said, "We will talk inside," and to the four guards, "Wait below until I come or unless I call. If I do, drop your burden and come at once."

I swung the door wide for her, then closed it in the guards' faces. I fumbled about the darkening hall, seeking a lamp, but she said, "Leave the house in gloom. We do not much enjoy looking at each other, do we?" So I led her into the front room, and we sat on facing chairs. She was a small, huddled figure in the dusk, but the threat of her loomed large. I poured and drank another copious draft of octli. If I had earlier sought numbness, the new circumstances made either paralysis or maniac delirium seem preferable.

"Laurel was one of the Texcaltéca girls given me to be my personal maids," said Malíntzin. "Today was her turn to taste the food served to me. It is a precaution I have been taking for some time, but unknown to the other servants and occupants of the palace. So you need not reproach yourself too harshly for your failure, Lord Mixtli, though you might sometime spare a moment's remorse for the blameless young Laurel."

"It is something I have been deploring for years," I said, with inebriated gravity. "Always the wrong people die—the good, the useful, the worthy, the innocent. But the wicked ones—and, even more lamentably, the totally useless and worthless and dispensable ones—they all go on cluttering our world, long beyond the life span they deserve. Of course, it requires no wise man to make that observation. I might as well grumble because Tlaloc's hailstorms destroy the nourishing maize but never a disagreeable thornbush."

I was indeed maundering, belaboring the self-evident, but it was because some still-sober part of my mind was frantically busy with a much different concern. The attempt on Malíntzin's life—and no doubt her intent to return the attention—had so far distracted her from noticing any unusual doings in The Heart of the One World. But if she killed me quickly and returned there immediately, she *would* notice, and she could yet warn her masters in time. Aside from my not being over-eager to die to no purpose, as the unfortunate Laurel had done, I was sworn to insure that Malíntzin would be no impediment to Cuitláhuac's plans. I had to keep her talking, or gloating—or, if necessary, listening to me plead cowardly for my life—until the night was full dark and there came an audible uproar from the plaza. At that, her four guards might rush off to investigate. Whether they did or did not, they would not much longer be taking orders from Malíntzin. *If* I could keep her with me, keep her occupied, for just a while.

"Tlaloc's hailstorms also destroy butterflies," I babbled on, "but never, I think, a single pestiferous housefly."

She said sharply, "Stop talking as if you were senile, or I were a child. I am the woman you tried to poison. Now I am here—"

To parry the expected next words, I would have said anything. What I said was, "I suppose I still do think of you as a child just turning woman . . . as I still think of my late daughter Nochípa. . . ."

"But I am old enough to warrant killing," she said. "Lord Mixtli, if my power is such that you deem it dangerous, you might also consider its possible usefulness. Why try to end it, when you could turn it to your advantage?"

I blinked owlishly at her, but did not interrupt to ask what she meant; let her go on talking as long as she would.

She said, "You stand in the same relation to the Mexíca as I do to the white men. Not an officially recognized member of their councils, nevertheless a voice they hearken to and heed. We will never like each other, but we can help each other. You and I both know that things will never again be the same in The One World, but no one can say to whom the future belongs. If the people of these lands prevail, you can be my strong ally. If the white men prevail, I can be yours."

I said, with irony, and with a hiccup, "You suggest that we mutually agree to be traitors to the opposing sides we have separately chosen? Why do we not simply trade clothes and change sides?"

"Know this. I have only to call for my guards and you are a dead man. But you are not a nobody like Laurel. That would imperil the truce that both our masters have tried to preserve. Hernán might even feel obliged to hand me over for punishment, as Motecuzóma handed over Cuaupopóca. At the very least, I could lose some of the eminence I have already won. But if I do not have you eliminated, I must forever be on my guard against your *next* attempt on my life. That would be a distraction, an interference with my concentration on my own interests."

I laughed and said, almost in genuine admiration, "You have the cold blood of an iguana." That struck me as hilarious; I laughed so hard that I nearly rocked myself off my low chair.

She waited until I quieted, and then went on as if she had not been interrupted. "So let us make a secret pact between us. If not of alliance, at least of neutrality. And let us seal it in such a way that neither of us can ever break it."

"Seal it how, Malíntzin? We have both proved ourselves treacherous and untrustworthy."

"We will go to bed together," she said, and that rocked me back so that I did slide off the chair. She waited for me to get up again, and when I remained sitting stupidly on the floor, she asked, "Are you intoxicated, Mixtzin?"

"I must be," I said. "I am hearing impossible things. I thought I heard you propose that we—"

"I did. That we lie together tonight. The white men are more jealous of their women than are the men even of our race. Hernán would slay you for having done it, and me for submitting to it. The four guards outside will always be available to testify—that I spent much time in here with you, in the dark, and that I left your house smiling, not outraged and weeping. Is it not beautifully simple? And unbreakably binding? Neither of us can ever again dare to harm or offend the other, lest that one speak the word which will doom us both."

At risk of angering her and untimely letting her get away, I said, "At fifty and four years old, I am not sexually senile, but I no longer lunge at just any female who offers herself. I have not become incapable, only more selective." I meant to speak with lofty dignity, but the fact that I hiccuped frequently between the words, and spoke them from a sitting position on the floor, somewhat diminished the effect. "As you have remarked, we do not even like each other. You could have used stronger words. Repugnance would better describe our feeling toward each other."

She said, "I would not wish our feelings otherwise. I propose only an act of convenience. As for your discriminating sensibilities, it is nearly dark in here. You can make of me any woman you desire."

Must I do this, I asked myself fuzzily, to keep her here and away from the plaza? Aloud, I protested, "I am more than old enough to be your father."

"Pretend you are, then," she said indifferently, "if incest is to your taste." Then she giggled. "For all I know, you really might be my father. And I, I can pretend *anything*."

"Then you shall," I said. "We will both pretend that our illicit coupling did take place, though it does not. We will pass the time simply conversing, and the guards can testify that we were together for a time sufficiently compromising. Would you like a drink of octli?"

I reeled away to the kitchen and, after breaking several things in the dark there, came reeling back with another cup. As I poured for her, Malíntzin mused, "I remember . . . you said your daughter and I had the same birth-name and year. We were the same age." I took another long drink of my octli. She sipped at hers, and tilted her head inquisitively to one side. "You and that daughter, did you ever play—games—together?"

"Yes," I said thickly. "But not what I think you are thinking."

"I was thinking nothing," she said, all innocence. "We are conversing, as you suggested. What games did you play?"

"There was one we called the Volcano Hiccuping—I mean the Volcano Erupting."

"I do not know that game."

"It was only a silly thing. We invented it ourselves. I would lie down on the floor. Like this." I did not exactly lie down;

I fell supine with a crash. "And bend my knees, you see, to make the volcano peak. Nochípa would perch up there."

"Like this?" she said, doing it. She was small and light of weight, and in the dark room she could have been anybody.

"Yes," I said. "Then I would wiggle my knees—the volcano waking, you see—and then I would bounce her—"

She gave a little squeak of surprise, and slid down to thump against my belly. Her skirt rucked up as she did so, and when I reached to steady her, I discovered that she wore nothing under the skirt.

She said softly, "And that was when the volcano erupted?"

I had been long without a woman, and it was good to have one again, and my drunkenness did not affect my capability. I surged so powerfully, so often, that I think some of my wits spilled with my omícetl. The first time, I could have sworn that I actually felt the vibration and heard the rumble of a volcano erupting. If she did too, she said nothing. But after the second time, she gasped, "It is different—almost enjoyable. You are so clean—and smell so nice." And after the third time, when she had her breath again, she said, "If you do not—tell anyone your age—no one would guess it." At last, we both lay exhausted, panting, entwined, and I only slowly became aware that the room had lightened. I felt a sort of shock, a sort of disbelief, to recognize the face beside mine as the face of Malíntzin. The sustained activity of copulation had been more than pleasurable, but I seemed to have emerged from it in a state of distraction, or perhaps even derangement. I wondered: what am I doing with *her?* This is the woman I have detested so vehemently for so long that I am now guilty of having murdered an innocent stranger. . . .

But whatever other thoughts and emotions rushed upon me in that moment of coming to awareness and at least partial sobriety, simple curiosity was the most immediate. I could not account for the lightening of the room; surely we had not been at it all night. I turned my head toward the light's source and, even without my crystal, I could see that Béu stood in the room's doorway, holding a lighted lamp. I had no idea how long she might have been watching. She swayed as she stood there, and not angrily but sadly she said:

"You can—do this—while your friends are being slaughtered?"

Malíntzin only languidly turned to look at Waiting Moon. I was not much surprised that such a woman did not mind being caught in such circumstances, but I should have expected her to make some exclamation of dismay at the news that her friends were being slaughtered. Instead, she smiled and said:

"Ayyo, good. We have an even better witness than the guards, Mixtzin. Our pact will be more binding than I could have hoped."

She stood up, disdaining to cover her moistly glistening body. I grabbed for my discarded mantle, but even in my confusion of shame and embarrassment and lingering drunkenness, I had enough presence of mind to say, "Malíntzin, I think you wasted your time and your favors. No pact will avail you now."

"And I think it is *you* who are mistaken, Mixtzin," she said, her smile unwavering. "Ask the old woman there. She spoke of *your* friends dying."

I sat suddenly upright and gasped, "Béu?"

"Yes," she sighed. "I was turned back by our men on the causeway. They were apologetic, but they said they could take no risk of anyone communicating with the outlanders across the lake. So I came back, and I came by way of the plaza to look at the dancing. Then . . . it was horrible. . . ."

She closed her eyes and leaned against the door frame and said, dazedly, "There was lightning and thunder from the palace roof, and the dancers—like some awful magic—they became shreds and pieces. Then the white men and their warriors poured out of the palace, with more fire and noise and flashing of metal. One of their blades can cut a woman in half at the waist, Záa, did you know that? And the head of a small child rolls just like a tlachtli ball, Záa, did you know that? It rolled right to my feet. When something stung my hand, I fled. . . ."

I saw then that there was blood all over her blouse. It was running along her arm from the hand that held up the lamp. I got quickly to my feet in the same moment that she fainted and fell. I caught the lamp before it could fire the floor matting. Then I lifted her in my arms, to carry her upstairs to bed. Malíntzin, leisurely picking up her clothes, said:

"Will you not even pause to thank me? You have me and the guards to bear witness that you were here at home and not involved in any uprising."

I stared coldly at her. "You knew. All the time."

"Of course Pedro ordered me to stay well out of danger, so I decided to come here. You wanted to prevent my seeing your people's preparations at the plaza." She laughed. "I wanted to make sure you saw none of ours: the moving of all the four cannons to the plaza side of the roof, for instance. But you must agree, Mixtzin, it was not a boring evening. And we do have a pact, have we not?" She laughed again, and with real amusement. "You can never again raise your hand against me. Not now."

I did not at all understand what she meant by that, until Waiting Moon was conscious again and could tell me. That was after the physician had come and tended to her hand, torn by what must have been one of the fragments discharged by the Spaniards' cannons. When he was gone, I remained sitting beside the bed. Béu lay, not looking at me, her face more wan and worn than before, a tear trickling down one cheek, and for a long time we said nothing. Finally I managed to say huskily that I was sorry. Still without looking at me, she said:

"You have never been a husband to me, Záa, and never let me be a wife to you. So your faithfulness to me, or your default of it, is not even worth discussing. But your being true to some—some standard of your own—that is another matter. It would have been vile enough if you had merely coupled with that woman used by the white men. But you did not. Not really. I was there, and I know."

Waiting Moon turned her head then, and turned on me a look that bridged the gulf of indifference which had for so long divided us. For the first time since the years of our youth, I felt an emanation of emotion from her that I knew was not a pretense or an affection. Since it was a true emotion, I only wish it could have been a more cordial one. For she looked at me as she might have regarded one of the human monsters in the menagerie, and she said:

"What you did—I think there is not even a name for it. While you were . . . while you were in her . . . you were running your hands over all her naked body, and you were murmuring endearments. 'Zyanya, my darling,' you said, and 'Nochípa, my beloved,' you said, and 'Zyanya, my dearest,' you said, and *'Again,* Nochípa!' you said." She swallowed, as if to prevent her suddenly being sick. "Because the two names mean the same thing, I do not know whether you lay with my sister or with your daughter, or with them both, or with them alternately. But this I know: both the women named Always—your wife and your daughter—they died years ago. Záa, you were coupling with the dead!"

It pains me, reverend friars, to see you turn your heads away, exactly as Béu Ribé turned hers away from me, after she had spoken those words that night.

Ah, well. It may be that, in trying to relate an honest account of my life and the world I lived in, I sometimes reveal more of myself than my closest loved ones ever knew of me, perhaps more than *I* might have wanted to know. But I will not retract or rephrase anything I have told, nor will I ask you to strike anything from your pages. Let it stand. Someday my chronicle may serve as my confession to the kindly goddess Filth Eater, since the Christian fathers prefer a shorter confession than mine could be, and they impose a longer penitence than I have life left to make it in, and they are not so tolerant of human frailty as was the patient and forgiving Tlazoltéotl.

But I meant to tell of that night's dalliance with Malíntzin only to explain why she is still alive today, although after that I hated her more than ever. My hatred for her was fired hotter by the loathing of me I had seen in Béu's eyes, and the loathing I consequently felt for myself. However, I never made another attempt on Malíntzin's life, though I had other opportunities, and in no way did I seek again to hinder her ambitions. Meanwhile, as it turned out, she had no cause to do me harm either. For, in subsequent years, as she rose high in the new nobility of this New Spain, I sank beneath her notice.

I have said that Cortés may even have loved the woman, for he kept her by him for some years longer. He did not try to hide her even when his long-abandoned wife, the Doña Catalina, unexpectedly arrived here from Cuba. When the Doña Catalina died within a very few months, some attributed it to a broken heart, some to less romantic causes, but Cortés himself convoked a formal inquiry that absolved him of any blame in his wife's death. Not long after that, Malíntzin gave birth to Cortés's son Martín; the boy is now about eight years old and, I understand, will soon go to Spain for his schooling.

Cortés did not put Malíntzin away from him until after his visit to the court of King Carlos, whence he returned as the Marqués del Valle, and with his newly acquired Marquesa Juana on his arm. Then he made sure that the discarded Malíntzin was well provided for. In the name of the Crown, he gave her a sizable land grant, and he saw her married in a Christian ceremony to one Juan Jaramillo, a ship's captain. Unfortunately, the obliging captain was soon afterward lost at sea. So today Malíntzin is known to you, reverend scribes—and to His Excellency the Bishop, who treats her most deferentially—as the Doña Señora Marina, Viuda de Jaramillo, mistress of the imposing island estate of Tacamichápa, near the town of Espíritu Santo. That town was formerly called Coátzacoálcos, and the island granted her by the Crown stands in the river from which the onetime slave girl One Grass once gave me a dipperful of water to drink.

The Doña Marina lives because I let her live, and I let her live because, for a brief while one night, she was ... well, she was someone I loved. ...

Either the Spaniards had foolishly been too eager to let loose their devastation in The Heart of the One World, or they had deliberately chosen to make their attack as wanton, punitive, and unforgettable as possible. For it had not yet been quite full night when they blasted with their cannons and then charged the crowd with swords and spears and harquebuses. They had killed or horribly wounded more than a thousand of the dancing women, girls, and children. But at that time of early dark, only a comparative few of our Mexíca warriors had infiltrated into the performance, so fewer than twenty of them had fallen, and not any of the commanding knights or the lords who had conceived the uprising. Then the Spaniards did not even go looking for the chief conspirators, to punish them; the white men, after their explosive emergence from the palace, merely withdrew into it again, not daring to be abroad in the wrathful city.

To apologize for my failure in not having eliminated Malíntzin I did not go to the war chief Cuitláhuac, who I supposed must be raging with fury and frustration. Instead, I sought out the Lord Cuautémoc, hoping he would be more sympathetic to my dereliction. I had known him ever since he was a boy, visiting my house with his mother, the First Lady, in the days when his father Ahuítzotl and my wife Zyanya still lived. At that time, Cuautémoctzin had been the Crown Prince, heir to the Mexíca throne, and it was only mischance that had prevented his becoming Uey-Tlatoáni before Motecuzóma was insinuated into that office. Since Cuautémoc was familiar with disappointment, I thought he might be more lenient about my not having prevented Malíntzin's warning the white men.

"No one holds you to blame, Mixtzin," he said, when I told how she had eluded the poison. "You would have done The One World a service in disposing of that traitress, but it does not matter that you did not."

Puzzled, I said, "It does not matter? Why not?"

"Because she did not betray us," said Cuautémoc. "She did not have to." He grimaced as if in pain. "It was my exalted cousin. Our Revered Speaker Motecuzóma."

"What?" I exclaimed.

"Cuitláhuac went to the officer Tonatíu Alvarado, you remember, and asked and was given permission to hold the Iztocíuatl ceremony. As soon as Cuitláhuac left the palace, Motecuzóma told Alvarado to beware of trickery."

"Why?"

Cuautémoc shrugged. "Injured pride? Vindictive spite? Motecuzóma could hardly have been pleased that the uprising was the idea of his underlings, and arranged without his knowledge, to be done without his approval or participation. Whatever his real reason, his excuse is that he will countenance no breaking of his truce with Cortés."

I snarled a filthy word, not generally applied to Revered Speakers. "What is our breaking of the truce, compared to his instigating the butchery of a thousand women and children of his own people?"

"Let us charitably assume that he expected Alvarado only to forbid the celebration, that he did not anticipate such a violent dispersal of the celebrants."

956

"Violent dispersal," I growled. "That is a new way to say indiscriminate slaughter. My wife, a mere onlooker, was wounded. One of her two female servants was killed, and the other has fled terrified into hiding somewhere."

"If nothing else," Cuautémoc said with a sigh, "the incident has united all our people in outrage. Before, they only muttered and grumbled, some of them mistrusting Motecuzóma, others supporting him. Now all are ready to tear him limb from limb, along with everyone else in that palace."

"Good," I said. "Then let us do so. We still have most of our warriors. Raise the city folk as well—even old men like me—and storm the palace."

"That would be suicidal. The outlanders have now barricaded themselves inside it, behind their cannons, behind the harquebuses and crossbows aimed from every window. We could not get near the building without being obliterated. We must engage them hand to hand, as originally planned, and we must wait to have that opportunity again."

"Wait!" I said, with another profanity.

"But while we wait, Cuitláhuac is packing the island with still more warriors. You may have noticed an increase in the traffic of canoes and freight barges plying between here and the mainland, apparently carrying flowers and vegetables and such. Concealed under that top cargo are men and arms—Cacáma's Acólhua troops from Texcóco, Tecpanéca troops from Tlácopan. Meanwhile, as we get stronger, our opponents may get weaker. During the massacre, all their servants and attendants deserted the palace. Now, of course, not a single Mexícatl vendor or porter will deliver to them food or anything else. We will let the white men and their friends—Motecuzóma, Malíntzin, all of them—sit in their fortification and suffer for a while."

I asked, "Cuitláhuac hopes to starve them into surrender?"

"No. They will be uncomfortable, but the kitchens and larders are adequately supplied to sustain them until Cortés gets back here. When he does, he must not find us overtly belligerent, holding the palace under siege, for he would need only to mount a similar siege around the whole island, and starve us as we starve them."

"Why let him get here at all?" I demanded. "We know he is marching hither. Let us go out and attack him in the open."

"Have you forgotten how easily he won the battle of Texcála? And he now has many more men and horses and weapons. No, we will not confront him in the field. Cuitláhuac plans to let Cortés come here unopposed, and find all his people in the palace unharmed, the truce apparently restored. He will not know of our imported and hidden and waiting warriors. But when we have him and *all* the white men within our confines, *then* we will attack—even suicidally, if necessary—and we will wipe this island and this whole lake district clean of them."

✠

Perhaps the gods decided that it was time Tenochtítlan had a change for the better in its communal tonáli, because that latest plan did work—with only a few unforeseeable complications.

When we got word that Cortés and his multitudinous force were approaching, everyone in the city, by command of the regent Cuitláhuac, determinedly assumed an outward semblance of untroubled normality, even the widowers and orphans and other kinfolk of the slain innocents. All three causeways were again bridged intact, and travelers and porters trudged and trotted back and forth across them. The canoes and barges that plied the canals of the city and the lake around the island were genuinely carrying innocuous cargoes. The thousands of Acólhua and Tecpanéca fighting men whom they had earlier ferried unnoticed, right from under the noses of Cortés's mainland allies, had been kept out of sight ever since. Eight of them, in fact, were living in my house, bored and impatient for action. Tenochtítlan's streets were as thronged as usual, and the Tlaltelólco market was as busy, colorful, and clamorous. The only nearly empty part of the city was The Heart of the One World, its marble pavement still bloodstained, its vast expanse traversed only by the priests of the temples there, who still performed their everyday functions of praying, chanting, burning incense, blowing the time-telling conch trumpets at dawn and midday and so on.

Cortés came warily, apprehensive of animosity, for he had of course heard about the night of massacre, and he would not expose even his formidable army to any risk of ambush. After skirting Texcóco at a prudent distance, he came around the southern lakeshore as before, but he did not take the southern causeway into Tenochtítlan; his men would have been vulnerable to an attack by canoe-borne warriors if they were strung out along the open span of that longest causeway. He continued on around the lake, and up its western shore, dropping off Prince Black Flower and his warriors, posting the big cannons at intervals, all of them pointed across the water at the city, with men to tend them. He marched all the way to Tlácopan, because the causeway from there is the shortest of the three approaches. First he and his hundred or so other horsemen galloped across it as if expecting it to be snatched from under them. Then his foot soldiers did the same, dashing across in companies of about a hundred men at a time.

Once he was on the island, Cortés must have breathed more easily. There had been no ambush or other obstacle to his return. While the people on the city streets did not greet him with tumultuous welcome, neither did they revile him; they merely nodded as if he had never been away. And he must have felt comfortably powerful at being accompanied by one and a half thousand of his own countrymen, not to mention that backing of his thousands of allied warriors camped in an arc around the mainland. He may even have deluded himself that we Mexíca were at last resigned to recognizing his supremacy. So, from the causeway, he and his troops marched through the city like already acknowledged conquerors.

Cortés showed no surprise at finding the central plaza so empty; perhaps he thought it had been cleared for his convenience. Anyway, the bulk of his force stopped there and, with much noise and bustle and wafting about of their bad odors, began to tether their horses, spread out their bedrolls, lay campfires, and otherwise settle down as if for an indeterminate stay. All the resident Texcaltéca, except for their chief knights, vacated the Axayácatl palace and also made camp in the plaza. Motecuzóma and a group of his loyal courtiers likewise made their first emergence from the palace since the night of Iztocíuatl—coming out to greet Cortés—but he disdainfully gave them no recognition at all. He and his newly recruited comrade in arms, Narváez, brushed past them and into the palace.

I imagine the first thing they did was to shout for food and drink, and I would like to have seen Cortés's face when he was served not by servants, but by Alvarado's soldiers, and served only moldy old beans, atóli mush, whatever other provisions remained. I would also like to have overheard Cortés's first conversation with Alvarado, when that sunlike officer told how he had so heroically put down the "uprising" of unarmed women and children, but had neglected to eliminate more than a handful of the Mexíca warriors who could still be a menace.

Cortés and his augmented army had come onto the island in the afternoon. Evidently he and Narváez and Alvarado remained huddled in conference until nightfall, but what they discussed or what plans they made, no one ever knew. I know only that, at some point, Cortés sent a company of his soldiers across the plaza to Motecuzóma's own palace, where, with spears and pry-bars and battering beams, they broke down the walls with which Motecuzóma had tried to seal up the treasure chambers. Then, like ants toiling between a honey pot and their nest, the soldiers went back and forth, transferring the treasury's store of gold and jewels to the dining hall of Cortés's palace. That took the men most of the night, because there was a great deal of the plunder, and it was not in easily portable form, for reasons I should perhaps explain.

Since it was our people's belief that gold is the sacred excrement of the gods, our treasurers did not simply hoard it in the raw form of dust or nuggets, and they did not melt it into featureless ingots or strike coins of it, as you Spaniards do. Before it went into our treasury, it went through the skilled hands of our goldsmiths, who increased its value and beauty by transforming it into figurines, gem-encrusted jewelry, medallions, coronets, filigree ornaments, jugs and cups and platters—all sorts of works of art, wrought in homage to the gods. So, while Cortés must have beamed with satisfaction to see the immense and ever growing pile of treasure his men were heaping in his hall, nearly filling that spacious chamber, he must also have frowned at its variety of shapes, unsuited for being loaded onto either horses or porters.

While Cortés thus occupied his first night back on the island, the city all around him remained quiet, as if no one paid any attention to the activity. He went to bed sometime before dawn, taking Malíntzin with him, and, in the most contemptuous manner, he left word that Motecuzóma and his chief counselors should stand ready to attend upon him when he woke and called for them. So the pathetically obedient Motecuzóma sent messengers early the next morning to call his Speaking Council and others, including myself. He had no palace pages to send; it was one of his own younger sons who came to my house, and he looked rather frayed and disheveled after his long immurement in the palace. All of us conspirators had expected such a message, and we had arranged to meet at Cuitláhuac's house. When we were gathered, we all looked expectantly to the regent and war chief, and one of the Council elders asked him:

"Well, do we obey the summons or ignore it?"

"Obey," said Cuitláhuac. "Cortés still believes he holds us helpless by holding our complaisant ruler. Let us not disillusion him."

"Why not?" asked the high priest of Huitzilopóchtli. "We are in readiness for our assault. Cortés cannot cram that whole army of his inside the palace of Axayácatl, and barricade it against us, as the Tonatíu Alvarado did."

"He has no need to," said Cuitláhuac. "If we cause him the slightest alarm, he can quickly make the entire Heart of the One World a fortification as unapproachable as the palace was. We must keep him lulled in false security only a little longer. We will go to the palace as bidden, and act as if we and all the Mexíca are still the pliant and passive dolls of Motecuzóma."

The Snake Woman pointed out, "Cortés can bar the entrances when we are inside, and he will have us hostage, too."

"I am aware of that," said Cuitláhuac. "But all my knights and cuáchictin already have their orders; they will not need my person. One of my orders is that they proceed with the various feints and movements, whatever the hazard to me or to anyone else who is inside the palace at the striking time. If you prefer

not to share that risk, Tlácotzin—or any of the rest of you—
I here and now give you leave to go home."

Of course, not a man of us backed away. We all accompanied Cuitláhuac to The Heart of the One World, and fastidiously made our way through the crowded and smelly encampment of men, horses, cooking fires, stacked weapons, and
other paraphernalia. I was surprised to see, grouped in one area
apart from the white men, as if they were inferiors, a contingent
of *black* men. I had been told of such beings, but I had never
seen any until then.

Curious, I briefly left my fellows to go and look more
closely at those oddities. They wore helmets and uniforms
identical to those of the Spaniards, but they physically resembled the Spaniards considerably less than I did. They were not
really *black* black, but a sort of brown-tinged black, like the
heartwood of the ebony tree. They had peculiarly flat, broad
noses and large, protuberant lips—in truth, they looked very
like those giant stone heads I once saw in the Olméca country—
and their beards were only a sort of kinky black fuzz, scarcely
visible until I was close to them. But then I was close enough
to notice that one of the blackamoors had a face covered with
angry pimples and suppurant pustules, such as I had long ago
seen on the white man Guerrero, and I hastily rejoined my
fellow lords.

The white sentries stationed at the Snake Wall entrance to
the Axayácatl palace felt us all over for concealed weapons
before they let us enter. We passed through the dining hall,
where there had grown up an indoor mountain of heaped and
tumbled jewelry, the gold and gems coruscating richly even
in that dim chamber. Several soldiers, who were probably supposed to be guarding the hoard, were fingering various pieces
and smiling at them and very nearly drooling over them. We
went on upstairs, to the throne room, where waited Cortés,
Alvarado, and numerous other Spaniards, including a new one,
a one-eyed man, who was Narváez. Motecuzóma looked rather
surrounded and beleaguered, since the woman Malíntzin was
the only other of his race in evidence until our arrival. We all
kissed the earth to him, and he gave us a cool nod of salute,
while he went on speaking to the white men.

"I do not *know* what the people's intentions were. I know

only that they planned a ceremony. Through your Malíntzin,
I told your Alvarado that I thought it wiser not to allow such
a gathering so close to this garrison, that perhaps he ought to
order the plaza cleared." Motecuzóma sighed tragically. "Well,
you know the calamitous manner in which he cleared it."

"Yes," said Cortés, through his teeth. His flat eyes turned
icily on Alvarado, who stood wringing his fingers and looking
as if he had endured a very hard night. "It could have ruined
all my—" Cortés coughed and said instead, "It could have
made your people our enemies for all time. What puzzles me,
Don Montezuma, is that it did not. *Why* did it not? If I were
one of your subjects and had suffered such maltreatment, I
would have pelted me with dung when I rode in. No one in
the city seems to show the slightest detestation, and that strikes
me as unnatural. There is a Spanish saying: 'I can avoid the
turbulent torrent; God preserve me from the quiet waters.'"

"It is because they all blame me," Motecuzóma said
wretchedly. "They believe I insanely ordered my own people
killed—all those women and children—and that I meanly employed your men for my weapons." There were actually tears
in his eyes. "So all my domestics left in disgust, and not so
much as a peddler of fried maguey worms has come near this
place since then."

"Yes, a most trying situation," said Cortés. "We must remedy that." He turned his face to Cuitláhuac and, indicating that
I should translate, said to him, "You are the war chief. I will
not speculate on the probable intent of that alleged religious
celebration. I will even humbly apologize for my own lieuten-
ant's impetuosity. But I will remind you that a truce still exists.
I should think it the responsibility of a war chief to see that my
men are not segregated in isolation, deprived of food and human
contact with their hosts."

Cuitláhuac said, "I command only fighting men, Lord Captain-General. If the civilian population prefer to shun this place,
I have no authority to command that they do otherwise. That
authority resides only in the Revered Speaker. It was your own
men who shut themselves in here, and the Revered Speaker
with them."

Cortés turned back to Motecuzóma. "Then it is up to you,

Don Montezuma, to placate your people, to persuade them to resume supplying and serving us."

"How can I, if they will not come near me?" said Motecuzóma, almost wailing. "And if I go out among them, I may go to my death!"

"We will provide an escort—" Cortés began, but he was interrupted by a soldier who ran in and told him in Spanish:

"My captain, the natives begin to congregate in the plaza. Men and women are crowding through our camp and coming hither. Not armed, but they look none too friendly. Do we expel them? Repel them?"

"Let them come," said Cortés, and then to Narváez, "Get out there and take charge. The order is: hold your fire. Not a man is to make any move unless *I* command it. I will be on the roof where I can watch all that occurs. Come, Pedro! Come, Don Montezuma!" He actually reached out for the Revered Speaker's hand and snatched him off the throne.

All of us who had been in the throne room followed them, running up the stairs to the roof, and I could hear Malíntzin breathlessly repeating Cortés's instructions to Motecuzóma:

"Your people are collecting in the plaza. You will address them. Make your peace with them. Blame every ill and calamity on us Spaniards, if you like. Tell them *anything* that will maintain calm in the city!"

The roof had been made a garden just before the first coming of the white men, but it had been untended since then, and had endured a winter besides. Where the ground had not been scored and furrowed by the wheels of the heavy cannons, it was a wasteland of dry soil, withered stalks, bare-branched shrubs, dead flower heads, and windrowed brown leaves. It was a most bleak and desolate platform for Motecuzóma's last speech.

We all went to the parapet that overlooked the plaza and, standing in a line along that wall, peered down at The Heart of the One World. The thousand or so Spaniards were easily identifiable by their glints of armor, as they stood or moved uncertainly among the twice as many Mexíca pouring into the area and converging below us. As the messenger had reported, there were both men and women, and they wore only their everyday dress, and they showed no interest in the soldiers or the unprecedented fact of an armed camp erected on that sacred ground. They merely made their way through the clutter, in no haste but with no hesitation, until there was a densely packed crowd of them right below us.

"The corporal was right," said Alvarado. "They bear no weapons."

Cortés said bitingly, "Just the kind of opponents you prefer, eh, Pedro?" and Alvarado's face went almost as red as his beard. To all his men present, Cortés said, "Let us step back out of view. Let the people see only their own ruler and lords."

He and Malíntzin and the others withdrew to the middle of the roof. Motecuzóma cleared his throat nervously, then had to call three times, each time more loudly, before the crowd heard him over its own murmurings and the noise of the camp. Some of the black dots of heads turned to flesh color as their faces lifted, then more and more of them. Finally the whole convocation of Mexíca were looking up, and many of the white faces as well, and the crowd noise subsided.

"My people . . ." Motecuzóma began, his voice husky. He cleared his throat again and said, loudly, clearly, "My people . . ."

"Your people!" came a concerted and hostile roar from below, then a confused clamor of angry shouts: "The people you betrayed!" "Yours are the white people!" "You are not our Speaker!" "You are no longer revered!" It startled me even though I had been expecting it, knowing that it had all been arranged by Cuitláhuac, and that the men in the crowd were all warriors only temporarily unarmed for the seemingly spontaneous community outburst of vilification.

I should say they were unarmed with ordinary weapons, for at that moment they all produced stones and fragments of adobe brick—men from under their mantles, women from beneath their skirts—and, still shouting imprecations, began hurling them upward. Most of the women's missiles fell short, and thudded against the palace wall below us, but enough others reached the roof to make all of us duck and dodge. The priest of Huitzilopóchtli uttered a most unpriestly exclamation when one of the rocks hit him on the shoulder. Several of the Spaniards behind us also cursed as rocks fell among them. The only man—I must say it—the only man who did not move was Motecuzóma.

He stood where he was, upright still, and raised his arms in a conciliatory gesture, and shouted above the noise, "Wait!" He said it in Náhuatl, "Mixchía—!" And then a rock hit him squarely in the forehead, and he staggered backward, and he fell unconscious.

Cortés instantly took command again. He snapped at me, "See to him! Put him at ease!" Then he grabbed Cuitláhuac by his mantle, and pointed and said, "Do what you can. Say anything. That mob must be calmed." Malíntzin translated to Cuitláhuac, and he was at the parapet, shouting, when I and two Spanish officers carried Motecuzóma's limp body downstairs and to the throne room again. We laid the unconscious man on a bench there, and the two officers ran out the door, presumably to fetch one of their army surgeons.

I stood and looked down at Motecuzóma's face, quite relaxed and peaceful despite the knot of bruise rising on his forehead. I thought of many things then: the events and occurrences of our simultaneous lifetimes. I remembered his disloyal defiance of his own Revered Speaker Ahuítzotl during the campaign in Uaxyácac . . . and his ignobly pitiful try at raping my wife's sister there . . . and his many threats against me over the years . . . and his spiteful sending of me to Yanquítlan, where my daughter Nochípa died . . . and his weakling vacillations ever since the first white men had appeared off our shores . . . and his betrayal of an attempt by braver men to rid our city of those white men. Yes, I had many reasons for doing what I did, some of them immediate and urgent. But I suppose, as much as for any other reason, I slew him to avenge his long-ago insult to Béu Ribé, who had been Zyanya's sister and was now in name my wife.

Those reminiscences went through my mind in only a moment. I looked up from his face and looked about the room for a weapon. Two Texcaltéca warriors had been left there on guard. I beckoned one over and, when he came, scowling at me, I asked for his waist dagger. He scowled more darkly, unsure of my identity or rank or intention, but when I made the request a loud and lordly command, he handed me the obsidian blade. I placed it carefully, for I had watched enough sacrifices to know exactly where the heart is in a human breast, and I pushed the dagger all the way to the extent of its blade, and Motecuzóma's chest ceased its slow rise and fall. I left the dagger in the wound, so only a very little blood welled up from around it. The Texcaltécatl guard goggled at me in horrified wonderment, then he and his companion hastily fled the room.

I had only just had time. I heard the uproar of the crowd in the plaza subside to a still wrathful but lesser rumble. Then all the people who had been on the roof came clattering down the stairs, along the hall, and into the throne room. They were conversing excitedly or worriedly in their different languages, but they fell suddenly silent as they stood in the doorway and saw and realized and contemplated the enormity of my deed. They approached slowly, Spaniards and Mexíca lords together, and stared speechless at the body of Motecuzóma and the dagger haft protruding from his chest, and at me standing unperturbed beside the corpse. Cortés turned his flat eyes on me and said, with ominous quietness:

"What . . . have . . . you . . . done?"

I said, "As you commanded, my lord, I put him at ease."

"Damn your impudence, you son of a whore," he said, but still quietly, with contained fury. "I have heard you make mockeries before."

I calmly shook my head. "Because Motecuzóma is at ease, Captain-General, perhaps all the rest of us may be more at ease. Including yourself."

He jabbed a stiff finger into my chest, then jabbed it toward the plaza. "There is a war brewing yonder! Who now will control that rabble?"

"Not Motecuzóma, alive or dead. But here stands his successor, his brother Cuitláhuac, a man of firmer hand and a man who is still respected by that rabble."

Cortés turned to look doubtfully at the war chief, and I could guess his thinking. Cuitláhuac might dominate the Mexíca, but Cortés had yet no domination over Cuitláhuac. As if also reading his thoughts, Malíntzin said:

"We can put the new ruler to a test, Señor Hernán. Let us all go again to the roof, show Motecuzóma's body to the crowd, let Cuitláhuac proclaim his succession, and see if the people will obey his first order—that we be again provisioned and served in this palace."

"A shrewd idea, Malinche," said Cortés. "Give him exactly those instructions. Tell him also that he is to make it unmistakably clear that Montezuma died"—he plucked the dagger from the body, and threw a scathing glance at me—"that Montezuma died at the hands of his own people."

So we returned to the roof, and the rest of us hung back while Cuitláhuac took his brother's corpse in his arms and stepped to the parapet and called for attention. As he showed the body and told the news, the sound that came up from the plaza was a murmur sounding of approval. Another thing happened then: a gentle rain began to fall from the sky, as if Tlaloc, as if Tlaloc alone, as if no other being but Tlaloc mourned the end of Motecuzóma's roads and days and rule. Cuitláhuac spoke loudly enough to be heard by the gathered people below, but in a persuasively placid manner. Malíntzin translated for Cortés, and assured him, "The new ruler speaks as instructed."

At last, Cuitláhuac turned toward us and gestured with his head. We all joined him at the parapet, while two or three priests relieved him of Motecuzóma's body. The people who had been so solidly packed below the palace wall were separating and making their way again through the cluttered encampment. Some of the Spanish soldiers still looked uncertain, and fingered their weapons, so Cortés shouted down, "Let them come and go without hindrance, my boys! They are bringing fresh food!" The soldiers were cheering when we all left the roof for the last time.

In the throne room again, Cuitláhuac looked at Cortés and said, "We must talk." Cortés agreed, "We must talk," and called for Malíntzin, as if he would not trust my translation without his own interpreter present. Cuitláhuac said:

"My telling the people that I am their Uey-Tlatoáni does not make it so. There are formalities to be observed, and in public. We will commence the ceremonies of succession this very afternoon, while there is still daylight. Since your troops have occupied The Heart of the One World, I and the priests and the Speaking Council"—he swept his arm to include every one of us Mexíca in the room—"will remove to the pyramid at Tlaltelólco."

Cortés said, "Oh, surely not now. The rain is becoming a downpour. Wait for a more clement day, my lord. I invite the new Revered Speaker to be my guest in this palace, as Montezuma was."

Cuitláhuac said firmly, "If I remain here, I am not yet the Revered Speaker, therefore I am useless as your *guest*. Which will you have?"

Cortés frowned; he was not accustomed to hearing a Revered Speaker speak like a Revered Speaker. Cuitláhuac went on:

"Even after I am formally confirmed by the priests and the Speaking Council, I must win the trust and approval of the people. It would help me gain the people's confidence if I could tell them exactly *when* the Captain-General and his company plan to depart this place."

"Well . . ." said Cortés, drawing out the word, to make plain that he had not himself given thought to that, and was in no hurry to. "I promised your brother that I would take my leave when I was ready to take the gift of treasure he offered to donate. I now have that. But I will need some time to melt it all down so we can transport it to the coast."

"That might take years," said Cuitláhuac. "Our goldsmiths have seldom worked with more than small amounts of gold at a time. You will find no facilities in the city for desecrating— for melting all those countless works of art."

"And I must not impose on my host's hospitality for years," said Cortés. "So I will have the gold carried to the mainland and let my own smiths do the compacting of it."

Rudely, he turned from Cuitláhuac to Alvarado and said in Spanish, "Pedro, have some of our artificers come in here. Let me see . . . they can take down these ponderous doors, and all the other doors throughout the palace. Have them build us a couple of heavy sledges to carry all that gold. Also order the saddlers to contrive harness for enough horses to drag the sledges."

He turned back to Cuitláhuac: "In the meantime, Lord Speaker, I ask your permission that I and my men remain in the city for at least a reasonable while. Most of my current company, as you know, were not with me during my earlier visit, and they are naturally most eager to see the sights of your great city."

"For a reasonable while, then," repeated Cuitláhuac, nodding. "I will so inform the people, and bid them be tolerant, even affable, if they will. Now, I and my lords will leave you, to begin the preparations for my brother's funeral and my own accession. The sooner we complete those formalities, the sooner I will be your host in truth."

When all of us who had been summoned by Motecuzóma left the palace, the Spanish carpenter-soldiers were eyeing the mountain of treasure in the downstairs dining hall, estimating its bulk and weight. We passed through the Snake Wall into the square and paused to watch the activity there. The white men moved about their various camp tasks, looking uncomfortably soggy, for the rain had become heavy. An equal number of our own men moved among the Spaniards, busy or managing to look busy, all stripped to their loincloths so the rain was not so much of a discomfort to them. Thus far, Cuitláhuac's plan was progressing as he had explained it to us—except for the unforeseen but by no means unfortunate demise of Motecuzóma.

All that I have recounted, reverend scribes, had been arranged by Cuitláhuac in every detail, long before our arrival in Cortés's presence. It had been at his order that the crowd of Mexíca men and women gathered to clamor outside the palace. It had been at his order that they then dispersed to fetch food and drink for the white men. But—what none of the Spaniards had noticed in the confusion—it was only the *women* in that crowd who had left the plaza at that command. When they returned, they did not again enter the encampment, but handed their trays and jars and baskets to the men who had remained. So there were no longer any women in the danger area, except for Malíntzin and her Texcaltéca maids, for whose safety we cared nothing. And our men were still coming and going, in and out of the palace, back and forth through the camp, dispensing meat and maize and such, bringing dry wood for the soldiers' fires, cooking in the palace kitchens, doing every kind of duty that would account for their being on the scene . . . and would keep them there until the temple conch trumpets signaled midnight.

"Midnight is the striking time," Cuitláhuac reminded us. "By then, Cortés and all these others will have become used to the constant traffic and the apparent servility of our nearly naked and clearly unarmed men. Meanwhile, let Cortés hear the music and see the incense smoke of v hat appears to be a jubilant ceremony preliminary to my inauguration. Find and collect every possible priest. They have already been told to await our instructions, but you may have to nudge them, since they, like the white men, will balk at having this rainfall wash them clean. Assemble the priests at the pyramid of Tlaltelólco. Have them put on the loudest, most firelit performance they have ever done. Also assemble there all the island's women and children and every man excused from fighting. They will make a convincing multitude of celebrants, and they should be safe there."

"Lord Regent," said one of the Council elders. "I mean, Lord Speaker. If the outlanders are all to die at midnight, why did you press Cortés to name a date for his departure?"

Cuitláhuac gave the o i man a look; I wagered that the old man would not much longer be a member of the Council. "Cortés is not such a fool as you, my lord. He certainly knows that I wish to be rid of him. Had I not spoken testily and insistently, he would have had cause to suspect a forcible ouster. Now I can hope he feels secure in my reluctant acceptance of his presence. I fervently hope he has no reason to feel otherwise between now and midnight."

He did not. But, while Cortés evidently felt no anxiety for the security of himself and his fellows, he apparently was most anxious to get the plundered treasury out of reach of its owners—or perhaps he decided that the rain-wet streets would make the sledges easier for his horses to pull. Anyway, despite their having to work in drenching rain, his carpenter-soldiers had the two crude land-boats hammered together not long after dark. Then other soldiers, helped by some of our own many men who were still making themselves useful to the Spaniards, carried the gold and jewels out of the palace and distributed them in equal piles on the sledges. Meanwhile, other soldiers used an elaborate tangle of leather straps to hitch four horses to each load. It was still some while before midnight when Cortés gave the order to move out, and the horses leaned into their leather webbing, like human porters bending against their tumplines, and the sledges glided quite smoothly across the wet marble paving of The Heart of the One World.

Though the bulk of the white army remained in the plaza, a considerable escort of armed soldiers went with the train, and they were led by the three highest-ranking Spaniards: Cortés, Narváez, and Alvarado. Moving that immense treasure was a laborious task, I grant you, but it hardly required the personal attention of all three commanders. I suspect that they all went because no one of them would trust either or both of the others to be in possession of all those riches, unwatched, even for a little while. Malíntzin also accompanied her master, probably just to enjoy a refreshing excursion after her long time spent in the palace. The sledges slid west across the plaza and onto the Tlácopan avenue. None of the white men evinced any suspicion at finding the city outside the square empty of people, for they could hear the throb of drums and music coming from the northern end of the island, and could see the low clouds yonder tinted red by the glow of urn fires and torchlights.

Like our earlier, unexpected opportunity to remove Motecuzóma as a possible obstacle to our plans, Cortés's unexpectedly sudden removal of the treasure was an unforeseen circumstance, and impelled Cuitláhuac to make his attack earlier than planned. Like Motecuzóma's demise, Cortés's precipitate move worked to Cuitláhuac's advantage. When the treasure train slithered onto the Tlácopan avenue, it was obviously taking the shortest crossing to the mainland, so Cuitláhuac could recall the warriors he had posted to man the other two causeways, and add them to his striking force. Then he passed the word to all his knights and cuáchictin: "Do not wait for the midnight trumpets. Strike *now!*"

I must remark that I was at home with Waiting Moon during these events I am recounting, for I was one of the men whom Cuitláhuac had charitably described as "excused from fighting": men too old or unfit to take part. So I did not personally witness the happenings on the island and the mainland—and no single witness could have been everywhere, in any case. But I was later present to hear reports of our various commanders, so I can tell you more or less accurately, lord friars, all the occurrences of what Cortés has ever since called "the Sad Night."

At the command to strike, the first move was made by some of those men of ours who had been in The Heart of the One World ever since the stoning of Motecuzóma. Their job was to loose and scatter the Spaniards' horses—and they had to be brave men, for never in any war had any of our warriors had to contend with any but human creatures. While some of the horses had gone with the treasure train, there still remained about eighty of them, all tethered in the corner of the plaza where stood the temple that had been converted to a Christian chapel. Our men untied the leather head straps that held the horses, then plucked burning sticks from a nearby campfire and ran waving them among the loosed animals. The horses panicked and charged away in all directions, galloping through the camp, kicking over the stacked harquebuses, trampling several of their owners and throwing all the other white men into a confusion of running and shouting and cursing.

Then the mass of our armed warriors poured into the square. Each of them carried two maquáhuime, and the extra weapon he tossed to one of the men who had already been long inside the plaza. None of our warriors wore the quilted armor, because it was not much protection in close combat, and would have been constrictive when sodden by the rain; our men fought wearing only their loincloths. The plaza had been but dimly lighted all night, since the soldiers' cooking fires had had to be sheltered from the rain by propping shields and other objects to lean over them. The running and plunging horses pounded most of those fires to pieces, and so disconcerted the soldiers that they were quite taken by surprise when our nearly naked warriors leaped out of the shadows, some slashing and chopping at any glimpse of white skin or bearded face or steel-wearing body, others forcing their way inside the palace Cortés had so recently quit.

The Spaniards manning the cannons on the palace roof heard the commotion below, but could see little of what was happening, and anyway could not discharge their weapons into the camp of their comrades. Another circumstance which worked in our favor was that the few Spaniards in the plaza who could lay hands on a harquebus found that it had got too wet to spit lightning and thunder and death. A number of the soldiers inside the palace did manage to use their harquebuses just once, but had no time to recharge them before our swarming warriors were upon them. So every white man and Texcaltécatl inside the palace was killed or captured, and our own men suffered few casualties in the process. But our warriors fighting outside, in The Heart of the One World, were not so quickly or entirely victorious. After all, the Spaniards and their Texcaltéca allies were brave men and trained soldiers. Recovering from their first surprise, they staunchly fought back. The Texcaltéca had weapons equal to ours, and the white men, even deprived of their harquebuses, had swords and spears far superior to ours.

Though I was not there, I can imagine the scene: it must have seemed like a war taking place in our Míctlan or your Hell. The vast square was only barely lighted by the remains of campfires, and those smoldering embers sporadically exploded into sparks as men or horses stumbled through them. The rain was still falling and making a veil which prevented any group of fighters from seeing how their fellows fared elsewhere. The entire expanse of pavement was littered with tangled bedding, the spilled contents of the Spaniards' packs, the remains of the evening meal, many fallen bodies, and blood making the marble even more slippery underfoot. The flash of steel swords and bucklers and pale white faces contrasted with the bare but less visible bodies of our copper-skinned warriors. There were separate duels taking place up and down the stairs of the Great Pyramid, and in and out of the many temples, and under the tranquil gaze of the innumerable sightless eyes of the skull rack. Making the whole battle even more unreal, the terrified horses still milled and reared and ran and kicked. The Snake Wall was too high for them to jump, but occasionally a horse would fortuitously find one of the wall's avenue openings and escape into the city streets.

At one point, a number of the white men turned and retreated to a far corner of the plaza, while a line of their comrades wielded their swords to keep our men from pursuing them— and that apparent retreat proved to be a clever feint. Those who fled had all snatched up harquebuses as they did so, and, during their brief respite from attack, they put dry charges from their belt pouches into the weapons. The swordsmen suddenly stood back, the harquebusiers stepped forward and all together discharged their lethal pellets into the crowd of our warriors who had been pressing them, and many of our men fell dead or wounded in that single roll of thunder. But the harquebuses could not again be charged before more of our men were pressing forward. Thereafter, the battle continued to be fought with stone weapons against steel weapons.

I do not know what made Cortés aware that something was happening to the army he had left leaderless. Perhaps one of the loose horses came clattering toward him through the streets, or perhaps it was a soldier escaped from the battle, or perhaps the first he heard of it was that one concerted thunderclap of the massed harquebuses. I do know that he and his train had reached the Tlácopan causeway before they knew of anything gone wrong. He took only a moment to decide what action to take, and there was no one to report later what words he spoke, but what he decided was, "We cannot leave the treasure here. Let us hurry it to safety on the mainland, then come back."

Meanwhile, that sound of the many harquebuses had also been heard all around the lake's nearer shores—by Cortés's camped troops and by our expectant allies alike. Cuitláhuac had instructed our mainland forces to wait for the midnight trumpets, but they had the good sense to move immediately when they heard that noise of combat. Cortés's detachments, on the other hand, had had no instructions. They must have jumped alert at the sudden sound, but did not know what to do. Likewise, the white men at the cannons set around the lakeshore had them already charged and aimed, but they could hardly send their projectiles flying into the city where their Captain-General and most of their comrades were in residence. So I suppose all of Cortés's mainland troops were simply standing, indecisive, staring bewildered toward the island dimly visible through the rain, when they were attacked from behind.

Around the whole western arc of the lakeshore, the armies of The Triple Alliance rose up. Though many of their best warriors were in Tenochtítlan fighting alongside our Mexíca, there were still multitudes of good fighters on the mainland. From as far south as the Xochimílca and Chalca lands, troops had secretly been moving northward and massing for that moment, and they fell upon Prince Black Flower's Acólhua forces camped about Coyohuácan. On the other side of the straits there, the Culhua attacked Cortés's Totonáca forces camped on the promontory of land around Ixtapalápan. The Tecpanéca rose up against the Texcaltéca camped about Tlácopan.

At about the same time, the beleaguered Spaniards in The Heart of the One World made the sensible decision to run. Some one of their officers seized a horse as it pounded through the camp, swung himself onto its back, and began shouting in Spanish. I cannot repeat his exact words but, in effect, the officer's command was, "Close ranks and follow after Cortés!" That gave the surviving white men at least a destination, and they fought their way from all the corners of the plaza to which they had been scattered, and they managed to bunch themselves in a tight pack which bristled with sharp steel. As a prickly little boar can roll itself into a ball of quills and defy even coyotes to swallow it, so that pack of Spaniards fought off our men's repeated assaults.

Still heeding the shouted directions of the one man astride a horse, they moved in that bristling clump backward toward the western opening in the Snake Wall. Several others of them, during that slow retreat, were able to catch and mount horses. When all those white men and Texcaltéca were outside the plaza, on the Tlácopan avenue, the mounted soldiers formed a rear guard. Their swinging swords and the pummeling hooves of the horses held back our pursuing warriors long enough for the men afoot to flee in the direction Cortés had gone.

Cortés must have met them on his own way back toward the city's center, for of course he and his treasure train had gone only as far along the causeway as the first canoe passage interrupting it, where they saw that the spanning wooden ramp had been removed, that they could not cross the gap. So Cortés alone rode back to the island, and there met the disorganized, ravaged remnant of his army, drenched with rain and blood, cursing their enemies and moaning over their wounds, but all fleeing for their lives. And he heard, not far behind them, the war cries of our pursuing warriors, still trying to fight past the barriers of horsemen.

I know Cortés, and I know he did not waste time asking for a detailed explanation of what had occurred. He must have told those men to stand fast there, where the causeway joined the island, to hold off the enemy as long as possible. For he immediately galloped back along the causeway to where Alvarado and Narváez and the other soldiers waited, and shouted for them to shove all the treasure into the lake, to clear the sledges and then shove them across the gap to make a bridge. I daresay everybody from Alvarado to the lowliest trooper raised a howl of protest, and I imagine Cortés silenced them with some command like, "Do it! Or we are all dead men!"

So they obeyed, or most of them did. Under cover of the darkness, before they helped to empty the sledges, many of the soldiers emptied whatever traveling packs they carried, and then crammed into their packs, inside their doublets, even down the wide tops of their jackboots, every scrap of gold small enough for them to steal. But the bulk of the treasure vanished into the lake waters there, and the horses were unhitched, and the men pushed the sledges across the break in the causeway.

By that time, the rest of the army was coming from the city along the causeway, not entirely voluntarily, being pressed backward along it as they fought our advancing warriors. When they had retreated to the point where Cortés and the others waited, the retreat halted momentarily, and the front ranks of the Spaniards and Mexíca came together in a toe-to-toe, standstill fight. The reason was that, although the causeway was broad enough for twenty men to walk abreast, not so many could fight efficiently side by side. Perhaps no more than the foremost twelve of our warriors could engage the front twelve of theirs, and the weight of our numbers in the rear ranks was of no avail.

Then the Spaniards suddenly seemed to give way, and fell back. But as they did so, they slid with them their sledge bridges, leaving our forward fighters teetering for balance on the edge of the sudden breach. One of the sledges, and several of our men, and several of the Spaniards too, fell into the lake. But the white men on the other side had little time to catch their breath. Our warriors were not heavily clothed and they were good swimmers. They began leaping deliberately into the water, swimming across the gap and climbing up the pilings below where the white men stood. At the same time, a rain of arrows came down on the Spaniards from both sides. Cuitláhuac had overlooked nothing; canoes full of archers were in the lake by then, converging on the causeway. Cortés had no choice but to make another fighting retreat. Since his horses were the biggest and most valuable and most vulnerable targets, he ordered a number of men to force the animals to plunge into the water, then to hang on to them as they swam for the mainland. Unbidden, Malíntzin jumped with them, and was hauled by a swimming horse to the shore.

Then Cortés and his remaining men did their best to make an orderly withdrawal. Those who had crossbows and workable harquebuses discharged them at random into the darkness on both sides of the causeway, hoping to hit some of the canoe-borne attackers. The other Spaniards, alternately wielding their swords and sliding the remaining sledge, crept backward from the more and more numerous warriors who were successfully crossing that first break in the causeway. There were two more canoe passages between Cortés and the Tlácopan mainland. The sledge served to get him and his men across the next one, but there they had to abandon their makeshift bridge because their pursuers also got across it. At the next gap, the white men simply fought and walked backward until they toppled off the brink into the lake.

Actually, that close to the shore, the water was shallow enough that even a man incapable of swimming could make his way to land by a sort of series of hops, keeping his head above water. But the white men wore heavy armor, and many of them were burdened with even heavier gold, and when they went into the water they flailed desperately to stay afloat. Cortés and their other comrades coming after them did not hesitate to step upon them in trying to leap across the breach. Thus many men who fell into the water sank, and the lowermost, I suppose, were stamped deep into the lake-bottom ooze. As more and more of the Spaniards fell and drowned, their bodies piled high enough to make a bridge of flesh, and it was by that means that the last surviving Spaniards got across.

Only one of them made the crossing without panic, with a flourish which our warriors so admired that they still speak of "Tonatíu's leap." When Pedro de Alvarado was pushed to the brink, he was armed only with a spear. He turned his back on his assailants, stabbed the spear into the heaving, drowning heap of his men in the water, and gave a mighty bound. Although he was heavily armored, probably wounded, and certainly weary, he *vaulted* across that gap from the near edge of the causeway all the way to the far edge . . . and to safety.

For our pursuing force stopped there. They had driven the last outlanders from Tenochtítlan into Tecpanéca territory, where they assumed the remainder would be killed or captured. Our warriors turned back along the causeway—where the boatmen were already bringing back and setting in place the missing spans—and on the way home, they did the work of Swallowers and Swaddlers. They picked up their own fallen fellows, and also those wounded white men who would live to serve as sacrifices, and with their blades they put a mercifully quick end to those Spaniards already near death.

Cortés and his accompanying survivors found a surcease from battle and a chance to rest in Tlácopan. The local Tecpanéca were not as good fighters as the Texcaltéca whom Cortés had quartered upon them, but they had attacked with the advantage of surprise, and they did know their own local terrain. So, by the time Cortés reached that city, the Tecpanéca had driven his Texcaltéca allies from Tlácopan north to Azcapotzálco and had them still on the run. Cortés and his companions had a time of reprieve in which to dress their wounds and assess their position and decide what to do next.

Among those still alive, Cortés at least had his chief underofficers: Narváez and Alvarado and others—and his Malíntzin—but his army was no longer an army. He had marched triumphantly into Tenochtítlan with something like one thousand five hundred other white men. He had just emerged from Tenochtítlan with fewer than four hundred—and about thirty horses, some of which had escaped from the plaza battle and swum all the way from the island. Cortés had no idea where his native allies were or how they were faring. The fact is that they too were in rout before the vengeful armies of The Triple Alliance. Except for the Texcaltéca, who were then being pushed northward away from him, all his other forces, which had been stationed along the lakeshore to the south, were at that moment being driven northward to where he sat exhausted and morose in defeat.

It is said that Cortés did just that. He sat, as if he would never rise again. He sat with his back against one of the "oldest of old" cypress trees, and he wept. Whether he wept more for his crushing defeat or for the lost treasure, I do not know. But a fence has recently been put around that tree where Cortés wept, to mark it as a memorial of "the Sad Night." We Mexíca, if we were still keeping histories, might have given a different name to that occasion—the Night of the Last Victory of the Mexíca, perhaps—but it is you Spaniards who write the histories now, so I suppose that rainy and bloody night, by your calendar the thirtieth day of the month of June in the year one thousand five hundred and twenty, will forever be remembered as "La Noche Triste."

✠

In many respects, that was a less than happy night for The One World too. The most unfortunate circumstance was that all our armies did not continue their pursuit of Cortés and his remaining white men and native supporters until they were slain to the last man. However, as I have said, the warriors of Tenochtítlan believed that their mainland allies would do just that, so they turned back to the island to devote the rest of the night to a celebration of what seemed a total victory. Our city's priests and most of its people were still engaged in that sham ceremony-of-distraction at the pyramid of Tlaltelólco, and they were only too pleased to move in mass to The Heart of the One World and hold a real ceremony of thanksgiving at the Great Pyramid. Even Béu and I, hearing the gladsome shouts of the returning warriors, left our house to attend. Even Tlaloc, as if better to watch his people's rejoicing, lifted his curtain of rain.

In normal times, we would not have dared to observe any kind of rite in the central plaza until every stone and statue and ornamentation had been newly scrubbed clean of every speck of dirt, every possible defilement, until The Heart of the One World shone bright for the gods' approval and admiration. But that night the torches and urn fires revealed the vast square to be a vast garbage heap. Everywhere lay dead bodies or parts of bodies, both white- and copper-skinned; also quantities of spilled entrails, gray-pink and gray-blue, hence indistinguishable as to origin. Everywhere lay broken and discarded weapons, and the excrement of frightened horses and of men who had incontinently defecated as they died, and the rancid bedding and clothing and other effects of the Spaniards. But the priests uttered no complaint about that foul setting for the ceremony, and the celebrants crowded in without showing too much disgust at the nasty things they trod on or in. We all trusted that the gods would not, that one time, take offense at the plaza's filthy condition, inasmuch as it was their enemies as well as ours whom we had defeated there.

I know it has always distressed you, reverend scribes, to hear me describe the sacrifice of any human beings, even the heathens despised by your Church, so I will not dwell on the sacrifice of your own Christian countrymen, which commenced when the sun Tonatíu began to rise. I will only remark, though it will make you think us a very foolish people, that we also sacrificed the forty or so horses which the soldiers had left behind—because, you see, we could not be sure that *they* were not also Christians of a sort. I might say, also, that the horses went to their Flowery Deaths much more nobly than did the Spaniards, who struggled while they were being undressed, and cursed while they were dragged up the staircase, and cried like children when they were bent backward on the stone. Our warriors recognized some of the white men who had most bravely fought them, so, after those men died, their thighs were cut for broiling and . . .

But perhaps you will not look so nauseated, lord friars, if I assure you that most of the bodies were without ceremony fed to the animals of the city menagerie. . . .

Very well, my lords, I will return to the less gala events of that night. While we were thanking the gods for the riddance of the outlanders, we were unaware that our mainland armies had *not* annihilated them. Cortés was still sulking miserably in Tlácopan when he was roused by the noisy approach of his other fleeing forces—the Acólhua and Totonáca, or what was left of them—being chased northward by the Xochimílca and Chalca. Cortés and his officers, with Malíntzin no doubt shouting louder than she had ever had to shout in her life, managed to halt the headlong rout and restore some semblance of order. Then Cortés and his white men, some on horseback, some walking, some limping, some in litters, led the reorganized native troops farther on northward before their pursuers caught up. And those pursuers, probably believing that the fugitives would be dealt with by other Triple Alliance forces beyond, or perhaps over-eager to commence their own victory celebrations, let the fugitives go.

Sometime about daybreak, at the northern extremity of Lake Tzumpánco, Cortés realized that he was closely trailing our allied Tecpanéca. And they, still on the trail of *his* allied Texcaltéca, were surprised and displeased to find themselves trudging along between two enemy forces. Deciding that something had gone amiss with the general battle plan, the Tecpanéca also abandoned their pursuit, dispersed sideways off the trail and made their way home to Tlácopan. Cortés eventually caught up to his Texcaltéca, and his whole army was again intact, though notably diminished and in dismal spirits. Still, Cortés may have been somewhat relieved that his best native fighters, the Texcaltéca—because they *were* the best fighters—had suffered the fewest losses. I can imagine what went through Cortés's mind then:

"If I go to Texcála, its old King Xicoténca will see that I have preserved most of the warriors he lent me. So he cannot be too angry with me, or account me a total failure, and I may be able to persuade him to give the rest of us refuge there."

Whether or not that was his reasoning, Cortés did lead his wretched troops on around the northern extent of the lake lands toward Texcála. Several more men died of their wounds during that long march, and all of them suffered greatly, for they took a prudently circuitous route, avoiding every populated place, hence could not beg or demand food. They were forced to subsist on what edible wild creatures and plants they could find, and at least once had to butcher and eat some of their precious horses and staghounds.

Only once in that long march were they again engaged in combat. They were caught in the foothills of the mountains to the east, by a force of Acólhua warriors from Texcóco still loyal to The Triple Alliance. But those Acólhua were lacking in both leadership and incentive to fight, so the battle was conducted almost as bloodlessly as a Flowery War. When the Acólhua had secured a number of prisoners—all Totonáca, I believe—they retired from the field and went home to Texcóco to hold their own celebration of "victory." Thus Cortés's remaining army was not further diminished too severely between its flight on the Sad Night and its arrival, twelve days later, in Texcála. That nation's lately converted Christian ruler, the aged and blind Xicoténca, did welcome Cortés's return and gave him permission to quarter his troops and to stay as long as he might wish. All those events I have just recounted, all working to our detriment, were unknown to us in Tenochtítlan when, in the radiant dawn after the Sad Night, we sent the first Spanish xochimíqui to the sacrificial stone at the summit of the Great Pyramid.

Other things happened at the time of that Sad Night which, if not sad, were at least to be wondered at. As I have told, the Mexíca nation lost its Revered Speaker Motecuzóma. But also the then Revered Speaker of Tlacopan, Totoquihuáztli, died in that city during the night's battle there. And the Revered Speaker Cacáma of Texcóco, who fought with the Acólhua warriors he had lent to Tenochtítlan, was found among the dead when our slaves did the grisly work of clearing the night's detritus from The Heart of the One World. No one much mourned the loss of either Motecuzóma or his nephew Cacáma, but it was a disturbing coincidence that *all three* ruling partners of The Triple Alliance should have died in the one afternoon and night. Of course, Cuitláhuac had already assumed the vacant throne of the Mexíca—though he never did get to enjoy the full pomp and ceremony of an official coronation ceremony. And the people of Tlácopan chose as a replacement for their slain Uey-Tlatoáni his brother Tétlapanquétzal.

The choice of a new Revered Speaker for Texcóco was less easy. The legitimate claimant was the Prince Black Flower, who should rightly have been the ruler anyway, and most of the Acólhua people would have welcomed him to the throne— except that he had allied himself with the hated white men. So the Speaking Council of Texcóco, in consultation with the new Revered Speakers of Tenochtítlan and Tlácopan, decided to appoint a man of such nonentity that he would be acceptable to all factions, yet could be replaced by whatever leader finally emerged as the strongest among the fragmented Acólhua. His name was Cohuanácoch, and I think he was a nephew of the late Nezahualpíli. It was because of that nation's uncertainty and division of loyalties and frailty of leadership that the Acólhua warriors attacked the fleeing forces of Cortés so halfheartedly, when they could have destroyed them utterly. And never again did the Acólhua manifest the warlike ferocity that I had admired when Nezahualpíli led them—and me— against the Texcaltéca those many years ago.

Another curious occurrence of the Sad Night was that, sometime during that night, the dead body of Motecuzóma disappeared from the palace throne room in which it last lay, and was never seen again. I have heard many suppositions as to what became of it—that it was viciously dismembered and chopped and minced and scattered by our warriors when they overran the palace; that his wives and children spirited the corpse away for more respectful disposition; that his loyal priests treated the cadaver with preservatives and hid it away, and will bring it magically to life again, someday when you white men have gone and the Mexíca reign once more. What I believe is that Motecuzóma's body got mixed in with those of the Texcaltéca knights who were slain in that palace and, unrecognized, went where theirs did: to the animals of the menagerie. But only one thing is certain. Motecuzóma departed this world as vaguely and irresolutely as he had lived in it, so his body's resting place is as unknown as the whereabouts of the treasure which vanished during that same night.

Ah, yes, the treasure: what is now called "the lost treasure of the Aztecs." I wondered when you would ask me about it. In after years, Cortés often called me in to help Malíntzin interpret while he interrogated many persons, each of them many times and in many interestingly persuasive ways, and he often demanded to know what *I* might know about the treasure, though he did not subject me to any of the persuasions. Many other Spaniards besides Cortés have repeatedly asked me and other former courtiers to tell them: of what did the treasure consist? and how much was it worth? and above all, where is it now? You would not believe some of the inducements I am still being offered to this day, but I will remark that some of the most persistent and more generously inclined inquirers are highborn Spanish doñas.

I have already told you, reverend friars, of what the treasure consisted. As to its worth, I do not know how you would appraise those innumerable works of art. Even considering the gold and gems simply in bulk, I have no way of reckoning their value in your currency of maravedíes and reales. But, from what I have been told of the great wealth of your King Carlos and your Pope Clemente and other rich personages of your Old World, I think I can declare that any man possessing "the lost treasure of the Aztecs" would be by far the wealthiest of all wealthy men in your Old World.

But where is it? Well, the old causeway still stretches from here to Tlácopan—or Tácuba, as you prefer to call it. Though the span is shorter now than it used to be, the farthest west canoe passage is still there, and that is where many Spanish soldiers sank from the weight of gold in their packs and doublets and boots. Of course, they must have sunk far into the ooze of the lake bottom in the past eleven years, and been even deeper buried by the silt deposited in those same years. But any man sufficiently greedy and sufficiently energetic to dive down and dig there should find many bleached bones, and among them many jeweled golden diadems, medallions, figurines, and such. Perhaps not enough to make him rank with King Carlos or Pope Clemente, but enough that he need never feel greedy again.

Unfortunately for any *really* greedy treasure seekers, the greater part of the plunder was thrown into the lake, on Cortés's orders, at the causeway's first acáli passage, the nearest to the city here. The Revered Speaker Cuitláhuac could have sent divers down to recover it afterward, and perhaps he did so, but I have reasons for doubting that. Anyway, Cuitláhuac died before Cortés could ask him, either politely or persuasively. And if any Mexíca divers did bring up from the lake the treasury of their nation, either they too have died or they are men of dedicated and exceptional reticence.

I believe the bulk of the treasure still lies there where Cortés had it jettisoned on that Sad Night. But when Tenochtítlan was later razed to the very ground and, after that, when the rubble was cleared for the city's rebuilding in the Spanish style, the unusable remains of Tenochtítlan were simply scraped to the sides of the island—partly for your builders' convenience, partly to increase the island's surface area. So the Tlácopan causeway was shortened by the encroachment of the enlarging island, and that nearest canoe passage is now underground. If I am correct in my estimation of where the treasure rests, it is somewhere deep beneath the foundations of the elegantly señorial buildings lining your avenue called the Calzada Tácuba.

Of all the things I have told of the Sad Night, I have not mentioned the one event that, all by itself, determined the future of The One World. It was the death of just one man. He was no one of any importance. If he had a name, I never heard it. He may have done nothing either praiseworthy or blameworthy in all his life, except to have his roads and his days end here, and I do not know whether he died bravely or cowardly. But during the next day's cleaning of The Heart of the One World, his body was found, cloven by a maquáhuitl, and the slaves made an outcry when they found it, because he was neither a white man nor one of our race, and those slaves had never seen such a being before. I had. He was one of those unbelievably black men who had come from Cuba with Narváez, and he was the one whose blemished face had made me shrink away when I saw it.

I smile now—ruefully and contemptuously, but I smile— when I see the swaggering and strutting of Hernán Cortés and Pedro de Alvarado and Beltrán de Guzmán and all the other Spanish veterans who now exalt themselves as "Los Conquistadores." Oh, they did some brave and daring deeds, I cannot deny it. Cortés's burning of his own ships on his first arrival in these lands has hardly ever been outdone, as an example of jaunty audacity, even by any caprice of the gods. And there were other factors that contributed to the downfall of The One World—not least the deplorable fact of The One World's turning against itself: nation against nation, neighbor against neighbor, finally even brother against brother. But if any one, single, solitary human being deserves to be honored and remembered with the title of El Conquistador, it is that nameless blackamoor who brought the disease of the small pocks to Tenochtítlan.

He could have given the disease to Narváez's soldiers during their voyage here from Cuba. He did not. He could have given the disease to them, and to Cortés's troops besides, during their march hither from the coast. He did not. He could himself have died of the disease before reaching here. He did not. He lived to visit Tenochtítlan, and to bring the disease to us. Perhaps it was one of those caprices of the gods, to let him do so, and there was nothing we could have done to avert it. But I wish the black man had not then been killed. I wish he had been among those of his fellows who escaped, so he could have shared the affliction with them, soon or later. But no. Tenochtítlan was ravaged by the small pocks, and the disease spread throughout the lake region, into every community of The Triple Alliance, but it never reached Texcála or troubled our enemies there.

In fact, the first of our city folk were beginning to fall ill even before we got the word that Cortés and his company had found refuge in Texcála. You reverend scribes doubtless know the symptoms and progress of the disease. Anyway, I long ago described to you how I had seen, many years earlier, a young Xiu girl die of the small pocks in the faraway town of Tihó. So I need only say that our people died in the same manner: strangling on the swollen tissues inside their noses and throats— or in some manner equally dreadful: thrashing and screaming in violent delirium until their brains could no longer stand the torment, or vomiting blood until their bodies were empty of blood, until they died more husk than human. Of course, I early recognized the disease and told our physicians:

"It is a common affliction among the white men, and they hold it of little account, for they seldom die of it. They call it the small pocks."

"If this is their small pocks," said one doctor, without humor, "I hope they never favor us with any larger. What is it the white men do to keep from dying of it?"

"There is no remedy. Or so they told me. Except to pray."

So thereafter our temples were crowded with priests and worshipers making offerings and sacrifices to Patécatl, the god of healing, and to every other god as well. The temple that Motecuzóma had lent to the Spaniards was also crowded, with those of our people who had submitted to baptism and who suddenly, devoutly *hoped* they had truly been made Christians—meaning they hoped that the Christian god of the small pocks would look on them as simulated white men, and so spare them. They lighted candles and crossed themselves and muttered what they could remember of the rituals in which they had received only slight instruction and to which they had paid even slighter attention.

But nothing stopped the spread of the disease and the dying of it. Our prayers were as futile and our physicians as helpless as those of the Maya had been. Before long, we were threatened with starvation as well, because our affliction could be kept no secret, and the mainland folk dreaded to come near us, so there was a cessation of the traffic of supply-carrying acáltin so necessary to our island's subsistence. But it was not much longer before the disease made its appearance in the mainland communities too, and, once it became evident that all of us of The Triple Alliance were in the same predicament, the boatmen resumed their freighting—or I should say, those boatmen did who were not yet stricken. For the disease seemed selective of its victims in only one particularly cruel respect. I never took sick with it, nor did Béu, nor did any of our contemporaries. The small pocks seemed to ignore those of our age, and those already ill of something else, and those who had always been of feeble constitution. Instead, it seized upon the young and strong and vigorous, not wasting its maleficence on any who for other reasons had not long lives to live.

Our having been stricken by the small pocks is one reason why I doubt that Cuitláhuac ever did anything about recovering the treasure sunk in the lake. The disease came upon us so soon after the departure of the white men—only days after we had cleaned up the litter they left, before we had begun to recover from the strain of the long occupation, before we had in any measure resumed our civic life where it had been interrupted—that I know the Revered Speaker gave no thought at that time to salvaging the gold and jewels. And later, as the disease became a devastation, he had other reasons for neglecting that task. You see, we were for a long while cut off from all news of the world beyond the lake region. Merchants and messengers of other nations refused to enter our tainted area, and Cuitláhuac forbade our own pochtéca and travelers to go elsewhere and possibly carry the contamination. I think it was fully four months after the Sad Night when one of our quimíchime mice posted in Texcála summoned up the courage to come from there and tell us what had been happening during that time.

"Know then, Revered Speaker," he said to Cuitláhuac and the others, including myself, who were eager to hear him. "Cortés and his company spent some while merely resting and eating ravenously and convalescing from their injuries and generally regaining their health. But they did not do so in preparation for continuing on to the coast, to go aboard their ships and leave these lands. They have been recuperating for one purpose only: to gather strength to make another assault upon Tenochtítlan. Now that they are up and active again they and their Texcaltéca hosts are journeying throughout all the country eastward of here, recruiting ever more warriors from tribes not over-friendly to the Mexíca."

The Snake Woman interrupted the mouse to say urgently to the Revered Speaker, "We hoped we had permanently discouraged them. Since we did not, we now must do what should have been done long before now. We must assemble all our forces and march against them. Kill every last white man, every one of their allies and supporters, every one of our tributary dissidents who has aided Cortés. And we must do it *now*, before he is strong enough to do exactly that to *us!*"

Cuitláhuac said wanly, "What forces do you suggest we assemble, Tlácotzin? There is hardly a warrior in any troop anywhere in The Triple Alliance who has force enough in both arms to lift his own blade."

"Excuse me, Lord Speaker, but there is more to tell," said the quimíchi. "Cortés also sent many of his men to the coast, where they and their Totonáca dismantled several of the moored ships. With toil and labor inconceivable, they have brought all those many and heavy pieces of wood and metal all the arduous way from the sea across the mountains to Texcála. There, at this moment, Cortés's boatmen are putting those pieces together to make smaller ships. As they did, you will recall, when they built the small ship here for the amusement of the late Motecuzóma. But now they are making many of them."

"On dry land?" Cuitláhuac exclaimed incredulously. "There is no water in the whole Texcála nation deep enough to float anything bigger than a fishing acáli. It sounds like insanity."

The quimíchi shrugged delicately. "Cortés may have been

demented by his recent humiliation here. But I respectfully submit, Revered Speaker, that I am telling truthfully what I have seen, and that *I* am sane. Or I was, until I decided those doings seemed ominous enough to warrant risking my life to bring you the news of them."

Cuitláhuac smiled. "Sane or not, it was the act of a brave and loyal Mexícatl, and I am grateful. You will be well rewarded—and then given an even greater reward: my permission to depart this pestilent city again as swiftly as you can."

So it was that we knew Cortés's actions and at least some of his intentions. I have heard many persons—who were not here at the time—speak critically of our apparent apathy or stupidity or deluded sense of security, because we stayed in isolation and did nothing to prevent Cortés's rallying of his forces. But the reason that we did nothing was that we *could* do nothing. From Tzumpánco in the north to Xochimílco in the south, from Tlácopan in the west to Texcóco in the east, every ablebodied man and woman who was not helping to nurse the afflicted was himself ill or dying or dead. In our weakness, we could only wait, and hope that we should have recovered to some degree before Cortés came again. About that, we had no delusions; we knew he would come again. And it was during that drear summer of waiting that Cuitláhuac made a remark, in the presence of myself and his cousin Cuautémoc:

"I had rather the nation's treasury lie forever at the bottom of Lake Texcóco—or sink all the way to the black depths of Míctlan—than that the white men should ever have it in their hands again."

I doubt that he later changed his mind, for he scarcely had time. Before the rainy season was over, he had fallen ill of the small pocks, and vomited up all his blood, and died. Poor Cuitláhuac, he became our Revered Speaker without the proper ceremonies of installation and, when his brief reign ended, he was not honored with the funeral befitting his station.

By that time, not the noblest of noblemen could be accorded a service with drums and mourners and panoply—or even the luxury of earth burial. There were simply too many dead, too many dying every day. There were no longer any available places left in which to bury them, or men to dig the graves for them, or time enough to dig all the graves that would have been necessary. Instead, each community designated some nearby wasteland spot where its dead could be taken and unceremoniously piled together and burned to ashes—and even that mode of mass disposal was no easy matter in the damp days of the rainy season. Tenochtítlan's chosen burning place was an uninhabited spot on the mainland behind the rise of Chapultépec, and the busiest traffic between our island and the mainland consisted of the freight barges. Rowed by old men indifferent to the disease, they shuttled back and forth, all day long, day after day. Cuitláhuac's body was just one among the hundreds ferried on that day he died.

The disease of the small pocks was the conqueror of us Mexíca and of some other peoples. Still other nations were defeated or are still being devastated by other diseases never known in these lands before, some of which might make us Mexíca feel almost thankful to have been visited only with the small pocks.

There is the sickness you call the plague, in which the victim develops agonizing black bulges in his neck and groin and armpits, so that he keeps continually stretching his head backward and his extremities outward, as if he would gladly break them from his body to be rid of the pain. Meanwhile, his every bodily emanation—his spittle, his urine and excrement, even his sweat and his breath—are of such vile stench that neither hardened physicians nor tender kinsmen can bear to stay near the victim, until at last the bulges burst with a gush of nauseous black fluid, and the sufferer is mercifully dead.

There is the sickness you call the cholera, whose victims are seized by cramps in every muscle of the body, randomly or all at once. A man will at one moment have his arms or legs wrenched into contortions of anguish, then be splayed out as if he were flinging himself apart, then have his whole body convulsed into a knot of torture. All the time, he is also tormented by an unquenchable thirst. Although he gulps down torrents of water, he continuously retches it out, and uncontrollably urinates and defecates. Since he cannot contain any moisture, he dries and shrivels so that, when at last he dies, he looks like an old seedpod.

There are the other diseases you call the measles and the

pease pocks, which kill less horrifically but just as certainly. Their only visible symptom is an itchy rash on the face and torso, but invisibly those sicknesses invade the brain, so the victim subsides first into unconsciousness and then into death.

I am telling you nothing you do not already know, lord friars, but did you ever think of this? The ghastly diseases brought by your countrymen have often spread out ahead of them faster than the men themselves could march. Some of the people they set out to conquer were conquered and dead before they knew they were the objects of conquest. Those people died without ever fighting against or surrendering to their conquerors, without ever even seeing the men who killed them. It is entirely possible that there are still reclusive peoples in remote corners of these lands—tribes like the Rarámuri and the Zyú Huave, for instance—who do not even yet suspect that such beings as white men exist. Nevertheless, those people may at this moment be dying horribly of the small pocks or the plague, dying without knowing that they are being *slain*, or why, or by whom.

You brought us the Christian religion, and you assure us that the Lord God will reward us with Heaven when we die, but that unless we accept Him we are damned to Hell when we die. Why then did the Lord God send us also the afflictions which kill and damn so many innocents to Hell before they can meet His missionaries and hear of His religion? Christians are constantly bidden to praise the Lord God and all His works, which must include the work He has done here. If only, reverend friars, you could explain to us why the Lord God chose to send His gentle new religion trailing behind the cruelly murderous new diseases, we who survived them could more joyously join you in singing praises to the Lord God's infinite wisdom and goodness, His compassion and mercy, His fatherly love of all His children everywhere.

By unanimous vote, the Speaking Council selected the Lord Cuautémoc to be the next Uey-Tlatoáni of the Mexíca. It is interesting to speculate on how different our history and our destiny might have been if Cuautémoc had become Revered Speaker, as he should have done, when his father Ahuítzotl died eighteen years earlier. Interesting to speculate, but of course fruitless. "If" is a small word in our language—tla—as it is in yours, but I have come to believe that it is the most heavy-laden word of all the words there are.

The death toll of the small pocks began to lessen as the summer's heat and rain abated, and finally, with the first chill of winter, the disease entirely let go its grip on the lake lands. But it left The Triple Alliance weak in every sense of the word. All our people were dispirited; we grieved for the countless dead; we pitied those who had survived to be gruesomely disfigured for the rest of their lives; we were wearied by the long visitation of calamity; we were individually and collectively drained of our human strength. Our population had been reduced perhaps by half, and the remainder consisted mainly of the old and infirm. Since those who died had been the younger men, not to speak of the women and children, our armies had been diminished by considerably *more* than half. No sensible commander would have ordered them into aggressive action against the massing outlanders, and their utility even for defense was dubious.

It was then, when The Triple Alliance was the weakest it had ever been, that Cortés once more marched against it. He no longer boasted any great advantage of superior weapons, for he had fewer than four hundred white soldiers and however many harquebuses and crossbows they still carried among them. All the cannons he had abandoned on the Sad Night— the four on the roof of Axayácatl's palace and the thirty or so he had posted around the mainland—we had pitched into the lake. But he still had more than twenty horses, a number of the staghounds, and all his formerly and latterly collected native warriors—the Texcaltéca, the Totonáca and other minor tribes, the Acólhua still following Prince Black Flower. Altogether, Cortés had something like one hundred thousand troops. From all the cities and lands of The Triple Alliance— even counting outlying places like Tolócan and Quaunáhuac, which were not really of the Alliance, but gave us their support—we could not muster one-third that many fighting men.

So when Cortés's long columns proceeded from Texcála toward the nearest capital city of The Triple Alliance, which was Texcóco, they took it. I could tell at length of the weakened city's desperate defense, and of the casualties its defenders inflicted and suffered, and of the tactics which eventually defeated it . . . but what matter? All that need be said is that the marauders took it. The marauders included Prince Black Flower's Acólhua, and they fought their fellow Acólhua warriors who were loyal to the new Revered Speaker Cohuanácoch—or, more truthfully, loyal to their city of Texcóco. And so it happened that, in that battle, many an Acólhuatl found himself wielding a blade against another Acólhuatl who was his own brother.

At least Texcóco's warriors were not all killed in the battle, and perhaps two thousand escaped before they could be trapped there. The troops of Cortés had assailed the city from its landward side, so the defenders, when they could no longer hold firm, were able to withdraw slowly to the lakeshore. There they took every fishing and fowling and passenger and freight acáli, including even the elegant acáltin of the court, and propelled themselves out into the lake. Their opponents, having been left no craft in which to pursue them, could only send a cloud of arrows after them, and the arrows did little damage. So the Acólhua warriors crossed the lake and joined our forces on Tenochtítlan, where, because so many people had lately died, there was ample room to quarter them.

Cortés would have known, from his conversations with Motecuzóma, if from no other source, that Texcóco was the strongest bastion city of our Triple Alliance, after Tenochtítlan. And, having conquered Texcóco so easily, Cortés was confident that the taking of all other and smaller lakeside cities and towns would be even easier. So he did not commit his whole army to that task, nor did he command it in person. To the mystification of our spies, he sent one entire half of his army back to Texcála. The other half he divided into detachments, each led by one of his under-officers: Alvarado, Narváez, Montejo, Guzmán. Some left Texcóco going northward, others southward, and they began circling the lake, along the way attacking the various small communities separately or simultaneously. Although our Revered Speaker Cuautémoc employed the fleet of canoes brought by the fugitive Acólhua to send those same warriors and our Mexíca to the aid of the beleaguered towns, the battles were so many and so far apart that he could not send enough men to any one of them to make any difference in the outcome. Every place the Spanish-led forces attacked, they took. The best our men could do was to evacuate from those towns whatever local warriors were left alive, and to bring them to Tenochtítlan as reinforcements for our own defense, when our turn should come.

Presumably Cortés, by means of messengers, directed the general strategy of his several officers and their detachments, but he—and Malíntzin—remained in the luxurious residence of the Texcóco palace in which I myself had once lived, and he kept the hapless Revered Speaker Cohuanácoch there too, as his compulsory host, or guest, or prisoner. For I should mention here that the Crown Prince Black Flower, who had grown old waiting to become Uey-Tlatoáni of the Acólhua, never did get that title and that eminence.

Even after the taking of the Acólhua's capital city, in which Black Flower's troops had played no small part, Cortés decreed that the inoffensive and uncontroversial Cohuanácoch should remain on the throne. Cortés knew that all the Acólhua, except those warriors who had for so long followed Black Flower, had come to loathe the once-respected Crown Prince as a traitor to his own people and a tool of the white men. Cortés would not risk provoking a future uprising of the whole nation by giving the traitor the throne for which he had turned traitor. Even when Black Flower groveled in the rite of baptism, with Cortés for his godfather, and in flagrant obsequiousness took the Christian name of Fernando *Cortés* Ixtlil-Xochitl, his godfather unbent in his resolve only sufficiently to appoint him lord ruler of three insignificant provinces of the Acólhua lands. At that, Don Fernando Black Flower showed one last flicker of his former lordly temperament, protesting angrily:

"You *give* me what already belongs to me? What has *always* belonged to my forefathers?"

But he did not long have to endure his dissatisfaction and debasement. He stormed out of Texcóco to take up his rule in one of those backwoods provinces, and arrived there just when the disease of the small pocks was also arriving, and within a month or two he was dead.

We soon learned that the marauding armies' Captain-General was lingering in Texcóco for other reasons than merely to enjoy a rest in luxury. Our quimíchime came to Tenochtítlan to report, not more mystification, but the news that the departed half of Cortés's force was returning to Texcóco, bringing on their backs or hauling on log rollers the many and various hulls and poles and other components of the thirteen "ships" that had been partially constructed on the dry land of Texcála. Cortés had stayed to be in Texcóco when they arrived, to oversee their assembly and launching upon the lake there.

They were not, of course, any such formidable things as the seagoing ships from which they had been fashioned. They were more like our flat-bottomed freight barges, only with high sides, and with the winglike sails that, we discovered to our dismay, made them far more swift than our many-oared biggest acáltin, and far more agile than our smallest. Besides the boatmen who controlled the vessels' movements, each carried twenty Spanish soldiers who stood on shelves behind those high sides. Thus they had the significant advantage of holding the height in any water battle with our low-slung canoes, and even stood high enough to discharge their weapons across our causeways.

On the day they made their trial voyage from Texcóco into the lake, Cortés himself was aboard the leading craft, which he called *La Capitana*. A number of our largest war canoes rowed out from Tenochtítlan and through the Great Dike, to engage them in the most open expanse of the lake. Each canoe carried sixty warriors, each of whom was armed with a bow and many arrows, an atlatl and several javelins. But on the choppy waters, the white men's heavier craft made much more stable platforms from which to discharge projectiles, so their harquebuses and crossbows were lethally more accurate than our men's hand-held bows. Besides, their soldiers had to expose only their heads and arms and weapons, so our arrows either struck in their boats' high sides or went harmlessly over them. But our men in the low, open canoes were exposed to the darts and metal pellets, and many of them fell dead or wounded. So the canoes' steersmen desperately tried to keep at a safer range, and that meant a distance too great for our warriors to fling their javelins. Before very long, all our war canoes came ig-nominiously home, and the enemy craft disdained to pursue them. For a while they almost gaily danced in intricate crossings and patterns, as if to show they *owned* the lake, before going back to Texcóco. But they were out again the next day, and every day after that, and they did more than dance.

By then, Cortés's under-officers and their various companies had marched all the way around the lake district, laying waste or capturing and occupying every community in their path, until at that time they had reassembled in two sizable armies, positioned on the headlands jutting into the lake exactly north and south of our island. It only remained for them to destroy or subdue the larger and more numerous cities situated around the lake's western shore, and they would have Tenochtítlan completely surrounded.

They went about it almost leisurely. While the other half of Cortés's army was resting in Texcóco, after its incredible labor of transporting those battle boats overland, the boats themselves went back and forth over the entire expanse of Lake Texcóco east of the Great Dike, clearing it of every other craft. They rammed and overturned, or they seized and captured, or they killed the occupants of every single canoe that plied the waters. And those were not war canoes: they were the acáltin of everyday fishermen and fowlers and freighters peaceably carrying goods from one place to another. Very soon, the winged battle boats *did* own all that end of the lake. Not a fisherman dared to put out from shore, even to net a meal for his own family. Only at our end of the lake, inside the dike, could the normal water traffic continue, and that did not continue for long.

Cortés finally moved his resting reserve army out of Texcóco, dividing it into two equal parts which separately made their way around the lake to join the other two forces poised north and south of us. And while that was being done, the battle boats breached the Great Dike. Their soldiers had only to sweep the length of it with their harquebuses and crossbows, and kill or rout all the unarmed dike workers who could have closed the flood-protection gates to impede them. Then the boats slid through those passages and were in Mexíca waters. Though Cuautémoc immediately sent warriors to stand shoulder to shoulder along the northern and southern causeways, they could not long repel the advance of the boats, which headed directly for the causeways' canoe passages. While some of the white soldiers cleared away the defenders with their hail of metal pellets and crossbow darts, other soldiers leaned over the boats' sides to pry loose and topple into the water the wooden bridges that spanned those gaps. So the battle boats got past the last barriers, and inside them, and, as they had done in the outer reaches of the lake, they cleared this end too of all water traffic: war canoes, freight acáltin, everything.

"The white men command all the causeways and the waterways as well," said the Snake Woman. "When they besiege the other cities on the mainland, we have no way of sending our men to reinforce those cities. What is worse, we have no way of getting anything *from* the mainland. No additional forces, no additional weapons. And no food."

"There is enough in the island storehouses to sustain us for some while," said Cuautémoc, adding bitterly: "We can thank the small pocks that there are fewer people to be fed than there might have been. And we have also the chinámpa crops."

The Snake Woman said, "The storehouses contain only dried maize, and the chinámpa are planted only with delicacies. Tomatoes and chilis and coriander and the like. It will be a quaint diet—poor men's tortillas and mush, garnished with elegant condiments."

"That quaint diet you will remember fondly," said Cuautémoc, "when your belly has Spanish steel in it instead."

With the boats keeping our warriors pent on our island, Cortés's land troops resumed their march around the western curve of the mainland and, one after another, the cities there were forced to surrender. First to fall was Tepeyáca, our nearest neighbor on the northern headland, then the southern promontory towns of Ixtapalápan and Mexicaltzínco. Then Tenayúca in the northwest, and Azcapotzálco. Then Coyohuácan in the southwest. The circle was closing, and we in Tenochtítlan no longer required quimíchime spies to tell us of what was happening. As our mainland allies fell or surrendered, numbers of their warriors survived to flee to our island, under cover of night, either coming in acáltin and managing to elude the patrolling battle boats, or sneaking across the causeways and swimming the gaps in them, or swimming all the long way across the water.

On some days, Cortés was astride his horse She-Mule, directing the implacable progress of his land forces. On other days, he was in his boat *La Capitana,* directing with signal flags the movements of his other craft and the discharge of their weapons, killing or dispersing any warriors who showed themselves on the shore of the mainland or on our island's truncated causeways. To fend off those harrying craft, we on Tenochtítlan contrived the only defense possible. Every usable piece of wood on the island was sharpened at one end, and divers took those pointed stakes underwater and fixed them firmly, angled outward, just under the surface of the shallows all about the island. Had we not done that, Cortés's battle boats could have come right into our canals and to the city's very center. The defense proved its worth when one of the boats one day moved close, apparently intending to tear up some of our food-growing chinámpa, and impaled itself on one or more of those stakes. Our warriors immediately sent flocks of arrows at it, and may have killed some of the occupants before they worked the boat loose and retreated to the mainland to patch it. Thereafter, since the Spanish boatmen had no way of knowing how far from the island our sharp stakes were planted, they kept a discreet distance.

Then Cortés's land troops began to find their cannons which our men had tumbled into the lake during the Sad Night—because such heavy objects could not be thrown very far—and they began retrieving them. The immersion had not, as we might have hoped, ruined the cursed things. They needed only to be cleaned of mud and dried and recharged to make them workable again. As they were recovered, Cortés had the first thirteen of them mounted, one apiece, in his battle boats, and those boats took up positions offshore of the cities where his troops were fighting, and there discharged their lightning and thunder and rain of man-killing projectiles. Unable to defend themselves any longer, when simultaneously beset from the front and from the side, the cities had to surrender, and when the last of them surrendered—Tlácopan, capital of the Tecpanéca, third bastion of The Triple Alliance—the encircling arms of Cortés's land forces met and joined.

His battle boats were no longer needed to support the troops ashore, but, the very next day, they were moving about the lake again and discharging their cannons. We on the island could watch them, and for a while we could not understand their intent, since they were aiming neither at us nor at any apparent targets on the mainland. Then, when we heard and saw the crash of a cannon ball's destructive impact, we understood. The heavy projectiles battered first the old aqueduct from Chapultépec, then the one built by Ahuítzotl from Coyohuácan, and they broke them both.

The Snake Woman said, "The aqueducts were our last connections to the mainland. We are now as helpless as a boat adrift without oars on a stormy sea full of evil monsters. We are surrounded, unprotected, fully exposed. Every other nearby nation which has not voluntarily joined the white men has been overrun by them and now does their bidding. Except for the fugitive warriors among us, there is no one but us—the Mexíca alone—against the entire One World."

"That is fitting," Cuautémoc said calmly. "If it should be our tonáli not to be victorious at last, then let The One World forever remember—that the Mexíca were the last to be vanquished."

"But Lord Speaker," pleaded the Snake Woman, "the aqueducts were also our last link to life. We might have fought for a time without fresh food, but for how long can we fight without drinkable water?"

"Tlácotzin," said Cuautémoc, as gently as a good teacher addressing a backward student. "There was another time—long ago—when the Mexíca stood alone, in this very place, unwanted and detested by all other peoples. They had only weeds to eat, only the brackish lake water to drink. In those dismally hopeless circumstances, they might well have knelt to their surrounding enemies, to be scattered or absorbed, to be forgotten by history. But they did not. They stood, and they stayed, and they built all this." He gestured with his hand to encompass the whole splendor of Tenochtítlan. "Whatever the end is to be, history *cannot* forget them now. The Mexíca stood. The Mexíca stand. The Mexíca will stand until they can stand no longer."

After the aqueducts, our city was the target of the cannons, those repositioned on the mainland and those mounted on the boats which constantly circled the island. The iron balls coming from Chapultépec were the most damaging and frightening, for the white men had hauled some of their cannons all the way to the crest of that hill and from there they could send the balls flying in a high arc so that they dropped almost directly downward, like great iron raindrops, on Tenochtítlan. One of the very first to fall in the city, I might remark, demolished the temple of Huitzilopóchtli atop the Great Pyramid. At which, our priests cried "woe!" and "awful omen!" and commenced to hold ceremonies that combined abject prayers for the war god's forgiveness and desperate prayers for the war god's intercession on our behalf.

Although the cannons continued that first thundering for some days, they did so only at intervals, and it seemed a most desultory attack compared to what I knew those cannons *could* do. I believe Cortés was hoping to make us concede that we were marooned and defenseless and inevitably to be defeated, to make us surrender without a fight, as he would expect any sensible people to do under those conditions. I do not believe he was showing any merciful compunction about having to slay us; he merely wanted to take the city intact, so he could present to his King Carlos the colony of New Spain complete with a capital that was superior to any city in Old Spain.

However, Cortés is and was an impatient man. He did not waste many days waiting for us to take the sensible course of surrender. He had his artificers construct light, portable wooden bridges and, using them to span the gaps in all the causeways, he sent heavy forces of his men running to the city in a sudden onslaught from all three directions at once. But our warriors were not then weakened by hunger, and the three columns of Spaniards and their allies were stopped as if they had run into a solid stone wall encircling the island. Many of them died and the remainder retreated, though not as quickly as they had come, for they were bearing many wounded.

Cortés waited for some days, and tried again in the same manner, and with even worse results. That time, when the enemy poured onto the island, our war canoes darted out and their warriors climbed onto the causeways behind the first waves of attackers. They kicked away the portable bridges and so had a goodly portion of the assault forces marooned *with us* in the city. The trapped Spaniards fought for their lives; but their native allies knew better what was in store, and fought until they were killed instead of captured. That night our whole island was lighted with celebratory torches and urn fires and incense fires and altar fires—the Great Pyramid in particular was brightly illuminated—so Cortés and the other white men could see, if they approached close enough, and if they cared to watch, what happened to their forty or so comrades we had caught alive.

And evidently Cortés did witness that mass sacrifice, or enough of it to put him in a retaliatory rage. He would exterminate all of us in the city, even if in the process he had to pulverize much of the city he wanted to preserve. He suspended his invasion attempts, but subjected our city to a vicious and unremitting cannonade, the balls being discharged from the cannons as rapidly and regularly as I suppose could be done without the cannons' melting from the prolonged exertion. The projectiles plummeted down on us from the mainland and whistled across the water from the circling boats. Our city began to crumble, and many of our people died. A single cannon ball could knock a sizable chunk out of an edifice even as massively built as the Great Pyramid—and many of them did, until that once beautifully smooth structure looked like a mound of bread dough gnawed and nibbled by giant rats. A single cannon ball could knock down one entire wall of a sturdy stone house, and an adobe house would simply go all to clods and dust.

That iron rain went on for at least two months, day after day, abating only at night. But even during the nights, the cannoneers would send three or four balls crashing down among us, at unpredictably irregular intervals, just to insure that our sleep was made uneasy, if not impossible, and that we had no chance to rest undisturbed. After some time, the white men's iron projectiles were used up, and they had to gather and employ rounded stones. Those were slightly less destructive to our city buildings, but they often shattered on impact, and their flying fragments were even more destructive to human flesh.

But those who died in that manner at least died quickly. The rest of us seemed doomed to a slower and more wretchedly dwindling death. Because the stores in the granaries had to last as long as possible, the dispensing officials doled out the dry maize in the meagerest amounts that would help sustain life. For a while, we were able also to eat the dogs and fowl of the island, and we shared the fish caught by men who sneaked out at night upon the causeways with nets, or out onto the chinámpa to dangle lines down among their roots. But eventually all the dogs and fowl were gone, and even the fish began to shun the island vicinity. Then we divided and ate all but the absolutely inedible creatures in the public menagerie, and the very rarest and most beautiful specimens, with which the keepers could not bear to part. Those remaining animals were kept alive—indeed, were kept in rather better health than their keepers—by being fed the bodies of our slaves who perished of hunger.

In time, we resorted to catching rats and mice and lizards. Our children, those few who had survived the small pocks, got quite adept at snaring almost every bird foolhardy enough to perch on the island. Still later, we cut the flowers of our roof gardens and stripped the leaves from the trees and made cooked greens of them. Toward the end, we were searching those gardens for edible insects, and peeling the bark from the trees, and we were chewing rabbit-fur blankets and hide garments and the fawnskin pages of books for whatever meat value might be extracted from them. Some people, trying to trick their bellies into thinking they had been fed, filled them by eating the lime cement from the rubble of broken buildings.

The fish had not left our neighborhood for fear of being caught; they left because our surrounding waters had become so foul. Though the rainy season was by then upon us, the rains fell during only a part of each afternoon. We set out every pot and bowl to catch it, and hung out lengths of cloth to be drenched and wrung, but, for all our efforts, there was seldom more than a trickle of fresh rainwater for each parched mouth. So, after our initial revulsion, we got accustomed to drinking the lake's brackish water. However, since there was no longer any means of collecting and carrying away the island's wastes of garbage and human excrement, those substances got into the canals, thence into the lake. Also, since we would feed none but slaves to the menagerie beasts, we had no way of disposing of our other dead except to commit their bodies to that same lake. Cuautémoc ordered that the corpses be shoved off the island only on its western side, because the eastern lake was the wider water and was more or less constantly refreshed by the prevailing east wind, thus he hoped that the water on that side could be kept less contaminated. But the seeping sewage and decomposing bodies inevitably dirtied the water on every side of the island. Since we still had to drink it when thirst drove us to it, we strained it through cloths and then boiled it. Even so, it knotted our guts with agonies of gripes and fluxes. Of our older people and young children, many died just from drinking that putrid water.

One night, when he could no longer watch his people suffer so, Cuautémoc called all the city's populace to gather in The Heart of the One World during that night's lull in the cannonade, and I think everyone who could still walk was there. We stood about the pits in what had been the sleek marble paving of the plaza, surrounded by the jagged upcrops remaining of what had been the undulating Snake Wall, while the Revered Speaker addressed us from partway up what remained of the Great Pyramid's shattered staircase:

"If Tenochtítlan is to last even a little longer, it must be no longer a city but a fortification, and a fort must be manned by those who can fight. I am proud of the loyalty and endurance shown by all my people, but the time has come when I must regretfully ask an end to your allegiance. There still remains one storehouse unopened, but only one. . . ."

The assembled crowd neither cheered nor clamored in demand. It merely murmured, but the combined sound was like the hungry rumbling of a very large stomach.

"When I unseal that store," Cuautémoc went on, "the maize will be shared out equally among all who apply. Now, it can provide every person in this city perhaps one last and very scant meal. Or it would suffice to feed our warriors slightly better, to strengthen them for fighting to the end, whenever that end shall come and whatever that end may be. I will not command you, my people. I will only ask that you make the choice and the decision."

The people made no sound at all.

He resumed, "I have this night had the northern causeway spanned so it can be crossed. The enemy waits warily on the other side, wondering why that has been done. I did it so that all of you who can depart, and will, may do so. I do not know what you will find yonder in Tepeyáca—food and relief or a Flowery Death. But I beg you who can no longer fight; take this opportunity to leave Tenochtítlan. It will be no desertion, no admission of defeat, and you will incur no shame in the departure. To the contrary, you will enable our city to stand in defiance a while longer. I say no more."

None went hurriedly or even willingly, all went in tears and grief, but they recognized the practicality of Cuautémoc's plea, and in that one night the city emptied of its old and its youngest people, its ill and crippled and infirm, its priests and temple attendants, all who could no longer be of use in combat. Carrying bundles or tumplined packs of what few most valued possessions they could snatch up as they left, they drifted northward through the streets of all four quarters of Tenochtítlan, began to converge in the area of the Tlaltelólco market, then formed a column crossing the causeway. They were met with no bursts of lightning and thunder at the northern end. As I learned later, the white men yonder were simply indifferent to their arrival, and the Texcaltéca occupying that position deemed those stumbling, emaciated seekers of refuge too scrawny even to be worth sacrificing as a celebration of victory, and the people of Tepeyáca—though themselves captives of the occupying forces—made them welcome, with food and clean water and shelter.

In Tenochtítlan there remained Cuautémoc, the other lords of his court and his Speaking Council, the wives and families of the Revered Speaker and some other nobles, several physicians and surgeons, all the knights and warriors still fit—and some few stubborn old men, myself among them, who had been in good enough health before the siege that we had not been severely weakened by it, and could still fight if necessary. There also remained the young women of fair health and strength and potential usefulness—and one elderly woman who, for all my urgings, declined to leave the sickbed she had occupied for some while past.

"I am less of a nuisance lying here," said Béu, "than being carried on a litter by others who can barely walk. Also, it has been a long time since I cared to eat much, and I can as easily eat nothing at all. My staying may earn me an earlier end to my tediously long illness. Besides, Záa, you yourself once ignored an opportunity to go safely away. It might be foolish, you said, but you wished to see the end of things." She smiled weakly. "Now, after all your foolishnesses I have put up with, would you refuse to let me share the one that will likely be your last?"

Cortés rightly concluded, from the sudden evacuation of Tenochtítlan and the skeletal appearance of those who left, that the remaining inhabitants must also have weakened considerably. So, on the following day, he sent another frontal attack against the city, though he did not do it quite so impetuously as he had done before. The day began with the heaviest rain of projectiles that had yet fallen on us; he must have worked his cannons very near their melting point. No doubt he hoped the we would still be cowering under shelter long after the devastating rain stopped. But even then, when the shore cannons desisted, he kept his battle boats hovering about the northern end of the island, discharging a barrage into that half of the city, while his foot soldiers streamed across the southern causeway.

They found us not cowering. Indeed, what they did find made the front ranks of white men stop so suddenly that the following ranks rather untidily piled up behind them. For we had posted, at each place where the invaders could arrive upon the island, one of the fattest men among us—well, at least plump, compared to the rest of us—and the Spaniards found him simply strolling there, contentedly belching while he munched on a haunch of dog or rabbit or some such meat. If the soldiers had seen it close, the meat was in reality an awful green from having been so long hoarded just for that gesture of ostentation.

But they did not see it close. The fat man quickly vanished, while a host of much leaner men suddenly stood up from the broken buildings and wreckage all about, hurling javelins. Though many of the marauders were felled in that moment, some pressed forward, only to meet other warriors armed with maquáhuime, and others quailed backward, where they were showered with arrows. All of them who survived that surprising and firm defense retreated even farther, all the way back to the mainland. I am sure they reported the apparition of the well-fed and still-feeding man—and I am sure Cortés laughed at that pathetic bit of bravado on our part—but they also reported, quite matter-of-factly, that the rubble of the city provided even better defensive positions for its occupants than the city would have done, had it been left entire.

"Very well," said the Captain-General, according to later report. "I had hoped to save at least some of it, for the amazement of our countrymen who will come later as colonists. But we will level it . . . level every standing stone and timber of it . . . level it until not even a scorpion has a hiding place from which to creep upon us."

Of course that is what he did, and this is how he did it. While the boats' cannons continued to pound the northern half of the city, Cortés wheeled several of his shore cannons along the southern and western causeways; they were followed by fighting men, some on horses, some on foot, accompanied by staghounds; and those were followed by many more men armed only with mallets and axes and prybars and battering beams. First the cannons were employed, to blow down everything possible in front of them, and to kill our warriors in hiding, or at least to keep them crouching harmlessly. Then the soldiers advanced into the area of devastation; when our warriors rose up to fight, they were ridden down by the horsemen or overrun by the foot soldiers. Our men fought bravely, but they were weak from hunger and half dazed by the cannonade they had just endured, and they invariably died or had to withdraw deeper into the city.

Some of them tried to remain undetected in their hiding places while the fighting swept on past them, hoping that when the enemy was later off guard they could make just one killing javelin throw or maquáhuitl stroke before they were slain. But none got that chance; they were always quickly unearthed; that was what the soldiers had brought the dogs for. Those huge staghounds could sniff out a man, however securely hidden, and if they themselves did not rend him apart, they disclosed his position to the soldiers. Then, as the area was cleared of defenders and danger, the working parties moved in with their tools of demolition, and they cleared whatever was left. They tore down houses and towers and temples and monuments, and they set afire everything that would burn. When they were done, there remained only a flat and featureless plot of ground.

That would be one day's work. On the following day, the

cannons would be able to advance unimpeded across that cleared area and batter a new portion, to be followed by the soldiers and the dogs, then the demolishers. And so, day by day, the city diminished a little more, as if afflicted by The Being Eaten by the Gods. We in the yet unafflicted sections of the city could stand on our rooftops and watch the progress of the leveling, and its approach toward us.

I remember the day the wreckers reached The Heart of the One World. First they amused themselves by shooting fire arrows at those tremendous feather banners which, although sadly tattered, still floated majestically overhead, and the banners, one by one, disappeared in flares of flame. But many more days were required for the destruction of that city within a city—the temples, the tlachtli court, the skull rack, the palaces and court buildings. Though the Great Pyramid was already a gnawed ruin, and could afford no stronghold or concealment worth Cortés's concern, he must have felt that, simply because it was Tenochtítlan's most magnificent and distinguishing symbol, it had to come down. It did not come down easily, even when swarmed over by hundreds of workmen with heavy steel tools, but at last it yielded, layer by layer, revealing the older pyramids inside it, each of them smaller and more crudely built, and they came down too. Cortés had his men work rather more gently and carefully when they began dismantling the palace of Motecuzóma Xocóyotl, for he obviously expected to find the nation's treasury reinstalled in the thick-walled chambers there. When he did not, he let the demolition proceed with a vengeance.

I remember also the burning of the great menagerie just outside the plaza's fragmented Snake Wall, for that day I was watching from the roof of a house close enough that I could hear the bellowing and roaring and howling and screeching of its occupants as they burned alive. True, the menagerie's population had been reduced by our having been forced to eat a good number of its occupants, but still there remained many wondrous beasts and birds and reptiles. Some of them may now be irreplaceable, should you Spaniards ever decide to build a similar showplace. For example, at that time the hall of animals exhibited a totally white jaguar, a rarity we Mexíca had never seen before and no one may ever see again.

Cuautémoc, well knowing the weakness of his warriors, had intended that they should merely fight a defensive withdrawal, delaying the enemy's advance insofar as possible, and slaying as many invaders as they could in the process. But the warriors themselves were so outraged by the desecration of The Heart of the One World that they exceeded their orders, and their anger gave them a surge of strength, and they several times emerged from the wreckage around the plaza, shouting war cries and pounding their weapons on their shields, to take offensive instead of defensive action. Even our women were infuriated and joined in, flinging down from rooftops nests full of wasps, and fragments of stone, and other things less mentionable, upon the despoilers.

Our warriors did kill some of the enemy soldiers and wreckers, and perhaps somewhat slowed their work of destruction. But a greater number of our men died in the doing so, and they were every time beaten back. Nevertheless, to discourage their harassment, Cortés sent his cannons continuing on to the north, blasting away more of the city, and his soldiers and dogs and work parties had to follow the cannons, to level what they left. It was because they moved on that they neglected to tear down this House of Song in which we sit today, and some few other buildings of no particular account in this southern half of the island.

But not many buildings were left, not anywhere, and those few stuck up from the prevailing wasteland like the last few, wide-apart teeth in an old man's gums, and my house was not among them. I suppose I should congratulate myself that when my house fell, I was not inside it. By that time, the city's entire remaining population was sheltering in the Tlaltelólco quarter, and in the very middle of it, to be as far as possible from the continuous barrage of cannon projectiles and fire arrows from the circling battle boats. The warriors and the stronger survivors lived in the open of the marketplace, and all the women and weaker folk were crammed into the houses already crowded by the neighborhood's resident families clumped together for refuge. Cuautémoc and his court occupied the old palace that had once belonged to Moquíhuix, the last ruler of Tlaltelólco when it was still an independent city. As a lord, I also was accorded a small room there, which I shared with Béu. Although she had again protested against being moved from her home, I had carried her thither in my arms. So, with Cuautémoc and many others, I stood atop the Tlaltelólco pyramid, watching, on the day Cortés's wreckers moved into the Ixacuálco quarter where I had lived. I could not see, through the clouds of cannon smoke and the dust of pulverized limestone, exactly when my own house went down. But when the enemy departed at the day's end, the Ixacuálco quarter was, like most of the island's southern half, a barren desert.

I do not know if Cortés was ever afterward informed of the fact that every wealthy pochtécatl of our city had in his house—as I did—a concealed treasure chamber. He clearly did not know at that time, for his work parties toppled every house indiscriminately and haphazardly, and, in the smoke and dust of each one's collapse, no one ever glimpsed the wrapped packets or bales of gold and gems and plumes and dyes and such, which got even more invisibly buried among the rubble and were later swept aside in the island's clearance and enlargement. Of course, even had Cortés scavenged every one of the pochtéca's valuables, they would have amounted to far less than the still-lost treasury, but they would yet have made a gift to astonish and delight his King Carlos. So I watched that day's devastation with some ironic satisfaction, even though, at the day's end, I was an old man poorer than the young child I had been when I first saw Tenochtítlan.

Well, so was every other Mexícatl still alive, including even our Revered Speaker. The end came not long after that, and it came quickly when it came. We had been for countless days devoid of every commodity that could be remotely regarded as food, and our very ability to move about, even to talk to each other, was enfeebled to listlessness. Cortés and his army, as relentless and numerous and voracious as those ants that strip whole forests clean, finally reached the Tlaltelólco marketplace and began tearing down the pyramid there, meaning that we fugitives were so huddled in what little space was left to hide that we scarcely had even a place to stand in comfort. Still Cuautémoc would have stood, if he had had to do it on one foot, but, after I and the Snake Woman and some other counselors had privately conferred, we went to him and said:

"Lord Speaker, if you are taken by the outlanders, the whole of the Mexíca nation falls with you. But if you escape, the rulership goes where you go. Even if every other person on this island is slain or captured, Cortés will not have bested the Mexíca."

"Escape," he said dully. "To where? To do what?"

"To go into exile, with just your closest family and a few of your chief lords. It is true that we no longer have trustworthy allies anywhere among the lands closest to here. But there are farther countries from which you can recruit supporters. It may be a long time before you can hope to return in force and triumph, but however long it may take, the Mexíca will still be unvanquished."

"What farther countries?" he asked, without enthusiasm.

The other lords looked to me, and I said, "To Aztlan, Revered Speaker. Go back to our very beginnings."

He stared as if I were mad. But I reminded him how we had, only comparatively recently, renewed our ties with our cousins of our first homeplace, and I gave him a map I had drawn to show him the way there. I added, "You can expect a hearty welcome, Lord Cuautémoc. When their Speaker Tliléctic-Mixtli left here, Motecuzóma sent with him a force of our warriors and a number of Mexíca families skilled in all our modern crafts of city building. You may find they have already made of Aztlan a miniature Tenochtítlan. At the very least, the Aztéca could be the seed kernels—as once before they were—from which to grow a whole new and mighty nation."

It took a good deal more persuasion to get Cuautémoc to agree, but I will not relate it all, since it all went for naught. I still think the plan should have succeeded; it was well conceived and executed; but the gods decreed that it should not. At twilight, when the battle boats ceased their day-long barrage and began to turn homeward toward the mainland, a goodly number of our men accompanied Cuautémoc and his chosen companions down to the edge of the island. They all got into canoes, and at a signal the many canoes paddled into the lake, all at once but each in a different direction, moving fast, appearing to be a sudden mass scurry for safety. The acáli carrying Cuautémoc and his abbreviated court headed for the little mainland bay between Tenayúca and Azcapotzálco. Since there were few if any habitations at that spot, it was presumably unguarded by any of Cortés's camps or sentries, and Cuautémoc should easily have been able to slip inland from there and keep going northwest to Aztlan.

But the battle boats, spying the sudden eruption of acáltin from the island, turned back and began to whisk busily about among them, seeking to determine if they really *were* in rout. And, by ill chance, one of the boat captains was astute enough to notice that one of the occupants of one canoe was rather too richly dressed to be a mere warrior. That boat dropped iron hooks, and grappled the canoe fast to its side, and hauled aboard the Revered Speaker, and carried him straight to the Captain-General Cortés.

I was not present at that meeting, but I learned later that Cuautémoc spoke, through the interpreter Malíntzin, saying, "I did not surrender. It was for my people's sake that I sought to elude you. But you caught me fairly." He pointed to the dagger at Cortés's belt. "Since I was taken in war, I deserve— and I request—the death of a warrior. I ask that you slay me now, where I stand."

Magnanimous in victory, or at least unctuous, Cortés said, "No, you did not surrender, and you have not ceded your rule. I decline to slay you, and I insist that you retain your leadership of your people. For we have much work to do, and I pray you will help me do it. Let us together build your city to a new grandeur, my esteemed Lord Cuautémoc."

Cortés probably pronounced it Guatemoc, as he always later did. I think I long ago mentioned, reverend friars, that the name Cuautémoc meant Swooping Eagle, but I suppose it was inevitable and even fitting that, after that day—by our calendar the day One Serpent of the year Three House; by your calendar the thirteenth day of August in the year one thousand five hundred twenty and one—our last Revered Speaker's name was ever afterward translated into Spanish as Falling Eagle.

✠

For some while after the fall of Tenochtítlan, life was not much changed in most of The One World. Outside the immediate area of The Triple Alliance, no other part of these lands had been so devastated, and there were probably many parts where the people were not yet aware that they resided not in The One World but in a place called New Spain. Though they were cruelly ravaged by the mysterious new diseases, they seldom saw a Spaniard or a Christian, so they had no new laws or gods imposed on them, and they went on with their accustomed ways of life—harvesting, hunting, fishing, whatever—as they had done through all the sheaves of years before.

But here in the lake lands, life was much altered, and it was hard, and it has never got easier, and I doubt that it ever will. From the day after Cuautémoc's capture, Cortés concentrated all his attention and energy on the rebuilding of this city—or I should say *our* energy. For he decreed that, since it was entirely the fault of us fractious Mexíca that Tenochtítlan had been destroyed, its restoration as the City of Mexíco should be our responsibility. Though his architects drew the plans, and his artificers oversaw the work, and his most brutal soldiers wielded the whips to make the work get done, it was our people who did the work, and we who supplied the materials, and if we would eat after our labors, it was we who had to provide the food. So the quarriers of Xaltócan worked harder than ever in their lives, and foresters laid naked the lakeside hills to cut beams and planks, and our former warriors and pochtéca became foragers and carriers of what foodstuffs and other necessities they could forcibly extort from the surrounding lands, and our women—when they were not being openly molested by the white soldiers, even raped before the eyes of all who cared to watch—were pressed into service as porters and messengers, and even small children were put to work mixing mortar.

Of course, the first things attended to were those most important. The broken aqueducts were repaired, and then the foundations were laid for what would be your cathedral church, while directly in front of it were erected the pillory and the gallows. Those were the first functioning structures in the new City of Mexíco, for they were much exercised to inspire us to unceasing and conscientious labor. Those who slacked at any job were strangled on the gallows, or were branded with the "prisoner of war" mark on the cheek and then were exposed in the pillory for the outlanders to pelt with stones and horse droppings, or they were broken by the whips of the overseers. But those who worked hard died almost as frequently as did the slackers, from such causes as being forced to lift a stone so heavy that they ruptured their insides.

I was far more fortunate then most, for Cortés gave me employment as an interpreter. With all the orders and instructions to be relayed from architects to builders, with all the new laws and proclamations and edicts and sermons to be translated to the people, there was more work than Malíntzin alone could manage, and the man Aguilar, who might have assisted to some degree, had long ago died in a battle somewhere. So Cortés engaged me, and even paid me a small wage in Spanish coin, in addition to giving me and Béu accommodation in the splendid residence—what had once been Motecuzóma's country palace near Quaunáhuac—which he had appropriated for himself and Malíntzin and his ranking officers and their concubines, and where he also kept under his eye Cuautémoc and his family and courtiers.

Perhaps I should apologize, though I do not know to whom, that I took employment with the white men, rather than die defying them. But, since the battles were all over, and I had not perished in the struggle, it seemed my tonáli ordained that for at least a while longer I should struggle not to perish. I had once been bidden, "Stand! Endure! Remember!" and that was what I determined to do.

For some time, a major part of my interpreting duties consisted in my translating Cortés's incessant and insistent demands to know what had become of the Mexíca's vanished treasury. If I had been a younger man, and able to work at any other trade that would have supported myself and my ever-ailing wife, I would right then have quit that degrading occupation. It required me to sit with Cortés and his officers, as if I were one of them, while they bullied and insulted my fellow lords, calling them "damned, lying, greedy, treacherous, clutching Indians!" I was especially ashamed of myself when I had to participate in the repeated interrogations of the Uey-Tlatoáni Cuautémoc, whom Cortés no longer addressed with unction or even the least respect. To Cortés's reiterated queries, Cuautémoc could or would say nothing but a disclaimer:

"To the best of my knowledge, Captain-General, my predecessor Cuitláhuac left the treasure in the lake where you threw it."

At which, Cortés would snarl, "I have sent down my best swimmers and yours. They find nothing but *mud!*"

And Cuautémoc could or would make only the rejoinder, "The mud is soft. Your cannons made the whole Lake Texcóco tremble. Any objects as heavy as gold would have settled ever deeper in that ooze."

I felt most ashamed on the day I had to watch the "persuasion" of Cuautémoc and the two old men of his Speaking Council who had accompanied him to that session of questioning. After I had many times translated those same words so many times exchanged before, Cortés exploded in a temper. He ordered his soldiers to rake from the palace kitchen's hearth three large bowls of embers, and made the three lords of the Mexíca sit with their bare feet in those smoldering coals while he again asked the identical questions and they, gritting their teeth against the pain, gave the identical replies. At last, Cortés threw up his hands in a gesture of disgust and stalked out of the room. The three cautiously stood up from their chairs and stepped out of the bowls and began gingerly to make their way to their quarters. The two old men and the younger one, doing their best to support each other, hobbled on their blistered and blackened feet, and I heard one of the elders moan:

"*Ayya,* Lord Speaker, why do you not tell them something else? *Anything?* I hurt unbearably!"

"Be silent!" snapped Cuautémoc. "Do you think *I* am this moment walking in a pleasure garden?"

Though I loathed Cortés and myself and our association, I refrained from any deed or remark that might arouse his displeasure and endanger my soft situation, because, within a year or two, there were many of my fellows who would happily have replaced me as Cortés's collaborator, and could adequately have done so. More and more of the Mexíca and other peoples—of nations both inside and outside The Triple Alliance—were hastening to learn Spanish and to apply for baptism as Christians. They did it not so much from servility as from ambition, and even necessity. Cortés had early promulgated a law that no "Indian" could hold any position higher than that of common laborer until and unless he was a confirmed Christian and proficient in the conquerors' spoken tongue.

I was already recognized by the Spaniards as Don Juan Damasceno, and Malíntzin was Doña Marina, and the other Spaniards' concubines were Doña Luisa and Doña María Immaculada and the like, and some few nobles succumbed to the temptation of the advantages of being Christian and speaking Spanish; the former Snake Woman, for instance, became Don Juan Tlácotl Velásquez. But, as might have been expected, most others of the onetime pípiltin, from Cuautémoc on down, disdained the white men's religion and language and appellations. However admirable their stand, it proved to be a mistake, for it left them nothing *but* their pride. It was the people of the lowest classes, and the lowest-born of the middle classes, and even slaves of the nethermost tlacótli class, who did besiege the chaplains and the missionary friars for instruction in Christianity, and for baptism with Spanish names. It was they who, to learn the Spanish tongue, eagerly gave their own sisters and daughters in payment to the Spanish soldiers who had enough education and intelligence to teach it.

Thus it was the mediocrities and dregs of society who, having no inborn pride to discard, freed themselves of the drudge work and got themselves put in charge of the drudges— who in an earlier day had been their superiors, their leaders, even their owners. Those upstart "imitation whites," as others of us called them, eventually were given posts in the increasingly complex government of the city, and were made the chiefs of outlying towns, even of several negligible provinces. It might have been regarded as praiseworthy: that a nobody could uplift himself to eminence; except that I cannot recall a single one who utilized his eminence for the good of anyone but himself.

Such a man was suddenly superior to all who had been his superiors and equals, and that was as high as his ambition reached. Whether he achieved the post of provincial governor or merely that of timekeeper at some building project, he became a despot over everyone under him. The timekeeper could denounce as a trifler or drunkard any workman who did not fawn on him and bribe him with gifts. He could condemn that workman to anything from a cheek brand to a hanging on the gallows. The governor could debase onetime lords and ladies to garbage collectors and street sweepers, while he forced their daughters to submit to what you Spaniards call "the rights of the señorío." However, I must in fairness say that the new nobility of Spanish-speaking Christians behaved equally toward *all* their countrymen. As they humiliated and tormented the formerly highest classes, so did they similarly mistreat the lower classes from which they themselves had sprung. They made everybody—except their own appointed superiors, of course—far more miserable than any meanest slave had been in years gone by. And, while the total reversal of society did not physically affect me, I was troubled by my realization that, as I told Béu, "These imitation whites are the people who will write our history!"

Though I had my own snug position in the new society of New Spain during those years, I can slightly excuse my reluctance to give it up on the ground that I sometimes could use my position to help others besides myself. At least once in a while, and if Malíntzin or one of the later-engaged other interpreters was not present to betray me, I could word my translating in such a way as to enhance the plea of some petitioner seeking a favor, or to mitigate the punishment of some accused malefactor. In the meantime, since Béu and I were enjoying free sustenance and lodging, I was able to hoard away my wages against the day when—perhaps through my own fault, or because of some visible worsening of Béu's condition—I should be expelled from my employment and from the Quaunáhuac palace.

As it happened, I left the position of my own accord, and it happened like this. By the third year after the Conquest, that impatient man Cortés was becoming impatient with his no longer adventurous role as administrator of many details and arbitrator of petty disputes. Much of the City of Méxíco had by then been built, and the building of the remainder was well under way. Then as now, about a thousand new white men arrived each year in New Spain—most of them, with their white women, settling in or about the lake region, carving out their own Little Spains of the best lands, and appropriating our sturdiest people as "prisoners of war" to work those lands. All the newcomers so swiftly and firmly consolidated their positions as overlords that any uprising against them was unthinkable. The Triple Alliance had become irreversibly New Spain, and was functioning, I gathered, as well as Cuba or any other Spanish colony—its native population subdued and resigned, if not notably happy or comfortable in that subjection—and Cortés appeared confident that his under-officers and his appointed imitation whites were capable of maintaining it so. He himself wanted new lands to conquer, or, more precisely, he wanted to view more of the lands he regarded as already his.

"Captain-General," I said to him, "you are already acquainted with the country between the eastern coast and here. The lands between here and the western coast are not greatly different, and to the north are mostly wastelands unworth the looking at. But to the south—*ayyo,* southward of here are majestic mountain ranges and verdant plains and impressive forests and, south of all, the jungle that is awesome and trackless and infinitely hazardous, but so full of wonders that no man should live out his life without venturing into it."

"Southward it is, then!" he cried, as if ordering a troop to move out that very moment. "You have been there? You know the country? You speak the languages?" I said yes and yes and yes, at which he did give a command: "You will guide us there."

"Captain-General," I said. "I am fifty and eight years old. That is a journey for young men of strength and stamina."

"A litter and bearers will be provided—and also some interesting companions for you," he said, and left me abruptly, to go and choose the soldiers for the expedition, so I had no chance to tell him anything about the impracticality of litters on steep mountainsides or in the jungle's tangle.

But I did not balk at going. It would be good to make one last long journey across this world, before my *very* last and longest, to the next. Though Béu might be lonesome while I was gone, she would be in capable hands. The palace servants knew her condition, and they served her tenderly and well, and they were discreet; Béu herself would only have to take care not to attract the notice of any of the resident Spaniards. As for me, old though I was by the calendar count, I did not yet

feel hopelessly decrepit. If I could survive the siege of Tenochtítlan, as I had done, I supposed I could survive the rigors
of Cortés's expedition. Given good fortune, I might *lose* him
there, or lead the train among people so revolted by the sight
of white men that they would slay us *all,* and I would then
have died to good purpose.

I was a trifle puzzled by Cortés's mention of "interesting
companions" for me, and, on the autumn day of our departure,
I was frankly astonished when I saw who they were: the three
Revered Speakers of the three nations of The Triple Alliance.
I wondered whether Cortés insisted on their coming along because he feared they might concoct some plot against him
during his absence, or because he wanted the people of the
southern lands to be impressed at the sight of such august
personages meekly following in his train.

They certainly made a sight to see, because their rich litters
were so often so unwieldy in so many terrains that the personages had to get out and walk, and because Cuautémoc had been
permanently crippled on that occasion of Cortés's persuasive
questioning. So, in many places along the trail, the local people
were treated to the spectacle of the Revered Speaker Cuautémoc
of the Mexíca limping and dangling from the shoulders of the
two others supporting him: on one side the Revered Speaker
Tétlapanquétzal of Tlácopan and on the other the Revered
Speaker Cohuanácoch of Texcóco.

But none of the three ever complained, even though they
must have realized, after a while, that I was deliberately leading
Cortés and his horsemen and foot soldiers along difficult trails
through country with which I was unfamiliar. I did it only
partly from the intent to make the expedition no pleasure trip
for the Spaniards, and the hope that they might never return
from it. Also, because it *was* to be my last journey abroad, I
had decided I might as well see some new country. So, after
taking them through the most rugged mountains of Uaxyácac,
then across the unlovely barrens of that isthmus between the
northern and southern seas, I took them northeast into the
swampiest interior of the Cupílco country. And that was where
at last, sick of the white men, sick of my association with
them, I went off and left them.

I should mention that, obviously to monitor the truthfulness of my own translating along the way, Cortés had brought along a second interpreter. For a change, it was not Malíntzin, since she was at that time still nursing her infant Martín Cortés, and I almost regretted her absence, for she was at least comely to look at. Her replacement was likewise a female, but a woman with the face and whine and disposition of a mosquito. She was one of those upstarts from the lowest class, who had become an imitation white by learning to speak Spanish and taking the Christian name of Florencia. However, since her only other language was Náhuatl, she was of no use in those foreign parts, except each night to service however many of the Spanish soldiers who had not been able to entice to their pallets, with gifts and the lure of curiosity, younger and more desirable local sluts.

One night in early spring, after having spent the day slogging through a particularly nasty and noisome swamp, we camped on a dry piece of ground in a grove of ceiba and amatl trees. We had eaten our evening meal and were resting around the several campfires, when Cortés came and squatted beside me and put a comradely arm about my shoulders and said:

"Look yonder, Juan Damasceno. That is a thing to be marveled at." I raised my topaz and looked where he pointed: at the three Revered Speakers sitting together, apart from the rest of the men. I had seen them sit like that many times on the journey, presumably discussing whatever is left to be discussed by rulers with nothing left to rule. Cortés said, "That is a sight infrequent enough in the *Old* World, believe me—three kings seated peaceably together—and it may never again be seen here. I should like a memento of it. Draw me a portrait of them, Juan Damasceno, just as they are, with their faces inclined toward each other in serious conversation."

It seemed an innocuous request. Indeed, for Hernán Cortés, it seemed unusually thoughtful, his recognition of a moment worth recording. So I willingly complied. I peeled a strip of bark from one of the amatl trees, and on its clean inner surface I drew, with a charred and pointed stick from the fire, the best picture I could make with such crude materials. The three Revered Speakers were individually recognizable, and I caught the solemnity of their faces, so that anyone looking at the picture could divine that they spoke of lordly things. It was not until the next morning that I had cause to lament having broken my long-ago oath never to draw any more portraits, lest I bring ill fortune upon those portrayed.

"We will not march today, my boys," Cortés announced, at our arising. "For this day we have the unhappy duty of convening a martial court."

His soldiers looked as startled and bewildered as I and the Revered Speakers did.

"Doña Florencia," said Cortés, with a gesture toward the smirking woman, "has taken care to overhear the conversations between our three distinguished guests and the chiefs of the villages through which we have passed. She will testify that these kings have been conniving with the peoples hereabout to mount a mass uprising against us. I also have, thanks to Don Juan Damasceno"—he waved the piece of bark—"a drawing which is incontrovertible proof of their being deep in conspiracy."

The three Speakers had thrown only a glance of disgust at the contemptible Florencia, but their look at me was full of sadness and disillusion. I leapt forward and cried, "This is not true!"

Instantly, Cortés had his sword out, the point of it against my throat. "I think," he said, "for these proceedings, your testimony and translation might not be entirely impartial. Doña Florencia will serve as interpreter, and you—you *will* keep silent."

So six of his under-officers sat as the tribunal, and Cortés presented the charges, and his witness Florencia provided the spurious supporting evidence. Perhaps Cortés had tutored her in advance, but I do not think that would have been necessary. Persons of her base sort—resentful that the world neither knows nor cares if they even exist—will grasp any chance to be recognized, if only for their egregious malignity. Thus Florencia seized that one opportunity to be noticed: by reviling her betters, and with seeming impunity, and before an apparently attentive audience which pretended to believe her. Dredging up her life-long indignation at her own nonentity, she spewed a torrent of lies and fabrications and accusations intended to make the three lords seem creatures more despicable than she was.

I could say nothing—not until now—and the Revered

Speakers *would* say nothing. In their disdain for the mosquito posturing as a vulture, they did not refute her vituperation or defend themselves or let their faces show what they thought of that sham trial. Florencia would probably have gone on for days, inventing even evidence that the three were Devils from Hell, if she had had the intellect to think of it. But the tribunal finally wearied of listening to her rant, and they summarily commanded her to desist, and then they just as summarily pronounced the three lords guilty of conspiring to revolt against New Spain.

Without protest or expostulation, only exchanging ironic farewells with each other, the three let themselves be stood in a row under a massive ceiba tree, and the Spaniards threw ropes over a convenient limb, and the three were hauled up together. In that moment, when the Revered Speakers Cuautémoc and Tétlapanquétzal and Cohuanácoch died, there also ended the last remaining trace of the existence of The Triple Alliance. I do not know the exact date of the year, because on that expedition I had not been keeping a journal. Perhaps you reverend scribes can calculate the date, for when the execution was concluded, Cortés shouted merrily:

"Now let us hunt, my boys, and kill some game and make a feast! Today is Meat Tuesday, the last day of Carnival!"

They caroused throughout the night, so I had no difficulty in slipping away from the camp unnoticed, and back the way we had come. In much less time than we had taken outbound, I returned to Quaunáhuac and to Cortés's palace. The guards were accustomed to my comings and goings, and they indifferently accepted my offhand remark that I had been sent home in advance of the rest of the expedition. I went to Béu's room and told her of all that had happened.

"I am now an outcast," I said. "But I believe Cortés is totally unaware that I have a wife, or that she is in residence here. Even if he were to find out, it is unlikely that he would wreak my deserved punishment on you. I must flee, and I can best hide among the crowds of Tenochtítlan. Perhaps I can find an empty hut in the laborers' low quarter. I would not wish you to live in such squalor, Waiting Moon, when you can stay and be comfortable here—"

"We are now outcasts," she interrupted, her voice husky but determined. "I may even be able to walk to the city, Záa, if you will lead me."

I argued and pleaded, but she would not be dissuaded. So I made a pack of our belongings, which were not many, and I called for two slaves to bear her in a litter, and we traveled over the mountain rim, back into the lake lands, and across the southern causeway into Tenochtítlan, and here we have been ever since.

✠

I bid you welcome once again, Your Excellency, after such long absence. Do you come to hear the conclusion of my narrative? Well, I have told it all, except for a little bit.

Cortés returned with his train about a year after I had left him, and his first concern was to put about the false story of the planned insurrection of the three Revered Speakers, and to show my drawing as "proof" of their collusion, and to proclaim the justness of his having executed them for that treason. It came as a shock to all the people of what had been The Triple Alliance, for I had not broached the news to any but Béu. All the people mourned, of course, and held belated funeral services of remembrance. They also, of course, muttered darkly among themselves, but they had no choice except to feign belief in the version of the incident told by Cortés. He did not, I might remark, bring back the perfidious Florencia to support his story. He would not have risked her trying to achieve another fleeting moment of recognition by publicly giving the lie to her own lies. Where and how he disposed of the creature, no one ever heard, or cared enough to inquire.

Surely Cortés had been angered by my desertion of his expedition, but that anger must have ebbed during the ensuing year, for he never ordered a hunt for me, or not that I know of. None of his men ever came seeking my whereabouts; none of his dogs were sent to sniff me out. Béu and I were left to live as best we could.

By that time, the marketplace of Tlaltelólco had been restored, though much reduced in size. I went there to see what was being bought and sold, and by whom, and for what prices. The market was as crowded as in the old days, though at least half the crowd consisted of white men and women. I noticed that most of the goods exchanged between my own people went by barter—"I will give you this gallipavo fowl for that pottery bowl"—but the Spanish buyers were paying in trade currency: ducados and reales and maravedíes. And, while they bought foodstuffs and other commodities, they also bought a great many things of only trifling use or decorative worth. Listening to them talk, I gathered that they were buying "quaint native handcrafts" to keep for their "curiosity value" or to send to their kinfolk back home as "mementos of New Spain."

As you know, Your Excellency, many different flags have flown over this city during the years since its reconstruction as the City of Mexíco. There has been Cortés's personal standard, blue and white with a red cross; and the blood-and-gold flag of Spain; and the one bearing the picture of the Virgin Mary in what I suppose are realistic colors; and the one with the two-headed eagle signifying empire; and others of significance unknown to me. In the market that day, I saw many artisans obsequiously offering for sale miniature copies of those various flags, well or badly done, but even the best did not seem to arouse any fervor among the browsing Spaniards. And I saw that not any of the tradesmen were offering similar replicas of our *own* proud symbol of the Mexíca nation. Perhaps they feared they could be charged with harboring sympathies contrary to peace and good order.

Well, I had no such fears. Or rather, I was already punishable for worse offenses, so I felt not much concern for trivial ones. I went home to our wretched little hut, and I made a drawing, and I knelt beside Béu's pallet to hold it close to her eyes.

"Waiting Moon," I said, "can you see this clearly enough to copy it?" She peered intently as I pointed to the various elements. "See, it is an eagle, with his wings poised for flight, and he perches on a nopáli cactus, and in his beak he holds the war symbol of intertwined ribbons. . . ."

"Yes," she said. "Yes. I can better make out the details, now that you have explained them. But copy it, Záa? What do you mean?"

"If I buy the materials, could you make a copy of this by embroidering with colored threads upon a small square of cloth? It need not be as exquisite as the pictures you used to make. Just brown for the eagle, green for the nopáli, perhaps red and yellow for the ribbons."

"I believe I could. But why?"

"If you can make enough such copies, I can sell them in the market. To the white men and women. They seem to fancy such curiosities, and they pay in coin for them."

She said, "I will make one, while you watch me, so you can correct me where I go wrong. When I have one done right, and can feel it with my fingertips, I can use it for a pattern to do any number of others."

And she did, and very nicely too, and I applied for a place in the market, and was allotted a small space, and there I spread a groundcloth, and on it I arrayed the replicas of the old emblem of the Mexíca. No one in authority came to molest me, or to make me take the things away; instead, many people came and bought. Most were Spaniards, but even some of my own race offered me this or that in barter, because they had thought they would never again see that reminder of who and what we had been.

From the start, many Spaniards complained of the design: "That is not a very lifelike snake the eagle is eating." I tried to tell them that it was not intended to be a snake, nor was the eagle eating it. But they seemed unable to comprehend that it was a word picture, the intertwined ribbons that signified fire and smoke, hence also signified war. And warfare, I explained, had constituted a great part of Mexíca history, whereas no reptile ever had. They said only, "It would look better with a snake."

If that was what they wanted, that was what they would have. I made a revised drawing, and helped Waiting Moon make from it a new piece of embroidery, which she used thereafter as her pattern. When inevitably other tradesmen at the market copied the emblem, they copied it complete with the snake. None of the imitations were as well made as Béu's, so my business did not suffer much. Rather, I was amused by the slavishness of the copies, amused that I had instigated a whole new industry, amused that *that* should be my concluding con-

tribution to The One World. I had been many things in my life,
even for a time the Lord Mixtli, a man of stature and wealth
and respectability. I would have laughed if anyone had told
me, "You will end your roads and your days as a common
tradesman peddling to haughty outlanders little cloth copies of
the Mexíca emblem—and a debased travesty of the emblem,
at that." I would have laughed, so I *did* laugh, as I sat there
day after day in the marketplace, and those who stopped to buy
from me thought me a jolly old man.

As things turned out, I did not quite end there, because the
time came when Béu's eyesight failed completely, and her
fingers also went, and she could no longer do the embroidery,
so I had to close my little venture into trade. We have lived
since then on the savings of coins we put by, though Waiting
Moon has often and fretfully expressed the wish that death
might release her from her black prison of boredom and immobility and misery. After a while of inactivity, of doing no
more than existing, I might have wished that release for myself
as well. But it was then that Your Excellency's friars found
me and brought me here, and you asked me to talk of times
past, and that has been diversion enough to sustain my interest
in living. While my employment here has meant an even more
dreary and solitary imprisonment for Béu, she has endured it
just so I would have someone to go home to, on the nights I
have gone home to that shack. When finally I go there to stay,
perhaps I shall arrange that it be no overlong stay for her and
me. We have no more work to do, or any other excuse for
remaining in the world of the living. And I might mention that
the last contribution we *did* make to The One World does not
now amuse me. Go to the Tlaltelólco market this day and you
will see the Mexíca emblem still for sale, still complete with
serpent. What is worse—why I am not amused—you will also
hear there the professional storytellers, now coiling that invented and excrescent snake into our most venerable legends:

"Hear me and know. When our people first came here to
this lake region, when we were still the Aztéca, our great god
Huitzilopóchtli bade our priests look for a place where there
stood a nópali, and upon it an eagle perched, *eating a
snake....*"

Well, Your Excellency, so much for history. I cannot change the pitiful little falsities of it, any more than I can change the far more deplorable realities of it. But the history I have told is the history through which I lived, and in which I had some part, and I have told it truthfully. I kiss the earth to that, which is to say: I swear to it.

Now, it may be that I have here and there in my narrative left a gap that Your Excellency would like bridged, or there may be questions Your Excellency would wish to put to me, or further details Your Excellency would desire on one subject or another. But I beg that they be postponed for a time, and that I be allowed a respite from this employment. I ask Your Excellency's permission now to take my leave of you and the reverend scribes and this room in what was once The House of Song. It is not because I am weary of speaking, or because I have said all that might be told, or because I suspect you may be weary of hearing me speak. I ask to take my leave because last night, when I went home to my hut and sat down beside my wife's pallet, something astounding occurred. Waiting Moon told me that she loved me! She said that she loved me and that she always had and that she still does. Since Béu never in her life said any such thing before, I think she may be approaching the end of her long dying, and that I ought to be with her when it comes. Forlorn things though we are, she and I, we are all we have.... Last night, Béu said she had loved me ever since our first meeting, long ago, in Tecuantépec, in the days of our greenest youth. But she lost me the first time and she lost me forever, she said, when I decided to go seeking the purple dye, when she and her sister Zyanya did the choosing of the twigs to see which of the girls would accompany me. She had lost me then, she said, but she had never ceased to love me, and never encountered another man she could love. When she made that astonishing revelation last night, an unworthy thought went through my mind. I thought: if it had been you, Béu, who went with me, who married me soon after, then it would be Zyanya whom now I would still have with me. But

that thought was chased away by another: would I have wanted
Zyanya to suffer as you have suffered, Béu? And I pitied the
poor wreckage lying there, saying she loved me. She sounded
so sad that I endeavored to make light of it. I remarked that
she had chosen some odd ways in which to manifest her love,
and I told how I had seen her dabbling in the magic art, making
a mud image of me, as witch women do when they would work
harm upon a man. Béu said, and she sounded sadder yet, that
she had made it to do me no hurt; that she had waited long and
in vain for us to share a bed; that she had made the image that
she might sleep with it and possibly enchant me into her embrace and into love of her. I sat silent beside her pallet, then,
and I thought over many things past, and I realized how un-
discerning and impervious I have been during all the years Béu
and I have known each other; how I have been more unseeing
and crippled than Béu is at this moment in her utter blindness.
It is not a woman's place to announce that she loves a man,
and Béu had respected that traditional inhibition; she had never
said it, she had disguised her feelings with a flippancy that I
had obstinately and always taken for scorn or mockery. She
had let slip her ladylike restraint only a few times—I remembered her once saying wistfully, "I used to wonder why I was
named Waiting Moon"—and I had refused ever to recognize
those moments, when all I need have done was hold out my
arms. . . . True, I loved Zyanya, I have gone on loving her, and
I always will. But that would not have been diminished by my
later loving Béu too. *Ayya*, the years I have thrown away! And
it was I who deprived myself; I can blame no one else. What
is more hurtful to my heart is the ungracious way in which I
deprived Waiting Moon, who waited so long, until now it is
too late to salvage even a last moment of all those misused
years. I would make them up to her if I could, but I cannot.
I would have taken her to me last night, and lain with her in
the act of love, and perhaps I could have done it, but what
remains of Béu could not. So I did the only thing possible,
which was to speak, and I spoke it honestly, saying, "Béu, my
dear wife, I love you too." She could not reply, for the tears
came and choked what little voice she has left, but she put out
her hand to mine. I squeezed it tenderly, and I sat there holding
it, and I would have entwined our fingers, but I could not even

do that, since she has no fingers. As you have probably already divined, my lords, the cause of her long dying has been The Being Eaten by the Gods, and I have described what that is like, so I would prefer not to tell you what the gods have left uneaten of the woman who was once as beautiful as Zyanya. I merely sat beside her, and we were both silent. I do not know what she was thinking, but I was remembering the years we have lived together, yet never together, and what a waste they have been—of each other, and of love, which is the most unpardonable waste there is. Love and time, those are the only two things in all the world and all of life that cannot be bought, but only spent. Last night, Béu and I at last declared our love... but so late, too late. It is spent, and cannot be bought back. So I sat and recalled those lost years... and beyond them, to other years. I remembered that night my father carried me on his shoulders across the island of Xaltócan, under the "oldest of old" cypress trees, and how I passed from moonlight to moon shadow and to moonlight again. I could not have known it then, but I was sampling what my life was to be—alternate light and shadow, dappled days and nights, good times and bad. Since that night, I have endured my share of hardships and griefs, perhaps more than my share. But my unforgivable neglect of Béu Ribé is proof enough that I have caused hardship and grief to others as well. Still, it is futile to regret or complain of one's tonáli. And I think, on balance, my life has been more often good than bad. The gods favored me with many fortunes and with some occasions to do worthwhile deeds. If I were to lament any one aspect of my life, it is only that the gods refused me the one last best fortune: that my roads and my days had come to their end when my few worthy deeds were done. That would have been long ago, but still I live. Of course, I can believe, if I choose, that the gods have their reason for that too. Unless I choose to remember that distant night as a drunken dream, I can believe that two of the gods even told me their reason. They told me that my tonáli was not that I be happy or sad, rich or poor, productive or idle, even-tempered or ill-tempered, intelligent or stupid, joyful or desolated—though I have been all of those things at one time or another. According to the gods, my tonáli dictated simply that I dare to accept every challenge and seize every opportunity to live my life as fully as a man can. In so doing, I have participated in many events, great and small, historic and otherwise. But the gods said—if they were gods, and if they spoke truly—that my real function in those events was only to remember them, and tell of them to those who would come after me, so that those happenings should not be forgotten. Well, I have now done that. Except for any small details Your Excellency might wish me to add, I can think of nothing more to relate. As I cautioned at the beginning, I could tell of nothing but my own life, and that is all past. If there is a future, I cannot foresee it, and I think I would not wish to. I recall the words I heard so many times during my journey in search of Aztlan, the words Motecuzóma repeated that night we sat atop the Teotihuácan pyramid in the moonlight, repeating them as if he spoke an epitaph: "The Aztéca were here, but they brought nothing with them, and they left nothing when they went." The Aztéca, the Mexíca—whatever name you prefer—we are going now, we are being dispersed and absorbed, and soon we will all be gone, and there will be little left to remember us by. All the other nations too, overrun by your soldiers enforcing new laws, by your lords properietors demanding slave labor, by your missionary friars bringing new gods, those nations also will vanish or change beyond recognition or decay into decrepitude. Cortés is at this moment planting his colonies in the lands along the southern ocean. Alvarado is fighting to conquer the jungle tribes of Quautemálan. Montejo is fighting to subdue the more civilized Maya of Uluümil Kutz. Guzmán is fighting to vanquish the defiant Purémpecha of Michihuácan. At least those peoples, like us Mexíca, will be able to console themselves that they fought to the last. I pity more those nations—even our ancient enemy Texcála—which now so bitterly regret what they did to help you white men hasten your taking of The One World. I said, a moment ago, that I could not foresee the future, but in a sense I already *have* seen it. I have seen Malíntzin's son Martín, and the ever increasing number of other little boys and girls, the color of cheap, watered-down chocolate. *That* may be the future: not that all our peoples of The One World will be exterminated, but that they will be diluted to an insipid weakness and sameness and worthlessness. I may be wrong; I doubt it; but I can hope that I am. There may be people somewhere in these lands, so remote or so invincible that they will be left in peace, and they will multiply, and then . . . aquin ixnéntla? *Ayyo,* I should almost like to live to see what could happen then! My own ancestors were not ashamed to call themselves The Weed People, for weeds may be unsightly and unwanted, but they are fiercely strong and almost impossible to eradicate. It was not until after The Weed People's civilization had flourished and flowered that it was cut down. Flowers are beautiful and fragrant and desirable, but they are perishable. Perhaps somewhere in The One World there exists, or will exist, another Weed People, and perhaps it will be their tonáli next to flourish, and perhaps you white men will not be able to mow them down, and perhaps they will succeed to what was once our eminence. It could even happen that, when they march, some of my own descendants will march among them. I take no account of whatever seeds I may have scattered in the far southern lands; the people there have been so long degenerate that they will never be anything else, not even with my possible infusion of Mexícatl blood among them. But in the north—well, among the many places I have dallied, there is still Aztlan. And I long ago realized the meaning of the invitation extended to me by that Lesser Speaker who was also named Tliléctic-Mixtli. He said, "You must come again to Aztlan, Brother, for a small surprise," but it was not until afterward that I remembered I had lain many nights with his sister, and I knew what the waiting surprise must be. I have often wondered: a boy or a girl? But this I know: he or she will not torpidly or fearfully stay behind in Aztlan, should another migration move out from there. And I wish that young weed all success. . . . But I maunder again, Your Excellency fidgets. If I have your leave, then, Lord Bishop, I will now make my departure. I will go and sit with Béu, and I will keep telling her that I love her, for I want those to be the last words she hears each night before she sleeps, and before she begins the last sleep of all. And when she sleeps, I will get up and go out into the night and I will walk the empty streets.

✠

EXPLICIT

The chronicle told by an elderly male Indian of the tribe commonly called Aztec, as recorded *verbatim ab origine* by

FR. GASPAR DE GAYANA J.
FR. TORIBIO VEGA DE ARANJUEZ
FR. JERÓNIMO MUÑOZ G.
FR. DOMINGO VILLEGAS E YBARRA
ALONSO DE MOLINA, *interpres*

FEAST DAY OF ST. JAMES, APOSTLE
25 *July*, A.D. *1531*

IHS
✠
S.C.C.M.

Sanctified, Caesarean, Catholic Majesty,
the Emperor Don Carlos, Our Lord King:

MOST Magisterial Majesty: from this City of Méxíco, capital of New Spain, this Day of the Holy Innocents, in the year of Our Lord one thousand five hundred thirty and one, greeting.

Please to forgive the long interval since our last communication, Sire. As Captain Sánchez Santoveña will attest, his courier caravel was much delayed in its arrival here, owing to contrary winds about the Azores and a long becalming in the doldrum latitudes of the Sargasso Sea. Hence we have only now received Your Magnanimous Majesty's letter directing us to arrange—"as recompense for his services rendered to the Crown"—that our Aztec chronicler be granted "for himself and his woman a comfortable house on a suitable plot of land, and a pension adequate to sustain them through their remaining lifetimes."

We regret to say, Sire, that we cannot comply. The Indian is dead, and if his invalid widow still lives, we have no idea where.

Since we had earlier inquired as to Your Majesty's pleasure

regarding the Aztec and what was to become of him upon the termination of his employment here, and since the only reply was an ambiguously long silence, we may perhaps be excused for having assumed that Your Devout Majesty shared this cleric's belief, often stated during our campaign against the witches of Navarre, that "to overlook heresy is to encourage heresy."

After waiting a reasonable while for any directive from you, Sire, or any expression of your wishes regarding a fitting disposition of the matter, we took the measure we thought eminently justified. We instituted against the Aztec a formal charge of heresy, and he was bound over for trial. Of course, had Your Forgiving Majesty's letter arrived earlier, it would have constituted a tacit royal pardon of the man's offenses, and the denunciation would have been dismissed. However, Your Majesty might reflect—could it not have been an indication of God's will, that the winds of the Ocean Sea delayed the courier?

In any case, we well remember our Sovereign's own oath, once declared in our hearing, that you were "ready to lay down your dominions, friends, blood, life and soul for the extinction of heresy." So we are confident that Your Crusading Majesty will approve of our having helped the Lord to rid the world of one more minion of the Adversary.

A Court of Inquisition was convened in our chancellery on St. Martin's Day. All protocol and formalities were carefully and strictly observed. There were present, besides ourself as Your Majesty's Apostolic Inquisitor, our vicar-general acting as President of the Court, our chief constable, our apostolic notary, and of course the accused. The proceedings occupied only the one morning of that one day, inasmuch as we were both the accuser and the prosecutor, and the accused was the sole witness called to testify, and the only evidence presented was a selection of quotations excerpted from the chronicle told by the accused and transcribed by our friars.

According to his own admission, the Aztec had embraced Christianity only fortuitiously, by happening to be present at that mass baptism conducted by Father Bartolomé de Olmedo many years ago, and he had submitted to it as casually as all his life he had submitted to every opportunity for sinning. But, whatever his attitude at that time—frivolous, inquisitive, skeptical—it could in no way abrogate the Sacrament of Baptism. The Indian called Mixtli (among innumerable other names) died in that moment when Father Bartolomé asperged him, and he was cleansed of all his actual sins and of original sin, and he was reborn blameless in the *character indelibilis* of Juan Damasceno.

However, during the years after that conversion and his professed confirmation of belief, Juan Damasceno committed many and diverse iniquities, most notably in making those comments derisive and derogatory of Holy Church, which he either slyly or brazenly expressed in the course of narrating his "Aztec history." Thus Juan Damasceno was charged and tried as a heretic of the third category: *i.e.*, one who, having embraced the Faith, having abjured all earlier sins, has subsequently lapsed into heinous error.

For politic reasons, we omitted from the denunciation of Juan Damasceno some of the corporal sins whose commission since his conversion he had admitted without the least contrition. For example, if we accept that he was (by existing folk law) "married" at the time of his admitted fornication with the woman then called Malinche, he was clearly guilty of the mortal sin of adultery. However, we deemed it would be imprudent for us to call *sub poena* the now respectable and esteemed Doña Sra. Marina Vda. de Jaramillo to testify in that regard. Besides, the purpose of an Inquisition is not so much to examine the particular offenses of the accused, as to ascertain his incorrigible tendency or susceptibility to *fomes peccati*, the igniting "tinder of sin." So we were satisfied to charge Juan Damasceno not with any of his carnal immoralities, but only with his *lapsi fidei*, which were numerous enough.

The evidence was presented rather in the form of a litany, with the apostolic notary reading a selected passage from the transcription of the accused man's own words, and then the prosecutor responding with the appropriate charge: *e.g.*, "Profaning the sanctity of Holy Church." The notary would lead with another question, and the prosecutor would respond: "Contempt and disrespect of the clergy." The notary would read again, and the prosecutor would respond: "Promulgating doctrines contrary to the Holy Canons of the Church."

And so on, through the whole roster of charges: that the accused was the author of an obscene, blasphemous, and pernicious book, that he had inveighed against the Christian Faith, that he had encouraged apostasy, that he had propounded sedition and lese majesty, that he had ridiculed the monastic state, that he had pronounced words which a pious Christian and a loyal subject of the Crown might neither speak nor hear.

All of those being most grave errors of Faith, the accused was given every opportunity to recant and abjure his offenses, though of course no recantation could have been accepted by the Court, inasmuch as all his heretical remarks had been taken down and preserved in writing, thus substantiating every charge against him, and the published word being inexpungeable. In any event, when the notary again read out to him, one by one, the selected passages from his own narrative: *e.g.*, his idolatrous remark that "Someday my chronicle may serve as my confession to the kindly goddess Filth Eater," and asked, after each such quotation, "Don Juan Damasceno, are those indeed your words?" he readily and indifferently conceded that they were. He posted no brief in defense or mitigation of his offenses, and when he was most solemnly advised by the Court President of the dire penalties he faced if found guilty, Juan Damasceno volunteered only one comment:

"It will mean I do not go to the Christian Heaven?"

He was told that that would indeed be the worst of his punishments: that he most assuredly would not go to Heaven. At which, his smile sent a thrill of horror through every soul of the Court.

We, as Apostolic Inquisitor, were obliged to advise him of his rights: that although an acceptable recantation of his sins was impossible, he could still confess and manifest contrition, thereby to be received as a penitent, and reconciled with the Church, and subject only to the lesser penalty prescribed by canon and civil law, *viz.*, condemnation to spend his remaining life at labor in Your Majesty's prison galleys. We also recited the standard adjuration: "You behold us sincerely afflicted at your culpable obstinacy. We pray that Heaven will endow you with the spirit of repentance and contrition. Do not grieve us by persisting in error and heresy; spare us the pain of being compelled to invoke the just but severe laws of the Inquisition."

But Juan Damasceno remained recusant, yielding not to any of our persuasions or inducements, only continuing to smile faintly, and murmuring something about his destiny having been decreed by his pagan "tonáli," a sufficient heresy in itself. Whereupon, the constable returned the accused to his cell, while the Court considered its judgment, and of course found for conviction, and pronounced Juan Damasceno guilty of contumacious heresy.

As provided by canon law, on the following Sunday his sentence was formally and publicly proclaimed. Juan Damasceno was brought from his cell and marched to the center of the grand plaza, where all the city's Christians had been commanded to attend and pay heed. So there was a large crowd, which included, besides the Spaniards and Indians of our several congregations, also the oidores of the Audiencia, the other secular officials of the Justicia Ordinaria, and the provisor in charge of the auto-de-fé. Juan Damasceno came wearing the sackcloth sanbenito garment of the condemned, and on his head the coroza straw crown of infamy, and he was accompanied by Fray Gaspar de Gayana bearing a large cross.

An elevated platform had been specially erected in the square for us of the Inquisition, and from that eminence the Secretary of the Holy Office read aloud to the crowd the official account of the offenses and charges, the Court's judgment and verdict, all of which was repeated in the Náhuatl language by our interpreter Molina, for the comprehension of the many Indians present. Then we, as Apostolic Inquisitor, preached the *sermo generalis* of sentence, remanding the condemned sinner to the secular arm for punishment *debita animadversione,* and routinely recommending that those authorities exercise mercy in the carrying out of that punishment:

"We find ourself bound to declare Don Juan Damasceno to be a contumacious heretic, and do pronounce him as such. We find ourself bound to remit, and thus do remit him, to the secular arm of the Justicia Ordinaria of this city, whom we pray and charge to deal with him humanely."

Then we addressed Juan Damasceno directly, making the obligatory last plea that he abandon his recusancy, that he confess and abjure his heresies, which penitence would at least earn him the mercy of a quick execution by garrotte before his body was relaxed to the fire. But he remained as obdurate as ever, smiling and saying only, "Your Excellency, once when I was still a small child I vowed to myself that if ever I were selected for the Flowery Death, even on an alien altar, I would not degrade the dignity of my going."

Those were his last words, Sire, and I say to his credit that he did not struggle or plead or cry out when the constables used the old anchor chain to bind him to the stake before our platform, and piled the faggots high about his body, and the provisor set the torch to them. Since God permitted and the man's sins deserved it, the flames consumed his body, and of that burning it pleased God that the Aztec should die.

We subscribe ourself our Gracious Sovereign's loyal Defender of the Faith, pledging our constancy in the service of God for the salvation of souls and of nations,

Bishop of México
Apostolic Inquisitor
Protector of the Indians

IN OTIN IHUAN IN TONÁLTIN NICAN TZONQUÍCA

HERE END THE ROADS AND THE DAYS

CEM-ANAHUAC
"THE ONE WORLD"

N

Tzumpanco
Lake Tzumpanco
Lake Xaltocan Xaltocan
Teotihuacan

Texcoco
Lake TEXCOTZINCO
Tenochtitlan Texcoco
TLALOCTEPETL
to Texcala
Tepepolco

Cuicuilco Ixtlahuaca Lake Chalco
Lake Xochimilco Chalco
Xochimilco IXTACCIHUATL

to Cholollan
One-Long-Runs

Miles POPOCATEPETL

Kilometers

Kilometers

Miles

One-Long-Runs

One-Long-Run = Approx
2 Statute Miles

Eastern or

Northern

Sea

Tihó

ULUUMIL

Uxmal

KUTZ

Kimpéch

Tzempoalan
Chalchihuacuecan

Xicalanca (MAYA

(OLMECA COUNTRY) CUPILCO COUNTRY) Chaktemál
Coatzacoalcos
COATZACOALI River of the
Tabasco'ob
COATLICAMAC Palemke

(HUAXYACAC CHIAPA GREAT RIVER CANYON TAMOAN
COUNTRY) Yaxchilán CHAN
'obeán Tzoztlan Chiapán Bonampak
Tecuantepec R. Semen Lakes of Tzalao
Nonbe Tonala (SOCONOCHO) (MAYA COUNTRY)
Pijijia QUAUTEMALAN

Tapachtlan

© 1980 A. hart/J. hemp

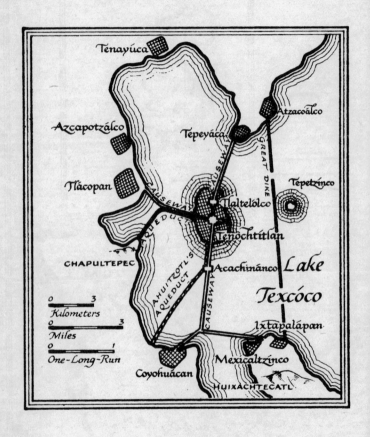

Tenayúca

Azcapotzálco

Tepeyáca

Atzacoálco

Tlácopan

CAUSEWAY

CAUSEWAY

GREAT DIKE

Tlaltelólco

Tepetzínco

AQUEDUCT

Tenōchtítlan

CHAPULTEPEC

AHUITZOTL'S
AQUEDUCT

Acachinánco

Lake

Texcóco

CAUSEWAY

Ixtapalápan

| 0 | 3 |
Kilometers
| 0 | 3 |
Miles
| 0 | 1 |
One-Long-Run

Coyohuácan

Mexicaltzínco

HUIXÁCHTECATL

On the following pages are details of Arrow
books that will be of interest.

A Selection of Arrow Books

☐ No Enemy But Time	Evelyn Anthony	£2.95
☐ The Lilac Bus	Maeve Binchy	£2.99
☐ Rates of Exchange	Malcolm Bradbury	£3.50
☐ Prime Time	Joan Collins	£3.50
☐ Rosemary Conley's Complete Hip and Thigh Diet	Rosemary Conley	£2.99
☐ Staying Off the Beaten Track	Elizabeth Gundrey	£6.99
☐ Duncton Wood	William Horwood	£4.50
☐ Duncton Quest	William Horwood	£4.50
☐ A World Apart	Marie Joseph	£3.50
☐ Erin's Child	Sheelagh Kelly	£3.99
☐ Colours Aloft	Alexander Kent	£2.99
☐ Gondar	Nicholas Luard	£4.50
☐ The Ladies of Missalonghi	Colleen McCullough	£2.50
☐ The Veiled One	Ruth Rendell	£3.50
☐ Sarum	Edward Rutherfurd	£4.99
☐ Communion	Whitley Strieber	£3.99

Prices and other details are liable to change

ARROW BOOKS, BOOKSERVICE BY POST, PO BOX 29, DOUGLAS, ISLE OF MAN, BRITISH ISLES

NAME...

ADDRESS...

....

....

Please enclose a cheque or postal order made out to Arrow Books Ltd. for the amount due and allow the following for postage and packing.

U.K. CUSTOMERS: Please allow 22p per book to a maximum of £3.00.

B.F.P.O. & EIRE: Please allow 22p per book to a maximum of £3.00.

OVERSEAS CUSTOMERS: Please allow 22p per book.

Whilst every effort is made to keep prices low it is sometimes necessary to increase cover prices at short notice. Arrow Books reserve the right to show new retail prices on covers which may differ from those previously advertised in the text or elsewhere.

Bestselling Fiction

☐	No Enemy But Time	Evelyn Anthony	£2.95
☐	The Lilac Bus	Maeve Binchy	£2.99
☐	Prime Time	Joan Collins	£3.50
☐	A World Apart	Marie Joseph	£3.50
☐	Erin's Child	Sheelagh Kelly	£3.99
☐	Colours Aloft	Alexander Kent	£2.99
☐	Gondar	Nicholas Luard	£4.50
☐	The Ladies of Missalonghi	Colleen McCullough	£2.50
☐	Lily Golightly	Pamela Oldfield	£3.50
☐	Talking to Strange Men	Ruth Rendell	£2.99
☐	The Veiled One	Ruth Rendell	£3.50
☐	Sarum	Edward Rutherfurd	£4.99
☐	The Heart of the Country	Fay Weldon	£2.50

Prices and other details are liable to change

ARROW BOOKS, BOOKSERVICE BY POST, PO BOX 29, DOUGLAS, ISLE OF MAN, BRITISH ISLES

NAME...

ADDRESS...

....

....

Please enclose a cheque or postal order made out to Arrow Books Ltd. for the amount due and allow the following for postage and packing.

U.K. CUSTOMERS: Please allow 22p per book to a maximum of £3.00.

B.F.P.O. & EIRE: Please allow 22p per book to a maximum of £3.00.

OVERSEAS CUSTOMERS: Please allow 22p per book.

Whilst every effort is made to keep prices low it is sometimes necessary to increase cover prices at short notice. Arrow Books reserve the right to show new retail prices on covers which may differ from those previously advertised in the text or elsewhere.

Bestselling General Fiction

☐ No Enemy But Time	Evelyn Anthony	£2.95
☐ Skydancer	Geoffrey Archer	£3.50
☐ The Sisters	Pat Booth	£3.50
☐ Captives of Time	Malcolm Bosse	£2.99
☐ Saudi	Laurie Devine	£2.95
☐ Duncton Wood	William Horwood	£4.50
☐ Aztec	Gary Jennings	£3.95
☐ A World Apart	Marie Joseph	£3.50
☐ The Ladies of Missalonghi	Colleen McCullough	£2.50
☐ Lily Golightly	Pamela Oldfield	£3.50
☐ Sarum	Edward Rutherfurd	£4.99
☐ Communion	Whitley Strieber	£3.99

Prices and other details are liable to change

ARROW BOOKS, BOOKSERVICE BY POST, PO BOX 29, DOUGLAS, ISLE OF MAN, BRITISH ISLES

NAME...

ADDRESS...

....

....

Please enclose a cheque or postal order made out to Arrow Books Ltd. for the amount due and allow the following for postage and packing.

U.K. CUSTOMERS: Please allow 22p per book to a maximum of £3.00.

B.F.P.O. & EIRE: Please allow 22p per book to a maximum of £3.00.

OVERSEAS CUSTOMERS: Please allow 22p per book.

Whilst every effort is made to keep prices low it is sometimes necessary to increase cover prices at short notice. Arrow Books reserve the right to show new retail prices on covers which may differ from those previously advertised in the text or elsewhere.